Philip S

A Commentary on the Holy Scriptures

Philip Schaff

A Commentary on the Holy Scriptures

Reprint of the original, first published in 1874.

1st Edition 2024 | ISBN: 978-3-36884-894-1

Verlag (Publisher): Outlook Verlag GmbH, Zeilweg 44, 60439 Frankfurt, Deutschland
Vertretungsberechtigt (Authorized to represent): E. Roepke, Zeilweg 44, 60439 Frankfurt, Deutschland
Druck (Print): Books on Demand GmbH, In de Tarpen 42, 22848 Norderstedt, Deutschland

A

COMMENTARY

ON THE

HOLY SCRIPTURES:

CRITICAL, DOCTRINAL AND HOMILETICAL,

WITH SPECIAL REFERENCE TO MINISTERS AND STUDENTS,

BY

JOHN PETER LANGE, D. D.,

PROFESSOR OF THEOLOGY IN THE UNIVERSITY OF BONN,

ASSISTED BY A NUMBER OF EMINENT EUROPEAN DIVINES.

TRANSLATED FROM THE GERMAN, REVISED, ENLARGED, AND EDITED

BY

PHILIP SCHAFF, D. D.,

PROFESSOR OF THEOLOGY IN THE UNION THEOLOGICAL SEMINARY, NEW YORK,

IN CONNECTION WITH AMERICAN AND ENGLISH SCHOLARS OF VARIOUS
DENOMINATIONS.

VOL. X. OF THE NEW TESTAMENT:

CONTAINING THE REVELATION OF JOHN, AND A GENERAL ALPHABETICAL
INDEX TO ALL THE VOLUMES OF THE NEW TESTAMENT.

———————

NEW YORK:

CHARLES SCRIBNER'S SONS,

743-745 BROADWAY.

THE

REVELATION OF JOHN.

EXPOUNDED

BY

JOHN PETER LANGE, D. D.,

PROFESSOR OF THEOLOGY IN THE UNIVERSITY OF BONN.

TRANSLATED FROM THE GERMAN BY
EVELINA MOORE.

ENLARGED AND EDITED BY
E. R. CRAVEN, D. D.,

PASTOR OF THE THIRD PRESBYTERIAN CHURCH AT NEWARK, N. J.

TOGETHER WITH A DOUBLE ALPHABETICAL INDEX TO ALL THE TEN VOLUMES OF THE
NEW TESTAMENT BY
JOHN H. WOODS, A. M.

NEW YORK:
CHARLES SCRIBNER'S SONS,
743–745 BROADWAY.

PREFACE BY THE GENERAL EDITOR.

WITH this tenth volume the New Testament Division of the American edition of LANGE'S *Biblework* is completed. The first volume (on Matthew) was published nearly ten years ago (October, 1864), seven years after the German original (1857). The remaining five volumes of the Old Testament Division have been distributed among competent American and English scholars, and will be published as soon as they are ready, without waiting for the German edition, which has been already anticipated in the recently published volume on the Minor Prophets. The completion of the whole series at no distant time, therefore, is placed beyond personal contingencies.

I have reason to be thankful to a kind Providence for life and strength, to my publishers for their energy, patience and perseverance, and to my forty-five contributors for their faithful and efficient co-operation in this laborious and complicated enterprise. I shall never forget the delightful associations with so many eminent Christian scholars, who, on my invitation, have made the treasures of foreign learning and the results of their own researches accessible to the English and American students of the Book of books. LANGE'S Commentary, we trust, will long be resorted to as a thesaurus of Biblical learning and piety from all ages and sections of the Christian Church.

This volume is devoted to the last and most difficult book of the Bible, the divine seal of the whole, the cross of crosses of commentators. The Apocalypse will not be fully comprehended until we see it in the light of the millennium and the new heavens on the new earth; nevertheless, even in its partial and imperfect understanding, it is continually fulfilling its noble mission as a book of hope and comfort in the Christian Church. The Jewish Prophets, in spite of all the obscurities and conflicting interpretations, served the same purpose under the Old dispensation long before they were fulfilled in the New. "How many passages in the prophets," says the genial HERDER, "are obscure in their primary historical references, and yet these passages, containing divine truth, doctrine and consolation, are manna for all hearts and all ages. Should it not be so with the book, which is an abstract of almost all prophets and apostles?" It has been such a manna especially in ages of trial and persecution, and will continue to instruct, to warn, to cheer, and to assure the Church militant of the final triumph of Christ—the Alpha and Omega of history.

Dr. LANGE, in this Commentary, which appeared in 1871 (302 pages), boldly meets the difficulties, and marks a considerable advance in the deeper spiritual apprehension of the Apocalypse and its mysterious symbolism. (*See his Preface.*)

The American edition has fallen into able and faithful hands. The translation of Miss EVELINA MOORE is all that can be desired.

The additions of Rev. Dr. CRAVEN greatly enhance the value of the work. He has paid minute attention to the textual department, making use of the latest critical labors of TREGELLES and TISCHENDORF.* He has throughout embodied the results of English scholarship, and of his own long-continued, careful and devout study of this book. We direct

---

* My thanks are due to Professor TISCHENDORF, who kindly forwarded me the advanced sheets of his text of the Apocalypse before they were published in the second volume of his eighth critical edition of the Greek Testament. May his health be restored to complete the Prolegomena of this invaluable work.

the reader's attention especially to his clear and condensed *abstracts of views* of the different classes of Apocalyptic interpreters, scattered throughout the volume, and to his original discussions of the following important points:

This volume contains also a double Alphabetical Index, verbal and topical, to the whole New Testament Division of the Commentary. It was prepared with great care and skill by Mr. JOHN H. WOODS, A. M., of Jacksonville, Illinois, and will be found almost indispensable in the use of any of the ten volumes which it covers.

PHILIP SCHAFF.

No. 42 BIBLE HOUSE, *New York,* }
            April 10th, 1874. }

PREFACE BY THE AUTHOR.

THROUGH the gracious assistance of God, the New Testament division of our *Bible-work* is now entirely completed, with the present Theologico-Homiletical Commentary on the Revelation of John.

In the treatment of this Book, I have considered it expedient to give particular prominence to the theoretical, critical and exegetical section;—a foundation of more than ordinary solidity being necessary in order to an ampler doctrinal and homiletical utilization of this Scripture, which has sustained such manifold wrenchings from one extreme to another.

The first thing requisite was to give a more elaborate and definite form to the theology of Apocalyptics; as it is possible to rectify the existent grand misapprehensions concerning the peculiar characteristics of Hebrew Art, in respect of its perfection in the forms of Eschatological Prophecy,—misapprehensions peculiar to the traditional Hellenistico-humanistic point of view,—only by bringing about a thorough understanding of the magnitude of the contrast between the summits of Hellenistic and Theocratic culture.

With this task was linked the necessity for fixing our gaze more intently upon the symbolical side of Apocalyptics, and for tracing the Apocalyptic symbolism of the New Testament back to the more or less conventionally defined Old Testament elements of Apocalyptics. Nothing save a system of Biblico-prophetic symbolism which shall be founded upon well-ascertained rules, can, on the one hand, terminate the endless hap-hazard conjecture in which exegesis is wont to indulge and which results in the attributing of significations the most motley to the allegorical figures of Scripture; and, on the other hand, insure the decided appreciation of the peculiar character of allegorical Scriptures.

If it be an unmistakable fact that a certain Book is of an allegorical character, it must appear simply inadmissible, in explaining it, to pitch upon interpretations *ad libitum*, without finding out the symbolical key to the work. But, again, to handle a prophetico-poetic Book, composed in allegories, as if it were a work of *literal* meaning, is, manifestly, an utterly unreasonable and mischievous procedure. If the interpreter be not aware of the heaven-wide distinction between an *explanation of an allegorical matter* and so-called *allegorical explanation*, his ignorance is an *intellectual calamity*. But if he do know very well that an allegorical composition should be explained *as such*, and if he, nevertheless, in order to illustrate certain school-opinions, torture that allegorical composition until its language seems to be that of the letter, his conduct is *a moral scandal*.

What though ten or twenty arbitrary and fanciful interpretations have attached themselves to an allegorical passage?—that circumstance does not in the least destroy its allegorical character; on the contrary. it serves but to recommend, in the most pressing manner, an inquiry after the symbolical analogies and the fundamental character of the prophecy. Despair as to exegesis as we find it, need not drive us to despair as to the text to which such exegesis has affixed itself. The so-called synchrono-historical interpretation of modern times, has shown, clearly enough, into what absurdities the latter despair may lead men. The allegorical character of the Apocalypse, in general, being established, the symbolical nature of its *numbers*, in particular, is at the same time proved; and the great lost labor of a chronological computation of the numbers,—that chronic malady of Apocalyptic exegesis,—is, so far at least as the principle is concerned, at an end.

Since the Apocalypses branch into a twofold genealogy, a canonical and an apocryphal, the further task of ascertaining, and eventually establishing, the canonical character of our Book, has presented itself to us. Presumptuous skirmishers in the field of criticism conceive that they can, without compromising themselves, rail at the bare supposition that there are canonical books,—reviling such an assumption as a lack of intellectual freedom. The term *canonical* was, however, originally applied to the Greek Classics. Now should any one essay to ridicule the idea of the Classics, he would hardly escape the charge of literary barbarism.

In respect of the *construction* of the Apocalypse, we adhere to the opinion that it is systematically arranged in cyclical collective pictures [pictures of the whole], which are always representative of the entire Course of the World down to the period of its End, and yet, in the succession which they are made to observe, are constantly advancing nearer to that End. The succession of these cycles, which are modified by the number Seven, is in exact correspondence with the movement, development and perfection of macrocosmical life,—*from within, outwards.* The Seven Churches, in their symbolical significance, constitute not simply an introduction to the Book ; as the kernel and centre of the World's history, they form the determinative fundamental idea of the Book. The Seven Seals constitute the history of the World, in relation to the Seven Churches. The Seven Trumpets follow, as Divine judgments upon, or penitential [exhorting to repentance] trumpets over, seven specific corruptions or forms of sin in the Church. Then ensue the Seven Thunders, as sealed life-pictures of the times of awakening, and of reforms, in the Church. Only in face of these powers of the world to come, can the Seven Heads of the Antichristian Beast develop;—the seven world-monarchies ending in the consummation of Antichristianity in the Antichrist;—the demonic reaction of world-history against the Kingdom of God. On the other hand, Antichristian evil, on its side, calls forth the Seven Vials of Anger, the judgments of hardening, the last of which unfolds into the three special judgments upon the Harlot, the Beast, and Satan, being afterwards summed up again in the General Judgment of the World. That this General Judgment then ushers in the Seventh Day, the eternal Sabbath of God, is a conclusion which the Seer has scenically portrayed rather than expressly declared; his particular reason for withholding such a declaration is probably to be found in the fact that he has at the outset, in the Prologue, announced the complete revelation of God in Christ as a revelation of the Seven Spirits in Christ, or in the fact that the number Seven results from the number Six.

Within the development of the Septenary, we, with others, have retained the division of the Book into Two Parts: *The World's Course to its End*, and *The End* itself.

In perfect consistency with this division, an earlier view is carried out, agreeably with which heavenly scenes precede the earthly occurrences. From beginning to end we find the entire sequence of troublous earthly times to be over-swayed by heavenly actions, by festal presentations of the Divine Council;—the gloomy Earth-pictures being thus ever ruled by radiant Heaven-pictures. The distinctions resulting from this law of the construction alone are qualified to dissipate the unclear and confused views which subsist in regard to the composition of the Apocalypse.

May our labor, under the blessing of the Lord, contribute somewhat toward the furtherance of an understanding of eschatological affairs; in particular, may it promote the wholesome and lively expectation of the Coming of Christ,—an expectation whose vocation it is, on the one hand, to subdue that indifferentistic spiritualism which disdains all knowledge of a real, eschatological Theology; on the other hand, to paralyze that fanatical separatism and spiritism which, in manifold respects, pervert the glorious prospects of the Church into ridiculous caricatures; and at the same time to disenergize the endless labors of formal chiliastic time-reckoners. * * * * * *

In general, we may regard the accomplishment of the *Bible-work* as a matter that has become independent of personal eventualities,—as a tolerably assured fact; and for this, in the name of Editors and Publishers, we offer thanks and praise unto the LORD, who hath helped us hitherto.

J. P. LANGE.

BONN, *November 1st*, 1870.

INTRODUCTORY NOTE BY THE AMERICAN EDITOR.

It is with devout gratitude to God that, after more than two years of labor, I find myself enabled to lay Lange's Commentary on the Apocalypse before the community. The publication has, much to my regret, been delayed far beyond the period originally contemplated. This delay was, in great measure, occasioned by a temporary indisposition, which, after the greater portion of the work had been placed in the hands of the printer, rendered expedient my absence for several months from the country.

Instead of presenting an extended Introduction, as originally designed, I confine myself to a brief statement of some of the difficulties, and one or two other matters, connected with the preparation of the work.

THE GREEK TEXT.

As is well known to scholars, the text of the Apocalypse is the most imperfect of the Recepta. Erasmus, for the preparation of this portion of his great and important work, had but one Manuscript, and that a cursive of (probably) the XII. Century. Not only was this MS. of but little, or rather no authority, but it was incomplete; gaps had to be supplied by re-translation from the Vulgate—the entire passage from the word Δαυείδ, ch. xxii. 16, to the close of the Book had to be thus prepared. The only copies of the Vulgate to which Erasmus had access were the corrupt printed editions then in common use. In addition to these sources of error, the work was so hurried through the press that several important mistakes of copyists found their way into the printed volume, where they have continued to the present day.

Even so late as 1844, Tregelles, when he first published his text of the Apocalypse, had access to but three uncial Codices, viz.: A., C., and the B. of the Apocalypse.* Of these, C. is probably the oldest, but, being a palimpsest, is defective in many parts—eight entire chapters of the Apocalypse are wanting.

It was not until the discovery by Tischendorf of the Sinaitic MS., generally known as ℵ., and the Porfirian, denominated P., both in 1862, that material was provided for a satisfactory emendation of the text. The recent great critical works of Tregelles and Tischendorf, based largely on these newly discovered Codices, did not appear until after the first part of this work was in the hands of the printer. Through the kindness of Prof. Tischendorf in furnishing advance sheets to Dr. Schaff, and of Prof. Abbott, of Harvard University, in allowing me the use of his copy of Tregelles' Apocalypse until I could obtain one from Europe, I was enabled not only to continue my labor with the aid of these all-important works, but also to correct that which I had already prepared.

An elaborate and valuable article on the "Greek Text of the Apocalypse," from the pen of the Rev. Thomas J. Conant, of Brooklyn, N. Y., may be found in The Baptist Quarterly, Vol. IV., pp. 129 sqq.

---

* This Cod. is not, as is supposed by many, the great Cod. Vaticanus. The Vaticanus, or B. proper, lacks the Apocalypse, which is supplied by an uncial of inferior value known as "the B. of the Apocalypse." In the following work this inferior Cod. is styled B*.; the few instances in which B. simple occurs, are errors.

THE VERSION.

The emendation of the text made necessary, of course, to a considerable extent, a revision of the English Version. But beyond this, I felt it to be proper to extend the revision. As is well known, the original translators inclined to the free use of synonyms—rendering the same Greek word by several English terms, and again rendering several Greek terms by the same English expression. For instance, in the New Testament the word *world* is employed to translate αἰών, αἰώνιος, γῆ, κόσμος, οἰκουμένη; and each of these terms has at least one other rendering; δύναμις, δυνατός, ἐξουσία, ἰσχύς, κράτος are continually confounded, as are also θυμός, ὀργή, etc. It has been my effort to give to each Greek term its proper English equivalent, and, as far as possible, to employ that equivalent uniformly. Certain verbal and grammatical inaccuracies have also been corrected. It is also proper to remark that the first-class marginal readings (those marked with a †) have almost invariably been adopted.*

It is proper to state that in my revision I was greatly indebted to the Version of Alford, and the Translation for the American Bible Union, by the late learned and lamented Rev. John Lillie, D. D., of Kingston, N. Y.

ADDITIONS.

Another great difficulty encountered by me was the selection of additional comments. No Book of the Bible has been the subject of so many and variant interpretations, by evangelical men, as the Apocalypse. More than *twenty-six* pages of Darling's *Cyclopædia Bibliographica* are filled with the mere titles of Commentaries on the entire Book or portions thereof. It was desirable to present, as far as practicable, the views of all classes of interpreters. That this might be done, a selection of the following representative authors was made, and abstracts of their views prepared, viz., Moses Stuart, Elliott, Wordsworth, Lord, Alford, Barnes, and Glasgow. Additions also were made from the writings of Sir Isaac Newton, Bishop Newton, Bush, Auberlen, Trench (*On the Seven Epistles*), Brown (*On the Second Advent*); and in the Homiletical Department from those of Matthew Henry, Scott, Bonar, Vaughan, and others. The additions to the Homiletical Department were made, during my absence from the country, by the Translator; they meet with my entire approbation.

---

* MARGINAL REFERENCE MARKS IN THE ENGLISH VERSION.

Three distinct marginal reference marks were employed by King James' Translators, indicating three entirely distinct classes of marginal readings, viz.: the *dagger* (†), the *parallel bars* (‖), and the *asterisk* (*). The *dagger* (†) was used when the *literal* rendering of the original term was placed in the margin and the opinion of the Translators as to its meaning was given in the text; the most conspicuous instance of this is in Is. xxvi. 4, where the margin gives "*rock of ages*," the literal rendering of צוּר עוֹלָמִים, and the text reads "*everlasting strength*." Where this mark appears, the marginal reading is always preceded by the abbreviation Heb. (Hebrew), Chald. (Chaldaic), or Gr. (Greek). The *parallel bars* (‖) were employed when the margin presented an *alternative* translation of the original, as in John xvi. 8, where the text reads "*reprove*" and the margin "*convince*." Where this sign was used by the Translators, the marginal reading was preceded by the conjunction Or. The *asterisk* (*) was used to indicate a marginal *comment* or *Scripture reference*, as in the titles to the Books of Job and the Psalms. This mark has almost entirely disappeared from modern editions of the English Bible, the *parallel bars* having been substituted in the majority of instances where the reference is to a *comment*, as in 2 Chron. xx. 36, and *letters* where it is to another Scripture.

The knowledge of the significance of these marks has almost entirely disappeared from the Church. As illustrations of the truth of this remark, reference need only be made to the almost universal disuse of the asterisk in our modern editions of the Bible; and the further fact that almost all the private publishing houses of Great Britain and America have substituted *letters* for the *dagger* and the *parallel bars*. This lapse of knowledge is doubtless due to the fact that King James' Translators published no statement as to the significance of the marks employed by them. They adopted them from the Geneva Bible, the Version in common use in Great Britain, merely substituting the *dagger* (†) for the double *dagger* (‡). The "Address to the Christian Reader" in the Geneva Bible contains a full explanation, and consequently, at the time of the publication of the amended (King James') Version, the significance of these signs was as well understood as that of the letters of the alphabet. Doubtless the Translators regarded a statement as unnecessary, not contemplating the fact that, in the absence of a perpetual reminder, knowledge of the meaning of such arbitrary signs would in a few generations pass away.

In the year 1871, the General Assembly of the Presbyterian Church in the United States of America, unanimously adopted a resolution requesting the Directors of the American Bible Society to publish, in their future editions of the Scriptures, a brief statement concerning the meaning of these marks, and also concerning the significance of words printed in capital and italic letters. The publication of such a statement would be of immense advantage to the students of the English Version.

CONCLUDING REMARKS.

It will be evident to the reader that I must be classed with those who are generally known as pre-millenarians. My views have been frankly expressed and supported, but I trust not offensively, and I have endeavored fully to present the views of those from whom I differ. My own views, it is proper to remark, are considerably modified by my peculiar hypotheses in reference to the Basileia, and the twofold Future Advent of Christ. On both these subjects extended Notes will be found in the body of the work.

With these general remarks, and with the fervent prayer that God will use this publication for His glory and the increase of knowledge in the Church, I submit it to the Christian public.

E. R. CRAVEN.

NEWARK, N. J., *April* 18*th*, 1874.

THE APOCALYPSE.

INTRODUCTION TO THE APOCALYPSE.

FIRST DIVISION.

GENERAL INTRODUCTION.

§ 1. THE APOCALYPSE IN ITS UNIQUENESS AND ITS KINDRED BEARINGS.

The canonical Scripture which forms the close of the New Testament, and of the Biblical Books generally, the Revelation of St. John, is not only a peculiar, but also an entirely unique phenomenon; a unique phenomenon in the very series of Biblical Books themselves, so that it can be said: As the Bible stands alone amongst the writings of the world, so does the Apocalypse stand alone amongst the writings of the Bible. It is thus doubly a unique book and that—by virtue of its essence, mysterious even to enigmatical obscurity—in a three-fold relation: in respect of its origin, its form, and its operation.

As to its origin, it is one of the most strongly authenticated of the Books of the Bible; authenticated by its superscription, its historical statements (chap. i. 9), and the historical evidences accompanying it. And yet, among the New Testament Antilegomena, or Scriptures whose reception into the Canon has been protested against, this very Book is the greatest Antilegomenon; ecclesiastically questioned in ancient times and the subject of theological dispute in more modern days.

Its form, however, conjoins a fullness of antitheses, of which many can conceive only as contradictions. A claim to the ripest New-Testamentalness, or Christian knowledge and freedom—united to the semblance of an Old Testament spirit of wrath, of a Judaizing tendency in general. Utterances of the highest ecstasy, of a contemplation the most direct, fully merged in the Divine revelation—framed in an expression apparently the result of an artistic culture and reflection the most exquisite. The richest fullness of Old Testament prophetic, evangelic and apostolic reminiscences,—and at the same time a prophetic originality which reminds us of the declaration, Behold I make all things new. An ideal peace which opens each new night-piece of earthly history with a pre-celebration of the heavenly, triumphant rule—conjoined to a feeling of human horror at the uncovered demonic abysses and the heavenly wrath-judgments. Finally, a work full of Greek elements of culture—in a form technically Hebrew, even in Hebraizing language.—All these antitheses announce a grandeur which, on a more cursory view, readily assumes the appearance of heterogeneousness. If we consider yet further that in the Apocalypse, still more than in the Epistles and Gospel of St. John, the severe expression of sublimity (here like a ghostly trumpet of judgment) is united to the simplest, pleasantest heart-words,—words sometimes of sympathy, sometimes of consolation and promise, so that the Book spreads itself out before us like the mantle of dusky night, broidered over with brilliant stars like jewels,—we shall understand the third mysterious feature of the Book, its even enigmatically marvelous operation.

Concerning the immediate operation of Christ Himself, we know that it was of a uniquely attractive and repellent character: those who came under His influence were attracted or repelled, in proportion to their spiritual affinity to, or alienation from, Him. The same truth continually obtains in regard to Christianity and also in regard to the Holy Scriptures. This two-fold operation, however, is inherent in the Apocalypse in a two-fold degree, and is there of so peculiar a sort as to be no longer the standard of simple piety. On the contrary, many men of piety and mark have been unable to accommodate themselves to the spirit of this Book, whilst the charm of its obscurity, giving promise, oft-times, of other revelations than the Gospel, has attracted impure and visionary minds. Still, every cavilling depreciation, as well as every fanatical misinterpretation, of this Book has for the most part betrayed a decided want—a want of that self-denying modesty which Socrates displayed in his treatment of the obscure writings of Heraclitus, or a want of that purity and integrity which never seek to supplement Christian knowledge through curiosity, secret-mongery and fantastical pictures of sensuous hope.

Thus, therefore, stands the mysterious tree of the Revelation before our eyes, unique of its kind. And yet, notwithstanding its uniqueness, or by reason of it, its roots are connected with great and varied spheres of literature. The Revelation, in respect of its intrinsic, apostolic wealth of light and life, is, as the last of the Biblical Books, intimately connected with them all. In respect of its prophetic and literary form, however, it stands in the centre of an extensive group of eschatological prophecies and apocalyptic writings, having common characteristic traits.

We shall arrive later at the general biblical kindred bearings of the Apocalypse; be it our next task to inquire into the whole phenomenon of Apocalyptics.

§ 2. ORIGIN OF APOCALYPTICS.

The origin of Apocalyptics—*i. e.*, by way of prefatory definition: the sum of those forms of revelation which have reference to an ethico-physical end of the world—is situate as high and as deep as the origin of religion itself.

The most general sphere of Apocalyptics is the religious view of the world; their more definite home, the theocratico-Christian view of the world; the most peculiar region of their origin, however, is prophetic Eschatology.

The general religious view of the world, underlying all the religious systems of the human race, knows of a *world-beginning*, resting upon Divine power and wisdom; of a *world-course*, whose physical side is conditioned upon the moral conduct of mankind (or of the gods even), and placed, by Divine decree, under Divine guidance; hence also of a *world-goal*, whose attainment Divine retribution accomplishes in the form of the *world's end*, on the one hand, and, on the other, of the *world's renewal*.

The *presageful* expectation of the end of the world, within the general sphere of religion, rests, on the one side, upon definite signs of that most general Divine revelation which lies at the basis of all religion (Rom. i. 19, 20); especially upon the religious interpretation of the transientness of earthly things, of the catastrophes of development, of the types of consummation;—reposing, on the other side, upon the human longing after the realization of ideals. But the more perfect a religious system is, the higher is its doctrine—in the form of prophecy—of the last things. This is true, for instance, of the Scandinavian Mythology.*

Purer in fashion, however, appears the expectation of a world-goal in that *believing* view of the world which is grounded upon the revelation of salvation; grounded first, in an imperfect shape, upon the basis of the Old Testamental, theocratic form of said revelation.

Yet in the Old Testament, the following premises are definitely declared:

1. The human world is, in respect of its plan [*Anlage*], a unitous humanity, and as it has a unitous foundation, so likewise it possesses a unitous destination to the Kingdom of God, and a unitous goal in a Congregation or City of God, which is to appear at the end of its development, being mediated by great moral conflicts and Divine judgments.

---

* Lücken, *Die Traditionen des Menschengeschlechts.* Münster, 1856, p. 376 sqq.

2. The whole physical sphere of humanity is engaged in a development unto perfection, which is entirely conditioned upon the ethical development of humanity.

3. This development is subject to the ideal plan of the Divine counsel and to the real supremacy of Divine guidance.

4. It is effectuated, however, not in accordance with laws of physical necessity, but in accordance with the ethical law of a reciprocity of action between the wisdom of God and the freedom of man; amid a preponderance of Divine governance, however, which makes even the contradictions of erring human wisdom minister to the eschatological world-plan.

5. The method of the Divine government of the world consists in its perfect ethical conditionality. Hence, the new *periods* of development are conditioned upon new *epochs;* instants of deliverance upon instants of judgment; the appearance of the world-goal upon the principle of the world-goal; the redemption upon the coming of the Messiah. Hence is evident the magnitude of the error of those who pretend to know of epochs without mediatory periods, or vice versâ;—of judgments without deliverances, or, finally, of the first coming of Christ without His second coming, or, like all Chiliasts,* of His second coming without the full *truth* and *reality* of the first.

6. The Old Testament has indeed with justice been denominated the religion of the future. Nevertheless, its prophecy and its longing, repose, for the most part, only in the expectation of the principial† Messianic Kingdom and the Messianic personality; but the universal renewal of the world which is bound up with this principle, emerges but in rarer and obscurer forms, although in respect of the idea, it is present in sufficient plainness.

With Christianity, this view of the world is perfected. Here mankind appears entirely as *a something that is in process of becoming*, which, in its maturity, shall know but *one* division—that, namely, into kernel and husk, wheat and chaff,—to the end that in its kernel it may glorify God as a perfected Church of God. Earth itself, with all its life-forms, is in an eminent sense a star of *becoming* [*i. e.*, growth, development], pointing off and up to stars of perfection and destined itself to become a star of perfection. Here [in Christianity] the human cosmos in its development is entirely conditioned upon the development of mankind; the development of mankind upon the development of the Kingdom of God; this latter upon the development of the sovereignty of Christ, from His first appearance in lowliness to His second appearing in glory. This entire movement, with its epochs and periods, ensues in accordance with the counsel, and under the guidance, of God. The first particular, therefore in which the New Testament is distinguished from the Old, is that the latter is pre-eminently the religion of the future, that the Theocracy gravitates outward toward the future point of the appearance of Christ and His Kingdom, whilst the New Testament is the religion of appeasement, in which believing humanity, in its glorified Redeemer, in its inner life, in the Holy Ghost, has already principially attained the goal of the world and thus already stands, internally, in the New Æon of perfection, existing meanwhile, in respect of its outward life, still in the Old Æon. Hence it is also that the Old Testament consists, in great measure, of prophetic books, while the New Testament has but *one* prophetic book. But even on New Testament ground, the religious yearning after perfection is not yet fully satisfied (Rom. viii. 19 sqq.). For to the perfect truth of life, the full reality of life appertains; this reality, however, must have passed beyond the painful contradiction between the internal and the external life, the internal and the external world, having become a reality in which the whole outward appearance is translumined by the life of the spirit. Therefore, also, does the individual Christian, together with all believing Christendom, long for the consummation; and all the objective and subjective goals of longing are summed up in the one aspiration with which the Apocalypse closes: Come, Lord Jesus. To this longing, and to it alone, is the Apocalyptic Revelation given.

The religious longing of humanity, awakened by the Spirit of God, has in general ever

---

* [It is difficult to conceive of the mode in which this imputation could be justified. Some Chiliasts may have held the opinion here attributed to them, but, most certainly, not *all;* nor is there any thing in the essential doctrines of Chiliasm to make this a necessary part of the system.—E. R. C.]

† [*Prinzipiell*—so far as principle is concerned.—Tr.]

been the human instrumentality of Divine revelation, of the self-communication of God in the prophetic contemplation of chosen men of God. The faithful of the primitive time addressed themselves, with their longing, to the obscurity of their own origin and the origin of all things; therefore the Spirit of God gave them a sufficient explanation concerning the Creator, the creation, the production and destination of man. But when this destination, in consequence of the fall, seemed utterly obscured and lost, the longing of the friends of God addressed itself entirely to the coming of salvation, and the Spirit of God gave them the promise of salvation in ever clearer traits: Victory over the Foe; rest from toil; blessing lifting above the curse; redemption from bondage. So soon, however, as a religious people had been converted into the typical people of the expectation and mediation of salvation, the longing directed itself to the Divine clearing up of the dark paths of the present, destined to be trod by men. This longing, likewise, did the Spirit of God answer, by giving the Law unto Moses. But the Law of the *Present*, in its outward figurativeness, was designed to kindle into flame the longing after the *Future* [*Zukunft*=future *and* coming] of the internal, essential Kingdom of God; and thus the longing of the Prophets, in the narrower sense of the latter term, took form, and the precursory appeasement of that longing was the Spirit of prophecy of and concerning Christ. As the fulfillment of prophecy lingered, however, all expectation of salvation was transformed into prayer, until the longing after salvation embodied itself, so to speak, in womanly receptivity. But as the mother of Jesus longed, with those about her, for the first coming of the Saviour, so, toward the end of the apostolic age, amid increasing signs of the great warfare of Antichristian powers against the Church of Christ, John longs for the second coming of his Friend. The Apostles, for the most part, had long since gone home to the Lord; the old friend of the Lord must wait so long in this world—under the act of persecution, wait as an exile on the rocky island—until at last was concentrated in him all the longing of the New Testament Church after Christ's coming; his yearning blazed up on the Lord's day, and thus the great prophetic disclosure concerning the coming of the Lord was apportioned to him.

Upon the basis of the general revelation of God through the creation and the conscience, arises the theocratic Christian revelation of salvation. This, in general, prophetic revelation begets again a revelation in the narrower sense of the term, viz., the prophetic disclosures concerning the future—the future of the Old and the New Covenant. Yet once more, however, within the prophetic Eschatology, there appears an entirely new, conclusive form of the Divine disclosures, and this form, the acme of all revelation, we call simply: Revelation, Apocalypse, because it is *the* revelation in the most eminent sense.

An unveiling of the future so vivid, that to the distempered vision of the reader it ofttimes became a new veiling.

§ 3. THE PECULIAR CONFORMATION OF APOCALYPTICS, IN THEIR DISTINCTION FROM THE GENERAL FORM OF PROPHECY.

The name Apocalyptics, in its peculiar signification, first took its place in Theology with the perception that the New Testament Apocalypse belongs to an entire group of writings, partly canonical, partly uncanonical, all of which, by peculiar marks in respect of purport and form, are recognizable as a separate species of prophetic or pseudo-prophetic literature, being distinct from every other species of sacred writings, even though they do not all appear under the name of Apocalypses.*

The name *Apocalypse* (ἀποκάλυψις) *disclosure, revelation,* has primarily a more general meaning. The verb, like the noun, denotes in general every *new* revelation of God, coming from Heaven, through the Spirit of God, either to the individual man or to the human race,—

---

* The newness of Apocalyptics as a branch of exegetical theology is evidenced by the fact that there is no article under that head either in Herzog's *Real-Encyklopædie* or in Schenkel's *Bibellexikon.* Hilgenfeld seems still to entertain the opinion that in the upbuilding of a system of Apocalyptics it is necessary to confound the canonical with the uncanonical forms of that species of writing (Introduction, p. 5). He says, p. 8, in his note: "What an unreasonable requisition upon science, to insist at the outset upon this hair-splitting separation betwixt canonical and uncanonical matter!" A requisition upon science that she should not, with a radicalism void of all spiritual taste, make a literary *Thohu Vabhohu* of the whole mass of scientific acquisitions, is surely well-founded, however. We have to do here simply with a peculiar kind of religious theocratic composition.

and that in respect both of the purport and form of such revelation; pre-eminently, however, in respect of its purport.

But now a two-fold distinction comes into view. In regard to purport, we have to distinguish the Apocalypse, as the primary form of revelation, communicated by God to the beholding or believing human spirit, or appearing in and by it (Rom. ii. 5; viii. 19; Gal. i. 12), from its secondary form, the revealing or publishing of the revelation (φανέρωσις, John ii. 11; 1 Cor. xii. 7). This material distinction, again, is connected with the formal distinction, in accordance with which the Apocalypse, in its primary forms of ideal *manifestation* or vision, is consummated, supplemented, by real manifestations or miraculous facts, whilst the secondary form as, in the first place, a development of principial points of revelation, finds its continuation in prophetic inspirations.

Every Prophet is called to be ■ Prophet by a fundamental Apocalypse which "rends" the heavens above him, developing itself subsequently in most manifold inspirations. These inspirations are, in the Prophet's own bosom, already revelations, (φανερώσεις); it is his province in his preaching to convert them into prophetic announcements for his cotemporaries, for the world.

But, once more, we have to distinguish the Apocalypse as a Divine fact, from its product, the Apocalypse as a human composition. The apocalyptic writing bears its specific name— which distinguishes it from all writings which are prophetic in a more general sense only— in accordance with a distinction which might at first sight be designated as conventional but which, upon closer inspection, is found to rest upon very decided distinctive marks.

The first mark respects *form*. The prophetic writings, in a more general sense, are collections of single prophecies, disposed with more or less order in regard to subject-matter, —in a word, anthologies; and their symbolic expression is transrupted by didactical sermons and exhortations [*Paränesen, παραινέσεις*]. In them, moreover, the source-points of the vision and the moral applications of the same, together with historical elucidations even, branch out very distinctly. An Apocalypse, on the contrary, is, on the one hand, the presentation of an uninterrupted succession of visions, following one upon another in cyclical divisions; on the other hand, a thoroughly unitous composition, a sacred work of art, whose style is, accordingly, altogether figurative or typical, even though it be based upon historical data; these historical data themselves attain a symbolical significance. The typical forms cease, however, to be purely individual [proper only to the person employing them— E. R. C.]; they assume the character of an historically conventional fixedness, *i. e.*, a theocratic science.

The second mark respects the *purport*. The prophetic anthologies proceed in the main, from the *present* onward, through a fragmentary series of Messianic pictures, to the Advent of the Messiah, and if they do advance beyond His simple appearance and sketch the fullness of the times in eschatological traits, those traits are nevertheless exceedingly few and far between. For the most part, the second coming of the Messiah coincides for them with His first coming, and the great gulf between the two becomes manifest only from particular features of the suffering Messiah, particular intimations of the "travail of the Messiah." On the other hand, the Apocalypses are eschatological from beginning to end. Not only the contrast between the suffering and glorified Christ, but also that between His first and second appearing, hence likewise that between Christ and Antichrist, nay, the contrast between the old and the new world, and consequently *the end of the world itself*, emerge boldly. In fact, the end of the world, or the course of the world, in its gravitation toward the end, forms the object upon which their gaze is concentrated — constitutes their peculiar point of view. This point of view they mediate, however, by a history of the world, eschatological in its modifications. The entire history of the world from the olden times, or from the first appearance of Christ, is in them unfolded in eschatological cycles, in which the entire course of the world is continually presented from different points of view—the cycles meantime progressing steadily toward the end. This type is, at all events, quite distinctly impressed upon the Apocalypse [of John]; and Hilgenfeld's denial of the fact is based upon a hampered rationalistic view of the narrow scope of this Scripture. It is, on the contrary, remarkable that the idea of a *universal history*—whose germ was contained in Genesis—here appears in full development, though in Hebrew theocratic form, whilst classical historiography was unable to attain to this universalism. We find later, in the Gnostics, a striving after a universal view of the world which should set at nought the barriers of history and of our earth—but which did not succeed in passing beyond fanciful and heretical forms.

With this latter mark, the third mark of the Apocalypses is connected. Originating, as they did, in the Divine pacification and consolation of elect prophetic hearts, whose ardent longing blazes brightly in times of great tribulation in the Kingdom of God, they are in like manner designed to instruct, to comfort, and to pacify, first the servants of God, and through them, the churches in times of *future* new and similar tribulations; nay, to transmute all signs of terror into signs of hope and promise: whilst the aim of ordinary Prophecies consists pre-eminently in the satisfaction of the needs of the *present* in regard to enlightenment, discipline, consolation, and exhortation. These latter are writings concerning the *future*, for the *present;* the others are writings which, passing over the *present*, are intended pre-eminently for the *future*. This fact is quite one-sidedly presented by Hilgenfeld: "They were meant to fill up the times when there was no revelation with substitutes of prophecy." The connecting link between Malachi and Christ was formed by the popular piety, longing, and hope of the true Israel, and not by pseudo-apocalyptic reveries.*

In proceeding to distinguish between genuine and spurious Apocalypses, we may put forth the general statement that the former contain a solution of the problem as to how the highest visions may be united to the highest forms of sacred art; the latter are at best poetic imitations, which, for visions, substitute compilations and extravagant fancies, and replace the theocratico-classical and mysterious artistic form with a manufactured and mystical *chiar' oscuro.*

§ 4. CLASSES OF APOCALYPTICAL WRITINGS.

Particulars concerning the development of Apocalyptics in general may be found in Lücke's work, the most prominent treatise on the subject: *Versuch einer vollständigen Einleitung in die Offenbarung des Johannes*, Bonn, 1848-52, p. 9-15. One of the first impulses to the Science of Apocalyptics was given in 1819, by the English Bishop Laurence, with his edition of Apocalyptic writings from the Ethiopian (Anabaticon of Isaiah; 4th Book of Esdras†);

---

* [The following remarks by Auberlen (Daniel and the Revelation, Eng. Trans. Edinburgh, 1856, p. 80) are worthy of highest consideration: "The name Apocalyptic (in the use of which we are justified by Rev. i. 1), already signifies that the divine communication and revelation are more prominent in the prophet than the human mediation and receptivity; for ἀποκάλυψις (revelation) signifies a divine,—προφητεία (prophecy, *Weissagung*) a human activity. Comp. Dan. ii. 22, 23, where it is said of God, that ' He revealeth (αὐτος ἀποκαλύπτει LXX.) the deep and secret things ; He knoweth what is in the darkness, and the light dwelleth with Him ;' and Rev. i. 1, 2, where the supernatural fact is three-fold. God gave the revelation to Jesus Christ, and He, through His angels, signified it to John for the purpose of further spreading it. All biblical prophecy, of course, is based on divine revelation, so that these two words designate, the one the subjective, the other the objective side of the same thing (see 1 Cor. xiv. 29, 30), and are sometimes used indiscriminately, as when John calls his Apocalypse, which is styled ' the revelation of Jesus Christ ' (Rev. i. 1), ' the words of this prophecy ' (Rev. i. 3). For this reason, however, a distinction is likewise made between the two expressions, and they are used as two distinct species of the same genus, according as the objective revelation, or the subjective prophetic inspiration, is more prominent. Thus St. Paul distinguishes them in 1 Cor. xiv. 6, ' either by revelation or by prophecy.' The prophet stands in connection with the outer world. He addresses words to the prince and the people, as in the Old Testament, to the congregation [Church], as in the New, words with which the Spirit of God, pervading the human spirit with His mighty influence, supplies him. But while the prophet *speaks* in the Spirit (comp. 1 Cor. xii. 3, ἐν πνεύματι Θεοῦ λαλῶν), the apocalyptic seer *is in* the Spirit, in his whole person (Rev. i. 10; iv. 2). The united activity of soul and body, which forms the link between man and the outward world, recedes altogether into the background, so that St. Paul, speaking of such a state from his own experience, can say he does not know whether he was in the body, or out of the body (2 Cor. xii. 2, 3). It is the spirit only, that which connects us with God and the invisible world, which is active, or rather recipient, in the apocalyptic state; for all proper human activity towards God can consist only in receiving. Here, where the object is not so much to influence the immediate contemporaries of the seer, as that the seer may receive disclosures for the benefit of all succeeding generations, he is alone with God while He reveals Himself, and perceives only what is disclosed to him from above, so the veil which hides the invisible world is drawn from off his spirit (ἀπο-καλύπτειν). ' The heavens were opened,' says Ezekiel (i. 1), ' and I saw visions of God.' This state is therefore called a trance," etc —E. R. C.]

† ["The classification of the four books which have been named after Ezra is particularly complicated. In the Vatican and other quasi-modern editions of the LXX., our (Eng. Apoc.) 1st Esdras is called the *first* book of Esdras, in relation to the Canonical book of Ezra, which follows it, and is called the *second* Esdras. But in the Vulgate, 1st Esdr. means the

this, indeed, was after Semler had availed himself of such Apocryphal apocalypses as were known to him in interpretation of the Revelation of St. John, being followed by Conradi, and, shortly after, by Eichhorn and Bleek; see Hilgenfeld, p. 4. Subsequent to Bishop Lawrence's work, Nitzsch, in the year 1820, sketched the idea of Apocalyptics. Lücke was spurred on in his task by the "report" of Nitzsch (1st edition, 1832). In 1833, A. C. Hofmann published a translation and exegesis of the Book of Enoch, with which he united a treatise upon the Apocalyptists of the olden time amongst the Jews and Christians, assuming the existence of a coherent whole, composed of apocalyptic literature, and commencing with the Book of Daniel. Quite a series of commentaries, from Ewald's commentary on the Apocalypse, down to the present time, have promoted the general views upon this subject (see Lücke, p. 14). The following work by Hilgenfeld especially belongs here: *Die jüdische Apokalyptik in ihrer geschichtlichen Entwicklung* [Jewish Apocalyptics in their historical development], Jena, 1857. In accordance with the main features of the two main Apocalypses of the Old and New Testaments, Auberlen, with his Daniel and the Apocalypse, Basel, 1857, likewise claims a place here. [English Translation, Edinburgh, 1856, a work of rare merit. —E. R. C.] In a more general sense, we mention here the Biblical Theologies, the Introductions to the New Testament, the books upon Eschatology and Chiliasm (particularly Conradi, *Kritische Geschichte des Chiliasmus* [Critical History of Chiliasm], II., p. 365; comp. 231, in the same vol.; III., 1, 60, 107). Note especially, however, the more or less comprehensive editions of Apocalyptic writings. Lücke dates the more distinct collections of apocryphal Apocalyptic writings from Gfrörer's *Prophetæ veteres pseudepigraphi*, 1840; although this publication did not contain Apocalyptic matter simply (the more ancient collections of Fabricius and Philo were not formed from the point of view which assumed the existence of a general system of Apocalyptics). Subsequently Tischendorf issued: *Apocalypses Apocryphæ Mosis, Esdræ, Pauli, Johannis, item Mariæ Dormitio*, Leipzig, 1866. Particular Apocalypses were discussed by Lawrence (see above), Nitzsch (*De testamentis* 12 *patriarch.*, Wittenberg 1810), Gieseler (*Vetus translatio latina Visionis Jesaiæ*, Göttingen, 1832), Hofmann (*Das Buch Henoch*, see above), Friedlieb (*Die Sibyllinischen Weissagungen* [The Sibylline Prophecies], Leipzig, 1852), Dillmann (*Das Buch Henoch*, 1853), Philippi (*Das Buch Henoch, sein Zeitalter und sein Verhältniss zum Judasbriefe* [The Book of Enoch, the time of its composition and its relation to the Epistle of Jude], Stuttgart, 1868; a monograph of sterling merit), Volkmar (*Das 4 Buch Esra* [second division of the Hand-Book of the Introduction to the Apocrypha], Tübingen, 1863), *et al.*

If it is with truth that we have designated the religion of Israel as the religion of the future, we may be permitted to designate Apocalyptics in particular as the vision of the future; partly as the actual prophecy, partly as the popular poetry of the future. Relatively, this applies again to the eschatological longing and hope of the New Testament faith, but particularly to the chiliastic-morbid Jewish-christian expectance of the future, in accordance with a condition of mind which looked for redemption more in the future Appearing of Christ than in the principial base-laying salvation of His first Advent.

The apocalyptical writings which have sprung up bearing these signs, are divided into the following classes:

    a. Old Testament canonical Apocalypses;
    b. Old Testament apocryphal Apocalypses;
    c. The New Testament Apocalypse;
    d. Jewish-Christian apocryphal Apocalypses.

a. Old Testament Canonical Apocalypses.

We have elsewhere (Comm. on Genesis, p. 36 [Am. Ed.] already stated that for the appearance of the apocalyptic form we go back far beyond Daniel. And this we do in accordance with the two principal marks of an apocalyptic writing; the formal mark—unity of

---

canonical Book of Ezra, and 2d Esdr. means *Nehemiah*, according to the primitive Hebrew arrangement, mentioned by Jerome, in which *Ezra* and *Nehemiah* make up two parts of the one book of Ezra; and 3d and 4th Esdr. are what we now call 1 and 2 Esdras."—SMITH'S BIB. DICT. TIT. ESDRAS.—E. R. C.]

composition; and the material mark—the expectation of an eschatological judgment, passing beyond simple Messianism (first Advent); an expectation in accordance with which we might regard the whole non-Christian Jewish people, in its eschatological expectancy, as a permanent, plastic appearance or embodiment of apocryphal Apocalyptics.

With respect to the Old Testament Books—composed, as they are, in accordance with a unitous idea, organically membered, and closing, consequently, with themselves—the phenomenon of the ideal, unitous, organic structure of the Books goes back far behind the first Old Testament apocalypses, to the beginning of Old Testament literature; and when criticism, whose existence is demanded by the very spirit of revelation, shall have outgrown its boyhood, in which, in slavish dependence upon the new, it gives chase, with slackened rein, to the newest, the fact will doubtless be recognized that—with the exception of redactions of original memorabilia—men have done the reverend Scriptures great wrong by this endless untwisting and patching together of the Biblical Books, on the hypothesis of the most spiritless book-making. One composition, at least, it is impossible to misjudge as a whole, even though it may receive damage in particulars—and that is the grand old Book of Job.

In the introduction to the Comm. on Genesis (see above) we have given our reasons for distinguishing an entire group of Old Testament Apocalypses, although not until Daniel does the species appear with features fully stamped.* The second part of Isaiah [ch. xl.—lxvi.] is a unitous composition, having its point of gravitation, manifestly, in the eschatological world-consummation—i. e., it has the sign of the Apocalypse. This is true no less of the appendix to the Prophecies of Jeremiah (chap. xlv.—lii.). The apocalyptic conclusion of Ezekiel (chap. xxxvii.—xlviii.), the whole Book of Zechariah in its indissoluble unity, and particularly the Book of Daniel—with the exception of the sections from chap. x. 1—xi. 45, and xii. 5-13, (see Comm. on Genesis, p. 38, Am. Ed.)—present, in form and purport, the Old Testament eschatological elements which in the original visions of the New Testament Apocalypse have arrived at their perfect significancy and configuration. "Among the minor Prophets we regard the Books of Obadiah, Nahum, Habakkuk and Zephaniah as Apocalypses, predominantly depicting, in unitous composition, the judgment upon Antichristianity in its symbolical preludes." (Genesis, p. 37. [Am. Ed.]).

b. Jewish Apocryphal Apocalyptics.

Hilgenfeld (*Vorwort* VIII.) is doubtless in error in viewing the whole Apocalyptics of Judaism as *a precursory history of Christianity*, and in believing that he has found in Essenism an offshoot of Jewish Apocalyptics which conducts us directly to the threshold of Christianity. This idea, which will allow of no distinction whatever between the theocratic and churchly main current and those turbid secondary streams which have their rise in the popular fancy, is based upon the ruling impulse of that school which pseudo-critically jumbles together all things in whose disposition a critical arrangement is to be found;—the same school which regards the Gnostics as presenting a peculiar stage in the development of true Christianity, and zealously labors against the distinction between canonical and apocryphal writings as a hereditary evil of Theology itself. Such confusions, growing out of a special tendency, are rarely to be met with to the same degree in any other department of science. Philology, for instance, is careful to avoid mingling together, without distinction, nay, with a fanatical levelling impulse, ancient classics and obsolete popular literature, to the production of endless trouble and great confusion.

Jewish apocryphal Apocalyptics have produced two writings which, in common, have a Jewish character—especially in their imitation of Daniel—and yet stand in decided contrast one to the other. The Jewish stock of the Sibylline books, interpolated and supplemented by Christians, namely the third book of Esdras,† has, like the book of the Wisdom of Solomon, an Alexandrian ground-tone; whilst on the other hand, the fourth book of Esdras, in its Hebrew-Pharisaic character, reminds us quite unmistakably of the book of Jesus Sirach. They possess in common the fundamental idea of the future victory of Judaism over the Gentile

---

* [Does not the prophecy of Balaam (Num. xxiv.) possess all the characteristics of the true Apocalypse?—E. R. C.]
† See Bleek, Hilgenfeld, Friedlieb.

world-kingdoms. This fundamental idea can be attributed to the Book of Daniel itself only by a false religious taste; in that prophecy it is not the restoration of the Theocracy, but an entirely new Heavenly Kingdom of the Son of Man which puts an end to the kingdoms of the world. In both writings (3 and 4 Esdras) the dwindling away of the expectation of a personal Messiah is unmistakable (see Hilgenfeld, p. 77, 78, 86, 221 sqq.; Volkmar, *Esra*, 260).

On the other hand, there is a distinction between the two books which accords with the contrast between the Hebrew-Jewish and the Alexandrian-Jewish character; in the fourth book of Esdras, the Pharisaic hatred of the heathen is unmistakably prominent—for instance, in the joy of the blessed at the spectacle of the wicked burning in everlasting flames (Hilgenfeld, p. 201)—; whilst the Sibyl is continually warning the heathen against the service of false gods, and finally anticipates the general instruction of the Gentiles and their conversion to Monotheism (Hilgenfeld, 87, 88). They are distinguished furthermore in that the Hebrew Messiah stands back of the Messianic upliftment of the nation above the Roman world-power, appearing only at the end of the world for judgment especially (Hilgenfeld, 220), while the Alexandrian Messiah is endowed with scarcely any distinctness of form.

Another distinctive mark is, that the Sibyl is glorified as prophecy come to the heathen from the theocratic source;—prophecy whose final aim, like that of Sophia [or Wisdom personified] in the Wisdom of Solomon, is the eschatological renewal of the world: while the Messianism of the fourth book of Esdras, as also of the book of Jesus Sirach, culminates in a growth of books or writings (Sirach xxiv. 23; 4 Esdras at the close: Esdras' 94 books [the English Version of the Apocrypha gives 204 (or nine hundred and four *Marg.*) as the number of the books that were written, 2.(4) Esdr. xiv. 44]; 24 open, 70 secret writings).

Neither is the contrast in the *form* of the prophecy to be overlooked. The Alexandrian Sibyl prophesies from an irresistible impulse, in *pathological* ecstasy (Hilgenfeld, 51), whilst the visions vouchsafed to Esdras are mediated by *ethical* conduct, fasting and praying, and thus their revelations can assume a conversational form.

According to Friedlieb, the Jewish Sibylline books came into being from the years 160 to 40 B.C. (according to Bleek, an older portion is cotemporary with the Book of Daniel (?), a later part having been produced, he thinks, about 40 B.C.). The time of the Jewish ground-form of the fourth book of Esdras is differently estimated by different exegetes. This disagreement of exegesis is based upon the interpretation of the exceedingly obscure vision of the eagle (dream-vision of the second night). Lawrence interpreted the twelve wings of the eagle as referring to the ancient history of the line of Roman kings and the more modern additions to it; Gfrörer conceived the wings to refer to twelve Roman emperors and associate-emperors [*Nebenkaiser*]. Lücke interpreted the eagle's three heads as significant of Sylla, Pompey, and Cæsar, as an arbitrarily conceived, successive triumvirate. Least tenable is the view of Hilgenfeld, who seeks to construe the Apocalypse of Esdras into a continuation of the Sibyl, without recognizing the contrast which it presents to the latter; declaring the eagle's twelve wings to be Alexander and the Egyptian kings who succeeded him. According to Volkmar (*Das vierte Buch Esra*, p. 338), the Jewish author wrote his Apocalypse in the autumn of the year 97, after the fall of Domitian. Contrary to this view is the fact that the second destruction of the Temple, in the year 70, is not mentioned in the book; Volkmar conceives it to be, "by way of disguise," "parallelized" with the first destruction, i. e., represented by, and along with, the first. Since the eagle, i. e., the Roman world-kingdom, comes to its end by a lion, i. e., the Jewish Messianic Theocracy, we can think, in interpreting this vision, of no time save that of the first Jewish insurrection previous to the destruction of Jerusalem, or that of the insurrection under Bar-Cocheba. But since, moreover, the destruction of Jerusalem is itself not mentioned, we are constrained to interpret the vision (whose obscurity is perhaps owing to the circumstances of the period) as referring to the first Jewish war. The first three feathers of the eagle are intelligible enough (Hilgenfeld, 205): Cæsar, Augustus, Tiberius. The following nine feathers are very dimly pictured; they denote imperial pretenders rather than actual emperors. The number twelve, consequently, is more a symbolico-ideal number than one to be historically identified and referred. Only a few of the mock emperors, like Galba and Otho, momentarily attain dominion. The greatest of the three heads of the eagle, which now awakes, makes an end of the feathers, takes the two other heads along with it, and shakes the whole earth; but suddenly disappears. Finally, the head on the right side devours that on the left, and is left alone until the roaring lion makes an end of it. Now, if this head on the right side were Jerusalem's great enemy, Vespasian, and the head devoured by it, Vitellius, we might go back for an interpretation of the middle head, which suddenly disappeared after shaking the whole earth, to Nero. In consideration of the dim and confused execution of the picture, the effort to interpret all the figures into a harmonious system is less requisite than inquiry into the spirit of the production as a whole; this is thoroughly consonant with the rancorous spirit of the pseudo-Messianic Jewish revolution. Ewald, after Conradi, has already set forth about the same view (see Hilgenfeld, p. 392, *note*).

In regard to the Book of Enoch, received by Hilgenfeld among the Jewish Apocalypses, we hold the argument of Philippi, who vindicates the original Christian character of the book, to be decisive.

On the other hand, the *Ascension of Moses* seems to form a supplement to the fourth book of Esdras, originating after the destruction of Jerusalem, for the uplifting of prostrate Judaism.*

c. The Apocalypse of John.

As the Book of Daniel became a pattern for the apocryphal Apocalypses of Judaism, so the Apocalypse of John has been the exemplar for all Christian Apocalypses. But upon the side of Christianity also, nothing but a lack of spiritual taste, *i. e.*, an unspiritual taste, can fail to recognize the distinction between canonical mysteries and apocryphal riddles, between a grandeur of forms in which order prevails, and an extravagance of forms over which confusion reigns.

d. The Christian (Jewish-Christian) Apocryphal Apocalypses.

These arrange themselves primarily into two leading classes: 1. Christianized: 2. Originally Christian Apocalypses.

As Christianized Apocalypses we may name the previously mentioned Jewish Apocrypha, the Sibylline books, and the Book of Esdras. Bleek, *Ueber die sibyllinischen Orakel. Theol. Zeitschrift von Schleiermacher.* De Wette und Lücke, Vol. I. 20; II. 172 sqq. Friedlieb, *Die sibyllinischen Weissagungen,* and Hilgenfeld, *Die jüdische Apokalyptik.*

Amongst the Jewish-Christian Apocrypha which are imitative of the Apocalypse, the principal composition is the Book of Enoch—an Ebionite Jewish-Christian production—for an examination of which the reader is referred to Philippi's work.

As the tissue of apocryphal, and, in many respects, heretical, fable has woven itself about the whole line of the most distinguished Biblical names and writings, so it is in especial with the bungling compositions of apocryphal authors. Most of them have issued forth from obscurity only to become again the prey of obscurity. We follow, in naming them, the Biblical thread:

1. Apocalypse of Adam (Lücke, p. 232).
2. The Book of Enoch, see above.
3. Apocalypse of Abraham. Ophitic. Lücke, 252.
4. Testaments of the Twelve Patriarchs, see above.
5. Book of Elias, *Hieronym. ad Sammachium, Ep.* 101.
6. Book of Esdras, (Christianized, see above).
7. *Ascensio Isaiæ Vatic.* (see Gfrörer, *Prophetæ Veteres Pseudepigraphi,* p. 1).
8. *Danielis,* Tischend., *Apocalypses* XXX.
9. *Apocalypsis Baruch (edidit Ceriani, Monumenta sacra, Mediolani,* 1866, see *Programm* of Dr. Joseph Langen, Bonn, 1867).

---

* A fragment of this lost book has recently been found. See Langen, *Das Judenthum in Palästina zur Zeit Christi* (Bonn, 1866, p. 2).

10. Apocalypse of Peter (Lücke, p. 240).

11. Two Apocalypses of Paul, see Tischendorf, p. XIV. (*Apocalypses Apocryphæ*). On one of these, see Tischendorf, p. 34.

12. Apocalypse of a Pseudo-John, Tischend., *Apocal.* XVIII.

13. Of Bartholomew (Tischendorf, *Apocalypses*, XXIV.).

14. Of Mary (Tischendorf, XXVII).

15. Of Stephen (Lücke, p. 247).

To these may be added some miserable works whose web extends over the post-apostolic period or falls within it. Relatively, *The Shepherd* of Hermas. The account of an Apocalypse of Cerinthus is dubious (Lücke, 247). Finally, an Apocalypse under the name of Methodius of Constantinople.

Later or more modern apocalyptic productions have scarcely any significance bearing upon the characteristics of ancient apocryphal Apocalyptics, which (according to Lücke) became extinct in the fifth century. In Gfrörer's collection the following are cited: *Vita Merlini. Galfridi Liber de Prophetiis Merlini. Fratris Hermanni Monachi Vaticinium. Prophetia Malachiæ de Summis Pontificibus.* Apocalyptic traits, however, are also visible in manifold form in the chiliastic writings generally.

§ 5. FIGURATIVE FORM OF APOCALYPTICS.

The Holy Scriptures are, throughout, a record of the Providence of God, as exercised in the establishment of His Kingdom; hence they are themselves overruled by His Spirit. From beginning to end, they rest upon the synthesis of the living word, mighty in deed, and the spiritually significant, speaking fact. Consequently they are acquainted, on the one hand, with no idle words; on the other hand, with no silent facts. From beginning to end, they set forth the Divine in the human, the spiritual in the sensible, the eternal in the temporal, the infinite in the finite, *i. e.*, they deal throughout in sense-imagery—being thus symbolical in the broader sense of the term.

This is true even of the historical portion of the Sacred Writings. The ideas which are reflected in the histories have re-acted upon the symbolism and mode of expression of the facts recounted. And thus Biblical history, by virtue of its matter-of-fact foundations, is distinguished from all heathen mythicism; by virtue of the ideal transparency or significancy of its facts, from all the pragmatism* of profane historiography. Whilst the latter circles for the most part between secondary causes and proximate designs, Biblical historiography has in view the supreme causes and supreme designs, and hence recognizes the media between cause and design—secondary causes and secondary designs—so far as it mentions them at all, in their universal significance; none the less in the light of Supreme Providence.

This same character of the Holy Scriptures occasions in the didactic writings the sententious form; in the poetic writings in particular, the wealth of figurative expression and the significance of the composition; its most powerful appearance, however, is in the prophetic writings. Here it converts historical items into symbols of the idea (for instance, *the king of Babylon*), and ideas into historical forms (*grass-eating lions*); as a consequence, it shuts up revelation from all common sensuous apprehension of it—for instance, for the mass of the later Jews—whilst it sets it in the brightest light for the disciples of the truth; a fact which holds true in regard to the parables of the Lord, according to Matthew xiii. 13.

The simple sense-image, however, in accordance with the fullness of life and life's illumination in the Holy Scriptures, branches out into three fundamental forms: ALLEGORISM, SYMBOLISM, and TYPISM.†

ALLEGORISM (*allegory* from ἄλλο ἀγορεύειν, to express something in words intended to

---

* [The German *Pragmatik*, which is here translated *pragmatism*, has the wide sense of the Greek word from which it is derived, and not the one-sided and purely offensive meaning of the English derivatives from πράγμα.—TR.]

† See the author's treatise: *Ueber die Beziehungen, welche zwischen der allgemeinen Symbolik und der kirchlichen Symbolik obwalten. Deutsche Zeitschrift für christliche Wissenschaft*, etc., 1855, Nr. 4–6.

convey a meaning other than their immediate one) is a form of imagery which, *in accordance with the semblance of outward similarity*, employs one phenomenon as the figure of another; imaging, especially, a more spiritual matter by means of a sensible phenomenon. The flowing element of allegory is the simple figurative expression, the *rhetorical metaphor* (the warrior, a *lion;* evil, a *weed*); an allegory is a *poetically* developed metaphor. It denotes its subject by *another which has a similar appearance.**

SYMBOLISM (σύμβολον from συμβάλλειν) unites a sensible image with a spiritual background, which latter is more or less *inwardly and essentially connected with* the phenomenon which furnishes the image. The uniting of the two sundered portions of a pledge of hospitality directly unites the pledge with hospitality itself. In general, however, the symbol is based upon the connection of the sign and that which it signifies; so that thus something moral or spiritual is denoted by something perceptible to the senses (a *scar*, for instance),—the higher by the lower; the combination may either be a conventional one (social connection) or it may be founded upon natural relations. The flowing element of the symbol is metonymy—the change of names; hence, the symbol is a fixed metonymy. It denotes a higher object — one, especially, which addresses itself to the mind—by a lower one, perceptible to the senses, yet akin to the first; in short, symbol may be expressed in one word—*the cognate.*

TYPISM, finally (τύπος, τύπτω), denotes the impression produced by a blow; a carving; a plan, sketch, or outline; consequently, the germ of a future form. It is the commencement-point, situate on the same line of development with the object denoted; a *real* prophecy, which fulfills itself in the future object, being, notwithstanding the ideal identity of essence, distinct from it in the substantial reality—like the shadow from the substance which projects it. The flowing element of the type is most prominent in synecdoche, which embraces not only the whole with a part, but also the fulfilment with the base-laying. The type relates to things ideally the same in essence, and really distinct, though, it may be, symbolically cognate; it denotes a *future* already subsisting germ-wise in the present.

The *allegory* is a *simple* image; the *symbol* is a *sense*-image; the *type* is a *fore*-image. [A *type* is a *symbol* in that it is a *sense*-image, but it is a peculiar kind of symbol;—it is always of the future (a *fore*-image); it is some person, act, or institution introduced by God into the ritual or history of His people, not only as prefiguring the antitype, but as having an ideal identity therewith—as being, in a sense, the representative thereof; as, for instance, the *priest*, the *sacrifice*, of the old economy.—E. R. C.]

It is also necessary, however, to make a distinction between these figures, the hasty coinage of poesy, and complete poetic elaborations of their character. The poetic elaboration of the allegory is the *fable* (for the most part, though not exclusively, that which avails itself of the animal kingdom in setting forth its ideas); the poetic elaboration of the symbol is the *parable*, though the latter may in detail likewise employ allegorical features; the poetic elaboration of the type is *prophecy*, from the formal stand-point (the *paramuthia* [that speech or discourse which encourages, exhorts, consoles—E. R. C.]).

Nearly related as these forms are, manifoldly connected as they may be in the more elevated productions of the mind—in historical, poetical, and prophetic works—the mingling of them is still inadmissible, whether it be in their three ground-forms—allegory, symbol, type—or in their three-fold gradation from element to form, from the simple form to the poetic application.†

Similarly, distinction must be made between the allegorical exegesis (which has ever been an instinctive supplement of the Christian mind to a Hellenistically shallow, grammatico-historical exegesis) and the exegesis of allegorical or allegorico-symbolico-typical writings;

---

* The most modern Natural Science allegorizes *nature* in a high degree, inasmuch as it deals pre-eminently with the outward similarities of created beings, at the expense of inner essential marks.

† It would lead us too far astray from our more immediate subject if we should attempt an exposition of the principle here laid down, together with an examination of extant theories and works upon symbolism—for instance, Bähr's excellent work upon the subject.

just as we distinguish between a poetic representation of the immoral and immoral representations.*

Upon Biblical ground, we have also to distinguish between *verbal*-prophetic and *real*-prophetic types.† We beg leave to designate, as the highest real types, the *mental* or *mood* types,‡ *i. e.*, Divine real prophecies, unconsciously uttered by men. The choice of the expression is of manifold importance here. The prophecy Gen. iii. [15] is significant of the Messianic Humanity [Christ]; the mental type denotes a unit. The same distinction obtains where the seed of Abraham is spoken of. Paul, Gal. iii. 16, has in mind the real mental type which significantly attaches to the Abrahamic promise. Pss. xvi. and xxii. and many other passages come under this head; especially, the virgin, Is. vii. In accordance with the above, mental types frequently constitute the envelope of verbal prophecies, and form the transition from real to verbal prophecy.§

As further regards *allegory* in particular, it is self-evident that the entire realm of evil can be symbolized only by allegorical figures—*i. e.*, figures of outward similarity—the world of nature not being related to evil; not even the creaturely serpent is so related, although it is the reflection of an extinct and ruder world-form ("in caverns dwells the dragons' ancient brood").

As, therefore, *allegorism* was requisite in the system of Sacred Writings, so, too, *symbolism* was necessary, since faith perceives in the visible world the phenomena of a higher and invisible one.

No less requisite, finally, was the *typical* presentation, as the Holy Scriptures of the Old Testament form the documentary evidences of a religion of the *future*, and in the New Testament also, the sacred writers pass from picturing the joy and satisfaction of the faithful in the Christ appearing in the form of a servant, and for the accomplishment of the work of redemption, to a longing for His glorious second appearance, and to the prophetic predescription of the same.

With all its figurativeness, however, Holy Scripture is far removed from a poetic fixation of images, which might degenerate into a spiritual image worship; the commandment, Thou shalt not make unto thee any image, is borne in mind throughout. For this holy word, characterized by Kant as sublime, excludes, not plastic and painted images simply, but also images of the fancy, mental figures and likenesses, insomuch as these, by an erroneous or servile fixation of ideas and attributes, might seem to render finite the Divine. Hence the bold change of imagery (*e. g.*, Ps. xviii.), a circumstance so surprising to a taste formed upon the Greek classics. This absence of fixation makes it possible for the Lion to

---

* A well-known critic of the Tübingen school reproached the author with interpreting the Apocalypse "allegorically." He should have said—interpreting it as an allegorical writing, in accordance with its character. The Tübingen school, which can allegorize the Pauline Epistles, takes a different view of matters in approaching the Apocalypse, and strives to apprehend it literally, thus hoping to make good a charge of Judaizing. Such proceedings are euphemistically denominated —tendency. After a similar fashion, Rothe confounds philosophic dogmatics and dogmatical philosophy.

† [A *real* prophecy, or *real* type, is a prophecy or type embodied in some person, act, event, which shadows forth some other person, act, or event, yet in the future. Thus, in the destruction of Jerusalem, we have a real type of the final destruction of the world. A *verbal* prophecy or *verbal* type, on the other hand, is a prophecy or type set forth in words simply.— E. R. C.]

‡ [*Gemüthstypus, Stimmungstypus. Gemüth* is a collective term for the affections, desires, impulses, will; it corresponds sometimes to soul, sometimes to mind, sometimes to heart. *Stimmung* denotes the disposition or (literally) *tuning* of a man; it may be used in a permanent or a transitory sense. In the latter sense it corresponds to the English *mood*. A *Gemüthstypus* or *Stimmungstypus*, then, is presented when the *inner man* of some individual is so worked upon as to prefigure the state of one who is yet to come. Pss. xvi., xxii. (as above cited) and xli. afford notable instances of the *Gemüthstypus.*—Tr.]

§ [The meaning of Lange in this somewhat obscure paragraph seems to be: The man himself in the mood in which he makes the unconscious (as to its prophetic nature) utterance, together with the utterance itself, constitute the complex type of the antitype in a similar mood, and making similar utterances. Thus, David uttering the 22d Psalm was a type of the suffering Messiah making similar lamentations. In such case the words spoken are not only typical, but verbally prophetic of that which is to be; and "form the transition from real to verbal prophecy."—It must be acknowledged, however, that it is difficult to reconcile this explanation with the references to Gen. iii., xvii., xxv., where the speaker is not an inspired man making utterances, of the prophetic nature and force of which he is unconscious, but Jehovah Himself (see *Comm. on Genesis*, p. 235, Am. Ed.).—E. R. C.]

denote Satan and also the Redeemer; because of it, a wisdom like that of the serpent can be recommended to the disciples; leaven can denote at once that which is worst (Matt. xvi. 6), and that which is most noble (Matt. xiii. 33); and the Christian sage can be represented under the figure of the unjust steward [Luke xvi.]. [Is it true that, in the parable referred to, the Christian sage is represented under the figure of the unjust steward? Is it not the fact that, from an example of worldly wisdom, our Lord would deduce instruction for His un-wise disciples?—E. R. C.]

It is true that the Biblical figures do assume, first in the historical and lyrical Scriptures, but particularly in the Apocalyptic region, a greater conventional fixedness. But this is the case, even here, within certain defined limits. And even here, the term *Beasts* may denote alternately the highest and the most debased (see Rev. iv. and xiii.).*

§ 6. THE FORMAL ELEMENTS OF APOCALYPTICS, OR THEIR SYMBOLICAL FIGURES. APOCALYPTIC SYMBOLISM AND ALLEGORISM.

Literature: Bähr, *Symbolik des mosaischen Kultus,* 2 Vols., Heidelberg, 1837. (A new edition is about appearing. In the Introduction, the history of ancient symbolic literature is discussed).   Nork, *Etymologisch-symbolisch-mythologisches Wörterbuch,* 4 Vols., Stuttgart, 1843–45. [Horne's *Introduction,* Vol. I., p. ii. (on the general subject of interpretation), Appendix, No. II. Fairbairn *On Prophecy,* Edinburgh, 1856. *Typology of Scripture,* by Fairbairn, Edinburgh and Philadelphia, 1859. *Daniel and Revelation,* by Auberlen, Eng. Trans., Edinburgh, 1856. *Theol. and Lit. Journal,* by D. N. Lord, New York, 1848, Articles, pp. 1, 10, and (especially) 177, and throughout the following years. *Premium Essay on Prophetic Symbols,* by Winthrop, New York, 1854.—E R. C.]

Since the Holy Scriptures nowhere concern themselves with school ideas, with anecdotes, with the pragmatism of worldly wisdom or worldly history, but with the life of man, placed, as it is, under the Providence of God as the supreme causality, and related to the final purposes of God, in accordance with the highest laws,—their aim thus being the representation of the infinite in the finite, the spirit-world in the natural world, — they have, on this very account, everywhere a symbolical side, a general symbolical character. The great misapprehension or *un*apprehension of this peculiar character results, on the part of some, in the conception of the matter-of-fact side of the Scriptures as pragmatically literal; on the part of others, in the stamping of their symbolical side as mythicism. The two tendencies are united in the fact of their turning the idiocratic Hebrew charism of revelation into a Græco-Roman one. Of course, the different Books of the Scriptures are symbolical in widely different degrees. As specifically symbolical in the broader sense, we have to consider the Apocalyptic writings.†

a. Symbolism of Numbers.

See the Art. *Zahlen [Numbers]* among the Hebrews, in Herzog's *Real-Encyclopædie.* Also *Zahl [Number]* in the *Biblisches Wörterbuch für das christliche Volk. Zahlen* in Winer's *Real-Wörterbuch,* Vol. II. Kliefoth, *Theologische Zeitschrift von Diekhof und Kliefoth,* 1862. Lämmert, *Zur Revision der biblischen Zahlensymbolik, Jahrbücher für deutsche Theologie,* 1864, I. 3. Bähr, *Symbolik,* I. p. 128 sqq. Kurtz, *Studien und Kritiken,* 1844, p. 315, sqq. [Brown, *Ordo Sæclorum,* London, 1844 (a most valuable work). Smith's *Dictionary of the Bible,* Title NUMBER. Auberlen, *Daniel and Revelation* (Eng. Ed.), pp. 131–141, 266, etc. White, *The Symbolical Numbers of Scripture,* Edinburgh, 1868.—E. R. C.]

One. The number of absolute unity, hence of Godhead, of omnipotence; of union, hence of power; of uniqueness or singleness, hence of individuality — of the mind at one with itself—of the one salvation "that is needful."

---

* [In the German Version, as in the English, the two words ζῶον (Rev. iv.), and θηρίον (Rev. xiii.), are erroneously rendered by but one term, *viz.:* *Thier* in the former and *Beast* in the latter. But is it not most strange that Lange, who recognizes the Scriptural distinction in the Commentary, should thus ignore it in the Introduction?—E. R. C.]

† Compare the author's lecture: *Ueber die Beziehungen welche zwischen der allgem. Symbolik und der kirchlichen Symbolik obwalten.* See above. *Comm. on Matthew,* p. 183, [Am. Ed.]

Two. The number of revelation, hence of creation; of nature, hence of life; of harmonious contrast, hence of marriage, of friendship. But also the number of discord, of war, of ruin, of death. The number of witnesses, of certainty.

Three (2+1). The specifically sacred number. The number of life at one with itself in harmonious contrast; *i. e.*, the number of *spirit* [*Geist*]; hence the number of the life that is in God.* The number of the absolutely living, three-fold Personality, hence of holiness; the number of the new life, the victoriously ended conflict, the Resurrection. But also the number of *unclean spirits* (the 3 frogs) and of *demoniacally great sufferings* (the 3 woes). Comp. the *Concordances. Three and a half* (the halved seven): the number of the apparent discontinuance of the Divine work (see Lämmert).

Four (2+2). The number of double contrast, hence the number of space, of the world; the number of the ground-forms of Divine Providence in the world.

Five (2+3, life moved by spirit). The number of the hand, of action, of freedom, of folly as well as wisdom, of motion, of the course of the world (five foolish and five wise virgins; five fingers upon the hand).

Six (3×2 and 2×3, the struggle betwixt spirit and nature). The number of weeks, of labor, of laborious service, of toil and need, of the endless toil of demonic self-annihilation. But also, in the sacred sense, the number of holy operations,—*the* sacred six whose unity is seven.

Seven (3+4 or 6+1). The number of the world as under the dominion of spirit; of completed work; of rest, of cessation from labor and keeping of holy-day, of the full development of light and life; of the full revelation of spirit, in good as well as in evil, hence the number of time. ["The number *seven* has a mystical and symbolical significance throughout Scripture, and especially throughout Prophecy, which, however, in no way lessens its chronological value. It is the sum of the number of God, *three,* and the number of the world, *four,* and is thus the number of the Divine in relation to the world, of the inward perfection of God, as manifested and viewed in His manifold works and judgments. Where this number prevails God is revealed, and *vice versâ.* The inward objective foundation of the law lies in the seven spirits of God, who are the mediators of all His revelations in the world (Rev. i. 4, iii. 1, iv. 5, v. 6). The outward manifestation of the dignity of this number begins as early as the first Book and first chapter of the Old Testament, where the work of creation is divided by it, whilst it prevails throughout the whole of the Apocalypse, the last Book of the New Testament. Cicero styles the number seven *rerum omnium fere nodus* (*Somn. Scip.* 5)." AUBERLEN, *Dan. and Rev.*, Eng. Ed., p. 133.—E. R. C.]

Eight (2×4). The number of the double world of the Cosmos, in the antithesis of Heaven and earth.

Nine (3×3). The number of the perfect movement of spirit, of renewal (the last simple number).

Ten (5+5). The number of numbers, hence the number of the completed course of time; of the full temporal development of life; the formal, worldly number of completeness. ["Ten is the number of what is human, worldly; it represents the fullness of the world's manifold activity and development. We may illustrate this by examples taken from our Book (Daniel) where the world-power issues in ten heads and ten horns (ii. 41, 42, vii. 7-24)." AUBERLEN, *Dan. and Rev.*, Eng. Ed., p. 133.—E. R. C.]

Eleven (6+5). The number of the decline of day, of evening, of the evening of the world; of the Church convulsed by the storm raging in the world (Judas and Simeon, or Dan, dropped out).

Twelve (3×4). The number of the spirit-world; hence the number of the *foundation,* the *mediation* and *consummation* of the Kingdom of God. The number of the plenitude of the charisms, as well as the number of the restored number of completeness. The real, heavenly number of completeness.

---

*See Lämmert, "Zur Revision," etc. See above.

Modifications of the Simple Numbers.

Fractions: $\frac{1}{2}$, $\frac{1}{3}$, $\frac{1}{4}$, $\frac{1}{10}$. A divided heart (James i. 8). Beginning of judgment (Rev. viii. 7 sqq.). The completion of satisfaction, atonement (Lev. v. 16). Theocratic tax (Gen. xiv. 20; Lev. xxvii. 30). Partial ruin (Rev. xi. 13). The half of seven, $3\frac{1}{2}$, the number of the Divine work and Kingdom as apparently at an end. The number of apparent hopelessness and despair, Rev. xi. 9, xii. 14; comp. Dan. xii. 7. This number is similar to the 42 months (Rev. xiii. 5), or the 1260 days (chap. xi. 3, xii. 6). This equal period of apparent disconsolateness is very differently apprehended by our believing contemporaries; opinions vary as to whether it should be reckoned as consisting of times, days, years, or months. Even to the human mind, one day can be as one year, and *vice versâ*.

Compounds.

4+3. Fortunes of the world and spiritual fortunes. The septenary of the Apocalypse divided into two portions. In general, completed destiny (Matt. v., the Beatitudes;* Matt. xiii., the Parables).

5+5. The entire evolutionary course of freedom in good and in evil (Matt. xxv. 1 sqq. 15).

7+1. Eight days. The round of life, in the antithesis of labor and rest, Luke ix. 28.

9+90. Luke xv. 4.

1000+600. Rev. xiv. 20. Comp. Düsterdieck, *Komm. zur Apocalypse*, p. 478. The number 1000 is an æon, and the number 600 a vast series.

Multiplications.

2×2. The world. 2×12. The 12 Elders of the Old and the 12 Elders of the New Covenant. The Theocratic and the Churchly Presbytery in a dynamic sense. The charisms of the Old and the New Covenant in their plenitude.

3×2. The new principle. The new. The priestly blessing, Num. vi. 24, 27. The thrice Holy ([Trisagion] Jehovah Sabaoth), Is. vi. — 3×40=120. The new Church, Acts i. 15.

4×2, or 8. The universe, an antithesis of the upper and the lower world.—4×3. God's world as a sanctified world. — 4×10. Course of the world, a generation.

5×2. The Church of God in respect of its genuine and spurious constituents, Matt. xxv. 1.

(6×100) 60+6. The number 666. The number of endless toil and self-consumption which fail to attain the goal of spiritual rest, hence the number of Antichrist.

7×4. The month, the real theocratic measure of time.

7×10. The seventy souls as the totality of Israel (Gen. xlvi. 27); the 70 disciples (Luke x.); 70 nations (Gen. x.). The fuller form 72=(6×12?). (The fullest number: 72×1000×2=144,000, Rev. xiv. 1). ["The number *seventy* is *ten* multiplied by *seven;* the human is here moulded and fixed by the Divine. For this reason the seventy years of exile are a symbolical sign of the time during which the power of the world would, according to God's will, triumph over Israel, during which it would execute the Divine judgments on God's people." AUBERLEN, *Daniel and Revelation* (Eng. Ed., p. 134).—E. R. C.]

8×10 (see Ps. xc.).

9 (?).

10×10. The worldly number of completeness. — 10×100. The chiliad, the æon.— 10×1000. The myriad, infinitude.

12×12, or 144. The elect of a period; these multiplied by 1000 : the elect of all times.

b. Symbolism of Colors.

Bähr I., p. 303 sqq. Friedrich, *Symbolik und Mythologie der Natur*, p. 426, 634, 671, 678. Winer, Art., *Farben* [colors]; *Bibl. Wörterbuch*, same article. The author's "*Vermischte Schriften*," Mörs, 1840, vol. I., p. 1, *Symbolik der Farben.* [Smith's *Bible Dictionary*, Title COLORS.—E. R. C.]

Colors are brought into view in the Scriptures with the idea of the rainbow; in this

---

* [Lange recognizes but *seven* Beatitudes in Matt. v., regarding the *eighth* and *ninth* as summations of the preceding. See *Comm. on Matthew*, p. 101, Am. Ed.—E. R. C.]

phenomenon, however, it is not the individual colors, as such, but the entirety which possesses a lofty symbolical significance for the theocratic faith, Ezek. i. 28.

But in the brilliant coloring of the Tabernacle, the symbolism of individual colors meets us in four separate colors (Ex. xxvi.). *White, blue* (yellow?), *purple, scarlet*.

The entire chromatic table of the Bible is drawn up by Winer, as follows : " No great variety of colors, natural or artificial, is presented in the Bible : besides white and black, (*a*) red is most frequently mentioned, in its varieties of brown-red (bay), crimson (purple-red), orange (minium); then (*b*) green; (*c*) pale yellow; (*d*) purple-blue (hyacinth-blue); (*e*) reddish or fox-brown; many of these appellations are indicative at once of the pigment used and its origin."

On the interpretation of colors in general, compare the works above cited.

In the canonical Apocalyptic writings, the glorious appearance of Christ, in which several colors combine, first demands our consideration: Rev. i. 13–16, comp. chap. x. 1, xiv. 14; xix. 11 sqq.; chap. xx. 11—the *white* throne; Dan. x. 5, 6.

Further, the color of the horses which are placed under the worldly authority of Christ, see Rev. vi. 2 sqq.; xix. 11-14; Zech. i. 8, vi. 2, 3.

Again, the brilliant coloring of the great harlot's attire, Rev. xvii. 4, xviii. 12, 16. The color of the dragon, chap. xii. 3; likewise the color of the horses of the horsemen of destruction, chap. ix. 17, comp. Jer. li. 7.

The Woman clothed with the sun, chap. xii. 1 (who divides into two opposite forms, meeting us, on the one hand, under the figure of the harlot, chap. xvi. 1, and, on the other hand, under the figure of the tried Woman, clothed with shining linen at the appearing of Christ, chap. xix. 8), comes forth at the end of the 1000 years as the Bride, adorned in the richest fashion, in the glory of God Himself, chap. xxi. 10, 11 sqq.

Those believers in Sardis, who have kept themselves from defilement, are clothed in *white* raiment, chap. iii. *White* is pre-eminently the color of innocence, purity, and righteousness, Rev. xix. 11, 14; but also that of spiritual age, maturity, perfection, eternity, of heavenly existence, of heavenly victory (the *white* hair, *white* horse, *white* throne of Him who was like unto the Son of Man; the *white* stone, the *white* garments). *White* has connected with it the clear brilliancy of snow and crystal, Matt. xvii. 2; Mark ix. 3; Rev. i. 14. Or, this color probably embraces those two symbols. See Rev. ii. 17, vi. 11, and other places. *Black* denotes, Rev. vi. 5, famine, distress, or simply suffering; thus, Job xxx. 28, 30; Cant. i. 5, 6. An effective contrast is presented Lam. iv. 7, 8. *Red* is of striking but also manifold significance. *Blood-red* (*crimson*) may, like blood itself, when taken in an active sense, denote war (Rev. vi. 4), murder (Rev. xii. 3), bloody victory (Is. lxiii.); but, in a passive signification, it may also denote a sacrificial death as the surrendering of life in blood (Lev. xvii. 11); the Atonement, with its propitiatory and cleansing power (1 John i. 7; Heb. ix. 22; Rev. vii. 14). *Purple*, on the other hand, is the color of royalty (Cant. vii. 5; Matt. xxvii. 28) or of kingly luxury and voluptuous ease (Luke xvi. 19). The Babylonian harlot decked herself with *purple* as a sign of her royal dignity, with *crimson* (*scarlet*) as a sign of her blood-shedding, with *gold* as a sign of her luxurious life. As the concrete form of *red* appears in blood, so the concrete form of *yellow* appears in gold. *Yellow* also, however, like *red*, separates into two distinct and diverse colors. *Pale yellow* is the color of expiring life, of death, of the kingdom of the dead (Rev. vi. 8); *golden* or *bright yellow* is the color of agitated, intensified, radiant life (Ezek. i. 4: Rev. i. 15); a spurious imitation of this last is presented by *minium*, the *yellowish red* of idols (Wisd. of Sol. xiii. 14). Allied to this *bright yellow* is the *red* or *fox* color, and, according to others, the *brown* of Zech. i. 8. [The German Bible gives, in this verse, " red, *brown* and white horses," instead of the *speckled* of the text and the *bay* of the margin of E. V.]. Two equally significant contrasts are formed by *sapphire blue*, the covenant color, the color of faithfulness, of heavenly stability (Ezek. i. 26), as, first, in antithesis to the *green* of the emerald, the color of the earth in her verdant spring-time, the color of hope, and, as the ground-tone of the rainbow *sub specie æterni*, the hue of heavenly promise (Rev. iv. 3); and, secondly, in antithesis to a *motley, speckled* tint (Ezek. xvi. 16), the hue of manifoldness or diversity, of instability, of change; a final

2

contrast to blue is presented by the *sombre, grey,* or *unclean* color of impurity, ashes, death (Job xxx. 19; Is. lxi. 3; Zech. iii. 3, and many other passages).

c. *Geometrical Figures. Forms of Measurement.*

The *quadrangular* form of Paradise, as the ideal blossom of the world, indicated by its four rivers, is reflected, in a secular aspect, in the four corners of the world, out of which the four winds blow (Dan. vii. 2); in a spiritual aspect, in the perfect square formed by the Holy of Holies (see Winer, *Tabernacle*) to which the imperfect square, the oblong of the Sanctuary, leads. The symbolical fulfillment of this square, from which the outer court has been cut off (Rev. xi. 2), is the City of God of the glorified world, the new Jerusalem (Rev. xxi. 2, 16); hence not merely a square, but, by reason of the height of the walls (which is to be symbolically understood), a perfect cube.

The quadrate of the earth is, however, enclosed by the circle of the earth (Is. xl. 22), the world by the circuit of the heaven (Job xxii. 14); the abyss is likewise encompassed by a circle (Prov. viii. 27)--the sphere of Divine Providence.

d. *Elements and Natural Phenomena.*

Air, earth, water, fire, ashes, hail, lightning, thunder, storm, earthquake.

Air is a symbol of life, of the region of life (1 Thess. iv. 17); hence the last judgment of hardening consists in the pouring out of the seventh vial of wrath into the air (Rev. xvi. 17), so that the sphere of life itself becomes a sphere of death. Air, as set in motion, or as *wind,* symbolizes the breath of spirit and the spiritual sphere; hence the prince of this world is said to rule in the air (Eph. ii. 2); and, in contrast to the *life-wind,* which is a symbol of the Spirit of God (Ezek. xxvii. 9; John iii.), the winds of wild and demonic spiritual currents storm over the sea of the life of the nations, exciting it to the production of Antichristian forms.

Water is subject to the *wind,* as the passive natural life is to the motory spiritual life; *water,* especially as the *billowy sea,* stands in distinct contrast to *earth* as the firm element of the world, to the *mountain* and, in a most special degree, to the *rock.* As earth, on the one hand, denotes the earthly, the becoming, the beginnings of life, the transitory (John iii. 31; 1 Cor. xv. 47), *the sphere of the becoming,* in antithesis to *Heaven, the symbol of the being,* of perfection, of the glory of God, so, on the other hand, it denotes the religious-moral institutions and regulations of God, the traditional spiritual firmament over against the water-floods of human life, regarded either in its natural inconstancy or as agitated by demonic powers (Ps. xciii.; Job xxxviii.). The true government of God within the sphere of the religious-moral order of things, the Theocracy, is a *mountain* of God upon earth, or rather a coronal of holy mountains (Pss. xv., xxxvi. 7, lxv. 6, cxxi. 1). Hence it is that the Theocracy, in its secularization into Jewish ordinance, could approve itself a mountain that lay, an apparently invincible obstacle, in the way of the Apostles' vocation; this same mountain, however, they were assured should by their faith be removed, nay, even be cast into the sea of nations (Matt. xvii. 20, xxi. 21). In consequence of this transposition of the Kingdom of God, there is a Christian order of things; it will be the sign of the last time, however, when the *beast out of the earth*—the old order of things—shall be sub-servient to the *beast out of the sea.* But though mountains depart and hills be removed (Is. liv. 10), yet will not God's mercy depart from His people; high above the mountains rises the eternal *Rock,* God Himself in His steadfastness and faithfulness (Deut. xxxii. 31, *etc.*). And, therefore, in the last time the *Mountain of the Lord* shall be higher than all mountains; the ordinance of the Kingdom in the Church of God shall be exalted above all other and human ordinances (Is. ii. 2).

Out of the *rock* of God's steadfastness, the *fountain* of undying life breaks forth. The *fountain* is the origin of life—of Divine life (Jer. ii. 13, xvii. 13) or of human spiritual life. All originalities, which make up the world's history, are *fountains;* in the midst is the *open fountain* of salvation (Zech. xiii. 1). From the fountains issue *brooks* and *streams,*—

tendencies, godly (Ezek. xlvii. 1 sqq.; *Shiloah*, Is. viii. 6) and ungodly (*brooks* [E. V.: *floods*] *of Belial*, Ps. xviii. 4); the character of the latter is that of stagnation, ending finally in the perfect stagnancy of the lake of fire. The *streams* empty into the *sea*, the great life of the nations (Dan. vii. 2; Rev. xiii.). The *sea* itself is, after the judgment, divided into two distinct and opposite seas—the *crystal sea* which, in spite of its fullness, its plenitude of life, is transparent, a pure spiritual life, clear as crystal (Rev. iv. 6)—and the *lake* or *pool of fire*, which, in spite of its great extent and its passionate, fiery storms, still remains a pool of absolute stagnation (Rev. xix. 20, xx. 14, xxi. 8).

Earth and *water* are still further to be considered as elements. The *earth* as a symbol of a rich and fruitful soil—in a spiritual as well as a material sense—in antithesis to dry, stony, and desert ground (Matt. xiii.); *water* as a symbol of vitalizing, refreshing affluences (Ps. i.). This latter element is likewise a symbol of cleansing, consecrative discipline (Ezek. xxxvi. 25), and of a penal judgment that leads through death to new life (1 Pet. iii. 21). The *water of the ocean* is, moreover, a symbol of the separation between this life and the beyond (Deut. xxx. 13), just as the *water of the flood* symbolizes the separation between the old and the new world. Both imports of *water* are presented, however, in a yet higher degree in *fire*—*fire* as the vital element (Is. iv. 5); *fire* as the refining and purifying * (Mal. iii. 3), the atoning (Lev. xvi. 27), transforming (2 Pet. iii. 10), and destroying element (Rev. xx. 9).

Under the head of natural laws and phenomena, the *antithesis of day and night* claims the first place. Both *day* and *night* have two aspects, for to the *day of life* (John ix. 4) the day of judgment corresponds (1 Cor. iii. 13), and to the *night of darkness*, full of secret works of wickedness (Rom. xiii. 12), the holy night of mystery corresponds (Luke ii. 8).

The *antithesis of light and darkness*, on the other hand, is less ambiguous. *Light*, as symbolic of truth, is opposed to *darkness*, as symbolic of falsehood (1 John i. 6, 7). Yet there is also a *holy darkness*, as there is a *holy night* (Ex. xx. 21).

The *sunshine* is rich in symbolical references, from the first blush of morning to the parting ray of evening (see the *Concordances* and Zech. xiv. 7). The *sun* can also smite, however (Ps. cxxi. 6; comp. xci). And so, in contrast to the *scorching, smiting, Oriental sun*, the *shadow*, sister to the night, is adopted as a symbol of the tranquillizing, protecting, and refreshing vital operations of God (Ps. xvii. 8, *etc.*).

Over against *the blue sky*, the symbol of eternal faithfulness (Ezek. i. 26), we find the *cloud*, as a medium of revelation and concealment (Ex. xiii. 21; xl. 34, *etc.*); as, likewise, the *rainbow*, as a medium of communication between heaven and earth (Gen. ix. 13; Ezek. i. 28; Rev. iv. 3). Again, we have the *cloudy darkness* (Ps. xviii. 9-11), and the *flying storm-cloud*, the latter, as denoting the chariot of God, being indicative of His stormy Providence, as seen in great events.

The *cherubim* of the cloud and storm government of God (Ps. xviii. 10) are accompanied by the *seraphim* of the Divine fiery rule (Ps. civ.; Is. vi.). These also were originally designated as cherubim—cherubim, however, who already wield the seraphic flaming sword (Gen. iii. 24).

We meet with *rain* under the import of times of blessing in a reference to the history of Elijah (Jas. v. 18). *Storm*, in its grand signification, as the crisis of the customary order of life (Dan. vii. 2; Luke xxi. 25), branches, on the one hand, into *thunder* and *lightning* (Pss. xi. 6, xviii.; Matt. xxiv. 27), on the other, into *hail* and (Rev. xvi. 21) *meteors*. The conjunction of judgment and salvation finds its climax in *fire from heaven* (Rev. viii. 10; history of Elijah—the chariot of fire).

Exceedingly significant are the conjunctions of the wonderful *shining of sun and moon*, and the great *hail storm* in the history of Joshua (Jos. x.). Likewise the Divine signs in the history of Elijah (1 Kings xix. 11 sqq.); the conjunctions of eschatological phenomena in the Lord's Eschatological Discourse (see the Synoptists); and especially the marking, in the Apocalypse, of decisive crises in the Kingdom of God by great natural crises. The voice

* [This property of fire is set forth in the very word *purify*, which, doubtless, comes to us, through the Latin, from the Greek πῦρ, *fire*.—Tr.]

of Christ is as the *sound of many waters* (Rev. i. 15); *i. e.*, it is perceptible from the life and operations of Christ in the stirrings of many nations. Particularly significant are the conjunctions: *lightnings, voices, thunders* (Rev. iv. 5); *voices, thunders, lightnings, earthquake* (chap. viii. 5); to these is added, in a third passage, a great *hail* (chap. xi. 19; comp. chap. xvi. 18). Manifestations of God; epochs, new periods; earth-shakings, catastrophes of judgment.

e. Symbolical Items Drawn from Natural History.

On precious stones, see my *Vermischte Schriften*, Vol. I., p. 15; Winer's *Bibl. Realwörterbuch* and the *Bibl. Wörterbuch* under the head of *Edelsteine* [Precious Stones]. Calwer, *Naturgeschichte* (Stuttgart, 1836). [Smith's *Dict. of the Bible*—TITLE, *Stones, Precious.*—E. R. C.]

As the Gospel of John, by virtue of its perfect ideal view of the world, is rich in natural symbolism, so likewise is the Apocalypse, especially in the symbolization of subjects drawn from natural history.

In the first place, the symbolism of the *twelve jewels* in the breastplate of Aaron is resumed in the description of the New Jerusalem (chap. xxi.). As the jewels in the breastplate reflect the Twelve Tribes of Israel in their peculiarities, so in the Apocalyptic jewels the foundations of the wall of the City are mirrored, *i. e.*, the complete number of the charismatic fundamental types of the eternal City of God; marked by the names of the Twelve Apostles. The *twelve jewels*, as foundations of the wall, are reflected in the *twelve pearls* that form the gates. The *pearls* stand toward the *jewels* as does Omega toward Alpha; they are the perfected lustre and splendor of appearance into which the charismatic foundations have developed; their perfection consists in the fact of their representing, in their quality of *gates*, on the one hand, the complete openness, universalism of perfect spiritual life, and on the other, its complete seclusion against everything that is base. This seclusion seems to be effected, however, only by a dynamically repellent agency which the pearls exercise of themselves (see chap. xxi. 25, 27).

The twelve jewels of the City of God are preceded by the three figurative jewels in the Theophany, chap. iv. 3. Particular prominence is given to the *jasper* stone. Its lustre, together with that of the *sardine* stone, characterizes the appearance of God Himself upon His throne; it is likewise expressive (as the most precious of all stones) of the glory of God which lightens His City, and so we find it again as the material of which the wall of the City is built, and as the first jewel of the foundations. Undoubtedly, therefore, it is not the ordinary jasper, but the diamond (see Düsterd., p. 216). The stones in Aaron's breastplate do not follow each other in the same order as those in the Apocalypse.

In the breastplate we have:

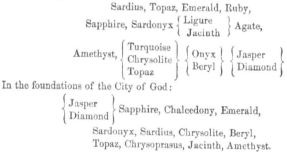

In the foundations of the City of God:

It is an unmistakable fact that the precious stones of the Apocalypse, chosen in accordance with the knowledge of antiquity, denote in general the elect of the City of God. As *twelve*, they indicate their numerical completeness (see chap. vii. and xiv.); as *shining with a common lustre*, their unity; as stones of *different hues*, their manifoldness; as *brilliant* stones, the glorification of this earthly life through the light of Heaven. It is, of course, not feasible exactly to combine the twelve Aaronic stones with the twelve sons and tribes of

Israel, or altogether to identify the Apocalyptic stones with the respective characteristics of the twelve Apostles, though many analogies may be found in both tables. The stones are, however, most highly significant as bearing upon the Christian doctrine of personality. They proclaim the fact that the individual is not relaxed and dissolved by the universal, but fixed and clarified. Since the jasper is described as the most precious of all stones, and compared with the transparent crystal, nay, spoken of as a crystal jasper, the ordinary jasper cannot be meant.´ See above.

As an image of the pure and crystallized solar ray, of faithfulness in motion, of motion in faithfulness — hence, of light — *gold* has an inalienable reference to the sun itself, consequently, to the symbol of the face of God, or Christ, *i. e.*, the manifestation of God's love.

As gold, however, it is indicative of the spiritual solar ray—a celestially pure and right tendency and motion. So, doubtless, the *golden girdle* denotes a preparation for holy motion (chaps. i. 13, xv. 6); the *golden treasure*, the *true* riches of active spiritual life (chap. iii. 18); the *golden crowns*, the perfecting of holy living in royal liberty (chap. iv. 4); the *golden censer*, the purity of the prayers ascending to heaven for the coming of the Kingdom (chap. viii. 3); the *golden vials* of wrath, the Divine purity and integrity in the course of the judgments (chap. xv. 7); the *golden streets* of the City of God, the sphere of holy life-motion (chap. xxi. 21).

Since the adornment of the harlot (chap. xvii. 4) is *worldly*, like the worldly merchandise brought to her by the merchants of the earth (chap. xviii. 12, 13, 14, 16), the passages referred to can contain nothing but a general allegorical symbolization of worldly show, in splendor, might, riches and pleasures, through the medium of precious stones, pearls, metals, products of the vegetable kingdom and works of art.

Together with the symbolical import of *earth* and *sea*, the symbolism of the vegetable world endows *trees* and all *green* things (chaps. vii. 3, viii. 7) with a like general significance. In accordance with well-known images in the Psalms (Pss. i. 3, xxiii. 2, xcii. 12) the *tree covered with verdure* is indicative of prosperity in human relations. In particular, we would note the two *olive trees*, chap. xi. 4, which recall the kindred passage in Zech. iv.; in the latter place, however, the olive trees afford nutriment to a *candlestick* in the midst of them, whilst in the Apocalypse the olive trees themselves are, at the same time, candlesticks, *i. e.*, not simply sources of Christian spiritual life, but likewise organs for the diffusion of the same. In the Old Testament passage, the prophetic and high-priestly offices seem to be intended, in their fructification of the kingly office; in the New, we regard the two olive trees as significant of the Christian Church and State. The *vine* of the earth (chap. xiv. 18), characterized as the object of the judgment harvest, doubtless denotes, in accordance with John xv. 1; comp. Ps. lxxx. 14, 15; Ezek. xv. 2, xix. 10, the entire human race in its higher destination; it is here contemplated, however, in that ironical perversion of its destiny of which it has in great part been guilty, bringing forth, it is true, *grapes* in abundance, yet grapes that have but the false semblance of love and joy, being fit only for the wine-press of wrath. On the other hand, the *trees of life*, chap. xxii., constitute an individual sign of the great superiority of the new Paradise to the old. The one possessed a single *tree of life;* the other abounds in *trees of life*, standing on either side of the river; it has thus an avenue of trees or organs for the eternal preservation and invigoration of life, and not only do these refresh the blessed the whole year through, with their twelve manner of *fruits*, but their *leaves* also are for the healing of the nations.

The animal kingdom has contributed more abundantly to apocalyptic symbolism than has the vegetable, and that not merely in simple forms but also in allegorical compounds; not merely to denote bestial and demonic impulses,* but also, in a remarkable degree, to illustrate the highest and holiest heavenly relations.

In general, the four *living shapes* or *beasts* before the throne of God, which we regard four fundamental forms of the Divine government,† primarily form a contrast to the

---

* Comp. the four beasts, Dan. vii., and the four bestial shapes, Ezek. i., Rev. iv. In the one place, demonic impulses; in the other, heavenly forms. [See *foot-note,** p. 14.—E. R. C.]

† See the author's *Leben Jesu*, Vol. I., p. 234.

beast out of the sea and to the beast out of the earth, *i. e.*, the true radical Antichrist and his prophet, the renegade from the old Christian order of things (chap. xiii.), and to the *dragon*, the ruler and inspiriter of them both (chap. xii. 3), Satan himself.

The *lamb* is the symbol of the suffering, and in suffering triumphant, Christ. This figure is employed throughout the Scriptures, from the paschal lamb (Ex. xii.) down; it receives special prominence at the hands of Isaiah (chap. liii.), and is also a favorite image in the Johannean writings (John i. 29; comp. 1 Pet. i. 19), particularly in the Apocalypse (chaps. v. 6, vi. 16, vii. 10, xii 11, xiv. 4).

The *horse*, in the Apocalypse as in Zechariah (chaps. i. 8, vi. 2, 3), is the symbol of a world-historical movement, or distinct fundamental forms of the course of the world.

The *eagle* (chaps. viii. 13 to xii.) has the significance of the horse, only in a higher degree. It denotes a ghostly or ideal and infinitely swift motion which (2 Sam. i. 23), as a rule, is directed towards light, the sun, heaven (Prov. xxiii. 5, xxx. 19; Is. xl. 31); wonderfully rapid in descent also, as the astonishingly swift catastrophes of judgment (Job xxxix. 30; Matt. xxiv. 28). Hence, the *eagle* is particularly fitted to denote the wonderful Providence of God, as exercised towards His people (Ex. xix. 4; Deut. xxxii. 11); or to symbolize mighty sovereigns (Dan. iv. 33), great military expeditions (Jer. xlviii. 40), great spiritual princes (Ezek. i. 10; Rev. xii. 14).

Highly remarkable and singular figures are the *three frogs* (Rev. xvi. 13). Their element— the swamp—their unanimity in the most perfect monotony, their loud nocturnal clamor and the emulousness with which they strive to outcry each other, are sufficiently characteristic features. Their number, however — three — denotes that they feign to be holy voices of the Spirit. They belong to the sphere of the *dogs*, which last, as Oriental *wild dogs*, are to be distinguished from the *little dogs* (Matt. xv.; Tob. v. 16, [xi. 4.] *Dogs* are a symbol of invincible *vulgarity*, associated though it may be with many gifts; of vulgarity in enjoyment (Prov. xxvi. 11), in possession (Sirach xiv. 2),* in a disregard for holy things (Psalm xxii. 16; Matt. vii. 6), in sensual impurity generally (Rev. xxii. 15). In a more general sense, therefore, they are also a symbol of baseness (2 Kings viii. 13). In connection with the *swine*, the *dog* denotes infinite activity and versatility (Eccl. ix. 4) in what is base and sordid, whilst the *swine* is expressive of a debauched hebetude in the like (2 Pet. ii. 22). The *serpent* bears sway over this domain, however; he is, in truth, serpent and swine in one, combining supreme demonic cunning with supreme bestial brutality; such is the *dragon*, *i. e.*, Satan.

Not images of *evil* itself [in the sense of wickedness or sin – Tr.], but images of the *ill* that is connected with evil, are the figures of the demonico-physical penal judgments; in the first place, the *locusts* that ascend out of the abyss (chap. ix. 3). These are allegorical figures: locusts that touch no green thing, but bite and torment men; illusive figures, like tormenting shapes created by the imagination: like horses, and yet not like horses; with things like crowns as of gold on their heads, and yet neither crowns nor gold; faces, as it were the faces of men, and yet not men's faces; their hair as the hair of women, and yet not women's hair; teeth like lions' teeth, and yet not lions' teeth; breastplates as the similitudes of iron breastplates; the sound of their wings as the sound of war-chariots; tails like scorpions' tails—all demonic phantasmagoria, hypochondria, forms of frenzy, self-tormentings of all kinds, such as make up the morbid dark side of the development of modern intellectual and spiritual life. Such is the appearance of these locusts, like the countless spawn of spiritual waste places—horses in their swiftness and strength; crowned with the phantasmal crowns of invincible phantasmal might; as human as though they looked through men's eyes; as effeminate as though clothed with women's hair; and yet, again, ferocious in strength, provided, as it were, with lions' jaws; mercilessly hard and unconquerable, guarded as with iron breastplates; venomous as though stinging with scorpions' stings; tormenting men five months, *i. e.*, through the measure of the whole course of the veriest temporality ([moon, month] measurer of time†), five times repeated, in accordance with the number of moral freedom—here, freedom in false self-destination.

---

* [The reference is manifestly incorrect. The one intended by the author cannot be discovered.—Tr.]
† [See Müller's *Science of Language*, Vol. I., p. 16.—Tr.]

Still more fearful is the aspect of the *tormenting spirits* of the sixth trumpet (chap. ix.); the locusts *tormented* men, but these *slay* the third part of men; the former are to the latter as countless swarms of grasshoppers to a serried host of twice ten thousand times ten thousand (200 millions) horsemen. The riders have breastplates of *fiery red*, *dark blue*, and *brimstone color* (*brimstone yellow*); the heads of the horses are like lions' heads, and out of their mouths issue fire, smoke, and brimstone, as though they were dragons of hell. Thus, the horses are worse than the riders, who seem only to guide them. The horses kill by the three agencies, *fire*, *smoke*, and *brimstone*, as by different plagues. Besides this power in their mouths, they have power in their tails; those resemble serpents, having serpents' heads, which harm men.

We must consider that the sixth trumpet has reference to the approaching end of the world. This consideration points to demonic Antichristian corruptions which burst forth from the Euphrates (not from *beyond* the Euphrates, whence a way is prepared for the kings, Rev. xvi. 12)—(from Babylon)—as Babylonish distractions. Mark first the close connection in which they stand, and their release for judgment, under four angels of judgment. Next their number—*two myriad myriads;* a two-fold immensity, to be referred, doubtless, to the antithesis of the two Antichristian beasts. Moreover, it is not the riders, the directors of the horses, who are the real devastators, but the terrible horses themselves, *i. e.*, wild and dreadful movements. Yet the riders are invulnerable; they have on breastplates corresponding in color with the deadly plagues that issue from the mouths of the horses; the flame-color with the fire, the steel-blue with the smoke, the brimstone-color with the brimstone. The men whom they kill, they kill not simply spiritually, but likewise physically; —with the fire of fanaticism; with the smoke of suffocating, negative self-consumings; with the brimstone of a morbid susceptibility for fire and suffocating glow. Thus are slain, snatched away into spiritual and bodily ruin, the *third part of men, i. e.*, a great portion of those under mental or spiritual excitement, representatives of the human number of spirit; the rest of mankind are mortally wounded by the bite of their serpent-like tails, yet they do not repent, either of their idolatry, or of their lawlessness (murder, *etc.*). The judgment is imminent.

If *heads* may be regarded only as symbolizing the real principles of definite tendencies, or as the intelligent originators of them (Gen. iii. 15; Ps. lxviii. 21), the seven heads of the dragon denote seven ground-forms of mischievous demonic principles; the perfect number, seven, being significant of the pretended holiness and Divine origin of these principles. The seven heads of Antichrist represent these principles in their historical development, showing how they finally have borrowed the most perfect semblance of Christianity whilst existing in the element of hatred towards Christ; ay, how they can appear like seven holy mountains of world-historical firmness and order (Rev. xvii.). As the dragon appears as a monster, and moreover as a liar and braggart, having ten horns upon his seven heads—the emphatic expression of the entire course of the world—so, too, does Antichrist wear the semblance of a monster, and that in a peculiar degree (Rev. xiii.). For the *horn* is, in general, the symbol of power, particularly historical, royal power (Rev. xvii 12). Still more monstrous, however, than the monster of Antichristianity, is the beast that comes up out of the earth; it has two horns [like a lamb], but it speaks as a dragon, *i. e*, not simply as Antichrist, but as the devil himself.

The fact that the *eyes* of the beasts ([living beings—E. R. C.] Rev. iv.) denote the consciousness of the spirit, His illimitable vision, requires no explanation. The *feet*, as figuring position (chap. x. 2), and the *hands*, especially the right hand, as figuring action, are also easily intelligible symbols.

The mention of these physical organs leads us to the contemplation of organic sufferings. Complete organic suffering constitutes the *corpse* (chap. xi. 9), the symbol of complete deadness and annihilation, accompanied by a certain continuance of the dead or slain form. But the *corpse*, on Biblical ground, is like tinder which has been extinguished but which a spark may re-ignite; it may revive again. And thus it is with the Kingdom of God, when all seems lost.

Evil also may receive a *deadly wound*, however, which for the time may be *healed* (Rev.

xiii. 3). Judgment that has taken up its dwelling within is more fell in its operation ; this is symbolized by the *sore* (Rev. xvi. 2, 11) ; it is that self-dissolution of life that begins with perfect hardening. But, in face of this death-power, we behold the wondrous life-power of the Kingdom of God, indicated by the *woman in travail* (chap. xii. 2). This last figure leads us to that department of symbolism which is connected with human life.

f. Human Relations.

In accordance both with the Apocalypse (chap. i. 13) and the Book of Daniel (chap. vii.), the human form, in its ideality, is specifically the form of Christ. As the Head of humanity, He is the essential and apparent Image of God; the Son.* He, therefore, not only embraces humanity and reveals Divinity (chap. x. 1), but also rules over and through the Cosmos (chap. i. 17, 18). Therefore, His eyes are like a flame of fire, and His voice like the voice of great waters (great hosts of peoples).

She who gave birth to Him is the *woman* clothed with the sun, whose footstool is the moon, and who is adorned with a crown of twelve stars. The Kingdom of God, or the ideal Theocracy,† bare Him in the radiant garment of the sun, *i. e.*, the revelation of God ; His Kingdom is elevated above the moon, *i. e.*, above the changes of time; it is adorned with the crown of twelve stars, the complete number of all the great bearers of Divine revelation, whilst the Church has seven stars (angels or ideal genii of individual churches or congregations) and the seven individual churches or congregations themselves do but reflect the glory of the Kingdom faintly, as seven candlesticks. The great spiritual adornment of the woman, however, reposes also upon a cosmical foundation : The sun, with its group of stars, constitutes the Christological Cosmos in the *narrower* sense.

The *travail* of the woman is doubtless indicative of the birth-pangs of the Messianic time. The Spirit in the Kingdom of God apprehends that Satan is desirous to devour the child, *i. e.*, He is the author of prophecy concerning the suffering Messiah (continuing it even into the New Testament: Simeon, John the Baptist, Mary of Bethany in the act of anointing Christ). He *desired to devour* Him ; this is the Death of Christ, changed into the Resurrection. The *child was caught up into Heaven*—the Ascension of Christ. Besides the immediate application of this fact, however, the self-same thing is continually going on in the history of mankind. Satan is continually desiring to devour every new birth of the Church. But the true Christendom, as the Church Triumphant, is ever being caught up into Heaven, whilst Satan is continually being more and more cast out of the Heaven of the spirit and the spirit-realm into the external world.

The *wilderness*, whither the woman flees, is not difficult of comprehension : it is the region of asceticism.‡ She is borne thither upon the *wings of the great eagle*. A super-terrestrial spirit of renunciation in heroic spirits — existing in a free form, even in the life of John—is the saving power that bears the New Testament Theocracy, the true Church, into the wilderness.

The *water-flood*, with which the serpent seeks to carry away the woman, is, in accordance

---

* [As the Head of humanity, He is THE MAN—"The last Adam," 1 Cor. xv. 45 ; as the promised *Seed*, Gen. iii. 15 (including the idea of Headship), He is the SON OF MAN.—E. R. C.]

† [By "the ideal Theocracy" Lange intended, beyond doubt, to indicate *the ideal* or *true Church*, continuing one and the same through all dispensations. (See *Comm. on Matthew*, p. 73, Am. Ed.) He could not have contemplated the Christian Church *as such*, since that was introduced by Him—in no sense "bare Him ;" and that he did not intend to indicate the Jewish Church *as such*, is made manifest by the subsequent reference to "the seven churches." Thus the Church is described by the preceding phrase as "the Kingdom of God." If this description be correct, "the Kingdom" had really come when Daniel *prophesied* concerning its *coming*,—when the Baptist heralded it as "at hand."—when our Lord taught His disciples to pray "Thy Kingdom come." For further remarks on the Kingdom of God, or the Basileia, the reader is referred to the Excursus on that subject under ch. i. 9.—E. R. C.]

‡ [Auberlen supports, by strong arguments, the opinion that *the wilderness* is symbolical of *the heathen lands* in which the Church took refuge when she was driven from Palestine. Elliott (*Horæ Apocalypticæ*, 5th Ed., Vol. III., p. 45) contends, in accordance with the author, that by *the flight* is symbolized, not a change of *place*, but a change of *state*. He differs from Lange, however, as to his explanation of that state, viewing it as implying "the *faithful* Church's loss of its previous character of *Catholicity* or *universality*, its *invisibility* in respect of *true Christian public worship, and destitution of all ordinary means of spiritual sustenance*."—E. R. C.]

with the idea of water-floods, a migration of a nation or nations (see Ps. xciii.). But the *earth*, that swallows up the flood, is the old order of things, conceived of not simply as secular authority, but likewise as legal and external Churchly authority. The forms of State and Church in the Middle Ages became victors over the flood of peoples in migration. Though it be true that the nations were partially influenced in their wanderings by a higher longing, it is nevertheless a fact that the first moving power of an Attila, for instance, was a demonically savage impulse; and, in every instance, the nations dashed themselves at first against the Church with a shock as of mighty waves.

It is an exceedingly note-worthy circumstance that the one *Woman* of whom we read in chap. xii. has, in the end of the days (chap. xvii., xviii., xix.), divided into the antithesis of the *Harlot* and the *Bride.** See above.

The *two olive-trees* of the interim are likewise introduced in the form of two personages endowed with miraculous power [the two *Witnesses*, ch. xi. 3–13]. They are able to shut Heaven, to inflict external and internal judgments upon men. In *the killing* of them, however, we behold the Antichristian destruction of Church and State. In their *dead bodies* we have a certain continuance of their exanimate forms. In their *resurrection*, at the expiration of three days and a half, *i. e.*, after the lapse of the resurrection period of three days—in the most hopeless hour, therefore—as also in their *ascension*, we see the exaltation of Church and State into the condition of the unitous form of the Kingdom. Here we behold the coming forth of the *Bride*. As the matured, free and unique heavenly Church upon earth, she stands opposed to Antichristianity.

Over against the olive-trees stand the *seven kings* and the *ten kings*, as Antichristian powers.

The starting-point for the explanation of these kings is formed by the fact that a precursory judgment, executed by the angel of the seventh vial of wrath, has divided the one great city of destruction into three parts (chap. xvi. 19). The first part is constituted by Babylon in the narrower sense of the term; she is connected with the seven kings, or the seven holy, or rather mock-holy, forms of the Antichristian world-power. The second part is formed by the Beast in the narrower sense of the term, represented by the ten kings of the democratic world-power. The third part is formed by the final rising of Gog and Magog, under the conduct of Satan himself (chap. xx.). The Babylonian Harlot is judged by the ten kings. The Beast, with the ten kings, is judged by the Parousia of Christ. The last anarchical rising is judged by fire that comes down from God out of heaven,—the fiery metamorphosis of the end of the world.

The *Woman* who at first fled from the dragon into the wilderness of a holy asceticism, seems to be again found in the wilderness, chap. xvii. But her asceticism is now holy in appearance only. The *Woman* has become a *Harlot*, and has seated herself upon the organ of Satan, the *scarlet*, *i. e.*, blood-colored, *Beast;* the Antichristianity of the last time. The beast is full of *names of blasphemy, i. e.*, central principles of impiety; its *seven* apparently spiritual *heads* or governments are in contradiction to the *ten horns* of worldly power. The woman, in her false pomp, also sits on *seven mountains, i. e.*, consecrated powers of order (see above, *Mountain*); and these are seven kings. It is, in the first place, declared concerning their unified personality, *i. e.*, the Beast itself: *It was, and is not, and shall ascend out of the abyss, and go into perdition.* This fact excites the wonder of the Christian world here, chap. xvii., and also according to chap. xiii. 3, where it is said: *The deadly wound of the Beast was healed.* The passages are unmistakably descriptive of Antichristianity in its continuance throughout the history of the world; in its heathen character it *was*, and received a deadly wound from Christianity; it arose again, however, an apparently Christian Antichristianity, and, in this character, as the perfection of wickedness, it is destined to go into perdition. Accordingly, by the *seven kings*, we are to understand, agreeably to the features presented in Dan. vii., seven world-powers, or phases of this gradually developing

---

* The author communicated the idea of this division of the one form of the Woman into two opposite forms to the late Dr. Auberlen, in a letter written, if we mistake not, subsequent to the issue of the first edition of his work on *Daniel and the Revelation.*

Antichristianity. We cannot assume that the Apocalyptist essentially differs from Daniel. It was necessary, however, for him to go beyond Daniel, in view, among other things, of the fact that Antichristianity would re-appear within Christianity ; hence he substituted a round, spiritual *seven*—taking for his point of departure the last kingly power—for the heathen, worldly *four* of Daniel. As a fifth power, which to the Israelites had become a world-power, he might regard the Antichristianity of the Herodians, or the Jewish Hierarchy itself in its diffusion over the world; as the sixth, the Roman empire of his own time as distinguished from ancient Rome. The other, it is declared, is not yet come; that is, the apparently Christian, Antichristian world-power. Upon this point the prophecy is brief, in perfect accordance with the laws of prophecy in contra-distinction to historic prediction.

The passage, chap. xvii. 11, has been combined with the declaration concerning the deadly wound of the Beast, chap. xiii. 3, for the purpose of presenting an absurd fable of heathen or Jewish popular life as the main motive of the great prophecy of a Christian Apostle.* The supporters of this view have failed to consider the serious injury which the adoption of such a popular error must necessarily inflict upon the entire Book. They are regardless of the distinction that exists between popular rumor and the opinion of morally cultured minds; between the generality of such minds and enlightened prophets of the Lord. Neither have they considered how impossible it is that the world-monarchies of Daniel, which invariably denote entire groups of kings, should here be converted into the names of single kings, of whom some are even highly insignificant. The confusion which such a proceeding would introduce into the Apocalyptic times is manifest.

It is deserting symbolical exegesis for literal interpretation to declare that the kings are real kings, instead of concrete world-powers ; or to seek to define the numbers *seven* and *ten* in accordance with chronologic historical dates. Neither can *Babylon* be significant of Rome in a literal sense, though Rome be the symbolical centre of Babylon ; and, notwithstanding the unmistakable allusion to Rome contained in the seven mountains (chap. xvii.), we must not be unmindful of the symbolic import attaching to the septenary, as well as to the figure of a mountain. When Christ is declared to be the Prince of the kings of the earth (chap. i.), the expression is manifestly a symbolically concrete term for the absolute-dynamical and dynamic-absolute dominion of the glorified Christ over all the world-powers of the earth. It is expressive of the dynamical principle of the personality, word, and Spirit of Christ, which principle overrules all materiality and all quantity. So, as the *Crown of life*, Christ Himself surpasses all the princely crowns or diadems of worldly dominion, and of spiritual victory in Heaven and on earth (Rev. ii. 10, *etc.*). It is also requisite that we should regard *city* as a symbolical term for a centre of human fellowship, whether the city of destruction (chap. xvi. 19) or the City of God (chap. xxi. 10) be intended. No less symbolical is the *temple*, chap. xi. 1. The exegetical assumption of modern critics that the last passage proves the Temple at Jerusalem to have been still standing at the time when the Apocalypse was written, affords another sign of the deep fall of these critics into a false literalism. The sharp distinction made by the Apocalyptist between the *temple* and the *outer court*, which last is not measured, but is given to the Gentiles that they may tread it under foot, is manifestly expressive of the distinction between the internal and the external Church, between the true, living congregation of God and a Christendom that is Christian in name only, being in essence truly heathen. It is an antithesis similar to that formed by the Kingdom of priests of the real spiritual life (chap. i. 6), and the merchants of the earth, who have been the intimate business friends of the false queen, just as the kings of the earth have been the associates of her revelry and debauchery. Again, in the *merchants* and *kings* we have, manifestly, two symbolic groups. One of these groups denotes all who have served and benefited the queen from self-interest; some of them being represented as egoists,

---

* See Düsterdieck, p. 439. Victorin, Corrodi, Eichhorn, Ewald, Lücke, De Wette, Bleek, Baur, Volkmar, and others, p 440; Düsterdieck opposes this idea. Weiss does the ▩▩▩ in his treatise in *Studien und Kritiken*, 1869, No. 1.

who drift upon the ocean of popular life. The other group is indicative of all who have occupied a relation of mutual support to the false world-power, the enslaver of humanity, the Woman,—lending her the worldly arm of despotism, with a view to being made strong by her through her enslaving of men's consciences.*

And now, in the midst of all these symbols, and in this out and out symbolical Book, what shall we say to those who ascribe a perfectly literal meaning to the term *Jews* † (chap. ii. 9, iii. 9), and who, upon this term, erect an entire house of cards, made up of false critical hypotheses concerning the New Testament? Very strong faith is requisite for the assumption that such critics are thoroughly in earnest in thus literalizing, particularly as the Apocalyptist himself characterizes those people who claim that they are the true Jews, as a synagogue of Satan. One would suppose that, previous to the Apocalypse, there never had existed a spiritual conception of Judaism (see Rom. ii. 29; Gal. iii. 29). No less worthy of rejection is the Judaizing, chiliastic interpretation of the passage descriptive of the *sealing* (chap. vii.) as referring to the national, external Israel. The Christians in the seven churches, which were in a great measure made up of Gentile Christians, must, we think, have better understood how to read a Christian symbolic Scripture than readers of this tendency, who hold that the congregation of believers who (as they suppose) are sealed towards the end of the world, are to be regarded as consisting purely of Jewish Christians. The above view would, moreover, necessitate the inference that precisely 12,000 should be sealed out of every tribe. Since the number twelve is the spiritual number of completeness, denoting the round fullness of the principial charisms of the life of Christ or the Kingdom of God, by the twelve thousand of each of the twelve tribes, the whole plenitude of charismatic forces in the development of the Kingdom of God is denoted; in the form of elect and tried souls, for such only are sealed. Since, however, this sealing has reference to the entire course of the seventh seal, *i. e.*, of the seven trumpets, the interpretation which refers it to a Jewish church subsisting at the end of the world, is utterly incorrect. These hundred forty and four thousand would, moreover, in the true evening of the world, seem to have emerged from their probationary state on the earth (chap. vii.) and to have attained to the triumphal state in Heaven (chap. xiv.). This time they appear as *"virgins,"* i. e., according to Rothe, celibates. Mark well, however, that, in adopting this interpretation, we have to conceive of them as 144,000 celibate Jewish Christians, assuming, moreover, that, on account of their celibacy, they have attained a more elevated position in Heaven. It is thus that the Apocalypse is handled, whilst, in simple accordance with Biblical style, the sealed Israel denotes the sealed New Testament people of God, consisting of Jewish and Gentile Christians; and the idea of " virgins " is sufficiently explained by moral predicates, especially the genuinely Johannean predicate of purity and truth (chap. xiv. 5). Neither is it to be supposed that the plenary number of the elect in the Church Triumphant in Heaven and of the elect on earth in the Church Militant, necessarily denotes the same individuals. The entire people of God is denoted by the symbolical name Israel. And though the *heathen* [nations], chap. xxii. 2, and elsewhere, form an antithesis to these Jews, that

---

* F. Baader: The despot and the hierarch play into each other's hands.

† [The remarks of the author proceed upon the assumption that the terms *Jews* and *Israel* can be " literally " (normally) applied only to the *natural* seed of Abraham. This was the old Jewish idea; an opinion repugnant to one of the first principles of the Abrahamic Covenant, which recognized *proselytes* as forming as integral a portion of Israel as the natural seed, Gen. xvii. 12, 13;—condemned by the Baptist in the declaration, " God is able of these stones to raise up children unto Abraham," Matt. iii. 9; Luke iii. 8;—and denied and disproved by the Apostle Paul in his Epistle to the Romans; conf. ii. 28, 29, iv. 10-17, ix. 25, 26, xi. 17-24. After the *breaking off* of the natural seed, and the *engrafting* of the new stock, there was, of necessity, a two-fold use of the terms. Sometimes, and in the most proper sense, they were applied to the covenanted seed (consisting of both the natural seed and proselytes—the Christian Church) who enjoyed the Divine favor, as in Rom. ii. 29; Gal. vi. 16; and sometimes to the community (consisting principally of the natural seed—the Jewish nation), which, as a community, had been " broken off," although it continued to hold covenant relations and is to be grafted in again. The former of these uses was not of course forbidden by the fact that the adopted seed were for the most part uncircumcised, since it is within the power of the institutor of a covenant to change the seal thereof, as has been done in the present case. No confusion can possibly arise from this double use of the terms, since the context always determines the special sense. Both these applications of the terms are *literal*, or more correctly speaking, *normal;* neither is, in any proper sense, figurative. The error of those contemplated by Lange consists, not in their contending for a literal application of the term, but in their ignoring the first and most important of its literal meanings.—E. R. C.]

term also is a symbolical expression for the, as yet, unredeemed, considered particularly as masses of peoples. Hence, therefore, it does not follow that the heathen [nations] and races [kindreds] and peoples and tongues, chap. vii. 9, with which the sanctification of the principle of nationality in the Kingdom of God is explicitly declared, form a subordinate complement to the 144,000 elect of Israel; this is the less tenable, since the so-called Gentile Christians are already in Heaven (chap. vii. 9), whilst the so-called Jewish Christians are still being sealed on earth; in antithesis to the 144,000 virgins standing upon the heavenly Mount Zion, whilst the heathen [nations] are still exposed to temptation on the earth (chap. xiv. 8). Further particulars we reserve for our EXEG. AND CRIT. NOTES *in loc.* Compare Düsterdieck, p. 274 sqq.

It would lead us too far if we should attempt to examine in detail all the human relations touched upon in the Apocalypse, in respect of their symbolical import, and we should also be obliged to repeat many of our explanations further on in this Commentary. Nevertheless, we present the following considerations under the following caption.

g. Human Ordinances, Affairs, and Relations.

The Lord's day [Rev. i. 10]. Sunday as the resurrection-day in the literal sense, and also at the same time as symbolical—the feast-day of the soul.

The trumpet [ch. i. 10]. The signal for the beginning of a new and holy Divine period; of a new Divine work; a new Divine war, judgment, and victory.

The book [*i. e.,* the *volume* or *roll,* ch. i. 11]. Divine decrees in a mysterious envelope.

The book of life [ch. xx. 12, 15]. The sum of those whose salvation is assured, being fixed by sealing, and founded upon election, calling, justification, and conservation amid trial and temptation.

The little book [ch. x. 8, 9, 10]. Prophecy relative especially to the end of the world. It is sweet in the mouth, the most delightful mystery, but agonizing in the belly, with its revelation of horrible depths of perdition and judgment.

The seven churches [ch. i. 11, *etc.*]. Types of the seven ground-forms in which the Church of Christ presents itself in secular and ecclesiastical history. [But, at the same time, literal churches. The view of the author seems first to have been advocated by Vitringa and Sir Isaac Newton.—E. R. C.]

The candlestick [ch. i. 12]. The Church as a light-bearer; like the star, a fountain of light issuing from the Lord, as the Primal Source.

The garment [ch. i. 13]. The festal high-priestly robe in a spiritual sense.

The altar [ch. vi. 9, viii. 3]. The symbol of all believing renunciation and devotion; not, however, in the coldness of indifference, but in the holy glow of a life of prayer.

Nicolaitans [ch. ii. 6, 15] *and Balaamites* [ver. 14]. The former are a type of all such antinomianism as is inwrapped in spiritual rational forms. *Jezebel* [ch. ii. 20] denotes the visionary, fanatic forms of antinomianism, whilst the Balaamites are indicative of sensually egoistic forms of the same.

Paradise. The new [ch. ii. 7]. The new world, as a world of new, imperishable fullness of life, reposing upon the consummation of the congregation of human spirits under the influence of the Divine Spirit.

Tree of life [ch. ii. 7, xxii. 2, 14]. Trees of life, of which not only the fruits, but also the leaves are productive of health. The full healing power of nature, freed from all restraint and conjoined with the healing power of Christ and Christian spiritual life; present in distinct organs and forms.

Synagogue of Satan [ch. ii. 9, iii. 9]. A perversion of the elements of revelation to the service of darkness; a perversion based upon theories, and propagandist in character.

The second death [ch. ii. 11, xx. 14]. An unending consciousness of death, that has become an unending form of life. A dying and an inability to die.

The hidden manna [ch. ii. 17]. See John vi. 32 ; the nourishment of the personal life, through the most intimate and personal vital communion with Christ.

The white stone [ch. ii. 17]. The eschatological justification in the judgment (Matt. xxv.), as a defence against every accusation and a removal of every stain. Christ's confession of His confessor, before His Heavenly Father.

The secret name [ch. ii. 17]. The mystery of a perfected, individually modified personal essence and self-consciousness.

The commission of fornication and the eating of things sacrificed to idols [ch. ii. 14, 20]. Lapse into worldly opinions, customs, society.—*Adulterers* [ver. 22]. Those laden with the guilt of apostasy. Spiritual renegades on the down-hill road to apostasy.

Cast into a bed [ch. ii. 22]. Sarcastic form of judgment. The vortex of antinomistical essence and perdition, changing from the semblance of Divine bliss to demonic torment.

The depths of Satan [ch. ii. 24]. An ironical designation of the mighty lies, or the apparent depths of knowledge reposing in the principles of Satanic denial.

The rod of iron (Ps. ii.) [ch. ii. 27, xii. 5]. The sceptre of Christ's rule as a sceptre of judgment ;—of such judgments as mediately proceed from His work. " I am come to kindle a fire."

Defiled garments ; White garments [ch. iii. 4, 5]. Antithesis of a spiritual appearance defiled by carnality (avarice, ambition, sensuality), and such a development of the spiritual mind as has ripened into the adornment of blamelessness before the world and before God.

The open door [ch. iii. 8]. Free spiritual ingress into the world in order to its conversion: a freedom of access mediated by the removal of traditional hindrances, and a Divinely effected susceptibility of souls for the testimony of Christ.

The key of David [ch. iii. 7]. The Potentate over the true communion of the Kingdom of God, having the power of reception and exclusion ; in accordance with the typical import of David, as the royal vicar of God in the old Theocracy.

The pillar in the temple of God [ch. iii. 12]. A man in Christ, whose importance is due to the fact that Christ has constituted him an ornament to His house, rather than that He has rested upon him a particle of the Temple's weight.

Behold, I come quickly [ch. iii. 11]. This *quickly* or *soon* is ever being more wearisomely protracted, in the judgment of modern exegetes ; but it is in reality ever growing *sooner*, in accordance with the eschatological expectation of a faith that can distinguish between a religious and a chronological date.

The crown [ch. ii. 10, iii. 11]. The glory of victory, liberty, dominion. *The Amen* [ch. iii. 14]. The personal centre and ultimate goal of all the promises of God and all the true religious hopes of humanity.

Cold, hot [Lange, *warm*], *lukewarm* [ch. iii. 15, 16]. Indifferent ; living ; inwardly inclined to indifference, by a constant wavering betwixt God and the world.

The supper [ch. iii. 20]. The festive solemnization of personal vital communion with Christ and the brethren ; as a feast at even, commemorative of the termination of earthly woe, and of an arrival at the eve of heavenly felicity.

The seven seals [ch. v. 1]. The seven dark enigmas of worldly history, unsolvable for the natural human mind ; rendered yet more terrible by the number six contained in them, which, to the worldly mind, gives them the appearance of endless woe ;* but endued with holiness and healing might by their union in the number seven.

The four riders [ch. vi. 2–8]. Christ as a rider, *i. e.*, as Lord over the world-historical movement corresponsive with Him ; the three following riders being His esquires, *i. e.*, absolutely and entirely subservient to the work of Christ.

Golden vials [ch. v. 8]. In form, holy, beauteous measures ; made of the gold of purity, faithfulness, and vital freshness.

---

* [This remark tends to the destruction of all confidence in the symbolical significance of numbers. If it be valid here, it is valid wherever *seven* occurs, since every seven contains six. On this platform every superior number contains all the symbolic significance of all the numbers inferior to it, which is to reduce the whole matter to an absurdity. These remarks, of course, do not extend to the *expressed* integers of composite numbers, as 6+1=7.—E. R. C.]

The new song [ch. v. 9, xiv. 3]. As the theocratic wonder, in word and deed, is the specifically *new thing* under the sun, and as consequently the redemption in Christ, as the New Testament, is the *principial* new world, so the new song is the celebration of the new world, as the anticipatory celebration of its perfected appearing.

The bow [ch. vi. 2]. Attribute of the first Rider. An agency effectual at a distance; sure, decisive, victorious operation.

The great sword [ch. vi. 4]. Attribute of War.

The balances and measures [ch. vi. 5, 6]. Attributes of Poverty and Death.

Appearance of the kingdom of the dead, or the group of the powers of death [ch. vi. 8]. Attribute of Death.

The souls under the altar [ch. vi. 9]. All martyrdom a sacrificial suffering for the sake of Christ, and an actual prayer for the coming of perfect retribution.

The seal of God [ch. vii. 2]. Positive confirmation and conservation of faithful souls amid the sorrows and temptations of the world; a fact and a consciousness in a unitous heroism.

Dan? The omission of Dan in the enumeration of the Twelve Tribes [ch. vii.]. This is a mysterious circumstance; one, however, which assuredly is not to be explained by placing the Danites in the category of outcasts. It is based rather upon a conventional Israelitish symbolism, being supported by the fact that a great portion of the Tribe of Dan emigrated at an early period. The number twelve, in which no Tribe is missed, shows that deficits in the Kingdom of God are speedily remedied, as was the case when Judas dropped out of the company of Apostles (see Acts i.).

The living fountains of waters (chap. vii. 17). See Ps. xxiii.; here, in the sense of final and perfect thirst-quenching.

The golden censer and the incense [ch. viii. 34]. Spirit and life of prayer.

Wormwood [ch. viii. 11]. Here, the image of a fatal water-miasma. Spiritual water miasms are moral corruptions, infecting reformatory efforts of, and for, the popular life.

The three woes [ch. ix. 12]. Why not seven? They appear as three specifically demonic and Antichristian sufferings, for the trial of the inhabiters of the earth. They are marked by the fifth, sixth, and seventh trumpets (chap. viii. 13).

The key of the pit of the abyss [ch. ix. 1]. The abyss is here hell itself; the pit of the abyss, the channel of such Satanic operations as earth is the subject of* (Matt. xiii. these operations are presented under the figure of *tares*—evil principles); the fact that the pit was shut is indicative of the preponderance of the holy counter-operations and institutions of the Kingdom of God; the *key* to the pit denotes the opening of the channel by means of liberty in the abstract, falsely understood,—the administrator of this liberty being an angel of judgment; the ascending smoke is significant of demonic operations which darken the sun of life, the heavenly world, and spread abroad an unheard-of amount of psychical sufferings, hypochondrias, mental and spiritual maladies, despair, and the like.

Worship of devils and idolatry (ch. ix. 20). In a general sense, the cowardly and hypocritical recognition of the power of evil, the homage offered to the geniuses of wickedness— a homage which, from time to time, makes its appearance, whilst it ever assumes mightier proportions—is a worship of the devil, in the broader sense of the term; it very readily unites with the grossest forms of idolatry,—especially figurative idolatry.

The measuring reed [ch. xi. 1]. Temple, altar, and worshippers are measured. The measuring reed of the spiritual life defines the true temple of worship, the true altar of renunciation, the congregation of true offerers of prayer. *The outer court, the heathen* [*Gentiles*] : the outside of the Church, false Christians. *The golden reed* (ch. xxi. 15), the Divine consciousness and heavenly precision in respect to the City of God.

Sackcloth as the garb of the two witnesses [ch. xi. 3]. Penitential robes. Gloomily austere phases of Christianity, in the forms of State and Church.

Power of the two witnesses. For instance, in pronouncing sentence of excommunication and outlawry; in declaring war and proclaiming peace.

---

* [Remarks on this and many other topics presented in the Introduction are reserved for the Commentary.—E. R. C.]

The great city called Sodom and Egypt [ch. xi. 8]. On the one hand, sensuality carried to a pitch directly contrary to nature; on the other, worship of the dead, asceticism and sorcery; carnality and demonicalness—the one aiding the other, and both forming the sign of the city of destruction.

The wrath of the heathen [nations], *and, in contrast, the wrath of God* [ch. xi. 18]. The two exercise a reciprocal action. Extreme excitement in the supposed autonomy of the heathenized nations, and extreme tension in the autonomy of God—the two in reciprocal agitation.

Worship of the dragon [ch. xiii. 4]. Similar to the worship of the devil. Cowardly homage offered to the illusive power and glory of Evil.

The tabernacle of God [ch. xiii. 6]. The communion of true believers. The Church in her inwardness and simplicity. See Acts xv. 15, 16; Amos ix. 11, 12.

Victory of the beast over the olive-trees [ch. xi. 7]. The apparent victory of Evil, gradually issuing in the victory of Good. And that above all, in the history of the crucifixion of Christ. The history of the crucifixion is the history of the cross. *The eschatological fundamental law*, chap. xiii. 10: If the Church take upon herself to wield the arms of the State, she must expect to have those arms turned against herself.

The image of the beast [ch. xiii. 14, 15]. The worship paid to the images of the Roman emperors may serve as an analogue for the worship of the ideals current in the world; for the glorifications and feasts in honor of Antichrist and Antichristianity. *The mark of the beast in the forehead and hand*, as the Antichristian mark of citizenship (vers. 16, 17). The heathen custom of branding slaves may furnish the analogous idea; the true mark of the beast, however, is doubtless a spiritual signature; the mark on the *brow* denoting perfect shamelessness, and that on the *hand* perfect wrong-doing.

666. *Six times and sixty times and six hundred times* [ch. xiii. 18]. Constant recurrence of the number six; hence the number of aimless work, of infinitely vain exertion and lost toil, which things are to reach their climax in the Man of Sin.

144,000 [ch. vii. 4, xiv. 1]. Twelve times twelve, or the number of the elect in all spiritual tribes or churches, multiplied by 1000 as the number of the æon of the whole Christian time-reckoning.

The voice [ch. xiv. 2]. The loud expression of a heavenly certitude. *The art of singing the new song*, ver. 4: the clear expression of heavenly bliss, an inimitable Divine art.

The virgins [ch. xiv. 4, 5]. It is evident from the context that they are chiefly characterized by integrity, purity, and truth.

The everlasting Gospel [ch. xiv. 6]. The Gospel in its first form extends from the first Parousia to the second; the everlasting Gospel extends from the second Parousia into endless æons. It is the Gospel of the final redemption through the final judgment.

The consummation of Babylon, the fall of Babylon [ch. xviii. *etc.*]. A royal law of the moral world. See Is. xiv. Jerusalem itself passed through a period of apparent bloom just prior to its destruction. The reign of Agrippa II.; the synagogues scattered everywhere; the proselytes and proselyte colonies; an apparently flourishing culture, and a national pride morbid in its excess.

The wine of wrath of fornication [ch. xviii. 3]. The wine of wrath, the judgment of God in the midst of the intoxication of fanaticism; the wine of the wrath of fornication, drunken exhilaration in the intoxication of apostasy.

The cup of His indignation [ch. xiv. 10, 11]. Lofty irony! Here expressive not so much of the Divine measure as of the visibility of this judicial dispensation.

The sickle [ch. xiv.] The instrument of judgment. The catastrophe which suddenly cuts short the old course of things.

The harvest [ch xiv. 15]. The fully matured judgment. [The harvest is properly the ripened crop—the peoples matured for judgment.—E. R. C.].

The wine-press [ch. xiv. 19, 20]. The crushing disaster accompanying the judgment and pressing from all crimes all their consequences; the process being at first attended, for the most part, with healing results (Is. lxiii. 3), but at the end being principally damning in its character.

The bridles of the horses, [ch. xiv. 20]. If the blood of the slain reaches to the bridles of the horses, it brings the horses, the organs of motion in the history of the world, to a stand-still ; the *course of time* is arrested. The space filled by the judgment is designated by the 1600 furlongs or stadia—that measurement being the length of Palestine, which symbolizes the whole world.

The song of Moses, and the song of the Lamb (ch. xv. 3). In the light of the New Testa-ment, the Old Testament becomes new, and the Law becomes another form of the Gospel.

The temple of the tabernacle of the testimony (ch. xv. 5). The inner and lofty primal region of the glory of God, and of His legislation.

The seven golden vials [ch. xv. 7]. As wrath is the lofty synthesis of righteousness and love, so the judgments of wrath are highly consecrate in respect of their sacred measures and their awful contents.

The Euphrates. The boundary line between the civilized and the barbarous world of antiquity ; on this side, Babylon (ch. ix. 14), on that side, the kings of the barbarian world (ch. xvi. 12). *Armageddon* (Zech. xii. 11, xiv. 4; Joel iii. 2, 12). Is there a reference to 2 Kings xxiii. 29, or Judges v. 19? See EXEG. NOTES. At all events, it is the place of the incipient judgment upon Antichristianity.

The golden cup in the hand of the woman [ch. xvii. 4]. Seduction in the guise of con-version to the truly holy. *The mother of harlots and abominations.* Not merely a harlot, but also a procuress in a spiritual sense.

The drunken woman [ch. xvii. 6]. The complete intoxication of consummate fanaticism.

The seven mountains and the seven kings [ch. xvii. 9, 10]. Seven forms of worldly civilization and worldly powers represented by the City of the Seven Hills.

The beast itself as the eighth king [ch. xvii. 11]. The beast, which is said to be *of the seven kings,* becomes itself the eighth king, through its intervals of existence. The heathen Antichristian world-power revives again in a Christian world-power.

The going forth out of Babylon [ch. xviii]. As the Christians went forth from Jerusa-lem when her judgment began. For the judgment is half immanent, — the intoxication of wrath.

The triumphal song and the lamentation [ch. xix. 1–7, xviii. 17–19]. The judgment in respect to its two sides ; their reflection in the Kingdom of light and the kingdom of darkness.

The sea-farers [ch. xviii. 17]. See above.

The merchants [ch. xviii. 11]. See above.

The millstone [ch. xviii. 21]. It is cast into the sea of the life of the nations, and now begins a storm that comes as a judgment upon the beast. The *smoke* (ver. 18), the dark and gloomy phenomena of judgment.

Amen; Hallelujah [ch. xix. 4]. Both real. God's prophecy, word and work sealed, and the eternal praise of God grounded thereon.

The Marriage of the Lamb [ch. xix. 7]. *Those called to the Marriage* [ver. 9]. See Matt. xxv. 1 sqq.

The Woman, the Bride [ch. xix. 7]. The perfected Church.

Her adornment [ver. 8]. The glorious appearance of her inner life.

The testimony of Jesus. Ch. xix. 10; Matt. x. 32; Luke xii. 8; Matt. xxv.

The name of Christ, His secret (ch. xix. 16; comp. ch. ii. 17; Matt. xi. 27).

The vesture of the Prince of victory (ch. xix. 13). His *blood* is, in the first place, the color of His personal, priestly righteousness.

The sword and the rod (ch. xix. 15). Justice and government.

The fowls (ch. xix. 17). Where the carrion is, *etc.*

The thousand years [ch. xx. 2–7]. See above.

The first resurrection (ch. xx. 4–6). The vernal bloom of the new spiritual humanity in its elect ones ; the foretoken of the general resurrection. *Excommunication and reception of the Gentiles* [ch. xxi. 26, 27]. A complete antithesis of dynamical operations of repulsion and attraction. [See Add. NOTE on the FIRST RESURRECTION in the Comment on ch. xx., pp. 352 sqq.—E. R. C.]

h. Terrestri-cosmical.

The antithesis of Heaven and earth appears throughout this Book in all its significance—a significance intimated as far back as Gen. i. 1 ; the region of the perfection of *heavenly being* extending over the region of *becoming*. Hence, throughout the Apocalypse, the heavenly triumphal feasts precede the conflicts of earth. When finally, however, the true Heaven in Heaven, the City of God, descends upon the earth, it is a sign that earth itself has been perfected into a centre of Heaven,—a centre of Christ's presence, of God's glory, of the perfected Church (ch. xx., xxi.).

Connected with the earth and its cosmical position are the notations of time. *The half-hour*, the smallest measure of time [in the Apocalypse],—a pause replete with expectation ; a moment of extremest tension. *The hour*, a great and unique period of decision (Luke xxii. 53) ; see the *last hour*, 1 John ii. 18. *The day*, symbol of day's work in its movement towards the end of the world, that great evening when labor is done. The 1260 *days*, the great period of the Church as a regulated course of things, arranged in days' works which are preparatory to the end of the world. *Three days and a half*, the fractional week ; the overpast time of resurrection and hope ; the time of extreme despondency. Amongst the diurnal seasons, *morning* and *evening* are especially significant. *Morning* as the cheerful dawn of a new period ; *evening* as a symbol of the end of the world (Ps. xxx. 5 ; Zech. xiv. 7). *Night*, as a symbol of darkness and misfortune (Is. ix. 2, xxi. 11), is possessed of peculiar grandeur and solemnity at *midnight ;* just at this awful climax, however, its higher import unfolds. *Night*—the time of secrecy (the darkness in the Holy of Holies) ; of conception and birth (Job iii.) ; of meditation (Ps. i. 2)—has been consecrated as a period of salvation, both by the first coming of Christ and by the expectation of His second Advent ; and the effulgence in the time of the consummation of all things is pictured as a higher union of day and night (Rev. xxi. 23. See below). If, however, the night be divided into *night-watches*, the conflict of the day is transferred, with increased hotness, to the night. *The week :* the little periodical alternation of seasons of darkness and light. The 70 *weeks*, seven times seven such revolutions of light and darkness to the consummation of the Messianic Kingdom. Thence, 62 *weeks* to the death of Christ (Dan. ix. 26). *One week*, the Apostolic age, with the destruction of Jerusalem in the midst of the week (ver. 27). Finally, 7 *weeks*, until the Messiah appears as King in His glory ; the New Testament time (ver. 25). *The month*, or the greater periodical revolution of time, as alternating seasons of light and darkness (42 months=1260 days). *The year*, the greatest symbol of the revolution of time, as an alternation betwixt diverse periods of conflict between light and darkness ; therefore the period of history,—a great day's work of God. *A thousand years*, a complete æon ; used especially to denote a transition-period culminating in the appearing of the æon of consummation at the second Parousia of Christ. The indefinite form—*three times and a half* (Rev. xii. 14)—is an involved [*mathematical*] term for the obscure form, *three days and a half*. Amongst the seasons of the year the symbol of *autumn* is particularly intelligible (Rev. xiv. 15). The symbolism of *spring* finds its most beautiful expression in the Song of Solomon, ch. ii. 11–13. As *summer* appears in connection with *autumn*, so *winter* is found in connection with *spring*. In regard to the change of day and night, we have already touched upon an antithesis which should not be overlooked ; *viz.*, that in the City of God of the new earth, the contrast of day and night is removed (ch. xxi. 25 ; xxii. 5—the region of eternal sunshine), whilst the damned are assigned to a region of change and of *becoming*,—a region where the contrast of day and night continues, where they are tormented day and night from æon to æon [ch. xiv. 11]. Not only does the change of day and night continue, therefore, but there is likewise a succession of different æons.

In respect to the earth's space-relations, the most prominent antithesis is that of *land* and *water*, *earth* and *sea*. *Earth* symbolizes life in its theocratic, ecclesiastic, or political organization (Pss. xciii. 1, xcvi. 10 ; Rev. xiii.). The *sea*, on the other hand, symbolizes the billowy life of peoples (Pss. lxv. 7, lxxxix. 9, xciii. 3, 4 ; Dan. vii. : Rev. xiii.). Accordingly, the *earthquake* is a shaking of all ancient authorities and regulations (1 Kings xix.

11, 12; Matt. xxviii. 2). The *stormy flood of ocean*, on the other hand, is a vehement agitation of national life — an onslaught, frequently, against the holy mountains, or *the* holy mountain of God (Pss. xv. 1, lxv. 7; Is. ii.). The second power [*mathematical*] of earth is the *mountain*,—high and highly consecrate order. The third power is the *rock*,—the Divine will, purport, Spirit, and design pervading the history of the world; everything striking against this rock is dashed in pieces (Deut. xxxii. 31, 37; Ps. xviii. 2; Is. viii. 14; Matt. xvi. 18. See above).

Christ's Kingdom is most significantly compared to a *stone* which detaches itself from a mountain—that is, the old Theocracy.

The import of the sea also is multiplied to a second and third power in the *abyss*, and the *pit of the abyss ;* in the complete unchaining of all national life and its connection with all demonic influences of hell. In the consummation, however, the sea of the unfreely flowing national life is to vanish from earth (Rev. xxi. 1), to form, in its precipitation, the *pool of fire*,—absolute stagnation in the form of passionate fermentation and commotion. The clear proceeds of land and sea, meantime, form the heavenly *sea of crystal*, wherein the infinite fullness, freshness, and movement of life are joined with infinite moral firmness and solidity, and ideal transparency and clearness.

Diminutive forms of the earth are, especially, *islands ;* the remote islands of secluded branches of peoples (Ezek. xxvii. 3, *et al. ;* Rev. xvi. 20).

Diminutive forms of the sea are *rivers*, or spiritual currents (spirits of the times, Is. viii. 6); and *springs*, or spiritual sources, creative personalities (Ps. xlvi. 4,* and other passages).

Individual Images.

The four corners of the earth [Rev. vii. 1, xx. 8]. Indicative of the uttermost ends of the earthly world; last and highest power [*mathematical*] of spiritual heathenism in antithesis to the Christian οἰκουμένη of the Millennial Kingdom. In connection with this, we have the term—

Gog and Magog [ch. xx. 8]. Symbolical designation of the Eastern barbarians as the last enemies of the Kingdom of God. See Ezek. xxxviii. and xxxix.

The mountain that fell, burning, into the sea [ch. viii. 8]. An old order of things which, blazing up in fanaticism, plunges into the service of absolute democracy. Poisoning of the popular life.

The third part of the waters become wormwood by means of the star " Wormwood." The embitterment of a great spirit results in the embitterment of many rivers, or currents of the age, issuing from many fountains, or original spirits or minds.

i. Siderial.

As Heaven in general is used as a symbol, in contrast to the symbolical import of earth (see *Terrestri-cosmical*, Rev. xii.), so the heavenly luminaries and signs, in particular, are exalted symbols.

Such is, above all, the *sun*. Considered by itself alone, it denotes the spiritual centre of the Cosmos, the revelation of God upon the earth ; finally, the appearing of Christ (Mal. iv. 2; Rev. x. 1).

As the companion of the sun, shining with its reflected lustre, the *moon* may, on the one hand, denote the Church ; as a symbol of change, however, and as a counterpart of the sun, it appears not to have been employed very extensively in this sense. The *stars*, considered apart, denote exalted spirit-forms, originally heavenly beings (Is. xiv. 12; Rev. i. 20).

In connection with the moon and stars, the sun appears (Rev. xii. 1) as the symbol of the Christian Cosmos, a local centre of the entire Cosmos ; at times it also, in this connection, symbolically represents the entire Cosmos.

---

* [We have to note a variation in translation here; the German Version reads thus: Nevertheless, the City of God, where the holy dwelling-places of the Most High are, shall still be joyful with her springs.—Tr.]

The *dawn* is a very obvious symbol for the rising of light (Is. lviii. 8); such likewise is the *morning-star*, the herald of the coming sun : they both particularly symbolize the rising of the Sun of righteousness within the heart (2 Pet. i. 19). Christ Himself, in His first Parousia, is related to His second Parousia as the Morning-star to the Sun and the great Day of Eternity.

All extraordinary signs in the Heavens are symbolical tokens that, with the spiritual development of mankind in the Church of Christ, a development continuing to the end of the world, there corresponds a cosmical development in the sphere of the world, so that these signs are to be regarded as signals on the heavenly heights telling of spiritual events of which earth is the scene (comp. Matt. xxiv. 29; Luke xxi. 25; Heb. xii. 26; Rev. vi. 12. The author's *Leben Jesu*, Vol. II., Part iii., p. 1276).

Special Items.

The sun black, the moon like blood, the stars falling, *etc.* (ch. vi. 12 sqq.). Cosmical import: metamorphosis of the old solar planetary system.

A burning star falls from Heaven upon the rivers and fountains [ch. viii. 10]. An apostasy in the spirit-world, having earth for its goal, and poisoning the third part of the mental and spiritual tendencies and original minds (like the burning mountain that falls into the sea, an authority that apostatizes from itself to the popular life).

The tail of Satan casts the third part of the stars of Heaven upon the earth [ch. xii. 4]. Great apostasy in the Kingdom of God, the spiritual Heaven. Transfiguration of spiritual powers into earthly pseudo-political forms.

Signs of the false prophet [ch. xiii. 13]. Illusive wonders. Magical miracles.* The two greatest signs : [1] He makes fire fall from Heaven *in the sight of men ;* according to human judgment. False imitation of Elijah ; misuse of the great ban.—[2] He gives a spirit to the image of the beast so that it speaks. The ideal of the beast, a demonic, forced and falsified caricature of public opinion.

The fire from God out of Heaven, which devours the Satanic host of Gog and Magog [ch. xx. 9]. The cosmical fiery metamorphosis of the earth at the end of the world, 2 Pet. iii. 10.

The new Heaven and the new earth [ch. xxi. 1]. The cosmical union of the two spheres of spirit—the one existing in this world, the other in the world beyond—as the appearance of the new and eternal city of God.

k. Sub-terrestrial Demonic Figures.

Hades (Sheol), the realm of the dead (ch. vi. 8), must be regarded as entirely distinct from the pool of fire, Gehenna, hell (ch. xix. 20, xx. 14, 15). The abyss (ch. ix. 2) seems to denote a transition-form. As Hades and the pool of fire are used symbolically, the former denoting the power of the realm of the dead even upon earth, and the latter signifying not merely the sphere of the damned, but also the manner of their spiritual existence—extreme turbulence of passion in the midst of extreme stagnation—so the abyss, likewise, has a symbolical import. It seems to denote the original region of psychico-demonic moods (ch. ix. 5); according to this, Abaddon or Apollyon should be regarded as the personification of God-deserted demonic melancholy and insanity.† The influences issuing from the abyss are, however, less pernicious than the pneumatico demonic corruptions which come from the Euphrates,—that is, from Babylon.

---

* [Do not the words of our Lord, Matt. xxiv. 24, and those of Paul, 2 Thess. ii. 9, imply that the miracles are to be real? The terms employed on both these occasions (σημεῖα and τέρατα) are those used to indicate the miracles of our Lord Himself. The phrase τέρασι ψεύδους (miracles of falsehood) of 2 Thess. ii. 9, does not necessarily mean aught else than miracles to confirm the "lie" (ψεύδει) which (verse 11) the Apostle declares that those who are deluded shall believe; and this seems to be its most natural interpretation. There can be little doubt that the signs and wonders (σημεῖον and τέρας.—LXX.) of which Jehovah warned His people, Deut. xiii. 1–3, were real miracles, which God would empower false prophets to work for the purpose of proving Israel.—E. R. C.]

† [See Excursus on Hades, under ch. xx. 13, 14.—E. R. C.]

A synagogue of Satan is spoken of in the epistle to Smyrna (ch. ii. 9), and in the epistle to Philadelphia (ch. iii. 9); a *throne of Satan* is mentioned in the epistle to Pergamus (ch. ii. 13); and we meet with the term "*depths of Satan*," *i. e.*, pretended depths, ironically so-called, in the epistle to Thyatira (ch. ii. 24). Satan himself appears (ch. xii.) as a *great red* (blood-colored) *dragon* (a union of serpent and swine). He has *seven heads*,—as if he were engaged in a spiritual work, holding forth the promise of a Sabbath—but *ten horns* of worldly power; he is thus characterized as a monster, yet nevertheless adorns himself with *seven crowns*,—in the semblance of holiness. *His tail drags the third part of the stars from Heaven, i. e.* not by intelligence, but by a wild vivacity, by his apparent power, he drags a multitude of spirits away with him,—not only in the angelic, but also in the human world; the latter is what is particularly meant here. For Heaven denotes also that Heaven on earth that consists of pure spiritual life, the centre of the Kingdom of God, the inner congregation of God. From Heaven *to the earth, i. e.*, a symbolical third part of human congregations, or individual churches, make use of the old established order of things (the *earth*) in the service of Satan. It is the intention of Satan to devour the holy *child;* not only is the child, however, personally rescued by being caught up to Heaven, but the universal Christ, also, of the inner congregation of faith, continues to find refuge in Heaven (*our citizenship is in Heaven* [Phil. iii. 20]), and from this Heaven of the pure spiritual Church, Satan is cast out by Michael and his angels (by the sovereign rule and authority of Christ and the operations of His Spirit). The woman finds refuge in the *wilderness*, in the unapproachableness of holy theocratic (not hierarchic) asceticism and renunciation; Satan's attempt upon her life is defeated by the *earth;* this, as the mighty spiritual and secular order of things, obtains the mastery over the floods of peoples with which Satan sought to overwhelm the Church. Thus, Satan's rage is powerless to reach either Christ or the essential Church; he, therefore, turns his efforts against Christians, as individuals (ch. xii. 17).

l. Sub-terrestrial and Terrestrial Demonic Forms.

In connection with the plenitude of heavenly, angelic appearances contained in the Apocalypse, the scantiness of its symbolism in reference to the demon-realm is very remarkable. In this point also it agrees perfectly with the Gospel of John, from which the healings of demoniacs are omitted. An explanation of both circumstances may probably be found in the fact that for John demonic beings retreated into the back-ground, leaving the more conspicuous place to demonic operations.

This very peculiarity lends additional distinctness to *Satan*, the principal demonic figure; to *Antichrist*, as his mature and world-historical organ in humanity,—the Bold or Wicked One, we may call him simply; and, as the organ of apostasy in the old religious moral world, to the *false Prophet*, whom we will call the Vile or Base One.

The human earth is under the influence of another cosmical region which has been the scene of a fall. The centre of this fall—a fall of spirits—is *Satan*, a fallen angel-prince; a *non plus ultra*, not of heavenly genius, but of talents originally worldly and still further secularized. The medium of demonic influence consists, not in magical operations, but in sympathetic, pseudo-spiritual operations; signals of false, pretended liberty. The bestial symbol of Satan is the *dragon*, as the union of serpent and swine.

Antichrist is the last and most perfect of the many Antichrists. He is neither the embodiment of evil (Daub, *Judas Iscariot*), nor a genius of evil, but man, deformed, through apostasy, into the most perfect organ of demonic worldliness in the working of mighty lies. His origin is the life of the nations demonically unchained—the *sea* (Rev. xiii.; Dan. vii.).

The *false Prophet* is the finished birth of worldliness in the secularized old theocratic, or rather hierarchico-political, order of things; he proceeds out of the *earth*. His tendency is to secure from Antichrist as large a share as possible of that universal dominion which is apparently devolving upon him; if possible, to trick him out of his booty; at all events to bear off a considerable portion of it out of the ruin of the old relations of things, by means of hypocritical homage to Antichrist, and by advancing his principles. The instrument which he makes use of for the furtherance of his ends is the false miracle, supported entirely by moral jugglery. His character, consequently, is that of true villainy, the type of which was Judas, who also thought to secure booty from ruin. His end is the pool of fire.

The insignia of Antichrist, or the demonic Beast, are similar to the insignia of the Devil himself. He, however, makes an open show of his insolence, and wears ten crowns instead of seven. He has also, in boldest despotism, set his crowns upon his horns. The diverse Danielic world-monarchies are united in him—the Leopard, the Bear, the Lion, hence, too, the fourth form, the monster (Dan. vii. 4–6). His apparent triumph is promoted by three things: first, by the healing of his deadly wound; secondly, by the boldness of his blasphemies (Rev. xiii. 5, 6); finally, by the accession of the great renegade, the false Prophet, the Beast of the earth, in whom the real spirit of the earth—i. e., of the old traditional order of things —accomplishes its apostasy. Yes, the Beast of the earth seduces "the earth" itself into worshipping Antichrist. The outward appearance of this Beast of the earth is characteristic; it is the form of the consummate hypocrite. He has two horns like a lamb [the Lamb?], but he speaks like a dragon [the Dragon?]. The wonders which he does, however, consist in jugglery; for only in a lying, magical way can he cause fire to fall from Heaven, and make the image of the Beast speak. His last and mightiest operation he effects by means of the ban of the mark. He completes the Antichristianity of the first Beast, as Judas completed the Antichristianity of the Jews.

m. Heavenly forms.

Heaven itself. In the concrete conception of the term, *Heaven* is the region of the absolute manifestation of God in the glory of Christ (ch. iv. 1 sqq.); in the spiritual acceptation, it is the region of the heavenly spirit-life, ideal Christianity (ch. xii. 7). Michael and his angels, *i. e.*, the sovereign rule of Christ in His organs, vanquishes Satan and his angels within the ideal Church (inward and outward foes). The consequence is, however, that Satan is cast upon the earth, *i. e.*, upon the earthly Churchly-political order of things.

Jehovah. God reveals Himself in the Apocalypse first as *Jehovah;* that is, as He Who is, Who was, and Who cometh (Rev. i. 4); this is in entire conformity to the believing expectation that His last manifestation will be in perfect unison with the Old and New Testament manifestations of Him. His manifestation is seven-fold in the *Seven Spirits* (see Isaiah xi. 2) that, as individual forms of the life of Christ, are all concentrated in the fullness of the Spirit resting upon the Son (ch. i.). This position of the Seven Spirits is likewise in accordance with the expectation of the perfect manifestation of Christ in seven forms throughout the ages. Then Jehovah appears as the *All-Ruler* upon the heavenly throne, and the glory of His throne and government is depicted anew, in symbolic traits. His appearance is described (ch. iv. 3); His heavenly Presbytery, the four and twenty elders (ver. 4); His manifestation or revelation (ver. 5); the celestially pure character and the operation of His government (the sea of glass) and the four fundamental forms of His government, the four beasts or living shapes (vers. 6–8). These glorify Him in the first place, for they are the fundamental forms of His government itself (ch. viii. 9). This actual glorification is reflected in the contemplation and praise of the elect heavenly spirits (vers. 9, 10). In His hand is the *sealed book* with the enigmas of the world's history (ch. v. 1). Furthermore, He appears as He that sitteth upon the throne, *i. e.*, the absolute Governor (ch. vi. 16). The prayers of the saints come *before God* (ch. viii. 4). Even the Angel who wears the features of Christ, swears by Him as the One who liveth from eternity to eternity, the Creator (ch. x. 6). He is in particular the *God of the earth* (ch. xi. 4), whose spirit of life re-animates the slain and faithful witnesses (ver. 11), proving Himself, by His raising of them, to be the God of Heaven, the Almighty One (ver. 17). His, also, is the Kingdom wherein the power of Christ rules (ch. xii. 10). He is the *Father* of Christ (ch. xiv. 1). He is, Himself, primarily the *Alpha and Omega*, the absolute Cause and the absolute End of all things; and He is the living unity of this antithesis as Jehovah, Who is, Who was, and Who cometh (ch. i. 8; comp. xxi. 6). But in union with Him, Christ also is Alpha and Omega, ch. xxii. 13 (i. 11).

In yet another passage [besides ch. x. 6] God the *Judge* is declared to be also the *Creator.*

Thus the Apocalypse, like the Gospel and Epistles of John, opposes the germs of Gnosticism (ch. xiv. 7). Hence, also, the *Song of Moses* and the *Song of the Lamb* accord in His praise [ch. xv. 3, 4]. His glory fills the heavenly Temple (ch. xv. 8). The last plagues are vials of His wrath [ch. xv. 1, 6, 7, xvi.]; and He it is Whose name men blaspheme on account of these plagues. He exercises absolute sovereignty over the world; He is ruler, therefore, even over evil, in that He turns it into judgment (ch. ix. 5, 14, xiii. 5, 15, xv. [xvi.], the judgment of impenitence, ch. xvii. 17). The rich doxologies of the Apocalypse are for the most part addressed to God, ch. iv. 8, 11 (comp. ch. v. 13, where the doxology of God is joined with that of the Lamb, the former, however, being placed first, ch. vii. 12, xi. 16, 17, xii. 10, xix. 1, 6); worship is likewise addressed to God. His is the Kingdom (ch. xix. 6); He executes the final judgment (ch. xx. 9, 12); from Him the new Jerusalem descends out of Heaven upon the earth and becomes the tabernacle of God, the Most Holy Place of His dwelling on earth itself (ch. xxi. 2, 3); He is the Beatifier (ver. 4). The relation betwixt God and the Lamb comes out distinctly in ch. xxi. 23, where it is declared that the glory of God lightens the City of God, and the Lamb is the light thereof; *i. e.*, Christ the visible image, the perceptible manifestation of God (see ch. xxii. 3, 5). As the God of the spirits of the Prophets, God is likewise the primal source of the Apocalypse itself (ver. 6).

Christ is adorned with all the features of the glorified God-manhood. The revelation of God is also the revelation of Christ. Grace proceeds from Him, as from Jehovah. His titles and traits combine His heavenly glory with His earthly work of redemption and salvation; chs. i. 5, 6, 11–18; v. 6–14; vi. 2; vii. 17; xi. 15; xii. 10; xiv. 1, 2, 14; xix. 11, 16; xxi. 23, xxii. 3. The motive of His glorification is everywhere His great work of redemption. This thought runs through the entire Book as its fundamental idea. He is the Lamb that was slain (ch. v. 6, 12); as Prophet, He is the Amen, the faithful Martyr (ch. iii. 14); as High-priest, He is the Atoner (ch. i. 5, vii. 14); as King, the Liberator or Redeemer (ch. v. 9), the Prince of the kings of the earth (ch. i. 5), the dynamical Prince of the world's history (ch. vi. 1); in the end appearing victoriously as such,—a King of kings and Lord of lords, Who has made His people a Kingdom of priests (ch. i. 6, v. 10, xix. 16); the most mysterious of all personalities (ch. xix. 12); in respect of His essential relation to the Father, the Logos of God (ch. xix. 13); in respect of His human nature, the Root of the race of David and the Morning-star of mankind (ch. xxii. 16).

The *Holy Ghost* is here glorified in concrete conceptions in the Seven Spirits; in the Spirit that takes possession of the spirit of the Prophet, becoming therein the spring of all visions (ch. i. 10, iv. 1, 2); He is also glorified as the principle of the certitude of eternal salvation and blessedness (ch. xiv. 13); and as the principle of the Church's longing for the Coming of her Lord (ch. xxii. 17). In accordance with the symbolical style of the Book, He also, like Christ Himself, several times appears in angelic form.

God's *seat* or *throne*, in its symbolical significance, requires no explanation. Since the Presbytery of Israel, like that of the Apostolic Church, consists of twelve persons, the *twenty-four elders* form a double Presbytery. This double Presbytery may, doubtless, be regarded as symbolically expressive of the choicest spirits, selected, on the one hand, from the human world, and, on the other, from the angelic world, and represented by the Patriarchs of Israel and the Twelve Apostles. We have elsewhere designated the *four living shapes* or *beasts* as fundamental forms of the Divine government.* Each of these Cherubim has six wings,— symbols of agitated, infinitely lively omnipresence. Each is covered with eyes, within and without,—symbols of omniscience and wisdom. They rest not day and night; they are ever conscious, moving, active, like the absolute rule of Divine Intelligence,—glorifying God continually as the Holy One and Jehovah.

Here, in the solemn company that surround the Almighty, *angels* are not immediately mentioned; in the progress of the action, however, they are brought in (ch. v. 11), and they appear throughout the Book as the media of God's government. For the designation of

---

* *Leben Jesu*, Vol. I., p. 235. Schleiermacher, p. 454, thinks that three more beasts [living-beings] are wanting, ch. vi., to complete the idea of the four beasts [living-beings], which interpret the first four seals. The four beasts [living-beings], however, refer to the fundamental forms of the world's history. [See Comment. on ch. iv. 6, p. 154.—E. R. C.]

personal angelic essences is connected with the idea that all manifestations and providences of God are, in a symbolical sense, angels. It is a mysterious circumstance that the principal angel of the Revelation, the Angel of Jesus Christ (ch. i. 1), likewise declares himself to be a personal angel (ch. xix. 10, xxii. 9). The prominence of angelic apparitions — in which Lücke pretends to discover a discrepancy between the Johannean Gospel and the Apocalypse —is primarily explained by the fact that we have here to do with an *epoch* of revelation, and that the final epoch, in which, as even the Gospels affirm, Christ is to appear in company with His angels [Matt. xxv. 31; Mark viii. 38. See *Comm. on John*, Am. Ed., p. 611.—Tr.]. The symbolical character of the Book must also be taken into account; in accordance with this, the spirits (heads?*) of the churches are called angels (ch. ii. and iii.). With the book of the seven seals, a strong angel makes his appearance, proclaiming the difficult problem of its unsealing (ch. v. 2). And now countless hosts of angels come forward, praising the Lamb (ver. 11). The four angels who hold the four winds of the earth (ch. vii. 1) are, we believe, symbols of the spiritual powers that hold the spirits of mankind in check; above them is set the Angel of Sealing, who, in accordance with the analogy of Scripture, is a symbol of the Spirit of God (ver. 2). He also is followed by a host of angels praising God (vers. 11, 12). Now the vision passes on to seven distinct angels who stand before God,—the angels of the trumpets—summonses to repentance, embodied in actual events (ch. viii. 2). Even these appear to be dependent upon the Angel who has in charge the prayers of t e saints. Here again, doubtless, we have a symbol of the Holy Ghost, Who, awhile ago, was represented by the Angel of the Sealing. An antithesis to the angels holding the four winds (ch. vii. 1) is formed by the four angels bound by the Euphrates, gloomy and mysterious forms which are identified with the judgment of the horsemen themselves (ch. ix. 15). That which constitutes them angels is not the character of personality, but the character of a Divine mission or the unity of four missions—corresponding to the whole world—of divine probational judgments. The absolute sovereignty of God over demonic darkness makes even Abaddon-Apollyon an *angel* of the abyss (ch. ix. 11).

Since the Parousia of Christ cannot yet be referred to in ch. x. 1, the mighty angel described there as bearing a complete resemblance to the image of Christ, is also, doubtless, a symbol of the Spirit of God. The Spirit of Sealing, the Spirit who represents the saints, by offering all their prayers before God, is also the Spirit of Prophecy concerning the approaching Coming of Christ. The Spirit of God has the little book of the eschatological Gospel in His hand. He over-rules the earth and the sea—stable order and the surging life of the nations. His voice is as the voice of a lion. Moved by Him, the seven thunders utter their voices; these thunders represent the entire course of reformations and missions in the Christian Church; a full revelation concerning these is withheld, because such revelation would encroach upon the free-agency of man. It is likewise the prerogative of the Spirit of God to swear, *i. e.*, to give certainty to the spirit of man. He is the author of New Testament prophecy (ver. 11). He distinguishes between the *Temple* of true worshippers and the *outer court* of the Church, which the Gentiles tread under foot (ch. xi. 1, 2). He it is Who causes the two olive-trees to be olive-trees, for oil is a symbol of the Spirit. That Michael, with his angels, in conflict with the Dragon and his angels, is indicative of the Spirit of Christ in His authoritative government, is to us an indisputable fact. The *eagle flying through Heaven* (ch. [viii. 13] xiv. 6) should likewise be noticed here as the angel of Apocalyptic Revelation to John himself, whose attribute the eagle has become. He flies through the midst of Heaven with his eschatological message, for this revelation flies through the whole sphere of the Christian spirit.

The Angel of Prophecy is succeeded by the Angel of the Church Triumphant (ver. 8); he is followed by the Angel of Judgment (vers. 9–11). The relation and conduct of the angels mentioned (ch. xiv. 14–20) is very mysterious. The form like unto the Son of Man, sitting upon the cloud and bearing the harvest-sickle, *i. e.*, commissioned to cut short the course of

---

* The Epistles are a component part of the Apocalypse itself, and not merely preparatory thereto. Hence th ir terminology, likewise, is symbolical—a fact unrecognized by Irvingism. It is not supposable that the *heads of the churches* should bear a relation to the *churches*, like that of *stars to candle-sticks*.

the world in order to judgment, is unmistakably Christ. The other angel, charged with the mandate to Christ, will then denote the message of the Father, Who hath reserved the time and the hour to Himself (ver. 15). Over against the specific *harvest* of Christ there is, however, also another harvest of condemnatory judgment. Accordingly, the fire-angel of the cosmical government of God, the angel who is [ideally] one with the altar of the universal sacrifice of the world in its old form (ver. 18) commands the angel who, in fellowship with Christ, executes the final judgment upon the earth, to thrust in his sickle also for the judgment of wrath. This latter angel with the sickle issues from the Temple (ver. 17); he appears further on (ch. xv. 6) to branch into the seven angels who dispense the vials of wrath. It is a very significant fact that these angels of judgment receive their vials from one of the four beasts [living-beings (ch. xv. 7)]; according to this, this individual life-form of Divine government intervenes between them and God. That the judgments executed are not blind events is shown by one of the seven angels, who acts as interpreter of these judgments (ch. xvii. 1, 7). This, therefore, is the Angel of Prophecy (ch. xiv. 15). Distinct from him is the Angel of Judgment itself (ch. xviii. 1 sqq.; comp. ch. xiv. 17). Somewhat obscurely the Prophecy goes back to the Angel of the Apocalypse in general (ch. xix. 9); again, however, we find the Angel of Prophecy (ch. xiv. 15, xvii. 1, 7), whilst after him the Angel of Judgment again appears (ch. xix. 17; comp. xviii. 1). His standing in the sun probably denotes the cosmical nature of the final judgment which he announces. The blessing of the renewal of the world attends upon the angel who shuts Satan up in the abyss (ch. xx. 1, 2). This angel has the same key that Christ has (ch. i. 18 —not to be confounded with ch. ix. 1). Subsequent to the consummation, as the union betwixt heaven and earth, we hear no more of angels until finally at the close, the Angel of the Revelation of Christ is again mentioned (ch. xxii. 8, [xxi. 9?]).

Angels alternate in a remarkable manner with heavenly *voices*. It is in accordance with the high ecstatic condition of the Prophet that the wonders of vision should be conjoined with wonders of hearing (ch. v. 2, 11, vi. 7, 10, viii. 13, x. 3, xiv. 6, 7, 9, 15, xviii. 2, xix. 17), or should alternate with them. The characterization of the heavenly voices is likewise significant. The first voice—and this is usual—introduces the vision. "I was in the spirit on the Lord's day, and heard behind me a great voice, as of a *trumpet*." The same voice further on resembles the sound of many waters (ch. i. 15). Again it is like a trumpet (ch. iv. 1). From the throne of God proceed lightnings and voices and thunders (ch. iv. 5), —holy revelations which become voices, voices which become thunders. A voice out of the midst of the four beasts (ch. vi. 6) causes the famine to appear as an infliction of specially conscious Divine dispensation. The prayers of the saints, having ascended to heaven, retroact upon the earth in voices and thunders, in lightnings and earthquakes (ch. viii. 5). Here preachings, words of thunder, precede the lightnings of new illumination and the shocks of mighty changes. A voice from the four horns of the altar (ch. ix. 13) directs, in conformity to this its origin, the immolation of a third part of mankind through the medium of a penal judgment (comp. ch. xvi. 7). It is in consequence of a heavenly voice that the Prophet eats the mysterious little book; the Holy Ghost quickens the word (ch. x. 8). A great voice from Heaven summons the two risen witnesses up to Heaven; a new and great revelation requires a new heavenly condition of State and Church in the form of the perfected Kingdom (ch. xi. 11, 12). Herewith are connected the great voices in Heaven announcing the dawn of the consummation (ch. xi. 15. Similarly the great voice, ch. xii. 10). At the opening of the Temple in Heaven, which now follows, a great hail accompanies the lightnings and voices and thunders and earthquakes (ch. xi. 19). The more detailed development of this latter figure (ch. xvi. 18, 21) makes the hail appear in the light of a great, terrible, and distressful decomposition of cosmical relations. The anticipatory celebration of the consummation in the heavenly Church of the elect is especially solemn (ch. xiv. 1 sqq.). Here the perfected life of nations, of geniuses or prophets, and of art, is united in the harmony of a new and lofty *song:* The voices of many waters, of a great thunder, and of harpers, singing a song that only the elect and holy company can learn. In yet fuller tones resounds the heavenly concert after the fall of the harlot, in anticipatory celebration of the marriage of the Bride (ch. xix. 1–7). It is also a heavenly proclamation that causes the writing of these words: *Blessed are the dead, etc.* (ch. xiv. 13); and how often have they been re-written! Again, the command to go forth from Babylon comes immediately as a voice from Heaven (ch. xviii. 4).

§ 7. PSYCHICO-PNEUMATIC MEDIA OF APOCALYPTICS.   APOCALYPTIC VISION.

a. Sacred Vision.

The Theology of the prophetic subjective form of this is wrapped in obscurity as yet.

Orthodoxism makes no distinction between objective phenomena addressing themselves to the common empirical perception of the five senses, and objective phenomena observable by the prophetic perception alone. Theosophy makes no distinction between the perceptive forms of the heathen mantic condition, in which man becomes the un-free, constrained tool of a mysterious influence, supposed to be of ghostly [spirit] origin—in a word between the pathologico-somnambulic form of perception—and the ethical ecstasy of the theocratic domain, in which the Seer is freed from the limits of common empiricism. Pantheistic rationalism makes no distinction between those salutiferous visions which are the sources of the higher life, yea, of the recovery of mankind, and fanatical hallucinations whose end is the mad-house (Strauss).

A result of the orthodoxistic confusion of ideas is the fact that the prophetic vision is regarded as merely one form of revelation among several; whilst, on the contrary, the vision is really the medium of all forms of revelation. This truth is expressed by the threefold development of the Hebrew terms denoting prophetic sight: [1] The Seer or Prophet (רֹאֶה); [2] The Proclaimer of new things (נָבִיא); [3] The Beholder or Seer (חֹזֶה).

The first thing that we shall premise relative to the subject of prophetic vision and also, in especial, of Apocalyptic vision, is the mysterious fact that a twofold form of con-sciousness is peculiar to the human soul,—a day consciousness, and a night consciousness. The latter forms the background of life, but is, however, generally veiled and hidden.

Our second premise is as follows: The liberation of the second consciousness was a thing of more ready occurrence when the nations were in their youth and filled with youth-ful presentiments, than whilst they were passing through the middle age of their develop-ment; a new liberation of this night-consciousness is in prospect for the time of perfect development.

It is a well-known fact that this second form of consciousness, the universal existence of which is betrayed by the most manifold signs, manifested itself among the Greeks in a *pathological* form (*manticism* [μαντεία, sooth-saying, divination]); this pathological form comes in contact with the *ethical* form only in the teachings of Socrates (*daimonism* [δαιμό-νιον]), being converted in the writings of Plato into a sort of theory; whilst on the line of Semitic tradition, the *ethical* form of vision has, amid the reciprocal action of Divine grace and the ethical struggling of elect spirits, been made the actual organ of revelation.

A polarity, therefore, meets us in all cases: a harmonious contrast of Divine manifesta-tions and human visions or transports—based, these latter, upon the being rapt out of the condition of ordinary consciousness (ecstasy). Without a Divine manifestation through the Holy Ghost, Who subserves Himself not only of natural phenomena and spiritual messengers, but also of the capacities and aptitudes of the human organism, there is no vision; without vision there is no Divine manifestation. Now although this contrast is harmonious and in-dissoluble in its nature, it is also one of great magnitude; it is, therefore, necessary for us to distinguish between forms of revelation which are predominantly *objective* and those in which the *subjective* element preponderates. The most objective form is that powerfulness of manifestation which reveals itself not only to the Prophets in the centre, but also, with a startling might, to profane individuals in their company (Moses in Egypt; Elijah on Mount Carmel; Christ in the Temple; Saul on the way to Damascus). The most subjective form of revelation is inspiration; such as traverses, unwaning, like a midnight sun, the conscious-ness of the Apostles. The perfect contrast is thus stated: the *objective* Divine novelty —the *wonder*, and the *subjective* Divine novelty—the *prophetic word* or the *preaching Prophet himself*.

Founded upon the psychological and historical conditions of revelation is the fact that its subjective forms can admit of augmentation to the richest degree, and diminution to a vanishing point. The beginning of revelationary vision is a *visional hearing* in a dream (Samuel); a form which is introduced by the natural-prophetic, significant *dream (e. g.,* Joseph's dream, Gen. xxxvii.), but must, however, be distinguished from that. The end of revelationary vision is an *Apostolic illumination,* the echo of which is heard long after in the Bath-kol.*

It results from the distinction of epochs and periods in the *inner*, pneumatic history of the world, that the miraculous forms of revelation become latent in the times of periodical development. From the universality of the prophetic aptitude in mankind (this is not saying as much as if we were to say—from the universality of the Christological [Theological?—E. R. C.] aptitude—comp. Acts xvii. 27), and from the momentousness of the human life, especially the Christian life, the expectation likewise results, however, that extraordinary and mysterious events will take place in all times.

Within the cycle of revelation the wonder of *hearing* develops into the wonder of *vision;* and the vision of the Seer, from whom the consciousness of the distinction betwixt empiric and prophetic sight is, as yet, absent, is developed in ghostly, historical events and visions, in the experience of which the consciousness of the distinction between this inward sight and common empiricism commences and continually increases.

But this suspense between prophetic experiences and the experiences of the five senses, does but constitute a transition between the incipient and the meridian point of prophecy. In the life of Abraham heavenly manifestation becomes a continual higher empiricism; he walks, like a holy child, on the borders of the spirit-world. In the life of Christ, on the other hand, the suspense between prophetic and ordinary vision is also done away with. His constant and every-day experience is for Him the recognized medium of an uninterrupted vision.

Not even the Apostles were able to walk on these heavenly heights of spirituality in this vale of earth. Christ walked in a faith that was, at the same time, sight; but the Apostles walked in faith, not in sight. Doubtless, however, their life of faith was founded upon, and interspersed with, moments of sight, whilst the intervals were filled up with the power of inspiration—a power which, indeed, for the moment and in particular relations, might sometimes be obscured [diminished]. On the other hand, however, there were also moments in the lives of the Apostles when momentary Divine manifestations were theirs in so rich and mighty a form as to develope into actual and lasting inspirations. The Sacred Writings were the issues of these forth-gushing springs.

On the meridian of a perfect union betwixt manifestation and inspiration, the canonical Apocalypse took its rise. It was based upon visions whose foundation was a burning longing for the Coming of the Lord; a longing awakened by the peculiar and oppressive character of the times, and cherished in minds that, by reason of their ideal nature, possessed a higher prophetic calling. Under the reciprocal action of this yearning and the Spirit of revelation, the visions took shape. In this longing, in the pangful attraction of love to the Coming of the Lord, the Old Testament Prophets could compete with the Apostles, and thus some of the former became, perforce, Apocalyptists. Each party excelled the other in some particular. The men of the Old Testament had not found satisfaction in the principially perfected redemption, as had those of the New Testament; their faith was pre-eminently hope; hence their longing in the face of the threatening of apparent ruin was more full of

---

* [We subjoin the following from Kitto's *Cyclopædia*. The whole article, which is too long for insertion here, is worthy of perusal. "BATH KOL (קוֹל בַּת, *daughter of the voice*). Under this name the *Talmud*, the later Targums, and the Rabbinical writers make frequent mention of a kind of oracular voice, constituting the fourth grade of revelation, which, although it was an instrument of Divine communication throughout the early history of the Israelites, was the most prominent, because the sole, prophetic manifestation which existed during (and even after) the period of the second Temple."—E. R. C.]

human passion, more darkly glowing, and their Apocalyptic productions were more richly colored, more manifold, more original. In the case of the Apostles, on the other hand, the New Testament longing developed gradually out of the most complete satisfaction drawn by faith from the principial redemption and overcoming of the world; the Apostles' longing was based upon this faith and soothed by it. And thus many passed away as martyrs in the first full enjoyment of the principial consummation; and in the case of a few only there was gradually developed a more distinct Apocalyptic vision (Peter, Paul). But one, John, the friend of Jesus, became the Seer and Prophet of His Advent in the truest sense. Hence the New Testament Seers continued scholars of those of the Old Testament in regard to Apocalyptical forms likewise. Whilst the latter were in advance of the former, so far as the painful pressure of unsatisfied longing is concerned, the former excelled in the universality, the spiritual clearness and fullness of their Apocalyptic views.

b. Sacred Vision in its Conjunction with Sacred Art; or Apocalyptic Composition.

The real problem of Apocalyptics is set forth in the question: How can visional ecstasy be conceived of as united to a calmly conscious, self-reflecting working of the materials gathered in such ecstasy into literary form and shape? The common prejudice is against such a combination. Not only ecstasy, but enthusiasm, or inspiration even, is regarded as forming a contrary antithesis to the reflective presentation of ideas or events and the artistic shaping of thought. Unconsciousness and *naïveté* of feeling are held to be requisite for the presentation of sacred matters. This opinion has a certain truth only as opposed to an over-nicety and artificialness of expression, affectation, false oratoricalness, and poetastery; it is, for the most part, however, itself biased by the mistaken idea that poetry and Prophecy must have a mantic ground-form. The example of poetry even, true, original and elevated poetry, exhibits a direct contradiction of this notion. There certainly does exist a distinction between the original conception of a poem and the artistic elaboration of it. But the mightier the conception, the richer the equipment of fundamental forms, poetic shapes and euphony that accompany it; besides, the original inspired contemplation of a subject continues, as a creative and formative power, throughout the entire calm, reflective and artistic process of elaboration. This is true of art in general; otherwise there could be no question of sacred art. Though we must, therefore, distinguish between the prophetic rapture, which can be so intensified as to cause the Prophet to sink, fainting, upon the earth, and the subsequent preaching of that which he has seen — yet the rapture is, in the first instance, as an ethical mood, fructified by the word of preaching, and in the word of preaching the continuous rapture attains its most complete expression. This fact is presented in the highest degree in the reciprocal operation of the mightiest manifestations and the calmest formative activity of inspiration, in which activity the original Divine voices shape themselves into the human word. Inspiration is in such perfect agreement with the most thorough deliberation and sober-mindedness that it may be clothed in all forms of true learning and pure art. This is true in the fullest degree of the Biblical Apocalypses; they are living syntheses of theocratic revelation and *Hebrew* art. The Johannean Apocalypse constitutes, in a three-fold aspect, the zenith of the canonical Apocalypses: first, it forms the zenith of eschatological vision; secondly, it forms the zenith of sacred art — art which is Hebrew, though breathed upon by the Greek spirit of measure and symmetry; and, thirdly, we behold in it the zenith of the union of vision and art. Thus it is in itself a typically prophetic presentation of the end of the world, in which the fullness of holiness shall appear in the full radiance of beauty — an intimidating and repellent mystery to the eyes of the profane world.

§ 8. FUNDAMENTAL TRAITS OF APOCALYPTIC COMPOSITION.

The fundamental traits of Apocalyptic composition are already indicated by the general character of sacred composition.

In respect of the inner side of this sort of composition, we distinguish the sacred motive;

the sacred design; and the sacred haste of execution from motive to design. In respect of the formal side, we distinguish the theocratic - world-historical foundation; the solemn language, replete with beauty, simplicity, and devotion; and the cyclical movement toward the goal in a series of original, circular pictures of the whole [*Gesammtbilder*=panoramas?].

If we apply ourselves directly to the tracing out of these features in the Apocalyptical Scriptures, we shall observe that, in respect of their *motive*, a world-historical state of necessity in the Church of God begets, within an elect and praying prophet-heart, that unique state of necessity to which Heaven opens;—opens, in order that, by the discovery of a glorious Messianic picture of the future, the fact may be revealed that the temporal necessity of the Church rests upon a Divine plan and is designed to lead to a triumph, the certainty of which is already rejoiced over in Heaven. Hence it is that, in the Apocalypse, every gloomy, distressful scene on earth is supported by a radiant, festive scene in Heaven, and analogies are found even in the Old Testament Apocalypses. Comp. Is. xl., xlix., lviii.; Ezek. xxxvii.

The *design* of the Apocalypse, both in the Old and the New Testament Scriptures, is practical in the higher sense of that term. It is intended that the Church of God — in the persons of His prominent servants, in the first place (Rev. i. 1)—shall receive, in chromatic rays, the requisite amount of light concerning the future, to enable her to find her way in situations of the greatest obscurity; it is likewise intended that she should possess a treasury of consolation at which she may always be able to quicken her longing, hope, patience, and perseverance, and, above all, her love: in this sense, Prophecy shall ever open more fully to her in accordance with her need, whilst it presents an impenetrable veil to the profane gaze of worldliness as well as to hypocritical chiliastic desires. This design is plainly revealed in the Apocalypse of John in a number of passages, and especially in the seven epistles and at the close; it is, however, the design of all Apocalypses. Comp. Is. xl. 1; Dan. xii. 10.

The holy *haste of execution*, its rapid gravitation to the final goal, is announced in the brevity of expression; the rapid succession of scenes; the ever new configurations of the end; and the strong expression of a presentiment of the end, to which the whole intervening period seems but a *brief* time. In consideration of the last-mentioned fact, it is a senseless proceeding to interpret the promises of a speedy fulfillment, *e. g.*, Rev. i. 1, as based upon a chronological error. That the Apocalypse intends the sayings concerning the speediness of the end in a religious sense, and not in an ordinary chronological signification, is proved by the ages which this same Apocalypse interposes between the stand-point of the Seer and the day of final decision (comp. 1 John ii. 18, "the last hour;" likewise Haggai ii. 6).

Revelation, in accordance with its theocratically world-historical character, takes in the entire breadth of the world, the entire length, height, and depth of its course, in a manner of which we find scarcely the faintest idea in classical historiography. This character is most clearly pronounced in the Apocalyptic Scriptures. The Book of Daniel presents a construction of the world's history agreeable to the predominant character of the pre-Christian time: the world-monarchies occupy the foreground of the picture until the Kingdom of Christ puts an end to them. In the Apocalypse of John, the entire history of the world is presented in the New Testament light: the Kingdom of God occupies the foreground, arrayed for the final decisive combats with the world-power, whose advances become constantly bolder and more threatening. Even in this Book, however, the vision of the seven seals (ch. vi.), and the figure of the Woman clothed with the sun (ch. xii.), as well as many another feature, carry us back to the old time before Christ. Manifold are the links connecting the Biblical Books in harmonious sequence, so that one Book rests not only upon the knowledge, but also upon the basis, of the preceding one. Thus, the Apocalypses are joined to all the foregoing Biblical Books; and as the whole of the Old Testament is reflected in the Prophet Daniel, so the Apocalypse of John presents the image of both the Old and the New Testament. Nay, more, this unique conclusion of the whole of the Sacred Writings is likewise the conclusion of their mysteries; in it, their very first Book, Genesis, is most clearly mirrored, thus imaging for us the Genesis of the first world in the Genesis of the second. Especially close, however, is the connection of the Apocalypse of the New Testament with the Apocalyptic Scriptures of the Old Testament; and that not in regard to the subject-matter alone, but also in respect of its figurative language and its art. The entire learning of the Old Testament, as well as the entire Eschatology of the Gospels and all other New Testament Books, is here reproduced in a perfectly original form; above all, we recognize here the elements of Eschatology presented in Isaiah, Jeremiah, Ezekiel, Daniel; as also those of Zechariah in particular, as well as the most manifold traits of other Prophets.

The solemn, devotional language of Holy Writ—language beautiful in its simplicity, and yet ghostly in its sublimity—is the property, in a peculiar degree, of all its Apocalypses; from the Apocalypse of Isaiah, through the Eschatologies of Jeremiah, Ezekiel, and Daniel, down to the Revelation of John. In the latter, however, we have, added to the Hebrew and Hebraizing expressions of the Prophet—who speaks in the spirit ($\dot{\epsilon}\nu\ \pi\nu\epsilon\acute{\nu}\mu\alpha\tau\iota$), not in the language of apostolic, didactic mediation ($\dot{\epsilon}\nu\ \tau\tilde{\omega}\ \nu\omicron\iota$)—a Christian Greek element, viz.: the hymn, which consists in lyrical outgushes and also in the most metrical domination of the material by the form. The general admiration excited by the diction of Habakkuk, and by the mysterious chiar' oscuro of Zechariah, is a well-known fact; it will be found, however, on examination, that Obadiah, Nahum, and Zephaniah also employ a language peculiarly Apocalyptical.

Of special moment for the true position of exegesis, is the cyclical movement of the Apocalypses, from the stand-point of the Seer to the final goal of the world. The least of the Apocalyptic Writings cannot, indeed, be affirmed to present such an arrangement, though even in them a similar organization is observable, in the division of the special topics of which they treat into rounded and distinct discourses. (Comp. the [Lange] Comm. on Obadiah, Nahum, Habakkuk, Zephaniah). On directing our attention to the greater Apocalypses, we find that the cyclical construction, in three stages, of the unitous Eschatology (Is. xl.—lxvi.), is marked both by the peculiar character of those stages (I. The restoration of Israel as the servant of God, including the promise of the Messiah, xl.-xlviii. II. The Messiah as the Servant of God, the suffering Redeemer of Israel, xlix.-lvii. III. The Messiah as the victorious Servant of God; and the consummation of the Kingdom of God (lviii.-lxvi.), and by their significant concluding formulas. In ch. xlviii. 22, we read: "There is no peace, saith the LORD, unto the wicked." In ch. lvii. 20, the terms are stronger: "But the wicked are like the troubled sea that cannot rest, whose waters cast up mire and dirt. [But] there is no peace, saith my God, to the wicked." Strongest of all is the close, ch. lxvi. 24: "And they shall go forth and look upon the carcasses of the men that have transgressed against [apostatized from] Me; for their worm shall not die, neither shall their fire be quenched; and they shall be an abhorring unto all flesh." This climax is, manifestly, a development of the final judgment—a development continually increasing in power, and pointing at last to the lake of fire spoken of in the Apocalypse, ch. xix. 20, xx. 10, 14. 15 (comp. Matt. xxv. 41).

The Eschatology of Jeremiah is unfolded in a series of pictures of judgment, beginning with ch. xlvi.* and closing with ch. li. 64. That this Eschatology forms a cyclical composition, is proved by the unitous line of judicial pictures and their close in the judgment upon Babylon, which also points to the fall of the antitypical Babylon (Rev. xviii.).

In the Eschatology of Ezekiel, three cycles are distinctly visible. I. The Vision of the Resurrection of Israel; the Union between Israel and Judah; and the Eternal Kingdom of the Messiah, as a revelation for the Gentiles (ch. xxxvii.). II. The Judgment upon the northeastern Antichrist, Gog in the land of Magog, the prince in Ros,† Meshech, and Tubal (chs. xxxviii. and xxxix.). III. The new Mystical Temple upon a high mountain in the land of Israel, the place of the Throne of the Incarnate Jehovah (ch. xliii. 6, 7); from this Temple, a stream, adorned on either side with trees of life, issues for the rejuvenation of the world (ch. xlvii.), chs. xl.-xlviii. Ezekiel's vision of the resurrection of Israel points to the first resurrection of the Apocalypse (ch. xx.). His vision of the judgment of Gog points to the Apocalyptic final judgment upon the last form of Antichristianity under the same

---

* Relatively, the Apocalypse of Jeremiah begins with ch. xlv., as we have stated in the Comm. on Genesis.

† [In the E. V., Ezek. xxxviii. 3, etc., the Hebrew expression רֹאשׁ נְשִׂיא is translated the chief prince; the entire expression may be rendered as above. See Robinson's Gesenius, under רֹאשׁ. The LXX. gives 'Ρώς.—E. R. C.]

name (ch. xx.). The new Temple upon the high mountain, with its river and trees of life, finds its final fulfillment in the City of God, with its paradisaical trees of life (Rev. xxi. and xxii.).

In regard to the Prophet Daniel, we have already remarked, in the *Comm. on Genesis* (Introduction [Am. Ed., p. 38]), that we consider the portions, (ch. x.–xi. 44. and ch. xii. 5–13), as an interpolation.* Irrespective of this interpolation, the work falls into two sections, each of which is composed of cyclical pictures. In the first part (ch. i.–vi.), Daniel appears as the interpreter of foreign oracles within heathenism itself; in the second part, he is no longer the expounder of obscure, dream-like, ghostly, Divine voices and writings within heathenism, but a Prophet of the clearer revelations of Jehovah for His people. In the first part, God's judgment upon the works of heathen arrogance and pride are unfolded, whilst pious men of Israel are wonderfully preserved and glorified; in the second part, the sufferings of the Kingdom of God under the final and the typical Antichristianity are portrayed, together with the triumph of God's Kingdom. Upon the Introduction, ch. i., in which the continuance of a holy Israel, in the midst of heathen temptations, is depicted as the basis of Prophecy and the foundation for the coming of the Kingdom of God, follow the oracles of the first part: *a.* Nebuchadnezzar's dream of the monarchy-image ; confirmation of the Messianic conclusion of the dream, in the preservation of the three men in the fiery furnace through the medium of the fourth Man among them, the "son of the gods" (chs. ii. and iii.). *b.* The dream of the tree that reached unto Heaven ; fulfillment of the dream in the humiliation of Nebuchadnezzar ; and his repentance (ch. iv.). *c.* The oracle in the banquet-room of Belshazzar, and the judgment upon his pride ; downfall of Belshazzar ; fresh exaltation of Daniel ; his apparent fall, and wonderful preservation in the den of lions (chs. v. and vi.). The second part reverts to the time of the first part. Daniel's own visions begin with the dream-vision of the four Beasts as forms of the four world-monarchies (ch. vii.) ; manifestly, the Israelitish pendant to the dream of Nebuchadnezzar (ch. ii.). The second vision of Daniel (ch. viii.) passes beyond the dream-form ; it manifestly presents the precursory, typical Antichristianity of Antiochus Epiphanes, which must by no means be confounded with the final Antichristianity sketched in ch. vii. 7, 8 ; a sufficiently distinct pendant to the fall of the mighty tree (ch. iv.) Daniel's third vision is even mediated by the Prophet's earnest prayer for Mount Zion ; it is, therefore, a highly developed form of the vision. It has reference to the import of the seventy weeks determined by Jeremiah, after which Jerusalem—in a thoroughly Messianico-eschatological sense—should be restored. We read the conclusion of the vision in the following connection : " And even to the summit [' double sense : to the uttermost, and to the top of the Temple'] come the abominations, the ravages, and until destruction, which is firmly decreed, is poured out upon the desolator" (see *Comm. on Matthew*, p. 425, Am. Ed.) [Dan. ix. 27]. But he shall set up his palace-tents between the sea and the mountain of the holy ornament, yet shall go on towards his end without deliverance [ch. xi. 45]. At that time, however, shall Michael arise, the great chief that standeth for the sons of thy people—it shall indeed be a time of tribulation, such as never was until that time, but, at the same time, thy people shall be delivered, all that are written in the Book of Life—and many that sleep in the dust of the earth shall awake, *etc.*" [ch. xii. 1 sqq.]. In this rounded form the vision constitutes a pendant to the ghostly writing on the wall in the banqueting-room of Belshazzar. With the abominable desecration of the vessels of the Temple, corresponds the abomination of desolation which reaches the summit (double sense [the uttermost, or]), the pinnacle of the Temple ; with the sudden fall of Belshazzar, corresponds the destruction that suddenly comes upon the desolator. At the same time, many features of the Book of Daniel point to the Apocalypse. The typical Antichrist of Dan. viii., who has already in ch. vii. appeared in the most general outlines of his antitype, points to the perfect antitype in the Apocalypse. The seventy weeks—which are to be interpreted symbolically, not chronologically—are thus divided (see the *Symbolism of Numbers*, above) : 1. Sixty-two weeks of the

---

* ["Compare, however, upon this point, Hengstenberg: *Authentie des Daniel.*" Note by Tr. of *Comm. on Genesis*, Am. Ed., p. 38.—E. R. C.]

troublous restoration of Jerusalem with streets and ditches, but in strait of times ; the time until the appearing and slaying of the Messiah. At the end of these weeks, *the Anointed, Who is not yet the Prince,* shall be cut off. 2. One week. *Appearance of the prince, who is not an anointed one.* Renewal of the covenant in this week for many, and, in antithesis, cessation of the sacrifice. Downfall of the Jewish State and worship. 3. Seven weeks to *the Anointed, Who is, at the same time, the Prince.* This is the shadowy sketch of the time from the destruction of Jerusalem to the Parousia of Christ, in which two features only are distinctly prominent: the renewed covenant of the many, on the one side ; the contrasted lasting desolation, on the other (the shortened days of tribulation, see *Comm. on Matthew,* ch. xxiv. [p. 425, Am. Ed.]).

With Daniel's symbolical reckoning of time, corresponds the symbolical reckoning of the Apocalypse (chs. xi., xii.) ; to the troublous time of the Theocracy in the sixty-two weeks, corresponds the travailing Woman, menaced by Satan (ch. xii.) ; to the slaying of the Messiah, corresponds His translation to Heaven. To the prince, who is a desolator, corresponds the whole development of New Testament Antichristianity. The appearance of the anointed Prince coincides unmistakably with the Parousia of Christ. In Daniel, however, the anointed Prince manifestly appears in the form of Michael. Finally, an antithesis corresponding to the antithesis of the times is formed by the fact that Daniel is commanded to seal up his writing (ch. xii. 4), whilst John receives an exactly contrary command (Rev. xxii. 10).*

We have already presented our views in regard to the unitous composition of those Prophecies that come under the name of Zechariah, in the Introduction to *Genesis* (p. 39, [Am. Ed.]). Not only the whole beginning of the disintegration of this Scripture into two parts—a procedure based upon a misunderstanding ;—not only the misapprehension of the manifest traits of a later Israelitish age in the second part, but also, in particular, the limitation of the Prophecies to the circumstances characterizing the time of the Prophet, without a due regard to the fact that he has throughout employed the circumstances of his time as symbols and types, has occasioned a permanent and increasing prejudice in favor of the division of the Book. We, however, in spite of a criticism which, though fully warranted in setting forth its peculiar views, is still in its youth, cling to the assumption that the whole Book forms a unitous Apocalypse ; its first part, depicting the coming of the Messianic Kingdom ; its second, the coming of the Messiah Himself ; types cyclically progressive being employed in each case. We regard the opening (ch. i. 1–6) as an introduction, instead of holding, with Köhler, that it forms the first section of the first part. The first vision (ch. i. 7–17) is promissive of the restoration of the Israelitish Theocracy. In connection with the second vision (vers. 18–21, Heb. text ii. 1–4), which announces the destruction of the four hostile powers that have scattered Israel,† it forms the *first* cyclical general picture. The third vision (ch. ii. 1–13, Heb. text ii. 5–17) depicts the immeasurable fullness and superb security of the inhabitants of the New Jerusalem ; with it, the fourth vision, the cleansing of the priesthood from its defilement, even to the point of the coming of the *Tsemach* ([E. V. Branch= Sprout] ch. iii. 1–10), must unite to form the *second* cyclical picture of the future. In the two sons of oil, the fifth vision sets forth the ramification of the Theocracy into the princely and priestly offices ; it is the duty of these offices, themselves being filled with the Spirit, to nourish the unitous candlestick of Israel, the light of the world, with the oil of the Spirit; keeping themselves, meanwhile, from the way of violence. Israel is to use no violence toward the Gentile world, but to maintain a severe discipline within ; accordingly, the sixth vision (ch. v. 1–4) is conjoined to the fifth (ch. iv.), thus presenting the *third* general picture in its two aspects.

---

* [" This prophecy is called *the Revelation,* with respect to *the Scripture of truth,* which Daniel was commanded *to shut up and seal, till the time of the end.* Daniel sealed it *until the time of the end;* and, until that time comes, the Lamb is opening the seals ; and afterwards the two witnesses prophesy out of it a long time in sack-cloth before they ascend up to Heaven in a cloud. All which is as much as to say that these Prophecies of Daniel and John should not be understood till the time of the end; but then some should prophesy out of them in an afflicted and mournful state for a long time, and that but darkly, so as to convert but few. But in the very end, the Prophecy should be so far interpreted ▬ to convert many." SIR ISAAC NEWTON.—E. R. C.]

† I now am doubtful as to whether the four world-monarchies ▬ intended by this, since the Prophet limits the work of the horns to the past.

According to the seventh vision (ch. v. 5–11) the theocratic domain is purified from all unrighteousness; a threatening antithesis to this is presented outside of the Theocracy, in the fact that this unrighteousness is set down in the land of Shinar. Hence, in the eighth, or last vision (ch. vi. 1–8), God's judgment upon the Gentile world is exhibited as going forth into all the quarters of Heaven; this, and the seventh vision, form the *fourth* cyclical general picture.

The conclusion of the first part, from ch. vi. 9 to ch. viii. 23, then unmistakably forms the transition to the second part, which consists of a cyclical series of typical representations of the Messiah.

In the first place, Joshua, the High-priest, is, by a solemn crowning, constituted a type of the coming Messiah, Who is to be at once Priest and King (ch. vi. 9 sqq.). Furthermore, the Prophet himself becomes a momentary and extraordinary type of the Messiah (ch. vi. 15 sqq.). Hence he decides the question which the Israelites put to the Priests, as to whether the extraordinary fasts of the exile should be continued; answering the inquiry for the Priests as well as the people, he declares that there is henceforth no ordinance of fasts; that the people are to observe the moral commandments of truth, mercy, and compassion, which, to their destruction, they formerly despised; now, however, judgment should be turned away from them, and, after the restoration of Israel, the fast-days should become joyful feast-days; yea, the salvation of Israel should be diffused amongst all nations (ch. vii. and viii.).

In this transition, the unitous picture of the time of the Messiah is laid before us. It is the programme of the second part, from ch. ix. to the close. Here, in this second part, the future of the Messiah is unrolled before our eyes in typical acts, representative of individual items in His career.

First type. Advent and appearance of the Messiah in poor and humble guise (ch. ix.; comp. Matt. xxi. 5; John xii. 15). Here the barren present and proximate future of the Prophet (Israel's restoration in antithesis to the judgments upon the neighboring Northern nations, — judgments, however, conducing to their conversion) become the basis of a prophecy concerning the Coming of the Messiah; the perspective of this prophecy is manifestly eschatological (vers. 13, 14 sqq.). This picture corresponds with the first vision (ch. i. 7–17.)

Second type. Jehovah's leading the people back out of the heathen world through the sea of tribulation or anguish may be the most obscure Messianic type of this series; its Messianic character is nevertheless sustained by the clearer types of chs. ix. and xi. The point of departure is the hope of a *universal* restoration of Israel, conjoined with a universal judgment upon the heathen; accordingly, this type corresponds with the second vision, the vision of the destruction of the horns (ch. x. We, like Neumann and Kliefoth, account vers. 1 and 2 as forming a part of this section).

Third type. The Messiah, typically represented by the Prophet, is *under*valued at thirty pieces of silver, *i. e.*, the absurdly cheap price of a slave (Matt. xxvi. 15; Ex. xxi. 32). The historical point of departure are the imminent judgments upon the shepherds in Israel (not the Gentile shepherds of the peoples, spoken of in the preceding section) who overshadowed the land like the cedars of Lebanon and the oaks of Bashan. With this type the third and fourth visions correspond, especially the filthy garments of Joshua (chs. ii. and iii.). The leading thought is that the Prophet, the Prophethood, takes the place of the unfaithful shepherds after Jehovah's destruction of the three shepherds * in one month; with his double staff (*Grace* [*Beauty*, Eng. Ver.] embracing the Gentile world, and the Theocratic *Band* uniting Judah and Israel) he [the Prophet—always as a type of Christ] feeds the flocks—the *sheep of slaughter* in company with the *poor* of the flock, for the sake of the latter;†

---

* In accordance with the context, none but Israelitish shepherds can be intended here; and, moreover, such as were destroyed in one (symbolical) month. If the month denote a short periodical change—the Babylonish captivity, for instance —those three false prophets might be meant upon whom Jeremiah proclaims judgment (ch. xxix. 22, 32), *viz:* Ahab, Zedekiah, Shemaiah. Are not, however, the three Old Testament offices intended, whose place the Messiah Himself assumes?

† [A variation in translation. The G. V. renders Zech. xi. 7, thus: And I took charge of the sheep of slaughter for the sake of the poor (wretched) sheep.—Tr.]

and even after his rejection, he is commanded to assume the same office (ver. 15) on account of the necessity for an offset and antithesis to the worthless shepherds yet to come.

Fourth type. The lamentation of all the families of Israel over the mortal suffering that they have inflicted upon the visible appearance of Jehovah, the Messiah, a result of the victory over all heathen, vouchsafed by Jehovah to the ideal Theocracy (ch. xii., particularly vers. 10–14). The very pre-supposition of this Prophecy is altogether eschatological; it is the expectation of the perfect fulfillment of the destiny of Jerusalem and Judah; the anticipation of a victory over all nations of the Gentiles—a victory conditioned upon the sanctification of Israel. Thus, it is a Prophecy, every feature of which is symbolical. With it corresponds the fifth vision, of the victory of Zerubbabel through the Spirit of God; and the sixth vision, of the sanctification of Israel (ch. iv. and v. 1–4).

Fifth type. Development of the period of the Spirit of God: prepared by a general mistrust of Prophets, the prophetic form of teaching, psychical inspiration, and the prophetic insignia—a mistrust occasioned by the many false prophets; introduced by the judgment, arising from that mistrust, which was visited upon the last and highest Prophet, and by the scattering of His flock (ch. xiii., especially ver. 7; comp. Matt. xxvi. 31). The two characteristics of this period are, first, the fountain opened for sin in Jerusalem—completed salvation, accessible for all: secondly, the destruction of all idolatry, even the most subtile; the destruction even of the extinct prophetic form; and the banishment of the unclean spirits from the land. This recalls the seventh vision (ch. v. 5–11), in which the unclean spirit, under the figure of a woman, is borne out of the holy land by flying women, whose wings are energized by the wind, *i. e.,* the Spirit.

Sixth type. Antichristianity in its temporary victory: and the appearing of the Lord for judgment. The new world. On the one side, the region of judgment, a region of absolute confusion, self-destruction, and withering; on the other, an absolute consecration of all life to God (ch. xiv., especially vers. 3–7). In this type the eighth vision, as a picture of the final judgment, is reflected; especially when regarded in its connection with the crowning of Joshua (ch. vi.).

The Book of Zechariah, with its symbols, particularly its horses, colors, horns, its measuring-line, its stone with seven eyes, its sons of oil, its roll, its forms of women, its *Shinar,* its crowns, its sea-waves and rivers, its pictures of judgment and deliverance, its appearance of Christ, and its glorious ideal of the new world (ch. xiv. 21), reminds us in many respects of the Apocalypse. It particularly resembles that Scripture, however, in its cyclical collective pictures, with their advance to the final eschatological form.

Apart from every other consideration, this universal appearance of the cyclical method in the Apocalyptic Books of the Old Testament is decisive against all interpretations of the Johannean Apocalypse, which, after the manner of secular historiography, aim at its resolution into periods following each other in chronologic succession.

The law of the cyclical method rests, first, on the peculiarity of all sacred literature, which aims at edification, not at the imparting of historical knowledge. Secondly, on the peculiarity of Prophecy, which has for its aim great and momentous facts, not particularities. Thirdly, on the peculiarity of the vision, which scans the succession of the ages in collective pictures forming a living, genetic chain.

§ 9. HEBREW ART IN COMPARISON WITH HELLENIC ART. MAGNITUDE OF THE CONTRAST. FATAL EFFECTS RESULTANT UPON THE MISAPPREHENSION OF IT.

When science shall have arrived at a perfect appreciation of the grand and world-historical antithesis between Judaism and Hellenism, between the Theocratic and the Humanistic tendency, then, and not till then, can Exegesis, Criticism, Theology in general, enter upon a new stage of development.

Until that time, Sacred History and Literature, being viewed from Hellenistic standpoints, must continue to endure manifold misrepresentations and even misusage.

For a long time the Biblical language was held in disesteem; the New Testament Greek,

4

especially, being looked upon .as a barbarous idiom, whilst the great contrast between the modes of mediation and the secularity of the Greek language, and the immediateness and spirituality of that mode of expression which lies at the basis of the New as well as the Old Testament were disregarded.   Neither was any distinction made between the blending of Greek and Hebrew in the traditional Alexandrian Greek of Scripture [of the Septuagint] and that grand linguistic formative process which came into operation on the basis of New Testament spiritual life, and continually exerted a creative energy in the production of new verbal, adjective, and substantive forms.   This fact was likewise the fertile source of a multitude of critical abortions.

Furthermore, until to-day, Biblical Historiography, as well as the Sacred History upon which it is founded, has been examined by a standard of ideas drawn from classical antiquity. Orthodoxy competed with neology in insisting upon the most rigidly literal acceptation of Scripture terms.   Indeed, neology is but following in the footsteps of orthodoxy, in maintaining now that the Bible inculcates the doctrine that the work of creation was completed in six astronomical days, *etc.*, though this in the case of neology is done in disparagement of the Scriptures, whilst the stragglers who bring up the rear of the older orthodoxy set forth the same views in praise of the Bible.

Thus it happens that the one class speak of perfectly literal historical reports ; the other class, of myths.   That the one class attribute the character of Greek pragmatism—such a conception of events as proceeds, in treating them from secondary causes and immediate human designs—even to the Biblical historic style ; whilst the other class handle a historiography that mounts to the Divine prime causality, and aims at portraying ultimate designs, in accordance with the ideas of common pragmatism, *i. e.*, omitting secondary causes.   True Biblical Historiography, however, in its character of historic symbolicalness, presenting, as it does, all individual actual items in the light of ideal and universal significance, passes between these two modes of procedure, like a living spirit between two sleeping sentinels.

The facts upon which Sacred History is based are treated by the one class as a long line of marvellous, *i. e.*, *purely* external Divine facts ; by the other, as a series of merely mental or spiritual, and in many cases morbid, conceptions.   The one class regard the subjective visions as utterly unreal items of revelation ; whilst the other class identify even objective visional perceptions of true Divine manifestations and heavenly appearances with the godless hallucinations of fantastical enthusiasts.   Sacred History, however, is throughout a Divine-human mystery ; a tissue of heavenly and earthly threads ; a line of points of union betwixt Heaven and earth ; betwixt the surest Divine deeds and facts and the innermost life of the human spirit in its æonic contemplation, averted from the world.   There has been no more absurd deliverance in modern times than the claim that a really risen Christ would have been obliged to show Himself on the streets of Jerusalem, or even to present Himself for examination before an academic committee.

If we look at both together, the facts and their presentation, a climax of critical absurdity has been reached in the turning of the inspired, original productions into conglomerates of the most external book-making.   And if, in other respects, this principle obtains, *viz.:* that the first and lower exigencies of man awakened language—*spoken* language, we mean—and the higher exigencies of his spirit gave rise to *written* language or literature— surely the next step would be to assume that the sublime prophetic and evangelic facts must, perforce, have been immediately fixed in written memorabilia.   If, however, the more ancient doctrine of inspiration despised such mediations, for the sake of heightening the miraculousness of inspiration—in this point, also, modern criticism is its heir.   It is to the interest of modern criticism to beget the opinion that a spiritless and superstitious literature had come limping a long way behind the sublime facts which it aspired to record.

The Hellenizing view is the product of the misapprehensive handling of the Prophets and the prophetic style.   For instance, it is a specifically Greek sentiment that the passion-picture of Isaiah liii. presents the ideal of the Jewish nation or even of the Prophethood. The Greek, indeed, knows of such ideals that hover above the School until they evaporate over the School-masters.   The Hebrew, on the other hand, beholds all his ideals in the form of fiery visions, in process of becoming actualities. Hence, his suffering Servant of God can be none but the Messiah in historic reality.

Finally, it is a well-known fact that the peculiar character of Biblical *Poetry* has been greatly depreciated, Greek models being made the standard of criticism. The critics have constantly sought for Greek images, the Greek or even the Germanic metre, even classical forms of poetic composition, finally, instead of being satisfied with kindred analogies and types.

People failed to recognize the immense antithesis between the *æsthetic* interest of the *beautiful* and the *ethical* interest of the *holy*. So, primarily, in reference to the poetic image. The Greek elaborates his image and worships its beauty. The Hebrew employs images for the sole purpose of corporealizing or illustrating thought, or conveying a clear idea of the contemplations and sensations of his spirit. Hence the great changes, as well as the immense circuit and bold use, of his images. Compare especially Pss. xviii. and xxii.*

The Apocalyptic Writings form the perfect point of union of Hebrew Prophecy and Poetry ; the acme of pure and original Hebrew art ; albeit, this dominant type of Hebrew art evinces its New Testament universalistic transfiguration in a plenitude of elements that recall the products of the Greek mind. As, however, in the first Genesis, the Bible begins with the most art-*less* form of Hebrew *Historiography*, so, in the second Genesis, at the close of the Apocalypse, it ends with the most art-*full* form of Hebrew *Visionography*, of Hebrew Apocalyptics. It is no wonder, then, that the Apocalypse must remain a sealed Book for all who read it with the spectacles of Hellenizing conceptions ; as, on the other hand, it will be a misleading meteor to all who pretend to read it with Chiliastic longings—to all who, with the allegorizing spirit of orthodoxism, look upon it as a historical painting in allegorical figures and colors, and based upon absolute inspiration.

As the specific characteristics of Hebrew art we would mention these three features : *Historical Dynamics ; Ideal Symbolism ; Ethico-pastoral Practice.*

---

* [See extract from TRENCH, in *foot-note*, p. 106.—E. R. C.]

SECOND DIVISION.

SPECIAL INTRODUCTION.

§ 1. THE APOCALYPSE OF JOHN AS THE CROWN OF ALL THE APOCALYPSES; THE WORTHY
CONCLUSION OF THE HOLY SCRIPTURES. AS THE SECOND GENESIS; THE GENESIS OF
THE NEW WORLD OF THE MANIFESTED KINGDOM OF GOD; THE WORLD OF PER-
FECTED SPIRITUAL LIFE IN THE CITY OF GOD; A WORLD WHOSE GENESIS IS MEDI-
ATED BY THE COMING OF CHRIST.

In the Apocalypse of John, Canonical Apocalyptics have found their ultimate and
highest expression, as well in a material as in a formal aspect.

In a material aspect, we have first to note the clearness of the laws of development, in
accordance with which the course of the world,* in its Christological modification, continually approaches its goal. Next we would call attention to the clearness of the dynamical
relations. In the midst of the synchronistic circle stands the Church, represented in the
Seven Churches, ruled over by Christ the Redeemer, as He walks through the Churches,
bearing the sword of His word. About the Church, for the furtherance of her life and of the
design which she is to accomplish, moves the collective Divine dispensation of worldly history, in its eschatological modification; represented in the *Seven Seals*. At the opening of
these seals, the history of the world is seen to be under the dominion of Him who rides upon
the white horse—even Christ as the Prince of victory. The sombre horsemen in His train—
Death and Famine, and the whole realm of the dead [Hades]—must, like esquires, serve
His purposes. And His all-sovereign might is manifested no less clearly in the martyrdom
of His witnesses throughout the course of history, and in the convulsions of the evening of
the world. From the *concursus* of the Church, and the sufferings of world-history, the
Seven Penitential Trumpets [trumpets calling to repentance] are developed;† from this very
circumstance of their origin, we should beware of regarding them as predominantly physical
events. The counterpart [*Gegenbild*] of the seven trumpets are the *Seven Thunders*, indicated
in the course of the sixth trumpet, or rather, in the introduction to the seventh. These
constitute the most mysterious side of the history of the Kingdom of God [Church]; a side
which, consequently, remains hidden, although, as a whole, it may be apprehended in the
mind of the *Son of Thunder*.‡ The preachings of repentance, in their totality, awaking,
as they do, on the one hand, *the Seven Thunders* (*Reformations*—we will call them), occasion
in the region of impenitence, on the other hand, the full manifestation of the *Seven-Headed
Beast* out of the abyss, the Antichristian powers. This, however, occasions in its turn the
pouring out of the *Seven Vials of Wrath*, or *judgments of hardening and destruction*, the last

---

* [For remarks on the term *world*, see Introduction by the Am. Ed.—E. R. C.]

† [This sentence is somewhat obscure. By the *concursus* (the original term reproduced) is meant, probably, the
pleading assemblage under the altar, brought to view in the opening of the *fifth seal*, ch. vi. 9–11 (and referred to, vii. 9,
14); and by *the sufferings of world-history* are intended the sufferings under the *sixth seal*, vi. 12–17. From the events
of these two seals are "developed," according to the hypothesis of Lange (see p. 83), those of the *seventh*, or of the *trumpets*, in the blowing of which is the unfolding of the seventh seal (viii. 1–6).—E. R. C.]

‡ [Rev. x. 3, 4. By Divine direction the *Thunders* were not written, but *sealed up*. Must not their meaning remain
hidden until set forth by the voice of another inspired Teacher?—E. R. C.]

of which develops into the actual final catastrophe. With the final judgment, Christ is fully manifested as the Prince of Victory. In the united lustre of the *Seven Spirits* He appears, for the purpose of opening the great Day of Judgment, which, as the great Saturday of a thousand years, begins with the judgment upon cultivated Antichristianity, and closes with the judgment upon the final rabble-Antichristianity, bringing in at last the eternal *Sunday*. The above are, manifestly, theocratically synchronistic circumstances, concentric circles.

With equal clearness the theocratic chronological succession of time is unfolded. The story of earthly affairs invariably has a heavenly scene for its point of departure; in the latter, the Divine counsel, the Divine foresight of coming events, the Divine celebration of victory, are presented in advance. On this brilliant ground, earthly phenomena develop themselves septenariously. At first they appear in four more general fundamental forms: the four churches: Ephesus, Smyrna, Pergamus, Thyatira; the four Apocalyptic horsemen; the first four penitential trumpets, embodied in facts affecting the earth and the human race; the four or five fallen heads of the Beast (or world-monarchies); * the first four vials of wrath which, like the first four trumpets, are restricted to the domain of man, yet verge upon the kingdom of demons.

The *four* fundamental forms are regularly followed by the last *three*, which lead us into the realm of spirits, and are thus indicative of the exceeding imminence of the final catastrophe. First, we have the *last three churches:* the dead, the living, the lukewarm church. The *last three seals:* the martyrs; the cosmical catastrophe; the seventh seal as the source of the trumpets. The *last three trumpets:* opening of the abyss; loosing of destructive powers; the seventh trumpet as the transition to the seven heads of Antichrist. The *last three* or *four heads of the Beast* (ch. xvii. 10).† The *last three vials of wrath:* demonic sufferings, seditions, and judgments, especially the judgment upon Babylon. The *seventh of the seven* generally forms the transition from one series, which it concludes, to the following series. Thus, the *seventh seal* is the point whence the *trumpets* issue; the *seventh trumpet*, the point at which the *seven-fold Antichristianity* is developed. The other transitions of this sort are less prominent, yet are implied by the context. The condition of the church of Laodicea is, unmistakably, a motive for the speedy coming of the Lord; and His coming begins in the vision of the seals.‡ Similarly, the Beast's *seventh* head, changing into the *eighth* (ch. xvii. 11), is the connecting-point for the *seven vials of wrath*, though the presentation of the vials is significantly intertwined with the presentation of Antichristianity. Apart from the fact that the number *six* is unfolded here in the number *six hundred and sixty-six*, with which the opening of the vials of wrath is connected in perfectly regular succession, the difficulty arising here in respect to the connection is solved thus: *the summary final judgment of the seventh vial of wrath*, ch. xvi., *is divided into three great separate judgments* (ver. 19): 1. The judgment upon precursory, absolute Antichristianity; the fall of Babylon or the great Whore, who is finally judged in the seventh head of the Beast, which head, however, reappears at last as the eighth head (ch. xvii. 1–xviii. 10). 2. The judgment upon the ten kings, or fully developed radical Antichristianity (ch. xix. 11–xx. 6). 3. The judgment upon the ultimate devilish-bestial Antichristianity of Gog and Magog (ch. xx. 7–15).

The greatest obscurity that spreads over the Apocalypse arises, doubtless, from the fact that the *seven thunders* (ch. x.) are not disclosed, but must, exceptionally, be sealed up (ch. x. 4), because it was inadmissible that the sketching of them should alter, as it necessarily would have done, the ethical character of their forthgoing in their own time. If, nevertheless, they be reckoned in, there are formed upon the foundation of the *Seven Spirits* united

---

* [The division of the Scripture is into *five* and *two*, Rev. xvii. 10; the division into *four* and *three*, hypothesized by Lange, here manifestly fails. The *three* heads spoken of in the following paragraph can be obtained only by regarding the *eighth* (ver. 11) as an independent division parallel with the *seven*, when manifestly it is either a transformation of the seventh (see Lange further on in the same paragraph), or a heading up in one of the entire seven.—E. R. C.]

† [See preceding note.—E. R. C.]

‡ [Is this more clearly set forth as a *motive* than was the declension of Ephesus (ii. 5) or Pergamus (ii. 16) or Sardis (ii. 3), or the faithfulness of Philadelphia (iii. 11)?—E. R. C.]

in Christ, seven churches, seven seals, seven trumpets, seven thunders, seven heads of the Beast, seven vials of wrath. One might conjecture that the Seven Spirits at the commencement of the Apocalypse were designed, as the first septenary, to complete the seven times seven; and that it was so designed, in accordance with the fact that the Christian Sunday precedes the week days. But, according to Hebrew typism, the number seven is the unity which is developed out of the number six; consequently, here also, doubtless, the seventh seven must be transferred in thought to the close.

In this great picture of the world's development, the dynamical relations of the Kingdom of God are in perfect keeping with its innermost relations, as has been already intimated. Heavenly scenes oversway earthly ones; Christ, in His heavenly, terrestrio-churchly spiritual power, oversways the Church; the Church oversways the world of history; the world of history oversways nature, the whole cosmos. Together with Christianity, Antichristianity waxes toward its complete ripeness. With the greatest universalism, such as embraces Heaven and Earth, Time and Eternity; such as brings into view, in the history of Christ's Church, the whole celestial world and all the demon-realm, there corresponds, in wondrous harmony, a wealth of concrete traits. These traits are composed of elements of homiletical warmth, doctrinal distinctness, and even deep religious philosophy—elements jointly characteristic of the Johannean mind, and agreeing with the tenor of the Johannean Gospel and Epistles.

As elements of religious philosophy and dogmatics we mention the following:
Ch. i. 4–6, 8, 13 sqq. Chs. iv., v., The Whole Heavenly Vision. Ch. vi. 1 sqq., 12 sqq. The Great Sealing, ch. vii. 1 sqq. 9. Ch. viii. 4. The Three Woes, ch. viii. 13. The Abyss and Apollyon, ch. ix. The Oath of the Angel, or the Divine Assurance in reference to the End of the World, to be found also in the heart of the Church itself, ch. x. 6. The *Little Book*, or the charm and dread of eschatological investigations, ch. x. 9. The Inner and Outer Church, ch. xi. 1, 2. The Olive Trees, ch. xi. The Woman clothed with the Sun, ch. xii. The Dragon, ch. xii. 3 sqq. The Twofold Antichristianity; The Mark of the Beast; The Number 666, ch. xiii. Mark of the Elect—readiness for suffering, sincerity, or simplicity, ch. xiv. The Everlasting Gospel (of the second Parousia); The Judgment of the World as a Harvest in a twofold sense, ch. xiv. 13 sqq. The Sea of Glass and the Lake of Fire. The sorest Divine Judgments in the hands of the Angels, measured in golden vials, ch. xv. Retribution for the Martyrs' Blood, ch. xvi. 5, 6. Blasphemies of the Hardened, vers. 11, 21. *Division of the one final judgment into three parts*, ch. xvi. 19. The Great Whore, chaps. xvii. and xviii. The Æons of Judgment, ch. xix. 3. His Name is called, The Word [Logos] of God, ch. xix. 13. His Vesture, dyed with Blood. Distinction in the Judgments, ch. xix. 20, 21. The Second Judgment. The Millennial Kingdom and the First Resurrection. The Third Judgment, ch. xx. The General Resurrection; The Final Judgment. The Book of Life, ch. xx. The Bride. The City of God, ch. xxi. The City of God,—absolutely Open; absolutely Shut (the Attraction of Salvation; the Ban of Dynamical Repulsion), ch. xxi. The River of Life and the Trees of Life of the New Paradise, ch. xxii. The Beholding of God, the Bliss of the Redeemed, vers. 4, 5; Christology. ver. 16.

The following are familiar as homiletical elements of great value: Ch. i. 17, 18. The Seven Epistles throughout, chs. ii., iii. The Doxologies, ch. iv. 11; v. 9, 10, 12, 13, 14; vii. 12; xi. 15 sqq. The Song of Moses and the Song of the Lamb, ch. xv. 3; xix. 1 sqq. Ch. v. 5. Ch. vi. 9–11. Ch. vii. 13–17. Ch. ix. 20, 21: Impenitence. Ch. xii. 9–11: The Judgment of Rejection, and Heavenly Blessedness; similarly, ch. xiv. 11–13. Ch. xviii.: The Cry of Triumph, Babylon is Fallen. The Merchants of Babylon. Desecrated Art, ch. xviii. 16, 22. Ch. xix. 9. Ch. xxi. 3–8. The City of God, ch. xxi. 22-27. Ch. xxii. 7: Behold, I come quickly, *etc.* The Time of Decision, ch. xxii. 11, 12. Alpha and Omega. *Without*, ch. xxii. 15. Divine Assurance and Human Longing in regard to the Coming of Christ. The Gospel in the light of Eschatology, ch. xxii. 17. Sanctity of the Book of Revelation, ch. xxii. 18, 19. Ground-tone of the Revelation: The Divine Promise, *I come quickly;* and the Human Prayer, *Even so, come, Lord Jesus.* The Benediction in view of the End of the World, ch. xxii. 21.

Passing to a consideration of the formal perfection of the Apocalypse, we must premise that the art of its construction has necessarily been brought into view in the preceding pages, along with the presentation of its material wealth. Categories of the construction : antithesis of the *heavenly*—branching into the world of spirits and the domain of œcumenical manifestations ; and the *worldly*—branching into the earthly-human and the ghostly-demonic. This antithesis unfolds itself more and more fully through the different dynamical cycles of the world's development. All these cycles start from a Christological beginning of the world, and touch, in closing, upon its end; the conclusion of each cycle, however, brings the end of the world nearer and nearer, until the Last Day unfolds its whole import in the Æon of a thousand years, forming, according to the grand conception of Irenæus, a bridge from the old world to the new.

What is true of the artistic construction of the Apocalypse in general, likewise holds good of its allegorical, symbolical, and typical single figures; of the wealth of its learned reproduction of ancient Apocalyptic figures, as well as of its original creations, and its treatment—partly fixed and partly free—of Apocalyptic images.

If we wish to gain a clear idea of the wealth of forms which the Apocalypse has woven, with the greatest art, into one magnificent tissue, let us fix our eyes more particularly upon *the grand similitudes, the rich maxims, the significant dialogues, the warm exhortations, the glowing prayers, the New Testament songs, the sublime doxologies* which it contains.

Thus, the Apocalypse is not a morbid Judaistic first-birth of a New Testament literature, as the Tübingen school has declared, but the noble and grand conclusion of Holy Writ; the crown of Canonical literature; as a Sacred Book, calculated, we might almost say, more for the readers of the last times, after those of the Apostolic Age, than for the readers of the Middle Ages, or of any mediate time whatsoever. It forms the conclusion, in the first place, of the Johannean Scriptures ; secondly, of the New Testament; thirdly, of the whole Bible. In a special sense, it closes Eschatological Prophecy; in the most special sense, it is the close of Canonical Apocalyptics. It is the mystery of the living union of the highest Theocratic-Christian Eschatology, with the perfection of Hebrew New Testament universal Christian art.

Constituting, on the one hand, as a Holy Scripture, the conclusion of the old records of Revelation, and having for its object the close of the old form of the world, it is, on the other hand, a *Pneumatic Genesis*. It regards the last woes of the old world as the birth-pangs of the new world, and unrolls this new world before our eyes as the new, second, Spirit-born creation; as the new Paradise; presenting it to us as a radiant and developed picture, with a perspective reaching into the furthest æons. Hence, the first Adamic Genesis is reflected in this second, Christological one; the earthly days of creation of the one are mirrored in the heavenly days of creation of the other. Together with this antithesis in the kindred subject-matter of both Scriptures, there appears a proportional antithesis in the kindred form of the two. The first Genesis is written with the stylus of child-like simplicity; and yet there is something sublime in this child-like form, on account of its adjustment to the great subject-matter, with a distinctly symbolical, anti-mythical consciousness. The last Genesis is written in the most finished, artistic style of Hebrew poetry ; in its case, however, the evangelic subject-matter, with its wealth of promises, permits—throughout the artistic form of the Book, replete with ghostly sublimity—the traits of a child-like warmth of feeling and simplicity to appear.

Passing to a consideration of special items, the creation of light on the first day is reflected in the lustre of the Seven Churches. The antithesis of Heaven and earth is reflected in the revelation of the glory of Heaven above the gloom of earth, anguished with the mysteries of the Seven Seals. The antithesis of land and sea—of the earth with its plants, and the sea with its waters—is reflected in the vision of the Trumpets. The appearance of the sun on the fourth day is reflected in the Angel like the sun, who comes down to earth. The demonic Beast, rising out of the sea, corresponds to the fifth day. The Beast out of the earth is the antitype of the sixth day. The Man of the sixth day, as well as his Paradise, is reflected in the festive Congregation of 144,000 perfected souls on Mount Zion ; his more perfect image, however, is visible in the Appearance of Christ, the New Man. So, too, the Paradise of the seventh day is reflected in the New Paradise. And this (the New Paradise) is likewise the perfect antitype of the seventh day, being the Sabbath of God, the eternal Sunday—allegations not applicable to the Millennial Kingdom, which does but precede this Sunday, like a great, Divine Saturday.*

Further particulars concerning the construction of the Apocalypse, see further on.

[The following sentence, the conclusion of the article on the Apocalypse in *Schaff's Hist. of the Ap. Church* (pp. 418-427),—a sentence replete with beauty as well as truth—is quoted as the fitting conclusion to this section: "The mystic John, the Apostle of completion, was, by his sanctified natural gifts, as well as by his position and experience, predestinated, so to speak, to unveil the deep foundations of the Church's life and the ultimate issue of her history ; so that in the Apocalypse the rejuvenated Apostle simply placed the majestic dome upon the wonderful structure of his Gospel, with the golden inscription of holy longing: ' Even so, come, Lord Jesus.' "—E. R. C.]

§ 2. GENUINENESS OF THE APOCALYPSE.   JOHN, AND THE JOHANNEAN SCRIPTURES.

The sudden and total change in the opinion of modern criticism concerning the genuineness of the Apocalypse, alone makes sufficiently manifest what our sentiments should be as to the infallibility of said criticism, and demonstrates the folly of those who suffer themselves to be overawed by its prejudices, as evinced in its premises, results, and dogmatic utterances. In one point, it is true, Lücke and, with him, the Schleiermacher school, and Baur and, with him, the so-called Tübingen school agree, namely, in the assumption that the man who wrote the Apocalypse could not have written the fourth Gospel.†

In the case of Lücke, apart from the influence of traditional and temporal prejudices, we may regard the absence of a comprehension of the fundamental diversity of Evangelico-didactic mediating forms and Apocalyptico-symbolic immediate forms, as one of the chief sources of his declaration against the authenticity of the Apocalypse ; though upon this diversity rests the difference between a form of language ‡ more purely Greek and that which possesses a more Hebraizing character, as well as the apparent difference in the eschatological ideas presented in the Gospel and the Apocalypse. Eusebius, in particular, with his presbyter John, has been a misleading guide in this connection.§

That which the prejudice of the Schleiermacher school-theology accomplished in Lücke's case was brought about in the case of Baur by the Hegelian school-philosophy, by which he was enslaved. In the application of the deductions of the Hegelian philosophy to the Apocalypse, however, Baur has far exceeded all the bounds of simple philosophical bias. We cannot comprehend how a theologian who showed himself prone to interpret purely historical writings (for instance the Epistle to Philemon) allegorically or symbolically, could, in dealing with a truly allegorico-symbolical writing, so completely turn the tables, and attempt to force upon this Book, of all others, a historical and literal signification. In thus doing, he sought, indeed, to establish a basis for his utterly false and infirm construction of history, alleging the Apocalypse to be the record of a presumptively narrow Ebionite Judo-Christianity. He has thus, however, with one stroke of his pen, utterly caricatured and robbed of dignity, not the Apocalypse only, but also the historical portrait of John, one of the finest in the gallery of great men.

The points of unity in the Apocalypse and the Gospel, as well as the Epistles of John, subsist, first, in the *subject-matter :* Agreement in the doctrine of the Revelation of God ; in the doctrine of Christ, especially as the Logos ; in the doctrine of the Kingdom of Light,

---

＊ Sander, likewise, characterizes the Millennial Kingdom as a fore-Sabbath.

† See the strong antithesis : *Entweder, Oder* [either—or] by De Wette and Lücke in Guerike, *Isagogik*, p. 534, note 2.

‡ See the author's *Miscellaneous Writings*, Vol. II., p. 173. On the indissoluble connection betwixt the individuality of the Apostle John and the individuality of the Apocalypse.—Lange's *Apostolic Age*, I. p. 88.

∥ See Guerike, *Die Hypothese von dem Presbyter Johannes als Verfasser der Offb.*, Halle, 1831. The author's *Hist. of the Apostolic Age*, I., p. 215. Guerike, *Isagogik*, pp. 534, 545, 605.—Zahn, *Ueber Papias, Stud. und Kritiken*, 1866, IV. (Hilgenfeld, 1867, I.). Riggenbach, *Joh. der Apostel und der Presbyter, Jahrb. für deutsche Theol.*, II. *Heft*, 1868, p. 319 sqq. See also the Appendix, p. 334, on an Essay by Dr. Milligan, in Aberdeen (London, 1867), [and Schaff: *History of the Ap. Church*, pages 418-427 (New York, 1853).—E. R. C.].

and the Kingdom of darkness; in the doctrine of Satan, of the Redemption, of the Church's gradual progress in development; finally, in the doctrine of Antichristianity, and in the doctrine of Eschatology in general. The fact that John does not give Antichrist the title of Antichrist, is indued with significance for those only who cannot accommodate themselves to the allegorical portrayal of Antichrist.

In conjunction with the above-mentioned material points of unity, we have the *idiocrasies of the Johannean images and expression*, the unitous character of which is apparent even through the contrast of the Evangelic and the Apocalyptic style. Christ, the Logos; the Light; the Lamb; the Redeemer, with His blood; the Bridegroom. The Church, the Bride. Christ's gifts, the water of life, manna, *etc.* Comp. Guerike, p. 549. In respect to the similarity of diction (in upholding which we submit that it is in perfect conformity to speech *ἐν πνεύματι* that, in its originally Greek, yet more Hebraizing expression, it should suffer the mother tongue of the Seer to be more apparent through it), Guerike's collection of examples, p. 550, note 1, may be compared. As to the alleged difference between the idiocrasies of the Gospel and Apocalypse, which, according to Lücke and others, occur in matter and form, the greater part of the spoils of these commentators are dependent upon the false literal apprehension of the Apocalypse, whereby a distinction is converted into a contradiction by the process of forcing a purely spiritual meaning upon the Gospel, and, on the other hand, grossly materializing the Apocalypse. Over and above the inner grounds for a belief in the genuineness of the Apocalypse, we have historical testimonies to its authenticity. These may be classified as direct and indirect.

Direct testimonies: Justin Martyr (*Dial. c. Tryph.* "'Ἀνήρ τις, ᾧ ὄνομα 'Ιωάννης, εἷς τῶν ἀποστόλων τοῦ Χριστοῦ.*"). Irenæus (*Hæres.* IV., 20, 11: *Sed et Joannes, domini discipulus in Apocalypsi;* and other passages). Clement of Alexandria (the *witness* of John, which is cited in *Stromata* IV., is in *Stromat.* II. denominated ἀποστολικὴ φωνή). The Muratorian fragment. *Advers. Marcion* III., 14: Tertullian (*Nam et Apostolus Joannes in Apoc.;* and other passages). Likewise, Origen, *etc.* See Kirchhofer, *Quellensammlung zur Geschichte des neutestamentlichen Kanons bis auf Hieronymus*, Zürich, 1842, p. 296 sqq.

Of almost equal weight are isolated indirect testimonies. The statement of Andreas, *Proleg. in Apoc.*, in regard to the testimony of Papias (on this compare the voluminous discussions). The statement of Eusebius in regard to Apollonius, *Hist. Eccles.* v. 18. To these add the Apocalyptic reminiscences in the *Shepherd of Hermas* and elsewhere (*e. g.*, in the letter of the church at Vienne and Lyons). On the strength of the general corroboration of the Apocalypse by historical testimonies, comp. besides Guerike, p. 533, and Langen, *Grundriss der Einl. in das Neue Testament*, Freiburg, 1868, p. 152, a number of Commentaries, especially that of Ebrard, p. 1 sqq. Deserving of special consideration is the fact that most of the witnesses to the authenticity of this Scripture stood in closest connection with the school and tradition of Asia Minor; this is particularly the case with Irenæus. Finally, we have the self-witness of the Apocalyptist, ch. i. 1, 2, 9, xxii. 8, and it is as little possible to set this aside as to do away with the tradition of the Apostle John on Patmos; on the contrary, each lends support to the other. Düsterdieck (p. 65) in vain seeks to invalidate this testimony. He even goes so far as to declare that this self-witness proves the Apocalyptist *not* to have been the Apostle John. The sum of the matter, however, is that Düsterdieck was unable properly to appreciate the import of the prophetico-symbolical style. What grounds are those that he puts forth! No trace of Apostolic authority in the seven Epistles! No trace of the intimate relation between the Apostle and the Lord! Of course the names of the Twelve Apostles, ch. xxi. 14, are likewise assumed to prove the non-Apostolic character of the Apocalyptic John. For other remarks of a similar nature, evidencing a lack of even an elementary understanding of symbolism, see p. 96 sqq.

It is demonstrable that the arguments adduced in denial of the genuineness of the Apocalypse are, as a general rule, rooted in misunderstandings and prejudices.* The most

---

* The presbyter Gaius of Rome. The Alogians (these, however, did not deny the authenticity of the Apocalypse). The Peshito (omission). Dionysius of Alexandria (inventor of the presbyter John). Eusebius, doubtful.

ancient prejudice regarded the Apocalypse as *chiliastic*, because Chiliasm was wont to lean for support upon the Apocalypse. True Chiliasm, however, consists not in the symbolical application of the number one thousand to the transition æon between the earthly and the heavenly world, but in the following particulars: 1. In a principial unsatisfiedness with the first Parousia of Christ, and a consequent transferring of the full principial redemption to His second Parousia; hence, in a subtilely carnal lust of outward appearance. 2. In the chronological computation of the times before the advent of the thousand years, literally understood; with a constant tendency to assign the termination of those times to as early a period as possible, *in a common chronological sense.* 3. In the idea that, in consequence of a gradual preponderance of the Kingdom of God in the outer world, there will arise, in *idyllic* wise, a Millennial Kingdom, sensuous, or even Jewish in form,* *before the Parousia* of Christ (comp. *Confessio August*, *Art.* XVII.), whilst Scripture holds in view a spiritualized Millennium, ushered in by a fearful *epic* catastrophe; a Millennium which is not to commence until *after* Christ's appearance, *i. e.*, after a single, final appearing, which shall then suffer no interruption whereby a *third* would be rendered necessary (as Stier, among others, assumed).†

The second prejudice,‡ represented by *Luther* (see Guerike, p. 531), did not find a sufficiency of orthodox dogmatism and doctrine of justification in this Scripture; nay, it even took offence at the vision form. The doctrine of justification by faith alone, laying, as it does, the foundation of salvation *in the forum of conscience* in view of the *first* Coming of Christ (Rom. iii.), cannot, without a slavish adherence to the letter of the great dogma, be transported to *the forum of the last judgment* in view of Christ's *second* Coming; this position is clearly proved by the Eschatological Discourse of the Lord, Matt. xxv. 31 sqq. The double meaning of the question concerning the relation of good works to salvation must be met by a strict distinction between *principial* and *eschatological* σωτηρία ? [salvation].

The more recent prejudice, represented by the greatest humanist of modern times, *Göthe*,‖ irrespective of its material estrangement from the Christian monotheistic purport of the Apocalypse, stood before this Scripture as before an enigmatical sphynx; and this was the case because minds occupying the summit of school Hellenism, are not in possession of the theoretic key to an understanding of a production which formed the summit of the Hebrew theocratic view.

The *Schleiermacher* prejudice (*Introduction to the New Testament*), in consequence of a one-sided spiritualism [*Spiritualismus*] ¶ that could not accommodate itself even to the Resurrection and Ascension of Christ, much less to the Eschatology, *i. e.*, the whole ideal realism, of the Apocalypse, was unable to settle to its own satisfaction the question of harmony between the Gospel and the Apocalypse; and this, especially, as the expressed opinions of Schleiermacher, in regard to the Apocalypse, betray a cognizance of it for the most part superficial.

The prejudice of *Baur*, finally (see Düsterdieck, p. 64), the worst of all prejudices, treated the Apocalypse as a monument of Ebionite Jewish-Christian narrow-mindedness.

---

* For an illustration of the most recent Judaizing interpretation of Scripture, comp. the idea which some English and German writings present of Israel's prerogatives at the end of the world, and of the restoration of Jewish rites.

† [Chiliasts, or Millenarians, do indeed defer the *full* redemption (the ἀπολύτρωσις) to the second coming of Christ (see Luke xxi. 28; Rom. viii. 23; Eph. i. 14, iv. 30); they, by no means, however, transfer the "full *principial* redemption" to that period. Lange seems to have contemplated, under this term, not the general class who are so styled by the English-speaking Church, but some peculiar section thereof. The essential doctrines of Chiliasm are: 1. The establishment of the Millennial Kingdom (political and righteous) in a glorious personal advent of Christ. 2. Two resurrections; the first, that of the righteous dead (or the specially faithful) at the establishment of the Kingdom; the second, a general resurrection at the close of the Millennial æon. Within the limits of these fundamental doctrines the different subordinate views, as is to be expected on such a subject, are many. See foot-note, on p. 62.—E. R. C.]

‡ Further particulars in regard to these prejudices, see below.

§ Time seems to have worked a conviction in the minds of many that it is a necessary part of Lutheran orthodoxy to regard the Millennial Kingdom as situate in the Middle Ages, as does Hengstenberg, or at least to deem this doctrine worthy of serious consideration.

‖ See Göthe's Letters to Lavater, published by Hirzel, Leipzig, Weidmann, 1833, p. 47.

¶ [See foot-note, p. 133.—E. R. C.]

That Dr. Hitzig endeavored to prove that John Mark was the author of the Apocalypse, is a fact that requires but a passing mention.

Addendum: Relative to the Life of John.

In respect to the personality of the Apostle himself, to the history of his life, and to his other writings, we refer to the Introduction to the *Commentary on the Gospel of John*, p. 3 sqq. [Am. Ed.].

We must supplement the sketch there given with the remark that Keim's assertion, to the effect that John never resided in Ephesus, has been conclusively refuted by Steitz in *Studien und Kritiken*, 1868, No. 3, p. 487: "The tradition concerning the activity of the Apostle John."

§ 3. TIME AND PLACE.

The point of departure for an investigation into the locality and time of the composition of the Apocalypse is given by the following passage in the introduction to this Book, ch. i. 9: "I, John, your brother and companion in tribulation, and in the Kingdom and patience of Jesus Christ, was in the isle that is called Patmos, for the word of God, and for the testimony of Jesus Christ."

It is a well-known fact that banishment for the sake of the Christian faith was a form of imperial violent justice, of whose exercise under Nero nothing is known; it was employed, however, by Domitian in company with other regular measures.* Neander (I. 51) is incorrect in denominating the order for the expulsion of the Christians from Rome, which was issued by Claudius in the year 53, and directed primarily against the Jews (Christians, of course, being relatively implicated), an order of banishment. Irrespective, moreover, of the fact that Nero's persecution of the Christians was mainly local, and, hence, necessarily affected two † Apostles who were sojourning in Rome at the time, but left unscathed an Apostle who can scarcely have been settled in Ephesus so soon, but was probably working quietly somewhere in the East ‡—irrespective of this fact, we repeat, it is in the highest degree improbable that Nero should have put two Apostles to death, and, when he did take hostile notice of the third, should have let him escape with a simple banishment to Patmos. Under Domitian, on the other hand, together with the execution of Christians, we meet with instances of their political banishment. This fact, alone, assigns the Scripture which we are examining, which manifestly originated on the basis of the Apostle's banishment to Patmos, to the time of Domitian.

Guerike has been persuaded by modern criticism § to depart from the traditional hypothesis that the Apocalypse was written under Domitian, and to transfer it to the time of Nero. The testimony of Irenæus, which, on account of its Johannean references, is of the greatest weight in this matter, runs thus (Vol. V., ch. xxx.): "The Apocalypse was beheld not long ago, but in the time of our own generation (near our own day), toward the end of Domitian's reign." This, Guerike (p. 62) interprets as having reference to Domitius Nero; as if, in the time of Irenæus, any man would have applied the name of Domitian to Domitius Nero. The reasons adduced by Guerike in favor of the origin of the Apocalypse in the time of Nero, are the issue, for the most part, of grand misunderstandings. Had Jerusalem been already destroyed, he declares, in the first place, the Apocalyptist would, in some manner, have referred to the fact. It was a most natural proceeding, however, in pursuance of the Lord's precedent, Matt. xxiv., to point forward to the destruction of the city, if that destruction had not already taken place. Just this is the case, he continues, with reference to those passages that treat of the Temple of God, ch. xi. 1, of the treading of the Holy City under foot, ver. 2, and of the partial destruction of the Holy City, ch. xi. 13. Here

---

* Dio Cassius, B. 67, "Domitilla." See Hengstenberg, pp. 31, 40.

† [Lange here assumes the residence of the Apostle Peter at Rome. For a full discussion of this subject, see Schaff's *Hist. of the Ap. Church*, p. 362 sqq.—E. R. C.]

‡ Why not in Pella, preparing for the settlement of the Christians there?

§ See authorities; for instance, note 3, p. 523. Baur, Lücke, Reuss, Thiersch.

Guerike falls entirely out of the symbolical apprehension of the Book, back into the literal historic understanding of it—a thing which has happened to so many exegetes on so many different occasions, giving rise to endless confusion. In accordance with the interpretation which we have just stated, it would be necessary, likewise, to understand the "Jews," ch. ii. 9, and iii. 9, literally, and, consequently, in company with the disciples of the Tübingen school, to regard the Apocalypse as an Ebionite production. It would, however, also be necessary to understand the passage cited, ch. xi. 2, as declaring that the Temple itself should be preserved, and only the outer court be abandoned to destruction; similarly, the Prophet would necessarily seem to declare that only the third [tenth? ch. xi. 13—Tr.] part of the city should be destroyed, and that by means of an earthquake, and not by the Romans; and also that only seven thousand men should perish on this occasion, and not hundreds of thousands. Again, the passage, ch. xvii. 11, "or, rather, vers. 7–12," is regarded as indicating the time of the composition of the Apocalypse to have been at least immediately subsequent to Nero. Here, also, the erroneous hypothesis shows a lapse into pure, and compared with the Apocalyptic view, shallow historicalness. The seven kings, it is asserted, denote the first seven Roman emperors; the eighth denotes the returning Nero (p. 525, note 2). Thus, Guerike, though apprehending the passage merely as a type, avows his faith even in this most absurd and untenable invention of modern criticism, viz.: that an Apostolic man such as John shared the vulgar and ridiculous popular superstition relative to the return of Nero.* Guerike likewise cites the Hebrew coloring of the Apocalypse in support of his views. He believes this to be an indication that the author of the work in question had not yet attained that command of the Greek, in writing, which he afterwards possessed. Even in regard to the manner of thinking, Guerike pretends to discover in the Gospel and the first Epistle of John an advance in pneumatical repose and clearness (see p. 530, especially the note). So soon as there is a thorough appreciation of the character of the Apocalyptic vision, in respect to the idiocrasy of the visionary mode of contemplation ἐν πνεύματι (1 Cor. xiv.), as well as in respect to the laws of Apocalyptic diction—which is as distinct from historical diction as the diction of the Greek tragic poets is from Attic prose—these ideas of an advanced literary and dogmatic culture of the Apocalyptist will—as unsupported misconceptions of the law of diverse styles, a law extant not only among the Hebrews, but also among the Greeks—be set down to the account of the prejudices of modern criticism.†

Let us review the historical testimonies concerning the time and place of the origin of the Apocalypse.‡ The principal testimony is that of Irenæus (Advers. Hæres., V., 30, 3; in Eusebius, Hist. Eccles., III., 18, see above). The testimony of Eusebius and Jerome is similar. Clement of Alexandria and Origen offer no contradiction. Clement says (Euseb. 3, 23, and Quis Dives, § 42): "As, after the death of the tyrant, he returned from the isle of Patmos to Ephesus." Origen (on Matt. xx. 22, 23) calls the tyrant "the king of the Romans." The testimony of Irenæus outweighs opposite and conflicting declarations: the declaration, namely, of the Syrian Apocalypse, followed by later exegetes (see Guerike, p. 61), to the effect that John was banished under Nero; and the declaration of Epiphanius, that his banishment took place under Claudius. Hengstenberg has shown in detail the correspondence of the contents of the Apocalypse to the time of Domitian, and the history of his

---

* The application of this popular romance to the criticism of the Apocalypse will ever remain a melancholy symptom of that narrow-minded desire for innovation peculiar to modern criticism. Modern critics believe that they make the biblical facts truly historical only by transporting them out of the visionary sphere of the elect, of the Apostles themselves, into the cloudy region of popular tradition—dragging them, as it were, from Tabor to the market-place. And it is even asserted that such a fable of the masses was a main motive of the Apoca'ypse, and that it is now the guiding-star to its chronology. Comp. against this view (as has been already recommended) Düsterdieck; also a Treatise by Weiss, in Theolog. Studien und Kritiken, 1869, Part 1st, entitled: Apokalyptische Studien. The value of Weiss' contribution is, however, considerably lessened by its support of the same prejudice that gave birth to the unlucky invention above mentioned. Even he maintains that it was a common supposition of the Apostolic period that the return of the Lord would take place in the then current age; and the recognition of this belief he declares to be the common property of modern Theology! The true cannon, that all Prophecy must take its departure from the history of the time in which it is given, is thus transformed into the erroneous canon that confines it to that time.

† Comp. the author's Apostolisches Zeitalter, Vol. I., p. 186.

‡ Das Apostolische Zeitalter, Vol. II., p. 448.—Guerike, p. 61 sqq.

time. He brings forward, in support of his position, these three traits especially, *viz.:* that martyrdom was already a fact of long standing in the memory of the Church; that a condition of the churches, such as is depicted in the Seven Epistles, warrants the assumption that those churches had already been in existence for a considerable time; and that the despotic rule of Domitian is plainly reflected in the description of the Beast.* Hengstenberg further pertinently remarks, that the opposite conclusions, which some profess to draw from individual passages of the Apocalypse, are attained only by affixing a literal interpretation to these passages, in contravention of the character of this symbolical Scripture.

In a *chronological* reference we have the following to remark. In accordance with the second Epistle to Timothy, we must necessarily suppose that Timothy was still the head of the Ephesian Church at about the time when a John, or a pseudo-John, is declared to have taken uvon him to write, in an episcopal character, to the whole diocese of this metropolis.†

The Apocalypse, therefore, belongs to the time of Domitian; and in respect of its visional origin, it came into existence on Patmos. Where it was *written*—whether in Patmos or in Ephesus—might appear doubtful. The circumstance that the Apostle despatches an epistle to Ephesus is, however, in favor of the assumption that he indited the Book whilst he was still on Patmos.

The darkest point amongst many dark points attaching to modern criticism, is the supposition that the popular Roman tradition setting forth the speedy return of Nero, as one who was not really dead, but only reported so to be, could have been weakly accredited by an Apostolic man such as the author of the Apocalypse is, perforce, admitted to be, and that it could have been made a principal item in his visionary task.

It is as little within the bounds of possibility that the Apocalyptist, as a mere successor of Daniel, should have contemplated by the *Great Beast* (Rev. xiii.), which embraces all the four Danielic beasts, *i. e.*, all the world-monarchies, a single king; or that he should have reduced a symbolical king, signifying an entire world-monarchy, to a single individual king.

§ 4. IMPORT OF THE APOCALYPSE.   ITS TWOFOLD OPERATION.

Though the Old Testament Prophets were forced lamentingly to cry: " Who hath believed our report, and to whom is the arm of the Lord revealed " (Is. liii. 1), still their word did not return void, but did substantially accomplish that whereto it was sent (Is. lv. 8–11). Though Jewish national pride did sensuously and chiliastically misinterpret the prophetic pictures of God's Kingdom, with disastrous effects for the great fanatical mass of the Jewish people, yet the elect of the nation have taken counsel of the prophetic Word concerning Israel's future, and have found it a compass in all times of darkness. It has lifted up and quickened their hope; it has inspired them with patience and perseverance in the sorest struggles; and, through the better understanding of its spiritual meaning, they have learned to find in its symbolical promises the true path of the future, and have thus been taught renunciation of the world and the abandonment of all sensuous hopes relative to the Kingdom. With the aid of the prophetic Word, the pious of Israel could familiarize themselves with the idea of a poor Messiah; of a Messiah who should, through suffering, attain unto glory. The prophecy of John the Baptist is founded upon the word of the Old Testament Prophets; and the like is true of the whole theocratic self-surrender and import of Mary. Nay, Christ Himself found a comforting confirmation of the rightness [appointedness] of the different stages of His life and passion in the Old Testament Prophecies, as is proved by the whole series of His references to the Old Testament. Thus, too, the Apostles, with the clearest spiritual vision, connected all their promulgations, doctrines, prophecies, and consolations with the Old Testament in general; more particularly, however, with the prophetic

---

＊ See Hengstenberg, I. p. 1. Lange's *Apostol. Zeitalter*, II., p. 452.

† In an ecclesiastical reference it is declared by many that a presbyter John, in Ephesus, took upon himself to despatch a grand exhortation to the seven churches, though the authority of presbyters was limited to the church to which they belonged.

word; and, finally, in the most special manner, with eschatologico-apocalyptic prophetic words—with passages in the second half of Isaiah; with Zechariah and Daniel.*

It is, consequently, to be expected that the Apocalypse should be destined to fill a similar place in the times of the New Covenant; that, in an analogous manner, it must, therefore, necessarily remain, for the majority of Christians, an obscure Book—a Book, not simply mysterious, but even enigmatical; that it should be an occasion to many of misunderstanding, of visionary and fanatical misinterpretation, as was the Old Testament Eschatology to the Pharisees; that it should become an offence to many, as were the Prophets to the Sadducees; and yet that it should continue to be, to the kernel of the Christian Church, a guiding-star over the path of the future, shining all the brighter for the gathering gloom of the times. Hence it follows that, in this its import and destination, it will be subject to constant development and confirmation in the days of the future.

It is said that the Chiliasm of the primitive age of Christianity was kindled and nourished by this Book. In the Thessalonian Church, however, chiliastic expectations developed themselves before there was an Apocalypse. And as surely as the second Epistle to the Thessalonians refuted such chiliastic fancies, so surely has the Apocalypse, with its grand perspective into a distant future of the Kingdom of God, and with its exhortation to martyr-patience, exercised a similar composing and purifying influence; whilst, on the other hand, throughout the actual martyr-period, it comforted, strengthened, and lifted up afflicted believers in the midst of their great temptations.

Possible though it was in the Middle Ages for men, in the most subtile chiliastic enthusiasm, to imagine that they had already reached the time of the Millennial Kingdom, yet, even then, the healthful counter-operation of the Apocalypse was not lacking. The signs of this Book gradually encouraged the firmer minds to make a bold stand against the boundless encroachments of the Hierarchy; and though false anticipations and wild extravagancies are to be met with at this time, as in the case of Frederick II. of Hohenstaufen, in the visionary and enthusiastic Franciscans, and many quiet thinkers and prayers, owing to the fact that they held Antichrist to be significant of the Papacy, still the large element of truth in the partly defective, partly erroneous exegesis of the time served to weaken the terrible spell in which priestly despotism held men's consciences, and, by means of the Mystics and the various forms which Protestantism assumed in the Middle Ages, to prepare the way for the Reformation. It was relatively a small thing for Boniface to fell the great oak of Thor, at Geismar, † in comparison with the boldness that was requisite finally to lay the axe to the tree of the conscience-despotism of the Middle Ages.

It is true that, in the period of the Reformation, a new chiliastic misunderstanding was inflamed by the coloring and images of the Apocalypse; a misunderstanding resident chiefly in the minds of the fanatical masses. Since that day there has been a constant growth of miniature chiliastic absurdities, the offspring of a sensuo-enthusiastic apprehension of the Apocalypse. But though ancient Protestant orthodoxy was fain to view the sombre times in which it was placed through so rosy a medium as to fancy itself in the midst of the Millennial Kingdom; though it recently, in the person of Hengstenberg, could even believe this Kingdom to be already past; and though, on the other hand, a rationalistic exegesis, under the pretence of according greater weight to the historical basis of this Book, has robbed it of its eschatological import, its high signification, as portraying the history of

---

* [Jewish national pride did, indeed, ignore those Prophecies which foretold an Advent of the Messiah in humiliation, and Jewish carnalism did misinterpret those which spoke of the future Kingdom as one of righteousness. With these errors Chiliasm has no sympathy. But Jewish piety never relinquished Israel's hope of a political Kingdom to be established on earth (in which righteousness should prevail). This hope Chiliasm also entertains. It is from a failure to distinguish between a *mere* political Kingdom, and a political Kingdom established and conducted on principles of righteousness and in which righteousness shall dwell, that much of the opprobrious denunciation of Chiliasm proceeds; as though one should charge upon the advocates of the doctrine of the resurrection of the body, that they contemplate a sensuous Heaven, and place the gratification of carnal lusts amongst the joys of the blessed. This failure to distinguish is akin to that of the Jews of our Saviour's day; although, it is admitted, it occurs at a different stand-point. It may also be observed, that a great system is not properly chargeabl- with the extravagancies of a few individual supporters. (See also the Excursus on the Basileia, p. 93 sqq., especially Part II.)—E. R. C.]

† [See Neander's *Church History*, Vol. III., p. 51 (Am. Ed.)—E. R. C.]

God's Kingdom; it has, nevertheless, worked out its destination in the centre of the evangelical congregations of the faithful, fostering the hope of better times; animating the cause of missions; stripping the idols of the modern day—for instance, the first Napoleon—of their magic lustre; and confirming more and more the lofty middle station of the faithful as between the hierarchic and anarchic minds of the most recent times.

Doubtless, in the future, the importance and influence of this Book will constantly increase with the increasing confusion and gloom of the times, with the increasing danger which they offer to sound and sober faith.

But, in considering the grand position which, as the New Testament Book of Futurity, the Apocalypse now occupies and shall continue to maintain, let us not forget the quiet influence which it has exerted as a word of God, opened here and there by one and another believer; a word embracing the past and every present, as well as the future; a word which has operated through all the Christian ages to the instruction and edification of the Church, and especially of individual, contemplative readers of the Bible; operated as an inexhaustible spring of instruction, and even of study, of consolation, of elevation, of warning, and direction.

It is, further, a wonderful fact that this most mysterious of all the Biblical Books seems destined to mediate, in its retroaction, an ever richer explanation of all Holy Scripture—above all, of the Prophetic writings, especially the Old Testament Eschatologies and Apocalypses.

Notwithstanding all this, the Apocalypse is not a popular Scripture. Its author is conscious, at the very beginning of his work, that his revelation is designed, primarily, only for *the servant of the Lord*, in a special sense; and though at the end he repeats the direction given him, that the Book shall remain unsealed (ch. xxii. 10), he is, nevertheless, convinced that, unsealed, it will be a sealed Book to many; that many will add to it and many take away from it. Accordingly, he has furnished the holy and glorious concluding Scripture of the Bible with an earnest warning, though he was unable to prevent men from ignoring the pure sense of even this warning word. Christ makes an entirely analogous provision in reference to the Law, Matt. v. 19 (comp. *Comm. on Matthew*, p. 110 [Am. Ed.]). He who augments the terrors of the Apocalypse by englooming additions, prepares for himself an additional burden of Apocalyptic plagues. But he who superficializes its prophecies, lessens his share in the great epic, triumphal joys of the Kingdom of God. If he have done this in innocent narrow-mindedness, an idyllic measure of joy may still be his; he may "sport with the lamb on the water's edge,"—he can have no conception of the joys of the lofty watch-tower. Even modern criticism, so one-sided in many respects, has felt itself constrained occasionally to make laudatory mention of the religious importance and influence of the Apocalypse, comp., *e. g.,* Reuss (*Die Geschichte der heiligen Schriften N. T.,* p. 146).

§ 5. VARIOUS INTERPRETATIONS OF THE APOCALYPSE.   HISTORY AND LITERATURE OF ITS EXEGESIS.

The history of the various explanations of the Revelation of John has been treated in detail in Lücke's work: *Versuch einer vollständigen Einleitung in die Offenbarung Johannis* [*Attempt at a Complete Introduction to the Revelation of John*], p. 950 sqq. Bleek also has given a somewhat circumstantial account of it in his *Lectures on the Apocalypse* [*Vorlesungen über die Apocalypse*], p. 23 sqq. De Wette has given a synoptical view of it in his *Commentary, Introduction*, p. 14 sqq.

In sketching briefly the essential points of Exegesis, we follow the plan of Lücke; without, however, sharing his views. In accordance with the fundamental principle that the situation of the Church has, in every age, exercised a decisive influence upon the interpretation of this Book, we distinguish: 1. The pre-Constantinian Martyr Era. 2. The Old Catholic Era, extending to the beginning of the Middle Ages, or to Gregory the Great. 3. The first and predominantly Theocratic half of the Middle Ages, to the time of Innocent III. 4. The second and altogether Absolutist-Hierarchical half of the Middle Ages, reaching to the

Reformation.   5. The period of Old Protestant Theology.   6. The Pietisto-Mystical period.
7. The Historico-Critical and Rationalistic period.   8. The Modern Time, as the period
of the most manifold antitheses and of incipient universal Apocalyptics.

I. *The Pre-Constantinian Period.*

Fundamental Thought: The Millennial Kingdom is to come; according to the chiliastic view, its coming is imminent. Here, however, we must disclaim the false idea entertained by Lücke, and many modern exegetes, who confound the expectation of a real, triumphant Kingdom of God, which, in a symbolical sense, is to last a thousand years, with Chiliasm proper. This fundamental error, alone, obscures the worth of the otherwise so valuable work of Lücke; its value is no less diminished by his modern definition of historical interpretation, according to which definition only the lower region of the people makes genuine history. Another faulty feature of his book is the failure to distinguish between symbolical and allegoristic interpretation, the latter of which invariably forms the complement of a false historical interpretation. Finally, we would call attention to his own misunderstanding of the idea of *recapitulation*, and his polemic against the misunderstood idea of the same.

The Chiliasm which was already germinant in the time of the Apostles (see 1 Thess.), which did not wait for the Apocalypse, which attained its rudest development in the Chiliasm of Cerinthus, was followed by the Church-historical Chiliasm of the Montanists. In antithesis to this last, the Apocalypse was rejected by the Alogians, and by Carius in Rome. It was recognized, indeed, by Origen, but allegoristically treated by him (allegorical it was of itself). Origen's disciple, Dionysius of Alexandria, denied that it was written by the Apostle John, yet admitted its canonicalness; he, however diminished its dignity and worth by assigning the authorship of it to the presbyter John, in which opinion he appears to have been timidly followed by Eusebius.

On the other hand, the realistic apprehension of Justin Martyr and Irenæus—the latter of whom is the most important authority concerning the Apocalypse of this period—with all its uncertainty in exegetical method, must, in respect of its sound churchly bent, be carefully distinguished from chiliastic notions;* so much the more, since Irenæus couches in symbolical terms his grand conception of the Millennial Kingdom as a *transition period* intervening between the form which the Kingdom of God wears in this dispensation and that which it will assume in the dispensation to come.

Hippolytus was akin to Irenæus. He was especially versed in Apocalyptic symbolism: he was, however, on the one hand more historical (literal) than Irenæus, and, on the other, because more historical, more allegoristic.

The Martyr Victorinus of Petabio (A. D. 303) coincides with this period so far as time is concerned; in point of fact, however, he forms the beginning of the following period.

Lactantius anticipated the arrival of the Millennial Kingdom at the end of the sixth series of a thousand years—soon, therefore (in about two hundred years); he believed that Rome should first fall, as also the dominion of Antichrist, who, according to him, was to come out of the East.

II. *The Old Catholic Time Down to Gregory the Great.*

Fundamental Thought: The Millennial Kingdom has already appeared with the Victorious Coming of Christ. There is still extant a Commentary on the Apocalypse written by Victorinus, bishop of Petabio, in Pannonia.† He regards the thousand years as an approximate designation of the time that should elapse from the first Coming of Christ to the end of the world. The details of his interpretation are somewhat grossly historical and allegoristic. *Yet he gives the first sketch of the cyclical mode of presentation, in contradistinction to the chronological method* (Lücke, p. 980). For a long time subsequent to him, the study of the Apocalypse was checked by the Dogmatics of the Synods, the criticism of Eusebius, *et al.*, and the Church's satisfaction with its connection with the State. "Not until the end of the fifth century did

---

* In opposition to Lücke, p 965.

† Whilst much, relating to this subject, that belongs to the former period, has been lost.

there appear among the Greeks the first connected and complete Commentary on the Apocalypse, written by Andreas of Cappadocia." This work is in many respects correctly symbolical; frequently, however, Origenistically allegoristic. Lücke censures its author for not referring ch. vi. 12 to the destruction of Jerusalem, and for "not even interpreting ch. xi. 1 sqq. as relating to the Temple at Jerusalem." Andreas' exegesis approaches more nearly to that of Lücke in ch. xi. 8 and xi. 13; but his refusal to interpret ch. xvii. 8 as having reference to the returning Nero, declaring that this notion is based upon unchristian γοητεία, Lücke considers as denoting a want of proper regard for historical truth! In some other respects, also, he evidences a more correct understanding of the Apocalypse than was possessed by Lücke (see Lücke, p. 987), e. g., in the assumption that the seven heads and mountains are seven world-kingdoms. Many points, we admit, are involved in perplexity and uncertainty, especially the sequence of events. He, also, placed the time of the Millennial Kingdom in the period intervening between the first Coming of Christ in the flesh and the coming of Antichrist.

The second independent Greek commentator is Arethas, who succeeded Andreas in the archiepiscopal chair of Cæsarea, in Cappadocia, in the sixth century.

In the Latin Church, Augustine and Jerome are the first whose views claim our attention; they wrote no Commentaries on the Apocalypse. Augustine's view of the "recapitulation" of the Apocalypse is a totally external one (Lücke, p. 994), like his analogous view of the days' works of creation.* He, too, regards the Millennial Kingdom as significant of the present rule of Christ. Jerome interprets allegorically, e. g., he makes the Holy City denote the present world. The Donatist Tichonius, a contemporary of Augustine, wrote a Commentary on the Apocalypse which, altered probably in conformity to the views of the Church, has been classed among the works of Augustine. Primasius and Cassiodorus made use of Tichonius. Primasius, likewise, favored the view of the parallel recapitulative style of the Apocalypse.† Cassiodorus also reckoned the Millennial Kingdom from the birth of Christ; he held the first Resurrection to be significant of Baptism.

"The view of the antithesis between the Church and the worldly State was now continually and increasingly pressed upon the Apocalypse."—LÜCKE.

III. *First and Predominantly Theocratico-Hierarchical Half of the Middle Ages to the Time of Innocent III.*

Fundamental Thought: The Millennial Kingdom threatens to come to an end in this period, with the advent of the year 1000 (*or, regarding the number as an approximate one, somewhat later*). The first commentators of this period are Bede and Ansbert. The former followed the method of Tichonius. Ansbert availed himself of the writings of Victorinus. He is in favor of the so-called *recapitulatio*, and (justly) declares the application of ch. xiii. 3 to Nero to be *absurd*. Next come Berengaudus, the Benedictine, Haymo, bishop of Halberstadt, and Walafried Strabo, in the ninth century; no one of these gives evidence of particular originality.

"The conventional interpretation of the Apocalypse, according to which the Millennial Kingdom was dated from the first Appearance of Christ, *etc.*, was productive, especially in the last decades of the tenth and in the beginning of the eleventh century, of a great movement in the Church. Men expected the speedy coming of Antichrist, and the end of the world." The end of the world did not come, and the delusion passed away. Now, however, the interpretation was modified into a symbolical acceptation of the number *one thousand*, as denoting an indefinite age.

Lücke leaves undecided the query as to whether the Greek exegete, Œcumenius, wrote a Commentary on the Apocalypse (Lücke, p. 992).

In the twelfth century, Richard of St. Victor produced a Commentary on the Apocalypse. In the thirteenth century, his example was followed by Albertus Magnus. The

---

* "*Multa dicuntur, ut mentem legentis exerceant.*"

† His interpretation of the name 666 is interesting (see Lücke, p. 997).

Commentaries attributed to Anselm of Canterbury and Thomas Aquinas belong to a later time. The mode of interpretation continues, as a whole, historico-allegoristic.

IV. *Second and Absolutist-Hierarchical Half of the Middle Ages from Innocent III. to the Reformation.*

Fundamental Thoughts : 1. *The Millennial Kingdom is soon to expire.* 2. *It is soon to arrive.* The method is the same as in the preceding period. Predominant practical and arbitrary application of the Apocalyptic predictions to the circumstances of the time.

" The prevalent custom of attributing to the Apocalypse imaginary allegorical and mystical meanings was the occasion of a growing abuse of this Scripture. Any historical condition of the Church whatsoever—every stand-point assumed by individuals or classes— every party aim, even—every curious inquiry into the future—every craving after it was be- lieved to be provided with its immediately corresponding Divine prophetic word of condemna- tion, of encouragement, or consolation—nay, it was even maintained that the Apocalypse furnished exact information in regard to the time of these various phenomena." (LÜCKE, p. 1005.)

" The Romish Church commenced this public abuse." Innocent III. declared that Mo- hammedanism was Antichristianity, and Mohammed the false prophet. Subsequently, the Hohenstaufens were called Antichristianity ; and, again, the heretical opposition was thus de- nominated. The opposition turned the tables. Gregory IX. first called Frederick II. the Beast of the abyss ; whereupon Frederick retorted by applying the same appellation to the Pope.

There is a celebrated interpretation of the Apocalypse from the pen of the Abbot Joachim of Floris, in Calabria.* From this and other writings of Joachim, the visionary and enthu- siastic party of the Franciscans fabricated the "Everlasting Gospel," after Rev. xiv. 6. This suggests the *Introductorius in Evangelium Æternum,* by *Frater* Gerhardus. (We mu t also mention the Postils on the Apocalypse, by John Peter de Oliva, A. D. 1297). The disposition of the Ages into the Kingdoms of the Father, the Son, and the Holy Ghost, forms the chronological clue of *Frater* Gerhardus' work ; according to him, the period of consummation begins with the year 1254. Joachim of Floris, however, construed the Apoca- lypse as, from its nature, it should be construed, *i. e.,* more or less cyclically (see Lücke, p. 1009). Joachim does not regard the Papacy itself as Antichrist ; Antichrist, he declared, was *mixtus* — compounded of the corruption of the Church, the enmity of the State to the Church, and Saracen and heretical opposition; "Rome, as the carnal Church, is the new Babylon ; the Papacy is, as Dante represents it, Antichristian only in its secularization " "Not merely the fanatical Franciscans, but also the Catharists, and Apostolicals, the Wal- denses, the Wicliffites, and Hussites, armed themselves with the Apocalypse as an offensive and defensive weapon against Rome and the Roman Papacy."

Both sides indulged in chronological computations, suiting them to their respective interests (see Lücke, p. 1010 sqq.). Nicholas de Lyra regarded the Apocalypse as a prophetic mirror of all history. Laurentius Valla and Erasmus explained only the verbal sense of the Apocalypse, avoiding deeper investigations; yet Erasmus, in one remark of his, hinted at an historical interpretation, as representative of the then existing time.

V. *Period of Old Protestant Theology down to the Appearance of Pietism.*

Fundamental Thought : The thousand years are past. Over against this orthodoxistic opinion, the Anabaptist view : *The thousand years have just dawned.* Method still litero-historical as a whole, in conjunction with allegoristic details. Prominent antithesis between the chrono- logical and the parallel disposition of the Apocalypse.

" The interpretation of Luther marks, in general, the spirit in which the Apocalypse was henceforth interpreted and used in the new Church. Down to more modern days, it be- longed to the churchly character of Protestant exegesis to regard the Apocalypse as a pro- phetic compendium of Church History ; the reference of its prophecy to the Antichristianity

---

* *Admiranda Expositio venerabilis Abbatis Joachim in Librum, etc.*

of papal Rome being looked upon as a settled thing. This is the spirit of almost all the Commentaries of the Reformed as well as the Lutheran theologians of this period. The only particular point of difference in them is, that some, like Luther, Chytræus, and the generality, assume an historical progress in prophetic development; whilst others, like Conradi, apply the law of parallelism to the Apocalypse, and assume a progress from the obscure to the plain. Only a few, like Theodore Beza and Joachim Camerarius, refrained from a prophetic interpretation, and directed their energies principally to a discussion of the verbal meaning and the immediate historical references of the Apocalypse." Lücke.

The interpretation of Luther, in the *Preface to the Apocalypse* (see Lücke, p. 1014), is very external and abortive; it is arranged to suit the facts of Church History. The thousand years, as he thinks, extend from the time of the Apocalyptist to Gregory VII. The Catholic interpretation of this period is akin to the Protestant, with the exception, of course, of a polemic resentment of the charge of Antichristianity (Lücke, p. 1019). Among the Catholic exegetes, we must mention Bellarmine, Ribeira, Alcassar (the latter, according to Hentenius and Salmeron, makes the following disposition of the Apocalypse: [1] Conflict of the Church of Christ with the synagogue, chs. v.–xi.; [2] with Roman heathenism, with worldly power and fleshly wisdom, chs. xii.–xix.; [3] Victory, repose, and glorification of the Church, chs. xx.–xxii.). Alcassar's follower was Cornelius à Lapide. His first Protestant opponent was David Parœus, whose system of interpretation was partly cyclical, partly chronological (according to Collado, Lausanne, A. D. 1551; he, however, took for granted a perfect parallelism between the seals, trumpets, and vials of wrath). *Leading idea:* The Apocalypse a drama. The summit of anti-papistical interpretation was reached in the Commentary of the fanatical Hoe von Honegg. An approach to the cyclical apprehension of the Apocalypse is marked by the synchronistic method of the English commentator Mede (first part of the Apocalypse: the fortunes of the Kingdom; second part: the history of the Church). Cocceius apprehends the Apocalypse as portraying the history of the Church.* Witsius, the antagonist of Cocceius, was in favor of the "recapitulation" theory. Grotius, according to Lücke's ideas, represented a great progress in exegesis; he explained the Apocalypse in the light of the historical events of its time, and of the time immediately subsequent to its composition. The Millennial Kingdom, he declares, commenced with the edict of Constantine, in the year 311. Hammond and Clericus interpret similarly. To this period belong also, on the one hand, the fanatical book of Eleonore Petersen; on the other, the explication of Bossuet, after Alcassar, Grotius, and Hammond. Bossuet applies the number 666 to Dioclesian; the loosing of Satan at the end of the thousand years, he thinks, has reference to the Turks and Lutheranism. The French Catholic exegetes, Le Maître de Sacy and Aubert de Versé, in point of characteristics, likewise belong to this period.

VI. *The Pietistic-Mystical Period.*

Predominant Fundamental Thought: The Millennial Kingdom is to come. Application of Apocalyptic chronology in a cabalistic, rather than a symbolical, sense.

The Spenerian hope of better times leaned for support on the Apocalypse; it marks the beginning of a turn in exegesis (Lücke, p. 1028). Even the important work of Vitringa ('Ανάκρισις, etc.) which Lücke does not sufficiently appreciate—once more placed Antichrist's appearance in the future, and found many followers (see the notes in Lücke, p. 1035). He restored the polemical interpretation of the Apocalypse against Rome—an interpretation which had been discarded by Grotius.

The more definite application of Apocalyptic *numbers* was commenced by the English exegete Whiston (a theologian and *mathematician*). He first declared that Christ's Coming should take place in the year 1715; and then transferred it to 1766. The great philosopher Isaac Newton was the author of *Observations on Daniel and the Revelation of John.* He supposed that the Revelation was written in the reign of Nero, and believed that it could be understood only so far as it was fulfilled; the grand revolution of things predicted in Rev. x. 7 and xi.

---

* Anton Driessen was a fantastical follower of this commentator; he flourished in the beginning of the eighteenth century (see Lücke, p. 1038).

12 had not yet come to pass, according to him. In complete contrast to Newton, the master of numbers, the theologian Albrecht Bengel, in various writings (Lücke, p. 1039), especially in the *"Erklärte Offenbarung Johannes,"* founded his interpretation particularly on the definition of the Apocalyptic numbers. On his elaborate and ingenious theory of numbers, comp. Lücke (p. 1040 sqq.) and Burk, *Leben und Wirken Bengels [Life and Labors of Bengel]* (p. 260 sqq.). In Bengel's exegesis historistic error walks hand in hand with chronistical misunderstanding. The Angel with the everlasting Gospel (ch. xiv. 6) was declared to be Johannes Arndt or his school. The Angel who announces the fall of Babylon (ch. xiv. 8) was thought to be Spener or his school. The Millennial Kingdom, it was said, was to begin on the eighteenth of June, 1836. Notwithstanding the impugnment of the Bengelian system, on the part of Pfeiffer and Kohlreiff principally, that exegete found admiring followers; by some, his system is conserved, with modifications, down to the present day. Lücke furnishes us with a record of his earlier disciples, p. 1044 (note 2; in reference to the diffusion of his system in England and Denmark, see p. 1045, note 1). The person who most overrated him was Œtinger, although the latter endeavored to combine the system of Bengel with the thoroughly chiliastic Apocalyptics of Swedenborg. The more recent followers of Bengel, forming an antithesis to the historico-critical and rationalistic mode of interpretation which has come in vogue since his day, are mentioned by Lücke, p. 1055. They are as follows: Michael, Friedrich Semler, Jung Stilling (*Siegesgeschichte*), Typke, Gerken, Opitz, Leutwein, Rühle von Lilienstern, Sander. A long series of writings, reaching down to the present time, are by Lücke regarded as offshoots of the Bengelian bent, p. 1055, note 4.

VII. *Historico-Critical and Rationalistic Period.*

Fundamental Tone or Key-note: Predominant Volatilizing of Apocalyptic Eschatology; especially the Prophecy of the Millennial Kingdom; amid a constantly gaining confounding of such Prophecy with Chiliasm.

The motive or inciting cause of the period which we are at present examining—a motive whose sketching by Lücke is not distinguished for clearness—was, negatively, that system of criticism which maintained that the Apocalypse consisted of purely supernatural predictions of Church History and church-historical numbers; and which applied such exegesis to the support of chiliastic extravagances. Positively, it was the felt need of a firm historical and psychological basis for the prophetic glimpses of futurity. The errors of this new critical bent were the issue, in part, of the delight which was occasioned by the novel historical stand-point — historical, it was believed, for the first time in a true sense. For the rest, these errors proceeded from doubt as to the Spirit of Prophecy, as to the authenticity of the Apocalypse, as to the demonic forms of the kingdom of darkness, and as to the reality of Biblical Eschatology.

According to Lücke, Abauzit of Geneva inaugurated this tendency in his *Essai sur l'Apocalypse.* "The Revelation, written probably under Nero, is nothing—according to its own profession—but *une extension de la prophétie du Sauveur sur la ruine de l'Etat Judaïque."* The German Wetstein was guilty of a curtailing and stinting of the Apocalypse, similar to that attempted by the French Swiss. According to Wetstein, Gog and Magog made their appearance in the rebellion instigated by Barcochba. Harenberg took sides with Abauzit, submitting, however, that the last four chapters of the Apocalypse are eschatological. He believed the Book to have been originally written in Hebrew. Semler * "thought that the true original spirit of the Apocalypse was Jewish chiliastic fanaticism."

On the common basis of a one-sided criticism, Herder formed an antithesis to Semler in this question as in other and more general respects. The contrast is exhibited in his work entitled: *Maran-Atha, das Buch von der Zukunft des Herrn, des Neuen Testaments Siegel.†* [*Maran-Atha; the Book of the Coming of the Lord: the Seal of the New Testament.*] The historical perspective of this book is, like that of Abauzit, barren and contracted in the

---

* For particulars relative to Abauzit and Semler, see Bleck, pp. 55-57.

† See Bleck, pp. 58, 59.

extreme: it consists of Jerusalem and the Jewish war. The formal treatment of the Apocalyptic theme, on the contrary, is enthusiastic, full of idealization, and appreciation of the figurative language of the Orient (see Lücke's commendation). Herder called the Apocalypse: "A picture-book, setting forth the rise, the visible existence, and the future of Christ's Kingdom in figures and similitudes of His first Coming, to terrify and to console." Hartwig, though the disciple of Herder, abandoned the Oriental view for the Greek, holding, with Paræus, that the Apocalypse was a drama. This dramatical view of the Scripture in question was subsequently fully carried out by Eichhorn. Others, taking a more general, poetical view of the Apocalypse, made metrical versions of it; of these the chief were those of Schreiber and Münter, and one by a follower of Bengel, Ludwig von Pfeil. The interpretation already advanced by many, according to which the Apocalypse depicted the downfall of Judaism and heathenism, and the tranquillity and glory of the Kingdom of Christ, re-appeared in the writings of Herrenschneider (*Tentamen Apocalypseos*). Johannsen, in his *Offenbarung Johannes*, set forth a similar view. Thoroughly novel and original, at variance both with the ancient Church-historical and the modern synchrono-historical view, is the book which appeared under the title of *Briefe über die Offenbarung Johannis. Ein Buch für die Starken, die schwach heissen*, Leipzig, 1784. [*Letters on the Revelation of John. A Book for the Strong, who are called Weak*]. "The [anonymous] author interprets all specials as generals, relative to the laws, arrangements and developments of nature and of the human life in general; amid, and according to, which laws, arrangements, and developments, God's Kingdom on earth shall one day be perfected." Kleuker maintained once more the eschatological signification of the Revelation (*Ueber Ursprung und Zweck, etc.* [*On the Origin and Design, etc.*]). On the other hand, Lücke mentions as followers of the bent of Herder and Eichhorn, Lange, Von Hagen, Lindemann Matthäi, Von Heinrichs (p. 1055).

VIII. *Modern Times as the Period of the most Manifold Antitheses and of Beginning Universal Apocalyptics.*

Fundamental Tone or Key-note: Gradual forthcoming to view of the Theocratic mode of presentation in historical Cycles and conventional Biblical and Apocalyptical Symbols; amid the working of Chiliastic, historistic, and neocritical Antitheses.

The first impulse to the furtherance of the study of the Apocalypse, by the study of Apocalyptic literature, was given by Corrodi in his critical history of Chiliasm, of which he had, however, no clear conception. With critical studies, in detail, on the literature of this subject, Bleek entered the lists as early as 1820* (Lücke, p. 1058). He was followed by Ewald, with his Latin Commentary, issued in 1828. Züllig's work, entitled: *Johannes, des Gottbesprachten eschatologische Geschichte* [*The Eschatological History of John, The man to whom God spoke*], combined great pretensions with the most limited field of view, restricting the prophecy of the Book to the destruction of Jerusalem; in its formal aspect, however, it furnished archæologico-apocalyptic material. Lücke closes the examination of the achievements of German Theology in this direction with the names of Tinius, De Wette, Hofmann, Hengstenberg, Thiersch. The first is designated as popular; his views occupy a middle station between the ancient and the more modern treatment of the Apocalypse. De Wette bears off the palm. The reactionary sentiments of Hengstenberg—to whose learning and achievements, in particular directions, special prominence is given—are, according to Lücke, conjoined with elements truly promotive of the growth of Apocalyptic science; for instance, the chapter on the time of the composition of the Apocalypse is an article of considerable value. It is a well-known fact, however, that Hengstenberg's Commentary (popularized by Dressel, and translated into Dutch by Schotel), has given marked offence by its false restoration of the obsolete view in regard to the Millennial Kingdom—as if it were already past. The refutations† of this view, however, have occasioned fresh vindications of it—effusions

---

* See Bleek, *Vorlesungen* [Lectures], p. 60.

† Hebart, *Für den Chiliasmus*, Nuremberg, 1859. Riemann, *Das 1000 jährige Reich gehört nicht der Vergangenheit, sondern der Zukunft an*, Gütersloh, 1860. *Die 1000 Jahre der Offenb. Joh., Evang. Gemeindeblatt für Rheinl. und Westf.*, 1861 (Nos. 12, 13). Rinck (H. Wm.), *Die Schriftmässigkeit der Lehre vom tausendjährigen Reich* (Elberfeld, 1866).

which seem to indicate that the doctrine in question is regarded as a choice and precious
item of genuine Lutheranism.*

Lücke has given utterance to an acknowledgment of the mediatory view of Thiersch
(in his work, *Die Kirche im apostolischen Zeitalter*, p. 251 sqq.) in terms more favorable than
could have been expected after his deliverances against the "recapitulation" theory.
Thiersch thinks that the Apocalypse, as a whole, should be regarded as a cyclical arrangement
of visions, and maintains that, in detail, it possesses the character of prefigurative types of
the development of the judgment of the world. Lücke's acknowledgment has almost the
aspect of assent.

In conclusion, Lücke glances at the most recent Apocalyptic Theology of the English
Church "on both sides of the water." He also submits a list—laying claim to our thanks
in so doing—of the most important English Apocalyptic works of modern times. This list,
communicated to Lücke by Dr. Geibel of Lübec, contains the following names: Whitaker,
Galloway, Woodhouse, Holmes, Fuller, Cunningham, Gauntlett, Tilloch, Culbertson, Croly,
Woodhouse again, Hutcheson, Jones, Irving, Addis (p. 1066 sqq.). Lücke gives special
prominence, however, to a work with which he is personally acquainted, *viz.*: Samuel Davidson's *Introduction to the New Testament, etc.*, 3 vols., London, 1848 to 1851.

Davidson distinguished a fourfold manner of apprehending Apocalyptic Prophecy.

1. *Preterists* The prophecies contained in the Apocalypse were fulfilled with the
destruction of Jerusalem and the fall of heathen Rome. This is the view of Bossuet, Grotius,
Hammond, Wetstein, Eichhorn, Ewald, De Wette, Lücke, and others, among whom is the
American expositor, Moses Stuart.

2. *Continuists.* The Apocalyptic prophecies are predictive of progressive history, being
partly fulfilled, partly unfulfilled. Thus, Mede, Brightman, Isaac Newton, Woodhouse,
Cunningham, Birks, Elliott (and many Germans).

3. *Simple Futurists.* According to these, only the first three chapters relate to the historical present of the Seer, all else having reference to the absolute future of the Lord's
Appearing. Thus, Burgh, Maitland, Benj. Newton, Todd, and others.

4. *Extreme Futurists.* Even the first three chapters of Revelation are a prophecy relative to the absolute future of Christ's Coming—being a prediction of the condition of the
Jews after the first Resurrection. Kelley, and some Irish authors.

Lücke's criticism of this system, see on p. 1068.

Davidson himself regards the Apocalypse as a prophetic poem of the Hebrew order, *i. e.*,
an Apocalypse. He justly maintains that the ages should be regarded as symbolical, not
chronological, periods. Notwithstanding this, however, he lays down a historical, not a
synchronistic, succession of prophecies: Jerusalem, heathen Rome, the heavenly Jerusalem;
viewing them, however, in the light of symbolical terms. He also judges the Millennial
Kingdom to have commenced with the conquest of heathen Rome, but makes it a period
of indefinite duration; in this particular he, in some measure, resembles Hengstenberg.

Lücke's work is supplemented in De Wette's *Commentary*, p. 14 sqq., by a number of
notices (representatives of Parallelism, p. 15; the exegetes Seraphinus de Fermo, Ubertinus de
Casalis, Lambert, Bullinger, Conrad, Jurieux, Launoi, Crocius, Matth. Hofmann, Calovius,
Lüderwald, Holzhauser, Franz, Baumgarten-Crusius). This catalogue of Apocalyptic literature is continued by Bleek; the work of this commentator, however, mingles views relative
to the authenticity of the Apocalypse with those which have reference to its contents.
Bleek embodies his own sentiments in the following propositions: 1. The Apocalypse was
not written by the Apostle John, but by John the Presbyter of Papias; 2. It is not, as
Eichhorn maintains, a general description of Christianity, as elevated above Judaism and
heathenism; but is intended to console and lift up the oppressed Christendom of its time
by pointing to the nearness of the Lord's return (by an error, then?); 3. The Parousia of
Christ is connected with the fall of heathenism, and especially of Rome, as the principal

---

Christiani, *Uebersichtliche Darstellung des Inhalts der Apokalypse.* The same, *Bemerkungen zur Auslegung der Apokalypse*
(Riga, Bacmeister). Volk, *Der Chiliasmus seiner neuesten Bekämpfung gegenüber*, Dorpat, 1869.
  * Althaus, *Diedrich*, two Treatises, "*Wider den Chiliasmus.*" Brunn, Keil, *Kommentar zu Ezechiel, etc.*

seat of heathenism ; the destruction of Jerusalem, on the other hand, forms no particular item in the prophetic delineation of this Scripture; neither do the visions of the first part of ch. ix. contain any reference to particular historical events of the Roman-Jewish war.

DE WETTE, in compiling his own *Commentary*, availed himself freely of the manuscript of Bleek (see Bleek, p. 62). De Wette sets forth the view which he himself entertains under three heads: 1. Nero, the Antichrist. 2. The occupation—not destruction—of Jerusalem, an event which, for the Apocalyptist, is still in the future (the scope of Apocalyptic prophecy, then, is narrower than that of the Eschatological Discourse of Christ, Luke xxi. 241). 3. The Millennial Kingdom, intervening between the conquest of Antichrist and the end, and commencing after the first Resurrection.

LÜCKE, besides viewing Rome as the new Babylon, maintains that Jerusalem presents an antithesis to the Kingdom of Christ, though he apprehends this antithesis in a less absolute sense (to which Bleek takes exception, *Beiträge zur Evangelien-Kritik*, p. 187, and *Studien und Kritiken*, 1855, p. 163).

After an exposition of the fundamental idea of his book, Bleek first introduces FR. SANDER (*Versuch einer Erklärung, etc.*). Sander supposed that 1847 was the decisive year when the Millennial Kingdom should begin. Chr. Hofmann's view, in " *Weissagung und Erfüllung*," pp. 300–378, is sketched on p. 66 of Bleek's work. Then follow Hengstenberg, Ebrard, Auberlen. Incidental mention is likewise made of Elliott and Gaussen. The editor of Bleek's *Lectures* has added an examination of the *Commentary* of Düsterdieck (Part XVI. of Meyer's *Commentary*).

The leading positions of CH. HOFMANN are as follows: The Apostle John was the author of the Apocalypse; he wrote in the reign of Domitian ; the prophecies form distinct series, which, in part, run parallel with each other. The *Woman*, ch. xii., is the Israelitish Church; the *Wilderness* is the land of Israel, in the last days, when that land shall again—according to the whole Judaizing school of Hofmann—become the seat of Sacred History. *Babylon* is Rome ; the *Seven Kings* are seven world-kingdoms. The *Beast out of the Abyss* is Antiochus Epiphanes !

HENGSTENBERG : John is the author of the Apocalypse; he wrote it in the time of Domitian. Its contents are : prophecies relative to world and Church history — principally fulfilled ; they are arranged in seven groups, supplementary to each other. The *Beast* is the God-opposed world-power ; it is portrayed in seven phases. The *Head wounded to Death* is the Roman world-power. The *Battle*, ch. xix., denotes the Christianization of the Germans ! The Millennial Kingdom is past, having begun with the Christianization of the Germans. We have no warrant for assuming that any reference is made to the Romish Church, or to Judaism, or to idolatry in the abstract ; but reference is had to the anti-Godly and anti-Christian temper of the world. No personal appearance of Antichrist is taught ; no first Resurrection, in the true sense of the term, but the bliss of believers in the other world is set forth. The liberation of Satan, the time of Gog and Magog, is significant of our own time, especially since 1848 (according to this theory, Satan would now not only be bound, but must even already be cast into the lake of fire).

EBRARD (conclusion of Olshausen's *Commentary*, Vol. VII.). He remarks, by way of preliminary, that his is the first attempt on record, distinctly and thoroughly to separate the interpretation of prophecy from the question as to its fulfillment (Bleek is of opinion that he has not zealously prosecuted this endeavor). His views are as follows:—
The *Seven Churches* have a typical significance for the later Church. The *Seven Heads of the Beast* are seven world-monarchies. The *sixth* head is the Roman world-monarchy. This Roman world-power is the *Beast that ascended out of the Sea ;* one with the *Whore* or *Babylon.*

The *Ten Horns* are the Germanic and Slavonic tribes of the migrating nations; these inflict a deadly wound on the Roman world-power, which, however, revives in the new Roman Empire. The Papacy itself is the *Beast that ascends out of the Earth, the False Prophet.* The *Seventh Head* are ten kings in the last time. Then ensues the kingdom of the personal Antichrist and the fall of Babylon ; finally, the return of Christ. The *Forty-two Months*== 1260 days (chs. xi. 2, 3, xii 6, xiii. 5) are a mystical term for the entire period from the·

destruction of Jerusalem by Titus to the conversion and restoration of the Jewish nation. Wonderful preservation of the corporeal Israel during the Antichristian time. The *two witnesses* are the Law and the Gospel. The 3½ *days*, ch. xi. 9, 11, like the 3½ *times*, ch. xii. 14, are equivalent to 3½ years.

AUBERLEN (*Der Prophet Daniel und die Offenbarung Joh.*, Second [German] Edition, 1857): Daniel forms the basis of the Apocalypse. The *Beast out of the Sea* is the world-power in general. The *Seven Heads* are seven world-monarchies. Conditional identification of the *Woman* in ch. xvii. 3, with the *Woman* in ch. xii. The *Flight of the Woman into the Wilderness* is the transfer of the Church of God from the Jews to the Gentiles, and its establishment at Rome. The *Harlot* is the secularized Church of God in the world; not *merely* the Catholic Church, though that is denoted in a special degree. The *Seven Mountains*, ch. xvii. 9, are seven great world-powers, though with allusion to Rome. The *Beast slain, as it were, to Death*, and thus having a similarity to Christ, is an externally Christian world-kingdom which bears the *Woman*, the *Harlot*. Hereby are denoted a secularized Christianity and a Christianized world (making mutual concessions: the mark of the Christian ages). The *Wound is healed;* this denotes the modern apostasy, the beginning of which appeared in the bestial outbreaks of the French revolution. The *Eighth Head* is the kingdom of Antichrist. The Millennial Kingdom and the first Resurrection are to be apprehended literally (in the Chiliastic sense, writes Bleek) and as future.

DÜSTERDIECK turns back into the track of the Schleiermacher spiritualistic school of Bleek, De Wette, Lücke, and others. His idea of the *ethical* conception of inspiration, *i. e.*, humanly conditioned inspiration, which he distinguishes from the *rationalistic* conception of Eichhorn and the *magical* (abstract supernatural) conception of Hengstenberg, seems to have led him to this stand-point; he, however, manifests an approach to Hengstenberg in regarding the form of the visions as a part of their substance.

In the most recent times, the cultivation of the Apocalyptic field has resulted in a very extensive literature. We distinguish: 1. Works which pertain preëminently to the criticism of Apocalyptics. 2. Theologico-critical Treatises. 3. Theological and theologico-practical Commentaries. 4. Monographs. 5. Chiliastic Monographs. 6. Edifying and homiletical matter on the whole Apocalypse and on individual sections.

1. With the general prefatory dissertations on Apocalyptics we may rank the most recent *Commentaries* on *Ezekiel, Zechariah*, and *Daniel*. In reference to the latter Apocalyptist, see the *Introduction* to the *Commentary on Daniel* (of the Lange series), pp. 20 and 45 [Ger. Ed.] (reference may also be had, at some future time, to the *Introductions to Ezekiel* and *Zechariah*). We have already examined the Apocrypho-Apocalyptic literature.

2. The theologico-critical Treatises include, above all, the articles in Theological Dictionaries, especially the article on the Revelation of John in Herzog's *Real-Encyklopädie*; further, Dissertations on the Last Things (Althaus, Luthardt, Gerlach, *etc.*). Works on the Biblical Theology of the New Testament, and on the Apostle John and his writings. Isolated writings: Wieseler, *Zur Auslegung und Kritik der Apok. Literatur*, 1. *Beitrag*, Göttingen, 1839. Dannemann, *Wer ist der Verfasser, etc.*, Hanover, 1841. Stern, *Einleitung*, Breslau, 1851. Hosse, *Die Prophetie der urchristlichen Gemeinde, oder der rechte Standpunkt der Betrachtung der Offenbarung St. Johannis* (*Monatsschrift für die Evang. Kirche von Rheinland und Westfalen*, 1853, No. 7). Rinck (Wilhelm Friedrich), *Apokalyptische Forschungen*, Zurich, 1853. *Das System der Apokalypse nach J. Medus v. Gräber* (*Evangelisches Gemeindeblatt*, 1861, No. 17 sqq.). Volkmar, *Eine neutestamentliche Entdeckung*, Zurich, 1862. Kelly, *The Revelation of John*, London, 1860. Luthardt, *Die Offenb. Johannis, übersetzt und kurz erklärt für die Gemeinde*, Leipzig, 1861. (*Idem, Die Lehre von den letzten Dingen*, 1861.) Delitzsch, *Handschriftliche Funde*, 1. *und* 2. *Heft*, Leipzig, 1861–62. Lämmert, *Zur bibl. Zahlen-Symbolik* (*Jahrbücher für deutsche Theologie*, 1864, p. 3 sqq.). *Idem, Die Cherubim der Heiligen Schrift*, *Jahrbb. für deutsche Theol.*, 1867, p. 587). Schröder, *Ueber die Auffassung der Offenb. Joh.* (*Ibid.*, 1864, p. 518). *Ibid.* Schmidt, *Die eschatologischen Lehrstücke in ihrer Bedeutung, etc.*, p. 577). Engelhardt, *Einiges über symbolische Zahlen* (*Jahrbb. für deutsche Theol.*, 1866, p. 301). Zahn, *Der Hirt des Hermas*, Gotha, 1868. Riggenbach, *Johannes der Apostel und der Pres-*

byter (*Jahrbb. für deutsche Theol.*, 1868, p. 319).   Löwe, *Weissagung und Weltgeschichte in ihrer Zusammenstellung.   Zugleich als Schlüssel, etc.*, Zurich, 1868.   Grau, *Ueber Inhalt und Bedeutung der Offenb. Joh.* (in the pamphlet: *Zur Einführung in das Schriftthum Neuen Testaments, fünf Vorträge*, Stuttgart, 1868).   Tischendorf, *Appendix Novi Testamenti Vaticani*, Leipzig, 1869.   Weiss, *Apokalyptische Studien* (in *Studien und Kritiken*, 1869, No. 1).*

3. Commentaries: Older writings, Heidegger, *De Babylone magna.*   Semler, Corrodi, Hartwig, Donker-Curtius, Rettig, Wünsch, Kleuker, Heinrichs, Laurmann, J. W. Grimm, Kolthoff, Matthäi, Scholz. See, besides, a list of older and more recent dissertations in Reuss, *Einleitung*, p. 152.   Holzhauser, *Erkl. der Offb. Joh. von den sieben Zeitaltern der Kathol. Kirche*, 1827.   Von Brandt, *Die Offb. erklärt*, Leipzig, 1845.   Schlipf, Backnang, 1847.   *The Second Epistle of Peter, etc., and Revelation, with Notes*, New York, 1854.   Stern, *Komment. über die Offb. des Apost. Joh.*, Schaffhausen, 1854 (Catholic theology).   Auberlen (1854–57, see above).   Hahn, *Leitfaden zum Verständniss, etc.*, Salon, 1851.   Christ. Paulus, *Blicke in die Weissagung der Offb. Joh.*, Stuttgart, 1857.   *Blicke in die Apok.*, Basle, 1857.   Gräber, *Versuch einer historischen Erkl. der Offb. Joh., mit besonderer Berücksichtigung der Auslegungen von Bengel, Hengstenberg und Ebrard*, Heidelberg, 1857 (a valuable work, apart from its chronologico-historical method. The same person wrote: *Das Jahr 1866 und die Offb. Joh.*, Elberfeld, 1867).   Düsterdieck, *Kommentar* (Part XVI. of Meyer's *Commentary*, 1859).   Benno, Cisterzienser, *Die Offb. Joh.*, München, 1860.   Vetter, *Die letzten Dinge der Offb.*, Breslau, 1860 (*Idem, Die Lehre vom tausendjährigen Reich*).   A. H. W. Brandt, *Anleitung zum Lesen der Offb. St. Joh.*, Amsterdam, 1860.   Sabel, *Die Offb. Joh., aus dem Zusammenhang der messianischen Reichsgeschichte ausgelegt*, Heidelberg, 1861.   Ewald, *Die Joh. Schriften*, 2 Vols., 1862 (Volkmar, also 1862).   Gärtner, *Erklärung des Propheten Daniel und der Offb. Joh., sowie der Weissagung von Hesekiels Gog* (*Hesekiels von Gog*), Stuttgart, 1863.   Kemmler, *Die Offb. Jesu Christi an Joh., etc.*, Tübingen, 1863 (*Chronological*, see Palmer's review of the work in the *Jahrbuch für deutsche Theologie*, 1863, p. 365).   Richter, *Kurzgefasste Auslegung der Offb. St. Joh.*, Leipzig and Dresden, 1864.   Holtzmann, *Die Offb. des Joh*, in Bunsen's *Bibelwerk*, 4 Parts, 1864.   Jessin, *Die Offb. des Joh.*, 1864.   Blech, *Erläuternde Uebersicht*, Dantzig, 1864.   *The Apocalypse Popularly Explained*, London, 1852.   Lämmert, *Die Offb. Joh. durch die Heilige Schrift für alle Bibelfreunde ausgelegt*, Stuttgart, 1864 (see the *Jahrbb. für deutsche Theologie*, 1865, p. 560, review by Palmer).   Pacificus, *Die Weissagungen, etc.*, Leipzig, 1864.   Heinrich Böhmer, *Die Offb. Joh. Ein neuer Versuch, ihr Dunkel zu lichten*, Breslau, 1866 (reviewed by Düsterdieck in the *Jahrbb. für deutsche Theol.* 1867, p. 127).   Fr. de Rougemont, *La Révél. de St. Jean, expliquée par les écritures et explicant l'histoire, précédée d'une brève interprétation des prophéties de Daniel*, Neuchatel, 1866 (the writings referred to by De Rougemont are by Nicolas, Von Orsbach, Faber, Jurieux, Newton, Digby, Guers, Elliott, Cunningham, Geymonat, Auberlen, Steinheil, N. von B., Vitringa, Lambert, Darby, Kelly, B. W. Newton, Mousseaux, Bossuet, etc.).   Riemann, *Die Offb. Joh. für das Christl. Volk, mit 3 Anhängen*, Halle, 1868.   H. W. Rinck, *Die Zeichen der letzten Zeit und der Wiederkunft Christi.   Erklärung der Hauptabschnitte der · Offb. Joh. für die auf ihren Herrn wartende Gemeinde*, Basle and Ludwigsb., 1868 (by the same, *Die Lehre der Heiligen Schrift vom Antichrist* and *Die Schriftmässigkeit der Lehre vom tausendjährigen Reich*).   Older works, particularly by Stilling, *Siegesgeschichten*, 1799.   *Nachtrag zur Siegesgeschichte*, 1805.   Rühle von Lilienstern, 1824.   Weigenmeier, Tübingen, 1827.   Sander, 1829.   Osiander, 1831.   Von Brunn (2 Parts, 1832).   *Schlüssel zur Offb. Joh. durch einen Kreuzritter.*   Fr. Von Meier, Karlsruhe, 1833.†

4. Monographs: Riemann, *Die Lehre der Heiligen Schrift vom 1000jährigen Reich und vom zukünftigen Reiche Israel* (in opposition to Diedrich), Schönebeck, 1858.   Flörke, *Die Lehre vom tausendjährigen Reiche*, Marburg, 1859.   Nepomuk Schneider, *Die chiliastische Doktrin und ihr Verhältniss zur Christlichen Glaubenslehre*, Schaffhausen, 1859.   Huschke, *Das Buch mit 7 Siegeln*, Leipzig, 1860.   Kraussold, *Ueber das tausendjährige Reich und die Offb.*

---

* Writings for and against Bengel's system, see the catalogues of literature. Opitz, *Kurze Uebersicht*, 1816. Tinius, *Der jüngste Tag*, Bautzen, 1836. *Idem, Die Offenb. Joh.*, Leipzig, 1839.

† Swedenborg, *Apocalypsis explicata secundum sensum spiritualem ed.* Tafel, Tübingen, *Verlags-Expedition*, 1862.

Joh., Erlangen, 1863. *Das tausendjährige Reich gehört nicht der Vergangenheit, sondern der Zukunft an* (in opposition to Hengstenberg), Gütersloh, 1866. *The Symbolical Numbers of Scripture*, by Rev. Malcolm White, Edinburgh, T. & T. Clark. *Christ's Second Coming, Will it be Pre-Millennial?* by D. Brown, Edinburgh. Fairbairn, *The Typology of Scripture*, 2 vols., 4th Ed., Edinburgh. Wemyss, *Clavis Symbolica;* or, *Key to the Symbolical Language of Scripture*, Edinburgh. Van Eldik, *Commentatio de septem Epist. Apoc.*, Lugd. Bat., 1827. Lämmert, *Babel, das Thier und der falsche Prophet*, Gotha, 1863. Hebart, *Für den Chiliasmus, ein Gutachten*, Nuremberg, 1859. Chantepie de la Saussaye, *De Toekomst. Vier eschatologische Voorlezingen*, Rotterdam, 1868. Christiani, *Bemerkungen zur Auslegung der Apok., mit besonderer Rücksicht auf die chiliastische Frage*, Riga, Bacmeister. Gottlieb, *Ursprung, Ausbildung und Ende der Erde*, Heidelberg, 1869.

5. Chiliastic Works : *Broschüren von* Zimpel (Schaffhausen, 1859, 1860, 1861; Frankfurt, 1866). Cumming, *Die grosse Trübsal* ([The Great Tribulation], Studal, 1862). [*Lectures on the Apocalypse, First and Second Series, etc.*]. Clöter, *Eine Heerde unter Einem Hirten im Königreich Jesu auf Erden vor dem jüngsten Tag*, Stuttgart, 1859. Charbonnel, 60 *Jahre noch und die Welt ist nicht mehr*, Stuttgart, 1850. Older works, by Petersen, Leutwein, Tübingen, 1821, 1830.

In reference to chiliastic writings, we would here again remark that it is necessary to distinguish, with a clear perception of Church history, between the Biblical doctrine of the Millennial Kingdom in a symbolical sense and actual Chiliasm. Some commentators—as, for instance, Schleiermacher—have fallen into the error of regarding the doctrine of this subject as set forth in the Apocalypse itself, as Chiliasm.

6. Works of an edifying and homiletical character: Literature on separate portions of the Apocalypse : Schmidt, *Ein Votum über die homiletische Behandlung der Apok.*, Stuttgart, Schober, 1867. Lucius, *Die Offb. Joh. in* 231 *Predigten*, Dresden, 1870. Bengel, 60 *Reden mit Pfeil's Liedern;* 60 *Gebete*, Tübingen, 1831. Roos, *Erbauliche Reden über die Offb. Joh.*, Tübingen, 1781. Idem, *Deutliche und zur Erbauung eingerichtete Erklärung, etc.* Hahn, *Erbauungsstunden über, etc.*, Stuttgart, 1795. Hermes, *Versuch zeitgemässer Betrachtungen, etc.*, Leipzig, 1801. Schulthess, *Homilien über die Offb. Joh.*, Winterthur, 1805. Idem, *Auslegung und christerbauliche Nutzanwendung, etc.*, Zurich, 1805. Frisch, *Apok. Kutechism.*, Winterthur, 1804. J. J. Hess, *Briefe über die Offb. Joh.*, 1843. Frantz, *Betrachtungen*, Quedlinb., 1838. Winkler, *Tägliche Betrachtungen*, Stuttgart, 1842. Spurgeon, *Stimmen aus der Offb. Joh.*, Ludwigsburg, 1862.

Poetical Literature on the Apocalypse : Pfeil, 1759 ; Schreiber; Lavater, *Jesu, Messias, oder die Zukunft des Herrn in* 24 *Gesängen*, Zurich, 1780; Münter, Copenhagen, 1784; Venator, *Die Offb. St. Joh.*, Darmstadt, 1846; in verse, Leipzig, 1864. Diedrich, *Die Offb. Joh. kurz erläutert*, Neu-Ruppin, 1865. Harms, *Die Offb. Joh., gepredigt nach einzelnen Abschnitten aus derselben*, Kiel, 1844. Wächtler, *Die Offb. St. Joh., für die christliche Gemeinde ausgelegt in Predigten*, 2 vols., Essen, 1855. W. Hoffmann, *Maranatha;* Part 2d, *Die Weissagungen der Apostel*, Berlin, 1858. Zuschlag, *Die Offb. Joh. in Bibelstunden*, Leipzig, 1860. Vetter, *Die Offb. St. Joh. auf Bibelstunden eingerichtet*, Breslau, 1859. Beckholz, Ludwigsburg, 1860. Guenning, *Blicken in de Openbaring*, 4 *deelen*, Amsterdam, 1867. Deutinger, *Die christliche Ethik nach dem Apostel Johannes; Vorträge über die Briefe und die Offb.*, Regensburg, 1867. Tomlin, *Scriptural and Historical Interpretation of the Revelation*, Macintosh, 1868. Bengel's *Offenbarungsgedanken. Aus den* 60 *Reden*, Stuttgart, 1867. Freybe, *Von unsers Herrn Christi Wiederkunft*, Parchim, 1868.

The Seven Epistles : Meister, *Pastoralbriefe des Sohnes Gottes.* Wichelhaus, *Die 7 Sendschreiben des Herrn, Predigten*, published by Sander, Elberfeld, 1827. Heubner, *Predigten über die 7 Sendschreiben*, 3d Ed., Berlin, 1850. Zorn, *Die 7 Sendschreiben und die 7 Siegel*, Bayreuth, 1850. Van Oosterzee, *Christus unter den Leuchtern. Uebersetzt von Petri*, Leipzig, 1854 (the title of the original Dutch work is : *Stemmen van Patmos*, Rotterdam, 1854. A new translation by Merschmann has recently been announced). Vetter, *Die 7 Siegel*, Breslau, 1859. Huschke, *Das Buch von* 7 *Siegeln*, Leipzig, Dresden, 1860. Roffhack, *Schöpfung und Erlösung nach Offb.* 4 *und* 5, Barmen, 1866.

The Seven Trumpets: Vetter, *Die 7 Posaunen*, Breslau, 1860.*
Antichrist (ch. xiii.): Comenius, *Cerberus Triceps*, Stockholm, 1641.   J. H. Hess, *Der
Antichrist*, Winterthur, 1831.   Viedebandt, *Die beiden Hauptparteien, Bibelstudien über Off b.
St. Joh., Kap. 12 u. 13.*
The Seven Vials of Wrath: Vetter, Breslau.
Chap. xvii.: *Geist der Zeit in seinen Werkzeugen und Folgen*, Stuttgart, 1848.   *Blicke in
die Vergangenheit, etc.* (chs. xi.-xix.), Elberfeld.
Chap. xx.: Röbbelen, 1861.   Seyfferth, *Das tausendjährige Reich*, New York.
Chaps. xxi. and xxii.: Ewald, *Die Herrlichkeit des neuen Jerusalems*, 2 vols., Bremen,
1738-40.

§ 6. SUPPLEMENTAL TO LITERATURE ON THE APOCALYPSE.

Having laid the preceding history of the exposition of the Apocalypse before our
readers, there remain but a few points to glance at, and those more especially of a general
character.

The literature on the Apocalypse, like that on the Canticles, is of immense extent.   The
charm of mystery, of the most significant images, of a language expressive of the strongest
feeling, as well as the piquancy of a striking singularity and an apparent sensuousness of
view, all these traits combine to assemble exegetes and ascetics, devout men and visionary
enthusiasts, allegorists, critics, and criticists of all kinds, before the sanctuary of these Books.
From the history of general exegetical literature alone, might be gathered an extensive history
of the literature on the Apocalypse.   We must limit ourselves here to a mention of the most
noted catalogues, the best synopses, and a few suggestive supplementary remarks.

According to Heidegger's *Enchiridion*, p. 661, the exegesis of the Apocalypse—apart
from Commentaries embracing the entire Scripture, or the whole of the New Testament—
seems to have been treated, principally, by Reformed and Catholic Theologians.   The *Biblical Archivarius* of Lilienthal, p. 707 sqq., however, shows that Lutheran Theologians have
likewise been extensively engaged in the interpretation of this Scripture; with especial
reference to the question of Chiliasm.   Still, the *Bibliotheca Theologica* of Walch, Part IV.,
p. 760 sqq., also represents the Reformed literature on the Apocalypse as particularly extensive.   Fuhrmann's *Handbuch der Theolog. Literatur*, Vol. II., 1st half, p. 343, presents but
a meagre account of the more recent literature on this subject (Vogel, Herder, Münter, Eichhorn, Sam. Gottl. Lange).   Two lists of the principal works on the Apocalypse are contained
in Wiener's *Handbuch der Theolog. Literatur*, p. 274 (on Daniel, p. 221), and in the first
supplement, p. 42 (Daniel, p. 35).   There are much more extensive lists in Danz' *Wörterbuch der Theol. Literatur*, pp. 53, 57 (Daniel, pp. 206-208) and in Supplement I. (reaching
to the year 1841-42), p. 6 (Daniel, p. 25).   The account of Apocalyptic literature is carried
down to the present day by the catalogues in Hagenbach's *Encyklopädie*, p. 190 (Daniel, p.
187); in Hertwig, *Tabellarische Uebersicht*, p. 77.   Guerike, *Isagogik*, p. 490.   Reuss, *Geschichte der Heiligen Schriften Neuen Testaments*, 4th Ed., p. 147 (Gnostic Apocalypses, p. 260.
Apocryphal Apocalypses, p. 270.   On Apocalyptic exegesis, pp. 576, 603).

On the Book of Daniel, Keil, *Einleitung ins A. T.*, p. 438.   Comp. also the articles on the
Revelation of John, and Daniel, in Herzog's *Real-Encyklopädie*.

The following Commentaries likewise furnish catalogues of literature: De Wette,
p. 22 sqq.   Olshausen, Ebrard, p. 15 sqq.

For more general lists, see Lange's Comm. on *Matthew*, p. 19 [Am. Ed.].   *John*, p. 46 sqq.
In Lücke's *Versuch einer vollständigen Einleitung*, there is much literary information in
the notes.†

[In Darling's *Cyclopædia Bibliographica*, London, 1859, there are more than 52 columns
consisting of the Titles of Special Works on the Apocalypse.—E. R. C.].

Armbruster, *Die 7 letzten Posaunen* (?) *oder Wehen* (!), Stuttgart, 1830.

† Antiquarian catalogues of Apocalyptic literature: Steinkopf in Stuttgart, Catalogue 18, 22, 29; Heckenhauer in
Tübingen, No. 34; Hanke in Zurich, No. 65; J. Moore, at Delft, Maske, Breslau, 91.

§ 7. GRAND MISCONCEPTION OF THE APOCALYPSE, AND THE REASON OF SUCH
MISCONCEPTION.

We are not referring now, primarily, to that misconception which the Apocalypse, as
a Biblical Book, must suffer in company with all other Biblical Books, or to that which,
as a Prophetic Book particularly, it shares with all Prophetic Books--the misconception
of unbelief;--we have reference at present to the misconception which it, specially, experiences at the hands, perchance, of earnest Christian men, or, it may be, of highly gifted
minds.

Passing by the misunderstandings of the old Alexandrian school—such as, for instance, were occasioned in the mind of Dionysius of Alexandria by the spiritualism
[*Spiritualismus*] of that school—three great instances drawn from the more modern
period, subsequent to the Reformation, will suffice fully to illustrate this surprising
fact. Three great men, of different tendencies, whose views we have already cited on
another occasion, measured their intellectual strength against the Apocalypse, and signally came short in the effort. We have reference to LUTHER, GOETHE, and SCHLEIER-
MACHER.

LUTHER says, in his *Preface to the Revelation of St. John*, 1522: "I suffer every one to
exercise his own judgment in regard to this Book of the Revelation of John. I have no
desire to tie any one down to my error or prejudice. I say what I feel. I judge this Book
to be neither Apostolic nor Prophetic, for more reasons than one. First and foremost, the
Apostles did not deal in visions, but prophesied in words, clear and direct, *etc*. My mind
cannot suit itself to the Book, and to me the fact that Christ is neither taught nor recognized in it, is good and sufficient cause for my low estimation of it," *etc*. Luther, in his
preface to the edition of 1534, considerably modified this indiscreet deliverance, conserving,
nevertheless, the expression of doubt (see Guerike, *Isagogik*, 531).

GOETHE gives utterance to the following sentiments in his *Letters to Lavater* (see foot-
note, p. 58): "I am a man of the earth, earthy; to me the parables of the unjust steward, the
prodigal son, the sower, the pearl, the lost piece of money, *etc., etc*., are more Divine (if aught
Divine there be about the matter) than the seven messengers, candlesticks, seals, stars and
woes." It may be seen from this sketch that Goethe did not plunge very deeply into the
study of the Apocalypse.

The opinion of SCHLEIERMACHER is particularly unfavorable (*Einleitung ins Neue Testament*. Vol. VIII. of his *Sämmtliche Werke*, p. 449 sqq.). This commentator perceives, as he
thinks, a lack of unitous connection in the Apocalypse; he discovers in it nothing but universal
plagues, represented under sensuous images to which he can attach no great religious value.
Viewing the Scripture in question thus one-sidedly, it seems to him a matter of indifference whether the visions be understood or not, and his inference is, that "even a thoroughly
correct interpretation of this Book would be productive of but little profit."

Schleiermacher delivered lectures on Church History, yet one grand fact seems to have
escaped his observation, *viz*., that, in the darkest times of the Church, the Apocalypse
contributed much to the maintenance of Christian hope and steadfastness. The circumstance that he regarded the Book as Chiliastic, in accordance with an exceedingly superficial
prejudice, is deserving of nought save a passing mention.

The cause of this misapprehension is far more evident in the case of Schleiermacher
than in the case of Luther. In the Apocalypse, as well as in the Epistle of James, Luther
seems to have missed the doctrine of justification. Schleiermacher, on the other hand, was
unable to accommodate himself to the Hebrew-symbolical style either of the above-mentioned Epistle or of the Apocalypse. He brought his Hellenizing mode of view to bear
upon these Scriptures in particular.

The criticism of the school of Baur has recently reached its meridian in the sphere of
the Protestant union. Under this head belongs: Schellenberg, *Die Offb. Joh. Ein Vortrag*,
Mannheim, 1867 (see the *Theol. Jahresbericht* for 1867, p. 179).

Any attempt to award a full measure of appreciation to the Holy Scriptures, particularly those of the Old Testament (Schleiermacher's misconception of that is well known)—the Prophetic Writings more especially, and hence most especially the Apocalypse—is still greeted with general coldness and disfavor; and the principal reason of this is, doubtless, the confounding of the Hebrew revelational style of writing, and the Græco-Roman intellectual style. For a more general treatment of this subject, we refer our readers to the introductory remarks on Apocalyptics.

§ 8. RULES FOR THE INTERPRETATION OF THE APOCALYPSE.

Under the caption: *The True Principles of Exegesis*, Ebrard (p. 27 sqq.) lays down the following canons:

1. The exegete is by no means to turn to those ' lights which Church History affords,' but is independently to interpret the given text, as such, in accordance with the general rules of exegesis.

2. The business of the exegete is not to query whether such and such a prophecy has been fulfilled; it is his simply to question—what is written here? *etc.*

3. Exegesis must be conjoined with a careful consideration of its roots in the Prophecies of the Old Covenant.

4. There must be a careful comparison of similar and dissimilar items.

5. Nothing should be symbolically interpreted which is not proved to be symbolical in the Apocalypse itself or by Old Testament visions. Nothing should be apprehended literally which is demonstrated to be a symbol.

6. In exegesis we are not to proceed from the external and formal sides of prophecies, but, on the contrary, always and everywhere from the subject-matter.

The result of these provisions is couched in the following terms: " That school which, in the Revelation of John, finds the fundamental points of Churchly development prophesied; which discovers in it neither conjectures and ideas, nor passages of Church-historical or eschatological detail, but real, true prophecy, is as yet in its infancy."

Such is, doubtless, the case. So far as exegesis is concerned, however, it can assuredly be productive of no harm, if we make use of such "exegetical illuminations" as Church History may offer, as well as examine into the fulfillment of prophecy, reserving to ourselves full liberty the while.

We need not here repeat the rules of general theological hermeneutics. If, however, we follow the progress of Apocalyptics, a series of definitions will result from the chain of developments—ranging themselves thus: 1. Revelation; 2. Prophecy—Messianic Prophecy, in particular; 3. Eschatological Prophecy, or Apocalyptics.

Parallel with these three material elements we find the following formal elements: 1. Historicalness in ideal significance; 2. Symbolical colors and forms in the service of holy, *i. e.*, objective-subjective, vision; 3. A Hebrew ground-form, which has thoroughly adopted the New Testament idea of universalism; or the perfect synthesis of the Hebrew art-form and Hellenic culture. Let us briefly examine the result.

1 *Revelation*. It is to be decided whether the Apocalypse really pertains to the sphere of Revelation. And, in handling this question, we must admit that a critical discrimination between genuine and non-genuine chronicles of Revelation is not an art of the most recent times only; far less is it the art of indiscriminately rejecting all that ecclesiastical criticism has won by dint of persevering labor through long centuries. It being, then, ascertained that our Apocalypse, regarded both as *a visionary fact, and as a written production*, belongs to the sphere of Revelation, it necessarily results that its character as a Revelation must be defended against the tendencies of deistic and pantheistic exegesis. And this most especially in respect to its fundamental idea—the foretokens of, and preludes to, the coming of the Lord for the perfect revelation of His Kingdom. In antithesis to this fundamental idea, the utter frivolity of fictitious motives, such as, for instance, the wretched Neronic tradition, should be shown up. The mere fact that it is ■ Revelation, proves that the Apocalypse consists neither of mere histories, for the satisfaction of idle curiosity or a profane thirst

for knowledge and love of science, nor of bare didactic conceptions, but of ideally significant facts appertaining to the Kingdom of God.

And here be it remarked that the present use of the term *historical* is calculated to mislead. Deism, in its day, bestowed the epithet of *historical* on that method which, for instance, constructed the Personality of Christ from Essenism, or translated the word *pistis* (πιστις) by *fidelity to conviction;* without questioning where, in the old time, the primeval source of all these things, whose novelty was but apparent, might be situate. In reality, the conception of an all-embracing, primitive cell was involved here. This hatred of the truly *new* and original is the property, in a still higher degree, of what are denominated modern times [*Neuzeit*]. Pantheistic rationalism regards Christianity as the product of a compound of Judaism and heathenism. The fact that both these were instrumental in preparing the way for Christianity, rationalism transposes into the assurance that they were the parents of it. Away with originalities!—seems to be the cry. Down, especially, with the highest of them, their peculiar stand-points, and aspects! History begins in the lowlands of humanity. —Then Gehazi must needs be more historical than Elijah, because he is so very human. Judas must be more historical than John. And, finally, the superstitious working up of the Neronic tradition must be more historical than the prophetico-original world-view of a John.

2. *Prophecy.* Prophecy, in the more general sense of the term, is the organ of the *new;* of the heavenly source-points of the Kingdom of God; of new words, new works. Prophecy, in the stricter sense, is the opening of new source-points within a sphere that had become historical—the sphere of individual, legal Judaism; the opening of source-points of theocratico-human universalism, of preludes to, and proclamations of, Christianity. This Prophecy is materially conditioned by contemporary inducements, formally conditioned by contemporary conceptions.

The fact that Prophecy has its points of departure in its own time must not lead us to conclude, however, that it is confined to its own time—least of all, to the errors of its time. What we have to conclude from this fact is that Prophecy, as the conditional disclosure of the eternal, which embraces the three periods—the past, the present, and the future—will be demonstrated to be the exegesis of the past, the pastorate of the present, and the guiding-star of the future, by means of its delineation of the fundamental traits of that future. Whilst it is said that Prophecy contemplates the future on a reduced scale in perspective concentration, it must be admitted that the religious measurement of time is totally distinct from the common chronological measurement. The difference is infinite between an Apostle's declaration: *The Lord cometh quickly,* and the same affirmation in the mouth of a Chiliast. The former does not *reckon;* he speaks forth his strong presentiment of the speedy Coming of Christ, because to him the history of the world is principially fulfilled; because he feels the Christologically winged, ever more rapid pace of its history to be a continual Coming of the Lord. But the Chiliast *reckons;** for to him and his impatience the interval between the first and second Advents of Christ is so much dead space. When, however, the chiliastic impulse begins to assume an authoritative tone with its chronology, the Prophetic and Apostolic spirit brings to light the critical sobriety of its consciousness, effecting this now by the designation of *seventy weeks,* now by a statement of other symbolical measures of time. Surely it is but a starveling branch in the midst of the Theology of the present day—this confounding of the religious dates of Prophets and Apostles with chiliastic determinations of times and seasons.

3. *Eschatological Prophecy.* The distinctive mark of Eschatological Prophecy is this: with the genuine characteristics of true perspectivity, it must reach to the second Parousia. Now a spiritualism [*Spiritualismus*] which regards the idea of the second Parousia as a chiliastic error, cannot fail to be dissatisfied with this claim. To such spiritualism the very idea of Apocalyptic Prophecy is itself a πρῶτον ψεῦδος. Upon these premises a lengthy strife as to details might be carried on; but we have here to do simply with the collision

---

* [A few may *reckon,* but not all —E. R. C.].

of opposite principles. It is, indeed, not every negation of the eschatological expectation that has a principial consciousness. Manifestly false, however, is every view that leaves the chariot of Ezekiel, near the first Parousia, deep in the sand of the common historical circumstances of his time. As it may be said with truth that the Baurian Theology causes the Christology of the "Jewish Apostles" to fall behind the Christology of an Isaiah, and makes the characters of the Evangelists and Apostles vanish like murky shadows behind the distinct and shining forms of the Prophecies; so, likewise, it is claimed that the New Testament Apocalyptist knew really less of the future than his brethren of the Old Testament, or at least that his writings reveal less than the eschatological discourses of the Lord and the Apostle Paul. If we have become truly acquainted with the mode of Old Testament Prophecy, we shall not look upon those fundamental traits of the eschatological future which are presented in the Apocalypse as a ground-plan of either Church or world-history; much less shall we be able to mistake the parallel points in the character of Apocalyptic Prophecy, or fail to recognize its cyclical progression.

4. *Historicalness in ideal significance, i. e., Hebrew theocratico-religious style.* This caption is expressive, on the one hand, of the reality of the historical basis of the Apocalypse (the personal Christ; the Redemption, the Church, the Kingdom of God, the kingdom of darkness, the Resurrection, etc.); on the other hand, of the ideal significance of that basis, which makes it impossible that the Apocalypse should anywhere be purely historical; hence, chs. ii. and iii. may not be restricted to the seven churches of Asia Minor ; chs. v. and vi. cannot have reference to periods of the Church's history; nor can ch. vii. and other passages be applied to the Jewish nation, etc.

5. *Symbolical colors and forms in the service of holy, i.e., objective-subjective vision.* If the *colors* are symbols, so too are the *forms.* And, consequently, so likewise are the numbers. It is unnatural, in a symbolical writing, to treat the numbers in accordance with either their common value or their literal value. Again, as it is necessary to distinguish betwixt symbols and dogmas, not taking for granted that a symbol—as, for instance, a beast, a lion—always denotes the same idea, but modifying the signification of the symbol by the context, so it is likewise necessary thoroughly to distinguish those visions which are produced by the Spirit of God from morbid subjective hallucinations, with which they now are often frivolously identified.

6. *A Hebrew ground-form which has thoroughly adopted the New Testament idea of Universalism; or, the complete Synthesis of the Hebrew Art-form and Hellenic Culture.* In the first place, we have to reject the common enthusiastic, as well as the common humanistic, notion which maintains the existence of a strife between the perceptions of immediate ecstasy, the mediation of those perceptions through the instrumentality of religious writings, aided by a knowledge of previously existing Holy Scriptures, and the framing of said perceptions in artistic forms. Secondly, we would controvert the notion which represents those moments of inspired conception and the moments when the mind, looking in upon itself, passes in review and commits to writing the treasures which have been entrusted to it, as mutually exclusive the one of the other. An ordinary knowledge of the nature of high poetic productivity should lead the critic beyond this sorry judgment. But the point upon which the greatest stress should be laid is this, viz. : that it is an hypothesis utterly contradictory of ethical psychology to suppose that exalted revelations could, by any possibility, have been poured into the vessel of narrow and impure folk-prejudices, folk-traditions, and fantastic extravagances. The wise man indeed says : Apples of gold in dishes [pictures] of silver, but never : Apples of gold in unclean earthen shards ! Again, the identification of Apocalyptic forms with forms of Greek poetry, or the dissection of the Revelation into various irreconcilable parts, or the non-appreciation of its unitous composition, is totally at variance with the idea of the Apocalypse.

According to Reuss (p. 147) the following leading tendencies have been developed in exegesis :

1. The Chiliastic tendency. This he should have divided into : (*a*) the true eschatological tendency ; and (*b*) its caricature, the really Chiliastic tendency.

2. The moral spiritualizing [*spiritualisirend*] tendency—more accurately defined: the religious-practical allegorizing tendency. This, however, may also be chiliastic.

3. The historizing tendency in various modifications: (*a*) Church-historical with polemic reference to the Papacy; (*b*) Political phases, in their relation to the development of the Kingdom of God; (*c*) Having reference only to the immediate period of the Jewish war.

4. Idealizing modernization of eschatological elements.

5. The purely historical tendency which is determined to insure the views of primitive times in full possession of their rights, and seeks to interpret the Book by them alone, without any regard to the views current in our own day. Reuss mentions Ewald, De Wette, Düsterdieck, Bleek, Volkmar, as representatives of this last tendency—a fact in itself sufficiently illustrative of his conception of the "purely historical."

Davidson's arrangement of systems, noted by us under § 5, is of greater value.

Auberlen distinguishes [*Daniel and Revelation*, p. 359 sqq., Eng. Ed.]: 1. *The Church-historical* view: Bengel, the English and French commentators; Elliott, Gaussen. 2. The view which conceives of the Apocalypse as portraying *contemporaneous history:* Ewald, De Wette, Lücke, *etc.* 3. The conception of it as descriptive of *the History of the Kingdom of God:* Von Hofmann, Hengstenberg, Ebrard—to this third class of exegetes Auberlen himself belongs.

This simple and attractive disposition, however, includes important varieties under its several rubrics. And beside the pure forms, there are also mixed forms of interpretation.

In accordance with our view of the style of theocratic revelation, we might lay down the following distinctions:

1. *Abstract historical view:* (*a*) Absolutely Divine Church and world-historical predictions; (*b*) Absolutely human combinations of contemporary history and popular prejudices; (*c*) Theosophic and chiliastic mixed forms, confusing—not reconciling—the two elements of which they are composed.

2. *Abstract idealistic view:* (*a*) Quietistic allegorizings for private edification; (*b*) Modern allegorizings as translations of theocratic concretes into deistic or pantheistic abstracts; (*c*) Chiliastic, mixed forms—Swedenborg and others.

3. *Concrete Christological forms:* (*a*) Cyclical view; (*b*) Rhapsodical view; (*c*) Mixed forms.

§ 9. CONSTRUCTION OF THE APOCALYPSE.

The Apocalypse, in respect to its formal side, constitutes the meridian of Hebrew poetry and art, embracing in its individual forms the most diverse elements. In respect to its constructive side, again, it is, in accordance with the character of all Apocalypses, a finished composition, a unitous work of art, as are the Biblical Apocalypses in general; beyond the circle of these, the same may be affirmed of the Book of Job, and, in a certain sense, of the Biblical Books throughout. If the laws of this construction be but recognized, the obscure Book of Revelation will present itself to our eyes as a radiant constellation, a symmetrical cathedral, built upon a plan of perfect clearness and transparency.*

In the first place, the Apocalypse is a unitous ideal representation, furnished, like the Gospel of John, with a Prologue and an Epilogue.

The Prologue of the Apocalypse relates to the revelation of the second Coming of Christ, imparted to the Apostle John for believers—the seven churches in particular. Similarly, the Prologue of the Gospel relates to the revelation of Christ's first Coming for the Jews, the disciples of John in particular. The Prologue is comprised in ch. i. 1-8.

In the Epilogue of the Apocalypse the Lord enacts certain definite regulations in reference to His Coming, as in the Gospel of John; here, however, He definitely proclaims His speedy approach, and in the stead of the two Apostles, Peter and John, He sets forth, on the one hand, the word of prophecy concerning His Coming, and, on the other hand, the Church's prayer for that Advent. The Epilogue is comprised in ch. xxii 6–21.

---

* Comp. Lange's *Apost. Zeitalter*, Vol. II., p. 464.

The fundamental idea or theme of the Apocalypse itself is: The near Advent of Christ, as the end of the world, in order to the perfect revelation of the Kingdom of God, or the transfiguration of the world into the Father's House, the City of God; considered in respect to its presages and signs, for the instruction, warning, strengthening, and elevating of the believing Church.

The mediation of Christ's Coming is developed agreeably to the idea of a great Divine week; this, as the week of the second creation—the creation of an eternal spirit-world—forms both a contrast and a parallel to the Divine week of the first creation, whose Sabbath was the consummation of the natural world in the appearance of the first man. The characteristic of the Apocalypse, therefore, is the number seven. Seven churches; seven seals, seven trumpets; seven thunders; seven heads of Antichrist, or seven mountains; seven vials of wrath; the seventh Day appears as the perfect revelation of the Seven Spirits in the glorified Christ.

As within each individual *seven*, within the *seven* churches, *seven* seals, *etc.*, a *quaternary* is set off against the following *ternary*—the *quaternary* forming the universal foundation; the *fifth* image, in the *ternary*, the special form of the crisis; the *sixth* the actual culmination of the crisis (the ἀκμή); the *seventh* image being the consummation or fruit of the foregoing ones, the bud of a following *septenary*—so it is with the arrangement of the *seven* principal items; here, too, a *quaternary* precedes the *ternary*. The *first four* images—the seven churches, seven seals, seven trumpets, and seven thunders—are descriptive of the course of the world as its approaching end; the *last three* images, on the contrary—the seven heads of Antichrist, the seven vials of wrath, and the seventh day, are descriptive of the end itself in its development from the judgment to the glorification of the world. In accordance with the above, the movement of the Apocalypse may be divided into two parts: the course of the world *to* the end, chs. i.-xi., and the course of the world *in* the end, chs. xii.-xxi*. We have only to remark that the fragmentary and mysterious sketch of the time of the seven thunders forms the transition from the first to the second half.

In accordance with the law of prophetic sight, the *individual items* of the *septenary* do not follow each other chronologically, like different historical periods (as Bengel and many others maintain); on the contrary, the *individual visions* are invariably *pictures of the whole course of the world*, characteristic of this course in its various aspects and dynamical relations, and linked together like rings. Accordingly, the seven churches, the pictures of Church-history, appear as the dynamical forerunners of the history of the world. The history of the world, in its seven seals, is the womb of those facts which pre-eminently preach repentance, *i. e.*, the seven trumpets. In the midst of the seven trumpets, the seven mysterious thunders are heard; these are, doubtless, spring and summer messengers for the rejuvenation of the Church. But over against the ever richer, purer, and riper development of Christianity, and almost outstripping it, the parallel development of Antichristianity is seen, the Beast with its seven heads. These seven heads call forth the final judgments, the judgments of hardening, poured forth from the vials of wrath; these judgments are to be carefully distinguished from the penitential trumpets [trumpets calling to repentance]. The last judgment of wrath signalizes the turning-point which brings with it the Coming of the Lord—the seventh day.

But though the seven principal items do not, as chronological sections, progress from the beginning to the final goal, yet there is an advance toward the end in the point of view which each predominantly exhibits. They gravitate toward the goal of the Coming of Christ. And, in this respect, the seven seals are more eschatological than the seven churches; the trumpets more eschatological than the seals, and so on. Nevertheless, the first item, the series of the seven churches, comes in contact with the end of the world, ch. iii. 20, 21, and even the last items, the vials of wrath, and the seventh day, reach back into the beginning of the Christian course of the world. See ch. xiii., the characteristics of the world-monarchies.

---

* [See Introduction by the American Editor—E. R. C.]

That which exhibits the construction in all its sublimity, however, is the idea of the absolute teleology of the Divine Government; the absolute and yet free sway of Divine Providence above a fluctuating liberty in the history of mankind, and over the demonic powers of hell; these hellish powers, with ever increasing boldness, induced by their apparent triumphs, are making constant advances against the Divine Rule, until, in the end, the complete unveiling and exhaustion of the Satanic kingdom results in the complete revelation of Heaven and the perfect appearing of the Kingdom of God, both Kingdoms grappling together at last in personal concentrations. This idea of the heavenly assurance of victory finds its expression in the fact that a heaven-picture invariably precedes an earth-picture; a heavenly pre-celebration of the victory of Christ is the invariable forerunner of the earthly crisis, of earthly strife and woe, the conflict of the Church Militant.

With the progress of these heavenly festivals of victory, in their eschatological succession, there is a corresponding progression in the forms of their revelation, i. e., the visions of the Apocalyptist. Thus, the one Apocalypse develops into a unity in the organic manifoldness of individual Apocalypses.

In accordance with the preceding remarks, the contents of the Apocalypse may be arranged as follows:

The *Theme* of the Book, which may be found in the conclusion of the Prologue, ch. i. 7, 8, is *the great Advent of Christ.* The Prologue itself characterizes the Book as the Revelation of the Coming of Christ, ch. i. 1–7, 8. The Epilogue proclaims the nearness and grand import of that Coming, ch. xxii. 6–21. The Apocalypse itself, therefore, begins with ch. i. 9, and closes with ch. xxii. 5. It falls into two parts: 1. The course of the world to the end of the world, chs. i. 9–xi. 14. 2. The end of the world to the glorification of the world, chs. xi. 15–xxii.*

THE PROLOGUE, Ch. i. 1–8.

PART I.—Course of the world to the end, or the future generally, as the Coming of Christ. The seven churches; the seven seals; the seven trumpets; the seven thunders, chs. i. 9–xi. 14.

1. The seven churches or lights. First day of creation: Let there be light, chs. i. 9–iii. 22.

    a. Heaven-picture. Heavenly appearance of Christ, and ideal forms of the Church; the stars in His hand; the candlesticks at His feet, ch. i. 9–20.

    b. Earth-picture. Earthly forms of the Church in the series of the seven churches; and the Lord in the spiritual coming of His word to them, chs. ii. 1–iii. 22.

        a. The first four churches in their conflict between light and darkness, pictures of the *developing* Church: The *active* church; the *martyr* church; the *mixed* church; the *enthusiastic* church.

        β. The three fundamental forms or aspects of the matured Church: The church *cold in death ;* the church *warm with life ;* the *dying and lukewarm* church (the world within; Christ without).

2. The seven seals or enigmas of world-history in its relation to the Church; unsealed by Christ. Or the second day of creation: Heaven and earth, chs. iv. 1–vi. 17.

    a. Heaven-picture. Heavenly aspect of world-history, chs. iv. 2–v. 14.

    b. Earth-picture. The unsealed seven (*i. e.,* the six, which develop into the seventh), ch. vi.

        a. First four seals. Universal fundamental aspects of world-history in its eschatological modification. *War, dearth,* and *mortality* under the *supremacy of Christ,* or the teleology of the Kingdom of God.

        β. The succeeding seals. Martyrdom of the Kingdom of God. Convulsions of the earthly cosmos. Dawn of the day of wrath.

---

* [See Introduction by the American Editor.—E. R. C.]

3. The seven trumpets, issuing from the seven seals. Third day of creation. Separation betwixt land and water, and appearance of vegetation, chs. vii. 1–ix. 21.

　　a. Heaven-picture. Sealing of the people of God in this present world, indicated by the sealing of the elect of the Twelve Tribes of Israel. Consummation of the people of God in the other world. Or the firmament of God (Ps. xciii.) in contradistinction to the billowy sea of world-history, ch. vii. 1–17.

　　b. Earth-picture. The seven (relatively six) trumpets. Or penal judgments, through the prayers of the saints converted into disciplinary sufferings in order to awakening, chs. viii. 1–ix. 21.

　　　　a. First four trumpets : Judgment upon the spiritual (and physical?*) earth. Upon the spiritual world-sea. Upon spiritual fountains and rivers. Upon spiritual celestial lights, in their outward appearance, ch. viii.

　　　　β. The two succeeding trumpets : Demonic psychical sufferings originating in the abyss, *as the first woe from the abyss ;* and pneumatic world-plagues, ch. ix. The second woe, completed in chs. x. and xi.

4. The seven thunders, or rejuvenizing voices delaying the trumpet of final judgment, the seventh trumpet (ὁ κατέχων; τὸ κατέχον). Fourth day. Appearance of the sun over earth and sea, chs. x. 1–xi. 14.

　　a. Heaven-picture. Heaven on earth in the sun-like radiance of the manifestation of Christ upon earth. Sealing of the seven thunders, ch. x. 1–7.

　　b. Earth-picture. Suggestive episodes of the time of the seven thunders. Eating of the little book. Measurement of the Temple, and separation of the outer court. The two olive-trees, or witnesses of Christ. Slaughter of them; their resurrection and ascension. Rise of Antichristianity, chs. x. 8–xi. 14.

PART II.—The end of the world, to the glorification of the world, chs. xi. 15–xxii. 5.

5. The Beast with seven heads, or Antichristianity. Fifth day of creation. Marine animals, chs. xi. 15–xiii. 18.

　　a. Heaven-picture, chs. xi. 15–xii. 17.

　　b. Earth-picture. The Beast out of the sea, or Antichristianity as developed out of national life. The Beast out of the earth, or Antichristianity as developed out of the old religious and secular order of things, chs. xii. 17–xiii. 18.

6. The seven vials of wrath, or judgments of hardening. Sixth day of creation, as the day of the appearing of the New Man from heaven, chs. xiv.–xx. 15.

　　a. Heaven-picture of the incipient judgment (general view), chs. xiv.–xv. 8.

　　b. Earth picture of the incipient final judgment (general view). The seven last plagues, ch. xvi. 1–21.

　　　　a. First four plagues. Judgment of hardening upon the earth; upon the sea; upon the rivers (spiritual currents); judgment of the transformation of the sunshine of revelation into fiery heat (comp. the first four trumpets).

　　　　β. Fifth and sixth vials of wrath. Judgment upon the seat of the Beast. Judgment of the loosing of the kings of the East (see the fifth and sixth trumpets).

　　　　γ. *The seventh vial of wrath, or the ramification of the one judgment into three judgments,* ch. xvi. 19–21.

　　　　a. Final judgment on the great Whore, executed by the ten kings, representatives of dechristianized national life, chs xvii. and xviii.

　　　　b. Final judgment on the ten kings, completed by the Appearance of Christ, chs. xix.–xx. 6.

　　　　c. Final judgment upon Gog and Magog, the last rabble-remnants of Antichristianity, incited to rebellion by Satan ; accomplished by fire from Heaven; the fire of the terrestrial metamorphosis, ch. xx. 7–15.

---

* This is contradicted by ch. ix.

A. First final judgment, or the judgment on the great Whore; absolute Babylon. A judgment of reprobation, chs. xvii. and xviii.

a. Heaven-picture of the reprobatory judgment on Babylon, ch. xvii.

b. Earth-picture. Fall of Babylon, ch. xviii.

B. Second final judgment, as a damnatory judgment upon the radical dominion of the Beast and the false Prophet, ch. xix. 1–21.

a. Heaven-picture. Pre-celebration of the visible appearing of the Kingdom of God, ch. xix. 1–16.

b. Earth-picture. Victory of Christ, at His appearing, over the Beast; and the result of victory; the Millennial Kingdom, chs. xix. 17–xx. 5.

C. Third judgment, or the fiery judgment on Satan himself, and the last anarchical rebellion instigated by him on earth, ch. xx. 6–15.

a. Heavenly pre-celebration of the consummation, ch. xx. 6–8.

b. Consummate victory over Satan and his kingdom on earth. The general resurrection and the general judgment, vers. 9–15.

7. The seventh day. As the day of the finished new creation, and the eternal new world, chs. xxi.–xxii. 5.

a. Heaven on earth, or the City of God, the new Paradise, ch. xxi.

b. Earth glorified to Heaven, or the Land of God, the Paradisaic world, ch. xxii. 1–5.

THE EPILOGUE, ch. xxii. 6–21.

APPENDIX.

A. SIGNIFICANT TERNARIES.

1. The last three churches; the last three seals; the last three trumpets; the last three kings; the last three vials of wrath.

2. The three woes.

3. The three frogs. (*a*) Out of the mouth of the Dragon; (*b*) out of the mouth of the Beast; (*c*) out of the mouth of the false Prophet.

4. The three parts of the great city, Sodom and Egypt, devastated by the seventh vial of wrath; and the ensuing three judgments: (*a*) Judgment upon Babylon; (*b*) judgment upon the Beast and the false Prophet; (*c*) judgment upon Satan, together with his last organ, Gog and Magog. The two or three [?] forthgoings of Antichristianity from the Euphrates.

B. PARALLELS OF THE SEVEN PHASES OF THE COURSE OF THE WORLD.*

In submitting, on the following page, parallels of the seven sevens, it is not with the intention of establishing a thorough analogy of the individual numbers in respect to their denotations; several such analogies will, however, appear—especially between the trumpets and the vials of wrath.†

---

* The visions of the fore-festivals in Heaven might be represented in a similar table.

† There is also a correspondence, by no means indistinct, between the Rider on the white horse and the first penitential judgment [judgment calling to repentance], as also the first judgment of wrath, upon the earth. To the rider on the red horse, the penitential judgment and the judgment of wrath upon the sea of nations correspond. To the black horse, or Dearth and Tribulation, the penitential judgment and the judgment of hardening upon streams and fountains. *i. e.,* intellectual tendencies and original minds, correspond. To the pale horse, or Death and Sheol, the judgment consisting in the obscuration of the Sun of Life, Revelation, corresponds. Under the quinary, the heavenly subtilty of the martyrs corresponds with the psychical and demonic subtilty of the plague of locusts, and the torments of the Beast himself. Under the senary, the eschatological earthquake corresponds with the loosing of the horsemen from Euphrates, and with the drying up of that river. That the seventh seal is productive of the seven trumpets, and that these, with the increased power of the seven thunders, occasion the manifestation of Antichristianity; and, finally, that Antichristianity induces the sending of the vials of wrath, are palpable facts. With the decomposition of the air, *as the separation of spirits,* of the seventh vial of wrath, the Parousia is also indicated.

PARALLELS OF THE SEVEN SEVENS.

The Seven Churches.	The Seven Seals.	The Seven Trumpets.	The Seven Thunders.	The Seven Heads of Antichrist.	The Seven Vials of Wrath as Judgments of Hardening.	The Seven Spirits Revealed in the Perfected Christ.
EPHESUS............	The Rider on the White Horse. Christ.	Penitential Judgment on the Earth.	(Reformations; Sealed. Significant Episodes	(The Two Beasts.) The Seven Kings.	Poured out on the Earth.	
SMYRNA............	The Red Horse. War.	Penitential Judgment on the Sea.	The Little Book.	First King	Poured into the Sea.	
PERGAMUS.........	The Black Horse. Dearth.	On the Rivers and Fountains.	Separation betwixt the Temple and the Outer Court.	Sec'd King	On the Rivers and Fountains.	
THYATIRA	The Pale Horse. Death. Power of Death.	Partial Darkening of Sun, Moon and Stars.	The Two Witnesses.)	Third King	Into the Sun.	
INTERVAL				F'rth King		
				Already fallen.		
SARDIS...............	The Martyrs.	Locusts out of the Opened Pit of the Abyss. Tormentors of Mankind.		Fifth King.	On the Seat of the Beast.	
PHILADELPHIA.	The Earthquake as a Presage of the End of the World.	Horsemen loosed from the Euphrates. Slayers of Mankind.		Sixth King, who is.	On the River Euphrates.	
LAODICEA	Seventh Seal as the Substance of the Trumpet or Penitential Judgments.	Seventh Trumpet: Announcement of the Last Penitential Judgment on Antichristianity.		Seventh King, who is to come.	Into the Air.	
				The Beast Himself as the Eighth King, ramifying into the Ten Kings.		

THE

REVELATION OF St. JOHN

AS THE

BOOK OF THE PROPHECY OF CHRIST'S COMING.

OR

THE REVELATION OF CHRIST TO HIS TRUSTED FRIEND, THE APOSTLE JOHN. THE
SECOND, HIGHER GENESIS, CORRESPONDING TO THE FIRST GENESIS, AS THE
BOOK OF GOD'S DAYS' WORKS IN THE THROES OF THE END OF THE OLD
WORLD, IN ORDER TO THE CREATION OF A NEW AND ETERNAL SPIRIT-WORLD,
AMID THE COMING OF CHRIST.

FIRST OR EXEGETICAL DIVISION.

PROLOGUE.

Chap. I. 1–8.

Comp. the Gospel according to John, Chap. I. 1–18; 1 John I. 1–3.

Ver. 1. THE REVELATION.—VER. 2. JOHN.—VER. 3. THE READERS IN GENERAL.—VER. 5. THE
IMMEDIATE READERS: THE SEVEN CHURCHES, AS SUCH—ALSO, HOWEVER, AS REPRESENTATIVES
OF THE CHURCH IN ITS TOTALITY. (THE GENERAL DEDICATION OF THE REVELATION TO THE SEVEN
CHURCHES MUST BE DISTINGUISHED FROM THE SEVEN EPISTLES, WHICH ARE NOT EPISCOPAL,
BUT PROPHETIC, ORIGINATING IN THE VISION AND FORMING A PART OF THE APOCALYPSE IT-
SELF.) — VERS. 4, 5, 6. GREETING AND BENEDICTION (GOD, JEHOVAH. THE SEVEN SPIRITS.
CHRIST, THE FAITHFUL WITNESS. HIS DIGNITY AND WORK. DIGNITY OF CHRISTIANS).—VERS. 7, 8.
ANNOUNCEMENT OF CHRIST'S COMING; THE THEME OF THE BOOK.

THE REVELATION OF ST. [om. ST.] JOHN THE DIVINE [om. THE DIVINE'].

Superscription.

1   The Revelation of Jesus Christ, which God gave unto him, to show unto his
servants things which [what things] must shortly [Lange: in swift succession] come
to pass; and he sent [sending] and [om. and] signified it [om. it][2] by his angel
2 unto his servant John: Who bare record [testified] of the word [Lange: Logos=
Word] of God, and of [om. of] the testimony of Jesus Christ, and of [om. and of][3]
3 all things that [whatsoever things] he saw.   Blessed is he that readeth,[4] [aloud] and
they that hear[4] the words[5] of this [the] prophecy, and keep those [the] things which
are written therein: for the time [Lange: decision-time][5] is at hand [near].

87

DEDICATION AND GREETING [WITH DOXOLOGY.]

4   John to the seven churches which are [om. which are]⁶ in Asia : Grace be [om. be]
unto you, and peace, from him which [who] is, [om. ,] and which [who] was, [om. ,]
and which [who] is to come [cometh]⁷ ; and from the seven Spirits⁸ which [that]
5 are before his throne ; And from Jesus Christ, who is [om. who is] the faithful witness, and [om. and] the first-begotten [first-born] of⁹ the dead, and the prince
of the kings of the earth.   Unto him that loved [loveth¹⁰] us, and washed¹¹
6 us from¹² our¹³ sins in his own [om. own] blood, and [ins. he] hath made us kings
[om. kings – ins a kingdom]¹⁴ and [om. and] priests unto [ins. his] God and his [om.
his] Father ; to him be glory and dominion forever and ever [into the ages of the
ages].¹⁵   Amen.

THE ANNOUNCEMENT.   THEME OF THE BOOK.

7   Behold, he cometh with [ins. the] clouds ; and every eye shall see him, and they
also [om. also] which [who] pierced him : and all kindreds [the tribes] of the earth
8 shall wail because of him.   Even so [Yea], Amen.   I am [ins. the] Alpha and [ins.
the] Omega, the beginning and the ending [om. the beginning and the ending,]¹⁶
saith the Lord [ins. God],¹⁷ which [who] is, [om. ,] and which [who] was, [om. ,]
and which is to come [who cometh], the Almighty [or All-ruler].¹⁸

TEXTUAL AND GRAMMATICAL.

¹ So the Rec. ; Cod. B.* has the Theologian [Divine] and Evangelist. [Lach., Alf., Treg., Tisch., with ℵ. C., give simply 'Αποκάλυψις 'Ιωάννου. The title of A. is lost.—E. R. C.]
² Ver. 1. ["Whether ἐσήμανεν has its object expressed in ἦν of this verb, or in ὅσα εἶδε of ver. 2, or whether the ob-
ject is to be supplied by a pronoun for ἀποκάλυψις, or for ἃ δεῖ γενέσθαι, or, lastly, whether the verb is used absolutely,
are questions, some of them at least, more difficult than important, into which we need not enter. A tr nslation, especially
of the divine oracles, ought not to be more explicit and determinate than the original.—No object is supplied by Wick.,
Tyn., Cran., Gen., Rheims,—Vulg., Syr.,—Erasm.. Vat., Castal., Cocc., Vitr.. Bos., Grenf., Lord, Kenr.'—NOTE OF DR.
LILLIE IN HIS TRANSLATION FOR THE A. M. BIB. UNION.—E. R. C.]
³ Ver. 2. The τε after ὅσα of the Rec. di turbs the sense, and is omitted, according to A. B.* C. ℵ.   There is also an
erroneous exegetical addition in [-o ue] minuscules.   Thus Düsterdieck.   [Omitted by Crit. Ed., generally.—E. R. C.]
⁴ Ver. 3. Ὁ ἀναγινώσκων καὶ οἱ ἀκούοντες   Unimportant variations and additions in minuscules.
⁵ Ver. 3. [Lach., Alf., Treg., Tisch. (1859) give τοὺς λόγους with A. C. P., Vulg., etc.; Tisch. (8th Ed.), with ℵ. B.,*
g ves τὸν λόγον.—E. R. C.]
⁶ Ver. 4. The words which are do not occur in the Edition of 1611.—E. R. C.]
⁷ Ver. 4. Variations: before ὁ ὢν τοῦ (on which see Delitzsch, Handschriftliche Funde), also θεοῦ, and instead of ὁ, ὅς.
[Rec. gives τοῦ before ὁ ὢν; B.* gives Θεοῦ; Lach., Alf., Treg. Tisch., with ℵ. A. C., etc., give simply ἀπὸ ὁ ὢν.   The last
mentioned reading is adopted in the text.   The translation is to come, although not erroneous, is obje tionable, as it is
l a le to have put upon it the erroneous meaning, is to be.   The Rheims, following the Vulgate, translates and which [who]
shall come.   (See Trench On the Epistles to the Seven Churches).   Still better is the translation given above.—E. R. C.]
⁸ Ver. 4. Πνευμάτων ἅ; B.* C.   The additions are explanatory. | Lach., Alf, and Tisch., read as above; for ἃ given by
B*. C., Treg. reads τῶν with ℵ. A.; Rec., in accordance with P., inserts ἐστιν after ἃ, which is omitted by ℵ. A. B*. C.,
etc.—E. R. C.]
⁹ Ver. 5. The ἐκ is omitted [by Crit. Eds. generally] in accordance with ℵ. A. B*. C.   [(Also by P. Vulg. Cop. Syr., etc.)
The German Vers. reads "from the dead.'   Rec. g.ves ἐκ.—E. R. C.]
¹⁰ Ver. 5. Τῷ ἀγαπῶντι, ℵ. A. B*. C.   [So re id Lach., Alf., Treg., and Tisch.—E. R. C.]
¹¹ Ver. 5. Λούσαντι according to B*. Vul *.; more Johannean than λύσαντι.   See, however, Düsterdieck.   [Lachm.,
Treg., and Tisch. (8th Ed.) give λύσαντι in accordance with ℵ. A. C.; Alford presents both readings (but brackets the o),
Λούσαντι, in accor lance with B*. P., Vulg. etc.   Tisch. (1859) gave Λούσαντι.—E. R. C.]
¹² Ver. 5. [Lach., Alf., Treg., Tisch. (8th Ed.) give ἐκ with ℵ. A. C. etc.; Tisch. (1859) gives ἀπό with P. B*.—E. R. C.]
¹³ Ver. 5. Ἡμῶν is better established than the omission of it.   [Lach., Treg., and T.sch., give ἡμῶν with ℵ. C. P. B.*;
Lach. (Min. Ed.) omits with A.: Al'ord bra kets.—E. R. C.]
¹⁴ Ver. 6. T e reading βασιλείαν established by ℵ*. A. C., etc., against βασιλεῖς [by Rec. and P., and βασίλειον by B*.
—E. R. C.]   'Ημᾶς established by ℵ. and B*. against ἡμῖν and ἡμῶν.   [Alf. and Tisch. read ἡμᾶς wit ℵ. b*. P. Vulg. (CL),
etc.; Lach. (Ed. Maj.) gives ἡμῖν in accordance with C., Alford cites in favor of this reading the following MSS. of the Vulgate—Amiat., Fuld., Harl., Toll.   Lach. (E l. Min.), and Treg., give ἡμῖν with A.   The correct reading of each word is exceedingly uncertain.—E. R. C.]
¹⁵ Ver. 6. [Lach. (Ed. Min.), Tisch. (1859), and Alf., omit τῶν αἰώνων with A. P.; Lach. (Ed. Maj.), Treg., Tisch. (8th
Ed.) and Lange retain it with ℵ. B* C., Vulg'ate.—E. R. C.]
¹⁶ Ver. 8. The unauthorized addi ion ἀρχὴ καὶ τέλος is explanatory.   [These words find no place in any one of the old
Codices.—E. R. C.]
¹⁷ Ver. 8. Κύριος ὁ Θεός against the Rec.   [They are given by Crit. Eds., with ℵ. A. B*. C. P., etc.—E. R. C.]
¹⁸ Ver. 8. [For the translation All-ruler see Add. Com. on ver. 8, p. 93.—E. R. C.]

EXEGETICAL AND CRITICAL.

a. THE SUPERSCRIPTION.

[In this section the nature, subject, and writer
of the Book are declared, and the importance of
the subject indicated by a benediction on those
who shall hear and read it in the spirit of obedience. (Altered from Alford).—E. R. C.]

See very rigorous revisions of the text by
Kelly.—On John the Theologian, see Biographies
of John.

Ver. 1. **Revelation** of Jesus Christ. Indicative not of the form of the B ok, but of its substance.   The Book likewise receives its title from
its subject-matter.   Inadequate conceptions of
the essence of the Apocalypse may be found in
the works of Bunsen and Holtzmann. ['Αποκά-

λυχις is employed in the New Testament as indicating—1. The disclosure *by word or symbol*
of that which *is* hidden or future, Rom. xvi. 25;
1 Cor. xiv. 6, 26; 2 Cor. xii. 1, 7; Gal. i. 12,
ii. 2; Eph. ii. 3; 2. The manifestation *in substance* of that which *was* hidden or future, Rom.
ii. 5, viii. 19; 1 Cor. i. 7; 2 Thess. i. 7; 1 Pet.
i. 1, 13; 3. Illumination (possibly) Luke ii. 32;
this meaning, however, may be resolved into the
first. It is manifest from the following δεῖξαι
that the term is here employed in the first of
these senses. The following from the Treatise
of Sir Isaac Newton is well worthy of consideration : "The Apocalypse of John is written in
the same style and language with the prophecies
of Daniel, and hath the same relation to them
which they have to one another, so that all of
them together make but one complete prophecy.
—The prophecy is distinguished into seven successive parts; by the *opening* of the seven seals
of the book which Daniel was commanded to
seal up; and hence it is called the *Apocalypse* or
Revelation of Jesus Christ." — E. R. C.]—Of
Jesus Christ.—*Genit.subj.* : Christ the mediatory
cause.—God, in the absolute sense, as the Father,
being the primal source of all things, is likewise
the fountain of Revelation. — [Which God
gave unto Him.—God, *i. e.* the Father : Christ,
the Mediator, knows not the times and seasons
(καιρούς, ver. 3) which the Father hath put in
His own power, save as they are revealed to Him.
Comp. Acts i. 7; Mark xiii. 32.—E. R. C.]
To show unto His servants.—Statement
of the purpose: To set before the eyes of the
servants of Christ. Hengstenberg : *the prophets.*
Ebrard: *believers.* These *servants* we hold to be
believers who are in a condition to discuss the
mysteries of the Apocalypse with the Church
proper.—Such things are to be shown as must
come to pass, in the sense of Providence, in
the Christian apprehension of the term. [*Must.*
" by the necessity of the divine decree. See ch.
iv. 1; Matt. xxi. 6, xxvi. 54; Dan. xi. 28."—
ALFORD.—E R. C.]
In swift succession [shortly] —Different
interpretations of ἐν τάχει. Ebrard correctly
interprets it as referring to the rapidity of the
course of the events prophesied.* Düsterdieck
maintains that this view is inconsistent with
ἐγγύς, ver. 3. But the καιρός is ἐγγύς, irrespective of the length of time consumed by what is
to come to pass. The whole course of the καιρός
has for its final component part a period of a
thousand years. The expression : *what shall
come to pass*, cannot, however, be paraphrased
by: what shall *begin* to come to pass. That
exegetical prejudice which is incapable of distinguishing between *religious* and *chronological*
dates, comes in play here (see Düsterdieck
against Vitringa and others). —'Εσήμανεν is a
modification of δεῖξαι, indicative of the signs

* [The contrary opinion as to the meaning of ἐν τάχει,
is ably set forth by ALFORD in the following extract : "The
context, the repetition below, ὁ γὰρ καιρός ἐγγύς, and the
parallel, ch. xxii. 6, followed *ib.* 7, by ἰδοὺ ἔρχομαι ταχύ, fix
this meaning (*before long*) here, as distinguished from the
other of *swiftly*, which indeed would be hardly intelligible
with the historic aorist γενέσθαι. This expression, as
De Wette well remarks, must not be urged to signify that
the events of apocalyptic prophecy were to be close at hand;
for we have a key to its meaning in Luke xviii. 7, 8, where
long delay is evidently implied."—E. R. C.]

employed, the symbolical representation.* It relates to Christ. [Christ is the sender; see ch.
xxii. 16.—E. R. C.] Hence, there is a change of
construction, according to Düsterdieck and
others.
Sending.† ἀποστείλας; absolute.—By His
angel (compare ch. xxii. 6) —In respect to the
various hypotheses concerning these words—the
angel of the Lord—Gabriel—the angel who accompanied the Apocalyptist, or who did but throw
him into his rapt state, *etc.*—we refer to the
Comm. on *Genesis*, p. 385 sqq. [Am. Ed.]. From
this Angel of Christ, in His universal form,
particular angelic appearances are to be distinguished. Düsterdieck regards the term as generic, signifying that particular angel of whom
Christ made use in each particular case. If we
assume the angelic visible appearance of Christ
to be the angel of the Apocalypse (comp. Acts
xii. 11, 15), we do indeed encounter a difficulty
in the fact that the angel designates Himself in
ch. xxii. 9, as σύνδουλος; doubtless, however, it
suffices to remark that He appears to the apostle
in the quality of an angel.‡
To His servant John.—Is it conceivable
that a presbyter John could have applied this
emphatic term to himself, so long as the memory
of the great Apostle John endured?
Ver. 2. Who testified.—According to Düsterdieck and many others (from Andreas of
Cæsarea to Bleek, Lücke, Ewald, II.) the whole
of verse 2d refers to nothing but the present
scripture. This supposition they hold to be in
nowise inconsistent with ἐμαρτύρησε. Not only,
however, is the Aorist thus rendered of no distinctive value, but the μαρτυρεῖν and μαρτυρία are
likewise deprived of their full weight. Neither
to a vision nor to the report of a vision could
these expressions be applied. We, therefore,
with many others—from Ambrosiaster to Eichhorn—refer this passage to what was known as
the earlier ministry of John; not simply to his
Gospel, but with Ebrard, to his whole evangelical and apostolic witness, corroborated by his
martyrhood, and familiar to his readers.§

* [This restriction of the meaning of σημαίνω is not in
accordance with the other instances of its use in the New
Testament (three of the five, it will be observed, being by
John), John xii 33, xviii. 32, xxi. 19, Acts xi. 28, xxv. 27.
In all these instances the *signifying* was by word and not by
symbol.—E. R. C.]
† [Lange translates, *in that he sent* (indem er Botschaft
sandte), a German idiom equivalent to the *sending*, with
which the E. V. in this translation is corrected.—E R. C.]
‡ [The comparison of Acts xii. 11 with 15, most certainly
does not show that by "the angel of the Lord," ver. 11, it
was intended to indicate in any sense "a visible appearance
of Christ." The disciples, manifestly, did not intend to
designate Peter himself by that which they styled *his angel*
—at the most, all they could have intended was his *spiritual
representative*, a person or thing distinct from himself. On
the supposition that by "the Angel of the L rd" it was
intended to designate some special representative of Christ,
he would be distinct from Christ, and, as a creature, would
represent himself as a σύνδουλος. On the supposition that
by the Angel was meant Christ Himself, it is impossible
satisfactorily to explain the language of ch. xxii. 9. The
explanation of Lange does not suffice. However He might
have appeared (either subjectively or objectively) to the
Apostle, it is impossible to conceive of Him as using the
language there attributed to the angel.—E. R. C.]
§ [As suggesting this view, see John xxi. 24; 1 John i.1, 2.
On the other hand, ALFORD writes: "The objections to Ebrard's reference are to me unanswerable. First, *as to its introduction with the simple relative* ὅς. We may safely say that,
had any previous writing or act been intended, we should
have had ὅς καί, or even more than this, ... Next, as to the

The Word of God (comp. ch. xix. 13).—Why should not the Logos be intended, as Ebrard and others maintain? [See the preceding extract.—E. R. C.] **The testimony** [*Zeugnisthat=witness-act*] **of Jesus Christ.**—Not *testimonium de Christo* (Lyra), and still less the angelic message of Christ. [See preceding extract.—E. R. C.] How natural it was for the Apostle, in his martyrhood, to think of Christ as the great Martyr (see ver. 5).—'Ὅσα εἶδε. Düsterdieck : The visions here described. Comp. against this view 1 John i. 1; Gosp. of John i. 14, xix. 35.—The expression embraces the whole witness of John concerning his whole view of the glory of Christ, in the grandeur of His deeds and demonstrations. **Ver. 3. Blessed is** [*or* be] **he.** [Comp. Matt. v. 3-11.—E. R. C.]—This conveys an idea of the importance of this book totally different from that which is represented by many moderns —Schleiermacher, for instance, in his Introduction to the New Testament. Düsterdieck affirms that this μακάριος has reference only to a participation in the kingdom of glory, and not to conservation in the conflicts which precede its establishment—as if the two ideas were separable.—**That readeth, and they that hear.** Representation of a religious assembly. If the *hearing* be intended to convey the idea of religious earnestness [comp. ch. ii. 6, 11, 17, 29, iii. 6, 13, 22, &c.—E. R. C.] thus being emphatic, why may not the *reading* be expressive of the same idea? [These words imply the duty of striving *to understand*—a duty still further implied by the following direction *to keep.* How can that be *kept* which is not *understood?* There are those who refrain from the study of unfulfilled prophecy, upon the ground that "the prophecies were not designed to make us prophets." This is true; but a prophet is one thing, and an understander of prophecy is another. There is, indeed, a curious prying into things not revealed, an effort to make determinate those times and seasons which our Lord has expressly declared are (for us) left indeterminate (comp. Matt. xxiv. 36; Acts i. 7). Such conduct, however, is entirely different from the reverential, prayerful study of the word as revealed. It should be remembered that our Lord rebuked the Jews and His disciples for not understanding the pro-

phecies relating to His first Advent, (comp. John v. 39, 46 : Luke xi. 52 ; Matt. xvi. 3 ; Luke xxiv. 25) ; and that His last great eschatological discourse was delivered that His people might be *fore-warned* (comp. Matt. xxiv. 4, 15, 24, 25, 33)— the implication, of course, being that it should be studied. It is not intended by these remarks to assert that a full and complete understanding of all prophecies will be attained to, by all who faithfully study ; their design is to set forth the duty of study. Doubtless, many things will remain dark to the most earnest students, even to the beginning of the end ; it may be confidently believed, however, that to such, much important knowledge will be vouchsafed which will be withheld from the negligent ; and, furthermore, that all knowledge expedient for them to possess will be granted.—E. R. C.]—**The words of the prophecy.** These eschatological predictions. —**And keep.** An edifying impression on the heart is not the sole thing intended here ; reference is had to the faithful holding fast of all things set down in this prophecy, and to a corresponding observation of the signs of the times. **For the decision-time.** This is not to be considered as relating to μακάριος, as Düsterdieck thinks, for the blessedness cannot refer to the future alone ; that time is intended when that which relates to the last things shall begin—hence ὁ καιρός. [The classical meaning of καιρός is *the right measure, the right proportion.* In the New Testament it is used to indicate a *time*, a *period ;* but it seems to carry with it its classical force of determinate proportion—it is a season fixed as to time of occurrence and duration. Comp. Matt. viii. 29, xiii. 30, xxi. 34, xxvi. 18, John v. 4 ; Acts i. 7, xvii. 27 ; Rev. xii. 14, *etc.* But what καιρός is here referred to ? Is it not, manifestly, the entire period, viewed as a unit, in which the things symbolically seen by the Apocalyptist should come to pass ?—a period *near* to the Apostle when he wrote ; to us, *present.*—E. R. C.]

b. DEDICATION AND GREETING [WITH DOXOLOGY].

The view of Hengstenberg and Ebrard,* who regard this dedication, from vers. 4-6, as relating only to the seven epistles, in antithesis to the established theory, is opposed to the organic simplicity of the book. The entire prologue belongs to the entire book, as does the entire epilogue. The seven churches, however, as the congregations of the first readers, represent the entire Christian reading-world ; just as the Gospel of Luke and the book of Acts composed by him, were not designed for Theophilus alone.

Ver. 4. John to the seven churches.—On the relation of the Apostle John to the Church in Asia Minor, comp. Church History. The fact that the seven churches formed an ecclesiastical diocese, extending from the metropolis of Ephesus to Laodicea, is intimated by the address of the Epistle to the Ephesians, taken in connection with Col. iv. 16. [It is difficult to perceive the *intimation.* Most certainly the fact that neighboring Churches are exhorted to exchange epistles directed to them respectively, does not imply that they belong to one diocese.—E. R. C.] On the accounts of John's labors in Ephesus, comp.

---

things witnessed. The words ὁ λόγος τοῦ θεοῦ κ. ἡ μαρτυρία 'I. Χρ. cannot with any likelihood be taken to mean 'the (personal) Word of God, and the testimony of Jesus Christ ;' for why, if the former term refer to Christ personally, should He be introduced in the second member under a different name? Besides, the words occur again below, ver. 9, as indicating the reason why John was in the island of Patmos ; and there surely they cannot refer to his written Gospel, but must be understood of his testimony for Christ in life and words: moreover, ἡ μαρτυρία 'Ἰησοῦ is itself otherwise explained in this very book, ch. xix, 10. But there is yet another objection to the supposed reference to the Gospel arising from the last words, ὅσα εἶδεν. First, the very adjective ὅσα refutes it ; for the Evangelist distinctly tells us, John xx. 30, that in writing his Gospel he did not set down ὅσα εἶδεν, but only a portion of the things which Jesus did in the presence of His disciples. . . . But still more does the verb εἶδεν carry this refutation. In no place in the Gospel does St. John use this verb of his eye witnessing as the foundation of his testimony. . . . But in this book it is the word in regular and constant use of the seeing of the Apocalyptic visions. . . . Taken then as representing the present book, τὸν λόγον here will be the aggregate of οἱ λόγοι, ver. 3 ; ἡ μαρτυρία 'I. Χρ. will be the πνεῦμα τῆς προφητείας, embodied in the Church in all ages."—E. R. C.]

---

* [Alford attributes to Ebrard the exactly opposite view. —E. R. C.]

Steitz. The reality of the septenary does not preclude its symbolical import.

Asia.—In the narrowest sense—proconsular Asia. See Winer and others. [See an exceedingly valuable and interesting passage in Conybeare and Howson's Life and Epistles of St. Paul, Vol. I. ch. viii. Also Smith and Kitto.—E. R. C.]

Grace be with you and peace.—As in the writings of the Apostle Paul principally. Comp. also 2 John iii.

From the: He is present, *etc.*—Declaration of the name of Jehovah, not an etymological analysis of it, as earlier exegetes imagined (see the citation of Bengel in Düsterdieck). The declaration *He is, He was, He cometh,* or *He is to come,* does not do full justice to the idea, for the word Jehovah signifies that God is ever present, *at hand,* for His people, as the faithful covenant-keeping God ; neither is this idea contained in the expression *who is,* etc. [Alford writes : "A paraphrase of the unspeakable name יְהֹוָה, resembling the paraphrase אֶהְיֶה אֲשֶׁר אֶהְיֶה in Exod. iii. 14, for which the Jerusalem Targum has, as here, *qui fuit, est, et erit :* as has the Targum of Jonathan in Deut. xxxii. 39; Schemoth R. iii. f. 105, 2 : 'Dixit Deus S. B. ad Mosen : Ego fui et adhuc sum, et ero in posterum.' Schöttg., Wetst., De Wette."—E. R. C.] On the [grammatical] imparity of this formula, and the attempts to smooth it down (τοῦ-ἦν-ἐρχόμενος), see Düsterdieck, page 100. [Trench, in his Com. on the Epistles to the Seven Churches, thus treats of "the departure from the ordinary rules of grammar: Doubtless, the immutability of God, 'the same yesterday, and to-day, and forever' (Heb. xiii. 8), is intended to be expressed in this immutability of the name of God, in this absolute resistance to change or even modification which that name here presents. 'I am the Lord ; I change not' (Mal. iii. 6), this is what is here declared."—E. R. C.] The name is no direct designation of the Trinity ; at most, it contains but an indirect allusion to the three economies.

From the seven Spirits.—See Is. xi. 2 ; Rev. iii. 1; iv. 5 ; v. 6. The seven Spirits burn like lamps [Germ. *Fackeln,* torches] before the throne, as Spirits of God, and are at the same time seven eyes of the Lamb. By this we understand seven ground-forms of the revelation of the Logos or heavenly Christ in the world (hence ideals of Christ; lamps of God ; eyes of Christ) ; neither, therefore, seven properties of the Holy Ghost, though the Spirit of God is their unitous life ; nor properties of God (Eichhorn) ; nor the symbolical totality of the angels (Lyra) ; nor the seven archangels, in accordance with the traditional view (of these archangels six only are grouped together on canonical and apocryphal ground) ; as in Is. xi. 2, the six spirits are merged in the unity of the septenary [*Siebenzahl*] ;* nor seven of the ten Sephiroth (Herder). We must likewise distinguish from these seven Spirits the

Spirit who speaks to the churches (ch. ii. 7, xi. 29); with reference to Zech. iii. 9, iv. 6, 10.*

Ver. 5. **From Jesus Christ.**—From Him also the blessing of grace and peace comes ; hence, to Him divine operations are attributable. [**Who is**].—The nominative, making a change in the construction, manifestly gives prominence to the three following designations of Christ as favorite Apocalyptic names. As God Himself, in an Apocalyptic view, is preëminently He Who is *present,* Who was *present,* and Who draweth *nigh* [*present*], so Christ is, first, the Great Martyr in a unique sense; secondly, the Conqueror of death ; thirdly, the Prince of the kings of the earth. In accordance with the sense, a τοῦ ὁ would be in place here also. These names, therefore, serve neither as a foundation for that which follows nor for that which precedes them, though it is not without reason that Ebrard parallelizes these three names of Christ with the following three soteriological operations. With the faithful Witness correspond the words : Who loveth us, etc. The three offices of Christ are likewise suggested here, though Düsterdieck disputes even this. We must remark that the reading λύσαντι would convert the high-priestly function into a kingly one.

The faithful Witness.—See ch. iii. 14 ; also ch xix. 11, xxi. 5, xxii. 6.—Düsterdieck apprehends this as intimating the fact that Christ is the Mediator of all divine revelation, and disputes the very reference in point ; viz. : to the fact that Christ, in the extremity of temptation under suffering, sealed the revelation of God with His testimony (Ebrard). The revelation of God is likewise enwrapped in both the following points; the *First-born and the Prince.* Other references [of the faithful Witness—TR.] either to the fulfillment of threats and promises, or to the truth of the apocalyptic words, pass by the fundamental idea. [The following comment of Richard of St. Victor, quoted by Trench, sets forth the truths involved in this appellation in great fullness : "Testis fidelis, quia, de omnibus quæ per Eum testificanda erant in mundo testimonium fidele perhibuit. Testis fidelis, quia quæcunque audivit a Patre fideliter discipulis suis nota fecit. Testis fidelis, quia viam Dei in veritate docuit, nec Ei cura de aliquo fuit, nec personas hominum respexit. Testis fidelis, quia reprobis damnationem, et electis salvationem

---

* [Michael, Gabriel, Raphael, Uriel, Sealthiel, Jeremiel. The doctrine of a true septenary of archangels was advanced in later times, though not so late as 1460. Comp. the note in Düsterdieck.—E. R. C.]

* [That created beings cannot be intended by *the Seven Spirits* is evident from their being mentioned between the Father and Jesus Christ, and also from their being regarded *as sources* of blessing. The view as to their nature advocated by Lange is inconsistent with their being associated with Persons, and their being named *with* and still more *before* Christ. Tr uch judiciously remarks : "There is no doubt that by 'the seven spirits' we are to understand not indeed the sevenfold operations of the Holy Ghost, but the Holy Ghost sevenfold in His operations. Neither need there be any difficulty in reconciling this interpretation, as Mede urges, with the doctrine of His personality. It is only that He is regarded here not so much in His personal unity, as in His manifold energies; for 'there are diversities of gifts but the same Spirit,' 1 Cor. xii. 4.—The manifold gifts, operations, energies of the Holy Ghost are here represented under the number seven, being as it is the number of completeness in the Church. We have anticipations of this in the Old Testament. When the Prophet Isaiah would describe how the *Spirit* should be given not by measure to Him whose name is the Branch, the enumeration of the gifts is sevenfold (xi. 2); and the seven eyes which rest upon the stone which the Lord had laid can mean nothing but this (Zech. iii. 9, cf. iv. 10 ; Rev. v. 6)."—E. R. C.]

nunciavit. Testis fidelis, quia veritatem quam verbis docuit, miraculis confirmavit. Testis fidelis quia testimonium Sibi a Patre neo in morte negavit. Testis fidelis, quia de operibus malorum et bonorum in die judicii testimonium verum dabit."—E. R. C.]

The First-born of the dead.—See Col. i. 18; 1 Cor. xv. 20.—The idea of the ancient Church, that the day of a man's death is the day of his higher birth, was founded upon fact in the history of Jesus, and upon the word of the apostles. [The reference however, to the title *First-born of the dead* was not to a glorification co-incident with death, but to the resurrection of Christ from the dead. Comp. Col. i. 18; 1 Cor. xv. 20, 23.—E. R. C.] Christ, according to the epistle to the Colossians, is the ἀρχή in a two-fold sense: the ἀρχή of the creation and of the resurrection; the latter is of course implied here, for the heavenly birth of Christ is the efficient cause of the resurrection of the dead (Eph. i. 19 sqq.).*

The PRINCE of the Kings.—In ch. xix. 16, He is called the KING of kings. There He has taken possession of the kingdom; in the beginning of the Apocalypse He has but unfolded the power and right of a king in a princely manner before the eyes of His people, and commenced to give proof thereof in the world; see Matt. xxviii. 18; Acts xiii. 33; Phil. ii. 6 sqq. Comp. Ps. cx.; Is. liii., and other passages. As the kingly principle, even now dynamically ruling over the kings of the earth, and destined in the end to prevail over the Antichristian powers also, He works on and ■■■ until His appearance as the King proper.

The three names jointly form the foundation for the truth of the facts of the Apocalypse. The whole of divine revelation, whose goal is a new world, is sealed by *the faithful Witness*; the principial foundation of its work of renewal—a deadly work to the old world—is in *the First-born*; it is continually at work and unfolding its royal power in *the Prince*.

From Him who loveth us.—According to Düsterdieck [the E. V., Lachmann and Alford], the doxological formula begins here. The doxology at the close of ver. 6, however, is independent;† it is founded upon all that has been previously affirmed of Christ. Düsterdieck rightly insists upon the significancy of the present [tense] form ἀγαπῶντι (ch. xxii. 17;‡ Rom. viii. 37). The real motive for the foundation of a new world is the loving glance of God and Christ at the men of God, who are to be the fruits of creation and redemption.

---

* On Düsterdieck's controversy with Ebrard in respect to ωδῖνες, Acts ii. 24, see the note in Düsterdieck, p. 113.

† [This position can be maintained only in defiance of all grammatical propriety. For obvious reasons, the datives ἀγαπῶντι and λούσαντι should be connected, not with the preceding genitives governed by ἀπό, but with the following αὐτῷ. The ‹olecism of ver. 4, can have no place here, ■■ the grounds of its existence are wanting; and, further, a similar solecism, were it in place, would give us ἀγαπῶν and not ἀγαπῶντι.—E. R. C.]

‡ ["The certainty that Christ continually loves His people is as significant, in the connection of the book, as the certainty that He is the Faithful Witness, etc. The Bride, rejoicing, comforts herself wi'h the coming of Him who loves her (Rev. xxii. 17; comp. Rom.viii.37"). DUESTERDIECK, p. 113. —TR.]

And washed us.—It is an unmistakable fact that one and the same root lies at the foundation of both λούειν and λύειν;* that the one involves the other, and that both are embraced in this concrete expression of Scripture. Nevertheless, the ideas of liberation from the *guilt* [reatus = liability to punishment.—E. R. C.] of sin and liberation from the *bondage* of sin are contra-distinguished, not only in doctrinal theology, but also in the Holy Scriptures. Now it is manifest that in ch. vii. 14, a liberation from guilt is meant; so likewise in 1 John i. 7. These analogies, as well as the consideration that an atonement for the guilt of sin lies at the foundation of a redemption from its power, add weight to the remark that the operation of Christ's blood is distinct from His special act of making us kings. We cannot, therefore, with Düsterdieck, find "substantially the same idea in both readings."

Ver. 6. A kingdom.—It is true that believers are, in a spiritual sense, kings as well as priests. They are true priests, however, through individual self-sacrifice. It is impossible for them, on the other hand, to exercise an individual government, thus encroaching upon the rights of Christian fellowship;—kings they can be only in the community of the Church. Hence there are material reasons, as well as documentary ones, for preferring the more difficult reading ἡμᾶς to ἡμῖν and ἡμῶν; though the abstract fact that Christians are spiritually possessed of kingly dignity is to be maintained; that fact is also supported by ch. v. 10 (βασιλεύειν). The term, then, denotes neither, on the one hand, *a people of kings*, nor, on the other: the subjects of the kingdom, for the essential element in this kingdom is that the members of it rule by serving and serve by ruling (Matt. xx. 25 sqq.) or the identity of sovereignty and subjection [serving. The ideas of *serving* and *subjection* are widely different.—E. R. C.] Christians, therefore, are ■ kingdom. because they are priests,—by virtue of a self-abnegation, heavenly in its purity. (On the Old Testament type, see Exodus xix.) [See Excursus at the end of the section.— E. R. C.]

To His God.—'Αυτοῦ "appertains to the whole term τῷ θεῷ καὶ πατρί." (Düsterdieck, against De Wette and Ebrard.) Believers are priests on the basis of the High-Priesthood of Christ, because, with reconciled consciences, they have immediate access to God in prayer for themselves and intercession for others (Rom. v. 2), in the spirit of self-surrender, giving proof of this spirit in their sufferings, and that not only as witnesses (Rom. xii. 1); these sufferings are of course (as Ebrard remarks in reference to Col. i. 24) to be distinguished from the perfect expiatory passion of Christ. "We find a kindred conception in ch. xxi. 22, where the new Jerusalem is represented as destitute of ■ temple." (Düsterdieck.)

To Him be.—According to De Wette and Düsterdieck, δόξα should be supplemented by

---

* [Liddell and Scott present both ΛΥΩ and ΛΟΥΩ as root words, the latter contracted from the old λοέω. They remark in ■ note under the latter—"Akin to Lat. luo, diluo, eluo, lavo, but hardly to the Greek λύω." (A similar note is appended to the former.)—E. R. C.]

ἐστί, after the manner of 1 Pet. iv. 11. A more obvious explanation of the ellipsis is in accordance with the sense of Rev. iv. 9, 11, and other passages. [Alford remarks: "The like ambiguity is found in all doxological sentences."—E. R. C.]

c. THE ANNOUNCEMENT. THE THEME.

Ver. 7. Behold, He cometh.—In the following words the Apostle announces *the theme* of his book with prophetic vivacity. *Behold, ἰδού* (see ch. xvi. 15). He directs the attention of his readers to a new and grand fact as one who himself beholds and wonders. This form is likewise met with in the Gospels.—*He cometh.* Not: He shall come. The strong Apocalyptic term *He cometh,* for *He cometh quickly,* is partly based upon the idea that He is continually coming—continually on the way. **With the clouds.**—Dan. vii. 13; Mark xiv. 62.—"Among the later Jews the Messiah is actually called the Cloud-Man" (Düsterdieck after Ewald). God also is said to have His dwelling among the clouds (Ps. xcvii. 2, xviii. 11). The cloud is, so to speak, a material symbol of the divine presence, or the divine mystery—partly veiling, partly revealing. [We are not to suppose, however, that the *declaration* "He cometh *with clouds*" is figurative. The clouds with which He will come may be symbolic, but they will be real. Of the literal fulfilment of a prophecy solemnly repeated by our Lord in His discourse on the Mount of Olives (Matt. xxiv. 30), and again to the High Priest, before the Sanhedrin, on the occasion of His trial (Matt. xxvi. 64; Mark xiv. 62); and referred to in the account of the ascension (Acts i. 9, 11);—all under circumstances that preclude the idea of figure;—there should be no doubts.—E. R. C.] **Every eye.**—All mankind; not believers simply (Matt. xxv. 32). **And they who pierced Him.**—According to Düsterdieck, this is significant of the Jews alone. The following sentence he renders: *and all the Gentiles shall wail because of Him.* This, however, does not accord with Zechariah xii. 10. Why should not those who at the first pierced the Lord be the mourners afterwards? And if a mere external historical meaning be attached to the former clause, the saying would apply to a few individual Jews only. The text leaves the question as to whether, and to what degree, repentance is involved, undecided. An element of judgment, startling to all, is enwrapped in the appearance of the Crucified One. Particular interpretations by Ebrard and Düsterdieck, see in the work of the latter, p. 116. The ἐξεκέντησαν appears also in John xix. 37. It was for the Apostle a point of the highest symbolical significance. [Alford makes the following important comment: "As there (John xix. 36) St. John evidently shows what a deep impression the whole circumstance here referred to produced on his own mind, so it is remarkable here that he should again take up the prophecy of Zechariah (xii. 10) which he there cites, and speak of it as fulfilled. That this should be so, and that it should be done with the same word ἐξεκέντησαν, not found in the LXX. of the passage, is a strong presumption that the Gospel and the Apocalypse were written by the same person."—E. R. C.]

Yea (ναί), **amen.**—Double assurance in the Greek and Hebrew. Ver. 8. **Alpha and Omega**—(ch. xxi. 6). —Indication of the *principle* and the *final goal* of all things, in a symbolism drawn from the Greek alphabet (see Rom. xi. 36). Hence the interpolated gloss by way of exegesis. The corresponding Jewish symbolism says: from א to ת. The deduction of the divine Essence from the revelation of that Essence in the world forms the foundation for the deduction of the divine Rule, in accordance with the divine Essence as revealed; and upon this latter deduction the certainty of that last thing is based.

The All-ruler.—It is not without reason that this expression παντοκράτωρ is of constant occurrence in the Apocalypse. It is one of the tasks of the last times to hold fast this assurance, notwithstanding all appearance to the contrary. [The Apocalypse is the only portion of the New Testament in which the word occurs, except in 2 Cor. vi. 18. It is, however, of frequent occurrence in the Septuagint, and to that book we must look for the determination of its meaning. In Job it is used to translate שַׁדַּי, the Almighty; elsewhere it is employed as the second member of the compound expression (κύριος παντοκράτωρ) which most frequently represents—not translates—the Hebrew compound צְבָאוֹת יְהוָֹה *Jehovah of hosts.* (Sometimes the second term is translated by τῶν δυνάμεων (Ps. xxiv. 10), τῶν στρατιῶν (Amos vi. 14), and frequently it is reproduced, σαββαώθ, as in Is. i. 9). Now, it is impossible to suppose that the Seventy regarded παντοκράτωρ as the Greek equivalent for צְבָאוֹת; the most natural supposition is that they looked upon the entire Hebrew expression as an ellipsis for צְבָאוֹת אֱלֹהֵי יְהוָֹה, which would give as the meaning of the Greek term one consistent with its etymology, viz.: *God of hosts.* This supposition is confirmed by the fact that, in several instances where the *three* terms occur, as in Jer. v. 14, xv. 16, xliv. 7; Amos iii. 13 (in this instance *four*), παντοκράτωρ is used to render the last *two.* From all these facts it is natural to conclude that it was used as a term expressive of infinite supremacy, including the two correlated ideas of universal dominion (God of hosts) and almighty power. This meaning, which is most in accordance with the classical and sacred usage of the words from which παντοκράτωρ is compounded, and which is consistent with every instance of its use in the New Testament, is, almost certainly, the meaning that should be attached to it.—E. R. C.]

[EXCURSUS ON THE BASILEIA, ver. 6.]

By the American Editor.

[The expression KINGDOM OF GOD (and its manifest synonyms, *Kingdom of Heaven,*[*] *The*

---

[*] [The phrase *Kingdom of Heaven* occurs only in the Gospel of Matthew. That it is strictly synonymous with *Kingdom of God* is manifest from the following comparisons—Matt. iv. 17 with Mark i. 14, 15; Matt. v. 3 with Luke vi. 20; Matt. xiii. 11 with Mark iv. 11, Luke viii. 10; Matt. xiii. 31 with Mark iv. 30, 31; Matt xix. 14 with Mark x. 14, Luke xviii. 16; Matt. xix. 23 with Mark x. 23, Luke xviii. 24. Matt himself uses *Kingdom of God* five times (vi. 33, xii. 28, xix. 24, xxi. 31, 43). It needs but a glance at these passages to perceive that he uses the phrase as synonymous with the one more frequently employed by him.—E. R. C.]

Kingdom, Kingdom of Christ, etc.) is of most frequent occurrence in the New Testament, and apparently of greatest importance. It is the phrase employed to designate that—(1) which the Baptist heralded (Matt. iii. 2); which our Lord, in the beginning of His ministry, proclaimed as at hand (Matt. iv. 17; Mark i. 14); (3) to the exposition of which His life before His Crucifixion was mainly devoted (Luke iv. 43, and the Gospels *pass.*); (4) concerning which He gave preëminent instruction throughout the forty days that followed His Resurrection (Acts i. 3); (5) which He sent forth His disciples to herald before His Passion (Matt. x. 7; Luke ix. 2; x. 9); (6) concerning which His ministers, after His Ascension, went everywhere giving instruction (Acts viii. 12; xiv. 22; xix. 8; xx. 25; xxviii. 23, 31; and the Eps.

It might naturally be supposed that some *one* objective would be represented by this oft-recurring and apparently important phrase, and yet there is no expression which the great mass of interpreters regard as having been used in so many varied and mutually exclusive senses. In some instances it is represented as designating something established on earth in New Testament times, either before the Crucifixion, or at the Ascension, or on the day of Pentecost; in others (and by the same interpreter), as something to be established in the future. Where it is regarded as indicating something already established — in some instances it is viewed as representing true religion in the heart; in others, the vital Church; and in others still, the apparent Church. Where viewed as designating something future — sometimes it is held to signify the millenial era on earth; and sometimes the Kingdom of glory in Heaven. Dr. Robinson, who may be regarded as a representative of the most numerous school of evangelical interpreters, and who, through his Greek and Hebrew Dictionaries, exerts a most powerful influence upon the theological thought of the ministry of this country, under the title Βασιλεία, thus writes: " We may therefore regard the kingdom of heaven, etc. in the New Testament as designating in its Christian sense, *the Christian dispensation*, or the community of those who receive Jesus as the Messiah, and who, united by His Spirit under Him as their Head, rejoice in the truth, and live a holy life in love and communion with Him. This spiritual kingdom has both an internal and an external form. As internal, it already exists and rules in the hearts of all Christians (it is then a *principle.*—E.R.C.) and is therefore present. As external, it is either embodied in the visible church of Christ, and in so far is present and progressive; or it is to be perfected in the coming of the Messiah to judgment and His subsequent spiritual reign in bliss and glory, in which view it is future. But these different aspects are not always distinguished, the expression often embracing both the internal and external sense, and referring both to its commencement in this world and its completion in the world to come." In his following digest of passages he gives instances of all these alleged uses. Now it is evident that a *dispensation*, a *principle*, and a *people actuated by that principle*, are distinct, mutually exclusive objectives. To

suppose that they were designated by one and the same expression, and that expression manifestly one of the most important in the Book of Life, is to attribute to the inspired writers a looseness in the use of language which, to say the least, would be thought strange in an uninspired teacher, and which, in the case of men writing under the influence of the Spirit for the instruction of the Church in all ages, is scarce conceivable. To such a supposition we should be driven only by most urgent considerations. The question naturally arises—Is there not some one objective which the expression may be regarded as indicating in each instance of its occurrence, and which objective shall satisfy all the demands of the expression—grammatical and contextual—in all its occurrences in the word of God? If such an objective can be set forth, it must, manifestly, be regarded as the one contemplated by the Spirit of the Lord. The writer believes that there is such an one—complex indeed, as is the objective of the term *Church*—but which, in all its fullness, may be regarded as designated by the expression wherever it occurs. —To the exposition of that objective this Excursus is devoted.

As preliminary, however, to this consideration of the *nature* of the Basileia (which, for the sake of precision, that *Kingdom of God* heralded by John and preached by Jesus will, in this article, be styled) it will be necessary to discuss another topic, viz.: *its futurity*. The generally received opinion that the Scriptures teach that it, in some one of its phases, was established in the days of our Lord, or shortly after His Ascension, lies at the basis of the prevalent idea as to its nature; and, consequently, until that opinion is at least shaken, and several of the texts which, almost without question, are assumed so to teach, are shown to have no such force, it cannot be expected that due weight will be given to those expressions which set forth its nature in language inapplicable to aught that now exists, or has ever existed, on earth.

I. THE FUTURITY OF THE BASILEIA.

Before presenting the scriptural argument it is proper to premise that—

(*a*). The fact that the natural Kingdom of God includes the earth as a revolted province, affords no proof that the Basileia prophesied by Daniel as future was established by Jesus. That natural Kingdom existed from the beginning.

(*b*). The mere fact that the existing order of things on earth—an organized Church, grace in the heart—can be spoken of as *a* Kingdom, does not imply that *the* Basileia has been established; a similar state of things existed when Daniel prophesied of the establishment of *the Basileia* as future.

With these remarks we proceed to the argument.

1. Our Lord and His Apostles at every stage of New Testament history referred to its establishment as future:

(1). Indefinitely as to accompanying event (only the leading passages will be cited): Jesus preached that it was *at hand* (i. e., not then established) Matt. iv. 17; Mark i. 14: He taught

His disciples to pray "Thy Kingdom come," Matt. vi. 10; Luke xi. 2: He sent them forth to preach the coming Kingdom, Matt. x. 7; Luke ix. 2, x. 9: near the close of His ministry He spake a parable for the instruction of those who thought it "should immediately appear" (μέλλει αναφαίνεσθαι), Luke xix. 11 : in the institution of the Supper He again and again referred to its futurity, Matt. xxvi 29; Mark xiv. 25; Luke xxii. 16-18, 24-30: it is declared that, after the Resurrection, "He opened their (the Apostles') understanding, that they might understand the scriptures" (Luke xxiv. 45), and also that "He was seen of them forty days, (and) speaking of the things pertaining to the Kingdom of God," Acts i. 3;—on the last day of His sojourn with them, they, illuminated and instructed, asked a question, "Lord, wilt Thou at this time restore the Kingdom unto Israel," evidently based upon the belief that it had not already been established, and He gave an answer that implied the correctness of that belief; is it conceivable either that they were mistaken, or that, if they had been, He would have so answered as to confirm them in their mistake? The Apostle James speaks of believers as *heirs* of a *promised* Kingdom, ii. 5 : Paul, of his being preserved unto God's heavenly Kingdom, 2 Tim. iv. 18; of *inheriting* the Kingdom, 1 Cor. vi. 9, 10, xv. 50; Gal. v. 21; Eph. v. 5; of his fellow-workers unto (εἰς) the Kingdom, Col. iv. 11: Peter exhorts believers so to walk that they might enter into the everlasting Kingdom, 2 Pet. i. 11.

(2). By representing it as synchronous with the second glorious Advent of the Messiah : This intimation was first given by Jesus just before the Transfiguration and after He had begun to show to His disciples that the first Advent was to be one of humiliation, comp. Matt. xvi. 21, 27, 28; Mark viii. 31, 38, ix. 1; Luke ix. 22, 26, 27. It is evident from a comparison of our Lord's last discourse (the Greek text) on the Mount of Olives (Matt. xxiv., xxv. ; Mark xiii.; Luke xxi. 5-33), with the LXX. of Daniel (vii. 9-27, ix. 27, xii. 1-13), that He had those prophecies in view throughout; and that He, as did Daniel (vii. 13, 14), connected the establishment of the Basileia with a future glorious Advent of the "Son of Man;" comp. Matt. xxiv. 3, 27, 30, 39, xxv. 1, 31, 34; Mark xiii. 26 ; Luke xxi. 27, 28 (and note especialey) 31 : see also 2 Thess. i. 5-10; 2 Tim. iv. 1. (There was probably an allusion to this in the institution of the Supper; comp Matt. xxvi. 29; Mark xiv. 25, Luke xxii. 16, 18, with 1 Cor. xi. 26).

2. Jesus implied that the offer of immediate establishment was withdrawn from the Jewish Church because of its rejection of Him, and that the establishment itself was postponed; comp. Luke xix. 41-44 (the weeping over Jerusalem and the accompanying remarks) with the subsequent addresses in the temple, Matt. xxi. 23–xxiii. 39, especially xxi. 42, 43, xxiii. 37-39. The preceding scriptures do not in themselves imply more than the withdrawal of the offer from the Jewish Church, in order to an immediate establishment amongst Jewish and Gentile converts; but, in connection with the words of Jesus referred to under the preceding head, the implication of an indefinite postpone-

ment becomes manifest. This view finds confirmation in the prediction of the *humiliation* of the Church until the day of Christ's glorious appearing, 1 Pet. iv. 13; (see also Acts xiv. 22; 2 Tim. ii. 12, iii. 12, etc.).

3. There is no critically undisputed passage in the Scriptures which declares, or necessarily implies, even a *partial* establishment in New Testament times (Rev. i. 6, is not contemplated in this argument, as the correct reading is uncertain).

The passages which have been referred to as proving the doctrine of a present establishment may be divided into two classes, viz. : those which it is alleged (1) logically imply it, (2) directly declare it. These will be examined in the order indicated. It should be distinctly noted that it is not denied that many of these passages are *consistent* with the hypothesis of a present establishment. All that is now claimed (save in reference to one or two of them) is that they are also consistent with the hypothesis of an entirely future establishment.

(1). Those passages which, it is alleged, logically imply a present establishment of the Basileia.

a. Those in which our Lord, and others, declare it to be *near* (ἐγγίζειν), as Matt. iii. 2, iv. 17, etc. Admitting that any reference to an argument to the distinction between prophetic and historic *nearness* would, in this connection, be out of place, it is enough to say that the offer of an immediate establishment, an offer subsequently withdrawn because of virtual rejection, fully satisfies all the requirements of the language referred to.

b. Those which declare that Jesus was a King, Matt. ii. 2, xxi. 5; John i. 49; xviii. 37, etc. Reference need only be made to the manifest distinction between a King *de jure* and a King *de facto*. He was *born* King of the Jews, and yet confessedly for thirty years He did not establish His Kingdom. A similar explanation may be given to the fact that believers are styled a βασίλειον ἱεράτευμα, 1 Pet. ii. 9. (The fact that He is now exalted to the throne of universal dominion, Eph. i. 20-22, no more proves that the Basileia is now established *on earth*, than did the universal government of God in the days of Daniel prove that *the Kingdom of God* was then established *on earth*. We must distinguish between a Kingdom *on* earth, and a Kingdom *over* earth—which includes earth as a revolted province.)

c. The exhortations of our Lord to "seek the Kingdom of God," Matt. vi. 33; Luke xii. 31. It is manifest that both these exhortations are consistent with the hypothesis of a future Kingdom—as though He had said, So act, that when the Basileia is established you may enter it. Indeed the contexts of both exhortations require that we should put that interpretation upon them : the one in Matt. follows the direction to pray "Thy Kingdom come" (ver. 10), and that in Luke is manifestly parallel with the exhortation to *wait* for an absent Lord (vers. 35-40).

d. The declaration "this generation shall not pass," etc., Matt. xxiv. 34; Mark xiii. 30; Luke xxi. 32. The term γενεά is one of the most indefinite in the Greek language. It is used to represent a *race* of men, a *generation* (of which three make a century, an *age* (see Liddell and Scott). Immediately after the preceding utterance our Lord declared that the time of His second coming was concealed (Matt. xxiv. 36); is it not probable that, in using this indefinite term, He did so *designedly*, that no note of time might be given? *e.* The declaration of Jesus, "There be some standing here," etc., Matt. xvi. 28; Mark ix. 1; Luke ix. 27. This, according to the opinion of Chrysostom and others (see Lange Comm. on Matt. xvi. 28), may find its fulfillment in the immediately following Transfiguration. In this event the Basileia was not merely symbolized, but in all its glory was for a moment set up on earth (comp. 2 Pet. i. 16-18).

(2.) The passages which, it is alleged, declare a present Basileia.

a. Matt. xi. 12; Luke xvi. 16. It is assumed that βιάζεται and ἁρπάζουσιν are taken in a *good sense*, as in the E. V. Against this assumption may be urged—(*a*) the established usage of the words: βιάζειν occurs in the New Testament only in the passages under consideration; in the LXX. it occurs (undisputed) *ten* times, it represents *rape* (Deut. xxii. 25, 28; Esther vii. 8), *the breaking through the barriers around Sinai* (Exodus xix. 24), *simple violence* (Sir. iv. 29; xxxi. 21; 2 Macc. xiv. 41), *urging* (Gen. xxx. 12; Judges xix. 7; 2 Kings v. 23); the leading idea of the word when applied to persons is, *inimical violence*; ἁρπάζειν occurs thirty-three times in the LXX., and (with possibly four exceptions) is always used in a bad sense; it represents the *violence* of the robber, the *ravening* of the lion and the wolf (Gen. xxxvii. 33; Lev. vi. 4, *etc.*); in the New Testament (besides the instance under consideration) it occurs, Matt. xiii. 19; John x. 12, 28, 29; vi. 15; Acts viii. 39; xxiii. 10; 2 Cor. xii. 2, 4; in all these instances the idea is that of *overmastering* force, and in the first four, which (with the one under consideration) are the only instances of its use by our Saviour, it indicates *sinful* force. (*b*) The unfitness of the terms, when used in a good sense, to represent the approach of a penitent sinner to Christ: the disciples were captives—not conquerors; (*c*) Their unfitness in a good sense, and their fitness in a bad sense, to represent the condition of things then existing. It is true that in the beginning of our Lord's ministry the people crowded around Him; but *few*, however, in the modern sense of the phrase, "entered the kingdom;" on the occasion indicated by Matt. xi. 12, the people were deserting Him (vers. 12-25), and their leaders were engaged in that system of opposition and persecution that culminated in His crucifixion. Must we not conclude that by these words our Lord intended to indicate that violent opposition to, and ravening upon, the offered kingdom in the person of Him, its representative, which resulted in the withdrawal of the offer (Matt. xxi. 43) and the fearful denunciations of Matt. xxiii. 13-39?

b. Matt. xii. 28; Luke xi. 20. The original in both cases is ἐφθασαν ἐφ' ὑμᾶς, not ἔρχεται (Luke xvii. 20), nor ἀναφαίνεσθαι (Luke xix. 11). "In the New Testament, with the exception of 1 Thess. iv. 15, (?) φθάνειν occurs only in the later, weakened sense of *reaching to*" (Lange Com. on 1 Thess., p. 43, E. V.) The phrase is

similar to the one in 1 Thess. ii. 16, where, manifestly, it was not designed to represent the wrath spoken of as *already poured forth* upon its objects—they were living men, but as *having reached unto, overhanging* them, comp. also Rom. ix. 31; 2 Cor. x. 14; Phil. iii. 16; 1 Thess. iv. 15, in all which, however, the prepositions are different. The passages under consideration aptly accord with the idea of a near approach of the Basileia to the Jews in the person of Christ, implying an offer of establishment which might be withdrawn; they are equivalent to the declaration of Luke x. 9, 11.

c. Luke xvii. 20, 21. This passage, probably, by the advocates of the prevalent theory of the Basileia, is regarded as their most important proof-text, both as to its *nature* and *present establishment*. In this portion of the Excursus, only its bearing on the latter of these points is to be considered. In the E. V. there is a difference in tense between the question of the Pharisees and the answer of Jesus—they asking, when the Basileia *should* come, and He answering, it *cometh* not with observation, it *is* within you—which necessarily implies a declaration of then existing establishment. This difference is altogether unauthorized—both the question and the answer are in the present; the question of the Pharisees should be translated "when cometh (ἔρχεται) the kingdom of God?" The question was asked in the vivid, dramatic present; it manifestly had reference to the future; it would be in defiance of every conceivable law of language to suppose that our Lord, in following the lead of His questioners, intended to indicate a different tense. The question and the answer are but illustrations of that law proper to all languages, but pre-eminently to the Greek, by which a *certain* future may be represented by a verb in the present; illustrations may be found, Matt. xxvi. 2 (after two days *is* the feast of the passover, and the Son of Man *is* betrayed, *etc.*); 1 Cor. xv. 42-44 (it is sown in corruption, it *is* [in the *future* resurrection] raised in incorruption), (see Jelf, Winer, Kühner, and grammarians generally). To the conclusion that the language of our Lord must be understood as having reference to the future, it may also be remarked, we are shut up by the following considerations: The supposition that He indicated an *existing* Basileia (*a*) implies that it was set up in (or among) the Pharisees; (*b*) disconnects His words from the immediately-following address to the disciples, whilst the contrary supposition brings them into manifest and beautiful connection therewith, and with His other utterances.*

---

* [Fully to appreciate this remark, we must appreciate the force of the terms παρατηρήσις and ἐντός. The former of these occurs nowhere else in the New Testament, and only in one disputed passage in the LXX. Its verbal root, h wever, occurs several times, and always has the force of close watching or observation (Mark iii 2; Luke vi. 7; xiv. 1; xx. 20; Acts ix. 24; Gal. iv. 10). In accordance with the meaning of the verb, the Lange Com. (Van Oosterzee) translates μετὰ παρατηρήσεως: "with or under observation," remarking "so that it can be recognized and observed by outward tokens, and that one could exclaim with assurance, Lo here! lo there!" The translation would be correct, and also, in the main, the accompanying remark. The latter, however, might be so modified as to distinctly set forth the twofold idea of observation—(1) as to *essence* (as that which in itself is visible), and (2) as to *manifestation* or *approach* (as the dawn, whose approach is with or under observation). With this modification: *no. under observation,*]

d. In this connection may be considered that class of passages which are regarded as teaching the doctrine of a present Basileia from their use of a *present* verb when mentioning it. (Reference is not now had to those in which there is aught *in the context* that apparently requires the hypothesis of a present kingdom—each of these receives an independent consideration). These passages are: all those parables which thus refer to the Basileia, Matt. xiii. 31, 33, 44, 45, 47, *etc.* ; also Matt. xi. 11 ; Rom. xiv. 17. These, it is admitted, are all consistent with the hypothesis of a present kingdom ; but, under the rule set forth under the preceding head, they are all grammatically consistent with that of a *certain* future establishment. That there is nothing in the nature of the Basileia as set forth in the parables to require the hypothesis of a present kingdom, but the contrary, will appear in the second general division of this Excursus.

e. Acts ii. 29-36. It is assumed by many that the *exaltation* of ver. 33 constitutes the *session on the throne of David* of ver. 30. But the assumption is wholly gratuitous. Nowhere in his sermon did the apostle declare the oneness of the two events ; and most certainly the exaltation there spoken of does not imply the session as already existing—it may be an exaltation begun, to culminate in a visible occupancy of the throne of David. (The visible establishment by an emperor of the seat of his government in the heart of a once revolted province, does not derogate from his dignity—does not imply an abdication of government in the rest of his empire.) But beyond this, not only is the assumption gratuitous ; it is against probabilities that amount to certainty. The apostle, be it remembered, was arguing with *Jews*, to prove that the *absent* Jesus was the Messiah (ver. 36) ; he was arguing with those, one of whose most cherished beliefs it was that the Messiah should occupy a

would mean either *without visibility* (as the wind), or *without the signs of gradual approach* (as the lightning). The strict meaning of *ἐντός* is *within, in the midst of*, as in Matt. xxiii. 36 ; that which is *ἐντός* men *individually*, is that which is internal to them individually ; that which is *ἐντός* them *collectively* (viewed as one whole), is that which is internal to them as a whole—in the midst of them—among them individually. This latter use of the term occurs Xenophon *Anab.* l. 10, 3—ἀλλὰ καὶ ταύτην ἔσωσαν (οἱ Ἕλληνες) καὶ ἄλλα ὁπόσα ἐντὸς αὐτῶν, *etc.* (see Alford *in loc.*) Now, remembering the close connection in the Jewish mind between the establishment of the Basileia, and the glorious coming of the Son of Man—a connection established by the prophecy of Daniel (vii. 13, 14), and not previously rebuked but approved by Jesus (Luke ix. 26, 27)—let any one hypothesize as the meaning of *μετὰ παρατηρήσεως with the signs of a gradual approach*, and of *ἐντὸς in the midst of*, and read the entire passage, vers. 20-30. The Pharisees ask our Lord "when cometh the Kingdom of God ?" He answers, "It cometh not with the signs of a gradual approach ; neither shall they say, Lo here, or Lo there, for lo the kingdom of God is in the midst of you." Then turning to His disciples He says : "The days will come when ye shall desire to see one of the days of the Son of Man, and ye shall not see it. And they shall say to you, Lo here, or there ; go not after nor follow. For as the lightning that lighteneth (flashing) from one part under heaven shineth to the other part under heaven (*comes not with the signs of a gradual approach*), so also shall the Son of Man be in his day," *etc.* Does not the very unity perceptible in the entire address—the vividness of the scene it presents—the manifest oneness of the doctrine with that elsewhere taught by our Lord, especially on the Mount of Olives—place the stamp of truth on the hypothesis ? Does it not become manifest that this passage, so far from teaching the doctrine of a present establishment of the Basileia, must be numbered amongst those that connect the establishment with the Second Advent ?—E. R. C.]

visible throne. To suppose that, under such circumstances, he should advance a doctrine at war with this belief without a word of explanation or proof, and that too in a sentence capable of an interpretation consistent therewith, is inconceivable. The interpretation suggested by the writer is confirmed not only by its consistency with the previous teachings of our Lord, but by the address delivered by the Apostle Peter shortly after, Acts iii. 19, 20. The literal translation of the passage referred to is as follows (see Lange *Com.* and Alford) : "Repent ye, therefore, and be converted, that your sins may be blotted out, in order that the times of refreshing may come from the presence of the Lord, and that He may send the Messiah Jesus, who was appointed unto you, whom the heavens must receive until the times of the restitution of all things," *etc.* It is also confirmed by the subsequent teachings of the apostle in his epistles ; comp. 1 Peter i. 4-7, 13 ; 2 Peter i. 11, 16 ; the κληρονομία and ἀποκάλυψις of the I Epistle are manifestly synonymous with the βασιλεία and παρουσία of the II.

1 Thess. ii. 12. The preposition in the Greek is *εἰς*. But since believers on earth are not yet in *glory*, the whole expression is manifestly proleptical, and the E. V. gives the translation, *unto.*

Col. i. 13. At first glance, the passage apparently teaches that believers are already translated *de facto* into the Basileia ; it may however legitimately be regarded as teaching a *de jure* translation. Not only does this interpretation bring the passage into harmony with the great mass of Scripture, but it seems to be required by the immediately preceding and succeeding contexts ; believers are not yet delivered *de facto* from the ἐξουσία of Satan (Eph. v. 12), nor have they yet received *de facto*, certainly not in completeness, the ἀπολύτρωσιν (comp. Luke xxi. 28 ; Rom. viii. 23 ; Eph. i. 14 ; iv. 30 ; see Lange Comm. *in loc.*).

Heb. xii. 28. The reception of the Basileia herein spoken of manifestly may be *de jure*. Believers on earth receive a sure title to their future possession.

II. NATURE OF THE BASILEIA.

When the Baptist and our Lord began to preach "the Kingdom of God is at hand," the subject of their discourse was no novelty. The Jews were then expecting the establishment of a Basileia, which had been foretold by the prophets. The phrases "Kingdom of God," "Kingdom of Heaven," do not indeed occur in exact form in the Old Testament ; cognate expressions, however, appear, which may be divided into two classes—(1). Those which refer to the natural Kingdom of God over the universe, Dan. iv. 3, 34, vi. 26 ; Ps. cxlv. 12, 13 ; (LXX. iii. 33, iv. 31, vi. 26 ; Ps. cxliv. 12, 13). (2). Those in which the then future Basileia of the Messiah was predicted, Dan. ii. 44, vii. 14, 27, (LXX. as Heb.) ; allied to the prophecies from which these citations are made, are Isa. xi., xxxii., lix. 20—lxvi. 24 ; Ps. ii., lxxii., *etc.* There can be no doubt that *the* Basileia foretold in the latter class was the one contemplated by Jesus, especially in view of the distinct reference to the prophecies of Daniel, and the quotations therefrom, in His great eschatological discourse on the Mount of Olives.

1. The apparent characteristics of the Basileia as deduced from a normal* interpretation of the prophecies referred to, are as follows:

It was a government to be established.— (1) in a glorious, visible advent of "the Son of man," Dan. vii. 13, 14; (2) in the συντέλεια τοῦ καιροῦ, Dan. ix. 27, xii. 4, 13; (3) after a period of great θλίψις, Dan. xii. 1, xi. 26, 27; (4) whose members should be *governors* (the subject nations were *under*, not *members of* the Basileia), Dan. vii. 18, 22, 27; (5) as œcumenical, Dan. vii. 14, 27, *et pass.* the other prophecies; (6) as political, in the proper sense of the term, as indicating an external government exercised, as are now merely human governments, over the persons and property of men, (*passim* the prophecies; (7) whose members should be the saints (spiritually holy ones) of the covenanted people of the preceding æon or καιρός, Dan. vii. 18, 22, 27 (comp. 27, ix. 27, xii. 4, 13); (8) in which righteousness (spiritual and external) should prevail, (*pass.* the prophecies).

Let it be observed concerning these characteristics—a. That no one is exclusive of any other; all may co-exist in one and the same objective. b. That if fairly deduced from the normal sense of the Old Testament Scriptures they are to be regarded as the true characteristics, unless it can be shown that the New Testament teachers declared that the prophecies are not to be normally interpreted, at least in reference to the points specified. c. That whilst the first six accord with those presented in what is universally recognized as the old Jewish scheme, the 7th and 8th are different—for *the Saints of the covenanted people*, the Jews substituted *the natural seed* of Abraham, and for *spiritual*, mere *ceremonial* righteousness.

2. Jesus and the other inspired New Testament teachers recognized the truth of the foregoing characteristics.

They did so not only by positive affirmation in respect to each one; but also by direct condem-

---

* [*Normal* is used instead of *literal* (the term generally employed in this connection) as more expressive of the correct idea. No terms could have been chosen more unfit to designate the two great schools of prophetical exegetes than *literal* and *spiritual*. These terms are not antithetical, nor are they in any proper sense significant of the peculiarities of the respective systems they are employed to characterize. They are positively misleading and confusing. *Literal* is opposed not to *spiritual* but to *figurative*; *spiritual* is in antithesis on the one hand to *material*, on the other to *carnal* (in a bad sense). The *Literalist* (so called) is not one who denies that *figurative* language, that *symbols*, are used in prophecy, nor does he deny that great *spiritual* truths are set forth therein; his position is, simply, that the prophecies are to be *normally* interpreted (i. e. according to the received laws of language) as any other utterances are interpreted—that which is manifestly literal being regarded as literal, that which is manifestly figurative being so regarded. The position of the Spiritualist (so called) is not that which is properly indicated by the term. He is one who holds that whilst certain portions of the prophecies are to be *normally* interpreted, other portions are to be regarded as having a *mystical* (i. e. involving some secret meaning) sense. Thus, for instance, Spiritualists (so called) do not deny that when the Messiah is spoken of as "a man of sorrow an t acquainted with grief," the prophecy is to be *normally* interpreted; they affirm, however, that when He is spoken of as coming "in the clouds of heaven" the language is to be "spiritually" (mystically) interpreted (see the quotation from Robinson in the introduction to the Excursus). The terms properly expressive of the schools are *normal* and *mystical.*—E. R. C.]

---

nation of the Jews for misinterpreting the Scriptures, where they substituted different doctrines, and by silence at times, as well as occasional affirmation, in respect to all those other points on which the Jewish belief accorded with them. (In the following exhibit, for purposes of compactness and distinctness in argument, the 7th and 8th of the characteristics will be considered first, and in the inverse order—the preceding notation, however, being preserved.)

(8). The Basileia was to be a government in which righteousness (spiritual and external) should prevail.

It is a universally recognized fact that the great mass of the Jews of our Saviour's day regarded all righteousness as consisting in ceremonial observance. Our Lord in rebuking this opinion, and in declaring to the people, "Except your righteousness shall exceed the righteousness of the Scribes and Pharisees ye shall in no case enter into the Kingdom of heaven," (Matt. v. 20), proceeded on the ground, not that the true meaning of the Old Testament had been hidden beneath a mystic veil which He came to remove, but that they had "made the law of God of none effect (i. e. had set aside its normal interpretation) through their (your) traditions" (Matt. xv. 6). Throughout the whole of His ministry, as lies on the surface of the New Testament, He taught the great doctrine previously taught by the prophets, that into the Basileia nothing impure should enter. (As to the *special* force, as bearing on this point, of the parables in Matt. xiii., xxii., xxv., see below.)

(7). Whose members should be the saints (spiritually holy ones) of the covenanted people of the preceding æon.

The Jews believed that the members of the Basileia were to be selected from the members of the covenanted people of the preceding æon, and on this point our Lord uttered no denial. He referred not merely to those then living as entering into the future Kingdom, but to Abraham, Isaac, and Jacob, as having a place therein, Luke xiii. 28. His teachings manifestly accorded with their beliefs. The Apostle Paul declared, "flesh and blood cannot inherit the kingdom of God," and, further, that upon those who remain upon earth until the coming of the Lord a resurrection change should pass (comp. 1 Cor. xv. 50-52 with 1 Thess. iv. 14-17), implying that those who inherit the Kingdom are the *changed* Saints of a former dispensation.

For the *Saints*, however, the Jews substituted *the ceremonially righteous*, and for the *covenanted* people, the *natural seed of Abraham*. Both these substitutions Jesus condemned, and that in accordance with the normal interpretation of the Old Testament. The former condemnation and its ground were virtually considered under the preceding characteristic.

As to the latter, the Baptist declared: "God is able of these stones to raise up children unto Abraham," Matt. iii. 9, and our Lord declared to the Chief Priests and Elders, "The Kingdom of God shall be taken from you, and given to a nation (ἔθνος=gentile people) bringing forth the fruits thereof," Matt. xxi. 43. Now, in making these declarations, Jesus and His forerunner were not uttering *new* revelations — they were proceeding on the platform of Old Testament Scripture, whose normal sense was ignored by the Jews. It is true that the covenant belonged pre-eminently to the natural seed of Abraham; yet, from the beginning, on the one hand, great branches of that seed had been cast aside; and, on the other, provision had been made for the reception of proselytes, and it had also been prophesied that in process of time Jehovah would call them His people ($\square\mathfrak{y}=\lambda a\acute{o}\varsigma$) who had not been His people, Hos. ii. 23. In that portion of the epistle to the Romans (ix.–xi.) in which the Apostle establishes the covenant relations of converted Gentiles, their true engrafting into the covenanted people (x. 17-21), he does not speak of it as a strange thing, but *argues* it as the fulfillment of prophecy, quoting the prophecy of Hosea above cited (ix. 24-26). Manifestly the New Testament teachers not merely approve this characteristic, but the Apostle Paul approves it as in accordance with the Old Testament.

(1). It was to be established in a glorious visible advent of "the Son of Man."

This is universally recognized as one of the most prominent doctrines of the Jews. If it had been an error, it is inconceivable that our Lord would not have rebuked it in terms as decided as those employed in reference to other errors. But on the contrary He affirmed it, and affirmed it, manifestly, as the fulfillment of the prophecy of Daniel (see under section 1, (2), of the I. division). The only instances in which it is claimed that He denied it (or spoke of a Basileia as coming in any other mode) are Luke xvii. 21, 22, and those few passages in which He referred to the Kingdom in the use of a present verb. The passage in Luke is best explained as being in harmony with His other teachings (see above), and the other passages, as we have seen, are grammatically consistent therewith.

(2). In the συντέλεια τοῦ καιροῦ (Dan. ix. 27, xii. 4, 13). This was directly taught and in manifest reference to the prophecy of Daniel, comp. Matt. xxiv. 3, 6, 13, 34; Mark xiii. 7; Luke xxi. 9, 31; see also Matt. xiii. 39, 40, 49, with context.

(3). After a period of great θλίψις (Dan. xii. 1, vii. 26, 27). Confirmed in the New Testament, Matt. xxiv. 21, 29; Mark xiii. 19, 24; 1 Pet. iv. 12, 13; 2 Thess. i. 4-7.

(4). The members to be governors (Dan. vii. 18, 22, 27). This was a doctrine never controverted by our Lord; but, on the contrary, He again and again so spake as to manifest that He took its truth for granted. See Matt. xix. 28, xxiv. 47, xxv. 21, 23; Luke xii. 44, xix. 17, 19, xxii. 29, 30. The counsel that He gave His disciples on the occasion of the ambitious request of the Sons of Zebedee, Matt. xx. 25-28, and the rebuke He administered at the Last Supper, Luke xxii. 24-27, cannot be understood as negativing that doctrine. His design on both these occasions was, not to teach that there should be no ruling in the Basileia, but to rebuke the ambitious spirit that seeks after authority for the sake of self, and to teach that the true idea of ruling is that of rendering service. This is evident from the fact that He presented Himself, the acknowledged Master, as their model; and

from the further facts that, on the first of the mentioned occasions, He implied that one was to sit on His right hand and another on His left (to share in superior authority), Matt. xx. 23, and that, in the latter, immediately after the rebuke, He declared to His Apostles that they should sit on thrones, Luke xxii. 29, 30. (See also 1 Cor. vi. 2, 3; Jude 14, 15; Rev. iii. 21, v. 10, xx. 6, xxii. 5.)

(5). As *œcumenical.* No one affirms that this characteristic was ever denied by our Lord. It was not, indeed, directly declared by Him that the saints should be associated with Him in the rule of *all the earth;* it was manifestly implied, however, in His evident reference to the prophecies of Daniel as of normal interpretation without any qualification, and in His association of His disciples with Himself in government, in connection with the known belief of the Jews. It seems to be directly affirmed, 1 Cor. vi. 2, 3; Jude 14, 15; Rev. xx. 6.

(6). As *political,* (*i. e.,* an external government exercised over the persons and property of men).

There can be no question as to the *apparent* teaching of the Old Testament on this point; all the prophecies bearing on the Basileia present the idea of an external, political government. And it is also universally admitted that the Jews were expecting such a kingdom of the Messiah, an expectation which was shared by the Apostles. It is utterly inconceivable that if they had been mistaken on this point, especially as their mistake was confirmed by the apparent teaching of the prophecies, the Great Teacher would not have distinctly undeceived them. And yet throughout His whole ministry He continually so spake as to leave them in error if they were in error. On the occasion of the Last Supper, He employed language which must have confirmed them in their belief on this point, Luke xxii. 29, 30,—a belief not shaken by His forty days teaching on the subject of the Basileia after His resurrection, as is evident from their last question, and in which He must have still further confirmed them by His answer, Acts i. 3-7. The alleged instances of His teaching a contrary doctrine will be considered in the following division.

III. Our Lord and His disciples taught no doctrine of *the* (or *a*) Basileia (either complete or inchoate) as lacking any one of the preceding characteristics.

It is alleged that this was done in those utterances in which the Basileia is spoken of in the use of a *present* verb, and also in Luke xii. 14; xvii. 20, 21; Matt. xiii. 31-52; John xviii. 36; Rom. xiv. 17. All these passages, it is contended, set forth a Basileia having a merely internal character. As to those texts whose force in this direction is derived merely from their grammatical form, we have seen that they are consistent with the idea of a future Basileia. We have also seen that Luke xvii. 20, 21, is consistent with the theory maintained in this excursus. The other passages will be considered in their order.

Luke xii. 14. "Who made Me a judge or a divider over you?" The kingdom had not then been established; our Lord at that time occupied simply the position of a teacher.

Matt. xiii. 31-52. It is contended that in the parables of the mustard seed and the leaven especially, Jesus taught concerning the Basileia, that it begins silently and imperceptibly in the heart and in the community, and gradually increases. The force of the argument is derived from the assumption that in these parables *the thing next to the verb of comparison* is that to which the Basileia is compared—that in one case it is compared to the mustard *seed*, and in the other to the *little* leaven which the woman hid. But if this rule hold good in one case, it must in all others; and under its operation we have the kingdom likened (ver. 24) to the *sower*, (ver. 45) to the *merchant-man*, (xx. 1) to the *householder*. (xxii. 2) to the *king*, etc. Manifestly, in all these instances, we must pass over the *next thing* to the verb of comparison, to seek for the object of comparison. Doubtless the true explanation of the phrase "the kingdom is likened, etc.," is the one given by Alford on Matt. xiii. 24, " *is like the whole circumstances about to be detailed,*" i. e., the entire parable presents a truth concerning the kingdom. With this explanation, unity as to the nature of the Basileia (which on the current interpretation is lacking) is brought into this whole series of parables, and these and all the other parables are brought into beautiful consistency with all the other teachings of our Lord. The series in Matt. may be regarded as setting forth that nothing impure, imperfect, or immature, can have place in the Basileia—in such case the good grain, the mighty tree, the thoroughly leavened lump, the treasure separated from the field, the pearl, the good fish, will represent it.

John xviii. 36. In this utterance, it is contended that our Lord intended to declare to Pilate that the kingdom He came to establish was not after the manner of the kingdoms of this world, i. e., not external, political. It is admitted that the utterance considered in itself will bear this interpretation; but it will also bear one consistent with the theory herein advocated, especially in view of the introduction of *νῦν* in the last clause of the verse, which may be regarded as a particle of time—My kingdom is not *now* established. Which of these interpretations are we to adopt? The one supposes that our Lord whispered into the ear of a heathen (neither the disciples nor the Jews were in the Pretorium, ver. 28), the great truth concerning His kingdom, which he had not only *concealed* from His disciples (hid from them in a bewildering enigma) but a few hours before on the solemn occasion of the institution of the Supper, Luke xxii. 29, 30: but which, also, He continued to *conceal* throughout the forty days of His subsequent continuance with them, during which time He is represented as "speaking of the things pertaining to the kingdom of God," Acts i. 3, and as opening "their understanding, that they might understand the Scriptures," Luke xxiv. 45! The other interpretation supposes

that He spake in consistency with His previous and subsequent teaching. Rom. xiv. 17. This passage is perfectly consistent with the hypothesis of a merely internal Basileia, but manifestly it is also consistent with the hypothesis of a perfectly holy external government. "Meat and drink" do not *necessarily* infer externality, they *may* refer to *mere fleshly enjoyment* which has no place in the Basileia as set forth in this excursus.

In conclusion of the whole subject it may be remarked:

(1). If it has been fairly shown that the great mass of Scriptures in which the term Basileia occurs, require as the objective thereof the one set forth in this excursus, then is it utterly illogical, from the possible force of a few scattered passages, which *may*, without straining, be interpreted in consistency with the others ; either, on the one hand, to deny the validity of the objective established, or, on the other hand, to hypothesize a second and variant objective—to conclude that the term was used ambiguously.

(2). The theory herein defended is not liable to the objection that it presents a " carnal " or " material " doctrine concerning the nature of the Basileia. Most certainly the doctrine is not " carnal " in the bad sense of that term, nor as teaching that gross flesh and blood shall inherit the kingdom ; nor is it " material " save so far as the doctrine of the resurrection of the body is so. It agrees with this latter doctrine in implying that the redemption of Christ respects the *body* as well as the *soul*, and also with the doctrine set forth in Rom. viii. 18-23.

(3). Much important matter bearing on this subject, connected with the scriptural use of the terms συντέλεια, παρουσία, ἐπιφάνεια, ἀνάστασις, παλιγγενεσία, ἀποκατάστασις, κληρονομία, ζωὴ αἰώνιος, has necessarily been passed over. Fully to discuss the subject in connection with all these terms would require a volume.

(4). If the foregoing reasoning be valid, increased doubt is thrown upon the reading ἡμᾶς βασιλείαν, ver. 6, of this chapter. Should, however, the now generally accepted reading be sustained, the passage may be rendered consistent with the theory herein supported by attributing to ἐποίησεν a proleptical, or rather *de jure*, force.

And, lastly, this excursus has been written in a spirit of deep conviction, but not, it is trusted, in one of dogmatism. The writer feels that any man should study so vast and important a subject with the deepest humility and self-distrust, and express his conclusions with the utmost modesty ; and he more keenly feels, as he finishes his work, than in the beginning, how unfit he is to grapple with it. If aught of dogmatism should have appeared in the expression of his views, he trusts that it will be attributed to the necessity of his situation, where brevity in expression is of prime importance.—E. R. C.]

PART FIRST.

THE COURSE OF THE WORLD TO THE END OF THE WORLD.

CHAP. I. 9—XI. 14.

SECTION FIRST.

The seven churches. Heaven-picture and earth-picture.

CHAP. I. 9—III. 22.

A.—THE IDEAL HEAVENLY LIFE-PICTURE OF THE CHURCH. HEAVEN-PICTURE OF THE SEVEN CHURCHES. STAND-POINT OF THE SEER.

THE GREAT VISION; FIRST, AS A BASIS FOR THE SEVEN EPISTLES TO THE SEVEN CHURCHES. HENCE ALSO AS THE BASIS OF THE FOLLOWING VISIONS (BECAUSE ALL THE VISIONS RELATE TO THE PERFECTION OF THE CHURCH AS REPRESENTED IN THE SEVEN CHURCHES).

CHAP. I. 9-20.

John in the spirit.

9 I, John, who also am [*om.* who also am]¹ your brother, and companion [fellow-partaker] in [*ins.* the] tribulation, and in the [*om.* in the]² kingdom and patience [endurance] of [in] Jesus Christ [*om.* Christ] [Lange: (in Christ)],³ was in the isle that is called Patmos, for the word of God, and for⁴ the testimony of Jesus Christ

10 [*om.* Christ].⁵ I was [Lange: transported] in the Spirit [spirit] on the Lord's

11 day, and [*ins.* I] heard behind me a great voice, as of a trumpet, Saying, I am Alpha and Omega, the first and the last: and, [*om.* I am Alpha and Omega, the first and the last: and,]⁶ What thou seest, write in [into] a book, and send *it* [*om.* *it*] unto the seven churches which are in Asia [*om.* which are in Asia];⁷ unto Ephesus, and unto Smyrna, and unto Pergamus, and unto Thyatira, and unto Sardis, and unto Philadelphia, and unto Laodicea.

Appearance of Christ in His glory.

12 And I turned [*ins.* about] to see the voice that spake [was speaking]⁸ with me.

13 And being turned [having turned about], I saw seven golden candlesticks; And in the midst of the seven⁹ candlesticks *one* like unto the [*the*]¹⁰ Son¹¹ of man, clothed with a garment down [reaching] to the foot [Lange: festal or priestly robe], and girt about [round at] the paps [breasts] [Lange: not as a working dress about

14 the loins] with a golden girdle.¹² [And] His head and *his* hairs *were* white like [*ins.* white] wool, as white [*om.* as white] as snow; and his eyes were as a flame

15 of fire; And his feet like unto fine brass [Alford: chalcolibanus],¹³ as if they burned [as if they had been burned, *or* as when burned] in a furnace [Lange: And his feet like unto a stream of molten metal, as it had become glowing¹⁴ in a furnace];

16 and his voice as the sound [voice] of many waters. And [: and] he [*om.* he] had [having] in his right hand seven stars: and out of his mouth went [going forth] a sharp two-edged [two-edged sharp] sword: and his countenance *was* [*om.* *was*] as the sun shineth in his [its] strength.

Convulsing and exalting effect.

17 And when I saw him, I fell at his feet as dead. And he laid his right hand upon
me, saying unto me [*om.* unto me],[15] Fear not; I am the first and the last : [*om.* :]
18 *I am* he that [*om. I am* he that] liveth, [and the living One ;] and [*ins.* I] was
dead ; [*om.* ;] and, behold, I am alive [living] for evermore, [into the ages of the
ages ;] Amen ; [*om.* Amen ;][16] and [*ins.* I] have the keys of hell and of [*om.* hell
and of] death [*ins.* and of hades].

John's prophetic calling and commission.

19 Write [*ins.* therefore][17] the things which thou hast seen, [;] and [both] the things
which are, and the things which shall be hereafter [are about to happen after
20 these] ;[18] The mystery of the seven stars which[19] thou sawest in [upon][20] my right
hand, and the seven golden [*om.* golden] candlesticks [*ins.* of gold]. The seven
stars are the [*om.* the] angels of the seven churches : and the seven candlesticks
which thou sawest [*om.* which thou sawest][21] are the [*om.* the] seven churches.

TEXTUAL AND GRAMMATICAL.

[1] Ver. 9. [Rec. inserts καί after ὁ; it is omitted in all critical editions, in accordance with all the leading Codices.—
E. R. C.]

[2] Ver. 9. [Rec. has ἐν τῇ with P. and a few minuscules; it is generally omitted in critical editions with א. A. B*. C., etc.
Vulg., etc.—E. R. C.]

[3] Ver. 9. Codd. א. C. [P.], Vulg., etc., read ἐν Ἰησοῦ; A., ἐν Χριστῷ.

[4] Ver. 9. [Lachmann omits διά with A. C., Vulg., etc.; Alford brackets it; it is found in א. B*. P., etc.—E. R. C.]

[5] Ver. 9. [Lachmann and Alford omit Χριστοῦ with א.¹ A. C. P., Vulg., etc.; it is found in א.³ᵈ B.*, etc.—E. R. C.]

Ver. 11. The addition ἐγώ εἰμι, etc. is not well founded. [It is found only in P. (which omits εἰμι) and a few minuscules; it is omitted in א. A. B*. C., Vulg., etc.—E. R. C.]

[7] Ver. 11. [Rec. gives ταῖς ἐν Ἀσία, with Vulgate (Clementine); all the Codd. omit, together with the Amiatinus and
other MSS. of the Vulgate.—E. R. C.]

[8] Ver. 12. [Critical Editors generally adopt ἐλάλει with א. B*. C., Vulg., etc.; Rec. with P. gives ἐλάλησε; A. gives
λαλεῖ.—E. R. C.]

[9] Ver. 13. [Lachmann omits ἑπτά with A. C. P., etc.; Alford brackets it; א. B., etc., agree with Rec. in giving it.—
E. R. C.]

[10] Ver. 14. [There is no article in the original. In justification of the retention of "*the*" (italicized) the following is
quoted from ALFORD: "In New Testament Greek we should be no more justified in rendering υἱὸς ἀνθρώπου in such a
connection as this "a son of man," than πνεῦμα θεοῦ, a spirit of God. That meaning would, doubtless, have been here
expressed by τοῖς υἱοῖς τῶν ἀνθρώπων."—E. R. C.]

[11] Ver. 13. The reading υἱόν Cod. B., etc., probably arose from the fear lest the apparition should not be taken for an
appearance of Christ.

[12] Ver. 13. Different forms : μαστοῖς Cod. C. [P.] Rec. and μαζοῖς Cod. A. [μασθοῖς, א.—E. R. C.].

[13] Ver. 15. [Alford transfers the Greek word χαλκολίβανον, its meaning not being known. See Exegetical Notes.—
E. R. C.]

[14] Ver. 15. The reading πεπυρωμένης corrected to πεπυρωμένῃ. Tischendorf [and Alford] in accordance with Codd.
B. A. and P., πεπυρωμένοι, relating to the feet, which gives no sense. Feet cannot be made to glow in a furnace, but the
lustre of gold ore is doubled when it appears glowing white in a glowing furnace. [Lachmann gives πεπυρωμένης, citing as
authorities A. and C., which Alford confirms, although he himself gives -οι; א. gives πεπυρωμένῳ (confirmed by Vulgate)
which, as a masculine or neuter dative, better agrees with Lange's idea. See Exeg. Notes.—E. R. C.]

[15] Ver. The μοι is utterly without authority.—E. R. C.

[16] Ver. 18. [א³ᵃ. and B*. give ἀμήν; א.¹ A. C. P. omit.—E. R. C.]

[17] Ver. 19. [א. A. B*. C. P., Vulg., and all recent critical editors, give οὖν.—E. R. C.]

[18] Ver. 19. [Alford (in accordance with Bleek and De Wette and others) translates this verse: "Write therefore
the things which thou sawest and what things they signify, and the things which are about to happen after these."
See Ex. Notes.—E. R. C.]

[19] Ver. 20. The Rec. and Tischendorf ὧν [also B*.]; A. C. [P.] give οὕς.

[20] Ver. 20. Ἐπί against ἐν. [A. gives ἐν τῇ δεξιᾷ.—E. R. C.]

[21] Ver. 20. [The Rec. reading ἃς εἶδες is supported only by P. and a few minuscules. Critical Editors, in accordance with
א. A. B*. C. omit it.—E. R. C.]

EXEGETICAL AND CRITICAL.

[Vers. 9-20. ALFORD: "Introduction to the
Epistles, Appearance of our Lord to St. John,
and command to write what he saw, and to send
it to the seven churches."—E. R. C.]

The entire section has a two-fold significance.
In the first place, as a heavenly action [an action
taking place in heaven], it lays the foundation
for the critical review of the seven churches in
the seven epistles. Secondly, it forms the basis
of the whole Apocalypse. We must observe,
however, that it is contrary to the text and to
all internal probability to suppose that the entire
series of visions, and even the recording of them,
took place in one day (Bengel, Hengstenberg

and others). In accordance with prophetic form,
John begins his book with the announcement of
his calling and commission; comp. Jer. i. ;
Ezek. i.

Ver. 9. **I, John.**—We find the same expression in ch. xxii. 8 ; comp. ch. i. 4. Düsterdieck:
"The conjunction of *ἐγώ* with the name is Danielic" (Dan. vii. 15, viii. 1, ix. 2, x. 2, xii. 5).
[TRENCH : "The only other writer, either in the
Old Testament or the New, who uses this style
is Daniel—'I, Daniel' (vii. 28, ix. 2, x. 2)."—
E. R. C.] It is, therefore, an apocalyptic form,
and it has been imitated by apocryphal apocalyptists. The conjunction of the name with what
follows signalizes the Apocalyptist as the living
mediator between God and the Church.

Your brother and companion. — This

companionship has its foundation in **Jesus**, in fellowship with Jesus. It is a companionship at first in tribulation; then in the glory of the kingdom; the great contrast being harmonized by endurance (Rom. viii.; 2 Tim. ii. 10, 12; 1 Pet.). To the suffering of affliction at the hands of the hostile world, as a suffering with Christ, for His name's sake, the principial possession of the glory of the kingdom corresponds, on which principial possession the hope of the perfect appearing of that glory is based. The goal is not attained, however, without endurance in Christ; see ch. xiii. 10, xiv. 12. ["As yet, however, while the tribulation is present, the kingdom is only in hope; therefore he adds to these, as that which is the link between them *and patience* (endurance) *of Jesus Christ;* cf. Acts xiv. 22, where exactly these same three, the tribulation, the patience, and the kingdom, occur. Ὑπομονή, which we have rendered 'patience,' is not so much the 'patientia' as the 'perseverentia' of the Latin; which last word Cicero (*De Invent.* ii. 54) thus defines: 'In ratione bene considerata stabilis et perpetua mansio;' and Augustine (*Quaest.* lxxxiii. qu. 31): 'Honestatis aut utilitatis causa rerum arduarum ac difficilium voluntaria ac diuturna perpessio.' It is indeed a beautiful word, expressing the *brave* patience of the Christian—βασιλὶς τῶν ἀρετῶν, Chrysostom does not fear to call it." TRENCH.—E. R. C.]

Was in the isle.—The Apocalyptist introduces himself to his readers under the aspect of his martyrdom [*Martyrium*], wherein they also participate, in that blessed fellowship of love and suffering, to which the Apostle Paul delighted to refer (see 2 Cor.). Düsterdieck thinks that this reference of "companion" to a suffering of affliction as a martyr is not admissible. The simple and obvious traditional reference of the following words: "for the word of God, etc." —to John's banishment to the Isle of Patmos, a fact attested by Church history, is disputed by De Wette, Lücke, Bleek, Düsterdieck. Διά, as they take it, indicates that John was on the island of Patmos in order that he might receive the testimony of Jesus. A marvellous idea, this, that John should have been obliged to travel from Ephesus to Patmos for the sake of receiving a revelation from Jesus! These commentators affirm that, according to the usage of the Apocalypse, the μαρτυρία Ἰησοῦ cannot mean witness *concerning* Jesus, as Ebrard and others suppose. "On the contrary, the genitive accompanying μαρτυρία is invariably a subjective genitive." In support of this view they cite: ch. i. 2, xii. 17, xix. 10, xx. 4, in connection with the passages ch. i. 5, xii. 11.* The Apocalyptist, however, manifestly regards the μαρτυρία of Jesus as a grand unitous fact, as that world-historical witnessing unto, and suffering for, the truth (John xviii. 37), in which Jesus stands in the midst of His people as *the faithful Witness,* but which all faithful believers participate in, by

virtue of the very fact that they testify *of Jesus.* For *testimony of* or *concerning Jesus* has a heavenly significance only through its being a testimony *with* Jesus of the whole revelation of God; as, on the other hand, a testimony *with Jesus* can not exist without a testimony *of* or *concerning Him.* [Believers, in filling up that which is behind of the afflictions of Christ (Col. i. 24), continue His witness—they witness both *with* and *concerning* Him.—E. R. C.] Moreover, it cannot be denied that this strained interpretation, which identifies the ideas of revelation and testimony, is in the interest of that criticism which seeks to set aside the authorship of the Apostle John. The expression, *was on the island,* permits a distinct discrimination between the time of the revelation itself, or the grand series of visions, and the time of the inditing of the scripture. Whether it follows, however, that, at the time of writing, the Apocalyptist was no longer on the island, is extremely doubtful. Various attempts to explain ἐγενόμην, see in Düsterdieck, p. 120. [ALFORD remarks: "When an *event* is notified with ἐγένετο, we express the meaning by 'came to pass:' when a *person,* we have no word which will do it;" and he continues on the same word, ver. 10: "Not merely '*I was,*' but '*I became.*'"— E. R. C.]

That is called Patmos.—The first readers of the Apocalypse were of course aware of this; doubtless, therefore, τῇ καλουμένῃ is not intended as an indication of the smallness of the island, but as a historical item for the more extended circle of readers. On the situation and character of the island (Patino or Palmosa), comp. the lexicons and works of travel.

Ver. 10. I was in the spirit, *i. e.,* transported out of the ordinary every-day consciousness, and placed in the condition of prophetic ecstasy [trance], Acts [x. 10;] xi. 5, xxii. 17, 1 Cor. xiv. 2. The contrast is: to be in one's right mind [the *ordinary* right condition of mind; or rather to be ἐν ἑαυτῷ.—E. R. C.] (Acts xii. 11), or to be and to speak in the *understanding* (νοῦς) [1 Cor. xiv. 14]. It is the contrast of reflecting consciousness, holding intercourse with the world through the medium of the senses, and of a higher, or rather, polarily opposed form of consciousness, in which direct spiritual contemplation predominates. By the spirit, therefore, we undoubtedly are to understand, not the Spirit of God (as Grotius and others maintain), but that spiritual life of man which stands contrasted with his relation to the world; which, as a prophetic state, is inconceivable without the operation of the Holy Spirit, and hence presupposes the more general life in the Spirit (Rom. viii. 9) as its basis.* [The expression is simply ἐν πνεύματι, the article does not appear. "That which is born of the Spirit, is spirit" (ἐκ τοῦ Πνεύματος πνεῦμά ἐστι), John iii. 6. The *ordinary* condition of the Christian, and the *extraordinary* condition of the prophet, are *spiritual* conditions produced by the Holy Spirit.—E. R. C.]

On the Lord's day.—Not transported by the Spirit of the Lord to the Last Day (Wetstein

---

* ["The usage of our writer himself in the passages where he speaks of death by persecution (vi. 9, xx. 4), show that with him διά in this connection is *because of, in consequence of.* De Wette naïvely says that had it not been for these parallel places such a meaning would never have been thought of here. We may as simply reply, that owing to those parallel passages it must be accepted here." ALFORD. —E. R. C.]

* Comp. my treatise on the two-fold consciousness in the *Zeitschrift für christliche Wissenschaft,* 1851, p. 342.

and others), for the *being in the spirit* is an independent idea, but on Sunday (Acts xx. 7; 1 Cor. xi. 20, xvi. 2). On the reference of this to Easter-day, and the ideas connected with this view, see Düsterdieck, p. 121. [Alford discusses the entire subject at considerable length.—E. R. C.]

And I heard behind me.—This represents, as Düsterdieck correctly remarks, the utter unexpectedness and surprisingness of the divine voice. Consequently, its pure and certain objectivity likewise. Various interpretations—as indicative of the *invisibleness* of God—of the position of the prophet, as on earth, *etc.*, see in Düsterdieck. That commentator, however, fails to recognize the reference to the fact that, in the region of prophecy, the auricular wonder generally precedes the ocular wonder; and after the latter has faded away, the tones of the former are still heard—a fact in perfect accordance with psychological relations. The Jewish popular notion that no man can see God without dying, can of course have no application here; it is itself, however, but a dark reflection of the actual fact that every first or greatest view of the glory of the Lord has so astounding an effect upon the prophet as to cast him to the earth (Is. vi. ; Jer. i. 6; Ezek. i. 28; Dan. viii. 17); thus it was here. Ebrard rightly gives prominence to the gradualness of the development of the visionary state.

As of a trumpet. — Düsterdieck remarks that this is a mere comparison without any particular significance. The trumpet, however, significantly opens the Apocalypse, as **a** signal of the last time; see 1 Thess. iv. 16 [Matt. xxiv. 31]. In Exodus xix. 19, it is the signal of the revelation of the law. According to Numbers x. 6, 7, the mere blowing of the trumpet was the signal for the gathering together of the congregation; the sounding of an alarm, on the other hand, being the signal for the breaking up of the camp—a distinction such as exists between the symbolical import of the peal of bells and the cannonade. This voice, according to Hengstenberg, proceeds from Christ Himself. Düsterdieck regards ch. iv. 1 as militating against this view. It is, manifestly, the visional trumpet of the visional form of the Angel of Christ, i. e. Christ Himself in His symbolical appearance.

Ver. 11. **Saying: What thou seest.**—Prophetic present.—**In a book** (βιβλίον).—Hengstenberg: Everything, to the end of ch. iii., is intended. Düsterdieck: The whole revelation is meant. Since this first, leading vision forms the foundation not only of the seven epistles, but also of the entire scripture, the latter view is established beyond a doubt. The commission to send the book to the seven churches devolved upon John immediately at the opening of the revelation in Patmos. This alone does not prove that the book was written on Patmos; nor, still less, that this author wrote it while in the ecstatic condition (as Hengstenberg affirms). But since it is not supposable that John made any unnecessary delay in writing down such great things, it is highly probable that the book was written during his stay on Patmos. It would seem as if the first ἐγενόμην were modified by the second, particularly when we consider the great contrast

between being in the spirit (πνεῦμα) and being in the understanding (νοῦς).

Send unto the seven churches.—Though the seven-foldness of the churches constitutes, as a sacred number, a symbolical type of the whole Church, this type is also founded upon a unitous organization of the diocese of Ephesus, to be inferred from the exchange of Paul's Ephesian cyclical epistle from [i. e., received by the Colossians *from.*—E. R. C.]. Laodicea and the epistle to the Colossians (Col. iv. 16).*— The order of the seven churches accords with their geographical position in respect to Patmos and Ephesus. Comp. the maps, ancient geography, and the travels of Schubert, Strauss, and others.

Ver. 12. **And I turned about.**—Effect of the voice. *To see the voice.*—The prophetic voice pre-supposes a speaker in the background, and to visional *seeing* a more general sense attaches. —**Seven golden candlesticks.**—These are the first things that he sees, for the whole Apocalypse treats of the future of the kingdom of God as represented by the Church. Seven candlesticks—"not one candlestick with seven arms" (Düsterdieck, in opposition to Grotius).

Ver. 13. **And in the midst** (ἐμμέσῳ).—The fact that Christ is always in His Church (Matt. xxviii. 20) and, indeed, *in the midst* of the seven candlesticks, is here symbolically displayed to prophetic contemplation. Herder has observed that every one of the seven epistles commences with a feature of this vision. On the candlesticks comp. Matt. **v.** 14-16. The appearance is directly signalized as an appearance of Christ by the apocalyptic sign, Dan. vii. 13, x 16-18. Why is the word ὅμοιος used? Hengstenberg; To indicate that the Person seen is no mere man. Lyra: To indicate that it is the Angel of Christ. Ebrard: The Danielic ⅀ (ch. vii. 13). The state of the case is simply this: Christ is called *the* Son of man, but is like *a* son of man (Rom. viii. 3 ; Phil. ii. 7). The Seer adopts the latter form as the original apocalyptic term, and the one corresponding to the mysteriousness of the phenomenon. Doubtless he was in part led to the use of this expression—Son of man—by the fact that it was Christ's own name for Himself; [It was one of the prophetic names of the Messiah—a name highly significant (see note*, p. 24), and the name adopted by Christ Himself.—E. R. C.]; and ὅμοιος is also in part expressive of the apostolic view that the *human* personality of Christ, in its glorification, is clothed with the splendor of *divine* majesty. The garment of Christ, the long talar (ποδήρης, reaching to the feet), denotes the High-priest; the golden girdle, the King. Christ is both these in the highest power, since He even makes His people kings and priests (ver. 6). He wears the girdle about His breast, not about His hips. Why is this? Ebrard's explanation is justly rejected by Düsterdieck (p. 124). It is well known that the girdle, when worn about the loins, denotes **a** preparedness for travel and, consequently, for labor ; surrounding the breast, it is an ornament, expressive of rest and festivity. The priests also wore their girdles thus, according to Josephus (see the citation in Düsterdieck).

---

* [See remarks on ver. 4, p. 90.—E. R. C.]

Ver. 14. **His head and His hairs.**—The head (pursuant to the irregular conjunction of terms) first appears under the aspect of the hair; since that, according to Oriental ideas, was the especial representative of its dignity. The whiteness of the hair is doubly characterized, the second image surpassing the first (Is. i. 18; Mark ix. 3). What does this whiteness denote? Cocceius: Purity from sin. Hengstenberg: Holiness and glory. De Wette: A celestial light [lucid] nature. Düsterdieck, with others: Eternity, in accordance with the appearance of the Ancient of Days, Dan. vii. 9;—with reference to Rev. i. 17, 18. In the history of the transfiguration and elsewhere, the white lustre certainly denotes the lucid or light-nature, in which eternity is conditioned by *purity* and *maturity* [together with the dignity and authority that (especially among the Orientals) belong to age—the Ancient of days.—E. R. C.], *perfection.* [Augustine (Exp. ad Gal. iv. 21): "Dominus non nisi ob antiquitatem veritatis in Apocalypsi albo capite apparuit."—E. R. C.]

As **a** flame (chap. xix. 12; Dan. x. 6).— Interpretations: Vitringa and others: Omniscience. Hengstenberg and others: Avenging justice. Ebrard: Holiness, consuming all that is unclean. Düsterdieck: Omniscience, directed, with holy wrath, against all that is unholy. De Wette: The translumining, consuming glance of heavenly light-essences (analogy: classical descriptions of the gods). It is significant that the eyes of flame re-appear in the epistle to Thyatira. The all-piercing glance of the Judge is specially directed to the distinguishing of mock-holy fanaticism, such as Jezebel's, from genuine spiritual life. The Greek term for pureness, sincerity, εἰλικρίνεια, is derived from the sun-ray [and the English *pure*, from πῦρ, fire. —Tr.]

Ver. 15. **His feet like unto fine brass** [or **molten gold**].—In the epistle to Thyatira this specification is conjoined with the eyes of flame. On the obscure χαλκολίβανον, comp. the lexicons, Ebrard, p. 138, and Düsterdieck, p. 126. The interpretations furthest from the point are: olibanum [*Erzweihrauch*, frankincense of deep hue] (Ewald); furnace ore [*Ofenerz*] (Hitzig); but neither is white ore [*Weisserz*, "a mixture of sulphuret of silver, sulphuret of copper, sulphuret of lead, and sulphuret of antimony."— Sanders' *Wörterbuch.*—Tr.] (Hengstenberg), or Lebanon ore (iron) [Ebrard], satisfactory. For what idea could readers living in Asia Minor connect with either of these? Züllig supposes χαλκολίβανον to be a provincial term peculiar to Asia Minor. Perhaps we should go back to λείβω, λιβάζω, λιβάς, λιβάδιον, and translate: fused copper [*Kupferguss*—a gush or flow of molten copper], glowing copper, heated in the furnace to a white glow, a golden stream, so that λίβανον may be a word unknown, indeed, to the lexicons, and yet a perfectly correct term for molten, white-glowing metal;* see ch. x. 1. According to De Wette, these feet, radiant with a fiery glow,

are significant only of brightness and splendor; according to Düsterdieck, they denote the down-treading of unholy foes, with reference to Ps. lx. 12; Is. lxiii. 6; Dan. x. 6. But as feet in themselves are instruments of motion, and as the golden-yellow hue denotes pure motion, so, especially, this metal, purified in the furnace, fluent and glowing with white heat, denotes the holiest motion. And hence, also, this characteristic of Christ is properly opposed to the unholy and mischievous motion of a fanatical Jezebel of Thyatira.

And His voice as the voice of many waters.—The *surging waters* represent the life of the nations. As the voice of Christ is, on the one hand, like a trumpet of God, it may, on the other, be heard in the sea-like roar of the voices of Christian nations. Whether the *many waters* admit of so simple a translation as "the majesty of ocean, calmly roaring" [*die Majestät des ruhig rauschenden Meeres*"] is doubtful.*

Ver. 16. **And having** (ἔχων) **in His right hand.**—The stars have, with exceedingly bad taste, been turned into jewels or rings (Eichhorn). ["Not *on* His right hand, as **a** number of jewelled rings, but *in* his right hand, as a wreath or garland held in it." Alford.—E. R. C.] The fact of His being able to lay the same hand on the head of John is contrary to the sensuous apperception, but not to the symbolical representation. That the stars are in His hand is expressive not simply of the fact that the churches are His property (Düsterdieck), but also that they are surrounded by His providence. We cannot, with Hengstenberg, regard this trait as pre-eminently expressive of His punitive power, though neither is that to be excluded. Nor is the element of comfort (Herder) pre-eminent. What is primarily taught is simply Christ's [property in, and] rule over His Church, a doctrine branching into consolation, admonition, and warning.

And out of His mouth.—This unpicturesque but symbolically pregnant combination is expressive of the fact that Christ overcomes the world with His word, as with a two-edged sword, Is. xi. 4; xlix. 2; Wisd. xviii. 15; 2 Thess. ii. 8. Christ's simple word is intended here; hence there is also a reference to the power of that word in so far as it is contained in the preaching of His servants (a point which Düsterdieck denies); even the testimony of each individual Christian is included, Eph. vi. 17. [The word of the Lord is almighty; by His word He acts—He creates, He overcomes, and He destroys. The last, or the last two, seem to be the facts, or facts, set forth by this figure.—E. R. C.]

And His countenance.—Düsterdieck translates: His appearance, declaring that in ch. x. 1, the word is πρόσωπον [instead of ὄψις]. But is it probable that different portions of the body would be described and the face, of all

---

* [Alford correctly remarks: "This word has defeated all the ingenuity of commentators hitherto. . . . If conjecture were admissible (which it is not), I conjecture in despair of any way out of the difficulty, suggest whether the word might not have been χαλκολιβαδίῳ, a stream of melted brass: ΔΙ having been read ΔΙ or Ν."—E. R. C.]

* [It is to be regretted that Lange does not give us the name of the author whom he quotes. If the above sentence was written in ridicule, it is singularly inappropriate. There is an internal calm, a "hiding of power," in that which is truly mighty when producing effects within its scope, that makes the expression "calmly roaring," when applied to the ocean, beautifully appropriate. As there is no sound on earth so majestic as the roar of ocean, and at the same time so suggestive of a hidden power, what figure so appropriate to represent the voice of the Almighty?—E. R. C.]

things, left out? And are we to suppose that the whole form shone as the sun, and yet that the white hair, the stars in the hand, and the white glow of the molten metal were perceptible in this dazzling radiance, whilst the face itself was invisible? Dan. x. 6, would then offer a diversity.—In its might.—The noon-tide blaze of the sun, unobscured by clouds or mist.*

Ver. 17. And when I saw Him.—Exodus xxxiii. 20; Is. vi. 5; Ezek. i. 28; Dan. viii. 17, x. 7. "The impression made by the appearance of the Lord is that of deadly terror, for because death is the wages of sin, no sinful man can stand before God and live" (Düsterdieck). In the first place, we must distinguish the pure meaning of Ex. xxxiii. 20 from the popular Jewish notion set forth in Judg. xiii. 22; the astounding and, possibly, well-nigh fatal effect which the appearance of the Heavenly and Holy One produces on sinful man does indeed remain; yet, as Ebrard justly remarks, it would be a very one-sided proceeding to regard this element of fear in view of death as the only one at work in the breast of the aged John. Was an element of rapture combined, an emotion of pleasurable fear, as the same commentator claims? At all events, the tremendous operation of the physiological and cosmical contrast is to be taken into account. Perfect spiritual sight is in itself a sort of death to this world (second consciousness), a state into which the seer is transported by a death-like convulsion, and a transportation from the earthly to the heavenly condition of existence is not conceivable without a metamorphosis. Comp. the history of the transfiguration and the resurrection. On the inconsistency which De Wette pretends to discover in this description, see Düsterdieck. Be it remarked only that this event signalizes the commencement of the visionary state and not its entire course.

He laid His right hand upon me.—See the miracles of Christ. According to Düsterdieck, the laying of the right hand upon John was but a friendly sign accompanying the aid actually given by the word of Christ. Unseasonable separation of the two sides of one act!

* [TRENCH: "The description of the glorified Lord, which has now been brought to a conclusion, sublime as it purely mental conception, but intolerable if we were to give it an outward form and expression, and picture Him with this sword proceeding from His mouth, these feet as burning brass, this hair white as wool, and the rest, may suggest a few reflections on the apocalyptic, and generally the Hebrew symbolism, and the very significant relations of difference and opposition in which it stands to the Greek. Religion and art for the Greek ran into one another with no very great preponderance of the claims of the former over the latter. Even in his religious symbolism the sense of beauty, of form, of proportion, overrules every other and must, at all costs, find its satisfaction. ... But with the Hebrew symbolism it is altogether different. The first necessity there is that the symbol should set forth truly and fully the religious idea of which it is intended to be the vehicle. How it would appear when it clothed itself in an outward form and shape, whether it would find favor and allowance at the bar of taste, this was quite a secondary consideration; may be confidently affirmed not to have been a consideration at all; for, indeed, with the one exception of the cherubim, there was no intention that it should embody itself there, but rather that it should remain ever and only a purely mental conception, the unembodied sign of an idea. I may observe, by the way, that no skill of delineation can make the cherubim other than unsightly objects to the eye. Thus, in this present description of Christ, sublime and majestic as it is, it is only such so long as we keep it wholly apart from any external embodiment."—E. R. C.]

Fear not.—The same words that ring through the Gospels.

I am the First, and the Last [ver. 18]. And the Living One.—The First: this, Christ is in a mediate sense, as the Father is the same in an absolute sense: He, Christ, is the principle of the world (Epistle to the Colossians) and the final goal of the world (Epistle to the Ephesians), especially of the Kingdom of God; and both these He is in the unity of the simple Living One, whose life and demonstrations of life go on from Alpha to Omega (ch. xxii. 13). The Living One does not directly signify ζωο-ποιῶν (Grotius) [it includes it, however.—E. R. C.]; but neither does it simply mean one who is alive; in power and effect it denotes Him who is the fountain of life, and who now restores life and animation to the paralyzed John.

And I was dead.—As Man, also, He is the Living One, Who, by His resurrection, has got death behind Him and under Him (Rom. vi. 9; Acts xiii. 34).

And behold, I am living.—He lives from æon to æon. This expression is significant of eternity—not, however, as a rigid unit, void of distinction and diversity, but as a series of peculiar and original conformations of the æon or the æons of the æons. The latter conception is one of infinite grandeur. As there is a heaven of heavens, i. e., as the uranic units unite into one more general unity, so there is an æon, composed, not of years, but of æons, and this æon, again, unfolds into a plurality. And Christ does not live passively into these æons, but as He who has the keys of death and Hades. Hell is not spoken of in this passage.

The keys denote authority—exclusive authority. Christ can redeem men from death and Hades, and can cast men into them; and He alone is possessed of this power, ch. iii. 7, ix. 1, xx. 1. And have these keys, through Peter's hands, been transmitted to the popes? The distinction between death and the realm of death occasions difficulty. We cannot think of death as a place to which keys give access. This place is Hades; see the articles on Sheol and Hades.* Thus both terms seem to express one and the same idea (De Wette); yet the Seer further distinguishes between death and Hades, ch. vi. 8; xx. 14. In the first passage, Death manifestly appears as the former lord of Hades, the previous possessor of its keys—Death is personified, therefore, as in Ps. ix. 13; Job xxxviii. 17. And it is personified because it had become an independent power, inasmuch as the natural spirit-life of humanity was powerless in its presence. Christ, in communicating to John a new and exalted consciousness of this His glory, not only raises him up again, but also endues him with that elevation of mind without which he would be unable to view the terrors of the last times.

Ver. 19. Write now [therefore].—Because thou art now freed from thy dread, and hast but to write of life's triumph over death. This verse, based upon verses 17 and 18, is in part a repetition of ver. 11 (Hengstenberg). What thou hast seen, is not limited to the vision intro-

* [See the Excursus on Hades under ch. xx. 14.—E. R. C.]

duced in ver. 12 (Düsterdieck), but includes what thou shalt have seen, i. e., the whole series of visions. The visions, however. relate first to what is, what now is (thus most commmentators, whilst Bleek, De Wette and others interpret ἃ εἰσίν in the sense of: *what it signifies*), and, secondly, to that which is to come. ["Two meanings of ἃ εἰσίν are possible. 1. *The things which are*, viz., which exist at the present time . . . 2. *What things they* (the ἃ εἶδες) *signify* . . . In deciding between these we have the following considerations: *a.* the use of the plural εἰσίν, as marking off this clause in meaning from the next, which has ἃ μέλλει γενέσθαι. If this latter is singular, why not this? Is it not because the μέλλει γενέσθαι merely signifies the future time, in which this latter class, *en masse*, were to happen, whereas this ἃ εἰσίν imports what these things, each of them severally, mean? And, *b.* this seems to be borne out by the double repetition of εἰσίν in the next verse, both times unquestionably in this (the second) meaning." ALFORD.—E. R. C.]

Ver. 20. **The mystery of the seven stars.** —This adjunct is of the highest moment in a two-fold aspect. In the first place, it gives us to understand that the whole apocalyptic prophecy *will really be a history of the seven stars and the seven candlesticks*; secondly, that the entire series of visions will consist of symbolical mysteries, not to be understood literally, requiring interpretation ; yet susceptible of interpretation through biblical means. The interpretation which Christ here gives by way of example, reminds us of the interpretation of the first two parables in Matt. xiii., also designed as a guide to the interpretation of the rest. Hence an angel of exegesis appears once more in the darker portion of the Apocalypse, ch. xvii. 7 sqq.; and at the close of ch. xiii., there is a fresh reference to the fact that we have to do with riddles. The mystery of the seven stars is that which is symbolized by them. *Sacrum secretum, per ipsas significatum* (Lyra). "A μυστήριον is everything that man is unable to understand by means of his own unassisted reason, and which can be apprehended only through divine showing and interpretation, such as immediately follow here" (Düsterdieck). But this definition is undoubtedly too narrow; or do commentaries on the Apocalypse pretend to be the direct result of divine notifications? A mystery is a deep-lying and concealed truth or fact, to be disclosed not by direct revelation, but by the Spirit of enlightenment in His own time, which time, however, God has always reserved to Himself, 1 Tim. iii. 16. Düsterdieck justly declares that the command to write this mystery is fulfilled throughout the book, "for the prophetic unfolding of the hope in the triumphant consummation of Christ's Church through His own return, rests upon the mystery of the seven stars in Christ's hand and the seven candlesticks amidst which He walks— *i. e.*, upon the fact that Christ is the all-powerful protector of His Church, the vanquisher of all its foes." [Lange seems to misapprehend Düsterdieck. The "divine showing and interpretation" spoken of by the latter is not necessarily an immediate divine influence upon the mind of each apprehender—as Lange evidently supposes him to mean. A μυστήριον, revealed immediately to one for the instruction of others, is revealed for all, and to all, who, under the ordinary enlightening operations of the Spirit, apprehend His instructions. It is generally supposed that the essential idea of a "mystery" is that of something *hidden*—that it ceases to be a "mystery" when it is apprehended. This is indeed the meaning of the term in ordinary language, and seems to be the one contemplated by Lange; it is not however the import of the term as employed in Scripture. There the essential idea is simply that of *something undiscoverable by mere human reason*—it is necessarily *hidden* until it is revealed, but the fact of being *hidden* does not enter into its essential character; it continues to be a "mystery" after it has been revealed, and after the revelation has been apprehended. Specifically, there are *hidden* mysteries, *revealed* mysteries, and (so far as individuals are concerned) *apprehended* mysteries. The symbolic relation of marriage to the union between Christ and His Church is as much a *mystery* now, as it was before the inspired Apostle announced it in the Epistle to the Ephesians (v. 32). And so with the mysteries of which the Apostles were stewards, comp. 1 Cor. iv. 1, with Matt. xiii. 11, 1 Cor. i. 26 ; the mystery of the *gospel*, Eph. vi. 19, of the *faith*, 1 Tim. iii. 9, *etc.* (See all the passages in which the term occurs ; the Greek term is invariably translated *mystery*, and the English word never occurs save as the translation of μυστήριον.)—E. R. C.]

The seven stars are angels.—This interpretation seems at first sight but to exchange one mystery for another ; we must consider, however, that in apostolic times the idea of angels was more intelligible than at the present day. Interpretations: 1. Heads, teachers, (Mal. ii. 7) ; either as bishops (ancient view) or as the whole ecclesiastical government of the church—the presbytery eventually, with the bishop at its head (Hengstenberg), Rothe: the bishop in idea). 2. The church itself (Andreas and others), or the personified church-spirit (De Wette: he identifies this church-spirit with the ἄγγελος ἔφορος). 3. The messenger of the church, *i. e.*, the delegate, who went to and fro between the church and the Apostle (Ebrard). John, however, could not write to this delegate, since it was he who took charge of all manuscripts ; neither is it probable that there was more than one delegate between John and the Church in Asia Minor.

If we consider the distance betwixt a star and a candlestick, we shall put both bishops and presbyteries out of the question, and above all, Irvingite wandering stars. We must consider, in the first place, that the epistles are addressed to the angels just as though they were addressed to the churches themselves. The angel receives praise and censure as the representative of the church. Again, he seems to be significant of the conscience of the church ; the church's reformation and awakening were to proceed from him. Now both these points coincide in the idea of the personified character or life-picture of the church (to be distinguished from the church-spirit ; comp. Acts xii. 15). It may indeed be objected that a symbol cannot be replaced by a symbol (Rothe). And certainly a symbol cannot be written to. But the ideal (in the sense of existing in idea, not in the sense of conforming to God's perfect idea) fundamental type of a Church is a reality in heaven and in the sight of God, as well as in the church's own disposition, and every amendment of a church must start from ■ laying hold on this fundamental type. It also results from this address that the letters are not episcopal, but apocalyptic. Episcopal letters Christ would, we believe, have left to John. It further results that the epistles form a constituent part of the Apocalypse, and not a mere introduction to it (Bleek); and, furthermore, that the churches are cited not simply as empirical congregations, but as seven universal types of the Church in all places and ages. That there is an empirical foundation for the epistles, is an unquestionable fact.

[NOTE ON THE ANGELS OF THE CHURCHES.— The subject of the Angels of the Churches is one of great interest, apart from the fact that it has an important bearing on the question of the government of the primitive Church. Beside the interpretations given by Lange, there are two others which it is most strange that he failed to mention—since the former was advocated by Origen, Greg. Nys., and Jerome, and in modern days by Alford; and the latter by Vitringa, Lightfoot, Bengel, and Winer. They will now be presented, and will be numbered in continuance of the interpretations given above. 4. Celestial angels, in some way representing the churches. 5. Officers in the primitive churches similar to the צִבּוּר שְׁלִיחַ (nuncius ecclesiæ) of the synagogue. The objection urged by Lange to the 3d view is insuperable; and to this may be added the fact that there is no evidence that any delegate from the churches waited upon John. The 5th view is supported only by ■ similarity in name—the title of the synagogue officer referred to may be translated: ἀγγελος ἐκκλησίας. It seems to be a fatal objection, however, that the Hebrew minister was one of the inferior officers of the synagogue (see Kitto's Cyclopædia, Tit. SYNAGOGUE), and the Angel of the Apocalypse, if ■ single person, must have been the chief ruler of the church. SCHAFF (Hist. of the Ap. Ch.) thus writes: "We must at the outset discard the view, that the angels here correspond to the deputies of the Jewish synagogues. ... For these had an entirely subordinate place, being mere clerks, or readers of the standing forms of prayers, and messengers of the synagogue; whereas the angels in question are compared to stars, and represented as presiding over the churches; nor have we elsewhere any trace of the transfer of that Jewish office to the Christian Church." The 2d view, the one advocated by Lange, viz.: that by angel was meant the church, or the personified character thereof—is liable not only to the objection mentioned by himself, but to the far stronger one, that the angel is clearly distinguished from the church (vers. 13, 16, 20). The arguments in favor of the 4th view may be abridged from Alford as follows: (1) The constant usage of this book, in which the word ἀγγελος occurs only in this sense; (2) the further usage of this book, in which we have, ch xvi. 5, the ἀγγελος τῶν ὑδάτων introduced without any explanation,

who can be none other than the angel presiding over the waters; (3) the expression of our Lord Himself, Matt. xviii. 10, together with Acts xii. 15, both asserting the doctrine of guardian or representative angels; (4) the extension of this from individuals to nations, Dan. x. 21; xii. 1; (5) the fact that throughout these Epistles nothing is ever addressed individually, as to a teacher, but as to some one person reflecting the complexion and fortunes of the church, as no mere human teacher or ruler could; (6) as against the objection that sin is charged upon the angel, "that there evidently is revealed to us a mysterious connection between ministering angels and those to whom they minister, by which the former in some way are tinged by the fates and fortunes of the latter. E. g., in our Lord's saying cited above (Matt. xviii. 10), the place of dignity there asserted of the angels of the little children, is unquestionably connected with the character of those whose angels they are," etc. As against this view it may be urged—a. that the preceding answer is not satisfactory—the citation does not support the assertion; and even if it did, it would afford no basis for the charging the sin of the churches upon the holy ministering spirits of God; and b. it is well nigh inconceivable that our Lord should have selected a human Apostle yet in the flesh, as His medium of communication with the blessed spirits who minister before His face. The first view is not only the most natural, but it is liable to the fewest objections.

The epistles are such as might properly have been addressed to the chief ruler or rulers of the respective churches, and would naturally have been addressed to them as representing their congregations. The sole difficulty arises from the use of the term angel. This, however, in view of the peculiar nature of the Apocalypse, should occasion no serious difficulty, and most certainly the difficulty is less in supposing an unusual application of the term, than is connected with any hypothesis that gives to the term a precedented meaning. No opinion is expressed as to whether by the angel was meant a single prelate, a bench of presbyters, or the moderator of ■ presbytery—a primus inter pares. These are questions which are not determinable from the passage before us, and which can be determined only from a discussion of the entire scriptural teaching on the subject of Church order—a discussion which cannot in this place be entered upon. (For valuable discussions of the subject of the Angels, see Neander, Kitto's Bib. Cyc., title BISHOP; Alford, Trench (: The Epistles to the Seven Churches), Onderdonk's Episcopacy tested by Scripture, Alexander's Primitive Church Offices, Killen's Anc. Ch., Schaff's Hist. of the Ap. Ch. and Hist. of the Chr. Ch., Vol. I.)—E. R. C.]

The seven candlesticks.—The churches as light-bearers. Their sevenfoldness is the ramification of the one seven-armed candlestick in the temple, symbolical of all revelation. "For this very reason the churches must represent the Church universal, or the kingdom of God" (?). DE WETTE.

Seven churches.—Are merely the seven churches in the empirical sense intended (Wolf; a singular variation by Harenberg, see in Düsterdieck), or have they a more general import? De Wette and many others are in favor of the latter view. In adopting the latter view, we must distinguish between the Church and the Kingdom of God, however. The question next suggests itself as to whether these types are to be chronologically apprehended and applied strictly to the different periods of the Church (Vitringa) ; or whether they are types of different conditions of the Church (Düsterdieck) ; or, finally, whether a combination of these two views is admissible (Ebrard) ; or, again, whether these types shall be realized in the last times exclusively (Hofmann). On these points, see the Introduction and the Notes on the Seven Epistles. We will but remark in passing, that the typical grouping of the ecclesiastical ground-forms of ecclesiastical life in a totality, composed of the sacred number seven, is evident ; the chronological arrangement unmistakably offers striking analogies—a circumstance which, however, must doubtless be referred to the fact that the outward consecution of these forms is based upon a considerable degree of inner ethical construction, nearly in accordance with the psychological law of oscillation. To that decrease of the first love, accompanying an honest zeal and activity, in Ephesus,

succeeds a re-inflammation of the Church under her martyrdom in Smyrna ; the mixture with the world which gained ground in Pergamus, amid all the faithful confession of the Church there, is followed by the reaction of a more active spiritual life in Thyatira, where even worldliness is induced to assume the garb of religious enthusiasm, which agitations, however, relapse into deep exhaustion, into a death-slumber, such as appears at Sardis; then, again, follows the reaction of faithfulness in the Church of Philadelphia, with its little strength; this reaction, however, cannot hinder the condition of final lukewarmness in the Church—a condition elsewhere described in the eschatological discourses and parables of the Lord.

[These variations, it may further be observed, occur in individual Christian experience, in the life of individual churches, and in the history of the Universal Church. And not only so, but they all find their illustrations in different portions of the Catholic Church of any one period. Though in each period the Church as a whole may predominantly present one of the seven types, yet illustrations of all the others may be found in different sections. (See add. note, p.139.—E.R.C.]

B.—EARTH-PICTURE OF THE CHURCH; OR THE REAL, EARTHLY WORLD-PICTURE OF THE SEVEN CHURCHES. THE SEVEN EPISTLES TO THE SEVEN CHURCHES.

CHAP. II. 1–29.

1. *The Metropolis.** [*Ephesus.*]

1 Unto the angel of the church of [in[1]] Ephesus write ; These things saith he that holdeth [*ins.* fast] the seven stars in his right hand, who [he that] walketh in the
2 midst of the seven golden candlesticks ; I know thy works, and thy[2] labor, and thy patience [endurance], and how [that] thou canst not bear them which [that] are evil: and thou hast tried [didst try[3]] them which [who] say[4] they are apostles,
3 and [*ins.* they] are not, and hast found [didst find] them liars: and hast borne [endurance], and hast patience [didst bear], and [*om.* , and] for my name's sake hast
4 labored [*om.* hast labored], and hast not fainted [become weary].[5] Nevertheless [But] I have *somewhat* [*om. somewhat*] against thee, because [that] thou hast left
5 thy first love. Remember therefore from [*om.* from] whence [Lange: from what height] thou art fallen,[6] and repent, and do the first works; or else [but if not] I will [*om.* will] come unto [Lange: upon] thee quickly [*om.* quickly[7]], and will

TEXTUAL AND GRAMMATICAL.

1 Ver. 1. Read thus in accordance with A. B*. C. [ἐν 'Εφέσῳ]; instead of the Rec. 'Εφεσίνης (which arose from too great haste [in transcribing]. See Delitzsch, *Funde*, p. 23). On the difference between τῆς and τῷ see Düsterdieck.
2 Ver. 2. The σου after κόπον, founded upon B*. [א.], *etc.*, is wanting in A. C.[P.], *etc.* Omitted by Tischendorf and Düsterdieck [also by Lachmann and Alford]. Analysis [and analogy] seems to be in favor of its retention.
3 Ver. 2. Instead of the Rec. ἐπειράσω (see Delitzsch, p. 24), according to the best Codd. [א. A. C. P. B*.] ἐπείρασας.
4 Ver. 2. Read Λέγοντας ἑαυτοὺς ἀποστόλους [with א. A. B.* C. P.; instead of the Rec. φάσκοντας εἶναι ἀποστόλους.—E.R.C.]
5 Ver. 3. Otherwise the Rec. See Düsterdieck. [The Rec. reads, Καὶ ἐβάστασας καὶ ὑπομονὴν ἔχεις, καὶ διὰ τὸ ὄνομά μου κεκοπίακας καὶ οὐ κέκμηκας. Alford gives a number of readings, and well remarks, "There is a seeming inconsistency in οἶδα τὸν κόπον σου . . . . καὶ οὐ κεκοπίακας, which caused those who were not aware of St. John's use of the last word (John iv. 6), to alter the sentence as in var. readd."—E. R. C.]
6 Ver. 5. The reading πέπτωκας [with A. B*. C., Lach., Treg., and Alf., instead of Rec. ἐκπέπτωκα with P. Tisch. gives πέπτωκες with א.—E. R. C.]
7 Ver. 5. Ταχύ not firmly established. See Delitzsch, p. 24 [supported by B*; om. by א. A. C. P., *etc.*—E. R. C.].

* Brandt: 1. "The Mother Church."

6 remove thy candlestick out of his [its] place, except thou repent. But this thou
   hast [Lange: retainest], that thou hatest the deeds [works] of the Nicolaitans,
7 which I also hate. He that hath an ear, let him hear what the Spirit saith unto
   the churches;[8] To him that overcometh [conquereth] will I give to eat of the
   tree of life, which is in the midst of [om. the midst of[9]] the paradise of [Lange:
   my[10]] God.

   2.* *The Martyr-Church persecuted by Judaism.* *Smyrna.*

8 And unto the angel of the church in Smyrna write ; These things saith the first
   and the last, which was [who became—ἐγένετο] dead [Lange: the First of the martyrs],
9 and is alive [revived] ; I know thy works[11] and [ins. thy] tribulation, and [ins.
   thy] poverty, (but thou art rich) and *I know* [om. *I know*] the blasphemy of them
   which [thy calumny from those who[12]] say they are Jews [Lange: and the calumny of those who say they are (true) Jews], and are not, but *are* [om. *are*] the
10 [a] synagogue of Satan. Fear none of [or not] those things [Lange: nothing of that[13]]
   which thou shalt [art about to] suffer : behold,[14] the devil shall [is about to] cast
   some of you into prison, that ye may be tried ; and ye shall have tribulation
   [Lange : a tribulation of] ten days : be thou faithful unto death, and I will give
11 thee a [the] crown of life. He that hath an ear, let him hear what the Spirit
   saith unto the churches ; He that overcometh [conquereth] shall not be hurt of
   [injured by] the second death.

   3.* *The Martyr-Church persecuted by Heathenism.* *Pergamus.*

12 And to the angel of the church in Pergamus write ; These things saith he which
13 hath the sharp [ins. two-edged] sword with two edges [om. with two edges] ; I
   know thy works, and [om. thy works and[15]] where thou dwellest, even [om. even]
   where Satan's seat [throne] *is :* and thou holdest fast my name, and hast not
   denied [didst not deny] my faith, even in those [the] days wherein [in which][16] Antipas *was* my faithful[17] martyr, who was slain among you, where Satan dwelleth.
14 But I have a few things against thee, because [that[18]] thou hast there them that
   hold [ins. fast] the doctrine of Balaam, who taught Balak[19] to cast a stumbling-block
   [Lange : a means of infatuation] before the children [sons] of Israel, to eat things
15 sacrificed unto idols [Lange : idol-sacrifices], and to commit fornication. So hast
   thou also them that hold the doctrine of the Nicolaitans [ins. in like manner],[20]
16 which thing I hate [om. which thing I hate]. Repent [ins. therefore[21]] ; or else
   [but if not] I will come unto thee quickly, and will fight [war] against them with
17 the sword of my mouth. He that hath an ear, let him hear what the Spirit saith
   unto the churches ; To him that overcometh [conquereth] will I give [ins. to
   him[22]] to eat [om. to eat][23] of the hidden manna, and will give [ins to] him a white
   stone, and in [on] the stone a new name written, which no man knoweth saving
   [except] he that receiveth *it.*

   [8] Ver. 7. The ἑπτά in Lachmann not tenable; [supported by A. C.; om. by אּ B*. P., Alford.—E. R. C.]
   [9] Ver. 7. Not: in the midst of the Paradise. [Rec. gives ἐν τῷ μέσῳ τοῦ παραδείσου; אּ. 8a. P. ἐν τῷ μέσῳ τῷ παραδείσῳ;
   אּ. A. B*. C, with Lachmann and Alford, give τῷ παραδείσῳ.—E. R. C.]
   [10] Ver. 7. The μου after θεοῦ has A. C. אּ. [P.,] against it, but all versions, Church fathers and theological considerations in its favor: [B*, Vulg. etc., give it; Lach., Treg., and Tisch. omit; Alford brackets.—E. R. C.]
   [11] Ver. 9. A. C., etc., omit τὰ ἔργα καὶ [also P., Lach., Treg., Tisch., and Alford; אּ. and B*. give it.—E. R. C.]
   [12] Ver. 9. [Rec. omits ἐκ with P.; it is given by אּ. A. C. B*., Lachmann and Alford.—E. R. C.]
   [13] Ver. 10. The other reading μή is strongly attested by A. B. C., Lachmann [and Alford]. μηδέν in Tischendorf is
   supported by versions, fathers, and minuscules. The subsequent text is in favor of it. [μηδέν appears in אּ, and P.—
   E. R. C.]
   [14] Ver. 10. δή is omitted [by אּ. A. C. P., Lachmann ; it is given by B* ; Alford brackets it.—E. R. C.]
   [15] Ver. 13. [Rec. gives τὰ ἔργα σου καὶ with B*.; omitted by אּ. A. C. P., Vulg., Æth., etc., Lachmann and Alford.—
   E. R. C.]
   [16] Ver. 13. Of this passage there are three readings: viz. ἐν αἷς [Rec. אּ. P.] αἷς [B*., Alford brackets]—and both
   omitted [A. C., Lachmann]. The omission may be due to the fact of the seeming inconsistency with the foregoing *hast not
   denied*, etc. [Treg., and Tisch. (8th ed.) omit.—E. R. C.]
   [17] Ver. 13. [A. and C. give a second μου after πιστός, also Lachmann, Alford brackets, which would give as the translation—my martyr, my faithful one. Treg., and Tisch. give the μου.—E. R. C.]
   [18] Ver. 14. The ὅτι before ἔχεις seems to be sufficiently corroborated by A. B*. and many others.
   [19] Ver. 14. Τῷ. Unimportant variations.
   [20] Ver. 15. Instead of ὁ μισῶ read: ὁμοίως [with אּ. A. B*. C., Vulg., Lachmann, Alford, Treg., and Tisch.—E. R. C.]
   [21] Ver. 16. The οὖν which is wanting in the Rec. has strong authorities in its favor. [אּ. P., Vulg. omit; it is given
   by A. B*. C., Lach., Treg., and Alf. Tisch. (8th ed.) omits.—E. R. C.]
   [22] Ver. 17. [This αὐτῷ omitted by אּ.—E. R. C.]
   [23] Ver. 17. Φαγεῖν is a late addition. [P. gives it; it is omitted by אּ. A. B*. C., Vulg., etc.—E. R. C.]

   * Brandt: 2. "The churches of the beginning, martyr-churches." [Smyrna and Pergamus.]

4.* *The Church stained by Idolatry.   Thyatira.*

18 And unto the angel of the church in Thyatira write; These things s ith the Son
   of God, who hath his[24] eyes like unto [as] a flame of fire, and his feet *are* like
19 fine brass [to chalcolibanus—(Lange : as white-glowing molten copper)]. I know
   thy works, and [*ins.* the] charity [love], and service, and faith [the faith, and the
   service], and thy [the] patience, [endurance of thee;] and thy works ; [*om.* and
   thy works;] and the [thy] last [*ins.* works] *to be* [*are*] more than the first.
   [Lange: thy love and thy faith, thy zeal in service and thy endurance in suffering
20 (and how[25]); thy last works are more than the first]. Notwithstanding [But] I
   have a few things[26] [*om.* a few things] against thee, because [that] thou sufferest [*ἀφεῖς*]
   that woman [thy wife *or* Lange : the woman[27]] Jezebel, which [who] calleth herself a prophetess, to teach and to seduce [and she teacheth and seduceth —Lange :
   and teacheth (applies herself to teaching) and seduceth][28] my servants to commit
21 fornication, and to eat things sacrificed unto idols [Lange : idol-sacrifices].   And
   I gave her space to [time that she might] repent of her fornication [*om.* of her
   fornication] ; and [Lange : but] she repented not [*om.* repented not—*ins.* willeth
22 not to repent of her fornication[29]].   Behold I will [*om.* will[30]] cast her into a bed,[31]
   and them that [those who] commit adultery with her into great tribulation, except
23 they repent of their [her (*αὐτῆς*)] deeds [works].   And I will kill [slay] her
   children with death ; and all the churches shall know that I am he which [who]
24 searcheth the [*om.* the] reins and hearts: and [Lange : , and that] I will give unto
   every one of you [to you, to each,] according to your works.   But unto you I say,
   and unto [*om.* and unto] the rest in Thyatira, as many as have not this doctrine
   [teaching] [Lange : these doctrines] and [*om.* and] which [such as[32]] have not
   known the depths of Satan, as they speak [say] ; I will [*or om.* will[33]] put upon
25 you none [cast not upon you any] other burden.   But that which ye have
26 already [*om.* already], hold fast till [until] I [*ins.* shall] come [Lange : until I
   come[34]].   And he that overcometh [conquereth], and [*ins.* he that] keepeth
27 my works unto the en 1, to him will I give power over the nations: And he shall
   rule [shepherdize] them with a rod of iron [an iron rod]; as the vessels of a
   potter shall [*om.* shall][35] they be broken to shivers [are shattered *or* he shattereth]:
28 even [*om.* even] as I [*ins.* also have[36]] received of my Father.   And I will give
29 [*ins.* to] him the morning star.   He that hath an ear, let him hear what the Spirit
   saith unto the churches.

CHAP. III. 1-22.

5.* *The Church for the most part Spiritually Dead.   Sardis.*

1   And unto the angel of the church in Sardis write; These things saith he that
     hath the seven Spirits of God, and the seven stars ; I know thy works, that thou hast
2 a[35] name that thou livest, and [*ins.* thou] art dead.   Be watchful [Become thou watch-
     ing], and strengthen the things which remain, that are ready [which were about][37]

[24] Ver. 18. Αὐτοῦ rests upon B. C. [P.], *etc.*   It is omitted by Lachmann and Düsterdieck.
[25] Ver. 19. Καί is omitted according to A. B. C., *etc.* [Lange is here mistaken ; καί omitted by the authorities cited,
and also by א. B*. P., Lachmann, Düsterdieck, Alford, is the one before τὰ ἔσχατα—which requires the translation given in
the text.—E. R. C.]
[26] Ver. 20. The addition ὀλίγα is omitted.   See Delitzsch, *Funde*, p. 22, No. 20. [א. gives πολύ; both are om. by A. B.*
C. P., *etc.*, and Crit. Eds. generally.—E. R. C.]
[27] Ver. 20. Γυναῖκα without σου or σου τήν, in accordance with C. א. Vulg. [σου is given by A. B*. Lachmann ;
Alford brackets.—E. R. C.]   *Thy wife* is probably a conjecture founded upon the supposition that the angel was the
bishop.
[28] Ver. 20. Καὶ διδάσκει καὶ πλανᾷ. A. C. א. See Delitzsch, No. 20, [also B*. P. and critical editors generally.—E. R. C.]
[29] Ver. 21. Καὶ οὐ θέλει μετανοῆσαι. [The reading of which the above is the translation is supported by א. A. B*. C.
P., Lachmann, Alford, Treg., and Tisch.—E. R. C.]
[30] Ver. 22. [A. C. Lach., Alford, Treg., and Tisch. give βάλλω ; א.³⁵ P., Vulg. βάλω.—E. R. C.]
[31] Ver. 22. Uod. A. φυλακήν—a gloss
[32] Ver. 24. Οἵτινες without καί. [Rec. gives καί with Vulg.; it is om. by א. A. B*. C. P., *etc.*—E. R. C.]
[33] Ver. 24. [Rec. with א. B. Vulg. gives βάλω ; A. C. P., Lach., Treg., Tisch., and Alf. give βαλῶ.   The former read ng is
probably correct.   An alternative translation is given.—E. R. C.]
[34] Ver. 25. [א. A. C. P., with Lach., Treg., Tisch., and Alf. give ἂν ἥξω ; B*. reads ἀνίοξω.—E. R. C.]
[35] Ver. 27. Συντρίβεται instead of the Future [with א. A. C.; B*. P. give συντριβήσεται.—E. R. C.]
[36] Ch. III. 1. The article τό before σνομα is omitted.
[37] Ver. 2. Instead of μέλλει, read ἔμελλον, according to A. C. *etc.* [א. P., Treg., Tisch.. and Alf.—E. R. C.]

* Brandt: 3. " The intermediate churches," externally unimpeachable, but inwardly fallen.   *a.* Lapsed into idolatry;
b. lapsed into spiritual death. (Both too strong). [Thyatira and Sardis.]

to die: for I have not found thy works [or any works of thine][38] perfect [completed]
3 before [ins. my[39]] God. ·Remember therefore[40] how thou hast received and heard
[heardest] and hold fast [keep[41]], and repent. If therefore thou shalt [dost] not
watch, I will come on [upon] thee[42] as a thief, and thou shalt not know what hour
4 I will come upon thee. [ins. But][43] Thou hast a few names even [om. even] in Sardis
which have not defiled their garments; and they shall walk with me in white: for
5 [because] they are worthy. He that overcometh [conquereth], the same shall [or
om. the same, and ins. thus (after shall)][44] be clothed in white raiment [garments];
and I will not blot [wipe] out his name out of the book of life, but I will confess
6 his name before my Father, and before his angels. He that hath an ear, let him
hear what the Spirit saith unto the churches.

6.* The Tried Church. Philadelphia.

7 And to the angel of the church in Philadelphia write; These things saith he that
is holy [the holy One], he that is true [the true One], he that hath the key of
David, he that openeth, and no man shutteth [shall shut[45]]; and [ins. he] shutteth
8 and no man openeth [shall open[46]]; I know thy works: behold, I have set [given]
before thee an open door [a door opened], and [which] no man can [is able to]
shut it [om. it]: for [Lange: . For] thou hast a little strength, and [Lange: ins.
yet] hast kept [didst keep] my word, and hast not denied [didst not deny] my name.
9 Behold, I will make them of the synagogue of Satan, which [who] say they are Jews,
and are not, but do lie; behold, I will make them [Lange: om. them] to come
[that they shall come] and [ins. shall] worship [Lange: fall down[47]] before thy
10 feet, and to [om. to—ins. shall] know that I have loved thee. Because thou hast
kept [didst keep] the word of my patience [endurance], I also will keep thee
from [Lange: through] the hour of temptation, which shall [is about to] come
upon all [om. all] the [ins. whole] world, to try them that dwell upon the earth.
11 Behold, [om. Behold,[48]] I come quickly: hold that fast which thou hast, that no
12 man take thy crown. Him that overcometh [conquereth] will I make a pillar
in the temple of my God, and [ins. out of it] he shall [ins. nevermore] go no more
[om. no more] out: and I will write upon him the name of my God, and the name
of the city of my God, which is [om. which is—ins. the] new Jerusalem, which cometh
down out of [from[49]] heaven from my God: [,] and I will write upon him [om. I
13 will write upon him] my new name. He that hath an ear, let him hear what the
Spirit saith unto the churches.

7.* The Lukewarm Church nigh unto Reprobation. Laodicea.

14 And unto the angel of the church of the Laodiceans [in Laodicea[50]] write; These
things saith the Amen, the faithful and true witness, the beginning [Lange: prin-
15 ciple] of the creation of God; I know thy works, that thou art neither cold nor
hot [Lange: warm]: I [om. I] would [ins. that] thou wert cold or hot [Lange:
16 warm]. So then [Lange: However] because thou art lukewarm, and neither cold
17 nor hot [Lange: warm], I will [am about to] spew thee out of my mouth. Because thou sayest,[51] I am rich, and increased with goods [Lange: yea, I have
become exceedingly rich], and have need of nothing; and knowest not that thou

[38] Ver. 2. [A. C. and Lachmann give ἔργα, without the article; א. B*. P. give τά; Alford brackets.—E. R. C.]
[39] Ver. 2. Μου is omitted by some manuscripts here as well as in ch. ii. 7, but has still stronger authorities in its favor
here than in the other passage. [The great authorities all support it; א. A. B*. C. P., Vulg.—E. R. C.]
[40] Ver. 3. [א. omits οὖν; Alford brackets; Treg., an I Tisch. give it.—E. R. C.]
[41] Ver. 3. Καὶ ἤκουσας καὶ τήρει is groundlessly objected to by Matth.
[42] Ver. 3. Ἐπι σέ an addition of the Rec. [א. B*., Vulg. (Clem. and Am.) give it; A. C. P. omit with Lachmann and
Alford, Treg., and Tisch. retain. The weight of ancient authority, as it seems to me, is in favor of retaining.—E. R. C.]
[43] Ver. 4. [א. A. B*. C. P. give ἀλλά.—E. R. C.]
[44] Ver. 5. Instead of οὕτος, read οὕτως, in accordance with A. C. etc. [also א.¹ Lach., Treg., and Tisch.; א.³ª B.* P. and Alf.
read οὕτος —E. R. C.]
[45] Ver. 7. [Rec. gives κλείει with Vulg.; Crit. Eds., with א. A. B*. C. P., give κλείσει.—E. R. C.]
[46] Ver. 7. [Ἀνοίξει, supported by א B*. Alford, Treg., and Tisch.; ἀνοίγει, by A. C. P., La h.—E. R. C.]
[47] Ver. 9. A C. א., ἥξουσι καὶ προσκυνήσουσι.
[48] Ver. 11. [Ἰδού is omitted by Crit. Eds., with א. A. B*. C. P., etc.—E. R. C.]
[49] Ver. 12. Καταβαίνουσα., A. C., etc.
[50] Ver. 14. [Crit. Eds., with א. A. C. P., give ἐν Λαοδικείᾳ.—E. R. C.]
[51] Ver. 17. [Lach., Treg., Tisch., with A. C., Vulg., give a second ὅτι after λέγεις; א. B*. P. omit; Alf. brackets.—E. R. C.]

* Brandt superscribes Nos. 6 and 7: The churches of the end; a. the beloved; b. the condemnable. Almost right!

art wretched, and miserable [the wretched and pitiable one[52]], and poor, and
18 blind, and naked: I counsel thee to buy of me gold tried in [burnt from
(Lange: purified by)] the fire, that thou mayest be [become] rich; and white
raiment [garments], that thou mayest be clothed [cover thyself], and *that* the
shame of thy nakedness do not appear [may not become manifest]; and [*ins.*
eyesalve to] anoint thine eyes with eyesalve [*om.* with eyesalve] that thou mayest see.
19 [*ins.* I, (Lange: (do thus).] As [as] many as I love, I rebuke and chasten: be zealous[53]
20 therefore, and repent. Behold, I stand at the door, and knock: if any man hear my
voice, and open the door, I will come in to him, and will sup with him, and he
21 with me. To him [*om.* To him—*ins.* He] that overcometh [conquereth] will I
grant [I will give (*ins.*) to him] to sit with me in [on] my throne, even as I also
overcame [conquered], and am [*om.* am] set [sat] down with my Father in [on] his
22 throne. He that hath an ear, let him hear what the Spirit saith unto the churches.

52 Ver. 17. The article before ἐλεεινός is not established. [It is given by Lachmann with A. B*.; omitted by ℵ. C. P.;
Alford brackets; Treg., and Tisch. omit.—E. R. C.]
53 Ver. 19. Ζήλευε in accordance with A. C., etc. [So Crit. Eds. generally.—E. R. C.]
54 Ver. 20. B*. and ℵ. read καὶ before εἰσελεύσομαι, against A. [P.], Lach. [Tisch. gives it; Treg. omits; Alf. brackets.
—E. R. C.]

EXEGETICAL AND CRITICAL.

GENERAL REMARKS ON THE SEVEN EPISTLES.*

In the use of the sacred number *seven* throughout the Apocalypse, we must note the indications
of a distinction between *four* and *three*. Düsterdieck remarks (p. 21) that in the case of the
seals and trumpets, the quaternary takes the precedence (this is additionally marked in the case
of the four riders by the parenthesis of the four
beasts; and in the vision of the trumpets, by
the fact that the last three are designated as
the three woes), and the trinary follows; in
the seven churches and the vials, on the other
hand, a *three* precedes the *four*. In the case of
the vials, Düsterdieck, not groundlessly, regards
the thought that we have presented as indicated
by the interlocution of ch. xvi. 5-7; though the
vials, in respect of their effects, may also be
perfectly well divided into *four* and *three*. The
first three epistles, according to this commentator (and Bengel, Ewald, De Wette and others,
p. 141), are distinguished from the last by the
form of the conclusion. In the first three epistles,
the admonition: he that hath an ear, etc., is followed by the final promise (ch. ii. 7, 11, 17),
whilst in the last four, such a promise precedes
the admonition (ch. ii. 29, iii. 6, 13, 22). This
variation is, we admit, well worthy of notice;
yet the inner marks of the churches favor the
distinction of four (mixed forms) and three (perfectly distinct forms). The fundamental forms
of the individual epistles have been presented by
Bengel, as follows (Hengstenb. I. p. 157): The
plan of the seven epistles is the same in all.
For in each we find: 1. An order to write to an
angel of a church. 2 A glorious title of Jesus
Christ [" taken for the most part from the
imagery of the preceding vision." ALFORD.—E.
R. C.]. 3. An address to the angel of the church:
wherein is contained *a.* a testimonial to the
mixed, the bad or the good condition of the angel;
an admonition to repentance or perseverance;
b. an announcement of what is to come to pass,
referring chiefly to the coming of the Lord. 4.
A promise to him that conquereth, together with
the word of awakening: he that hath an ear, etc.

"The *titles* put forth by the Lord at the beginning of each letter are most illustrious, as is also
indicated by the words: these things saith—the
Supreme Majesty,—like the Old Testament: *thus
saith the Lord.*"

"The *address* in each epistle consists principally
of plain and perspicuous expressions. In the
promise, on the other hand, the Spirit deals more
in figurative expressions. In the *address*, the
Lord Jesus speaks principally and primarily to
the churches then existing in Asia Minor, especially and particularly to their angels. The
promise speaks in the third person *of* those who
conquer—both in those first times and also in the
ages after them."

"Amongst the seven angels of the seven
churches there were two, the one at Ephesus and
the one at Pergamus, in a mixed state; and two,
those at Sardis and Laodicea, were extremely corrupt. Not only the latter two, whose whole condition was bad, ch. iii. 3, 19, but also the former,
who were defective in some particular respect,
ch. ii. 5, 16, are recommended to repent. And
so at Thyatira the adherents of Jezebel are admonished to repentance—the woman herself willing not to repent, and the angel of the church
having no need of repentance so far as he
himself is concerned, ch. ii. 21, 22. The condition of two of the angels, those at Smyrna
and Philadelphia, was good; hence they needed
no admonition to repentance, and are only
encouraged to persevere. There is no mixed
or good or bad state whose pattern might not be
found here, as well as apt and salutary doctrine
therefor. Though a man were as dead as the
angel of the church at Sardis, or as flourishing
as the one at Philadelphia and the aged Apostle
John himself, this book suiteth his case, and the
Lord Jesus hath somewhat to say to him therein."

"In the seven epistles there are twelve *promises*. In the third, fourth, and sixth, there is
a two-fold promise, and in the fifth a three-fold
promise; each one of the promises being distinguished by a particular expression: I will
give, I will not blot out, I will confess, I will
write.—The promise to him that overcometh
[conquereth] is declaratory, sometimes of the
enjoyment of the most precious boons, sometimes
of immunity from the extremest misery. The

one is included in the other, and when a part of the blessedness and glory of the victor is expressed, the whole should be understood, ch. xxi. 7. That part is particularly expressed which relates to the virtues and deeds referred to in the address.—Some things contained in these promises are not again expressly mentioned in the Revelation; as, for instance, the manna, the confession of the victor's name, the name of the New Jerusalem written upon the victor, the sitting upon Christ's throne. Some things bear a resemblance to what is afterwards declared concerning Christ Himself; viz. the secret name, ch. xix. 12; the shepherdizing of the nations, ch. xix. 15; the Morning Star, ch. xxii. 16. Some things are expressly mentioned again in their proper place; as the tree of life, ch. xxii. 2; immunity from the second death, ch. xx. 6; the name in the book of life, ch. xx. 12, xxi. 27; the abiding in the temple of God, ch. vii. 15; the name of God and of the Lamb on the righteous, ch. xiv. 1, xxii. 4." BENGEL.

The *fundamental idea* of all the seven epistles is the fundamental idea of the Apocalypse itself—the Coming of the Lord. The arrangement is the epistolary form in apocalyptic sublimity: superscription, substance, conclusion. The superscriptions have the common form of Christ's self-designation, with the prophetic announcement: τάδε λέγει (Amos i. 3, etc.); they present the various attributes of His majestic appearance as described in ch. i. The distribution of the attributes harmonizes with the churches. For Ephesus, the metropolis: the seven stars and seven candlesticks. For Smyrna, the martyr church, He that was dead and is alive again. For Pergamus, where Satan's seat is: the sharp, two-edged sword. For Thyatira, where the spirit of fanaticism is rampant: the eyes as flames of fire, and the feet like a glowing stream of molten metal. For dead Sardis: the Possessor of the Seven Spirits (of life) and the seven stars. For faithful Philadelphia: the Possessor of the keys of David, the Opener of a door to the church. For Laodicea, as for Ephesus, a more general designation of Christ, yet under the name of the Amen, Who certainly fulfills His threats. The attributes also correspond with the commendations, admonitions, and threats, i. e., with the criticisms and the promises. In the criticisms, praise and blame are sometimes united; and where praise predominates (as in the case of the first four churches), the first place is given to it; where censure predominates, it has the first place (Sardis). So in one case we find praise exclusively (Philadelphia), and, in another, only censure (Laodicea). The promises are always promises of entire blessedness in concrete terms, such as are appropriate to the condition, conduct, and conflict of the church. Ebrard remarks that the first four promises are taken from consecutive items of Old Testament history (Paradise, death, manna, David); the last three relate to the final establishment of the Kingdom (p. 157). The epistle proper is grounded upon the Lord's complete knowledge of the state of the church (οἶδα, etc.). This is followed by a portraiture of the church and the award of praise and blame; next follows the prognosis, the prediction of good or danger; finally, the

application: admonition, threat, consolation. The conclusion is a specific conditional promise, accompanied by the exhortation to hear the words of the Spirit; amid constant reference to the Coming of the Lord.

[See an exceedingly able and interesting article on "The Seven Churches of the Apocalypse," in Schaff's *History of the Apostolic Church*, p. 427 sqq.—E. R. C.]

FIRST EPISTLE. EPHESUS.

Chap. ii. 1-7.

Ver. 1. **Ephesus** was the metropolis of proconsular Asia; not merely in a political, but also in an ecclesiastical sense. It is placed at the head of the seven churches as the actual see of John, Hengstenberg remarks; a proposition which is groundlessly denied by Düsterdieck. On Ephesus, see Winer, *Das Wörterbuch für das Christliche Volk*, and Books of Travel.* [Conybeare and Howson's *Life and Epistles of St. Paul*, Schaff's *History of the Apostolic Church*, Kitto's *Bib. Cyc., etc.*—E. R. C.] At the present day, the only remains of this once pleasant city are some ruins and the village of Ajosoluck. The church was founded by Paul (Acts xviii. 19, xix. 1). On its Pauline period, see the Commentaries on Ephesians and 1 Timothy. Because Timothy was the head of this church for a time, Alcasar, Cornelius à Lapide, and others, have regarded him as the angel of the church. This opinion was held even in opposition to the traditional notion, according to which John was the successor of Timothy.

That holdeth [fast].—Κρατῶν, stronger than ἔχων, ch. i. 16. Düsterdieck thinks it involves the idea of Christ's ability to cast the stars out of His hand. [The idea is that of holding with power, comp. John x. 28.—E. R. C.] We must distinguish, however, between stars and candlesticks (ver. 5, ch. iii. 1). The stars, perhaps, are "graven in His hand."

Who walketh.—"The περιπατῶν resembles the passage ch. i. 18." It is a stronger expression, however. [The idea presented seems to be that of one who walks about to trim the lamps. According to the opinion of Sir Isaac Newton. E. R. C.] Ebrard justly refers this more general designation of Christ, in respect of His relation to the churches, to the metropolitan character of Ephesus. Düsterdieck does not recognize this reference.

Ver. 2. [I know=οἶδα.—Knowledge concerning, not approval, is indicated by this term; the same word is used in reference to the church of Laodicea, ch. iii. 15. The commendation spoken of below is to be gathered from the context and not from this term.—E. R. C.]—**Thy works**.—With reference to ver. 4, it may seem a strange thing that He should begin with a commendation of the works of the church. Yet they are commendable, though not exactly heroic deeds against false teachers, as Hengstenberg maintains. The active zeal of the church may have formed a contrast to the heathen mysticalness and moonstruck character of the city. The form of the works branches first into labor or toil, and perseverance or endurance. It is thus [as perse-

* Also Lange's *Apostol. Z-italter.*

verance or endurance] that we translate ὑπομονή in this place, since the word cannot be a mere repetition in ver. 3. ["This word κόπος, signifying, as it does, not merely labor, but labor *unto weariness*, may suggest some solemn reflection to every one who at all affects to be working for his Lord, and as under his great Task-Master's eye. This is what Christ looks for, this is what Christ praises in His servants." TRENCH. — "Κόπος and ὑπομονή form the active and passive sides of the energizing Christian life. The omission of the σου after τὸν κόπον, serves to bind the two together in one. They are epexegetic, in fact, of ἔργα; cf. 1 Cor. xv. 58," etc. ALFORD.— E. R. C.] — With this zeal in the life of the Church, a healthy polemical system corresponds, which may also be divided into two forms. In the first place, the church cannot bear bad men —this means, of course, in the domain and mask of religion — and, secondly, it even dares, by means of a Christian proving of spirits, to unmask men giving themselves out as apostles, and to show them to be liars. False teachers, manifestly, are meant [see Acts xx. 29, 30]; men assuming to possess apostolic authority, whether they appeared in the guise of inspired persons, or as Judaizing traditionalists. According to Düsterdieck, this saying would be meaningless after the destruction of Jerusalem. It is well known, however, that in all ages of the Church persons have appeared who have laid claim to apostolical authority. Düsterdieck thinks that these men were tried by their works pre-eminently; but false apostles should be pre-eminently, though not exclusively, tried by their doctrine. [Comp. 1 John iv. 1–3.—E. R. C.]

Ver. 3. **And that thou hast patience** [endurance]. — Here follows the third commendation of the church, for its good conduct under suffering; this also is exhibited under two aspects—suffering in general, for Christ's name's sake, and steadfast endurance under these sufferings. [There can be little doubt that the alteration of the text in this passage is due to an apparent inconsistency between οἶδα τὸν κόπον σου, and οὐ κεκοπίακας (see *Textual and Grammatical*). There is a world-wide distinction between being weary in the *flesh* (a mark of faithfulness in working) and being wearied in *spirit* (a mark of faithlessness), which, doubtless, the Apostle designed to indicate, and which the alterers failed to grasp.—E. R. C.]

Ver. 4. [**I have against thee.** — The unauthorized introduction of *somewhat* into the E. V. weakens the force of the rebuke — which, as it came from the mouth of Jesus, was unqualified. Trench well remarks: "It is indeed not a '*somewhat*,' which the Lord has against the Ephesian Church; it threatens to grow to be an 'every thing;' for, see the verse following, and comp. 1 Cor. xiii. 1–3."—E. R. C.]—**That thou hast left thy first love.**—This reproach is a contrast and counterpoise to all previous praise, almost outweighing it, in fact. Some of the different interpretations of this first love are characteristic. The two following are antithetic in their nature: Calovius understands the words as signifying a watchful zeal for the purity of the word of God (*i. e.*, doctrine), while Eichhorn, on the other hand, thinks that the church

is charged with a want of clemency in the judgment of the false teachers. Grotius understands the passage as referring to a defective care for the poor. Ebrard thinks it indicates a diminution, not of love to Christ, but of Christian brotherly love. Düsterdieck will not allow that the words bear a comparative meaning, but maintains that the first love was actually lost. If it were completely lost, as love, the church's Christianity were at an end. What Düsterdieck means, however, is the maiden form of love, with reference to Züllig, Hengstenberg, and Jer. ii. 2. But the Spirit of Revelation cannot have intended to say that the first bridal or blossom-like form of development of Christian life must be permanent. Neither can brotherly love be called the first love, in comparison with love to Christ; nor can we suppose it possible for the former to vanish whilst the latter remained. Least of all is it assumable, after the commendations bestowed, that the church was lacking in its care for the poor. According to the presentation of the contrast in the epistle, there was, manifestly, in proportion to a flourishing outside show of churchly life, an incipient lack of inwardness and fervor—i. e., a lack of true divine knowledge, of habitual prayerfulness, warmth, contemplativeness; in a word, just those traits began to be lacking whose deficiency became more and more perceptible, not before the destruction of Jerusalem, but toward the end of the first century. Such a deficiency may be connected with a morbid prosecution of Christian works; as, for instance, is the case in our own time, even in evangelical circles. In a time when three important Lutheran ecclesiastical schools no longer sound the depths of the Lutheran doctrine of justification, and the religious expectation of the speedy coming of the Lord is almost universally exchanged for a chronological error, we have a practical illustration of what it is to have left the first love. [The words seem scarce to require a comment. The obvious reference is to the loss of that glowing, all-absorbing love to Jesus, as a personal Saviour, which at the first constrained them to devoted service (comp. Eph. iii. 16–19, iv. 15, 16). This view is borne out by the following verse, where the decay of love is followed by the decay of works of righteousness. See also Jer. ii. 2 sqq.—E. R. C.]

Ver. 5. **Whence thou art fallen.**—From what a height of ideal Christian life (comp. the writings of the Apostles and the works of the apostolic fathers).

And repent.—In reference to this fall, inward reflection is needed—a new internalization of Christian character. And thus, **do the first works** does not mean, do yet more outward works, but, do the living inward works on which all sound Christianity rests. [The reference doubtless was to both inward and outward works —to the internal works of love and faith, and to the bringing forth of fruits meet for repentance in the outward life. The "first works" do not mean *more* ritual observances, yet they do include such *outward works* as are described, Eph. iv. 17, to the end of the Epistle.—E. R. C.]

But if not.—The magnitude of the threatened punishment shows that the internal condition of the church is exceedingly bad. The grand trouble is that it is travelling a downward road. If the inward life be once neglected, and replaced or covered up by an external zeal for works, the false movement, if not corrected by repentance, goes on to spiritual death. This fact is demonstrated by the history of the mediæval Church, and by that of the modern evangelical awakening. [Not only was the internal condition of the church bad, but also the external. It is to be feared that many Protestants confound externality with *mere* externality, and so lose sight of vital truth. True religion has an outside as well as Pharisaism—an outside which differs from the latter not only in that it is more scriptural, but also in that it is broader, more complete. It may be indeed narrower in a merely ritual direction, but, in all other respects, it is more extensive. It should ever be remembered that our Lord exhorted, "Let your light so shine before men that they may *see* your good works," Matt. v. 16, and that the Apostle Paul presented it as one of the characteristics of true Christians that they are "*zealous* of good works," Tit. ii. 14. The Pharisees, in losing internal piety, *narrowed* the field of external religion; they placed it altogether in ceremonial observances; in tithing mint, anise, and cummin (which was a duty) and in other *uncommanded* rites, and ignored the weightier matters of the law, Matt. xxiii. 23. They omitted not merely the internal graces of judgment, mercy, and faith, but the actions proceeding from these graces. The mark of a decaying church is not an external zeal for works, but a zeal for works in a contracted, often an uncommanded field, whilst the broad surrounding territory of Christian duty is left uncultivated. This, doubtless, was the condition of the Ephesian church.—E. R. C.]

I come upon thee.—Properly, **unto** thee (σοί). (The ἐπὶ σέ of ch. ii. 3 is similar. Both forms are expressive of the unexpectedness of the coming.)

Will remove thy candlestick.—Since the church is also itself called the candlestick (ch. i. 20), the following explanation readily suggests itself: *efficiam, ut ecclesia esse desinas* (Aret.); or, if the angel be regarded as the bishop: I will take from thee thy church, thy position (Zeger)—the ordinary expression for which, however, would be: I will remove *thee*. The interpretations of Grotius and Ewald are also inadequate. But since the candlestick is here distinguished from the church, it doubtless denotes the Christian quality of the church, consisting, according to the Christian saying, of light and life. History teaches us what becomes of the dead body in the case of such a removal of the soul. This passage suggests a reference to the perfect desolation of Ephesus, as compared with Smyrna and Philadelphia.

Ver. 6. **But this thou hast.**—Properly, doubtless: thou still retainest. The sign of hope presented in ver. 3 is again and more distinctly set forth. Hate cannot be resolved into *disapprove* (as De Wette interprets); it is, however, to be referred to the works of the Nicolaitans—not to them personally (Lyra). The *dogmata* lying at the foundation of the works, are doubtless also intended, though not exclusively, as Calovius supposes.

Nicolaitans.—A sectarian tendency in the Apostolic Church, on which comp. Church history and the Encyclopædias.* It is obvious from the epistles themselves—1. That they form a contrast to "*the Jews*" in Smyrna and at Philadelphia [ch. ii. 9], ch. iii. 9; and, on the other hand, 2. That they are akin to, and, in practice, even identical with, the Balaamites at Pergamus, ch. ii. 14, and the school of Jezebel at Thyatira, ver. 20.† We distinguish three opinions in regard to the Nicolaitans: 1. The Catholic tradition representing the deacon Nicolas, Acts vi. 5, as the founder of the sect; 2. The correction proceeding from Clement of Alexandria, stating that from a misunderstanding of an utterance of Nicolas, the doctrine that the lusts of the flesh must be indulged had been derived; 3. The assumption, since Heumann, that the term Nicolaitans is a symbolical expression; in support of this hypothesis it is alleged that the Greek word *Nicolas* means *conqueror of the people;* the Hebrew *Balaam*, *devourer of the people;* the two, in symbolical unity, signifying religious seducers of the people (analogous is the Antichrist Armillus, ἐρημόλαος [desolator, ravager of the people]). From the Epistle of Jude, ver. 11 (comp. 2 Pet. ii. 15), we see that the name of Balaam had previously been symbolically employed in reference to antinomistic corrupters of the people. The apocalyptic symbolism might take advantage of this fact, freely translating the name. In this case, however, the Apocalyptist would most probably have made one name suffice him; and so the tradition of the misuse of the name of Nicolas does not seem to be altogether unfounded. It is possible that one and the same antinomianism branched into three forms: 1. A *doctrinal* form (Nicolaitans); 2. A *worldly-wise* form (Balaamites); 3. A *spiritualistic* form (Jezebel). "The Nicolaitans are, undoubtedly, not identical (Hengstenberg) with the κακοί mentioned in ver. 2; yet they certainly do belong to those bad people." (Düsterdieck.) On the confusion of opinions, see the last-named commentator. The reference of the false apostles [ver. 2] to "the Apostle of the Gentiles and his adherents," is presumptuous and even audacious.

Ver. 7. **He that hath an ear,** i. e., the organ of hearing; here in a spiritual sense. The singular is more significant, our plural [Luther's version has *Ohren*, ears] more popular and emphatic. [**Let him hear.**—Hear in the sense of *heed*, as in Matt. xviii. 15–17, xiii. 18 (comp. with 15).—E. R. C.]

The Spirit.—The Holy Spirit, as the Spirit of Christ and the inspiration of the Prophet.

<hr/>

* See Lange's *Apostol. Zeitalter*, II. 525. [Also, Schaff's Hist. of the Apost. Church, p. 671, sq.—Alford *in loc.*—E. R. C.]

† [The sole reason that can be drawn from the epistles for distinguishing them from " the Jews " is that they are separately mentioned—when, had they been the same, or allied, we should expect the fact to be declared. A similar and still stronger reason exists for distinguishing them from the Balaamites, arising from the fact that they are separately mentioned in *the same epistle*, and that without a word that could lead us to suppose that they were not distinct sects. No conceivable reason arises from the Scripture for connecting them with the followers of Jezebel. To those, indeed, who hold that the Nicolaitans were allied to the Balaamites, must also hold that they were allied to the school of Jezebel, since it is manifest that the last two were similar, comp. ii. 14 with 20.—E. R. C.]

Düsterdieck justly gives prominence to the fact that John's personality is in no way abrogated, but glorified, by his ascription of what is said, to the Spirit.

To him that overcometh [conquereth]. —The same exhortation at the close of all the seven epistles denotes the victory of a steadfast life of faith over the temptations and trials indicated, and over all adverse things in general. [It also implies that the Christian life, throughout the entire period covered by the seven epistles, is to be one of conflict. It pre-supposes the warfare and the preparation of Eph. vi. 10-20. —E. R. C.]

Will I give.— The *give* is emphatic, meaning—not *bestow a portion*—but *grant power, authorize*.

Of the tree of life.—A reference to the new Paradise (see chaps. xxi., xxii.). To eat of the trees of life, the heavenly-earthly antitypes of the tree of life in the first Paradise. An emphatic promise of eternal life, of the enjoyment of eternal nourishment to eternal rejuvenation. Since the lack of the first love is a lack of life, the promise of heavenly life is a fitting one.

In the paradise of [My] God.—(John xx. 17). The word *My* has been objected to (see the TEXTUAL NOTES) probably because it was thought to militate against the Divinity of Christ. But even in glory. Christ can call the God Who, as the Faithful One, will so transcendently abide by His faithfulness, *His God*, in order to denote the infinite certainty of infinite promise. [Similar expressions occur, John xx. 17; Eph. i. 17; Rev. iii. 12. As the *Fons Deitatis*, the Begetter, the First Person of the Trinity is at once the God and the Father of the Divine Son.—E. R. C.]

SECOND EPISTLE. SMYRNA.

Vers. 8–11.

Ver. 8. **Of the church in Smyrna.**— This city is situated on a harbor of the Ægean sea, and is flourishing even to this day. See the Real-Encyclopædias and Books of Travel. Letters of Ignatius, Polycarp, Church Histories.

"Many, particularly Catholic exegetes, *etc.*, also Calovius and Hengstenberg, have regarded Polycarp as the angel of Smyrna." [Altered from Düsterdieck.—TR.] This assumption is based upon the false theory in regard to the angel.

[These things saith the first and the last, *etc.*—" Being addressed, as this epistle is, to the Church exposed, and hereafter to be still more exposed, to the fiercest blasts of persecution, it is graciously ordered that all the attributes which Christ here claims for Himself should be such as would encourage and support His servants in their trial and distress." TRENCH. —E. R. C.]

Who became dead.—This self-designation of Christ harmonizes with the martyr-state of the church. **[And revived.**—"The words (both clauses of this designation) seem to point to the promises in vers. 10, 11." ALFORD.—E. R. C.]

Ver. 9. **Thy tribulation.**—This has reference to sufferings from persecution—shame and distress — extending even to imprisonment and death (ver. 10 sqq.)

And poverty.—It is more probable that this has reference to the spoiling of the church's goods (Heb. x. 34, Primas. and others), than to the helplessness of originally poor persons, in contrast to rich Jews, able to bribe the government (Hengstenberg).

But thou art rich.—In heavenly goods (ch. iii. 18; Eph. i. 3; Matt. vi. 20. [v. 11, 12], *etc.*) Soul-elevating contrast. (Πολύκαρπος, Hengstenberg!)

And (I know) thy calumny.—This calumny,* as addressed to heathen, might be an accusation of riotousness and sedition (Acts xvii. 6); as addressed to Jews or Jewish Christians, it might be an accusation of apostasy from the Law or from Ebionite Christianity. It is a query whether real Jews are intended here (most commentators),or Judaizing Christians (Vitringa and others). The two readily made common cause, however, in taking offence at the free development of Christianity, and the Prophet might reproach them both with not being genuine Jews, *i. e.*, believers on the Messiah (comp. the Epistle of James). Hence, even if the Apocalyptist were speaking of real Jews, he would take the word in a higher, symbolical sense; we would remark in this connection, that, in the Gospel of John, on the other hand, the word Jews denotes, in the historical sense, Judaizers. Ch. iii. 9, however, seems to be more in favor of the supposition that Jewish Christians are intended. Though it cannot be denied that, in many cases, the Jews incited the heathen to the persecution of Christians, we cannot suppose (with Düsterdieck) that, at the beginning of the Jewish war, the Jews, who were almost all insurrectionists, could have accused the Christians, who were peaceable citizens, of anything like insurrection or sedition.†

A synagogue of Satan.—Cutting oxymoron. Not a synagogue of the Lord (Num. xvi. 3 and elsewhere), but the extreme opposite of that. As Antichristian adversaries of the church's Christianity (see James ii. 2). Düsterdieck recalls Hosea iv. 15: Bethel ▪ Bethaven. [ALFORD referring to TRENCH: *New Testament Synonyms*, § 1, thus writes: "He (Trench) brings out there how ἐκκλησία, the nobler word, was chosen by our Lord and His Apostles for the assembly of the called in Christ, while συναγωγή, which is only once found (James ii. 2) of a Christian assembly (and there, as Düsterd. notes, not with τοῦ Θεοῦ, but with ὑμῶν) was gradually abandoned entirely to the Jews, so that in this, the last book of the Canon, such an expression as this can be used. See also his Comm. on the Epistles to the Seven Churches." It is to be observed that συναγωγή was not *gradually abandoned*, but was at once relinquished. As a term relinquished by true Israel, it might be applied to an assembly either of those clinging to Judaism, or of an heretical Christian sect.—E. R. C.]

Ver. 10. **Fear none of those things which**

---

* [The translation given in the text—*thy calumny from those, etc.*—is more nearly in accordance with the Greek than the *E. V.*—E. R. C.]

† [May it not be that our Lord used the term "Jews" in its highest sense, as indicating the true Israel (see note on p.27.)? This explanation gives obvious and special force to the entire expression, "who profess themselves to be Jews, but they are not, but a synagogue of Satan."—E. R. C.]

thou shalt suffer.—The **prison** is indicative of persecutions on the part of the magistracy, which, however, in persecuting, is unwittingly the devil's servant (see ch. xii.). Düsterdieck: "The meaning of the name (διάβολος, slanderer) should not be emphasized here (contrary to Züllig and Hengstenberg) ; otherwise we should expect to find ὁ διάβ. in ver. 9, and ὁ σαταν. in ver. 10." Still, the idea of the adversary (Satan) takes precedence of the idea of the slanderer (devil), and the incarceration of the pious is a practical slander. [**Behold, the devil is about to cast some of you into prison,** *i. e.*, through his influence upon the minds of magistrates, as he influenced the Sabeans and Chaldeans against Job (i. 15, 17). This passage agrees with other Scriptures, in teaching not merely the personality of the devil (Satan), but also that his permitted power over the world and members of the Church, though weakened, is still continued. Comp. Luke xxii. 31; 1 Thess. ii. 18, 2 Thess. ii. 9; Eph. vi. 11, 12; 1 Pet. v. 8, *etc.*—E. R. C.] **That ye may be tried.**—Though *temptation* on the part of the devil is at the same time a *testing* or *proving* on the part of God, here the devil's tempting to apostasy is intended. Three terms for the devil are presented here, therefore: *enemy, accuser, tempter.*

Tribulation ten days. — The numeral is not to be taken literally (Grot.), and denotes neither a *long* time (à Lapide and others), nor a *short* time (De Wette and others, [Alford, Trench]), but a divinely meted, periodical world-time, according, however, with the minor measure of the worldly life of Smyrna—numbered days; *i. e.*, the period of the expiration of the old world-time in Smyrna; which period, if we regard it as thus meted and modified by days, may undoubtedly appear a short time. Interpretations: 1. Ten days are equivalent to ten years. The persecutions under Domitian or Decius. 2. The ten persecutions of the Christians (Ebrard). This time of persecution must be distinguished from the universal time of tribulation of the Church, ch. xiii. 5 (42 months=1260 days, ch. xi. 3, xii. 6=3½ times, ch. xii. 14).

Be thou faithful.—Γίνου is significant—pointing to a long and perilous way.

Unto death. — The faithfulness must be the faithfulness of the martyr, who is ready even for death; a faithfulness exceeding the persecutions. This exhortation may be beautifully generalized thus: be faithful *until* death. [The two ideas of *unto* and *until* death are conjoined. Be faithful, though faithfulness lead to death; be faithful until you die.—E. R. C.]

The crown of life.—1 Pet. v. 4. Τὸν στέφ. τ. ζωῆς. Düsterdieck: *Genit. apposit.* See, in opposition to this, the Lange *Comm. on James* i. 12, p. 47 [Am. Ed.]. "The *summum* of life as life's prize of honor." Genitive of appertinency, therefore. Various interpretations: Züllig: The royal crown of the faithful. Hengstenberg figuratively: The most precious thing. Düsterdieck, correctly: The figure of the victor's crown, taken from the competitive games. [The question here is as to whether the στέφανος spoken of is the *diadem* of the king, or the *wreath* of the victor. In favor of the latter interpretation may be urged that the term is στέφανος, and the further fact, that the promise is to the *victor*. This, at first glance, may seem to settle the question. It will not be denied that, according to strict classical usage, διάδημα represents the crown of the king, and στέφανος that of the conqueror in the Grecian games. It should be remembered, however, that at this very time the crown of the Roman Emperors was the στέφανος —(See Elliot, *Hor. Apoc.*, Vol. I., p. 136 sq.), the symbol at once of victory and dominion. The question is as to the force of the term in the New Testament. Διάδημα occurs but three times, Rev. xii. 3, xiii. 1, xix. 2; the word everywhere else translated *crown* is στέφανος. In 1 Cor. ix. 25 and 2 Tim. ii. 5, there is, manifestly, reference to the wreath of the victor; but, on the other hand, the crown placed on the head of Jesus in mockery of His claim to be a King, was styled στέφανος, Matt. xxvii. 29, *etc.;* (see also Rev. iv. 4, 10, vi. 2, xiv. 14, where the crown of the ruler is referred to). A consideration of these Scriptures establishes the conclusion that, in the New Testament, this term, like the English *crown*, is used to designate both the *diadem* and the *wreath.* This conclusion is confirmed by the well-known fact concerning the Roman Emperors above alluded to. From this point of view there can be little doubt that the στέφανοι of the glorified saints are the symbols at once of their *victory* in the contest of earth, and of their *authority* as kings in the Kingdom of Heaven.—E. R. C.]

Ver. 11. **He that overcometh [conquereth].**—The promise corresponds with the address and charge. *Overcoming* is here the concrete victory over temptation in the persecutions announced; a victory founded, as it necessarily must be, upon a general victory over evil. — To such a victor, invulnerableness against the second death is assured.

The second death.—A designation of damnation (ch. xx. 6, 14, xxi 8), with reference to Jewish Theology (see Düsterdieck, De Wette, Wetstein, Buxtorf). This, therefore, is indirectly the surest promise of eternal life. The more certain the first death seems to be, the more surely will the one assailed by it receive an entrance into that free realm, where all is imperishable and unfading, where death is a thing of the past. [See the Excursus on Hades, p. 364. —E. R. C.]

THIRD EPISTLE. PERGAMUS.

Vers. 12–17.

Ver. 12. **Pergamus** or Pergamum in Mysia; formerly a royal residence; later, a principal city of Roman Asia. This was the city of Æsculapius, as Ephesus was that of Diana. It is now called Bergamo. There are many ruinous remains of the old city. See the Lexicons and Books of Travel.

The sharp, two-edged sword. — Here, too, the attribute of Christ corresponds with the situation of Pergamus; see ver. 16. The sharp sword is, however, not an instrument of external penal judgments, but the organ of the Spirit's judgments (see Eph. vi. 17; John xvi. 8).* It was an hypothesis of Lyra, that the epistle was addressed to a bishop named Carpus.

---

* [The term in Eph. vi. 17 is, not as here, ῥομφαία, but μάχαιρα; and surely that single passage (neither term occurs

Ver. 13. Satan's throne.—The same idea is made prominent at the end of the verse: *where Satan dwelleth.*—Double recognition is made of the church's faithfulness, on account of the perils of the place in which it is tested. Interpretations of the term *throne of Satan:* 1. Worship of Æsculapius, whose symbol was the serpent (= devil, Grotius, and others). 2. Acme of idolatry (Andreas and others). 3. Dwelling-place of heathen and Nicolaitans (Calovius and others). 4. Extreme of persecutions (Ewald and others). 5. Museum of Pergamus (Zornius). Pergamus being the seat of the supreme court, it was natural that it should be the central point of persecution (Ebrard). Düsterdieck also mentions this supposition, without giving it its due weight. It has reference, indeed, to a later period of the first century, when persecutions began to be judicial. [TRENCH judiciously remarks: "All which we can securely conclude from this language is, that from one cause or another, these causes being now unknown, Pergamum enjoyed the bad pre-eminence of being the headquarters in these parts of the opposition to Christ and His Gospel. Why it should have thus deserved the name of 'Satan's throne,' so emphatically repeated a second time at the end of this verse, 'where Satan dwelleth,' must remain one of the unsolved riddles of these Epistles."—E. R. C.]

And thou holdest fast My name.—Revelation and knowledge of the essence and governance of Christ. Düsterdieck, on the other hand, in accordance with a widely diffused and inevident interpretation: The true objective Person of Christ, together with its riches and glory. The same expositor denies that confession is intended, as De Wette maintains. The church has already given proof of this, its holding fast of the name of Jesus, in a time of tribulation and martyrdom, when it was tempted to deny and would not.*

My faith; *i. e.,* belief in Christ, resting upon His faithfulness. Objective genitive; ch. xiv. 12, and other passages. Comp. Rom. iii. 25, 26. [This interpretation is not required by the con-

struction. Πίστις may be regarded as having been used concretely, as in Jude 3. *etc.*, and the genitive as that of the source.—E. R. C.]

In which Antipas.—We follow the reading αἷς, supported by Cod. B. and adopted by Griesbach.* This reading has been objected to, probably on the ground that the church generally was faithful. Accordingly, αἷς has been omitted —a proceeding which gave rise to still greater difficulties, on which comp. Düsterdieck (p 158). Again, an explanatory ἐν has been prefixed to αἷς. On the plays upon the word Antipas, comp. Düsterdieck ('Αντί-πας, against all; Anti-papa, or ἰσότατρον == Athanasianism; Pergamus == Alexandria). De Wette: "A certain Antipas (Antipater) must have suffered martyrdom in Pergamus some time previously." The later martyrologies announce that in the time of Domitian, Antipas, bishop of Pergamus, was killed by being placed in an iron image of a bull, heated red-hot. Tertullian mentions the martyr Antipas, taking the name, most probably, from our passage. Eusebius (*Hist. eccles.* iv. 15) cites three other martyrs of Pergamus. Hengstenberg conjectures that the symbolical name, *against all* (Saskerides†), denotes Timothy. Ebrard ironically expatiates upon this view (p.174). Consistent symbolical interpretation may lead to attempts at the interpretation of names; but consistent symbolical interpretation does not demand that the names of the seven cities should also be interpreted.

Ver. 14. A few things against thee.—We must not regard this as a *litote* and understand the opposite to what is said (Heinrich).

Thou hast there them.—Members of the church are intended, but not the whole church. It has not completely purified itself from these people; has been negligent in church discipline.

Who hold the doctrine of Balaam—Persistently hold it fast, κρατοῦντας. The combination of the history of Balaam, Num. xxii. 25 sqq., and the story of the avenging war of Israel against Midian, ch. xxxi., served for a foundation to a Jewish tradition to the effect that Balaam taught Balak how, by the institution of idolatrous sacrificial feasts, he might entice the Israelites to fornication and thus corrupt them.‡ It was a doctrine, not in the sense of a system, but as a maxim. And whilst Balaam hoped for outward gain, and the Nicolaitans, on the other hand, were following an Antinomian principle, we find, together with the coincidence of the two names, a certain difference which we have previously pointed out.

[**To cast a stumbling-block before the children of Israel, to eat idol offerings.**— "There are two words which claim here special consideration, σκάνδαλον and εἰδωλόθυτον. Σκάνδαλον, a later form of σκανδάληθρον. . . . and σκανδαλίζω . . . occur only, I believe, in the Sacred Scriptures, the Septuagint and the New

---

In John xvi. 8) affords too narrow a basis upon which to build any hypothesis as to the general use of even the latter word—most certainly nothing can be gathered from it as to the symbolic force of ῥομφαία. The most natural interpretation of ῥομφαία (comp. ver. 16, i. 16, vi. 8, xix. 15, 21) is that it is symbolic of the destroying power of Christ's word —it implies external penal judgment; (see also Isa. xi. 4; 2 Thess. ii. 8). A comparison of the declaration of the following verse, "where Satan's throne is," with 2 Thess. ii. 8, where it is declared that "the Lord shall consume with the Spirit (*i. e.,* sword) of His mouth. . . . him, whose coming is after the working of Satan," may shed light upon the use of this designation in this connection.—E. R. C.]

* [The Am. Ed. would suggest that, by the expression *My name* in this place, and in ch. iii. 8, is meant *Christ Himself* in all His offices. Two meanings of the term ὄνομα seem to prevail in the New Testament. 1. The verbal expression (title) which designates any person or thing, as in Matt. i. 21, x. 2, *etc.* 2. The personality itself, as in Matt. xii. 21; John i. 12, ii. 23; Acts iii. 16 (*bis.*), iv. 12; Rom. x. 13. *etc.* To this class belongs the term when it occurs in such phrases as (1) *for My name's* sake (Matt. x. 22, etc.) *i. e.,* for *My* sake; (2) *in My* (or *Thy*) name (Matt. xxiv. 5; John xvii. 12, *etc.*, as the representative of *My* (or *Thy*) personality. A third sense is probably found, ch. iii. 1, where it seems to indicate *reputation*; this sense, however, may be resolved into the first. The meaning assigned by Lange is unsupported by argument and is altogether unprecedented. The meaning suggested above is in accordance with a prevalent use of the term, and is consistent with the context.—E. R. C.]

* [" As the shorter text runs (omitting αἷς, and probably also if we read the rais of the Cod. Sin., 'Αντιπας is regarded as indeclinable, which circumstance has apparently led to all the perplexing varieties of reading." ALFORD.—E. R. C.]
† Why not : *offering resistance—the whole man ?*
‡ [" Certainly it is not expressly asserted in Num. xxxi. 16, that it was *Balak* whom Balaam advised to use this agency against Israel; but the narrative almost implies it. Balak was in power, and was the most likely person to authorize and put in force the scheme." ALFORD.—E. R. C.]

Testament, and in such writings as are immediately dependent upon these (see Suicer, S. V.); being almost always in them employed in a tropical sense; Judith v. 1, Lev. xxix. 14, are exceptions. Σκάνδαλον is properly a trap (joined often with παγίς, Josh. xxiii. 13; Ps. cxl. 9; Rom. xi. 9), or more precisely that part of the trap on which the bait was laid, and the touching of which caused the trap to close upon its prey; then generally any loop or noose set in the path, which should entangle the foot of the unwary walker and cause him to stumble and fall; σκάνδαλον == πρόσκομμα (Rom. xiv. 13) and σκανδαλίζειν == προσκόπτειν (Matt. iv. 6; Rom. ix. 32); and next, any stone or hindrance of any kind (Hesychius explains it by ἐμποδισμός), which should have the same effect (1 Pet. ii. 7). Satan, then, as *the* Tempter, is the great placer of 'scandals,' 'stumbling-blocks,' or 'offences,' in the path of men; his sworn servants, a Balaam, or a Jeroboam (1 Kin. xiv. 16), are the same consciously. All of us unconsciously, by careless walking, by seeking what shall please ourselves rather than edify others (1 Cor. viii. 10), are in danger of being the same; all are deeply concerned in the warning of Matt. xviii. 7. Εἰδωλόθυτον is a New Testament word to express what the heathen sacrifices were, as they presented themselves to the eye of a Christian or a Jew, namely things offered unto idols. The Gentiles themselves expressed the same by ἱερόθυτον (which word occurs 1 Cor. x. 28, according to the better reading, St. Paul there assuming a Gentile to be speaking, and using, if not an honorable, yet at any rate, a neutral word), or by θεόθυτον, which the Greek purists preferred." TRENCH.—E. R. C.]

Ver. 15. **So hast thou also.**—De Wette explains καὶ σύ as indicative of a comparison with Ephesus. Düsterdieck remarks: "It either refers to Balak, or, which is more probable, to the ancient congregation of the children of Israel. Yet this too would be a reference to Balak." This fact, at all events, is indicated; viz.: that in Pergamus, as well as elsewhere, two kindred forms of Antinomianism occur. It is also intimated that the sect-name of the Nicolaitans had its own independent origin in a misinterpretation of the doctrine of Christian liberty. This lax tendency, on the ground of a misunderstood liberty, was springing up in Rome and Corinth at the time of the Pauline Epistles to the Christians of those cities; it had attained further development at the time of the pastoral Epistles, and subsequently received, among the methodical Anomians, the sect-name of Nicolaitanism. At the time of the Epistle of Jude and the Apocalypse it was illustrated by the Old Testament history of Balaam, an etymological kinship of names aiding this comparison. This is more probable than the supposition that the Greek name is a mere translation of the Hebrew Balaam. The practice of the different factions of Antinomianism (Balaamites, Nicolaitans, the fanatical school of Jezebel) amounted to the same thing, viz.: disorderly conduct under the cloak of liberty; the first specific mark of this disorderliness being a participation in heathen sacrificial banquets; the second, connected with the first, a sexual laxity amounting to actual unchastity.

Ver. 16. **Repent, therefore.** — This repentance, as the painful self-prostration and stirring of the church, must result in its cleansing from Nicolaitanism. ["This command is addressed not only to the Nicolaitans, but to the Church, which did not, like that of Ephesus, hate them, but apparently tolerated them." ALFORD. — E. R. C.]

But if not.—The threat appears much milder than that addressed to Ephesus.

I will come unto thee, i. e., upon thee. How?

And will war against them.—This act will be a humiliation for the church, inasmuch as it accomplishes directly, without the church's instrumentality, what the church itself should effect—thus suspending, to a degree, the church's authority, and making it appear in the light of a dependent church, taking away its independence. But how shall this be done? Grotius: Prophets are to accomplish what the bishop has neglected to do. Calovius; The Lord will act through another bishop. The fact is, the Lord comes to the slothful individual church with the spirit of the metropolitan church; and, when it becomes utterly sluggish, He comes to it with theocratico-hierarchical authority, or by means of separatist contrasts.

With the sword of My mouth.—This is indicative of a spiritual conflict and victory through the word and the Spirit of God. It has no reference, therefore, to the avenging sword which came upon the misguided Israelites (Ewald, De Wette, and others); particularly, in view of the contrast between the Old and the New Covenant. The sword of the angel that stood in the way of Balaam can scarcely come into consideration, for this reason, if for none other—because that passage in the life of Balaam preceded his actual sin.*

Ver. 17. **Of the hidden manna.**—The victor in Pergamus is the recipient of two promises which, however, constitute a substantial unity. The hidden manna stands contrasted with the impure communion of idolatrous sacrifices, and hence, as well as in accordance with the Johannean idea (John vi.), characterizes the enjoyment of the highest, heavenly communion with Christ and the holy and blessed, as the partaking of a manna which is hidden as yet—perhaps like that which was kept for the Jewish Sabbath—or as the mystery of the inner life of blessedness. With this manna, **the white stone** with the **new name** corresponds. The white stone is that acquittal in the judgment which shall be based upon a recognition of the verification and righteousness of the new life; and the new name is the distinct individual personality of the new life; every beatified spirit has a particular and unique consciousness of this personality—a consciousness known, in this uniqueness, to none but the recipient himself (ch. xix. 12).

Different interpretations of the manna: The Lord's Supper; Spiritual refreshments; Justifica-

---

* [See note on ver. 12. The interpretation of Lange, in this and the preceding paragraph, requires us both to regard that which was manifestly spoken of as a threat against the persistently unrepentant, as a promise of highest blessing; and to take Ἀολεμεῖν in the altogether unnatural and unprecedented sense of indicating the convincing influence of the Spirit. Comp. comment on ver. 12.—E. R. C.]

tion; The manna in the Ark of the Covenant, which has been hidden since the destruction of the Temple; Christ; Heavenly bread. ["There can, I think, be no doubt that allusion is here made to the manna which, at God's express command, Moses caused to be laid up before the Lord in the sanctuary (Ex. xvi. 32–34; cf. Heb. ix. 4). This manna, as being thus laid up, obtained the name of 'hidden' . . This 'hidden manna' . . . represents a benefit pertaining to the future Kingdom of glory. . . . I would not indeed affirm that this promise has not prelibations which will be tasted in the present time. . . The words imply that, however hidden now, it shall not remain hidden evermore; and the best commentary on them is to be found at 1 Cor. ii. 9; 1 John iii. 2." TRENCH.—E. R. C.]

Interpretations of the *white stone:* The glorified body; Analogue of the names on the breastplate of the High Priest—priestly dignity, therefore; A reference to the heavenly reward; *Tessera hospitalis;* The stone used in casting lots for succession in the priestly function; The glory of victory.

The two meanings which attached to the white stone among the Greeks, viz.: acquittal in judgment and the award of some rank or dignity—are, manifestly, most intimately connected. Justification in the final judgment must, however, be distinguished from the justification of faith, though the two are connected and agree in the possession of a negative and a positive element (*absolutio; adoptio* in the principial sense; in the sense of consummation).

Interpretations of the *name:* The name of God; Consecrated to God; Son of God, or elect person. Most commentators: The victor's own name. This is *new* as the pure expression of the new, heavenly life, in antithesis to the old conventional name, meaningless in many cases, and often a name of shame.

[The remarks of Trench (*Ep. to the Seven Churches*, pp. 170–181) on *the white stone* and *the new name* are worthy of the highest consideration. He repudiates the idea that these symbols "are borrowed from *heathen* antiquity," declaring that "this Book moves exclusively within the circle of sacred, that is of Jewish, imagery and symbols; nor is the explanation of its symbols in any case to be sought beyond this circle." Following Züllig (*Offenb. Johannis*, Vol. I., pp. 408–454), he suggests that the ψῆφος λευκή may be, not a white pebble, but the Urim and Thummim —probably a diamond, a precious stone shining white. The "*new name written, which no man knoweth saving he that receiveth it (the stone),*" he identifies with the *new name* of Christ ch. iii. 12, and suggests that it was symbolized by what was written on the Urim (probably the holy Tetragrammaton) which no one knew except the High Priest to whose charge it was committed.— E. R. C.]

FOURTH EPISTLE. THYATIRA.

Ch. ii. 18–29.

Ver. 18. **Thyatira.**—In Lydia, between Pergamus and Sardis, a provincial city; now called Akhissar. See the Encyclopædias and Books of Travel. Lydia was a woman of Thyatira, Acts xvi. 14. This Lydia may be referred neither to

the loving zeal of the church nor to Jezebel (Düsterdieck). For a mention of wavering views in regard to the elements of the church and worthless views concerning the bishop, see Düsterdieck.

[The **Son of God.**—"Our Lord thus names Himself here, in accordance with the spirit of that which is to follow; ver. 27 being from Ps. ii., in which it is written, 'The Lord hath said unto me, *thou art my Son,*'" (ALFORD); comp. vers. 26, 27, with Ps. ii. 8, 9. The reason of the reference to Ps. ii. may possibly be found in a comparison of ver. 20 with Ps. ii. 1–3, and the history of Jezebel, 1 Kings xvi. 31; 2 Kings ix. 37. The Jezebel of the Old Testament was a heathen, a king's daughter, and a queen; she took counsel against the Lord, and seduced the people of God to iniquity. This interpretation requires us to suppose that the Jezebel of ver. 20 occupied a position analogous to that of her Old Testament type. Symbolically (on the hypothesis that the churches represent different ages of the Universal Church) she may represent a world-power, professedly converted and assuming the position of a teacher, introducing idolatry and impurity into the Church,— E. R. C.]

His eyes like as a flame of fire.—With reference to the fanaticism in Thyatira. His eyes pierce through the sphere of spirit, and perceive the impure motives of all fanaticism, be it hierarchic or sectarian, ascetic or libertine; and this with a view to making it manifest and judging it.*

And His feet.—He, "Who, with His feet like unto brass, tramples on all that is unclean and inimical." (Düsterdieck.) This, however, is not the way in which fanaticism is judged. It is made manifest in its nothingness by the feet of Christ, in their holy, glowing motion, passing over its imbecility and worthlessness and resolving them into themselves. To the extent that this nuisance is the originator of moral scandals, it is broken in pieces with the iron sceptre as heathenish (ver. 27).

Ver. 19. **I know thy works.**—These are subdivided into four fundamental traits: *love and faithfulness*—the one showing itself in a loving *service* to those requiring help; the other manifested in *steadfastness* under persecutions and temptations. To these is superadded the fact of the church's growth—that its last works are more than the first. The opposite of Ephesus (Düsterdieck).

Ver. 20. **But I have against thee.**—There is a connection between the very vitality of the church of Thyatira and the fact that it suffers itself to be dazzled by the fiery semblance of life in the fanaticism of Jezebel and her followers; that it is unwatched on that side.

The woman Jezebel.—As the Anomians were formerly traced back to Balaam, so here they are traced to Jezebel, the wife of Ahab, 1 Kings xvi. sqq.

* [The sins of Jezebel and her followers can hardly be styled "fanaticism;" they were lapses into idolatry and impurity (see note on ver. 20). The eyes of flame are not only indicative of spirit-searching power (ver. 23) but also of the wrath of the Son of God, the Husband of the Church, flaming against those guilty of spiritual, as well as physical, adultery.—E. R. C.]

The individual traits of the description call for the conclusion that Jezebel was a religious fanatic, who claimed to be a prophetess and had founded a school of Antinomianism, in which an impure intercourse of the sexes was reduced to a religious system, and clothed in the garb of pious enthusiasm. The name is symbolical, but scarcely the sex of the person. It should be observed that the seduction to fornication occupies the foremost place in this instance, and that much more stress is laid upon it than upon the eating of idolatrous sacrifices.* Here, therefore, we have the primitive type of a story that has been often repeated by isolated Gnostic sects even down to the present day.

Other interpretations: 1. Jezebel was the wife of the bishop (Grotius and others); hence the reading τὴν γυναῖκά σου. 2. Heresy personified, or the Nicolaitan false teachers (Vitringa, Hengstenberg, and others). 3. A woman really called Jezebel (Wolf, Bengel). 4. The Jewish synagogue (Züllig).

The fornication to which the Old Testament Jezebel was the seducer, was connected with the service of Baal and Astarte; Jezebel had brought the worship of these gods with her from Sidon and propagated it in Israel (see 2 Kings ix. 22, and other passages). Hengstenberg conjectures that the ancient Jezebel was a demonically inspired prophetess of Baal.

Ver. 21. And I gave her time.—Ebrard groundlessly takes this in a present sense; rendering it thus—from this time she shall have yet another respite for repentance.—She has not made use of her respite; **she willeth not to repent.**—The disorder, therefore, has already lasted some time, and though the church, as a church, has suffered its continuance, admonitions to repent have not been wanting. We need not conclude from this, however, that John has previously issued a written reprimand (Ewald. Nor does John here speak as a bishop).

Ver. 22. Behold, I cast her into a bed.—The punishment, whose prefacing with *behold* indicates its severity and speediness, is, in its ironical expression, conformable to the sin; just as the cup of intoxication is poured out for the intoxicated. A bed of torment corresponds with the bed of fornication.

According to Lyra and others, κλίνη denotes the punishment of Hell; while most commentators regard it as indicative of the bed of sickness, with reference to Ps. xli. 3. [A bed of sickness, physical and symbolical, the result of her own impurity, may be intended.—E. R. C.] But whether such a menace of sickness is intended to be conveyed here is exceedingly doubtful. By the bed we understand an insulated sectarianism, in which Jezebel and her followers

will be the instruments of their own destruction; the threatened casting into this bed, therefore, we apprehend as a threat of excommunication, to be executed by the Spirit of the Lord in and along with the church (1 Cor. v. 3 sqq.), if she do not thoroughly repent.* We emphasize as follows: Behold, I cast *her* into a bed, and *those* that commit adultery with her—**into great tribulation.**—"For the destruction of the flesh," St. Paul says. After its excision from the church, the school, as a sect, must necessarily be given over to eccentricity, discord, the pangs of remorse, and despair, to say nothing of the disgrace which would attach to it, and the censure of the world.

Those who commit adultery with her.—The fornication is now characterized as adultery, for together with the actual occurrences of this sort, religious apostasy, previously present in germ, is thus symbolically designated; in this case, it is apostasy from Christ and from the Spirit of His Church. *With her.* In fellowship with her; as her companions and followers.

Except they repent.—An ultimatum preceding excommunication, such as was addressed to the false teachers in the Galatian Church, Gal. i.

Of her [αὐτῆς=] **works.**

Ver. 23. And I will slay her children.—According to Grotius and others, these are actual children of fornication—as such, however, they could not be the objects of so severe a threat. According to Düsterdieck and many others, they are the previously mentioned companions of Jezebel, the μοιχεύοντες. Ebrard: "The Jezebel brood, in which iniquity threatens to propagate itself in time to come." These children are plainly distinguished from the immediate companions of Jezebel, both by name and by the form of the threatened punishment. They are the second generation of disorderly sectarianism, in which the whole power of spiritual and physical death becomes manifest; and there is an unlimited perspective into futurity in the threat—hence it is declared that **all the churches** shall know this Divine judgment.

With [Lange: **By the power of**] **death.**—Sin, when it is finished, bringeth forth death (Jas. i. 15). Explications of ἐν θανάτῳ: 1. Death is Hell: 2. Pestilence (Septuag. Ezek. xxxiii. 27); 3. The Hebrew formula: מוֹת־יוּמָת, as the penalty of adultery, Lev. xx. 10. Düsterdieck urges cogent reasons against the supposition, entertained by Hengstenberg, that the passage in Leviticus is alluded to. Ἐν signalizes θάνατος as the instrument of killing—hence, as deadly power. [" A strong Hebraistic expression, meaning that he would certainly destroy them." BARNES.—"Others find a reference to the two sweeping catastrophes which overtook the Baal priests and votaries at exactly that period of Jewish history to which the mention of Jezebel here points (1 Kings xviii. 40; 2 Kings x. 25). To me it seems no more than a threat that their doom should be a signal one, that they should

---

*[It is true that "the seduction to fornication occupies the foremost place," but it is intimately conjoined with the eating of things sacrificed to idols. This conjunction, together with the distinct reference to the Old Testament Jezebel, implies that the fornication itself was connected with idolatry. Now, whilst it is conceivable that Christian fanaticism (i. e., fanaticism starting from Christianity) may have assumed the form of an improper intercourse of the sexes, it is utterly inconceivable that it could have assumed that of idolatry. Far better is it to regard Jezebel as a heathen at heart, and those seduced by her, as errorists led astray by her heathen teaching, than as fanatics. She may indeed have been a *heathen*, but not a *Christian*, fanatic.—E. R. C.]

*[The *Church* excommunicates; the woe here threatened is one that Christ Himself threatens and inflicts. Excision from the visible Church is not necessarily implied, but rather that spiritual corruption and death which follow a withdrawal of the influences of the Spirit.—E. R. C.]

not die the common death of all men, nor be visited after the visitation of all (Num. xvi. 29), but leaving the precise manner of that doom undefined." Trench.—E. R. C.]
And all the churches shall know.— Düsterdieck: "Every Divine judgment upon the world is a manifestation of the Lord's glory, resulting, in accordance with the Divine intention, in the advancement and strengthening of believers in knowledge." —They *shall know*, especially, that God is the Holy One, that He is pure Light, and that He knows and judges all impurity, even when arrayed in the closest semblance of holiness.

All the churches — congregations — in the whole Church. We can say, with Grotius, "The Asiatic churches, if we only do not apprehend them externally, but as types of the whole Church."

That I am He.—The absoluteness of God is here indicated, from the special point of view that it is He who tries and searches the reins and hearts, the whole inner life, and the innermost disposition of man. ["This is clearly a claim to Omniscience, and as it is the Lord Jesus who speaks in all these epistles, it is a full proof that He claims this for Himself." Barnes.— E. R. C.] Grotius and Bengel make a distinction in the concrete unity of the expression, interpreting *loins* as the lusts or passions, *hearts* as the thoughts; this is in opposition to the unitous sense of the passage, in which, at the utmost, a harmonious contrast is indicated.

To you, to each.—Address to the guilty ones. Within the more general chastisement, the judgment upon each individual shall be proportioned to his works. [According to your works.—"This promise, or this threat, for it may be either (is it not both?—E. R. C.) is one which we commonly keep at this time too much in the background; but it is one which we should press on ourselves and others with the same emphasis wherewith Christ and His Word presses it upon us all (Ps. lxii. 13; Matt. xvi. 27; Rom. ii. 6; Job xxxiv. 11; Prov. xxiv. 12; Jer. xxii. 19). It is indeed one of the gravest mischiefs which Rome has bequeathed to us, that in a reaction and protest, itself absolutely necessary, against the false emphasis which she puts on works, unduly trusting therein to share with Christ's merits in our justification, we often fear to place upon them the true; being, as they are, to speak with St. Bernard, the '*via regni*,' however little the '*causa regnandi*;' though here too it must of course never be forgotten that it is only the good tree which brings forth good fruit; and that no tree is good until Christ has made it so." Trench.—E. R. C.]

Ver. 24. But unto you I say, [the rest in Thyatira, *etc.*—The *and* of the E. V. is omitted; see Text. and Gram. Notes.—E. R. C.]. Address to individuals who, as such (not as members of the church as a body), are guiltless. They are characterized by two marks. First, they have not this erroneous doctrine; and, secondly, they have hitherto not known the pretended depths in it *as depths of Satan*, as they express themselves now that their eyes are opened. The objectionableness of the doctrine in question was clear to them, but not its Satanic depth, its nature, and

operation—ruinous to souls, poisoning the words of truth, fatal to spiritual life.

Interpretations: These false teachers boasted that they knew the depths of Satan (Neander, Hengstenberg). These false teachers, like the Gnostics, boasted that they knew the depths of life and, especially, of the Godhead; but the Apocalyptist sarcastically reverses this boast by intimating that their pretended depths are depths of Satan (Grotius and many others).

"As they say," according to Vitringa, refers purely to *the depths*; this restriction, however, seems somewhat violent, and it is more probable that the innocent individual members of the church have themselves now recognized the greatness of the evil, and sarcastically handle the claim of the false teachers.

["It was the characteristic of the falsely called γνῶσις to boast of its βάθεα, or depths, of Divine things. . . . We may safely therefore refer the expression οὐκ ἔγνωσαν τὰ βάθεα to the heretics spoken of. But it is not so clear to whom, as their subject, the words ὡς λέγουσιν are to be appropriated; and, again, *whose* word τοῦ σατανᾶ is, whether that (1) of our Lord, (2) of the heretics, or (3) of the Christians addressed. If ὡς λέγουσιν belongs to the *Christians*, then the sense will be, that they, the Christians, called the βάθεα of the heretics, the βάθεα τοῦ σατανᾶ, and were content to profess their ignorance of them. So Andr., Areth., Heinr., Züllig, Ebrard: and so far would be true enough; but the sentence would be left very flat and pointless, and altogether inconsistent in its tone with the solemn and pregnant words of the rest of the message. If ὡς λέγουσιν belongs to the *heretics*, we have our choice between two views of τοῦ σατανᾶ: either (1) that the heretics themselves called their own mysteries τὰ β. τοῦ σατανᾶ. But this, though held by Hengst., and even by Neander . . . as a possible alternative, and recently by Trench, can hardly be so, seeing that the words surely would not bear the sense thus assigned to them, viz.: that they could go deeper than and outwit Satan in his own kingdom: and seeing, moreover, that no such formula, or any resembling it, is found as used by the ancient Gnostic heretics: or (2) that the ὡς λέγουσιν applies only to the word βάθεα, and that, when according to *their* way of speaking, τοῦ θεοῦ should have followed (cf. 1 Cor ii. 10), the Lord in indignation substitutes τοῦ σατανᾶ. This has been the view taken by most commentators, e. g., Corn.-à-Lapide, Ribera, Grot., Calov., Wetst., Vitr., Bengel, Wolf, Eichhorn, Ewald, De W., Stern, Düsterd. And, it appears to me, that this alone comes in any measure up to the requirements of the passage, in intensity of meaning and solemnity, as well as in veri-similitude." Alford. See, as representing other views, Trench and Barnes *in loc.*—E. R. C.]

I cast not upon you any other burden. —Our first effort must be to gather the meaning of the *other burden* from the epistle itself. The sinful toleration of Jezebel must now be exchanged for the opposite course, *i. e.*, the excommunication of the false teachers, unless they repent. And this, indubitably, is a painful and heavy task, a *burden*; the Apostle will, however, lay none other on the church.

Explanations: 1. No other suffering than that which ye already bear (Bengel and others); including the threats (Ewald). 2. No other obligation than the one indicated—to prohibit the eating of idolatrous sacrifices, *etc.*, Acts xv. 28. Not the entire Mosaic law, therefore. The former of these interpretations is too indefinite, the latter too far-fetched.* Equally valueless is the interpretation of Grotius: *Jactant illi se rerum multarum cognitione, eam a vobis non exigo* (gnosis, then, is the ἄλλο βάρος!); Bengel: As Jezebel was burden enough to them; Eichhorn gives a still different explanation, see De Wette.

By the following promise, we see what they are to do. They are to combat the new heathenism arising in that sectarian school; and to wield the iron sceptre of the Messiah, in accordance with the promise, yet in a spiritual sense.

Ver. 25. **But that which ye have.**—The ἔχειν is to be converted into a κρατεῖν in the manner indicated.

Hold fast (have more than ever). Seek to hold it fast in its whole consistency. They need not, therefore, work themselves up to another stand-point, but must consistently work out their actual spiritual life (ver. 19). ["The aorist is more vivid and imperative than would be the present; it sets forth not so much the continuing habit, as the renewed and determined grasp of every intervening moment of the space prescribed." ALFORD.—E. R. C.]

[**Until I shall come.**—"The ἂν gives an uncertainty when the time shall be, which we cannot convey in our language." ALFORD.—E. R. C.]

Ver. 26. **And he that conquereth.**—The promise, in this case also, is in perfect harmony with the tenor of the epistle. The overcoming is modified here by the keeping of Christ's works to the end, or to the goal of the works themselves in their perfect consistency. In τηρεῖν, we find, on the one hand, the acknowledgment that they occupy the right stand-point, and, on the other, the demand that they should keep it pure, after the example of Christ, and as His instruments. Together with the eschatological goal, therefore, reference is had to the ideal goal of perfect Christian development. The works of Christ, which are particularly meant, however, are here those of purifying severity, ver. 27. The works of His people must in their purity be *His* works, and this in antithesis, also, to the works of Jezebel.

Power over the nations [heathen].—This, according to Düsterdieck, is to be fulfilled, "when the βασιλεία is set in operation at the Coming of the Lord." A one-sided adjournment of the promises to the day of the Parousia, in accordance with Meyer's method. It is apos-

tolic doctrine that the Parousia does not bring the beginning of the blessedness and glory of the new life, but their final consummation. It is so with the preceding promises and so with this. The power of Christianity over the heathen world, which power is to be perfected at the end of the world, begins with the victorious power of the Christian spirit over heathen works and ways.*

Ver. 27. **And he shall rule** [shepherdize] **them with an iron rod.**—Neither can the wielding of an iron sceptre be adjourned to the end of the world. This sceptre unmistakably denotes the element of severe discipline in the shepherdizing of the flock; a preponderance of spiritual power over the carnal mind (see the parable of the leaven) is also expressed by the antithesis of the iron sceptre and the earthen vessels dashed in pieces by it. Of course, the dashing in pieces is a spiritual act, and one that is performed only in proportion to the resistance offered.

Düsterdieck, in consequence of his peculiar views, fails to recognize the element of truth in Grotius' explanation: *Evolvam illum in gradum Presbyteri, ut judicet de iis, qui non Christiane, sed ἐθνικῶς vivunt;* and ῥάβδ. σιδ. = *verbum dei, cujus pars est excommunicatio.* Düsterdieck likewise denies that there is any reference to the conversion of the heathen, either separately or in connection with the idea of the future royal rule.

Shepherdize [ποιμαίνειν] is the Septuagint rendering of רֹעֵם, Ps. ii. 9. Alcasar regarded the iron rod as significant of the bishop's staff or crosier. "Brightman thought it denoted the power which Protestant princes have exercised over popish cloisters," *etc.*, (De Wette).

As I also.—The personal Christ as the entire Christ in His Church.

Ver. 28. **And I will give him.**—The morning-star is to be a recompense of that *purity* which is the fundamental requirement of the whole epistle. According to 2 Pet. i. 19, the *morning-star* symbolizes the full dawn of the New-Testament day. According to Rev. xxii. 16, Christ, on the way of His speedy Advent, is the bright Morning-star. The promise, therefore, is that the pure and unadulterated Christian, as a victor over fanaticisms, shall, in advance of others, behold the morning-star of new time, the last time, the Coming of the Lord, as if that morning-star were his own; nay, he shall even point to the morning-star as the object of his prophecy. He shall stand "in the morning radiance of eternity," in the full enjoyment of Christian hope, Christian progress, the true ante-celebration of the Coming of Christ.

Interpretations: 1. The glorified body of Christ; 2. The devil, with reference to Is. xiv. 12; 3. The king of Babylon; 4. Christ; 5. The *gloria illustris*, the heavenly δόξα; starry radiance.

["It is observable that it is not said that He

---

* [The view thus characterized is supported by a comparison of the sins of the Jezebelites with Acts xv. 28, 29. In that passage abstinence from these very sins is enjoined, *viz.:* ἀπέχεσθαι εἰδωλοθύτων ... καὶ πορνείας, and is characterized as a βάρος in almost the same language here employed. In support of the view advocated by Lange, it must be admitted, are the words of our Lord, ver. 20, "thou *sufferest* that woman," *etc.*, implying the duty of casting her out of the church. The reason assigned for this interpretation in the following paragraph is futile: The "iron sceptre" was not promised to the Church Militant, as an organism, but to individuals; and not to individuals in the present state of conflict, but to those who, at "the end," should appear as conquerors (vers. 25-27).—E. R. C.]

* [That Christianity possesses a power over the heathen world is not denied; the power, however, is not that of "the iron sceptre" (ver. 2)—the power of government. The adjournment of these promises to the day of the Parousia is in accordance with the express language of Christ Himself. See the preceding note, and the Excursus on the Basileia, ii.; (comp. Luke xix. 17).—E. R. C.]

would *make* him *like* the morning-star, as in Dan. xii. 3, nor that he would be compared with the morning-star, like the king of Babylon, Isa. xiv. 12; nor that he would resemble a star which Balaam says he saw in the far distant future, Num. xxiv. 17. The idea seems to be, that the Saviour would give him something that would resemble that morning planet in beauty and splendor — perhaps meaning that it would be placed as a gem in his diadem and would sparkle on his brow—bearing some such relation to Him Who is called 'the Sun of Righteousness,' as the morning-star does to the glorious sun on his rising. If so, the meaning would be, that he would receive a beautiful ornament, bearing a near relation to the Redeemer Himself as a bright Sun—a pledge that the darkness was past—but one whose beams would melt away into the superior light of the Redeemer Himself, as the beams of the morning-star are lost in the superior glory of the Sun." BARNES.—E. R. C.]

FIFTH EPISTLE. SARDIS.

Ch. iii. 1–6.

Ver. 1. **Sardis**, once the wealthy capital of Lydia, and the city of Crœsus, is now a poor village, bearing the name of Sart. An earthquake took place here during the reign of Tiberius. Melito was bishop of Sardis about the middle of the second century. For particulars, see Commentaries and Books of Travel.

From the description given of the church, it appears that its members, with the exception of a small remnant, were almost entirely secularized. Though occupying a correct position in respect of creed and worship—having the name of life, therefore—the faith of the church was a dead faith, and its life of that worldly form which is always accompanied by the most manifold moral defilements. Yet the reproach of death is not absolute; otherwise, there could be no question of a part that was in danger of dying or, still less, of a vital strength that should re-animate this part, the elements of which strength the angel must find in the church itself.

"Ewald's conjecture, that the Christians of Sardis had, on account of their heathenish life, not been molested by the heathen, and that this is the reason why the epistle does not speak of θλίψις and ὑπομονή, is scarcely in accordance with the text." (DUESTERDIECK). Even if [as Dü-sterdieck avers] "the church had enough of the semblance of Christianity to preclude the friendship of the heathen," there is no foundation for the assertion that Ewald's conjecture is not in accordance with the text, save the bare fact that it is not expressly laid down in the text.

That hath the seven Spirits of God.— The seven fundamental forms of the revelation of Christ, in the seven fundamental forms of the working of God's Spirit, with Whom He (Christ) is anointed without measure; corresponding to the seven stars or fundamental forms of the Church. Why is Christ thus described here? Explanations: Because of His omniscience, penetrating the innermost recesses (De W. and others). But this would be a repetition of the idea set forth by the eyes like a flame of fire (see Thyatira). Un-

limited power to punish and reward (Hengstenberg). But the Seven Spirits are not Seven Spirits of judgment. They denote the *holy all-sidedness* of Christ and Christianity, here as opposed to the *false all-sidedness* of a sham Christianity, which is conformed to the world. Inasmuch as they are indicative of the *fullness of the Spirit of Christ*, they are proclaimed to a church which, from its lack of spiritual life, is at the point of death. Bengel: The Seven Spirits have reference to the vital forces which Christ proposes to communicate to the church.

[By the Seven Spirits, as was set forth in the note on ch. i. 5, we must understand the Holy Ghost, "seven-fold in His operations." Christ is spoken of as having the Spirit, not because in the days of the flesh, as the Son of man, He was anointed with the Spirit without measure (John iii. 34), but because, as the Son of God, the Spirit of God is His Spirit (Rom. viii. 9), and because He sends the Spirit (John xv. 26, xx. 22; Acts ii. 33), Who acts as His representative (John xv. 18, 26). In reference to the fitness of the assumption of this designation in the address to the Angel of the Church of Sardis, Trench well remarks: "To him and his people, sunken in spiritual deadness and torpor, the lamp of faith waning and almost extinguished in their heart, the Lord presents Himself as One having the fullness of all spiritual gifts; able therefore to revive, able to recover, able to bring back, from the very gates of spiritual death, those who would employ the little last remaining strength which they still retained, in calling, even when thus *in extremis*, upon Him." — E. R. C.]

And the seven stars.—The Spirits and stars are contrasted here. The seven stars must receive their vital light from the Seven Spirits; these latter are also the source whence Sardis must draw its light.* ["Since the *stars are the angels of the seven Churches*' (i. 20), we must see in this combination a hint of the relation between Christ, as the giver of the Holy Spirit, and as the author of a ministry of living men in His Church (Eph. iv. 7-12; John xx. 22, 23; Acts i. 8, xx. 28)." TRENCH.—E. R. C.]

Thy works, that thou hast a name.— We are not to read : *and* that thou, *etc.* Düsterdieck interprets: From thy imperfect works I know that thou, *etc.* The meaning of the passage, however, is, doubtless — the sum of thy works is sham Christianity.

A name.—Several have interpreted this as referring to the fortuitous name of the bishop (Zosimus, *etc.*), or to his office. Others have better interpreted it by referring it to the outward semblance of the church. ["*In name*" (BARNES) ; "*Nominally*" (ALFORD); *thou hast the reputation.*—E. R. C.]

Thou livest.—In accordance with the conception of life in Christ. ["The word *life* is a word that is commonly employed in the New Testament to denote religion, in contradistinction from the natural state of man, which is described as *death* in sin." BARNES.—E. R. C.]

And thou art dead.—Spiritual deadness, as spiritual sleep, indulged in to the furthest

* Comp. Ebrard's polemical suggestion, p. 572. See Düsterdieck, p. 178.

extremity which admits of a waking; hence the admonition of ver. 2. Our passage, particularly, proves that the state of the angel represents the state of the church.

Ver. 2. **Become thou watching.**—This is a stronger term than the simple *awake*. Watchfulness or wakefulness must become as much an attribute of the angel's life as sleep—carelessness, indifferentism—is now.

And strengthen the things which remain.—Here also we must take the angel in his connection with the church. It does not mean, therefore, the remaining good in thy soul (Bengel); nor, the rest of those in the church; but the dying, though not yet dead, life which constitutes the vitality hitherto possessed by the church. Novatianism could only have written: *the ones who remain* [τοὺς λοιποὺς], and it is true that, from another point of view, there would necessarily be a reference to *persons* as constituting the remainder (Ezek. xxxiv. 4). The present passage, however, treats of the general edification of the church, not directly of the special cure of souls. The "official conception" of the angel regards τὰ λοιπά as representative of the laity (Hengst.).

[ALFORD thus writes: "The latter view (that τὰ λοιπά refers to persons), is taken by (Andr., Areth., as reported in Düsterd., but not in Catena) Calov., Vitr., Eichh., De Wette, Stern, Ebrard, Düsterd., Trench, *et al.* And there is nothing in the construction to preclude the view. But if I mistake not, there is in the context. For to assume that the λοιποί could be thus described, would surely be to leave no room for those mentioned with so much praise below, in ver. 4."—E. R. C.]

For I have not found thy works perfect [completed].—*Good* works are not the only ones intended here—at the best, they are still *imperfect*, as a matter of course; nor is the external conduct in general referred to; but the actual collective works as phenomena of the spiritual condition: they are not *complete* before Christ's God; in His light and judgment they lack the impress of the New Testament spirit, the stamp of principial perfection in the purity and sincerity of love. *Pure, ripe, rich* are the predicates of Christ's works and of Christian works in Him.

["The word here employed is not that which we commonly render 'perfect;' not τέλεια, or πεπληρωμένα: so that the Lord contemplates the works prepared and appointed in the providence of God for the faithful man to do as a definite sphere (Eph. ii. 10), which it was his duty and his calling to have *fulfilled* or *filled to the full*, the same image habitually underlying the uses of πληροῦν and πληροῦσθαι (Matt. iii. 15; Rom. xiii. 8). This sphere of appointed duties the Sardian Angel had not fulfilled; not, at least, '*before* God;' for on these last words the emphasis must be laid. Before himself and other men his works may very likely have been '*perfect*,' indeed we are expressly told that he had '*a name to live*,' ver. 1, etc." TRENCH.—E. R. C.]

Ver. 3. **Remember, therefore.**—Not only the reception of the Gospel on the part of the church (how *received*), but also its character as Gospel (how *heard*), is specified by πῶς. In each connection there is a reference to the qualitative nature of living Christianity. The dege-

neration of the subjective keeping of God's word is accompanied by a degeneration of the objective form of truth; orthodoxy itself, when dead, becomes heterodoxy; Thus, not only the receiving, but also the thing received, must be traced back to original (principial) vitality. Dead orthodoxy sinks the doctrine in doctrines, the primary articulation in derived articles. The result of right remembrance, which always constitutes the essence of true repentance, will be a compliance with the following commands.

["This may refer either to some peculiarity in the manner in which the Gospel was conveyed to them—as by the labors of the Apostles, and by the remarkable effusions of the Holy Spirit; or to the ardor and love with which they embraced it; or to the greatness of the favors and privileges conferred on them; or to their own understanding of what the Gospel required, when they were converted. It is not possible to determine in which sense the language is used, but the general idea is plain, that there was something marked and unusual in the way in which they had been led to embrace the Gospel, and that it was highly proper in these circumstances to look back to the days when they gave themselves to Christ." BARNES. "The charge against Sardis is not a perverse holding of untruth, but a heartless holding of the truth; and therefore I cannot but think that the Lord is graciously reminding her of the heartiness, the zeal, the love with which she received the truth at the first." TRENCH.—E. R. C.]

And hold fast and repent.—The distinctions of Bengel are not applicable to this passage (see Düsterdieck).—True holding and keeping is a constant seizing and holding fast; here, a renewed seizing and holding fast that lead to repentance. The significance of the perfect εἴληφας, as contrasted with the aorist ἤκουσας, indicated by Ewald, would have greater weight if λαμβάνειν did not denote the manner of the subjective appropriation.

[**Hold fast.**—"1. The truth which thou didst then receive; 2. What remains of true religion among you. Repent in regard to all that in which you have departed from your views and feelings when you embraced the Gospel." BARNES.—E. R. C.]

If, therefore, thou dost not watch.—Stress is again laid upon the main matter, and ▪ threat connected with its non-observance. The threat itself corresponds with the command. To spiritual sleepers the Lord, as Judge, always comes as a thief in the night (Matt. xxiv. 42). *Spiritual sleepers have lost all perception, by their spiritual senses, of the threatening signs of the development of judgment unto its catastrophe.* As this applies to the judgment at the end of the world, so it also holds good in regard to all preliminary judgments upon whole congregations as well as upon individual souls. Even though there may be an obscure presentiment of judgment, the proximity and actual hour of it take its objects by surprise; the hour is hidden from the sleepers, and the judgment comes upon them in as strange a form ▪ a thief.

Ver. 4. **But thou hast a few ▪▪▪▪▪▪ in Sardis.**—The Lord's righteous verdict always distinguishes between the guilt of communities and the guilt or innocence of individuals; here also the distinction is made. The contrast which the persons indicated in the text present to the dead mass of the church, makes them appear as living members, known to the eye of the Lord by name [comp. John x. 3]; after being made to prostrate themselves under the general verdict, they are relatively excepted from that verdict as individuals.

["In most cases, where error and sin prevail, there may be found a few who are worthy of the Divine commendation; comp. Rom. xi. 4." BARNES.—E. R. C.]

Which have not defiled their garments. —This sentence is not *absolute* praise, inasmuch as it is simply negative; still it is *great* praise, inasmuch as the individuals referred to have withstood the general infection. On the various one-sided explanations of *the garments* (the body, as the garment of the soul; the conscience; the righteousness of faith, the baptismal robe), also Ebrard's interpretation, see Düsterdieck [this commentator regards all such special interpretations as an unwarrantable straining of the text.—TR.]. But neither must we stop at the general conception, *maculari per peccatum* (Lyra), against which Aretius and Vitringa have insisted upon the ideas of life and its actions, or confession and morals. The divine sharp-sightedness of the Lord is proved by the fact that among the Sardians who have the semblance of life, He perceives their defilement or non-defilement by the mere appearance of their life, by their actions. If the works of the majority, in their negative aspect, were formerly characterized as not complete, not perfect, here they are indirectly characterized as polluted, defiled by the filth of worldliness, of earthly-mindedness, of heathenishness; thus Christ passed sentence upon the pious-mouthed Pharisees, judging them from their very words. And so the spotted garments do really refer to the polluted consciences, and, symbolically, to the defiled baptismal robe.

["That *'white raiment'* there [ver. 5] is the garment of glory—this the garment of grace. That incapable of receiving a stain, being part of an inheritance which, in all its parts, is ἀμίαντος (1 Peter i. 4); this, something to which σπίλοι (Eph. v. 27; James iii. 6), μιάσματα (2 Peter ii. 20), μολυσμοί (2 Cor. vii. 1), can only too easily adhere. . . . This, itself a wedding garment (Matt. xxii. 11, 12), but not *necessarily* identical with the fine linen, clean and white, the righteousness of saints (Rev. xix. 8), is put on at our entrance by baptism into the Kingdom of grace; that at our entrance by the resurrection into the Kingdom of glory." TRENCH. "There can be little doubt that the simpler and more general explanation is the right one; viz.: who have not sullied the purity of their Christian life by falling into sin." ALFORD. So also BARNES.—E. R. C.]

And they shall walk with Me in white. —The reward of these is appropriate to their conduct, yet far superior to it. "The white robes, with their 'bright hue of victory' (Bengel), are peculiar to the inhabitants of Heaven (ver. 5: ch. vi. 11; vii. 9; xix. 8). Those who keep their garments undefiled in this earthly life, shall walk with Christ (μετ' ἐμοῦ, compare

Luke xxiii. 43; John xvii. 24) in white robes, living, thus adorned, *in statu gloriæ immortalitatis* (N. de Lyra), before the throne of God and of the Lamb, in the full and blessed enjoyment of fellowship with Him" (DUESTERDIECK). On a reference of the promise to the Israelitish sacerdotal dress, see Düsterdieck.

Because they are worthy.—Here also we learn, in accordance with Scripture, to distinguish between the righteousness of faith in the court of the Spirit and the repentant conscience, and righteousness of life in the tribunal of the Judge of the world (ch. xvi. 5); recognizing the fact, however, that the latter is always conditioned upon the former.

["They have shown themselves worthy to be regarded as followers of the Lamb; or they have a character that is fitted for Heaven. The declaration is not that they have any *claim* to Heaven, on the ground of their own merit, or that it will be in virtue of their own works that they will be received there; but that there is a *fitness* or propriety that they should thus appear in Heaven." BARNES. "God's word does not refuse to ascribe a worthiness to men (Matt. x. 10, 11; xxii. 8; Luke xx. 35; xxi. 36; 2 Thess. i. 5, 11); although this worthiness must ever be contemplated as relative and not absolute. . . . There are those who '*are worthy,*' according to the rules which free grace *has*, although there are none according to those which strict justice *might have* laid down." TRENCH.—E. R. C.]

Ver. 5. He that conquereth shall thus be clothed in white garments.—The ever-recurring term ὁ νικῶν has here the special meaning of victory over temptation emanating from the subtle worldly-mindedness and slumbrous spirit of the church. The faithful in Ephesus had to overcome the temptation of excess in external works, amid which the first love grew cold. Believers in Smyrna had to overcome the trial of persecutions unto death. Believers in Pergamus were to overcome anomianism. Believers in Thyatira must be victorious over fanaticism. The Philadelphians were tried with Judaism, and the Laodiceans, finally, had the temptation to self-righteousness to surmount. The richer expression, *he shall thus be clothed, etc.*, gives prominence to the free act of grace in the righteous recompense; as does also the clause:

And I will not [Lange, never (οὐ μή)] wipe out his name.—His name was entered in the Book of Life simultaneously with his calling and conversion. Such names may, however, be wiped out—a destiny awaiting many in Sardis.* But the names of the conquerors shall never be wiped out.

The figurative expression, **book of Life**, borrowed from the registers of the living citizens of a community (see Düsterd.), like the idea of calling, is not always used in exactly the same sense; sometimes it predominantly denotes the actualized ethical relation of man to God (Ps. lxix. 28; Is. iv. 3; Dan. xii. 1; Rev. xx. 12; xxi. 27); sometimes it is pre-eminently significant of the relation and conduct of Divine grace to man (Ex. xxxii. 32; Ps. cxxxix. 16;

* [It is not *asserted* in this passage that the names of any who shall finally perish were ever entered in the Book of Life, nor is it *necessarily* implied.—E. R. C.]

Rev. xvii. 8); and sometimes the predominant idea is that of the concrete unity of the two elements which we have mentioned, the reciprocal relation of which is always implied (Phil. iv. 3; Rev. xiii. 8).*

But I will confess his name.—Third promise. The recurrence of the *name* is significant. It is the mark of a dead church-life that only a collective Christianity remains, that Christian *names*, pronounced personalities, are lacking. In Sardis, however, there are still a few such names; and these the Lord will confess by name as His own, before God His Father, and before the angels of God—in the most glorious circle of life, therefore. Highest glorification of the highest definiteness of their personal life! [Comp. Matt. x. 32; Luke xii. 8.—E. R. C.]

["It is a very instructive fact, that everywhere else in the epistles to all the churches, save only to this and to Laodicea, there is mention of some burden to be borne, of a conflict either with foes within the church or without, or with both. Only in these two nothing of the kind occurs. The exceptions are very significant. There is no need to assume that the church at Sardis had openly coalesced and joined hands with the heathen world; this would in those days have been impossible; nor yet that it had renounced the *appearance* of opposition to the world. But the two tacitly understood one another. This church had nothing of the spirit of the Two Witnesses, of whom we read that they 'tormented them that dwelt on the earth' (Rev. xi. 10), tormented them, that is, by their witness for a God of truth and holiness and love, Whom the dwellers on the earth were determined not to know. . . . The world could endure it because it too was a world." TRENCH.—E. R. C.]

SIXTH EPISTLE.   PHILADELPHIA.

Ch. iii. 7–13.

Philadelphia, like Sardis, was situated in Lydia, about thirteen hours' journey southeast from that capital. It derived its name from its builder, the Pergamese king, Attalus Philadelphus. Though frequently visited by earthquakes, the city still exists under the Turkish name of Alah Shehr, a living monument of the faithfulness of Divine promises in the midst of ruins. Comp. the Encyclopædias and Books of Travel. On its church-historical reminiscences see Düsterdieck. In Philadelphia, as in Smyrna, there was a "synagogue of Satan," *i. e.*, an association of Judaistic enemies of Christianity, in opposition to which the epistle, whose images are theocratic throughout (see Düsterdieck), signalizes the church as the true people of God.

Ver. 7. These things saith the Holy [One], the True [One].—The Lord's self-designation is here in perfect accordance with the theocratic idea of God, and that in reference

* [The phrase: βίβλος (τῆς) ζωῆς, occurs Phil. iv. 3; Rev. iii. 5; xx. 15, and βιβλίον τῆς ζωῆς, xiii. 8; xvii. 8; xx. 12; xxi. 27. (Cf. xxxii. 2; Dan. xii. 1, probably refer to the same, although the word ζωῆς does not appear; and possibly Ps. lxix. 28, and Is. iv. 3, may have a similar reference.) In all these passages it is manifest that the simple hypothesis of a register (figurative, of course), of those who are to inherit eternal life, satisfies every contextual requirement.—E. R. C.]

to the question as to which is the true people of God. The description is connected as a whole with the import of the Son of Man, ch. i. 13, in accordance with Dan. vii.

The Holy One.—The specific predicate of the God of Israel, the Sanctifier to Himself of a peculiar people—or a people of possession (see 1 Peter i. 15, 16). "Christ, rejected and blasphemed by the synagogue of Satan, is nevertheless, simply and plainly the Holy One, the true Messiah and Lord of the Church" (Düsterdieck). The personal manifestation of the God of Israel, the Founder of the Theocracy. Düsterdieck (p. 186) cites a number of instances of the misapprehension or ignoring of this obvious reference. [Comp. Luke i. 35; Acts iii. 14. "Christ claims here to be ὁ Ἅγιος, the Holy One; cf. Acts ii. 27; xiii. 35; Heb. vii. 26. In all these passages, however, ὅσιος, not ἅγιος, stands in the original; nor are these words perfectly identical, though we have but the one word, 'holy,' by which to render them both. The ὅσιος, if a man, is one who diligently observes all the sanctities of religion; anterior, many of them, to all law, the '*jus et fas*,' with a stress on the latter word. If applied to God, as at Rev. xv. 4; xvi. 5, and here, He is One in whom these eternal sanctities reside; who is Himself the root and ground of them. The ἅγιος is the separate from evil, with the perfect hatred of the evil. But holiness, in this absolute sense, belongs only to God; not to angels, for He chargeth His angels with folly (Job iv. 18), and certainly not to men (Jam. iii. 2; Gen. vi. 5; viii. 21). He then that claims to be '*the Holy One*'—a name which Jehovah in the Old Testament continually claims for Himself—implicitly claims to be God," etc. TRENCH. "As opposed to the συναγωγή τοῦ σατανᾶ below." ALFORD.—E. R. C.]

The True One.—In the New Testament, the term, "the true" [*der Wahrhaftige*, ἀληθινός, veritable, see *Comm. on John*, p. 460, Am. Ed.—E. R. C.] denotes not only the fulfillment of Old Testament prophecy (2 Cor. i. 20), but also the substance of the Old Testament shadowy sketches (John i. 17). Accordingly, the attribute ἀληθινός is related to ἀληθής, and founded thereupon; the two epithets are contra-distinguished, however, by the pre-eminence of the idea of substantiality, of true spiritual life, in ἀληθινός. Comp. the series of interpretations cited by Düsterd. The blasphemies of the Jews who refused to see in the Lord aught but the hanged one"—hence, a false Messiah—are correctly pointed out by Hengstenberg as the antithesis to ὁ ἀληθινός. As Christ is personal holiness as the realized fundamental idea of the Old Covenant, so He is also the True in the sense of the fulfillment and essential consummation of the Old Testament, the perfect essential form of the Messiah.

["We must not confound ἀληθινός (=verus) with ἀληθής (=verax). God is ἀληθής (=ἀψευδής, Tit. i. 2), as He cannot lie, the truth-speaking and truth-loving God; with whom every word is Yea and Amen; but He is ἀληθινός, as fulfilling all that is involved in the name God, in contrast with those which are called gods. . . . That is ἀληθινός, which fulfills its own idea to the highest possible point. . . . Nor is ἀληθινός only, as in this case of God, the true as contrasted with the absolutely false; but as contrasted with the subordinately true, with all imperfect and partial realizations of the idea; thus Christ is φῶς ἀληθινόν (John i. 9; 1 John ii. 8), ἄρτος ἀληθινός (John vi. 32), ἄμπελος ἀληθινή (John xv. 1); there is ■ σκηνὴ ἀληθινή in Heaven (Heb. viii. 2). In each of these cases, the antithesis is not between the true and the false, but between the perfect and the imperfect, the idea fully and the idea only partially realized; for John the Baptist also was a *light* (John v. 35), and Moses gave *bread* from Heaven (Ps. cv. 40), and Israel was ■ *vine* of God's planting (Ps. lxxx. 8), and the *tabernacle* pitched in the wilderness, if only a figure of the true, was yet pitched at God's express command (Ex. xxv.)." TRENCH.—E. R. C.]

That hath the key of David.—The key of the house of David was kept by the steward of his house; it was the province of this official to grant or deny access to the king, and to decide all questions of presentability at court. According to Is. xxii. 22, the key was given to Eliakim, after being taken from Shebna.* This key to the perfected theocratic Royal House, the House of the Messiah, the Messianic Kingdom, is now held by Christ the Messiah Himself (not by a steward); He and He alone decides, first, by His word and Spirit in the Church, and, again, by His authoritative rule in the world, the question as to who belongs to the people of God. And thus He forms in His Church the contrast to the synagogue of Satan. That which the Judaists would exclude, He includes; what they would include, He excludes. The difference, however, is that their communion, like their excommunication, is a mere delusion, whilst His acts have absolute reality. When He opens, none can shut; the world cannot take away His peace—no, not even from the martyr. When He shuts, none can open: the sentence of judgment which He by His Spirit executes in the spirits of men, can be invalidated by no fanatical self-delusion, or deception on the part of others.

["Christ teaches us here that He has not so committed the keys of the Kingdom of Heaven, with the power of binding and loosing, to any other, His servants, here, but that He still retains the highest administration of them in His own hands." TRENCH. Is not "emphasis" to be laid on "the ὁ ἔχων"—the "steward" may *hold* the key, subject to the authority of the Master, the latter alone can be said to *possess* it? This view supports the interpretation of Düsterdieck given below.—E. R. C.]

Various interpretations. Christ alone opens the Holy Scriptures; Lyra.† The cross of Christ *instrumentum omnipotentiæ*; Alcasar. That supreme power which is the property of the Lord, Matt. xxviii. 18; Düsterd. and others. Christ, as Lord and King of the Kingdom, admits into it and excludes from it (Düsterd., Hengst., and others).

Ver. 8. I know thy works.—We do not, with Bengel and others, pass over the next word ἰδού, *etc.*, and find a specification of the works in the

subsequent ὅτι, *etc.*; but neither are they "destitute of further qualification" [Düsterd.]; on the contrary, they contain the motive of the following: Behold I have given [δέδωκα, *etc.*]; they are consequently an expression of full recognition.

Before thee a door opened.—Does this mean: The door into the Kingdom of God is opened for the church, though the Judaists would fain shut it, or is it a door to successful activity?* The former apprehension, with various modifications, is supported by Bengel, Hengstenberg and others (see Düsterd.), whilst most commentators favor the latter conception, interpreting the passage as referring to the church's opportunity for missionary labors. Düsterdieck declares in favor of the latter view, with reference to ver. 9. The connection may also be thus construed, however: So far from thine adversaries being able to shut the door upon thee, they shall be constrained to turn to thine open door themselves. If we translate thus: Behold, I have determined that the door shall stand open before thee, we include both particulars, and it generally proves that that church which itself enters into the Kingdom of God draws in others with it.†

For thou hast little strength.—This must not be understood as indicative of spiritual weakness (a lack of miraculous gifts, Lyra), but of the external smallness or insignificance of the church (Düsterd., *et al.* ["The words 'little strength' may refer either to the smallness of the *number*; . . . . or it may refer to the spiritual life and energy of the church—meaning that, though feeble, their vital energy was not wholly gone. The more natural interpretation seems to be to refer it to the latter." BARNES. It may refer to either of these, or both; conjoined with their lack of temporal wealth.—E. R. C.]). Though thou hast little strength ["not as E. V., 'a little strength,' thereby virtually reversing the sense of the words: μικρὰν ἔχεις δύν. importing '*thy strength is but small*,' and the E. V. importing '*thou hast some strength*,' the fact of its smallness vanishing under the indefinite term '*a little*,' . . . and (using that little well)." AFORD.—E. R. C.]—The sense is, though thou hast little strength, Thou didst keep, *etc*. [This idea of the German, weakened by the parenthesis, must be preserved.]

Thou didst keep My word, *etc*.—The church has already proved its faithfulness by confessing Christ in tribulation; therefore the Lord will grant it spiritual success exceeding the measure of its external power.

Ver. 9. Behold, I will make them [Lange: ■ give (δίδωμι) that some] of the synagogue of Satan.—Here also that community

---

* [Is. xxii. 22. (LXX.) Δώσω αὐτῷ τὴν κλεῖδα οἴκου Δαυὶδ ἐπὶ τῷ ὤμῳ αὐτοῦ, καὶ ἀνοίξει καὶ οὐκ ἔσται ὁ ἀποκλείων, καὶ κλείσει καὶ οὐκ ἔσται ὁ ἀνοίγων.—E. R. C.]

† [There is no connection between this key and "the key of knowledge," spoken of Luke xi. 52.—E. R. C.]

9

* [Prof. Stuart advocates ■ third interpretation, viz.: (as presented by Barnes) " that they had before them an open way of egress from danger and persecution."—E. R. C.]

† [The view of Düsterd. (Alford, Trench) and others requires more than this—it demands that the door opened should be between the church and the unconverted; comp. (as referred to by Trench) 1 Cor. xvi. 9; 2 Cor. xi. 12; Acts xiv. 27; Col. iv. 3. It is true that Christ does open that door; but is not the door which He unlocks with the key of David that which leads into the Kingdom of Heaven? As King, He bursts open the gates of His enemies. Ver. 9 can hardly be regarded as supporting the view of the text: being "made of the Synagogue of Satan," and "falling down before the church" (not worshipping before God), are not the results of *the open door* to the unconverted, referred to in 1 Cor. xvi. 9, *etc*.—E. R. C.]

of Judaism which assumes to be the true Israel,* is denominated a synagogue of Satan, with the same energy with which the Johannean Gospel opposes Judaism. Even from this community of demonic adversaries, the church shall win some souls. Here, too, the διδῶμι has more the appearance of an enactment than of a gift. He makes a disposition of these few already; subsequently He causes them to come.

And fall down before thy feet.—As it was prophesied in the Old Testament that the Gentiles should be converted and come unto Zion to the Jews, so here it is predicted that the Judaizing Jews shall in their conversion come to the Church of Christ as the true Zion. Even the προσκυνεῖν, as an expression of homage, and, at the same time, humiliation before the Church of Salvation and of the presence of the Lord, is heard in the following prophecies: Ps. lxxii. 9; Is. ii. 3; xlix. 23; lx. 14; Zech. viii. 20. On the misinterpretation of this passage in favor of the Catholic Hierarchy, see Düsterd., p. 192.†

And to know that I have loved thee.—Ἠγάπησα denotes a continuous love, begun in the past. Düsterd. refers this demonstration of love to the death of Christ, in which case Philadelphia would only represent the Church total. Others interpret the word as indicative of the superiority or excellence of the Philadelphian church. De Wette: That I have known thee to be a faithful church. Both considerations must, however, be recognized in their unity: That My love to thee has become manifest in thy life of faith. The recognition of Christ is implied with the recognition of the church, and as the real motive of the latter. Düsterdieck gives prominence to the thought that the Jews shall know the love of Christ as manifested in His death upon the cross, whilst now they still blaspheme Him as a crucified malefactor.

Ver. 10. Because thou didst keep the word of My patience [endurance].—Düsterdieck makes the pronoun μου relate, not to τῆς ὑπομ. alone (like Ewald, De Wette, Hengstenberg and others), but to the whole conception τὸν λόγ., etc. (with Grot., Eichhorn and others). But the reading: *My word of patience*, gives rise to obscurity, suggesting the thought that the words of other teachers have glorified patience. There

---

* [See foot-note to chapter ii. 9.—E. R. C.]

† [There can be no doubt that there is special reference here to the prophecies of Is. xlix. 23, lx. 14; and there can be little doubt that a *conversion* is implied in these prophecies. The conversion, however, is not that of the present missionary era of the Church—that which follows the preaching of the Gospel to the unconverted through the "open door" alluded to in 1 Cor. xvi. 9, etc.;—during which time the converts are at once admitted into the Church. It is a conversion which is consequent upon the subjection of the nations to the established Basileia.—On Is. xlix. 23, J. A. Alexander thus comments: "The addition of these words, 'face toward the earth,' determines the meaning of the preceding verb (LXX. προσκυνήσουσι) as denoting actual prostration, which is also clear from the next clause, where the licking of the dust cannot be naturally understood as a strong expression for the kissing of the feet or of the earth, in token of homage, but is rather like the biting of the dust in Homer, a poetical description of complete and compulsory prostration, not merely that of subjects to their sovereign, but of vanquished enemies before their conquerors (comp. Micah vii. 17; Ps. lxxii. 9)." A *conversion* is implied in this passage under consideration, it is true; but that which was directly contemplated in this *threat of the Lord* is *subjugation*. See also preceding note, and the Excursus on the Basileia, pp. 93 sqq.—E. R. C.]

---

are also different explanations of this apprehension of the sentence. The word which, among other things, prescribes patience (Heinrich); The word which bestows and demands patience (Düsterd.). Isolated utterances of Christ, recommending patience—Christian patience (Hengstenberg. This interpretation approximates the other).

[Barnes: "My word commanding or enjoining patience, that is, thou hast manifested the patience which I require." Trench: "Better, however, to take the whole Gospel as '*the word of Christ's patience,*' everywhere teaching, as it does, the need of a patient waiting for Christ, till He, the waited-for so long, shall at length appear." The translation, *constancy* or *endurance*, or *steadfastness*, is altogether to be preferred; the idea of *patience* is rather that of *uncomplaining submission under trial*—in this sense it is a misnomer to speak of the ὑπομονή of Job, Jam. v. 11.—E. R. C.]

The word of the patience of Christ is also variously interpreted as the word of My passion, My constancy (Calov.). The word which, as the word concerning the cross, demands, in respect of its purport and in respect of the obligation which it imposes, steadfastness such as is peculiar to Christ and His people (Vitringa). We read: The word ripened in persecution into a word of perseverance, to the martyrs' testimony [*martyrium*], to confession. Hence: Thou hast kept my word in the fiery trial of temptation and opposition, when the word *concerning* the cross became a word *of* the cross;—the word in the beauty and power of the cross. The Holy Scriptures contain multiplied references to ὑπομονή; particularly Rev. ii. 2, 3, 19; xiii. 10; xiv. 12 [Luke viii. 15; xxi. 19; Rom. ii. 7; v. 3, 4; viii. 25; xv. 4, 5; 1 Thess. i. 3; 2 Thess. iii. 5; Heb. x. 36; xii. 1; James i. 3, 4, etc.—E. R. C.]

I also will keep thee.—Three-fold interpretation: [1] Thou shalt be excepted from the hour of temptation. [2] Thou, with all the faithful, shalt be preserved from the plagues of unbelievers. [3] Thou shalt be kept through exterior temptation; it shall not become to thee an internal temptation to apostasy (Vitringa, Hengstenb., and others). Düsterdieck: "The expression τηρ. ἐκ must be distinguished from τηρ. ἀπό."

From the hour of temptation.—The *hour* of *temptation* is the culminating point in the time of temptation (Luke xxii. 53), the moment of the crisis. In general, doubtless, the severe conflicts of faith which the Church must undergo previous to the Coming of the Lord (see ver. 11) are here intended, as bringing with them the danger of apostasy.

More particular definitions: The preservation represented ch. vii. 3 sqq. (Ewald, De Wette); the tribulations of Antichrist (Primasius); in addition to these, the plagues of the sixth angel (Bede).—Needless limitations.

False modifications: The persecutions under Nero (Grotius), Domitian (Lyra), Trajan (Alcasar and others).

[A πειρασμός is aught that tends to cause to swerve from the right (either in feeling or action), whether it be a promise, an allurement, a prophecy of evil, a threat, a persecution, or an affliction (see Luke iv. 13; viii. 13; xxii 28, 40, 46; Acts xx. 19; 1 Cor. x. 13; Gal. iv. 14; 1 Tim. vi. 9; 1 Peter i. 6; iv. 12, etc.). It is so styled because it is a trial, a test, of faith or the spirit of obedience. The hour of temptation (testing) is doubtless that special period referred to, 1 Pet. iv. 12 (τῇ ἐν ὑμῖν πυρώσει πρὸς πειρασμὸν ὑμῖν γινομένη), and by our Lord, Matt. xxiv. 21, 22; (a period both of testing and of punishment—primarily, however, of the former). This special period, be it observed, is distinguished from the period of ordinary πειρασμοί referred to 1 Peter i. 6, and Matt. xxiv. 4-13. It is also to be observed that the promise is not of preservation in trial, as was the promise to Peter, Luke xxii. 32; but of preservation from (ἐκ) the hour or period of trial (comp. 2 Peter ii. 9). The idea of this promise seems to be, that as the Philadelphians had continued steadfast throughout the period of ordinary testing, they were to be exempted from those extraordinary πειρασμοί which were to come upon the world.—E. R. C.]

Which is about to come upon all the world [οἰκουμένη].—Though it is relatively true that the Roman empire was the οἰκουμένη [Grot., Vitr., Stern, etal.],* it must here symbolize the whole of the inhabited world. This is indicated by the next clause.

To try them that dwell upon the earth. —According to Düsterdieck, "the mass of mankind in antithesis to believers, redeemed out of all peoples." The following passages are cited in illustration of this view: ch. vi. 10; xi. 10; xiii. 8, 14. It results from ch. xiii. 8, however, that the inhabitants of the earth are more or less identified with unbelievers only on account of the great majority of the latter over believers. It is true that the temptation comes, as a judicial infliction, only upon the unbelieving; yet the tempting fact comes, as a rigorous trial, upon believers also, in order to their confirmation. This result they owe to Divine preservation.

Ver. 11. I come quickly —Constantly recurring announcement, designed for the awakenkening and terrifying of foes and the consolation and elevation of the pious. We would again insist upon the fact, that it is no definition of time in the common chronological sense; it is to be apprehended in an exalted religious sense. The term ταχύ always involves the surprisingness of the coming, as unexpected, sudden, terribly early and terribly great.

Hold that fast which thou hast.—See ch. i. 3; ii. 25; xxii. 7. Cherish the charism peculiar to thee. The ever new reproduction and more thorough acquisition of the thing possessed is expressed, together with the holding of it fast (Matt. xxiv. 13). Here the charism of steadfastness in the faith is denoted. ["Whatever of truth and piety you now possess." BARNES.—E. R. C.]

That no man take thy crown.—That no man despoil thee of the victor's wreath.† that awaiteth thee at the goal; i. e. that none cause thee to lose it. Not, therefore, in the sense of

* [There is no authority for this limitation of the prime reference of οἰκουμένη (comp Matt. xxiv. 14; Luke iv. 5; Acts xvii. 31; Rom. x. 18; Heb. i. 6; Rev. xii. 19; xvi. 14). —E. R. C.]

† [Στέφανος=that which is at once the wreath of the victor and the crown of the king. See note on ch. ii. 10.—E. R. C.]

another's coming before and winning it in the church's stead (Grot.). Μηδείς, however, represents the power of temptation, finally concentrated in Antichrist, with reference to the competitive contests of antiquity.

Ver. 12. A pillar in the temple.—The distinct promise corresponds again to the distinct conduct of the church : 1. A pillar in the spiritual Temple of God; 2 An eternally consecrate inmate of the Temple; 3. Adorned with the three-fold inscription : a. With the name of God ; the complete expression of perfect religiousness. b. With the name of the City of God ; the complete expression of perfect ideal churchliness. c. With the name of Christ ; the complete expression of perfect Christliness, which embraces in one both the foregoing considerations. This promise will, of course, not be perfectly fulfilled until the Coming of the Lord ; yet we cannot, with Düsterdieck, regard its fulfillment as exclusively subsequent to the second Advent. Düsterdieck not only denies the reference of the promise to the Church Militant alone (Lyra, Grot., and others), but he even disputes its application to it and the Church Triumphant (Vitringa and others). ["The promised reward of faithfulness here is, that he who is victorious would be honored as if he were a pillar or column in the Temple of God. Such a pillar or column was partly for ornament, and partly for support, and the idea here is, that in that Temple he would contribute to its beauty and the justness of its proportions, and would at the same time be honored as if he were a pillar which was necessary for the support of the Temple."—BARNES. ALFORD judiciously observes: "It is no objection to this view (substantially the one set forth above) that in the heavenly Jerusalem there is no Temple, ch. xxi. 22 ; but rather a corroboration of it. That glorious City is all Temple, and Christ's victorious ones are its living stones and pillars. Thus, as Düsterdieck well remarks, the imagery of the Church Militant 1 Cor xiii. 16 sqq.; Eph. ii. 19 sqq.; 1 Peter ii. 5 sqq., is transferred to the Church Triumphant, but with this difference, that the saints are no longer the stones merely, but now the pillars themselves, standing on their immovable firmness." This passage is but one of many which set forth the pre-eminence of the victorious saints of the present dispensation, in the future æon of blessedness and glory. They are the ἀπαρχή, the first fruits, Jas. i. 18; Rev. xiv. 4; the bride, Rev. xxi. 9; kings in the Kingdom then to be established, Rev. ii. 26; iii. 22; priests in the holy congregation, Rev. i. 6; v. 10; xx. 6; pillars in the heavenly Temple. (See also note on ch. ii. 26.)—E. R C.]

And he shall nevermore go out. (Καὶ ἔξω οὐ μὴ ἐξέλθῃ ἔτι.)—The pillar shall not be put out, according to Ewald and others. But there is doubtless a change of figure. The victor can no more fall away or be separated from the blessed fellowship of God. His secure position in the eternal Temple as a pillar, for firmness and beauty, is only equalled by his sure establishment therein as an inmate. [Continued purity, and exemption from association with anything impure, seem to be emphasized by the use of ἔξω; comp. ch. xxii. 15.—E. R. C.]

Hengstenberg justly says, that this applies to every Christian, for to be a Christian is to be a victor. The inscription also refers to the victor, not to the pillar, see ch. xiv. 1. On the reference of the name of Jesus to Jesuani, Jesuitæ, see Düsterdieck's note, p. 197.

An analogue of the three names in Jewish Theology, see in Düsterdieck, p. 198. **Which cometh down out of heaven.—** See ch. xxi. As the Church in this world is ever growing more spiritual, so the Church in the other world is constantly becoming more real, more corporeal, until its perfect worldly appearance is consummated in the resurrection. [See under ch. xxi. 1-3.—E. R. C.]

As the three names, in close connection with the Trinity, are expressive of a three-fold manifestation of the Divine image in the beatified one, so they also denote a three-fold appertinency or consecrateness on his part.

[**And I will write upon him the name of my God.—**"Christ will write this name of His God upon *him* that overcometh—not upon *it*, the pillar. It is true, indeed, that there were sometimes inscriptions on pillars, which yet would be στῆλαι, rather than στῦλοι; but the image of the pillar is now dismissed, and only the conqueror remains. In confirmation of this, that it is the person, and not the pillar, whom the Lord contemplates now, we find, further on, the redeemed having the name of God, or the seal of God on their foreheads (vii. 3; ix. 4; xiv. 1; xxii. 4), with probable allusion to the golden plate inscribed with the name of Jehovah which the High Priest wore upon his (Exod. xxviii. 36-38). In the 'Kingdom of priests' this dignity shall not be any more the singular prerogative of one, but the common dignity of all."

TRENCH.—**And the name of the City of my God.—**"What the name of this City is, we are told Ezek. xlviii. 35: 'The Lord is there.' Any other name would but faintly express the glory of it; 'having the glory *of God*' (Rev. xxi. 11, 23). He that has the name of this City written upon him is hereby declared free of it. Even while on earth he had his true πολίτευμα ἐν οὐρανοῖς (Phil. iii. 20; see Ellicott thereon), the state, city or country to which he belonged was a heavenly one; but still his citizenship was latent; he was one of God's hidden ones; but now he is openly avouched, and has a right to enter in by the gates to the City (xxii. 14)." TRENCH. —**And . . . . My new name.—**"This '*new name*' is not 'The Word of God' (xix. 13), nor yet 'King of kings and Lord of lords' (xix. 16). It is true that both of these appear in this Book as names of Christ; but at the same time neither of them could be called His *new* name; the faithful having been familiar with them from the beginning; but the '*new name*' is that mysterious and, in the necessity of things, uncommunicated and, for the present time, incommunicable name, which, in that same sublimest of all visions, is referred to: 'He had a name written, that no man knew but He Himself' (xix. 12); for none but God can search out the deep things of God (1 Cor. ii. 12; cf. Matt. xi. 27; Judg. xiii. 18). But the mystery of this new name, which no man by searching could find out, which in this present condition no man is so much as capable

of receiving, shall be imparted to the saints and citizens of the New Jerusalem. They shall know even as they are known (1 Cor. xiii. 12)." TRENCH.—E. R. C.]

[The following extract from Gibbon's *Decline and Fall* (ch. lxiv.) will be read with interest in this connection: "Two Turkish chieftains, Sarukhan and Aidin, left their names to their conquests, and their conquests to their posterity. The captivity or ruin of the *seven* churches of Asia was consummated; and the barbarous lords of Ionia and Lydia still trample on the monuments of classic and Christian antiquity. In the loss of Ephesus, the Christians deplored the fall of the first angel, the extinction of the first candlestick, of the Revelation; the desolation is complete; and the temple of Diana, or the church of Mary, will equally elude the search of the curious traveller. The circus and three stately theatres of Laodicea are now peopled with wolves and foxes; Sardis is reduced to a miserable village; the God of Mahomet, without a rival or a son, is invoked in the mosques of Thyatira and Pergamus; and the populousness of Smyrna is supported by the foreign trade of the Franks and Armenians. Philadelphia alone has been saved by prophecy, or courage. At a distance from the sea, forgotten by the emperors, encompassed on all sides by the Turks, her valiant citizens defended their religion and freedom above four-score years; and at length capitulated with the proudest of the Ottomans. Among the Greek colonies and churches of Asia, Philadelphia is still erect, a column in a scene of ruins; a pleasing example that the paths of honor and safety may sometimes be the same."—E. R. C.]

SEVENTH EPISTLE.   LAODICEA.

Ch. iii. 14-22.

Our Laodicea was situated on the river Lycus in Phrygia Major, in the neighborhood of Colosse and Hierapolis: it was a large and rich commercial city. Bearing earlier the name of Diospolis, and then of Rhoas, it received its subsequent appellation in honor of Laodice, the Queen of King Antiochus II. In the year 62 this city, like Colosse and Hierapolis, was destroyed by an earthquake, but was speedily rebuilt. An insignificant town called Eskihissar, surrounded by ruins, now forms the last trace of its existence. Laodicea was the last of the seven churches; hence, a circular letter to these (the Epistle to the Ephesians) had, on reaching this city, arrived at its final destination, and from there an exchange could readily be effected between it and the Epistle to the Colossians (Col. iv. 16). Notwithstanding this, Winer still talks of a lost letter from Paul to the Laodiceans.[*] The bearer of the seven epistles, having gone northward from Ephesus through Smyrna

---

[*] [There are three opinions concerning the destination of the Epistle to the Ephesians: 1. That it was addressed specifically to the church in Ephesus; 2. That it is the Epistle to (from—ἐκ) Laodicea mentioned Col. iv. 16; 3. That it was a circular letter for all the churches of Asia Minor. For full discussions of the entire subject see Com.bene and Howson's *Life and Epistles of St. Paul*, Alford, Eadie, Hodge, the Lange *Comm. on Ephesians* (Am. Ed.), *etc.* The evidence in favor of the last two opinions is of the most meagre character.—E. R. C.]

to Pergamus, turned southward to Thyatira, Sardis, Philadelphia and Laodicea; thus traversing a trivium and a quadrivium.* For further particulars, see Encyclopedias, Books of Travel and Geographical works. "A bishop and martyr of Laodicea, called Sagaris (A. D. 170), is mentioned by Eusebius, H. E. iv. 26; v. 24; even Archippus (Col. iv. 17) is named as bishop (*Const. Apost.* viii. 46) Each has been regarded as the angel of the church; and in the expression ἡ ἀρχὴ τ. κτ., ver. 14, Hengstenberg has even discovered an allusion to the name of Arch–ippus as the most influential leader of the church at Laodicea." (DUESTERDIECK.) A curious discovery, certainly! Colossians ii. does not distinctly prove, as Düsterdieck assumes, that in Paul's time the Laodicean church, as well as that at Colosse, was in danger from erroneous theosophic doctrines, though Vitringa, with astonishing acuteness, maintained that there were traces of such things in the very epistle that we are examining (Düsterdieck, p. 199). The spiritual condition of the church may be clearly gathered from the epistle addressed to it, but cannot be explained from the external circumstances of the church itself.

Ver. 14.† **These things saith the Amen.**— Here also a harmony of all parts may be taken for granted at the very outset. The central point of all the terms contained in the epistle lies, manifestly, in the false self-gratulation of the Church as expressed in ver. 17. In the first place, such a morbid assurance of completeness, involving a cessation from striving, and even from aspiration—such a conviction of having arrived at a state in which all need is done away with (πεπλούτηκα)‡—does not arise in a healthy condition of faith, for even on the firm ground of the peace of reconciliation, such a condition implies—nay, is itself—a longing and striving after perfection (the true righteousness of faith, an agonizing after righteousness of life).

But, again, this assurance of completeness and consequent stoppage of all exertion does not spring into existence where there is a mere legal holiness of works; the goad of the law is constantly rousing those under its bondage—or, at least, the worthier portion of them—from the false repose to which they, for a moment, may have yielded, and urging them on. Spiritualism [*Spiritualismus*].§ however, is always and every-

where thoroughly satisfied, whether it appear in a mystical form, declaring, I too am a son of God, or in a rationalistic guise, affirming that there is no such thing as a son of God, no such thing as the Atonement. Spiritualism [*Spiritualismus*] has the property of not being warm, because it has no spiritual [*geistlich*] blood, no social, historical or personal life; but neither is it cold, for it has its religious views and opinions, its party even, for which it can, for a time, be enthusiastically or fanatically hot. It does not, however, grow warm for the living fellowship of God and the Church of God. Now this spiritualism [*Spiritualismus*] may, in Laodicea, as well as elsewhere, have been based upon the antecedents of theoretical, theosophic heresies; at the writing of the epistle, however, these heresies were a vanishing point in the background; the enthusiastic soarings in the clouds had been succeeded by the reactionary fall of satiety and lukewarmness. Hence the word of revelation does not directly attack theoretical errors of the church, but its practical appearance, so specifically modified, however, that we perceive the epistle to be also aimed at the germs of the church's corruption latent in the background.

The self-designation of Christ is the first instrument for the accomplishment of the design we have just stated. The Amen, the faithful and true [genuine] Witness, the Originator (ἀρχή, see Col. i. 18) of the creation and redemption.* He is the *Amen* as the perfect and complete personal conclusion of the revelations of God, beyond Whom there can be no angelic or philosophic or spiritualistic [*spiritualistisch*] revelations,†—the focus of the Divine sun of revelation, through Whom alone true vital heat is to be got. He is the faithful and essential, perfectly historical and real *Witness* of the truth, in face of Whom the inflated illusions, images and systems of spiritualism [*Spiritualismus*] must vanish away. He is the living, personal *Principle* of the whole creation; hence there is no principial life of spirits or spirit outside of that cosmical order of the Kingdom which is comprehended in Him.

With this description of Christ, the description of the church corresponds. Its works are specifically merged in its character, and this character is lukewarmness—not lukewarmness as positivism, however, but as a double negation: neither cold nor warm. If the church were cold, if it were a stranger to Christ, like the heathen, or even if it cherished a positive antipathy against Him, He would not approach it in the character of a Judge; it might yet become warm. It has just enough Christianity to come under condemnation, but not sufficient to attain to blessedness, for the reason that it is not warm.

* [Of all this there is not one particle of evidence.—E. R. C.]
† [On this and several following pages, Lange presents a general view of the epistle. Special exegetical comments and additions may be found pp. 135 sqq.—it. R. C.]
‡ [The marvellous compendiousness of the German language is forcibly illustrated here. Six words present all that our translation has given in the space comprised within the last period and πεπλούτηκα, with the exception of θ on the first place," which in the German occurs further on. We cite the pregnant six: *Ein solches krankhaftes Fertigsein und Bedürfnisslosgewordensein*. Perhaps it is but fair to remark that the final octosyllable is composed of a substantive, an adjective, a participle, and an infinitive.—FR.]
§ [Lange seems to have employed this word, coined from the Latin as a generic representative of the doctrines of those who deny the necessity of an external atonement, r-relation and ordinances—affirming that the spirit of a man is sufficient unto itself. In this sense it includes the wildest mystics and the baldest rationalism. The only English word by which it can be rendered is *spiritualism*. The use of this term, however, is objectionable, as it is

already employed in English in two or three different senses. As far as possible to avoid confusion, whenever it and the allied words *spiritual, spiritualist*, occur, the originals will be printed in brackets as above.—E. R. C.]
* [See comments and additions on pp. 135 sqq.—E. R. C.]
† [This comment seems to be based on a *modern* use of the term *Amen*. As it forms the *conclusion* of our prayers it has come to be employed, both in German and English, as a word expressive of *conclusion*. No such meaning, however, properly belongs to it. Nor is there any reason to suppose that, in the days of the Apostles, it was ever employed in this special conventional sense.—E. R. C.]

This condition, in its approximation to eternal hopelessness, wrings from the Judge Himself, in His blessed majesty, a sigh that seems laden with a human grief: O that thou wert cold or warm!—Again, the condition of the church is illustrated by the figure of lukewarm water, which, when drunk, causes nausea: *I am about to* (not yet: I will) *spew thee out of my mouth;* *i. e* reject with lively indignation and repulsion.

Not cold, not warm, but lukewarm. This attitude toward the Lord, His word and His Church, is based upon the church's conduct toward itself, upon its spiritual [*geistlich*] pride. This pride is likewise expressed three-foldly: I am rich—I have become rich to excess or satiety —I have need of nothing (or, as it may also be rendered, *no person*, no Saviour, no fellowship). The first declaration is expressive of the church's self-deception in imagining that it can be rich independently. In the second declaration, the church intimates, that in some way or other (by an arcanum or a would-be new idea) it has become rich, and that its wealth is forever an accomplished fact. In the third declaration, the fearful consequence is announced: it has need of nothing more; it is subjectively free from all heavenly and earthly props; its satiety is the complete caricature of the blessedness of true faith, having an imaginary exaltation in an imaginary omniscience. Its false self-appraisement is met by the annihilating sentence of the Lord:

Thou knowest not.—Ignorance, and that in relation to the most immediate and necessary knowledge—ignorance of its own condition; ignorance in its most aggravated form—self-blinding, constitutes the basis of its wants. The church (represented by her character, her masculine life-picture) knows not that she is, on the one hand, *the* wretched one, the specific bearer of the burdens of a salvationless state; and, on the other, the one pitiable above all others, on whom, also, the Lord wills yet to have pity in consideration of her ignorance (see Luke xxiii 34). The three fundamental traits of this woful picture are: *poor* and *blind* and *naked;* *poor* in reference to the true riches of life; *blind* in reference to truth and knowledge; *naked* in reference to the utter want of a truly spiritual [*geistlich*] appearance in genuine good works or signs and evidences of the inner life.

The counsel of the Lord is in harmony with the situation. The church is admonished to buy all that she lacks of Him. For of Him alone can the beggar buy—buy for nought (Is. lv. 1), and yet *buy,* inasmuch as it is only under moral forms and conditions that the free gift is received; its reception implies the surrender of a whole world of counterfeit value, and thus there is a difference between its bestowal and the actual giving of alms to a beggar. The first proffer is that of *gold*—gold purified by fire; the heavenly riches of righteousness, in the sterling quality of the fidelity of faith; purified by the fire of tribulation, and thus proven to be genuine gold. The spiritualist [*Spiritualist*] dares not expose his gilded fancies to the fire of tribulation. The church's nakedness is the second thing provided for—in advance of her

blindness; and this is, doubtless, because a modicum of sight is pre-supposed in the first and second acts, and because it is high time that the manifestation of *the shame of her nakedness,* appearing, as it necessarily will, in moral scandals, should be averted by demonstrations of Christian life, in *white garments,* which are connected with the gold of faith. Then comes the *eye-salve* of truth, in order to the gaining of true and perfect sight in Christian knowledge, from which the spiritualist [*Spiritualist*], in his false conceit of knowledge, is most remote. The severe utterance of the Lord is next exempted from all suspicion of partyism, party-strife or school-wrangling. The truth of Christ, under whatever aspect it is viewed, always turns to rebuke when it encounters falsehood; and the very fact of its rebuking and chastening is designed to teach the person thus exercised, that the love of Christ has not yet given him up, and that, on the contrary, it would fain win him by these means of rebuke and chastening—that it is thereby calling him to repentance.

Ver. 20. **Behold, I stand at the door.**— With the peculiar species of sinfulness in the condition of the church, the peculiar form of repentance corresponds. An obliteration of the consciousness of man's liberty of election is partly the cause, partly the effect of spiritualism [*Spiritualismus*]; the nerve of moral freedom is paralyzed, and the sense of moral greatness, as exemplified in the history of the world, is obscured. Therefore Christ—Who has not for a long time been *in* this high-flying spiritualism [*Spiritualismus*]—stands at the door of the soul and knocks. He finds the door shut; still He does not burst it in; He knocks and begs for admittance. In face of this conduct of the royally Free, the unfree should rouse him from his palsy. *If any man.*—This, indeed, is not to be *expected* of the mass of blinded ones, yet it may be *hoped* of individuals.

If any man hear My voice.—There is help for any one who still has an ear for this—for the affectionate tone, the loving call of Jesus' voice. Amid his spiritual [*geistig*] waverings betwixt light and darkness, his heart, constantly declining, as it is, into an indifference to personal love, is not yet quite dead. This is proved by the fact of his opening the door to the Lord, by his reception of the personal Christ as his Friend and Saviour. And what then ? With the peculiar modification of repentance, the peculiar modification of grace corresponds. The subsequent word of promise is, assuredly, meant for all who are converted, but especially is it intended for the returning spiritualist [*Spiritualist*].

I will come in to him and will sup with him.—In the case of the spiritualist [*Spiritualist*], above all, the new life must take the form of the most intimate communion, of personal fellowship with the Lord. This communion is primarily Christ's supping with him; his heart, his property, his bread henceforth belong to the Christian fellowship. But the higher form of this new life is that *he,* on his part, sups with Christ, that he becomes a participant in His blessed, heavenly life. And though the general reference here is to the meal of vital communion, the restoration of the spiritualist [*Spiritualist*] will also be particularly evidenced in a proper appreciation of the Lord's Supper, the social Christ, a Sacrament which he has before despised in his imagined self-sufficiency.

In this epistle, as in all the others, the concluding promise to the victor is in perfect harmony with all that has gone before.

Ver. 21. **To him that conquereth will I grant to sit with Me on My throne.**—The *throne* of Christ is the glory of His Kingdom—the *sitting on His throne*, the personal vital possession of this glory; the sitting *with Him* on this throne is, therefore, the co-enjoyment of this highest definiteness of perfected personal life. This future forms the extremest contrast to the expectation of the spiritualistic [*spiritualistisch*] indifferentist who holds that he is to be swallowed up in the waves of the general, impersonal world-essence.

But the promise unfolds still greater glories: **And sat down with My Father.**—We can imagine nothing concerning a fellowship in God's personal exaltation above the world, above the transitoriness, unfreeness, and imperfection of the world. The words at the head of this paragraph, however, unmistakably form the culminating point of the contrast to the nihilistic views of the indifferentistically lukewarm mind, the positive counterpart of the negative Buddhistic Nirvana.

The solemn conclusion appeals for the last time to the organization, the capacity, the destination of man; for the last time to man's freedom and to the first stirrings of freedom in hearing and obeying; for the last time to the high calling of the Christian—to *hear what the Spirit saith to the churches*. The words this time have a seven-fold weight, for they form the conclusion not only of the last letter, but of all the foregoing epistles likewise.

The more general import of Christ's declaration, Behold, I stand at the door, is this, *viz.*, that the last epistle sketches the last form of the church, and touches upon the Parousia.

After this general consideration of the final epistle, we present, briefly, the following exegesis of particular points:

Ver. 14. **The Amen.** 2 Cor. i. 20.—["Referring, as is the case in every epistle, to some attribute of the speaker adapted to impress their minds, or to give peculiar force to what He was about to say to that particular church. . . . The word *amen* means *true, certain, faithful*; and, as used here, it means that He to whom it is applied is eminently true and faithful. What He affirms is true; what He promises or threatens is certain. Himself characterized by sincerity and truth (2 Cor. i. 20), He can look with approbation only on the same in others; and hence He looks with displeasure on the lukewarmness which, from its very nature, always approximates insincerity." BARNES. It may also be observed that a state of lukewarmness is a state of indifferentism, of partial unbelievingness. The lukewarm hear as though the promises and threats of their teachers were as vain as the wind. It was most appropriate that the Great Teacher should endeavor to arouse the Laodiceans to heed His words, by an epithet declara-

tive of His sincerity, and the truth and certainty of His declarations.—E. R. C.] The Hebrew expression is, doubtless, thoroughly akin to the subsequent Greek terms (Bengel and others); yet there is a distinction between absolute certainty and absolute faithfulness and actuality, and we have here no mere climax (Düsterdieck).—See Düsterd. on unsupported interpretations.

[**The faithful and true Witness.**—"He is '*the Witness, the faithful and the true*,' in that He speaks what He knows, and testifies what He has seen. The thought is a favorite and ever-recurring one in the Gospel of St. John (iii. 11, 32, 33); but does not appear in any other. . . . Of the two epithets, the first, πιστός, expresses His entire trustworthiness. The word is employed in the New Testament, as elsewhere—now as trusting or believing (John xx. 27 : Acts xiv. 1), now as trustworthy or to be believed (2 Tim. ii. 22 ; 1 Thess. v. 27 ; 1 John i. 9). Men may be πιστοί in both senses, the active and the passive, as exercising faith, and as being worthy to have faith exercised upon them. God can be only πιστός in the latter. . . . It will be seen that the *truthfulness* of Christ as a Witness is asserted in the πιστός, not, as might at first sight be assumed, in the ἀληθινός that follows, or at least in it only as one quality among many. Christ is a μάρτυς ἀληθινός (not ἀληθής), in that He realized and fulfilled in the highest sense all that belonged to a witness. Three things are necessary thereto. He must have been αὐτόπτης ; having seen with his own eyes that which he professes to attest. He must be competent to relate and reproduce this for others. He must be willing faithfully and truthfully to do this. These three things meeting in Christ, and not the presence of the last only, constitute Him a '*true* Witness,' or one in whom all the highest conditions of a witness met." TRENCH.—E. R. C.]

[**The beginning** (ἀρχή) **of the creation of God.**]—[1] The *principle* of the creation; see Col. i. 15.—False interpretations: [2] The Prince [*Fürst*, first] of the creation; [3] The Founder [*Fürst*, first] of the creation; [3] The new creation, the Church; [4] The first and most glorious Creature of the creation. See John i. 1 sqq. [The first of the preceding views, the one adopted by Lange, is the one advocated by Alford and Trench. Their arguments as against the 4th, or Arian, view, are embodied in the following extract from Barnes. Both these distinguished commentators cite, as supporting their opinions as to the use of the term ἀρχή, many passages from Apocryphal and early Christian authors. TRENCH writes as follows: "For the use of ἀρχή in the sense and with the force which we here demand for it as '*principium*,' not '*initium*' (though these Latin words do not adequately reproduce the distinction), comp. the *Gosp. of Nicod. c.* 25, in which Hades addresses Satan as ἡ τοῦ θανάτου ἀρχὴ καὶ ῥίζα τῆς ἁμαρτίας; and further, Dionysius, the Areopagite (c. 15) : ὁ Θεός ἐστιν πάντων αἰτία καὶ ἀρχή; and again, Clement of Alex. (*Strom.* iv. 25) : ὁ Θεὸς δὲ ἄναρχος, ἀρχὴ τῶν ὅλων παντελῆς. These, and innumerable other passages, abundantly vindicate for ἀρχή that active sense which

---

* [The word *competent* is a better translation. The idea of the original seems to be best brought out in the phrase : *the Witness, the faithful and the competent.*—E. R. C.]

we must needs claim for it here." BARNES, who adopts the 2d of the above views, presents the entire subject in the following powerful language: "The phrase here used is susceptible, properly, of only one of the following significations, viz.: either (a) that He was the beginning of the creation in the sense that He caused the universe to begin to exist, that is, that He was the author of all things; or (b) that He was the first created being; or (c) that He holds the primacy over all, and is at the head of the universe. It is not necessary to examine any other proposed interpretations, for the only other senses supposed to be conveyed by the words, that He is the beginning of the creation in the sense that He rose from the dead as the first fruits of them that sleep, or that He is the head of the spiritual creation of God, are so foreign to the natural meaning of the words as to need no special refutation. As to the three significations suggested above, it may be observed, that the first one—that He is the author of the creation, and in that sense the beginning, though expressing a Scriptural doctrine (John i. 3; Eph. iii. 9; Col. i. 16), is not in accordance with the proper meaning of the word here used—ἀρχή. The word properly refers to the commencement of a thing, not its authorship, and denotes properly primacy in time, and primacy in rank, but not primacy in the sense of causing anything to exist. The two ideas which run through the word, as it is used in the New Testament, are those just suggested. For the former—primacy in regard to time—that is properly the commencement of a thing, see the following passages where the word occurs: Matt. xix. 4, 8; xxiv. 8, 21; Mark i. 1; x. 6; xiii. 8, 19; Luke i. 2; John i. 1, 2; iii. 11; vi. 64; viii. 25, 44; xv. 17; xvi. 4; Acts xi. 15; 1 John i. 1; ii. 7, 13, 14, 24; iii. 8, 11; 2 John 5, 6. For the latter signification—primacy of rank or authority—see the following places: Luke xii. 11; xx. 20; Rom. viii. 38; 1 Cor. xv. 24; Eph. i. 21; iii. 10; vi. 12; Col. i. 16, 18; ii. 10, 15; Tit. iii. 1. The word is not, therefore, found in the sense of authorship, as denoting that one is the beginning of anything in the sense that he caused it to have an existence. As to the second of the significations suggested, that it means that He was the first created being, it may be observed (a) that this is not a necessary signification of the phrase, since no one can show that this is the only proper meaning which could be given to the words, and therefore the phrase cannot be adduced to prove that He is Himself a created being. If it were demonstrated from other sources that Christ was, in fact, a created being, and the first that God had made, it cannot be denied that this language would appropriately express that fact. But it cannot be made out from the mere use of the language here; and as the language is susceptible of other interpretations, it cannot be employed to prove that Christ is a created being. (b) Such an interpretation would be at variance with all those passages which speak of Him as uncreated and eternal; which ascribe Divine attributes to Him; which speak of Him as Himself the Creator of all things. Compare John i. 1–3; Col. i. 16; Heb. i. 2, 6, 8, 10–12. The third signification, therefore, remains, that He is 'the beginning of the creation of God,' in

the sense that He is the Head or Prince of the creation; that is, that He presides over it so far as the purposes of redemption are to be accomplished, and so far as it is necessary for those purposes. This is (a) in accordance with the meaning of the word, Luke xii. 11; xx. 20, et al., ut supra, and (b) in accordance with the uniform statements respecting the Redeemer, that 'all power is given unto Him in Heaven and in earth' (Matt. xxviii. 18); that God has 'given Him power over all flesh' (John xvii. 2); that all things are 'put under His feet' (Heb. ii. 8; 1 Cor. xv. 27); that He is exalted over all things, Eph. i. 20–22. Having this rank, it was proper that He should speak with authority to the church at Laodicea."—E. R. C.]

Ver. 15. **Thy works.**—Works are of value only as indications of the character of the persons performing them. Lukewarm hearts, lukewarm works, and vice versâ. [See comments on ch. ii. 2.—E. R. C.]—[**That neither cold nor hot** (Lange: warm)] —The application to this passage of the distinction between the perfectly righteous, the perfectly unrighteous, and those occupying a middle position, is misleading; far more applicable is Dante's description of the sinners peopling that portion of Hell which lies immediately beyond the direful portal—wretches too bad for Heaven, and even for Hell; i.e., the present passage of Scripture speaks of qualitative not of quantitative things. Most certainly the warm one is he who hangs upon the Lord, for only a personal relationship of love to Jesus, and conduct actuated by that love, make warm life. Whilst De Wette and others regard ψυχρός as the antithesis to ζεστός, Düsterdieck, with Hengsten. and others, justly insist that the antithesis is a vacillating middle conduct. Düsterdieck's positive definition of coldness as enmity and resistance to the Lord, such as were manifested by Saul of Tarsus, is, however, as incorrect as Hengstenberg's theory concerning a cold person who is painfully sensible of his coldness. The antitheses are: the believer—the non-believer—and in the midst, the half-believer, who in his inmost soul is already an unbeliever. [I would, etc.—"Ὄφελον, properly the second aorist of ὀφείλω, but now grown into an adverbial use (= utinam), has so far forgotten what at the first it was, as to be employed promiscuously in all numbers and persons; cf. 1 Cor. v. 8; 2 Cor. xi. 1. It governs an indicative, not an optative, here (ἧς not εἴης, is the right reading), inasmuch as the Lord is not desiring that something even now might be, but only that something might have been. In form a wish, it is in reality a regret." TRENCH. But in what respect is a lukewarm worse than a cold condition? The author just quoted answers the question thus: "Best, I think, . . by regarding the 'cold' as one hitherto untouched by the power of grace. There is always hope of such an one, that, when he does come under those powers, he may become a zealous and earnest Christian. He is not one on whom the grand experiment of the Gospel has been tried, and has failed. But the 'lukewarm' is one who has tasted of the good gift, and of the powers of the world to come, who has been a subject of Divine grace, but in whom that grace has failed to kindle more than the feeblest spark. The pubficans and harlots were 'cold,' the Apostles 'hot.' The Scribes and Pharisees, such among them as that Simon in whose house the Lord sat and spake the parable of the fifty and the five hundred pence (Luke vii. 36–47), they were 'lukewarm.' It was from among the 'cold' and not the 'lukewarm,' that He drew recruits."—E. R. C.]

Ver. 16 The figure is unmistakably derived from the nauseating effect of lukewarm water when taken into the mouth. [The figure is indicative of most fearful woe, namely, utter rejection by Christ as loathsome.—E. R. C.] The μέλλειν must be distinguished from a positive θέλειν.

Ver. 17. I am rich.*—This is not, as a number of commentators suppose, to be referred to the earthly wealth of the flourishing emporium of Laodicea, though the connection between external riches and the danger of an inward conceit of riches cannot be ignored. Comp. the Old and New Testaments. The fancied wealth of spiritual goods is, therefore, the thing intended, in accordance with most commentators. [" So far as the language here is concerned, this may refer either to riches literally, or to spiritual riches. . . . It is not easy to determine which is the true sense, but may it not have been that there was an allusion to both, and that, in every respect, they boasted that they had enough ?" BARNES. —E. R. C.] Note the climax: πλούσιός εἰμι, etc., [see p. 134.]

And knowest not.—This is no mere simple self-delusion; it is marked in its character, being an aggravated ignorance, over against a supposed multiplied knowledge.—That thou, even thou.—ὁ ταλαίπωρος—the wretched one, par excellence.

Ver. 18. I counsel thee.—The "dash of irony" which Ebrard discovers in this expression, may consist in the fact that Christ does not here approach the spiritualistic [spiritualistisch] indifferent in His historical authority, because such an one has loosed the bond of historical obedience. He meets him on the ground of his false liberty. If he will not obey the voice of the Lord, he must still hear the language of truth.† Perfectly analogous to this form is the further declaration: Behold, I stand at the door—a hint to the Church in her dealing with [self-] emancipated spirits [emanzipirte Geister].‡

* [Trench would connect this verse with the preceding: "placing a colon at the end of ver. 16, and a full stop at that of ver. 17."—E. R. C.]

† [" There is a certain irony, but the irony of Divine love, in these words. He who might have commanded, prefers rather to counsel; He who might have spoken as from Heaven, conforms Himself, so far as the outward form of His words reaches, to the language of earth. To the merchants and factors of this wealthy mercantile city, He addresses Himself in their own dial ct." TRENCH. "There is a deep irony in this word. One who has need of nothing, yet needs counsel on the vital points of self-preservation." ALFORD. Is it not better, as more consistent with the character of the compassionate and long-suffering Saviour, to suppose that there is no irony here? The language, couched indeed in the commercial dialect of those addressed, is such as a loving Father, yearning over indifferent and ungrateful children, might use to win th m to better things.—E. R. C.]

‡ [By this expression, Lange doubtless would indicate those who, in his own language, might better be styled (self-) emancipated spiritualists. The adjective emanzipirt has, when employed in certain connections, the meaning of self-emancipation—thus an emanzipirte Frau, is a woman who has freed herself from conventionalisms—as we say in English, a strong-minded woman.—E. R. C.]

To buy.—There can be no question of an actual purchase by a meritum de congruo; for Laodicea is poor and naked, and the thing to be procured is gold. Yet the usual Protestant idea —the church must simply surrender her self-conceit; that is the purchase-price (Vitringa, Bengel, and others)—conceals in some measure the true relation of things. Such a surrender invariably presupposes an advance toward the Saviour in penitence and self-denial.* According to Ebrard, the Lord's counsel should be followed invertedly; first, eye-salve, then raiment, then gold. There are substantial grounds, however, for the order given. The gold purified in the fire, the fidelity of faith, tested in temptation and trial (Hengstenberg, fides; à Lapide, caritas; Düsterd., spiritual good things; Ebrard, good fruits). [Is it not the righteousness of Christ, imputed to him who believes, by virtue of which the possessor becomes rich (comp. Rom. v. 15–18; 2 Cor. viii. 9)?—E. R. C.]

White garments.—Throughout the Apocalypse, these represent the victorious adornment of that righteousness of life which is based upon the righteousness of faith. Hence they are not of like meaning with the gold (Düsterd.), nor do they denote the subjective purification of the heart (Ebrard), which cannot be seen as can white garments. [May not the reference be to the entire righteousness of sanctification (holiness of heart and life) produced by the Spirit? The garments of the Saints are white within as well as without.— It may here be remarked, that it is utterly vain to expect that any one material figure should set forth a spiritual truth in all its phases.— E. R. C.] The eye-salve, κολλούριον (the classic form is κολλύριον), is likewise differently explained (as the word of God, the gift of the Holy Spirit Who enlightens).

Ver. 19. Ἐγώ.—After the Lord's apparent self-coördination with the church, His high and sovereign personality emerges once more to view. This is the case here, however, especially in order to the expression of the fact, that His rebuke and chastening are pure love, and that His love can chasten and punish; and all this in contrast to the loose and anti-personal nature of indifferentism, which perverts love into laxity, accounts punishment as harshness, and utterly sunders the two. [Comp. Heb. xii. 5–13; Prov. iii. 12.—E. R. C.]

As many as I love.—Düsterdieck justly insists, in opposition to Vitringa, that this does not apply merely to the better portion of the church.

[I rebuke and chasten.]—The relation of ἐλέγχειν and παιδεύειν is in harmony with Christian liberty. The sinner must first suffer himself to be convicted, intellectually corrected; then grace begins to exercise an affectionate discipline over conscience and life.

* [And so it might be said, that any advance presupposes a previous advance. There must be a beginning of spiritual activity somewhere. This surrender, this giving up the tinsel of one's own righteousness, is essentially involved in that living faith which rests upon Christ alone for salvation, and which is the beginning of spiritual activity.— E. R. C.]

[For a full discussion of the force of ἐλέγχειν, see *Lange on John* xvi. 8 (Am. Ed., pp. 472 sqq.). Trench writes that it is "more than ἐπιτιμᾶν, with which it is often joined; see my (his) *Syn. of the N T.*, § 4. It is so to rebuke, that the person rebuked is brought to the acknowledgment of his fault, is convinced, as David was when rebuked by Nathan (2 Sam. xii. 13)." This definition will scarce bear the test of thorough exegesis. It is manifest that in the use of the term Matt. xviii. 19, an *acknowledgment* of sin is not contemplated, but the contrary. The word is one which expresses the act of an agent, and not the effect of that act upon its object; it is such a presentation of the truth as leaves the object without excuse for not believing (comp. John viii. 46; xvi. 8; 1 Cor. xiv. 24; Eph. v. 11, 13; 1 Tim. v. 20; 2 Tim. iv. 2; Titus i. 9, 13; ii. 15; Heb. xii. 5; Jas. ii. 9). The necessary consequence of *rebuke* thus defined may, indeed, be a dim, inchoate perception of the right, but not necessarily that completed *judgment*, that *conviction*, which involves an *acknowledgment* even to self; and even this perception is not necessarily contemplated in the use of the term. (In John iii. 20; viii. 9; the only other passages in which the term occurs, its use is peculiar. In the latter the man was his own rebuker—*conviction* preceded *rebuke*; in the former, the idea is somewhat similar—here a dim perception of the fact of sin leads the transgressor, *instinctively*, to avoid the light which will clearly manifest his unworthiness.) The term παιδεύειν is also too much restricted by Trench, and apparently by our author. The former writes: "Παιδεύειν, being in classical Greek to instruct, to educate, is in sacred Greek to instruct or educate *by means of correction*, through the severe discipline of love," etc. This is the meaning of the English word *chasten*, which was used by our translators to render the word whenever, in their judgment, the παιδεία was castigatory (1 Cor. xii. 32; 2 Cor. vi. 9; Heb. xii. 6, 7, 10; see also παιδεία in Heb. xii. 5, 7, 8, 11; and παιδευτής, Heb. xii. 9); but it is by no means the established sacred usage of the original term. That *fatherly* correction was not always contemplated, see Luke xxiii. 16, 22 (and *perhaps* 1 Tim. i. 20); that *castigation* was not always implied, see Acts vii. 22; xxii. 3; 2 Tim. ii. 25; Titus ii. 12; also παιδεία, Eph. vi. 4; 2 Tim. iii. 16; and παιδευτής Rom. ii. 20. An *apparent* force is given to the remark of Trench from the frequent recurrence of the word (and its allies) in Heb. xii., where it appears *eight* times out of the *twenty-one* instances of its New Testament use. These, however, in an exegetical point of view, constitute but one appearance. It appears in only *thirteen* independent passages; in *three* of these only do the contexts require us to limit its specific meaning to the training of *castigation* (Heb. xii. 5–10; 1 Cor. xi. 32; 2 Cor. vi. 9—possibly *four*, if we include 1 Tim. i. 20); and in *seven* this specific meaning is excluded by the context (see above). The classical force of the word is retained in the Scriptures. Its proper meaning is to *discipline*, to *educate*; and into this education enter all the elements of spiritual training. Παιδεύειν includes ἐλέγχειν. A context may, indeed, limit

the education spoken of to one specific kind. In such case only have we a right to regard it as limited. In the passage under consideration, in which sin is referred to, doubtless, chastisement was contemplated; but we should not suppose that chastisement *alone* was in the view of the Divine speaker. This very epistle entered into the παιδεία.— E. R. C.]

[Be zealous, therefore, and repent.— "This word (ζήλευε), through ζῆλος connected with ζέω and thus with ζεστός (ver. 15), is chosen as the special word of exhortation, with special reference to the lukewarmness," etc. TRENCH. "Be earnest, strenuous, ardent, in your purpose to exercise true repentance, and to turn from the error of your ways." BARNES.—E. R. C.]

Ver. 20.—This verse also makes part of the special word to Laodicea; it is not, therefore, an epilogue to the whole (Vitringa). Yet the entire proceeding here described forms a picture which closes the preceding epistles and touches upon the approaching Parousia.

The door.—Generally interpreted, the door of the heart, the knocking being referred to the word of God, the Holy Ghost, special visitations. [Compare Song of Sol. v. 2–6.—He *knocks* in every incident of providence—in every act of παιδεία—that produces the thought of Himself in the mind.—E. R. C.] The door of the heart however, is *the personal liberty*. The standing before this door is expressive of three things: 1. Christ is not in the heart of the lukewarm; 2. He recognizes the liberty of shutting Him out which the lukewarm person possesses; 3. He makes a positive assault up n that unfreeness which lies in the abuse of liberty. The Lord's knocking in the last time is a synthesis of the threatening presages of judgment and His word. According to Bengel, the promise, *I will sup with him*, must be understood of the earthly life; *he with Me*, of the heavenly. The promise, however, distinguishes in a general manner a lower and higher grade of spiritual life (Martha, Mary). Our passage has nothing to do with the figure of the Marriage; it treats of the establishment of a personal intimate relationship between Christ and the individual church, or, better, the individual soul. [Compare John xiv. 21–23.—E. R. C.]

Ver. 21. The promise, in its special greatness, certainly corresponds to the special greatness of the victory to be gained by the Laodicean (Ebrard); in its peculiar nature, however, it also forms a contrast to the destruction whence he must tear himself. According to Düsterdieck, this promise is merely the greatest and last. But as the final promise it points, with peculiar expression, to the all-embracing, consummate victorious form of the heavenly glory. Düsterdieck justly discards the distinction of different thrones of the Father and the Son (Calov.), referring to the oneness of the throne in ch. xxii. 1. [Is it not a promise of *kingship* in the Basileia (comp. Dan. vii. 27; Matt. xxv. 21; Luke xxii. 30; and the Excursus on the Basileia, p. 93 sqq.)?—E. R. C.]

SUPPLEMENTARY REMARKS ON THE HISTORICAL REALIZATION OF THE PROPHETIC CHURCH-PICTURES.

We wish, first of all, to establish the following points:

1. The seven epistles are by no means *episcopal* letters designed as an introduction to the Apocalypse: they are *prophetic* letters, constituting the first part of the Apocalypse itself, and forming a foundation for the whole.*

2. Hence, the life-pictures of the seven churches are not merely historical portraits of the Apostolic Church (issued through an episcopal medium, but of prophetic depth and form); they are also prophetic types of churchly conditions, which shall hold good until the end of the world.

3. Still, we should bind ourselves to the general chronological Church-historical conception of the Apocalypse if, in the succession of these pictures, we were to pretend to discover distinct periods of Church history.†

4. Notwithstanding this, the Prophetic Spirit has, out of the synchronistic coördination of the seven Asiatic churches, indubitably made an ideal succession which, in its beginning and end, is at the same time unmistakably historical. For Ephesus is manifestly a picture of the Church toward the end of the apostolic time, whilst Laodicea pictures it as it shall be in the last time, according to the fundamental traits of that time, as predicted Matt. xxiv. 37 sqq. And thus individual attempts at exposition, conceiving of the seven churches as historical periods, may be worthy of notice; in any case, the ideal foundation, the prophetic view of a spiritual world-historical process of development, such as we have sketched above, must be retained. The attempts themselves, however, are by their disagreement characterized as mere attempts.

The construction of the Catholic Theologian Holzhauser is incorporated by Haneberg in his *History of Biblical Revelation*, p. 690:

1. Ephesus: End of the apostolic age. 2. Smyrna: Time of the martyrs. 3. Pergamus—Confession of faith: Time of the great Church fathers, from the fourth to the sixth century. 4. Thyatira—Laudable condition: Time of the Church's domination, from Justinian to Charlemagne; warning (?) against worldliness—Jezebel. 5. Sardis: Semblance of Christianity; the prevailing condition of the Church at the present time. 6. Philadelphia—Destitute of exterior power, yet witnessing a faithful confession: Perhaps our immediate future. 7. Laodicea, *i. e.*, people's judgment: The end.

* [Are they not, on Lange's own hypothesis, both episcopal and prophetic? Epi-copal, as coming from the great Shepherd and *Bishop* of souls (1 Pet. ii. 25) to the individual churches in Asia Minor primarily addressed; and also to those portions of the Church throughout the ages respectively prophesied concerning, through the medium of these individual churches as types.—E. R. C.]

† [We should so bind ourselves, if we pretended (as we endeavored) to discover *only* such distinct periods. If it be recognized that all the types may be exemplified at any one time, although only one predominantly, there is no such binding. Manifestly when these epistles were written, all the types existed as realities; but, almost certainly, the existing Ephesus represented the predominant character of the then extant Church. See ADDITIONAL NOTE, beginning in the following column, and paragraph 4 above.—E. R. C.]

Sander furnishes a Protestant pendant to this: 1. Ephesus: Like Holzhauser. 2. Smyrna: As above. 3. Pergamus: Period from Constantine the Great to the middle of the eighth century. 4. Thyatira: From the middle of the eighth century to the Reformation. 5. Sardis: Time of dead orthodoxy, from the end of the sixteenth century to about the latter half of the eighteenth. 6. Philadelphia: Church of Brotherly Love, signalized by the phenomena of Pietism, Herrnhutism, Methodism. 7. Laodicea: Picture of the final period.

We can affirm with certainty that the seven life-pictures are continued side by side through all ages of the Church; now one, and now another, predominating; one prevailing at this place and another at that. There have been illustrations of the figure of Jezebel in all ages. And were there no Philadelphia in the very last time, where would the Lord find His Bride?

[ADDITIONAL NOTE ON THE HISTORICO-PROPHETIC CHARACTER OF THE SEVEN CHURCHES.—As to the nature of the Seven Churches, there are three (logically) possible hypotheses. I. The Historic—that they were *merely* seven churches in Asia Minor; II. The Prophetic—that (having no proper historic character, as existing when the Apocalypse was written), they represent *merely* seven ages of the Church; III. The Historico-prophetic—that they were seven churches then existing, but also typical of seven periods of Church history. The generic Historico-prophetic hypothesis is divisible into two species: 1. The *simple* Historico-prophetic—that merely seven prophetic periods were indicated; 2. The *complex* Historico-prophetic—that seven periods were indicated in which all the typ·s should be exemplified, one exemplification however being predominant in each period, in the order indicated. There have been few, if any, supporters of the II. hypothesis: nearly all commentators who have advocated the prophetic character of the churches, have admitted that the types were realized in the churches mentioned. It is probable, also, that there are no advocates of the I., or Historic, hypothesis, who do not also admit that the seven historic churches were, in some sort, representative of churchly conditions that should be exemplified throughout all periods of the present dispensation. Thus Trench (who, in an exceedingly able Excursus at the end of his work on *The Epistles to the Seven Churches*, opposes the III., or what he styles the "Periodist," hypothesis, admits that 1. "These seven epistles, however, primarily addressed to these seven churches of Asia, were also written for the edification of the Universal Church;" 2. "These seven churches of Asia are not an accidental aggregation, which might just as conveniently have been eight, or six, or any other number; that, on the contrary, there is a fitness in this number, and that these seven do in some sort represent the Universal Church; that we have a right to contemplate the seven as offering to us the great and leading aspects, moral and spiritual, which churches gathered in the name of Christ out of the world will assume. . . . (But) though not exhaustive, . . . they give us on a smaller scale ὡς ἐν τύπῳ, the grander and more recurring features of that life (the new life which Christ brought into the world) ; are not fragmentary, fortuitously strung together ; but have a completeness, a many-sidedness, being selected probably for this very cause ; here, perhaps, being the reason why Philadelphia is included and Miletus past by ; Thyatira, outwardly so insignificant, chosen, when one might have expected Magnesia or Tralles. . . . That these churches are more or less *representative* churches, and were selected because they are so ; that they form a complex within and among themselves, mutually fulfilling and completing one another ; that the great Head of the Church contemplates them for the time being as symbolic of the Universal Church, implying as much in that mystic *seven*, and giving many other indications of the same.'' It is also probable that there are few, if any, who adopt the first species of the Historico-prophetic view, all the advocates of this generic hypothesis adopting more or less completely the second—the one designated in this note as *complex*. This latter specific view, is the one that will be advocated in this paper ; as there is no danger of confusion it will be styled simply, *Historico-prophetic.*

In order to the complete establishment of this hypothesis, three points must be proved: 1. That the Seven Churches are representative of the Universal Church. 2. That they are representative of different forms of Church-life, each of which is always existent, to a greater or less degree, in every period of Church-history. 3. That they are, in their order, representative of the predominant characteristics of the Church in seven periods of her history between the writing of the Apocalypse and the second Advent of Christ.

1. The proof of the first of these points is ably set forth in the language of Trench, quoted above. The following, however, is presented as a more complete *exposé* of the facts upon the view of which the truth of this proposition may be concluded, *viz.:* The nature of the Apocalypse as a Book for the Universal Church (chs. i. 1-3 ; xxii. 6–20 [16]); the mention of the *seven churches* in *immediate connection* with an Introduction contemplating the Universal Church (comp i. 1–3 with 4) ; the choice of the number *seven* (the sacred, mystic number, symbolic of completeness), when there were other, and in some instances, more prominent, churches in the geographical district ; the manifest parallelism of the *seven* candlesticks and the *seven* stars, with the *seven* Spirits of God, ch. i. 4; iii. 1 ("the Holy Ghost sevenfold in His operations" in the Church), and with the *sevenfold* description of the person of Christ, ch. i. 14-16 ; their being symbolized by the seven-branched candelabrum of the Tabernacle (itself, doubtless a symbol of the one light-giving Church, manifold in its branches) tended by the Great High Priest, ch. i. 13 ; ii. 1 (see Notes); the characteristics of the respective churches which set forth every conceivable form of Church-life, each being the complement of all the others, as is each beam of the seven colored rainbow ; the constant call throughout the epistles for *all* to hear and (*heed*) the things said unto the churches, a call manifestly contemplated, and in essence resumed, in the conclusion of the Book, where the address is unquestionably to the Universal Church (ch. xxii. 6-20) ; all these

things are inconsistent with the idea that ch. i. 4–iii. 22, is an unnoted episode, in which *merely* seven churches (and these not, all of them, the most prominent even in their own geographical district) should have been addressed ; but, on the other hand, require the hypothesis that, whilst the seven churches specified were specifically addressed, they were selected and addressed as types of Church-life then existent, and that should continue to exist until Christ should come again.

2. An *à priori* probability as to the truth of the second point—*viz.*, that each of these forms typified a form existent in every period of Church history—arises from all that has been said under the preceding head. Manifestly, they were all existent, in the apostolic age, in the churches specified ; and the most cursory view of history is sufficient to show that these churches have always had their analogues—in every age, there has been *somewhere*, a Philadelphia, a Sardis, a Laodicea.

3. The proof of the third point—*viz.*, that the Seven Churches are, in their order, representative of the predominant characteristics of the Church in the seven periods of her history—is based entirely on observation of history. On this point TRENCH, after stating objections to the hypothesis, remarks : " But all such objections, with all those others which it would only be too easy to make, might indeed be set aside or overborne, if any marvellous coincidence between these epistles and the after-course of the Church's development could be made out ; if history set its seal to these, and attested that they were prophecy indeed ; for when a key fits perfectly well the wards of a complicated lock, and opens it without an effort, it is difficult not to believe that they were made for one another. But there is nothing here of the kind.'' He admits that " there are two or three fortunate coincidences here between the assumed prophecy and the fact. . . . Smyrna, for instance, represents excellently well the *ecclesia pressa* in its two last and most terrible struggles with heathen Rome ; so too for such Protestant expositors as see the papacy in the scarlet woman of Babylon, the Jezebel of Thyatira appears exactly at the right time," *etc.* His principal objection—*viz.*, that resemblance fails between the church of Philadelphia and the churches of the Reformation, in that the latter suffered the " *open door* " set before them " to so great an extent to be closed again "—is based altogether upon his own interpretation of the *open door*—that it was to *the heathen.* If by this be understood an *open door* to the Kingdom of Heaven (see Note on ch. iii. 8), which had been previously closed by those who made void the law of God by their traditions (comp. Matt. xxiii. 13 ; Luke xi. 52), the coincidence becomes no less striking than in the case of Smyrna. And if by Jezebel is understood, not the scarlet woman of the Papacy, but a world-element brought into a position of power in the Church by the unholy marriage of Church and State—in time assuming the position of a teacher and introducing heathen abominations (see Note on ch. ii. 20), the coincidence between Thyatira and the period following the union becomes more striking than as presented above.

The scheme set forth in the following paragraph, which, as to the great periods indicated, is substantially that of Vitringa, is suggested for consideration. It may here be remarked that, upon the supposition of the truth of the hypothesis, it does not necessarily follow that the different periods should have distinctly defined termini ; it is rather to be expected that, like the colors of the rainbow, the characteristics of adjacent periods, manifestly distinct in their central portions, should blend into one another at each beginning and end.

EPHESUS : The Church of first love, but declining—the primitive era extending to a time between the date of the Apocalypse and the Docian persecution, A. D. 250. SMYRNA : the Church faithful in trial—the period of persecution extending from near the beginning of the third century to about A. D. 312. PERGAMUS : The Church beginning in persecution (martyrdom of Antipas), subsequently brought under the protection of the world-power (dwelling [κατοικειν= secure habitation] where Satan's throne is), earnest in working and faithful in the confession of essential truth, yet having those who, like Balaam, taught the world-power to seduce to heathen customs—the period beginning at the close of persecution. A. D. 312, and extending through the era of Constantine to about A. D. 700. (This was the period of Athanasius, Basil, Ambrese, Jerome, Augustine, Chrysostom ; of the protests against Arianism and Pelagianism ; of the first five Œcumenical Councils ; and also of the introduction of pompous ceremonies and image worship, after the manner of the heathen.) THYATIRA : The Church of earnest working, yet of unholy union with the world-power, in which the State itself, as an authority and a permitted teacher, established heathen rites—a period intimately connected with the former, yet in its culmination different ; having its roots, indeed, in the era of Constantine, but, as a distinct period, really beginning with the transformation of alliance into marriage with the State, culminating in the era of Charlemagne, and running on until lost in the period typified by Sardis, at some time before A. D. 1200. (This was a period of great charities and extensive missionary operations in Britain and throughout northern, central and eastern Europe, and yet of unholy union with, and subjection to, the civil power. In the West, the right of patronage was developed, the right of kings to confirm and invest bishops was established, and that of the emperor to confirm the election of the Pope ; in the East the subservience of the Church was still more complete. Heathenish customs, which at the first seemed to have been adopted

out of compliance with the world, now became, especially in the East, a matter of state control. On the subject of image worship, Gieseler well remarks that "orthodoxy changed according to court caprice ; " it was abolished by Leo Isauricus, A. D. 726 730, but restored by the infamous Irene, who, A. D. 787, summoned a Synod at Nice, which, under her authority and influence, decreed in its favor ; again under imperial authority, it was abolished, and again restored by the Empress Theodora, who, A. D. 842, instituted a yearly festival [ἡ κυριακὴ τῆς ὀρθοδοξίας] in commemoration of its establishment [see Gieseler's Church History, Period III. D v. 1; and Historians generally on Century VIII]. This was an extended period in which ample space was given for repentance.) SARDIS : The Church of uncompleted works, of mere ritual observances, of spiritual death : in which, however, a few living souls were found—the period blending with the spiritual declensions of the preceding, and extending through the dark ages to the Reformation. This was a period in which true religion was confined almost entirely to small and oppressed bodies, as the Paulicians, Albigenses and Waldenses. PHILADELPHIA : The faithful Church, to be preserved, before whose members was set an open door to the Kingdom—a period beginning with the " morning star" of the Reformation," near A. D. 1400, and extending in appreciable degree to the present time. LAODICEA : The outwardly prosperous, but lukewarm Church. Has not this period already begun ? That this is a day of unequaled outward prosperity for the Church is acknowledged by all. Is it not also a period of lukewarmness even in Protestant lands? It is true that this is a time in which, as compared with the absolute works of former days, great schemes of Christian beneficence are in operation. Spiritual warmth, however, is to be estimated, not by the absolute amount of work performed, but by the proportion which that amount bears to ability. The existing schemes of beneficence are sustained and operated by only a portion of the nominal Church ; and still further, they bear a scarce appreciable proportion to the ability even of the portion nominally engaged in them. In point of fact, are not these schemes the work of the Philadelphia which, still preserved, is embusomed within the increasing Laodicea ?*—E. R. C.]

* [SIR ISAAC NEWTON presented a peculiar prophetic scheme. He referred the seven churches to the times of the fifth and sixth seals, which he placed between the periods of the division of the Empire under Dioclesian, A. D. 285, and A. D. 378. All these churches, he held, were destroyed, with the exception of Smyrna and Philadelphia, which were continued as the two Witnesses of ch. xi. 3.—E. R. C.]

SECTION SECOND.

The Seven Seals.

Chap. IV. 1—VI. 17.

A.—IDEAL HEAVENLY WORLD PICTURE CONCERNING THE SEVEN SEALS. STAND-POINT OF THE SEER IN HEAVEN. THE HEAVENLY WORLD AS THE ARCHETYPE AND FINAL GOAL OF THE EARTHLY WORLD.

Chap. IV. 1—V. 14.

a. Translation of the Seer to Heaven.

1　　After this [these things] I looked [saw[1]], and, behold, a door was [om. was] opened [set open] in heaven : and the [that] first voice which I heard was [om. was] as it were of [om. it were of] a trumpet talking [speaking] with me; [,] which said [saying[2]], Come up hither, and I will show thee things which must be here-
2　after [after these things]. And [om. And[3]] Immediately I was in the Spirit [spirit] :

b. The Throne, the Sitter thereon, and His Government.

And, behold, a throne was set [stood[4]] in heaven, and one sat on the throne [upon
3　the throne[5] one sitting].[6] And he that sat [the one sitting] was [om. was[7]] to look upon [in appearance] like a jasper and a [om. a] sardine stone : and there was [om. there was] a rainbow round about the throne, in sight [appearance] like unto
4　[om. unto] an emerald. And round about the throne were [om. were] four and twenty [twenty four[8]] seats [thrones] : and upon the seats [thrones] I saw [I saw][9] four and twenty [twenty-four[8]] elders sitting, clothed in white raiment [garments] ; and they had [om. they had[10]] on their heads crowns of gold [golden crowns].
5　And out of the throne proceeded [go forth] lightnings and thunderings and voices [voices and thunders] :[11] and there were [om. there were] seven lamps of fire burning

---

TEXTUAL AND GRAMMATICAL.

[1] Ver. 1. [B*. gives εἴδων.—E. R. C.]

[2] Ver. 1. Instead of λέγουσα [Rec., P. א⁵ᵃ.], read λέγων, [with א.] A. B*., Lach., Words., Alf., Treg., and Tisch.—E. R. C.]

[3] Ver. 2. The καὶ before εὐθέως is not firmly established, according to א. A. [B*., etc.; P. gives it. Lach., Words., Alf., Treg. and Tisch., omit.—E. R. C.]

[4] Ver. 2. [The original is ἔκειτο, the literal translation of which would be lay ; the English idiom requires stood.—E. R. C.]

[5] Ver. 2. 'Επὶ τὸν θρόνον, comp. Düsterdieck, p. 209. [Rec., with P., gives τοῦ θρόνου ; א. A. B*., Lach., Words., Alf., Treg., and Tisch.—E. R. C.]

[6] Ver. 2. [" This ord r is retained by the Latin and German Verss., Syr., It., Fr., S., —Daub., Woodh., Sharp., Treg., Kenr." (Alford). Dr. Lillie :—E. R. C.]

[7] Ver. 3. Against the ἦν, before ὅμοιος [given by Rec., P. and Vulg.], Codd. א. A. B*.

[8] Ver. 4. Each time εἴκοσι τέσσαρες without καί. It is a perplexing question whether the second twenty-four is connected with the thrones or with the elders. The thrones, however, have their number from the elders—not vice versâ. The τοὺς before the twenty-four elders [with B*.] would certainly be premature here. [The correct reading of this entire passage is exceedingly doubtful. The Rec. gives καὶ κυκλόθεν τοῦ θρόνου θρόνοι εἴκοσι καὶ τέσσαρες· καὶ ἐπὶ τοὺς θρόνους εἴδον τοὺς εἴκοσι καὶ τέσσαρας πρεσβυτέρους καθημένους. All the authorities omit καὶ before τέσσαρες in both instances, and also εἴδον. In the first sentence Lach. and Tisch., with א. and A., give θρόνους, Words., Tisch., and Treg., with B*., give θρόνους, Words., Alf., Treg., with B*. give θρόνοι· also with P., omit the second τοὺς; Lach. and Alford, with A., read ἐπὶ τοὺς εἰκ. τέσσ. θρόνους πρεσ. καθ. Cod. א. omits all the words between ἐπὶ and τέσσαρες inclusive. In the judgment of the Am. Ed the reading of א is to be preferred ; in The reading of Treg. (which Lange supports) is adopted in the translation.—E. R. C.]

[9] Ver. 4. [" All the recent editors reject εἴδον on the authority of A. B., ... I recommend that this reading be followed, but, in order to mark the change of construction, would leave I saw in italics, as a supplement, extracted from the ἰδοὺ of ver. 2. See Win. § 64, 3. 1." Dr. Lillie's Notes, etc.—E. R C]

[10] Ver. 4. The ἔσχον before ἐπὶ τ. κ. unfounded. [It is omitted by א. A. B*. P., and critical authors generally.—E. R. C.]

[11] Ver. 5. [The order φωναὶ καὶ βρονταὶ is given by Lach., Words., Alf., Treg., Tisch., in accordance with א. A. B*. P.—E. R. C.]

6 before the throne,[12] which are the[13] seven Spirits of God. [;] And [and] before the
 throne *there was* [*om. there was—ins.* as it were] a sea of glass [glassy sea][14] like
 unto crystal : and in the mid-t of the throne, and round about the throne, *were*
7 [*om. were*] four beasts [living-beings[16]] full of eyes before and behind. And the
 first beast [living-being] *was* [*om. was*] like a lion, and the second beast [living-be-
 ing] like a calf [bullock[16]] ; and the third beast [living-being] had [having] a [the]
 face as[17] [*ins.* of] a man, and the fourth beast [living-being] *was* [*om. was*] like a
8 flying eagle. And the[18] four beasts [living-beings] had each of them [each one of
 them having][19] six wings [*ins.* apiece[20]] about *him* [*om.* about *him*][21] ; and *they were*
 [*om. they wer*—*ins.* round about and within were][22] full of eyes within [*om.* within] :
 and they [*om.* they] rest [*ins.* they have] not [*ins.* by] day and [*ins.* by] night, saying, Holy, holy, holy,[23] Lord God [*ins.* the] Almighty [*or* All-ruler[24]], which [who]
9 was, and [*ins.* who] is, and [*ins.* who] is to come [cometh]. And when [whenso-
 ever] those [the] beasts [living beings] [*ins.* shall] give glory and honor and thanks
 to him that sat [sitteth] on [upon] the throne, who [to him that] liveth for ever
10 and ever [into the ages of the ages], the four and twenty elders [*ins.* shall] fall
 down before him that sat [sitteth] on [upon] the throne, and [*ins.* shall] worship
 him that liveth for ever and ever [into the ages of the ages], and [*ins.* shall[25]] cast
11 their crowns before the throne, saying, Thou art worthy, O Lord [our Lord and
 God],[26] to receive [take] [*ins.* the] glory and [*ins.* the] honor and [*ins.* the] power :
 for thou hast created [didst create] all things, and for thy pleasure [on account of
 thy will] they are [were[27]] and were created.

CHAP. V. 1—14.

c. *The Sealed Book of the World's Course. Lamentation and Comfort touching the Sealed Book with the*
Dark Enigmas of the World's History.

1   And I saw in [upon] the right hand of him that sat [sitteth] on [upon] the
 throne a book [scroll] written within and on the back [*or,* without[28]] side [*om.*

12 Ver. 5 [Alford brackets αὐτοῦ after θρόνου, in accordance with B*. Lach., Treg., and Tisch., omit with א³ª. A. P.—
E. R. C.]
13 Ver. 5 [Alford brackets τα in respect of its omission by B*. ; Lach., Words., Treg., Tisch. give it with א²ª. A. P. and
Rec.—E. R. C.]
14 Ver. 8 [B*. and Rec. omit τὰ. —E. R. C.] The adjective is retained here by Latin and German Verss., Dt.; Wakef., Woodh., *etc.* (Comp. Horace,
Carm. IV. 2, ' *Vitreo* . . *Ponto ;* ' and Milton, *P. L.* VII. 619 : ' The clear *hyaline,* the *glassy* sea ')." Dr. Lillie's *Notes, etc.*
—E. R. C.]
15 Ver. 6. [' The E. V. ' *beasts* ' is the most unfortunate word that could be imagin-d. A far better one is that now
generally adopted, ' *living-creatures ;* ' the only objection to it being that when we come to vers. 9, 11, we give the idea, in
conjoining ' living-creatures ' and *created* (ἔκτισας), of a close relation which is not found in the Greek." Alford.—
E. R. C.]
16 Ver. 7. [" Μόσχος is not necessarily to be pressed to its proper primary meaning, as indicating the young calf in
distinction from the grown bullock ; the LXX. use it for an ox generally, in Exod. xxii. 1 ; Lev. xxii. 23 ; also Exod. xxix.
10, and Gen. xii. 16." Alford.—E. R. C.]
17 Ver. 7. The reading ὡς ἀνθρώπου in accordance with A., *etc.* Cod. א. reads otherwise still. [Cod. א. reads : ὡς
ὅμοιον ἀνθρώπου ; Wordsworth, with B*, omits ὡς ; Alford brackets ; Lach., Tisch., and Treg. read with A.—E. R. C.]
18 Ver. 8 [B*. and Rec. omit τὰ. —E. R. C.]
19 Ver. 8. The reading : ἓν καθ' ἓν αὐτῶν ἔχον. [Lachmann, as Lange. Alford, and Tisch., give ἓν καθ' ἓν αὐτῶν, with
A. P.: (B*. also gives ἓν καθ' ἓν, ut omits αὐτῶν) ; Wordsworth follows the Rec., ἓν καθ' ἑαυτὸ ; Tregelles, with A. and
Vulg., gives ἓν ἕκαστον αὐτῶν. Alf., Treg., and Tisch , with A , give ἔχων ; Lach. and Words., with B*., ἔχον ; א. Rec.
Vulg., εἴχον. The readings of Treg. are adopted in the translation.—E. K. C.]
20 Ver. 8. [For the force of ἀνά, see Winer, § 49. b.—E. R. C.]
21 Ver. 8. [There is great difference amongst critical editors as to the connection of κυκλόθεν. Treg. agrees with Rec.
in connecting it with the preceding πτέρυγας ἕξ ; Lach., Words., Alford, Lillie, Tisch., with Vulg. and Lange, connect with
καὶ ἔσωθεν. Lillie thus supports the latter arrangement (*Notes, etc.*) : " (1) Assuming ἔχον or ἔχων and γέμουσιν to be
the true r-adings, the structure of the whole verse is simplified ; (2), the other arrangement does not harmonize with the
cherubic appearances before referred to, ver. 7 ; (3), and might have precluded the Seer's minute observation of the other
features (vers 6, 7), which first caught his eye ; while, (4), the construction proposed is apparently required by the ἔμπροσθεν and ὄπισθεν of ver. 6 : and, (5), is that adopted by Vulg., Fr., 8.; Grot., Hamm., Bong., Sch., Wordsworth." Cod.
B*. has, after κυκλόθεν, καὶ ἔξωθεν.—E. R. C.]
22 Ver. 8. [For the unauthorized γέμοντα of the Rec., all the modern critical editors, with א. A. B*. P., Vulg., *etc.*, read
γέμουσιν.—E. R. C.]
23 Ver. 8. [The ἅγιος occurs *nine* times in B*., and *eight* times in א¹.—E. R. C.]
24 Ver. 8. [See *Additional comment* on ch. i. 8, p. 93.—E. R. C.]
25 Ver. 8. [Lach., Words., Alf., Treg., Tisch. give βαλοῦσι (ν) with א**. A., Am., Fuld. ; βαλλοῦσι is given by א*. B*.;
Vulg. (Cl.) reads *mittebant*.—E. R. C.]
26 Ver. 11. According to A. B*., *etc.* [Lach., Words., Alf., Treg., Tisch., with א. A. B*., read ὁ κύριος καὶ ὁ θεὸς ἡμῶν (א.
prefixes κύριε, and B*. subjoins ὁ ἅγιος) : P gives κύριε ὁ θεὸς ἡμῶν. Lange translates : *our Lord and our God.*—E. R. C.]
27 Ver. 11. [The Rec. εἰσι agrees with P. Lach., Words., Alf., Treg., Tisch., with א. A. B*., read ἦσαν. B*. gives our
ἦσαν ; on this Alford remarks : " The remarkable reading οὐκ ἦσαν is worth notice, ' by reason of Thy will they were not,
and were created,' *i. e.,* ' they were created out of nothing.' But besides the preponderance of authority the other way,
there is the double chance that οὐκ may have arisen from the preceding ου (σου), and that it may have been an escape from
the difficulty of ἦσαν.'—E. R. C.]
28 Ver. 1. The reading : ὄπισθεν so far as the sense is concerned, the same as ἔξωθεν. [Lach , Words , Alf., T eelles,
Tisch., with א. A., give ὄπισθεν ; ἔξωθεν is given by B*., Vulg., *etc* ; the reading : ἔμπροσθεν καὶ ὄπισθεν in א., Origen,
etc.—E. R. C.]

2 side], sealed [*ins.* up] with seven seals. And I saw a strong angel proclaiming with [in[29]] a loud [great] voice, Who is [*is*[30]] worthy to open the book [scroll], and
3 to loose the seals thereof [of it]? And no man [one] in heaven, nor in [upon] earth, neither [nor] under the earth, was able to open the book [scroll], neither [nor even][31]
4 to look thereon [upon it]. And I wept much,[32] because no man [one] was found worthy to open and to read [*om.* and to rea t][33] the book [scroll], neither [nor even]
5 to look thereon [upon it]. And one of the elders saith unto me, Weep not: behold, the Lion [*ins.* that is][34] of the tribe of Juda, the Root of David, hath [*om.* hath] prevailed [conquered] to open[35] the book [scroll], and to loose [*om.* to loose][36] the seven seals thereof [of it].

d. The Lion as the Lamb.

6 And I beheld [saw], and, lo, [*om.*, and, lo,][37] in the midst[38] of the throne and of the four beasts [living-beings], and in the midst of the elders, stood [*om.* stood] a Lamb [*ins.* standing], as [*ins.* if[39]] it had been [*om.* it had been] slain, having seven horns and seven eyes, which[40] are the seven Spirits of God sent forth[41] into
7 all the earth. And he came and took the book [*om.* the book[42]] out of the right hand of him that sat [sitteth] upon the throne.

e. Worship of the Lamb.

8 And when he had taken the book [scroll], the four beasts [living-beings] and [*ins.* the] four *and* twenty [twenty-four] elders fell down before the Lamb, having every one [each] of them [*of them*] harps[43] [a harp], and golden vials full of odours [in-
9 cense], which are the prayers of [*ins.* the] saints. And they sung [sing] a new song, saying, Thou art worthy to take the book [scroll], and to open the seals thereof [of it]: for thou wast slain, and hast redeemed [didst buy] us [*or om.* us[44]] to God by [with] thy blood out of every kindred [tribe], and tongue, and people, and na-
10 tion; And hast made [didst make] us [them[45]] unto our God[46]kings [a kingdom[47]] and priests:[4] and we [they] shall[48] [*or om.* shall] reign on [upon *or* over][50] the
11 earth. And I beheld, and I heard [*or ins.* as[51]] the [*or* a] voice of many angels

[29] Ver. 2. In accordance with **A. B***. [**א**.], *etc.*, ἐν(φωνῇ). [So also Lach., Words., Alford, Treg., and Tisch.; Rec. with P., Vulg., *etc.*, omits ἐν.—E. R. C.]

[30] Ver. 2. The ἐστιν aft.r τίς is omitted, which throws a stronger emphasis on ἄξιος. [It is omitted by critical editors generally, in accordance with **א**. A. P., *etc.*; Rec., with Vulg., inserts it *before* ἄξιος, and B*. *after* that word.—E. R. C.]

[31] Ver. 3. [Wordsworth and Alford give οὐδέ three times; Lachmann and Tregelles give οὐδέ οὐδέ, οὔτε, with A.; Tisch., with B*., gives οὔτε thrice; and **א**., οὔτε twice, omitting the intermediate. See also Winer, ₂ 55 b (d.)—E. R. C.]

[32] Ver. 4. Πολὺ instead of πολλά, in accordance with B*. [πολὺν]. **א** [P.], *etc.*

[33] Ver. 4. Καὶ ἀναγνῶναι is omitted. [So Lach., Words., Alford, Treg., Tisch., with **א**. B* P., *etc.*—E. R. C.]

[34] Ver. 5. The ὤν is omitted. [So all the recent critical editors, with **א**. A. B*. P., *etc.*—E. R. C.]

[35] Ver. 5. The reading ἀνοίξαι, in accordance with A. [**א**.] and many others, against ἀνοίγων [B*.]. (*Cl.*).—E. R. C.]

[36] Ver. 5. [Lach., Words., Alf., Treg., Tisch., with A. B*. P., Amiat., *etc.*, omit λῦσαι, which is given by Rec., **א**., Vulg.

[37] Ver. 6. The clause καὶ ἰδοὺ, supported by B. [?], *etc.*, is also supported by the context. The Seer wishes to prepare his readers for an unexpected, great and new vision. It seems most hazardous to erase the two words. [B*. d es not support the clause. It is omitted by Lachmann, Wordsworth, Alford, Tregelles, Tisch., with **א**. B*., *etc.* A. and Vulg. give it.—E. R. C.]

[38] Ver. 6. [Lange translates: "the middle point." Alford translates: "the midst," commenting: "the words seem to indicate the middle point before the throne."—E. R. C.]

[39] Ver. 6. [For the translation *as if*, see Robinson under ὡς. B. a; Kühner, ₂ 312, 6.—E. R. C.]

[40] Ver. 6. Unimportant variations, see in Düsterd. [**א**. A. and Vulgate give οἱ; Tischendorf, with B*., gives ἅ.—**■**. R. C.]

[41] Ver. 6. The reading ἀποστελλόμενα has B., and the sense, in its favor. [So Wordsworth; Alford and Tischendorf read ἀπεσταλμένα, with **א**.: Lach. and Treg., ἀπεσταλμένοι, with A.—E. R. C.]

[42] Ver. 7. Without βιβλίον. [Lach., Alford, Tregelles, and Tisch., with **א**. A., omit τὸ βιβλίον; Wordsworth gives it; B*. gives τήν.—E. R. C.]

[43] Ver. 8. [Modern editors, with **א**. A. B*. P., give κιθάραν.—E. R. C.]

[44] Ver. 9. Against the insertion of ἡμᾶς are Cod. B. [?], *etc.* Still more opposed to it is the context, for ἡμᾶς would refer to the living-beings as well as to the elders. Hence we should read αὐτούς in ver. 10 also, in accordance with Cod . A. B., *etc.* [Lachmann, Wordsworth, Alford, and Tisch., with A., omit ἡμᾶς; Tregelles, with **א**. B*. P., Vulgate, *etc.*, gives it. It is marked above as doubtful.—E. R. C.]

[45] Ver. 10. [Critical editors, with **א**. A. B*., give αὐτούς.—E. R. C.]

[46] Ver. 10. Τῷ Θεῷ ἡμῶν, omitted by A., is probably connected with the foregoing variations. [Lachmann and Alford, with A., omit; Wordsworth, Tregelles, Tischendorf, with **א**. B*. P., Vulg., *etc.*, give the expression.—E. R. C.]

[47] Ver. 10. Βασιλείαν. [Lachmann, Alford, Tregelles, and Tisch., with **א**. A., give βασιλείαν; Words., with B*., *etc.*, read βασιλεῖς.—E. R. C.]

[48] Ver. 10. [Cod. **א**. reads ἱερατείαν.—E. R. C.]

[49] Ver. 10. Βασιλεύουσιν. [Lachmann, Wordsworth, Alford, Tregelles, with A. B*., read as Lange. Tischendorf, with Cod. **א**. Amiat., Fuld., Tol., Harl., gives βασιλεύσουσιν; the Vulgate (*Mem.*) requires βασιλεύσομεν. The weight of ancient authority seems t me to be about equally divided between the *present* and the *future* forms. The conditi n of those who utter the song *in heaven*, together with the promise to the saints of *future* authority upon and over the earth, in my judgment, require the *future*.—E. R. C.]

[50] Ver. 10. [For the force of ἐπί with the gen., see Winer, ₂ 47, a.—E. R. C.]

[51] Ver. 11. [Tregelles and Tischendorf, with **א**., give ὡς before φωνήν; Lachmann and Wordsworth, with A. B*. (corr.), P., Vulgate, *etc.*, omit; Alford brackets.—E. R. C.]

round about [around[52]] the throne, and the beasts [living-beings], and the elders: and the number of them was ten thousand times ten thousand [myriads of myriads], and 12 thousands of thousands; Saying with a loud voice, Worthy is the Lamb that was [hath been] slain to receive [take] [*ins.* the] power, and riches, and wisdom, and 13 strength, and honor, and glory, and blessing. And every creature which [that] is[53] in heaven, and on [upon] the earth,[54] and under the earth,[55] and such as are in [upon[56]] the sea, and all [things[57]] that are in them, heard I saying, [*ins.* To him that sitteth upon the throne and to the Lamb, *be*] Blessing [the blessing], and [*ins.* the] honor, and [*ins.* the] glory, and [*ins.* the] power [might], *be* unto him that sitteth upon the throne, and unto the Lamb [*om. be* unto him that sitteth upon the throne, and 14 unto the Lamb] for ever and ever [into the ages of the ages]. And the four beasts [living-beings] said, Amen. And the four *and* twenty [*om.* four *and* twenty][58] elders fell down and worshipped him that liveth for ever and ever [*om.* him that liveth for ever and ever][59].

52 Ver. 11. [Recent editors, ℵ. A. B*. P., Vulgate, *etc.,* give κύκλῳ.—E. R. C.]
53 Ver. 13. Without ἐστιν. [Lachmann, Wordsworth, Alford, Tregelles, Tischendorf, with ℵ. A. B*., omit ἐστιν after ὅ (ℵ. τό); Tregelles and Tischendorf omit it also after θαλάσσης with ℵ.; Lachmann and Alford give it in the latter place with A. B*. P.; Wordsworth, with B*. P., reads ἃ ἐστι.—E. R. C.]
54 Ver. 13. [Recent editors, with ℵ. A. B*. P., *etc.,* give ἐπὶ τῆς γῆς.—E. R. C.]
55 Ver. 13. [ℵ. omits ὑποκάτω τῆς γῆς, which is given by A. B*., Vulgate, *etc.*—E. R. C.]
56 Ver. 13. [Recent editors give ἐπὶ τῆς θαλάσσης, with A. B*. P.; ℵ. and Vulg. give ἐν τῇ θαλάσσῃ.—E. R. C.]
57 Ver. 13. [Lachmann, Alford, Tregelles, Tischendorf, with ℵ. P., read πάντα; Wordsworth and Lange read πάντας, with Vulgate; (Tregelles claims A. for πάντα, Alford cites it as reading πάντας); B*. reads πάντα καὶ πάντας.—E. R. C.]
58 Ver. 14. [Εἴκοσι τέσσαρες, which is supported by the Vulgate (*Clem.*), *etc.,* is omitted by critical editors, with ℵ. A. B*. P., Amiat., Fuld., *etc.*—E. R. C.]
59 Ver. 14. This addition is not based even upon minuscules.

EXEGETICAL AND CRITICAL.

[PRELIMINARY NOTE ON THE SYMBOLISM OF THE VISION.]

By the American Editor.

[The question—What did the Apocalyptist behold?—is one of great interest and importance. It is almost universally admitted, that he did not look upon the *real* Heaven and *real* angels. The scene he beheld was *symbolic.* But what is a symbol? What are the classes of symbols? What relation do they bear to the objects symbolized?

It is not designed in this note to discuss the whole subject of Symbolism. For this, the writer does not feel himself to be, at present, prepared; neither has he time or space for so great a work. He would, however, present certain views which may prove helpful to a more thorough appreciation and understanding of the Apocalypse than at present obtains, and which also may be of use as preparatory to that complete discussion of the entire subject, which, in the not distant future, must be made.

A *Symbol* may be defined to be a *substantial* (*real* or *apparently real*) *sense image of some other object.* Ordinarily, in the enumeration or classification of symbols, not only are *substantial objects* given, but also *attributives* (such as acts, effects, relations, *etc.*), and *chronological periods* and *numbers.* These latter, for scientific purposes, are better classed as symbolic *attributives, periods* and *numbers,* contemplating under the term *Symbol* only *substantial* (*real* or *apparent*) objects.

Symbols are of two essentially distinct classes, viz.: *material* and *visional.* The former are *material* things, such as the Tabernacle, the Mercy-Seat, the Candlestick, and the Cherubim of the Tabernacle, the Water of Baptism, and the Bread and Wine of the Lord's Supper. *Visional Symbols* are those images, having the appearance of substantiality (*simulacra*), beheld

10

in ecstatic vision. The latter were the objects beheld by the Apocalyptists (Daniel, Ezekiel, John), and concerning these alone is it designed, in the present note, particularly to treat. It is here proper to remark, however, that whilst scientific arrangements of these two classes of symbols based on their nature will be somewhat different, those based on a consideration of their relations to the ultimate objects represented will be precisely similar, as will appear.

As has just been hinted, Symbols may be classed on two essentially distinct principles: *first,* in respect of their *nature ;* and, *secondly,* in respect of their *relations to the ultimate objects symbolized.*

The former, which, so far as the writer is aware, is the only classification that has been attempted, is exceedingly important; it is absolutely essential to a complete presentation of the subject of Symbolism. The following, adapted to meet the special views of the present writer, from Winthrop's *Essay on Prophetic Symbols,* pp. 16 sqq. (and therein credited to Lord's *Theological and Literary Journal,* Vol. III., pp. 688 sqq.), is presented for consideration.*

I. LIVING CONSCIOUS AGENTS.
  1. Intelligent, (1) the *Ζῶα,* Rev. iv. 6, 8, 9; (2) Angels; (3) Men, *etc.*
  2. Unintelligent, (1) Brutes; (2) Monster Animals.

II. DEAD BODIES, such as the *slain witnesses,* Rev. xi. 8–11.

III. NATURAL UNCONSCIOUS AGENTS OR OBJECTS; as the earth, the sun, the moon, stars, mountains, *etc.*

IV. ARTIFICIAL OBJECTS IN ORDINARY USE: as candlesticks, crowns, swords, harps, *etc.*

___

* [This table was prepared with special reference to Visional symbolization. It should be noted, however, that in *form* it presents a classification, not of Visional Symbols themselves, but of the apparent elements thereof; by the *Visional Symbol* must be understood the *simulacrum of*

A still more important classification, however, is to be made in respect of the relations existing between the symbol and the *ultimate object* symbolized. The following, which does not profess to be more than tentative, is presented for consideration.

The symbols (*simulacra*) beheld by John and the other Apocalyptists are at once divisible into two classes: *Immediate* and *Mediate* The former *immediately* represent the *ultimate* object contemplated, as the *simulacra* of Heaven, the Elders, the Angels; the latter represent the ultimate through the *medium* of some other object, as *Christ* is represented by the Simulacrum of a *Lamb*, and a *church* by that of a *candlestick*. This distinction is clearly implied in the narrative of John. Sometimes he wrote as though he directly beheld the ultimate objects; he saw Heaven, the Throne, and Him who sat thereon, and the Angels: and again he wrote, not as beholding the ultimate, but some object that represented it; he saw, not Jesus, not the Holy Spirit, but a Lamb representing the former, and Seven Lamps the latter. In the descriptive language of the Apocalyptist, the *simulacra*, which formed the common elements of the entire vision, were, so to speak, eliminated, and he wrote as though he directly beheld the things which the *simulacra* represented,—sometimes the ultimate object, sometimes the intermediate object that denoted the ultimate. In the former case, the *eliminated simulacra* were *immediate*; in the latter, *mediate*. In reference to the latter class, we occasionally find the Seer interpreting the symbol as in Rev. i. 20, " The *seven stars* are (*i. e.* represent) the Angels," *etc*. This was not always done, because, generally, it was *unnecessary*, as in the case of the *Lamb slain* representing Christ. It was done, however, with sufficient frequency to indicate the law.

Immediate symbols are divisible into *two* orders, *viz*.: (1) *Similar*, where the *form* of the *simulacrum* corresponds with that of the ultimate, as where the *simulacrum of a man* symbolizes a *man;* (2) *ideal*, where the *form* is not an image of the *form of the ultimate*, but is an *ideal image* (not, however, a likeness of some other known object) expressive of the *qualities of the ultimate*, as the (probably) ideal *simulacra* of the angels. *Mediate* symbols may be divided into *three* orders, *viz*.: (1) *individual*, where the *simulacrum* indicates an individual ultimate, as where the Lamb indicates Christ; (2) *classical*, where it indicates a class of individuals, substantial entities regarded as one whole, as where the *simulacrum* of a *candlestick* symbolized a *church*, and that of a *woman*, the *universal Church;* (3) *aberrant*, where the simulacrum (always *appa-*

rently substantial) indicates as its ultimate, not a *substantial*, but an *ideal* entity, as where the *simulacrum of a* sword indicates justice ; and that of a horseman, war or pestilence.

From the preceding classification we deduce five orders of symbols, which may be designated with sufficient clearness as follows: I. Immediate-similar; II. Immediate-ideal; III. Mediate-individual; IV. Classical; V. Aberrant.*

All the *attributives of symbols* (qualities, actions, relations to other symbols, *etc.*) are themselves symbolic, *i. e.* they represent some *attributive* of the ultimate object. They are of two kinds: *Similar* and *Ideal*. *Similar*, when some similar attributive is denoted, as where the walking, standing, speaking, of the symbol denotes that the individual symbolized walks, stands or speaks; *Ideal*, when something dissimilar is indicated. Thus *the opening of the Seven Seals by the Lamb* is *Ideal*; it denotes, not an actual opening of seals by Christ, but a disclosure of the previously concealed purposes of God. It may be observed that this division is analogous to the general divisions of the symbols themselves, given in the preceding foot-note. It may also be remarked that in the case of Classical and Aberrant Symbols, all the attributives are necessarily *Ideal*.

Numbers as applied to symbols, whilst they cannot properly be classed as attributives, have a like division. They are either *Similar*, denoting a like number as applied to the ultimate, or *Ideal*. *Chronological periods* may be in like manner divided.

One important fact in reference to Visional Symbolization should here be distinctly noted, as its non-recognition has resulted in much confusion. A *simulacrum* may *immediately* represent a *Material symbol*. Thus, for instance, in the real world, a *throne* is a *real thing*, even though it be at the same time a *Material Symbol* of established sovereignty. Now in the *Visional* symbolization of a palace and its furniture, the simulacrum of *the throne* would be an *Immediate* Symbol: it would designate a really existent substance. *The throne in the palace* would be a *Material Aberrant* symbol indicating sovereignty. The *simulacrum of that throne* would be a *Visional Immediate* symbol representing, primarily, a real throne. Such a *Visional* symbol, it should be remarked, would legitimately suggest that which the *Material* Symbol represented, and, under certain circumstances, might be designed to suggest it. From these observations it follows that a *Visional* Symbol may perform the double office (1) of *immediately* symbolizing a *Material* Symbol as a substance, and (2) of *aberrantly* representing that which the Material symbol was designed to set forth.

the thing *specified* therein. With certain modifications the table may be regarded as presenting a classification of *Material Symbols*. These are of two distinct, though parallel, orders: the *first*, embracing those *real* existencies that are themselves employed as Symbols—as the *lamb* of sacrifice, the *bread* of the Lord's Supper; the *second*, consisting of material *images* (of real or ideal existencies) that are thus employed—as the *image* of the flying fiery serpent, the *Cherubim of the Tabernacle*. The above table presents a complete classification of the *first* of these orders, in so far as it is a classification of *real* existencies that have been employed as Symbols; it bears to the *second* order a relation precisely similar to that which it bears to Visional Symbols.— E. R. C.]

* [These orders may be more scientifically deduced as follows : There are four *general* respects in which every symbol is related to its ultimate object, *viz*.: as to (1) manner of representation, (2) correspondence of nature, (3) form, (4) number; and in each of these respects it must be related in one of two alternative modes. Its relation must be in view of (1) *manner of representation*, either *Immediate* or *Mediate* ; (2) *correspondence of nature*, either *Correspondent* or *Aberrant* ; (3) *form*, either *Similar* or *Ideal* ; (4) *number*, either *Individual* or *Classical*. From a combination of these general divisions there would result, theoretically, *sixteen* distinct orders of symbols. Several of these, however, would

The effort will be made to apply the principles set forth in this Note in additional notes and comments throughout the remainder of the Commentary.—E. R. C.]

SYNOPTICAL VIEW.*

Chs. iv. and v.

THE SEVEN SEALS.

The Vision of the Seven Seals embraces the history of the world,† reposing upon the foundation of the Divine counsel and government. This history is represented in its constant gravitation toward the end. It is, on the one hand, in its fearful form, the riddle of all riddles, a book sealed seven-fold; but, on the other hand, unsealed by the Lamb of God, by Christ and the spirit of His cross, it appears as the foundation of the Church's history, as the history of the Kingdom of God [Church]. Its Sovereign Ruler is the Rider on the white horse,‡ behind Whom the other terrible horsemen must ride as esquires. It is thus dynamically governed by the Christian idea or, rather, the personal Christ; its object being the renewal of mankind by the connection of all human suffering with the redemptive crucial suffering of the Lamb. The Lamb, as It had been slain, is the central Personality, in the infinite life-giving operation of Its central suffering. As is the relation of the Logos to the world, of Christ to the human and spiritual world, so is the relation of Christ's suffering to all the sufferings of humanity, down to the very depths of Sheol [Hades]. Accordingly, the vision, in respect of the celestial foundation which it constitutes, is the archetype of the world's history—not its precursive counterpart, in accordance with Jewish ideas. See Düsterdieck, p. 211. The picture of the world's history, again,—especially its history in New Testament times—ch. vi., is the foundation of external Church history, in respect of its eschatological bearings; whilst the Church, in respect of its inner relations as exhibited in the seven Churches, is the ideal *prius§* of world-history. On the *seven seals* rest

be impossible of realization. Thus a symbol at once *Aberrant* (*i.e.* differing in *nature* from its object) and *Natural* (*i. e.* similar in *form*) is inconceivable. And of those that are *possible* of realization, several have no exemplification in the Scriptures. The five orders given above (all of which are exemplified in the Apocalypse) are here reproduced, an enumeration of the general divisions to which each belongs being given in the parenthesis.
 I. Immediate-similar (Immediate, Similar, Correspondent, Individual).
 II. Immediate-ideal (Immediate, Ideal, Correspondent, Individual.
 III. Mediate-individual (Mediate, Ideal, Correspondent, Individual).
 IV. Classical (Mediate, Ideal, Correspondent, Classical).
 V. Aberrant (Mediate, Ideal, Aberrant, Individual).
     —E. R. C.]
 * [Additional comments, save in a few special instances, are reserved for EXPLANATIONS IN DETAIL, on pp. 150 sqq.—E. R. C.]
 † [If by *world* is meant the present *æon* or *dispensation*, extending to the Second Advent and the complete establishment of the Basileia, this statement is manifestly true, since the *seventh seal* includes the *trumpets* and the *vials*. If, however, by *world* is contemplated the *earth*, as the scene of life and activity, the statement cannot be accepted. See Introduction by the American Ed, also Lange on ch. i. 1, p. 156.—E. R. C.]
 ‡ [For other interpretations of the Rider on the white horse, see *Comm.* on ch. vi. 2, p. 171.—E. R. C]
 § [Lange reproduces this term from the Latin. As there was no German word that could express his idea, it is hardly possible that an English term can be found.—E. R. C.]

the *seven trumpets;* on these, the *seven thunders,* and against these last, the opposition of the *seven-headed dragon* rears itself, calling forth, in its turn, with its two *seven-headed* [?] Antichristian organs, the *seven anger-vials of judgment;* the vials of anger being, as the end of the old world, the preliminary condition of the new.

The effort to decide whether John beheld the whole series of visions in an unbroken succession, or whether prophetic sight ceased between the individual visions, and he set down by parcels that which he had seen only in part (Bengel and others), is the result of a rather literal conception of the Apocalypse. The latter view overlooks the grand unity of the vision in its totality, a unity which is even distinctly expressed in chap. i., and without which the lively connection of the whole could be comprehended only through the assumption of *immediate* inspiration. On the other hand, the opposite theory ignores the freedom of the symbolic expression; in accordance with which the conception, given in its fundamental outlines on one Sunday, might be further developed in, with and amid its setting forth in writing, being continually accompanied by prophetic evidence.*

The sublime Heaven-scene of chs. iv. and v., introduced by the words, μετὰ ταῦτα εἶδον, is the type of all subsequent Heaven-scenes. And like the rest, it is, as a Heaven-picture, the preliminary condition of the earth-picture; in the sense, that is, of an absolute Providence of the Personal God—a Providence overruling the progress and development of freedom in the world, in their human and demonic aspects, in the might of *light and right* (Urim and Thummim), in order to the carrying out of judgment to the victory of salvation.

Single Features of the Heaven-Scene.

The *Open Door in Heaven* is the full unfolding of the Apocalyptic revelation even unto its deepest heavenly foundation. In the first stage of vision, Christ came to the Seer on earth, clarifying the condition of the Seven Churches, already historically familiar to John, into a type of all future fundamental forms of the Church. In this new stage of vision, Christ transports John to Heaven itself: this higher power of vision is signalized by the words: *Immediately I was in the spirit.*

The *Throne of God* needs no explanation: it denotes the absolute firmness of His government.† He *sits* upon the Throne—an ex-

 * [It is somewhat difficult to determine from this passage what view Lange adopts. The most natural hypothesis seems to be that John beheld the visions like the unfoldings of a panorama (see the frequent recurrence of the phrase μετὰ ταῦτα εἶδον, ch. iv. 1; vii. i. 9; xv 5; xviii. 1; xix. 1, and similar expressions through the Book); and that he wrote as he beheld, or in the possible intervals of vision (see ch x. 4, where it is recorded that after hearing the thunders, he was about to write, but was forbidden). The latter part of this hypothesis is not inconsistent with the idea that, after the completion of the entire vision, he wrote at leisure a full account of what he had seen and heard, on the basis of the notes he had previously taken.—E. R. C.]
 † [See PRELIMINARY NOTE on p. 145 sqq., especially the concluding paragraph on p. 145.
 [Is not this symbol, primarily, significant of a *Throne in Heaven*—some glorious seat in the Heaven of Heavens where Jehovah specially manifests His glory? Secondarily, it is indicative not merely of the "firmness" of the Government of God, but of the fact thereof. The *Throne*—the visible seat

pression of His glorious assurance of victory. He sits upon the Throne as the Unique One, the Mystery of mysteries; and yet recognizable as the exalted Personality. He is also more particularly characterized by His symbolic appearance. The *jewels*, as such, denote the most noble life, light and imperishability in one. If we suppose the *sardius*, as the *carnelian*, the *flesh-colored* stone, to be expressive, not of the divine penal righteousness—indicated by the hue of fire—but of God's eternal relation to humanity through Christ, it is probable, that the *jasper* is significant of the Divine Essence in the abstract, in its symbolical appearance everywhere manifest as essential light; and according to this, the *diamond*,* and not the ordinary *jasper*, is undoubtedly intended.

The *Rainbow*, whose arch surrounds the Throne, is indicative of the fundamental tone of God's government; judgment issuing in salvation—covenant faithfulness, an attribute previously expressed by the rainbow of Noah. Amongst the colors of this rainbow, *emerald* [green] is pre-eminent; and it is to this that it is likened [ch. iv. 3]; Divine promise demands human hope.

The *Occupant of the Throne* is immediately surrounded by the *twenty-four Elders*, the ideal representatives of the Old and New Testament Theocracy, human spiritual princes; in respect of their symbolical *number :*† representing the ramifying foundations of the Old and the New Covenant in the adornment of their heavenly perfection—*clothed in white raiment :* and by their *golden crowns*—the sign of their imperishable royal freedom [and authority], won by surrender to God—attested in God as His heroes (Israel=combatant of God).

Before the Throne *the whole governance of God* is manifest. His alternate operations are *lightnings*, and *voices*, and *thunders;* lightnings of heavenly wonders, forming epochs on the earth; *voices*, in which the fundamental idea of these lightnings becomes manifest; and far-reverberating *thunders*, as periods of the rejuvenescence, extension and development of the Kingdom of God [Church].

These operations are conditioned, however, by the *Seven flaming Lamps* [Torches] before the Throne, the Seven Spirits of God, as Fundamental Forms of the personal and permanent Life-Revelation of God in His Logos or the eternal

Christ, or as the Seven Fundamental Forms of the revelation of the Holy Spirit (see s. xi.)* In pursuance of this manifestation of God, the *ideal world* is spread out before His Throne ;—a *sea*, clear like crystal; infinitely swelling and agitated life ; yet in its appointedness harmonizing with the Divine will—as in crystal life is fixed and transparent, like light ; infinite liberty in infinite appointedness.

The foundation of the operations of God in the moral kingdom before the Throne are the *four Life-forms* (beasts) [*Living-beings*] about the Throne ; the four Fundamental Forms of Divine Governance in the universal world generally—also in the creatural world.† For the number of the world is *four ;* the number of the Kingdom of God is *seven* (see below, on the four beasts [Living-beings]). These Life-forms are *full of eyes before and behind* (as also within and without, see ver. 8). That is, the Divine Governance is a thoroughly conscious rule; an absolute looking back upon the foundations and events of life, an absolute looking forward to the aims of life and their preliminary conditions; a perfect insight into the profoundest vital causes, as well as a perfect outlook upon the uttermost vital phenomena. A figure of omniscience in its undying motion over the world, in the consciousness of the Divine Governance. The *lion* appears in this figure as the mighty governance which overcomes all things, the dynamical principle in its irresistible forth-breakings. The *bullock* or *ox* appears as the principle of all sacrifice in the world, the principle of suffering in the creatural life (monstrously perverted into a conflict for existence). The *human face* represents the principle of humanity, relatively pervading the whole world ; this Life-form is expressive of the concentration of the infinite in a likeness of the most conditioned finite life. The *flying eagle* appears as that ideal tendency toward some central sun which not only pervades the planets and comets, but is expressed in the motion of our sun itself; that tendency which is the mystery of all motion—a mystery manifested in its most peculiar essence in the higher tendency of the spirit-world toward the Sun of all life (*I go to the Father*). In a more general sense, however, motion is the property of all four Life-forms [Living-beings]. Each has *six wings* ; for *six* is the number of restless activity in Heaven, of restless labor on earth, of restless self-frustration in the abyss. Hence it is said: *the beasts [Living-beings] have no rest day and night.* Their non-repose, however, consists in the festal work of glorifying God. They glorify Him as the thrice Holy One, Who preserves the purity of His own personality, and works unto purification in all His providential operations throughout the creatural and spiritual world. As the Holy One, He is the *All-Ruler*, Who repels every temptation to an impersonal line of conduct. And at the same time He is *Jehovah* (*Who was, etc.*), Whose covenant faithfulness aims in all ages at the establishment in love of a pure life-kingdom of personal beings.

Now follows the representation of an *antiphony*

---

of the Sovereign—is the symbol of established government. On earth Jehovah now governs, and the fact becomes evident to those who wisely consider; but it is not *patent*: it is in measure hidden beneath the veil of what we style the *laws of nature*. In Heaven, however, it is *immediately* manifest that He upholds those laws, and governs in, and through, and above them.—E. R. C.]

* [So also Ebrard conjectures. Wordsworth thus writes: "The *Jasper* (says Victorinus) is like *water ;* the *Sardine* is like *fire;* and thus these stones seem to represent God's Majesty and Justice as seen in His judgments—that of the *flood*, and that of the *fire* of Sodom and of the Last Day. Or, rather, the union of these two colors; the one of a brilliant and lively hue; the other of a deeper, fiery and darker hue, may perhaps be designed to symbolize the union of Mercy and Glory, with Justice and Majesty in the Godhead, especially in the Gospel dispensation (Rom. iii. 26). Similarly there is a combination of brightness and fire in Ezekiel's Vision (Ezek. i. 4), which also displays the Rainbow (i. 28)."—E. R. C.]

† [See additional comment under ch. iv, 4, p.152 .—E. R. C.]

* [See on ch. i. 4, p.91 —E. R. C.]

† [See on ch. iv. 6, p.154—E. R. C.]

between the beasts [Living-beings] and the Elders. The beasts [Living-beings] have the initiative; for the adoration of the human spiritual princes, the Elders, rests upon the Fundamental Forms of the Divine rule in the world; that Divine Governance which actually redounds to the praise and glory and thanks of Him that sitteth upon the Throne, Who liveth for ever and ever. The Elders fall down before the Throne in humility and reverence, and worship; they cast their crowns at God's feet as a sign that unto Him alone belongs honor, and utter their doxology. It agrees with the doxology of the beasts [Living-beings], with the exception that in the case of the Elders we have δύναμις instead of εὐχαριστία, thanksgiving resolving itself into a glorification of the Divine almighty power. But the Elders further give the reason of their praise, and it is noteworthy that they speak of an ideal existence of things preceding the actual creation of them.

This vision of God's glory in His government of the world constitutes the general basis of the special vision of the world's history. The history of the world is embraced in a book-roll [scroll] in the hand of God; the leaves of which are sealed with seven seals. The book [scroll] must, doubtless, contain seven leaves; otherwise all the seals would of necessity be loosed at once.* At every new leaf of the roll, a fresh seal is encountered; but if the leaf be unrolled, it is found to be written upon both sides. Thus, in God's sight, the history of the world is complete, like a book [scroll]. Its course is septenarious, for its design is holy. But it is a sealed book [scroll]; its whole contents are made up of perplexing and disturbing enigmas. And no being is able to unravel this fearful history, to throw light on the gloom-enwrapped fate of the world. None in the angelic world is able to do this, none in the human world, none in the world of departed souls. Not one can so much as try to look upon the book, to examine whether he can open it. The cry of the strong angel is not simply dramatic; it must be made evident that no spiritual power would have solved the riddle of the world's history, if Christ had not solved it with His cross.

And I wept much, says the Seer. A simple yet sublime expression of the feeling and thought of what the world's history would be, had not Christ's cross and victory unveiled it.† The

weeping Seer is comforted by one of the Elders (for the redemption belongs to humanity), who points him to the glorious victory of Christ (ch. v. 5). The cross must, of course, be perfected in the resurrection; the Lamb that was apparently overcome must be manifested as the triumphant Lion, for only thus might He loose the seals of the world's history. As the Lion of Judah, Christ possessed the lion nature in the highest sense, as the Master of self-denial and self-conquest (Gen. xliv. 33, 34); and the depths of His royal essence are expressed in the announcement that He is the Root of David, the truly real fundamental idea and fundamental impulse of Davidic glory in the centre of humanity.* This Root is significant of the deepest human cause of life; this Lion denotes the most spiritually mighty human appearance. Then the new wondrous vision within a vision is prefaced by the words: I beheld, and lo!

In the midst of the Throne, i. e., directly in front of God, surrounded by the circle of beasts [Living-beings], and by the circle of Elders, there appears a Lamb, as it had been slain—the Man, with the lineaments of absolute patience and the traits of mortal suffering—suffering surmounted, it is true, yet in its effects enduring forever. The attributes of the Lamb, symbolically defined, are seven horns, the sum of holy powers (Matt. xxviii. 18), and seven eyes, the seven Spirits or spiritual manifestations of the one Spirit of God, which are continually going forth from the Lamb into the world. This apparition comes and receives the book [scroll] from the right hand of God. Two things are indicated here: first, the self-presentation of the Lamb upon the summons of the angel; secondly, the fact that He is really to loose the seals. And hence the grand chorus of praise is not postponed until after His action. In reference to His work, the Elders need not await the doxology of the Divine powers of the world. A new song bursts forth from beasts [Living-beings] and Elders in one grand unison. This song relates to the new creation, the redemption. The redemption [Erlösung] is the loosing [Lösung] of all seals, and the Redeemer [Erlöser] alone is worthy to perform this work. The beasts [Living-beings] and Elders base their praise upon the Redeemer's death on the cross (slain), and the effects of that death. He thereby out of all peoples bought a people for God, the New Testament people of the peoples, making of them a Kingdom of Priests who, in dynamical operation, even now, in all their yielding, may, by means of the same, reign on earth. This song of praise in the centre of the heavenly congregation, is echoed in a grand antiphony betwixt the angelic world, on the one hand, and the creatural world, on the other. The doxology of countless angel hosts, forming the remoter circle round the beasts [Living-beings] and Elders, comes first. Their homage is sevenfold, in harmony with the holy throng. The worship of the creatures is fourfold, in accordance with the number of the world. We have here an antiphonal song of praise from all beings, reminding us of Ps. cxlv.

[* Not necessarily. A roll might receive seven seals on either of the flat ends, each seal holding together the edges of a number of the revolutions of the parchment. In such case all the seals would be visible, and any one might be broken without breaking the others. Of course, in the unrolling, the seal nearest to the circumference would have first to be broken, and so on toward the centre. Nor would there be any difficulty in reading such a roll, written within and without, if the writing were in transverse columns, from edge to edge—the entire scroll being turned (longitudinally) when the bottom edge was reached. In this case the portion read would have to be re-rolled in one hand, as the unread portion was unrolled in the other.—E. R. C.]

† [Does not the explanation take for granted that the Seer understood something of the future history before the unrolling? Alford's explanation, in which he agrees with Lyra, seems to be better: "It had been promised to him, ch. i. 1. that he should be shown future events; and now it seemed as if this promise were about to be frustrated by the lack of one worthy to open the Book, ... and his tears burst forth in the earnestness of disappointed desire after the fulfillment of the promise."—E. R. C.]

* [See on ch. v. 5, p.167—E. R. C.]

In a didactical aspect, the *song* is expressive of the fact that the effect of Christ's triumph pervades the entire world of spirits, on the one hand, as an extension of His glory (Eph. i; Phil. ii.) ; and that, on the other, it ushers the whole creatural world into the process of glorification, to be consummated in the Palingenesia (Rom. viii.). The four Life-forms or beasts [Living-beings] can only say *Amen* to this, for therein is the effort of their governance fulfilled. But for the Elders this blissful contemplation is an incentive to unutterable prostration and worship.

EXPLANATIONS IN DETAIL.

Ch. iv. 1. Compare the introductory remarks by Düsterdieck, p. 211. Especially the distinction between the Jewish view of the heavenly preludes (a Divine council with the angels) and the Christian idea. Also the difference of the formulas : μετὰ ταῦτα εἶδον and καὶ εἶδον.*
On the disputed question as to whether John always beheld and wrote down the visions separately, see above [p. 147]. The literal conception is pressed on either side.
[**After these things**.—The reference here is to the order of the visions. It does not necessarily follow that the events symbolized were to be subsequent to those previously set forth.—E. R. C.]
[**I saw**, "not *I looked*, as in the E. V ; not the directing of the Seer's attention, which discovers the door to him, but the simple reception of the vision which is recorded." ALFORD.—E. R. C.]
A door set open in Heaven.—Explanations : Heaven is conceived of as a vault ; as a Temple ; as the Palace of God (Düsterd.). In accordance with the connection, however, the *door* here denotes the disclosure of the highest revelation, and, hence, the insight of John (De Wette). The *voice* is expressive of the heavenly inspiration and legitimation of this view. It distinguishes the real ecstasy of the Seer from an enthusiastic and fanatical exaltation.
[**Set open**.—"Observe here the perfect participle, the door had been opened and was *standing open*. The veil of the heavenly Holy of Holies had been removed by Christ (Heb. x. 19,

---

* [The passages in Düsterdieck specially referred to are as follows:

"On comparing the description, ch. iv., with Rabbinical conceptions, such as *More Nevoch.*, II. 6; '*Non facit Deus quicquam, donec illud* INICITUR *fuerit in familia superiori*,' and *Schir Haschirim* R. fol. 93; '*Non facit Deus quicquam, nisi autea de eo* CONSULTAVERIT *cum familia superiori*' (in Wetstein), we can not overlook the essential difference consisting in the fact that the Johannean view is a pure development of Old and New Testament fundamental truths, whilst the Rabbins had but a corruption of those truths (contrary to Wetst., Eichh., Heinr., Ew., *et al.*.) For the *familia superior*, which is represented by the Rabbins as taking part in the council of God, has, according to John, but to worship God and to magnify the counsel together with the works of God; and the visions beheld by John, in which the things to come are prefigured to him, being in the spirit, are by no means that heavenly prelude of earthly events which the Rabbins conceive of (comp. Wetst.; '*Ex mente Judæorum, quæ in terris eventura sunt, in cœlo eorum consessu angelorum prius manifestantur atque* REPRÆSENTANTUR ')."

"The formula μετὰ ταῦτα εἶδον marks the beginning of a new vision, and that a greater or more important one (chs. vii. 1; xv. 5; xviii. 1), whilst the formula καὶ εἶδον introduces the manifold individual features which present themselves in the course of a greater main picture (v. 1, 6, 11; vi. 1, 5, 8, 9, 12; viii. 2, 13, *et al.*)."—E. R. C.]

---

20), and Heaven was laid open to the view." WORDSWORTH.—E. R. C.]
[The Apocalyptist saw *Heaven, i. e.*, he saw an *Immediate* symbol thereof. As to the fact that Heaven is a *place*, there should be no doubt. It is, indeed, unquestionable that the term Οὐρα-νός is sometimes employed to denote the *sky*, as in Matt. xvi. 2, 3, and sometimes so used as to be consistent with the idea of a mere *state*, but it is also again and again employed in the didactic Scripture, as indicating a glorious and blessed *place*, where God specially manifests His glory, to which the Saviour ascended after His resurrection, and which is to be His abode until His second appearing in glory. (Comp. Acts i. 10, 11 ; iii. 21 ; vii. 55, 56 ; Rom. x. 6 ; 2 Cor. xii. 2 ; 1 Thess. iv. 16, *etc.* See also the Excursus on HADES, p. 364). It can scarce be supposed, however, that the symbolic display of the vision took place in this central home, this Holy of Holies, of the universe. This supposition is not required, as some may suppose, by the language. It is manifest that, throughout the Book, the Seer employs similar expressions where the object of vision was not the thing described, but a *simulacrum* thereof, as in ch. xiii. 1, where he declares that he " saw a beast rise up out of the sea." And still further, precisely the same form of expression is employed, Rev. xxi. 1 (" I saw a new Heaven and a new earth "), when the real objects referred to were not, at the time of the vision, existent—all that he could then have beheld were their *simulacra*. But was the symbol *similar* or *ideal?* On this point it is impossible to speak with certainty ; and, perhaps, it is improper in any degree to speculate. It may be remarked, however, that it by no means follows (as some seem to suppose) from the fact that the complex symbol beheld by John resembled the Tabernacle as to form and arrangement, that it must have been purely *ideal*. On the contrary, it is not improbable that the Tabernacle—the earthly dwelling-place of Jehovah, fashioned by Moses after the pattern shown him in the Mount (Ex. xxv. 40 ; xxvi. 30) —may have been a *material* symbol of the Heavenly Temple, not only *Immediate*, but, so far as the earthly can resemble the heavenly, *similar*.—E. R. C.]
Ver. 2. **Immediately I was in the spirit**. —'Εὐθέως, without a conjunction, forcibly expresses the instantaneous translation of the Seer, thus denoting a high enhancement of the first stage of visionary sight. The text, therefore, forms a new step in comparison with the first *I was in the spirit*, ch. i. 10.* The prototypes of this visionary celestial Throne-picture, 1 Kings xxii. 19 ; Is. vi. ; Ezek. i. ; Dan. vii. 9, have been perverted by the Jews into monstrous allegories. See Düsterdieck, p. 214, the extract from the *Pirke*, R. Elieser, as given by Schöttgen. "*A dextris ipsius est vita, a sinistris mors*." This recalls a kindred idea of Milton's.
The θρόνος ἔκειτο is interpreted in a variety of ways (breadth of the Throne, Bengel ; its resting upon the cherubim (!), Hengsten.) The fact of its establishment in the highest sense is doubtless enwrapped in the κεῖσθαι.†

---

* [See on ch. i. 10, p. 101.—E. R. C.]
† [See foot-note,† p. 147.—E. R. C.]

Upon the Throne *One* sitting.—Not an indefinite designation, but an expression of the loftiest mystery. The Jewish dread of uttering the name of Jehovah (Ewald and others) can hardly have any application here, since the Seer has several times given utterance to that name in a developed form. Herder's explanation is irrelevant: "the soul has no image, language no word whereby He may be called." According to Düsterdieck and some elder commentators, He who sits upon the Throne is not the Triune God, but the Father. This is a misapprehension of the symbolical nature of the distinctions. [May there not be an allusion here to a visible Manifestation of the Glory and Presence of Jehovah similar to the Shekinah, which, in the Tabernacle, beamed from the Mercy-seat (the Throne), from between the Cherubim? For comments on the *Throne*, see p. 147.—E. R. C].

Ver. 3. **Like a jasper stone.**—See the Introduction, pp. 20, 21 [and also p. 148]. The true jasper is sometimes greenish, sometimes of a reddish hue, but not τιμώτατος and κρυσταλλίζων, as this jasper is described, ch. xxi. 11. Hence those exegetes who apprehend the word as expressive either of the ordinary jasper, or of a peculiar and unknown sort, are justly opposed by those who are of opinion that the diamond is intended. See Düsterdieck, pp. 216, 217. Compare likewise the various interpretations of the stones as there given.

And a rainbow.—It is a mooted question whether the *iris* is to be apprehended as a *rainbow*, or merely as a *bow;* whether it encircled the Throne vertically or horizontally. As the light of the sun is refracted in its journey toward the earth, so the refraction of absolute Light can be conceived of only in its direction toward the world, *i. e.*, toward the Seer primarily. Yet the bow, as a bow, can appear only in a vertical form. Green, the color of promise, is a dominant color even in the real rainbow, and it is not without reason that Ebrard (p. 222) and others have apprehended it as forming an antithesis to the hues of the precious stones which denote attributes of the Divine Essence itself. It is not indicated, however, that this circular radiance has its origin in the lustre of the jewels. It is possessed of an independent symbolical meaning; the revelation of God in the world is always, conditionally, at the same time a concealment. A tempering of the Divine radiance (Züllig) lies in the colored appearance of the Divine manifestation, whether a pillar of fire, a pillar of cloud, or a cloud is the instrument of presenting the highest glory to the gaze of imperfect human beings. The bow can, of course, be no true rainbow, since the most sublime refraction of light is intended here; though it cannot be concluded that John had a distinct idea of a heavenly ether in contra-distinction to the grosser atmosphere of earth.

["The *rainbow*, composed by the joint influences of shower and sunshine, is an emblem of Divine severity, blended with Divine love; a symbol of the dark shower of Divine judgment illumined by the bright beams of Divine Mercy. Comp. the vision of Ezekiel, i. 28. The Bow is a record of the *deluge*, in which the world was drowned for sin, and speaks of sunshine after storm; and of the Divine Promise that the world should never more be destroyed by *water;* and yet it is also a silent memento of *another* judgment (see Gen. ix. 13--16, and 2 Pet. iii. 7." WORDSWORTH. The *iris* is but the manifestation of the different hues which *perfect light* assumes when in connection with gross matter. Since *perfect light* is the highest symbol of the Divine Excellence, what so significant of that excellence in its relation to the creature world (disintegrated, so to speak, into what we style different attributes) as the many-colored rainbow? Alford is of opinion that the entire bow was *green*—the shape, and not the prismatic coloring, being indicated by the term *rainbow.* — E. R. C.]

Ver. 4. **Twenty-four thrones.**—According to De Wette, the twenty-four thrones must be conceived of as "a few degrees lower" than the Throne of God. If we bring earthly ideas in play here, "a few degrees" would not be sufficient to indicate the distinction. The definition of the twenty-four Elders is an index to the ecclesiastical and theological stand-points of the different exegetes; they have been interpreted as follows: *cardinals* (Lyra); *priests* (Alc.); *pastors* (Calov.); *true heads of the Church, and pastors* (Vitringa); *the crown of the human race* (Herder the humanist); *angels* (Hofmann)—in accordance with an exaggerated Angelology. Rinck similarly; *Old Testament dignities* ([*Würden*=dignities?] Beng.); *New Testament martyrs* (Eichhorn); half, *representatives of teachers,* half, *representatives of hearers* (Volkmar; not quite democratic enough, since the hearers must necessarily preponderate over the *clergy*). The *number* of the Elders being composed of *twice* twelve, Bleek and others have groundlessly regarded it as indicative of a twofold representation of Jewish and Gentile Christians. Ebrard justly remarks, in opposition to this view, that such a division has no Biblical foundation; whilst Düsterd., on the other hand, erroneously cites ch. vii. 4, 9, in support of the same opinion, though the real antithesis in the passage quoted is—not Jewish Christians and Gentile Christians, but— the Church Militant, and the Church Triumphant. Yet Düsterdieck himself gives the preference to the preponderant interpretation of many commentators, according to whom the twenty-four Elders represent the Old and New Testament Church, or the Twelve Patriarchs of Israel, and the Twelve Apostles. De Wette shows a thorough misapprehension of the symbolism employed, in insisting upon the unworthiness of individual Patriarchs. And thus an adverse argument has been founded upon the names of the Twelve Apostles, ch. xxi. 14. In perfect analogy with this symbolism is the fact that the conquerors on the sea of glass sing "the song of Moses and the song of the Lamb." By this, as well as by the twenty four Elders, the complete harmony of the Old and the New Covenant is expressed. The fact that Jehovah is immediately surrounded by Elders, entirely corresponds with the symbolical significance of the theocratic Presbytery. The Elders represent the purest, richest, and ripest spirits in their Divine likeness and their acquaintance with the counsel of God. In this idea originated the Talmudistic Judaistic ac-

counts of the Elders before the Throne of God
(see Hengst., p. 270; Düsterd., p. 219).

[Düsterdieck thus writes: "The twenty-four
Elders whom John sees sitting on the thrones
which are placed around the Throne of God are
the celestial representatives of the whole people
of God, just as in Isaiah xxiv. 23, Elders (Ancients) are conceived of as the earthly heads
and representatives of the whole Church."*
This view, which is confirmed by a comparison
of Deut. xxxi. 28 with 30, does not exclude, but
confirms, the further idea that the *representative*
Elders were also (individually) *chief* Rulers in
the Kingdom of God. The idea of superiority
in rule was distinctly recognized by Jesus (see
the EXCURSUS ON THE BASILEIA ii. 2 (4), p. 99).
The fact that these Elders are *Rulers* is set forth
by their sitting on *thrones* and wearing *crowns*
(see below). The suggestion of Barnes in explanation of the *number* of the Elders is worthy
of consideration, viz.: that it was in reference
to the *twenty-four* courses of the Jewish Priesthood (see 1 Chron. xxiv. 3-18). On this view
the *twenty-four* Elders are not only Superior
Kings, but the Chief Priests, the Heads of the
priestly courses of the glorified Israel.†—
E. R. C.]

* [Düsterdieck also quotes, as bearing upon the passage
cited from Isaiah, the following passages quote i by Schöttg.
and Hengst. from *Tanchuma* (fol. 48): "*Tempore futuro
Deus S. B. gloriam senioribus tribuit. Dixerunt quoque Rab-
bini nostri: faciet sibi Deus S. B. consessum seniorum suo-
rum.*" Also the following in reference to Dan. vii. 9:
"*Tempore futuro Deus S. B. sedebit et Angeli dabunt sellas
magnatibus Israelis, et illi sedent. Et Deus S. B. sedet cum
senioribus tanquam princeps senatus et judicabunt gentiles.*"
—E. R. C.]

† [In the Additional Comments above, the Am. Ed. has
written as adopting the generally accepted view that the
Elders belong to the glorified Church. He would, in this
place, deferentially suggest for consideration another hypothesis. The evidence for the current view rests solely on
the formerly accepted text of the doxology in which the
Living-beings and the Elders are represented as uniting (ch.
v. 10, 11). Criticism has shown that, in this instance, the
text of the Recepta is specially corrupt; it has established
the fact, that the ἡμᾶς and βασιλεύσομεν of ver 10 are corruptions of αὐτούς and βασιλεύουσιν (or βασιλεύσουσιν),
and has rendered probable (*certain* in the opinion of Lange,
Alford and Tischendorf) the further fact, that the ἡμᾶς of
ver. 9 is an interpolation. It is well nigh certain (from
t xtual criticism alone) that the doxology was raised in view
of the general fact of redemption, and not of the personal
redemption of those who united in it—that it affords no
evidence that any who joined in its utterance were themselves the subjects of redemption. Apart from this doxology,
there is no evidence that the Elders in any way connected with the Church; on the contrary, all the indications
of the Apocalypse are opposed to the idea. Although they
are several times mentioned, it is never as representing the
redeemed, as being amongst them, or as joining in their
hallelujahs. When they are represented as *sitting on thrones*,
the souls of the martyrs—certainly the *noblest portion* of the
redeemed, even if that throng were not intended to represent the whole body of the saved—were *beneath the altar*
(comp. chs. iv. 4 with vi. 9). And where, if not amongst the
martyrs, are the Princes of the glorified Israel to be sought?
When the great multitude of the redeemed stood before the
Throne and raised their hallelujah, the Elders stood, not
with them, but with the Living-beings and the Angels, offering a separate worship and uniting in a separate hymn
of praise (ch. vii. 9-12). On this august occasion one of the
Elders is represented as addressing the Seer, not as a representative of the glorified Host, but as a spectator of their
glory; and as a mere *spectator* (he spoke of *them*, not of *us*),
he gave information concerning their past and future history
(ch. vii. 13-17). In the doxology that burst forth from the
Living-beings and the Elders immediately on the announcement of the complete establishment of the Kingdom of the
Messiah on earth, there was no allusion to any personal
participation in the rewards that should be bestowed on
(human) prophets and saints (ch. xi. 15-18). Again, when
the Lamb at the head of the hundred and forty-four thousand

The *white robes* and *golden crowns* are not
merely symbols of the martyrs or confessors in
the narrower sense; they are expressive of
perfect righteousness of life in its negative and
positive aspects. [The *crowns*, doubtless, are
significant of their kingly authority (see above;
also additional comment on ch. ii. 11) —E. R. C.]

Ver. 5. **And out of the Throne go forth
lightnings.**—[See SYNOPTICAL VIEW, p. 148.—
E. R. C.] According to Düsterdieck, the *lightnings, voices* and *thunders* symbolize the omnipotence of God, especially that almighty power
which is exercised in judgments (similarly
Hengstenberg [also Alford and Barnes.—E. R.
C.]). This interpretation is connected with the
one-sided apprehension of the precious stones as
symbolizing the essence of God. This too special interpretation contrasts with the too general
explanation of De Wette. "In ver. 5 the mighty
and vital influence of God over nature is represented; in vers. 6-8 nature itself, or the realm
of *the living*, is symbolized in the four cherubim;
in vers. 9-11, finally, the harmony of creation
and redeemed humanity is represented; and
thus God, in His living activity and reality, is
exhibited" (De Wette). Similarly Ebrard, who
describes God's Throne as a "laboring, effer-
vescent volcano."*

On theocratic ground the *lightnings* are still
less a purely terrific conception than in the
Scandinavian-Germanic mythology (the hammer
of Thor). With reference to the *lightnings* of
Sinai, comp. Deut. xxxiii. 2, 3. The Coming of
the Son of Man shall be like a mighty flash of
lightning. Thus the *lightnings* of the whole
New Testament manifestation are for the defence
of the faithful people of God, being terrible only
to His foes, Zech. ix. 14. They are, therefore,
wonders of revelation [Divine manifestation?—
E. R. C.].

The history of Christ's Baptism and Transfiguration demonstrates that *voices* are a sequence, in definite ideas and truths, of Divine
revelations—revelations of salvation, in particular; in general, they are the first of the Divine
forms of revelation. Even God's *voices*, His revelation truths, have a judicial as well as an
evangelical side, Gen. iii. 10.

The last remark applies equally to the *thunder.*
This denotes the grand effect of revelation [Divine
manifestation] in judgment and deliverance. Thus
the typical redemption of Israel was effected by a
mighty *thunder* which, at the same time, brought

stood on Mount Zion (where should the Princes of Israel
have been but with that company?), the Elders and the
Living-beings stood apart by the Throne, and *before*
(not by) them the *new song of the redeemed* was sung (ch.
xiv. 1-5).

The writer would ask, Do not these facts go far to confirm
the independent conclusions of criticism as to the true text
of the doxology in ch. v. 10, 11? And do they not tend to
establish the conclusion, that the Elders were not Princes or
representatives of the glorified Church, but Princes of the
heavenly hosts—of unfallen spirits? And it may also be
asked, if this view does not give a unity to this Heaven
scene, and to all the scenes of the Apocalyptic visions,
entirely lacking on the hypothesis generally accepted.—
E. R. C.]

*[The following view of Wordsworth can hardly be ac-
cepted as a complete explanation: "This adjunct (thunders)
confirms the opinion that St. John is here speaking of God's
word. Thunder is the voice of God. St. John himself, as
a preacher of God's word, was named by Christ 'a son of
thunder.'"—E. R. C.]

down judgment on the head of Israel's foes, Ps. lxxvii. 18, 19. Job finds his prostrating judgment, but also his reconciliation, in a grand *thundering* of God, chs. xxxviii.-xl. As thunder accompanied the giving of the Law, so the voice which answered Christ's prayer in the Temple, the prayer with which He consecrated Himself to death for our redemption, was accompanied by a tone as of *thunder*. And the more tremendous the wrathful judgment announced in the thunder, according to Jer. xxv. 30, the more distinct is its proclamation of a new redemption for the people of God; comp. Joel ii. 11. As Elijah, like Moses, was an Old Testament *son of thunder*, ascending to Heaven in a fiery storm, so two of the greatest Apostles of the New Testament were *sons of thunder*. And how glorious is the description of the seven-fold thunder of God in Psalm xxix., the festal thunder-Psalm! This, therefore, is the sense in which we apprehend the *thunders* of God; they are heavenly, uncheckable, redemptive revelations, accompanied by judgments—in other words, reformations.

And seven Lamps [torches]* **of fire burning before the Throne.**—[See SYNOPTICAL VIEW, p. 148.—E. R. C.] We cannot refer the participle καιόμεναι to the preceding ἐκπορεύονται; for the *Lights*, as such, do not issue forth like *lightnings*, and the Spirits of God do not proceed from His Throne, but from Himself. By the Seven Spirits that, according to ch. i., stand between Jehovah and Christ, and, according to ch. v. 6, go forth into all lands, we understand the seven fundamental forms of the revelation of the Holy Ghost through Christ, according to Is. xi. 1, or the seven archangelic forms of Christ.

["These seem to represent the Holy Spirit in His seven-fold working: in His enlightening and cheering as well as His purifying and consuming agency. So most Commentators."—ALFORD. The idea of the *seven-fold* influences of the Holy Ghost is thus set forth in the ordination hymn of the Church of England:

"Come, Holy Ghost, our souls inspire,
 And lighten with celestial fire;
 Thou the anointing Spirit art,
 Who dost Thy *seven-fold* gifts impart."

It may here be remarked, that in the view of the Am. Ed. (see PRELIMINARY NOTE, p. 145 sqq.) the *simulacrum* of the *Seven Lamps* constitute one (compound) *Mediate-individual* Symbol of the Holy Ghost; the *division* being significant of His manifold energies, and the *seven-fold* division, of the completeness, the perfection of those energies.—E. R. C.]

According to De Wette, the Seven Spirits are significant of the Spirit of God as the principle of physical and spiritual life, through Whom the inner influence of God over nature and mankind operates. According to Ebrard, also, the Spirit of God, in all His distinct properties, is denoted, in so far as He rules over the creation. According to Hengstenberg, on the other hand, the πυρός—fire being invariably used in the Apoca-

lypse to designate the Divine wrath (? comp. ch. xv. 2)—here denotes the Spirit of God or of Christ with a limitation, *i. e.*, "in so far as His operations are productive of ruin, are punitive, destructive." To this view Düsterdieck justly opposes the remark, that the Apocalyptist is speaking of *torches* (λαμπάδες). This word is doubtless expressive of the enlightening effect of God's Spirit.

The contrast between the *lightnings, voices, thunders*, which issue forth from the Throne, and the *lights* which are stationary before it, has been explained by De Wette in a manifold way. He suggests the dogmatical distinction of manifestations and inspirations, the distinction between the evangelical history and the outpouring of the Holy Ghost. The *thunder* slowly dies away in the great echoes of the world's history; but the *light* [λαμπάς] becomes a morning star in the heart—in the realm of the interior history of the Kingdom, therefore; and when the Spirit can complete His judgment as the Spirit, that judgment becomes a redemptive judgment.

Ver. 6. **Before the Throne as it were a glassy sea** [sea of glass].—[See SYNOPTICAL VIEW, p. 148.—E. R. C.] The meaning of this is easily gathered from the two items, *sea* and *crystal*—national life and transparent, spiritualized creaturality. Hence the interpretation of Aretius comes very near the point: *cœtus ecclesiæ triumphantis*. Similarly Ebrard, p. 225. The interpretations—some of which are quite singular—of this passage are also, in many respects, characteristic. We cite some of them: Baptism (the baptismal basin); the Holy Scriptures; the perishable world; the smooth and shining heavenly pavement; the atmosphere; or more abstract conceptions (*certa dei voluntas, etc.*). See Düsterdieck, p. 223. In ch. xv. 2 the crystal brightness of this sea is mingled with fire, or the appearance of fire, either because the victors have, in many ways, passed through the fire, or because the victorious Church contains the principle of the fire of the universal judgment. Düsterdieck, referring to Rinck, maintains that the crystal-like sea is identical with the crystal-like river of ch. xxii.; but this view is untenable. The purity, transparency, spirituality of this sea is doubly asserted when it is declared to be both *glassy* and *like crystal*. According to Hengstenberg, the crystal sea is another image of the judgments of God. "Opposed to the flood of human wickedness is the great flood, the broad ocean of Divine judgments."

[The following from Alford is worthy of highest consideration: "Compare, by way of contrast, ἡ καθημένη ἐπὶ (τῶν) ὑδάτων (τῶν) πολλῶν, the multitudinous and turbulent waters, ch. xvii. 1. In seeking the explanation of this, we must first track the image from its Old Testament earlier usage. (*He compares* Exod. xxiv. 10; Ezek. i. 22, *and* Job xxxvii. 10). If we are to follow these indices, the primary reference will be to the clear ether in which the Throne of God is upborne; and the intent of setting this space in front of the Throne will be to betoken its separation and insulation from the place where the Seer stood, and, indeed, from all else around

---

* ["*Seven torches of fire:* λαμπάς in this Book does not mean a *lamp* (see viii. 10), but a *torch* (comp. John xviii. 3); and these seven torches or flambeaux of fire burning before the Throne are contrasted with the Star which *fell* as a *torch from* Heaven (viii 10); comp. *Wetstein* I., p. 507; and *Trench, Syn. N. T.*, p. 193.' WORDSWORTH.—E. R. C.]

it. The material and appearance of this pavement of the Throne seem chosen to indicate majestic repose and ethereal purity. . . . It is the purity, calmness, and majesty of God's rule which are signified by the figure." Wordsworth, who adopts the idea that the *sea of glass* was symbolical of the glorified Church, thus writes: "Sea, in this Book, represents the element of tumult and confusion in this lower world (see xiii. 1). But here, by way of contrast, there is in the *heavenly* Church **a** sea of *glass*, expressive of smoothness and brightness, and *this* heavenly sea is of *crystal;* declaring that the calm of Heaven is not like earthly seas, ruffled by winds, but is *crystalized* into an *eternity of peace.*"

Here, it may be asked, may not the *glassy sea* be an *Immediate* symbol, indicating a real pavement in the real Heaven spreading out before the Throne; but at the same time *aberrantly* significant of the unapproachable grandeur of Him who sits upon the Throne, and (perhaps) of the peace, stability, and brightness of His rule? Similar questions might be asked in regard to other symbols, which generally are explained as merely *Aberrant.—*E. R. C.]

In the midst of the Throne and round about the Throne four living-beings [Lange: life-forms].—[See SYNOPTICAL VIEW, p. 148; and also ADDITIONAL NOTE ON THE LIVING-BEINGS, by the Am. Ed., p. 161 sq.] According to Eichhorn, Ewald I., and Hengstenberg, "the hinder part (of the eagle, and the human figure, as well as the others?) of the four ζῶα lay under the Throne, whilst the upper portion of them projected from beneath it and rose above it." "An idea which, for the sake of its unsightliness, if on no other account, should not be imputed to John. According to Ebrard, the Throne is transparent, and the ζῶα move within it and issue forth from it." (DUESTERD.) IDEM: "One on each side of the Throne, and each in the middle of its respective side." If the Throne be significant of the Divine sovereign rule, the beasts [Living-beings], as individual Fundamental Forms of this government, must issue neither from the foot nor from the summit of the Throne, but from its mid-height, as from the centre of the Divine governance; see above. According to Bengel and Hengstenberg, the four beasts [Living-beings] are emblems of nature or the earth, or of the creation, according to Düsterd.* According to Ebrard, they are *the creative powers* of God Himself, by means of which He exercises a sovereign sway throughout creation (like the lightnings, *etc.*). Against Ebrard's interpretation of the beasts [Living-beings] as representatives of the fourfold *powers* of God, see Düsterdieck, p. 228. The contrast, moreover, is by no means clearly defined.

The germ of the representation of the four Fundamental Forms of Divine Providence is contained in Gen. iii. 24. It is a view which, in constant process of development, runs through the whole of the Sacred Writings; see Ex. xxv. 18; Ps. xviii. 10; (comp. Ps. civ. 4; Is. vi. 2);

Ps. xcix. 1; Ezek. i. and x., *etc.* Riehm, *De natura et notione Cheruborum*, 1861. Lämmert, *Die Cherubim der Heiligen Schrift*, Jahrbb. *für deutsche Theologie*, 12, 4, p. 587. The latter starts from the passage Heb. ix. 5, from the term *Cherubim of glory.* He beholds in the figure of the Cherubim "symbolical representations of the sovereign glory of God, keeping His holy law, overthrowing all that is hostile to Him, but rescuing all that have His laws before their eyes." The explication of the beasts [Living-beings], p. 615, reminds us of Ebrard's interpretation; it offers no inducement to us to depart from our own view as given above. We, therefore, regard the *ox* as expressive of the spirit of sacrifice; the *lion* as expressive of the spirit of irruptive victorious courage; the *human figure* as expressive of the spirit of human and humane sympathy; and the *eagle* as expressive of the spirit of ideality, of striving after the realization of the ideal (see *Leben Jesu*, I., p. 234; *Dogmatik*, 603). Different interpretations: The four Evangelists (whose attributes they certainly are, but not their original symbols); the four cardinal virtues; the four patriarchal churches; the four greatest fathers of the Church; the four mysteries of faith, *etc.* The *quaternary* is manifestly the number of the world. The *six wings* likewise demand consideration; the *eyes*, all about, *as well as within* (directed inward); the *restless motion*, by day and by night, in eternal praise of the thrice Holy One. The *senary* of the wings is *six* in a good sense; restless activity which in its unity makes up the festal *septenary* (see John v. 17). The *wings* are symbolical of the absolute motion of the Divine governance toward higher and highest goals. The *eyes* represent the omniscient rule of Divine Providence, immanent in the life of the world, conscious on all sides. With an absolute *round*-look corresponds an absolute *in*-look, expressive of the contemplative concentration and unity of the Divine omniscience. According to Hengstenberg, the *eyes* are expressive of the permeation of the whole world by spirit; according to Düsterd., they are significant of wakefulness by day and night (of creatural beings?*); whilst the *wings*, as he thinks, denote the dependence and subjection of the creature. The *praise* continually offered by the four Life-forms, the Trisagion, reminds us of the song of praise of the Seraphim (Is. vi.), though it does not follow from this that the Cherubim and the Seraphim should be identified, as Lämmert thinks. These two symbolical angelic groups are undoubtedly connected; yet they also form an antithesis (Ps. civ. 4). See Com. on *Genesis*, p. 241 sq. [Am. Ed.]). Their *hymn* is expressive of the fact that the governance of God, in all its forms, redounds to His praise; to the praise of the glory, the glorious personality of God, Who is Jehovah, in an *involved†* expression (*Who was, etc.*), and Lord of Hosts (Sabaoth), as the *All-Ruler*, in an *involved* expression also.

---

* DE WETTE: These four creatures, as pre-eminent, the first two for strength, and the two others for knowledge, are representatives of all creatures (*creatures—*that rest not day or night?).

* [Yes. Comp. ch. vii. 15, where the redeemed are represented as serving by day and by night (i. e., continually) in the Temple. To the blessed spirits, braced by the atmosphere of Heaven, perpetual service is perpetual rest.—E. R. C.]

† [Mathematically involved. E. R. C.]

Vers. 9-11. [See SYNOPTICAL VIEW, p. 148 sqq.]. "With the representatives of the creation, the four beasts [Living-beings], the twenty-four Elders, the representatives of redeemed humanity, unite in the praise of God" (comp. De Wette, Hengstenberg, Ebrard). The contrast here presented, however, is not that of creation and redemption ; neither is a union of voices intended. On the contrary, the *actual* eulogy of God in the Forms of His government, wakes the antiphony of praise on the heights of the human spirit-world. The future, ὅταν δώσουσιν, is declared by some commentators to be a pure future ; whilst others apprehend it in a frequentative signification—*when* they. or *as often as* they. [This latter view is adopted by Wordsworth, Alford, Barnes, *etc.* See Winer, § 42, 5.—E. R. C.] The relation of priority, as pertaining to the song of praise of the Life-forms [Living-beings], is, however, also enwrapped in the term. They must strike the first notes. It is doubtless indicated, moreover, that there are particular epochs of praise.

Ver. 9. **Give** is a genuine theocratic term: to return that which is beheld or experienced, to its Author, as a spiritual sacrifice.

Glory and honor.—Düsterdieck: Recognition of the glory and honor peculiar to the Lord, "whilst καὶ εὐχαριστίαν denotes directly, without metonymy, the thanks (Hengstenberg) offered by the creature." This under the supposition that the ζῶα are creatures. If, however, they be Ground-forms of the Divine glory or δόξα in its governance, τιμή may denote the objective side of this governance *over* human souls, and εὐχαριστία its subjective side *in* human souls. Comp. the Doxologies, ch. v. 12, 13; vii. 10, 12; x. 6.

To Him that sitteth upon the Throne. —In face of all the terrors of the last times, the Spirit of this prophecy is not afraid that the Throne of God will ever totter. As God lives into the æons of the æons, *i. e.*, into the great æons which are composed of lesser æons (analogue of the Heaven of Heavens), and lives absolutely, so He survives all enemies upon whom the first and second deaths shall prey.

Ver. 10. **The twenty-four Elders fall down—cast [down] their crowns.**—An expression of enthusiastic reverence, prostration, self-abasement, in the recognition of the fact that to Him alone belongeth honor. [It is also expressive of their voluntary and grateful recognition of the fact that as *Rulers* they are subject to Him—that their authority is derived from, and continually dependent upon, Him.—E. R. C.]

Ver. 11. [**Thou art worthy to take.**—"The original signification of the word (λαμβάνω) is twofold ; one, *to take*, the other, *to receive*" (LIDDELL and SCOTT). Is not the fact that it was here used in the former of these senses, indicated by the exchange of δύναμις for the εὐχαριστία of ver. 9? Jehovah *receives* the *thanks* which His creatures *give* ; He *takes* the *power* that can be given Him by none. So far as δόξα and τιμή are concerned, there is an *essential glory and honor* which He *takes* and *holds*, and there is also an *ascriptive glory and honor* which His creatures may *give* and which He *receives*.—E. R. C.]

The glory.—The Elders say: τὴν δόξαν κ. τ. λ.,

because they are responding in a degree to ver. 8 (Bengel and Düsterd.) They seem antiphonally to translate the εὐχαριστία into δύναμις; why is this? DÜSTERDIECK: The representatives of the creature must necessarily and justly return thanks, but the Elders looked upon the work of creation with a certain objectivity. See against this view ch. xi. 17. Even thanksgiving is a δύναμις given of God (*da quod jubes*).* [See the preceding paragraph.—E. R. C.]

[**For Thou hast created all things** (τὰ πάντα=the *all things*, the *universe*).—The Elders here assign the reason why they esteemed Jehovah "worthy to take the glory, and the honor, and the power." Κτίζειν, like the Hebrew בָּרָא, which in the LXX. it is often used to translate, has not the distinctive meaning, *to create ex nihilo* ; in 1 Cor. xi. 9, for instance, it manifestly has the signification : *to form out of previously existing substance*. It may, however, be restricted to the former meaning by the context, and this is clearly the case in this present instance—to *make the all things*, must mean to *create* them. And that this is the meaning, is confirmed by the following sentence (see below).—E. R. C.]

And on account of Thy will (not: *by Thy will*). — ["Because Thou didst will it, ... they were, *i. e.*, they *existed*, as in contrast to their previous state of non-existence, . . . and received it (existence) from Thee by a definite act of Thine, ἐκτίσθησαν." ALFORD after DÜSTERD.—E. R. C.] It is the teleologically higher conception that all things have come into being in order to the fulfillment and glorification of the Divine will (Rom. xi. 36). "Ἦσαν is generally regarded as synonymous with ἐκτίσθησαν." Düsterdieck makes this distinction : *they were*. and thus it is that they were—*they were created*. Almost the same idea again! Nic. de Lyra ingeniously distinguishes the eternal counsel of God and the actual creation. Grotius, with equal ingenuity, distinguishes birth and regeneration. Taking creation and redemption together, the doxology says : for the fulfillment of Thy will, they finally were, and were created (received their shape and impress) with a view to this ultimate design (see Rom. ix., comp. also Ebrard, p. 231).

Ch. v. 1. [**And I saw.**—"Notice that from the general vision, in the last chapter, of the heavenly Presence of God, the scene is so far only changed that. all *that* remaining as described, a particular incident is now seen for the first time, and is introduced by καὶ εἶδον." ALFORD.—E. R. C.]

Ver. 1. **On the right hand of Him that sitteth upon the Throne.** —[See SYNOPTICAL VIEW, p. 149]. For a discussion of ἐπὶ τὴν δεξιάν, in opposition to Ebrard's view, see Düsterd., p. 234. ["The right hand was open, and the book *lay on* the open hand." ALFORD.—E. R. C.]

A scroll.—The book [scroll], βιβλίον, was in the Hebrew form of a *roll* (not in the form of a Roman document, as Huschke maintains).

[In answer to the question, "What is represented by this Book?" Alford presents *seven* different opinions, which may be condensed as fol-

---

* [The prayer of Augustine (*Confess.*, Lib. x. 29): "*Da quod jubes, et jube quod vis.*"—E. R. C.]

lows: 1. The Old Testament, or the Old and New conjoined (Orig., Euseb., Epiphan., Hippol., Victor., August., Tichon., Bede, Hilary, Jerome, Joachim, Greg. the Great, Haymo, Ansbert). 2. Christ Himself (Hilary [?], Heterius, Paschasius). 3. *Libellus repudii a Deo scriptus nationi Judaicæ* (Wetstein). 4. *Sententiam a Judice et patribus ejus conscriptus in hortos ecclesiæ conceptam* (Schöttgen and Hengstenberg). 5. That part of the Apocalypse which treats of the opening of the seven seals, chs. vi.–xi. (Alcasar). 6. The Apocalypse itself (Corn. a-Lap.). 7. *"Divinæ providentiæ concilium et præfinitio, qua apud So statuit et decrevit facere vel permittere, etc."* (Areth., Vitringa, Mede, Ewald, De Wette, Stern, Düsterd., *et al.*). The last he declares to be, in the main, his own view. See also SYNOPTICAL VIEW.—E. R. C.]

Within and on the back.—The idea of a great leaf-roll, covered with writing on both sides, is here presented. Similar descriptions in classical literature; see in Düsterd. ["According to ancient usage, a parchment roll was first written on *the inside*, and if the inside was *filled* with writing, then the *outside* was used, or back part of the roll; and if that also was covered with writing, and the whole available space was occupied, the book was called *opistho-graphos* (written on the *back-side*; Lucian, *Vit. Auction.* 9, Plin. *Epist.* iii. 5). or written '*in aversâ cartâ,*' *Martial,* viii. 22." WORDSWORTH.—E. R. C.]

The book [scroll] has no vacant places, for the world's history is great, and in Heaven everything is foreseen even to the very end. The explanation of the whole passage is by no means as easy as Düsterdieck and others seem to think. It is not easy to demonstrate how a single leaf could be unsealed without the simultaneous loosing of all its seals, or how the loosing of a single seal could have freed only a single division of the leaf.* And therefore we, with Vitringa (De Wette?) and others, adopt the idea of seven membranes or leaves, of which each one was separately sealed. Further, we reject the view which conceives of the book [scroll] as directly embracing the whole Apocalypse. It of course embraces it *implicite*, but *explicite* its contents are exhausted with the sixth chapter, inasmuch as the seventh seal, on being opened, gives place to a new vision and introduces a new group of pictures. We can, indeed, say that as the seven churches preside over the seven seals, so the latter preside over the seven trumpets; nevertheless, not only do trumpets and seals form distinct groups, but the seals, as forms of secrecy or mystery, constitute a perfect antithesis to the trumpets. We must particularly note here the idea of the *seal* (secrecy and security at once, Is. xxix. 11, *etc.*); that of the *sevenfold* seal (a sevenfold and hence sacred involution of both considerations); the idea of the *book* [scroll] (Ex. xxxii. 32; Ps. cxxxix. 16, etc.); finally, the idea of the *writing on both sides.*

"The idea that the βιβλίον is the Old Testament (Victorinus), or the whole of Sacred Writ, containing the New Testament within and the Old Testament without (Primas., Bede, Zeger)

is founded upon mere guess-work." DUESTERDIECK. Our comment upon this is that the contents are made known by the unsealing.

Ver. 2. **And I saw a strong angel** (*ἰσχυρόν*).*—To the world of Angels the world of the contrast of guilt and grace is a mysterious region (1 Pet. i. 12). Even to the *strong* Angels it is mysterious. And an anxiety is felt in the heavenly realms for a solution of this dark enigma of earth. Now, the research of the whole non-Christian spirit-world in regard to the great enigma of the world's history might itself be called a *mighty Angel*. The longing of all spirits and all men cannot solve this enigma, and it sends out its demand for a solution into the universe. And hence beneath the unmistakable proclamatory office of the strong Angel, whose voice must pierce the whole world (Vitringa and others), we hear the cry of the entire world of spirits for the coming of the looser of the seals. Without this loosing [*Lösung*] there can be no complete releasing [*Erlösung*], redemption, as, on the other hand, the loosing is conditioned by the releasing [or redemption]. According to De Wette and Hofmann, the loosing of the seals is at the same time the execution of that which is sealed. But a great part of the book [scroll] is referable to the economy of the Father—not to that of the Son: we have reference especially to the red, the black, and the pale horse. Even the Rabbinic declaration: *non facit Deus quidquam, donec illud intuitus fuerit in familia superiori,* does not lead to the assumption which we have indicated.†

Who is worthy?—The history of the world in its eschatological tendency is unsealed only by the perfect ethical power resident in the Lamb.

To open the scroll and to loose the seals of it. — Is this a *hysteron-proteron* (De Wette)? We think not. The undertaking is first spoken of as a whole, and then its details are entered into. And, moreover, it is highly probable that there was something that bound the book [scroll] together as a whole.

Ver. 3. **Or under the earth.**—All this is in perfect accordance with the real circumstances of the case. The angels know not sin; the spirits in Hades and the demons (*under the earth*) know not grace; and sinful men know not the depths of the contrast between sin and grace. According to Düsterdieck, the place under the earth denotes, not demons (Vitringa), but only departed souls. Why should demons be excluded, since they, most of all, are positively blind in regard to the issue of things?‡

* ["The epithet ἰσχυρόν is by no means superfluous, but corresponds to the φωνῇ μεγάλῃ below, which, as appears by what followed, penetrated Heaven and earth and Hades."— ALFORD. This is one of the passages which indicate that there are grades of angelic beings.—E. R. C.]

† [That the *loosing* involved the *symbolic execution* of that which was sealed, seems to be clear. John beheld in vision (by symbols) that which was afterwards *to be* (in reality); (comp. ch. vi. 1 with the frequent recurrence of εἶδον). The fact stated by Lange cannot invalidate this conclusion. The "economy of the Father" was, so to speak, the platform on which the actions of the Son were wrought; in order to the unfolding of the latter there must have been, of necessity, an unfolding, to some degree, of the former, just as in the unfolding of a *writing* there must be the unfolding of the parchment on which it is inscribed.—E. R. C.]

‡ [See Excursus on Hades, p. 364 sqq.- E. R. C.]

And no one was able.—This takes for granted numberless attempts.

Nor even [neither] to look upon it.—Düsterdieck: "The seeing resultant upon the opening; hence, the seeing within it." This would be a great deal and would lie beyond the opening, whilst it is intimated that the inspecting precedes the opening. Most creatures dare not so much as look well at the problem, and none thoroughly recognizes it as a Divine book.

Ver. 4. **And I wept much.**—Hengstenberg, who is apt to see judgment everywhere, has even accused the weeping John of weak faith (p. 302); upon which view Ebrard sarcastically expatiates. It is particularly remarkable that Hengstenberg can conceive of a pusillanimous weeping as compatible with a condition of inspired vision. In this vision, John the Seer sees himself weeping as a bishop, and the weeping bishop has a right to weep. How could he receive a communication concerning the whole history of the world—a communication which exalted the most terrible things, war, famine, death's rule in the world's history, the great martyr history, and the dread trumpet tones of the world's evening, into one triumphal procession of Christ—how could he, we repeat, receive such a disclosure without tears? Perfect faith in the glorified Christ in the centre of the world did not exclude the law that the universal consequences of His glorification must be unfolded in a grand sequence of stages, amid the most painful apostolic and reformatory struggles!*

Ver. 5. **One of the Elders.**—The spirit of literalism has given birth to unsupported definitions of this Elder as Matthew or Peter (of course it is taken for granted that one or the other of these Apostles is already glorified).

Behold.—This, according to Düsterdieck, has reference to the beholding of the Lamb, in ver. 6.

The Lion of the Tribe of Judah, the Root of David, hath conquered.—John is to see, as he never has done before, the full consequence of Christ's victory in its relation to the grand enigma of the world's history.

Interpretations: 1. Christ has obtained the power of opening the book (ἐνίκησεν ἀνοῖξαι, Bengel, Ewald and others). 2. Absoluteness of Christ's victory (Ebrard and others). The text is, however, no mere declaration of Christ's worthiness to open the book. The opening of all seals is the consequence of absolute victory. For the sealing is a judgment,‡suant upon the darkening of the mystery of the world into an obscure and forbidding enigma by sin.† Consequently, victory over the power of

---

* [As in the SYNOPTICAL VIEW, Lange here takes for granted that the Seer knew *before the disclosure.* He wept, not because of the woes that were to be (of these as yet he knew nothing), but because no one was found worthy to open the seals—to make the disclosure. See SYNOPTICAL VIEW and *foot note,* p. 149.—E. R. C.]

† [What is the proof of this assertion? And if it be true in reference to men, how came the scroll to be sealed in reference to sinless angels? It should be remarked in continuance, however, that there can be no doubt that the right and power of the God-man to open the seals, which is but a mode of representing His supreme authority over all things, is the result of His victory over the power of darkness and sin and death.—E. R. C.]

---

darkness is the condition of the loosing of the seals.

The Lion of the Tribe of Judah.—The promise of the Protevangel to the effect that the Seed of the woman should crush the serpent's head, was further modified by the prophecy which constituted Judah the typical conqueror, the victorious Lion (Gen. xlix. 9). The fact that in the passage cited Judah was designated merely as a type, is brought out in our text by the additional clause: **the Root of David.** These latter words are explicative of the further explication of the type, in respect of its genealogical kernel, in David, the warlike and victorious prince; in other words, it is intimated, that the Incarnation of Christ was the innermost motive power of the Christological significancy of David (Is. xi. 10), and consequently that the type of the Lion of Judah has found its true fulfillment.

The whole designation of Christ is a profound Christological saying, which neither refers alone to the human descent of the Saviour (Düsterdieck), nor to His Divine nature simply (Calov.). A reference to the hewn-down stem of the Davidic house, in accordance with Is. xi 1, is applicable here only as a collateral thought. [Alford thus comments: "*The root of David* (comp. Rom. xv. 12 with Is. xi. 1, 10), *i. e.* the branch or sucker come up from the ancient root, and so representing it: not as Calov., *al.*, the Divine root which brought forth David, to which Vitringa also approaches very near: for the evident design here is to set forth Christ as *sprung from* the tribe of Judah and lineage of David, and His victory as His exaltation through suffering."—E. R. C.].

Ver. 6. **And I saw [Lange: And lo*] in the midst of the Throne.**—[See SYNOPTICAL VIEW, p. 149]. The vision of the Seer expands, and lo! Christ appears, in wondrous contrast to the ideas which a Judaistic conception of the Lion of Judah, the ideal David, might entertain. This contrast is strikingly brought out (after Bengel) by Ebrard: "Now comes this Lion, the Mighty One, Whom none is able to resist,—the Victor *par excellence.* How terrible must be His aspect! But lo! a Lamb (ἀρνίον) appears in the stead of the Lion, and that ὡς ἐσφαγμένον. This is the battle whereby the Lion has overcome, *viz.*: that He has suffered Himself to be slain as a Lamb. It is only in the omnipotence of all-suffering love that the greatness of omnipotence could be proved."

Superfluous interpretations of the diminutive ἀρνίον see cited by Düsterdieck. ["The use of ἀρνίον, the *diminutive,* as applied to our Lord, is peculiar to the Apocalypse. It is difficult to say what precise idea is meant to be conveyed by this form. . . . . Possibly, as De W., it may be to put forward more prominently the idea of meekness and innocence." ALFORD. As there was manifestly an intended contrast between the *announced* Lion and the *appearing* Lamb, may it not have been intended to bring out more vividly, not merely His meekness and innocence, but His extreme natural feebleness? — E. R. C.]

---

* [See TEXTUAL AND GRAMMATICAL NOTES.—E. R. C]

The Lamb stands in the middle of the space enclosed, on the inner side, by the Throne and the four Life-forms [Living-beings], and on the outer side by the circle of Elders. Thus Düsterdieck, De Wette, Hengstenberg, whilst Ebrard, on the other hand, conceives of the Lamb as seated in the midst of the Throne, and also in the midst of the circle of Elders. "A truly monstrous idea," observes Düsterd., who justly cites the Hebrew בְּרָךְ־בִּין.* This arrangement, moreover, distinctly proves that the four Life-forms are not four representatives of the creature, but that they can be only four Ground-forms of the Divine governance which is embraced in the Lamb, as are also the Seven Spirits which, therefore, likewise stand between God and Christ.† [" The words (ἐν μέσῳ) seem to indicate the middle point before the Throne; whether on the glassy sea (De Wette) or not does not appear; but certainly not on the Throne, from what follows in the next verse. Ἐν μέσῳ is repeated as ἀναμέσον in Levit. xxvii. 12, 14." ALFORD.—E. R. C.]

[Standing.—"The Lamb is here represented as standing, as having been slain (comp. Isa. liii. 7; Jer. xii. 19). Although Christ was slain, yet He stands. He was not overthrown. On the contrary, by falling He stood." WORDSWORTH.—E. R. C.]

As it had been slain.—Düsterdieck, in accordance with many others: "As one whose still visible scars indicate its having once been slain." The completion of the Biblical delineation of the Lamb, see ch. i. 18.

Seven horns and seven eyes.—See the SYNOPTICAL VIEW [p. 149]. Comp. the Concordances. Seven world-historical manifestations of Christ in forms of power; seven world-historical manifestations in forms of spirit (the Lights). Against the combination made by Bede and others, according to whom the seven horns as well as the seven eyes are included in the explanation—which are the Seven Spirits, etc.—see Düsterd., p. 242. The Spirits here do, undoubtedly, seem to be manifestations of the spiritual life of Christ in the narrower sense of the term, and should, we think, be apprehended as Spirits of truth, knowledge. In accordance with their position in ch. i., however, they also represent the specific mighty governance of Christ;‡ Michael, among the Archangels, appears as the symbol of His mighty rule. The septenary denotes perfect holy working, as the number three is significant of holy being.

* [Düsterdieck's comment, in our opinion, has special reference to Ebrard's conception of the Lamb i as sitting. It is thus that he quotes and italicizes Ebr rd: "Das Lamm erscheint mitten im Thron, so dass es zu gleicher Zeit im Centrum der vier lebenden Wesen und im Centrum der aussen herumsitzenden, einen weiten concentrischen Kreis bildenden, 24 Aeltesten sitzt." He then gives utterance to the comment cited by Lange: "eine wahrhaft ungeheuerliche Vor-tellung (with this addition—the italics are our own—): das Lamm mitten im Throne sitzend." Lange, by his peculiar representation of Ebrard's view and his suppression of the italics in sitzt, and also by his immediate introduction of the Hebrew term, which Düsterdieck does not cite in direct connection with Ebrard, makes the latter commentator the author of an utter absurdity, viz., the assumption that the Lamb could sit in two places at once.—TR.]

† [See Additional Note on the Living-Beings, p. 161 sq.—E. R. C.]

‡ [See comment and additional foot-note under ch. i. 5, p. 91.—E. R. C.]

Sent forth.—See Zech. iv. 10.

[Seven horns.—"The horn is the well-known emblem of might; comp. 1 Sam. ii. 20; 1 Kings xxii. 11; Pss. cxii. 9; cxlviii. 14; Dan. vii. 7, 20 sqq., viii. 3 sqq.; ch. xvii. 3 sqq. The perfect number seven represents that all power is given unto Him in Heaven and earth, Matt. xxviii. 18. And seven eyes, etc., which eyes represent the watchful, active operation of God's Spirit, poured forth through the death and by the victory of the Lamb, upon all flesh and all creation. The weight of the whole sentence lies in the predicative anarthrous participle, ἀπεσταλμένα. As the seven burning lamps before the Throne represented the Spirit of God immanent in the Godhead, so the seven eyes of the Lamb represent the same Spirit in His sevenfold perfection, profluent, so to speak, from the incarnate Redeemer; busied in His world-wide energy; the very word ἀπεσταλμένα reminding us of the Apostolic work and Church." ALFORD.—E. R. C.]

Ver. 7. And He came.—Expressive of the calmest decision and certainty. Since the great action of the Lamb is in question, εἴληφεν can not be reduced to a passive receiving. Λαμβάνειν has in general in the New Testament a considerable ethical weight.

Ver. 8. When He had taken; ὅτε ἔλαβεν.—[See SYNOPTICAL VIEW, p. 149.] In* place of the antiphony, ch. iv. [8, 11], sustained by the four Living-beings and the Elders, in praise of the Creator and the creation, we have here a three-fold choral song in glorification of the Redeemer, the Redemption, and that transfiguration of the obscure and gloomy history of the world issuing from the Redemption. The order of succession in this chorus is very significant. First resounds the song of praise of the four Life-forms [Living-beings] and the Elders; then the song of the Angels (Eph. iii. 10; 1 Pet. i. 12); after that the song of all creatures (Ps. cxlviii.; Rom. viii.). If the four Life-forms [Living-beings] were representatives of nature, nature would here twice strike up the song of praise, in one case in advance of the Angels. It may, indeed, be questioned: how can the four Life-forms [Living-beings] fall down before the Lamb if they denote Fundamental Forms of the Divine governance? But we might also query: how can Christ send forth the Seven Spirits that yet do stand between God and Him? All these manifestations, however, are, as individual forms of revelation, subordinated to the Lamb in His unity and in the unity of His highest decisive deed; and that with the expression of the freest homage. And the real beginning of every creaturely song of praise must proceed from Divine operations themselves.

[Fell down before the Lamb.—They render to Him Divine honor; comp. ch. iv. 10.—E. R. C.]

Having every one a harp [lute].—The playing upon the cither or harp is limited to the Elders; the Greek reads: ἔχοντες ἕκαστος. On the difference between the cither and the harp,

*[The proper place of this paragraph would seem to be under the following verse. As however, there are allusions in it to this verse, the Am. Ed. has not felt at liberty to transpose it.—E. R. C.]

see Winer, MUSICAL INSTRUMENTS. See ch. xiv. 2; xv. 2. [Also Kitto's *Cyclopædia*, and Smith's *Dict. of the Bible.*—E. R. C.]

And golden vials* full of incense.— Each cither, or lute, is proportioned to the individual who holds it, and belongs to him alone; the golden vials are alike; hence the plural in the case of the latter, though each might have his vial as well as his lute. These vials are full of incense, and the explanation reads: αἱ εἰσιν αἱ προσευχαὶ τῶν ἁγίων. Though αἱ may by attraction relate to θυμιάματα, it is more probable that its reference is to the vials, since these forms, these measures of precious metal (intrinsic value) are an essential part of the matter. ["Aἱ might well have θυμιαμάτων for its antecedent, being feminine to suit προσευχαί below; but it is perhaps more likely that φιάλας is its antecedent—each vial being full of incense." ALFORD. So also Wordsworth. Far more natural does it seem to refer the αἱ, with Barnes, to θυμιαμάτων, thus bringing the passage into correspondence with Ps. cxli. 2, "Let my prayer be set before Thee as incense," and with the apparent meaning of the incense offered in the Temple.—E. R. C.]

Here, too, commentators violate common sense in the effort to grasp both items [the *harp* and the *vial*] at once. Ebrard: The κιθάρα is supported by the knees and operated upon by one hand (without its falling?), whilst the other presents the φιάλη. Düsterdieck: "In the right hand the vial, whilst the left holds the cither." How then could they play? The like arrangements of Biblical facts are of frequent occurrence; for instance, De Wette makes the Lamb stand on the sea of glass. Symbolism gives both attributes to the Elders without insisting upon the idea that each one manages both harp and vial at each and every instant. Hengstenberg remarks that the harps, in conjunction with the songs of praise, refer chiefly to praise, and the golden vials to supplicatory prayers.

On the ungrounded application of the passage to the establishment of the Catholic doctrine of the intercession of saints, or to the support of the practice of invoking their intercession, compare Düsterdieck, p. 244. Luther did not deny, he says, that the members of the Church Triumphant pray for those of the Church Militant. The text, however, does not exactly bear upon this point.† That which we gather from the

* ["The word *vial*, with us, denoting a small, slender bottle with a narrow neck, evidently does not express the idea here. The article here referred to was used for offering incense, and must have been a vessel with a large, open mouth. The word *bowl* or *goblet* would better express the idea, and it is so explained by Prof. Robinson, *Lex.*, and by Prof. Stuart, *in loc.*' BARNES. The criticism is undoubtedly correct. Since, however, the word *vial* is so inwrought into the religious literature and thought of the English speaking people, and as no material interest is affected by its retention in the text, it is deemed expedient to retain it. Similar remarks might be made in reference to the retention of the term *harp.*—E. R. C.]

† [From this passage Stuart derives the opinion that prayer is offered by the redeemed in Heaven. (See Barnes, *in loc.*) This doctrine cannot be regarded as established by this Scripture; it is however, consistent with it, and seems naturally to flow from it. It may further be said that the doctrine referred to does not involve the utterly unscriptural idea that prayer may be offered to glorified saints, nor is it inconsistent with aught els where taught in the Word of God.—E. R. C.]

words under examination, is that the prayers of the saints on earth are inclosed in the holy measure of the golden vials; that they are by the ideal Church divested of their earthly, unbounded, and immoderate affections. As God beholds all mankind in the most special sense in Christ, so, too, He views the earthly Church in the light of the ideal Church, which is its aim. It is justly remarked, in this connection, that the twenty-four Elders are symbolical forms.* On the other hand, the view of Hengstenberg and Bengel, who understand the saints already in Heaven to be included in our passage, is productive of confusion.

In reference to these prayers, the posture of the Elders is different from that of the Angel with the censer, ch. viii. 3. That Angel seems to gather the prayers of the saints together, and to supplement them precisely as the Holy Ghost is declared to do in Rom. viii. 26. The prayers are thus made perfectly acceptable, and hence the same exalted Angel takes charge of the granting of them, filling the emptied censer with fire from the altar, *i. e.*, with flames of the Divine judgment of the Spirit, and pouring its contents upon the earth—a proceeding productive of voices, and thunders, and lightnings, and earthquake, stirring forces which promote the process of consummation going on in the earth.

Vers. 9–14. [See under ver. 8, p. 158.] Let us first compare this first choir with the second and third, and then examine the three anthems.

The second choir is composed of Angels, the heavenly host (1 Kings xxii. 19). *And I beheld and heard*, says the Seer. This does not mean: he saw, *that is*, he heard; but it probably indicates that the survey of the infinite array of spirits recedes behind the distinct perception of their song. The circular arrangement of this celestial army first demands our notice; all of the vast array are related to the little inner circle, that centre of the history of salvation. Observe next their infinite number: myriads consisting of myriads, and thousands consisting of thousands. According to Bengel, the addition of the smaller numeral denotes a limitation of the whole number; according to Hengstenberg, it indicates that distinctions vanish in the case of immense numbers. Düsterdieck, on the other hand, says: ' The anti-climax (comp. Ps. lxviii. 17) signifies that the first and greater number is not sufficient."

Ver. 13. **And every creature.**—["The chorus of assenting praise from creation itself.' ALFORD.—E. R. C.] The third choir is formed of the sphere of creatures generally, in four divisions or regions (Bengel). The *three*-fold division in Phil. ii. 10 has reference exclusively to the spirit world; the *four*-fold division here, with its world-numeral, relates to creatures in general. As the spirit-world is already represented in the first two choirs, we cannot, with Alcasar, regard the term *in Heaven* as referring to Christians. As the song of praise of this choir is a matter-of-fact one, à-Lapide's explanation, to the effect that sun, moon and stars are meant (included), is not to be rejected. The heavenly

* [See *foot-note* on p. 152.—E. R. C.]

beings, as well as beatified saints (Düsterd.), are represented in the first and second choirs. In respect to the *earth*, Düsterdieck regards all other creatures as intended together with men. It is justly denied that demons (Vitringa) are here denoted by the creatures *under the earth*; reference is had to the realms of the dead [to *Hades*, where *demons* are not (see Excursus on Hades, p. 364 sqq.).—E. R. C.].

Upon the sea.—On Patmos John had a lively view of creatures which live *upon* the sea rather than *in* it; we have reference particularly to sea-birds and flying fish.

The first choir [vers. 9, 10] represents the whole knowledge of the New Testament, and magnifies it in a *new song*. From the wording of the song it would seem that the four Life-forms joined in it. As, however, the anthem is sung to the music of the harps, and the harps are the property of the Elders, the above assumption becomes somewhat dubious. But then the question arises: how can the Elders sing of the redemption without including themselves if they too have a part in it? Be it observed that an Apocalyptic Heaven-picture always has reference to a subsequent earth-picture. Thus our song of praise relates to ch. vi., especially to the Martyrs amid the sufferings of the earthly time. They are ransomed to God with the blood of the Lamb by the redemption. And these very ones who in the earth-picture appear under the altar as souls of the slain, crying for recompense, appear in the Heaven-picture as the Kingdom of God, the Kingdom of true Christian kings who already (dynamically) reign upon earth—not merely *shall reign* (βασιλεύουσιν in accordance with Cod. A. etc.*). They reign on earth as God's Kingdom, but not as individual kings; yet their common rule on earth is mediated by their individual priesthood.† As a matter of course, the Elders do not exclude themselves from the redemption; their expression, however, is concrete in reference to the Church Militant on earth.‡ The worthiness of the Lamb to unseal the book [scroll] is deduced from His redemptive act; and justly so, for it alone solves the enigmas of the world's history. [Is not the reason rather, that, by His redemptive act, He has conquered to become "Head over all things" (comp. Phil. ii. 8, 9; Eph. i. 20-22)?—E. R. C.]

The Elders sing a new song§ (*sing*), for the

redemption is a matter of their enraptured experience. The Angels, on the other hand, are moved by adoration and sympathy; therefore they **say with a loud voice**, in a sort of *recitative*, as we understand it. The collective creatures of the universe, again, are simply described as **saying**. This *saying* is, of course, also doxological.

Again, the song of the Angels [ver. 12] is in harmony with their stand-point. For them, the idea of the redemption recedes behind that of holy suffering. Because the Lamb was *slain*, *i. e.* humbled Himself to such a degree, He is worthy to receive majesty (*i. e.* glory and dominion) in the spiritual world such as is exalted far above that which is possessed by even them, the Angels (Eph. i.; Phil. ii.). This majesty unfolds itself in three predicates of inner essence and three of outward appearance. The exalted Christ is, in the first place, *rich* in life; secondly, He is the *wise* Governor of His great Kingdom; and, thirdly, He possesses all requisite *power*. Hence, in the first place, He is worthy of all infinite *honor*; secondly, His dominion is an apparent spiritual *glory*; and, thirdly, His *praise* is sung by the whole world of spirits.*

The song of the creature-world rightly refers to the Creator, Him who sitteth upon the Throne. But even the creature-world is acquainted with *Christ's* import to the creation. For it, however, the *death* of Christ recedes, giving place to the calm ground-tone of His Logos rule. He is magnified with the Enthroned One as the Lamb. And in harmony with the world-numeral *four*, the creatures utter four eulogies.

The sublimest doxology of all is the ascription of *praise* [*blessing*] in the region of conscious creatures. Next comes the ascription of *honor* from all living things. Next, the loveliness and magnificence of all beautiful creations in the Cosmos [*glory*]. The conclusion is formed by the glorification of God's *power* in the whole universe. And thus it is to be into the æons of the æons, say the creatures. They speak thus, first, because they are under the law of temporality, and have a sense of the greatness of eternity; and, secondly, because they are destined to an eternal development reaching into the æons.

Finally, it is exceedingly significant that the four Life-forms [Living-beings] utter an Amen to the whole heavenly cultus, while the twenty-

---

* [See Textual and Grammatical.—E. R. C.]

† [The idea that the Saints are to *reign as mere subjects* (*i. e.* to be *kings without authority over others*) seems to be inconsistent with (1) the essential idea of *reigning*, which is to *exercise authority over others*; (2) the express intimations of the word of God; comp. Dan. vii. 22, 27; Luke xxii. 29, 30, *etc.* (see Excursus on the Basileia ii. 1, (4), (6), p. 98). The requirements of the first of these positions might apparently be satisfied by saying that the glorified saints, being freed from the dominion of Satan and sin, are *to reign over themselves*. The requirement of the second, however, cannot thus, even in appearance, be satisfied. If it be asked, Over whom are the Saints to reign? it may be answered, (1) *Some*, as *superior Rulers*, over their brethren (see Luke xxii. 29, 30, *etc.*); and (2) *all*, as kings, over the human races to be born after the establishment of the Basileia, and, perchance, over other races throughout the universe. Speculation as to this last point, however, not only as to *answer*, but as to *question*, should be restrained.—E. R. C.]

‡ [See *foot-note* to ver. 4, p. 152.—E. R. C.]

§ [*Sing*.—" Why *present*? Is it because the sound still lingered in his ears? Or, more probably, as describing their special and glorious office generally, rather than the mere one particular case of its exercise?" Alford.

New song.—" *New*, in the sense that it is a song consequent upon redemption, and distinguished therefore from the songs sung in Heaven before the work of redemption was consummated. We may suppose that songs of adoration have always been sung in Heaven; . . . but the song of redemption was a different song, and is one that would never have been sung there if man had not fallen, and if the Redeemer had not died." Barnes.—E. R. C.]

* [The above arrangement of the particulars of the ascription seems to the Am. Ed. not only to have no foundation in the text, but to be inconsistent therewith; for (1) the force of the single article placed before the first particular is to bind all together as one word (so Bengel and Alford); and (2) δύναμις cannot be regarded as a *generic* term (meaning *majesty*), inclusive of those that follow as representatives of *specific* excellencies. The true idea seems to be that we have here a *seven-fold* (indicating *completeness* or *perfection*) ascription of glory.—E. R. C.

four Elders, falling down, are plunged in adoration.

In regard to the seven eulogies of the Angels, Bengel thinks that they should be uttered like one single word, on account of the one article at the beginning; he also regards them as referring to the seven seals. We prefer to take them as different views of the spirit-world.

The hypothesis that the four Life-forms utter the Amen on account of their comparatively *meaner position* (an idea of Hengstenberg's) needs but a passing mention.

[ADDITIONAL NOTE ON THE LIVING-BEINGS (ch. iv. 6).—It is generally conceded, that the *Zōa* are the same as the heavenly Cherubim of the Old Testament. Not only is the term (*Zōa*) the one that is employed by Ezekiel, ch. i. 5 (LXX.), to designate those whom he afterwards declared to be the Cherubim, ch. x. 1 sqq., *etc*; but the *general appearance*, the *position*, and the *office* of the Living-beings of both Testaments are the same (comp. Rev. iv. 6–8; Ezek. i. 5–10; x. 1 sqq. See also the description of the Seraphim, Isa. vi. 2, 3, with whom many of the most judicious commentators identify them). On the subject of their *nature*, however, there is great diversity of opinion. It is generally agreed that they are *Mediate* symbols; but beyond this there is unexampled diversity. They have been explained as—1. *Individual-mediate* symbols of (1) the Four Evangelists, (2) the Four greatest Fathers of the Church, *etc.* 2. *Classical* symbols of (1) the Church Militant (Mede and Elliot), (2) the Ministers of the Church on earth (Daubuz), (3) eminent Ministers and Teachers of every Age (Vitringa), (4) glorified Saints who have been raised to special eminence (Lord), (5) Saints who are to attend Jehovah as Assessors in the Judgment (Hammond), (6) the Church Triumphant (Bush), (7) the forms of animated nature (Alford). 3. *Aberrant* symbols of (1) Divine Attributes (Stuart), (2) the Four Cardinal Virtues, (3) the Four Fundamental Forms of Divine Government (Lange), *etc.*

This diversity indicates utter uncertainty in the mind of commentators as to the Scriptural idea of the Cherubim. This uncertainty, in the judgment of the Am. Ed., is due *primarily* to the corrupted form of the doxology in ch. v. 9, 10; and is itself, in great measure, the cause (not the *result*) of that confusion of thought which prevails in the Church on the entire subject of Symbolism. The effort will be made to show the truth of both these positions.*

It will be generally admitted, that the *apparent* force, not only of the Heaven-scene set forth in chs. iv. v., but of the language and descriptions of the entire Apocalypse is (1) to place the Living-beings on the same platform *as to reality of existence* with the Elders and Angels (if these are *symbols*, then are the *Zōa* symbols; if these are *real persons*, then so are the *Zōa*); and (2) to suggest the idea, in reference to all

* [It should here be remarked that, to prevent confusion, the generally accepted terminology will be used throughout this argument. The hope may also be here expressed, that, as incidental results of the argument, the importance of a classification of symbols similar to the one given in the Preliminary Note (p. 145 sqq), and of the employment of a scientific terminology, will be apparent.—E. R. C.]

these objects, that they are heavenly *Persons*. (The idea that the Angels and the Cherubim are *persons* seems also to be implied throughout the Old Testament; the Elders, at least by that name, are not mentioned therein.) Whilst, however, it is generally conceded that the Angels and Elders are *persons*, it is also generally held that the *Zōa* are *mere symbols*. Whence arises this apparently unauthorized variance?

This question cannot be answered by a reference to the admitted fact that the objects immediately beheld by the Seer (the *simulacra*) were *symbols*. This, *in a sense*, is true; but (1) it ▨▨▨ also true in the case of the Angels and the Elders; it consequently does not explain the *variance;* and (2) it is not true that the simulacra beheld by John were symbols in the sense in which that term is ordinarily employed—in the sense, for instance, in which the *Lamb* was the symbol of Jesus. There is an ambiguity here, resulting from the generally unappreciated fact that there are two essentially distinct classes of symbols. A moment's reflection should convince any ▨▨▨▨ that whilst the *Lamb* was a symbol of Christ, there was back of this in the *vision of the Lamb itself*, the same distinction of *simulacrum* and *object of representation* that existed in the vision of the *Zōa*. In the vision of the *Lamb* not only was there a double symbolization, but a symbol of one class was charged upon that of another. The meaning of the writer may be made clear by the following diagram:

JOHN SAW—

I. A *simulacrum*, representing ...... { an Angel.
                                        { Zōa.
II. A *simulacrum*, representing a *Lamb*, representing *Christ*.

By this diagram the fact and importance of the distinction between *Immediate* and *Mediate* symbols, presented in the Preliminary Note, p. 146, is made *visibly* manifest. In ordinary language (and in ordinary *thought*) the *simulacrum* drops entirely out of view, and the Seer is said to behold, not the *simulacrum*, but the object it represents.

Nor can the variance be explained by a reference to the probable fact that the *simulacra* of the *Zōa* were ideal *as to form*. It is probable that the *simulacra* of the Angels were also ideal; and it is *certain* that the undescribed Form upon the Throne was so—we do not thence conclude that the BLESSED ONE whom that Form indicated (ch. iv. 2, 3) must have been a *Symbol*. (And here becomes manifest the importance of the distinction between *Similar* and *Ideal* Symbols. See p. 146.)

Nor, again, is it in the least supported (not to say *explained*) by the admitted fact that mere (*Mediate*) Symbols are introduced into the Heavenscene—as, for instance, the *Lamps* symbolizing the Holy Spirit, and the *Lamb* representing Christ; for (1) these are not associated with the Angels, Elders, and *Zōa*, as the Angels, Elders, and *Zōa* are associated with each other; and (2) the symbol of the *Lamps* was declared to be a symbol by the fact that it was *explained*, and that of the *Lamb*, the previously recognized symbol of Christ, needed no explanation—in the case of the *Zōa* there is no intimation, either in this narrative, or any where else in the Scriptures, that they symbolized any thing.

The only satisfactory explanation of the variance is the one suggested above, viz.: that if the Zôa did take part in a doxology that ascribed *their redemption* to Christ, whatever be the *apparent* force of the implications of Scripture to the contrary, they *must* be symbols either of *individual redeemed men*, or of *classes of redeemed men*. And so, in effect, commentators must have argued in the days when the text of the *Recepta* was universally accepted. And thus the idea became established in the Church that the Cherubim, the Zôa, *could not* be heavenly persons—that they *must* be mere symbols.

But what do they symbolize? On this point there is not the slightest intimation given in the Word of God. The whole matter seems relegated to the imagination of commentators. The proof of these assertions is to be found, not only in the multitudinous and contradictory explanations given by able men, but in the entire lack of Scriptural evidence adduced as supporting any specific view. On the platform of the Recepta, the Zôa are the Sphynx of the Bible.

It should here be observed that the very necessity of adopting a conclusion in this important instance, in the face of the apparent implications of the language and scenic descriptions of the Scripture, together with the entire lack of Scriptural explanation of the (supposed) symbol, necessarily precludes any true scientific investigation of the subject of Symbolism. Such an investigation can be made only on the basis of those *implications* which the compelled conclusion virtually declares to be deceptive, and of those *explanations* which in the most important instance manifestly do not exist. The idea that the Zôa are mere Symbols plunges the whole subject of Symbolism into inextricable confusion—it involves the further idea that the entire symbolization of the Scripture is without order, at least without order discoverable by us.

It may, however, be remarked by some that our author is free from the alleged trammels of the Recepta; he accepts as genuine that form of the doxology which does not imply that those who united in it had any necessary connection with the redeemed race, and yet he regards the Living-beings as *Symbols*. In answer it may be said, that every observer of the course of human thought must have perceived that a generally established idea will often, in measure, linger, even in the mightiest minds, after the foundation on which it was reared has been swept

away. To this, it is with the greatest deference suggested, may be due the position of Lange on this subject. He saw clearly (the fact is *patent*) that the correction of the doxology released him from the necessity of regarding the Zôa as symbols of human beings, and he took a forward step; but, reared under the influence of the universally accepted idea that the Living-beings *must be* mere symbols, and not perceiving the *concealed* truth, that the corrected doxology logically releases from this position also, he failed to take a second. The step he has taken is a mighty one in advance. It is preparatory, if not essential, to another, viz., that the Zôa are not Symbols at all—not *Symbols* of the Fundamental Forms of Divine Government, but personal Ministers thereof. This view, which subsidizes all of truth that our author has with so much power and beauty elaborated, is respectfully submitted for consideration. It is submitted in the belief that, upon reflection, it will be seen to be, not only more consistent with the apparent force of Scripture language and description than the one presented by Lange, but also absolutely essential to a consistent scientific scheme of the great subject of Scripture Symbolism.

The ideal forms of these glorious ministers of Jehovah, who stand nearest the Throne, are doubtless symbolic. So far as those forms are common to all, they are doubtless symbolic of their common attributes of knowledge, wisdom, and power; and so far as they are peculiar, they are representative of their peculiar characteristics and ministries. The question is suggested for consideration, whether the key to their respective ministries (ministries in accordance with their characteristics, as symbolized by their personal appearance) may not be found in the characteristics of the four seals, at the opening of which they respectively officiated. (See foot-note on p. 179).

In conclusion, it may be remarked, concerning the number *four* attributed to them, that *two* hypotheses are possible. The *first*, that it is natural, i. e., indicative of the actual number of these heavenly Ministers in the realms of Nature; the *second*, that it is *ideal*, drawn from the precedent symbolic number of nature (*four*), and thus symbolic of their relation to nature. The judgment of the writer inclines to the adoption of the former of these, both because of the relation of the Zôa to the first *four* seals, and because this view manifestly presents a reason why *four* should have been selected as the number of nature.—E. R. C.]

B.—EARTH-PICTURE. UNSEALING OF THE SEVEN SEALS. (THE OPENED SEVEN
SEALS IN HEAVEN AND THE SEVEN FUNDAMENTAL FORMS OF THE
WORLD'S COURSE ON EARTH.)

THE DARK EARTHLY WORLD IN THE LIGHT OF THE HEAVENLY WORLD.

Chap. VI. 1-17.

1. Predominantly Human History of the World.

Vers. 1-8.

1   And I saw when the Lamb opened one of [from among] the seals, and I heard, as
it were the noise of thunder [om., as it were the noise of thunder], one of the four
beasts [living-beings] saying [ins. as a voice of thunder], Come and see [om. and
2 see]! And I saw, and behold a white horse: and he that sat on him had [having]
a bow ; and a crown was given unto him : and he went [came] forth conquering,
and to [om. to—ins. that he might] conquer.

3   And when he had [om. had] opened the second seal, I heard the second beast
4 [living-being] say [saying], Come and see [om. and see].   And there went out
[came forth] another horse that was red : and power was given [om. power was
given] to him that sat thereon [upon him] [ins. it was given to him[2]] to take peace
from the earth, and [ins. in order] that they should [shall[3]] kill [slay] one another:
and there was given unto him a great sword [μάχαιρα].

5   And when he had [om. had] opened the third seal, I heard the third beast
[living-being] say [saying], Come and see [om. and see].   And I beheld [saw],
and lo [behold] a black horse ; and he that sat on him had [having] a pair of
6 balances [balance] in his hand.   And I heard [ins. as it were[4]] a voice in the
midst of the four beasts [living-beings] say [saying], A measure [chœnix] of wheat
for a penny [denarius], and three measures [chœnixes] of barley for a penny
[denarius] ; and see thou hurt not [om. see thou hurt not] the oil and the wine
[ins. injure thou not].

7   And when he had [om. had] opened the fourth seal, I heard the voice of the
8 fourth beast [living-being] say [saying[5]], Come and see [om. and see].   And I
looked [saw], and behold a pale horse : [,] and his name that sat on him was
Death [and the one sitting upon him, his name Death], and Hell [Hades] followed
[was following] with him.   And power was given unto them over the fourth part
of the earth, to kill with sword [ῥομφαία], and with hunger, and with death, and
with the [ins. wild] beasts of the earth.

2. World-history in its Predominantly Spiritual Aspect, or the Martyr-history of the Kingdom of God as the core of World-history.

Vers. 9-11.

9   And when he had [om. had] opened the fifth seal, I saw under the altar the souls
of them that were [have been] slain for [on account of] the word of God, and for

10 [on account of] the testimony which they held [had]: and they cried with a loud
[great] voice, saying, How long [Until when] O Lord [Ruler], [ins. the] holy and
true, dost thou not judge and avenge our blood on them that dwell on the earth?
11 And white robes were [a white robe was]⁶ given unto every one of [om. every one
of] them [ins. to each]⁷; and it was said unto them, that they shou'd rest yet for [om.
for] a little⁸ season [time], until their fellow servants also and their brethren, that
should [who are about to] be killed as [ins. also] they were, should be fulfilled
[fulfill it (the time),—or have been completed (as to number)]⁹.

8. _The Sixth Seal._　_An Earthquake as a Presage of the End of the World._
VERS. 12-17.

12　And I beheld [saw] when he had [om. had] opened the sixth seal, and, lo, there
was [om. lo, there was] a great earthquake [ins. took place]; and the sun became
13 black as sackcloth of hair, and the [ins. whole¹⁰] moon became as blood. And the
stars of heaven fell unto the earth, even [om. even] as a fig tree casteth¹¹ her
untimely figs, when she is [om. when she is—ins. being] shaken of [by] a mighty
14 [great] wind. And the heaven departed as a scroll when it is [om. when it is]
rolled together [up]; and every mountain and island were moved out of their
15 places. And the kings of the earth, [ins. and the chief captains,] and the great
men, and the rich men, and the chief captains [om. and the chief captains], and the
mighty [strong] men, and every bond man, [om. ,] and every [om. every¹²] free man,
16 [om. ,] hid themselves in the dens [caves] and in the rocks of the mountains; and
said [they say] to the mountains and [ins. to the] rocks, Fall on [upon] us, and
hide us from the face of him that sitteth on the throne, and from the wrath of the
17 Lamb: For the great day of his [or their¹³] wrath is come; and who shall be [is]
able to stand?

⁶ Ver. 11. [Critical editors generally, with אּ. A. B*. C. P., give ἐδόθη and στολή.—E. R. C.]
⁷ Ver. 11. [The reading αὑτοῖς ἑκάστῳ generally adopted in acc. with אּ. A. C. P.—E. R. C.]
⁸ Ver. 11. Μικρόν is to be retained in acc. with אּ. A. C. [P.].
⁹ Ver. 11. [Alf., Treg., Tisch., with אּ. B*. P., give πληρώσωσιν; Gb., Lach., Words., with A. C., read πληρώθωσιν.—E. R. C.]
¹⁰ Ver. 12. [Lach., Alf., Treg., Tisch., with אּ. A. B*. C., insert ὅλη.—E. R. C.]
¹¹ Ver. 13. [Tisch. gives βάλλουσα with אּ. Lach., Words., Alf., Treg., read βάλλει, with A. B.*C. P.—E. R. C.]
¹² Ver. 15. The second καί was not well founded, interpolated for the sake of clearness. [It is generally omitted in acc. with A. B.*and C.—E. R. C.]
¹³ Ver. 17. [Treg. and Tisch. give αὐτῶν with אּ. and C.; Lach., Words., and Alf., αὐτοῦ with A. B*. P.—E. R. C.]

EXEGETICAL AND CRITICAL.

SYNOPTICAL VIEW.*

This second eschatologico-cyclical world-picture is as simple, clear, and intelligible in its
fundamental features as the first, the world-picture of the Seven Churches. It seems to be the
special prerogative of a chronological Church-
historical exegesis to close it up again with seven
seals and to involve it in the obscurity of night.
Through the Lamb's opening of the seals, the
darkest book has become most clear—the book
of the world's history, in its enigmatical fearful and gloomy phenomena. The very fact that
the book is _sealed_ is a ray of light for us; the
highest hand has shut it up, intending that it
shall presently be opened. Another hopeful
fact is that the Seals are _seven_, i. e., the riddle is
a holy one, and when it reaches its final term it
shall meet with a festal solution. The loosing
of the very first seal sheds a joyful light over

the whole dark history of the world. The Rider
upon the white horse rides at the head of all the
others. The mere fact that the train is one of
horsemen calms our apprehensions; the horses
denote the rapid movement of great phenomena
of life or death; no one of these phenomena
hangs stationary over the world. They all, in
their riders, have their governors. Wild though
the course of some may seem on earth, their
management, their direction, their career, and
their limit are fixed in Heaven. But at the
head of all is the Rider on the white horse. He
is the Prince, the rest are esquires. Thus all apparently fatal events must serve His purposes,
and those purposes are full redemption and its
diffusion through the world—not yet judgment, as
at His forthcoming in ch. xix. 11. The _horse_ of the
first Rider is _white_; holy and pure as heavenly
light is the dynamical fundamental movement
which governs all other and more conspicuous
movements. The Rider is Christ [see p. 178];
to Him, therefore, to His power, His rule, all
subsequent facts are subject; not only the three
riders, His servants, but also the facts of the
fifth, sixth, and seventh seals, the latter of which
embraces all items subsequent to its opening.
His _bow_ is the bow with the sure arrows of the
word; His _wreath_ or _crown_ is the diadem of His
principial victory over all the power of the
world and of darkness, and when He, notwith-

standing, again goes forth to conquer, it is in order to the necessary development and consummation of His principial conflict and victory in a grand succession of world-historical conflicts and victories. He has no need of many attributes; a leading attribute is this: that the three other riders are not *before*, but *behind* Him.

The figures of the following three symbolical riders are, manifestly, so general in their conception, that it ▨▨▨▨▨ altogether arbitrary to limit War, Dearth, or the Power of Death, to particular times. Manifestly, we have here before us dark forms that traverse the .whole stage of the world's history. From this running back into pre-Christian times, it results that Christ also, the Rider on the white horse, surmounted all historical bounds in the dynamical operation of His Coming, even in those pre-Christian times. A further sequence is that these powers [War, Dearth, Death] have been possessed of the eschatological bent from the very beginning, and have been gravitating toward the end —the judgment. And how could it be otherwise, when the final judgment must adjust the difference between the *doing* of wrong and the *suffering* of it in *war ;* when, further, it must strike the balance between those who have revelled in *wine* and *oil* and those who have starved on the scanty measure of *wheat* and *barley* in *dearth ?* Death is eschatological from the outset. Still, the complete appearance of *Christ* at the head of the horses proves that we are dealing pre-eminently with forms of the Christian time, and that, too, ▨▨ the last time.

The *second* horse is of *the color of blood*. His rider is *War ;* War as a totality, in its most fearful form—not merely the war of self-defence, of the vindication of rights, but rather that dark power to which it is granted to *take peace from the earth*, to set on foot a reciprocal slaughtering on countless battle-fields, and in pride and wantonness to flaunt the *great sword*, the symbol of all deadly instruments down to the present day. It does not say, to take away peace from time to time, for the intervening times of peace are so problematical, so penetrated with warlike commotions and apprehensions, that perfect peace is in reality taken away until the advent of eternal peace.

The *black* color of the *third* horse is that of mourning, here especially of *hunger* and *anxiety ;* of that scarcity of bread which forms a part of the world's dark history in all times and places. Pauperism, moreover, is inclined to see and to paint all the circumstances of life black—far blacker, indeed, than they are in reality. Dearth, however, is scarcely half a direct dispensation of God, to be referred purely to the failure of crops; it is no more so to be regarded than war or death as to be classed under the head of purely natural phenomena. Dearth is at least half a result of the social exaggeration of the distinction between the rich and the poor. For the most indispensable necessaries of life, wheat and barley, must pass through the scales of the rider and through ▨ rigorous valuation. According to this valuation, a *denarius*, the entire day's wages of a man, suffices only for his own support, if he buy *wheat* (one *chœnix* of *wheat*, the eighth part of ▨ *Scheffel* or Ger-

bushel [nearly ▨ quart, English measure.— E. R. C.], for a denarius); whilst even if he buy *barley*, there remains but ▨ little, over and above his own allowance, for a very small family (*three chœnixes* of *barley* for ▨ denarius). This rigor is all the more noticeable since the means of enjoyment and adornment, oil and wine, principally used by the rich, remain untouched. Certainly then, this human exaggeration of a divinely appointed contrast is an act which will have to be accounted for equally with violent war, and only the subordination of the third horseman to the power of the first makes, primarily, an ideal compensation ("to the poor the gospel is preached")—it is not ordained that apostasy should be preached to them, however), which toward the end becomes real. Comp. Matt. xxiv. 7.

In connection with this dispensation of Dearth it is especially remarkable that it is announced by a *voice out of the midst of the four beasts* [Living-beings]. This, doubtless, denotes that all four beasts [Living-beings] are particularly concerned in it [see p. 179]. That which the *lion*, on the one hand, as the mighty power, institutes, is compensated by the *ox*, on the other hand —self-sacrificing and devoted love. And the *eagle*-like soarings of the spirit above earthly circumstances, are supplemented by the *human figure of humanity*.

The *fourth* horse is of ▨ *pale* color, light yellow, and its rider, whose name is expressly declared, is *Death*. The whole kingdom of the dead, *Hades* itself, is in his train. As he himself is an esquire of Christ, so he also, in accordance with his mighty power, has himself an esquire, namely, Hades. This is expressive of the fact that the power of *historical* Death, ▨▨ ▨ consequence of sin, reaches down into the realm of the dead, in its dark compartment; and light is also thereby shed upon the Old Testament doctrine of Sheol. Whilst, in accordance with other passages, the gates of the Kingdom of the Dead open wide and covetously towards the actors upon this stage of life (Matt. xvi. 18), here their effect appears in the midst of the stage of the world itself. Thus much there is no difficulty in understanding, namely, that the human idea of the domain of the dead does preach repentance, on the one hand, but that it also is indirectly productive, on the other hand, of ▨ fatal effect of great power and extent (1 Cor. xv. 32; Heb. ii. 15). If it be true that every epidemic draws countless victims into its whirlpool by the mere workings of sympathetic fear, the like is true of the power of Death as a totality. The exhalation of shadowy, terrific and spectral images rising from Sheol goes like the breath of sickness and death over the earth, carrying contagion with it; and this entirely irrespective of real retro-actions of the other world. The pale, yellow color of the horse (*pallida mors*) points to the element of fear ▨▨ well ▨▨ to the hue of a dead body.

And yet to the united action of Death and Hades, power is given over only the *fourth part* of the earth. Pure mortality in the abstract almost seems to be distinguished from this doom of death; at least there is also a euthanasia; a blessed dying with Christ and according to Christ.

Four is the number of the world; the *fourth part,* therefore, we believe to be the specifically *worldly part,* which is given over to the world [see p. 174], as, on the other hand, the *third part* (ch. viii. 7), as a part bearing the number of *spirit,* is indicative of *spiritual circumstances,* of events transpiring in the spirit-world.

The worldly powers of Death are also *four* in number: the *sword, hunger, death, beasts.* The import of the *sword* here manifestly passes beyond that of the great war-sword; it embraces all forms of violent death. *Hunger,* likewise, as a particular power of death, passes beyond Dearth. And no less does specific *Death,* in the shape of great pestilences desolating the world (λοιμοί, Matt. xxiv. 7), exceed the ordinary forms of death. Whether rapacious animals, simply, are meant by the *beasts of the earth,* or whether there is at the same time a reference to those mysterious and hurtful animal powers which are being discovered in these modern times in the form of parasites of all kinds, we do not venture to decide. The point of departure for clearer glimpses was certainly already in existence; together with a knowledge of the noxious herb, men possessed a knowledge of the worm and its destructiveness (Hos. v. 12).

Another point which we wish clearly to bring out is this: that the four horsemen are successively announced by one of the four beasts [Living-beings]. The first beast [Living-being] is signalized by its announcement of the First Horseman, Christ, in a *voice like thunder.* This fact decides the whole sequence. Understanding, as we do, by the four beasts [Living-beings] the four Fundamental Forms of God's rule over the world, we claim that their task is completed with the presentation of the four more general fundamental forms of worldly history itself as comprised in the four horsemen [see p. 179]. We cannot, therefore, with Schleiermacher, conjecture that the Seer lacked beasts [Living-beings] for the following seals. Manifestly, a turning-point occurs just here; the forms of the cosmical course of the world are succeeded by the forms of cosmical spiritual history.

First comes *the history of the Martyrs* in its whole extent, though predominantly New Testamental and eschatological. The Seer beholds them as *souls under the altar.* The world would fain have sacrificed them as curse-offerings to Moloch, as Caiaphas desired to do with the Prince of Martyrs Himself (John xi. 50); they themselves, however, have with their faithful testimony sacrificed themselves to God. In this generalness, their sacrifice comes under the head of the burnt offering; the *altar* is the centre of the sacrificial system, as the altar of burnt sacrifices; here, in respect of its ideal import as appearing in the vision, the symbol of all voluntary sacrifice of life under the hand of hostile powers, in faithful testimony to, and confession of, the truth. They appear as *souls,* for the world has violently deprived them of bodily appearance; it must be evident from their appearance that they have been slain on account of their faithful confession. In their confession they have been faithful at once to the Logos of God and to the subjective witness in their own breasts. And thus they are united, a congrega-

tion of souls, belonging to the other world, yet far removed from Sheol,* which meanwhile is careering over the earth.

Now though the spirit of the Martyrs is shown in Stephen's prayer: "Lord, lay not this sin to their charge," the instinct of justice which lies enwrapped in the suffering of wrong, in shed blood (that of Abel, for instance, Heb. xii. 24), in the full perception of the terrible calumnies perpetrated on just men, of the darkenings of the truth, of the caricatures of the gospel of love and mercy on the part of persecutors, is not in the slightest degree done away with by this prayer. And in this sense, with the ghostly severity of truth, they cry with a loud voice, saying: *Lord, the holy and true.* As the *Holy* One, God owes it to Himself to repay; as the *True* One, having given them His word as the word of life, He has put Himself under obligations to them to repay. [See foot-note, p. 175 sq.—E.R.C.]

The terms employed have other and primary bearings, however. The Martyrs address God (not Christ; Grot. and others) by the unusual name of Δεσπότης, because they must needs bleed under the sword of earthly despots or tyrants, and in contradistinction to their unholy despotism, exercised under cover of lying and arrogant pretensions, they call Him the *holy and true* (genuine) *Despot.*

Thus a mighty pressure and urgency of grief, a cry for heavenly justice, rises ever stronger from the depths of worldly and psychical life up to the Throne of righteousness, though mitigated and pacified by the spirit of the Atonement, the blood that speaketh better things than that of Abel. *How long dost Thou not judge?* Though God's judgment goes on incessantly through the depths of life, the great wrong-suffering of the Martyrs requires a restitutory final judgment before the whole world. And in hungering after this justice, the great interval may seem a right long one, a hard trial of patience (μακροθυμίαν, Luke xviii. 7) to all human perception. The fact that they anticipate the avenging of their blood as a consequence of the Divine judgment, and hence call upon God as the Avenger of blood, has nothing in common with a malignant and hateful animosity. The avenging of blood is the religious and moral popular fountain of criminal justice; criminal justice, therefore, in its true shape, is the form into which the avenging of blood has ever developed under the influence of civilization. Where criminal justice is so perverted into its opposite, as to appear as a system of judicial murder of the worst kind, in demonic hostility to Divine justice, in the sufferings and executions of the Martyrs, there the cry for God's avengement of blood as the Divine Fountain of Justice which men have utterly denied, follows almost as a logical consequence.

But why should vengeance for former bloodguiltiness be taken upon those "that dwell on the earth"? Those who now, as inhabitants of earth, belong to and are attached to earth, the old blood-stained tragical order of things, are, as accessories in guilt, placed under the consequences and further development of guilt (Matt. xxiii. 32 sqq.).

---

* [See the Excursus on HADES, p. 364 sqq.—E. R. C.]

This holy instinct of justice, however, is appeased in a two-fold manner. First, a *white robe* is given to each one. In the other world, therefore, they are clothed with the adornment of innocence and righteousness. And so bright are these white robes that even in the history of this world they constantly become more distinctly visible, more admired and more honored; think of the white robes of a Justin, a Polycarp, a Huss, a Savonarola, and many thousand other faithful witnesses. Again, the Martyrs are further comforted by the assurance that *their period of waiting is nearing its end*, while, as a period of waiting, it is itself under a holy decree, in accordance with which the Martyr-history must attain its completion, the number of Martyrs must be filled up. Herein is the indirect announcement that the season of martyrdom is not yet at an end; that martyr sufferings assume diverse forms throughout the ages, yet continue to be even to the end a fundamental condition of the healthful development of the world's history, as the history of the Kingdom. The great company of their fellow-servants and brethren, the necessity of suffering in this world and of patience in the other, the glorious aim of a suffering together with Christ (Rom. vi. 4; 2 Tim. ii. 12), elevate them to an exalted standpoint, from which the perspective of the great and glorious retributive judgment momentarily becomes clearer and more complete. So far as His perfect rehabilitation before the world is concerned, even Christ in His glory must wait until His great Epiphany.

In the grandest contrast, the history of the Martyrs is immediately confronted with *the beginning catastrophe of the final judgment* in the opening of the *sixth* seal [see p. 179]. It is as certain that a cosmical change is here indicated as it is that such is the case in the Eschatological Discourse of the Lord, Matt. xxiv. 29 sqq., though the figures may have their spiritual back-ground as well. With the *great earthquake*, the first final convulsion of terrestri-cosmical things is announced. The *sun*, wrapped in obscurity as in a penitential garment, is the actual sun; the *moon*, red as blood, is the literal moon; for what we have here is not a predominantly spiritual history, like ch. viii. 7 sqq., but the—ghostly, it is true—*finale* of this world's history, and to the theatre of this history our sun belongs. As a matter of course, the occurrences in the sun and moon are to be understood phenomenally. Even now there is no man that dies, to whom the sun is not at the last clothed in the garb of mourning, whilst his senses sigh for "more light." The same remark applies to the falling of the *stars* from Heaven. Like every genuine catastrophe, this final catastrophe, above all, seems to make its appearance quite abruptly; hence the stars fall from Heaven as the unripe figs of a fig-tree, suddenly shaken by a storm, fall to the earth. The figure recalls that of "the thief in the night," the "days of Noah," and "the coming of the flood." The Holy Scriptures are thoroughly at home in the law of catastrophes The *fall of the stars* also can primarily be understood only phenomenally, for there would not be found room on the earth for them all. But a cosmical change in the astral

region belonging to the earth is, doubtless, also indicated. Nay, in reference to the condition of this earth, the metamorphosis is as total as if the old Heavens vanished like the contents of a scroll that is rolled together (Is. xxxiv. 4); and this on the basis of the *earthquake*,—in consequence of a crisis in which the entire old form of the solid *land*, with the *mountains*, and the entire old form of the *sea*, with the *islands*, pass away.

But the spiritual back-ground of the changes set forth in the picture of the convulsed earth and star-world also becomes manifest. This spiritual back-ground consists in a convulsion of the old order of things: in a darkening of the old sun, the time of grace of the economy of salvation; in a transformation of the ancient luminary of night, who-se silver radiance filled the night with peace, into a bloody, fiery phenomenon, for a sign that slumber is at an end (Matt. xxvi. 45); in a perfect confusion of those earthly relations and spirit-constellations which have hitherto subsisted; and in the wreck of all views of the world conditioned upon the senses. All this is still more prominent in the effects of the great convulsion of things. A general terror at the presages of judgment seizes men of all ranks and conditions. *Kings* first; they have most to lose. Then *princes* [great men] and *chief captains* [principal men of war] are specified in their contrast [civil and military eminence]. Then the *rich* and the *mighty* Finally, together with the *freemen*, the *slaves*. The range of view, therefore, extends far beyond an absolute democracy. In the perspective of the *day of wrath*, slaves equally with freemen, appear loaded with guilt and convulsed with apprehension, for it stands to reason that without the servilism of the laity there could be no hierarchs, and without the servilism of political slaves no despots could subsist. When all are said *to hide themselves in the clefts and in the rocks of the mountains*, we are reminded of the overthrow or removal of the mountains, spoken of before. That, however, all slavish souls would fain find refuge in the ruins of the old order of things; nay, that they would rather share in their destruction than step into the bright presence of the great day, lies in the nature of the grand contrast between their worldly life and the judgment of which they are on the eve. The convulsion described will, however, as a mighty convulsion of souls, be universal (Luke xxi. 25, 26); ay, a *holy trembling* (as set forth in the *Dies Iræ**), shall pass over even the servants of God, for whom the day of judgment is the day of final redemption (Luke xxi. 28). Hence the appeal of the unprepared to the mountains and rocks: *Fall on us, and hide us from the face of Him that sitteth on the throne, and from the wrath of the Lamb.* The economies of the Godhead seem to have changed, in accordance with the great change of the times. The face of God the Father, the perfect light of His revelation, acts like a judgment of the Spirit, similarly to the face of Christ in His earthly pilgrimage. The wrath of the just and right-

---

* [" *Quantus tremor est futurus,*
Quando Judex est venturus,
Cuncta stricte discussurus."—E. R. C.]

God is now committed to the Lamb, *i. e.*, He is to execute the actual judgment of separation. It is a judgment under the sign of wrath, because it comes as the final decision, after the days of forbearance and long-suffering (Rom. ii. 5), upon an infinite accumulation of guilt. Wrath, as the synthesis of love and righteousness—the latter having the leadership—is manifested in positive inflictions of death (Ex. iv. 14, 24; Ps. xc. 6). With the wrath of the Lamb, the danger of the second death is revealed (Matt. xxv. 41). *For the great day of His wrath is come* (see Zephaniah), *and who is able to stand?* Here we perceive the tone of worldly-mindedness, which sees only wrath in judgment, not judgment in wrath. The day of wrath is characterized as a super-human death-doom. Of a distinction between the blessed and the damned, these exclamations know nothing. For the fact that the words that we are examining have a bearing not upon the dogmatical deliverances of Augustinian theologians, nor upon the terrors of conscience with which all human spirits may be smitten at the dawning of the great day, but upon the outbreaks of a mere slavish anguish of men of the world—an anguish that knows of no blessed existences—is evident from the expressions of despair which precede the final saying. It is the worldliness of the old world in its death-thought.

[ABSTRACTS OF VIEWS OF LEADING MODERN ENGLISH AND AMERICAN COMMENTATORS. *By the Am. Ed.*—It was pertinently remarked by Barnes at the beginning of his comments on this chapter: "It is at this point that interpreters begin to differ, ... here commences the divergence towards those various, discordant, and many of them wild and fantastic theories, which have been proposed in the exposition of this wonderful Book." The Am. Ed. deems it expedient at this point to introduce abstracts of some of the views which have been put forth by leading English and American divines in recent times. His own view will be presented in an Additional Note at the close of the Explanations in Detail, on p. 178. sq.

ELLIOTT.—This author is the most distinguished (English) advocate of what Lange styles the *Chronological Church-historical* school of interpreters. He has favored the Church with four large volumes on the interpretation of the Apocalypse, replete with extended, rich and varied learning on the subject of which it treats. (*Horæ Apocalypticæ*, 5th Ed., London, 1862.) One of the chief excellencies of his work, is his constant citation of the infidel historian Gibbon, thus striving to elucidate prophecy, by a historical record prepared by an opponent of the truth of the inspiration of Scripture. He identifies the *Horses* of the first four seals with the Roman Empire, under different appearances in different times, and the *Riders* with the Emperors of those times. He regards the period of the first *six* seals as extending from the date of the Apocalypse (which he fixes at A. D. 95 or 96) to A. D. 395, the year in which Augustine was elevated to the See of Hippo. The character of this period he describes as from the stand-point of the Seer: "The coming temporary prosperity and the decline and fall of the Empire of heathen

Rome." He divides the period as follows: *First Seal:* From the accession of Nerva to the incipient deterioration of the government under Commodus (A. D. 96-183). *Second Seal:* From the close of the preceding to the accession of Diocletian (A. D. 183-284). *Third Seal:* The time of distress from excessive taxation following the Edict of Caracalla. (This æra overlaps the preceding, as Caracalla was assassinated A. D. 217; Elliott assigns no date of its close.) *Fourth Seal:* The period of fearful mortality from War, Famine, Pestilence, and Wild Beasts (A. D. 248-268). *Fifth Seal:* The 'Æra of Martyrs," —the Diocletian persecutions (A. D. 303-312). *Sixth seal:* (Part I.; ch. vi. 12-17).—The *politico-religious revolution* of the time of Constantine, which involved the destruction of the political supremacy of heathenism (A. D. 323); (Part II.; ch. vii.).—The æra of *general* religious deadness, and *special* religious life (that of the 144,000 sealed ones), extending from the time of Constantine to that of Augustine.

BARNES, the distinguished American commentator, is mentioned in connection with Elliott, from the fact that he agrees with him in his general principles of interpretation. The scheme he adopts is precisely similar to that of Elliott, so far as the first five seals are concerned. In reference to the *Sixth*, however, he presents the following as descriptive of its events. "It is, in one word, the impending judgments from the invasions of the Northern hordes of Goths and Vandals threatening the breaking up of the Roman Empire; . . . the tempest of wrath that was, as it were, *suspended* yet on the frontiers, until the events recorded in the next chapter (vii.) should occur, then bursting forth in wrath in successive blasts, as denoted by the first four trumpets of the *seventh* seal (ch. viii.), when the Empire was entirely overthrown by the Goths and Vandals. The precise point of time which, I suppose, this seal occupies, is that succeeding the last persecution."

MOSES STUART, the eminent Professor in the Theological Seminary at Andover, held, as is well known, the view that the Apocalypse was written before the destruction of Jerusalem, and that the prophecies of *the greater portion thereof* (to the close of ch. xix.) had *special and immediate* reference to the period closing with that event.*

* [The views of this distinguished commentator have been by many strangely misunderstood and misrepresented. He has been understood as holding that the *entire* Book has reference to events that have long since occur ed, and yet in his comment on ch. i. 1, he writes "Now, although the closing portion of the Revelation relates, beyond a doubt, to a distant period, and some of it to a future eternity," etc. He is also by many understood as teaching that the first portion had reference *only* to events preceding the destruction of Jerusalem, and yet the opening paragraph of his Introduction (Vol. I., p. 9) contains this sentence (the italics being his own): " It lies upon the very face of the whole composition, I mean the prophetic part of it, that *the coming and completion of the Kingdom of God or of Christ*, or, in other words, *the triumph of Christianity over all enemies and oppiners, its universal prevalence in the world for a long series of years, and its termination in an endless period of glory and happiness*, constitute the main theme of the writer, and is indeed the almost exclusive subject of his contemplation." In § 9, entitled " *Object of the Book*" (Vol I.. p. 155), he writes. " *The final and complete triumph of Christianity over all enemies, and the temporal and eternal glory and happiness to which this triumph leads the Church*, or, still more briefly, as Lücke has stated it, ' *the coming and completion of the Kingdom of God*,' is the gene-

He entitles his special Introduction to chapters vi.-xi. (Vol. I., 138 sqq.) " FIRST CATASTROPHE, OR OVERTHROW OF THE JEWISH PERSECUTING POWER;' declaring therein, "Nothing, in my apprehension, can be further from a correct mode of interpretation than a mere historical and literal application of any of the symbolic part of the Apocalypse. The prophetic portion is all *symbolical picture;* but not such a picture as to constitute a regular history of wars and calamities. In its very nature, most of it is *generic,* and not individual and specific." He continues, in reference to the Seals (p. 151), " The first four seals indicate the assembling and preparing of an awful array commissioned against the enemies of the Church. ... A mighty conqueror bedecked with the emblems of victory leads on the hosts of destruction. These hosts, armed with deadly weapons, follow him. Then, in the train comes *famine,* commissioned against the enemy, and, in the rear of famine, march Death and Hades, the allied tyrants of the under world; while the ravenous beasts of the earth, waiting to devour the corpses of the slain, close the terrific procession." Concerning the Fifth Seal he continues (p. 159), " The awful array, symbols of the work of destruction about to be accomplished, have been summoned, have taken their places, and formed the ranks of the army. Before marching into the battle their ardor is now to be excited. In accordance with the design of rousing up powerful sympathies on such an occasion, the persecuted and slaughtered Martyrs are presented, lying covered with blood at the foot of the altar where they have been sacrificed, and crying aloud to the God of Justice to take cognizance of their wrongs and vindicate their cause." And, again (p. 163), "On the opening of the sixth seal, the sun and moon are darkened; the stars fall from heaven; the heavens themselves are rolled away with a mighty wind; and all the people of the land to be smitten are filled with terror and amazement, and fly to the rocks and mountains for refuge from the dreaded invasion which is about to be made." He explains the celestial phenomena foretold as portending, according to the ideas of those addressed, merely " *calamitous events.*"

WORDSWORTH regards the Seals as representing "a prophetic view of the history of the Christian Church, from the first Advent of Christ to the end of the world;" not however in successive eras, the one closing as the other begins. The Rider on the white horse he identifies with Christ, and He "is followed in the second, third, and fourth seals by another (hostile) Power, riding on three horses in succession." This Power is Death (Satan), who, in the *second* place makes an assault by *persecution;* in the *third,* by *heresy,* producing *spiritual famine;* in the *fourth,* by various workings: (1) barbarian incursions (ρομφαίᾳ, the barbarian sword), (2) heresies and schisms producing spiritual *famine* and death (λιμῷ and θανάτῳ), (4) heathen Rome.

ric theme of the Revelation." And, again, in § 28 ("*Apocalypse designed for the Church in every Age.*" Vol. I., 478), we find the following. " I regard the Apocalypse as containing matter which is *a τύπος of all that is to happen in respect to the Church.* I regard the whole Book as (a) particular illustration of a general principle—of a generic truth."—E. R. C.]

Papal Rome, the Romish hierarchy—τὰ θηρία τῆς γῆς. The opening of the *fifth* seal unveils the condition of the faithful departed, in the intermediate state, in Paradise. "The *sixth* seal reveals the crisis of greatest suffering for the Church; it is the Friday of *her* Passion Week. But it is also the eve of the *Sabbath* of *her* rest."

ALFORD regards the openings of these seals as corresponding "to the various arrangements of God's Providence, by which the way is prepared for the final opening of the closed book of His purposes to His glorified Church." He classes together the *first four,* viewing "these four visions as the four solemn preparations for the Coming of the Lord, *as regards the visible Creation,* which the four Living-beings symbolize." In his own language, "The whole Creation demands His coming. Ἔρχου is the cry of all its tribes. This cry is answered *first* by the vision of the great Conqueror (not Christ Himself, but only a symbol of His victorious power) Whose arrows are in the hearts of His enemies, and Whose career is the world's history. The breaking of this first seal is the great opening of the mystery of God. This, in some sense, includes and brings in the others. The others . . . hold a place subordinate to this. They are, in fact, but exponents of the mysteries enwrapt within this conquering career: visions of the method of its being carried out to the end in its operations on the outward world." The *Second* Seal he regards as representing "the reign of the *sword* (WAR) as one of the destined concomitants of the growing and conquering power of Christ, and one of the world long and world-wide preparations for His Coming." The *third,* as Famine, limited, however, "in his desolating action, by the command given, that enough is to be reserved for sustenance," i. e., (as Lange) Dearth. The *fourth,* as destroying influences,—sword, famine, pestilence, wild beasts. These seals he believes "to be contemporaneous, and each of them to extend through the whole lifetime of the Church," although he admits "that they may receive continually recurring, or even ultimate fulfilments, as the ages of the world go on, in distinct periods of time, and by distinctly assignable events." The opening of the *fifth* seal brings to view the souls of the martyred saints, and the cry for the Coming of the Lord is now from them. The opening of the *Sixth* Seal he regards as intimating "(ch. vi. 12-17) Immediate approach of the great day of the Lord, Matt. xxiv. 29, (vii. 1-8); gathering of the elect out of the four winds Matt. xxiv. 31, (vii. 9-17); vision of the whole glorified Church, Matt. xxv."

LORD (*An Exposition of the Apocalypse,* New York, 1847) identifies the *Riders* with different classes of Ministers: I. "The pure teachers of Christianity at large." II. "Diocesan Bishops," by whom, as he alleges, there was "a usurpation of powers which Christ has not authorized, an interception thereby of religious peace from the earth, and, finally, a compulsion of men to apostasy, to confer on and perpetuate their usurpation." III. Philosophic, mystic, and ritualistic teachers, who "reduced the Church to a destitution of the means of spiritual life, analogous to the dearth of bread produced by oppressive exactions in the Empire." IV. "Met. opolitans, Archbishops, and other superior prelates of the fourth and subsequent ages, and especially the Patriarchs of the Greek and the Popes of the Latin Church. . . . It was at this period, and under the promptings and guidance of those great Prelates, that the Church first formally apostatized from the faith and worship enjoined in the Gospel, and embraced a false religion." Hence followed, he contends, spiritual *pestilence* and *death*. In respect of the other seals: the V. As a Heaven scene, symbolizing the appearance of the martyrs in the presence of God, and their reception by Him. "It contains no note either of the commencement or close of the period to which it belongs. The whole representation, however, indicates that it is late in the reign of Antichrist. . . . Its period is doubtless during the ravages of the *fourth horseman*," etc. He represents as follows the VI.: "The events denoted by the symbol are such as must naturally occupy a long period. A political convulsion subverting one form of government and instituting another is itself the work of years. The change of the sun to black, and the moon to blood, denote, not their extinction and disappearance, but their conversion from an agreeable and salutary to a dreaded and disastrous agency; and the change of the new rulers, which it denotes, from justice to oppression, and exercise of a tyrannical sway, requires quite a considerable period. It is subsequently that the fall of the stars takes place, by which their dejection from their stations is symbolized. And the final disappearance of the heavens, the removal of the mountains and islands, and the promiscuous flight of rulers and subjects from the presence of the Lamb, are to follow at a still later period. The first three of these great events have undoubtedly already taken place" (the French revolution, the conversion of the Republic into despotism, the overthrow of that despotism). Then a period, during which the sealing of ch. vii. takes place; then "the annihilation of the civil governments, the Advent of the Son of God, and a resurrection of the saints." —E. R. C.]

EXPLANATIONS IN DETAIL.

Ch. vi. 1, 2.

VISION OF THE FIRST SEAL.

Ch. vi. 1. The literal system is at much trouble to settle upon an adequate conception of the opening of the single Seals and the succession of the single visions. The individual leaves of the book are, manifestly, books in themselves; and the individual books open not into leaves with dead figures, but into living pictures. Each new leaf is a new world-scene, illuminated by a light from the open Heaven. Heinrich's idea, according to which the six pictures are found upon the unsealed sides of the book, see in Düsterdieck. According to Düsterdieck, the opening of each separate Seal denotes a separate vision; this view is in opposition to the vital connection of the different items. According to Bengel, the two groups of *four* and *three* are so divided that the *first four* refer to *visible* things, and the *last three* to *invisible* things. On Alcasar's wonderful allegory, see Düsterdieck. There is no reason

for referring the four beasts [Living-beings] or Life-forms by name to the four Seals. The general relation between the Life-forms and the Seal-pictures is expressed, not thus: the Seal-pictures are expressed, not thus: the creation, on the one hand, and the Seal-visions on the other; but thus: the Fundamental Forms of the Divine governance, on the one hand, and on the other, the fundamental forms of worldly history. From καὶ εἶδον ὅτε, Düsterdieck draws the inference that the opening of the Seals was not itself the subject of vision. It is merely necessary, however, to distinguish between the emphasis falling upon the new and leading fact, the forth-coming figure, and that which after the foregoing narrative is more a matter of course, viz.: the acts of opening. Düsterdieck likewise maintains that the hearing of the voice forms no part of the εἶδον. In regard to this, we would remark that the visions in general branch into voices and visible appearances. According to this, the εἶδον of ver. 1 will be universal, branching subsequently into a manifestation for the ear, ver. 1, and one for the eye, ver. 2 (καὶ εἶδον). According to Düsterdieck, the thunder-tone of the voice is to be taken for granted in the case of all four voices after its mention in connection with the first voice; Hengstenberg, on the other hand, justly insists upon the peculiar significance of the first voice.

Düsterdieck cannot positively deny that the formula **come and see** is not only rabbinic but also specifically Johannean. His declaration that John's nearer approach is required is void of meaning, since a visional appearance is referred to. For the reasons here intimated, we regard the reading which omits the *see* as an improper correction.

The weight of evidence of the Codd. is about equally divided as to the reading (see TEXTUAL AND GRAMMATICAL). Unless, therefore, some new uncial MS. be discovered, having special claims to confidence, we must form our conclusions as to the genuine text from collateral considerations. The fact that "Come and see" is more Johannean than the simple "Come" (if it be a fact), has no bearing on the question at issue, which is, What did John hear? and not, How was John in the habit of expressing *himself?* If it has any weight, it is rather in support of the hypothesis of interpolation, since a copyist would be more likely to insert a word, that he might bring a sentence into accordance with the style of his author, than to omit a word when the omission would involve a departure from that style.

[If the address of the Living-beings was to the Seer, nothing can be gathered as to its *form*, since, manifestly, it might have been either *Come and see*, or the abbreviated *Come;* if, however, it was to the Symbols, or to Christ, then it must have been simply *Come*. That it was not to John, Alford thus argues: "Whither was he to come? Separated as he was by the glass*y* sea from the Throne, was he to cross it? And where shall we find the simple verb ἔρχεσθαι used absolutely in such a sense, 'Draw near,' without ὧδε or some such particle? Compare also the place where the Seer is to go and take the little book (ch. x. 8), and see how different is the whole form of expression." To this it may be added, Was not the Seer already at the point of vision? Why then was he called to draw nearer? Why the *repeated* call? Are we to suppose that he went back to his former position after the breaking of each Seal? Why the voice of *thunder?*

The view of Alford, however, as to the object of the call is liable to serious objections. He writes: "In interpreting so unusual a term of address, surely we should begin by inquiring whether we have not the key to it in the Book itself. And in this inquiry, are we justified in leaving out of consideration such a verse as ch. xxii. 17, τὸ Πνεῦμα καὶ ἡ νύμφη λέγουσιν Ἔρχου κ. τ. λ., and the following ἀμὴν ἔρχου, κύριε Ἰησοῦ, *ib.* ver. 20? This seems to show, in my mind, beyond a doubt, what, in the mind of the Seer, the remarkable and insulated exclamation ἔρχου imported. It was a cry addressed, not to himself, but to the Lord Jesus; and as each of these four first Seals is accompanied by a similar cry from one of the four living beings, I see represented in this four-fold ἔρχου the groaning and travailing together of creation for the manifestation of the sons of God, expressed in each case in a prayer for Christ's coming." This view, it must be admitted, is beautifully consistent with Alford's hypothesis, that the Zōa symbolize the different classes of animated beings, and could it be sustained by independent considerations (indeed, were it consistent with other considerations), would give great support to that hypothesis. The objections to it are: 1. In that it lacks any express reference to Jesus, it is altogether unexampled and unnatural as an address to Him. 2. The comparison of ch. xxii. 17 with 20. does not in the least support it; the call of ver. 17 is manifestly to the *water of life* mentioned in the last clause; and vers. 17 and 20 belong to entirely distinct divisions of the Book, the object of the ἔρχου of the latter being fixed by the immediately preceding Ναὶ ἔρχομαι ταχύ (see *in loc.*). 3. A voice of *thunder* is a voice of *command,* and not of *prayer.* Far better does it seem to the Am. Ed. to regard these voices as *commands* issuing from the ministers of God in nature (or, on the hypothesis of Lange as to the nature of the Zōa, from the Forms of God's Governance in nature). This view, of course, involves a special hypothesis as to the meaning of the four Riders, for which see Additional Note on p. 178 sq.—E. R. C.]

Ver. 2. **And I saw, and behold, a white horse.**—"The horses of the heroes of Roman triumphs were white" (Düsterdieck, p. 258). The single triumph of Christ, as set forth here, has in ch. xix. 14 extended through the Church Triumphant; it appears as an array of victorious hosts on white horses.

The *horses* [of the Seals] may not be specially identical with those of Zech. i. 8; yet they are in general related to them, as Divine *sendings* which proceed over the earth (Zech. i. 10). The *chariots* (Zech. vi. 1 sqq.) seem to denote the same *sendings* in involved forms of destiny. The *Rider* is here characterized by the *bow*—not the *sword.* This distinction, according to Düsterdieck, has no symbolical significance. Such an inference, however, should not be drawn from the abortive interpretations offered,

as especially the absurd one of Wetstein, who makes the *bow* indicative of a Parthian king. Doubtless the bow's property of being effective at a distance (as is the case in modern times with *fire-arms* of every description) is the true ground-idea of the picture. Düsterdieck's remark, that possibly the *arrows* spoken of in Ps. xlv. 6 were present to the mind of the Seer, excuses the interpretation of Vitringa and others, according to whom the *arrows* that have to be supplied denote Christ's numerous Apostles and Evangelists. Here, however, the unity of the Rider and the unity of His bow are the main thing; and inasmuch as arrows are to be taken for granted as accompanying the bow, we are to understand them as signifying, not persons, but the lightning-like spiritual operations issuing from Christ Himself, and traversing the whole earth (Zech. ix. 14). Thus the weapons which Satan employs are *fiery darts,* Eph. vi. 16.

In opposition to Züllig and Hengstenberg, Düsterdieck maintains that στέφανος here (as 1 Cor. ix. 25) denotes only the *wreath* of a warrior—not the *crown* of a king. But there is a peculiar meaning in the wreath which adorns the brow of Him who is described as victorious over the whole earth. And though a wreath might be given to the Warrior in advance, as a promise of victory, as Düsterdieck maintains, the white horse would scarcely be given Him in advance also. That He, therefore, "already goes forth as a νικῶν," does not mean simply that His purpose ἵνα νικήσῃ will assuredly be attained; it denotes, rather, that He is the *Victor* absolutely, that He *has conquered* and *will conquer.* The *principal* victory of Christ through His death and resurrection, and the development of that victory into universal victory, could not be more pertinently represented. Düsterdieck himself comes to a similar conclusion a little further on.

The upholders of the Church-historical and world-historical interpretation necessarily make a special chapter out of the first Rider.

EBRARD: "We pass over those purely allegoristic interpretations according to which this rider is Caligula or Trajan (Bengel and others; consult, however, Düsterdieck's note on this, p. 255), or war (Herder, De Wette), or the victory of evangelical preaching (Cyr. and others), or the word concerning Christ (Hofm.), or the fall (Berengaud.), and more of the same sort."

DE WETTE, without any foundation, even contrasts the mounted figure of Christ in ch. xix. 11 with the horseman in this passage.

HENGSTENBERG recognizes the figure as that of Christ. But what a Christ! Here also He goes forth only to execute judgment upon a godless world. Judgment and ever judgment! Here Christ rides forth for the development of the triumphs of salvation. In ch. xix. He goes forth in order to the triumph of judgment. Ebrard also remarks here: Christ is a warrior on horseback in reference to the hostile world. According to Ebrard, John has a view of earth from his station in Heaven, having been previously transported to Heaven. But the book of destiny with its earth-pictures is opened in Heaven.*

* [For the view of the Am. Ed. see Additional Note, p. 178.
[Alford, in the main, agrees with Lange in the interpreta-

Vers. 3 and 4.
VISION OF THE SECOND SEAL.

Come [LANGE: **and see**]. From this it appears, it is claimed, that after the disappearance of the first Rider, John drew back and resumed his original place (Düsterdieck). According to Ebrard, he retired from the book during the interim. And this proceeding must necessarily be repeated yet two more times. Then, however, according to this literal apprehension of the passage, in which it is forgotten that we are in the midst of the whole vision, John would remain standing before the book after the opening of the fourth and fifth Seals.* Neither can we regard the second figure as the form of "personified bloodshed" [Düsterdieck]. There are yet other forms of bloodshed (see ver. 8); here its warlike form is intended. Concerning the bloody hue itself there can be no doubt (2 Kings iii. 22).

_____

tion of this symbol. There is a difference, however, which is set forth in his answer to the question: "*Who is the Rider* on this white horse?" He writes: "We must not, in reply, on the one hand, too hastily introduce the Person of our Lord Jesus Himself, or, on the other, be startled at the objection that we shall be paralleling Him, or one closely resembling Him, with the far different forms which follow. Doubtless, the resemblance to the Rider, ch. xix. 11 sqq., is very close, and is intended to be very close. The difference, however, is considerable. There He is set forth as *present* in His triumph, followed by the hosts of Heaven: here, He is working in bodily absence, and the rider is not Himself, but only a symbol of His victorious power, the embodiment of His advancing Kingdom as regards that side of its progress where it breaks down earthly power and makes the kingdom of the world to be the Kingdom of our Lord and of His Christ."

[Elliott (followed by Barnes) supports his view (see p. 168) as follows: He begins his discussion of the general subject of the Seals with the *a priori* probabilities that the Apocalyptic *horse* symbolized a *nation*, and that this nation was the *Roman*. He contends that, under this hypothesis, on the comparison of the symbols with the established facts of history, such unity and significance become apparent as to establish the truth of the hypothesis. (And it must be acknowledged, that if the unity and significance be as he claims them to be, it will be difficult to invalidate his conclusion.) He, then, in reference to the description of the character of the even s of this particular seal (ver. 2, the *crown* and the *white* color of the horse, indicating *triumph* and *prosperity*) asks: "Did not this answer very notably and distinctively to the *general state* and *history* of the Roman Empire for eighty or ninety years succeeding John's banishment? that is, from Domitian's death, A. D. 96, throughout the successive reigns of Nerva, Trajan, Hadrian, and the two Antonines, until the accession of Commodus, etc.?" In answer to this question, he refers to Gibbon's description of this period (vol. i., chs 1., ii), quoting the following from the second chapter of the great History: "If a man were called upon to fix the period in the history of the world during which the condition of the human race was most happy and prosperous, he would, without hesitation, name the period which elapsed from the death of Domitian to the accession of Commodus." He strives to confirm his hypothesis by reference to the στέφανος and the *bow* of this Rider; showing that during this period of Roman history the στέφανος, and not the διάδημα, was the crown of the Emperor, and that Nerva, who was a Cretan by extraction (his *great-grandfather* was probably a Cretan! see *Hor. Ap* Vol. I., p 116, notes 2 and 3), was properly represented with a *bow*, which was the symbol of a Cretan.—E. R. C]

* [The *call* must have had some significance. If addressed to John (and it must have been if the καὶ βλέπε or ἴδε be genuine), it is inconceivable that it should have meant anything else than that he should *go forward;* and the thrice-repeated call implies that he must have retired after each opening. The further conclusion of our Author, however (which he seems to have presented in ridicule), is by no means necessary; the Seer, after the opening of the *fourth* Seal, might have retired, as he must have done after the opening of all the preceding. The necessity (on the supposition of the genuineness of the *Rec.*) of this advancing and retiring is among the considerations that go to establish the fact of interpolation (see Add. Comment on p. 170 sq.).—E. R. C.]

_____

Special references:* To the Jewish war (Grotius, Wetstein, Herder. *etc.*); to the persecutions of the Christians (De Lyra and others); to Antichristianity, its rider being the Devil (Calov.); to the Roman empire (Vitringa); or the world-powers (Stern). The figure is correctly apprehended as general by some others (Hengstenb., Ebrard, Düsterd.).

Vers. 5 and 6.
VISION OF THE THIRD SEAL.

The *black* color of the third horse does not, according to Düsterdieck, indicate the mourning occasioned by the dearth, but trouble and vexation in general. It is not to be expected, however, that among colors of specific meaning, *white*, *red*, and *pale-yellow*, we should find one so general in its import, embracing all troubles. In Job xxx. 30 the blackness of the skin is connected with the drying up of the bones. The following passage in Lamentations, however, ch. iv. 8; 9, is particularly significant: "But now their visage is dark with blackness [A. V.: blacker than a coal; *marg. read.:* darker than blackness], so that they are not known in the streets; their skin cleaveth to their bones, and they are as dry as a stick. It fared better with those that were slain by the sword than with those *whom hunger slew, etc.*" Nothing can be plainer than that the black color spoken of in the third Seal-vision is likewise that of hunger. ["The color is indicative of the mournful nature of the employment of the rider." ALFORD. —E. R. C.]

Ver. 5. A balance.—Hengstenberg: "The balance comes into consideration merely as a symbol of dearth or scarcity. For according to the subsequent verse the fruits of the earth are not weighed out, but measured." Where there is a superabundance, there is no counting and measuring, Gen. xli. 49: but where a thing is weighed out, there is none too much of it. Fundamental passages are Ezek. iv. 10: "And thy food which thou shalt eat (shall be) by weight, twenty shekels a day;" and ver. 16: "Moreover, He said unto me, Son of man, behold, I will break the staff of bread in Jerusalem; and they shall eat bread by weight and with care."

_____

* [Elliott and Barnes regard this Seal as symbolizing that long period of war and bloodshed which, commencing shortly after the accession of Commodus, extended to the accession of Diocletian (A. D. 185 or 6-284). As descriptive of this period, they make many citations from Gibbon, and (Elliott) the following from *Sismondi* (*Fall of the Roman Empire*, Vol. 1.): "With Commodus' death commenced the third and most calamitous period. It lasted ninety-two years, from 192 to 284. During that time thirty-two Emperors and twenty-seven pretenders to the Empire alternately hurled each other from the throne by incessant civil warfare. . . . Ninety-two years of nearly incessant civil warfare taught the world on what a frail foundation the virtue of the Antonines had reared the felicity of the Empire." They support this hypothesis by such considerations as the following: (1.) All the symbols, the *red* color of the horse, the peace *taken away*, the *killing*, the *great sword*, indicate a state of war; (2) the *taking away* of peace indicates that it was a state of war following a period of peace; (3) the μάχαιρα —the Roman battle-sword, not ῥομφαία as in ver. 8), that it was a state of *civil* war; (4) the *sword given to the rider*, that the *causal agency* in the state of war should be "those whose fitting and distinctive badge was *sword-bearing*," *i. e.* "the military."

[Wordsworth, who holds that the Rider is Satan making his *first* assault *by persecution*, writes: "This is the exposition which all the ancient interpreters have given of this Seal." On this point, however, he presents only one direct testimony from the *Catena*.—E. R. C.]

These passages rest upon Lev. xxvi. 26. [So also Elliott, Alford, etc. The last-named continues: "Some, as, e. g., Woodhouse, have defended the meaning 'yoke' for ζυγόν. But surely the question is here decided for ▇▇ by Ezek. xlv. 10 [LXX.]: ζυγὸς δίκαιος, κ. τ. λ., where the same words occur in juxtaposition. The assertion of Mr. Barker, in his strictures on Elliott's Hor. Ap., that ζυγός in the sense of balance absolutely is very rare, is sufficiently answered by the proverb ἀκριβέστερος ζυγοῦ, by Diog. Laert. viii. 18. . . . . Where a word can thus be used figuratively, in common sayings, its literal sense cannot be so very rare."—E. R. C.]

Ver. 6. And I heard as it were a voice.—[See Text. Notes]. Gloomy cry, gloomy dispensation! It resounds in the midst of the four Life forms. That is, all four participate in it. [This is not, by any means, a necessary conclusion; the voice more probably proceeded from one, but which one is not specified.—E. R. C.] It is not, however (as Hengstenberg maintains), a piece of intelligence which concerns the representatives of the living beings on earth (in which category Hengstenberg places the Cherubim).

"The first half of the cry," says Düsterdieck, "sounds as when something is offered for sale" (Winer). But during a scarcity, produce is not cried for sale. On the other hand, a dearth is limited by a taxation of bread. The taxation here indicated issues from the midst of the four Living-forms.

Hengstenberg: "A measure, chœnix, of wheat is designated by Suidas as the daily maintenance of a man (ἡμερήσιος τροφή). A denarius was the usual day's wages of a man, according to Matt. xx. 2." The dearth fixed by this taxation is certainly no famine as yet; moreover, as a permanent and universal suffering is denoted, the figure of famine would be an exaggeration. Hengstenberg thinks that "if a man should eat barley bread, the usual food of the common people (comp. John vi. 9, 13), which is three times as cheap as wheat bread, he and his family might make shift to live." Possibly they might, if the family was a very small one. [So also Elliott, Alford, Barnes, etc.—E. R. C.]

An unmeaning remark is that of Bengel, who observes that barley and wheat (see on the contrary, Ex. ix. 31, 32) ripen earlier than oil and wine. Hence there would be only a moderate dearth, because the later productions would succeed better. Still less should the contrast be obliterated by the declaration that the greatest economy should be observed in regard to oil and wine likewise (Rinck). The most utter misinterpretation is found in Ewald's assumption that the oil and wine remained uninjured in a sort of mockery. Though oil and wine are not, in the strictest sense, articles of sustenance, they are—even in the East, where they are more common—articles of luxury and enjoyment, and the oppressiveness of the contrast lies in the fact that the rich, who can also easily pay for the dear wheat, have their special luxuries at a proportionably cheap rate. Similar contrasts run through social life down to the present day.

Special interpretations:* The famine under Claudius (Grotius and others); famines in a more general sense (Calov., etc.); the black horse, false brethren whose works are black (Bede); dearth of spiritual nourishment (Vitringa, [Wordsworth and Lord]); heretics (à-Lapide); personified heresies (Stern). For additional fanciful interpretations, see Düsterdieck.

Vers. 7 and 8.
VISION OF THE FOURTH SEAL.

It is not without purpose and effect that of the fourth rider it is expressly said that his name is Death. In this stress upon the name, we might find it indicated that Death is only so called on earth; that he is not really death, but sleep, according to the name whereby faith knows him; nay, that he is even a cosmical birth so far as the name by which he is known in the other world is concerned. The context, however, seems more to favor the idea that he here appears in the light of a terrific object, whom all men call by name, by his dread title. Death here appears as the specific death-power, as a historically aggravated mortality (see Ps. cx.). Hence he cannot be reduced to a specific form of death, pestilence, for instance, as Eich-

a [Elliott and Barnes identify the events of this seal (see p. 168) with the period of distress following the edict of Caracalla, ante A. D. 217. Both these authors refer largely to Gib on; the latter quotes (from Lord) the following from Lactantius (De Mort Pers-c, ch. xxiii.) as furnishing "a painful but most appropriate illustration:" "swarms of extactors sent into the provinces and cities filled them with agitation and terror, as though a conquering enemy were leading them into captivity. The fields were se arately measured, the trees and vines, the flocks and herds numbered, and an examination made of the men. In the cities the cultivated and rude were united as of the same rank. The streets were crowded with groups of families, and every one required to appear with his children and slaves. Tortures and lashes resounded on every side. Sons were gibbeted in the presence of their parents, and the most confidential servants harassed that they might make disclosures against their masters, and wives that they might testify unfavorably of their husbands. If there were a total destitution of property, they were still tortured to make acknowledgments against themselves, and, when overcome by pain, inscribed for what they did not possess. Neither age nor ill-health was admitted as an excuse for not appearing. The sick and weak were borne to the place of inscription, a reckoning made of the age of each, and years added to the young and deducted from the old, in order to subject them to a higher taxation than the law imposed. The whole scene was filled with wailing and sadness. In the mean time individuals died, and the herds and the flocks diminished, yet tribute was none the less required to be paid for the dead, so that it was no longer allowed either to live or die without a tax. Mendicants also e sce ed, where nothing could be wrenched, a d whom misfortune and misery had made incapable of farther oppression. These the impious wretch affecting to pity, that the might not suffer want, ordered to be assembled, borne off in vessels, and plunged into the sea." He adds: "Were we now to represent these things by a symbol, we could scarcely find one that would be more expressive than that of a rider on a black horse with a pair of scales, sent for th under a proclamation which indicated that there would be a most rigid and exact administration of severe and oppressive laws, and with a special command, addressed to the people, not for the purposes of concealment, or from opposition to the government, to injure the sources of revenue."

[Wordsworth thus writes: "The imagery of the Apocalypse is derived from ancient Hebrew prophecy. The ground-work of its language here is that of Hosea xii. 7, concerning Ephraim. Ephraim in the Apocalypse is a representative of enmity to Judah, the Church of Christ. And Hosea thus describes Ephraim: He is a merchant; the balances of deceit are in his hand, he loveth to oppress; the characteristic of Heresy is to be a merchant, and it bears a balance in its hand. 'The Rider,' says Augustine, (?) 'has a balance in his hand, for he professes that he is teaching equitably, and yet he is doing wrong.'"—E. R. C.]

horn supposes. Besides, all Hades follows him, and Hades is not populated by pestilence solely. Hades on earth is the whole terrific retro-action of the Kingdom of the Dead on the race of mortals; it does not, therefore, denote the inhabitants of Hades (Eichhorn, Ebrard); otherwise the earth would be peopled with ghosts. Hengstenberg even tries to make Hades the place of torment, the abode of the damned, after the mediæval fashion, in accordance with his ruling view (p. 339). It is not said, however, that Gehenna spreads itself over the earth. Düsterdieck, moreover, justly remarks that general plagues are treated of here; not special plagues of unbelievers.

The color of the horse is χλωρός, the yellowish green of the fresh-springing verdure, and the greenish yellow of decay; the latter is the symbol here.

On the meaning of the *fourth part*, see above. It might be said—*all* men are mortal; but the fourth and pre-eminently worldly part is swept away by an aggravated mortality. In the Prophets, also, the four dark species appear as leading forms of punishment, viz.: the sword, hunger, death (in this special sense contagion [רֶבֶר, see Düsterdieck, p. 262], of which, again, pestilence is a particular form), and evil beasts (Lev. xxvi. 22; Ezek. xiv. 21). (Another explanation of the *fourth part*, see in Ebrard, p. 249.)*

[ALFORD: "The enumeration comprehends the '*four sore judgments*' enumerated in Ezek. xiv. 21, and in the same terms (LXX.): τὰς τέσσαρες ἐκδικήσεις μου τὰς πονηράς, ῥομφαίαν, καὶ λιμὸν, καὶ θηρία πονηρὰ, καὶ θάνατον. This fixes the meaning of this second and subordinate θανάτῳ as above" (*i. e.*, "*pestilence* ").—E. R. C.]

Special interpretations†: The mortal suffer-

ings in the Jewish war (Wetstein and others); the pagan Romans under Domitian (Lyra); migration of nations (Huschke); death-bringing heresy (Bede and others [Wordsworth]); the Saracens (Vitringa).

Vers. 9, 10, 11.

VISION OF THE FIFTH SEAL.

Ver. 9. **Under the altar.**—[" Ὑποκάτω τοῦ θυσιαστηρίου, i. e., at the foot or lower part of the altar, where the victim was laid whose blood had been shed." STUART.—E. R. C.] "Two altars are mentioned in Revelation; namely, the golden altar of incense, and the altar of burnt-offering, which is not called golden. The former is denoted in ch. viii. 3. 4; ix. 13; the latter in ch. xiv. 18; xvi. 7. [Here it can be only the altar of burnt-offering that is meant. For this, as being the more public of the two, accessible and open to the view of all, is always the one intended in Scripture, and especially in the Revelation, when the altar is simply mentioned (comp. ch. xvi. 7). And here we can the less think of any other than it, as on it alone were the bloody offerings presented, and only under it could the blood be found, or the souls of those that had been slain."—(E. R. C.)] (? Hengstenberg). On the embarrassments in which the literal exegesis finds itself in striving to account for the position of the souls under the altar, and for their visibility, see Düsterdieck, p. 264. IDEM: "The reason why the souls are conceived of as *under* the altar, is found in the fact that the blood of sacrifices, as which the

---

* [The Am. Ed. must here express his dissatisfaction with every explanation that he has seen of the *fourth part*; nor can he propose an interpretation satisfactory to himself. In his judgment, there is here either an undiscovered corruption of text, or else a knot in symbolism which it is reserved for some future commentator to unravel.—E. R. C.]

† [ELLIOTT and BARNES regard this seal as indicating the period (A. D. 243-268) embracing the reigns of Decius, Gallus, Æmilianus, Valerian and Gallienus. Concerning this period, as to its *general* characteristics, they quote from Gibbon the following: "From the great secular games celebrated by Philip to the death of the Emperor Gallienus, there elapsed twenty years of shame and misfortune. During this calamitous period, every instant of time was marked, every province of the Roman world was afflicted by barbarous invaders and military tyrants, and the wearied empire seemed to approach the last and fatal moment of its dissolution." In reference to *particular* things (the quotations are made from Barnes) we have the following: The *sword* (ῥομφαία—the *barbaric sword*): This " was the period of the *first* Gothic invasion of the Roman Empire; the period when those vast hordes . . . . invaded the Roman territories from the East, passed over Greece, and made their appearance almost, as Mr. Gibbon says, within sight of Rome. . . . . As one of the illustrations that the ' *sword* ' should be used by ' *Death* ' in this period, we may refer to the siege and capture of Philadelphia. ' A hundred thousand persons are reported to have been massacred in the sack of that great city ' " (*Gibbon*). [*Hunger*: "This would naturally be the consequence of long continued wars, and of such invasions as those of the Goths. Mr. Gibbon says of this period: ' Our habits of thinking so fondly connect the order of the universe with the fate of man, that this gloomy period of history has been decorated with inundations, earthquakes, uncommon meteors, preternatural darkness, and a crowd of prodigies, fictitious or exaggerated. But a *long and general famine* was a calamity of a more serious kind. It was the inevitable consequence of rapine and oppression, which extirpated the produce of the present, and the hope of future harvests.' " Vol. I., p. 159.

[*Pestilence*: "Of the pestilence which raged in this period

Mr. Gibbon makes the following remarkable statement, in immediate connection with what he says of the famine: ' Famine is almost always followed by epidemical diseases, the effect of scanty and unwholesome food. Other causes must, however, have contributed to the furious plague, which, from the year two hundred and fifty to the year two hundred and sixty-five, raged *without interruption in every province, every city, and almost every family in the Roman empire*. During some time, five thousand persons died daily at Rome; and many towns that had escaped the hands of the barbarians were entirely depopulated,' i. 159."

[*Wild beasts*: "These are formidable enemies in the early stages of society, and when a country from any cause becomes depopulated. . . . Though not adverted to by Mr. Gibbon, there *is* a record pertaining to this very period which shows that this was one of the calamities with which the world was then afflicted. It occurs in Arnobius, *Adv. Gentes*, *lib.* i. p. 5. Within a few years after the death of Gallienus (about A. D. 300), he speaks of *wild beasts* in such a manner as to show that they were regarded as a sore calamity. . . . 'When were wars waged with wild beasts, and contests with lions? Was it not before our times? When did a plague come upon men poisoned by serpents? Was it not before our times?' "

[WORDSWORTH comments as follows: "The word used in the seal for *sword* is different from that in ver. 4, and properly signifies a *Thracian sword*, ... The *Beasts of the Earth* here, are *savage powers* exercising an *earthly* dominion for *earthly ends*. . . . Observe the article here, *the* Beasts, showing that although they have not yet been mentioned, they are present to the Divine fore-knowledge, and will be described more fully in later parts of the Apocalypse. . . . These words, *the Beasts of the Earth*, thus introduced, connect the *time* of the *seal* with the time of *other* prophecies in other portions of the Apocalypse. The words thus used in this book may be called *chronological catch-words*. They serve to rivet prophecies of contemporaneous events, to mark identity of subject, as well as sameness of time. . . . We find on examination that the word θηρίον, *Beast*, is used in no less than *thirty-seven* places of the Apocalypse, and *always* in a special sense, signifying a *particular power*; we may therefore reasonably infer that the word is used in the same sense in *the passage now before us*. This seal, therefore, presents a compendious view of the sufferings which the Church of Christ would have to endure from the *various* workings of the Evil One."—E. R. C.]

martyrs are accounted, was poured out at the foot of the altar." He rightly adds, in opposition to Züllig and Hengstenberg, that it does not follow from this that by the *souls*, nothing but the *blood* is here intended. The altar is, by most commentators, regarded as the altar of burnt-offering [so Wordsworth, Elliott, Alford, Barnes, etc.—E. R. C.]; only De Wette incorrectly apprehends it as the altar of incense, in accordance with ch. viii. 3.

[WORDSWORTH: "The imagery of this vision is derived from the sacrificial service of the Temple (Ex. xl. 29); 'the blood of the victims being received by the sacrificing Priest in a vessel was *poured out at the foot of the altar*' (Jahn, *Archæol.*, § 377); see Lev. iv. 7, viii. 15; Isa. xxix. 1). The sacrificial word (ἐσφαγμένων), here rendered *slain*, is the same as is applied to Christ, the True and Faithful *Martyr*, the Lamb slain (see v. 6, 9, 12, xiii. 8), and to the Martyrs (in xviii. 24). This imagery had been already adopted by the Apostle St. Paul at Rome, on the eve of his own martyrdom; 'I am already being *poured out*,' etc. (2 Tim. iv. 6)."—ALFORD: "The representation here, in which they are seen *under the altar*, is simply symbolical, carrying out the likening of them to victims slain on the altar. Even as the blood of these victims was poured under the altar, and the life was in the blood, so their souls are represented as under the symbolical altar in Heaven,* crying for vengeance, as blood is often said to do."—BARNES: "John saw these souls *as if* they were collected under the altar—the place where the sacrifice for sin was made—offering their supplications. Why they are represented as being there is not so apparent; but probably two suggestions will explain this: (*a*) The altar was the place where sin was expiated, and it was natural to represent these redeemed martyrs as seeking refuge there; and (*b*) it was usual to offer prayers and suplications *at* the altar, in connection with the sacrifice made for sin, and on the ground of that sacrifice. The idea is, that they who were suffering persecution would naturally seek a refuge in the place where expiation was made for sin, and where prayer was appropriately offered."—E. R. C.]
On account of the word of God and on

account of the witness which they had.— The *testimony*, according to the ancients, De Wette, and Bleek, is the testimony concerning Christ; according to Hengstenb., Ebrard, Düsterd., it is the testimony (objective or subjective?) which the martyrs have received from Jesus. Düsterdieck says: "This view is demanded, irrespective even of the parallelism of the foregoing τ. λόγ. τ. ϑ. by the clause ἣν εἶχον, which presupposes that the μαρτυρία which the martyrs *had*, had been in the first instance by them *received*, namely, from the true or original Witness, Jesus Christ." There is an exegetical obscureness here. The *testimony* is a specific term. The gospel which a man receives from Christ is not in itself a specific testimony or witness. It becomes *testimony* by faithful confession; and then, doubtless, Christ confesses Himself to the man by whom He is confessed. Here, however, the *holding fast* of confessors to their confession is denoted. ["The testimony is one *borne by them*, as most commentators; not one *borne to them* by the faithful Witness, as Düsterdieck and Ebrard, most unnaturally; for how could the testimony borne to them before the Father by Christ (so Ebrard) be the cause of their being put to death on earth?" ALFORD.—E. R. C.]

Ver. 10. **They cried** (ἔκραξαν).—According to Ebrard, the *souls*; according to Hengstenberg, the *slain*. The grammatical reference, it is true, is to the latter; but the *slain* are the *souls*. In this vision Hengstenberg, after a more general view of all that goes before it, falls entirely into the church-historical interpretation, and speaks of catastrophes which hold out a prospect of the final judgment. All the seal-visions, from the first on, progress toward the final judgment; and this is assuredly true, therefore, of the vision of the martyrs in particular. Toward the actual end of the world, however, quite different forms of persecution take the place of *slaying*, see ch. xiii. 17.

According to Hengstenberg, the *souls of the slain* are not their spirits as existent in the other world, but their animal souls, identical with the blood, and destroyed in death along with their bodies; he, therefore, apprehends the description as purely poetical; or, rather, he gives a purely prosaic interpretation.*

---

* [There is no altar of *burnt offering* in Heaven; the only altar there is that of *incense*. In the symbolic Tabernacle, the altar of *burnt offering* was placed in the open court, before the *vaòs* (the true Temple) and in the way to it; and so, doubtless, in the Apocalyptic vision. In the judgment of the American Editor, the outer altar was symbolic of the *Earth* as the platform of service (*i. e.* sacrifice in its broadest sense) offered unto God *as the condition of entrance into the Holy Place*. For the *sinful* creature, this serv ice involves *sacrifice* in the sense of suffering and death. The perfect service, involving the voluntary endurance of suffering and death, which is the efficacious condition of the sinner's entrance into Heaven, was offered by the Second Adam; and yet those united unto Him are called to a service like His—a service of obedience, involving *sacrifice* in the narrower sense, the sacrifice of burnt offering. It was in respect of this that the Apostle desired, not only for himself, but for all believers, that they might know the *fellowship of Christ's sufferings*, and be made *conformable unto His death* (comp. Phil. iii. 10 with 17). In *the restitution of all things*, doubtless, this earth will be brought into the Holy Place, and the brazen altar of *burnt offering* will become a golden altar of *incense* (Rom. viii. 21, ch. xxi. 3, 4), but until that day the earth will remain, before the Temple, an altar of *sacrifice*. The scene that the Seer beheld was (in the first part) an earth scene during the present æon, in which he beheld the true followers of the Lord partaking in the sufferings of their Head. (See Add. Note. p. 178.)—E. R. C.]

* [It becomes an exceedingly interesting and important question whether Hengstenberg is not right. He writes: "The *Souls* of the martyrs, in ver. 9, are not the souls in the intermediate state, as expositors commonly suppose; the *souls* (ψυχαί) are meant, of which it is said in the Old Testament that they are the blood—the animal souls (see, for example, Gen. ix. 5, [the term here translated *life* is in the LXX. ψυχή]); they are murdered souls; but the blood itself might as well have stood, and in ver. 10, indeed, is actually put instead of the souls here. This is plain from comparing the original passage, Gen. iv. 10, where the blood of Abel cries to God from the ground. (Züllig: 'Only a dramatizing of the thought; your blood demands vengeance, according to Gen. iv. 10, ix. 5, etc.' [LXX.]) It is in accordance with the phraseology of the Old and New Testaments, in which everywhere the *spirits* (πνεύματα) only, not the *souls* (ψυχαί) of the *departed* are spoken of—see my *Comm. on the Psalms*, Vol. III., p. 87 (Trans.). It is shown by a comparison of the parallel passage, ch. xx. 4, where the discourse is of the *souls* (ψυχαί) of those who have been beheaded for the testimony of Jesus, and where the Prophet sees them live again. It is plain, finally, from the fact that the *souls* were seen un der the altar, in reference to Levit. iv. 7 (comp. v. 9), 'And the whole blood of the bullock shall he pour out at the bottom of the altar of burnt offering, which is before the tabernacle of the congregation.' Accordingly, s nce the place under the altar has nothing to do with *souls* in the higher sense,

The souls invoke the Lord as ὁ δεσπότης ; i. e., the LORD in His absolute power' and authority. They doubt not that He is able immediately to bring the course of the world to a conclusion. The human soul in extreme distress is always prone to appeal to this power. Düsterdieck [also Alford], not without reason, brings out the special reference of the Divine title to the δοῦλοι, as indicated in our text by the σύνδουλοι. The application of ἀληθινός to God's faithfulness to His promise (Vitringa, Bengel and others) is opposed by Düsterdieck. The word certainly does primarily denote the true, essential Lord; this, however, is not to the exclusion of an appeal to His faithfulness. [See on ch. iii. 7.—E. R. C.]

Them that dwell on the earth.—Antithesis to the servants of God. In demonstration of the ethical nobility of the longing uttered by the martyrs—a longing which contained neither a culpable impatience nor a desire for revenge—Bede has remarked: "*Non hæc odio inimicorum, pro quibus in hoc sæculo rogaverunt, orant, sed amore æquitalis, qua ipsi judici ut prope positi concordant*" (Düsterdieck).

To Bengel's observation: "They are concerned for the honor of the holiness and truth of their Lord;" we must add that, for that very reason, they are also concerned for justice and their own justification.

Ver. 11. **And a white robe was given unto them, to each.**—This express singular is very significant. Each soul in particular is justified. According to Hengstenberg, this is but an illustration of their felicity, for the benefit of John and the Church. "According to ch. iii. 4, 5, and vii. 14, the *white robe* constitutes the attire of all the blessed, and they, as such, enter into glory immediately upon their departure out of this life. Accordingly, the words, *was given*, cannot refer to the bestowment itself, but to the consciousness of the Seer." Düsterdieck opposes this hypothesis of a 'poetical fiction," but also combats the view of Bengel, who supposes that some particular thing over and above eternal salvation and blessedness is intended. "White *stolæ*, or long white robes, are an excellent adornment and high honor." Vitringa's interpretation is, indeed, a more valuable one: "The cause of these martyrs shall be publicly vindicated in the Church, and they shall be recognized and extolled as sharers in the glory and Kingdom of Christ, their cause having for a time appeared in a dubious light." Bossuet, in accordance with the import of the white robe amongst the Romans, seems to regard it here as indicative of a special expectancy of the resurrection. Martyrdom is certainly a special candidateship for glory; yet, according to the mean-

ing of the white robe elsewhere in the Apocalypse, Vitringa appears to us to have presented the true signification of the present passage.*

[ALFORD: "The *white robe*, in this Book, is the vestment of acknowledged and glorified righteousness, in which the saints walk and reign with Christ, comp. ch. iii. 4, vii. 13 sqq. *al.* This was given to the martyrs; but their prayer for vengeance was not yet granted. The Seer saw in vision that this was so. The white robe was not actually bestowed as some additional boon, but seemed in vision to be thus bestowed, because in that vision one side only of the martyrs' intermediate state had been presented, viz.: the fact of their slaughter and their collective cry for vengeance. Now, as over against that, the other more glorious side is presented, viz.: that though the collective cry for vengeance is not yet answered, yet, individually, they are blessed in glory with Christ, and waiting for their fellows to be fully complete."—E. R. C.]

That they should rest.—According to Bengel and De Wette, ἀναπαύσωνται means a cessation from crying; according to Hengstenberg, it denotes the repose of the blessed, the rest from the toils and conflicts of life, with reference to ch. xiv. 13. This too, then, would be a mere poetic description. As in the humanly conditioned world of feeling, the impulse of justice and the impulse of mercy modify each other, and the latter especially appeases the former (James ii. 13), so too the impulses of longing in view of the Divine purpose and end of the world are appeased by the impulse of patience in view of the Divine plan of the world. Patience must supplement longing, Rom. viii. 17, 25. The consolation of them, by pointing them to the end of their earthly sufferings, is an independent affair, and its place is not here. The first word of comfort that would be spoken to a man who had been slain would not be—thou art now freed from all trouble [?]. The instinct of justice is æonic, and extends into eternity; this Kant saw.

[WORDSWORTH: "They enjoy the rest and refreshment of Paradise (Luke xxiii. 43), and are in Abraham's bosom (Luke xvi. 22). Therefore, as the Apocalypse says, '*Blessed* are the *dead* that die in the Lord . . . for they (that they may [shall]) *rest* from their labors, ch. xiv. 13.'"—ALFORD: "Not merely *abstain from their cry for vengeance*, be quiet; but *rest in blessedness*, see ch. xiv. 13; Dan. xii. 13."—BARNES: "That is, that they must *wait* for a little season before they could be avenged as they desired."—E. R. C.]

Yet a little time.—" Bengel's reckonings in regard to the length of the 'χρόνος' suffer shipwreck on the right reading χρ. μικρόν" (Düsterdieck). The term *time* in itself is the indefinite form of the future softened for patience by the epithet: a *little* time, as also by the idea of the *chronos* as the legitimately expiring period leading to the καιρός. Then, again, the purpose of the waiting is stated: ἵνα πληρωθῶσιν, etc. That their full number may be made up. Wolf, Ebrard, Düsterdieck, De Wette: That their career might be completed, or that they might be com-

---

we can only understand by the souls (ψυχαί) the *animal souls*, which perish with the body." According to this interpretation, it is the blood, the murdered lives, of the saints that calls to God for vengeance. And this idea is far more in accordance with what we are taught concerning the character of the redeemed than the one commonly received. There is no incongruity in the supposition that the *blood* of martyred Stephen, like that of Abel, should have called upon God to avenge it; but we cannot entertain the thought that the *spirit* of him who, like Jesus, departed with a prayer for forgiveness, should, immediately after his departure, have raised the cry, Lord, avenge me, punish my murderers.—E. R. C.]

* [Does not a comparison of this verse with ch. vii. 9, 13, 14, indicate that the *white robes* have reference to a *heavenly condition*, and not to an *earthly vindication*?—E. R. C.]

pleted [in the sense of dying, or of moral perfection ; De Wette thinks either may be intended. —Tr.]. Similarly Hengstenberg, in accordance with the reading πληρώσωσι. In opposition to Bengel's view, Hengstenberg remarks : "One must be very full of Judaistic notions to pretend to understand by the *fellow-servants*, future martyrs from among the Gentiles, and by the *brethren*, martyrs of Israel." Being slightly scholastic, however, is not always being Judaistic. Bengel had overcome the Judaistic tendency to a greater degree than many another man. According to Düsterdieck, against De Wette, the numeric completeness has reference only to the *future* martyrs. But neither can these constitute a separate class, according to John's view. [Alford: "*Shall have accomplished* (scil. *their course*). Considering that this absolute use of πληροῦν, without an object following, is an ἅπαξ λεγόμενον, it is strange that Ebrard and Düst. should designate πληρώσωσιν as an explanatory reading for πληρωθῶσιν. If this latter be read, then we must render: *shall have been completed* (in number); a meaning found Luke xxi. 24; Acts vii. 23, 30; ix. 23; xxiv. 27; comp. also Col. ii. 10, which suggests another reason for altering to -θῶσιν."—E. R. C.]

The vision of the fifth seal has also been particularized. In the martyrs crying for vengeance, Vitringa discovered the Waldenses. Bengel interposed a chronos=1111⅑ years between the Apostolic martyrs that cry for vengeance and the martyrs of the future; thus he also struck upon the Waldenses—not, however, at the beginning, but at the end of the chronos.*

On isolated allegorizing interpretations of the words, *souls under the altar*, see Düsterdieck, p. 265.

Vers. 12–17.
VISION OF THE SIXTH SEAL.

Ebrard and Düsterdieck maintain with perfect truth that the end of the world is depicted in this vision [so also Wordsworth and Alford. See Add. Note, p. 178.—E. R. C.]. And thus for the second time the cyclical structure of the Apocalypse is established. But as the condition of Laodicea and the Lord's standing before the door did but lightly touch upon the end, so the present cycle does indeed advance, yet in such a manner as to leave abundance of room for the following cycles. And this inasmuch as it is essentially confined to the cosmical indications of the beginning catastrophe. Our passage reproduces the parallels in the Eschatological Discourse, Matt. xxiv. 29, 30, in a prophetically

developed form. The second vision has its foundation in Matt. xxiv. 6; the third and fourth visions have theirs in ver. 7; and the fifth in ver. 9. [This sketch, manifestly true in all the particular parallels mentioned, leaves entirely out of view, as will be observed, any parallel to the leading figure, the false Christs of ver. 5. See Add. Note.—E. R. C.] Hence, all allegoristic interpretations which deny the reference of the fifth seal to the end of the world, making the vision consist of intermediate forms or more general features, are to be rejected. Prominence, however, must be given to the fact, that the Seer here beholds only the signs of the *comical* end of the world and the effects of those signs, whilst with the seventh seal, or in the trumpet cycle, chs. vii. and viii., the *spiritual* signs and events are revealed. By this fact exegesis is conditioned, as has been previously intimated. Hoffmann did not understand this sequence when he judged that nothing but a description of the new world could follow this delineation of the day of wrath. See Ebrard on this, p. 261. Whilst Ebrard gathers from our text that the whole firmament, the entire structure of the world, *shall be destroyed and cease to be*—a view which exceeds every Biblical limit, even 2 Pet. iii.—Düsterdieck, on the other hand, justly makes mention of the visional form of the revelation, though that, indeed, does not preclude the reality of the individual features as symbolically presented.

Ver. 12. **A great earthquake.**—See ch. xi. 13; xvi. 18; viii. 5. In all these passages, however, the context must decide whether the terrestrial or the social and spiritual import predominates.

[" We have no word but *earthquake* for σεισμός; but it does not, by any means, cover the meaning. For here the *heavens* are shaken (against Düsterdieck), and the sea, and the dry land. See Hag. ii. 6, 7, and . . . Heb. xii. 26, 27." Alford.—E. R. C.]

As sackcloth of hair, Is. l. 3.

The moon like blood, Joel ii. 31.

The heavens rolled together, Is. xxxiv. 4.

The kings, *etc.*, Matt. xxv. 32. "Kings are filled with anguish in common with the meanest slave" (Düsterdieck). This ought, properly, to be transposed, since the meanest slave has outwardly the least to lose.

Ver. 17. In the cry of the terrified and trembling ones to the mountains and rocks, the thought that they seek death (Hengstenberg, Ebrard, Düsterdieck) is not the primary idea conveyed by the text. They seek absolute concealment from the face of God and the wrath of the Lamb, from judgment, in their despairing repentance. And the meaning of this is, we admit, that this present life is so transformed for them into an invasion of the terrible *beyond*, that they now picture even that *beyond* as more endurable in reality than the life which they now live. Düsterdieck rightly characterizes these exclamations as representative of the utterances of unbelievers.

Special interpretations :* as applying to the

---

* [Elliott and Barnes identify this Seal with the persecution under Diocletian (A. D. 303–312). They both give copious extracts from Gibbon and other historians. The latter quotes from Gibbon as follows : " Galerius at length extorted from him (Diocletian) the permission of summoning a council, composed of a few persons, the most distinguished in the civil and military department of the State. It may be presumed that they insisted on every topic which might interest the pride, the piety, the fears of their sovereign in the destruction of Christianity, i. 318." " It would have been an easy task, from the history of Eusebius, from the declaration of Lactantius, and from the most ancient acts, to collect a long series of horrid and disgustful pictures, and to fill many pages with racks and scourges, with iron hooks and red hot beds, and with the variety of tortures which fire and steel, savage beasts, and more savage executioners, could inflict on the human body, i. 326."—E. R. C.]

* [Elliott and Barnes identify this Seal also with great periods in Roman history (see p. 168).
[The former, who regards the period indicated *in this chap-*

12

Jewish war, especially the destruction of Jerusalem (Grotius and others); 'to intermediate historic spiritual events in the Church (Bede, Vitringa and others); particularly to the darkening of prophecy and law (Böhmer), to Christ blasphemed (the darkened sun), etc. See Düsterdieck, p. 269. On similar allegorizings by Hengstenberg, see Ebrard, p. 258.

[ADDITIONAL NOTE ON THE FIRST SIX SEALS.]
By the American Editor.

[Every proposed scheme of the Seals must be tried on its own merits, and that only which at once meets the requirements of the individual symbols, which preserves the unity of the whole system of symbolization, and which manifestly lies parallel with the established facts of history, should be accepted.

It is an essential element in the scheme of Stuart, which represents the visions as having had their *primary* fulfillment in the events which terminated in the destruction of Jerusalem, that the Apocalypse should have been written before that event. This opinion is, in the judgment of the writer, successfully controverted by Lange (see Introduction, p. 59 sqq.) and many of the ablest Commentators. But even if that opinion be correct, and if the visions did find *a* fulfillment in the events referred to, it seems rational to regard that fulfillment as only typical, in itself prophetic of one greater and more complete. We cannot suppose, in view of ancient history alone, that the tremendous imagery, either of our Lord's eschatological discourse, Matt. xxiv. 5-31, or of the Seals (which seem to lie parallel with the portion of the discourse referred to), should have had relation *merely* to the events that preceded and accompanied the victory of Titus. Still less, in view of the course of history since the destruction of Jerusalem and the manifest accordance of the symbolization therewith, can we avoid the conclusion that the latter was a forecasting of the former. Stuart himself, it will be observed (see Foot-note, p. 168), does not deny the validity of this conclusion.

The schemes of Wordsworth and Lord, whilst they have many things in them that have the appearance of truth, do not, even where the

*ter as that in which the political power of heathenism was destroyed, supports his view as follows: By the earth he understands the " Roman earth " (vol. i., p. 103); by the firmamental Heaven above this Apocalyptic earth, "the ruling department in the dominant polity;" and by its luminaries, "the actual rulers and governing powers therein" (vol. i., pp. 103, 236 sq.). From this point of view he writes concerning this vision: "It surely betokened some sudden and extraordinary revolution in the Roman Empire, which would follow chronologically after the era of martyrdoms depicted under the Seal preceding; a revolution arising from the triumph of the Christian cause over its enemies, and in degree complete and universal." These conditions he finds fulfilled in the great revolution under Constantine—a revolution concerning which he quotes Gibbon as writing (vol. v.): " The ruin of the Pagan religion is described by the Sophists as a dreadful and amazing prodigy, which covered the Earth with darkness and restored the ancient condition of chaos and of night."

[BARNES fixes upon a different period, viz.: A. D. 365-410 He writes: " The design of these verses (15-17), in the varied language used, is evidently to denote universal consternation and alarm—as if the Earth should be convulsed, and the stars should fall, and the Heavens should pass away." He quotes largely from historians to show that these figures met their most complete fulfillment in the period closing with the destruction of the Empire by the Goths and Vandals.—E. R. C.]*

presentation of historical facts is correct, satisfy the requirements of the Symbols.

Of the many historical views that have been presented, those of Elliott and Barnes have by far the greatest appearance of probability. But even these are liable to serious objections. 1. They fail in presenting *well-defined* historical periods. The historical hypothesis calls for *successive* periods which, although they may blend into each other at each beginning and close, shall be distinctly marked as satisfying the symbols in their central portions. The *first* and *second* periods presented by these Commentators (I. A. D. 96-184; II. 184 or 193-284) are well-defined (and to a considerable extent satisfy the symbols), but beyond these all is confusion. The *third* period does not begin at or near the termination of the *second*, but is embosomed within it, beginning *before* A. D. 217, and running on indefinitely; the *fourth* period is embosomed within the *third* (A. D. 243-268); the *fifth* (A. D. 284-310 or 312) does not begin on the termination of the *fourth*, or even of the *third*, but of the *second*. 2. Both these schemes present utterly unsatisfactory explanations of the *Sixth Seal.* We feel that the awful figures of this vision—a trembling Universe, the sun darkened, the moon as blood, the stars of Heaven falling to the earth—are not satisfied by the merely terrestrial convulsions that terminated in, either the destruction of the political power of Paganism, or the sack of Rome.

The hypothesis, advocated by Lange and Alford, that the first five Seals are synchronous, beginning, as to their development, at the date of the Apocalypse and continuing to the present time, is, in the judgment of the writer, correct, as is also the further hypothesis, that by the Riders on the *second, third* and *fourth* horses are meant respectively *War, Dearth* and *Aggravated Mortality.* He must, however, express his dissatisfaction with the interpretations of both these distinguished Commentators of the Rider on the *first* or white horse. Lange identifies this Rider with Christ. A special objection lies against this view, viz.: that it requires us to regard as mixed together symbols of entirely different orders. As the symbols of the second, third and fourth visions are *aberrant,* and as all the surroundings lead us to group the four Horsemen together, it seems natural to suppose that the first symbol should be *aberrant* also. Far better is the supposition of Alford, who, ignoring the consideration just mentioned, supports his interpretation that this Rider is not the personal Christ, but Christianity, by language quoted in the *Foot-note* on p. 171 sq.

But even this modified hypothesis is liable to serious objections. In the first place, it represents Christianity as wearing the *golden* crown, whilst those who profess it are represented in the *fifth* Seal as victims falling under the hand of *the dwellers upon earth.* The *crown* of this Rider calls for *recognized sovereignty* in the world, and it is not satisfied by what is called the *spiritual kingship* of the Sons of God. There is a sense in which Christ was a King in humiliation; but the only crown He wore on Earth was the Crown of Thorns. It is the teaching, not only of the fifth Seal, but of the didactic portions of Scripture, that, throughout the present dispensation, His true followers, as pilgrims and sojourners here, must be partakers of His humiliation. Another objection to this view is, that it places Christianity in apparent subordination to God's ministers in nature (see last paragraph of the *Add. Comment* on p. 170 sq.). It is at the call of the *Zōa* that the four Riders come forth. The unity of the complex symbol seems to demand that each one of the Riders should act in one of the realms of God's *natural* government.

There is an hypothesis which, in the judgment of the writer, satisfies all the requirements of the entire symbolization, and which brings that symbolization into harmony with the other teachings of the Scripture and the facts of history, *viz.*: that the Rider on the white horse symbolizes mere *Human Culture*, or, to adopt the current term, *Science*.

From the beginning, Science has gone forth in triumph, conquering, and that he may conquer; amongst "the dwellers upon earth" he is the acknowledged and crowned King; his *bow*, like that of Apollo, is far-sounding and far-reaching. He has proclaimed himself, and now in louder and more triumphant tones than ever is proclaiming himself, to be the true deliverer of men from woe. And yet throughout the long period of his reign, though he has ministered much to intellectual and material advancement, he has been unable to abolish war, and dearth, and aggravated mortality, and the *true* followers of Jesus have been opposed and persecuted—sometimes with the sword and faggot, sometimes with less apparent, but not less real instrumentalities. As the *servant of Christ*, Science has been in the past, and will be more gloriously in the future, one of the grandest instrumentalities for human development and blessing; but, as an independent king, he is a *mock Christ*.

This hypothesis, which is consistent with historical facts, satisfies the Symbols of the first vision, and brings them into unity with those which follow; it places the first Rider in the same order of Symbols with the others; it places him in a realm of nature; it is consistent with the implications of the fifth Seal; it is in harmony with the teachings of the didactic Scriptures as to the condition of the Church throughout the present dispensation; and, lastly, it brings the entire vision into parallelism with the eschatological discourse of our Lord (Matt. xxiv.), in which He forewarned His disciples that in the future before His second Advent there should be (1) false Christs, ver. 5; (2) wars, vers. 6, 7; (3) dearth, ver. 7; (4) aggravated mortality, ver. 7; (5) persecutions, vers. 9, 10; (6) to be followed by fearful commotions and woes preceding the Advent, vers. 15-30; (7) the Advent, vers. 30, 31.*

In the opinion of the writer, the *fifth* Seal, as

---

to its first part (vers. 9, 10), is an *Earth* scene representing the condition of the true followers of Christ (or at least the most faithful portions thereof) during the period of His absence. That this is to be a condition of humiliation and suffering, comp. 2 Tim. iii. 12; Matt. xxiv. 8, 9; John xv. 18-24; xvi. 1-4, 19-22; Rom. viii. 18-23, 35, 36; Gal. iv. 29; Phil. i. 27-30; 1 Thess. ii. 11-15 with iii. 3, 4; 2 Thess. i. 4-7; 2 Tim. ii. 3, 12; Heb. xii. 1-5; xiii. 13, 14; James i. 2, 3, 12; v. 7-11; 1 Pet. i. 6, 7, 11, 13; ii. 12, 21; iv. 1, 12-14, *etc.** As to its second part (ver. 11), it describes the condition of their departed spirits (see *Foot-note*, p. 176).

The events of the *sixth* Seal it seems most reasonable to regard as subsequent to those of the preceding Seals—indeed as still future. Even on the hypothesis that the fearful convulsions therein foretold are to be regarded as symbolic of revolutions in the realm of human government, it may be asked: Have there as yet been such revolutions as satisfy the tremendous symbols? And beyond this—Doubtless, fearful convulsions in human affairs were in the view of our Lord (Matt. xxiv. 29) and of the Seer (vers. 12-16); but can we regard their words as referring *only* to such convulsions? If the earth quaked, and the rocks rent, and the sun was darkened, when the God-man died (Matt. xxvii. 45, 51, *etc.*), is it not rational to expect, in view of such prophecies as those referred to, that similar portents will precede or accompany His Second Coming in glory?

That the sixth Seal heralds and introduces the End of the Æon and the Coming of the Lord for the Establishment of the Basileia, there can be no doubt; that in any proper sense it can be said to usher in the Final Consummation, the Advent of the Lord for Final Judgment, is exceedingly questionable (*Add. Notes*, p. 339 sqq.). It brings us to the very Appearing of the Lord; but here, that Advent and its accompanying and succeeding events are not described. We are again brought to the same event at the blowing of the *Seventh Trumpet*, ch. xi. 15; and again ch. xiv. 11. The full description, however, is reserved until the close of all the collateral visions ending in that event; it is presented to us chs. xix. 11; xx. 6.—E. R. C.]

---

* [As against the position taken above, may be urged the present exemption of the Church from persecution. This suggests the question, whether this exemption may not be the result of undue conformity to the world—a conformity exemplified in the case of the Church of Laodicea, ch. iii. 15-17. The only texts in the New Testament with which the writer is acquainted, militating against the truth of his position are such as 1 Tim. iv. 8; Matt. vi. 33; xix. 29; Mark x. 30. These texts, it is urged, promise temporal prosperity to true Christians. It is to be remembered, that they had immediate respect to *primitive* believers—to those to whom the Saviour directly declared that the world would hate and persecute them. The first passage cited was addressed to that very minister to whom it was declared (2 Tim. iii. 12) "All that will live godly in Christ Jesus shall suffer persecution." To suppose, therefore, that these texts imply a promise of *temporal* prosperity and freedom from persecution is to place them in direct antagonism with the general run of inspired utterance; and not only so, but it is to suppose the utterance of a promise that manifestly never was fulfilled in the case of those to whom it was primarily given. All the passages can, without straining, be regarded as implying the promise of *spiritual* prosperity in the midst of temporal adversity. Thus, and thus only, can they be brought into harmony with the declarations of prophecy and the facts of history.—E. R. C.]

---

* [The four realms of nature brought to view on this hypothesis are (1) human intellect, (2) government, (3) the processes ministering to growth and nourishment, and (4, possibly) the atmosphere as the seat of those influences which minister to health and disease. Is it not possible that the ideal forms of the *Zōa* may have relation to these realms of nature: the *Human figure* to the first, the *Lion* to the second, the *Ox* to the third, and the *Eagle* to the fourth?—E. R. C.]

SECTION THIRD.

The Seven Penitential Trumpets, issuing from the Opening of the Seventh Seal.

CHAP. VII. 1—IX. 21.

A.—IDEAL HEAVENLY WORLD-PICTURE OF THE SEVEN PENITENTIAL TRUMPETS.
THE IDEAL, INVINCIBLE CHURCH.   ITS ESTABLISHMENT AS THE CHURCH MI-
LITANT BY THE SEALING OF THE ELECT IN THIS WORLD; ITS CONSUMMATION
WITH THE FOUNDING OF THE CHURCH TRIUMPHANT IN THE OTHER WORLD.
PREPARATION FOR THE LOOSING OF THE SEVENTH SEAL.

CH. VII. 1—17.

1   And[1] after these [this[2]] things [om. things] I saw four angels standing on [upon]
the four corners of the earth, holding the four winds of the earth, that the wind
should [may] not blow on [upon] the earth, nor on [upon] the sea, nor on [upon]
2   any tree.[3]   And I saw another angel ascending from the east [sun-rising], having
the [a] seal of the living God: and he cried with a loud [great] voice to the four
angels, [ins. those] to whom it was given to hurt [injure] the earth and the sea,
3   saying, Hurt [Injure] not the earth, neither [nor] the sea, nor the trees, till we
4   have sealed[4] the servants of our God in [upon] their foreheads.   And I heard the
number of them which were [om. them which were—ins. the] sealed : and there
were sealed [om. and there were sealed] a hundred and forty and four thousand
[ins. sealed] of all the tribes [out of every tribe] of the children [sons] of Israel.
5   Of [Out of] the tribe of Juda w·re sealed [om. were sealed] twelve thousand [ins.
sealed[5]].   Of [; out of] the tribe of Reuben were sealed [om. were sealed] twelve
thousand.   Of [; out of] the tribe of Gad were sealed [om. were sealed] twelve
6   thousand.   Of [; out of] the tribe of Aser were sealed [om. were sealed] twelve
thousand.   Of [; out of] the tribe of Nephthalim were sealed [om. were sealed]
twelve thousand.   Of [; out of] the tribe of Manasses were sealed [om. were sealed]
7   twelve thousand.   Of [; out of] the tribe of Simeon were sealed [om. were sealed]
twelve thousand.   Of [; out of] the tribe of Levi were sealed [om. were sealed]
twelve thousand.   Of [; out of] the tribe of Issachar were sealed [om. were sealed]
8   twelve thousand.   Of [; out of] the tribe of Zabulon were sealed [om. were sealed]
twelve thousand.   Of [; out of] the tribe of Joseph were sealed [om. were sealed]
twelve thousand.   Of [; out of] the tribe of Benjamin were sealed [om. were sealed]
twelve thousand [ins. sealed].

9   After this [these things] I beheld [saw], and, lo [behold][6], a great multitude,
which no man [one] could number, of [out of] all nations, and kindreds [tribes],
and people [peoples], and tongues, stood [standing][7] before the throne, and before

---

TEXTUAL AND GRAMMATICAL.

[1] Ver. 1. The Καὶ uncertain.   [Words. and Tisch. give it with אֶ. B*. P.; Lach. omits with A. C., Vulg.; Alf. and Treg.
bracket.—E. R. C.]
[2] Ver. 1. The reading τοῦτο preponderates.   [Critical Editors read τοῦτο with אֶ. A. B*. C.; Cod. P., Vulg., etc., give
ταῦτα.—E. R. C.]
[3] Ver. 1. Τι δένδρον, more significant than πᾶν δένδρον.   [Gries., Words., Lach., Treg., Tisch. (Ed. 1859) read τι with
B*. C., Vulg.; Tisch. (8th Ed.) gives πᾶν with אֶ. P.; Alford brackets τι.—E. R. C.]
[4] Ver. 3. [The reading σφραγίζωμεν is without authority.   All the Critical Editors with אֶ. A. B*. C. P., etc., σφραγί-
σωμεν.—E. R. C.]
[5] Ver. 5. In the best Codd. ἐσφραγισμένοις is given only at the beginning and at the close (vers. 5 and 8).
[6] Ver. 9. The Καὶ ἰδού is doubtful.   In a material aspect also, inasmuch as the whole chapter treats of one general
vision.   [Words., Alf., Treg., Tisch., give καὶ ἰδοὺ with אֶ. B*. P.; Lach. omits with A., Vulg.—E. R. C.]
[7] Ver. 9. [Words. and Alf. read ἑστῶτας with B*.; Cod. C. gives ἑστώτων; Lach., Treg., Tisch. (and Lange, see in loc.),
with אֶ. A. P., etc., ἑστῶτες.—E. R. C.]

10 the Lamb, clothed with white robes, and palms in their hands; and [*ins.* they] cried [cry] with a loud [great] voice, saying, [*ins.* The] salvation to [*or, is* with] our God which [who] sitteth upon the throne, and unto [*or, is* with] the Lamb.
11 And all the angels stood [were standing⁸] round about [*om.* about] the throne, [*om.* ,] and about [*om. about*] the elders and the four beasts [Living-beings], and [*ins.* they]
12 fell before the throne on their faces, and worshipped God, saying, Amen : [*ins.* the] blessing, and [*ins.* the] glory, and [*ins.* the] wisdom, and [*ins.* the] thanksgiving, and [*ins.* the] honor, and [*ins.* the] power, and [*ins.* the] might [strength], *be* [*or om. be*] unto our God for ever and ever [into the ages of the ages]. Amen.

13   And one of the elders answered, saying unto me, What are [*om.* What are] These which [who] are arrayed in white robes [*ins.* , who are they]? and whence came
14 they?   And I said unto him, Sir [My⁹ lord], thou knowest. And he said to me, These are they which came [that come] out of [*ins.* the¹⁰] great tribulation, and [*ins.* they] have [*om.* have] washed their robes, and made them¹¹ white in the blood
15 of the Lamb.   Therefore [On this account] are they before¹² the throne of God, and [*ins.* they] serve him day and night in his temple : and he that sitteth on the throne shall dwell among them [σκηνώσει ἐπ' αὐτούς, shall spread his tabernacle over
16 them]¹³.   They shall [*ins.* not] hunger no [any] more, neither [*ins.* shall they] thirst any more ; neither [οὐδὲ μή]¹⁴ shall the sun light [πέσῃ, fall] on them, nor
17 any heat [καῦμα, burning heat].   For the Lamb which is in the midst of the throne [τὸ ἀνὰ μέσον τοῦ θρόνου] shall feed [shepherdize] them, and shall lead them unto living [*om.* living] fountains of waters [*ins.* of life¹⁵] : and God shall wipe away all tears [every tear] from their eyes.

⁸ Ver. 11. Different readings see in Düst. [Lach., Alf., Treg., Tisch. give εἱστήκεισαν with ℵ. A. B*. P. (ℵ. A. P., however, give ἱστ–. ℵ. also gives–κισαν, and B*. –κησαν.—E. R. C.]
⁹ Ver. 14. There is a μου after κύριε according to B*. C., *etc.* [Μου is given by Words., Alf., Treg., Tisch., with ℵ. B*. C. P., Vulg., *etc.* ; it is omitted by A. 1, *etc.*—E. R. C.]
¹⁰ Ver. 14. The article is significant. The reading of Lachmann omits it. [Words., Alf., Treg., Tisch., give ἐκ τῆς θλίψεως τῆς μεγ., with ℵ. B*. P., *etc.*; Lach. gives ἀπὸ θλίψ. μεγ., with A. (Tisch. does not mention A. as presenting this reading).—E. R. C.]
¹¹ Ver. 14. "Their robes " [τὰς στολὰς αὐτῶν] in accordance with minuscules.
¹² Ver. 15. [Tisch. (Ed. 1859) gave ἐπὶ τῷ θρόνῳ with B*.; Cod. ℵ. A. P., *etc.* (according to Treg. and Tisch.) give ἐπὶ τοῦ θρόνου; Words., Alf., Treg., Tisch. (8th Ed.) give ἐνώπιον τοῦ θρόνου, the ἐνώπιον being apparently without authority. (Alf. claims for it ℵ. and A., and cites P. as agreeing with B*. The Am. Ed. cannot but suggest that the true reading is as given by ℵ. A. P., the ἐπί (with the genitive) having the force of *before* or *near* (see ROBINSON'S *Lex.* under 'Επί, I. a. (β), and Winer, § 47, g. (c)).—E. R. C.]
¹³ Ver. 15. [Lange translates " will settle abidingly (in His glory of manifestation) o er them." See EXPLANATIONS IN DETAIL, p. 192, and also a most valuable note by Schaff in the Lange *Comm. on John* (TEXT. AND GRAM.) i. 14, p. 71. The idea here seems to be that God will spread His own special dwelling-place over them; this includes the idea that He will dwell among them.—E. R. C.]
¹⁴ Ver. 16. [Alford and Tisch. (1859) read οὐδ' οὐ μή; Tisch., Treg., with ℵ. A. P., *etc.*, read as above.—E. R. C.]
¹⁵ Ver. 17. The reading ζωῆς. [So all modern Critical Editors, with ℵ. A. B*. P., Vulg., *etc.*—E. R. C.]

EXEGETICAL AND CRITICAL.

SYNOPTICAL VIEW.*

The literal, allegorictical exegesis, with its chronological interpretation, has covered this section [ch. vii.] in particular, together with the corresponding eighth and ninth chapters, with confusion and obscurity. It should be premised, first of all, that chapters vii.–ix. constitute a whole, representing the essential form of the history of the Church in this world *in respect of its spiritual aspect*, in its connection with the history of the Kingdom of God, or the New Testament history of religion. [See p. 192 sq.] If the *seven churches* were portraits of the Church in its spiritual *and* world-historical aspects; if, further, the *seven seals* were characteristic of the world-historical side of New Testament times ; so now in the *seven trumpets* the New Testament history of religion, as the spiritual side of New

* [Additions may be found under EXPLANATIONS IN DETAIL.— E. R. C.]

Testament times, is exhibited, or, in other words, the Church is portrayed in its transcendent nature as militant and triumphant. It will appear, as we proceed, that the reference is purely to spiritual matters ; let us meantime direct the attention of our readers to the characteristic of the section as presented in the concluding words ch. ix. 20, 21. The dark side on the entire period is the worship of demons, devilish spirits, and this dark side is divided into religious idolatries and moral enormities. As the sections throughout the Apocalypse unfold into the antithesis of Heaven-pictures and earth-pictures, so it is with the present one. If it be objected that the sealing of the 144,000 souls does not take place in Heaven, but on earth, we respond that to the Apocalyptist, Heaven and earth are not purely local terms, as is evident, moreover, from chaps. xii. and xxi. Even the Son of Man Himself walks on earth, amid the candlesticks, according to ch. i. We must, therefore, once for all, distinguish *Heaven on earth* from *the earthly form of the Kingdom of God*. And this Heaven on earth is in this case the kernel of the Church

Militant, the plenary number of the sealed elect, from whose ranks are issuing, ever and anon, those victor-trains of parting souls that form the Church Triumphant in the world beyond the grave. Thus is framed the conception of the Heaven-picture of the ideal Church as a whole; as branching into the two stages of the Church Militant and the Church Triumphant (ch. vii. 1-8; 9-17). The contrasted earth picture of the Church is characterized by the *trumpets* themselves. We continue to designate these as *penitential* Trumpets, though prominence should also be given in the first place to the more general signification of the *trumpetings*, as figuring the sudden warlike or dramatic appearance of worldly spirits and spiritual errors, both of which, however, serve as an admonition to repentance, to the marrow of the Church. [See p. 212 sqq.]

With the chronological and literal conception referred to, correspond the most considerable misunderstandings which attach to this chapter. Above all, the chapter should not be regarded in the light of an episode. Neither should it be considered as a special promise to the Jewish people. If we hold fast to the idea of the organic completeness and unitedness of the Apocalyptic narration, such an episode, which would be destructive of all connection, is inconceivable. As, furthermore, the seventh chapter, as the basis of the *seven Trumpets*, must perfectly coincide with the following two chapters, it cannot be reduced to a section of the last time.

So far as the Jews are concerned, those commentators are entirely at odds with the text who teach that the Jews in a literal sense are intended here. As surely as the New Jerusalem of ch. xxi. cannot denote a new Jewish city; as surely as the term *Jews*, as used in the *seven epistles*, denotes the very opposite of Judaists, namely, the true spiritual Israel; just so surely are the people of Israel, here, representative of the whole body of the people of God. It can be affirmed only that converts from Israel are included.

Or are the 144,000 souls, standing, according to ch. xiv., on Mount Zion, other chosen ones, though these here mentioned likewise appear as sealed? Or are the former, also, only Jews after all? And being Jews, are they virgins in the literal sense, as Rothe maintains; celibates, such as are found so seldom amongst the Jews? And has the scene so far changed that, whilst in our passage the Church in this world consists purely of Jews, but in the other world is made up of all nations, Gentiles predominating, therefore,—in ch. xiv., on the other hand, the Gentiles upon Mount Zion, *i.e.*, in the same region in which they, in ch. vii., occupy the foreground, are displaced by the Jews?—In every case, we answer *no*.

Be it observed moreover, that if the symbolical significance be lost sight of in the leading matter, the Twelve Tribes must also be taken literally; as also the 12,000 of every Tribe; the omission of the Tribe of Dan, and everything else. And this, apart from the essential absurdity that during this whole period of sealed Jewish Christians, there should be no account made of sealed Gentile Christians on earth.

And here arises the question, why the New Testament Church should be symbolized by the Jewish Tribes; its kernel by sealed individuals belonging to those Tribes. This question is at once satisfactorily settled if we do but glance back at the prophetic representation of the destiny of Israel. The people of Israel is the typical *servant of God*, His elect, whose office it is to disseminate His law amongst the Gentiles (Is. xlii., xliii., *etc.*), before the *Servant of God* in the truest and fullest sense of the term, the Messiah, is spoken of. The New Testament, again, takes up this typical import of Israel, but only decisively to transfer it to the spiritual Israel, the New Testament faithful people, or people of faith (Matt. viii. 11; Rom. ii. 28; ch. iv. 11, 12; Gal. iv. 26). In our passage there was abundant motive for going back to the symbolical name of Jews, and to the symbolical import of the Twelve Tribes in particular, since the position of the spiritual Israel in regard to spiritual heathendom—whose pressure into the Church the Apocalyptist foresaw—was to be marked.[*] We would observe, in this connection, that John, in accordance with ideal theocratic notions, regarded even Judaistic forms of corruption as a special formation of heathenism. Precautionary measures were virtually taken against misunderstanding, in the fact that the Seer made those who were sealed in this world re-appear, in their consummation in the other world, as an innumerable throng *out of all nations*. [See p. 193.] What we have here, therefore, is not a special scene from the last time, but an entirely new cycle of the whole New Testament time which, as a whole, is eschatological;—a heavenly portrait of the ideal Church.

The vision begins with the apparition of the four Angels that stand upon the four corners of the earth, holding the four winds of the earth, that no wind may blow upon the earth, nor upon the sea, nor upon any tree.

We have recognized the *earth* as the theocratic order or institution; here it is the New Testament order of things, as presented, first, in the Church alone, branching out, subsequently, into ecclesiastical and political life. On the four corners of this earth, where it comes in contact with the old world — from the direction of heathenism, consequently—the four winds arise. The four winds are the fundamental forms of those worldly time-currents which threaten the ruin of the Church (Dan. vii. 2; Eph. iv. 14). These time-currents must be loosed when their time comes, for a particular work is appointed them; on this very account, however, they are, as Divine dispensations, held by Angels, that they may not break loose *before* their time and destroy the *earth, i. e.*, the young Church; the *sea*, or Christian national life, which is not yet strong; or individual Christians that, like all sorts of *trees* of God ($r l$) have begun to grow up (Ps. i.). [See p. 187.]

When another Angel appears, forbidding the four Angels to injure the earth, or the sea, or individual trees, until he shall have sealed the servants of God, there is presented, in the antithesis of two chronological sections of time, the antithesis of the bound and the loosed winds,

---

[*] [See *foot-note* † on p. 27.—E. R. C.]

a spiritual antithesis; that, namely, of the sealed, over whom the four winds have no power, as contrasted with the injured earth, the injured sea, and the injured trees. The temporal distinction, however, has likewise its own independent signification; the winds are never loosed until the kernel of the faithful is firmly established.

The nature of the other Angel, ascending from the rising of the sun, is determined by the idea of the sealing. Since the conception of justification has suffered such decay in the evangelical Church, it is not to be wondered at that our Theology has in still greater measure lost the idea of *sealing*, although the latter was prefigured in the Old Testament (Ezek. ix. 4), whilst it appears distinctly in the New Testament as the idea of the eternal fixation of Christian character, to preserve it from the danger of apostasy (Rom. v. 4, δοκιμή; James ii. 21; Eph. i. 13). [See p. 186.]

With justification, the new life of faith is principially decided; it is necessary, however, that it should be historically proved and fixed, just as it was necessary that Abraham's faith should be *proved* (see James ii. 21; comp. ver. 23). Now this *proving* [or verification] is called, in its relation to the simple trials of life, *proving*; in its spiritual import, over against the temptations to apostasy, it is denominated *sealing*; Ezekiel symbolized it by a mark on the forehead. It is the mark of a spiritually quick and faithful confession, which the tempter, the spiritual murderer, passes timorously by.

It will hardly be supposed that the Apocalyptist had a lower conception of the sealing than the Apostle Paul; consequently, the Angel of sealing can be significant only of the Holy Ghost. [See p. 187.] He ascends with *the rising of the sun; i.e.*, the life of Jesus Christ, in His glorification, results in the sending of the Holy Ghost. His seal is the seal of the living God; no letter, no form, no fancy:—nothing but the life of the living God, Whose personal manifestation is consummated in the glorification of Christ, begets in pure and honest souls such a homogeneous Divine life as, in its matured form, victoriously withstands all the winds and storms of worldly history (1 John v. 4). For, after the sealing, all the four winds must have been suffered to sweep over them; otherwise it could not be said of them: they are come out of the great tribulation. Nay, sealing is itself a confirming against great temptation.

Again, this Angel has power, with a mighty voice to put his veto on an untimely loosing of the four winds. This is the power of mighty operations of the Spirit of God, checking for a while the currents of the spirit of this world; *e. g.*, by this power heresies were restrained throughout the entire Apostolic age.

Then follows the *sealing* itself. This is too great and too extended for the Apocalyptist to describe the view of the acts themselves; he, therefore, hears the number of the sealed. And the mere number is a leading point; it is a predetermined plenary number, the whole harvest of God (Matt. iii. 12), the whole inheritance of God. [See p. 193.] The winds may take their part, the chaff (Ps. i.; Matt. iii.); the whole wheat harvest is secured to the Lord. We

scarcely need remark that the predestination indicated corresponds with religious and moral conditions. If it were not so, the sealed must have brought the mark on their foreheads into the world with them.

The plenary number of the sealed is 144,000. For all charismatic ground-forms of the life of faith are represented by the Twelve Tribes; whilst the 12,000 souls out of every Tribe represent the whole ramification of each ground-form into its twelve modifications, and the whole harvest of this fullness of the Divine Spirit and human spirits, through the entire Christian course of the world, as symbolized by 1000 years. In proportion to the historical extension of the Tribes, the number 12,000 is exceedingly small; this fact, however, agrees with all the declarations of the New Testament [in regard to the proportion of the saved].

The order of the Tribes gives rise to several queries. Why is the Tribe of Dan wanting here, whilst in the blessing of Moses the Tribe of Simeon was left out? Why is Simeon here even set over Levi? Why is Manasseh distinguished from Joseph, and why is Ephraim merged in Joseph? It would almost seem as if the Tribes had been mingled together promiscuously, in order to ward off every Judaistic conception from the figure. At all events, the perfect equalization of the Tribes is itself not without significance. A Jew would have expected preference to be shown to the Tribe of Judah; he would, however, have anticipated that the Tribe of Levi would have the priority over all. Levi, however, is placed amongst the later Tribes; the prerogatives of the Old Testament priesthood are at an end (Bengel). We shall revert later to the Christian and Jewish traditions in regard to the omission of the Tribe of Dan. As this Tribe early left its inheritance (Jud. xviii.), and conquered the city of Laish, which, probably, was subsequently included in the domain of Naphthali, the Israelitish genealogy merged it in Naphthali (see 1 Chron. iv. sqq.); and the Tribe the rather lost its symbolical significance, since it had damaged it, not merely by the surrender of its tribal seat, but also in other ways (by idolatry). And yet from none of these things need we conclude that the future Antichrist is to issue from it, or that it has died out. In all New Testament times, the Twelve Tribes have been represented only by Judah, Benjamin, Levi, and remnants of the other Tribes, and it is not known exactly where the great mass of the Ten Tribes are. The thing which the Apocalyptist had in view was a symbolical *twelve*, on a historical basis. Possibly the motive for this substitution of the venerable name of Joseph for Ephraim was, that a disturbing allusion to the falling away of Israel might be avoided. Amid all the seeming confusion of the Tribes, in which no distinction is made between the sons of Jacob's lawful wives and the sons of his concubines, it is still in harmony with the theocratic idea that Judah should head the list and Benjamin conclude it.

If we essay now to divide the entire table by the number *three*, as the number of spirit, into *four* times *three*, we have, *first*, two sons of Leah and one of her maid: Judah, Reuben, Gad;

we have, *secondly*, Leah's adopted son, Aser, Rachel's adopted son, Nepthalim, and Manasseh, the first-born of Joseph; the *third* triad is formed by Leah's sons, Simeon and Levi, and her adopted son, Issachar; in the *fourth* group, Zabulon is conjoined with Joseph and Benjamin, the late offspring of Leah with the late offspring of Rachel.

On a general survey, the thought forces itself upon our mind that the vision, in its symbolistic enumeration of the Twelve Tribes, has obliterated every semblance of a legal prerogative;— apart from Judah's place of honor, which, again, was symbolically significant of the dignity of Christ.

In the 144,000 sealed ones, the assurance is given that the Church shall in all ages have a heart or kernel firm as a rock; an invisible congregation of *sealed ones*, against whom every power of temptation, or every storm of the four winds, must break. Our eyes are not permitted to behold this kernel, this choicest and innermost part; for this reason, among others, — because many apparent forms of Christian heroism are delusive and fall (the young men fall and the youths faint, *etc.*), whilst insignificant and humble characters, or such as are disguised in worldly forms, step into the breach at decisive moments. Furthermore, we do not readily recognize and honor God's heroes in a strange attire, as, for instance, when they appear in the Middle Ages in monkish garb, or, in the eighteenth century, in the garment of critical humanism. Enough, the *Rock* is ever there, and though the gates of the abyss lift themselves up against it, they shall be confounded; and that *Rock* is Christ in His elect. The fact that these chosen ones are numbered, like the Einheriar [heroes] of Odin in the Northern mythology, points to the conclusion that the reference is not to all pious souls, indiscriminately, or in a body, but to those only who constitute the support of the Church, as is evident also from the description of the 144,000 in ch. xiv., and from the second scene of our vision, the picture of the Church Triumphant.

It is tacitly assumed that the *four winds* have been *loosed* subsequently to the sealing. Their effect, however, is not described until we come to the *seven Trumpets*, and then the figures are changed. Yet it is declared of the triumphant throng: these are they that come ([or, *the coming ones*] οἱ ἐρχόμενοι) out of the great tribulation (ver. 14). The throng is not secluded in Heaven, but is constantly receiving new additions. We have here, therefore, no picture of the Church Triumphant *in its perfection;* we see it in the period of its *growth*, during the entire course of New Testament times. Hence, too, this Church Triumphant presents the most diverse contrasts to the sealed on earth. It is a multitude so great that none can number it; because, in the first place, it increases every instant by the arrival of those who have died in the Lord; and, further, because not only the sealed heroes of God, but all the blessed make their appearance here. It is a multitude out of all the nations and tribes and peoples and tongues. That there are blessed Israelites in this throng, is a matter of course; and it is just as evident that the name Jews, in the picture of the Church Militant, is the symbolical title of honor of the heroes of the New

Testament people of God. They who compose this multitude appear as the antitype of the sealed, *i. e.*, the invincible on earth; they *have overcome*. They have left the storms of earth behind them; they stand before the Throne, to whose Occupant they owe their general redemption from the woes of earth; and before the Lamb, to Whom they owe their specific redemption. The *white robes*, with which they are clothed, are significant of their victory; the *palms* in their hands denote the eternal festival that has begun for them. Their maturity is evidenced in part from the fact of their ascribing their whole salvation to the grace of God, glorifying not simply the government of the Father, but also that of the Lamb; not simply the government of the Lamb, but also that of the Father, and praising the latter first. Their *song* is a unitous, mighty harmony, at which the Angels in the grand circle surrounding the Elders and the Living-forms, fall upon their faces and worship. The *Amen* which they utter, proclaims the unison of the whole spirit-world with that redemption of which earth is the scene (Col. i. 20); and their present understanding of the great fact so long hid from their gaze (Eph. iii. 10; 1 Pet. i. 12) is expressed in their *doxology*. In accordance with their universal stand-point, they merge the praise of the Lamb in the general praise of God. It is evident from the praise which they render, that the world of spirits and the world of blessed humanity have become one congregation of God. The *sevenfoldness* of their ascription of praise has been referred, not without reason, to the antithesis of the *seven Thunders;* at all events, the whole New Testament Divine week, the entire accomplishment of the work of redemption is herein symbolized. In the first two dicta lies the general verdict, the praise of the spirits, corresponding with the glory of God. The two following dicta are declarative, on the one hand, of the wisdom of God; and, on the other, of the thanksgiving of the spirits. In the following two, mention is made of the honor, the honorableness, which God has given to His people, and with it is extolled the power or majesty to which they owe this honor. That, however, which has finally snatched the redeemed out of all tribulation, is the eschatological mighty ruling of God. And for this He is worshipped, in accordance with all these terms, into the æons of the æons; all the ground-tones of the world's history, and of the history of salvation form themselves into this eternal hymn, resounding henceforth without end throughout the æons.

The conversation next ensuing between one of the Elders and the Seer himself, reviews the spiritual career through which the blessed ones of Heaven passed on earth. The Elder seems to answer the question contained in the astonishment of the Seer by first questioning him as to whether he knows who the white-robed ones are and whence they come. Though the Seer himself cannot be uncertain in regard to the general facts of the case, he desires a heavenly assurance as to the earthly extraction of the blessed. He, therefore, replies: Thou knowest. The response of the Elder embraces both questions: Who are they? and whence come they? For they are sufficiently characterized by the statement that they *came out of the great tribulation* of all earthly trials and temptations; that they have escaped from it; and that, with a full sense of the inherent natural impurity of their *garments*,—which are significant of their form of life—they have *washed* them — washed them and *made them white in the blood of the Lamb*. We cannot conceive of blood as making garments white, but in the conception of salvation, the Atonement in Christ makes them white as snow. Here, then, righteousness of faith and righteousness of life are evidently united. In accordance with this is their exaltation (διὰ τοῦτο; comp. Phil. ii. 9). They are *before the Throne of God*, happy in the contemplation of His governance. They *serve Him day and night in His Temple*. This is the eternal, real Divine service of the priestly race: they have become absolutely devoid of will, and strong in will in their God. The glory of God is extended permanently over them, just as, in a typical manner, it was outspread over the Ark of the Covenant in the Holy of Holies. All their longings, all their needs are satisfied; their *hunger* and their *thirst* are forever appeased; *i. e.*, they are in the enjoyment of all heavenly blessings, whilst they are free from every annoyance from the earthly sun and every heat of the day. They are thus complete negatively and positively. They have reached the highest point of that experience which falls to the lot of God's people even on the earth, according to Ps. xxiii. The Lamb in the midst before the Throne is their Shepherd, Who feeds them and leads them to the water-springs of life. And, again, together with their positive felicity, their negative blessedness is expressed in a few glorious and comforting words: God Himself (their Leader through the vale of tears) shall wipe away every tear from their eyes. The highest heavenly consolation for every sad experience is theirs, in the warmest human form, as if consoling love were for them transformed into pure maternal tenderness. Every tear! Every tear of every sort! God shall wipe it away as a mother does with her child. The blessed, then, may come into the heavenly world with a tear in their eyes, a child-like question as to the way that God has led them.

[ABSTRACT OF VIEWS, ETC.]
By the American Editor.

[ELLIOTT says, concerning the two visions of this chapter, that they "together constitute the second part of the sixth Seal" (see p. 168). The period he places between the destruction of the political power of heathenism and the year 395. This period he sets forth as satisfying the symbols, in that it was one in which—1. "The *threatening tempest of barbarians*, which so soon subverted the Roman greatness, being just during the Constantinian era 'repelled or suspended on the frontiers'" (quoting Gibbon iii. 97); 2. "The great mass of the professedly Christianized population of the Roman world" were "Christians in profession only;" 3. Through the instrumentality of faithful ministers, Jesus gathered an elect portion for Himself from the corrupt mass. The first vision (vers. 1-8) he regards as "figurative not of events cogniza-

ble in real life by mortal eyes, . . . but of certain *invisible and spiritual actings* by Jesus Christ, whereby to constitute and mark out for Himself an election of grace;" the second (vers. 9-17) as indicating that the view of Christ's true Church . . . . embraced the far future, ... as well as the present; the perpetuation of this true Church in its integrity . . . ; and, in fine, the realization by the whole collective body of its many successive generations, and by each and all of its individual members, of the blessedness of accomplished salvation and the glory of the beatific vision."

BARNES agrees with Elliott, substantially, as to the *period* of the first vision, carrying it on, however, to the sack of Rome, A. D. 410. By the *sealing* he understands the affixing "some mark, sign or token" (1) "by which they who were the people of God would be known;" (2) "that would be conspicuous or prominent, *as if* it were impressed on the forehead;" (3) "appointed by God Himself;" (4) that "would be a pledge of safety." What this *sealing* is, he does not directly state. His language is such as to induce the belief, that he regarded it as, possibly, two-fold: (1) *Christian profession*, in view of which multitudes were saved in the destruction of Rome by Alaric, and (2) the "influence" "of the doctrines of grace" selecting and designating those who were "the 'true servants of God' among the multitudes who professed to be His followers." The process of *sealing* he regards "as continued throughout the long night of Papal darkness." The second vision (vers. 9-17) he regards as "an episode having no *immediate* connexion with what precedes or with what follows." "The scene is transferred to Heaven, and there is a vision of *all* the redeemed—not only of the 144,000, but of all who would be rescued and saved from a lost world."

STUART regards ch. vii. as an *episode* indicating the care of God for His people, and their safety in the time of destruction.

WORDSWORTH treats of the whole chapter as an *episode*, without directly declaring that it is so. He regards the first vision as relating to "the 'blessed company of all faithful people' gathered together from all parts of the world and constituting the Church universal, redeemed by Christ's blood, and sealed by His Spirit," *etc.*; the second vision he regards as relating to the same Church glorified and triumphant.

ALFORD directly declares that the whole chapter is an *episode;* the first vision representing "the sealing of the elect on earth;" the second, "the great final assemblage of the saints in Heaven." Concerning the first vision, he declares that it "stands in closest analogy with Matt. xxiv. 31. . . . The judgment of the great day is in fact going on in the background." Concerning the *nature* of the sealing, he expresses no opinion; as to its *intent*, he argues that (1) "it was to exempt those sealed from the judgments which were to come on the unbelieving," and (2) "it appropriates to God those upon whom it has passed."

LORD connects the visions with the *sixth* Seal. Under his comments on this Seal, he writes: "Betwixt that fall (of Bonaparte in 1815) and the final subversion of the governments of the earth, denoted by the passing away of the heavens, a period intervenes during which the sealing symbolized by the next vision is to take place." In this vision (ch. vii. 1-8), he regards the "winds" as indicating "multitudes and nations roused to passion, and uniting in a violent demolition of political and social institutions;" the symbol of the sealing as denoting "that the servants of God, ere the whirlwind of ruin begins, are to be led to assume a new attitude towards the apostate Church, and usurping civil rulers, by which, and in a manner never before seen, they are to be shown to be indubitably His true people. . . . The sealed and the witnesses (ch. xi. 13) are undoubtedly the same." The scene of the second vision he declares to be the Divine presence. "The innumerable multitude stand before the throne of God and the Lamb, and are undoubtedly the redeemed raised from the dead, publicly accepted and exalted to the station of heirs of God and joint heirs with Christ in His Kingdom" (the resurrection here referred to is the first—that of "the holy dead").—E. R. C.]

EXPLANATIONS IN DETAIL.

To regard ch. vii. as an *episode*, with Eichhorn and others, and even Düsterdieck, is almost as incorrect as to assume, in accordance with Vitringa, that it constitutes the second and third parts of the sixth Seal; according to this view, the true contents of the sixth Seal, as described in ch. vi., would form but the third of it.

The discussions relative to the *purpose* of the *sealing* show the obscurity that has crept over the idea of sealing—an idea so familiar to the New Testament, and introduced even by the Old Testament. Düsterdieck justly combats the view of many exegetes (especially à-Lapide, Ebrard), according to which the sealing here denotes an insurance against threatening penal judgments. The New Testament sealing secures against that temptation to apostasy which is enwrapped in the penal judgments, and thus conditionally, we admit, annuls the penal judgments so far as the sealed are concerned, although they pass through them. And hence the *signs*, σημεῖα, Ex. xii. and Ezek. ix., have a typical relation to this passage; a fact which Düsterdieck denies, notwithstanding his correct apprehension of the idea of sealing (p. 280).

[Is not the *sealing* the impressing upon believers the *name*, *i. e.*, the image of God the Father and the Son (comp. ch. xiv. 1), or, in other words, is it not their *sanctification?* This interpretation well agrees with all the instances in the New Testament, in which it is said that believers are *sealed* (see 2 Cor. i. 22; Eph. i. 13; iv. 30). Barnes writes: "It would be something that would be conspicuous and prominent, *as if* it were impressed upon the forehead. It would not be merely some *internal* sealing, or some designation by which they would be known to themselves and to God, but it would be something *apparent*, as if engraved on the forehead." Sanctification, although internal as to its origin, becomes apparent in the whole carriage of the man; it shines forth from him. No figure of it, as *apparent*, could be more striking than that of

a *seal* placed upon the *forehead*—the noblest and most prominent portion of the physical man.

[The *intent* of *sealing* is, first, to make manifest the fact of ownership, and, secondly, to secure. Both these ends are effected by the *sealing*, as interpreted above; and furthermore, it may be remarked, the safety of that portion of the sealed who may remain on earth during the period of *the great tribulation* is insured, whether we regard that tribulation as resulting from special judgments, inflicted by personal ministers of God, or from the influx of fearful temptations. In the former case, it is secured, as was that of the Israelites in the last great judgment inflicted upon the Egyptians, by the sprinkled blood of the paschal lamb; in the latter, by the spiritual strength inwrought by the Spirit of sanctification.—E. R. C.]

With the manifold misapprehension of the sealing, a non-appreciation of the universal import of this section is connected. Hence have arisen false specializations, as *e. g.*: the flight of the Christians to Pella (Grot. and others). All the Jews down to the final judgment (Heinrich). All the servants of God at the end of the days (De Wette). Hengstenberg, however, interprets the passage more correctly than would appear from Düsterdieck's notice of his views (p. 277). He writes as follows: "The sealing, as a symbolical act, is enclosed in a particular epoch of time; it takes place, once for all, before the commencement of the plagues with which the godless world is judged. *The root idea, however, is this: that God protects His own in the midst of all the judgments that sweep over the godless world.*—The sealing has reference to the entire duration of the Christian Church, until its final *consummation*; to the entire duration of the *world*, to its final *destruction* (?). It has, therefore, not yet lost its significance."

The relation of the second part of the chapter (from ver. 9 to the close) to the first part has been defined in harmony with the individualization of the section. The innumerable multitude of Christians, ver. 9, has reference to the Christians in Syria, according to Grotius. It forms a portion of the 144,000; a portion that have perished despite the sealing, according to Heinrich. It is also declared to be identical with the 144,000. Düsterdieck makes an ingenious attempt to answer the question why only believing Jews (as he supposes) are represented as sealed. If, however, it were really true that sealed Jewish Christians were alone intended here, the charge of Volkmar and others, that the Book is Judaistic, would not be so easily set aside. Ebrard affirms, that Israel alone is spoken of here, "not because the Gentile Christians then existing together with it are excluded from this congregation of Israel, but because they must be conceived of as adopted into it." This reminds us of a generally diffused school-idea, according to which Israel is, at the end, yet to obtain legal prerogatives; though it was to its pretension to such prerogatives that its apostasy was owing. The simple antithesis of the elect, as the kernel of the Church in this world, and the innumerable blessed, as the constituents of the continually increasing Church in the other world, is entirely overlooked. Even Düsterdieck limits the 144,000 to Jews. A special reason for this is the fact, that the Twelve Tribes are mentioned by name. As if the very Tribes had not a typical or symbolical meaning! Let the full consequence of Israel's symbolical import be gathered from the Prophets, Evangelists, and Apostolic writings, and Düsterdieck's arguments in favor of Bengel's view—viz., that in vers. 1–8 only Israelitish believers are intended, whilst ver. 9 has reference to blessed spirits from all nations, from the Gentiles and the Jews—will excite nothing but astonishment. On special distinctions see Düsterdieck, p. 280.

Ver. 1. **Four angels.**—These are neither four world-kingdoms (Bede), nor ostensible Angels of Nature (De Wette), nor bad Angels (Calov.), nor distinct personal Angels, but symbolical angelic forms, like the Cherubs at the entrance of Paradise; denoting here all God's providential arrangements in regard to the forth-breaking of the spirit or winds of temptation.[*] "In the Angels who restrain and loose the winds, the idea that the salvation of the elect and the perdition of the wicked (?) come from God alone has, as it were, assumed flesh and blood. Comp. the similar symbolical representation in ch. ix. 14, 15" (Hengstenberg). The commentator just quoted also shows that the winds in Scripture are symbols of Divine judgments (p. 177); and it is thus that he apprehends them here. In the New Testament, however, they are also symbols of opinions, of false doctrines, Eph. iv. 14 (comp. Hos. viii. 7), and this meaning is by far the more probable one here.[†] Ebrard truly remarks, that the conception of the four corners of the earth does not necessitate the idea that the earth is a four-cornered plane. The four corners characterize the whole earth-world in respect of its spiritually dark side, the heathen earth. The Seer is already accustomed, like the Christian Church at a later period, to conjoin the idea of heathenism (Paganism) with the idea of a coming from the uttermost corners of the earth. And in this Ezekiel preceded him with his prophecy concerning Gog and Magog—a prophecy which John himself takes up (ch. xx.). According to Hengstenberg, the four winds denote, "that the storms of Divine judgments are to burst upon the earth from all sides." Düsterdieck maintains that the winds are to be taken simply as actual storm-winds, just as in ch. vi. 12 a real earthquake should be understood. Misunderstanding is driven to its utmost stretch when it is proposed to take the figures of an allegorical book literally, and when, on the other hand, the law-abiding explanation of these allegorical

figures is denominated allegorical interpretation. With equal justice might it be said, that the sower of Matt. xiii. is a real sower, and that the spiritual interpretation of him is allegorical exposition. However abortive most of the interpretations of such allegorical figures may be, they are so only because they have not sufficiently regarded the key which is offered by the poetical and prophetico-symbolical style of expression. Our remark applies, for instance, to Bengel's explanation of the earth as Asia; the sea as Europe; the trees as Africa. Yet other interpretations see in Düsterdieck. Hengstenberg quite rightly understands the sea as denoting the sea of nations. Here, however, the sea should be apprehended in the better sense of the term, as symbolizing Christian national life, because it is possible for it to be injured; it cannot thus be understood, however, in cases where the harm proceeds from it, as Dan. vii. 2 and Rev. xiii. Hengstenberg thinks that the trees denote kings or magnates; trees and grass, the lofty and the lowly. We prefer, in this passage, to apprehend the trees in accordance with Psalm i., the grass in accordance with Psalm xxiii., since it is not neutral things that are spoken of as being injured, but positively good things.

[May there not be here a double symbolization—the storm directly significant of a convulsion that is to shake the real earth and sea, and that symbolic of convulsion in the whole fabric of human society? Our Lord connects together storms in the physical and social worlds as preceding His Coming (Luke xxi. 25–28), and the whole imagery of the Apocalypse leads to the idea that such storms will be connected in reality.—E. R. C.]

Ver. 2. **And I saw another angel.**—Vitringa, with perfect justice, regarded this other Angel as significant of the Holy Ghost. Düsterdieck considers it too great a digression from the text to regard him even as an Archangel (Stern), or as Christ (Calov., Hengstenb.). The term certainly is ἄγγελος, and not Holy Ghost; but outside of Apocalyptic symbolism, it is the Holy Ghost Who seals. [The Holy Ghost, doubtless, is the efficient sealer; but may not the Angel be a symbol of the instrumentalities by which He seals?—E. R. C.] This Angel undoubtedly says in ver. 3, **the servants of our God;** but he must, necessarily, speak as an Angel and he also includes with himself, as Hengstenberg correctly reminds us, the four Angels first spoken of. [The inclusion is possible, but not necessary.—E. R. C.]

Ascending from the sun-rising.—Even this, we are told, contains nothing but the "significant" intimation, "that the Angel who comes on an errand of blessing, with the guarantee of life eternal" (Angels, then, are possessed of such power!), "rises from the side whence light and life are brought by the earthly sun." Düsterdieck, with reference to Hengstenberg (?), Ebrard, Volkmar and others. The words, then, contain a modern poetical figure, and nothing more, though Scripture speaks of the rising of the Sun of righteousness (Mal. iv. 2; comp. Luke i. 78; Hengstenberg, p. 382 sqq.). Düsterdieck rejects a

---

[*] [LORD regards the Angels as (Classical) Symbols of "the authors and propagators of those (disorganizing) opinions; the fomentors and directors of the violences to which they excite." There is nothing in this opinion inconsistent with the fact that they are under the direction of God, since the wicked are His hand, and He restrains the remainder of wrath (comp. Ps. xvii. 14; lxxvi. 10).

[ALFORD remarks: "This (that they are simply Angels) is all that is declared to us in the text, and it is idle to inquire beyond it. All allegorizing and all individualizing interpretations are out of the question."—E. R. C.]

[†] [See preceding foot-note.—E. R. C.]

number of interpretations similar to his own (p. 284).

A seal of the Living God.—This term does not denote merely that the "seal *belongs* to the living God;" it means, rather, that *it secures a life corresponding to the living God*—the new life of believers. Hence God is termed the *living* God. According to De Wette, the expression means that God is the true God, and hence that His seal is the valid one. According to Hengstenberg, Düsterdieck and others, the meaning is, that God, as the Living One, is also the bestower of life. Our passage treats of the *insurance* of a life already given, as is always the case when sealing is spoken of. Together with the idea of *insuring*, the idea of *property* is included. These two conceptions really cannot be separated; he who seals anything, secures it to himself. Without this reference of insurance to ownership—of which Hengstenberg can find no certain example in Scripture—sealing, as such, would have merely the import of a mechanical fastening. But even a lock is not purely and simply a mechanical impediment.

"According to the hypothesis of several exegetes, the seal bore the name of *Jehovah.* Such commentators refer to ch. xiv. 1, where the elect are described as having the Name of God written on their foreheads, *etc.* It is to be observed, that Ezekiel (ch. ix. 4) merely speaks of a *mark*, without further qualification. This fact alone should prevent us from going beyond what is expressly stated in the text" (Hengstenberg). Others have conjectured that the *seal* bore the sign of the cross. Düsterdieck, on the other hand, concludes, from the omission of the definite article, that we are at liberty to suppose that God has different seals for different purposes. The Apostle Paul, however, seems to know of but one purpose in the sealing of the servants of God.*

And he cried with a great voice.—This, according to Hengstenberg, denotes the decidedness of the command. Other interpretations see in Düsterdieck, p. 286. We understand by it the mighty counter-working of apostolic Christianity against the incipient breaking loose of spiritual heathenism upon the Church.

To whom it was given.—We find no pluperfect in ἐδόθη; for it is not until the sealing that such power is given them. Previous to the sealing, the four Angels were just as much designed for the restraining of the winds as they afterwards were for the loosing of them, for they were the angelic purpose and the angelic measure of the winds themselves (Ps. civ. 4).

To injure the earth.—'Αδικεῖν is to be apprehended in the more general sense of *doing harm to.*† A strange perversion of the sense is

shown in the interpretations of Bengel, Herder and Rinck, according to whom the *holding* of the winds should be regarded as an injury, because they have a *cooling* or a *dispersing* effect. The ἄχρι in ver. 3, irrespective of anything else, decides in regard to the meaning. It even precludes the assumption that harm would result only in case the winds were loosed too soon. After the sealing, the injuring really ensues; though the loosing of the storms is not literally narrated, it is actually accomplished with the sounding of the seven Trumpets.

Till we have sealed.—The general apprehension of the plural as indicating that the Angel has assistants who are not mentioned, may have another direction given to it in the assumption, that the four Angels themselves are the assistants of the Angel who issues the command. This view is justly upheld by Hengstenberg, though Düsterdieck opposes it. For the repression and limitation, as well as the co-operation of temptation, of trial, of tribulation from without, are alike necessary in order that man may inwardly attain to his sealing. As, however, a certain degree of temptation is the condition of sealing, so there are also degrees of temptation which would be irresistible, were it not for the previous sealing. And this is the idea presented here. Hence the four Angels must first take a negative part in the sealing by holding the four winds in check for a time. Calovius' application of the plural to the Trinity, see noticed by Düsterdieck.

The servants of our God.—In the Old Testament all the pious are, in a general sense, *servants of God*, in accordance with His Thorah [law]. In a special sense, however, the people of Israel, or pious Israelites, are His servants, being organs of God, designed for the diffusion of His light, His law and His salvation over the whole earth (Is. xlii. 1). In the most special sense, therefore, the Messiah is His Servant (Is. liii.). On account of the contrast of sonship and the slavish servitude of legalists (Rom. vi.), the term *servant* occupies a less conspicuous place in the New Testament. The διάκονος of God is a *servant* who is familiar with his Master's purpose, and serves voluntarily. The high and honorable name of δοῦλος, however, gradually and significantly re-appears, and the δοῦλος of Christ is also the δοῦλος of God (Tit. i. 1; Rev. i. 1). The true servants of God are those in whom Israel's destiny is fulfilled; those who, in and with Christ, represent, as the kernel of the Church, God's light and law on the earth.* And these, some exegetes would

---

* [The Apostle Paul, when he wrote of sealing, was writing, not as a prophet, but of a matter then existent. The fact that but one kind of sealing (or a sealing having but one purpose) then existed, or may exist throughout the greater portion of the Christian era, does not exclude the possibility that in "the last days" another kind may be employed.—E. R. C.]

† [The use of ἀδικεῖν, the proper meaning of which before an accusative is *to do wrong to* (comp. Matt. xx. 13; Acts vii. 26, 27, *etc.*) favors the idea of Lord, that the four Angels are symbolic of evil men, or, at least, the idea that they signify *evil agencies.* No valid objection can be urged against this

opinion from the fact, that "*it was given*" to them to injure, since it is the prerogative of God to use even the evil as His instruments; that which is a wrong from them, is no wrong from Him Who permits, uses and restrains them (comp. Acts ii. 23).—E. R. C.]

* [Therefore no less than *six* words in the Greek Testament which in the German Version are rendered *Knecht*, and in the English (with one additional) *servant*. The word generally and correctly so rendered is δοῦλος, the ordinary LXX. rendering of עֶבֶד. It cannot with propriety be said, that it occupies a less conspicuous place in the New Testament than its equivalent in the Old. In the Gospels, in direct address to the disciples and in descriptive parables, our Lord used it more than fifty times; it is applied twenty five times to Christians in other portions of the New Testament. It is a term generally employed by the Apostles in the introductions to their Epistles as descriptive of their own

fain persuade us, are Jewish Christians exclusively! "De Wette," says Ebrard, "wrongly refers to ch. xiv. 1 in proof of the incorrectness of the view which makes the sealed ones of ch. vii. Jewish Christians. In his opinion the 144,000 sealed ones of ch. vii. re appear in ch. xiv., being generally designated in ver. 3 as redeemed from the earth.—We shall see, in due time, that the 144,000 introduced in the latter chapter have nothing whatever to do with those of ch. vii."* And yet in each case the number and qualification [the mark on the forehead] are the same! The identity of individuals is, of course, not the material point: what we contend for is the identity of the idea: viz. of the 144,000 as the stand-holders of the people of God, the pillars of the Temple.

On their foreheads.—Düsterdieck: "The mark received by the servants of the Beast is—like the mark of slaves in ordinary life—impressed upon the right hand or the forehead (ch. xiii. 16; xiv. 9; xx. 4); the servants of God bear the seal and the name of their Lord on their *foreheads* alone. The fact that this is the most conspicuous place (Aret., Bengel, Stern and others) is a sufficient reason only in the case of the servants of the Beast; with the servants of God, the material point is, rather, that the noblest part of the body should bear the sacred mark." Again, there is no recourse to the Scriptural bases of the idea. Why does Aaron bear the name of Jehovah upon his *frontlet* (Ex. xxxix. 30; xxviii. 36), and upon his *breast-plate* the name of the children of Israel? The breast encloses the *secret* of faith; but the forehead *manifests* the confession, the stand-point, the symbol, the colors and standard (Rom. x. 10). When it is said of the house of Israel: It hath hard foreheads and obdurate hearts ([they are stiff of forehead and hard of heart] Ezek. iii. 7), not only is the like substance of unbelief expressed, but also an antithesis of form. The

relation to Christ; see Rom. i. 1; Phil. i. 1; Titus i. 1; Jas. i. 1; 2 Pet. i. 1; Rev. i. 1. With still less propriety can it be affirmed, that there was any relinquishment of the term because of "the contrast of sonship and the slavish servitude of legalists." In the very chapter to which our Author refers as presenting that contrast (Rom. vi.) δοῦλος is employed as a generic term applicable to both the righteous and the wicked (ver. 16), and the verb δουλόω is twice applied to Christians (vers. 18, 22); and in the beginning of that very Epistle Paul styled himself a δοῦλος. [In the primitive sense of the term, all creatures are the δοῦλοι of God; as applicable to Christ and Christians, it carries with it the idea of *voluntary subjection to Him as Master, Owner* (comp. Eph. vi. 16). Ordinarily, this *subjection* implies *ministration* (in the ordinary sense of that word), because God commands His δοῦλοι (having the opportunity) to minister. It is not implied, however, that *doulos*, nor is it always implied in fact : God sometimes calls His δοῦλοι to *serve* by patient acquiescence in circumstances which forbid them to *minister*—"they also *serve* who only stand and wait." The position of Lange is based upon the altogether unauthorized (occasional) translation of διάκονος by the German *Knecht* (=the English *servant*). Not only are these words radically distinct as to meaning, but in the New Testament one is never used as exegetical of the other, and, still further, never are Christians, *as such*, styled the διάκονοι of Christ. The only instance which can be, even apparently, adduced as negativing the last assertion is John xii. 26; but even there, manifestly, the idea present to the mind of our Lord was *personal* ministration. For a full discussion of the meaning of δοῦλος and διάκονος see Cremer's *Biblico-Theological Lexicon of N. T. Greek (translated from the German);* Edinburgh (T. & T. Clark), 1872—a most valuable work.—E. R. C.]

* [For a counter statement see Additional Note, p. 193.—E. R. C.]

expression: Thy forehead against their forehead, is precisely a case in point. The symbolical sense of the words is unmistakable (see Ez. iii. 8, 9).

Vers. 4-8. As the loosing of the storms is not described further on, neither is the very act of sealing now depicted. John heard the number of the sealed. Why "probably from the other Angel" (De Wette, Ebrard)? The visional hearing is the finest sensorium for the most secret and profound revelation (see 2 Cor. xii. 4). And there are here but three general points: Israel; the number, 144,000; each Tribe furnishing a twelfth of this number. On the number itself, see the *Introduction,* p. 16. The equality of the number 12,000 for each Tribe is, according to Düsterdieck, expressive of the idea that all have an equal share in the Divine gift of grace—none, however, of right. But if the Twelve Tribes, like the Twelve Apostles, be significant, as an organic totality, of the manifoldness of the different gifts of grace, the meaning of this equality will be, that the round sum and plenitude of every species of churchly gifts of grace is assured to the eternal Kingdom of God.

The enumeration of Levi amongst the Twelve Tribes has been pertinently explained by Bengel as follows: "The Levitic ceremonies being done away with, Levi is again placed on an equal footing with his brethren." Now if, Levi being included, Manasseh and Ephraim—the latter under the name of Joseph—retain their places in the catalogue, the result must be thirteen Tribes. In order to avoid this, the vision omits the Tribe of Dan.

On violences against the text, see Düsterdieck, p. 289. As also on the play upon the name of Manasseh; the ancient conjecture, that Antichrist is to come out of Dan (with reference to the figure of the serpent, Gen. xlix. 17!); the reference to the idolatry of the Danites; also the reference to the Jewish tradition, representing the Tribe as being extinct, with the exception of a single family. Düsterdieck himself thinks that the omission of Dan is to be explained on the ground of the Tribe's having become extinct. We refer to the general view of the chapter presented above.* The Tribe of Simeon was also in danger of being left out on account of its partial emigration and its partial fusion with Judah (see 1 Chron. iv.; comp., with reference to Simeon, Deut. xxxiii. According to Düsterdieck, Issachar, too, is here left out).

On the promiscuous order of the sons of the different wives, and its design, as expressive of the co-ordination of all believers, see Hengst., p. 398 sqq.

For a table of the different occasions when the Twelve Tribes are mentioned, see Ebrard,

* ["He must have had an important special reason for leaving out the Tribe of Dan; and this could only be a theological one. We find the key in such passages as ch. xiv. 4, where it is said of the 144,000 : 'These are they who have not defiled themselves with women (i. e., sins [or rather idolatry=spiritual adultery]), for they are virgins,' ch. xxi. 27; ch. xxii. 14. Almost the only remarkable fact which is to be found in the history of the Danites is, that after having got possession of the land, they introduced into their territory a false worship (Judges xviii.), which continued through centuries." HENGSTENBERG.—E. R. C.]

p. 266 (Gen. xxix. 30; Gen. xlix.; Num. i.; Num. ii.; Deut. xxvii.; Deut. xxxiii.; ·Ezek. xlviii.) On an error in the Cod. Sin. see Düsterdieck, p. 290. [Gad and Simeon are omitted; Joseph and Benjamin, transposed.—E. R. C.] Ver. 9. As a matter of course,—De Wette to the contrary, notwithstanding—the section which now follows forms, in connection with the preceding section, one general picture.* ["The vision seems to be transferred from earth to Heaven; for the multitudes which he saw appeared BEFORE THE THRONE, i. e., before the Throne of God in Heaven. The design seems to be to carry the mind forward quite beyond the storms and tempests of earth—the days of error, darkness, declension and persecution—to that period when the (entire) Church should be triumphant in Heaven." BARNES.— E. R. C.]

A great multitude.—The elect in this world are numbered; the blessed in the other world are innumerable. This one antithesis makes a rent both in the Calvinistic doctrine of predestination and in the system of its antagonists, which fails to recognize the element of truth in the doctrine of election. It might be supposed, that the distinction consists in the fact that the 144,000 sealed ones are significant merely of the last Christian generation, whilst the blessed are congregated out of all generations. But even the sealed denote the whole sum of steadfast Christians out of the most diverse Christian ages. An antithesis must have been formed in the Seer's perception by the fact, that he only heard on earth of a host whose ranks were closed, whose number was complete, whilst in Heaven he actually saw a whole train of constantly augmenting masses. The constituent element of the contrast can, however, lie only in the distinction between the chosen servants of God who have to withstand the storms of the kingdom of darkness on this earth, and the whole fullness of blessed souls, amongst whom there are also children, who have entered into bliss. In ch. xiv. this antithesis again makes its appearance; and that in stronger terms and as continuing in Heaven itself, without detriment to the blessedness of all.

According to Düsterdieck, the difference is contained in the circumstance, that the sealed are of Israel exclusively, whilst the great multitude are gathered out of all nations. According to Ebrard, the distinction consists in the fact, that the former are the Christians still on earth in the last time, being, therefore, pre-eminently Jewish Christians; whilst the latter are all the blessed in the other world, being, therefore, pre-eminently Gentile Christians. According to De Wette, the distinction consists in the fact, that the former are representative of an elect number, in antithesis to the rejected, whilst in the latter case there is no such antithesis.†

Standing before the Throne.—The nominative ἑστῶτες,‡ remarkable in connection with

the accusative περιβεβλημένους [see TEXT. AND GRAM.], seems, together with ὄχλος, to be dependent upon ἰδού, thus supporting the reading indicated; it may be explained, however, by the irregularity of the Apocalyptic style.

Standing before the Throne, and before the Lamb.—Contemplation of the two-fold and yet unitous source of their felicity, in God's providence and Christ's suffering; this contemplation is at once the continuance and the perfection of their bliss.

["Of all nations.—Not only of the Jews; not only of the nations which in the time of the sealing vision had embraced the Gospel, but of all the nations of the earth. And kindreds —φυλῶν.—This word properly refers to those who are descended from a common ancestry, and here denotes a race, lineage, kindred. . . . And peoples—λαῶν.—This word refers properly to a people or community as a mass, without reference to its origin or any of its divisions. And tongues—languages.—This word would refer also to the inhabitants of the earth with respect to the fact, that they speak different languages . . . not as divided into nations; not with reference to their lineage or clanship; and not as a mere mass without reference to any distinction, but as divided by speech. The meaning of the whole is, that persons from all parts of the earth, as contemplated in these points of view, would be among the redeemed." BARNES. —E. R. C.]

The white robes are the attire of victory. ["The emblems of innocence or righteousness, uniformly represented as the raiment of the inhabitants of Heaven." BARNES. Comp. chs. iii. 4; vi. 11; and especially ver. 14, where the symbol is explained.—E. R. C.] The palms are signs of peace and festivity. From these the inference has been drawn that a heavenly Feast of Tabernacles or harvest is indicated (Züllig, Hengstenberg, p. 403, with reference to Zech. xiv. 16). "The palms, as a symbol of victory, attribute an activity to the redeemed which is not pertinent here, where everything subserves to the praise of God's transcendent redeeming grace" (Hengstenberg). As if any principial contradiction were involved therein! It cannot be disputed, however, that the Israelitish Feast of Tabernacles might form the point of departure for the present figurative representation. [The palm was the symbol of victory amongst the Greeks, but not amongst the Hebrews. With the latter (in the Feast of Tabernacles) it was the memento of trials from which they had been delivered—it was the symbol of salvation (comp. Lev. xxiii. 39-44). The remarks of Trench on ch. ii. 17 (the last quoted), p. 85, are applicable here.—E. R. C.]

Vers. 10-12. With a great voice.—Now follows the doxology of the Church Triumphant, rejoicing in its deliverance from the great tribulation of the Church Militant. The mighty voice is the expression of the great, common, unitous feeling of all the redeemed at their complete redemption. Σωτηρία denotes the whole redemptive salvation, as principial and final σωτηρία [deliverance from sin (comp. Matt. i. 21) and woe.—E. R. C.]. "Grotius erroneously interprets ἡ σωτηρία metonymically (=gratias ob

---

*[Why "as a matter of course," when separated from the preceding section by the strong disjunctive phrase, μετὰ ταῦτα εἶδον? See on ch. iv. 1 (and foot-note), p. 150; also Additional Note, p. 193.—E. R. C.]

† [See Additional Note, p. 193.—E. R. C.]

‡ [See Additional Note, p. 193.—E. R. C.]

acceptam salutem). The thanksgiving consists rather in the fact, that the σεσωσμένοι ascribe the σωτηρία given them to their God as the σωτήρ'' (Düsterdieck). This, then, is, after all, equivalent to converting the σωτηρία into a thank-offering.* The Apocalyptic doxologies have in all cases a similar profound meaning. They give back to God in thanks and praise that which He has first bestowed.

Ver. 11. And all the Angels.—Here personal Angels are spoken of. Whilst the symbolical Angels are restraining the storms on earth, it is said of this heavenly choir: *all* the Angels.

Were standing.—The celebration of the fact of redemption summons them all around the Throne. They first ratify the song of praise raised by the throng of blessed human spirits, by their deep adoration and their *Amen*. Then they also give expression to their angelic stand-point in contemplating the redemption. We apprehend their doxology from the Christological point of view, so that three harmonious antitheses form a group of *six*, which, with a mighty finale, becomes a *septenary*. See the SYNOPTICAL VIEW.

Vers. 13–17. The ensuing explanation of the foregoing vision reminds us of a similar scene which occurs in ch. xvii. 7. The conversation here, manifestly, serves to give additional distinctness and effectiveness to the hortatory and consolatory idea of the vision.

Ver. 13. And one of the Elders answered.—An Elder speaks; what he says is an *answer* according to Hebrew usage. No explicit question preceded his reply; it had, however, an interrogative cause, consisting, doubtless, in the question enwrapped in the astonishment of the Seer. An Elder, as a representative of redeemed humanity, is the fittest interpreter of the scene depicted.† "The dialogistic form, with its distinctness and liveliness, serves to mark the point in question" (Düsterdieck).

These who are arrayed in white robes, who are they? and whence came they?—He does not mention the token of the *palms*—a circumstance which demonstrates more clearly his desire to give prominence to the great marvel: so many men of a sinful race—countless men—in the garb of innocence. Yes, countless *holy* men! How is it possible? Here the question *qui genus? unde domo?* (see Düsterdieck) acquires quite a unique significance.

Ver. 14. Lord, thou knowest.—This mode of address—lord or sir—is, in its more general sense, a term of respect. *Thou knowest.* Ebrard: "I, indeed, know; but thou knowest far better." Düsterdieck and others: "I know not, but I should like thee to tell me."

Both, of course, are aware that these blessed ones are *men*, and that they come from earth. Even John knows great things concerning the redemption and its effect. But notwithstanding this, it continues to be a question with him, what the nature of this vision of innumerable

sanctified human beings, clad in snow-white raiment, is. He is battling with sin, like Elijah of old, and though it is with a New Testament experience of salvation that he is waging this conflict, still the view of the Elder is on a higher plane than his own, just as the voice that told of the seven thousand faithful Israelites was exalted above the conception entertained by Elijah. The wealth of the heavenly fruits of the Gospel passes even the ethical conception of a John. The train of the blessed is an endless festal line; they come and come. Hence the answer:

These are they that come [Lange:— **These are the ones coming**].—And the answer to the question, Whence come they? is at the same time a reply to the inquiry as to who they are. All who suffered, fought and conquered in the great tribulation through which every Christian, from the beginning of the ages of the Cross down to the end, has to pass. According to Düsterdieck, the great tribulation of the last days is alone intended. He also thinks that the comers are to be regarded as "on earth as yet."

Out of the great tribulation.—This expression has, doubtless, an eschatological bearing; not, however, in the sense which Düsterdieck attributes to it, citing Ebrard in support of his view, though the last-named commentator says: "The great tribulation can be only that *general* one, which had begun in John's time, and which is to continue until the ἐκδίκησις at Christ's return." On the other hand, Bengel's interpretation of the great tribulation, as significant of all the Adamic trouble and toil of Earth, is, undoubtedly, too general, or, rather, it is altogether wrong, since the tribulation begins only with the conflicts of faith. This is the first *historical* fundamental feature of the blessed: they have passed happily through this great tribulation. The historical conflict, however, is based upon the inward fact:

And they washed their robes, *etc*—Quite characteristically Johannean is this more definite apprehension of the Atonement in the innermost centre of the expiation. Equally characteristic the Catholic mediæval idea, held by Bede and Lyra, of the purifying power of the blood of the martyrs; Ewald himself, in his earlier publication, espoused this view (see Düst., p. 295). "Hengstenberg's distinction of the *washing* from the *making white*, and his application of the former to the forgiveness of sins and of the latter to sanctification, is contrary to the nature of the figure. A washing whereby the garments have become white, is denoted" (Düsterdieck).

[NOTE ON THE GREAT TRIBULATION.—Daniel (xi. 1) prophesied of a "trouble" (θλῖψις) to occur in the last days in the following language: (LXX.) καὶ ἔσται καιρὸς θλίψεως, θλίψις οἵα οὐ γέγονεν ἀφ' οὗ γεγένηται ἔθνος ἐν τῇ γῇ, ἕως τοῦ καιροῦ ἐκείνου. He also declared "at that time thy people shall be delivered (σωθήσεται)." The evident implication of the Prophet is that this θλῖψις shall not be visited upon the people of God, but upon men of the world. Our Lord (manifestly referring to this prophecy, for He uses its very phraseology) speaks of the same

---

* [The ascription, according to the view of Düsterdieck, *implies* thanks; but is not thereby converted into a *mere* thank-offering. It implies *thanks*, because it is an ascription of *praise* in view of benefits conferred.—E. R. C.]

† [See *foot-note* † on p. 152.—E. R. C.]

θλῖψις, describing it as great. His language is (Matt. xxiv. 21); ἔσται γὰρ τότε θλῖψις μεγάλη, οἵα οὐ γέγονεν ἀπ' ἀρχῆς κόσμου ἕως τοῦ νῦν, οὐδ' οὐ μὴ γένηται. This θλῖψις immediately precedes the Coming of the Son of Man (ver. 30); and there can be no doubt that the period thereof is that of the vengeance predicted Luke xxi. 22, whose special woes the disciples were exhorted to labor to escape by faithfulness (ver. 36). In the Epistle to the Church of Philadelphia, the same tribulation, doubtless, was alluded to as "the hour of temptation (πειρασμός)," which should "try them that dwell upon the Earth" (worldlings), but from which the faithful should be "kept" (Rev. iii. 10). It seems hardly possible to avoid the conclusion, that when, in connexion with the Coming of the Lord, a tribulation was spoken of to John, which, in the very words of Jesus, is emphasized as "the tribulation, the great one" (οἱ ἐρχόμενοι ἐκ τῆς θλίψεως τῆς μεγάλης), the Seer must have understood by it the very tribulation predicted by Jesus. Two objections, possibly, may be urged against this view, viz.: that (1) the redeemed are said to come out of (ἐκ) the tribulation; (2) this interpretation involves that the innumerable white-robed throng consists only of those who were on earth at the beginning of the tribulation. Concerning the former of these, it may be said, that the force of ἐκ is not necessarily that the delivered should have been actual participators in, or sufferers from, that from which they are delivered, see chs. ii. 11; iii. 10; xviii. 4; John x. 39; Acts xv. 29; 2 Cor. i. 10; Gal. ii. 13; 2 Tim. iv. 17; 2 Pet. ii. 9, etc. The second objection disappears on the supposition, that the winds, which are to bring on the great tribulation, have been threatening, but are withheld, throughout the entire preceding period, until the sealing and gathering of the elect; on this supposition, all the redeemed who have died throughout the preceding ages have gone up from that which is constantly threatening (see under ch. iii. 10, and also Additional Note, on p. 193).

[There can be little doubt that the prophecy of our Lord, Matt. xxii. 15-22; Luke xxi. 20-24, found its first or typical fulfillment in the destruction of Jerusalem; it should be remembered, however, that, previous to that destruction, "the Christians, remembering the Lord's admonition, forsook Jerusalem and fled to the town of Pella, . . . where King Herod Agrippa II. . . . opened to them a safe asylum" (Schaff's Hist. Ap. Ch., p. 391). It may be asked, if the flood, the destruction of Sodom and Gomorrah, and the destruction of Jerusalem, are not types of the great tribulation, and if the deliverance of Noah, of Lot, and of the Church of Jerusalem, are not, at the same time, types of the deliverance of the Saints (comp. 2 Pet. ii. 5-9)?—E. R. C.]

Ver. 15. On this account are they before the throne.—[They are in Heaven; see the extract from Barnes, p. 185.—E. R. C.] Perfectly Johannean: 1 John iii. 2. And all this Grotius soberly refers to the Christians in Pella!

And serve Him day and night.—The heavenly life has itself become a priestly service of God, being, moreover, as a spiritual life, ele-

vated above the change of day and night (ch iv. 8; v. 8; xxii. 3). [The heavenly life is not one of mere enjoyment, but of continued, active service.—E. R. C.]

And He that sitteth on the throne shall spread his tabernacle over them [Lange: shall settle abidingly over them]. —Σκηνώσει is difficult to translate. Hengstenberg's translation: to tabernacle, is objected to by Ebrard on philological grounds. The expression μετ' αὐτῶν, ch. xxi. 3, is different from the present term ἐπ' αὐτούς. In ch. xxi. 22 it is declared concerning the City of God: I saw no Temple in it: God Himself is its Temple. There is, then, a development of blessedness in the other world. Whatever interpretation we may give to the passages in question, it is a thought of unique grandeur, that the glory or Shekinah of God, once veiled by the pillar of cloud and fire, and, outside of distinct prophetic manifestations, regularly revealed only in a figurative form to the High Priest in the Holy of Holies (of the Tabernacle), is now, in a permanent and apparent glory, to sink down from the Throne upon the blessed and spread itself out over them. See Matt. v. 8; 1 Cor. xiii. 12; comp. Lev. xxvi. 11; Is. iv. 5; Ezek. xxxvii. 27. ["It is exceedingly difficult to express the sense of these glorious words, in which the fulfillment of the O. T. promises, such as Levit. xxvi. 11; Isa. iv. 5, 6; Ezek. xxxvii. 27, is announced. They give the fact of the dwelling of God among them, united with the fact of His protection being over them, and assuring to them the exemptions next to be mentioned." ALFORD.—E. R. C.]

Ver. 16. They shall not hunger any more. —Ps. xvii. 15.

Thirst.—Is. lv. 1; Ps. cvii. 9. Hunger and thirst, and the satisfaction of both these needs, are, throughout the Scriptures, the fixed figures of spiritual circumstances. As the body is a fixed symbol of the soul, so the conditions of bodily existence and satisfaction are a fixed symbol of the corresponding spiritual conditions. [If the vision was of the post-resurrection condition of the Saints, there was more than the figure of spiritual supply in these words. The bodies raised from the dead shall experience no want or pain.—E. R. C.]

The sun.—Ps. cxxi. 6; Ps. xc. and other passages. The oriental sun, in its overpowering effects; a type, also, of overpowering reality in daily life.

Any burning heat, (καῦμα.)—Heat of the hot wind, of the burden of the day, of fever, etc.

For the Lamb.—Is. xlix. 10. "He that hath mercy on them." ["Ihr Erbarmer," their Compassionator.] From Him that shows mercy or that pities, comes the Spirit of mercy; He perfects His manifestation in the spirit of the Lamb, personal and complete meekness, and founds a congregation of infinitely deep and firm peace. On the expression: τὸ ἀνὰ μέσον τοῦ θρόνου, comp. Düsterdieck, p. 297. The meaning is probably this: that Christ, by His invincible meekness, has risen to the centre of the Divine government. As the meek are to possess the kingdom of the earth, so the Meek

One par excellence has attained the sovereignty over Heaven and earth at the right hand of the Father and in His Name, Matthew xxviii. 18; Phil. ii.
Shall shepherdize them.—Ps. xxiii.; John x.
And God shall wipe away every tear from their eyes.—Is. xxv. 8; Rev. xxi. 4.

[ADDITIONAL NOTE ON THE VISIONS OF CH. VII.]
By the American Editor.

[That chap. vii. is independent of what precedes (although, of course, related to it), is evident from the disjunctive phrase, μετὰ τοῦτο εἶδον, with which it commences (see *footnote,* p. 190); and that it consists of *two* independent visions, is also evident from the similar phrase with which the second vision is introduced, ver. 9. These visions are here introduced as proper to this stage of the complex narrative. They do not, properly speaking, constitute an *Episode,* because they enter as materially into the revelation of things future as do the events under the Seals. They are not placed under the Seals, because the matters set forth were not *concealed* from the heavenly hosts (the *withholding* of the tempest of wrath, the *sealing,* and the *gathering of the redeemed* in bliss), but had been in process of development for a long time, possibly from the days of Abraham or even those of Abel.*

The 144,000 of the first vision the writer identifies with those of ch. xiv.; in his judgment the *number* and the almost certain reference to the Seal upon the forehead in ch. xiv. 1, place this beyond a peradventure. But if this identification be correct, then the *Sealed* constitute a peculiar portion of the redeemed, eminent for faithfulness and nearness to Christ: "They are the *first-fruits,* the ἀπαρχή, unto God and to the

Lamb" (ch. xiv. 3-5). This fact seems also to be indicated by the *number,* which is one of perfection, which may well indicate, not merely completeness as to number, but the peculiar excellence, both in character and condition, of the whole body. They are selected from the tribes, the *denominations,* of the nominal Israel, the visible Church of God (possibly the Jewish as well as the Christian—the latter being the legitimate successor of the former, Rom. xi. 17, 18). By the *sealing* the writer understands (probably) a peculiar Christ-likeness impressed upon the sealed by the sanctifying influences of the Holy Ghost (see p. 186). The *period of the sealing* he regards as extending throughout the whole Christian dispensation, and possibly back to the institution of the visible Church in Abraham, during the whole of which periods the winds of Divine wrath were restrained.*

The second vision contemplated, not (or not *merely*) the ἀπαρχή, but the whole body of the redeemed (probably exclusive of the ἀπαρχή). This innumerable company was composed of individuals of all *ages*—*ante* as well as *post*-diluvian; of all *races*: it included, probably, that innumerable host of infants (more than one half of the entire human family), and those others amongst the nations, who, influenced by the Spirit by modes unknown to us, have been renewed and saved by the blood of the Atonement.

The manifest points of difference between the two companies have already been alluded to; they may, however, be arranged as follows: the one was innumerable, from all nations, *the whole body of the redeemed*; the other was a (comparatively) small, definite number, from Israel (the Church), the *first-fruits.* It may be asked, if another point of difference is not suggested by the ἑστῶτες of ver. 9; there the general throng are represented as *standing before the Throne,* but the promise to the faithful of the Church is that they themselves shall be *enthroned* with Jesus (comp. chs. iii. 21; xx. 4).—E. R. C.]

* [The *Seals* symbolize the concealment from angelic and human view of *certain* (not *all*) events in future history. Probably, at the date of the Apocalypse, both Angels and men expected the immediate return of Christ to earth. The eschatological predictions of our Lord (Matt. xxiv., *etc.*) up to the point of His promised appearing seemed to have been fulfilled (and *typically* they had been fulfilled) in the destruction of Jerusalem. It is probable that neither Angels nor men dreamed that centuries, or even months, of false Christs, wars, famines, pestilences, persecutions, would intervene before the earthly establishment of the promised Kingdom; and hence the importance of the *unloosing* of the Seals. But however these things might be hidden, the *sealing* of believers and the *gathering of departed Saints in Heaven* were not concealed from any. These were events that for years (or centuries) had been going on, and their continuance until the resurrection (whenever, or after whatsoever events, that might be) was revealed and secured by the *open* promise of God. In the visions of ch. xiv., the Seer had a view of what had been openly progressing under the view of Angels, and the fact of whose future progress had already been revealed.—E. R. C.]

* [If by the *sealed* the *first-fruits* are meant, they cannot be regarded as consisting merely of those who shall be on Earth just before the *great tribulation.* Not only is it repugnant to reason and sensibility to shut out from that glorious company the Apostles and Martyrs, but we are expressly taught, that the primitive Christian's formed a portion of the ἀπαρχή (Jas. i. 18), and the Apostle Paul assures us, that those who are alive at the Coming of the Lord shall not *take precedence* of those who sleep (1 Thess. iv. 14–17). Nor does it seem proper to exclude from the company of the faithful the Father of the faithful and that noble host described in Heb. xi., of whom it is impliedly declared that, though without us they are not made perfect, with us they shall be perfected (Heb. xi. 40).—E. R. C.]

B.—EARTH-PICTURE OF THE SEVEN PENITENTIAL TRUMPETS, ISSUING FROM THE OPENING OF THE SEVENTH SEAL.

CHAP. VIII. 1—IX. 21.

1. *Opening of the Seventh Seal.*

CHAP. VIII. 1-6.

1   And when he had [*om.* had] opened the seventh seal, there was [ἐγένετο=supervened] silence in [*ins.* the] heaven about the space of [*om.* the space of] half an hour.
2 And I saw the seven angels which [who] stood [stand[1]] before God; and to them
3 were given seven trumpets.   And another angel came and stood at [*or* before[2]] the altar, having a golden censer; and there was given unto him much incense, that he should offer *it* with [*or* add *it* to[3]] the prayers of all [*ins.* the] saints upon the
4 golden altar which was [*is*] before the throne.   And the smoke of the incense, *which came* [*om.* , *which came*] with [to *or* for][4] the prayers of the saints, ascended
5 up [*om.* up] before God out of the angel's hand.   And the angel took the censer, and filled it with [from the] fire of the altar, and cast *it* [*om. it*] into [upon] the earth : and there were [supervened] voices, and thunderings [thunders,and voices],
6 and lightnings, and an earthquake.   And the seven angels which [who] had the seven trumpets prepared themselves to [*om.* to—*ins.* that they might] sound [trumpet].

2. *First four Trumpets.   Predominant human spiritual Sufferings under the figure of Sufferings in Nature.*

VERS. 7-12.

7   The first angel [*om.* angel[5]] sounded [trumpeted], and there followed hail and fire mingled[6] with blood, and they were cast upon the earth : [*ins.* and the third part of the earth was burnt up,][7] and the third part of trees was burnt up, and all green grass was burnt up.
8   And the second angel sounded [trumpeted], and as it were a great mountain burning with fire was cast into the sea : and the third part of the sea became blood;
9 And the third part of the creatures which were in the sea, and had life [ψυχάς] died ; and the third part of the ships were destroyed.
10   And the third angel sounded [trumpeted], and there fell a great star from [*ins.* the] heaven, burning as it were [*om.* it were] a lamp, and it fell upon the third

TEXTUAL AND GRAMMATICAL.

[1] Ver. 2. [For the ▩▩ of the perf. and plup. of ἵστημι as an intransitive present and imp., see Grammars and Lexicons generally.—E. R. C.]

[2] Ver. 3. [Ἐπί with the genitive; see TEXT. AND GRAM. on ch. vii. 15 (Note 12). Lange explains: "ἐπί—bending over;" Alford translates: *over.*—E. R. C.]

[3] Ver. 3. [This alternative translation of δώσει ταῖς προσευχαῖς is adopted from the margin of the E. V. For this, or an equivalent, sense of δίδωμι see Robinson's *Lex.* (d). For a full discussion of this phrase, see Dr. Lillie's Notes.—E. R. C.]

[4] Ver. 4. [See Winer, § 31, 6. c.; Lillie explains: "'Incense belonging to, designed for,' the *case* here answering to with the latter of two nouns in construction."—See also EXPL. IN DETAIL *in loc.*—E. R. C.]

[5] Ver. 7. [All the recent editors, with א. A. B*. P., *etc.,* omit ἄγγελος.—E. R. C.]

[6] Ver. 7. [Tisch. (8th Ed.), with א. P., gives μεμιγμένον; Lach., Alf., Treg. (and Tisch., 1859), with A. B*., μεμιγμένα. —F. R. C.]

[7] Ver. 7. Καὶ τὸ τρίτον τῆς γῆς κατεκάη, omitted by the Rec. in acc. with minuscules. [Given by א. A. B*. P., *etc.*—E. R. C.]

11 part of the rivers, and upon the fountains of [*ins.* the⁸] waters; And the name of the star is called Wormwood: and the third part of the waters became⁹ wormwood: and many [*ins.* of the] men died of [from] the waters, because they were made bitter.

12 And the fourth angel sounded [trumpeted], and the third part of the sun was smitten, and the third part of the moon, and the third part of the stars; [,] so as [*om.* so as—*ins.* that] the third part of them was [might be] darkened, and the day shone not [might not shine]¹⁰ for **a** [the] third part of it, and the night likewise [in like manner].

3. *Last three Trumpets.   Predominant demonic Sufferings—in figures of Nature perverted into Unnaturalness.*

CHAP. VIII. 13—IX. 21.

13 And I beheld [saw], and [*ins.* I] heard an angel [eagle¹¹] flying through the midst of heaven [in mid-heaven], saying with a loud [great] voice, Woe, woe, woe, to the inhabiters of [them that dwell upon] the earth by reason of [*ἐκ*] the other [remaining] voices of the trumpet of the three angels, which [who] are yet [about] to sound [trumpet]!

CHAP. IX. 1–21.

a.   Fifth Trumpet.   First Woe.

VERS. 1–12.

1 And the fifth angel sounded [trumpeted], and I saw **a** star fall [fallen] from [*ins.* the] heaven unto [upon] the earth: and to him was given the key of the bot-

2 tomless [*om.* bottomless¹²] pit [*ins.* of the abyss].   And he opened the bottomless [*om.* bottomless] pit [*ins.* of the abyss]¹³; and there arose [ascended] a [*om.* a] smoke out of the pit,¹⁴ as the [*om.* the] smoke of a great furnace; and the sun [*ins.* was darkened] and the air were darkened [*om.* were darkened] by reason of [*ἐκ*] the

3 smoke of the pit.   And there came [*om.* there came] out of the smoke [*ins.* came forth] locusts upon the earth: and unto them was given power, as the scorpions of

4 the earth have power.   And it was commanded [said to, *ἐρρέθη*] them that they should [shall] not hurt [injure] the grass of the earth, neither [nor] any¹⁵ green thing, neither [nor] any¹⁵ tree; but only those [the] men which [who (*οἵτινες*)]

5 have not the seal of God in [upon] their [the¹⁶] foreheads.   And to them it was given that they should not kill them, but that they should [shall] be tormented¹⁷ five months: and their torment *was* [is] as the torment of **a** scorpion, when he

6 striketh [it hath stricken] a man.   And in those days shall men seek death, and shall not find¹⁸ it; and shall [*ins.* earnestly] desire to die, and death shall flee [fleeth¹⁹] from them.

7 And the shapes of the locusts *were* like unto [*om.* unto] horses prepared unto battle; and on [upon] their heads *were* [*om.* *were*] as it were crowns like gold, and

8 their faces *were* [*om.* *were*] as the [*om.* the] faces of men.   And they had hair as

⁸ Ver. 10. Τῶν ὑδάτων; comp. Delitzsch, p. 32.   [So all the recent editors with א. B*. P.   This entire clause (*after rivers*) **a** om. by A.—E. R. C.]

⁹ Ver. 11.   The Rec. gives γίνεται in acc. with minuscules.

¹⁰ Ver. 12.   [Alf., Treg. and Tisch., with א. A., give φάνῃ.—E. R. C.]

¹¹ Ver. 13.   The reading ἀγγέλου has the best Codd. against it; for particulars see Düst. [Alf., Treg., and Tisch., w th א A B*, give ἀετοῦ; P., however, reads ἀγγέλου.—E. R. C.]

¹² Ch. ix., ver. 1.   [The translation "*bottomless pit*" is altogether without justification.   By it, an important fact of revelation is concealed from the readers of the E. V. (see EXCURSUS ON HADES p. 304 sqq.)—E. R. C.].

¹³ Ver. 2.   The words Kαὶ ἤνοιξεν τὸ φρέαρ τῆς ἀβύσσου are groundlessly assailed.   [All the recent editors give these words with A. P., Vulg. (*Cl.*, *Fuld.*, *Harl.*² *Tol.*²); they are om. by א. B*., Vulg. (*Am.*, *Harl.*, *Tol.*), etc.—E. R. C.]

¹⁴ Ver. 2.   Some Codd. omit καπνὸς ἐκ τοῦ φρέατος [ὡς].   [These words are om. by 1, 35, 41, 87 (see Tischendorf).—E. R. C.]

¹⁵ Ver. 4.   [For this rendering of πᾶν **a**-e Winer, § 26, 1, *first par.*   (The μή is here connected with the verb, the οὐδέ being a mere continuance of the negation.)—E. R. C.]

¹⁶ Ver. 4.   Tisch. [1859] gives αὐτῶν.   [Tisch. (8th Ed.) and Treg. omit with א. A. P., *Am.*, *Harl.*, etc.; C d B*. gives it; Alford brackets.—E. R. C.]

¹⁷ Ver. 5.   [Lach., Words., Alf., Treg., Tisch., give βασανισθήσονται with א. A. P., etc.   Lange reads βασανισθῶσι with B*.—E. R. C.]

¹⁸ Ver. 6.   Kαὶ μὴ εὕρωσιν, Cod. A. [P], etc.   [So Lach. and Tisch. (1859); Tisch. (8th Ed.), Alf., Treg., give εὑρήσουσιν with א. B*.—E. R. C.]

¹⁹ Ver. 6.   The reading φεύγει.   [So Alf., Treg., Tisch., with A. P.; **a** reads φύγῃ and B*. φεύξεται.—E. R. C.]

9 the hair of women, and their teeth were as *the teeth* of lions.   And they had breastplates, as it were [*ins.* iron] breastplates of iron [*om.* of iron] ; and the sound of
their wings *was* as the [a] sound of chariots of many horses running to battle.
10 And they had [have] tails like unto [*om.* unto] scorpions, and there were [*om.*
there were] stings [*ins.* ; and] in their tails: and [*om.* : and—*ins. is*] their power[20]
11 *was* [*om. was*] to hurt [injure] men five months.   And they had [have] a king over
them, *which is* [*om. which is*] the angel of the bottomless pit [*om.* bottomless pit—
ins. abyss], [;] whose [his] name in the [*om.* the] Hebrew [,] tongue *is* [*om.* tongue
is] Abaddon, but [; and] in the Greek tongue [*om.* tongue—*ins.* he] hath *his* [the]
12 name Apollyon.   [*ins.* The] one woe is past [hath passed] ; *and*, [*om. and*,]
behold, there come [*ins.* yet] two woes more hereafter [*om.* more hereafter—
ins. after these things].

b. *Sixth Trumpet.   Second Woe.*

Vers. 13-21.

13   And[21] the sixth angel sounded [trumpeted], and I heard a [*or* one (μίαν)] voice
14 from the four[24] horns of the golden altar which is before God, saying to the sixth
angel [,] which had [the one having[23]] the trumpet, Loose the four angels which
15 [that] are bound in [at] the great river Euphrates.   And the four angels were
loosed, which [that] were [had been] prepared for an [the] hour, and a [*om.* a]
day, and a [*om.* a] month, and a [*om.* a] year, for to [*om.* for to—*ins.* that they
16 should] slay the third part of [*ins.* the] men.   And the number of the army
[armies] of the horsemen [cavalry[24]] *were* [*was*] two hundred thousand thousand
17 [two myriads of myriads]: and [*om.* and[25]] I heard the number of them.   And
thus I saw the horses in the vision, and them that [those who] sat on them, having
breastplates of fire [fiery] and of jacinth [hyacinthine], and brimstone [sulphure-
ous]: and the heads of the horses *were* as the heads of lions; and out of their
18 mouths issued [goeth forth] fire and smoke and brimstone [*or* sulphur].   By these
three [*ins.* plagues[26]] *was* [*om.* was—*ins.* were slain] the third part of [*ins.* the] men
killed [*om.* killed], by the fire, and by [*om.* by[27]] the smoke, and by [*om.* by[27]] the
19 brimstone [*or* sulphur], which issued [went forth] out of their mouths.   For their
[*om.* their—*ins.* the] power [*ins.* of the horses][28] is in their mouth, and in their tails:
for their tails *were* [*are*] like unto serpents, and [*om.* and] had [having] heads, and
20 with them [these] they do [*om.* do] hurt [injure].   And the rest of the men [,] which
[who] were not killed [slain] by these plagues [,] yet [*om.* yet] repented not [did
not even[29] repent] of the works of their hands, that they should not worship devils
[the demons], and [*ins.* the] idols of gold, and [*ins.* of][30] silver, and [*ins.* of][30] brass,
and [*ins.* of][30] stone, and of[30] wood ; which neither can [can neither] see, nor hear,
21 nor walk: Neither repented they [And they did not[31] repent] of their murders, nor
of their sorceries, nor of their fornication, nor of their thefts.

---

[20] Ver. 10. The reading of Lach. and Tisch. after Bengel.   [Also of Words., Alf., Treg., κέντρα, καί έν ταίς ούραίς αύτών
ή έξουσία αύτών άδικήσαι; א. A. B*. P. give καί after κέντρα and omit it after the first αύτών; א. A. P. have ή έξουσία αύτών ;
B*. reads έξουσίαν έχουσιν; B*. inserts τού before άδικήσαι, which is omitted by א. A. P.   There are other minor variations
of less authority.—E. R. C.]
[21] Ver. 13. [א. omits καί; B*. not only omits in this place, but inserts before μετα ταύτα in preceding verse; in acc.
with this, the correct pointing would be a period after *woes*, the translation running, *And after these things, the sixth Angel, etc.*—E. R. C.]
[22] Ver. 13. Τεσσάρων was omitted probably because it was regarded as superfluous; Düst. suspects it of being an
interpolation. [Lach., Treg., omit with א.* A. 28, 79, Am., Fuld., etc. Tisch. inserts with B*. P., etc.; Alford brackets.—
E. R. C.]
[23] Ver. 14.   A. B. [א. P.], etc., ὁ έχων;   comp. Delitzsch with ref. to Tisch., p. 33, also p. 32 (No. 10).
[24] Ver. 16.   Codd. A. B. [א. P.], etc., τού ἱππικού.
[25] Ver. 16.   [Καί is gener lly om. in acc. with א. A. B*. P., etc.—E. R. C.]
[26] Ver. 18.   [Recent editors generally insert πληγών, with א. A. B. C. P., etc.; C. omits τών, and א. omits τριών.—
E. R. C.]
[27] Ver. 18.   [The έκ before καπνού is given by C. P., Vulg. (Cl.) and om. by א. A. B*., Vulg., Am., Fuld., etc ; that before
θείου is given by P., etc.; א. A. B*. C. Vulg , etc ; critical editors generally omit both.—E. R. C.]
[28] Ver. 19.   [Lach., Alf., Treg., Tisch., with א. A. B*. C. P., Vulg., etc., give ή γάρ έξουσία τών ἱππων; Words. also αύτών.—E. R. C.]
[29] Ver. 20.   [Tisch. and Alf. give ούδέ with א. B*.; Lach. and Treg., ούτε with A. P.;   Gb., Sz, Tisch. (1859), ού with
C.   For the rendering above (ούδέ), see Win. § 55, 6 (*foot note* 2).—E. R. C.]
[30] Ver. 20.   ["The repetition, if not required in order to prevent ambiguity, is the most convenient compensation for
the omission of the article." Dr. Lillie.—E. R. C.]
[31] Ver. 21.   The reading ού [καί ού μετενόησαν].

EXEGETICAL AND CRITICAL.

SYNOPTICAL VIEW.

The *trumpet* calls to war; the *trumpet* summons the congregation to assemble. Both points are embraced by the vision of the Seven Trumpets; it is the vision of the experiences of the Church as the Church Militant; the vision of her conflict in her spiritual assailments and perils.* This spiritual conflict of the Church is evident from each individual feature of the vision. The prayers of all the Saints: the *third*, as a diminution of *three*, the number of spirit; the opening of the abyss; the horsemen, coming from the great river Euphrates, *i. e.* from the sphere of Babylon; the slaughter of mankind, effected by their demonic horses; and the impenitence still remaining after all these plagues —everything is indicative of spiritual circumstances.

These spiritual circumstances are, moreover, of such a nature that they can be overcome only by a mighty effort of Heaven itself; by a tension of the heavenly spirits in meditation, prayer and intercession. Hence there is *silence* in Heaven. Praise seems to grow dumb in Heaven itself. Heaven *prays* in consideration of the conflicts which are before the Church on earth. The heavenly *hour* is the decisive hour of the whole crisis; the entire *half* of this hour is employed in the celestial hallowing of the conflict of the Church Militant.

In the mean time, the *seven Angels*, with the trumpets which are given them, stand waiting. The *other Angel*, whose task it is to give a heavenly completeness to the earthly and imperfect prayers of the Saints is, doubtless, in accordance with Rom. viii. 26, the *Spirit of Prayer*, in connection with the symbolical *intercession of Christ*. In this character he approaches the heavenly *altar of incense*. His instrument is the *golden censer* — the heavenly purification and measurement of the prayers which ascend to Heaven mingled with pathological turbidity and eccentricity (comp. the μετριοπαθεῖν of Christ the High Priest, Heb. v. 2). The *incense* given to him is offered upon the *golden altar of incense* before the Throne, and the smoke of it rises up and completes the imperfect prayers of the Saints before God.

By the retro-active power of this heavenly sacrifice of prayer, the earth is consecrated for her struggle: the Angel pours the *fire of the altar*, with which he has filled the censer, upon the earth. Then from the heavenly fire of prayer there issue on earth *voices* and *thunders* and *lightnings* and an *earthquake*: holy ideas and words, holy preachings and alarm-cries, holy illuminations and spiritual judgments, result in holy convulsions of the human world. Thus is set on foot a victorious counteraction against the onsets just beginning. Though seven terrible corruptive and destructive agencies are now, one after another, let loose against the earth, we must remember that the providence of God has encircled them with angelic might; that in Heaven they are transformed into seven grand dispensa-

* [See ADDITIONAL NOTE, p. 212 sqq., on this statement, and on the entire Synoptical View.—E. R. C.]

tions; and that they are announced by *Trumpets*, which summon the Church to the conflict— summon her to resistance, by repentance and by a closer serriment in collectedness of spirit and in the life of Christian fellowship.

First Trumpet-blast.

The *first Trumpet* sounds, and hail, mingled with fire and blood, falls upon the earth. This is, unmistakably, the dispensation of carnal zeal, of sensuous piety, of fanaticism (Luke ix. 54), which falls upon the *earth*, *i. e.*, the churchly form of the Kingdom of God (Ps. xciii.). The *hail*, or the icy coldness of men's souls toward true spiritual life, corresponds with the *fire* of superstitious passions (see Nitzsch, *System*, p. 39); and the fire is continually more and more mingled with *blood*, as is demonstrated by the first appearance of fanaticism in sacred history, Gen. xxxiv., and, further, by all kindred records, especially by the superstitious persecutions of heretics in the history of the Church. This unholy fire consumes *the third part of the earth, i. e.*, the Church, or, in a universal sense, legal order; *the third part of the trees* (Ps. i.), *i. e.* pious personalities; and *more than the third part of the green grass:* the *entire* soul-pasturage of the Christian flock (Ps. xxiii.) is more or less scorched and blasted, being converted partly into hay, partly into ashes.

Second Trumpet-blast.

The *mountain*, which is next introduced, is not a real mountain, but the *appearance* of a great burning mountain, rushing, like a giant meteor, through the air, as though hurled, by some mighty hand, upon the *sea*. This, manifestly, is the deceptive semblance of a great Divine ordinance, which, changed by the flames of bigot passion into a self-consuming crater, is inflicted, as a Divine judgment, upon the *sea* or national life. The *third part of the sea* is *turned to blood* by means of religious wars and abominations of all kinds springing from fanatical party spirit. The further consequence is that the *third part of the creatures* in the sea perish, and the *third part of the ships* are destroyed. The poisoning of Christian national life by the false fire-mountain destroys a third part of the healthful and gladsome popular life, and a third part of all human intercourse, blessing and prosperity. Whole nations, states and vital branches of the state are, so far as their spiritual existence is concerned, in good part ruined. History affords abundant illustrations of these Apocalyptic words.

Third Trumpet-blast.

From *Heaven*, from the kingdom of spirit, a *great star falls*, a real spiritual luminary, *burning like a torch, i. e.,* like a great and brilliant world-light. If we contemplate its spiritual fall, we cannot fail to perceive, that it is the personified likeness of false liberty, of the fanaticism of negation, rushing upon us under the semblance of a new enlightenment for the world. For it falls upon the *third part of the rivers, i. e.* more general spiritual tendencies, or *currents*, as they are called at present (Is. viii. 6; xxxv. 6); it falls also upon the *fountains* (Prov. xxv. 6), *i. e.*, creatively original minds, whence the currents proceed.

When it is said that the name of the star is called *Wormwood*, the idea immediately strikes us that it is indeed that embitterment by which —as in the history of Julian—a great portion of the heavenly knowledge-life, the enfranchising spiritual reform, is corrupted and transformed from a quietly shining heavenly star into a burning torch that falls from Heaven, and, instead of truly enlightening, poisons the fountains and currents of spiritual life. Thus a third part of the spiritual water of life, in society, culture and literature, is turned into a water of death, a soul-destroying partyism, sedition and sectarianism, inflicting even bodily death upon many men, by mortally embittering them (comp. Heb. iii. 8; Ex. xvii. 7; Num. xiv. 22; Deut. vi. 16).

Fourth Trumpet-blast.

A *third part of the Heaven of spiritual life* is *closed*, and thus the *opening* of the *abyss* at the blast of the fifth Trumpet is prepared. The *third part of the sun is smitten; i. e.*, the third part of the sun of revelation is concealed and made of none effect by the united darkness of positive and negative fanaticism—superstition and unbelief. In like manner the *third part of the moon* is smitten. Together with the bright day-life of Christian knowledge, the night-life of the spiritual repose and peace of souls is, in a great degree, obscured; the spiritual life of nature, we might say, in accordance with Mark iv. 27.

Thus, too, the *third part of the stars* is smitten; in spite of all the advances of astronomy, the joyous upward gaze of immortal souls into the heavenly home of the eternal Father-house (John xiv. 2) declines with many even to utter extinction. And it is in perfect accordance with the laws of polarity, that, together with the true day-life of the spirit, the true night-life of the heart, especially in the intercourse of spirits, has suffered great loss.

By this great spiritual obscuration of sun, moon and stars—an obscuration which, though on the one hand partial, is, on the other hand, lasting—preparation is made for the first of the three great woes. This woe, together with its successors, is heralded by an *eagle* which John sees and hears, by reason of the rustling of his wings, flying through the lofty midst of Heaven; an eagle proclaiming with a mighty voice a *three-fold woe* upon the inhabitants of the earth —a woe coming with the last three Trumpets. As the *horse* denotes regular rapid historic motion, so the *eagle* is indicative of a vehement and mighty movement toward a great catastrophe. This eagle flies along the meridian altitude of Heaven, thus being visible down to the very horizon, besides being able to descry the coming woes with his piercing glance, and to make himself heard by all with his mighty voice. Thus the eagle is indicative of the lofty and rapid flight of the seer-spirit over the earth, with its sharp outlook upon the catastrophes of the last times. It is the very genius of Apocalyptics, the eagle of John. That it does not denote the final judgments themselves (as Hengstenberg

maintains), is evident from the fact, that it distinguishes them from itself as the three woful times of the future. In spite of its lofty eagle nature, it seems to suffer in human sympathy with the inhabitants of the earth, upon whom the judgments are coming.

Thus the way is prepared for the

Fifth Trumpet-blast.

Again a *star* falls from Heaven upon the earth, or, rather, it has already fallen when John sees it. If the previous falling star was the genius of all carnal levity, it is followed quite naturally by the genius of demonic gloom, the second Janus-face of the more general spiritual corruptions in Christian and, especially, modern times. This star receives the *key* to the *pit of the abyss*. The abyss is, undoubtedly, not equivalent to Sheol, or the realm of the dead, in the general sense of that term; but neither is it the same as Gehenna, in the full sense of that word is identical with the lake of fire. It is the hell-like or demonic region of the realm of disembodied and unembodied spirits—a region of torment, bounded on the one side by the brighter portion of Sheol and on the other by Gehenna (the remarks on p. 30 must be modified by the present comments; see p. 35). [See Excursus on Hades, p. 364 sqq.—E. R. C.]

It is declared, ch. xvii. 8, that the *Beast* ascends out of the abyss and goes into ἀπώλεια; ch. xx. 3, *Satan* is cast into the abyss; after the final revolt, however, he also is cast into the *lake of fire*, to which the Beast and the false Prophet have previously been banished. In the present passage, mention is made of the same demon-region which, 2 Pet. ii. 4, is, through the medium of a verb, indirectly designated as Tartarus.

The *pit of the abyss* is manifestly the connecting channel by means of which the region of tormenting demons holds communication with the earth and with human life. It corresponds with the partial closure of Heaven. Not all of Heaven is closed; not all of the abyss is let loose upon the human world, but the connecting channel between earth and the abyss is now, in a mode entirely new, thrown open. As the revelation of Heaven, on its side, extends into the human world of spirit, so it is also with the pit of the abyss: it is opened in the demonic depths of the human psychical life itself through a demonic sympathy with the spirits of the abyss.

The genius of a God-estranged gloom is the *star* that opens the pit; the *key* in his hand is hopelessness, the more general form of despair. As the opening of the gloomy demonic death-realm below began with the darkening of the Gospel above, it is not in the modern world alone that a spirit of gloom has pressed into the Christian world. Rather, the origin of the sombre abysmal moods in Christendom is to be found in the land of the *cultus* of the dead, the *cultus* of graves—in Egypt. Again, during the whole of the Middle Ages we must distinguish between the *monk's garb*, assumed by all Christian confederations, and the specific *spirit of monkery* in its dark form. In the course of time the latter has continually been assuming darker and darker forms, until in the modern world it touches its other and worldly extreme.

Substantially, however, the two extremes of gloom amount to about the same thing; they are connected in a decided estrangement from the Gospel, from inwardness, as well as in a fanatical racing and chasing, and in absolute fancifulness, whether in a religious or an irreligious garb.

The first result of the opening of the pit of the abyss is the thick-rising *smoke*—spiritual derangement exhibiting itself in a gloomy play of the fancy, darkening more than ever the *sun* of truth and consciousness and the clear *air* of prospect and hope. Then *locusts* break forth out of the smoke;—demonic hobgoblin forms, not eating grass, as do *locusts*, but, like *scorpions*, stinging men. They have no power over the objective region of genuine spiritual life—over the grass of the soul's pasture, the verdure of new life, the trees of God by the rivers of water; their power is over those men who have not the seal of God on their foreheads. It is, therefore, manifest that good men, awakened men, well-meaning men, in a more general sense, may be exposed to them. Even those men, however, whom they successfully attack, they cannot directly kill; they have power only to *torment* them *five months, i. e.*, to rob them of spiritual liberty, indicated by the numeral *five*, through a series of minor changes of time or of the moon. And in those days—those gloomy days of ancient and, especially, modern despair—*men shall seek death and not find it; death shall even seem to flee before them.* This does not exclude individual suicides on the extreme of these self-tormentings; in general, however, these gloomy soul-moods are below the level of the feeling of, and pleasure in, life. And what an array of phantoms, or mere semblances full of contradictions, do these tormenting spirits of modern soul-suffering constitute! The description of the text very significantly proclaims them to be nothing but fantastical and airy visions (see p. 22).

The phantasmagoria image forth, as *war-horses*, strong and passionate moods; they transform themselves into *heads*, wearing superb and kingly *crowns*, radiant with the semblance of *gold*; then they put on a *humane face*, as of man, and even assume a sentimentally soft deportment, indicated by the *hair as of women*, whilst yet they bite as though they had *lions' teeth*. But above all, they love to disguise themselves as grand warlike phantoms; they appear in breast-plated war-hosts; their wings thunder like war-chariots charging to the battle; and with their fanciful terrors they change the world of Christian brotherhood more and more into a grand complex of camps. The venomous sting of these locusts is in their *tails*, which are like the tails of scorpions, the emblems of the evil spirit. Thus, too, the still worse power of the monsters of the *sixth* Trumpet lies not only in their *mouths*, but also in their *tails*. The meaning of this fact is, doubtless, that their effects increase and intensify toward the end; they make themselves felt particularly in the pains and painful consequences of party-trains. Their power is limited, however, and the Seer

again brings into view its terminus, *five months*.

These demons of torment are, moreover, not isolated apparitions; they form a mysterious complex, a unity wherein, on the one hand, their fearful power lies, and, on the other, its limitation is contained. As Hades constitutes a unitous realm of the dead, governed by Death personified; and as the kingdom of evil, as beyond this life, is concentrated in Satan, whose manifest organ in this world is Antichrist, so, in the midst between Hades and the domain of Satan, the Abyss lies; this also is under the rule of a *king*, called, in Hebrew, *Abaddon*, and in Greek, *Apollyon*—the destroyer, waster. This king, in accordance with the distinct region and operation belonging to him, is the genius of despair, which must be regarded as specific destituteness of good or salvation, specific destruction. The two names doubtless signify, likewise, that the Hebrew form of his spoiling of souls is different from the Greek form; in the one case, he is wont to appear in the form of demonic possession; in the other, in that of melancholy madness. In view of all this, however, this whole terrible sphere of psychical torments must be clearly distinguished from the ethico-demonic plagues appearing at the sound of the *sixth* Trumpet.

This one woe passes; but it is the forerunner of two others which are still worse.

Sixth Trumpet-blast.

On account of the importance of what follows, this trumpet-blast is supplemented by a *voice*. The voice issues from the *horns of the golden altar*. Horns are symbols of protective power; the horns of the *altar of incense*, therefore, are significant of the perfect security of that spiritual life which proceeds from a life of prayer perfected in Heaven. In this sense the voice cries: Let loose! the Church is armed. Thus Christ Himself says: "It must needs be that offences come, but *woe*," etc. (Matt. xviii. 7; comp. 1 Cor. xi. 19). The following treats, doubtless, of offences in the strictest sense of the term—*tares* (see Matt. xiii. 88, 39). *Loose the four Angels by the great river Euphrates.*

With a grand assurance of victory, the vision brings out two fundamental features in the infliction of religious-ethical offences upon the earth. They appear at the start as *four bound Angels.* As emphatically as they, as offences, belong to the kingdom of darkness and are representative, in respect of the numeral *four*, of the spirit of the world (like the *four beasts* of Dan. vii.)—just so certain is it that they are *bound* by God's providence, and are unable prematurely to break forth to destroy His souls, and that, under angelic power, under the power of the four Angels who, according to ch. vii., hold them bound, they must, as dispensations of God, themselves go forth for judgment, when the time comes, as His messengers. In respect of their inmost essence, they may be representative of four fundamental forms of the Satanic essence and worldliness; they are, however, fundamental forms disguised as angels of light (2 Cor. xi. 14; 2 Thess. ii). Thus all heresies, at their first appearance, claim to be truths in a higher form of knowledge, and also operate as powerful lies through the admixture of elements of truth. Schleiermacher, perchance, might have found his four ground-forms of heresy symbolized here, had he properly appreciated the Apocalyptic style.

Again, though these offences seek to press forth in their quiet preparedness, they are conditioned by their Divinely ordained time as to hour, day. month and year; as to the *hours* of decisive conflict, the *days* of their apparent victory, the *moons* of their periodic change, and the *years* of their collective domination. As it is their natural tendency to kill men (John viii. 44), such is likewise their mission, inasmuch as they are instruments of judgment. Their *murders*, however, are spiritual murders; they deprive the third part of mankind of their spiritual life and prosperity.

After the portrayal of their peculiar essence, these fundamental forms vanish behind the prodigious train of horsemen forming their concrete appearance. What Bürger said of the dead [in the ballad of *Lenore*] is true also of erring spirits: they ride, and ride fast. One would think that a *myriad* might have been enough; but as a curse generates a curse, so the erring spirits is productive of more of its kind, even to *myriads of myriads*. The circumstance that the enormous number is twice given, may have its foundation in the fact that errors are divided into positive and negative ground-forms or extremes.

The concrete numeric form employed by the Seer does not, therefore, gain by its resolution into two hundred millions. The Seer heard their number and could never forget it in its importance.

In these images of *cavalry* the *horses* themselves are the main thing. In ch. vi. the horses are but the bearers, in symbolical colors, of the acting riders; here, on the contrary, only the horses seem to be actually operative; the riders work merely as weak directors of the movements of their steeds and by their symbolical *breast-plates* and *colors*. Is the intimation intended that these *riders*, heretics, are, in many respects, not so bad as their *horses*, death-breathing heresies? Or is it suggested that the horses ordinarily run away with them; that they speedily lose control over the movements originated by themselves? Possibly both thoughts are intimated. At all events, they all, without exception, are strongly mailed against the darts of truth, of sincerity and soberness of spirit, for fanatics are chips of one block, though not in a predestinarian sense; there is among them a good deal of talent, ambition, ardor and a strong impulse of self-consciousness; but little genius, soul, piety and reverence. The *colors* of their breast-plates correspond with the fatal operations of their horses. The *fire* of fanaticism, so prone to be mingled with blood; the *smoke* of gloomy and confused mental disorders, already resolved into vapor; and the *brimstone* of still unused fuel floating about—how could the fundamental forms of *false-lightism* be more fitly characterized!

Again, the horses have *heads* as the *heads of lions*. Their arrogance, their aggressive ap-

pearance, assumes the semblance of true lion-heartedness, of genuine leonine strength. It is natural that their fatal operations issue from their *mouths*, though these may also, in a figurative sense, work by means of the pen. Besides the power in their mouths, they have power in their *tails*. These *tails* are still worse than those of the locusts of the fifth Seal: they are not like scorpions, but like *serpents*, which, after the manner of serpents, do harm with their heads. It is, perhaps, not out of the way to suppose that the Seer designed giving prominence, along with the direct dogmatic injuries, to the pernicious moral effects of offences or false principles; for thus they have a two-fold mortal agency—through head and tail. It is in the nature of the thing that an inestimable amount of bloodshed follows in the train of spiritual murders.

The Seer finally brings out the melancholy fact with which this cyclical world-picture closes; which is also, be it understood, a characteristic universal picture of the last time. The *rest of the men*, who were not killed by these plagues, are those who have not, through ■ fall into heresies, lost all spiritual life. In this respect, therefore, they offer a contrast to the others; yet even they have not suffered themselves to be roused to repentance. They are divided into two ranks, composed of those who are guilty in a religious point of view pre-eminently, and those whose guilt is pre-eminently moral—both ranks, however, being connected.

The principal offence of the one side is, that they are subject to the *works of their hands*, i. e., thoroughly externalized, sunk in externalisms, of which they do not repent. *Demon-worship*, a subtile service of devils—thus runs the terrible superscription, beneath which a pompous image-worship is set forth—*idolatry* with figures of gold, of silver, of brass, of stone, and of wood. The absolute irrationality of this idolatry is noticed by the Apocalypse as well ■■ by the Old Testament. These idols can neither see, nor hear, nor walk; they are, therefore, less than the beasts.

On the other side, the chief superscription is that of *murder*—something which well corresponds with the service of the Devil: the individual forms—*sorcery, fornication, theft*—are at all events connected with this fundamental form. *Sorcery* [*Magismus*], in its most general import, is the duskiest side of immorality; it has a wide domain, from conscious impieties to ecclesiastical mechanisms. *Fornication* is a chief sin of heathen grossness under the mask of Christian culture. *Theft* understands sublimating itself into the most subtile and underhand forms of swindle and fraud.

We would submit the following general observations:

We have seen that the *Seven Times Seven* which forms the foundation of the Book, stands in a natural sequence. The same remark was applied, in particular, to the *seven Churches*. Again, if we examine the *seven Seals*, we cannot fail to recognize the naturalness of their sequence: war, dearth, all sorts of death, especially pestilence, martyrdom, earthquakes. The same remark holds good, furthermore, in regard to the

Trumpets : 1. Fanaticism ; 2. A fanaticised community-life ; 3. Negative embitterment : 4. Darkening of revelation and of the life of salvation ; 5. Penitential demonic psychical sufferings ; 6. Demonic mental or spiritual disorders, heresies—preparatory to apostasy.

[ABSTRACT OF VIEWS, ETC.]

By the American Editor.

[ELLIOTT regards the Trumpet-septenary as included in the *seventh* Seal, and also this Septenary as chronologically consecutive on that of the six Seals preceding. The Period of the *first six* Trumpets (to the close of the *First Part* of the *Sixth*, ch. ix. 21)* he regards as extending from A. D. 395 to 1453, including "the destruction of the Western Empire by the Goths, and the Eastern Empire by the Saracens and Turks." The *half hour's silence in Heaven* (ch viii. 1) he interprets as "the stillness from storms" in "the aerial firmament ;" *i. e.,* a continuance, for a brief period, of the calm brought to view, ch. vii. 1 ; by the *incense offering* he understands the presentation of the prayers of the *Sealed* before God by Jesus, the great High Priest. The Trumpets he regards as fulfilling the uses of the trumpets under the Levitical law, which uses he represents as two: (1) "as regarded the *Israelites,* to proclaim the epochs of advancing time ;" (2) "during *war-time,* and as regarded *their enemies, . . .* to proclaim war against those enemies as from God Himself (Num. x. 1-10)." The *first four* Trumpets he, in common with other interpreters, regards as intimately connected together ; and he understands by them the four Gothic ravages which ended in the subversion of the Western Empire. He contends that during the period of these ravages the Roman world was, in fact, divided into *three* parts, *viz.* the *Eastern* (Asia Minor, Syria, Arabia, Egypt) ; the *Central* (Mœsia, Greece, Illyricum, Rhœtia) ; the *Western* (Italy, Gaul, Britain, Spain, Northwestern Africa) ; and that the *third* or Western part was destroyed. The *first* Trumpet (ch. viii. 7): (A. D. 400-410) the Era of Alaric and Rhadagaisus. The *second* (vers. 8, 9) : (A. D. 429-477) the Era of Genseric, to whom "was allotted . . . the conquest of the *maritime provinces* of Africa and the islands." The *third* (vers. 10, 11) : (A. D. 450-453) the Era of Attila who, as a "baleful meteor," "moved against the *Western* provinces along the *Upper Danube,* reached and crossed the *Rhine* at Basle, and thence tracing the same great frontier *stream* of the West down to Belgium, made its valley one scene of desolation and woe ;" thence directing his steps to "'the European *fountains of waters*' in the Alpine heights and Alpine valleys of Italy." The *fourth* (ver. 2): (about A. D. 476 or 479) the Era of Odoacer, by whom "the *name* and *office* of *Roman Emperor of the West* was abolished," and "thus of the Roman imperial *Sun,* that *third* which appertained to the *Western* Empire was eclipsed, and shone no more." By the *Angel (Eagle)* flying through mid-heaven (ver. 13), he understands the public "forewarnings of coming woe" that

prevailed throughout the period from the death of Justinian, A. D. 565, to the rise of Mohammed and the Saracens—forewarnings in (1) the warning utterances of eminent fathers of the Church (Sulpitius Severus, Martin of Tours, Jerome, Hesychius, Evagrius, Theodoret, and especially Gregory the Great) ; (2) the generally diffused idea that the end of the world was approaching ; (3) the threatening "outward state and aspect of things." The *fifth* Trumpet (ch. ix. 1-11) : the *Saracenic* woe beginning with the public announcement by Mohammed of his alleged mission, A. D. 512, and extending through one hundred and fifty years (five prophetic months, ver. 5) to A. D. 762, when, in the establishment of Medinat al Salem (City of Peace) as the capital of the Saracenic Empire and the following tranquillity, occurred what Daubuz calls "the *settlement* of the locusts."* The *sixth* Trumpet, Part I. (vers. 13-19) : the *Turkish* woe, extending from January 18th, A. D. 1057, the day on which the Turcomans went forth from Bagdad on their career of victory, to the day on which the investiture of Constantinople was completed, to May 16th, A. D. 1453 (*i. e.,* 396 years, 118 days= the prophetic year, month and day, ver. 15).†

BARNES agrees substantially with Elliott as to the periods of the Trumpets, and the nature of the judgments inflicted under them. He differs in certain points of interpretation, as will be seen under EXPLANATIONS IN DETAIL.

WORDSWORTH regards the description of the *seventh* Seal as closing with ch. viii. 1, to be resumed in the glories set forth in chs. xxi., xxii.; and maintains that the Seer then proceeds to portray the Divine judgments, *from the beginning,* on the enemies of the Church, under the Seven Trumpets. The Trumpets are prefaced by the prayers of the Saints (vers. 3, 4), in answer to which the judgments are sent forth (vers. 5, 6). The Trumpets correspond with the woes inflicted upon Egypt (Ex. ix. 23-26), and to the sevenfold encircling of Jericho (Josh. vi. 1-20) ; the first six are *preparatory* denunciations, warning, calling to repentance, and preparing for the *seventh* which will convene all nations to the general judgment. The *first* (ver. 7) is a retributive sequel to the *second* Seal, and represents the woes which fell upon the Roman Empire in the fourth century, when it was smitten by a hail storm from the *North* (the Gothic invasion). The *second* (vers. 8, 9) : the uprooting and destruction of Imperial Rome (which had been as a great Volcano) by the Goths, Vandals and Huns. The *third* (vers. 10, 11) : heretical teachers (represented by the *fallen star*), who embittered the waters of Holy Scripture. (" In the *Seals* heresy is represented as a *trial* of the Church ; in the *Trumpets* it is treated as a *judgment* inflicted on (godless) men for sins.") The *fourth* (ver. 12) : "a prophecy of the great prevalence of errors, defections, apostasies and confusions in *Christendom,* such as abounded in the Seventh Century." The *fifth* (ch. ix. 1-11) : the Mohammedan (Saracenic and Turkish) woe. The *sixth* (vers. 13-21) : "This vision has revealed . . . that the Holy Scriptures (*four-fold*

* [Elliott regards the *Second Part* of the Sixth Trumpet ▓▓ extending through ch. xt. 13.—E. R. C.]

* [To Daubuz, according to Elliott, is due the above explanation of the one hundred and fifty years.—E. R. C.]
† [For particulars, see EXPLANATIONS IN DETAIL.—E. R. C.]

Gospel), though *bound as captives* for a time, would be *loosed* by the command of God, and that they would traverse the world like an innumerable army. And although they are . . . . ministers of salvation unto many, yet the Vision has declared, that the Holy Scriptures would be like instruments of punishment and death to the enemies of God." (!) ALFORD regards the *seventh* Seal as having its completion in ch. viii. 5; the preparation for the Trumpets, however, he looks upon as "evolved out of the opening of the seventh Seal." The first *four* he regards as connected together by "the *kind* of exercise which their agency finds" —"the plagues indicated by them" being "entirely exercised on *natural objects.*" The *fifth* and *sixth* are in like manner connected; the plagues being inflicted on *men*—the former by *pain*, the latter by *death*; the *seventh* forming rather the solemn conclusion to the whole than a distinct judgment of itself. He affirms (1) that the series of visions reaches forward to the time of the end, and (2) that the infliction of the plagues is *general*, no particular city nor people being designated as their object. He assigns no date for the beginning of the Trumpets, and leaves us in doubt as to whether he regarded them as in the process of development or still future.

LORD apparently regards the *seventh* Seal as closing with ch. viii. 5; the *silence* was symbolic of a short period (1) of contemplation, submission and faith amongst Angels and the Redeemed in Heaven, and (2) of quiet on Earth—the period of repose intervening between the close of persecution, A. D. 311, and the commencement, near the close of that year, of the civil wars by which Constantine was elevated to the throne; the *voices*, etc. (ver. 5), symbolize the agitations and revolutions which attended the elevation of Constantine and the subversion of Paganism. His interpretation of the Trumpets is substantially that of Elliott and Barnes.

GLASGOW* represents the *seventh* Seal as comprehending the Trumpets. The period of *silence* he identifies with the seven and a half days from the Ascension to Pentecost, the *smoke of the incense* with the Intercession of Christ, the *fire thrown on the land* with the effusion of the Holy

* [(*The Apocalypse Translated and Expounded:* JAMES GLASGOW, D.D., Irish Gen. Ass. Prof. of Oriental Languages, etc. Edinburgh: 1872.) The Am. Ed. regrets that the above-mentioned valuable Co mentary was not received in the United States until after a large portion of this work w s in print. He subjoins an abstract of Dr. Glasgow's scheme of the Seals. They were all synchronous as to their opening: I. Christ; II. Apostate Judaism; III. Greek and Roman Paganism; IV. Gnosticism; V. Martyrs of the old Economy; VI. General Commotion: the *sun* (the Church) was darkened at the death of Christ, the *moon* (the political government of the Jews) suffered a total eclipse, from which it never emerged, the *stars* (the rulers of the Synagogue) lost their light, the *heaven* (the Jewish Church) passed away, the *mountains* and *islands* (the provincial governors in Judea and those whom they represented) fell, *kings* and *magnates* (the nations they represented) were oppressed with the wrath of God (ch. vii. is not a description of any prophetic times or successive events, but of the condition of the Lord's people worshipping, serving and blessed). VII. As above.

[The important objections to this scheme are, first, that *in fact* it places the events of the *sixth* and *seventh* Seals *before* the others; and, se ondly, that it *reveals* to John as things to "be hereafter" (ch iv. 1) events that had taken place in connection with the Crucifixion, the Ascension and the Pentecostal Effusion of the Spirit.—E. R. C.]

Ghost. The Trumpets he regards as successive: I. The woes ending in the destruction of the Jewish state, one third of the people being destroyed by the Roman army. II. The expatriation of the Jews after the revolt under Barcochba (the mountain burning with the wrath of God cast into the sea of the pagan empire). III. Usurpation of Prelacy. IV. Arianism promoted by Constans and Constantine. V. The Mohammedan woe (Saracens and Turks). VI. The *four bound Angels* are kings, popes, inquisitors, and councils, previously kept in restraint, but who are now loosed to slay *the third part of the men, i. e.* true Christians—the period of persecution beginning A. D. 1123, and extending to the Reformation.—E. R. C.]

EXPLANATIONS IN DETAIL.

Ch. viii. 1. Half an hour.—"The anxious expectancy of the inhabitants of Heaven" (Düsterdieck). Classical, but not Biblical: *Stupor cœlitum* (Eichhorn. Similar interpretations see in Düsterdieck, p. 299). Vitringa: The whole purport of the *seventh* Seal is: *ecclesia in pace!* Similar interpretations see in Düsterdieck, p. 301. Hengstenberg offers a most remarkable interpretation: Silence of Christ's enemies (in Heaven!). We regard Düsterdieck's polemic against the idea that there is a recapitulation in this place also, as utterly wrong; especially do we object to his unconditional rejection of Lyra's interpretation, viz. that nothing but the Church's battle against heretics is depicted, though it is true that this explanation would be applicable only to the sixth Trumpet, if heresies proper were alone involved. The fact that there is a difference between a supposed anxiety in Heaven and a readily intelligible tension of spirit and prayerful mood in the same blessed place needs no further exposition. See the SYNOPTICAL VIEW.

[For different views of the *σιγή* see Add. Note, p. 201 sq. Bishop Newton (after Philo) calls attention to the fact, that "while the *sacrifices* were made (2 Chron. xxix. 25-28), the voices and instruments and trumpets sounded; while the priest went into the Temple to burn incense (Luke i. 10), all were silent, and the people prayed to themselves." (See also 2 Chron. xxix. 29). This silence was, so to speak, *intensified* on the great day of Atonement when, at the offering of the incense and the sacrifice, all save the High Priest withdrew from the Sanctuary (see Levit. xvi. 17; also Kitto's *Cyc.*, Articles ATONEMENT [DAY OF] and INCENSE). It was said to the souls under the altar in answer to their cries (the cries of their blood for vengeance), that they should rest until the full number of martyrs (or the time of martyrdom) had been completed (ch. vi. 9-11). On the completion of the number, or the time (it matters not which, for they would be completed together), the Seer beheld in symbolic vision the offering, by the Great High Priest, of their *prayers* (doubtless inclusive of the cry of the blood of their sacrifice), together with the incense of His own merits before the Throne—it was fitting that during that highest offering every creature sound, even that of praise, should be hushed in Heaven.—E. R. C.]

Ver. 2. And I saw.—This scene, depicted in vers. 2-6, can have taken place only in the pause of the σιγή. Heaven is sunk in prayerful silence; it is also, however, busy preparing to encounter the ill effects of the events which transpire at the blast of the *seven Trumpets*. According to Ebrard, this scene of preparation takes place *after the silence:* according to Düsterdieck, the silence ceases with ver. 5, since there we read of *thunder* and *voices*. (Further on, however, he also makes the σιγή end with ver. 6.) But these latter are but the general consequences of the *sacred fire* cast upon the earth.

The seven Angels who stand [Lange: **stood**] **before God**; not who *stepped* [took their stations] before God (Luther). But neither is the reference to seven Angels who, by preference, stand permanently before God (Düsterdieck; Archangels, De Wette; *the seven Spirits*, Ewald). They are, undoubtedly, the Angels of the seven Trumpets (Ebrard, Hengstenberg), and the article—*the* seven Angels—has reference to the presupposition that these seven stand ready, waiting their Divine commission. With Hengstenberg, the idea of the seven Archangels shifts into that of Angels whose number is modified by that of the Trumpets.

Seven Trumpets.—See above. For an archæological treatise on the Trumpets, see Hengstenberg, p. 432 sqq. [Eng. Trans., p. 395 sqq.].

Ver. 3. Another Angel.—"The *other* Angel, like the one mentioned in ch. vii., is to be regarded as a real Angel," says Düsterdieck. The meaning of this is, that the Apocalypse is not to be treated as a symbolical Book in this passage either. Hengstenberg, also, at first regards the Angel here described as occupying merely the position of a carrier, although he subsequently remarks that he is nothing but a symbolical figure. Manifestly, the former view is in opposition to the text. This Angel ministers at the heavenly altar of incense. For it is to such an altar alone that the present passage refers, as Grotius and others maintain; not to an altar of burnt-offering, as is the opinion of Hofmann and Ebrard.

The question might well be asked: What idea should we connect with a heavenly altar of burnt-offering?* The altar of incense is quite another thing. Comp. Düsterdieck's polemic against Hofmann and Ebrard, p. 305.

The attribute of this Angel is the *golden censer;* by the heavenly *incense* which he burns, the prayers of all the Saints on earth are perfected. This Angel can even pour the holy *altar fire* upon the earth and waken voices, thunders, lightnings and earthquake. Can an *Angel* do all this? Such forced literalism should surely not bear the name of *historical* interpretation. If consistently retained, it would here of necessity lead to the Roman Catholic idea of angelic mediation. The inquiry *is* historical as to who is elsewhere in Scripture to be regarded as the perfecter of earthly petitions, by heavenly intercession or by the heavenly administration of prayer. The result of such inquiry precludes

the possibility of this Angel being taken for any but *Christ*, in accordance with Bede, Böhmer, and many others (1 John ii. 1), or the *Holy Ghost* (Rom. viii. 26). It might, however, also be maintained, that the heavenly perfecting of human prayers is generally represented by a symbolic angelic form (Grotius: *angelus precum ecclesiæ*).

A golden censer.—On λιβανωτός see the lexicons.

There was given unto him much incense. — Much of the spirit of prayer, of heavenly renunciation and heavenly confidence.

[Of what was the *incense* of the Tabernacle symbolic? In seeking an answer to this question, it should be remembered that it was compounded of the most precious spices, that in its normal condition it was *most holy* (Ex. xxx. 34-36), but at the same time inefficacious for its peculiar uses until consumed by fire from the altar of burnt-offering; thus consumed, however, it was that without which the High Priest could not enter the Holy of Holies to offer the blood of the Atonement (Lev. xvi. 12-14), and with which every morning and evening was sanctified (Ex. xxx. 7-9). What *can* it symbolize but the excellencies of the God-man, *most holy* in their normal condition, but made effluent and efficacious for atonement and sanctification only by fire from the Altar of Sacrifice?—E. R. C.]

That he should add it to the prayers.—Ταῖς προσευχαῖς has been differently interpreted to mean: *as* the prayers; *in* the prayers; or *among* them. The attempt has also been made by emendations and constructions to improve the simple sense, that this incense was *intended* for the prayers of the saints, that is, for their heavenly supplementation and perfection (Vitr., Calov. and others).

Upon the golden altar.—This, according to Ebrard, is the altar of incense, whilst, on the other hand, the altar mentioned elsewhere, in vers. 3 and 5, is an altar of burnt-offering. The altar of burnt-offering in ch. vi. 9 should not be cited in support of this view, for that is to be found, in a symbolical sense, on earth. If, however, this description of a golden altar before the Throne be applied to the idea of the Temple, the *golden altar* is the Ark of the Covenant, ch. xi. 19. The *Ark of the Covenant* was really an *altar*, and that the third and holiest; it was also *golden*. According to Lev. xvi. 12— a passage misconstrued by Ebrard, p. 281; see in opposition to him Düsterdieck, p. 305—the offering of incense was, on the great Day of Atonement, made over the Ark of the Covenant in the Holy of holies.*

* [The American Editor is unable to find the slightest foundation for the assertion, that the Ark of the Covenant was an Altar. Most certainly it is not implied in ch. xi. 19; and the *off-ring* of Lev. xvi. 13 was *before* the Lord, and consequently *before* the Ark, which supported the Mercy-seat. That, in the second reference, the ascending cloud of incense *covered* both the Mercy-seat and the Ark, most certainly does not imply that the *offering* was made either upon or over the latter; and also, manifestly, if it implies this in the case of the latter, it must also in that of the former, and so the reference proves not only that the Ark, but that the Mercy-seat was an Altar! It is inconceivable that the Ark should, in the Divine intent, have been an Altar without

Ver. 4. **And the smoke . . . . ascended.**
—EBRARD: "The prayers of the Saints had ascended long before this; but had hitherto not been heard." This relation between earthly prayers and heavenly intercessions, or perfectings, cannot possibly, however, be thus parted into separate times.* The human prayers are, as it were, swallowed up by the smoke of the heavenly incense, whose attributive destination is "to the prayers of the Saints;" in this form, the smoke rises before God—locally speaking, this can mean only: over the Ark of the Covenant. Thus is the perfect acceptability of the prayers expressed. Their acceptance and answering is also, however, symbolically set forth.

Ver. 5. **And the Angel took the censer.**
—He fills it with fire from the altar of incense, and casts the fire upon the earth. Thus, rightly, Düsterdieck. Ebrard, on the other hand, is of opinion, that he must have taken the fire from the altar of burnt-offering, and then have set the censer down upon the altar of incense. Hence the fire, he thinks, is indicative of the flame in which the martyrs were burned, and is to be regarded as a fire of judgment. It is not to be wondered at that Hengstenberg even here finds a close connection between the fire of prayer and the fire of zeal which shall consume the adversaries. According to him, the silence in Heaven itself is but a silence of the annihilated enemies of God upon earth (p. 424 [Eng Trans., p. 392 sq.]). Here, however, we have to do with the heavenly fire of Divine providence, which, having perfected the prayers, is now become a fire of saving grace. By its being cast upon the earth, the earth is rendered capable of bearing the judgments now following; by no means, however, are these voices, thunders, lightnings and earthquake significant of the judgments themselves. Comp. the voices, Matt. iii. 17; xvii. 5; the thunder, John xii. 29; the earthquake, Matt. xxviii. 2; Acts iv. 31; xvi. 26.

[The fire with which the incense was ignited was taken from the altar of burnt-offering (Lev. xvi. 12); it is probable, however, that the coals cast upon the earth were taken from the golden altar, where the incense had been consumed: the fire of sacrifice which made effluent the virtues of Christ for the blessing of His people is poured back on earth for vengeance.† The

following explanation is suggested in Kitto's Cyc. (Art. INCENSE), which is worthy of consideration: "A silver shovel was first filled with live coals (at the altar of burnt offering), and afterwards emptied into a golden one, smaller than the former, so that some of the coals were spilled (Mishna, Tamid, v. 5, Yoma, iv. 4)." It is possible that this Temple custom may have been reproduced in the vision; the preceding explanation, however, seems the more probable. —E. R. C.]

Hengstenberg regards the earthquake as "the presage of imminent great revolutions." But, be it observed, the earthquake was induced by *fire from Heaven,* which can here properly be said only of reformations. [?]

For general observations on the first four Trumpets, see Düsterdieck, p. 308.

Vers. 6, 7.

FIRST TRUMPET.

Ver. 7. **Hail and fire, mingled with blood.**—Comp. Ex. ix. 24; Joel ii. 30. Düst.: "To explain allegorically all that John now sees," i. e. to assume that the Apocalypse is a symbolico-allegorical Book,["is an undertaking, which, there being no ground for it whatever in the text, can lead to nothing but arbitrary guess-work."].* By sticking to the letter of the text, on the other hand, we arrive at the conclusion, that *the third part of the earth* (the *surface* of the earth, with all that is thereon) is burnt up, "and, still more, the *third part of the trees* and *all the grass* upon the whole earth." All the abortive interpretations in the world cannot make us abandon our conviction that the Apocalypse has an allegorical meaning.† Düsterdieck cites Bede: *Pœna gehennæ;* Grotius: *Judæorum obduratio* and *iracundia sanguinaria* (not bad!); Wetstein: *Arma civilia, etc.,* p. 310. Sander, better than many others, interprets the figure as significant of the fire of false devotion, joined with bloodshed, placing the same, however, in the definite period of the

---

any distinct declaration of the fact in the Pentateuch; and not only so, but the supposition is inconsistent with the ideas manifestly attached to both the Ark and the Altar. The former, containing the moral law, was the foundation of the Divine Throne; the latter was the platform of human service.—E. R. C.]

* [Is it not absolutely necessary for us to hypothesize a certain kind of separation? The prayers of saints are always acceptable to God, and are always accepted by Him, through the merits of Christ; but, though accepted, they are not always efficacious for the *immediate* procurement of the results asked for, even where the bestowment of those results is in the Divine purpose. For ages the entire Church Militant upon the earth have, day by day, offered the prayer for the complete establishment of the Kingdom of Righteousness, and yet the bestowment of the object of that prayer has been deferred (comp. ch. vi. 10, 11). These prayers have, in a sense, so to speak, been gathered up by Jesus, and in due time they will be urged before the Throne with the incense of His intercession, and the answer will be bestowed. —E. R. C.]

† [Barnes is of opinion that, "by casting the *censer* upon the earth," "it is designed to show that, notwithstanding

the prayer that would be offered, great and fearful calamities would come upon the earth, . . . *as if* the prayers were not heard any longer, or as if prayer were now in vain."— E. R. C.]

* [The portion within the brackets is supplied from Düsterdieck, Lange having ended the quotation with an "*etc.*" before his own comment.—E. R. C.]

† [The question is not whether the Apocalypse has an allegorical meaning—that is admitted by all—but as to whether *everything* in it is always allegorical, or rather *mediately* symbolical. This, it would seem, our Author himself does not always claim; for he admits, and must admit, that sometimes when Heaven and Earth and Angels are mentioned, the *real* Heaven and Earth and *real* Angels are intended, and that always when God is spoken of, the Divine Being is designated. Indeed, it seems scarcely possible to construct an allegory in which some portion of the figures will not be *natural;* and most certainly the union of the Natural with the Symbolic appears everywhere else throughout the prophetic Scriptures. The following examples are taken from an excellent article on this subject by Elliott (*Hor. Apoc.* Vol. I., p. 357 sqq.): Ezek. xxvii. 26. "In this passage Tyre is symbolized as a ship, and Nebuchadnezzar as the destroying wind that shipwrecked it; yet the chorographic phrase: *in the midst of the seas,* designates the literal locality of the situation of Tyre, and the '*East,*' that of the kingdom of Nebuchadnezzar with respect to it." Ps. lxxx. 8, 11: "Thou hast brought a *vine* out of *Egypt.* . . . It sent out its boughs into the *sea,* and its branches unto the *river.*" Here, "though the *vine* is symbolic, yet the *Egypt, sea* (Mediterranean), and *river* (Euphrates) are all notoriously literal." See also Ezek. xxxii. 2-16; Jer. iii. 6; Is. lvii. 5, *etc.*—E. R. C.]

time succeeding Constantine. The *Kreuzritter* thinks the migration of nations is referred to. Paulus believes that a great scarcity and famine is intended (the soil and vegetation being particularly involved in the dispensation). Gärtner thinks there is a reference to Arianism.

[By this Trumpet, Elliott and Barnes understand the desolation of the Western Empire by the Goths under Alaric and Rhadagasius (see p. 201; where also Elliott's exposition of "the third part" may be found). These commentators regard their hypothesis as confirmed by the fact, that the nature of one of the elements of the plague (*hail*) indicates it as coming from the North, and the further fact that it was upon "*the land*" indicates that it was to fall on the continental provinces. Both these conditions were fulfilled in the invasion contemplated. Bishop Newton, who previously presented this view, farther supports it by the following extract from Philostorgius, a historian who wrote in this period: "The sword of the barbarians destroyed the greatest multitude of men; and among other calamities, dry heats with flashes of flame and whirlwinds of fire occasioned various and intolerable terrors; yea, and hail greater than could be held in a man's hand fell down in several places, weighing as much as eight pounds (*Hist. Ecc.* l. ii. ch. 7)." He also quotes from Claudian, who, in his poem on this very war, (*De Bello Getico*, ver. 173), compares the invaders to a *storm of hail.—E. R. C.*]

Vers. 8, 9.

SECOND TRUMPET.

See Jer. li. 25; Ex. vii. 20.

"The text," remarks Düsterdieck, "contains nothing of an allegorical nature." And this though the literal apprehension admits of positively no well-founded conception. The above-cited commentator quotes, in illustration of the allegorical interpretation, Bede: *Diabolus, etc.*, *in mare sæculi missus est;* Grotius: The mountain is the *arx Antonia* in Jerusalem; Hengstenberg, who, he says, "entertains, in general, the view, that all the Trumpet-visions except the last are representative of the same thing, viz. war;" Ebrard: The volcanic, Titanic energy of egoism, *etc.* Ebrard likewise supposes that the *mountain* is a volcano (like the Throne of God, ch. iv.), which, by reason of its inward raging violence, plunges into the sea (ἐβλήθη is subversive of this view). Düsterdieck believes the ὡς to be indicative of the fact, that only a mass of fire resembling a great mountain is intended. But since the *mountain* is always significant of a fixed and permanent order of things. ὡς merely denotes that this mountain lacks the reality of the spiritual mountain nature. The same truth is involved in the fact, that the mountain is *on fire*, and that hence, to counteract its conflagration, it is thrown into the sea. Christian history is acquainted with many such burning mountains, which, by reason of fanaticism, have incurred judgment—beginning with the destruction of Jerusalem, the fall of Judaism, the casting of which into the sea of nations resulted in a considerable empoisonment of national life. Similarly, not only have states sub-

sequently fallen—as, for instance, the Eastern Roman Empire—but also a series of dynasties, being become a prey to fanaticism, have been hurled from their proud eminence. Sander holds that the Arian controversies are here predicted. The *Kreuzritter* regards the passage as expressive of the maritime supremacy of the Roman Empire; while Gärtner maintains that the erroneous doctrines of the Orient, and Islam, *etc.*, are denoted. In short, every variety of arbitrary interpretation attaches to the passage. [For other views, see on p. 201 sqq.— E. R. C.] *

Vers. 10, 11.

THIRD TRUMPET.

Ver. 10. There fell a great star from the Heaven —The literal apprehension brings with it such queries as these: whether the *star* itself were devoted to perdition, or whether perdition consisted but in the falling of the star; how one star could fall upon so many streams and springs; and how it is that *wormwood*, which is not a deadly poison, can here have such bitter effects. Düsterdieck remarks, à *propos* of the last question, that *natural* wormwood is not meant here, immediately breaking out again into a polemic against allegorizing expositors, *i. e.*, expositors of allegories.

We cannot deny that the most aimless and arbitrary play of interpretation again meets us at this passage. Pelagius, Arius (H. W. Rinck thinks Arius is here intended—a view which is also held by Renan, Strauss, Schenkel and their associates), Romulus Augustulus and Gregory the Great file past us in accordance with more ancient conceptions of the *great star*, whilst the synchrono-historical interpretation advances the Jewish fanatic Eleazar (Düsterdieck, p. 313). According to Ebrard, the star is, "as it were, the natural spirit of bitterness, the power of bitterness or embitterment, sent down by God in visible concentration, so to speak, as a judgment upon the earth." Sander construes the star as false asceticism, monkish morality, constantly developing after Constantine's time. According to Paulus, apostasy is intended. According to Gärtner, "the adulterations of doctrine by the Romish bishops and priests" (thus the *Kreuzritter*).

Even the *external* form of the star has been the subject of a superfluity of conflicting conjectures: it has been represented as a shooting-star of great magnitude (Züllig, Ewald); a comet (Wetstein); a "great star" in the literal sense of the words (Düsterdieck). On the *import* of the star see Dan. xii. 3; Jude 13. On the *fountains* see Prov. xiii. 14; xiv. 27; xviii.

---

* [Elliott and Barnes suppose that this plague relates to the ravages of the Vandals under Genseric. The latter thus writes: "The symbol of a blazing or burning mountain, torn from its foundation and precipitated into the ocean, would well represent this mighty nation moved from its ancient seat and borne along toward the *maritime* parts of the Empire." The former confines the conquest to "the *maritime provinces* of Africa and the *islands*—all, in short, that belonged to the Western Empire in the Mediterranean. Both refer largely to Gibbon and other historians to show that the Vandals were principally a *naval* power, and that their ravages were confined to the maritime provinces and islands of the Mediterranean, and to the destruction of the fleets of the Empire. two of which were completely destroyed. —E. R. C.]

4; xxv. 26. On the *rivers* see 2 Kings v. 12;
Isa. viii. 6; Ezek. xlvii. 1. [See also pp. 201 sq.
—E. R. C.]*

Ver. 12.

FOURTH TRUMPET.

The third part of the sun —It is necessary here to lay special stress upon the fact,
that in treating of the Trumpets we have to do
with spiritual affairs—not with natural phenomena. It is, therefore, somewhat superfluous
to ask whether a *natural percussio* of the sun
(after the Rabbins) or a *supernatural* one (in accordance with Wolf) be meant; whether a *temporal* third of the luminary (in accordance with
Ebrard) or a *local* third (in accordance with
Düsterdieck) be intended.

These ideas, since they have no symbolic
significance, are not to be pressed; the idea,
however, that the *third part* of the *brightness* of the luminary is smitten or done
away with (according to Bengel, Böhmer and
others) is, as we think, the true one. This is
to be understood, in the first place, as touching
the *effect* of the luminary, and it must be limited
to its *general* effect in time; it should not be
taken as an effect prejudicial to every individual
Christian. Thus, when the *third part* of the
sunshine is extinguished, this fact corresponds
with the loss of the third part of the capacity
of the human spiritual vision for taking in the
sunlight—the third part of man's love and kinship to spiritual sunlight. The thing meant is
a more general obscuration of the light of revelation; an obscuration conditioned upon human
guilt and modified by a fraction of the numeral
of spirit. But as amid this obscuration there
are those for whom *all three thirds* of the sun are
smitten—men walking in the darkness of night
—so, on the other hand, there are those who
have the full light of the firmament. The censure which De Wette and Düsterdieck cast upon
the Seer as having "unnaturally" followed out
the uniformity existing between the third of the
luminary and the third of the day or night-time,
rests only upon a prejudice in favor of the sensuous conception of the passage, *i. e.*, upon a failure
to recognize its symbolicalness. Ebrard qualifies his interpretation of the *third* as a *temporal*

---

* [Barnes and Elliott (and historical interpreters generally) understand by the events under this Trumpet the
ravages of the Huns under Attila. A brief abstract of the
views of the former was presented on p. 201. The latter
writes: "It is not a lurid meteor (lurid, pale, ghostly) that
is here referred to, but a bright, intense, blazing star—emblem of fiery energy, of rapidity of movement and execution,
of splendor of appearance—such as a chieftain of high en-
dowments, of impetuousness of character, and of richness of
apparel, would be. In all languages, probably, a meteor
flaming through the sky has been an emblem of some splendid genl s causing or threatening desolation and ruin; of a
warrior who has moved along in a brilliant but destructive
path over the world, and who has been regarded as sent to
execute the vengeance of Heaven." All these points he
finds realized in Attila, whose common appellation is "the
Scourge of God." He finds a further confirmation of his
view in the facts that (1) "the principal operations of Attila
were in the region of the Alps (*the fountains of waters*) and
on the portions of the Empire whence the *rivers* flow down
into Italy;" (2) "at least a *third* part of the Empire was
invaded and desolated by him;" (3) "the meteor seemed to
be *absorbed* in the waters: their power (the Huns') seemed
to be concentrated under Attila, he alone appeared as the
leader of this formidable host; and when he died, all (their)
concentrated power was dissipated." (A full detail of the
career of Attila may be found in Gibbon, chs. xxxiv., xxxv.)
—E. R. C.]

third with the remark: "This is conceivable in
the vision; scarcely so in reality. Here also
therefore, the vision must contain a prophetic
symbol." He adds: "Hengstenberg is, as
usual, ready with his allegorical application of
the vision to anxious and gloomy times of war.
Vitringa, by the *sun*, apprehended the Roman
Emperor; by the *moon*, the Patriarchs [ecclesi-
astical]; by the *stars*, the bishops; by the *whole
vision*, Arianism, together with the migration of
nations, *etc.*" Other interpretations see noted
in Düsterdieck, p. 314: The troubling of the
Church by false brethren, heresy, Islam, political disorders, Goths and Vandals, *etc.* Sander
justly remarks: "No *positive* operation of hostile powers, no distinct and single perverted
tendency is here spoken of; it is something
purely *negative*—a suppression of light, a reces-
sion of truth, subsequent to the operation of
the three perverted tendencies already mentioned" [first three Trumpets]. He thinks
this condition belongs to the time of the Middle
Ages. The *Kreuzritter* makes this Trumpet refer
to the operations of Mohammedanism. Gärtner
finds the *Beast from the abyss* here indicated—the
sovereignty of the people, which is to set up a
false religion. Grüber interprets the *obscuration* as significant of the stoppage of the machine
of state, the disturbance of magistratic affairs.
The reverse of this dismal darkening see in Is.
xxx. 26. The opposite of the latter idea see in
Is. xxiv. 23, and again in Is. xiii. 10. On the
symbolism of the *sun*, Mal. iv. 2. For the figure
of the *moon*, Gen. xxxvii. 9 may not be without
significance. Feminine nature, natural life,
nocturnal consciousness: kindred ideas. The
Kreuzritter applies the *darkening of the moon* to
the darkening of natural wisdom, science, civilization and culture, by Mohammedanism. Düsterdieck thinks the *first four* Trumpets have reference to cosmical foretokens of the end of the
world, in accordance with Matt. xxiv. 29. [See
also pp. 201 sq.—E. R. C.]*

---

* [Barnes and Elliott refer this prophecy to the Era of
Odoacer, by whom the *name* and *office* of the Roman Emperor
of the West were abolished. In support of this view, Barnes
thus writes: "Of the effect of the reign of Odoacer, Mr.
Gibbon remarks: 'In the division and decline of the empire,
the tributary harvests of Egypt and Africa were withdrawn;
the numbers of the inhabitants continually decreased with
the means of subsistence; and the country was exhausted
by the irretrievable losses of war, famine and p stilence.
St. Ambrose has deplored the ruin of a populous district,
which had been once adorned with the flourishing cities of
Bologna, Modena, Regium and Placentia. Pope Gelasius
was a subject of Odoacer; and he affirms, with strong exaggeration, that in Æmilia, Tuscany, and the adjacent provinces, the human species was almost extirpated. *One third*
of those ample estates, to which the ruin of Italy is originally imputed, was extorted for the use of the conquerors'
(ch. xxxvi.). Yet the light was not *wholly* extinct. It was
'a third part' of it which was put out; and it was still
true that some of the forms of the ancient constitution were
observed—that the light still lingered before it wholly passed
away. In the language of another (Elliott, *Hor. Apoc.,* Vol.
I., p. 383 sqq.), 'The authority of the Roman name had not
yet entirely ceased. The Senate of Rome continued to assemble as usual. The consuls were appointed yearly—one
by the Eastern Emperor, one by Italy and Rome. Odoacer
himself governed Italy under a title (that of *Patrician*),
conferred on him by the Eastern Emperor. There was still
a certain, though often faint, recognition of the supreme
imperial authority. The moon and the stars might seem
still to shine in the West, with a dim, reflected light. In
the course of the events, however, which rapidly followed in
the next half century, these too were extinguished. After
above a century and a half of calamities unexampled almost,
as Dr. Robertson most truly represents it, in the History of

Ver. 13.

Ver. 13. **An eagle.**—DE WETTE: "An angel in the form of an eagle." (Thus other commentators.) There is no need arbitrarily to augment the symbolical angelic forms. According to De Wette, μεσουρανἡματι here, as in ch. xiv. 6, means *through the midst of Heaven.* But the passage cited forms part of ■ Heaven-scene, whilst the one which we are now examining occurs in the midst of an Earth-scene. Düsterdieck rejects the opinion set forth by Ewald in his first Comm., *viz.,* that the middle space betwixt the vault of Heaven and the Earth is intended, but seems to think that his [Düsterdieck's] own explanation—through the meridian altitude of Heaven—is identical with that of De Wette. (Of course, Düsterdieck's interpretation must be taken approximatively, the zenith being only a point, affording no space for the flight of an eagle.) [De Wette, it would seem, uses the term "Heaven" in the sense of the place of God's visible presence, whilst Düsterdieck employs the word as significant of the firmament above us.—TR.]

The Three Woes have reference to the subsequent three Trumpets; they are, therefore, entirely new calamities, exceeding the former ones. They come as visitations upon the human race; they are *woes* in the strict sense of the term, however—as bringing destruction—only to the earthly-minded *dwellers upon the Earth.*

Interpretations: EBRARD: "The world has become a putrefying carcase; the *eagle* of judgment flies along, croaking (?) his thrice-uttered *oùai.*" Referring to Matt. xxiv. 28. (Similarly Herder, Böhmer, Volkmar.)

HENGSTENBERG: The *eagle* here forms a contrast to the *dove*, John i. 32. "Whether the *oùai, woe*, is intended to recall the croaking of the *raven*, as Hofmann supposes, we will not undertake to decide."

"According to JOACHIM, the *eagle* is Gregory the Great." The same, then, who, according to another, was represented by the *falling star.*

DE LYRA applied the *eagle* to John; it is certain that it is Johannean, as a symbol of Apocalyptic prophecy. (Similarly the *Kreuzritter*, p. 430.) [See also on pp. 201 sq.—E. R. C.]

Chap. ix. 1.

FIFTH TRUMPET, OR THE FIRST WOE.[*]

Ch. ix. 1. I saw a star fallen from the Heaven to the Earth.—Its fall is done; it

Nations, the statement of Jerome—a statement couched under the very Apocalyptic figure of the text, but prematurely pronounced on the first taking of Rome by Alaric—might be considered at length accomplished: *Clarissimum terrarum lumen extinctum est*—The world's glorious *sun* has been extinguished; or, as the modern poet (Byron, *Childe Harold*, Canto IV.) has expressed it, still under the Apocalyptic imagery:

"She saw her glories star by star expire,"

till not even one star remained to glimmer in the vacant and dark night.'" The passage from Robertson (*Charles V*, pp. 11, 12) is: "If a man were called on to fix upon a period in the history of the world during which the history of the human race was the most calamitous, he would without hesitation name that which elapsed from the death of Theodosius to the establishment of the Lombards in Italy."—ε. R. C.]

* [Elliott and Barnes, in accordance with Bishop Newton and many other historical interpreters, understand by this

has fallen hither from Heaven to judgment, Luke x. 18; Is. xiv. 12. A *star*—therefore not an *Angel* (Eichhorn); either good (Bengel) or bad (Düsterdieck); certainly not the *devil* (Bede, against which view ch. xii. 9 militates). According to Düsterdieck, the ideas of *star* and *Angel* are confluent (Ps. ciii. 21; Jer. xxxiii. 22). Here, however, where distinct symbols or conceptions are treated of, the two forms must be kept separa'e. If we suppose the *locusts* to be phantasies originating in psychical gloom, we may take the *star*, which has fallen from Heaven, to be repentance without faith, or the sorrow of this world—so-called Cain or Judas repentance—or the remorse and penance of religious self-torment, whether clothed in ■ more ancient and mediæval or ■ more modern form. Comp. John xiii. 30; 1 John iii. 21.

Trumpet the woes under the Saracenic invasions. They support this view by considerations such as the following: 1. The admixture of the *human* with the *bestial* (vers. 7, 8) seems to imply, that the agents in this woe were men. 2. It is implied, that they were actuated by a false religion by vers. 1-3, 11. 3. That they were symbolized by *locusts* (ver. 3) indicates (1), that they were from the *Orient*, Arabia especially (see an exceedingly able article by Elliott [*Hor. Apoc.*, Vol. I., pp. 420 sqq.] on "The *Local Appropriateness* of Scripture Symbol"); (2) that they ravaged in numerous and immense armies as succeeding swarms; (3) their destructiveness. 4. The peculiarities of appearance presented vers. 7-10 are strikingly significant of the Saracens: (1) *like unto horses*, they were principally horsemen; (2) *crowns like unto gold*, their peculiar head-dress—*turbans* adorned with gold (Elliott) or yellow (Barnes); (3) *faces like men*, bearded; (4) *hair like women*, they wore their hair (unlike other military nations) long. ("In that most characteristic of Arab poems, *Antar*—a poem composed at the time I speak of—we find the mustache and the beard, the long hair flowing on the shoulders, and the turban also, are specified: i. 340; 'He adjusted himself properly, twirled his *whiskers*, and folded up his hair under his *turban*, drawing it *from off his shoulders:*' i. 169; 'His hair *flowed down his shoulders:*' iii. 117; 'Antar cut off Maadi's *hair* in revenge:' ii. 325; 'We will hang him up by his *hair:*' ii. 4; 'Thou *foul-mustachioed* wretch!'" Elliott); (5) *teeth like lions*, their ferocity; (6) *breastplates as of iron*, "Sale's *Koran* ii. 104, 'God hath given you coats *of mail* to defend you in your wars'" (Elliott). 5. The addition of the *scorpion* (also pointing to the Orient) *sting*, ver. 10, indicates (1) that their agency was to be on *men*, and not as the simple locust figure would have indicated, on *vegetation*, ver. 4. (It was the command of the Caliph Aboubeker, the father-in-law and successor of Mohammed, in accordance with the spirit of the Koran, issued to the Saracens on the invasion of Syria, "Destroy no palm trees, nor burn any fields of corn; cut down no fruit trees, nor do any mischief to cattle, only such as you kill to eat." *Gibbon*, ch. li.); (2) that it was to be ■ *tormenting*, not an utterly destructive, agency, ver. 5 (the sting of the *scorpion* is exceedingly *painful*, but not ordinarily *fatal*, see Books of Travel generally. In reference to the nature of this woe, as thus appropriately symbolized, the following is extracted from Barnes):

[" As applicable to the conflic's of the Saracens with Christians (Christendom, the external Church), the meaning here would seem to be, that the power conc ded to those who are represented by the locusts was not to cut off and to destroy the Church; but it was to bring upon it various calamities to continue for a definite period. . . . In respect to this, some remarkable facts have occurred in history. The followers of the False Prophet contemplated the subjugation of Europe and the destruction of Christianity from two quarters—the East and the West—expecting to make ■ junction of the two armies in the North of Italy, and to march down to Rome. Twice did they attack the *vital* part of Christendom by besieging Constantinople; first, in the seven years' siege, which lasted from A. D. 668 to A. D. 675, and secondly, in the years 716-718, when Leo the Isaurian was on the imperial throne. But on both occasions, they were obliged to retire defeated and disgraced. Gibbon, iii. 461 seq. Again, they renewed their attack on the West. Having conquered Northern Africa, and Portugal, and extended their conquests as far as the Loire. At that time they designed to subdue France, and having united with the forces which they expected from the East, they intended to make ■ descent on Italy, and complete the conquest of Europe. This

To him was given, *etc.*—It is the *key* of the pit of the Abyss, and is given 'him only after his fall. Repentance was in Heaven at first, but, through want of submission, fell to Earth, a *fallen star*, receiving now the melancholy ability to open the pit of the Abyss, the demonic domain of the lower realm of the dead. On the Abyss, comp. the *Lexicons*. The pit, φρέαρ, denotes the mouth of the Abyss ; the mouth being significant of the close connection and readily opened communication between human psychical life and the demonic domain.

Different interpretations of the *star* see in De Wette, p. 102 :—(Lyra) : Valens ; (Grotius) : Eleazar ; (Herder) : Menahem, the son of Judas. The Abyss : the fortress Masada. Abaddon : Simon, the son of Gorion. A singular interpretation is given by Alcasar : the Mosaic Law.

According to Hengstenberg, the *star* is an ideal person, a line of rulers, the last and grandest form being Napoleon. Sander : Mohammed and his Islam. Gärtner : Arius. The *Kreuzritter* : The hierarch ; he regards the *ascending smoke* as enthusiasm and fanaticism.

[Barnes (on ch. viii. 10) : "A *star* is a natural emblem of a prince, of a ruler, of one distinguished by rank or by talent. See Num. xxiv. 17 and Isa. xiv. 12. A star falling from Heaven would be a natural symbol of one who had left a higher station, or of one whose character and course would be like a meteor shooting through the sky." And *in loc.:* "This denotes **a** leader, a military chieftain, **a** warrior. In the fulfillment of this, we look for the appearance of some mighty prince and warrior, to whom is given some power, as it were, to open the bottomless pit, and to summon forth its legions."

[Alford : "The reader will at once think on Isa. xiv. 12 : 'How art thou fallen from Heaven,

purpose was defeated by the valor of Charles Martel, and Europe and the Christian world were saved from subjugation. Gibbon iii. 4 seq. 'A victorious line of march,' says Mr. Gibbon, 'had been prolonged above a thousand miles, from the rock of Gibraltar to the mouth of the Loire; the repetition of an equal space would have carried the Saracens to the confines of Poland and the highlands of Scotland. The Rhine is not more impassable than the Nile or the Euphrates, and the Arabian fleet might have sailed without a naval combat into the mouth of the Thames. Perhaps the interpretation of the Koran would now be taught in the schools of Oxford, and her pulpits might demonstrate to a circumcised people the sanctity and truth of the revelations of Mahomet. The arrest of the Saracen hosts before Europe was subdued, was what there was no reason to anticipate, and it even yet perplexes historians to be able to account for it. 'The calm historian,' says Mr. Gibbon, 'who strives to follow the rapid course of the Saracens, must study to explain by what means the church and state were saved from this impending, and, as it should seem, inevitable danger.' 'These conquests,' says Mr. Hallam, ' which astonish the careless and superficial, are less perplexing to a calm inquirer than their cessation—the loss of half the Roman empire than the preservation of the rest' (*Middle Ages* ii. 3, 169). These illustrations may serve to explain the meaning of the symbol—that their **g** and commission was not to annihilate or root out, but to annoy and afflict. Indeed, they did not go forth with a primary design to *destroy*. The announcement of the Mussulman always was, 'the Koran, the tribute, or the sword,' and when there was submission, either by embracing his religion or by tribute, life was always spared. 'The fair option of friendship, or submission, or battle,' says Mr. Gibbon (iii. 387), ' was proposed to the enemies of Mahomet.' Comp. also vol. iii. 453, 456."

[6. The length of the woe, *five months*, *i. e.* the prophetic calendar) *one hundred and fifty years*—the precise length of the Saracenic invasion (see abstract of Elliott on p. 201; and also the Note on *Prophetic Days*, p. 260.—E. R. C.]

O Lucifer, son of the morning!' And on Luke x. 18: 'I beheld Satan as lightning fall from Heaven.' And doubtless as the personal import of the *star* is made clear in the following words, such is the reference here. We may also notice that this expression forms a connecting link to another place, ch. xii. 9, in this Book, where Satan is represented as cast out of Heaven to the Earth. . . . It is hardly possible, with Andr. Ribera, Bengel and De W., to understand a *good Angel* by this fallen star." Elliott agrees with Alford in regarding his star, whom he looks upon as the inspirer of Mohammed. (For other views see on pp. 201 sq.)—E. R. C.]

Ver. 2. And he opened the pit of the abyss.—The **smoke**. The region of the evil conscience in the realm of the dead is a region of self-burning, like Gehenna, whence the smoke of torment ascends. The Seer knows of a retroaction of the gloomy feelings of this region on the Earth, the more since this region is even to be found in the back-ground of an unfree human soul-life in this world. Hence there results **a** *great darkening* of the sun and air.

Ver. 3. Locusts.—Old Testament types, Ex. x. 12–15; Joel i. and ii. In antithesis to natural locusts, which desolate vegetation, these locusts leave unharmed all *green things*, attacking solely *those men who have not the seal of God.*

The scorpions of the earth.— (Of the *earth;* De Wette : in antithesis to the *abyss.*) See the article *Scorpion* in Winer, particularly the distinction between the Oriental and the Italian species.

Interpretation of the *locusts:* Longobards, Vandals, Goths, Persians, Mohammedans, Jewish zealots. Bede and others: The raging of heretics. The Pope and the monks: or, Luther and the Protestants (ancient Protestant exposition—in opposition to Bellarmin and others), *etc.* Hengstenberg: Martial hosts, see Düsterdieck, p. 328. "He who, like Hebert (*Die zweite sichtbare Zukunft Christi*, Erlangen, 1850), looks for the literal fulfillment of all these visions, expecting, for instance, the actual appearance of the *locusts* described in ver. 1 sqq.,* certainly does more justice to the text than any allegorist ; by reason of a mechanical conception of inspiration and prophecy, however, he fails to recognize the distinction betwixt real prophetic matter and poetic forms" (Düsterdieck). Remarkable words, if we consider that by allegorists are understood such as regard the Apocalypse as a Book of allegoric figurative forms.

Ver. 5. Not kill them, but that they shall be tormented [Lange: torment **them**].—This trait is characteristic; it runs through ver. 6: *They shall seek death and not find it.* In itself, this torment is not spiritual death as yet ; it is, however, so great as to make men weary of life.

Five months.—The reference of the *five*

* "The fact that such creatures have never yet been seen should not make us conclude, that they never can or never will come. In the last times many things, till then unheard of, shall come to pass—much hitherto unseen shall greet mortal vision." Thus Hebert. This mode of apprehension, however, has nothing to do with inspiration, as Düsterdieck thinks, but with literal exegesis.

months to the popular idea that locusts are wont to appear during the five months from May onward (Düsterdieck, p. 323 [Alford]), does not preclude the symbolical significancy of the number. Here, too, manifold guesses have been hazarded. See De Wette, p. 102; Düsterdieck, p. 321; Ebrard, p. 294; Sander, p. 70. Vitringa thought he had found the key to the mystery in the following formula: Each day of each month=one year. Bengel defined the month as 15 $\frac{5}{6}$ years. Hengstenberg saw in the number 5, as the number of *incompleteness*, the sign of *half*. Thus: "A long time, but not the longest."

Ver. 6. **Seek death.**—"A terrible counterpart to the ἐπιθυμία of the Apostle, springing from the holiest hope" (Düsterd.).

Vers. 7-10. **Like horses.**—The likening of the *locusts* to *horses* see likewise in Joel i. and ii. **As crowns.**—Ewald: The *antennæ*. Düsterdieck and others: A jagged elevation in the middle of the thorax (?). Hengstenberg: The sovereign people. We must not overlook the fact, that the figures are modelled from the idea, as is often the case in the Gospel parables. **Their faces ▄▄ the faces of men.**—Hengstenberg cuts the knot: "Virtually they really were the faces of men." Undoubtedly if they were troops of cavalry!

Ver. 8. **Hair ▄▄ the hair of women.**—Hengstenberg: Suffering their hair to grow at will, uncut and untended. Ebrard: "Mild and gentle womanly faces." By this he understands, not inaptly, those women whom, as history shows us, the spirits of the abyss employ as tools to decoy many fools. Yet the text does not speak of women's *faces*.

As the teeth of lions.—To terrify—not to bite with. Hence the interpretation of Calov. and others is wrong: The false doctrines and blasphemies with which heretics have rent the orthodox Church. Düsterdieck thinks their *desolating voracity* is symbolized; this quality, however, should not be portrayed here.

Ver. 9. **As iron breastplates.**—Their thoraxes. **The sound of their wings.**—Comp. Joel ii. 5.

Ver. 10. **Tails like scorpions.**—Does this mean that their tails themselves are like scorpions (Bengel and others); or that they, like scorpions, have tails (Düsterdieck)? The analogy of ver. 19 seems to favor the former supposition. But as we must adhere to the general idea of the locusts, the latter view is the more probable.

Ver. 11. **And they have a king over them.**—According to Hengstenberg, this king is identical with the fallen star. And certainly it is impossible not to perceive a close affinity between them. If, however, we regard the fallen star, a faithless remorse and penitential self-torment, as the *beginning* of the plague of locusts, their king surely must be regarded as its *consummation*—the genius of absolute self-torment. This symbolical king must likewise be distinguished from Satan, for whom Grotius and others take him. The comment: An angel who is, in a peculiar manner, the head of the Abyss (Bengel and others) throws no light on the subject.
14

Abaddon.—See the *Lexicons*, article אֲבַדּוֹן. It occupies in the Old Testament the same relation to Sheol as in the writings of the Rabbins to Hell. [See Excursus on Hades, p. 364.—E. R. C.]

Apollyon.—With reference to ἀπόλλεια. John had himself beheld the truest type of the whole locust plague in the development of Judas, in reference to whom it must be said that even suicide is a seeking of death and not finding it. [See Excursus on Hades.—E. R. C.]

Ver. 12. **Behold, there come.**—On the singular, ἔρχεται, see Düsterdieck. De Wette reads ἔρχονται, with Cod. B. and others. The following two woes are, according to the arrangement of the Seer, *intensively* as well as *extensively* greater. The climax, *intensively* viewed, may be stated as follows: Penitential self-torment; the spiritual death of heresy; consummate apostasy. *Extensively* defined: An infliction of torment upon such men as have not the seal of God; an infliction of death upon the third part of men; and, moreover, double hurtfulness; an apparent general fall into destruction by the reception of the mark of the Beast. See ch. xiv. 9-11.

Ver. 13 sqq.

SIXTH TRUMPET, OR THE SECOND WOE.*

In consequence of the omission of the utterances of the seven Thunders, ch. x., the esoteric sketch of the cycle in question is incorporated in the *sixth* Trumpet. *And this makes it possible to regard the sixth Trumpet as a double Trumpet.*

---

* [Elliott and Barnes, in accordance with Bishop Newton and many other distinguished historical interpreters, understand by this Trumpet the Woe of the Turkish invasions (see pp. 201 sq.). The following is an abstract of the alleged parallelism between the prophecy and history, in view of which this view has been adopted and supported. (In the arrangement of the points, the plan of Barnes has been, in great measure, followed.) 1. *The place of departure:* ver. 14 declares this to be the Euphrates; it is a well known fact, that the Turks went forth from this river on their career of conquest. 2. *The four Angels*, ver. 14: Barnes explains this by referring to the fourfold division of the old Turkish Empire, previous to the *outpouring* on the remains of the Roman Empire, into *four* Kingdoms—Persia, Kerman, Syria and Roum (*Gibbon*, ch. lvii.); [Elliott discards this and all similar divisions, and suggests that the *propriety* of the figure as indicating that there would be a *general* outpouring, in correspondence with the *four winds* which are the proverbial representatives of *all* winds, or else (b) as indicating that the *tempest Angels* (ch. vii. 1) *loosed* in the Saracenic woe were subsequently bound at the Euphrates. 3. *The preparation*, ver. 15: the Turkish Empire, having its seat about and to the East of the Euphrates, had long been growing in power and fitness to subdue the Eastern Roman Empire; long before their attack upon the latter, they had become the most powerful nation on the earth (see *Gibbon*, ch. lvii.). 4. *Bound and loosed*, vers. 14, 15: It is a matter of surprise that the powerful Empire which had subdued the East should so long have refrained from moving westward; it would seem as though they had been *restrained* by some superior power. 5. *The material of their armies:* ver. 16 implies that this was *cavalry*, the well known principal element of the Turkish hosts. 6. *Their numbers:* ver. 16, *two myriads of myriads;* the Turkish armies were *immense*. Gibbon says (ch. lvii.): "The *myriads* of Turkish horse overspread a frontier of six hundred miles, *etc.*" (It is probable, if this hypothesis be correct, that the *number* relates to the entire number engaged throughout the period of the invasions.) 7. *The numeration:* by *myriads*, ver. 16: it is one of the peculiarities of the Turks to speak of numbers, not as we do, by *thousands*, but by *tomans* (myriads), "so that it is not without his usual propriety of language that Gibbon speaks (as in the quotation in the preceding division) of 'the *myriads* of Turkish horse'" (Elliott). 8. *Their personal appearance:* ver. 17, "breastplates *fiery, hya-*

It is half the Trumpet of heresies; half the Trumpet of *beginning* apostasy.` Hence the *second woe* is continued through ch. x. to ch. xi. 14. Hence, also, it results that the *second woe* is in two stages. At the end of the first stage, men do not repent of the works of their hands, ch. ix. 20; at the end of the second stage, there is at least a repentance of fear, ch. xi. 13. Still it must be observed that the section consisting of chs. x. and xi. to ver. 14 is representative of an entirely new cycle—a cycle connected with the preceding section only from ch. xi. 7. The connection between the two consists in the fact, that in ch. ix. we have to do with *the spiritual end of the course of the world;* in ch. xi. 7 sqq., with *the spiritual beginning of the end of the world.* Thus at the revelation of the consummate offence, the precursory offences form themselves into a unit. See 2 Thess. ii. 7, 8.

Ver. 13. **A voice from the four horns.**—

Not from God, "behind the altar." The four horns of the altar denote the complete, all-sided protective power of the altar. From the same altar on which they prayers of the saints were perfected (ch. viii. 3-5), the signal that they have been heard goes forth. The earth is now, in its sealed ones, prepared by voices and thunders and lightnings and an earthquake of the spiritual life; the greatest temptations may, therefore, now be let loose. The distinction between these new and great temptations and the foregoing ones is at the same time expressed. That which the voice from the horns of the altar says, is, of course, to be traced back to Divine decision. According to Düsterdieck, the misapplication of the horns to the four Gospels (Zeger and others) may have even occasioned the reading—*four* horns. Nevertheless, *four,* as the number of completeness, is not devoid of significance in a correct apprehension of the passage.

cinthine and *sulphureous;*" Daubuz remarks: "From their first appearance, the Ottomans have affected to wear warlike apparel of *scarlet, blue* and *yellow.*" 9. *The heads of the horses as the heads of lions,* ver. 17; indicative (1) of their strength and fierceness—these were well-known characteristics of the Turkish cavalry; (2) not only of the *characteristics,* but of the *titles* of the *heads* or *leaders;* Gibbon writes (ch. lvii.): "The name of Alp Arslan, the *Valiant Lion,* is expressive of the popular idea of the perfection of man; and the successor of Togrul Bey displayed the fierceness and generosity of the royal animal. He *passed the Euphrates,* and entered Cæsarea, *etc.*" Elliott remarks (vol. i., p. 498): "This kind of title, which reminds one of those of the American Indians, seems to have been common among the Turkmans. So *Kizil-Arslan,* the *Red Lion,* a chief contemporary with Togrul Bey; and again *Kilidge Arslan* (*Noble Lion*) *etc.*;" and again he writes (p. 510): "So Rycaut on *the Turks,* ch. xxi.: 'The Turks compare the Grand Seignor to the *lion,* and other kings to *little dogs.'*" 10. *Out of their mouths, etc.,* ver. 17 Barnes remarks: "This is just such a description as would be given of an army to which the use of gunpowder was known. Looking now upon a body of cavalry in the heat of an engagement, it would seem, if the cause were not known, that the horses belched forth smoke and sulphureous flame;" the use of fire-arms by the Turks in their invasion of the Eastern Empire is one of the established facts of history. 11. *The destructive agency,* ver. 18: Not only did the Turks use *fire-arms,* but to this agency, more than to aught else, was their success due, as appears from the following remarks of Gibbon in reference to the siege of Constantinople, ch. lxviii.: "Among the implements of destruction he (the Turkish Sultan) studied with peculiar care the recent and tremendous discovery of the Latins; and his artillery surpassed whatever had yet appeared in the world. A founder of cannon, a Dane or Hungarian, who had almost starved in the Greek service, deserted to the Moslems, and was liberally entertained by the Turkish Sultan. Mohammed was satisfied with the answer to his first question, which he eagerly pressed on the artist: 'Am I able to cast a cannon capable of throwing a ball or stone of sufficient size to batter the walls of Constantinople? I am not ignorant of their strength; but were they more solid than those of Babylon, I could oppose an engine of superior power: the position and management of that engine must be left to your engineers.' On this assurance, a foundry was established at Adrianople, the metal was prepared, and at the end of three months Urban produced a piece of brass ordnance of stupendous and almost incredible magnitude; a measure of twelve palms is assigned to the bore; and the stone bullet weighed above six hundred pounds. A vacant place before the new palace was chosen for the first experiment; but to prevent the sudden and mischievous effects of astonishment and fear, a proclamation was issued that the cannon would be discharged the ensuing day. The explosion was felt or heard in a circuit of a hundred furlongs; the ball, by the force of gunpowder, was driven about a mile; and on the spot where it fell, it buried itself a fathom deep in the ground. . . . . The same destructive secret had been revealed to the Moslems, by whom it was employed with the superior energy of zeal, riches and despotism. The great cannon of Mohammed has been separately noticed—an important and visible object in the history of the times. But that enormous engine was flanked by two fellows almost of equal magnitude; the long order of the Turkish artillery was pointed against the walls; fourteen batteries thundered

at once on the most accessible places; and of one of these it was ambiguously expressed that it was mounted with one hundred and thirty guns, and that it discharged one hundred and thirty bullets. From the lines, the galleys, and the bridge, the Ottoman artillery thundered on all sides; and the camp and city, the Greeks and the Turks, were involved in a cloud of smoke which could only be dispelled by the final deliverance or destruction of the Roman empire." In view of such historical facts, Elliott remarks: "It was to 'the fire and the smoke and the sulphur.' to the artillery and firearms of Mahomet, that the killing of the third part of men, *i. e.,* the capture of Constantinople, and by consequence the destruction of the Greek empire, was owing." 12. *Power in their tails,* ver. 19: on this Elliott remarks: "A *horse-tail* to denote a ruler! Strange association! Unlikely symbol! Instead of symbolizing authority and rule, the *tail* is in other Scriptures put in direct contrast with the *head,* and made the representative rather of the subjected and the low. Besides which, it is not here the lordly *lion's* tail, but that of the *horse.* Who could ever, *à priori,* have conceived of such an application of it? And yet among the Turks . . . that very association had existence, and still exists to the present day. . . . It is the ensign of *one, two* or *three horse-tails* that marks distinctively the dignity and power of the Turkish Pasha." Barnes remarks: "The image before the mind of John would seem to have been that he saw horses belching out fire and smoke, and—what was equally strange—he saw that their power of spreading desolation was connected with the *tails* of the horses." 13. *The number,* the third part of the men. ver. 18: this Elliott explains as indicating the overthrow of the Eastern, or *one-third* of the entire, Empire. Barnes writes: "No one in reading the accounts of the wars of the Turks, and of the ravages which they have committed, would be likely to feel that this is an exaggeration; it is not necessary to suppose that it is literally accurate." 14. *The time of continuance—a day, hour, month and year,* ver. 15: this period in the prophetic calendar, on the ordinary hypothesis of regarding the prophetic year as consisting of three hundred and sixty days, would equal three hundred and ninety-one years and thirty days. Elliott, however, calls attention to the fact, that the term employed is not the prophetic καιρός, but ἐνιαυτός; he therefore hypothesizes that the Julian year was intended, and thence deduces as the period contemplated, reckoning twelve hours to the prophetic day (comp. John xi. 9), three hundred and ninety-six *years,* one hundred and eighteen *days.* The Turks, according to Abulfeda, went forth from Bagdad on their career of Western conquest on the 10th of *Dzulcaad A. H.* 448, which corresponds with *January 18th, A. D.* 1057; from this to *May* 29th, 1453, the date of the fall of Constantinople, is three hundred and ninety-six *years,* one hundred and thirty days; or counting to May 16th, the day on which the investment was completed, the *fortieth* day of the siege, we have the exact prophetic period. Concerning the *fortieth* day, we have the "unintended expository words of Gibbon): 'After a siege of *forty days,* the fate of Constantinople could be no longer averted.'" 13. *The effect,* vers. 20, 21: It is notorious that, previous to the Turkish woe, nominal Christendom was sunk in a condition of (1) *demon worship* (the invocation of saints), (2) *idolatry* (image worship), (3) *murders* (bloody persecutions), (4) *sorceries* (incantations and pretended miracles), (5) *fornications* (abounding impurities), (6) *thefts* (indulgences, masses, *etc.*); and it is equally notorious that this woe was not followed by general repentance.—E. R. C.]

Other interpretations of the *four horns* see in Düsterdieck, p. 332. How important it is that the trials should not break out before their set time, appears from the fact, that the Angel of the sixth Trumpet may loose the four bound Angels only upon a higher order. The same truth is demonstrated by the co-operation of the sixth Angel. Offences *must* come.

[The following, abridged from Elliott (Vol. I., pp. 481 sqq.), is worthy of consideration: "When a voice of command issued from the Throne, or some divinely commissioned Angel, it was an intimation that it originated from God; but when proceeding from some other local source, it was indicated that the locality whence the voice proceeded was one associated with sin to be punished (comp. Gen. iv. 10; xxxi. 38; Isa. lxvi. 6; Hab. ii. 11; James v. 4). So here, a cry commissioning judgment from the mystic incense Altar indicates that that Altar had been a scene of special sin. But this explanation is only partial. It would seem as if guilt had been contracted in respect of some ritual in which the *horns* of the Altar were concerned. There were *three* such services in the Mosaic ritual. The first two were the *occasional atoning services* for sins of ignorance; the third that of the *Annual Atonement*. In all these cases, some of the blood of the sacrifice was put on the *horns* of the Altar (comp. Ex. xxx. 10; Lev. iv. 3-7, 13-18; xvi. 1-18). It was thus that Hezekiah made atonement for Israel after its apostasy under Ahaz (see 2 Chron. xxix. 20-24). This rite of Atonement having been performed, the promised reconciliation with God followed. From the Temple, and Altar, and each blood-bedewed horn of the altar, a voice, as it were, went forth, not of judgment, but of mercy; instead of summoning destroying armies against Judah from the Euphrates, it staid them (comp. 2 Chron. xxxii. 21; Isa. xxxvii. 33, 34). Thus direct was the contrast between Israel's case under Hezekiah, and that of Christendom as here figured. And now when, after the judgments of successive Trumpets, the Seer heard a voice denouncing judgment yet afresh from the *four horns* of the *golden Altar*, what could he infer but this, that in spite of the previous fearful rebukes of their apostasy, neither the priesthood nor the collective people, at least of this third of Christendom, would have repented. More particularly, as the rite had special reference to the sins connected with the incense Altar itself, it was to be inferred that *those* sins would be persisted in: to wit the abandonment of Christ in His character (1) of the one great propitiatory Atonement, and (2) of the one great Intercessor; and thus the sin would be graven even on *the four horns of the golden Altar*, and their one and common voice, or that of the intercessorial High Priest from the midst of them, would pronounce the fresh decree of judgment: 'Loose the four Angels to slay the third part of men.'"—E.R.C.]

Ver. 14. **Loose the four angels.**—The number *four* being the number of the world, the *four* symbolical *angels* represent the collective spirit of the world, collective heathenism, in its infection of Christianity and transformation of Christian truths into powerful lies, 2 Thess. ii. These angels are, therefore, neither bad angels

(Bede, Düsterdieck and others), nor good ones (Bossuet), nor destroying ones (De Wette. Ebrard), if, by such, *personal* beings are understood. As *symbolic* forms they are, beyond question, *evil* spirits—yet in angelic shape; as it were in the angelic shape of the one Satanic mask of an Angel of light (2 Cor. xi. 14) in four world-forms. Different interpretations of the *quaternary* see in Düsterdieck, p. 333.

At the great river.—We doubt not that the hither bank of the great river Euphrates has an import similar to that of Babylon, yet without coinciding with Babylon. Babylon is a peculiar configuration of the spiritual river Euphrates; that *river*, the general basis and condition of Babylon—*spiritual* Babylon as the sphere of *historical* Babylon.

Different interpretations: Parthian armies against the Romans; Roman armies against Jerusalem; Tartars, Turks (the *Angels* being their commanders). The Euphrates, the Tiber; Babylon, Rome (Wetstein). The Euphrates, the border of Abraham's land, or of the Roman empire.

According to Düsterdieck, the mention of the Euphrates is merely schematical [*schematisch*], as the region whence plagues usually came in the Old Testament—the Assyrians, for instance. Insignificant enough!

Ebrard: "Almost all ancient Protestant exegetes discover in this passage a prediction of Mohammedanism. Grotius, Wetstein, Herder, Eichhorn and others think it prophetic of the army of Titus, which destroyed Jerusalem. De Wette, with Züllig and Ewald, occupies the ground of 'fancy.'"

In opposition to these historical conceptions, a just reference has been made to the supernaturalness of the martial hosts portrayed. Düsterdieck will not listen to any allegorical apprehension of this supernaturalness, and so, according to him, these armies are still more incomprehensible than those of the locusts. According to Gärtner (p. 465), the two hundred millions of horses are two hundred millions of devils—hosts of Satan, amongst whom the fanatical faith of Islam, symbolized, as he contends, by the Euphrates, originates. The horsemen are such men as are borne away by the horses.

Ver. 15. **The four angels were loosed.**—The resistance hitherto made by the power of truth is withdrawn.

Prepared for the hour, *etc.*—Beautifully expressive of the certainty that these trials, like all hateful things in the world, have their appointed time, and that time only, Luke xxii. 53.

To slay the third part of men.—Only spiritual slaying can be meant here, as is further indicated by "the third part," *three* being the number of spirit, ch. viii. 7-12.

Ver. 16. **And the number.**—*Two hundred millions* [*two myriads of myriads*]. He did not himself count the hosts, but heard the number through the voice of prophecy; this fact makes the number more than ever significant. It being impossible to conceive of an army of this size, Bengel has added together all the Turkish armies of more than two centuries; Hengstenberg sees an allegorical collective designation of all armies in the number; whilst Düsterdieck takes it as schematical [*schematisch*]—that is to say, denoting, like the army, nothing definite. But, manifestly, the *number* itself is allegorical. The *myriad* is indicative of an enormous number; the formula, *myriad times myriad*, denotes the infinite productivity of the figures; and, finally, the *binary* is significant of an antithesis, either of positive and negative offences, or of dogmatical and ethical heresies.

Ver. 17. **And thus I saw the horses.**—In the vision, he adds, probably because the monstrosity of their appearance necessitates a slight reminder of the fact that we have here to do with allegorical forms; an assumption which Düsterdieck, in his horror of allegory, endeavors to refute.

And those who sat on them.—The *horses* are of prime importance (see above); their *riders*, however, are first described. In this place the riders bear the colors of the horses, as the horses the colors of the riders in ch. vi.

Having breastplates.—According to Bengel and others, the *riders* are here referred to; according to Düsterdieck and others, the words, *having breastplates*, refer to both *horses* and *riders*. This view is contradicted, in the first place, by the impossibility of putting the idea into execution; and, furthermore, by the antithesis between the colors of the breastplates and the destructive stuff issuing from the mouths of the horses. Many hypotheses have been founded on the *colors* of the breastplates, see Düsterdieck, p. 337. On ὑάκινθος see Ebrard. He conjectures that this color was dark brown; it cannot but be seen, however, that it must correspond with the color of smoke. Düsterdieck would have it that "dark red" is the corresponding color.

As the heads of lions.—Not actual lions' heads. A cruel and terrific aspect cannot be meant by this, according to Düsterdieck, because it " would undoubtedly correspond better with the allegorical exposition."

It is likewise denied that there is an allegorical meaning to **fire, smoke, and brimstone.** The combination is, most certainly, found in volcanos *in natura*. The significance of these forms, however, appears from the following other passages: ch. xiv. 10, 11; xix. 20; xxi. 10. For different interpretations, see Düsterdieck. The view of Calov, who finds the three substances associated in the Koran, is particularly striking. Other singular exegeses are those of Grotius (burning torches), Hengstenberg and Bengel (the murderous spirit and wanton destructiveness of soldiers). It is worthy of note that the same materials which compose the erring spirit of this world, create the hellish torment of the next: the fire of fanaticism; self-dissolution in ambition and self-seeking; demonic irritability—inflammability.

Ver. 19. **For the power of the horses.**— They are hurtful in a two-fold manner; with their *mouths* and with their *snake-like tails.* Their principal power, however, is in their mouths. On the futile application of this double figure to the fable of two-headed serpents or *amphisbænæ* (Wetstein, Beng., Herder), see Düsterd.

Other interpretations: Bengel: Reference is had to the turning of the Turkish cavalry, to the sudden detriment of their pursuers.

Hengstenberg interprets the hurtful power in the tails as significant of the insidious malignity of martial hosts; for fiery wrath, warlike terrors, and the like, pervade the visions of the *fifth* and *sixth* Trumpets particularly, according to him.

Grotius: The tails are indicative of foot soldiers [on the backs of the horses, behind the horsemen].

Sander: They dragged the teachings of their false prophet behind them.

Volkmar has even applied this passage to the kicking out of the horse behind.

The after-effects of all heresies consist in the fact that they poison morals and manners, introducing a destructive element into Christian social life especially, and thus issuing in psychical and physical evils.

Ver. 20. **And the rest of the men, who were not killed by these plagues.**—The Seer distinguishes between the specific destruction of a third of mankind by the fatal horses and the general corrupt condition of the human race. **Repented not.**—Comp. ch. xvi. 11. Their conversion should show itself in a specific abstinence from religious and moral transgressions. The **works of their hands**, therefore, do not directly denote their whole conversation and walk, but those characteristic sins in which, of a truth, their whole walk was reflected. It has been maintained that *idols* are thereby indicated, as their own manufacture (Hengstenberg, Düsterdieck); but the first object—τὰ δαιμόνια—stands in the way of this view. This first object is, indeed, of prime importance to the Seer. The meaning is as follows: subtile demon-worship, symbolized by subtile idol-worship offered to images of the most diverse materials; see 1 Cor. x. 20. **Which neither see,** *etc.*—Compare the analogous passages in the Old Testament [Pss. cxv. 4-7; cxxxv. 15-17; Is. xlvi. 7; Jer. x. 5; Dan. v. 23].

Ver. 21. **Of their sorceries.**—The *poison-mingling,* as the word might likewise be understood, is already contained in the preceding **murders.**

EBRARD: "Sorcery is to be understood as seductive enchantments." The reason alleged in support of this view, *viz.,* that true sorcery is a sin against God, whilst the present passage treats of injuries inflicted by man upon his brother man, is, however, of insufficient weight. All gross (poison-mingling) and all refined sorcery is conjoined with injury to one's neighbor. The terms are, doubtless, symbolical throughout; Gal. v. 20. " It is clear that the author is thinking of heathen." De Wette (similarly Düsterdieck). Truly, the author regards all the things mentioned, even in respect of their most subtile conception, their most subtile manifestation in Christendom, as heathenish.

[ADDITIONAL NOTE ON THE SEVENTH SEAL AND THE TRUMPETS.]

By the American Editor.

[The very position of the *Seventh Seal,* separated as it is from the others by the visions of chap. vii., should lead us to suppose that it is *sui generis;* and a careful consideration of its development supports and enforces this supposition. The most rational hypothesis, as it seems to the Am. Ed., is that it includes the Trumpets and the Vials; there is no strong disjunctive at the beginning of either ver. 2 or 6, such as would certainly have been employed had the Seal closed with ver. 1 or 5, and no such disjunctive occurs until ch. xviii. 1. This hypothesis is not only in accordance with the manifest indications of the phraseology, but it avoids the supposition that a Seal was *opened* without any thing being revealed under it, and it also gives unity to all that follows, and to the whole complex vision.

In the view of the writer, the opening of the first *five* Seals discloses the general course of history to the time of the second Advent—false Christs, war, dearth, aggravated mortality, together with the persecutions of the saints; the opening of the *sixth* reveals the events immediately preceding the Advent (see pp. 178 sq.); the *seventh* is the Seal of Judgment (also terminating in the Advent), in which, under the Symbol of Seven Trumpets (indicating the *going forth* of Jehovah against the enemies of His people, comp. Num. x. 9; xxxi. 6; Josh. vi. 4, 5; 2 Chron. xiii. 14; Jer. li. 27, *etc.*), are revealed the woes to be visited upon the sinful and persecuting world-power;* the last Trumpet develops into the seven Vials.†

That the opening of the Seal was to be *delayed*, is consistent with God's dealings in judgment—sentence against an evil work, ordinarily, is not executed speedily (Ecc. viii. 11); and not only so, but it is intimated, (ch. vi. 10, 11), that there should be delay until a certain *period* (or *number of martyrs*) should be completed.

The *length* of this period of delay being unrevealed, the time of the beginning of the Trumpet-blasts can be determined only by the occurrence. It becomes a most interesting and important question: Have any of these blasts been given, or are they all still future? The writer must acknowledge that, after a careful consideration of the principal views that have been presented, he has been constrained to the conclusion that the scheme of interpretation advocated by Elliott and Barnes is substantially correct (see foot-notes on pp. 205 sqq.). The points of resemblance between the symbols and the events of history, especially as portrayed by the infidel Gibbon, are too many, too striking, and too exact, to allow the thought that they are merely fortuitous. It would seem as though God had raised up the great historian just mentioned to perform a work for the Bible and the Church,

which could not have been so effectually performed by a friend—at times it seems as though he were writing history, purposely for the elucidation of prophecy. The language of Barnes in reference to the correspondence between the events of the *sixth* Seal and the history of the Turkish invasion, as described by him, may be equally applied to the correspondence between the entire series of symbols and his descriptions of all the invasions which historical interpreters have adduced as fulfilling these symbols: "If Mr. Gibbon had *designed* to describe the conquests of the Turks as a fulfilment of the prediction, could he have done it in a style more clear and graphic than that which he has employed? If this had occurred in a *Christian* writer, would it not have been charged on him that he had shaped his facts to meet his notions of the meaning of the prophecy?"

It must be acknowledged that there are difficulties connected with this interpretation; that there are some points where the symbol and the event adduced as realizing it, do not seem exactly to harmonize. It may be remarked that, in view of the imperfection of our records of history, and the partial ignorance of individual interpreters, even of that which is imperfectly recorded, such discrepancies are to be expected—indeed, it is matter of surprise that they are not more numerous and important. In fact, one of the influences that led the writer to adopt, in the main, the scheme of Elliott, was the exhibit of objections by Alford. Thoughts, such as the following, arose in his mind: If these are the only objections that can be adduced by an acute and learned opponent, they are tantamount to an acknowledgment that in the far more numerous and important matters presented in the scheme, there is complete resemblance between the Symbol and the event; and if this be so, either these discrepancies will disappear on a more thorough investigation of our historical records, or else they will serve to show that on the points at issue our records are themselves imperfect. The first of Alford's objections is to Elliott's interpretation of *the third part* (see p. 201). He remarks, "It is fatal to this whole class of interpretations that it is not said: *the hail, etc.*, were *cast on a third part*, but that the destruction occasioned by them *extended to* a third part of the earth on which they were cast. And this is most expressly declared to be so in this first case by *all green* grass being destroyed, not a third part of it" (ch. viii. 7). Now, Elliott's hypothesis concerning the *third part* is deduced from a most careful comparison of ch. viii. 7–12 with the acknowledged facts of history. It is notorious that four successive hordes of enemies did, in the Fourth and Fifth centuries, burst upon the Roman Empire, their ravages being almost entirely confined to *a third*, or the *Western division*, thereof; and it is manifest, also, that these ravages did, as to their general features, most strikingly fulfil the requirements of the symbolization—the *first* invasion being on the inland provinces, the *second* on the maritime portions, the *third* on the rivers and fountains, the *fourth* affecting the governors, the *luminaries* of that third part (see pp. 205 sq.). In view of the general agreement, which is like that

* [These judgments, in the opinion of the Am. Ed., commenced after the Woman had become the *Harlot*—after the unholy alliance between the Church and State. See on ch. xvii.—E. R. C.]

† ["There were to be *seven Trumpets* sounded, and under the seventh Trumpet *seven Vials* poured out. The numeral resemblance of these to the seven trumpet blasts sounded on seven successive days against the ancient Jericho, and which were followed on the seventh day by seven compassings of its walls, till on the last the wall fell down, and entrance was given to Israel into that first city of the promised Canaan (Josh. vi. 3–16)—this interesting resemblance, I say, has been noticed by Ambrose Ansbert in old times, and in more modern times by Vitringa, and other Apocalyptic interpreters after him. It almost seemed as if some power were marked out hereby as the New Testament Jericho; whose dominion opposed, and whose overthrow would introduce the saints' enjoyment of the Heavenly Canaan." ELLIOTT, Vol. I., p. 349.—E. R. C.]

of the mountain shadows on the bosom of the Lake of Geneva and the mountains themselves, it seems legitimate to conclude that the symbol shadowed forth the fact, and that *the third part* of the former was designed to indicate (when the event should occur) *the third part* of the smitten empire. If this be so, then, when it is said that hail fell upon the earth, we may understand the prophecy as meaning that it fell upon *that third part;* and, be it observed, there is no undue straining of language in such an interpretation, for certainly there is no disagreement between a prophecy that Great Britain shall be smitten, and the fact that Scotland receives the blow. And still further, by the third part of the trees and all the grass, we may understand the trees and the grass of that smitten third part.

Another objection is that Elliott's scheme fails to give any satisfactory explanation of the exemption of the *sealed* from the torment of the fifth plague (ch. ix. 4). So far as Elliott is concerned, the objection is well taken. This does not imply, however, that an explanation cannot be given consistent with the scheme. Whilst historical records do give us the general information that the citizens of those countries which had been the seat of the old Roman Empire did suffer fearfully from the Saracenic invasions, they are almost totally silent as to the fate of individuals; from *historical investigation* it is impossible to determine who were the sealed, and what was their condition during the ravages of the Saracens. Alford writes: "In the very midst of this corrupt Christianity, were at that time God's elect scattered up and down; and it is surely too much to say every such person escaped scathless from the Turkish (Saracenic) sword." If from other points of resemblance between the Symbol and the Saracenic woe (and there are many such which cannot be challenged, see pp. 207 sq.), the identity between the object of prophecy and that woe can be established, then it is not "too much to say," especially in view of the absence of all proof to the contrary, that God did, according to His promise, preserve His *sealed* ones from the *torment* which was visited upon the unsealed.

Another objection is brought against Elliott's interpretation of the *crowns like unto gold* (ch. ix. 7). "Elliott tries to apply it to the *turban;* but granting some latitude to the στέφανοι, the ὅμοιοι χρυσῷ, will hardly bear this. The appearance of a turban, even when ornamented with gold, is hardly *golden.*" True; but a *yellow* turban (Barnes) might be described as *like to gold.* Certainly Alford, who interprets *fiery* and *sulphureous* (ver. 17) as meaning *red* and *light-yellow,* should have no objection to this explanation.

Alford again writes: "I cannot forbear noticing, as we pass, the caprice of historical interpreters. On the command *not to kill* the men, *etc.,* in ch. ix. 5, Elliott says: '*i. e.,* not to annihilate them as a political Christian body.' If then the same rule of interpretation is to hold, the present verse (6) must mean that 'the political Christian body' will be so sorely beset by these Mohammedan locusts, that it will desire to be annihilated, and not find any way. For surely it cannot be allowed that the *killing of*

men should be said of their annihilation as a political body in one verse, and their *desiring* to die in the next, should be said of some thing totally different, and applicable to their individual misery." The propriety of the criticism of the distinguished commentator may be allowed, and yet it be shown to have no force against the historical scheme. In chs. l.–lii. of the immortal history of Gibbon, we have described the rise, the conquests, and the decline of the Saracens. In the grand features of history as therein set forth, we perceive the similarity to the complex symbol of ch. ix. 1–11. Prominent amongst these features is the fact that though the Mohammedan conquerors *tormented,* they never totally *destroyed* the political combinations of Christendom. In Europe they were as an invading army encamped—they were never able to take Constantinople; although they ravaged the country around Rome, they were restrained from the capture of the Imperial City; in their advance upon Christendom from the Pyrenees, they were driven back by Charles Martel. Even in Spain, where for centuries they held dominion, they never completely extinguished either the Spanish nationality or the organized Church. In Syria, where their first conquests in Christendom were made, although their sceptre has passed away to the Turks, we still find nominally Christian communities substantially as they were organized in the days of the Saracens. "After the revolution of eleven centuries, the Jews and Christians of the Turkish Empire enjoy the liberty of conscience which was granted by the Arabian Caliphs. . . . . . All the oriental sects were included in the common benefits of toleration; the rank, the immunities, the domestic jurisdiction of the patriarchs, the bishops, and the clergy, were protected by the civil magistrate. . . . . . The captive churches of the East have been afflicted in every age by the avarice or bigotry of their rulers; and the ordinary and legal restraints must be offensive to the pride or the zeal of the Christians" (*Gibbon,* ch. li.). From the beginning, these communities have been *tormented,* but not *destroyed.* And not only so, but from the days of the Caliphs their preservation as organized communities, having a peculiar dress, has been in accordance with the policy of their rulers—they are thus more easily kept in subjection, and are separated from Moslems as inferior and tributary. The very preservation of these communities has in all time subjected them to *torment,* to official exaction and popular contumely and persecution. Is it not most natural to suppose that as *political communities* they have desired annihilation?

The last objection urged by Alford is against Elliott's interpretation of ch. ix. 19. "Well may Mr. Barker say (*Friendly Strictures*): 'An interpretation so wild, if it refutes not itself, seems scarcely capable of refutation.' Happily, it does refute itself. For it is convicted, by altogether leaving out of view the power in the *mouths,* which is the principal feature in the original vision; by making no reference to the serpent-like character of these tails, but being wholly inconsistent with it; by distorting the canon of symmetrical interpretation in making the *heads* attached to the tails to mean that the *tails* are symbols of authority, *etc.*" The force of the criticism is admitted, and yet, like the preceding, it bears not against the historical scheme. The following is suggested as possibly the true explanation of the verse alluded to. On opening Webster's *Dictionary* we find the following as the second definition of *Basilisk:* "In *military affairs*, a large piece of ordnance, so called from its supposed resemblance to the serpent of that name, or from its size. This cannon carried an iron ball of 200 pounds weight, but is not now used." Such were the cannon with which the Turks moved to the assault of Constantinople. These long, serpent-like instruments of destruction, dragged breach foremost in the rear of the companies that served them, might well have been described in symbol as *tails, like unto serpents having heads;* and the power by which the Turkish armies breached the walls of Constantinople, and thus subjugated the Eastern third of the old Roman Empire (ch. ix. 18), was in these *tails* and the *mouths* of these heads.

It should be remarked, in conclusion, that the resemblance contemplated in this Note is not merely between the individual symbols and the events which have been adduced as fulfilling them respectively, but it is a resemblance between the entire series regarded as a whole, and the entire course of history—it extends to the relations of the symbols to each other, their succession and mutual proportions.—E. R. C.]

SECTION FOURTH.

The Seven Thunders, or Seven Sealed Divine Voices; the mystery of mysteries, as mediatory of the end of the world.

CHAPTER X. AND CHAPTER XI. 1–14.

(Transition to Part Second.)

A.—VEILED HEAVEN-PICTURE OF THE SEVEN THUNDERS.

CHAP. X. 1—11.

a. The Angel of the Time of the End.

1 And I saw another[1] mighty [strong] angel come down [descending] from [out of] heaven, clothed with a cloud: and a [the[2]] rainbow *was* [*om. was*] upon his head, and his face *was* [*om. was*] as it were [*om.* it were] the sun, and his feet as 2 pillars of fire: and he had [having[3]] in his hand a little book [scroll] open [opened]: and he set his right foot upon the sea, and *his* [the] left *foot* [*om. foot*] 3 on [upon] the earth, and cried with a loud [great] voice, as *when* [*om. when*] a lion roareth: and when he had [*om.* had] cried, [*ins.* the] seven thunders uttered [spake] their voices.

b. The seven Thunders as mysterious Mediations of the Time of the End.

4 And when[4] the seven thunders had [*om.* had] uttered [spake] their voices [*om.* their voices],[5] I was about to write: and I heard a voice from [out of—*ins.* the] heaven saying unto me [*om.* unto me],[6] Seal up [*om.* up] those [the] things which the 5 seven thunders uttered [spake], and write them not. And the angel which [that] I saw stand [standing] upon the sea and upon the earth lifted up his [*ins.* right[7]]

TEXTUAL AND GRAMMATICAL.

1 Ver. 1. Ἄλλον is groundlessly omitted by some minuscules. [It is omitted by B*. and P. Critical Editors give it with ℵ. A. C.—E. R. C.]
2 Ver. 1. The article is firmly established. [Critical Editors generally give it with ℵ.[1] A. B*. C ; Rec. *et al.* omit with 1. 7. P.—E. R. C.]
3 Ver. 2. [Crit. Eds. generally give ἔχων with ℵ. A. B*. C. P., *etc.*—E. R. C.]
4 Ver. 4. Cod. ℵ. reads ὅτα [instead of ὅτε]. An exegetical substitution.
5 Ver. 4 An addition of the Rec. [Om. by crit. Eds. with ℵ. A. B. C. P., *etc.*—E. R. C.]
6 Ver. 4. [Lach., Alf., Treg., Tisch., with ℵ. A. B*. C. P., *etc.*, omit μοι ; Lange retains.—E. R. C.]
7 Ver. 5. An omission of the Rec. [Given generally in acc. with ℵ. B*. C. P. ; omitted by A.—E. R. C.]

6 hand to [*ins.* the] heaven, And sware by him that liveth for ever and ever [into the ages of the ages], who created [*ins.* the] heaven, and the things [*ins.* in it] that therein are [*om.* that therein are], and the earth, and the things [*ins.* in it] that therein are [*om.* that therein are], and the sea,⁸ and the things [*ins.* in it] which are therein [*om.* which are therein], that .there should be [*om.* there should be] time
7 [χρόνος] [*ins.* shall be] no longer [*or* not yet (οὐκέτι ἔσται)] : But in the days of the voice of the seventh angel, when he shall begin [should be about] to sound [trumpet], [*ins.* is also finished] the mystery of God should be finished [*om.* should be finished], as he hath [*om.* hath] declared [*ins.* the glad tidings (εὐηγγέλισεν)] to his servants the prophets.

c. Second, new Calling of the Seer, in order to the symbolical Preparation and symbolical Annunciation of the Time of the End.

8   And the voice which I heard from [*ins.* the] heaven [*ins. I heard*] spake [speaking⁹] unto [with] me again, and said [saying⁹], Go *and* [*om. and*] take the little book
9 [scroll] which is open [opened (τὸ ἠνεωγμένον)] in the hand of the angel which [that] standeth upon the sea and upon the earth.   And I went [*ins.* away] unto the angel, and [*om.* and] said unto [saying to *or* telling] him, [*om.* ,—*ins.* to] give¹⁰ me the little book [scroll].   And he said [saith] unto me, Take *it*, [*om. it,*] and eat it up ; and it shall make [*om.* make—*ins.* embitter] thy belly bitter [*om.* bitter], but [*ins.*
10 in thy mouth] it shall be in thy mouth [*om.* in thy mouth] sweet as honey.   And I took the little book [scroll] out of the angel's [*om.* angel's] hand [*ins.* of the angel], and ate it up ; and it was in my mouth sweet [*om.* sweet] as honey [*ins.* ; sweet]: and as soon as [when] I had eaten it, my belly was bitter [embittered¹¹].
11 And he said [they say]¹² unto me, Thou must prophesy again before [*or* concern' ing¹³] many peoples, and nations, and tongues, and kings.

⁸ Ver. 6. Καὶ τὴν θάλασσαν [καὶ τὰ ἐν αὐτῇ] is omitted by א*. [and also by A.—E. R. C.]
⁹ Ver. 8. [Critical Editors give λαλοῦσαν and λέγουσαν with א. A. B*. O. P., etc.—E. R. C.]
¹⁰ Ver. 9. [Critical Editors generally give δοῦναι with א. A. B. C.; Rec., with P., gives δός.—E. R. C.]
¹¹ Ver. 10. [Cod. א. gives ἐγεμίσθη.—E. R. C.]
¹² Ver. 11. The reading, λέγουσιν, although strongly attested, might have originated in a consideration of the co-operation of the voice and the Angel. [Lach., Alf., Treg., Tisch., with א. A. B., give λέγουσιν ; λέγει is supported by P. The former reading, against Lange, is adopted above.—E. R. C.]
¹³ Ver. 13. [For the force of ἐπί with the dative, see WINER, § 48, c., and the grammars and lexicons generally. The Am. E l. has inserted the alternative translation in deference to the distinguished authorities by whom it is supported. In his own judgment, the proper translation is *before* (possibly in a *hostile* sense), ▬ in his opinion, it should be, Heb. x. 28. In confirmation of this opinion in the case in Hebrews, it should be noted that those condemned to death under the Mosaic law, were executed *before* (*in the presence of*) the witnesses. (Comp. Deut. xvii. 6, 7 ; xiii. 6–9 ; Acts vii. 58).—E. R. C.]

EXEGETICAL AND CRITICAL.

SYNOPTICAL VIEW.

The picture of the prevailing impenitence of the generality of men, or of the ruling world as a whole, leads (as in Matt. xxiv. 37) to the announcement of the end of the world itself. The end of the world is brought on, however, not simply by the development of human corruption into a readiness for judgment, but, rather, by the development of the Kingdom of God over against man's corruption, and, most of all, by the development of the conflict between the two.

It was to be expected that the Apocalypse would contain a revelation of the history of the Kingdom of God, its development, advances and reforms. And this revelation was made to the Seer in the voices of the seven Thunders. But the Prophet was commanded to seal those voices; he was forbidden to write them. This trait is, unmistakably, a special sign of the Divine origin of our Book ; no imitator, no apocryphal apoca-lyptist would have thought of this holy silence, and still less would he have consented to observe it.

The fact that the Thunder-voices betoken a new revelation, an advance of the Kingdom of God, and, relatively, a *reform*, is proved by the *thunders* of Sinai; by the *thunder* which heralded God's answer to Job (ch. xxxvii. 2) ; the de-scription of Israel's redemption amid *thunder* and lightning in the prophecy of Zechariah (ch. ix. 14) ; the voice of *thunder* over Christ as He prayed in the Temple (John xii. 28)—the voice which said : I have glorified My name, and will glorify it. A reference to the charismatical ele-ment, in the name of the *Sons of Thunder*, is also appropriate here.   [See *foot-note* ‡, p. 52.—E. R. C.]

Now why was the unfolding of this bright side of the Kingdom of God, the succession of seven holy reforms, not written ? Schleier-macher regrets the omission of a revelation of this sort. The Spirit of revelation wisely with-held it. The Seer might *hear* the seven Thun-ders ; but the *writing* of them might have been prejudicial to the free development of New Testament times. The example of the gross misinterpretations of Old Testament prophecy lay at the door. Moreover, this was not to be a section of prophecies, in the more general sense of the term, but a closed [*geschlossen*] Apocalypse. Yet the Seer was permitted to communicate a few features, in exoteric form, which fill up this space.

The Heaven-picture of this cosmical and ecclesiastic history of the seven Thunders is opened by the appearance of a *strong Angel*, Who descends from Heaven clothed with a cloud—the rainbow above His head. These attributes strongly resemble the picture of Christ at His coming, as elsewhere portrayed (ch. i. 15; Dan. x. 6); the last terms—*His face as the sun, and His feet as pillars of fire*—being particularly suggestive of the appearance of Christ in the first chapter. We may, therefore, say that the same relation which is sustained by the Angel of the Lord, in the Old Testament, to the first Parousia of Christ, is borne by this Angel to His second Parousia. It is the manifestation of the New Testament figure of Christ in the foretokens of His power. This Angel, in the might and victorious confidence of His appearance, reminds us of the Archangel Michael; as the author of the seven Thunders or reformations, He suggests the dispensation of the Holy Ghost. There is also a close connection between the seven Spirit-forms of the Holy Ghost (Is. xi. ; Rev. i.), and the seven revelation-forms of Christ in archangelic shapes (1 Thess. iv. 16). Christ's reformatory breaches through the old form of the world are, in their personal features, conflicts and victories of the Archangel Michael (ch. xii. 7) ; in respect of their ideal effects of Divine origin, they are Pentecostal seasons of the diffusion of the Holy Ghost.

But as this strong Angel is related to the approaching end of the world, so also is the *little book* in His hand thereunto related. Three books are associated in the Apocalypse. The first is the book of the course of the world, in its relation to the end of the world (ch. v. 1). The last is the book of life, as the book of God's Church which is to be perfected at the end of the world (ch. xx. 15 ; xxi. 27). Between these two, comes the book of the world's end, the revelation of the events of the approaching end of the world. The first book was closed with seven Seals; this book, on the other hand—a *little* book, because the last things shall come in the quick succession of a catastrophe and epoch—is unrolled, *opened*. Relatively it is reflected in the everlasting Gospel (ch. xiv. 6), the Gospel as the glad tidings of the final σωτηρία with which a blissful *eternity* begins—in contradistinction to the Gospel of Salvation in the midst of *time*. For the tidings of the last day are to believers a Gospel themselves ; not, indeed, really another one (ἕτερον, Gal. i. 6), but the final metamorphosis and glorification or spiritualization of the first Gospel, Luke xxi. 28.

The Angel *sets his right foot upon the sea, and his left upon the land*. The right one on the sea, for it is from the sea, from surging, popular life, that the last and mightiest crises arise, ch. xiii. That Antichristianity which is from the earth will be a secondary affair.

The setting of His feet on the sea and on the land denotes, not simply and in general His power over the whole earth, but also, particularly, His power over the two opposite fundamental forms of its spiritual life—earth and sea; theocracy and world.

His cry is a *great* one; His voice as that of a *lion*. The *lion*, from of old, is significant of the warlike and victorious epochs or transruptions of the Kingdom of God in the history of the world, Gen. xlix. 9. When Satan goes about as *a roaring lion*, he does but imitate the voice of the true Lion. He gives utterance to a lie as to his power and as to his courage. The lion-voice of the triumphant Christ then seems immediately to branch out into the seven Thunders of His reformatory witnesses. The fact that these Thunders are, in the most special degree, mediatory of the end of the world, is evident from all that follows; why their voices, their ideal revelations were *not written*, we have seen above. Here a very special *sealing* takes place, for reformers must walk by faith, not by sight. The result, however, is summed up by the Angel in His dread oath concerning the imminent end of the world. A more powerful expression of the assurance of the Divine Spirit, the confidence of prophetic faith, in regard to the approaching end, could, we venture to assert, scarcely be conceived of. The right hand of the Angel is lifted toward Heaven. The oath is an oath by Him Who liveth from eternity to eternity, and Who, as the Creator of all things, defines the measure and limit of all creaturely vital movements toward the end. Mark xiii. 32. There shall be no more *time* (χρόνος [*Zeitfrist*=respite]) ; from the term defined by the Angel. *i. e.*, from the opening of the seventh Trumpet, the catastrophe of the end of the world shall begin. They are *days*, *numbered* days—the times of the voice of the seventh trumpet. In those days, the *mystery of God*, the specific mystery of the Father (Mark xiii.), shall be fully accomplished.

The fact that the time of the seven Thunders forms the transition to the final period of the world, *i. e.*, also to the Second Part of the Apocalypse, is evident from the circumstance that the section of the seven Thunders can be inserted between the sixth and seventh Trumpets, whilst a complete and minute survey of the section leads to the expectation that the Antichristian time must follow directly upon the seventh Thunder. Another proof that a general turn in affairs now takes place, is involved in the fact that the same voice from Heaven that spoke to the Seer in ver. 4, as well as at the beginning (ch. i.), now commands him to take the little book out of the hand of the Angel. The Angel gives him the book, directing him, at the same time, to eat it (comp. Ezek. iii. 2), and telling him that it will cause him bitter pain in his belly, but will in his mouth be sweet as honey. The Seer forthwith experiences the truth of the Angel's words.

Apocalyptic things have a wondrous charm. To the honey-like sweetness of the little book in the mouth, that enormous mass of literature testifies, which is engaged in the eating of it. But whoever has, with some degree of understanding, appropriated the little book, is greatly pained within him by its startling perspectives and images. A termination is then put to all idyllic conceptions of the future and the end of the world.

But by the eating of the book the Seer is doubly as much a Prophet as before. As he has prophesied concerning the course of the world, down to its end, so he must now prophesy of the end itself, *in* the course of the world, in accordance with the words: *Thou must prophesy again, concerning many peoples, and nations, and tongues, and kings.* The universal peoples' life is now to form the foreground of his prophecy. By way of preliminary, however, an Earth-picture is annexed to this commission, in which the general effect of the seven Thunders is reflected. That is, it forms, in its conjunction with the seven Thunders, the transition from the course of the world to the end of the same.

[ABSTRACT OF VIEWS, ETC.]
By the Am. Editor.

[ELLIOTT regards the entire section, ch. ix. 20—xi. 15, as referring to "The Reformation, as occurring under the latter half of the Sixth Trumpet: including the antecedent history, and the death, resurrection, and ascension, of Christ's two sackcloth clothed Witnesses;" the whole period extending from "A. D. 1453–1789." He interprets ch. x. as indicating the beginning of the Reformation—the strong Angel is Christ, His *adornment* in antithesis to the *antichristian* claims of the Popedom; the *opened little scroll*, the opened Bible; the *Seer* himself the symbol of Luther and the reformed clergy; the *sweetness in the mouth*, the delight following the personal reception of the opened Gospel; the *embittering*, the woes following the promulgation before peoples, *etc.*; the prophesying *again*, the resumption of evangelical preaching, which had been almost entirely relinquished; the *seven Thunders*, the Papal bulls; the *sealing*, the non recognition, publication, and action upon those bulls as of authority. The *Angel's oath* he interprets as follows: "*There shall be time no longer extended, viz.*, to the mysterious dispensation of God which has so far permitted the reign of evil, including the power of Papal Rome's mock thunders; the seventh Trumpet's era being its fixed determined limit—"For in the days of the seventh angel, when he shall sound, the mystery of God shall be finished."*

BARNES, as to the general interpretation of ch. x., agrees with Elliott, save that in reference to the *Angel's oath* he adopts the view put forth by the latter in his earlier editions, *viz.*: "That the time (of the consummation) should not yet be; but in the days, *etc.*"

STUART writes: "The impression made on my own mind by ch. x. is, that the design of it is to show in an impressive manner that the vision respecting this book with seven Seals (ch. v.) is just now at its close, that nothing more remains but the sounding of the seventh and last Trumpet, and that this shall speedily take place, οὐκέτι χρόνος ἔσται, ver. 6. With this seems also to be joined another object, *viz.*, to introduce this final catastrophe with all the solemnity and de-

monstration of its importance, which the nature of the case seemed to require. The destruction of the Temple and City of God, and also the destruction of the Jewish nation, were events such as cannot often happen, and when they do, it is intended that they shall make a deep impression. The new commission which John receives (ver. 11) seems to be a circumstance which obviously contributes to show, that his former vision of the sealed book was now at its close or completed, and that he needed new directions for the further discharge of prophetic duty. The contents of the book are not sealed. He devours them, *i. e.*, he reads them with avidity, in order that he may know what they contained; and then he is told, that he must prophesy again *respecting* many nations and people, and tongues and kings. Thus, when the last or seventh trumpet shall have sounded, his task will still proceed; while the scene is entirely changed in respect to those whose destiny is predicted." Concerning the seven Thunders he remarks, "What was declared in the voice of thunder was ominous of the catastrophe near at hand. *Entire* silence (represented by the *sealing*) is neither commanded nor observed. . . . What the seven Thunders most probably declared *fully* to John, he is restrained from writing down, *etc.*"

WORDSWORTH regards the *Angel* as representing Christ, the items of description setting forth His excellencies; the *seven Thunders*, as signs of His power and indignation, representing the consummation of God's judgments; the *little scroll* as containing a prophetic episode *unrolled* by Christ; the *eating* as indicating, that the Seer made it his own; the *oath* as implying "that there shall be no longer any *delay* or respite for repentance to the wicked, or postponement of reward to the righteous, *save only* in the days of the *last* Angel;" the *act of swearing* as indicating that on account of the overflow of iniquity, even in the Christian Church, the world would begin to doubt the truth of Christ's universal sovereignty, and as designed to put an end to such doubts.

ALFORD regards ch. x. 1—xi. 14, as "episodical and anticipatory." This section, which relates to things still future, he represents as consisting of two episodic visions, that of the *Little Book*, and that of the *Two Witnesses.* In respect of the former, he regards the *Angel* as an angelic minister of Christ; the *symbols* with which he is accompanied (those which surrounded the Throne of God in ch. iv. 2 sqq.) as betokening "judgment tempered with mercy, the character of his ministration, which, at the same time that it proclaims the near approach of the completion of God's judgments, furnishes to the Seer the book (*little scroll*) of his subsequent prophecy, the following out of God's purposes of mercy." In his judgment the meaning of the Thunders, whilst they form a complete portion of the Apocalyptic machinery, is not revealed, and is by us undiscoverable. The χρόνος of the oath he regards as that of ch. vi. 11; the *intent* of the oath being to declare that the delay there referred to is at an end.

LORD regards the *Angel* as representing the Ministers of the Reformation; the *seven Thunders* as denoting violent expressions of thought and

---

* [The interpretation of the *oath* above is that given in the 5th edition. In this edition Elliott writes, "Another proposed interpretation, 'that the time shall yet be,' which in my earlier editions I adopted from other preceding interpreters, appears to me on reconsideration to be on grammatical grounds inadmissible; since I cannot find authority for ἔτι meaning *yet* in that sense of our English word *yet* or as *yet.*"—E. R. C.]

passion by those addressed ("one of the first and most violent of these thunder utterances was a false pretence to inspiration, and expression of the persuasion that the period had arrived for the final overthrow of Antichrist and establishment of the Redeemer's millennial Kingdom "); the *solemn oath* of the Angel, as a response to these thunder voices, designed to correct their error, denoting the answer by Luther and the reformers, from Scripture, to errorists, showing that the time of the millennial Kingdom was *not yet to be*; the *Seer* as symbolizing the reformed Church, to which the ministry extended the open Gospel symbolized by the *little scroll;* the *prophesying* as indicating the fulfilling by the members of the Church "the office of witnesses for God in the presence of Antichristian rulers and nations."
GLASGOW.—The *period* indicated by the vision of ch. x. is the beginning of the Gospel age; the *Angel* is Christ; the *voice as a lion roaring* is Christ's commission to preach; the *seven Thunders* are the voices of the disciples proclaiming the truth; the *direction to seal the Thunders* indicates that *the* proclamations of the Church are not inspired and therefore not to be incorporated in the Canon; the *oath* implies a term and end of the seven Thunders; the *opened scroll* is the Bible (the revealed Word of God), the reception of which is sweet to the taste, and yet fills the Christian soul with sadness; the declaration "*Thou must prophesy, etc.*," announces the communication of the New Testament prophetic gift, to the ministry symbolized by John, and the extension of the prophetic commission as to all people.—E. R. C.]

EXPLANATIONS IN DETAIL.

Ver. 1. This is as little the beginning of an inter-scene as ch. vii. Some confusions resulting from the misapprehension of those who so regard it, see in Düsterdieck, p. 342. Likewise curious discussions concerning the stand-point of the Seer. If he was transported to Heaven in ch. iv. 1, how could he see the Angel come down from Heaven? De Wette has rightly limited that more definite transportation to Heaven to the contemplation of the heavenly Throne-scene. Düsterdieck "retains," with Ewald, "the heavenly stand-point." According to this, John must finally have come down to earth with the heavenly Jerusalem. Hengstenberg has remarked, with justice, that there is no question of exclusive localities here.* [ALFORD remarks —" The place of the Seer rest continues in Heaven," calling attention to the fact that, in ver. 9, he is represented as *going away* (ἀπῆλθον), *i. e.*, from his former place.—E. R. C.]
Another strong angel.—The *other* Angel is distinguished as the *strong* one from the foregoing Angels of the Trumpets. It does not follow from the ἰσχυρόν that he should be specially distinguished from the ἰσχυρός of ch. v. 2 (after Bengel and others). We have called this Angel the angelic image of Christ, preceding His speedy Parousia. This, undoubtedly, is not, in the strictest sense, Christ Himself, as Bede and many others maintain; but neither is the conception

* ["The presence of John in Heaven must be understood *positively—not exclusively.*" Hengstenberg.—TR.]

of a mere Angel that which is presented in the text (in accordance with Düsterdieck and others). Düsterdieck: "The very style of the oath (ver. 6) is inappropriate to Christ." Bengel remarks, on the other hand: "The Apocalypse makes a distinction throughout between the Father and Christ."
Clothed with a cloud.—"The *cloud* characterizes the Angel as a messenger of Divine judgment" (comp. ch. i. 7; Hengstenb., Ebrard [so also Alford]). It has, however, a much more general significance, as is evidenced by the cloud at the Transfiguration and the Ascension. It denotes, in general, the mysterious veiling of the Divine and heavenly glory from the human eye on earth.
[And the rainbow upon his head.— "The (ἡ) well known, ordinary, rainbow; indicating, agreeably with its first origin, God's covenant of mercy." ALFORD.—E. R. C.]
[And his face ▬ the sun.—See chs. i. 16; xviii. 1. Indicative not merely of His manifested glory, but of His light-giving, life-giving power. The *sun* in the solar system is the noblest and most glorious symbol of Christ in His relations to the Universe.—E. R. C.]
▬▬ feet ▬ pillars of fire.—This feature, also, is interpreted as indicative of judgment, as in ch. i. 15. An antithesis to the **rainbow** is, doubtless, presented. That, however, is not simply a token of covenant grace in general; it is also a sign or guaranty of ▬ continuing existence of the world until the end. Here too, then, it is a sign that the end of the world has not yet arrived. The sun-like radiance of the face denotes, like the revelation of God itself, both grace and judgment. Düsterdieck very correctly observes that the end of the world embraces both judgment and redemption. Aretius applies the *cloud* to the incarnation of Christ—Christ's flesh.
Ver. 2. **In his hand a little scroll.**—Bengel: In his left hand, see ver. 5. Why a *little* book [scroll]? See above. Three different expositions are cited by Düsterdieck, p. 346. [ALFORD: "That (the seven sealed scroll) was the *great* sealed roll of God's purposes; this but one portion of those purposes." GLASGOW: "This book applies to the whole contents of the Bible, which, though the greatest of books in character, truth, beauty, and importance, is comparatively a *small* Book in bulk, and thus adapted for use, translation, circulation, and universal perusal."—E. R. C.]
Opened.—It is open, as the unrolled conclusion of the book opened by the Lamb.
Sea and earth neither denote simply that the tidings brought by the Angel are for the whole earth (De Wette), nor are they significant merely of power over the whole earth (Ewald); the expression likewise embraces the contrast of sea and earth in their symbolical import. Christianity recognizes the truth and the falsehood on both sides of the contrast—ecclesiastical authority and political national life—and rules, without party-spirit, over both parties.
Interpretations of the antithesis: Bengel: Europe and Asia. Hengstenberg: The sea of peoples and the cultivated world, *etc.*—All of which Düsterdieck denominates *allegorizing.*

Ver. 3. **With a great voice.**—According to Bengel, the purport of the voice is given in ver. 6; according to Düsterdieck, its purport cannot be determined. We regard it as the unitous source of the seven Thunders; hence it is as little definitely intimated as the purport of these. The "threatening character" [Ewald, Düsterd.] of the cry is interpolated in the description. **The seven thunders.**—The symbolical idea of the *thunder* is presupposed by the *Son of Thunder.* The number of the Thunders is distinctly stated—*seven*—being the number of a full cycle (designated by us as the cycle of the Reformations). The article accompanies the expression of this definite totality. The Old Testament type of the Divine manifestation is most distinctly contained in the seven Thunders, Ps. xxix.

Different interpretations of the seven Thunders and their purport: Seven roaring heavens; seven Spirits of God; identical with the seven Trumpets; the oracles of the Prophets; the blessed mystery of the new world (Hofmann); curses; the seven crusades; seven future acts of God; terrible judgments on the persecutors of the Church. [For other interpretations see Abstract of Views on pp. 218 sq.—E. R. C.]

Ver. 4. **And when the seven thunders spake.**—They have, therefore, a verbal purport, as distinct and diverse revelations. "In accordance with the command, ch. i. 11, John was about to write what the thunders had spoken." **I was about to write,**—*i. e.*, he entertained this idea in the vision—an idea, however, which would have been the basis of the future act. **A voice from heaven.**—From this also it is evident that the Seer was no longer thinking of himself as in Heaven. He was but momentarily in Heaven, by virtue of a special, higher transportation of his spirit. Düsterdieck strangely supposes that he was still in Heaven, but that the voice sounded from the interior [*Tiefe*, depth] of Heaven. ["From this it does not *follow* that the Seer is on earth, any more than in ver. 1." Alford. Had the Seer been in Heaven, it is evident that he must thus have spoken to indicate that the voice came not *from Earth*, but *with authority.*—E. R. C.]

Seal.—According to Hengstenberg, this has reference merely to this place (in the Book!). For various and, in part, curious explanations of the commandment not to write the voices, see Düsterdieck, p. 350.

Ver. 5. **Lifted up his right hand.**—Gen. xiv. 22; Dan. xii. 7. Symbolism of the sacred, heavenly consciousness and certainty of the oath; see Deut. xxxii. 40 and other passages. ["Jesus, the faithful and true Witness, has here left, for the guidance of His people, a pattern according to which they should be adjured when called to give evidence in a court of justice—not by the idolatrous act of kissing a book, but by lifting the right hand in appeal to the living and true God, that what they speak is truth." Glasgow. —E. R. C.]

Ver. 6. **By him that liveth.**—God the Father, by virtue of His economy, alone has knowledge originally of the time and hour of the Parousia (Matt. xxiv. 36); this knowledge He has here communicated to the New Testament "An-

gel of the Lord." Every χρόνος or period closes with a καιρός or epoch; and this is particularly true of the final age.

Interpretations: Simply the cessation of time; cessation of the time of grace; a chiliastic measure of time—a *non-chronus* (! Bengel: Close of the non-chronus—between 1,000 and 1,100 years —the year 1836); most commentators: the commencement of the fulfillment of the mystery of God; see Düsterdieck, pp. 351 sqq.—" The time of the seventh Trumpet."

[The view of Alford, *viz.*, that the χρόνος is that of ch. vi. 11, seems to the Am. Ed. to be the true one. It was there declared to the souls under the altar that they should rest ἔτι χρόνον. The season referred to, manifestly, was that of world domination — to be followed by the avenging of the martyrs. In this passage the Angel declares, Ὅτι χρόνος οὐκέτι ἔσται.* It seems hardly possible to avoid the conclusion that those χρόνοι are one and the same. And this interpretation is in accordance with truth elsewhere revealed. It would seem as though the judgments under the first six Trumpets, although the beginnings of coming woe, are rather judgments calling to repentance. The *avenging*, properly speaking, does not take place until the last Trumpet. This the writer supposes to be the period of *the great tribulation*— a *tribulation* from which the Saints are to be exempt, a *period* in the beginning of which their humiliation is to end (comp. Matt. xxiv. 21, 22; Luke xxi. 36; Rev. iii. 10; see also *Add. Com.* under ch. vii. 14). Then is finished the *μυστήριον* (see *Add. Comm.* on ch. i. 20) the glad tidings of which had been declared to the Prophets (ver. 7).†—E. R. C.]

Ver. 7. **In the days of the voice.**—The fact that *days* are still spoken of, after the cessation of time has been proclaimed, can be explained by the distinction of χρόνος and καιρός, but not, with De Wette, by the remark that the stand-point of the vision is not strictly preserved.

The mystery of God.—The mystery of the last things, announced by the Prophets; in a

---

* [According to Middleton *On the Greek Article* I. 3, 3 (referred to by Elliott, Vol. II., pp. 125 sq.) the absence of the definite article is supplied by the fact that the copula is the verb substantive (see Acts xxiii 5; John v. 9; John xix. 14; Mark xi. 13; John v. 1).—E. R. C.]

† [It is well worthy of consideration whether there is not a connection between this section of the Apocalypse and 1 Cor. xv. 51, 52. It is difficult to imagine that in two Books, both written under the inspiration of the Holy Ghost, the manifest parallelism between the μυστήριον and the last σάλπιγξ and the *glad tidings* announced in the one, and the μυστήριον and the last σάλπιγξ and the *glad tidings* referred to in the other, should have been merely fortuitous. Nor is there aught in the events described under these *last Trumpets* to forbid our regarding them as one and the same. Certainly there is nothing inconceivable in the idea that the period of vengeance upon the persecutors of the saints, should be that in which the heirs of the *first resurrection* should be raised from the dead, and, together with living saints, be removed to some place of safety (see Excursus on the *First Resurrection*, ch. xx. 5, 6). It may also be remarked that this hypothesis does not involve the idea that the Apocalypse was written *before* the Epistles to the Corinthians. It should be remembered that the Trumpets were introduced into the Apocalyptic vision, in full accordance with the imagery of preceding Scripture, as indicating the *going forth* of Jehovah for the deliverance of His people, and for the execution of judgment upon their enemies. It should therefore excite no surprise that the Apostle Paul should, under the inspiration of the Spirit, have referred to a period as that of the *last Trumpet*, which in the more complete revelation to John should be so described.—E. R. C.]

wider sense the eschatological mystery of the world's history. According to Düsterdieck and many ancients, only Old Testament Prophets are here intended; we cannot see, however, why the Prophets of the New Testament, and consequently Christ Himself, should be excluded. The grand fulfillment of this prophecy is immeasurably dwarfed by a reference of it to the emancipation of the Christians from the oppression of the Jews (Grotius, Eichhorn). [See under ch. i. 20; and also preceding *Foot-note.*—E. R. C.]

Ver. 8. **Go.**—He is to go to the Angel. Of course this means in idea, in the vision. He is boldly to draw near the opening of the terrible new revelation. As the Angel is standing on earth, so the person commanded to approach him has his station there also. According to Düsterdieck [and Alford], the Seer was still in Heaven.

Vers. 9, 10. **And I went,** *etc.*—According to Düsterdieck, the *eating* of the *little book* is not allegorically intended. And yet by accepting the interpretation of Beza: *insere tuis visceribus et describe in latitudine cordis tui,* with reference to Ezek. ii. 8; [iii. 1–3;] Jer. xv. 16, he does admit that the passage has an allegorical sense. ["To *eat* is, in various Eastern languages, expressive of receiving. (See Jer. xv. 16; Ezek. iii. 1; Job xxiii. 12; Ps. xix. 10). The reception of Divine truth is a mental and spiritual exercise, sustaining and developing the higher nature as food does the body." GLASGOW.—E. R. C.]

The Angel says, in accordance with his view of the operation of the little book:

It shall embitter thy belly, but in thy mouth it shall be sweet as honey.

The Seer, on the other hand—from the standpoint of the eater—says:

Ver. 10. **It was in my mouth as honey, sweet: and when I had eaten it, my belly was embittered.**—Learned discussions on this antithesis, see in Düsterdieck, p. 355. Bengel has even harmonistically inferred a double sweetness—before and after the bitterness. Besides the false interpretation of Heinrich, the interpretations of Herder, Bede, Vitringa and Hengstenberg come under consideration; with the last of these commentators, Düsterdieck himself agrees. The distinction between the first reception and the subsequent digestion, or investigation, is represented. Düsterdieck pertinently refers to the similar experience of Ezekiel (ch. iii. 3; comp. ch. ii. 10); the explanation which he accepts is also the best. ["The Angel, dwelling on the most important thing, the working of the contents of the book, puts the bitterness first; the Evangelist in relating what happened, follows the order of time." ALFORD.—E. R. C.]

Ver. 11. **And they say** [Lange: **he said**] **unto me.**—On the plural, see the *Textual Notes.* The passage ch. xii. 6 is no parallel.

Thou must.—It makes a false antithesis to refer the *δεῖ* exclusively either to his internal obligation, caused by his eating of the book, or to the objective command of the Angel, since the two are closely connected.

Prophesy again.—The prophecy of the *end* of the world, now following, is thus distinguished from the prophecy hitherto given, concerning the *course* of the world (Grotius, Hengstenberg, Düsterdieck, Ebrard).

Erroneous interpretations: Antithesis to the old Prophets (Bengel). *Again, i. e.,* after returning from exile (Bede, *et al.*).

[**Prophesy again before (or concerning) many peoples,** *etc.*—For the views of the Am. Ed. as to the correct rendering of the preposition, see TEXT. and GRAM. *"Prophesying.* In the Scriptural sense of the word, a *prophet* is one who speaks for another, as Aaron is called the prophet or *spokesman* of Moses. 'Thou shalt speak unto him, and put words into his mouth, . . . and he shall be thy spokesman,' Ex. iv. 15, 16; or, as he is called, vii. 1, *thy prophet.* The prophets of God, therefore, were His spokesmen, into whose mouth the Lord put the words which they were to utter to the people. To *prophesy,* in Scripture, is accordingly, to speak under Divine inspiration; not merely to predict future events, but to deliver, as the organ of the Holy Ghost, the messages of God to men, whether in the form of doctrine, exhortation, consolation, or prediction." HODGE, *Com. on 1st Corinthians,* ch. xi. 4. This interpretation of the word is consistent with the idea that the prophesying here referred to was that of the ministry of the Reformation, symbolized by the Seer, before peoples, *etc.;* or with the cognate and perhaps truer idea that the Apostle was to prophesy again—his ministry being resumed and carried on by them. (See, however, the following Add. Note.) —E. R. C.]

Difficulties of construction, arising from an imperfect distinction between Heaven-pictures and Earth-pictures, see cited by Düsterdieck, p. 357. Also a quantity of abortive applications of the chapter, the fault of which applications, however, does not lie in "the allegorical interpretation" in the abstract—i. e., the correct assumption of the allegorical character of the text. Thus, the strong Angel is declared to be: The Emperor Justin; Justinian; the evangelical preachers; the Pope. The little book [scroll] is called: The Codex Justinianus; the New Testament.

On the relation of the two books (ch. v. and the present chapter), we refer to the *Synoptical View.* Diverging opinions concerning them are that they are: (*a*) identical; (*b*) altogether different; (*c*) that the second is a distinct part of the first book; (*d*) that it is a repetition of the first.

[ADDITIONAL NOTE ON THE VISION OF THE ANGEL WITH THE LITTLE BOOK].

By the American Editor.

[The Am. Ed. inclines to the opinion of Elliott, that the period contemplated by this vision is that of the Reformation. On this hypothesis all the symbols (with one exception subsequently noticed) are beautifully appropriate and significant—the *Angel,* clothed with symbols indicating excellencies falsely claimed by the antichristian Papacy, representing Christ; the *Seer,* the ministry of the Reformation proclaiming the truth, as the prophets of Christ, before peoples and nations, and tongues and kings; the *open book,* the Bible opened by Christ, *sweet* to the taste of those who receive it by reason of the instruction and assurance of salvation that it affords, and yet producing *sorrow* both in its study and in the faithful promulgation of its truths. The truth of this hypothesis seems to be confirmed (1) by the position of the vision following the second woe—if that represent the Turkish invasion, then this would aptly indicate the following Reformation; and (2) by the *à priori* probability that such a glorious event as the Reformation would not be unnoticed in the Apocalyptic visions, and unless this vision indicate it, it is unnoticed.

[The writer must acknowledge, however, that there is much in the vision that seems to demand a still future fulfillment—especially *the oath* of the Angel (see above) which apparently contemplates a speedy sounding of the seventh Trumpet; and also the declaration to the Apostle that *he* is to prophesy *again*. This declaration, which is not satisfied by the fact that he continued his Apocalyptic narration, seems hardly to be satisfied by the hypothesis that he resumed his prophecy (symbolically) in the preaching of the Reformers. May it not be that there is here an indication that the Seer is personally to be one of the two *prophesying* Witnesses of the succeeding vision (see ch. xi. 3-10, especially 8, 9, 10)?—E. R. C.]

B.—INTIMATIONS FROM THE EARTH-PICTURE OF THE SEVEN THUNDERS. FEATURES OF THE PREPARATIVE REFORMATORY RENEWAL OF THE EARTH; OR TRAITS OF THE OPERATION OF THE SEVEN THUNDERS WHICH, IN THEMSELVES, WERE SEALED.—IN CONCLUSION: THE FIRST AND PRECURSORY ANTICHRISTIANITY; OR THE BEAST FROM THE ABYSS, THE DEMONIC REALM OF THE DEAD.

CHAP. XI. 1–14.

a. The Inner and the Outer Church.

VERS. 1, 2.

1 And there was given me a reed like unto a rod: [,] and the angel stood, [*om.* and the angel stood,—*ins. he*][1] saying, Rise, and measure the temple [ναόν] of God and
2 the altar, and them that worship therein [in it]. But [And] the court which is without [outside of] the temple [ναοῦ] leave [cast] out,[2] and measure it not [it shalt thou not measure]; for it is [was] given unto the Gentiles: and the holy city shall they tread under foot forty *and* [or and] two months.

b. The Two Witnesses. The Ideal Church and the Ideal State.

VERS. 3–12.

3 And I will give *power* [*om. power*] unto my two witnesses, and they shall prophesy a thousand two hundred *and* threescore [sixty] days, clothed in sackcloth.
4 These are the two olive trees, and the two candlesticks standing[3] before the God
5 [Lord][4] of the earth. And if any man [one] will [wills][5] hurt [to injure] them, fire proceedeth [goeth forth] out of their mouth, and devoureth their enemies: and if any man [one] will hurt [shall will][6] to injure] them, he must in this manner
6 [thus must he] be killed. These have [*or ins.* the][7] power to shut [*ins.* the] heaven, that it [*om.* it—*ins.* rain (ὑετός)] rain [βρέχῃ] not in [during][8] the days of their prophecy: and have power over [*ins.* the] waters to turn them to [into] blood, and to smite the earth with all plagues [every plague], as often as they [*ins.* shall]
7 will. And when they shall have finished their testimony, the beast [wild-beast] that ascendeth out of the bottomless pit [*om.* bottomless pit—*ins.* abyss] shall make war against [with] them, and shall overcome [conquer] them, and [*ins.* shall] kill

TEXTUAL AND GRAMMATICAL.

[1] Ver. 1. The reading of the Rec., *and the Angel stood and said*, is without sufficient foundation. [Cod. B*. gives καὶ εἱστήκει ὁ ἄγγελος; Critical Eds. generally omit, and also give λέγων with A. B*. P., instead of λέγει, acc. to א*.— E. R. C.]
[2] Ver. 2. [Treg. and Tisch. give ἔξωθεν with א°. A.; Alf. ἔξω with B*. Cod. א*. reads ἔσω and P. ἔσωθεν.—E. R. C.]
[3] Ver. 4. The reading ἑστῶτες with A. C. א. [א*. B*. P.] and others.
[4] Ver. 4. Κυρίου in acc. with A. B*.C.[א. P.], not Θεοῦ.
[5] Ver. 5. The reading θέλει. [So Crit. Eds. with א. A. B*. C. P.—E. R. C.]
[6] Ver. 5. [Treg. and Tisch. give θελήσῃ with א. A.; Gb., Sz., Lach., Alf., Tisch. (1859), θέλει.—E. R. C.]
[7] Ver. 6. [Lach. gives τὴν with A. C. P.; Tisch. omits with א. B*.; Alf. brackets and Treg. marks with *.—E. R. C.]
[8] Ver. 6. [Mod. Crit. Eds. give τὰς ἡμέρας with א. A. B*. C. P. See Lange, EXP. IN DETAIL.—E. R. C.]

8 them. And their dead bodies [corpse⁹] *shall lie* [*be*] in [upon] the street [broad-
way¹⁰] of the great city, which spiritually is called [is called spiritually] Sodom
9 and Egypt, where also our [their¹¹] Lord was crucified. And they [*men*] of the
people [peoples] and kindreds [tribes] and tongues and nations shall [*om.* shall¹²]
see their dead bodies [corpse] three days and a half, and shall not [*om.* shall¹³ not]
suffer [*ins.* not] their dead bodies [corpses] to be put in graves [a sepulchre].
10 And they that dwell upon the earth shall [*om.* shall¹⁴] rejoice over them, and make
merry,¹⁵ and shall [*or om.* shall¹⁶] send gifts one to another; because these two
11 prophets tormented them that dwelt on [dwell upon] the earth. And after [*ins.*
the] three days and a half the Spirit [a spirit] of life from God entered into them,¹⁷
and they stood upon their feet; and great fear fell upon them which saw [those
12 who beheld] them. And they [*or* I]¹⁸ heard a great voice from [*ins.* the] heaven saying unto them, Come up hither. And they ascended up to [into—*ins.* the] heaven
in a [the] cloud; and their enemies beheld them.

c. The Judgment.

VERS. 13, 14.

13 And [*ins.* in] the same [that] hour was there [there was] a great earthquake,
and the tenth part of the city fell, and in the earthquake were slain [*ins.* names]
of men seven thousand : and the remnant were [became] affrighted, and gave glory
to the God of [*ins.* the] heaven.
14 The second woe is past; *and,* [*om. and,*] behold, the third woe cometh quickly.

⁹ Ver. 8. [Lach., Alf., Treg., Tisch., give τὸ πτῶμα with A. B*. C.; Lange, and Rec. τα πτώματα with ℵ. P. In v. r. 9,
first occurrence, ℵ. also gives the singular; P. alone, the plural: in the second occurrence all the Codd. give the plural.—
E. R. C.]
¹⁰ Ver. 8. [See EXPLANATIONS IN DETAIL.—E. R. C.]
¹¹ Ver. 8. Instead of ἡμῶν, read αὐτῶν. [So Modern Crit. Eds. generally with ℵª. A. B. C. P.; Rec. *et al.* read ἡμῶν
with 1; ℵ*. omits both.—E. R. C.]
¹² Ver. 9. [Lach., Words., Alf., Treg., Tisch., give βλέπουσιν with ℵ. A. B*. C. P., Gb., Sz.; Lange, βλέψουσιν with
Vulg., *etc.*—E. R. C.]
¹³ Ver. 10. Ἀφίουσιν. [So Eds. generally with ℵ. A. C. P., *etc.*—E. R. C.]
¹⁴ Ver. 10. [Lach., Alf., Treg., Tisch., give χαίρουσιν with ℵ. A. B*. C. P.—E. R. C.]
¹⁵ Ver. 10. Εὐφραίνεται. [So Modern Eds. with ℵ. A. C. P.—E. R. C.]
¹⁶ Ver. 10. [Tisch. reads πέμπουσιν with ℵ*. P.; Lach., Words., Alf., Treg., Tisch. (1859), Lange, πέμψουσιν, with ℵ°.
A. C.—E. R. C.]
¹⁷ Ver. 11. Ἐν αὐτοῖς. See Düst. [Tisch. so giv s with A.; Treg. reads αὐτοῖς without ἐν with C. P. (he cites A. as
reading ἐπ' αὐτοῖς); Alf. brackets ἐν; ℵ. B*. read εἰς αὐτούς.—E. R. C.]
¹⁸ Ver. 12. The reading ἤκουσαν was probably preferred *as* apparently the more natural one. [So Lach., Alf., Treg.,
Tisch., with ℵ. A. C. P., Vulg., *etc.* Gb., Tisch. (1859), Lange, give ἤκουσα with ℵ.° B. (Treg. cites P. as giving the latter
reading.)—E. R. C.]

EXEGETICAL AND CRITICAL.

SYNOPTICAL VIEW.

The first figure that we meet with in this
chapter could scarcely be plainer; nothing save
a lapse into the misapprehensive literal conception could, from this passage, ch. xi. 1, 2, draw
the conclusion that the Temple in Jerusalem
was still standing at the time of these visions.
The Temple has always been a symbol of the
visible form under which the Kingdom of God
has appeared, *i. e.* the Theocracy at first, and,
later, the Church; and even the Temple of Ezekiel most distinctly presents this typicalism
(especially in the features of the mystical stream,
ch. xlvii. 1, and the voice of the Lord, ch. xliii.
7). In general, the mystical Temple of Ezekiel
seems to constitute a form which is transitional to
the Temple of the Apocalypse, in accordance with
the symbolical circumstances. The Holy of Holies has become one with the Holy Place, because the time of reconciliation has come; and,
on the other hand, the outer court has spread
into a number of outer courts, because it must
become a place for all nations; comp. Matt. xxi.
13; Is. lvi. 7. This significance and grandeur

of the outer court particularly appears in the
picture presented in the Apocalypse. Its contrast to the Temple is likewise strongly set
forth. The Prophet is to *measure* the *Temple*,
but *not* the *outer court*. The Temple of Ezekiel
is also measured, ch. xl. But the City of Jerusalem itself is described as an immeasurable
place in the Prophecy of Zechariah, ch. ii. 1 sqq.
In the Apocalypse, the measured Temple expands into the measured City of God (ch. xxi.
15); the unmeasured or immeasurable outer
court expands into the ideal domain of the
world and the nations, out of which all glory
shall be brought into the Holy City (Rev. xxi.
24; xxii. 2).

The Temple itself, then, must be measured; a
reed is given to the Prophet that he may measure it. The Spirit of God in the Church has
within Himself and in the Prophet a consciousness that the inner, essential Church is a Divine
definity, chosen by God and known to Him—*not*
a passing cloud, a drifting, shifting, transitory
object. That which is here expressed by *measure*, is twice declared by the *number* 144,000
(chaps. vii. and xiv.). So the Northern Mythology claims that the heroes of Odin are numbered.

A still more remarkable circumstance is that the *Altar* also is measured—the Altar of incense —the whole domain of holy prayer-life. And, humanly speaking, this belongs to the most conscious consciousness of God—to the inmost intuition (*innersten Erinnerung*) of the Church.

Finally, the *worshippers* in the Temple are to be measured. For the spiritual nature and development of every individual believer, the degree and the species of his glory, are known to God; they repose upon the individual capacities and disposition of each believer, as determined from eternity, his free agency being in nothing impaired (see Matt. vi. 27).

In antithesis to these Divine fixities, an immeasurable indefiniteness is reserved for the outer court. There can be nothing hostile in the direction to *cast it out;* the words can be expressive only of the decree that it is not to be measured along with the Sanctuary, that the consciousness of its externality is to be made permanent. For in its very quality of an outer court, it already lies outside of the Temple; and, furthermore, the direction: *cast it out* (on the milder or more general signification of ἐκβάλλειν, see the *Lexicons*) is modified by the words: *measure it not.* And why not? *For it is given to the Gentiles.* This does not mean merely, because the throng of the Gentiles—of such as are not subjective, living Christians—is immeasurable, but also because their assembly is fluctuating; because the outer court denotes the vestibule to the Sanctuary—a preparation for entrance into the Sanctuary. Of course, so long and in so far as the Gentiles are Gentiles, they *trample on* the outer court, as is also declared concerning the impenitent Jews, Is. i. They are loungers, street-walkers [*Pflastertreter*] in a religious sense; their outer court is the entire Holy City, i. e., the Church as an external body; they are they who, according to another figure, "stand all the day idle in the market." In the Christian service of the Sanctuary, they constitute the ebbing and flowing mass; they may, as a pious man once paradoxically expressed himself, sit in the way of the truly devout. Their theological knowledge consists partly of gross popular conceits, partly of spiritualistic mist. In confession, they strain the Divine word, in one direction, into a literal ordinance, and relax it, in the other direction, until nothing but an uncertain sentiment remains. In matters of practical piety, they are either violently active or inconstant and wavering. In all cases, the *treading of the outer court* is the leading feature of their devotions.

In regard to the import of the *forty-two months*, Düsterdieck and others believe, that they are connected with "the type of the duration of the down-treading of the Holy City by Antiochus Epiphanes." That, however, lasted but three years (see 1 Macc. iv. 59; comp. ch. i. 55). Moreover, the different designations of the theocratic time of tribulation (a time, two times, and half a time, Dan. vii. 25; xii. 7), according to times, years, months or days, are not without a mutual connection (see *Introduction,* p. 16). The forty-two months are the times of the pilgrimage of Christianity through the world, bearing the cross of suffering—suf-

fering inflicted on the internal Church through the external Church. These times are defined as forty-two little periods of change.

The second picture, in the history of the *Two Witnesses,* treats of another antithesis—that of the Christian Church and the Christian State. For the voice of the Lord which, in the text, so simply speaks of His two Witnesses, we, in face of the many marvels which have here been found, conceive of as setting forth the antithesis of the Christian Church and the Christian State; and this in accordance with the original passage in the Prophecy of Zechariah, on which the present passage is founded. The candlestick of Israel, the light and law of the Theocracy (Zech. iv. 2), receives its oil from the two olive-trees, or sons of oil, standing at the right and left of it (vers. 3 and 4). Now then, as they stand before the Ruler of the whole Earth, are, according to the context (ch. iii.), Joshua, the High-Priest, the typical representative of the future Church, concerning whom it is expressly declared, that he stands before the Angel of the Lord, and Zerubbabel the governor, the typical representative of the future State, distinguished by like dignities (ch. iv. 6, 7).

Many, no doubt, will regard this conception as too home-spun—not sufficiently ingenious or anecdotical. But, let us further remark, the removal, through the Man of Sin, of the *hindrance* to Antichristianity—the κατέχον (2 Thess. ii. 6), or κατέχων (ver. 7)—coincides precisely with the removal of the two olive trees [*German, sons of oil*] through the medium of the Beast out of the abyss.

The two Witnesses of God *prophesy.* To prophesy is to aid in opening for the Kingdom of God a way into the future, by declaring the signs of the future.[*] True advances, developments and reforms, are prophecies in act. All sound dogmas of the Church, as well as all sound laws of the State, are prophecies. Both Witnesses prophesy *clad in sackcloth*—in the penitential garb of the Church Militant and of the State, which latter is engaged in an incessant struggle with the ungodly spirit of the world. Here the movement continues through an uninterrupted chain of days' works—*one thousand two hundred and sixty days.* The time is equal to the forty-two months, but is viewed from an entirely different point; the whole Church and the whole State, in their higher aspect, are denoted here. As, however, Church and State are distinct under the new dispensation, their oil no longer flows together in one candlestick; both are *olive* trees [oil-trees]; both, also, are candlesticks. Again, they *stand before the God of the earth;* i. e., they unitedly represent firm, historic order, authority,—symbolized by the earth. Both have retained somewhat of the Old Testament character, the Elijah nature; and they are, manifestly, drawn after the type of Elijah. When they desire to injure any one, *fire goeth forth out of their mouth.* This can, of course, only be spiritual fire; just as the sword issuing from the mouth of the Lord, is but a spiritual sword. Nevertheless, it is a fire of judgment; it *devoureth their enemies.* The death that they inflict upon those who offend them, cannot be apprehended as the spiritual death in order to the new life; at least social death must be understood—exclusion from religious communion and civil fellowship, practiced in the Middle Ages under the great and gloomy forms of outlawry and excommunication. Their *power to shut the Heaven, that it rain not*, is most strongly suggestive of Elijah; whilst their power *over the waters, to turn them into blood, and to smite the earth with every plague, as often as they shall will*, recalls the wonders done by Moses in Egypt.

They can shut Heaven. The meaning of this is, they can check and withhold the blessings of the Spirit.

To turn the waters into blood, is to darken the currents of national life through wars and bloodshed.

To smite the earth with every plague, means to curtail the blessing of the historical authority or order of things in every way, and to convert it into a curse. *As often as they shall will*, adds the Seer, thereby indicating a great development of despoticalness and autocracy in their power.

Can it be supposed, we ask, that toward the end of the New Testament economy, two persons could appear as Prophets, having power to answer personal grievances with devouring fire? Or having power, at their own discretion, to bring forth in nature such wonders of judgment, and inflict them upon the earth? The Church and the State, however, have, in a symbolical sense, acted after precisely the Old Testament fashion here described, and that, with such a mingling of their qualities, as though they had done all things in common. They have likewise, in respect of their fundamental tendency, prominently set forth by the Seer, *prophesied, i. e.*, served the cause of development; and they have been *Witnesses* of God—representatives of His light and justice.

The predominantly Old Testament character of the past and present fulfillment of their mission, undoubtedly aids in cutting short the time of their testimony and in facilitating the triumph of the Beast over them. In consequence of the severity—in many respects excessive—of their rule, as manifested, particularly, in the form of the mediæval excommunication, and the military and judicial system of the same period, a two-fold Helot rancor, an ecclesiastical and political resentment, has ineffaceably impressed itself on the memory of the agitated life of the nations, bringing near the fatal time at which the *Beast* of Antichristianity may *ascend out of the abyss*.

Be it observed that Antichristianity passes through three climactic stages before attaining to perfection; exhibiting itself first in the form of the Beast out of the *abyss*, next in that of the Beast out of the *sea*, and finally in that of the Beast from the *earth*. The Beast out of the abyss possesses, as yet, no positive popular and human apparent form, much less the complete mock-holy semblance of the Lamb, possessed by the Beast from the earth; it first comes forth, as a bodiless spirit, from the abyss, in the power of a predominantly demonic spirit of the times, or party spirit. This spirit has ascended from the abyss, *i. e.*, the demonic region of the realm of the dead, which

15

constitutes a transition-form to the final hell. In this respect he is suggestive of the spirit of gloom which arose from the abyss at the fifth Trumpet. And from the fact of this resemblance, it results that he does not necessarily appear in the naked forms of lawlessness [*Anomismus*]. There is a gloomy churchly form which is subversive of the true Church, and a passionate state-form which undermines the true State. If we have recognized in the two Witnesses the intimate union between Church and State, as respects the bright side of both institutions, it becomes evident that their absolute disagreement must speedily be followed by self-dissolution. The true spirit of the Church can, indeed, long curb the wantonness of the State; the true spirit of the State can long protect the Church against a false ecclesiastical system. But mankind has already seen the false Church-form in conflict with sound State principles, and *vice versâ*. And mankind must finally see the Church ruined by the State, the State by the State, because in the case of each, sombre party-spirit has taken the place of right principles.

The Beast, then, shall *make war with* the two Witnesses—not merely a word and pen war, but also the war of social breach. He shall *conquer them* in *public opinion*, as men say, and complete his triumph by *killing* them. They are killed when destroyed as to their true principles —when the masses rule over faith and worship [*Kultus*] in the Church, over morals and culture in the State; or when, in the State, the last trace of kinship with the Church is destroyed through principial Atheism, and the last trace of political or social discipline and duty has disappeared from the Church. Then are they killed, even though their outward forms continue to exist, like the shades of departed substances, as, for instance, the forms of the Roman Republic under the first Emperors.

It is most significantly said: *their corpses lie in the street of the great city*. Their bodies, therefore, are not formally buried and put out of sight; they remain in the public street of the great city, under the eyes, and amid the surging to and fro, of a society fundamentally anarchical.

The great city itself is called *Sodom and Egypt*. Sodom is the symbol of perfect unnaturalness; Egypt is the symbol of a magical natural science and deification of nature. The two extremes, in their abominable coalition, are the Janus heads of a world which, in her deification of nature, is fundamentally at variance not only with God, but also with the kernel or inmost essence of nature itself.

There, adds the Seer, *their Lord was crucified*. The crucifixion of Christ was itself the result of a coalition of the spiritual unnaturalness of Judaism—self-murderous, in the killing of its Messiah—and the heathen world, which had fallen into sorcery [*Magismus*] and an intellectual cultus of nature.

Thus, as the murderess of Christ, Jerusalem may be the type of this great collective city, Sodom-Egypt; that the real Jerusalem itself is intended, can be supposed only under the erroneous system of an anti-symbolical, so-called historical treatment of the Book. With the symbolical name Jerusalem, however, another collective city, Babylon, might easily correspond. Some of the men, better disposed ones, who still have a remnant of influence left, individuals of the *peoples and tribes and tongues and nations*, shall in the meantime keep their dead bodies in view for *three days and a half*—not permitting them to be put into sepulchres; assuredly, in the hope of their revival. But the time rich in promise, the time of resurrection, the *three days* (Hos. vi. 2), pass away without affording any comfort; the corpses lie there until the hour of despair, indicated by three days *and a half*. And precisely this fact is a cause of delight to those who *dwell on the Earth*, or cling to the Earth in her earthiness—the earthly-minded ones. They *rejoice* over the apparent destruction of the two Witnesses; they hold feasts and contemplate further festivities; mutual greetings, in the way of presents or compliments, are exchanged, falling, particularly, to the share of the great utterers of public opinion, we doubt not.

The reason for all this is as follows: *These two Prophets tormented them that dwell upon the Earth.* Churchly rule [*Norm*] and civil law have always, to the true men of this world, who have made themselves at home on the Earth, been as a troublesome fanaticism, only disciplinary and tormenting.

But the people who watched their dead bodies have not sorrowed in vain. Finally, out of the horror of the human heart, full of a religious-moral anguish, a super-terrestrial power developes. It is thus not without instrumentality that, in the most disconsolate hour, the flame of the ecclesiastical and the political spirit rises again bright and heavenly, with united brilliancy and glorified beauty; that *a spirit of life from God* penetrates the corpses, so that they again *stand upon their feet*, prepared for war and victory, offering defiance to the whole apostate world, and diffusing great spiritual terror over all with whom they come in contact.

But they are not commissioned to fight again the former conflict; in the Kingdom of Spirit, they have triumphed through their defeat, like Christ their Lord. Therefore they hear, or the Seer hears, a great voice from Heaven saying to them: *Come up hither.*

But how can the Christian Church and the Christian State have assigned to them an ascension more glorious than that of Elijah—similar to that of Christ Himself? Nitzsch says: "Church and State shall, in their consummation, be swallowed up in the unity of the Kingdom of God." Let us particularly consider the following in this connection:

Their *ascension* is their exaltation above the former historical, in part pedagogical, forms, into the ideal form of a pure spiritual fellowship. They ascend into Heaven even whilst still on Earth, by being transported into the realm of pure spirit, of perfect fellowship with God. When, however, it is declared, that a *cloud* envelops them, there takes place a gathering and separation of this perfected congregation of God, this Bride of Christ, from the unbelieving world (Matt. xxiv. 31); and, no less, an alteration of her condition, to meet the heavenly glorification—an alteration characterized as an "attaining" [*Entgegenkommen*=coming towards] "the resurrection" (Phil. iii. 11); as a being "changed" (1 Cor. xv. 51); as a being "caught up into the air to meet the Lord" (1 Thess. iv. 17).

Their *enemies* must be spectators of their beginning glorification.

The hour of their glorification, however, becomes an hour of judgment for the world. The separation of the congregation of God from the world is followed by a *great earthquake;* all the relations of the old human society are shaken and mingled confusedly together by the separation of the salt of the Earth. Thus a great reaction is awakened in the better elements of the ungodly world. The *tenth part* of the godless city falls in the earthquake. *Ten*, as perfect development, realized freedom, is also perfect will, decided tendency. Thus, with the fall of the tenth part of the Antichristian world, the back-bone of that world is broken; henceforth it is a confused mass, anxiously expectant of the end. This change is especially brought about, however, by the fact that *seven thousand names of men*, or men of name, are *slain* in their names by the earthquake. Without doubt, the reaction of the terrified peoples has been directed with special fury toward their leaders, who, as seducers, by *thousands*, as spirits, by *seven* (Matt. xii. 45), have promised men the seventh day—the peoples' holiday. Above all, their names, shimmering with a deceptive lustre, are given up to scorn and destruction.

Whilst we must not forget that a cyclical life-picture of the entire New Testament time is here presented to us, neither should the fact be overlooked, that the conclusion of this time is characterized as the *second woe*—the intermediate one therefore—that which forms the transition from the first to the third woe; and it is in accordance with this fact that we must seek to determine the eschatological import of the present section.

We have seen that the second woe has presented itself in the grand succession of heresies (religious and ethical), which run through the entire Christian time; the time of this woe, therefore, coincides with that of the activity of the two Witnesses; it forms the reverse of their dispensation (Matt. xxiv. 26). It has likewise been found that the third woe begins with the seventh Trumpet, as the time of ripened Antichristianity, with features historically developed and determined.

The second woe is, therefore, a peculiar conformation of the times, consummated at the defeat of the two Witnesses and continuing until the period of positive Antichristianity. Its characteristic feature is the tremendous rocking of affairs beginning with the bursting forth of Antichristianity. The authorities and guardians of Church and State seem at last to be everlastingly destroyed; the better disposed are but individuals from all parts of the world who, in a manner, keep watch by the bodies of the slain, whilst the ruling party celebrate the excited festivities of an utterly secularized party-spirit. Then, however, by reason of the separation and gathering of the Church of God, a reaction again takes place; the power of the godless city is shaken by the glorious precursory appearing of the congregation of the Kingdom and by the altered sentiments of many of her inhabitants— in whom the change, however, bears the predominant character of a repentance of fear, and can therefore give way to the full manifestation of Antichristianity in the third woe. This period of a purely Antichristian spirit of the times, without final consolidation, is, in more *general* descriptions, included together with the *final* revelation of Antichrist, *e. g.* 2 Thess. ii. 8. The manifestation of wickedness [or the Wicked One—*des Boshaften*] has its gradations, as has already been intimated. This time seems to be more definitely characterized by the Beast, which is transformed into the eighth king (ch. xvii. 11), and which forms the transition from the *seven* kings of the old world of authority to the *ten* kings of absolute democracy.

We must, further, not overlook the fact, that even the second woe touches the end of the world, and that even the third woe, the revelation of Antichristianity, reaches back into the old time. In this connection, we would again call to mind the law of the cyclical circles; they ever present total world-pictures, though observing a continual progression toward the end of the world and illustrating always a different aspect of the world.

A feature worthy of notice is that the Beast of this second woe ascends out of the same abyss whence, after the fifth Trumpet, the smoke, accompanied by the swarm of locusts, arose; that, on the other hand, it precedes the third woe of consummate Antichristianity, just as the judgment upon Babylon (chs. xvii. and xviii.) precedes the judgment upon the Beast (ch. xix.).

We have, then, in ch. xi., the Earth-picture of the Christian visible world, in respect of its all-sided historic conformation in good and evil; above all, in respect of the conflict, waxing ever more pronounced, between ecclesiastical and political *nomism* [*Nomismus*] in the good sense of the term, on the one hand, and the *antinomism* or *anomism* of false liberty, or the modern spirit of the times, on the other hand—a conflict finally conducting, in part, to the ripe antithesis betwixt the Kingdom of God and the world, and ending, in the world itself, with the most extreme fluctuations.

[ABSTRACT OF VIEWS, ETC.]
By the American Editor.

[ELLIOTT and BARNES regard vers. 1, 2, as properly belonging to the preceding section (the latter part of ver. 2 being transitional to the following section) and as indicating the *Re-Formation* of the Church by those whom the *Seer* symbolized. The Temple, in the widest sense of the term, (inclusive of the Sanctuary and all the Courts) they interpret "as symbolic of the *Christian Church Universal:* the *Holy of Holies* . . . representing that part of it . . . gathered into Paradise; the *remainder of the Temple* . . . the Church on *Earth*, the *Holy Place*, ... as figuring the Church in respect of its *secret spiritual worship and character*, . . . the *Altar-court* . .

the Church in respect of its *visible and public worship*, ... the *outer or Gentile court* is the symbolic scene of the adscititious members from out of heathenism." The bestowment of the *rod (Elliott)*, as denoting "the *royal authorization* of those whom St. John here represented . . . in the work of the Scriptural *re-formation* of the Church;" the direction to *measure*, coupled with the *casting out*, as implying, 1. The *defining* of those who alone could rightly be considered as belonging to Christ's Church ("such as in public profession and worship recognized that cardinal point of the Christian faith which the Jewish Altar and Altar ritual-worship symbolized, viz. *justification by the alone efficacy of Christ's propitiatory sacrifice*");—2. The *exclusion* or *excommunication* of "the Romish (and Greek?) Church . . . as apostate and heathen;"—the recognition of those excluded as within a *Court* of the Temple, as indicating that those excluded "would continue to appear for a time attached as an appendage to the Church visible." By the *Witnesses* they understand the unbroken series of upholders and proclaimers of truth, divided as follows: (1) The earlier Western Witnesses, such as Serenus of Marseilles in the early part of the 8th Century, the Anglo Saxon Church, Agobard, Claude of Turin, *etc.;* (2) the Eastern line, consisting of the Paulicians arising about A. D. 653; (3) the United Eastern and Western lines, during the 11th and 12th Centuries; (4) the Waldenses* and Albigenses origina-

* [Elliott (Vol. II., *Appendix*) gives at length, and in the original, the *Noble Lesson* of the Waldenses. This work, written about A. D. 1170, presents the *Witness* of the Waldensian Church to the truth. He gives, Vol. II., pp. 390–396, translations from this, and from one of their later works entitled *Antichrist*. So valuable and interesting is the latter as indicating the position of that remarkable people in reference to Rome, and as *witnessing* against her, that the extract presented by Elliott is here reproduced. (The last paragraph is as presented by Barnes.)
"Antichrist is the falsehood (doomed to eternal damnation), covered with the appearance of the truth and righteousness of Christ and His spouse . . . being administered by false apostles; and defended by one or other arm (i. e., the spiritual and secular arm). . . . Thus it is not a certain particular person, ordained in a certain grade, office, or ministry, considering the thing generally; but the falsehood itself, opposed to the truth, with which however it covers itself, adorning itself *outwardly* with the beauty and piety of Christ's Church, of Christ Himself, His names, offices, scriptures, sacraments. The iniquity of this system, with all his ministers, higher and lower, following it with an evil and blinded mind—such a congregation, taken together, is called Antichrist, or Babylon, or the Fourth Beast, or the Harlot, or the Man of Sin, the Son of Perdition.
"His *first* work is, that the service of *latria*, properly due to God alone, he (Antichris) perverts unto himself and to his works, and to the poor creature, rational or irrational, sensible or insensible; as, for instance, to male or female saints departed this life, and to their images, bones, or relics. His works are the *sacraments*, especially that of the *eucharist*, which he worships equally with God and Christ, prohibiting the adoration of God alone.
"His *second* work is, that he robs and deprives Christ of the merits of Christ, with the whole sufficiency of grace, righteousness, regeneration, remission of sins, sanctification, confirmation, and spiritual nourishment; and imputes and attributes them to his own authority, to his own doings, or to the saints and their intercession, or to the fire of purgatory. Thus he *separates the people from Christ*, and leads them away to the things already mentioned; that so they may seek not the things of Christ, nor through Christ, but only the work of their own hands; not through a living faith in God, and Jesus Christ, and the Holy Spirit; but through the will and the works of Antichrist, agreeably to his preaching that man's whole salvation depends on his works.
"His *third* work is, that he attributes the regeneration of the Holy Spirit to a dead outward faith; baptizing child-

ting about A. D. 1170; (5) the Churches of the Reformation.—They interpret: (1) The 1260 *days* as indicating 1260 *years;* (2) the *olive-trees* and *candlesticks*, that they were to consist of both *ministers* and *churches;* (3) the number *two* that they were to be, (*a*) a number *competent* to bear witness (comp. Deut. xvii. 6; xix. 15, *etc.*), (*b*) a *small* number, (*c*) possibly the original division into *two* lines, Eastern and Western ; (4) their being *clothed in sack-cloth,* that they were to witness in the midst of grief and persecution ; (5) their *power* (Barnes), (*a'*) over those who should injure them, to *devour them with fire,* their doctrines and denunciations, which would resemble consuming fire (resulting ultimately in Divine judgment); (*b*) to *shut heaven,* that spiritual blessings would seem to be under their control. ("During the ages of their ministry, there was neither dew nor rain of a spiritual kind upon the earth, but at the word of the Witnesses. There was no knowledge of salvation but by their preaching—no descent of the Spirit but in answer to their prayers; and as the Witnesses were shut out from Christendom generally, a universal famine ensued," *Seventh Vial;* (*c*) over the *waters*, that the wars, commotions, *etc.*, which have followed the attempts to destroy them, and which have caused rivers of blood to flow, would *seem* to have been in answer to their prayers; (6) the *war* against them, the war of extermination waged in particular against the Waldenses ("from the year 1540-1570 . . . no fewer than *nine hundred thousand* Protestants were put to death by the Papists in different parts of Europe."—*Barnes*) ; (7) the *Beast* (the fourth Beast of Daniel. Dan. vii.), the Papacy ; (8) the *death,* the apparent destruction of the Witnesses at the Lateran Council (to which all dissentients had been summoned and at which none appeared) when, May 5, A. D. 1514, the Orator of the Council proclaimed to the Pope from the pulpit, "*Jam nemo reclamat, nullus obsistit!*" "There is an end of resistance to the papal rule and religion; opposers there exist no more :" and again "The whole body of Christendom is now seen to be subjected to its *Head,* that is to Thee." (Quoted by Elliott, Vol. II., p. 450); (9) the *not permitting their bodies to be buried,* "that they should be treated with indignity *as if* they were not worthy of Christian burial," (it was decreed that heretics should be denied Christian burial by the

---

ren in that faith, and teaching that by it is the consecration of baptism and regeneration, on which same faith it (he) ministers orders and the other sacraments; and on it founds all Christian religion.
"His *fourth* work is, that he rests the whole religion and sanctity of the people upon his Mass; for leading them to hear it, he deprives them of spiritual and sacramental manducation.
"His *fifth* work is, that he does every thing to be *seen*, and to glut his insatiable avarice.
"His *sixth* work is, that he allows manifest sins without ecclesiastical censure and excommunication.
"His *seventh* work is, that he defends his unity, not by the Holy Spirit, but by the secular power.
"His *eighth* work is, that he hates, persecutes, makes inquisition after, and robs and puts to death the members of Christ.
"These things and many others, are the cloak and vestment of Antichrist; by which he covers his lying wickedness, lest he should be rejected as a heathen. But there is no other cause of idolatry than a false opinion of grace, and truth, and authority, and invocation, and intercession; which this Antichrist has taken away from God, and which he has ascribed to ceremonies, and authorities, and a man's own works, and to saints, and to purgatory.'—E. R. C.]

Lateran Council, A. D. 1179; again, 1215, by Gregory IX.; and by Pope Martin, 1227); (10) the *broad place* (or *way*) of the City, (*Elliott*) the Council above mentioned, representing the whole Roman power, gathered in Rome; (11) the *rejoicing, etc.,* the special rejoicings after every new victory over "*heretics*," and especially at the close of th Council mentioned in sect. (8)—(see Elliott, Vol. II., pp. 454 sq.); (12) the *resurrection after three days and a half,* the renewal of witness by Luther—Luther posted his theses at Wittemberg, Oct. 31, 1517, *i. e., three years* and 180 *days* after May 5, 1514, when the Orator of the Lateran Council (see above in 8) proclaimed *heresy* to be *extinct;* (13) the *ascension,* the deliverance of the Church's of the Reformation from persecution and into positions of prosperity and influence; (14) the *earthquake,* the Reformation—"That religious revolution which astonished and *convulsed* the nations of Europe" (*Lingard*, quoted by Barnes); (15) the *fall* of the *tenth* part of the City, the falling away from Rome of, (*Barnes*) a considerable portion of her power, (*Elliott*) England, one of the *ten* Papal kingdoms; (16) the *slaying* of seven Chiliads, (*Elliott*) the separation from the Roman power of the Seven United Provinces of Holland—(*Barnes*) the proportion of those who *perished* in Europe in the wars consequent on the Reformation; (17) the *remnant affrighted,* the alarm of, (*Elliott*) the *remnant* of Papists in Protestant countries, (*Barnes*) the entire unconverted portion of the Roman City; (18) *gave glory to God,* (*Elliott*) praise was given by the Witnesses, (*Barnes*) the unconverted stood in awe at what God was doing.

STUART understands vers. 1, 2, "to prefigure *the preservation of all which was fundamental and essential in the ancient religion,* notwithstanding the destruction of all that was external in respect to the Temple, the City. and the ancient people of God." The vision of the Witnesses he interprets as symbolizing "that God would raise up faithful and well endowed preachers among the Jews, at the period when the nations were ready to perish ; that those preachers would be persecuted and destroyed ; and after all that the Christian cause would still be triumphant."

WORDSWORTH regards (vers. 1, 2) the *Temple* and *Altar* (of incense) as symbolizing the true Church ; the *reed* as the Scriptures ; the *measuring* as an act "of *appropriation* and of *preservation* (Num. xxxv. 5; Jer. xxxi. 39; Hab. iii. 6; Zech. ii. 2), and also of *partition* and *separation,* (2 Sam. viii. 2)" ; "in this vision of the Apocalypse, the last written of all the Books of Holy Scripture (the completion of the Canon or *measuring rule*), St. John receives the reed from Christ and measures the Church." The two *Witnesses* he understands as indicating the Church (called *two* as consisting of both Jews and Gentiles), enlivened and enlightened by the two Testaments (the two *olive trees*); their *persecution, death,* etc., that the history of Christ will be reproduced in the history of His Word and Church. The *Beast* and *City* he interprets as Barnes and Elliott.

ALFORD remarks, "No solution at all approaching to a satisfactory one has ever yet been given of any one of these periods. This being so, my principle is to regard them as being still among things unknown to the Church, and awaiting their elucidation by the event." Concerning the *Witnesses* he remarks on ver. 6, "All this points out the spirit and power of Moses combined with that of El'as. And undoubtedly it is in these two directions that we must look for the two witnesses or lines of witnesses. The one impersonates the law, the other the Prophets. The one reminds us of the Prophet whom God should raise up like unto Moses; the other of Elias, the Prophet who should come before the great and terrible day of the Lord." As to whether the prophecy is to be fulfilled by *individuals* or *lines of witnesses*, he does not attempt to decide.

LORD writes as to the *measuring of the Temple*, "The *rod* is the symbol of the revealed will of God; . . . the *Holy of Holies* . . . the scene in which God visibly manifests Himself, Christ intercedes, and the Cherubim, the representatives of the redeemed, serve in His presence; so the *other sanctuary* symbolizes the place or places on earth in which the true worshippers offer Him the public worship which He enjoins. The *Altar* on which incense, the symbol of prayer, was offered, represented the Cross of Christ, the instrument of His expiation, and thence of reconciliation and access to God. . . . To *measure the Temple*, then, was to seek and learn the truths taught in the Scriptures, and symbolized first by the *inner sanctuary*, . . . and next . . . by the *outer sanctuary*, respecting the *place* or *places* on earth which He has appointed for the worship which He enjoins on His people, respecting the *expiation* on which they are to rely, . . . and respecting the *ministers* who conduct the worship He enjoins. . . . The *court*, which was on the *outside*, . . . denoted the station of the congregation of visible worshippers; . . . to *reject it as no part of the Temple*, was therefore, to reject the body of the nominal or visible, as not true worshippers; and the direction to reject it was equivalent to the prophecy that the *nominal* was not to be a *true* Church. . . . The command to measure the Temple was addressed to *the Apostle* doubtless as representing the same persons as he symbolized in the prediction that he must again prophesy before peoples, *etc.*" On the subject of the Witnesses, he agrees as to their *nature*, substantially, with Elliott and Barnes; their death, resurrection, and ascension, however, he regards as still future and as literal. The 1260, and three and a half, *days*, he interprets as symbolic of years.

GLASGOW refers the measuring to Apostolic times. "The *Apostles* (symbolized by *John*), by inspiration, gave laws of discipline and of morals, for receiving or excluding candidates for members. Thus they *measured* the *House* and *City* of God. And they measured the *Altar* by teaching the doctrine of the one sacrifice offered by Christ, and of His intercession, and of His government on the mediatorial throne; and they measured the *worshippers*, by supplying the patterns and rules of duty, and thus furnishing the means of distinguishing the Lord's peculiar 'people' from His enemies." The *outside* court he interprets substantially as Elliott; the *trampling* of the City, as the predominance "of what Neander and Killen have called 'the Catholic system.'" The *Witnesses* he also interprets as symbolizing

the Paulicians, Waldenses, *etc.*; he begins the Witness, however, with the protest of the Novatians about A. D. 253, and thus concludes the 1260 days (or years) of prophesying *in sackcloth* (or affliction) in A. D. 1514. He adopts the opinion that the declaration made May 5th, 1514, in the Lateran Council, referred to above, denotes the death and exposure of the dead bodies of the Witnesses. On other points of interpretation he agrees generally with Elliott.—E. R. C.]

EXPLANATIONS IN DETAIL.

Düsterdieck holds, with us, that the present section really closes with ver. 14. [With Elliott and others, the Am. Ed. regards vers. 1 and 2 as connected with the preceding chapter. See Additional Note, p. 182.—E. R. C.]

Ver. 1. And there was given me a reed. —After the analogy of Old Testament propheticosymbolical transactions; see Is. viii. 1, and many other passages, particularly in the Prophecies of Jeremiah and Ezekiel.

Given.—*By whom?* The indeterminateness denotes that nothing in the symbolism is dependent upon this feature. The *literal* interpretation would fain define the giver.

A reed.—Ezek. xl. 3; Rev. xxi. 15. [**Like unto a rod.**—"The word ῥάβδος, rod, is coupled three times in the Apocalypse with the adjective σιδηρᾶ (ii. 27; xii. 5; xix. 15). And in the same places it is coupled also with the verb ποιμαίνειν, to tend, as a shepherd does. The idea is thus suggested of a *pastoral staff*." WORDSW.—E. R. C.]

Saying [Lange: **Whilst it was commanded**].—Λέγων—indefinite form. Bengel explains, grammatically but not symbolically: the κάλαμος.

Measure the Temple.—The Temple in Jerusalem had long since been measured; it, however, is not what is meant here. Neither, indeed, is the measuring to be taken literally. The *worshippers*, also, are to be measured, *i. e.*, precisely determined. In Ezek. xl. 3 sqq., the measuring of a symbolical Temple is spoken of, whilst Rev. xxi. treats of the measurement of the symbolical City of God.

According to Düsterdieck and many others, the *measuring* here denotes exemption from destruction; the above-mentioned commentator supposes that the *treading under foot* of the outer court is indicative of actual destruction. Yet the very passages that he cites [in connection with the *measuring*]—Amos vii. 7; Hab. iii. 6—have reference to destruction, and the idea that the outer court was destroyed, but that the Temple and the worship continued to subsist, is utterly futile, as is in general the so-called historic application of the passage to the Temple at Jerusalem. Düsterdieck calls the interpretation of the Temple as the true Church of God, allegoristic! One-sided, we admit that it is, to interpret the measuring of the Temple as indicative of a reconstruction of the Church, or to apply the contrast between the Temple and the outer court, in which contrast the chief weight of the similitude lies, to the contrast between the evangelic Church and Catholicism; in opposition to the latter exposition, Catholic exegetes distinguish between good Catholics and excommunicated persons. [See the ABSTRACT OF VIEWS, etc., pp. 227 sqq.—E. R. C.] The altar.—The Altar of incense. The Altar of burnt-offering stood in the outer court. [Elliott and Barnes regard the Altar as that of *burnt-offering*. It must be acknowledged that the language apparently points to the three great divisions of the Temple enclosure—the ναός or Sanctuary, the θυσιαστήριον or *altar (court)*, and the court *outside* the Sanctuary, *i. e.*, the court of the Gentiles. Of these courts, that of the Gentiles alone entirely surrounded the Sanctuary; the inner court merely enclosed it on three sides: the latter, from both its local and spiritual relations to the Sanctuary, could not so well be described as *outside* (τὴν αὐλὴν τὴν ἔξωθεν τοῦ ναοῦ), as the former.—E. R. C.]

In it (ἐν αὐτῷ).—These words might be referred to the *Altar of incense*, inasmuch as all *prayers* do, in a symbolical sense, ascend from the Altar of incense; most exegetes, however, make them relate to the Temple.* The main thing, here as elsewhere, is the contrast presented to those without. John is thought even here to have in view the imminent destruction of Jerusalem, differing, however, from the eschatological prophecies of the Lord by predicting a preservation of the Temple, and placing the faithful Jewish Christians therein! (comp. also De Wette, Lücke, p. 354).

Ver. 2. And [Lange: But] the court which is without the Temple.—On misapprehensions of the outer court, by Luther, Vitringa, Ewald, see Düsterdieck.

Cast out.—Eichhorn, correctly: *Profanum declara.*

Given unto the Gentiles [*heathen*].—[On the New Testament force of τὰ ἔθνη see Cremer's *Biblico-Theological Lexicon* under ʼΕθνος. The following is extracted: " It is a peculiarity of New Testament, or, indeed, of Bible usage generally, to understand by τὰ ἔθνη, πάντα τὰ ἔθνη, *those who are not of Israel*, opp. υἱοὶ ʼΙσραήλ, ʼΙουδαῖοι, Acts ix. 15; xiv. 2, 5; xxi. 11, 21; xxvi. 20; Rom. ii. 24; iii. 29; ix. 24, 30, 31; xi. 25; 1 Cor. i. 23; Gal. ii. 15: οἱ ἐκ περιτομῆς; Acts x. 45: περιτομῆ; Gal. ii. 9 (cf. Eph. ii. 11): γένος; 2 Cor. xi. 26 parallel; οἱ κατάλοιποι τῶν ἀνθρώπων, Acts xv. 17. In this sense the word corresponds to the Hebrew נ (LXX. sometimes=λαός, *e. g.*, (Josh. iii. 17; iv. 1), which signifies primarily nothing but a *connected host, multitude*. . . . Τὰ ἔθνη are *the peoples outside* of Israel—the totality of the nations, which, being left to themselves (Acts xiv. 16), are unconnected with the God of Salvation, Who is Israel's God; Acts xxviii. 28; Eph. ii. 11, 12; Rom. xi. 11, 12; Gal. iii. 8, 14; 1 Thess. iv. 5; Eph. iii. 6; Matt. xii. 21. Left to themselves and to their own will, they stand in moral antagonism to the Divine order of life, Eph. iv. 17; 1 Pet. iv. 3, 4; 1 Cor. x. 20; xii. 2; Matt. vi. 32; Luke xii. 30; cf. Matt. xviii. 17; they

are not in possession of the revealed law. Rom. ii. 14; cf. ix. 30; nor are they bound to the rules and laws of Israelitish life, Gal. ii. 12, 14, 15. It is this moral-religious lack that renders so significant the emphasis laid on the ὑπακοὴ πίστεως, on the part of the ἔθνη, Rom. i. 5; xv. 18; xvi. 26. . . Whether in the Apocalypse ἔθνη is opposed to Israel, or, as it appears to me, to the New Testament redeemed Church, must be left to commentators to decide. Rev. ii. 26; xi. 2, 18; xii. 5; xiv. 8; xv. 3, 4; xvi. 19; xviii. 3, 23; xix. 5; xx. 3, 8; xxi. 24, 26; xxii. 2." See *foot-note†* on p. 27.—E. R. C.]—[Given unto.] —Düsterd.: They shall lodge therein as victors, trending the outer court and the entire Holy City. Bengel—better, at least: The outer court is not measured, because an unthought-of throng of Gentiles shall one day worship therein. But something more than a mere future is contemplated. De Wette and others: The bloody sacrificial service, consummated on the altar of burnt-offering, shall cease.

Ver. 3. My two Witnesses.—According to Düsterdieck, these must be personal individuals. Personal individuals possessing the characteristics described cannot be pointed out as existing at the time of the destruction of Jerusalem, or as living on through the entire Cross-æon of the Church down to the end of the world. According to Düsterdieck and others (p. 382), these two witnesses are Moses and Elijah; according to Stern and others, they are Enoch and Elijah; even Luther and Melanchthon have been suggested. According to Ebrard, they are symbols of authorities, powers, which, however, he pertinently enough defines as Law and Gospel. Since the Witnesses can be witnesses of *Christ* only, the term, *My* witnesses, is elucidative of the strong Angel mentioned in the foregoing chapter [who spoke to John, ch. x. 9, 11, and whom Lange apparently regards as still speaking]. [See ABSTRACT OF VIEWS, pp. 227 sqq., and ADD. NOTE, pp. 232 sq.—E. R. C.].

I will give.— *What* He gives them, is declared by what follows; δώσω, therefore, need not be supplemented by conjectures.

Sackcloth, as a penitential dress, Jer. iv. 8; Jon. iii. 5; Matt. xi. 21. [As a garment of *affliction*, see Gen. xxxvii. 34; 2 Sam. iii. 31; xxi. 10; 2 Kin. vi. 30; Esth. iv. 1, 2, 3, 4; Job xvi. 15; Pss. xxx. 11; xxxv. 13; lxix. 11; Isa. iii. 24; xv. 3; xx. 2; Jer. xlviii. 37; xlix. 3; Amos viii. 10.—E. R. C.]

Ver. 4. The two olive trees.—The Seer, as an accomplished symbolist, has descried in the olive trees of Zech. iv. perfectly admissible types of New Testament affairs. On αἱ...ἑστῶτες, see the remark in Düsterdieck. [" As the olive-tree furnished oil for the lamps, the two trees here would seem properly to denote ministers of religion; and as there can be no doubt that the candlesticks, or lamp-bearers, denote churches, the sense would appear to be that it was through the pastors of the churches that the oil of grace which maintained the brightness of those mystic candlesticks, or the churches, was conveyed. The image is a beautiful one, and expresses a truth of great importance to the world:—for God has designed that the lamp of piety shall be kept burning in the churches by truth supplied

---

* [With equal propriety may they refer to the Altar court, if that be meant by the θυσιαστήριον. And indeed the introduction of this clause seems to point to this interpretation of the Altar, as only priests worshipped in the Sanctuary —the people worshipping in the court. On the other hand, however, it may be contended that, as all true Christians are priests, their proper place of worship is the Sanctuary. —E. R. C.]

through ministers and pastors." BARNES.—
E. R. C.]
Before the Lord of the earth.—The Lord
is the unitous authority of the *earth* or the theocratic institution—which formerly branched into
Joshua and Zerubbabel, and now ramifies into
State and Church. Ebrard interprets the Old
Testament *Lord of the whole earth* as indicative
of the king of Persia, and regards the corresponding New Testament expression as significant of the ruler of this world.
Vers. 5, 6. "The individual lineaments of
this description, especially in ver. 6, are borrowed from the history of Elijah and Moses.
This reference—admitted by all expositors—to
the miracles of those old Prophets (miracles
which are in no wise allegorically understood)
of itself renders it highly improbable that the
description of the present passage is allegorically intended" (Düsterdieck). Most original
logic, this! As if historical facts, and especially such as have since their very occurrence
assumed a symbolical coloring, might not be
employed in allegorical descriptions. A slight
examination of the New Testament will speedily
convince us that such is not the case. [See the
quotation from Alford, p. 229.—E. R. C.]
Fire goeth forth out of their mouth.—
Jer. v. 14. The reference to 2 Kings i. 10 is by
Düsterdieck considered of doubtful propriety,
because Elijah calls down fire *from Heaven.* But
even this fact might be paraphrased, in the prophetic style, as follows: fire proceeded out of
his mouth, Sirach xlviii. 1. If, however, we
take the words, *out of their mouth,* and *fire,* literally, we have "a fearful reality" (Düsterd.).
This is called *historical exegesis.* The spectator
of such fire-works might possibly say: a *dubious*
reality—magic; such an one would be able to
set his mind at rest only by echoing the verdict
of Rothe: "God is an adept at sorcery."
Ver. 6. **Power to shut Heaven.**—1 Kings
xvii. 1.
During [Lange: **For**] **the days.**—If the
words, *for the days of their prophecy,* denote the
time of their entire activity, and that with reference to the 3½ years of drought predicted by
Elijah, the time of this entire activity would need
to be reduced to ordinary years—and this is not
practicable. We, therefore, apprehend the passage thus: for the days *fixed by* their prophecy.
Over the waters.—Ex. vii. 19.
With every plague [Lange: **With all**
(manner of) **plagues**].—Reference to the
Egyptian plagues generally. According to Düsterdieck, it is inadmissible to interpret even these
features allegorically, *i. e.,* to apprehend them
as allegorical. Whilst the interpretation of
Bede—making the *power to shut Heaven* the
potestas clavium—may be too restrictedly ecclesiastical, the more general application of the
passage to the *withholding of the rain or blessing of the Gospel,* is certainly removed beyond
the objection urged against it, *viz.:* that in case
of its acceptance, it would be necessary to apprehend 1 Kings xvii.; James v. 17; Ex. vii.
sqq. figuratively also; and this, apart from the
fact that even these passages are not to be taken
in so naked a Græco-historical sense as many
seem to suppose.

Ver. 7. **Finished their testimony,**[*] **the
wild-beast,** *etc.*—Preliminary and more general symbolization of Antichristianity. This
one Beast branches into two Beasts in ch. xiii.
Vers. 8-10. **In the broad-way**[†] [Lange:
street] **of the great city.**—The literal method entails the apprehension of the fact that
the bodies remained lying in the City, in accordance with the ancient conception of the great
impiety of suffering corpses to remain unburied.
The question arises here, however: are the individuals (ver. 9) of (all) **the peoples** identical with the persons mentioned in ver. 10, who
are described in general terms as *the inhabitants
of the earth,* and are, therefore, enemies of the
Witnesses? The text plainly distinguishes between the two classes. There is, then, in any
case, a two-fold interest which is subserved by
the leaving of the corpses unburied—a hostile
and a friendly interest. In ver. 9 it is declared:
βλέπουσιν ἐκ τῶν λαῶν, *etc.*
"That the *great* City is identical with the *Holy*
City, where the ναὸς τῶν θεοῦ stands (ver. 1 sqq.),
and that it is, therefore, none other than Jerusalem, is evident from the context" (Düsterdieck).
Even the literal interpretation is forced to admit
that *Sodom and Egypt* (see Is. i. 9; Ezek. xvi. 48)
is a "spiritual appellation," the fact being expressly set forth in the text. Yet this appellation
is robbed of the greater part of its force, when
the attempt to exhibit a distinction (Hengstenberg's, for instance: *Egypt* has reference to religious corruption, *Sodom* to bad morals) is swept
aside, with the declaration that the only point of
importance is that in which Sodom and Egypt
are essentially *one,* viz.: perfect hostility to the
true God, His servants, and His people.
The great City.—As the so-called historical
interpretation regards the present passage as
significant, throughout, of the real Jerusalem
(Ewald, Bleek, De Wette, Düsterd., *et al.*), the
following question arises: Why is the City called
the *great,* and not the *holy?* Discussions of this
question are submitted by Düsterdieck, p. 370.
The question does not present itself at all to a
more correct exegesis—one that appreciates the
symbolical import of the passage. It is something of a leap to discover, like Calov., here, in
the City of Jerusalem, Babylon—in Babylon,
Rome—in Rome, papal Rome. Undoubtedly,
this great City of Jerusalem is, in essentials, of
like import with the great City of Babylon (in
the more general sense of the latter, ch. xvi.
19); but the context contains a reason for the
fact, that the City is *here* indirectly called *Jerusalem,* as the city where the Lord was crucified,
and *there, Babylon.* Here, namely, it represents
the symbolically modified Theocracy, or Divine
establishment, embracing Church and State, as
a mock-holy *fallen* Theocracy; there, it repre-

[* [Lord translates: *And when they would finish their testimony, etc.*; and comments: "The Witnesses *would* finish
their testimony before the close of the 1260 years, doubtless
under the apprehension that it was no longer to be necessary; that the great changes wrought in public opinion, and
in the condition of the apostate Church by judgments on it,
divested it of its dangerous power, and insured its speedy
overthrow; and that they might therefore turn from the
mere endeavor to maintain the truth in opposition to it, to
the happier task of proclaiming it to those who had never
yet heard the glad tidings."—E. R. C.]
† [See Kitto's *Dict. of the Bible,* Title STREET.—E. R. C.]

sents the centre of the open Antichristian spirit of the world.—The meaning of the great City is more generally apprehended by Ebrard, p. 342.* Different interpretations of the *three and a half days* see in Düsterdieck, p. 371. A short time; the time during which Christ lay in the grave; the time which exceeds the term during which corpses should remain above ground; analogous to ver. 2; Chiliastic computations of the number.

Ver. 11. And after the three days and a half, a spirit of life, etc.—*Materially* [as distinguished from *grammatically*], Hengstenberg's interpretation of πνεῦμα ζωῆς as *the Spirit of life* cannot be incorrect [Düsterdieck to the contrary, notwithstanding], since this spirit proceeds from God.—A form of peculiar significance : εἰσῆλθεν ἐν αὐτοῖς.

Great fear.—The usual effect of great Divine wonders, angelic appearances, spiritual operations, and especially of the wonder of resurrection.

Ver. 12. And they ascended, etc.—Suggestive of the ascension of Elijah and, still more, of Christ's ascension.

Vers. 13, 14. And in that hour.—That is, the events narrated took place simultaneously with the ascension of the two Witnesses and were co-operative therewith. According to Düsterdieck, not even this *earthquake* should, as Ebrard maintains, be symbolically apprehended as an extraordinary event. In respect of the numbers, we refer to the SYNOPTICAL VIEW. Ebrard's interpretation, see p. 347; comp. Düsterdieck, p. 374.

In spite of the invincible difficulties which lie in the literal apprehension (the outer court destroyed; the Temple, and even the worship therein celebrated, continuing; the two Witnesses vomiting fire; Christ prophesied the *destruction* of Jerusalem—the Seer narrates its visitation by an earthquake, etc.), Düsterdieck, supported, we must own, by notable predecessors, believes that this apprehension is in all points firmly established against the symbolical apprehension. An allegorical text, however, does not cease to be allegorical for the simple reason, that a multitude of wrong interpretations have attached themselves to it. Arbitrary interpretation is not conquered by cutting the Gordian knot and plunging into the absurdities of literalism; that which is requisite and able to overcome it is a more precise and accurate determination of the symbolical expressions and conceptions of the Old Testament. Such a determination at once dispatches the following collection of arbitrary expositions presented by Düsterdieck, p. 375.

Vers. 1 and 2 are, according to Bede, prophetic of the institution of the festival of Church consecration by Pope Felix. The *two Witnesses* are, according to Lyra, Pope Silverius and the Patriarch Mennas; or, according to others, the *testes veritatis;* or the Waldenses; or Huss and Jerome; or Luther and Melanchthon. The *Beast out of the Abyss* is the Imperial general Belisarius, or the Pope. The *Temple* is the true Church; the *outer court*, bad Christians, etc. Similar chronological computations see in Düsterd 's note, p. 376.

In reality, however, most of the so-called allegorists essentially occupy the same standpoint with the historical expositors after Lücke, Bleek, Düsterd. and others; both have in view particular historic facts, literally defined; only, according to the allegorists, these particularities are actual, inspired prophecies, veiled in figures. Modern supporters of the historical view have found some portions of the veil indispensable; they, moreover, divide the prophetic items into truths and errors.

With all Düsterdieck's fondness for literalism, however, he decidedly rejects the rationalistic interpretation, p. 377 sqq. See likewise his further examination of the symbolical exegesis as represented by Hengstenberg.

[ADDITIONAL NOTE ON THE SECTION.]

By the American Editor.

[In the judgment of the American Editor, vers. 1-8 (or 7) are connected with the vision of the preceding chapter—vers. 2-8 (or 7) containing an *address* made to the Seer during that vision, in which the work and death of the Witnesses are *verbally* described to him. The *vision* of the Witnesses begins with ver. 9 (or 8). It will be perceived that at that point the phraseology changes; the Seer no longer rehearses what another told him; he describes what he himself beheld. If this opinion be correct, the *Apocalyptic stand-point* of John at the vision beginning ch. x. 1, was probably at the period of the death of the Witnesses; in the explanatory narration beginning ch. xi. 8, the narrator described as *future* that which *was to be;* but in the description of the *vision*, John describes as *past* and *present* that which (in symbol) he so beheld.

THE WITNESSES.— *Who are they?* Barnes has well declared concerning the passage which describes them: "This is, in some respects, the most difficult portion of the Book of Revelation." There are many points in the description which seem to favor the idea that they are, as is contended by Elliott, Barnes, etc., the long line of protesters against a heathenized Christianity; there are other points, however, in which we feel that, on this hypothesis, the symbols are but inadequately satisfied; the miraculous powers ascribed to them, for instance and especially, seem to demand something which the history even of the Waldenses does not fully supply. The thought has arisen in the mind of the writer, that possibly here, as in some of the Old Testament prophecies, and probably in those concerning Antichrist (see ADD. NOTE, p. 339), the symbols may have a double objective—respecting (1) *two lines of witnesses* which are to be consummated in (2) *two individual witnesses,* in whom they are to be fully (as Immediate-similar Symbols) realized. On this hypothesis (possibly) *the lines* would prophesy throughout the twelve hundred and sixty *years* of initial Gentile trampling; the *individuals* throughout twelve hundred and sixty *days* of consummate trampling (the *three and a half years*—twelve hundred and sixty days, during which *the lines* would lie as dead), and then be literally slain, and lie unburied for three and a half days.

On the general hypothesis that *lines of witnesses*

---

* [For an exceedingly able argument designed to show that Rome was probably referred to by the Apocalyptist, see Barnes *in loc.*—E. R. C.]

(either primarily or exclusively) are intended, two questions arise, *viz.*, What is the period of their *rise?* and what of their *death?* These questions are so intimately associated that they cannot with propriety be considered separately; they constitute one complex subject. On this subject there are *three* particular hypotheses set forth by those who adopt the *day-for-a-year* theory: 1. That of Elliott, that they began in the Paulicians about A. D. 653; were slain at the Lateran Council, May 5th, 1514; arose again in Luther, Oct. 31st, 1517; and still continue their testimony. 2. That of Glasgow, who agrees with Elliott as to the period of their death, but who places their beginning about A. D. 253, in the Novatian protest. 3. That of Lord, who substantially agrees with Elliott as to the period of their beginning, but who places their *death* in the future. Of these hypotheses, the first seems to the writer to be clearly inadmissible; the comparison of vers. 3 and 7 requires that we should place their death at the close of the twelve hundred and sixty days of their testimony. There is much to commend the earlier period *of beginning* advocated by Glasgow. Manifestly, there is much in history to support the idea that *a death* of the Witnesses did occur at the Council referred to—a death followed by a resurrection *three and a half years after* in the rise of the Reformers; and it is certainly a question whether, twelve hundred and sixty years before, *a trampling* of the Church by the previously invading Gentiles did not begin in the almost unconditional restoration of the *lapsi*—a resto-

ration against which the Novatians *in sackcloth* protested. But, on the other hand, this hypothesis not only assumes a doubtful *terminus a quo*, but it fails to provide for the present time when, manifestly, there exists just such *a trampling* as then existed, and likewise a similar *witnessing.*

The writer would suggest ▪▪ a possible solution of the difficulty, that there was contemplated (1) an *initial* trampling of the outer court beginning about A. D. 253, followed by a *typical* death of the Witnesses in 1514; (2) ▪ *more complete* trampling beginning, perchance, in the introduction of image worship, to be followed by a *more complete* death in the future; (3) the whole to be consummated, as indicated above, by the prophesying and death of individual Witnesses. As to the *measuring*, the writer agrees with the general opinion of the commentators whose views he has presented above. That opinion may be most completely set forth in the language of Wordsworth: "The action of measuring is one of *appropriation* and *preservation*, and also of *partition* and *separation*." This act, possibly, was initially and typically performed at the Reformation; probably it will be more fully performed in the future, when the *casting out* (the *excommunication*) of those who trample the outer court will be proclaimed by an *individual* (or a *class*) directly commissioned for this purpose by the Great Head of the Church. May not this event be coincident with the call to the people of the Lord, who may still remain in Babylon, to come out of her (ch. xviii. 4)?—E. R. C.]

PART SECOND

THE END OF THE WORLD.

[CH. XI. 15—XXII. 5.]

SECTION FIFTH.

Developed Antichristianity. The seven-headed Dragon and his Image [*Erscheinungs-bild*]: the seven-headed Beast.

CH. XI. 15—XIII.

A.—THE HEAVEN-PICTURE ABOVE THE ANTICHRISTIANITY ON EARTH ; OR THE PRECURSORY TRIUMPH OVER THE DRAGON, AND HIS FALL FROM HEAVEN TO THE EARTH.

CH. XI. 15—XII. 12.

a. Pre-celebration of the Victory.

CH. XI. 15—19.

15   And the seventh angel sounded [trumpeted] ; and there were great voices in [*ins.* the] heaven, saying, The kingdoms [kingdom][1] of this [the] world are [is] become *the kingdoms of* [*om. the kingdoms* of] our Lord [Lord's], and of [*om.* of] his Christ
16   [Christ's] ; and he shall reign forever and ever [into the ages of the ages].   And the[2] four and twenty [twenty-four] elders, which [who][2] sat [sit][3] before God on
17   [upon] their seats [thrones], fell upon their faces, and worshipped God, Saying, We give thee thanks, O Lord God Almighty [*or* All-ruler[4]], which [who] art, and [*ins.* who] wast, and art to come [*om.* , and art to come][5] ; because thou hast taken to
18   thee [*om.* to thee] thy great power, and hast reigned.   And the nations[6] were angry [wroth], and thy wrath is come, and the time of the dead, that they should [*om.* , that they should—*ins.* to] be judged, and that thou shouldest [*om.* that thou should-est—*ins.* to] give [*ins.* the] reward unto thy servants the prophets, and to [*om.* to] the saints, and them that [those who] fear thy name, [*ins.* the] small and [*ins.* the great][7] ; and shouldest [*om.* shouldest—*ins.* to] destroy them which [those who] destroy the

---

TEXTUAL AND GRAMMATICAL.

[1] Ver. 15. The plural of the Rec. is based upon a misapprehension of the passage. [Modern Critical Editors read ἐγέ-νετο ἡ βασιλεία with ℵ. A. B*. C. P. *Vulg., etc.*   The Rec. is supported by only 1, 7.—E. R. C.]

[2] Ver. 16. [Lach. omits the οἱ in both instances, the former with ℵ*. A., the latter with A. B*., *etc.*; Alf. brackets both ; both are given by Treg. and Tisch., the former with ℵ*. B*. C. P., the latter with ℵ. C. P.—E. R. C.]

[3] Ver. 16. [Gb., Treg., Tisch. (8th Ed.) give κάθηνται with ℵ* et ª. B*. C., *etc.*; Lach., Tisch. (1859), Alf., καθήμενοι with A. P.—E. R. C.]

[4] Ver. 17, [See *Add. Comm.* on ch. i. 8, p. 93.—E. R. C.]

[5] Ver. 17. The third item is here om. by the best Codd. [Modern Crit. Eds. om. with ℵ. A. B* C. P., *Am., Fuld., Harl.,* etc.—E. R. C.]

[6] Ver. 18. [See *Add. Comm.* on ch. xi. 2.—E. R. C.]

[7] Ver. 18. On an erroneous accusative in Cod. A., and in some others, see Düsterdieck. [Lach., Alf., and Treg., with ℵ*. A. C., read τοὺς μικροὺς καὶ τοὺς μεγάλους ; Tisch., with ℵᶜᶜ. B*. P , gives τοῖς μικροῖς, κ. τ. λ.—E. R. C.]

19 earth. And the temple of God [*ins.* which *was* in the heaven][8] was opened in heaven [*om.* in heaven], and there was seen in his temple the ark of his testament [covenant] : and there were lightnings, and voices, and thunderings [thunders], and an earthquake, and [*ins.* a] great hail.

CH. XII. 1–12.

b. The Theocracy. Christ. The Churches of the Wilderness, or Church of the Cross.

1 And there appeared [*om.* there appeared] a great wonder [sign ($\sigma\eta\mu\varepsilon\tilde{\iota}o\nu$)—*ins.* was seen] in [*ins.* the] heaven ; a woman clothed with the sun, and the moon under her feet,
2 and upon her head a crown of twelve stars : And she being with child cried [crieth][9], travailing in birth [*om.* in birth], and pained [tormented] to be delivered
3 [bring forth]. And there appeared [was seen] another wonder [sign] in [*ins.* the] heaven ; and [,] behold [,] a great red [$\pi\nu\rho\rho\acute{o}\varsigma$] dragon, having seven heads and ten horns, and [*ins.* upon his heads] seven crowns [diadems] upon his heads [*om.* upon
4 his heads]. And his tail drew [draggeth][10] the third part of the stars of [*ins.* the] heaven, and did [*om.* did] cast them to the earth : and the dragon stood before the woman which [who] was ready to be delivered [about to bring forth], for to devour her child as soon as it was born [that, when she should bring forth, he might
5 devour her child]. And she brought forth a man child [male son ($\upsilon\grave{\iota}\grave{o}\nu$ $\check{a}\rho\sigma\varepsilon\nu$ [11])] who was [is ($\mu\acute{\varepsilon}\lambda\lambda\varepsilon\iota$)] to rule [shepherdize] all [*ins.* the] nations with a rod of iron [an iron rod] : and her child was caught up [away ($\dot{\eta}\rho\pi\acute{a}\sigma\theta\eta$)] unto [to] God, and
6 to [to] his throne. And the woman fled into the wilderness, where she hath [*ins.* there][12] a place prepared of [by ($\dot{a}\pi\acute{o}$)[13]] God, that [*ins.* there] they should feed [may nourish][14] her there [*om.* there] a thousand two hundred *and* threescore [sixty] days.

c. Establishment of the Church Triumphant in the Heaven of the inner Spirit-life on Earth. Freedom of the Invisible Church.

7 And there was [$\dot{\varepsilon}\gamma\acute{\varepsilon}\nu\varepsilon\tau o$] war in [*ins.* the] heaven : [,] Michael and his angels fought against [warring with][15] the dragon ; and the dragon fought [warred] and his angels,
8 and [*ins.* they] prevailed not ; neither was their place found any more in [*ins.* the] hea-
9 ven. And the great dragon was cast out [thrown down ($\dot{\varepsilon}\beta\lambda\acute{\eta}\theta\eta$)], that [the] old [ancient] serpent, [*ins.* that is] called the [*om.* the] Devil, and [*ins.* the] Satan [*or* adversary], which deceiveth [that seduceth *or* misleadeth ($\dot{o}$ $\pi\lambda\alpha\nu\tilde{\omega}\nu$)] the whole world [inhabited world ($o\iota\kappa o\nu\mu\acute{\varepsilon}\nu\eta\nu$)] : he was cast out [thrown down] into [unto] the
10 earth, and his angels were cast out [thrown down] with him. And I heard a loud [great] voice saying in [*ins.* the] heaven, Now is come [*ins.* the] salvation, and strength [the power], and the kingdom of our God, and the power [authority] of his Christ : for the accuser of our brethren is cast [thrown] down, which accused [that accuseth]
11 them[16] before our God [*ins.* by] day and [*ins.* by] night. And they overcame [conquered] him by [on account of] the blood of the Lamb, and by [on account of] the word of their testimony ; and they loved not their lives [life ($\psi\nu\chi\acute{\eta}\nu$)] unto the [*om.* the]

---

[8] Ver. 19. The reading $\dot{o}$ $\dot{\varepsilon}\nu$ $\tau\tilde{\omega}$ $o\dot{\nu}\rho\alpha\nu\tilde{\omega}$. [Alf. om. $\dot{o}$ with א. B.; Treg. and Tisch. give it with A. C. P., *etc.* Crit. Eds. generally give $o\dot{\nu}\rho\alpha\nu\tilde{\omega}$ without the add. of $\check{a}\nu\omega$ ▪ in א*.—E. R. C.]

[9] Ch. xii. 2. The reading $\kappa\alpha\grave{\iota}$ $\check{\varepsilon}\kappa\rho\alpha\xi\varepsilon\nu$ is probably an alteration of the original reading. [Alf., Treg. and Tisch. read $\kappa\rho\acute{a}\zeta\varepsilon\iota$ with א. A. P.; Tisch. (8th Ed.), Lach. (maj.), prefix $\kappa\alpha\acute{\iota}$ with א. C.; Tisch. (1859), Lach. (min.), Treg., omit with A. B*. P.; Alf. brackets ; Lach. reads $\check{\varepsilon}\kappa\rho\alpha\zeta\varepsilon\nu$ with C.; B*. gives $\check{\varepsilon}\kappa\rho\alpha\xi\varepsilon\nu$.—E. R. C.]

[10] Ver. 4. The imperfect is probably an alteration. [The reading $\sigma\nu\rho\varepsilon\iota$ is unquestioned.—E. R. C.]

[11] Ver. 5. Codd. A. C. give the reading $\check{a}\rho\sigma\varepsilon\nu$ instead of $\check{a}\rho\rho\varepsilon\nu a$. [So Crit. Eds. generally. א. and B*. give $\check{a}\rho\rho\varepsilon\nu a$ (B*. $\check{a}\rho\varepsilon\nu a$).—E. R. C.]

[12] Ver. 6. "$O\pi o\nu$ $\check{\varepsilon}\chi\varepsilon\iota$ $\check{\varepsilon}\kappa\varepsilon\tilde{\iota}$. [Alf. and Tisch. give $\dot{\varepsilon}\kappa\varepsilon\tilde{\iota}$ with א. A. B*. P., *etc.*; Rec. Lach. and Treg., omit with C. 1, *etc.*—E. R. C.]

[13] Ver. 6. [Crit. Eds. give $\dot{a}\pi\acute{o}$ with א. A. O. P.; B*. reads $\dot{\nu}\pi\acute{o}$.—E. R. C.]

[14] Ver. 6. [Lach. and Alf. give $\tau\rho\acute{\varepsilon}\phi\omega\sigma\iota\nu$ with A. P.; Gb. and Tisch. (1859), $\dot{\varepsilon}\kappa\tau\rho\acute{\varepsilon}\phi\omega\sigma\iota\nu$ with B*; Treg. and Tisch. (8th Ed.), $\tau\rho\acute{\varepsilon}\phi o\nu\sigma\iota\nu$ with א. C. For the N. T. use of $\iota\nu a$ with the Ind. Prs., see Winer, § 4, par. 3.—E. R. C.]

[15] Ver. 7. We follow the best authenticated, although difficult and venturesome reading $\tau o\tilde{\nu}$ $\pi o\lambda\varepsilon\mu\tilde{\eta}\sigma\alpha\iota$. [Crit. Eds. give $\pi o\lambda\varepsilon\mu\tilde{\eta}\sigma\alpha\iota$ with א. A. B*. C. P., Gb., Sz., Lach., Tisch. (1859), Treg. prefix $\tau o\tilde{\nu}$ with A. C. P.; Tisch (8th Ed.), omits with א. B*.; Alf. brackets. Winer (§ 44, 4) confesses his inability to explain the construction, and thinks it probable that there is a corruption of the text. Alford comments : "The construction is remarkable, but may easily be explained as one compounded of ($\tau o\tilde{\nu}$) $\tau\grave{o}\nu$ M. $\kappa\alpha\grave{\iota}$ $\tau o\grave{\nu}\varsigma$ $\dot{a}\gamma\gamma$. $\alpha\dot{\nu}\tau o\tilde{\nu}$ $\pi o\lambda\varepsilon\mu\tilde{\eta}\sigma\alpha\iota$ (in which case the $\tau o\tilde{\nu}$ depends on the $\dot{\varepsilon}\gamma\acute{\varepsilon}\nu\varepsilon\tau o$ as in Acts x. 25) and $\dot{o}$ M. $\kappa\alpha\grave{\iota}$ $o\grave{\iota}$ $\dot{a}\gamma\gamma$. $\alpha\dot{\nu}\tau o\tilde{\nu}$ $\dot{\varepsilon}\pi o\lambda\acute{\varepsilon}\mu\eta\sigma\alpha\nu$. In the next clause it passes into this latter." Lillie, assuming the correctness of the text ($\tau o\tilde{\nu}$ $\pi o\lambda\varepsilon\mu\tilde{\eta}\sigma\alpha\iota$) prefers " to construe $\dot{o}$ M $\kappa\alpha\grave{\iota}$ $o\grave{\iota}$ $\dot{a}\gamma\gamma$. $\alpha\dot{\nu}\tau o\tilde{\nu}$ as absolute nominatives, with the participle of the substantive verb understood." This gives a construction equivalent to the one adopted above. For other explanations see Winer and Lillie.—E. R. C.]

[16] Ver. 10. There is an unimportant difference between $\alpha\dot{\nu}\tau\tilde{\omega}\nu$ and $\alpha\dot{\nu}\tau o\nu\varsigma$. [Alf. and Tisch. read the latter with A. P.; Treg., the former with א. B*. C.—E. R. C.]

12 death. Therefore rejoice, *ye* heavens, and ye that dwell in them. Woe to the inhabiters of [*om.* the inhabiters of][17] the earth and of [*om.* of] the sea! for [because] the devil is come down unto you, having great wrath [anger], because he knoweth that he hath but a [*om.* but a] short [little] time.

[17] Ver. 12. The reading τοῖς κατοικοῦσιν is a gloss. [It is supported only by 1.—E. R. C.]

EXEGETICAL AND CRITICAL.

SYNOPTICAL VIEW.

Here, manifestly, the beginning of the End commences, and, consequently, the second division of the Apocalypse. It begins with the heavenly pre-celebration of the victory over the Dragon—Satan—and over his representative on earth—the Beast, *i. e.*, Antichrist. This pre-celebration is linked to the blast of the seventh Trumpet. A striking turn in the description is found in the fact, that the Spirit of prophecy does not make the seven-headed Beast appear immediately upon the blast of the seventh Trumpet, as the seven Trumpet-Angels emerged from the seventh Seal. In like manner, the vision of the seven Seals might not directly follow the picture of the seventh Church; nor, furthermore, can the seven Vials of wrath be immediately linked to the seven heads of Antichrist, and this irrespective of the fact, that these [the heads] constitute, in the first place, a unitous phenomenon. If it had been designed that the seven Thunders should be particularly set forth, they would have followed upon the seventh Trumpet, whilst the seventh Thunder would have been succeeded by the announcement of the Antichristian time. The sealing of the seven Thunders, however, necessitated a modification of the outward consequence of the septenaries; nor could the new Divine manifestations issue from the preceding bad human conditions, but could only follow them as judgments.

From the seventh Trumpet *great* or powerful *voices* proceed. Not *one* voice, but a chorus of voices—and those, *mighty* voices—concordantly proclaim the great victory

This is, manifestly, an expression of the strongest assurance of victory, developed in the very face of the emergence of Satan and his Antichrist.

This assurance of victory *in Heaven* is also an assurance of victory in the *spirit-realm* of the Kingdom of God *in this world, i. e., in the invisible Church*. It is a fundamental feature of the Kingdom of God, that this assurance of victory has been in process of more and more glorious development from the Protevangel down to the consummation of the New Testament (1 John v. 4). And, indeed, with the death and resurrection of Christ the victory is, in principle, decided, so that there is no longer question save as to the full development of the principle into the visible appearance.

But in what manner do the voices proclaim the victory? *The kingdom of the world is become our Lord's and His Christ's, and He shall reign to the æons of the æons.* The position of Christ toward God the Lord is economically modified here, because the kingdom relationship is involved (see 1 Cor. xv. 25-27). Since we must distinguish between a

Kingdom of power, possessed by God from the beginning, and a Kingdom of His Spirit's sovereignty in spirits, founded by His grace in Christ, to which, however, the kingdom of darkness stands opposed—an anarchy of spirits, under the lying power of Satan—the point in question here can be nought but the synthesis, already accomplished in principle, of the Kingdom of power and the Kingdom of grace. It is a Kingdom of God over the world, which is at the same time a Kingdom over hearts; or a Kingdom over hearts which, from the invisible Church, goes forth, in dynamic operation, through all the world, finally spreading through the worlds of space, as through the æons of time.

At the close appearing of this Kingdom, the kingdom of darkness is destroyed. With the mere announcement of this absolute Kingdom is conjoined the absolute *thanksgiving* of pious humanity in the evening of the world; pious humanity as represented by the *twenty-four Elders*, the Presbytery of the Theocracy and the Presbytery of the New Testament Kingdom of God, both of which institutions have had so much to suffer from the oppressions of the kingdom of darkness. [See *foot-note*†, p. 152.—E. R. C.]

They, lying upon their faces, rightly return thanks to *God* as the *All-Ruler*, Who now *has taken to Himself—i. e.*, brought into full operation—*His great power*. In these words a grand theological revelation is contained. From the beginning of the world's history, but, above all, in the humiliation of Christ, in His cross, and His cross-bearing Church, God has so greatly restrained His power, in the maintenance of the liberty, thereunto opposed, of moral agents, and in the service of love, as to make it seem as if He had laid that power aside. Now, however, that the seed of liberty has gradually matured, having sprouted up partly on the right hand side, partly on the left hand side, He can unchain His full majestic power, and He has begun His absolute royal rule.

The first mark of this turn in the current of affairs is peculiar; it has almost the aspect of a contradiction. *The heathen* [*nations*] *have become wroth*, it is declared; the power of darkness seems just now to be more than ever at liberty. But as, in the second Psalm, the strongly emphasized *to-day* marks the very date of the general rebellion against Jehovah and His Anointed as the date of the anointing and institution of His Son—as the date of the crucifixion of Christ became the date of His exaltation likewise—so it shall be at the time of the last great apostasy; even above the wrath of the heathen and simultaneously with it, the revelation of *the wrath of God* appears.

The wrath of God is destination to death (Ex. iv. 14; comp. ver. 24; Ps. xc). The suicidal death-choice of the old world, in its apostasy from the living God, brings the judgment of the Divine destination to death directly upon this old world. The living have become a prey to death; the dead, on the other hand, revive. *The time of the dead,* when it is their turn to have justice done them, *has come;* the retributive judgment must be held, in which God *gives to His servants their reward, i. e.,* the final perfect and solemn restoration, which forms the antithesis to all the ignominy and sorrow of their historic life.

And here the Old Testament *Prophets* and the New Testament *saints* are beautifully linked together; and with them, all the *God-fearing,* who have kept the *name* of God—their knowledge of God—sacred; all, both *small* and *great,* in the whole sphere of God's Kingdom. For they all had to suffer from the destroyers of the *earth*—of Divine order on Earth, as well as of Nature and Earth in the literal sense.

But the time of compensatory retribution is likewise the time of punitory retribution: the destroyers of the Earth must themselves *be destroyed.*

The judgment is consummated amid the complete revelation of that idea of justice by which it is put in execution. Hence *the Temple of God in the Heaven is opened, i. e.,* the radiant archetype of the Kingdom of God on Earth is revealed in its ideal and dynamical authority for mankind. The *Ark of the Covenant* in this Temple becomes visible; the heavenly rule [*Norm*] of the condemning law, as well as of the real redemption, is made known to all the world.

Nor is the radiant appearance all; it produces, as a vital phenomenon, in the richest manifestations of its powers, *lightnings,* or revelations of the Spirit; *voices,* or Divine words and thoughts; *thunders,* or lively stirrings of soul; *earthquake,* or convulsions of the old world; and *a great hail,* as a symbol of the conflict betwixt Heaven and Earth: fire and cold issue from the disclosure of the heavenly spirit-world at the end of the world.

And now the history of Antichristianity on Earth is prefigured by the history of it in Heaven. Here *Heaven* is manifestly the pure celestial sphere of spirit and of spirits, the background of all occurrences in that general history of the world which is visible to all. A *great sign* appears in this Heaven. A *Woman,* the Kingdom of God, modified by the feminine receptivity of the human mind, is seen. She makes her appearance in the unity of the Old Testament Theocracy and the New Testament Kingdom of Heaven; she is adorned with the *sun* of revelation; with the *moon,* as a symbol of nature, in its subserviency to the Kingdom of God (and also as symbolizing the change of times), *under her feet;* and a *crown of twelve stars upon her head*—the adornment of a plenary number of elect spirits appertaining to her. The Seer has deeply felt the conflict of the transition from the Old Covenant to the New, as is proved by the words: *And she, being with child, crieth, etc.;* the Lord's people, together with Himself, have experienced these throes of the Messiah (see John xvi. 21). This sign is accompanied by another: *Behold, a great fiery-red Dragon. In Heaven!* how is this possible? Heaven is that realm of spirit and of spirits in which Christ overcame Judas (see the author's *Leben Jesu,* Book ii., p. 1328), without the observation

of mere historical men, in their external world; hence, it is the spiritual back-ground of worldly history. In this Heaven, the great red Dragon appears; the winged primeval serpent, at once serpent and swine; signalized as a monster, not only by the *fiery* hue of the murderer, but also by the *seven heads,* and especially by the disproportion between the seven heads, or the caricature symbol of holy intelligence—not to say of a Holy Spirit—and the *ten horns* or the symbols of worldly power; the *heads* only are adorned with *diadems,* thus making the worldly power appear as unauthorized might, obtained by artifice. Farther on, the Dragon, the *ancient serpent* (Gen. iii.), is expressly called the *Devil* and *Satan* (ver. 9; ch. xx. 2). These seven heads of the Dragon are not to be identified with the seven heads of the Beast, nor are they to be referred to historical shapes; they are seven spiritual deformities which ape the seven Spirits, or ground-forms of the Spirit.

It is declared concerning his first exertion of violence: *His tail draggeth the third part of the stars of the Heaven, and cast them upon the Earth.* This cannot be regarded as significant of the apostasy of a portion of the angels, since the angels of the Dragon are spoken of, further on, as still in *Heaven.*

The passage should rather be interpreted in accordance with ch. viii., particularly ver. 10.

The third part of the spirits designed as *light-bearers* in the human Heaven are, by the violent oscillations of the demonic tail—overpowered, that is, by the impressions of apparently irresistible vivacity and might—swept from the Heaven of spiritual purity, and cast upon the Earth; made subservient to worldly-mindedness, in order to the more thorough transformation of God's Earth (Ps. xciii.) into an Earth estranged from God. The preliminaries to the crucifixion of Christ were, in particular, the fruit of this act of the Dragon. Fallen stars constituted the government of Palestine and the majority of the Sanhedrin; even the Messianic hopes of the Jews were satanically empoisoned. In the face of Christ's appearance, however, the machinations of the Dragon concentrate themselves; for Christ is the glorification of the personal God, of love in the love-kingdom of personal life, by means of an absolutely worthy personal conduct; Satan, on the other hand, is the seducer and accuser of men, who tends to sink the whole world in worldliness—to plunge the personal kingdom into the service of impersonal things, by means of the lying perversion of his own true creaturely essence into the semblance of a false divinity.

Shamelessly, therefore, the Dragon takes his stand before the Woman who is about to be delivered, that he may *devour her child.* Thus was the power of evil concentrated in Israel at the very moment when Christ, in respect of His historical descent from the eternal congregation of God, extending through the Theocracy and the Church, was about to be born.

But the new-born Child is a *man—the Man,* simply (Is. ix.)—destined, in the words of the Old Testament (Ps. ii.), to *rule* [*shepherdize*] *the nations with a rod of iron;* ordained to the government of the world in redemptive and judicial righteousness—for Satan, therefore, unattainable in His essence (John xiv. 30). His own name for Himself is *the Son of Man*, in the highest sense. Pilate calls Him *the Man* [*ὁ ἄνθρωπος*=*Mensch*, human being]. The vision calls Him *the Man* [*Mann* (*υἱὸν ἄρσεν*)], in the highest sense of the term. And here, in accordance with the spiritual, æonic aspect of the history, there is no special reference to the *sufferings* of Christ; His death itself forms a part of His elevation above every assault of Satan; hence it is declared: *her Child was caught away to God and to His Throne.* This exaltation (Phil. ii. 6 sqq.) is at the same time the foundation of the Church Triumphant in Heaven and on Earth.

Of the Woman it is said, that she *fled into the wilderness*. She is the same who bore Christ—hence, the Old and New Testament Church in undivided unity. The *wilderness*, prepared for her by God as a place of shelter,* exhibits a transformation similar to that presented by the cross. As the cross, from the tree of the curse, has become the symbol of salvation, so this wilderness, from being the abode of demons (Lev. xvi. 22; Matt. iv.; xii. 43), was changed into a refuge from the Arch-demon. This wilderness is the perfect New Testament renunciation of the world, which makes the Church on Earth, in respect of its invisible kernel, like unto the Church in Heaven. The entrance thereto is baptism into the death of Christ (Rom. vi.); its external form is asceticism; its security is courage for the cross; its verdant oases are the triumphs of the martyrs. The *time of residence* in this wilderness is modified after the measure of the New Testament trial-time; not in the form of the *change* of times (ch. xi. 2), but in that of uninterrupted days' works — *twelve hundred and sixty days* (ch. xi. 3). In regard to the Woman herself, the notation of time is more obscure, less definite, and gloomier: a time, two times, a half time (ch. xii. 14; Dan. xii. 7)—running, we may say, into apparently endless helplessness or destitution (Luke xviii. 1).

The succeeding scene is most wonderful. The theatre of this *war in Heaven*—a conflict marvellous when considered merely in the abstract—is, we believe, the spiritual and spirit world of the Church Invisible—not, however, the Heaven of Christ's glory.

The *nature* of the conflict is equally remarkable: *Michael and his angels* (as the attacking party) *war with the Dragon; but the Dragon also wars, and his angels* (as the resisting party). We have shown elsewhere that the Archangel Michael is an image of Christ victoriously combatant. Christ is an Archangel in His quality of Judge; and He appears as Judge, not only at the end of the world, but also in the preservation of the purity of His Church (Acts v. 1 sqq.; 1 Cor. v. 1 sqq.). That Christ has His angels also—those that war with Him—not merely in the evening of the world, but from the beginning, is a fact which

John has previously intimated in his Gospel (ch. i. 51); they are the principles and spirits which are with Him absolutely. And so the Dragon also has his angels, his assistants. Since the foundation of Christ's Church, Christian and Antichristian principles have been warring with each other—primarily, in spiritual, intellectual and ethical forms (John xiv. [xv.?]).

These battles are not simply central general combats, but a sum of great single conflicts. Michael wars; the angels war; the Dragon wars, and his angels. But, with them, he is defeated.

Why is it so concisely declared: *they prevailed not?* Be it observed, in the first place, that the *principal* victory of Christ has already taken place, and that the *final* historic victory cannot yet be intended. But Satan is totally defeated, in so far as respects the fact, that the New Testament Heaven, in its central essence, is thoroughly purged from him and his angels; *in Heaven their place is no more found.* That is, as the Church Triumphant is now established in Heaven, so, in correspondence with it, the Church on Earth has also a place that is purified from all Satanic essence—the sphere of pure Christian spiritual life, the communion of saints. Out of this Heaven, therefore, is cast the *great Dragon,* the *ancient Serpent* (the demonic seducer of Adam); the *Devil* and *Satan,* as the slanderer and enemy of mankind (Job ii.), who has continually changed the conception: man is sinful and wicked—into the calumniatory sentence: he is fundamentally bad; and this, on account of his success in approving himself *the seducer of the whole world.*

When it is declared, that the whole Satanic troop is cast upon the Earth, in company with its leader, it cannot be necessary to apprehend the declaration in an astronomical or local sense. Expelled from the *inner* Church, Satan now directs his whole assault against the *outer* Church. The wheat of Christ's field remains pure; but the field, as such, becomes impure: the enemy sows his tares amongst the wheat.

The foundation of the holy Church, the communion of saints, is an infinitely glorious achievement. A *great voice* pronounces the hymn of victory; it is a single, common triumphant consciousness of all the heavenly throng. Now there is founded, with Christ and through Him, a pure, eternal Heaven, which descends from Heaven to Earth. And with the pure Church, the New Testament Kingdom of Heaven is established, in which God reigns with three attributes: He has taken upon Himself the *salvation* —the perfect and *final* redemption from all evil; He has, further, taken to Himself the *power* over redeemed souls, and has called in the current of worldly affairs as-co-operative in redemption (Rom. viii.); and, consequently, He has finally assumed the real *Kingdom* of His Spirit as a sovereignty over all good spirits. The attribute of *Christ* is, henceforth, the *authority,* the executive power (*ἐξουσία*). Such is the constitution of the Kingdom (ch. xi. 15).

How all this has come to pass, is intimated in the following words. The negative term runs thus: *the accuser of our brethren is cast down, who accuseth them before our God by day and by night.*

The temptations to despair, which Satan brought to bear upon the consciences of men, subsequent to his seduction of them into sin, are annihilated, throughout the whole realm of faith, by the sure and perfect peace of reconciliation (comp. 1 John iii. 20; Heb. ii. 15).

And they conquered him by [on account of] the blood of the Lamb, is the reason assigned for their victory ; for it is upon the triumph of Christ that the triumphs of Christians are grounded. Their heart-victories, however, have become intellectual victories likewise, through the word of their testimony; and victories of their entire life, because they loved not their life unto death, when martyrdom was the price of adherence to the truth (Matt. xvi. 24, 25).

Therefore rejoice, ye Heavens, and ye that dwell (take up your abode) in them—such is the festal conclusion. Heaven spreads out into a plenitude of Heavens (John xiv. 2), and these Heavens become peopled with blessed conquerors.

A terrible contrast to the above is presented by the last words : Woe unto the inhabiters* of the earth and of the sea. The danger is heightened for the world-church of external order and authority, as well as for the surging popular life and the fluctuations of society. For the Devil, as the poisoner of the truly historical powers, has made their common destruction his aim. He has great anger; the principle of demonic worldly-mindedness is excited—the more, as it is a final paroxysm, or because he knoweth that he hath little time.

The fact that the Heaven-picture continues to this passage, is proved, among other things, by the concluding hymn (vers. 10–12).

[ABSTRACT OF VIEWS, ETC.]
By the American Editor.

I. Ch. xi. 15-19.

[ELLIOTT regards ver. 14 as setting forth the cessation of the Turkish woe—the period of ~cessation beginning with the battle of Lepanto, A. D. 1571, and extending to the peace (humiliating to Turkey) in 1791, between Turkey on the one side and Russia and Austria on the other. He connects this "second half" of the Turkish woe with the visions of ch. x. 1–xi. 13, as follows : It was just after the "slaying of the third part of men" (ch. ix. 18), i. e., the fall of Constantinople—and the ineffectiveness of the catastrophe to induce repentance (see p. 210, foot-note), that the Covenant Angel descended (ch. x. 1)—betokening the Reformation (see p. 218); and also it was just after the fall of the tenth part of the City and the seven Chiliads (ch. x. 13), i. e., the political earthquake following the Reformation (see p. 228), that the announcement of ver. 14 was made. (The beginning of this earthquake he places about A. D., 1569 ; the battle of Lepanto was fought A. D. 1571.) Vers. 15–19 he interprets as a general Heaven-picture of the last time (including the establishment of Christ's Millennial Kingdom), the development of the great events of this vision being deferred until after "the parenthetic Visions" in chs. xii.–xiv.

BARNES regards the description of the events of the seventh Trumpet as closing with ver. 18; the period extending to the establishment of the Millennial Kingdom, and the vision closing the series of visions beginning at ch. v. 1. He regards ver. 19 as commencing "a new series of visions, intended, also, but in a different line, to extend down to the consummation of all things. '

STUART : "One powerful and bitter enemy of Christianity is now, or is speedily to be, put down. The judgments of Heaven, which had been so gradually proceeding, and seemingly so slow, are immediately to be consummated. The triumph of Christianity over opposing and embittered Judaism is to be completed. 'Their place and nation are now to be taken away.' The progress of the Gospel can no longer be stayed by them."

WORDSWORTH agrees with Barnes in regarding this section as closing the first series of visions, and with commentators generally, in regarding it as referring to the last time.

ALFORD : (Ver. 14). "Transitional—The episodical visions of chs. x. 1-11, xi. 1-13 are finished ; and the prophecy refers to the plagues of the sixth Trumpet, ch. ix. 13-21. These formed the second woe, and upon these the third is to follow (vers. 15–19). But in actual relation and detail it does not immediately follow. Instead of it, we have voices of thanksgiving in Heaven, for that the hour of God's Kingdom and vengeance is come. The Seer is not yet prepared to set forth the nature of this taking of the Kingdom, this reward to God's servants, this destruction of the destroyers of the earth. Before he does so, another series of prophetic visions must be given regarding not merely the dwellers on the earth, but the Church herself, her glory and her shame, her faithfulness and her apostasy. When this series has been given, then shall be declared in its fullness the manner and the process of the time of the end."—"Notice (1), that the seventh Seal, the seventh Trumpet, and the seventh Vial, are all differently accompanied from any of the preceding series in each case ; (2) at each seventh member of the series (a) we hear what is done, not on earth, but in Heaven (chs. viii. 1 ; xi. 15; xvi. 17) ; (b) we have it related in the form of a solemn conclusion (with slight variations), ἐγένοντο βρονταὶ κ. τ. λ., chs. viii. 5; xi. 19; xvi. 18 sqq. ; (c) we have plain indication in the imagery or by direct expression, that the end is come, or close at hand, by (a) the imagery of the sixth Seal, and the two episodes preceding the seventh Seal, (β) the declaration here ἦλθεν ὁ καιρὸς τῶν νεκρῶν κριθῆναι, (γ) the Γέγονεν sounding from the Temple and the Throne on the pouring out of the seventh Vial; (3) all this forms strong ground for inference, that the three series of visions are not continuous, but resumptive ; not indeed going over the same ground with one another, either of time or of occurrence, but each evolving something which was not in the former, and putting the course of God's providence in a different light. It is true that the Seals involve the Trumpets, the Trumpets the Vials ; but it is not mere temporal succession, the involution and inclusion are far deeper," etc.

LORD : The seventh Trumpet is to be followed

---

* [In the Text (see ver. 12 and note 17) our author properly omits these words.—E. R. C.]

by 1. The assumption by the Redeemer of the dominion of the earth in a new and peculiar relation as its King, and the commencement of a visible and eternal reign. 2. The *resurrection*, and *public adoption as heirs of the Kingdom*, of all saints who have suffered the penalty of death; and the acceptance and reward of all living saints. 3. The destruction of the apostate powers, the Wild-beast, False Prophet, *etc.* This Trumpet is cotemporaneous with the seventh Vial (comp. ver. 19 with xvi. 18 sqq.); the lightnings, voices, *etc.*, denoting excitements, commotions, and revolutions among the nations, and the descent on them of judgments. The opening of the inner Temple and the exhibition of the Ark (ver. 19), denote, probably, that the *mysteries* of the former administration are finished, and that thenceforth the reasons of the Divine procedure are to be understood.

GLASGOW regards the prophecy of the period of the seventh Trumpet as contemplated in only ver. 15. This period he holds to begin with the Reformation and to extend "through all the period of the Vials." "The Trumpet declares the Kingdom to be Christ's, and goes on to announce the events by which all rebels are to be brought to submission or extinction." The *voices* he interprets as "The voice of Jesus through the instrumentality of ecclesiastical voices. They are the voices of Luther, Zwingli —all the Reforming preachers." He explains the expression: "His Christ's," as relating to the Church (see EXPL. IN DETAIL). Vers. 16, 17 describe a Heaven scene (at the *opening* of or *throughout* the period?); ver. 18, an Earth scene at the beginning of the Reformation. Ver. 19, he refers to the day of Pentecost, when "Peter and the other apostles, by preaching, 'opened the door of faith instrumentally!'" (See EXPL. IN DETAIL.)

II. *Ch. xii.* 1-12.

[ELLIOTT: With this section this author regards PART IV. of the Apocalypse as beginning, including chs. xii., xiii., and xiv. This PART presents a "supplemental and explanatory history of the Rise, Character, and Establishment of the Beast from the Abyss, or Popedom; with its chief Adjuncts; and the contrasted Impersonation of Christ's faithful Church." The vision of this section he holds to be *retrogressive*. By the *Travailing Woman* he understands Christ's true visible Church, in the *heaven* of *political elevation* (invested with Christ as the *Sun of Righteousness;* the *moon*, representing the *civil authority*, under her feet; the *stars*, ecclesiastical ministers, recognized as dignified authorities before the world); bringing forth *with pain* (the Diocletian persecution) a *son who is to rule*, *etc.*, i. e., producing children who, united and multiplied into a nation, are to be raised to dominant political power; (this elevation being first accomplished under Constantine, to whom, according to Ambrose, was given the title "Son of the Church"). The *Dragon* he interprets as *the Roman Empire* as *a persecuting power hostile to Christianity.* He presents the following indications as to the time of the *birth* and effort to *destroy:* (1) not until after the close of the Second century, as it was

then that the *dragon* was first used as a Roman ensign; (2) not until the time of Diocletian, as it was then that the *diadem* was first assumed as one of the imperial insignia; (3) the *drawing* by the *Dragon* of a *third part* of the stars of *Heaven* indicates that though he was still in the *political heaven*, his power was diminished to a third part of the Imperial power, and this occurred about A. D. 313, when in two divisions of the Roman Empire, Europe and Africa (under Constantine and Licinius), *Christianity was in the ascendancy*, but in the third, Asia (under Maximin), *Christians were still exposed to persecution;* (4) this was the period of the termination of forty weeks (280 prophetic days from Pentecost) of the Church's gestation. The attempt *to destroy* he explains by (1) the persecution of Maximin (see Gibbon ii. 489); (2) the apostasy of Licinius, A. D. 323, and the following persecutions. The *catching up of the child to God and His throne* he regards as the elevation of Constantine, *as an avowed Christian*, to the undivided throne of the Roman Empire, and the consequent establishment of Christianity, after the defeat of Licinius at the battle of Adrianople, A. D. 323 (see Gibbon and historians generally). (For the explanation of the *flight of the Woman*, see the following abstract, p. 258.) The *war in Heaven* he regards as indicating the struggle of Paganism for re-elevation to political power under Licinius and *Julian the Apostate*, and the *throwing down* of the Dragon (or Satan, who inspired them) as the final downfall of Paganism, *primarily* in the defeat of Licinius, and *finally* in the death of Julian in the Persian War, A. D. 363. Vers. 10-12 (1st clause) he interprets as the *Church's* song of victory in the "*symbolic Heaven* of political elevation and power." The last clause of ver. 12 he regards "as a detached and solemn notification by the *dictating prophetic Spirit* of some woe on the Roman Empire soon about to follow," reference being had "primarily, to *heretical* persecutors *within* the Church and Empire; and, secondarily, to the *Gothic.* scourge."

BARNES agrees, in the main, with Elliott. His most important variations are as to—1. *The adornment of the Woman:* by the *moon under her feet* he understands "the ancient (Jewish) and comparatively obscure dispensation now made subordinate and humble; and by the *twelve stars*, "the usual well-known division of the people of God into twelve parts." 2. *The war in Heaven:* he writes, "Another vision appears. It is that of a contest between Michael, the protecting Angel of the people of God, and the great foe, in which victory declares in favor of the former, and Satan suffers a discomfiture, *as if* he were cast from Heaven to Earth."

STUART interprets (1) the *Woman* as the Church ("not simply as *Jewish*, but in a more generic and theocratic sense, *the people of God*") at the period of Christ's birth; (2) the *child* as Christ Himself; (3) the *dragon* as Satan inspiring Herod, Judas and other persecutors; (4) the attempt to destroy as the massacre at Bethlehem and the other assaults on our Lord; (5) the *catching up to Heaven* as the Ascension; (6) the *War in Heaven* (the lower heaven, the *air*) as a struggle between good and bad spirits, "according to the usual popular modes of conception;"* (7) "the words of the voice in Heaven (ver. 10 sqq.) are to be regarded mainly as *anticipative* of victory in respect to the future, grounded on a reminiscence of victory with regard to the past."

WORDSWORTH regards ch. xii. as a "Prophetic View of the History of the Church relatively to Rome" (vers. 1-12, relatively to *heathen* Rome). "The Woman in this vision is the Christian Church; she appeared in *Heaven*, for her origin is from above; she is *clothed with the Sun*, for Christ is the *Sun* of righteousness; she has the *moon under her feet*, because she will survive the changes of this world; she has on her head a *crown of victory* (στέφανος); the crown of *twelve stars* indicates the *Twelve Apostles*." The *Dragon* is the Old Serpent, who is called in this Book the Dragon, see vers. 9, 15, 16, where the names *Satan, Devil, Dragon* and *Serpent* are interchanged; the *Dragon* is also described here as having Seven Heads, etc.; *diadems* are symbols of *royalty; horns* are emblems of *power* (Luke i. 69); the number *seven* represents completeness, and combined with the number *ten* (*ten horns*), it connects this manifestation of the Dragon with the display of his power, **as** wielded by the *fourth* great Monarchy, that of Rome." He refers the *Male Son* primarily to Christ, secondarily to

the people of Christ; the *rod of iron* is Christ's *word*, the Holy Scriptures, and by it the *male children*, the masculine spirits of Christ's Church, are endued with power from Him to *rule the nations* and *overcome the world.*" (On the flight of the Woman see the Abstract on p. 261.) Concerning the *war in Heaven*, he writes: "St. John now *reverts* to an earlier period, in order to recite the *antecedent* history of the Dragon, and to explain the circumstances under which he was led to persecute the Woman, and he traces that history till it is brought down, in ver. 14, to the same point as in ver. 6, namely, to the escape of the Woman in the Wilderness; Satan is displayed as he was before his fall from Heaven."

ALFORD regards the vision of this chapter "as introductory to the whole imagery of the latter part of the Apocalypse," and holds that "the principal details of the present section (chapter) are rather *descriptive* than *strictly* prophetical." By the *Woman* he understands "the Church, the Bride of God, and, of course, from the circumstances afterwards related, the Old Testament Church, at least at this beginning of the vision;" by the *Dragon*, the Devil ("he is πυρρός, perhaps for the combined reasons of the *wasting* properties of *fire*, and the *redness of blood;*" the *seven crowned heads* represent "universality of earthly do-

---

[STUART gives, in the Appendix of his Commentary on the Apocalypse, an elaborate Excursus on this subject, of which the following is an abstract.

I. *Good Angels.*

1. They are very numerous, Dan. vii. 10; Ps. lxviii. 17; 2 Kings vi. 16, 17; Heb. xii. 22; Matt. xxvi. 53; Jude 14; Rev. v. 11.

2. They accompany the Divine Majesty and the Saviour, and take part in all the peculiarly glorious displays which they make, either in the way of mercy or of judgment. (1). At the giving of the Law, Deut. xxxiii. 2; Ps. lxviii. 17; Heb. ii. 2; Acts vii. 53; Gal. iii. 19. (2). At the destruction of Jerusalem, Matt. xxiv. 30, 31. (3). At the final judgment, Matt. xiii. 39-41; xxv. 31; 1 Thess iv. 16; 2 Thess. i. 7-9.

3. They are guardians—(1). Of the Lord Jesus, Luke i. 11-20, 26-38; Matt. i. 20, 21; ii. 13, 19, 20; iv. 11; John i. 51; Luke xxii. 43; Matt. xxviii. 2-7; Mark xvi. 5-7; Acts i. 10, 11. (2). Of individuals, Matt. xviii. 10; Gen. xxxii. 1; 2 Kings vi. 17; Ps. xxxiv. 7; Acts xii. 7-15; Heb. i. 14. Of nations and kingdoms, Ex. xiv. 19; xxiii. 20; xxxiii. 2; Num. xx. 16; xxii. 22-35; Josh. v. 13; I-a. lxiii. 9; Dan. x. 5-13, 20, 21; xi. 1; Zech. i. 8-14; iii. 1, 2; xii. 1; Jude 9. From all this it is apparent that not only the Jews had other nations—that not only Jesus and the saints, but *little children* have their guardian angels.

4. They are employed as special ministers for executing Divine justice. See many of the preceding passages; also Gen. xix. 1-23. comp. with xviii. 1, 2; Ex. xii. 23; Josh. v. 13, 14; 2 Sam. xxiv. 16, 17; 2 Kings xix. 35; Acts xii. 23; Rev. vii.-xi.; xvi.

5. They seem to watch over and govern the different elements, Rev. vii. 1, 2; xiv. 18; xvi. 5, (prob. 7); xix. 17; (also probably Ps. civ. 4; Heb. i. 7).

6. They were regarded as intercessors, Job. xxxiii. 23; Zech. i. 12, 13. In Rev. viii, 3 an Angel takes his station by the altar in Heaven, and presents " much incense .... with the prayers of all saints." (He endeavors to show, by copious extracts from Jewish and contemporary Christian writings, that John is not singular in his alleged meaning in Rev. viii. 3. This view, be it observed, does not involve the utterly unscriptural idea that Angels may themselves be invoked.)

II. *Evil Angels.*

1. These are numerous, Matt. xxv. 41; xii. 26; Mark v. 9.

2. They were originally good, but fell from their first estate, 2 Pet. ii. 4; Jude 6.

3. One is more distinctly marked and made very prominent. He is called (1). Satan (שָׂטָן), the *adversary*, Job i. 6-12; ii. 1-7; 1 Chron. xxi. 1; Zech. iii. 1, 2; Matt. xii. 26; Mark iv. 15; Luke xxii. 3; Acts v. 3; Rom. xvi. 20, *etc.* (2).

The *Tempter*, Matt. iv. 1-11; xiii. 19; Luke xxii. 3. 53; Acts v. 3; 1 Cor. vii. 5; 1 Thess, iii. 5; 2 Cor. xi. 3; Rev. xii. 9; xx. 2, 8, 10. (3). The *Destroyer* ('Απολλύων), Rev. ix. 11. (4). The *Devil* (ὁ διάβολος), the accuser, calumniator. This designation is too frequent to need references.

4. The extent of Satan's power, together with that of other evil spirits (*demons*), is very great, 2 Cor. iv. 4; John xii. 31; John xiv. 30; Eph. vi. 12; Col. i. 13; Rev. xii. 17; xx. 8. (This extensive influence is the result of corruption in men, rather than of any irresistible power in Satan, Jas. iv. 7; 1 Pet. v. 8, 9; Eph. iv. 27.)

5. *Place* of evil spirits before the general judgment. (1). The *Abyss.* This word means *without bottom, unfathomable*. The idea of the Hebrews respecting it was that of a deep, dark pit or chasm, which was, or might be, closed up, and where darkness perpetually reigned; hence Jude 6, " angels .... kept in perpetual chains under *darkness,*' i. e., in the deep and dark abyss. See also 2 Pet. ii. 4; Luke viii. 31; Rev. ix. 1, 11; xvii. 8; xx. 1-3 (his, ver. 9, is styled φυλακή). (2). *Deserts*, Isa. xiii. 21; xxxiv. 14; Rev. xviii. 2; Matt xii. 43. (3). The *air*, Eph. ii. 2; vi. 12.

6. They are sometimes employed as executioners of Divine justice or chastisement, Job i., ii; 1 Kings xxii. 21-23; 1 Cor. v. 5; 1 Tim. i. 20.

The Excursus concludes with the following: " Is angelic interposition unworthy of the Godhead? What then are the laws of nature, and all the intermediate agencies by which the Maker of Heaven and earth carries on His designs and accomplishes His purposes? On the other hand, I can conceive of no more magnificent and ennobling view of the Creator and Lord of all things, than that which regards Him as delighting to multiply, even to an almost bounded ex- tent, beings made in His own image, and therefore rational, and moral, and immortal, like Himself. How different from representing Him as the Master of a magnificent puppet- show, all of which He manages by m rely pulling the wires which His own hand! To make Him the only real agent in the universe, and all else as mere *passive* recipients of His influence, is to take from Him the glory that results from the creation of numberless beings in His own image—beings which reflect the brightness of their great Original. It is this intelligent and rational creation in which John lives, moves, thinks, and speaks. The mind, as viewed by him, is filled with ministers swift to do Jehovah's will. They stand before His throne; they preside over nations; they guide the sun in his shining course; the moon and stars send forth radiance at their bidding; the very elements are watched over by them; even infants are committed to the guidance of presence-angels; and 'the Angel of the Lord encampeth round about all that fear Him.' Such is the Universe, which the God Who is, and was, and is to come has created and governs; and ami t the contemplation of productions and arrangements such as these, John wrote the glowing pages of the Apocalypse."—E. R. C.]

minion;" "the magnitude and fury of the *Dragon* are graphically given by the fact of its tail ... sweeping down the stars of heaven"); by the *child*, "the Lord Jesus, *and none other*" ("the exigencies of this passage require that the *birth* should be understood literally and historically, of that Birth of which all Christians know;" (see also EXPL. IN DETAIL, ver. 5). Concerning the *war*, he writes: "The war here spoken of appears in some of its features in the Book of Daniel, ch. x. 13, 21; xii. 1 (also Jude 9) ... Satan's being cast out of Heaven to the Earth is the result not of the contest with the Lord Himself, of which it is only an incident leading to a new phase, but of an appointed conflict with his faithful fellow angels led on by the Archangel Michael." (See also EXPL. IN DETAIL.) In conclusion he writes: "I own that I have been led ... to think whether after all the *Woman* may represent, not the *invisible* Church of God's true people, which under all conditions of the world must be known only to Him, but the *true visible Church*: that Church which in its divinely prescribed form as existing at Jerusalem was the mother of our Lord according to the flesh, and which continued as established by our Lord and His Apostles, in unbroken unity during the first centuries, but which, as time went on, was broken up by evil men and evil doctrines, and has remained, unseen, unrealized, her unity an article of faith, not of sight, but still multiplying her seed, those who keep the commandments of God and have the testimony of Jesus, in various sects and different countries, waiting the day for her comely order and oneness again to be manifested —the day when she shall 'come up out of the wilderness, leaning on her Beloved;' when our Lord's prayer for the unity of His people being accomplished, the world shall believe that the Father has sent Him. If we are disposed to carry out this idea, we might see the great realization of *the flight into the wilderness* in the final severance of the Eastern and Western churches in the seventh century, and the flood cast after the Woman by the Dragon in the irruption of the Mohammedan armies. But this, though not less satisfactory than the other interpretations, is as unsatisfactory. The latter part of the vision yet awaits its clearing up."

LORD. "The *Woman* is the representative of the true people of God; ... her sunbeam robe, her station above the moon, and her crown of stars, bespeak her greatness, conspicuousness, and majesty; ... her cry and labor to bear, denote the importunate desire and endeavor of those whom she symbolizes to present to the empire one who should, as their son, rise to supreme power, and rule the nations with an iron sceptre, etc." "The *great red Dragon* symbolizes the rulers of the Roman Empire; the *seven heads* denoting the seven species of the chiefs of its ancient government; the *ten horns* the chiefs into which its western half was divided on its conquest by the Goths; ... its sweeping its tail through the sky, dragging one-third of the stars, and casting them to the earth, represents its violent dejection of one-third of the Christian teachers from their stations by imprisonment," etc. By the *child* he understands CONSTANTINE; and his being *caught up to God and His throne* he takes as de-

noting "both (1) that he was rescued in an extraordinary manner from the attempts of the Pagan Emperor to destroy him, and exalted to supreme power in the Empire; and (2) that he became in that station a usurper of the rights of God, and an object of idolatrous homage to his subjects." "That the Woman fled into the desert, signifies that the people of God, wholly disappointed in their expectation of a more favorable rule from monarchs professing to be Christian and exposed to greater evils than they had suffered from their pagan persecutors, were compelled, in order to safety, to retire from the nationalized Church into seclusion." (See also Abstract on p. 262.) Concerning the *war*, he writes: "Michael and his angels are symbols of believers in Christ, who gain a victory by faith in His blood, by proclaiming His word, and by submitting to martyrdom rather than swerve from fidelity to Him. ... Satan* and his angels, on the other hand, symbolize antagonists of believers, who endeavor by contradiction to countervail, or by persecution to prevent, their testimony and to maintain the supremacy of idolatry. ... The period of this war was the period of the persecutions by Diocletian, Galerius, Maxentius, Maximin, and Licinius; and the victory, that change of feeling that rendered persecution and paganism itself unpopular, prompted Constantine to espouse the cause of the Christians, and finally led to the rejection of paganism as the religion of the State." "The *chant* (ver. 10) was uttered by the victors, and indicates that the Church was to regard .. (the victory) as insuring the speedy Advent of Christ, and commencement of His millennial reign. The *heavens* summoned to rejoice are the *new heavens*, the symbol of the risen and glorified saints; ... they who *dwell* in those heavens are the sanctified nations who are to live under their sway; ... the *land* and the *sea* ... denote the nations at rest and in agitation anterior to the establishment of that millennial kingdom." "That the *dejection* of Satan and his angels was to be a *woe to the earth*, indicates that the decline of the pagan party into a minority was to exasperate its priests and rulers, and lead them to more violent measures, to overwhelm their antagonists, and reinstate themselves in authority."

GLASGOW regards the *Woman* as denoting the *invisible Church*; the *Child*, all the regenerated children of God, the *assumption of the Child*, the elevation of the members of the Church invisible to a heavenly status; the *Dragon* ("the seven headed monster, with his sixth head now fully developed "),† the heathen empire; the *attempt*

* [Lord distinguishes between the *great Dragon* of ver. 3, and the *great red Dragon* of ver. 6, identifying the former with Satan.—E. R. C.]

† [GLASGOW: "The pagan empire occupied the place and character of all the heads developed and gone. ... Various enumerations of them (the heads) have been propounded. That which bears most verisimilitude is: 1. Egypt ... 2. *Palestine* or Arabia (Amalek, Idumea, *etc.*) ... 3. *Assyria* .. . 4. *Babylon* ... 5. *Persia* ... 6. *Yavan*, or Hellas, dating from Alexander's conquest of Persia, B. C. 331, and comprehending Greece and Rome, until Paganism fell, and which, when it became complete, assumed the nature and received the name of Dragon. 7. *Rome*, which began first with Constantine, who adopted Byzantium as his capitol, B. C. 323, and thus led the way to the rise of that new or second Roman empire, called Θηριον, *the monster with seven heads* (the first six represented by the last) and ten horns." (See *footnote* †, p. 272.)—E. R. C.]

to devour, the persecution of the Church begun, in a public and national sense, in A. D. 51, under Claudius, but in an indirect sense in Herod's massacre of the babes; the *flight* (ver. 6, distinguished from that of ver. 14), the banishment of Christians in the first persecution, A. D. 51. The *war* he interprets as the intellectual and polemical warfare waged between Jesus (Michael) and His ministers (Quadratus, Aristides, Justin, *etc.*), and Satan and his ministers (Celsus, Porphyry, Diocletian, *etc.*), resulting in the *defection,* i. e., the destruction of Pagan supremacy under Constantine. The *hymn* (ver. 10) he regards as that of Christians raised to the Heaven of ecclesiastical superiority; the *woe* (ver. 12) as implying that Satan instigated the pagan priesthood to resist Christianity to the utmost, and also that after Constantine, Arianism prevailed.

AUBERLEN.* "Woman and Beast form manifestly the same contrast as in Daniel the Son of Man and the Beasts. . . . In both cases it is the *human* which is opposed to the *bestial,* only with Daniel in *male,* with John in *female* shape. Daniel beholds the *Man,* the *Bridegroom,* the *Messiah;* because he looks into the time when Christ shall reappear visibly and establish His Kingdom upon earth. John, on the other hand, within whose horizon lies, to speak at present only in a general way, the time before the second advent, beholds the *Woman,* the *Bride,* the *Congregation of God* in the world. He beholds her in the figure of a *Woman,* and this symbolism is not confined to the Apocalypses, but is a consummation of the whole *usus loquendi* of the Old and New Testaments. It begins in the Pentateuch . . . (for example Ex. xxxiv. 15; Lev. xvii. 7; xx. 5. 6; Num. xiv. 33; xv. 39; Deut. xxxi. 16; xxxii. 16, 21). We find a further development of this view in the writings of the Prophets . . . (Isa. i. 21; l. 1; liv. 1; Jer. ii. 2, 20, 23–25; iii. 1; Ezek. xvi., xxiii.; Hos. i., *etc.*). In the New Testament the same expression is used by John the Baptist (John iii. 29). Thus from the very outset Christ is introduced in the place of Jehovah; in the time of fulfillment Jehovah became Jesus Christ, as His name manifests, ὁ Κύριος, the Lord. He Himself calls Himself the Bridegroom (Matt. ix. 15). . . . We meet the same view in the Apostolic Epistles (Eph. v. 23–32, comp. with Gen. ii.) . . . All this the Apocalypse sums up in one word, *Woman* (xii. 1). The characteristic of *woman,* in contradistinction to that of *man,* is her being subject (Eph. v. 22–24), the surrendering of herself, her being receptive. And this is in like manner the characteristic of man in his relation to God, and receiving from Him. . . . Humanity, in so far as it belongs to God, is the *Woman;* therefore it is said of Christ, the Son of the woman (xii. 5), that He is a Male-Son. True, He is born of a *woman;* . . but at the same time, He is the Son of God, and as such His relation to the Church is that of Husband to Wife. . . . This is the simple meaning of the addition of *male* to *son,* apparently pleonastic. . . . Beside Him no man dare deny his receptive, woman-like position; for they who imagine to have life in themselves, who separate themselves

from God, rise against Him, and, trusting to stand in their own strength, sink to the level of *irrational beasts.* The proud nature-strength of man is not of a manly, but of a beastly kind; it is nothing but the brute force of the beast. . . . The choice of symbols is (not) accidental or arbitrary, but based on the essential characteristics of *Woman* and of the *beast.* . . . *Woman* and *Beast* designate the Kingdom [Church] of God, and the kingdom of the world, not only in this or that period of their development in time; but also in general universality." By the *male-son,* this commentator understands (as above) CHRIST; by the *Woman,* at the period of Christ's advent, *"the congregation of God in its Old Testament shape;"* by her *adornments*—the *sun,* the supernatural Divine light borne by her; the *moon under her feet,* heathenism vanquished and conquered by her; the *crown of stars,* the twelve-fold division of Israel (continued in the twelve-fold New Testament shape, ch. xxi. 12). The *wilderness* he regards as indicating the *heathen world* whither the Church fled from Canaan; *"the flight of the Woman into the wilderness* is nothing else but the passing away of the Kingdom, [Church] of God from the Jews, and its introduction among the Gentiles: Matt. viii. 11, 12; xxii. 43: Acts xiii. 46, 47; xxviii. 25–28." ("The *Acts* of the Apostles gives us a grand comment upon this in the description it contains of the Church's migration from Jerusalem to Rome. . . . The Church's life is nourished by the kind ministrations from on high; she lives in the *wilderness,* even as Israel on manna from Heaven; . . . but though she finds no nourishment, yet she finds a refuge and an asylum in the Gentile world, even up to this day.") Concerning the *war in Heaven* (vers. 7–12) he writes: "We cannot possibly find anything else but a description of the fact, known to us from other parts of Scripture . . . that the Prince of this world is judged by the completion of Christ's work of reconciliation. . . . There are three stages of the conflict of Christ and Satan. The *first* is the temptation of Christ in the wilderness; . . . (the *second,* the assault upon) those who were near Christ, in order to oppose the Saviour's work; the *third,* in which the victory is consummated, is the sufferings and death, the resurrection and ascension of Jesus. (What Paul expresses in Col. ii. 15, in a didactic form, John saw in a prophetic vision. The devil is now cast out of Heaven after the Son is raised to the throne of God, ver. 5. The Archangel Michael is appointed the executor of the judgment. For according to Dan. x. 13, 21; xii. 1, he, among the high angelic Princes, is the Angel to whom is entrusted the defence of God's Church against the opposing powers in the invisible world of spirits.)" Vers. 12 sqq. he regards as setting forth the *second period** in the history of Satan

---

* [Although this distinguished author cannot be classed with English and American commentators, it is deemed proper here to present an abstract of his views.—E. R. C.]

* [Auberlen holds that the history of Satan and evil spirits "consists of an ever deeper downfall, in *four* gradations or periods. The *first* extends to the first coming of Christ (ver. 8 (ἔτι) presupposes that hitherto up to the ascension of Christ, *the demons were in Heaven* like the other angels, and that like them, they influenced Earth from their abodes in Heaven, in which there are many mansions. See Job i. 6; ii. 1; 1 Kings xxii. 19–22; Zech. iii. 1, 2). The *second* period is from Christ to the commencement of the Millennium; then Satan is cast out of Heaven to earth, where he exercises yet free power. . . . The *third* period embraces the millennium.

during which, having "lost his power and place in Heaven, and chiefly for this reason, because (ὅτι) he *can no longer accuse men before God,*" "he concentrates all his strength (by *temptation* and persecution) to ruin as many souls as possible." (See also *in loco.*)—E. R. C.]

EXPLANATIONS IN DETAIL.*

Ch. xi. 15. **Great voices.**—Voices simple are prophecies. In view of the hasty movement of the Kingdom of Darkness toward the revelation of Antichristianity, Heaven is filled with the triumphant and prophetic presentiment that now the judgment upon the dark kingdom and, consequently, the appearance of Christ's Kingdom, are near. "The question—to whom did these voices belong?—need neither be asked nor answered" (Düsterdieck). For various insignificant hypotheses on this subject. see Düsterdieck. This commentator also rightly discards the limitations of the circuit of the seventh Trumpet (Hengstenberg: it embraces vers. 15–19 ; Ebrard : vers. 15–18), and, in connection with others, maintains the proleptical import of the voices. On the other hand, the interpretation of the words:

In the Heaven, as indicative that John is still in Heaven, reposes upon a comprehensive misapprehension of the structure of the Book. **The kingdom of the world.**—Simultaneously with the Satanic and Antichristian uprising, the imminent emergence of the Kingdom of Christ is decided (Matt. xxvi. 64 ; comp. Ps. ii.)—as beginning, however, with dynamical operations which are in constant process of development, and do not become perfectly apparent until the end, at the Parousia.

Is become our Lord's.—Rapturous feeling of the Christian consciousness, in face of the *apparent* rule of the Beast who is about to come forth.

He shall reign.—See Dan. vii. 14. **Our Lord's and His Christ's.**—Careful observation of the economical relation.

Vers. 16, 17, 18. **The twenty-four Elders.** —These, therefore, are distinguished from the voices ; doubtless, however, as forming the concentrated acme of them. The prophecy concerning the Kingdom of God likewise assumes a stronger expression. *First,* in the circumstance that the Elders **fell upon their faces** (see ch. iv. 10 ; v. 8, 14 ; vii. 11 ; xix. 4). The contemplation of the sublime, thrills us with a sense of our own littleness and nothingness ; the adoring and admiring consideration of the sublime, triumphant Divine rule, in its moments of grandeur, casts angels and men upon their knees. In the twenty-four Elders we see, as ever, the elect representatives of the human race. [See *foot-note* †, p. 152.—E. R. C.]

The *second* element in which the *prophecy of the Kingdom* presents a stronger tinge. is the *form* of their adoration : they **give thanks,** in the loftiest assurance of spirit ; they regard what is to come as already decided. "*They give thanks,* not because they regard themselves as participants in the great power and government of God (Hengstenberg), a conception which is as remote from the subject here as in ver. 15" (Düsterdieck). As remote, in the sense of hierarchical superiority, and as near, in the sense of humble co-heirship with Christ. Furthermore, the feeling that God is the **All-Ruler** assumes additional prominence, and the *future* of His consummate sovereignty has become *present* —hence the omission of ὁ ἐρχόμενος.

Because Thou hast taken, *etc.* — In the economy of grace, God had suffered human spirits to pursue their own way in liberty, emptying Himself, as it were, of His power, even to the semblance of impotency (Christ on the cross), that He might then make conquest of souls in this their liberty, and educate them to salvation. Now, however, this economy of salvation is ended, and God brings His whole authoritative sway into active and visible operation again.

Thirdly, there is a particular grandeur in the sign by which the Elders recognize the turning-point of the times. This sign consists in the fact that **The nations** [Lange: **heathen**] **were wroth.**—In the very wrath of the revolt, the apostasy of the heathen—and also of the Christian peoples, which have, by apostasy, become heathen again,—the Seer—as, approximately, the singer of Ps. ii. (particularly in the *to-day* that exegetes have misunderstood)—perceives that the *wrath of God* is on the point of executing its judgment. Not only has He arisen "against the wrath of His enemies," but *in* the very wrath of His enemies, the judgment of *His* wrath is revealed. Undoubtedly, however, the wrath of God first issues forth, *in full revelation,* in the *Vials of wrath* [or *anger*]* which follow upon the wrath of the heathen under the domination of the Antichristian Beasts.

The time of the dead.—We understand this, not as significant of the judgment upon the awakened dead, ch. xx. 12, with Düsterd., but as indicative of the satisfaction imparted to the pious dead by the judgment upon living transgressors (see ch. vi. 10, 11). This judgment is two-sided : first, it *gives reward* to all the *servants of God,* and that in all proportionate degrees : to *Prophets, saints,* even to simple *God-fearing* men—and not only the *great,* but also the *small.* This reward does not necessarily begin with the heavenly glory ; the most affecting reward is satisfaction, vindication of honor, justification. Hence the second side of the judgment, the antithesis :

To destroy those who destroy the earth. —The latter expression recurs in ch. xix. 2. It is in every respect highly significant, whether by *earth* we understand the theocratic Divine institution, or the basis thereof, the cosmos, which, in all points of its ideal destinations, is laid waste by the enemies of the Lord, even in the direction of an ungodly civilization.

The enemy is bound; and as he was cast out of Heaven to Earth, he is now cast into the bottomless pit [pit of the Abyss] and rendered harmless, Rev. xx. 1–3. After having been let loose for a little while, he is, *fourthly,* judged and cast for ever and ever into the lake of fire (Rev. xx. 7-10; Matt. xxv. 41 ; 1 Cor. vi. 3). Thus the whole history which the Apocalypse gives of Satan, is a continual succession of his being cast out, hurled down (βληθῆναι, xii. 9 ; xx. 3-10)." —E. R. C.]

* [Special comments are reserved for the Add. Note, p. 250 sq —E. R. C.]

* [See note 20, p. 275; and *foot-note* on p. 276.—E. R. C.]

Düsterdieck refers τοῖς δούλοις to the *Prophets* only, apprehending τοῖς φοβουμένοις as a summary expression for the entire mass of the godly. The distinction of Bengel, adopted by Hengstenberg, accords better, however, with New Testament usage; namely, the *servants of God* and the *God-fearing*—by *servants* understanding the *saints* together with the *Prophets*. Nor must the antithesis, *the small and the great*, be confounded with the same antithesis in ch. xiii. 16 and xix. 18—interior relations being contemplated here.

Ver. 19. **And the Temple of God which was in the Heaven was opened.**—Herewith begins the heavenly fulfillment of the preceding festal prophecies.

The Heavenly Temple is the archetype of the earthly Temple (see Ex. xxv. 9 and 40); it is, therefore, the ideal Kingdom of God. The Church Invisible, then, begins to become visible; even the *Ark of the Covenant* in the Holy of Holies is seen. The meaning of this is, we believe: the ideal import of the holiness of the law and the truth of the redemption becomes a matter of Christian knowledge manifest to all the world. Hence, also, there proceed from this great ideal appearance *lightnings*, and *voices*, and *thunders*, and *earthquake*, and *a great hail* —all kinds of awakening and vitalizing convulsions of the spiritual world. They commence with *lightnings*, with grand radiations of new illumination, and close with a great *hail*, in which the grand conflict of hostile winds with the heavenly spring-wind in the spiritual atmosphere seems to be set forth. So far as the idea of the heavenly Temple, the heavenly Ark of the Covenant, etc., is concerned, we may remark that the Jewish axiom cited by Düsterdieck [see p. 150 and *foot-note.*—E. R. C.]: *quodcunque in terra est, id etiam in cœlo est*, does not stand on the same footing with the Jewish tradition to the effect that the lost Ark of the Covenant had been transported to Heaven. On the confusions of construction attaching to vers. 18 and 19, see Düsterdieck, p. 388.

The different expositions of the present section follow the lead of the various conceptions of the whole Book. According to the *Church-historical* view, reference is had to the conquest of the Goths and other Arians by Narses (Lyra). According to the *synchrono-historical* view, we have an announcement of the truth, that access to the heavenly Sanctuary is open to all through Christ (Herder), or a reference to the destruction of Jerusalem (Eichhorn), or to Barcocheba (Grotius). According to Hofmann, the law has now received its due through the medium of the judgment; therefore, the Ark of the Covenant, which contains the law, can now appear. According to Hengstenberg, the Ark of the Covenant appears, because the Covenant now meets with its visible realization. Similarly Düsterdieck. Sander better explains: "The testament [covenant] which the Lord made with His Church and, particularly, with Israel, becomes manifest in all its glory; to many, profound glimpses into the mysteries of the covenant are vouchsafed," etc.

Ch. xii. 1. "If that judgment upon Antichristianity, which the Lord comes to execute,

is to be represented in exact completeness and reasonableness [*Begründung*=state of being based upon just and sufficient reasons.—TR.], not only must the deepest Satanic foundations of Antichristianity as a whole be laid bare but, likewise, the most essential shapes in which this radically Satanic Antichristianity appears in the world, must be depicted" (Düsterdieck).

A great sign was seen in the Heaven.—According to Ebrard, this means simply a *symbol*. Hengstenb. is of the same opinion. Düsterd. strives to distinguish this symbol from other figures, which, he declares, are in no whit allegorical in their nature; he, however, cites, in illustration, no figures that are *not* allegorical; for *dearth*, for instance, in ch. vi., is assuredly presented in an allegorical figure. Hengstenberg, on the other hand, superfluously suggests that John is continually seeing only *signs*.

Be it observed, in the first place, that the Seer here speaks of a *great* sign; and, furthermore, that the *Woman* cannot be intended as a symbol of the Church or the Theocracy simply in and for herself; but that her *condition* forms an important element in the symbolism. The great sign in Heaven presents, in a highly striking picture, which is no mere symbol, but a historical life-picture or parabolical phenomenon (an entire composition of single symbols), the whole spiritual conflict betwixt the Kingdom of God and the kingdom of Satan—a conflict which is at the same time a presage of the imminent emergence of Antichristianity, to do battle against Christianity in this present visible world.

A woman.—In reality, only three explanations are possible here:

1. The *Woman* (as the Bride of the Lord, in accordance with a standing Biblical view, based upon deep and essential spiritual relations, the contrast of spiritual receptivity and spiritual creative power) is the Christian Church (Bede *et al.* to Bengel *et al.*), or, particularly, the Christian Church of the last time (à Lapide, Stern, Christiani). The attempt has been made to remove the contradiction which makes the Christian Church the mother of Christ, by saying that by the birth of the Messiah we are to understand the birth of Christ in believers; or even by declaring that His birth is His return to judgment (Kliefoth).

2. The *Woman* can be only the Old Testament Church of God, the true Israel (Herder *et al.* to Düsterdieck). Ebrard even apprehends by the *Woman*, the *natural* people of Israel *qua* possessor of the promises.

3. The *Woman* is the Old and New Testament Church of God in undivided unity (Victorinus to De Wette, Hengstenberg, Auberlen). The fact that the Woman cannot be referred to the *New Testament Church* alone, results clearly from ver. 5; that the Christian Church did not bear Christ. Holding fast the identity of her in the *Heaven* and her in the *wilderness*, neither can the Woman be significant of the *Old Testament Church* by itself, since the same Woman lives on in the wilderness throughout the New Testament period of the cross. The *unity* of the Old and the New Testament Church of God lay, doubtless, much nearer to the contemplation of John

than to that of an exegesis whose view is, in many respects, too exclusively fixed upon externalities. Though it is impossible that John could have apprehended the Woman as *Mary* herself, yet the fact was most closely present to his consciousness that this Mary, whose bodily offspring Christ was, was the final concentration of the Old Testament Theocracy—the Theocracy which, in respect of its inner essence, spiritually gave birth to the Messiah, and which, in respect of this inner essence again, continued, as the Kingdom of God, in a new and New Testament shape.

But who then are the λοιποί of ver. 17? queries Düsterdieck. This we shall touch upon later.

Clothed with the sun.—It is an obvious fact that the *sun* is a symbol of the Divine revelation of salvation; comp. Mal. iv. 2; also Ps. xix., where the sun is spoken of in connection with the law, *i. e.*, revelation. The distinct reference of the sun to the historic Christ, which many have sought to establish (Bede, *etc.*), is not pertinent here, because Christ is the Son of the Woman. According to Hengstenberg, the sun is the glory of the Lord; but with the glory of the Lord, the Lord Himself is clothed (Ps. civ. 1, 2).

So far as the **moon** is concerned, Diana of the Ephesians was well known to the Apostle as a symbol of *nature*, and to readers of Asia Minor there was something peculiarly striking in the circumstance that the Seer represents the moon as appearing **under the feet** of the Woman whose clothing was the sun. The symbol of Isis also denotes nature. Thus Constantine saw the cross over the *sun*, because in his time the latter was adored, as a symbol of the nature-divinity, by a sublimated heathenism, and particularly in his own family.

The figure of the **moon** has likewise been variously interpreted—as significant of: Worldly glory (Bede); the light of the Old Testament (Grotius); the light of Church teachers, in so far as that is derived from Christ (Calov.); the light of the Turkish crescent (Bengel; to make this true, however, half of the moon must be invisible. The same commentator regards the *sun* as the Christian Empire!); created light (Hengstenberg; the same looks upon the *sun* as significant of uncreated light); pale night with her half (?) moon-light (Ebrard). Poetic description (Düsterdieck).

A crown of twelve stars.—*Twelve* is the number of completeness; the *crown*, as a wreath or garland [prize], is an ornament which has been obtained by a struggle; the *stars* are the elect spirits of the Kingdom of God (Dan. xii. 3). The number *twelve* has been taken literally, and, in accordance with the whole interpretation, referred either to the twelve Apostles (Vitringa, *et al.*), or to the twelve Tribes of Israel (De Wette, *et al.*).

Ver. 2. **And she, being with child, crieth.**—Several grand contrasts successively appear here. First, the Woman in her heavenly garb of light; then the same, crying out in the pains of a hard travail and menaced by the hellish Dragon. Again, the Woman in her simply beautiful and sublime raiment of light, over against the Dragon in the startling forms and

glaring colors of demonico-bestial unnaturalness. Furthermore, the *third part* of the *stars* of Heaven; swept away and cast down by the tail of the Dragon. Next, the Son lifted up to the Throne of God, and the mother sheltered in the retirement of the wilderness. The *crying Woman* represents the sufferings of the true Israel at the time of Christ's crucifixion—sufferings of which John had the deepest experience.

Ver. 3. **Another sign.**—The sign is not only the symbolical form of the Devil, as the prince of darkness, the adversary of the Kingdom of God, the murderer of man and mortal enemy of Christ, but also a presage of the imminent outburst of the Antichristian power. The allegorical figure of the *serpent*, originally significant of Satan, was blended, even upon Israelitish ground, with the figure of the crocodile or leviathan; in Jewish tradition, together with the *features* of the dragon of story, it received the *name* thereof, especially through the mediation of the Septuagint (δράκων=תנין and לויתן). Though the dragon, in the narrower sense, has, in accordance with passages in the Psalms, been represented as king of the sea and of marine animals (like the Midgard serpent in Scandinavian mythology), he also occupies the position of a hostile ruling power toward the Earth; and the present figure in the Apocalypse symbolically indicates that which in the Gospel of John is denoted by "the prince of this world" (John xii. 31; xiv. 30; xvi. 11). Greek mythology elevated the dragon, subsequent to its killing by Hercules, into a constellation, situated near the polar star, and embracing several stars in its folds. Jewish tradition elaborated the original figure of a serpent into a dragon with seven heads (see De Wette, p. 127).—Even in Christian story, the dragon-slayer, under different names (Michael, St. George), occupies an important place.

A great red [Lange: fiery red] dragon.—Πυῤῥός, the designation of the color, is looked upon by many as blood-color, in accordance with ch. vi. 4, and considered as referring to him who, from the beginning, has been the murderer of man (John viii. and 44), and who now seeks to kill, in particular, the Son of the Woman also. Ebrard combats this interpretation, maintaining that blood-red and fire-red are two different things, and that fire is a symbol of destruction and ruin. The fire-hue certainly is susceptible of several shades, from pale to brownish red. In ch. vi. 4, blood-color is unmistakably indicated. In the Neronic persecution, John had, moreover, become acquainted with the prelude to those stakes at which, since then, the hues of blood and fire have so often mingled.

Seven heads and ten horns.—"The picture is not to be conceived of (with De Wette) as so utterly without taste, as if on *four* of the heads there were *one* horn and on the remaining *three, two* horns, but (with Bengel, *et al.*) as having *ten* horns on *one* of the heads." This is said to be proved by ch. xvii. 5, 9, 12; but the horns of Satan must not be identified with the horns of the Beast. Neither is it possible for us to see how one head with ten horns could, beside these, carry a crown likewise. A correct appreciation of the symbolism, however, will leave the disposition of the *ten horns* amongst the *seven heads* to exegetical controversy. The appearance is *designed* to be monstrous, however. By many, a wrong leap is taken from the figure of the heads and horns of the Dragon to the heads and horns of the Beast (see Düsterdieck, p. 395; Ebrard, p. 355; Hengstenberg, p. 603), although the Seer himself has taken sufficient pains for their distinction. The *seven heads* of Satan are not, in the abstract, to be divided into historical phases, any more than are the seven archangelic forms, or the seven Spirits, that, from the Throne of God, go forth into all lands, to be thus distributed. In the case of the seven heads, the septenary bears the import of the whole Satanic *week*, so to speak—in its continuance, as a plenary number of lying works, from the beginning of the Satanic labor in Paradise : this week, with its demonic days' works, gives promise of a new Paradise, an absolute witches' Sabbath *—which, however, shall be celebrated in the *lake of fire.*

The same emphasis must be laid upon the symbolical element in the case of the *ten horns ; i. e.,* neither are they to be identified with the ten kings who appear as ten horns of the Beast. *Ten* is the complete course of the world; *ten horns* are the complete world-power, here, indeed, appearing as lying powers. This circumstance [of their falsity] is manifest in the fact that Satan has three more horns than crowns. In more ancient times Vitringa, at least, pointed out the difference of equipment between the Dragon and the Beast ; the same has been done in modern times by De Wette. Ancient exegetes have, moreover, taken the difference for granted, by referring the *seven heads* of the Dragon to seven bad spirits, or the whole number of bad spirits ; to seven capital vices, or the seven deadly sins : or by apprehending, by the *ten horns,* the ten sins against the ten commandments; or worldly power; or the multitude and might of the demons.

According to Hofmann, the *seven heads* symbolize the *non-unitous* power of Satan; according to De Wette, they are a symbol of wisdom—that is to say, of consummate cunning. In the Indian mythology, the members of the divine forms are multiplied, for the purpose of portraying the superhuman greatness of the qualities indicated.

Erroneous historical interpretations see cited by Düsterdieck : Diocletian, the one head with ten horns. Düsterdieck himself : the Roman empire [*imperium*], *etc.* Düsterdieck, p. 395 ; De Wette, p. 127.

The *Heaven,* in which the Dragon makes his appearance, can be neither the antemundane Heaven of the angel-world—since the fallen angels did not immediately fall to *earth*—nor the Heaven in which the glorified Christ is enthroned. That which is intended, therefore, is the Heaven that Christ has instituted on earth—the invisible Church, the Communion of saints —into which Satan, as a Dragon, has found entrance, just as, long ago, he pressed into Paradise.

* [Witch—s' Sabbath (*Hexensabbath*) : "the festive conventicle of witches and spirits, for the indulgence of wild uproar and dissolute mirth." SANDERS' *Wörterbuch.*—TR.]

Ver. 4. **And his tail,** *etc.*—De Wette : "The strength of dragons is resident in their tails, *Solin.,* ch. xxx. in Wetstein." *Three* is the number of spirit. A *third* is a fraction in reference to spiritual things. The significance of the *third* has already been set forth in ch. viii. From the one star of embitterment, of mere.y germinant apostasy, an apostasy of the third part of the stars, *i. e.,* the spiritual Church-heaven, has resulted. These stars are, by the lashings of the Satanic tail, by the magic of an apparently prodigious vital power, cast from Heaven to earth, *i. e.,* from being stars of the invisible Church, they become demonic organs of the external Church and of Christian political order.

The reference of the stars to angels (Vitringa, *et al.,* Ebrard) is most erroneous : further on, the Dragon himself, *together with his angels,* is found still in Heaven. The division of the stars into two classes, based upon their reference to churchly teachers (Grotius, *et al.*), and to believers or saints (Alcasar, *et al.*), is inadmissible. According to Ewald, the action of the Dragon's tail constitutes merely a poetic trait—being indicative of eagerness for combat. Düsterdieck also reduces the description, in essence, to a poetic picture. Other interpretations see quoted by the last named commentator, p. 398.

And the Dragon stood [*trat*=stepped— took his stand].—According to Pliny viii. 3, dragons move in an upright posture. Comp. Wetstein, De Wette.

Ver. 5. **A male son.**—Jer. xx. 15. The strong expression of the manfulness of the Child by the neuter ἄρσεν, is not merely explanatory of His destination, in accordance with Ps. ii. 9, to **shepherdize** (in accordance with the Sept.) **all the nations with a rod of iron** (Düsterd.); it also contains a slight intimation of the fact that Christ has, by His resurrection, frustrated the attempt of Satan to devour Him. De Wette totally denies the emphasis in the apposition ; Düsterdieck, unnecessarily, discovers an announcement of the shepherdizing of Antichristian nations in *judgment.*

Manifestly the Messiah is here denoted in the literal sense of the term—not in any metaphorical sense whatsoever. This truth, however, does not invalidate the typicalness of the facts set forth : the people of Christ, in whom He is born on earth, are, like Him, themselves caught away into Heaven, through the medium of suffering and death, from Satan's plots for their destruction.

Manifold interpretations of the words, as referring to the Christ born of the Church, from Bede onward, see in Düsterdieck, p. 400, De Wette, p. 128 (Christians ; Constantine the Great : the Nicene confession ; the Roman Church ; Christianity, *etc.*).

["These words (who is to shepherdize all the nations, *etc.*), cited verbatim from the LXX. of the Messianic Psalm ii., and preceded by the ὅς of personal identification, leave no possibility of doubt who was here intended. The man-child is the Lord Jesus Christ, *and none other.*' ALFORD. See also the abstract of Auberlen, p. 243, and the ADD. NOTE, p. 250 sq.—E. R. C]

And her child was caught away.—*Sub*

specie æterni, the sufferings of Christ, as instigated by Satan, down to His very death upon
the cross, are a baffled machination, resulting in
the consummation—opposite to that desired—of
His exaltation to the Throne of God. De Wette
pertinently cites the words of Jesus (John xiv.
30): The prince of this world hath nothing in
Me. Mark also his comment on the "absurd
interpretation" of Grotius concerning the
translation of Christ, on the hypothesis that
the Roman Church is meant. On the same
hypothesis of a mystical birth of Christ, Lyra
spoke of the liberation of the Church, and Eichhorn of its growth. The fact that the actual
history of the humiliation and exaltation of Jesus (hence also the fact of the Ascension) under-
lies the Apocalyptic description, is vainly denied
by Düsterdieck; he himself subsequently admits it, in a certain degree, by saying that the
historical actuality serves merely as a firm, concrete substratum for the idea.

Ver. 6. **And** [Lange: **But**] **the woman
fled into the wilderness.**—On the repetition
of this passage, see above. The *wilderness* becomes a place in the heavenly region itself by
its perfect symbolico-ideal import: heroic abne-
gation of the world. On the term designating
the *period* of retirement in the wilderness, see
Symbolism of Numbers in the Introduction.
Also De Wette, p. 121. In commenting on *the
wilderness*, exegetes have referred to the wandering of Israel through the wilderness; the sojourn
of Elijah in the wilderness; the flight of the
parents of Jesus to Egypt; withdrawal from the
world and renunciation of it; the flight of the
Christians into the wilderness; the flight of
the Christians to Pella, *etc.* Even waste-lying
Palestine is mentioned (by Hofmann) as the
wilderness in which the Woman, who is still
fleeing, will one day arrive (!).

De Wette calls the interpretation of the *flight*
as the flight of the Christians into the wilderness, "pettily literal"—a comment which is
ungrounded, since in that flight the external
fact originally coincided with its inner significance—as was the case in regard to Christ's sojourn in the wilderness.

[AUBERLEN supports his view that by the *wilderness* is meant the heathen world (see p. 243),
by considerations such as the following: "It is
by flight that the Woman comes into the wilderness. If we remark whence she flies, we shall
also find whither. It is before the persecutions
of the Devil, through Herod, and in general
through the Jews. But whither does she fly? . .
Undoubtedly from the Jews to the heathens.
Therefore it is that, in this passage, the attribute given to Christ elsewhere, that He will rule
the heathen with an iron sceptre (ii. 27; xix.5;
Ps. ii. 9), is expressly mentioned. From the
time of His ascension, the heathen are given to
Him as His field; thither His Church, persecuted by the Jews, takes her refuge (from Acts
viii. onwards). There God has prepared a
place for her to be sheltered and nourished. . .
This signification . . . is corroborated by the
prophetic *usus loquendi*. We know that Canaan,
as the seat of all temporal and spiritual blessings of God, is called the land of glory, of plea-
santness, *etc.* (Jer. iii. 19; Ezek. xx. 6, 15; Dan

xi. 16, 41; viii. 9). The land of the heathen,
on the contrary, is a wilderness, because for-
saken by the fullness of Divine life and strength.
As God dwells and reveals Himself in the *land
of glory*, the demons dwell in the *wilderness*
.(Matt. xii. 43; Mark i. 13; Lev. xvi. 21, 22;
Isa. xxxiv. 14); they are the rulers and princes
of the heathen world (1 Cor. x. 20; Rev. ix. 20).
Hence, when Israel is exiled to Babylon, it is
said to be in the *wilderness* (Isa. xl. 3; xli. 17-
19; xlii. 10-12; xliii. 19, 20," *etc.*—E. R. C.]

Vers. 7-12. Expulsion of Satan from the Heaven of the spiritual Church, the communion of
saints.

"The assumption that the Dragon pursued
the Child even to the Throne of God, and that
this was the cause of the conflict that arose in
Heaven (Eichhorn, Herder, De Wette, Stern), is
not only utterly without foundation in the context, but is also incompatible with what is
stated in ver. 5" (Düsterdieck). The commentator from whom we have just quoted, will,
however, listen to no conjectures as to the signification of this *Heaven*, and calls even Bede's explanation (which is also that of Primasius and
others), *in ecclesia*, "allegorical interpretation."

Ver. 7. **War in the Heaven.**—Treatises on
the difficult reading which we meet with here,
see in De Wette (p. 131; Düsterd., p. 404). [See
TEXT. AND GRAM.—E. R. C.]

Michael.—We read this as in apposition to
the war in Heaven. The *war in Heaven* is the
eternal, holy, and warlike opposition against the
Satanic Kingdom; an opposition represented by
Michael, the warlike form of Christ, a form
which also manifests itself in His Church as the
spirit of discipline.

"The view of Vitringa, of which Hengstenberg is an earnest advocate, that Michael is not
an *Angel* (according to Dan. x. 13; xii. 1, the
guardian Angel of the Old Testament people of
God; according to Jude 9, an Archangel), but
Christ Himself, or, as Hengstenberg prefers to
say, the *Logos*—suffers shipwreck at the very
outset—irrespective of the passage Jude 9,
where the express title ὁ ἀρχάγγελος, according
to Hengstenberg, no more contains a proof
against the divinity of Michael than the utterance of our Lord, John xiv. 28, bears testimony
against the homoöusia of the Son—in the impossibility of regarding the Michael of ver. 7
and the Child of ver. 5 as one and the same
person" (Düsterd.). Within the range of sensuous apperception this is, undoubtedly, impossible; in Christology, however, Christ can, at
the same time, be a child, in Bethlehem, and the
Son of God, in universal relations and manifestations. We take it that Michael, in accordance
with the difficult reading, is, from the outset,
Christ in warlike array against Satan, and that
hence it is that the angels of Michael are appointed to be angels of war against the Kingdom
of Darkness. The very designation of Michael
in Jewish Theology as the συνήγωρ, or advocate
of the pious, in opposition to the κατήγωρ, is expressive of the assumption that Michael is no
mere angel. [See *foot-note*, p. 241.—E. R. C.]

Ver. 8. "Hofmann, Ebrard and Auberlen pre-
posterously dogmatize on this verse, maintaining
that it presents the idea that until then (until

the Ascension of Christ, ver. 5, Auberlen [see pp. 243 sq.]; during the whole 'world-period,' *from* the Ascension, Ebrard) Satan and his angels have really had *their place* in *Heaven*. In the presentation of this view, reference is had to the appearance of Satan before the Lord, Job i., in the sense of an historical fact, and from Zech. iii. it is shown that Satan's occupation in Heaven is that of *accusing*" (Düsterd). Ebrard even assumes that during the whole world-period of the 1260 days, Satan has a right to appear before God as the accuser of the people of Israel, etc., p. 365.

We have already called attention to the conciseness of the expression: **they prevailed not; neither was their place** (as a permanent position) **found any more in the Heaven**

Ver. 9. **And the great Dragon was thrown down** [Lange: **cast out**], *etc.*—A solemn and comprehensive expression, declaratory of the expulsion of Satan, hence also of his lying arts and motives, from the Church of God, the kernel of humanity. First, *the* symbolical term : **the ancient serpent**. The *great Dragon*, as the mortal enemy of Christ, long ago began his murderous sport as the *ancient serpent*. The serpent of Paradise has become the great Hell-dragon. And, similarly. in accordance with his true essence, the fiend has, from being the **Devil**, or *slanderer* and *accuser* of mankind, become its unmasked *foe*, **Satan**. Although known in, and *cast out* from, *Heaven* under these titles, he resumes his old courses in the *world* as the *seducer* of the whole world. In antithesis to the holy kernel of the Church of God, he now becomes, more truly than ever, the seducer of the world.

He was thrown down unto the earth.—That is, not out of the cloud-heaven upon the terrestrial globe, but out of the inner Church upon the external Church and the ecclesiastico-political institution. It is a truth supported by historical data, that the antithesis of the external Church to the inner spiritual Church of faith has, in many impure, egotistical organs of the former, been the cause of the more perfect development of the hypocritical world-spirit in hierarchical and sectarian forms. The second clause of the sentence, therefore—

And his angels were thrown down with him, must not be regarded as relating purely to demonic powers of the other world. The declaration concerning the angel of Satan, who buffeted the apostle Paul [2 Cor. xii. 7], is suggestive of the hatred of Jewish or Judaizing fanaticism; and such fanaticism was also at work in the rise of the synagogues of Satan, of which the Apocalyptist speaks.

Vers. 10–12. The song of triumph over the liberation of the invisible Church, the communion of saints, from the deceptive arts of Satan and his angels.—This song is expressive of the great contrast betwixt the inner and the external Church—a contrast as great as that between Heaven and earth, nay, between wheat and tares, though, notwithstanding it, the Church in its totality continues to be a unitous organic phenomenon until the end of the world. Hail to the one! Woe to the other!

Ver. 10. **Now is come** (ἐγένετο) **the salva-tion and the power and the Kingdom of** [Lange: **with**] **our God**.—These words, difficult in an exegetical point of view, are explained by the assumption of a traditional antithesis. In this holy region, which is purged from all Satanic works, but one *salvation* is known, which, as principial and final σωτηρία, is *with God* alone. Here, therefore, there is no condition of the forgiveness of sins, or of the going home to the Father through human mediation. Here the mighty rule of God alone prevails, and the Church is purely and alone His Kingdom, in which the authority of no other ruler is of any account. The rule of the Divine authority, however, is mediated singly and only by the pure and infallible mighty rule of Christ.

For the accuser (κατήγωρ) **of our brethren is thrown down.**—Satan is, on the one hand, the *seducer* of the natural life to levity by the sophism, that sin is nothing, and on the other hand, the *accuser* of the spiritual life, and the deluder into melancholy, by the sophism, that sin is unpardonable ; in both aspects, he is the *calumniator* of man before God, in the declaration that man is worthless to the very core. As *seducer*, he endeavors to rule in the world ; as *accuser*, he seeks dominion in the Church. So long as men's consciences are unperfected (Heb. ix. 9, 14), so long are they in fear of death (Heb. ii. 14, 15); and just so long are they not free from the power of the accuser, as exercised through hierarchs and sectarian heads of parties. If, however, the *accuser* be but decidedly cast out of the sanctuary by means of the perfect peace of the reconciliation, then is salvation found here alone with God, and all the might of hypocrites influenced by Satan is here broken. But how has this Divine freedom in the peace of God been brought about?

Ver. 11. **They conquered him on account of** [Lange: **by virtue of**] **the blood of the Lamb.**—The appropriation of the reconciliation in the death of Christ was, at the same time, a being baptized, with Him, into His death, resulting in their joyful confession of Him. [ALFORD: "They conquered by virtue of that blood having been shed ; not as in E. V., '*by* the blood,' as if διά had been with the genitive. The meaning is far more significant ; their victory over Satan was grounded in, was a consequence of, His having shed His precious blood ; without that, the adversary's charges against them would have been unanswerable. It is remarkable, that the rabbinical books give a tradition that Satan accuses men all days of the year, except on the day of Atonement. Vajikra Rabba, § 21, fol. 164. 3, in Schöttgen."—E. R. C.]

The word of their testimony. In the consistent bearing of this testimony, **they loved not their life unto death**; they were, in respect of the posture of their hearts, *ideal* martyrs, even though *real* martyrdom should not have been required of them. That the Heaven on earth is here intended throughout, is evident from the fact that the great voice in Heaven says: *The accuser of our brethren is thrown down*. Thus do the blessed in the Heaven beyond, speak of the sealed in this present world.

Interpretations of the heavenly *brethren:* As the Angels; the twenty-four Elders; the perfected saints in the other world. According to Ebrard, the *voice* proceeds from the whole number of individual Israelites who are converted throughout the period of the 1260 days; by the *brethren* in this world, he understands Israel as converted at the end of the world-period.

Ver. 12. **Therefore rejoice, ye heavens.** —Significant plural. The dwellers in the Heaven *beyond* this life, as well as the dwellers in the Heaven *in* this life. Düsterdieck combats the declaration of Hengstenberg, that the saints on earth are included in this apostrophe (in accordance with Phil. iii. 20; Eph. ii. 6). The former commentator regards the inhabitants of Heaven as proleptically celebrating the victory, yet future, of their brethren. This explanation is foreign to the context, and does not hold fast the antithesis.

Woe to the earth and the sea.—Even here Bengel looks upon earth and sea as significant of Asia and Europe. Düsterdieck utterly rejects every "allegorical interpretation," and thus the two unreconciled propositions stand contrasted: WOE TO THE EARTH (with the Accusative)—"Satan is made a conquered foe even for believers *on earth*" [Düsterdieck's comment on ver. 11.—TR.].* If the *terrestrial orb* were meant, in its merely literal sense, the mention of the *sea* would be superfluous. Hengstenberg rightly refers the *sea* to the sea of nations, and thus, here also, a contrast to it is formed by the *earth* as the theocratic institution and order, as ecclesiastical and, relatively, ecclesiastico-political authority.

The devil is come down unto you.—Even within the sphere of the earth there is an *above* and *below*. The devil, after being cast down, makes pretence of a voluntary descent, as a sort of Mentor, to the pastors of the earth and the agitators of the sea.

Having great anger.—The animosity of the kingdom of darkness and its prince is heightened by the presentiment of its imminent judgment—a presentiment conditioned by the sense of its vileness.

Little time.—We cannot identify καιρός with χρόνος, as if the whole time from the Dragon's expulsion from Heaven to the coming of the judgment were intended, as the "time of Antichrist," or, according to Bengel, the period from the year 947 to 1836. The καιροί of Satan do not run through the whole Chronos of the Church of the cross; they emerge from time to time only, as particular moments of apparent triumph for the kingdom of darkness, even though Satanic temptations pervade all times; see Luke xxii. 53. Here, therefore, the kingdom of darkness, in its deepest demonic foundation, as represented by Satan himself and his angels, appears first as an ultramundane spiritual kingdom—which, however, in its onslaughts against

the Kingdom of God and His Anointed, begins, in the centre of the Theocracy in this world, as, subsequently, in the periphery of the Church, to belong to this world. Satan already has his instruments in this world, as prefigured by his organs in the specific Antichristian sphere, the Beast out of the sea and the Beast from the earth. The attributes of this hellish triad are attributes of falsehood and hypocrisy. The Dragon has *seven heads*, the sea-Beast has seven heads; and whilst the *plurality* of heads announces the monster, the *septenary*, as holy, seems to cover this drawback; it is the number of holy days' works, promissory of an entrance upon the eternal Sabbath, the new Paradise. In still more hypocritical guise, the Beast from the earth appears; he has *two horns* like the lamb. This is the pseudo-Christian figure which comes to the aid of the Antichristian shape, by means of which the latter succeeds in obtaining perfect apparent victory. The consummate hypocrisy of this second Beast forms a contrast to the insolent boldness of the Beast out of the sea. The *ten horns* of Satan are themselves indicative of complete earthly worldpower, as well as the *ten horns* of the first Beast; but the former wears the *crowns*, a sacred *seven*, with the semblance of legitimacy, upon his heads, whilst the Beast has *ten* crowns, which he boldly sets upon his horns, as manifest signs of his usurped revolutionary power. This hellish triad agree, however, in blasphemous speech; even the *Lamb* speaks as a Dragon.*

[ADDITIONAL NOTE ON THE SECTION.]

By the American Editor.

[In the judgment of the writer, this Section is divisible into two parts. The first, ch. xi. 15–18, presents the doxology of the heavenly host† in view of the events of the seventh and last Trumpet, which events are immediately in order to the establishment of the Millennial Kingdom, and issue in that establishment. At the first blast of the Trumpet this doxology is begun. The *second* part, ch. xi. 19–xii. 12, forms the introduction to the development of the events of the Trumpet. Ch. xi. 19, like the preceding doxology, may indicate purely a Heaven-scene in which, under circumstances of inexpressible grandeur, the Divine purposes in fulfillment of the promises of the Covenant will be unveiled to the inhabitants of Heaven; or it may betoken a fearful convulsion, shaking Heaven and Earth, which will inaugurate, and perhaps be continued throughout, the period of this Trumpet.

The Woman and the Dragon.

The writer adopts the view, that the *Woman* symbolizes the True Church; and the *Dragon*, Satan, or more probably the host of evil spirits under the leadership of Satan (possibly one-third of the original number of blessed spirits, ch. xii. 4). He regards them as Classical Sym-

---

* [The precise position of Düsterdieck is, that ver. 11 contains a proleptical celebration of the future victory of earthly believers, whilst ver. 12 rather reverts to the actual condition of affairs, proclaiming *joy* to the Heavens and the dwellers therein, on account of the victory over the Dragon; but *woe* to the earth and all its inhabitants—even to believers, since it is theirs now to make good the triumph proleptically rejoiced over, and to fight the raging Dragon, even though Satanic temptations pervade all times; see therefore, is not quite so irreconcilable as would appear from Dr. Lange's statement of the case.—TR.]

* The hypothesis earlier advanced by Bleek, to the effect that the Book originally closed with ch. xi., has since been declared by himself to be untenable (*Apok.*, p. 126; *Beiträge*, p. 81). This dispatches the note in Hengstenberg I., p. 589.

† [For the writer's views concerning the *Elders* see footnote to p. 152.—E. R. C.]

bols (see p. 146), as also the *male Son* of ver. 5, representing the ἀπαρχή (see below). He cannot adopt the conclusion that the vision is *retrogressive*. This seems to be forbidden by the phraseology of the Apocalyptist. There is here no strong disjunctive (καὶ μετὰ τοῦτο εἶδον) as in the beginning of the account of the intercalated vision of ch. vii., not even the *secondary* disjunctive καὶ εἶδον (see ADD. NOTE, p. 193; and *footnotes*, pp. 150, 190); the whole narrative flows on as though the Seer were describing one continuous scene. And not only so, but there is nothing to *require* an unannounced and unprecedented break in the description at this point, and still further, as will appear, the idea that the actions ascribed to these symbols occurred *after* the blowing of the *seventh* Trumpet gives a unity to the whole description unattainable on any other hypothesis.

As to the *adornment* of the Woman, the writer adopts the general view set forth by Lange (pp. 237, 246), understanding, however, by the *crown of twelve stars* the dignified position and completeness of her ministers. (On the number *twelve*, see p. 15; and for an inspired exposition of the *stars*, ch. i. 20.) He has formed no decided opinion as to what is symbolized by the *seven crowned heads* and the *ten horns* of the Dragon. He would suggest, however, that this symbolization may have been employed because of the relation of Satan to the *seven-headed and ten-horned Wild Beast* (the World-power, developing in *seven* Empires, the last being divided into *ten* kingdoms, see p. 272), which he inspires, which is his earthly representative and instrument. On this hypothesis, the Dragon appropriately wears the crowns on all his *heads*, as the one inspirer and ruler of all; but the Wild-beast is introduced as wearing the crowns upon his *horns* (ch. xiii. 1) as indicative of the time of his appearance on the Apocalyptic platform.

By the *male Son*, the writer understands the ἀπαρχή, who, with Christ, their Elder Brother and Head, are to rule all nations with an iron sceptre (comp. ch. ii. 26, 27; iii. 21; xx. 4, 6; Matt. xix. 28; Luke xxii. 29, 30; 1 Cor. vi. 3; see also ADD. NOTE, p. 193). In one point of view (exclusive of Christ), this body constitutes the *Bride* of the Lamb, and is so symbolized, ch. xxi. 2, 9; but in another (as forming one body with Christ—a body of which He is the Head, the Root, the King, the Elder Brother, the Husband) it may appropriately be styled the *male Son*. The *travail* of the Woman commenced with the Advent of Jesus, and from that time until the present the Dragon has continually stood before her striving to destroy her offspring, which continually has been caught away from

his grasp to the Throne of God. She is brought into the field of Apocalyptic vision in the *last time*, when her long labor is near its end. John behold the completion of the birth, the last assault of the Dragon, and the completed deliverance of the male Son from his attacks. Then the completed body, the ἀπαρχή, the 144,000, delivered from Satan and the woe that is to come upon *them that dwell upon the Earth*, stand in safety, with their Head, on Mount Zion (comp. vers. 5, 12; Luke xxi. 35, 36; Rev. iii 10; vii. 4, 14; xiv. 1—5; see also NOTE ON THE GREAT TRIBULATION, pp. 191 sq., and ADD. NOTE, p. 193).*

The *War in Heaven* the writer also refers to the period of the seventh Trumpet. It may, indeed, have begun on, or before, the Ascension of Jesus; but for reasons already given, we must conclude, that it comes into the view of the Seer as waged to its completion under this Trumpet. As additional reasons for this opinion may be urged the following: 1. The declaration concerning the Dragon following his dejection, "he knoweth that he hath *little* time," ver. 12; the time accorded could not have been characterized as *little* if the dejection occurred at either the Ascension of our Lord or the establishment of Christianity under Constantine. 2. The declaration that the woe following the dejection should be visited upon *the Earth*. This seems to point to the period of the *great tribulation* (see above; and also 2 Thess. ii. 8-13, comp. with Matt. xxiv. 21—24, in which the last and most violent outburst of Satanic malice is directly connected with the *great tribulation*). The writer adopts in the main the views of Auberlen as to the *nature* and *place* of demons; holding, however, that the dejection is still future; that when it takes place, the hosts of evil spirits being concentrated on Earth, the fulfillment of the last quoted prophecies, which lie parallel with the remaining portions of this vision, will begin.

By the *flight of the Woman into the Wilderness*, the writer thinks it probable, is intended the removal of the vital Church to some earthly retreat of seclusion and safety. By the *victory* of ver. 11 he understands not that of Michael, but the victory of the Saints whom the Dragon *persecuted* and *accused*.—E. R. C.]

* [An objection to the interpretation given above may arise in the minds of some from the fact, that after the dejection of the Dragon to Earth, he is represented as making war with the *remnant* of the Woman's seed, v. r. 17. The writer will here only remark, that in his mind there is a growing conviction, but that it consists of a select portion of them—the special y faithful. He regards ver. 17 (τῶν λοιπῶν τοῦ σπέρματος αὐτῆς) as strongly confirmative of this view. See ADD. NOTES, pp. 193 and 291.—E. R. C.]

B.—THE DRAGON UPON THE EARTH; OR, CHRISTIANITY, AND, OPPOSED TO IT, ANTICHRISTIANITY, IN ITS DEVELOPMENT AND IN THE TWO GROUND-FORMS OF ITS MATURITY; THE BEAST OUT OF THE SEA AND THE BEAST OUT OF THE EARTH.

Chap. XII. 13—Chap. XIII. 18.

Chap. XII. 13–18.*

a. The Dragon and the Prelude of Antichristianity.

13 And when the dragon saw that he was cast [thrown] unto the earth, he persecuted
14 the woman which [who] brought forth the man *child* [male *son*]. And to the woman were given [*ins.* the[1]] two wings of a [the[2]] great eagle, that she might fly into the wilderness, into her place, where she is nourished [*ins.* there] for [*om.*
15 for] a time, and times, and half a time, from the face of the serpent. And the serpent cast out of his mouth [*ins.* after the woman] water ▬ a flood [river] after the woman [*om.* after the woman], that he might cause her[3] to be carried
16 away of the flood [river][4]. And the earth helped the woman ; and the earth opened her mouth, and swallowed up the flood [river] which the dragon cast out
17 of his mouth. And the dragon was wroth with [concerning[5]] the woman, and went [departed] to make war with the remnant of her seed, which [who] keep the commandments of God, and have the testimony of Jesus Christ [*om.* Christ][6].
18* And I [he][7] stood upon the sand of the sea, [.]

Chap. XIII. 1–18.

b. The Antichrist out of the Sea of Nations.

1 And [*ins.* I] saw a beast [wild-beast] rise up [ascending] out of the sea, having seven heads and ten horns [ten horns and seven heads][8], and upon his horns ten crowns [diadems], and upon his heads the [*om.* the] name [names[9]] of blasphemy.[;]
2 and the beast [wild-beast] which [that] I saw was like unto a leopard, and his feet were [*om.* were] as *the feet* of a bear, and his mouth as the mouth of a lion : and the dragon gave him his power, and his seat [throne], and great authority
3 [ἐξουσία].[:] And I saw [*om.* I saw][10] one of [from among] his heads as it were [*om.* it were—*ins.* if] wounded [slain][11] to death ; and his deadly wound [or the wound of his death] was healed : and all the world [the whole earth] wondered after the beast

TEXTUAL AND GRAMMATICAL.

[1] Ver. 14. [Tisch. inserts *ai*, with A. C. P.; Treg. marks with *; Alf. brackets; it is omitted by 𝕭. B*.—E. R. C.]
[2] Ver. 14. [Alf., Treg., Tisch., insert τοῦ before ἀετοῦ ; it is omitted by 𝕭.—E. R. C]
[3] Ver. 15. [Gb. and Sz. read ταύτην with P. 1, 7, instead of αὐτήν, given by Modern Eds. with 𝕭. A. B*. C.—E. R. C.]
[4] Ver. 15. [An unusual compound adjective is here employed, ποταμοφόρητον ; the literal translation of the sentence is, *that he might make her river-borne.*—E. R. C.]
[5] Ver. 17. [" The ἐπί presents the Woman ▬ the ground and occasion, not as the immediate object, of the Dragon's wrath. Comp. Matt. xviii. 3; Mark iii. 5, *etc.;* and see Winer, § 52, c." Lillie's *Notes.* Winer, § 52. c. (*c*), gives ἐπί in this place the force of *over.*—E. R. C]
[6] Ver. 17. [Modern Editors omit Χριστοῦ with all the Greek Codd.; it is given by the Vul. *Cl.*, om. by *Am.* and *Fuld.*; Lange retains.—E. R. C.]
[7] Ver. 18. This reading is given by 𝕭. A. C., *Vulg., etc.* The Rec. ἐστάθην (retained by B*. [P.], *etc.*, Gb., Tisch., *etc.*), has the internal connection against it. The standpoint of the Seer is immovable ; the scenes he beholds are movable. [The reading of Lange, with which Lach., Alford, and Treg. agree, is adopted.—E. R. C.]
[8] Ch. xiii. 1. According to 𝕭. A. B*. C. [P.], *etc.*, the κέρατα are mentioned first ; and indeed they are more striking here than the heads ; the natural sequence, preferred by the Rec., would here be inappropriate.
[9] Ver. 1. The plural ὀνόματα is given by [𝕭.], A. B*., and many others. Düsterdieck regards it as interpretative, but it might also be supposed—*one* Beast, *one* name. [Treg. and Tischendorf give the plural; Alford gives ὄνομα with C. P.—E. R. C.]
[10] Ver. 3. Inserted for the sake of clearness. [It is omitted by Crit. Eds. with 𝕭. A. B*. C. P. 1, *Am., Tol.*; it occurs in Vulg. *Cl.* Doubtless the μίαν is governed by the εἶδον of ver. 2 ; the Seer beheld the Wild-beast ascending with a wounded head. Ver. 2 i-, in ▬ sense, parenthetical and subsidiary to ver. 1.—E. R. C.]
[11] Ver. 1. The marginal reading of the E. V. (*first-class*, marked †) is here adopted. See section on *Marginal Readings* in the Special Introduction, by the Am. Ed.—E. R. C.]

* [The notation of Lange and of Critical Editors of the Greek Testament is here adopted. That which is here styled ▬ 18 is the first clause of *ch.* xiii. 1 of the English Version. See Note 7 above.—E. R. C.]

4 [wild-beast]. And they worshipped the dragon which [*om.* which—*ins.* because
   he] gave power [the authority (τὴν ἐξουσίαν)] unto the beast [wild-beast] :[12] and
   they worshipped the beast [wild-beast], saying, Who *is* like unto [*om.* unto] the
5 beast [wild-beast]? [*ins.* and] who is able to make [*om.* make] war with him? And
   there was given unto him a mouth speaking great things and blasphemies ;[13] and
   power [*om.* power—*ins.* there] was given unto him [authority (ἐξουσία)] to continue
6 [act[14]] forty *and* [*om. and*] two months. And he opened his mouth in blasphemy
   [unto blasphemies][15] against God, to blaspheme his name, and his tabernacle, and[16]
7 them that dwell [those who tabernacle] in [*ins.* the] heaven. And it was given unto
   him to make war with the saints, and to overcome [conquer][17] them : and power
   [authority (ἐξουσία)] was given him over all kindreds, and tongues, and nations
8 [every tribe, and people[18], and tongue, and nation]. And all that dwell upon the
   earth shall worship him,[19] whose names are not [*every one* whose name[20]] hath not
   been] written in the book of life of the Lamb [*ins.* that hath been] slain [*or ins.*,][21]
9 from the foundation of the world. If any man [one] have [hath] an ear, let him
10 hear. He that leadeth into [If any one *is* for] captivity shall go [*om.* shall go—*ins.*,]
   into captivity [*ins.* he goeth][22] : he that killeth [if any one shall kill][23] with the
   sword [*ins.*, he] must be killed with the sword. Here is the patience [endurance]
   and the faith of the saints.

c. The Antichristian False Prophet, as the last Product of the Earth—i. e., the Ancient Order of Things—
in its Lapse into Antichristianity.

11 And I beheld [saw] another beast [wild-beast] coming up [ascending] out of the
12 earth ; and he had two horns like a lamb, and he spake as a dragon. And he
   exerciseth all the power [authority (ἐξουσία)] of the first beast [wild-beast] before
   him, [in his presence ;] and [*ins.* he] causeth [maketh][24] the earth and them which
   [that] dwell therein [in it] to [*om.* to—*ins.* that they should] worship the first beast
   [wild-beast], whose deadly [*om.* deadly] wound [*ins.* of his death] was healed.
13 And he doeth great wonders [signs], so that [*or in order that also* (ἵνα καί)][25] he
   maketh [may make] fire come down from [*ins.* the] heaven on [unto] the earth in
14 the sight [presence] of men, and deceiveth [seduceth *or* misleadeth (πλανᾷ)]
   them that dwell on the earth by *the means of* [because of] those miracles [the
   signs] which he had power [it was given to him] to do [work] in the sight [pre-
   sence] of the beast [wild-beast] ; saying to [telling] them that dwell on the earth,
   that they should [*om.* that they should —*ins.* to] make an image to the beast [wild-
15 beast], which [who[26]] had [hath] the wound by a sword, and did live [lived]. And

12 Ver. 4. [The Am. Ed. leaves unaltered the *pointing* of Vers 3 and 4, in the E. V. On this subject critical editors are
widely at variance. That pointing which, in his judgment, will most correctly present the entire passage, is as follows:
*And one from among his heads as if slain to death. And the wound of his death was healed ; and the whole earth wondered
after the wild-beast, and they worshipped the dragon because he gave the authority unto the wild-beast, and they worshipped
the wild-beast, saying, etc.*—E. R. C.]
13 Ver.5. We give the *plural* in acc. with the Rec., N. C. Opposed to this we find the *singular*, and the reading
βλάσφημα. [Treg. and Tisch. (8th ed.) Lange, which reading is adopted above; Gb. and Tisch. (1859), give βλασφημίαν
with B*. P. ; Lach. and Alford, βλάσφημα with A.—E. R. C.]
14 Ver. 5. [For this translation of ποιῆσαι, see Robinson *sub voce* 2. (b). Lange translates *schalten.*—E. R. C.]
15 Ver. 6. [Crit. Eds. read εἰς βλασφημίας with N. A. C. The singular is given by B*. P.—E. R. C.]
16 Ver. 6. [Lach., Alford, Treg., Tisch. (8th ed.) omit καί with N[1]. A. B*2. C.; Lange and Tisch. (1859) retain (as above)
with N*. B*. P., Vulg.—E. R. C.]
17 Ver. 7. The first half of this verse is omitted in A. C. [P.], *etc.*, and is discarded by Lach. Codd. N. B. and versions
[Vulg., Cop., Æth.] give it. The omission is to be explained by the repetition καί ἐδόθη. [Alford, Treg., Tisch. retain.
Against such authorities the Am. Ed. dares not remove the sentence from the text, although he regards the internal evidence as favoring the judgment of Lachmann.—E. R. C.]
18 Ver. 7. [Crit. Eds. insert λαόν with N. A. B*. C. P.—E. R. C.]
19 Ver. 8. The reading αὐτόν in acc. with A. B*. C., *etc.*
20 Ver. 8. Several unimportant variations here. Tisch. [Alford, Treg.] gives οὐ οὐ γέγραπται τὸ ὄνομα κ. τ. λ. [Some
Eds. give τὰ ὀνόματα with N. P.—E. R. C.]
21 Ver. 8. [It is doubtful from the text whether or not a comma should here be introduced. Lange omits. For a presentation of his views and those of other commentators, see under EXP. IN DETAIL, pp. 268sq.—E. R. C.]
22 Ver. 10. For various readings, see Tisch. and Düsterd. [Lach. (ed. maj.), Alford, Tisch., with A., give εἴ τις εἰς
αἰχμαλωσίαν, εἰς αἰχμαλωσίαν ὑπάγε ; Treg., with N. B*. C., gives εἰς αἰχμαλωσίαν only once ; Lange seems to adopt the
reading of the Rec.—E. R. C.]
23 Ver. 10. [Treg. and Tisch. give ἀποκτενεῖ δεῖ with B*. C. P. ; Alford reads ἀποκτανθῆναι with A.—E. R. C.]
24 Ver. 12. Καὶ ποιεῖ, N. A. C. [P.], Lach. [So Alf., Treg., Tisch. (8th ed.). Tisch. (1859), καὶ ἐποίει with B*.—E. R. C.]
25 Ver. 13. [WINER writes, § 53, " In the defective diction of the Apocalypse, ἵνα is apparently used once, xiii. 13, for
ὥστε or ὡς, after an adjective including the notion of intensity : *magna miracula*, i. e., tam magna, *ut, etc.*" The Am. Ed.
must express his dissatisfaction with this unprecedented, though generally accepted, translation—the more especially, as,
in his judgment, the ordinary force of the particle gives a good sense.—E. R. C.]
26 Ver. 14. The striking reading ὅς in A. B*. C. [P.], is probably based upon an exegetical interpretation of the Beast.
[N. 1. *etc.*, give ὅ. The reading ὅς, which Alford, Treg., Tisch. adopt, is clearly to be preferred.—E. R. C.]

he had power [it was given to him] to give life [or ■ spirit²⁷ (πνεῦμα)] unto the
image of the beast [wild-beast], that the image of the beast [wild-beast] should
both speak, and cause that²⁸ as many as would [should]²⁹ not worship the image of
16 the beast [wild-beast] should be killed [slain]. And he causeth [maketh] all, both
[om. both—ins. the] small and [ins. the] great, [ins. and the] rich and [ins. the]
poor, [ins. and the] free and [ins. the] bond, to receive [om. to receive—ins. that
they should give³⁰ them] ■ mark in [on] their right hand, or in [on] their foreheads
17 [forehead]: and [or om. and]³¹ that no man might [one should be able to] buy
or sell, save [but] he that had [hath] the mark, or [om. or] the name of the beast
18 [wild-beast], or the number of his name. Here is wisdom. Let him that hath understanding count the number of the beast [wild-beast]: for it is the number of a
man ; and his number is Six hundred threescore [and sixty] and [om. and] six.³²

²⁷ Ver. 15. [The Marg. Read. (†) of the E. V. is *breath*. This meaning is altogether unprecedented in the New Testament.—E. R. C.]
²⁸ Ver. 15. Lachmann, in acc. with A. [P. 7, Vulg. *Cl.* and *Fuld.*], reads ἵνα before ὅσοι. [This reading is also given by
Treg.; Alford brackets ; Tisch. and Lange omit with א. C., *Am., etc.* The Am. Ed. has not felt at liberty to alter the
generally accepted reading, although he is inclined to adopt the opinion of Lach and Treg. If the ἵνα be genuine, the
translation will be, "*the image of the wild-beast should both speak and act, in order that as many as,*" etc.—E. R. C.]
²⁹ Ver. 15. [Lach., Tisch. (1859), Alford, Treg. read προσκυνήσωσιν, with A. B*. P.; Tisch. (8th ed.), -ουσιν with א.
—E. R. C.]
³⁰ Ver. 16. [Crit. Eds. give δῶσιν with א*. A. B*. C. P.; 1 reads δώσει ; 7, δωσῶσιν ; 26, 95, Λαβῶσιν.—E. R. C.]
³¹ Ver. 17. Lachmann, in acc. with C., omits the καί without sufficient reason. [Tisch. (8th ed.) omits with א*. C. 6,
Tol., etc.; Tisch. (1859), Treg. give it with א*. A. B*. P., Vulg. (except *Tol.*), etc. ; Alford brackets.—E. R. C.]
³² Ver. 18. [Tisch., Treg. read χξϛ with B*. 1, 6, *etc.* (Tischendorf's Ed. of B*. gives χξϛτ); Alford ἑξακόσιοι ἑξήκοντα
ἑξ with A. Cod. א., instead of the ἑξακόσιαι of A., reads -ιαι ; and P. 7, -ια. Cod. C. gives ἑξηκόσια δέκα ἑξ—E. R. C.]

EXEGETICAL AND CRITICAL.

SYNOPTICAL VIEW.

PREFATORY REMARKS ON THE RELATION OF
CH XIII. TO CH. XVII.—*It has already been remarked that the figure of Satan and his seven heads*
(ch. xii.) *must not be identified with the figure of
Antichrist and his seven heads. Neither must the history of the rule of Antichristianity, primarily set forth
as a whole* (ch. xiii.), *be identified with the judgment
upon the first third of Antichristianity, the Harlot,*
(ch. xvii.). *Consequently, the details also* (chs.
xiii. *and* xvii.), *especially the parallels of the seven
heads, may, indeed, be regarded as similarities, but
are not to be treated as identities. This remark applies particularly to the deadly wounding of one of
the Beast's heads* (ch. xiii.) *and the temporary disappearance of the Beast* (ch. xvii.)—*a disappearance certainly resultant upon the wounding. All
those combinations that are grounded upon the identity of these two items, which are connected as cause
and effect, fall to pieces when subjected to a more
precise and circumstantial exegesis. It is impossible
to overlook the antithesis, that, in the total history
of Antichristianity* (ch. xiii.), *the False Prophet. the
spirit of a fallen Hierarchy, is subservient to the Antichristian political World-power, whilst in the history
of partial Antichristianity* (ch. xvii.), *the Woman
rides upon the Beast, although the Beast at last
destroys the Harlot. Comp. Ebrard, pp. 377 and
455.*

Above all, we would remind our readers of the
fact that we have another entire cyclical world-
picture before us, viewed under the aspect of
Antichristianity ; it is no more petty section of
Roman history, comprised, as some would have
it, between the years 1 and 70 A. D. Further,
the following definite antithesis is distinctly evident : As the *Beast out of the sea* represents the
whole of historical worldly political Antichristianity, as embraced, however, in its final consummate appearance—so, likewise, the *Woman*, contrasted with the *Beast*, is not, so to speak, a

particle of the Kingdom of God, still less the
Jewish people, but *the whole Old and New Testament* Kingdom of God, and this too with reference
to the *final* form of the *Old* Testament, in which
the Mother appears, and to the *final* form of the
New Testament Church, which divides into the
two forms of *Harlot* and *Bride*, finally appearing
as the Bride.

Our Earth-picture is in three sections. In the
first, the devilish essence has obtained no human
shape, but already operates by summoning to its
aid human masses which unconsciously serve it.
In the second section, it has fashioned an organ
unto itself in the appearance of the Beast out of
the sea. In the third section, it has even made a
Beast from the earth, a production of the old
Theocratic order of things, subservient to the
sea-monster, and hence, indirectly, ministrant
to itself.

The beginning of the first section plainly shows
that here the Earth-picture commences which
corresponds with the Heaven-picture, for in ver.
14 ver. 6 is repeated. Here however, we have
the amplificatory statement: *to the Woman
were given the two wings of the great eagle,
that she might fly into the wilderness.* The great
eagle may be relatively understood of worldly
powers, if the context require such an apprehension, as for instance in Ezek. xvii. 3, 7. When,
however, the term is ■■ free from limitation as
we find it here, our thoughts are led back to the
redemption of Israel from Egypt, when Jehovah
bare the people on *eagle wings* (Ex. xix. 4) ; and
we are the more forcibly reminded of that event,
since Israel, also, found refuge from the pursu-
ing Pharaoh far out in the *wilderness.* If Jehovah Himself is not to be here understood, the
thing signified is His redemptive providence, in
its powerful, swift and lofty flight, unattainable
for all earthly pursuers. The fact that the
wings must be *two* in number requires no elucidation ; it is, however, somewhat remarkable
that the Woman receives the wings herself and
becomes ■ *flying* Woman. Thus did the young

Church of Christ fly from Jerusalem to Pella; and thus in every subsequent persecution it has fled deeper into the *wilderness* of solitude, of concealment, of renunciation, of foreign countries;* thus it finally fled literally into the wilderness of hermitry and monasticism. For the *wilderness* forms, in general, a contrast to the worldly region of secular life, just as the wilderness into which the Eagle bore Israel formed a contrast to Egypt. The Middle Ages afford a symbolical representation of these flights, in the development of monkish forms, of constantly increasing strictness, in face of every new advance of secularization;—back of these figures, however, lies the fact that the Church has ever fled deeper into the hiding-place of world-renunciation. Here is her *place*, where she is *nourished*. And how she has been nourished with heavenly strength, has been shown by the Mystics of the Middle Ages as well as by the Martyrs of the Reformation.

The *time* of her sojourn in the wilderness, or the time of the Church of the Cross, is, as has already been observed, obscurely designated in a twofold manner—by the number $3\frac{1}{2}$ and by the indefinite form of *times*.

Thus she is nourished *from the face of the Serpent*. Even the serpent of hierarchical despotism scarce observed how the Church was nourished inwardly with powers of the world to come [Heb. vi. 5].

But the abode of the Woman does not remain hidden from the Serpent, who *casts out of his mouth water as a river, that he might cause her to be carried away*. In the parable of the mustard seed, Christ had described the development of the seed into a tree-like shrub, which the birds would mistake for a real tree, and make their nests in its branches; John could already see the beginnings of the fulfillment of this prophecy in the pressing of foreign elements into the living Church. In his quality of Seer, however, he had the broadest and most extensive view of this whole inundation of the Church by the Græco-Roman world, by the migrations of nations, by its baptism with many peoples. For it is an irrefragable fact that *waters* are indicative of surging national life (Ps. xciii. 3, 4); consequently, the *river* here denotes a violent flux of national life against the essential Church, and the *casting of this water out of the mouth of the Dragon* forces the inference of a diabolical background to this tremendous onset. We cannot, of course, deny the fact that an opposite attraction to the light had its share in influencing the Germanic peoples, especially, in their migrations; this, however, does not invalidate a truth clearly unfolded in the migrations of the Huns, the Vandals, the Turks, and the Mongols, in their perilous onset against the Church. And, moreover, the Germanic nations were urged on and swept away by the dark lust of conquest of the Huns. But *the earth helped the Woman by opening her mouth and swallowing up the river*. It was the *earth* as a Divine institution, in the double form of the pedagogical *Church* of the Law, striking back into the Old Testament, and the

Christian *State*, which subdued the flood of barbarous nations through the medium of a Theocratic education.* Numbers xvi. 32 can hardly, merely on account of the similarity of expression, be cited here as analogous.

The rage of the Evil One is, indeed, only heightened by this discomfiture; it, however, takes another direction. The Dragon, *angry concerning the Woman*, departs to make war "with the remnant of her seed." These are designated as truly pious persons: they *keep the commandments of God, and have the testimony of Jesus Christ*. The explanations of them as brethren of Christ, or Gentile Christians, or Zionites, are not satisfactory. It would seem nearer the truth to say that they are the individual Christians who, collectively, form the Woman (Bleek *et al.*), if the text did not make a decided distinction between the Woman, or the Kingdom of God in its visible appearance, and these isolated children of the same. And here it is a natural proceeding to glance back from the striking expression οἱ λοιποί (comp. ch. iii. 2) to the significant typical expression of the Prophets: *the remnant* ([residue, remainder] שְׁאֵרִית שְׁאָר; Is. x. 20-22; xi. 11; xxviii. 5; Amos ix. 12; Micah ii. 12; iv. 7; vii. 18, *etc.*). There has been a storm of judgment, in the assaults of the Dragon upon the Woman, at the end of which there is but a remnant of individual Christians left, who are true servants of God and martyrs of Christ. The *Woman* has had to submit to an alliance with *the earth*; the *essential Church* has had to consent to an alliance with the Theocratic ecclesiastico-political form. In consequence of this alliance, the Church has itself become more akin to the earth, and a distinction has arisen between her visible totality and her living children. Subsequently she is herself partially represented by the earth. In the last time, therefore, Satan instinctively directs his attacks only upon the vital Christianity of individual Christians. He may gain many a victory in combat with them; for how many separatists and sects fall a prey to diabolical deceit. As a whole, however, they resist him, and this urges him on in the direction of the *sea*, the social life of the nations.

Accordingly, *he stands upon the sand of the sea*. Here he appears to vanish—only, however, to arise in his moral creature, the *Beast out of the sea*, positive Antichristianity. The fact that here, as well as Dan. vii. 2 sqq., the sea represents the life of the nations, is proved not only by the consistent import of this symbol, but also by the agreement of the idea in respect of the ascending Beast. The fundamental thought is thus —that always a demonic *ruling power* issues from a spiritual *anarchy* of excited national life, and rests thereupon. It does not follow from this that we already have to do with a democratic form of Antichristianity. The decisive passage where we are to seek for light is the scene ch. xvi. 19. After the out-pouring of the seventh Vial of wrath, the one great city, Sodom-Egypt (ch. xi. 8), is divided into *three*

---

* Christians as emigrants to Bohemia, Poland, Germany, Prussia, America—a long story. See Matt. x. 23.

* In connection with the general fulfillment of this prophecy, reference may be made to the slaughter of the Huns, the victory of Charles Martel, and, in general, to the triumphs of Christendom in the East and West over Mohammedanism.

parts, and the one judgment branches into three judgments—the judgment upon specific Babylon, executed by the ten kings (chs. xvii., xviii.); the judgment upon the ten kings, executed through the Parousia of Christ (ch. xix.); and the judgment upon Gog and Magog as the host of Satan, executed through the intervention of God with fire from Heaven (ch. xx. 9). Hence it is evident that in the present bestial figure, those three potencies are still undivided—Antichristian absolute despotism, democracy and anarchy. That the decidedly *worldly* character of the Beast is expressed, is evidenced by his coherence with the Danielic world-monarchies; and, no less, by his hostile antithesis to the Theocratico-churchly Woman, and his distinction from the False Prophet from the earth. Still, the three groundforms of Antichristianity already peep forth from our unitous figure, and among them, of course, the first ground-form, Babylon, appears. That a great *Beast of prey* is intended, is evident from the attributes of the Beast as well as from his peculiar designation (θηρίον not—ζῷον). With these attributes, he appears as a unitous compound of the Danielic beasts, yet in an original modification. The *ten horns* of the fourth Danielic Beast come in view here. In the stead of the *four* Beasts, however, we have the *one* Beast, and that not with *four*, but with *seven* heads, because here the centre of gravity falls in the New Testament time, beyond the vision of Daniel. The Beast has, moreover, become civilized with the times. In the vision of Daniel, the *lion* occupies the foreground; here, the general aspect of the Beast is pied, like the less formidable *leopard*—variegated with hierarchic and despotic colors. Of the Danielic *bear*, the Johannean Beast has retained the *ursine feet*, on account of his ungainly appearance, or his fatal embraces. Of the *lion*, the *mouth* remains (see 1 Pet. v. 8). Thus compounded, he is still more of a monster than the fourth Danielic Beast; and his monstrosity is still further increased by the fact of his union of the *seven* spirit-like and apparently holy *heads* with *ten horns* of worldly authority—a disproportion which distinctly proclaims that his authority is to be regarded as bestial arbitrariness, and not as reposing upon actual spirit-might; this fact is also evident from the circumstance that he has set his *crowns* not on his *heads*, but, more shamelessly than Satan himself, on his *horns*. On the other hand, the *heads* have on them *names of blasphemy*, different forms of rebellion against the Divine-human government of God, and against the God-man Himself (Dan. vii.; 2 Thess. ii.).

The *Dragon* seems desirous of being completely merged in this his representative. He gives him (the *manner* of the giving is intimated John xiii. 27) his magical *power*, *i. e.* his lying power; his *throne* or his terrific ruler-glory, intimidating to all that is cowardly and base on Earth; and his *authority* as a ruler (see Matt. iv. 9; 2 Cor. iv. 4).

Manifestly, this collective appearance of Antichristianity reaches back into the Old Testament; in this it resembles the collective appearance of the Kingdom of God, in the form of the Woman (ch. xii). As, however, the main his-

tory of the Woman falls in the New Testament time, so it is with the full revelation of Antichristianity, which even tapers at last into the consummate figure of Antichrist (vers. 17, 18).

And now we come to the hardest knot of the Book. The point of departure for our consideration is the *mark*, or recognition-sign (χάραγμα), the real *symbolum* of the congregation of the Beast. Every one who chooses to belong to this congregation must bear this sign about him, either on his *forehead* or on his *hand*. After the analogy of branded slaves, he must bear the Antichristian slave-mark on himself as a sign that he belongs to the Beast—indirectly to the Dragon—and that he has not fallen under social excommunication, like the confessors of Christ. Now is this mark to be apprehended literally or figuratively? The particulars seem to favor the literal apprehension of it. Either on the forehead or on the hand—either in ordinary writing or in number-writing.

Forehead and *hand*, however, are themselves intelligible symbols; and, consequently, the sign on the *forehead* seems to denote the *Theocratic* impiety of open confession of the prince of enmity to God and Christ, whilst the sign on the *hand* is apparently significant of the *practical* impiety of open atheistical audaciousness; thus a contrast is formed, as if the complete dogmatics and ethics of Satanic superstition and unbelief were intended.

But, though the spiritual deportment is the main thing, the instantaneous recognizability of the spiritual state is conditioned on a definite symbolum. This symbol consists of the Antichristian party-name, corresponding to the generic name of Christian. The devil-worshipper calls himself after the name of the Beast who rules him; either plainly, without circumlocution, or in numeric writing.

In the declaration: *here is wisdom*—however, it cannot be meant that the Seer designs depossiting here in a riddle the central point of all the wisdom of revelation. The like expression recurs, more plainly, in ch. xvii. 9: *Here is the understanding that possesses* [is master of] *wisdom*—in accordance with what follows after, the skillful, holy, intelligent ability to recognize the Antichristian power, or rightly to apply the Apocalyptic sign to the corresponding historic phenomenon. In this, therefore, wisdom will approve itself. *Wisdom* alone will not answer; *understanding* alone would be still further from the mark. But whosoever has the right understanding of wisdom will *reckon the number of the Beast, or transpose the ideal marks of the Beast into historic marks.*

The Seer next furnishes the key. The *number* of the Beast is, in the first place, the number of an unknown *man*. It runs through a line of precursory Antichrists down to the last specifically consummated Antichrist. The standing sign, however, is the demonic side of Antichrist, and this is signalized by the number *six hundred sixty-six*. By an absolute unrepose and toil, by the absolute denial of the approaching Sabbath or Golden Age, and by an absolute aimlessness and abortiveness, or self-consumption, we are to recognize the features of Antichrist. Where these appear in demonic perfection, there is

Antichrist (comp. Is. xlviii. 22; lvii. 21; lxvi. 24). To *compute* the number of the Beast means, therefore, to determine the human unknown Antichrist in accordance with the stationary and revealed traits of the demonic nature of Antichrist, with the understanding of wisdom (not the understanding of a prying and calculating curiosity).*

Between the general form of Antichristianity and its summing up in the last Antichrist, a highly significant consideration presents itself. One of *the heads* of the Beast appears as *wounded to death;* but the deadly wound becomes whole again. Such a wounding could proceed only from Christianity. We have, however, carefully distinguish the fact, that Christ Himself, in the kingdom of spirit, has bruised the serpent's head (the life-principle of the seven heads)— from the fact that historic Christianity inflicts a deadly wound upon the Antichristian world-power in the distinct head of the pagan-Roman world-monarchy,—a wound which, in this present world's history, can be *healed.* This item coincides precisely with the apparent vanishment of the Beast that was and is not and shall be, as represented by the *seventh* head (ch. xvii. 8-10.—See *Int.*, pp. 25 sq.). Since that healing, *all the Earth* has been *wondering after* the Beast. Since within Christianity itself an Antichristian power has unfolded in many and diverse forms, having even partially *matured* its principles, the generality of men, especially such as are hangers on of authority *à tout prix*, have become accustomed to divide their hearts, and at the rupture of light [truth] and falsehood, right and might, with superstition and cowardice to pay homage to the lying power, making, for the most part, only symbolical reverences to Christianity. This is *worshipping the Beast,* and it is also, indirectly, a subtile devil-service—a worshipping of the *Dragon.* For that which has converted Satan into an Ahriman, an evil deity, for such men, is the fact that he has *given power* to the Beast; this he has accomplished by means of an impious policy of craft and violence—a policy which, starting from Italy especially, attained such fearful terroristic development in the Middle Ages. In reference to the Dragon, they worship Godless principles; in reference to the Beast, they worship his incomparableness and irresistibility. Vast pomp and inexorable hardness compose the social cement which, ever more and more, threatens to convert the majority of men into an idea-less, anti-ideal mass—the method which would succeed in giving mankind an animal training, were it not that it has a Divine kernel before which all the might of Satan must be confounded. So secure is Divine Providence in face of the Beast, that it gives him *a mouth* for all boasting and blas-

phemy, i. e., for all self-exaltation and derision of Divine truth, of Christian principles. For precisely this is the Divine method of sifting, as exhibited in the history of the world ; thus the elect must become manifest, and thus the chaff must be separated from the wheat. To this end, therefore, *authority* is given to him, power to do what seems good to him for *forty-two months.* This, again, is the whole time of the Church of the cross—not, however, in the form of times or of days, but in the form of *months* [moons], like the abandonment of the outer court to the Gentiles (ch. xi. 2); the greatest vicissitudes and fluctuations thus being indicated. Meanwhile, this Antichristianity is perfecting itself against the end. Finally, there is an open manifestation of audacity ; the Beast *blasphemes God,* and that in a threefold manner : he blasphemes His *name,* or revealed religion; His *tabernacle,* or His vital, simple, unadorned Church ; and His *children,* the men of the Spirit [or men of spirit, *i. e.,* spiritually-minded men], who *dwell in Heaven:* in his blaspheming against them that dwell in Heaven, a blasphemy against the hope of a hereafter is involved. It is also given him even *to make war with the saints and to overcome them.* For the combat is conducted before the undiscerning, appearance-seeking and party-spirited world, and here, almost invariably, it is the Stentor voice, arrogance and false pathos that decide; and the result is all the more certain since extraordinary magical and terroristic aids are on the side of the Beast, extending even to all terrors of violence and tricks of craft. Thus there is vouchsafed him an extension of authority over *every tribe, and people, and tongue, and nation.* Now it is an unmistakable fact that this ideally unitous might has hitherto, in its actual exercise, been only approximately unitous, although the phenomena of the gradual realization of such a unity occasionally appear in formidable powers. But with the development of the Antichristianism might, corresponds the homage of all *who dwell upon the earth,* the true slaves of the old ordinances and the old earth, further characterized as those whose *names are not written in the Book of Life of the Lamb slain from the foundation of the world.* The meaning of this is—they lack the Divine trait of a believing aptitude for suffering, of willingness to suffer for the truth, to suffer with Christ.

The highly significant words now following, to which the arousing challenge is prefixed, "if any man hath an ear, let him hear," may primarily conduce to the comfort of believers amid the persecutions which the Beast prepares for them. The Old Testament law of the strictest retribution, in spite of that misunderstanding which regards it as abrogated in the social affairs of life, because it is thus abrogated, by a higher law, in the Kingdom of Love, of personal relations, re-appears at the close of the New Testament in all its freshness, nay, in sharper outlines than before. We refer our readers to the original text and the attempt of the translation to reproduce it.* The retribution will correspond in each case to the fault.

---

* The verb [ψηφίζειν] means not merely to reckon, but also to judge (pass sentence), decide, adjudge. We have already rejected the unsymbolical, though usual, hypothesis of an ordinary number. Such an hypothesis fails to recognize the symbolical character of the Apocalypse. It is an impossibility that the Seer should have regarded it ■■ ■ mark of Christian wisdom, and that in an extraordinary degree, either to propose or to decipher such a numeric puzzle. In ch. xvii. 9 likewise, wisdom will approve itself, not in refinements of calculation, but in a religious-moral judgment, aided by a reference to Old Testament symbolism.

---

* [The translation of Lange is: "*Wenn jemand eine Gefangenschaft* betreibt, *der treibt sich in die Gefangenschaft*

Believers are to comfort themselves with these words in their sorrows. The words are, also, however, designed for their instruction, for even well-meaning, pious zeal has, in manifold ways, violated the law of *the patience* [*endurance*] *of the saints.* Often are the sufferings of a later Christian generation expiations of ancient trespᵥses, committed in a sphere in which the *patience* [*endurance*] and the *faith* of the saints alone win the victory. Here appears the vital law which lies at the foundation of the patience and faith of the saints. The more prominence is given to this law, inasmuch as just these excesses of pious zeal to which we have referred, are connected with the contrast which now comes to view with the appearance of the *second Beast,* that arises from the *earth.* This *Beast from the earth,* the supreme issue of the spirit of corrupt theocratic authority, the spiritual extract of the fallen hierarchy, is a still more hateful monster than the Beast out of the sea. He is personified baseness, for he denies his origin, *the consecrated earth of God.* He is personified *hypocrisy,* for he has *two horns like a lamb,* and he *speaks like a dragon;* he is, therefore, still worse than the Beast out of the sea, in Satanic falseness, in Satanic hate. He is, likewise, personified *hollowness,* in that he begins to imitate the deeds of the first Beast. Finally, he is personified *reprobacy,* in that he becomes an eye-servant of the first Beast, changing from a prophet of God into a prophet of Antichrist. The prototype of such "arch-rogues" was *Judas,* when he became subservient to the enemies of Christ, himself excelling them in depravity.* Even in earlier Judaism such traitors made their appearance, especially in the time of the Maccabees, when Simon, Jason, Menelaus and the like figured (2 Macc. iv.). In reality, Caiaphas, in his relation to the Romans, belongs to this class. Throughout the Christian ages such perfidies have been repeated: there was a rank growth of them in the French revolution in particular. Even our own time betrays a peculiar disposition to the production of such subjects. The approach to the bridge of treason is, however, visible at *all* times in such tendencies ᴀᴇ seek to obliterate, as far as possible, the contrast between God and the world, sin and grace, inwardness and outward show. But at all events, the master of false prophecy is yet to come—the vice-Antichrist, acting ᴀᴇ the deputy [*Scherge*] of the head Antichrist, and seeking to save at least his thirty pieces of silver out of the wreck of his former system. Thus, therefore, the *False Prophet* enters the service of Antichrist; his office, henceforth, is to gain adherents for his master. He it is who also prepares *the earth* for apostasy. A special motive which he urges

to induce men to become worshippers of the Beast, is the fact that *his deadly wound is healed.* This, in his sense, signifies that the operation of Christianity is exhausted—that Christianity has outlived itself—Biblical, pristine Christianity is at an end. This false, counterfeit *lamb* does *great signs,* and would even, in appearance, imitate the former Church-ban by a ban of nature, and make *fire fall from Heaven.* Here, especially, we perceive the heavenly integrity of the former Son of Thunder, who once desired to make fire fall from Heaven upon a Samaritan city. He now knows to what such a proceeding would lead, and knows that God has reserved to Himself the right in the final judgment to let fire fall from Heaven on the Satanic mob (ch. xx.). The signs, however, which the false lamb really executes, to the seduction of men, will be lying signs, like the cause which he serves—or, at all events, grandiose magical arts.* The greatest sign is the infatuation of men into making an *image* to the Beast—to the Beast, moreover, as presenting the mockery of Christ's resurrection, as having been wounded to death, and as having revived again—i. e., to the invincible, immortal Beast. It is a slight reminder of the sin of Aaron, that the men must make the image, but the False Prophet himself gives it a *spirit,* so that the image of the Beast can *speak.* Thus, in fine, the theory, science, poetry, and art of Antichristianity speak just as does this Beast himself in his practical shape. The declaration that the tendency of the image was to cause that all who would not worship the Beast should be *killed,* is doubtless to be taken ᴀᴇ referring to social death; and matters even arrive at such a pass that those who refuse their countenance to the Beast are, by his godless company, who have adopted an absolutely anti-symbolical *symbolum,* completely excluded from social intercourse, ᴀᴇ indicated by *buying* and *selling.* Thus there is already prepared, by the world, that separation which Christ, at His coming, shall judicially consummate.

[ABSTRACT OF VIEWS, ETC.]
By the American Editor.

[ELLIOTT: The dejected *Dragon* (Satan) persecutes the *Woman* (*the true, primitive, orthodox, catholicly united Church*), also fallen from Heaven (*her first figured state of elevation and glory*), by inciting against her (1) *Arian* emperors (Constantius, A. D. 337-361; Valens, A. D. 364-378); (2) *temptations to superstition:* (3) the *Arian-Pagan* Gothic flood (see below). The *flight into the wilderness* indicates a change, not of *place,* but of *state;* it implies "the *faithful* Church's (gradual) loss of its previous character of *Catholicity* or *Universality,* its *invisibility* in respect of true Christian public worship and destitution of all ordinary means of spiritual *sustenance.*" (For the period of the Wilderness-state, ch. xii, 14, see below with ch. xiii. 5.) The *two wings of the great eagle,* the assisting and protecting influence of the Eastern and Western divisions of the *great, eagle-symbolized,* Roman Empire united under Theodosius the Great; these wings were *given to her:* Theodosius was not only a *Church-*member, but appears to have been a truly pious

---

hinein. Wenn jemand mit dem Schwert tödten will, der muss selber (schon) mit dem Schwert getödtet sein;" which may thus be rendered: "If any one driveth a captivity, he driveth himself into captivity. If any one will kill with the sword, he must himself (his very self) be killed with the sword."—E. R. C.]

* Here we have a striking Johannean trait. Not one in the circle of the disciples of Jesus penetrated so early and so deeply the demonic inclination to treason as John. And thus, doubtless, Judas became for him the type of the False Prophet. The way in which he several times strikes upon the idea of making fire fall from Heaven, is likewise characteristic of the Son of Thunder.

* [See Add. Comment on ch. xiii. 13, p. 270.—E. R. C.]

man.* The *flood cast out of the serpent's mouth*, the Arian-Pagan Gothic invasions (a double idea suggested: (1) what flows from the *mouth* is *doctrine*, good or bad, Prov. xviii. 4; xv. 28; (2) *floods* are a constant Scripture metaphor for the *invasion of hostile nations*, Isa. viii. 7; Jer. xlvi. 7; Ezek. xxvi. 3; Nahum i. 8, *etc.;* see also, with the double sense, Ps. cxliv. 7); such was the fury of this flood as "to sweep away all the political bulwarks of the Roman authority before it; and thus might well have been deemed sufficient to sweep away also the Christian Church and Christianity itself, the professed religion of the Empire." *The earth helped, etc.:* "In those continuous and bloody wars of which the Western world had been the theatre, the barbarous invading population was so thinned, so absorbed, as it were, into the land they had invaded, that it needed their incorporation as one people with the conquered to make up the necessary constituency of Kingdoms. And in this incorporation, not only was much of their original institutions, customs and languages absorbed, but their religion altogether. . . . So the *Arianism* of the invading flood, as well as its Paganism, was seen no more. It was absorbed, as it were, into the soil, and had disappeared." The *Beast from the sea* (ch. xiii. 1) is one with (1) the *Beast from the Abyss* (ch. xvii. 3); (2) the *little horn* of Daniel's *fourth wild Beast* (Dan. vii. 7, 8, 19-24); (3) St. Paul's *Man of sin* (2 Thess. ii. 1-12); (4) St. John's *Antichrist* (1 John ii. 18-22; iv. 3; 2 John 7), and symbolizes the PAPAL EMPIRE (the *sea* representing the *flood of invading Goths*): the *seven heads* signify (1) *seven hills* (of Rome), ch. xvii. 9; (2) "the number of *different successive governing heads* of *bestial character—forms of government* —which (not *another Beast or Empire*, but) the *same individual seven-hilled Roman Empire* would be under from first to last, from its early origin to its final destruction; there being here premised, however, . . . that the *seventh* head visible on the Apocalyptic Beast would be, in *order of existence*, its *eighth* (ch. xvii. 11),"† they (*five*

having fallen at the time of the Apocalypse, xvii. 10) represent (*a*) Kings, (*b*) Consuls, (*c*) Dictators, (*d*) Decemvirs, (*e*) Military Tribunes, (*f*) the στέφανος crowned Emperors beginning with Augustus (the head then existing), (*g*) the διάδημα Emperors beginning with Diocletian,* (this head received its *deadly wound* in the edict of Theodosius, suppressing Pagan worship, which edict, according to Gibbon, ch. xxviii., "inflicted a *deadly wound* on Paganism," but revived or sprouted again as an *eighth* head, *viz.:*) (*h*) the Popedom—professedly Christian, but essentially heathen: the *ten horns* represent the ten kingdoms into which the Western Empire was divided (and which gave their power and strength unto the Beast, ch. xvii. 12, 13), *viz.*, (1) the Anglo-Saxons, (2) the Franks of Central France, (3) Alleman-Franks of Eastern France, (4) the Burgundic Franks of South-eastern France, (5) the Visigoths, (6) the Suevi, (7) the Vandals, (8) the Ostro-Goths in Italy, (9) the Bavarians, (10) the Lombards; (with changes, "the number *ten* will be found to have been observed on from time to time, as that of the Western Roman or Papal Kingdoms"): the Beast and the ten horns receive their power at *one and the same time* (μίαν ὥραν, ch. xvii. 12), *i. e.,* from about A. D. 430-530; *three horns* plucked up before the Beast (Dan. vii. 8), the subjection of the Vandals, Ostrogoths and Lombards to the temporal power of the Pope (A. D. 533-755, in which last year was Pepin's *donation* of the Exarchate of Ravenna—a *donation* confirmed and enlarged by Charlemagne, A. D. 774, which completed *Peter's Patrimony*); *blasphemies*, as Christ's Vicar assuming all his offices as Prophet, Priest and King; *worshipped* (ch. xvii. 4, comp. 2 Thess. ii. 4), the Pope seats himself "on the day of his consecration upon *God's high Altar* under the dome of St. Peter's, there to receive the adoration of his Cardinals," and "in the eighth century it was Gregory the Second's boast to the Greek Emperor, 'All the kings of the West reverence the Pope as a God on Earth'"

---

* ["First, to him (Theodosius), alone of Roman Emperors from Constantine to Charlemagne, the title has attached—*deservedly* attached, to use Gibbon's expression—of 'THEODOSIUS THE GREAT.' Next it was his lot, alone of Roman Emperors after its bipartition by Valentinian, to unite the two divisions of the Empire, the Eastern and the Western, which now, let it be noted, in the very coinage of the Empire seemed to be figured as *wings*, under his own sway. Further, it was pre-eminently his character to use all this, his imperial power, success and greatness, as a protector and nursing father to the orthodox Church of Christ. As Gibbon says, 'Every victory of his contributed to the triumph of the Christian and catholic faith.' Indeed, not the *professing orthodox Church* alone (contradistinctively to the *Arian*) might claim Theodosius as a friend and protector; but Christ's true Church also, included in the former. For none, I think, can read his history without the impression of his real personal piety. See his character as sketched by Milner."—ELLIOTT, Vol. III., pp. 55 sq.
[The patent objection to this exposition is, that it is difficult to conceive how the influence of Theodosius could have assisted the flight of the Church *into the wilderness* as that symbol is explained by Elliott; it would seem as though his influence must rather have tended to an *escape from it*.—E. R. C.]
† ["His (the Angel's) meaning in this (xvii. 11) is easily seen, in so far as the symbol itself is concerned, by reference to the statement . . . of ch. xiii. 3, that one of his heads appeared to have been wounded to death by a sword, but that his deadly wound was healed. For a fresh head had evidently sprouted up in place of the preceding one cut down—a *new* seventh in place of the *old* seventh; so that the last

head visible on the Beast, though *visibly the seventh*, was, in point of chronological succession, the *eighth*. It was thus, indeed, that the Beast, under its new and last head, became what the Angel called it, 'The Beast that was, and is not, and yet is' (καὶ παρέσται—and shall be present), ch. vii. 8; it having by that deadly wound been annihilated in its immediately preceding *draconic* form; and through the fresh-sprouted head, revived in its new or *ten-horned* bestial form. I said the *next preceding draconic* form, because it is stated, that *the Dragon yielded to it* (the Beast), on its emergence from the sea, 'his power and *his throne* and great authority.' So that the transition from the *draconic* state of Rome and its empire to the *ten-horned bestial* was direct, and without any other form or head intervening, according to the Apocalyptic representation." ELLIOTT, vol. iii., p. 115.—E. R. C.]
* [Elliott calls attention to the fact, that although the *title* of the sovereign remained the same, the nature of his office was entirely changed after Diocletian. He writes: "On turning to Gibbon . . . and glancing at the Index of Contents, ch. xiii., . . . both the *fact* and the *symbol* that we seek arrest the eye connectedly, even as if placed there for the very purpose of illustrating the Apocalyptic enigma: 'Diocletian *assumes the diadem*, and introduces the *Persian* ceremonial. *New form of administration.*'—The notice thus summarily given is explained and enlarged on in the history (ch. xiii). The transition of the Roman Empire from its *imperial* or *sixth* head, introduced by Augustus, to a new and *seventh* introduced by Diocletian, is thus distinctly declared: 'Like Augustus, Diocletian may be considered as *the founder of a new empire*,' and the change is then illustrated somewhat fully, as affecting alike the *official dignity of the Prince governing*, and the *constitution and administration of the Empire governed*."—E. R. C.]

(*Gibbon;* see also Secular and Ecc. Histories). The *two-horned Beast* represents the *Papal Clergy* united under the Pope in his ecclesiastical character as Western Patriarch, and acting so as to support his usurpation as Vicar of Christ: (1) *he has horns like a lamb, and speaks as a dragon,* i. e. under pretence of preaching the Gospel, he elaborates a denial of Christ: (2) *he exercises all the power and authority of the first Beast before* (i. e. as responsible to) *him,* the grand characteristic (assumed) power of the Pope—that of *the keys*—is delegated to the clergy; (3) *signs,* the assumption by the clergy of the power to work miracles: (4) *causing them that dwell on the Earth to worship,* the entire influence of the clergy exercised to support the usurped claims of the Pope. The *Image of the Beast* symbolizes the *Papal General Councils,* which virtually *represented* the Head of Antichristendom,* (1) it was the *two-horned Beast* (the papal clergy) that said to them who dwelt on the Roman Earth, that they should *make the image* (constitute a General Council); (2) *it was given to this Beast to give breath to the image,* etc.—it was the peculiarity of the General Councils that on *matters ecclesiastical* the clergy should *alone* have voice; (3) *the Image was made to be worshipped*—these Councils claimed to pronounce *infallibly* on questions of religion and faith; (4) the Image caused as many as would not worship it *to be put to death*—the Councils anathematized and excommunicated all who would not submit to their decrees. The *name* is, the one suggested by Irenæus, Λατεινός—the numerical value of the constituent letters of which is (λ, 30 + a, 1 + τ, 300 + ε, 5 + ι, 10 + ν, 50 + o, 70 + ς, 200 =) 666; the imposing on men the *mark,* etc., is causing the inhabitants of the Roman Earth to devote themselves to the Papal Antichrist, and this both in *profession* (forehead) and *action* (hand), even as *soldiers* to their *emperor, slaves* to their *master, devotees* to their *god.*—The *period* of the *Beast's continuance* as a persecuting power, ch. xiii. 5, and of the *wilderness-state* of the Church, ch. xii. 6, is twelve hundred and sixty prophetic days or years: the *primary* terminus *a quo* of this period is *the promulgation of Justinian's Code and Decretal Epistle to the Pope,* A. D. 529-533; the *secondary* epoch is the Decree of Phocas, A. D. 604-608; the *primary* concluding terminus, A. D. 1789-1793, "the epoch by which a blow was dealt to the Papal power from which it has never recovered." (In reference to the *secondary* concluding terminus, Elliott calls attention to the fact, that Daniel (xii. 11, 12) foretells a supplemental period of *seventy-five* years which he (writing in A. D. 1861) suggested was probably to be added to that terminus in A. D. 1864-8. Writing in A. D. 1868 (Postscript to Preface, Vol. I.), he claims that the Bull of the Pope for the Convocation of an Œcumenical Council, issued in that year, in that it does not invite Sovereigns to sit in that Council, is "an admission of the *completed* end-

* [As to the *fitness* of the symbol (εἰκων), Elliott writes: "The figure has been parallel to the chief exemplifications that history offers of *national representation* by *deputies.* So e. g. of the British Parliament. Says Burke: 'The virtue, spirit and essence of a *House of Commons* consists in its being the express *image* of the feelings of a nation,'" etc.— E. R. C.]

ing of the period of the kings of Western Christendom spiritually subjecting the power of their kingdoms to him; that is, of the completed ending of twelve hundred and sixty years." The *present* he regards as the *supplemental* period, to close about A. D. 1943.*

BARNES: (Ch. xii. 13-17). Satan (after his failure to destroy the Church through Pagan persecutions, see p. 240), "puts forth his power and manifests his hostility in another form—that of the Papacy. . . The Church is, however, safe from *that* attempt to destroy it, for the *Woman* is represented as fleeing to the wilderness (some place of refuge—possibly the retreats of the Waldenses, deserts, monasteries, *etc.*), beyond the power of the enemy, and is there kept alive. Still filled with rage, though incapable of destroying the true Church itself, he turns his wrath, under the form of Papal persecutions, against individual Christians."—(Ch. xiii.) The first Beast is the one (secular) Roman power contemplated as made up of ten subordinate kingdoms, which "combined in itself all the elements of the terrible and the oppressive, which had existed in the aggregate in the other great empires that preceded it." The *second* Beast is the Papacy considered as a spiritual power, putting on the apparent gentleness of the

* [Elliott at this point (vol. iii., p. 260 sqq.) presents an elaborate argument, of which the following is an abstract, against the *Day-Day,* and in favor of what he styles

THE YEAR-DAY PRINCIPLE.

I. The presumptive *á priori* evidence.
1. From *the nature of prophetic symbols.* The Apocalyptic prophecies, to which the controversy relates, are confessedly *symbolic* prophecies (save that of the Two Witnesses, which some contend to be literal). In such prophecies (which are pictures in miniature), it is reasonable to expect that a proportion of scale will be observed between the *symbol* and the *thing symbolized,* in *time* as well as in other respects.
2. From God's declared purpose of making the near approach of the consummation evident at the time of its approaching; yet, till then, so hidden as to allow of Christians always expecting it. This seems to require that, when prophesying concerning times, a *chronological cypher* should have been employed.
3. From the probability that this *cypher* would be a *day* for a *year.* We find similar cyphers employed Dan. ix. 24-27 (Elliott contends that יָמִים שָׁבֻעַ, there meaning *hebdomad,* when by itself, always means a *week*—seven days); Ezek. iv. 1-6; Analogies. Num. xiv. 34; Lev. xxv. 2-4.
II. The direct evidence.
This arises from the fact, that the periods of so many prophecies interpreted on the Year-day principle have proved correct. He refers to his interpretations of the periods of the Saracenic woe, p. 201; the Turkish woe, p. 201; the Witnesses, p. 228; the Woman travailing in birth, p. 240, and sojourning in the Wilderness, p. 260; the ten-horned Beast's time of prospering, p. 260.
III. Objections. (Only the more prominent will be mentioned.)
1. The alleged *novelty* of the principle as one unknown in the Church from the days of Daniel to those of Wickliffe. *Answer:* The fact is not as alleged. From the days of Cyprian, this principle in reference to *some* prophecies has been adopted.
2. The alleged discrepancies and unsatisfactoriness of Apocalyptic expositions based on this principle. *Answer:* Wrong applications of a principle, resulting in discrepancies, do not militate against the principle itself, if it be supported (as this is, see under II.) by manifest coincidences.
3. The alleged necessary participation of all in communion with the Church of Rome throughout twelve hundred and sixty years (many of whom we have reason to believe were true Christians) in the curse and perdition of Babylon as set forth ch. xiv. 9-11. *Answer:* The chronological position of the warning which contains the threatening of woe is at the very end of the period of twelve hundred and sixty years, after the fall of Babylon (xiv. 8), and therefore after the call of ch. xviii. 4.—E. R. C.]

lamb, but at the same time possessing the spirit of the Dragon. The *deadly wound* of the first Beast indicates that the Roman civil and secular power was *so* waning (in consequence of the invasion of the Northern hordes) as to be in danger of extinction ; the *healing* symbolizes the restorative and preservative influence of the Church of Rome upon the secular empire. The *secular* power thus preserved is to continue 1260 prophetic days or years—*blaspheming* (by its (1) arrogant claims, (2) assumed authority in matters of conscience, (3) setting aside Divine authority, (4) impious declarations in derogation of the Divine claims); *persecuting* (*e. g.*, the Waldenses, Albigenses, *etc.*), but at last shall (1) *go into captivity,** (2) come to an end in blood. —The *image of the Beast* symbolizes the civil government *strongly* resembling the old Roman dominion, which the spiritual power of the Papacy caused to exist, depending for its vital energy on the Papacy, and in its turn, lending its aid to support the Papacy.†—In reference to the *name* and *mark* of the Beast, Barnes agrees with Elliott.

STUART : (Ch. xiii.). The *first* Beast symbolizes the *Pagan* Roman Empire; the *second*, the Pagan Priesthood ; the *deadly wound* of one of the heads, the death of Nero, one of the *seven* Kings of Ch. xvii. 10, 11 ; the *restoration*, the belief of a reappearance of that emperor (!) ;‡ the *image*, the statue erected to him as a god; the *forty-two months*, the period of the Neronic persecution (from November, A. D. 64 to June,

---

* [" This is yet, in a great measure, to be fulfilled ; and as I understand it, it discloses the manner in which the Papal *secular* power will come to an end. It will be by being subdued, so that it might *seem* to be made captive, and led off by some victorious host. Rome now is practically held in subjection by foreign arms, and has no true independence; perhaps this will be more and more so as his ultimate fall approaches." BARNES. (This was written A. D. 1851.)—E. R. C.]

† [Barnes finds the fulfillment of this Symbol in the re-establishment of the Roman Empire under Charlemagne. He quotes the following from Gibbon, ch. xlix.: " The title of patrician was below the merit and greatness of Charlemagne ; and *it was only by reviving the Western empire* that they could pay their obligations, or secure their establishment. By this decisive measure they would finally eradicate the claims of the Greeks; from the debasement of a provincial town the majesty of Rome would be restored; the Latin Christians would be united under a supreme head in their ancient metropolis; *and the conquerors of the West would receive their crown from the successors of St. Peter. The Roman Church would acquire a zealous and respectable advocate ;* and, under the shadow of the Carlovingian power, the bishop might exercise, with honor and safety, the government of the city." To this he adds the following remark : " All this seems as if it were a *designed* commentary on such expressions as these : 'And he exerciseth all the power of the first Beast, ... saying to them that dwell on the earth that they should make an image to the Beast which had the wound by a sword and did live; and he had power to give life unto the image of the Beast,'" *etc.* He also subjoins the coronation oath of the Emperor from Sigonius: " I, the Emperor, do engage and promise, in the name of Christ, before God and the blessed Apostle Peter, that I will be a protector and defender of this holy Church of Rome, in all things wherein I can be useful to it, so far as Divine assistance shall enable me, and so far as my knowledge and power can reach."—E. R. C.]

‡ [Stuart devotes a long Excursus to the establishment of this opinion. He writes: " I do not say that John meant to convey the impression that Nero would actually revive, and reappear on the stage of action ; for this I do not believe. But thus much I am compelled to believe, . . . that John here recognizes, and intends that others should recognize, Nero, by pointing to an individual respecting whom reports were everywhere current, such as have been exhibited above."—E. R. C.]

A. D. 68) ; the *name*, קֶסַר נְרוֹן, the letters of which give the number 666.

WORDSWORTH : " The *Two Wings* are emblems of the Two Testaments ; . . . the Church flies on their pinions in her missionary course through the *wilderness of this world.*" The *flood* and the *help of the earth*, he interprets as Elliott.—(Ch. xiii.) He agrees with Elliott in the exposition of this chapter, with the following exceptions : By the *seven heads* he understands (ch. xvii. 10, 11) " the kingdoms which were successively absorbed within the circle of the Roman Empire, . . . the (1) Babylonian, (2) Medo-Persian, (3) Greek, (4) Syrian, (5) Egyptian, (6) Roman Heathen Imperial . . . (7) Imperial power of Germany." By the *wounding*, the ceasing of the imperial power in the abdication of Augustulus —it is not said that the *Head* was restored, but that the wound of the *Beast* was healed (ver. 12), the Beast lived on in the Papacy. By the *image*, " the *personification* of the Papacy, in the visible form of the Pontiff for the time being."

ALFORD : (Ch. xii. 13-18.) The figure of the *wings* is taken from Old Testament expressions in reference to the flight of Israel from Egypt (Ex. xix. 4 ; Deut. xxxii. 11). " We must not understand (by) the *Woman*, the invisible spiritual Church of Christ, nor (by) her *flight into the wilderness*, the withdrawal of God's true servants from the eyes of the world. . . I own that considering the analogies and the language used (in reference to Israel in the desert), I am much more disposed to interpret the *persecution of the Woman by the Dragon*, of the various persecutions by Jews which followed the Ascension, and her *flight into the wilderness*, of the gradual withdrawing of the Church and her agency from Jerusalem and Judea, finally consummated by the flight to the mountains on the approaching siege. . . And then the *river* . . . might be variously understood—of the Roman armies which threatened to sweep away Christianity— or of the persecutions which followed the Church into her retreats, but eventually became absorbed by the civil power turning Christian—or of the Jewish nation itself, banded together against Christianity wherever it appeared, but eventually itself becoming powerless against it by its dispersion and ruin—or, again, of the influx of heretical opinions from the Pagan philosophies which tended to swamp the true faith. I confess that not one of these seems to me satisfactorily to answer the conditions ; nor do we gain any thing by their combination. . . . As to the *time* indicated by the 1260 days, or 3½ years, the interpretations given have not been convincing, nor even specious." See also the extract from Alford on p. 242. He concludes his section with the words: " This latter part of the vision yet waits its clearing up."—Chap. xiii.) *The first Beast* is one with the four Beasts of Daniel and that of ch. xvii. ; he symbolizes the aggregate of the empires of this world as opposed to Christ and His Kingdom ; the seven *heads* are (1) Egypt, (2) Nineveh, (3) Babylon, (4) Persia, (5) Græcia, (6) Rome, (7) the *Christian Empire* beginning with Constantine ; the *wound.ng* (with Auberlen), the *conversion* of the empire to Christianity, by virtue of which the Beast in his proper essence, in the fulness of his opposition

to God and His saints, ceases to be; the worship,
etc., "are a sort of parody on ascriptions of
praise to God (Ex. xv. 11; Ps. xxxv. 10; lxxi.
19; Is. xl. 18, 25; xlvi. 5, etc.): they represent
to us the relapse into all the substantial elements
of Paganism of the resuscitated empire:" the
forty-two months, the well-known period of the
agency of Antichrist. The second Beast, identical with the false Prophet of ch. xix. 20, is the
reviver and upholder of the first; in reference
to the first, he is (1) identical as to genus, (2)
diverse in origin, (3) subsidiary in zeal and action;
he symbolizes the sacerdotal persecuting power,
Pagan and Christian, which, gentle in its aspect
and professions, was yet cruel in its actions.
The Image, the statue of the Emperor, which
every where men were made to worship: "it is
not so easy to assign a meaning to the giving life
and speech to the Image. . . The allusion probably is to some lying wonders permitted to the
Pagan priests to try the faith of God's people.
We cannot help, as we read, thinking of the
moving images, and winking and speaking pictures, so often employed for purposes of imposture by their far less excusable Papal successors." Vers. 16, 17 point to the commercial
and spiritual interdicts which have, both by
Pagan and by Papal persecutors, been laid on
non-conformity. Concerning the name and number, he writes in the Prolegomena, §5, 32: "It
(Λατεινός) is beyond question the best solution
that has been given; but that it is not the solution, I have a persuasion amounting to a certainty." (See also in loc.)

LORD: (Ch. xii. 13-17.) "The Dragon who
followed the Woman symbolizes the Pagan priests
and their abettors; . . their following after her
denotes their attempt to join her society by a
profession of Christianity." "The Serpent . . .
was not the Devil who fought with Michael, but
the Monster Dragon of seven heads (see p. 242),
. . . it represents the rulers of the Roman Empire from the elevation of Constantine." The
gift to the Woman of the wings, denotes that supernatural aids were granted her, viz.: graces
that formed a part of herself; the river, the
flood of false doctrines and superstitious rites
introduced by Constantine and his successors;
the earth, the people generally, who eagerly embraced the adulterated religion, and who by their
exulting reception of it so occupied the attention
of the rulers as to allow the dissentients to
escape; the retreat from the face of the serpent,
the flight of the true Church to a place unknown
(the Waldenses, etc.); the anger of the serpent, the
continued disposition to destroy; the making
war with the remnant, the persecution of isolated
dissentients; the time, times, and half a time,
twelve hundred and sixty years.—(Ch. xiii.)
The first Beast symbolizes "the Gothic rulers
who established governments in the Western
Empire during the Fifth century, and their successors and subjects to the present time;" the
symbols of the first part of ver. 2. that this government unites in itself the agility of the
leopard, the strength of the bear, and the merci-
lessness and voracity of the lion; the head receiving the wound was the last—the wounding
denotes the slaughter of all Christian heirs to
the throne and the accession of Julian the apos-

tate; the recovery, the restoration of the Christian succession in Jovian; the worship, etc., of
vers. 3, 4, that the populace (1) entertained for
their rulers awe and admiration, (2) and, regarding them as having acquired the rights of
the old Roman Emperors, acquiesced in their assumptions in matters of religion; the great
things and blasphemy, usurpations of authority
over Divine rights, laws, etc.; ver. 7, the persecutions of the Albigenses, Waldenses, etc.; vers.
9, 10 predict the slaughter and vassalage of all
who should attempt to deliver themselves from
religious tyranny by force (exemplified in the
history of all persecuted peoples); the forty-
two months denotes 1260 years of domination (the
terminus a quo being about A. D. 597 or somewhat later).* The second Beast indicates the
"hierarchy of the Italian Catholic Church
within the Papal dominions;" the earth whence
he came, the population of the empire under a
settled government; the two horns, twofold rule
(civil and military)—lamb-like (apparently for
ornament and defence), dragon-like (aggressive,
insatiable, merciless); ver. 12 (first part), that it
exercises the same power (civil and military) as the
first Beast, and contemporaneously (issuing and
executing decrees, making war, etc.); ver. 12 (second part). the leading of the populace to submit to
blasphemous usurpations of the emperors; vers.
13, 14, the pretended miracles of the priesthood.
The Image symbolizes the Papal Kingdom which
the priesthood established—"the union of their
several national churches into a single hierarchy,
and subjection of them to the Pope as their supreme legislative and judicial head, after the
model of the ancient civil Empire under Constantine," etc. The Name is Λατεινός, whose letters give the number 666. Vers. 16, 18 indicate
excommunication and outlawry for non-conformity.

GLASGOW: (Ch. xii. 13-18.) Ver. 13. When
Satan could not prevent the external prosperity
of the Church, he diffused the poison of heresy.
Ver. 14. The second flight of the Woman; the
great eagle is the fourth Zōa of chap. iv;† the
flight to the desert indicates expatriation (in the
valleys of Piedmont, etc.); the time, etc., the prophetic period of 1260 years (beginning about
A. D. 607).‡ Vers. 15-17, as Elliott.—(Ch. xiii.)

* [Lord's EXPOSITION was published in 1847.—E. R. C.]
† [Glasgow recognizes in the Zōa "The official and representative ministrant agencies commissioned by the Lord Jesus; and comprehensively all His people, when actively
serving Him for the good of man." According to him, the
Lion symbolizes "that like Judah of old will be the Christian people of the Gospel age, rising paramount to and sub-
duing all the nations of the earth; the Ox, the ministers
and people of Jesus" as (1) "sufferers of persecution," (2)
abounding in "works of faith and labors of love;" the Face
of a Man, the "people of God as bearing the image of Christ"
—especially ministers; the Flying Eagle, "three great facts
realized in the agencies employed by Jesus in His Church:
(1) the means and power given them of escaping from the
rage of their persecuting enemies; (2) their movement to
distant places in bearing the gospel message; (3) their study
of the prophecies, and their having 'their life hid with Christ,'
the Rock of Ages."—E. R. C.]
‡ [Glasgow remarks: "It is worthy of being noted that
there is in all these, as in prophetic dates generally, a margin of three or four, sometimes as many as seven, years,
within which limit an event may be reckoned some few years
earlier or later." (He might also have call d attention to
the fact that some prophecies have a double—an initial and
consummate—objective, and consequently will have a two-
fo d beginning and ending.) He brings together some even a
that have for their period 1260 years, as follows:

This is not a new vision, but a continuation of the preceding—the Dragon that sank down in the sea (ch. xii. 18) emerges in a new form and with a new name; this Beast (see p. 242) emerges from the sea, i. e., "of the Arian Goths and northern Pagans, and remnant Pagans of the Empire." For his expositions of the *heads*, see p. 242; in his interpretation of the *horns* he agrees with Elliott, p. 259. The *wounding* denotes the fall of the Western Empire, partially in A. D. 476. and more completely A. D. 493—this fall did not imply a total cessation of the imperial power; the imperial laws and principles were so adopted by the barbarian conquerors that ultimately a new Roman Empire sprang to life from the contused head of the old (the *restoration*). The transition of the Beast from the Dragon-form spanned over the time from Constantine to Justinian; the *forty-two months* were allotted to him after the healing of the mortal stroke, and their beginning (A. D. 529-532) was marked by the institution of the Benedictine Order, and the publication of the Code of Justinian. The *second Beast* is the Papal hierarchy (*generally* on this subject he agrees with Elliott). The *Image*—(*sic*)—"this we at once recognize in the temporal power of the Pope, and the territory called Peter's Patrimony, granted by Pepin in A. D. 754; to which may be added the creation of cardinals, who are at once priests and temporal lords;" (this image of the monster has not the term of 1260 prophetic days assigned to it; the *giving of spirit* to it was fulfilled in the summoning of Western Councils—by these it both spoke and acted. The *Name* and *number*, Λατεινός, is *one*, though not the *sole*, solution of the problem. (He presents the following, all bearing on the Latin Church : Βενέδικτός, Ἰταλικὴ ἐκκλησία, Εὐπορία, Παράδοσις, Ἔσπερος ἀββᾶ, רֹאשׁ לְקַהֵל, *Vicarius Filii Dei*, *Vicarius generalis Dei in terris, etc.*).

AUBERLEN : (Ch. xiii.) This writer in many points agrees with Elliott, and his views have to a considerable extent been adopted by Alford, Glasgow and others. According to him : The *first Beast* represents the world-power ; The *seven heads*, (1) Egypt, (2) Assyria, (3) Babylon, (4) Medo-Persia, (5) Greece, (6) Rome, (7) the Germanic-Sclavonic Empire ; the *wounding*, the conversion to Christianity of the *seventh* head ;*

[A. D. 67+1260=1327, from the Woman's flight under Nero, until the setting up of a rival Pope by Louis of Bavaria, which gave a measure of relief—synchronous with the birth of Wickliffe, and the rise of Marsilius of Padua.
[A. D. 254+1260=1514, from the usurpation exercised by Cornelius, Bishop of Rome, to the death of the Witnesses (see p. 229).
[A. D. 292+1260=1552, from the beginning of the Galerian persecution to the Peace of Passau and the establishment of Protestant freedom.
[A. D 311+1260=1571, from the election of Coecilianus Bishop of Carthage leading to the Erastian interference of the Emperor, to the granting of liberty of conscience to Protestants in France, and the Pope's excommunication of the Protestant Sovereign of England.
[A. D. 529+1260=1789, from the institution of the Benedictine Monks, and the publication of Justinian's code, to the beginning of the French Revolution.
[A. D. 607+1260=1867 (8), from the decree of Phocas, to the Spanish Revolution, which brought down the last of the ten horns.—E. R. C.]
* ["St. John beholds 'one of the Beast's heads, as it were slain unto death, and the wound of his death was healed' (xiii. 3, 12, 14). This deadly wound of one of the world-kingdoms reminds us of what Daniel saw (Dan. vii. 4) with

the *healing*, the apostatizing of the Christian head (this is the *eighth* head of ch. xvii. 11, the *Antichristian Kingdom* in the strict sense ;* probably a *person* †); the *ten horns* denote ten

regard to the King of Babylon: 'I beheld till the wings thereof (of the lion) were plucked, and the King received the upright posture and the heart of a man.' We know that hereby the humiliation of Nebuchadnezzar's high-soaring haughtiness is indicated, and his sub-sequent con ersion to the living God. A similar change passes over one of the Apocalyptic heads of the Beast. It is not changed into a human head, but it receives a wound to death, and is thus rendered innocuous. The Kingdom of this world, for which this head stands, does not truly turn to the living God, so that its beast-nature is changed into a human one, as was the case with Nebuchadnezzar; but it does not develope its beast-like, brutal, God opposed character, so fully as the six others ; for a time it divests itself of its anti-Christian character. It appears ὡς ἐσφαγμένον, as if slain ; and the remark has been justly made, that this expression is chosen purposely, in order to point out an outward resemblance between the Beast and the Lamb, which John beholds (ch. v. 6), likewise ὡς ἐσφαγμένον. The second Beast was like the Lamb, because it had two horns like a lamb (xiii. 11.); the first is like the Lamb in having a deadly wound. Hence we must not expect, even of the Beast, of the world-power itself, that its development to the end will be in an exclusively heathenish form ; it is to be Christianized externally ; nay, for a time, it will appear to be altogether dead, and to have passed out of existence ; and yet it will be in existence, and not have ceased to be *Beast*." AUBERLEN, p. 297.—E. R. C.]
* ["The deadly wound is thus healed : The Beast which received it recovers life and returns, but now not only from the sea, but out of the Abyss, whence it drew new Antichristian strength of Hell (xiii. 3, 12, 14 ; xvii 8; xi. 7). The Lord Jesus has expressed the same progression (Matt. xii. 43-45). The Christian Germanic world apostatizes from Christianity ; the old, God-opposed, and anti-Christian beast-nature asserts itself with new power and gains the ascendancy ; a new heathenism breaks in upon the Christian world. A heathenism which is worse, more demoniac, more of the nature of the bottomless pit, than the ancient one, for it, as represented by the first heads of the Beast, was only an apostasy from the general revelation of God in nature and conscience (Rom. i. and ii. 14), whereas this heathenis is an apostasy from the full revelation of Divine love in the Son (comp. Matt. xi. 41. 42); it is refined, intensified heathenism, to which the words shall be addressed : 'Remember from whence thou art fallen !' (ch. ii. 5). This prophecy is not confined to the Revelation ; it is the same apostasy (ἀποστασία) of which St. Paul speaks in 2 Thess. ii. 3, and which he sees culminate in Antichrist, the Man of Sin, the son of perdition. And in describing the evil times of the last days (2 Tim. iii. 1 sqq.), the Apostle delineates the character of the men who shall live then, in a manner which reminds us of his characteristics of the heathens (Rom. i. 29); thus he foresaw a new heathenism within Christendom. For it is evident that he speaks of Christendom ; his expressions—apostasy, 2 Thess. ii. 3 ; *some shall depart from the faith,* 1 Tim. iv. 1 (comp. 2 Tim. iii. 5; iv. 3, *etc.*)—plainly show it. What is peculiar to the Apocalypse is the clear juxtaposition of the Harlot and the returning Beast. The Lord Jesus (Matt. xxiv. 4, 5, 11, 23-26) and the Apostles speak of false doctrine, seduction, apostasy, more in general terms, whereas the Apocalypse distinguishes between two kinds of apostasies, Jewish and heathenish, of the Church and of the world; the pseudo-Christianity of the Harlot, and the anti-Christianity of the returning Beast. The latter is the world divested of all Christianity ; the former, the world, adopting Christianity, or Christianity adapting itself to the world." AUBERLEN, pp. 300 sq.—E. R. C.]
† ["It cannot be proved with absolute certainty that a *personal* Antichrist will stand at the head of the Antichristian Kingdom, for it is possible that the eighth, like the preceding seven heads, designates a kingdom, a power, and not a person, and the same may be said concerning the Antichristian horn described by Daniel. But the type of Antiochus Epiphanes is of decisive importance, for this personal enemy of God's Kingdom is described in the eighth chapter of Daniel, as a little, gradually increasing horn, just as Antichrist is spoken of in the seventh. And this is corroborated by the Apostle Paul (2 Thess. ii.), who describes Antichrist (ver. 4) with colors evidently furnished by Daniel's sketch of Antiochus, and who calls him, moreover, the *Man* of sin, the *Son* of perdition, which, if explained naturally, must refer to an individual (comp. John xvii. 12, where the same expression, ὁ υἱός τῆς ἀπωλείας, is used of Judas). In favor of the same view may be adduced, likewise, analogies in the history of the world ; the previous world-kingdoms had extraordinary persons as their heads, Nebuchadnezzar, Cyrus, Alexander the Great,

kingdoms into which the last head is to be divided (this division is still future). The *second Beast* is identical with the *False Prophet* of ch. xix. 20, and with the *human eyes* of the *little horn* f Dan vii. 8; the *first Beast* is a *physical, political*—*this* a *spiritual* power, the power of doctrine and knowledge, of intellectual cultivation, of ideas; he arises from the *earth*, i. e., the civilized, consolidated, orderly world; he comes in a Christian garb and name, *the horns of the lamb*, but with the spirit and speech of the Dragon (comp. Matt. vii. 15); the *Image* which the False Prophet causes to be made (the historical substratum of which is in the image in Dan. iii., and the statues of the Roman Emperors, to which divine worship was paid), denotes the deification of the world and the world-power—this is the new heathenism, sinking back into the deification of nature and humanity, of which it cannot. be predicted what forms of folly and bestiality (Rom. i. 22 sq.) it shall yet assume; with this enhancement of idolatry, seem to be connected new demonic mighty operations, according to ver. 15. Vers. 15-17 contain a prophecy that all public intercourse will be on condition of receiving the *mark of the Beast* (which is significantly contrasted with the *Seal* of the servants of God, ch. vii. 3 sqq.), and that *true believers* will be given into the hand of Antichrist for persecution, as is intimated, Dan. vii. 21, 25 ; Matt. xxiv. 9.*—E. R. C.]

The spiritual and universal character does not exclude individual personal representatives. Every spiritual tendency has its distinguished representatives, and when it has reached its perfection, produces its representative κατ᾽ ἐξοχήν. Hence Anti-Christian tendencies produce different Antichrists; and it is a sober historical view, when Christianity maintains that these separate Antichrists shall, some future day, find their consummation in an individual, far excelling them in the intensity of his evil character (Lange I. c. 374)." AUBERLEN, pp. 304 sq.—E. R. C.]

* [According to Auberlen the *healing of the first Beast* and the exercise of the special power of the *second*, set forth in ver. 12, have already begun. He writes: " The return of the Beast is represented, or at least prepared in that principle, which, since A. D. 1789, has manifested itself in beast-like outbreaks, and has since then been developed both extensively and intensively. This principle has appeared in various forms, in the Revolution; in Napoleon, despotism sanctioning revolution, proving, at the same time, that the Beast, even in this shape, can carry the Harlot; in Socialism and Communism. But we may yet expect other manifestations."——' It will not be denied by any one who views the events of the two last centuries with enlightened eyes, that also the prediction of the false prophecy has begun to be fulfilled. Unconverted Paganism passed over by degrees into the Chur h dur ng the first centuries, and this mixing of Christian and Pagan elements produced Roman Catholicism. Then came the Reformation, dissolving this illegitimate union, and restoring pure Chri-tianity; and hence, it was natural, that in 'he succeeding centuries, Heathenism should likewise appear more naked, undisguised, and decided, and should attack Christianity again, but at first only with spiritual weapons. The Antichristian element, which before was under a Christian guise, now came forward with increasing openness, and manifested itself as the false prophecy, as false doctrine, the spiritual power of seducing ideas, which are based on a view of the world, radically false and opposed to God, but which spread and eat as a canker, under the name of philosophy, enlightenment, and civilization (2 Tim. ii. 17). It is a fact, that the Beast's coming to life again and its new power, whereof we spoke above, is called forth, accompanied and strengthened by the influence of the False Prophet exactly as it is described in Rev. xiii. 13 sqq. It is evident and palpable, that the philosophic principle of the autonomy of the human spirit, and the corresponding theological principle of Rationalism, that Idealism and Materialism, Deism, Pantheism, and Atheism, are all the products of the same spirit, the essence of which is apostasy from the fundamental principles of Christianity, alienation from the living and holy God, deification of the creaturely, is exactly what is meant in the Apocalyp e by

EXPLANATIONS IN DETAIL.

Ch. XII. 13. He persecuted the woman. —First he persecuted her *Child*, the holy Christ Himself; now he persecutes the *Woman*, the institution of the Kingdom of God; subsequently, when the Woman has, in respect of her outward appearance, allied herself with *the earth*, he persecutes her inner essentiality—that which is later to appear as the *Bride*—in her *remaining children*. That the *earth* must, equally with the *wilderness*, be symbolically apprehended, is required by the consistency of the description.

Ver. 14. The two wings.—The saving providence of God is represented, in *eagle-like flight*; the Church has so intimately appropriated this providence, that it may be said that the *eagle-wings* are given her, Rom. viii. 28-37. As the deliverance on eagles' wings, into the wilderness, is suggestive of *Israel's* deliverance, so, also, an entrance into the heavenly *Canaan* is in view; not, however, the Judaizing prospect of the external leadership of a Jewish Church at the end of the world.*

Where she is nourished.—The beginning of this fact had arrived even in the ancient days of John—with the flight to Pella. The typical element in the miraculous nourishment of Israel in the wilderness is here touched upon. She is nourished (and thus preserved) **from the face of the serpent** (Bengel, Ewald, *et al.*). That the *wilderness* is to be apprehended in a symbolical sense, is manifest from the fact that the Woman, whilst in it, is unattainable for Satan, although elsewhere earthly wildernesses are designated as a favorite abode of evil spirits. The Serpent, therefore, sends a *stream of water out of his mouth* after the escaped Woman.

Vers. 15, 16. Water as a river.—That is, in the form of an apparently incessant current. Düsterdieck vainly labors to fix upon the interpretation of the torrent of *water* as a torrent of *nations* an allegorical character. It is the simple historico-philological explanation of a very pronounced allegorical figure; whilst, on the other hand, the general application of the figure to *pressing dangers*, or the citation of billows of death and streams of destruction (Ps. xviii. 4), is meaningless in this connection, it being the intention of Satan not to *kill* the woman outright, but to **cause her to be carried away of the river**—possibly, only to cause her "to float with the current" (ποταμοφόρητον). The divergent specializations of the stream of nations do, indeed, rest upon ill-advised and arbitrary guesswork, practised in conformity to the theory of Church-historical predictions (persecutors; wicked men and evil demons; heretics; Saracens ;

worshipping the Beast. Indeed, even in a literal sense, in the present day, 'bestiality is the ideal of thinkers.' But even where this extreme point has not yet been reached, the False Prophet is powerful enough. What is bringing thousands from Chri-tianity, and preventing others from coming to a belief in a full and true Chri-tianity, is nothing else but respect for these intellectual powers which rule in these days, for modern Science and Culture." (These quotations have been made from the Edinburgh Trans. of the first edition of Auberlen, pp. 304, 311 sq.)—E. R. C.]

* [In accordance with his view that this vision relates to that which is still future (see ADD. NOTE, pp. 250 sq.), the Am. Ed. regards this definite symbol (the two wings of the great eagle) as having reference to an object that cannot now be identified. For his views concerning the *wilderness*, see concluding paragraph on p. 251.—E. R. C.]

Ewald: a sore peril menacing the fugitive Christians by the Jordan! See Düsterdieck). Düsterdieck's objections against the general reference of the water-stream to streaming nations (p. 418) are based upon a continuous misapprehension of allegorical modes of expression. He asks: " Can it be said that the Germanic peoples came, like a flood, out of the jaws of Satan, and were swallowed up by the earth ?" It may, assuredly, be assumed that in the first motions of the migrations of nations, especially in the rising of the Huns, demonic impulses were at play; and, similarly, it may be asserted that the Theocratic order of the Mediæval Occident overcame the hostile torrent of barbarians.

And [Lange: But] the earth.—Neither the application of this figure to the cultured Roman world (Auberlen) or to another opposing worldly power (Hengstenberg), nor the reference of it to the cleaving Mount of Olives (Zech. xiv. 4), in accordance with the opinion that the *final* Antichristian time is here exclusively spoken of (Ebrard), corresponds to the explicit character of this Old Testament type.

Ver. 17. And the dragon ~~was~~ wroth.—Since the Dragon has already been wroth against the Woman, an increase of wrath is here expressed, developed in the conflict with the Woman. Hence the reading: ἐπί in conjunction with τῇ γυναικί is significant. The preposition ἐπί with the dative may, indeed, simply denote the object of an action, but it often signifies: *concerning, on account of, about,* and this is most frequently the case with verbs that indicate an emotion of the mind (as here). Satan becomes so incensed *concerning the combat* with the Woman that he now departs, *etc.*

With the remnant.—See above. A copious treatise on this point see in Düsterdieck, who, however, by these *remaining ones* apprehends, with Züllig. the Zionites (?) on earth.*

Ver. 18. And he stood.—[See TEXT. AND GRAM., Note 7.—E. R. C.] According to De Wette and many others, the reading ἐστάθη is exegetically impossible. In reality, however, the reading of the Recepta, ἐστάθην, for which there is less authority, is far less possible. See above. Since a demonic operation upon the *sea of nations* is in question, Satan takes his station upon the *sandy* shore, a place where the earth is *flat* and the sea *shallow.* A contemporaneous appearance of the *Dragon,* on the sand, and the *Beast,* above the waves of the ocean, is not declared; the Dragon vanishes as the Beast inspired by him makes his appearance.

Ch. XIII. 1.† Ascending out of the sea.—See the *Introduction.* Out of the sea of nations: Many interpreters from Victorinus down. Out of Europe (! Bengel); out of the Italian insular kingdom (Ewald). The sea is the sea and nothing more, Düsterdieck declares, just as the earth is the literal earth—why, then, are not also the Beasts literal beasts ?

A wild-beast.—Doubtless, only the God-opposed, Antichristian world-power can primarily be intended—eschatologically concentrated and modified, however (Auberlen, Hengstenberg). One-sided, therefore, is the interpretation of the Beast as *pagan* Rome (from Victorinus to Bleek and many others) ; and equally one-sided is the application of it to papal Christian Rome (Vitringa, Bengel, *et al.*). The import of the figure, undoubtedly, does not gravitate backward to heathen Rome, but, in accordance with its eschatological tendency, forward to Christian Rome. Heathen Rome can be but visible in one of the *seven heads;* and the like is true of Christian Rome, or, rather, the ecclesiastico-political Rome of the Middle Ages. The Beast is ἀναβαῖνον through a long period. With the circumstance that the terrestrial ocean embraces the earth, the fact that the *Beast from the earth* does not appear as co-regent with the *Beast out of the sea,* but as his vassal, must not be confounded, as in Düsterdieck.—The Beast, as θηρίον, is to be distinguished from ζῶον; the word is indicative of a bestially ferocious nature, see Dan. vii. 1.

Ten horns.—See the *Introduction.*

Seven heads.—Interpreted as seven world-periods; or seven persecutions of Christians; or seven Antichristian world-powers. Hengstenberg defines these powers as follows (ii. 13): The Chaldean, Medo-Persian, Greek and Roman kingdoms. The first and second heads he looks for as existing before the Chaldean empire. Consequently, "only *Egypt* and *Assyria* can be thought of." The sixth kingdom, he affirms, is that of Rome, in accordance with ch. xvii. 10; the seventh endures, as he believes, until the cessation of the God-opposed power, and passes into the *ten horns* or God-opposed kings. We have taken the liberty of apprehending the seven heads otherwise (p. 25 sq.). In the first place, it is, in all probability, to be taken for granted that the Apocalyptist retains the four world-monarchies of Daniel. In accordance with his manner of constructing the *seven,* he then follows up the pre-Christian *quaternary* with a *ternary,* beginning with the Christian era. John would be more apt to include the Herodian kingdom in his system of heads than Egypt or Assyria. With Christianity, pronounced Antichristianity first began — began primarily, in the Herodian forms,* and continued in the new phase of the Christ-opposed Roman *empire,* as distinct from the Danielic vision of the Roman *republic.* With the application of the Beast to *pagan* Rome, a manifold explanation of the *seven heads* has been connected (the seven hills with ten kings, seven emperors with ten prefects). With the reference of the Beast to *papal* Rome, Vitringa conjoined an enumeration of seven principal forms of Roman government, from kings and consuls to the pope ; by the *ten horns* he understood ten kingdoms subservient to the papacy, from the French kingdom to the Polish (see Düsterdieck). Pursuant to the interpretation of the Beast as the pagan Roman empire, Düsterdieck, in accordance with others (see Bleek, p. 326), makes of the *ten horns with ten crowns* ten Roman emperors; 1. Augustus; 2. Tiberius; 3. Caligula; 4. Claudius; 5. Nero; 6. Galba; 7. Otho; 8. Vitellius; 9. Vespasian; 10. Titus. The *tenth,*

ª Züllig regards the eight kings as Edomitish princes.

corresponding to the *seventh head*, is, he declares, still future [to the Seer]. His exposition of the relation between the ten horns and seven heads may be found p. 432. The whole, therefore, according to his view, is a petty repetition of the history of the time, clothed, in an illusory manner, in prophetico-symbolic form. It is not to be denied that the self-deifications of Roman emperors (Düsterdieck, page 58) were types of Antichristian blasphemies.

Names of blasphemy.—It is neither assumable, with Züllig, that the individual heads bore frontlets, on each of which was inscribed one letter, the whole number making together the inscription:

קֹדֶשׁ לַיהוָה (although the antithetic reference to the frontlet of the High Priest, Holiness to Jehovah, is certainly ingenious)—nor that upon every head the same blasphemous name was written, according to Düsterdieck and others. Why should not a sevenfold form of Antichristian self-deification, corresponding to the seven world-powers, be intended? Bede refers to the name Augustus; Bengel conjectured that the name Papa was intended; Hengstenberg suggests the name of Christ, ch. xix. 16.

Ver. 2. And the wild-beast that I saw was like, *etc.*—The Beast is a compound of the four Danielic Beasts, Dan. vii. 4; amongst these, however, we regard the fourth Beast as the Roman world-kingdom, since the third Beast (ch. vii. 6) has the same number as the Greek world-kingdom (ch. viii. 8)—four wings, four heads, four horns. It is entirely incorrect, on the other hand, to identify the eschatological anti-theocratic horn (ch. vii. 8) with the precursory anti-theocratic horn (ch. viii. 8). Be it observed, however, in this connection, that the fourth Beast in Daniel, as the real eschatological Beast, embraces, together with the vision of the Roman kingdom, the entire series of world-powers, as coinciding, in perspective, with that kingdom. The ground-color of the Apocalyptic Beast is *variegated*, as was formerly the color of the Greek kingdom in its division. The fact that, with John, the four kingdoms have become one kingdom, rests upon the depth of intuition by which he has perceived the unitous demonic foundation of the world-kingdoms. The circumstance that the ten horns of the fourth Danielic Beast find their parallel in the ten horns of the Apocalyptic Beast, which embraces all the world-kingdoms, reposes upon the common symbolism of the number *ten* and the *horns*, by which a perfectly developed and organically ramified world-power is expressed. Amongst the different interpretations of the individual bestial forms, that of Cocceius is particularly interesting: *Varii coloris. Ad hanc bestiam enim pertinent Christiani servientes episcopis et aliud principium fidei constituentes, item Ariani, Musulmanni,* etc.

And the Dragon gave him, etc.—After this inauguration, the Dragon seems to retire from the scene. His representative now comes forward. The Devil has vanished from theology, philosophy, and popular consciousness, but Antichrist is present, in whom the genius of the former secretly lives on. To him is transferred, first,

the *demonic* **power,** the true method of combining falsehood, hatred, and the breath of death into a magical agency. Then he has, secondly, the *demonic* **throne,** *i. e.*, there is henceforth a centre of diabolical evil in this present world. Thirdly, great *demonic* **authority** is committed to him; he has despotic and anarchical organs enough.

Ver. 3. One from among his heads as if slain [Lange: **wounded**]. — That the Apocalyptist could ascribe the wounding to death of a head of the Antichristian power only to the operation of Christ's victory, or to Christianity in its assumption of its visible place in history (Hengstenberg), but not to the migration of nations (Calov., Auberlen, De Rougemont, *et al.*), ought to be understood without further dissertation. Nothing save the ὡς could lead us to doubt that such was the fact, and that only if the word be regarded as indicative exclusively of mere empty appearance. The expression, however, does not mean that the wound itself was mere semblance, but that the probability of its inflicting death upon the head, and so, indirectly, upon the Beast, seemed to be mere semblance. The wound was, doubtless, principally mortal (as is evident from the expression: ἡ πληγή τοῦ θανάτου αὐτοῦ, vers. 3 and 12—each time referring to the Beast itself), but, so far as outward appearance was concerned, it seemed soon after to be healed, the Antichristian power of this head reviving. Now whilst the ancient Protestant exegesis referred this power, exclusively, to Rome (see Calov., Cocceius, Nikolai, Vitringa, Bengel, in Düsterdieck, p. 438), Düsterdieck maintains the limitation of the seven heads to seven Roman kings. A *quid pro quo*, he declares, is ascribed to the Apocalyptist when it is asserted that "he represents the holy Roman Empire as the revived world-kingdom of pagan Rome;" such an assertion, he states, is incompatible either with historical truth or with a sound conception of Biblical prophecy. We certainly are not willing to conclude, with Auberlen and others, from ὡς ἐσφαγμ., that an *apparently* Christian life and essence are ascribed to the healed* head. The explanation of Hengstenberg is as follows: ὡς ἐσφ., as in the case of the Lamb, means that the slaying was accompanied by real death, but was now perceptible only by the scar, the Beast having become alive again; —this interpretation, also, may be dispatched with the remark that there is a wide difference between the risen Christ and the apparent restoration of the Antichristian Beast. We may safely leave the "*holy* Roman Empire" its measure of holiness, without, on the one side, with Rothe, regarding the Christian State as the heir of the goods of the Church, or with Hengstenberg, locating the Millennial Kingdom in the Middle Ages; but also without, on the other hand, shutting our eyes to the fact that the mediæval system of government, in its theocratic, ecclesiastico-political character, abandoned itself more and more, in the constraint which it

---

* [Lange seems here to misapprehend Auberlen. It is to the *wounded* head that *the* latter ascribes an apparent Christian life; the wounding consists in the partial destruction of the *beastly* nature. See Abstracts of Auberlen, p. 265 sq. —E. R. C.]

exercised over men in matters of faith, in the Inquisition, in Machiavelism, in papistic and despotic forms of world-empire, to ungodly, worldly, and demonic principles. In the face of this great fact, Düsterdieck arrives at the following interpretation: "The *death-wound* was given to the (fifth [?]) head by the death of Nero and the immediately following interregnum, *etc.* The *healing* of that death-wound took place when Vespasian, the founder of a new race of emperors, restored the empire, as its actual possessor, to its ancient strength and vitality." Far be it from us to deny that Düsterdieck has performed a meritorious act in refuting that miserable invention—first appearing in the obscure sphere of Victorinus—which regards the fable concerning the risen Nero as here transformed into an Apocalyptic prophecy (see Düsterd., p. 439 sqq.); he has, however, not accomplished the refutation without inconsistency, for if the Apocalyptic *king* be only a literal king, the *wound* can not be situate in Nero, and the *healing*, on the other hand, in Vespasian. Comp. the Introduction to this Commentary, pp. 26 and 60. Explanations by Grotius and Züllig, see in Düsterdieck, p. 439, as also a special reference to the Popes, by Vitringa, in the note on p. 438. Sander thinks the wounded Beast is Gregory VII. Gräber, more appropriately, regards the wounding as the Reformation; in a certain degree, the Reformation does pertain to the death-stroke which the Beast received at the entrance of Christianity into the world.

And the whole earth wondered.*—This applies to the increasingly general despair as to the truth of the victory of Christ and the Christian principle—a despair which is confronted by a sovereignty and an external glory of the world-power which continually become more imposing. To this wonderment and admiration all converts of despotism and particularly of the hierarchy, who have turned their backs on Christianity, specially testify.

Ver. 4. **And they worshipped the dragon.**—The history of gross and subtile devil-service here arrives at its meridian. Most certainly the exclamation: **Who is like unto the wild-beast, and who is able to war with him?** does bear the appearance of a liturgy of this new demonic *cultus*, of "a blasphemous parody of the praise with which the Old Testament congregation celebrated the incomparable gloriousness of the living God (comp. Is. xl. 25; xliv. 7, *etc.*"). Duesterdieck. The commentator from whom we have quoted seems, however, to apprehend everything that is said in regard to a worship of the Devil, rather literally; hence he cannot approve of the utterances of Cocceius, according to whom such worship may be offered by the adherents of the papacy. But what is it to offer the most decided personal conviction to a worldly apparent power, let that power be of a hierarchical or a political nature? In every village where demonic villainy has become such a power that no one dares any more stand up for right and truth against it, there a subtile devil-service reigns, even though the

people who indulge in it may still frequent the house of God.

[The verb προσκυνέω is the one elsewhere employed to denote the outward worship that should be offered only to God. See ch. iv. 10; v. 14; vii. 11; xiv. 7; xv. 4; xix. 4, 10; xxii. 8, 9 (ch. iii. 9 may seem to be an exception to the general rule; but even there the reference is to a *grovelling in the dust* as before a superior being). The reference here, and in vers. 8, 12, 15; xiv. 9, 11; xvi. 2; xix. 20; xx. 4, probably is to the payment of Divine honors. These prophecies have almost certainly been fulfilled, either typically or consummately, in the *worship* offered to the Pope.—E. R. C.]

Ver. 5. **And there was given unto him.** —An actual *giving*, in the ordinary sense of the term, is not intended, but a perfect *abandonment*, as a positive Divine destination to judgment. The στόμα of the Beast, employed by him for blasphemy, is even itself to be regarded as a product of world-historical culture. The specifically *great* mouth may, in a formal aspect, be conceived of as an excessively cultivated mouth, practised in the rhetoric of deceit. Its manifestation in **speaking great things**, words of outrageous arrogance, of self-glorification (2 Thess. ii.), is in close correspondence with its **blasphemies**. In all great world-kingdoms, political and hierarchical, this polarity of godlessness appears. The great words of the King of Babylon (see Is. xiv.) were followed by the great words of the successors of Cyrus; these, by the self-deification of Alexander and the anti-theocratic machinations of Antiochus Epiphanes. To the last, finally, succeeded the vain-glorious vaunts and apotheoses of pagan (see Düsterdieck, p. 58) and mediæval Rome, the echoes of whose last word are even yet resounding in all the churches and on all the thrones of Europe. The typical expression of this art of blasphemies is found in Dan. vii. 20 and 25. The time which is there granted to the last king for his blasphemy is defined in the form: a time, two times, a half time. Here, the authority of the Beast continues for **forty-two months**. These periods are not to be chronologically calculated; still less are they to be conformed to each other; the distinction lies in the choice of form. The *forty-two months* constitute a changeful time of tribulation, in which the number of rest and joy is continually crossed by the number of toil and distress (7×6).

Ver. 6. **Unto blasphemies against God.** —The blasphemies noticed in ver. 5 are here more particularly explained, and that with exceeding pertinence.

To blaspheme (first) **His name.**—In the more general sense, religion itself; in the more special sense, His revelation, especially His complete revelation in Christianity. The Beast retains a remnant of religious idea sufficient to make a god of himself (Antichristianity=pseudo-Christianity).

(Secondly) **His tabernacle.**—That is, the Church of God, the true, living Church, mentioned in Amos, ch. ix. 11, 12, as the house of God of the λοιποί out of all nations, in antithesis to the splendid edifice of the Temple. According to Düsterdieck, Heaven is meant. But how

---

* [The German word (*bewundern*) includes the idea of admiration.—Tr.]

should Heaven, as distinct from God and from those who dwell in Heaven, be an object of irreligious hate? Possibly it might be thus conceived of by those systems which regard the Earth alone as a place of spiritual life, and to which the idea of the stars as symbols of a local existence beyond this life is repugnant.

The third blasphemy is, however, itself the blasphemy against the life beyond. With **those who tabernacle in the heaven**, not only is God's work of grace in Christians who are yet in this world blasphemed, as a recognized reality, but the inhabitants of the world beyond are themselves, likewise, blasphemed as vain shadows, or as men who, for a phantom hope, have sacrificed their pretensions to this present life.

As, to the *Name* of God, the Beast opposes his own self deification, so, to the *Tabernacle* of God, he opposes God's desecrated Temple (2 Thess. ii. 4), and so, finally, to the vital *Heaven* of the blessed Church of Christ and to the hope of that Heaven, he opposes the present world, made empty and of no account by atheism and communism.

Ver. 7. **To make war with the saints, and to conquer them.**—Observe the grand integrity and boldness of the vision. The victory will, indeed, be only an apparent victory, for before God it is the saints who shall remain victors (ch. xii. 11); it is not necessary to conclude from this, however, that the Beast will *conquer* them merely by violence, by imprisonment, exile, death, and all sorts of θλῖψις (Düst.; similarly De Wette and others). We question whether those are the methods of triumph of Antichristianity in the last days. At all events, *killing* is not spoken of previous to ver. 15. In the war of words, also, and the conflict of opinions, the Beast is able to conquer the saints, before an auditory fully given over to the spirit of the times. Even the religious disputations of the time of the Reformation may give us a preliminary idea of the magic of the loudest voices, of bold assurances, of disputatious arts, in presence of a sympathizing audience. Not merely the awkward utterances of an uncalled pious zeal, but also ripe testimonies to the truth, may, in great modern world-circles, be seemingly demolished by so-called witty jests. But when, in the future, public opinion, the press, the forms of mental intercourse in general, shall lapse more and more into what may be the ungodly tendency of the day, the tongues of truth and of love, of men and angels, may, in the end, be drowned by an impious majority of voices. The elect, of course, who are of the truth, will, doubtless, always recognize the voice of truth.

Authority was given him over every tribe, *etc.*—In connection with morbid universalism, a morbid particularism, on the other hand, is developed; the principle of nationality, which, in its ancient morbid form, preferred the isolation of the heathen nations to the principle of humanity, appears again in a modern morbid form; in this latter form, by the excessive stress which it lays upon *tribes*, it disintegrates the nation and the state; by an exclusive stress upon the *people* (for instance, the Italian or the Russian), it disintegrates the Church;

and it results in making of the conflict of *languages* (whose common notions are increasingly denied) an eschatological Babel, and, by the fanatical battle of *races* [*nations*], puts an end to the conflict between the Kingdom of God and the kingdom of darkness. The relative authorization of the principle of nationality in the Kingdom of God has been earlier expressed in the Apocalypse (ch. v. 9; also, it is probable, ch. 9). The fixedness of the four forms (φυλή, *etc.*; also ch. xiv. 6) manifests, at the same time, their authorization. Hence we have particularly to consider the distinction of λαός (עַם) cultured people, primarily Israel) and ἔθνος (גּוֹי a nationality, nation or race). At the last, this classification is perturbed, as it appears, by the agency of Antichristianity (ch. xvii. 5).

Ver. 8. **And all that dwell upon the earth.**—The *dwelling on earth* is the common characteristic of the different modern heathendoms: all who have made themselves at home in *this* world simply and exclusively. [The expression: "they that dwell upon the Earth" (οἱ κατοικοῦντες ἐπὶ τῆς γῆς) here, and elsewhere (ch. iii. 10; vi. 10; viii. 13; xi. 10 *bis*; xii. 12; xiii. 8, 12, 14 *bis*; xiv. 6; xvii. 2, 8) might be translated *worldlings*. It designates such as are in antithesis to those whose *conversation is in Heaven*, who live as *pilgrims and sojourners* here. —E. R. C.]

Shall worship him (προσκυνήσουσιν).—Αὐτόν is rightly referred by Düsterdieck,—against Hengstenberg, who understands by it the king, ch. xvii. 11—to the chief subject ὁ δράκων, with the remark that the future form corresponds with such a reference ["(comp., on the other hand, ver. 4): as the activity of the Beast, in respect of its decisive part, is still in the future (comp. ver. 7, where it is first Divinely given to the Beast what it shall do), so also is the worship of the Dragon thereby induced still future." DUESTERDIECK.—TR.]. There continually develops more and more fully, along with the enthusiastic veneration of the Antichristian power, a conscious bowing of the knee before the *Satanic* principles which lie at the foundation of that power (slander, murder, absolute egoism) and before the *Dragon* himself.

Every one whose name, *etc.*—Thus a contrast is found—not merely in a general way, but betwixt man and man—between the worshippers of the Dragon and those whose names are written in the book of life. This *writing* here denotes that security of the people of God which is expressed in ch. vii. by the *sealing*. And now the following question arises—Shall we read: **Written in the book of life of the Lamb that hath been slain from the foundation of the world** (Vulg., Bede, *etc.*), as the immediate reference of the closing words [ἀπὸ καταβολῆς κόσμου] seems to demand, or: **written from the foundation of the world in the book of life of the Lamb that hath been slain** (Grotius, Bengel, Hengstenberg, Düsterdieck, *et al.*), as seems to be decidedly indicated by the passage, ch. xvii. 8? It cannot, however, be denied that 1 Pet. i. 19, 20, supports the former and more ancient apprehension, as does also the Johannean utterance in the Gospel of John, ch. xvii. 24. Both apprehensions of the passage contemplate the first, and hence the last, cause of the security of God's people in that election which took place before the foundation of the world, and which has therefore prevailed since the foundation of the world. But as the pre-appointment of the glory of Christ was at the same time a pre-appointment of His death, and was conditioned, in its manifestation, by the foreview of His holy conduct, so the election of believers, *in its manifestation*, is conditioned by their faithfulness, in accordance with ch. xx. 12 (κατὰ τὰ ἔργα αὐτῶν). We, therefore, have to do with a mysterious synthesis of eternal personal foundation and disposition and a morally free verification [of said foundation and disposition]—neither with the one alone, in a predestinarian sense, nor with the other exclusively, in an Arminian sense. There is a decided lack of clearness in the following deliverance of Hengstenberg: "When temptation has attained its highest degree, nothing holds out against it save the eternal election *based upon the atonement in Christ*." Since both explanations are, materially, equally warranted, the more obvious course is to prefer the older exposition. And what shall we gain by so doing? Those who are written in the book of the Lamb that was slain from the foundation of the world, are such as form a contrast, in respect of their disposition and conduct, to those who *dread and shun suffering ;* for by a dread of suffering, the greatest genius that mankind has ever seen may lapse into subtile cowardice, and thus fall under the dominion of the world and Antichristianity. Comp. Rom. vi. 3. The central point of those who are *ready for suffering*— the martyrs, who, precisely as such, are invincible—is formed by the *Lamb*, Who was mystically *slain from the foundation of the world,* and Who, from the very fact of His being thus slain, is the Prince of life, with Whose victory the ideal, eternal *book of life* is actualized.

["These last words (ἀπὸ καταβολῆς κόσμου) are ambiguously placed. They may belong either to γέγραπται, or to ἐσφαγμένον. The former connection is taken by Hammond, Bengel, Heinr., Ewald, Züllig, De Wette, Hengst., Düsterd. But the other is far more obvious and natural : and had it not been for the apparent difficulty of the sense thus conveyed, the going back so far as to γέγραπται for a connection would never have been thought of. . . . The difficulty, however, is but apparent : 1 Pet. i. 19, 20, says more fully the same thing. That death of Christ which was foreordained from the foundation of the world, is said to have *taken* place in the counsels of Him with Whom the end and the beginning are one." ALFORD.—The *foreordination* of an event is one thing, its *occurrence* is another. In like manner as the above, it might be said that, as the destruction of the world was foreordained from the foundation of the world, the world has been destroyed from its foundation. In the judgment of the Am. Ed., the *manifest* difficulty of the sense conveyed by the connection advocated by our author and Alford, together with ch. xvii. 8, not only jus'ify, but require, the connection with γέγραπται.—E. R. C.]

Vers. 9, 10. **If any one is for captivity** [LANGE: **If any one driveth a captivity**], *etc.*—Whosoever *hears* this declaration with the

right hearing of faith, is perfectly comforted as well as perfectly warned. In God's world, a perfect system of retribution obtains. Just as elsewhere the depth of the suffering and the wrong-suffering of Christ is made the measure of His exaltation, so here the greatness and the manner of wrong-doing—especially in the Antichristian persecution of believers—are constituted the measure of future retributional suffering. In the form of the legal *jus talionis*, this is a thoroughly matter-of-fact and indefeasible vital law. So much so, that the Apostle speaks elliptically, as if he were quoting a perfectly familiar paragraph from the Law: εἴ τις εἰς αἰχμαλωσίαν, *etc.* DUESTERDIECK: "Volkmar regards the threat of the sword as directed against Nero." *Of course,* where the Apocalyptic Seer declares a profound and general vital law, there—according to Volkmar—an uncanonical, Christian poet of the people slyly doubles up his fist against Nero.* This reminds us of the kicking cavalry horses, ch. ix. 19.

[The declaration seems to be the announcement of a general law in reference both to Saints and the ungodly. In reference to the Saints, it is a declaration that if they resist persecution with carnal weapons, they shall perish by the sword. And has not this been exemplified in the history of the Albigenses and Waldenses, and others who have taken up the sword in their own defence? In reference to the persecuting world-power, it is a declaration that though for a season it may prosper, in the end it shall be destroyed with violence. The reception of this truth, which is but one phase of the more general truth, "Vengeance is Mine, I will repay, saith the Lord," Rom. xii. 19, manifests the *faith* and gives strength for the *endurance* of the Saints.— E. R. C.]

Here is the endurance [LANGE: **patience**] *etc.*—Does this mean : here must the patience and faith of the saints show themselves (DE WETTE), or: "here is patience existent; here are the foundation and the source of it" (DUESTERDIECK)? The meaning may also be, however: here is the objective mark of the saints, the vital law which has become embodied in them. The suffering of wrong without doing wrong, in the assurance that the wrong-doing rebounds upon its author, in accordance with the law of retribution—this universal ordinance established by God in this world, appears principally in the cross of Christ and is continually further manifested in the *endurance* and *faith* of the saints. Thus, eschatological *wisdom* appears in the right understanding of the number of the Beast, ver. 17, and thus the wise man's understanding of eschatological symbolism, in particular, is evident in the right understanding of the *seven heads* of the Beast, ch. xvii. 9.—Here is the *source* or *fountain :*—this would be saying too much, inasmuch as Christ is the fountain, Who, verily, has drawn His constancy from the depths of that Divine law. On the o'her hand, the challenge : here let the patience and faith of the saints give evidence of themselves, would be saying too little. Here, therefore, appears *the idea* which is realized in the life of the saints.

* [*Da macht' nach Volkmar ein unkanonischer christlicher Volksdichter gegen den Nero eine Faust in der Tasche.*]

Ver. 11. **Another wild-beast.***—The *False Prophet*, according to chs. xvi. 13; xix. 20: xx. 10; Iren. v. 28, (2). According to Düsterdieck and many who preceded him (Victorinus, Grotius, De Wette, Hengstenberg), the pagan Roman prophethood is here intended—that paltry system of augurs. "The many references to papal Rome (Cocceius, Calov., Vitringa, *et al.*)" are, according to Düsterdieck, precluded [by the application of vers. 1-8 to the Roman empire.—Tr]. The Augurs, then, had hypocritically imitated the lamb-like character of Christ! [Düsterdieck denies that there is any special reference to Christ as the Lamb, whilst he admits that there may be an allusion to the idiocrasy of pseudo-prophethood as set forth in Matt. vii. 15.—Tr.] **Out of the earth.**—Of this, various interpretations have been given, all of which regardlessly pass by the Old Testament symbolism; the Asiatic continent (Bengel and Ewald); earthliness or worldliness (Hengstenberg); as near as may be, meaningless (Düsterdieck); ἐκ τῆς γῆς signifies: out of that which "has already become firm soil" (Ebrard after Vitringa and Hofmann).

Two horns like a lamb.—We do not translate, like *the* lamb, since the Lamb, in the eminent sense of the term (ch. v. 6), has seven horns; the present description, however, like that unique Lamb, goes back to the phenomenon of the *lamb generically considered;* the Beast counterfeits the nature of the lamb. The *two horns,* therefore, are not to be placed in the category of a defect, in accordance with Ebrard: "the Beast (ver. 11) has but two horns, and is thus distinguished, as a natural beast, confined within creaturely limits and boundaries, from that other Lamb." According to this, he is innocent enough. But since he *speaks* as the *Dragon,* he is scarcely all right, notwithstanding his two horns. Hengstenberg's conjectures respecting the two horns, see in Ebrard. The former commentator looks upon them as denoting the hidden might of the wisdom of this world! The lamb has his two horns simply for self-defence, and yet he speaks as the Dragon, as though he had ten horns. Are there not such lambs? See Matt. vii. 15. According to Düsterdieck, the speaking like the Dragon is indicative of the crafty speech of the deceiver and seducer, Gen. iii. ; but the Dragon's speech is not merely crafty, like that of the serpent, as is evident from the whole of the present chapter.

Special interpretations: Vitringa: The two horns are the two mendicant orders of friars. Hammond: Double priestly power of miracles and prophecy. Ver. 12. **And he exerciseth.**—Ποιεῖ. In magical *poesy* he imitates all the power of the first Beast *in presence of that Beast,* thus preparing the earth and the dwellers thereon to *worship* the first Beast, whose wound was healed. The ἐνώπιον αὐτοῦ cannot mean that he has from the outset voluntarily regarded himself as the vassal of the first Beast; his subserviency to him was not originally contemplated and does but gradually result from the operations of the second Beast. His mode of action being terrestrial, must eventually devolve upon the first Beast, and finally,

the second form, as a matured *Beast from the earth,* becomes the conscious False Prophet of the Sea-Beast.

Ver. 13. **Great signs.**—Not real miracles, but ostensible, illusive wonders. The tendency is that he would even [seem to] **make fire come down from the Heaven in the presence of men.** That is, the acknowledgment of spectators. Without doubt, this is an imitation of Elijah, in the sphere of the superstitious view of men. Agreeably to the conception of superstition, the fire of the Inquisition stakes fell from Heaven. A controversy between Hengstenberg and Düsterdieck on the subject of ἵνα, see in the Commentary of the latter, p. 452. Misunderstanding of the passage. It might, indeed, be said that an a true Elijah goes before the true Christ, so a pseudo-Elijah goes before the pseudo-Christ.— False applications to the Pentecostal feast and to Solomon, see noted in Düsterdieck.

[The term σημεῖα (see also Matt. xxiv. 24; 2 Thess. ii. 9) is the same that is generally employed to designate the miracles of Christ. In both the additional passages referred to, τέρατα occurs, and in the second δυνάμεις. And not only so, but the connection of ποιεῖν with σημεῖα is the form of expression commonly used by John to designate the working of miracles (see John ii. 11, 23; iii. 2; iv. 54; vi. 2, *etc.*). In view of these facts, together with a consideration of Deut. xiii. 1, 2, (where *genuine* σημεῖα and τέρατα seem to be referred to) and the solemn warning of our Lord, Matt. xxiv. 24, 25, it seems, to the Am. Ed., scarce possible to avoid the conclusion that the miracles foretold are genuine. The implication of Deut. xiii. 1-5, seems to the writer to be that miracles *alone* are not evidence of Divine commission, that God may permit their being wrought for the purpose of *testing* His professed followers; and that the claims of one who offers miracles as a proof that he speaks by Divine inspiration, are to be further tested by the accordance of his teachings with extant Revelations. The last clause of 2 Thess. ii. 9 cannot be alleged as an objection to this view, since the τέρασι ψεύδους (*wonders of falsehood*) may well be interpreted as τέρατα in confirmation of the ψεύδος mentioned in ver. 11.—E. R. C.]

And he seduceth (or misleadeth).—Düsterdieck: "The wonders are an actual means, (Matt. xxiv. 24);"—as powerful lies, or lying powers, we would add.—Telling them that dwell on the earth to make an image to the wild beast.—Duesterd.: "The images of the deified emperors. The statues of Augustus and Caligula erected to them in the character of gods." The Seer is not speaking of an image of the first Beast in the abstract, but of the image of that Beast in his quality of having the wound by the sword and reviving. This can be only an idealized, theoretical and poetical likeness of the regenerate heathen world power—a likeness which has diffused itself in the pagan deification of power, in hero-worship, image-worship and external *cultus* and popular superstition—a unique image of the pre-Christian world-power in many images. The image of the Beast is, therefore, the re-appearance of heathenism, or the heathen world-power, in the Christian world; and it is the False Prophet who

---

* [See the Add. Note, p. 272 sq.—E. R. C.]

causes the erection of this Image. Ay, he even knows how to communicate a sort of apparent life to the image of the first Beast.

Ver. 15. **And it was given to him to give a spirit,** etc.—A kind of *spirit* suitable to the kind of *image;* an appearance of unitous spirit-life, for modern heathenism as the image of ancient heathenism. It is impossible by this to understand the cultivation of humanism—practised by later Byzantinism and the Romanism of the Fifteenth century,—as the acme of the civilization of ancient heathenism. The image of the heathen world-power is spoken of—the reflection of that world-power, in copy, within Christendom. The fundamental features of this image are: abstract authority, corresponding with abstract superstitious democratism—the design being abstract uniformity. At first, the second Beast claimed all this for himself, but, in accordance with the nature of the case, he was all the time playing into the hands of the first Beast, and has now, in the last eschatological time, entirely gone over to the service of the latter. The medium by which life is counterfeited in the image is the power to *speak.* "Ver. 15 must not be apprehended as significant of a 'spiritual speaking' of pagan images of gods (in opposition to Hengstenberg, who remarks that the heathen, in his image of a god, objectified his own intuitions [*Anschauungen*], and that with a liveliness which attested itself in the allegations of actual speech on the part of those images]; this trait of the description rather contains a suggestion of what is reported concerning divine images which are said really to *speak* (comp. Grotius, Ewald II.; the latter also refers to the deception of the people by means of talking images of the Virgin); and John seems to take for granted the reality of such demonic wonders" (DUESTERDIECK). Disregard of the symbolicalness of the expression leads to such an assumption as the above, which virtually charges John with superstition. The image of the Beast can really *speak.* But as the image itself is a fundamentally false, new-heathenish, romantic system, so its *speaking* is the art of the fundamentally false and dazzling phraseology which is in the service of that system.

And cause that as many as should not worship the image of the wild-beast should be slain.—We understand this *slaying* in an eschatological sense, and regard it as signifying social annihilation—privation of oral, legal, social [in the more restricted sense of the term] life [=influence, efficiency]. The analogies discoverable in the heathen mode of procedure against Christianity (DUESTERD., p. 453—letter of Pliny to Trajan: worship of the imperial image), consisting in the infliction of capital punishment, may have served as the starting-point of the text. The first great type of the uniformity-image was the tower of Babel. The first image which men were commanded, on pain of death, to worship, was the symbol of the first heathen world-power—the golden image of King Nebuchadnezzar, at Babylon (Dan. iii.).

Vers. 16, 17. **And he maketh all.**—The False Prophet operates upon all. This fact of his universal operation is emphatically set forth by a threefold antithesis: **the small and the great,** etc. The end for this universal company upon which the False Prophet has been working, is the Antichristian symbolism; they assume the mark of appertinency to the Beast (ch. xiv. 9, 11; xvi. 2; xix. 20; xx. 4). The terrible earnestness and decisiveness of this self-assignment of men to the Beast, and the distinctness with which the Seer foresees this formation of a perverted congregation of Antichristian confessors, are evident from his frequent recurrence to this fatal *symbolum.* We cannot perceive why Düsterdieck should regard the view of Grotius and others, who maintain that this idea is reminiscent of the heathen custom of stigmatizing slaves and soldiers, and thus signalizing their appertinency to their masters, as at variance with Hengstenberg's view, that the χάραγμα will be a species of confession. The exclusive operation of the token is expressly brought out. Here, also, it is perfectly obvious that the Seer did not intend that his words should be taken literally. For it is impossible to overlook the fact that both the *forehead* and the *hand* have a symbolical significance in the Scriptures. The frontlet of the high priest, with its inscription; the expression: forehead against forehead, Ezek. iii. 8, 9; and similar passages afford sufficient evidence that the mark on the forehead imports a confession; whilst the mark on the hand is no less expressive of a practical tendency. See SYNOP. VIEW. Consummate effrontery and consummate mutinousness—by these attributes, the members of this Church of the Beast shall recognize each other, and accordingly consign to social death those who are unmarked, not simply excommunicating them, but also civilly outlawing them. A fanatical Protestant interpretation of the χάραγμα by Coce., see in Düsterd., p. 454.

Ver. 18. **Here is wisdom.**—The wisdom of God, like the wisdom of men, relates to the ends and aims of life. Hence Christianity, towards the end of the world, is more and more a vocation to wisdom, to the trying of spirits, especially to the recognition of the signs of the Antichristian spirit. Herein wisdom must show itself (see SYNOP. VIEW). Wisdom, however, is to be learned in learning to calculate the number of the Beast. That this can be no problematical, chiliastic reckoning, in the true sense of that term, we may rest assured, by reason of the origin of the recommendation ["Let him that hath understanding," etc.] with the Spirit of prophecy.

Various explanations of the number 666:

1. According to Hofmann (*Schriftbeweis*, ii. 2, p. 702), John himself was ignorant of the reference of the number to a determinate personality, having merely seen and written the number (similarly Luthardt, *Die Offenb. Joh.*, p. 53). In reality, however, Hofmann pledges himself to the following solution: It will be the Greek enemy of the Old Testament Church of God, who will return to this earthly life in order to the destruction of the New Testament Church.

2. The difficult solution of the puzzle will be found in the future (Iren., Andr., *et al.*).—With Nos. 1 and 2, No. 3 is connected, which is as follows:

3 The number denotes a distinct human individual (Bede, Grotius, et al.).

4. The expression, ἀριθμὸς γὰρ ἀνθρώπου, denotes that the interpretation of the letters is to be determined in accordance with their conventional numeric value (which must be translated back into letters); the number must be referred, agreeably to ordinary human custom, to a name (Wetstein, De Wette, Hengstenberg, Düsterdieck, et al.). "That this is no easy operation is manifest from the history of the interpretation of this passage, which exhibits (comp. Wolf, Curæ; Heinrichs, Excurs. vi.; Züllig, Excurs. ii.) hundreds of attempts at a solution of the problem, etc." (Düsterdieck).

5. Interpretations looking off from the personal reference; amongst these, that of Bengel —666 years—is specially worthy of notice (Düsterdieck, p. 457).

Vitringa and Hengstenberg refer the number to the Hebrew name Adonikam (the Lord ariseth), because the Adonikam mentioned in Ezra ii. 13 had 666 sons. Hengstenb. gives a better alternate interpretation, in accordance with which the number 666, as a world-number, falls short of the Divine number Seven. In this sense, Luthardt contrasts the number 666 with 888, the number appearing in the Sibylline books as the number of the name of Jesus. By the employment of the Greek, the Hebrew and the Latin alphabet, the most diverse names have been arrived at (Nero, Diocletian, Luther, Calvin, names of Popes, the Jesuits, Napoleon, Balaam, Cæsar, Rome, etc., see Düsterdieck, p. 459. A quantity of chiliastic computations of time and other definitions, see noted in Ebrard, pp. 391, 392; De Wette, p. 139 sqq.). Calov., Eichhorn, De Wette, Ebrard, Düsterd., and others, have, after Irenæus, declared themselves in favor of the name λατεῖνος. And thus, according to them, the great mystery amounts, after all, only to such a generality as the Roman world-kingdom.*

[ADDITIONAL NOTE ON THE SECTION.]
By the American Editor.

[For reasons given in the preceding Add. Note (pp. 250 sq.), the writer regards the entire scene described in ch. xii., as having its consummate fulfillment in events under the seventh Trumpet—the blowing of which is yet future. In continuance, he would remark that to him it seems scarcely possible that (according to Lord) the flight of the Woman mentioned in ver. 6, should be different from that of ver. 14. He supposes that after the mention of the flight in ver. 6, an account of the Dragon is given, which in ver. 14 reaches the same incident. In vers. 15, 16 are foretold Satan's attempt, immediately following the flight, to destroy, and its frustration; ver. 17 declares his subsequent purposes of destruction; and in ch. xiii. are described the instrumentalities by which he endeavors to accomplish these purposes.

The position here taken, that the visions of this section have immediate respect to events still future, in which they are to be consummately

fulfilled, is not inconsistent with the further idea that they may have already had a typical fulfillment. The course of history is often a foreshadowing, through long ages, of that in which it is to be consummated; and, in such case, a prophecy which has immediate respect to that consummation, will have a secondary (though previously fulfilled) relation to the foreshadowing events. Many of those prophecies which had an immediate respect to the Messiah, found a typical fulfillment in Israel. The many coincidences brought to view by Elliott and others, forbid the thought that in this section there is no reference to the Church of Rome; but, on the other hand, the circumstances of the vision, together with the manifest fact that the fulfillment claimed in the past is to so great an extent shadowy and incomplete, compel the conclusion that the consummate fulfillment is yet future.

The Beasts and the Image (ch. xiii.).

The writer adopts the opinion that the first Beast symbolizes the world-power, or rather that portion of the world-power within whose domain the Church has had existence, and is substantially (i. e., ■■■ to the object symbolized) identical with the statue of Dan. ii., the Beasts of Dan. vii., and the scarlet colored Beast of ch. xvii.; the heads representing the seven universal* Sovereignties that have exercised temporal authority over the Church, viz.: (1) the Egyptian, (2) the Palestinian, or the Assyrian, (3) the Babylonian, (4) the Medo-Persian, (5) the Grecian (the five fallen heads, ch. xvii. 10), (6) the Roman (the one existing at the date of the Apocalypse), and (7) one that is yet to arise.†

By the wounding the writer understands, not only with Auberlen the nominal conversion of one of the heads, but also its ceasing to be as a universal Sovereignty; and by this wounded head he understands, not the seventh, as does Auberlen, but the sixth or Roman. They are notorious facts of history, (1) that the Roman head was conquered (at least nominally) in the person of Constantine, and (2) that shortly after the period of Constantine the one Roman sovereignty ceased to exist. The imperial power was divided amongst the sons of Constantine, and though again united, it was again divided, and finally in the death of Theodosius it ceased to exist as a unit—and from that day to the present there has been no universal go-

---

* [Universal, i. e., in reference to what may be styled the area of the Church. No human government, since that of Noah, has been universal, in the more extensive sense of that term.—E. R. C.]

† [Daniel presents only the Sovereignties that were to bear rule in and after his day—his fifth power being presented in the feet of the Statue (ch. ii. 33, 41-43), and in the ten horns and little horn of the fourth Beast (ch. v i. 7, 8, 20, 24, 25). The view of John sweeps over the entire period of the Church's history, and embraces the two persecuting powers that had preceded Daniel. Glasgow, in his identification of the heads (see foot-note, p. 242), mentions the Palestinian as the second, and the Assyrian as the third. This cannot be correct, as it would imply that six heads had fallen at the date of the Apocalypse, which is directly counter to ch. xvii. 10. Auberlen omits the Palestinian, and reckons the Assyrian as the second, on the authority of Jer. l. 17 sq. Is it not more probable that the Seer contemplated the Assyrian and Babylonian as one head—the third, and the Palestinian as the second? Most certainly this power, ■■ represented by the Philistines (or the Arabian horde), may well be regarded as one of the persecuting heads.—E. R. C.]

vernment within the area of Christendom. The Empire established in Charlemagne cannot be regarded either as the continuance of the sixth head, or as the seventh, since it never extended over the field of the Eastern Churches, and indeed not entirely over that of the Western. If the seventh head is in its universality analogous to that of the six that preceded it, we must look for it in the future.

It is with extreme hesitation that the Am. Ed. ventures to write any thing concerning prophecy ▨ yet unfulfilled. He dares not dogmatize, and he scarcely ventures to suggest what he regards as the possible outline of the future as portrayed in Apocalyptic symbols.

Did ch. xiii. stand alone, the probable interpretation would be that the Beast is to arise from the sea of the nations with the seventh head not only fully developed, but analogous in form to those that preceded it, i. e., under one fully established and visible imperial government, the ten horns indicating ten subordinate kingdoms. A comparison, however, of this chapter with Dan. vii. and ch. xvii. suggests a different hypothesis. May it not be that in the first arising of the Beast the head is to be found in a confederation of the ten horns or kings (themselves wearing the diadems), which confederation is to be subsequently developed into an empire? May it not be that the Image, vers. 14, 15, is the Little Horn of Dan. vii. 8, 24, 25, before whom three of the original horns are to be plucked up, and who is to attain to supremacy over the others—the eighth head of ch. xvii. 11, who is of the seven—in whom the Beast is to be finally and completely "headed up," and who is the personal Antichrist, the Man of Sin and Son of Perdition. On this hypothesis the second Beast (vers. 11–14), the False Prophet (ch. xix.

20) may represent a class of teachers (perchance an apostate ministry of Christ [comp. Matt. vii 15], possibly to be consummated in an individual) under whose influence he shall arise, and be anointed and supported, who shall develop into the seventh complete head.

Of the prophecy as interpreted above, we have had a typical fulfillment in the history of the Western Empire. Although wounded unto death, the beastly nature of the world-power has continued throughout the ages. In the West we find the temporal power continued in ten kingdoms, which, under the instigation of the great adversary, might be regarded as confederate in the oppression of the true body of Christ. Under the influence of the Romish priesthood, the Pope—an image of the old Roman emperors—arose; before him three of the original horns were plucked up, and in process of time he attained to a real supremacy over the whole of Western Christendom (see Abstract of Elliott, p. 259). This Image of the old Roman Empire is now, it is true, shorn of his temporal. and in great measure of his spiritual, supremacy; but, in conclusion, it may be asked if it be not possible that he, under the influence and support of an apostate ministry, may yet develop into the seventh and consummate head of the Beast (the eighth head of ch. xvii. 11).

As to the number of the Beast, the writer agrees with Alford (see p. 262). As to the 1260 days, it may be remarked that in the typical fulfillment of the prophecy it may indicate a period of years—in the consummate fulfillment a period of days, or weeks, or months, or years. Properly the symbol indicates 1260 periods of time; what those minor periods are, can be determined only by the event, or at least in the period of fulfillment.—E. R. C.]

SECTION SIXTH.

(First Division.)

The End-judgment in general.   The Judgment of Anger.   The Seven Vials of Anger.

CHAP. XIV. 1—XVI. 21.

A.—THE IDEAL HEAVENLY WORLD-PICTURE OF THE LAST JUDGMENT; THE ANGER-VIALS IN GENERAL.

CH. XIV. 1—XV. 8.

1. *The solemn Festival of the Elect.   The Church Triumphant high above the Anger-Judgments of Earth.*

1   And I looked [saw], and, lo [behold], a [the][1] Lamb stood [standing][2] on the
       mount Sion, and with him a hundred forty and four thousand, having [ins. his
2   name and][3] his Father's name written in their foreheads. And I heard a voice
       from [ins. the] heaven, as the [a] voice of many waters, and as the [a] voice of a

TEXTUAL AND GRAMMATICAL.

1 Ver. 1. [Crit. Eds. give τό, with ℵ. A. B*. C.; it is omitted by P. 1, 28, etc.—E. R. C.]
2 Ver. 1. Instead of the Rec. ἑστηκός, ℵ. A. C. [P. 79] give ἑστός. [B*. gives ἑστώς.—E. R. C.]
3 Ver. 1. His against the Rec. [Lange reads αὑτοῦ twice, but ὄνομα only once. Alf., Treg., Tisch., read τὸ ὄνομα αὑτοῦ καὶ τὸ ὄνομα τοῦ πατρὸς αὑτοῦ with ℵ. A. B*. C.; 7, 16, 98, with Lange, omit the second τὸ ὄνομα; P. and 1 read ▨ Rec.—E. R. C.]

18

[*om.* a] great thunder : and [*ins.* the voice which][4] I heard the voice [*om.* the voice

3 —*ins.* was as][4] of harpers harping with their harps : And they sung [sing] as it were [*om.* as it were][5] a new song before the throne, and before the four beasts [living-beings], and the elders : and no man [one] could [was able to] learn that [the] song but [except] the hundred *and* forty *and* [*om. and*] four thousand, which

4 [that] were redeemed [bought] from the earth. These are they which [who] were not defiled with women ; for they are virgins. These are [*are*] they which [who] follow the Lamb whithersoever he goeth [may go].[6] These were redeemed [bought] from among men, *being* the [*om. being* the—*ins.* a] first-fruits [first-fruit] unto God

5 and to [*om.* to] the Lamb. And in their mouth was [*ins.* not] found no [*om.* no] guile [falsehood]: for they are without fault [blameless] before the throne of God [*om.* before the throne of God].[7]

2. *The Three Angels of the Annunciation of the Final Judgment.*
a. *Announcement of the Final Judgment as the Eternal Gospel.*

6 And I saw another[8] angel fly [flying] in the midst of heaven [mid-heaven], having the [an] everlasting gospel [,][9] to preach [declare glad tidings (εὐαγγελίσαι)] unto[10] them that dwell [sit][11] on the earth, and to every nation, and kindred [tribe], and

7 tongue, and people, Saying with a loud [great] voice, Fear God, and give glory to him ; for the hour of his judgment is come: and worship him that [who] made [*ins.* the] heaven, and [*ins.* the] earth, and the[12] sea, and the [*om.* the] fountains of waters.

b. *Announcement of the Final Judgment for the Destruction of Babylon.*

8 And there [*om.* there—*ins.* another, second[13] angel] followed another angel [*om.* another angel], saying. [*ins.* Fallen, fallen, is] Babylon [*ins.* the great][14] is fallen, is fallen, that great city [*om.* is fallen, is fallen, that great city],[14] because she [*om.* because she—*ins.* who][15] made [gave] all [*ins.* the] nations [*ins.* to] drink of the wine of the wrath [anger *or* rage][16] of her fornication.

c. *Announcement of the Final Judgment upon the Wicked.*

9 And the [*om.* the—*ins.* another,][17] third angel followed them,[18] saying with a loud [great] voice, If any man [one] worship [worshippeth] the beast [wild-beast] and his image, and receive [receiveth] *his* [*or* a] mark in [on] his forehead, or in [on]

10 his hand, The same [he also] shall drink of the wine of the wrath [anger] of God, which is [hath been] poured out without mixture into [*or* mingled unmixed in][19] the cup of his indignation [wrath (ὀργή)] ; and he shall be tormented with fire and brimstone in the presence of the [*om.* the][20] holy angels, and in the presence of the

11 Lamb : And the smoke of their torment ascendeth up [*om.* up] for ever and ever [into ages of ages] : and they have no [not] rest [*ins.* by] day nor [and by] night, who worship the beast [wild-beast] and his image, and whosoever [if any one] re-

---

[4] Ver. 2. [Alf., Treg., Tisch., read καὶ ἡ φωνὴ ἣν ἥκουσα ὡς with ℵ. A. B*. C. ; P. reads, καὶ φωνὴν ἥκουσα ὡς.—E. R. C.]

[5] Ver. 3. The reading of ℵ. B*. [P.], *etc.*; A. C., *etc.*, read ὡς ᾠδήν. [Tisch., as Lange, omits ; Alf. and Treg. bracket.—E. R. C.]

[6] Ver. 4. [Lange and Tisch (8th Ed.) read ὑπάγῃ with ℵ. B*. P. ; Lach., Alf., Treg., Tisch. (1859) ὑπάγει with A. C. 7, *etc.*—E. R. C.]

[7] Ver. 5. This clause is wanting in the best codices. [So modern Crit. Eds. with ℵ. A. B*. C. P. 1, *etc.*—E. R. C.]

[8] Ver. 6. [Lange, Treg., Tisch., read ἄλλον with ℵ*. A. C. P., Vulg., *etc.*; Gb. omits with ℵ*. B*.; Alf. brackets.—E. R. C.]

[9] Ver. 6. [The pointing is that of the Vulg., Treg., Lillie, *etc.*—E. R. C.]

[10] Ver. 6. Codd. A. C [ℵ. P.] give ἐπὶ before καθημένους.

[11] Ver. 6. [Modern Crit. Eds. give καθημένους with ℵ. B*. C. P. Vulg., *etc.* Lach. (min.), κατοικοῦντας with A.14, *etc.*—E. R. C.]

[12] Ver. 7. [Tisch. (8th Ed.) gives τήν with ℵ. B*.; Lach. Alf., Treg., Tisch. (1859) omit with A. C. P. 1, *etc.*—E. R. C.]

[13] Ver. 8. [Crit. Eds. give δεύτερος in acc. with almost all the Codd.—E. R. C.]

[14] Ver. 8. [Modern Crit. Eds. read Ἔπεσεν ἔπεσεν Βαβυλὼν ἡ μεγάλη ; the insertion of ἡ πόλις is without authority —E. R. C.]

[15] Ver. 8. In accordance with A. C., *etc.*, ἥ. [Ὅτι is given only by 1 and 36.—E. R. C.]

[16] Ver. 8. [For the rendering *anger* see Note 29 below. It is, however, exceedingly questionable whether, by reason of its connection with *wine* and *fornication*, θυμός has not, in this place, a peculiar idiomatic force, and should not be translated *rage*. See Note 29 below.—E. R. C.]

[17] Ver. 9. In accordance with A. B* C. [P.] *etc.*

[18] Ver. 9. [Crit. Eds. generally read αὐτοῖς with Ovpr.; Lange reads αὐτὰ with A.—E R. C.]

[19] Ver. 10. [The E. V. presents the *idiomatic*, though not the *literal*, translation of the Greek. Alford remarks : "From the almost universal custom of mixing wine with water, the common term for preparing wine, putting it into the cup, came to be κεράννυμι ; hence the apparent contradiction in terms here."—E. R. C.]

[20] Ver. 10. [Treg. and Tisch. (8th Ed.) give ἀγγέλων ἁγίων (without τῶν) with ℵ. C. P., *etc.*; B*. prefixes τῶν; Tisch (1859), Alf. read τῶν ἀγγέλων with A.—E. R. C.]

12 ceiveth the mark of his name. Here is the patience [endurance] of the saints : [,]
here *are* they that [*om.* here²¹ *are* they that—*ins.* who] keep the commandments of
God, and the faith of Jesus.

d. Deliverance concerning the Godly.

13 And I heard a voice from [*ins.* the] heaven saying unto me [*om.* unto me]²², Write,
Blessed *are* the dead which [who] die in the Lord from [*om.* from] henceforth :
Yea, saith the Spirit, that they may [shall] rest²³ from their labours ; and [for]²⁴
their works do [*om.* do] follow [*ins.* with] them.

3. The Three Angels of the Beginning Execution of the Final Judgment.
a. The Judgment, or Harvest, of the Earth itself.   The Chief Harvest, or the Harvest of the Blessed.
(Matt. iii. 12 *a.* Ch. xiii. 43.)

14 And I looked [saw] and behold a white cloud, and upon the cloud *one* sat [sitting]
like unto the [a] Son of man, having on [upon] his head a golden crown (στέφανον),
15 and in his hand a sharp sickle.   And another angel came [*ins.* forth] out of the
temple, crying with a loud [great] voice to him that sat on [the one sitting upon]
the cloud, Thrust in [Send forth (πέμψον)] thy sickle, and reap : for the time
[hour] is come for thee [*om.* for thee]²⁵ to reap ; for the harvest of the earth is ripe
16 [has become dry].   And he that sat on [the one sitting upon] the cloud thrust in
[cast (ἔβαλεν)] his sickle on [upon] the earth ; and the earth was reaped.

b. The Harvest of Anger, or the Judgment upon the Wicked (Matt. iii. 12 ; cb. xiii. 42).

17 And another angel came [*ins.* forth] out of the temple which is in [*ins.* the] heaven,
18 he also having a sharp sickle.   And another angel came [*ins.* forth] out from [of]
the altar, which had [*om.* which had—*ins.* having]²⁶ power [authority (ἐξουσία)] over
[*ins.* the] fire ; and cried with a loud cry [great voice] to him that had [the one
having] the sharp sickle, saying, Thrust in [Send forth] thy sharp sickle, and
19 gather the clusters of the vine of the earth ; for her grapes are²⁷ fully ripe.   And
the angel thrust in [cast] his sickle into [unto] the earth, and gathered the vine of
the earth, and cast *it* [*om. it*] into the great²⁸ winepress of the wrath [anger] of God.
20 And the winepress was trodden without the city, and blood came [*ins.* forth] out
of the winepress, even [*om.* even] unto the horse [*om.* horse] bridles [*ins.* of the
horses], by the space [*or* to the distance] of a thousand *and* six hundred furlongs
[stadia].

4. Preparation, in Heaven, for the Judgment.
Cн. XV. 1–8.
a. The Ideal Preparation.

1 And I saw another sign in [*ins.* the] heaven, great and marvellous, seven
angels having the [*om.* the] seven last [*om.* last] plagues [*ins.* the last] ; [,] for
2 in them is filled up [finished] the wrath [anger]²⁹ of God.³⁰   And I saw as it were
a [*ins.* glassy] sea of glass [*om.* of glass] mingled with fire : and them that had

²¹ Ver. 12. The second ὧδε is unfounded. [Crit. Eds. omit with א. A. B*. C. P. Vulg., *etc.*; it is given by 1. 7, *etc.*—
E. R. C.]
²² Ver. 13. [Lach., Alf., Treg., Tisch., omit μοι with א. A. B*. C. P. Am., Fuld., *etc.*; Lange gives it with 1, 28, 36, *Clem.*,
etc.—E. R. C.]
²³ Ver. 13. [Crit. Eds. give ἀναπαήσονται w th א. A. C. (B*. and 1 also give ἀναπαύσονται) ; P. gives ἀναπαύσωνται.—
E. R. C.]
²⁴ Ver. 13. [Lach., Alf., Treg., Tisch. (8th Ed.) give γάρ with א. A. C. P. Vulg., *etc.*; Lange and Tisch. (1859) read δέ
with B*.—E. R. C.]
²⁵ Ver. 15. Σοι is omitted by the best Codd. [by א. A. B*. C. P. Vulg.—E. R. C.]
²⁶ Ver. 18. The article ὁ is omitted by א. B*. [P.] ; the omission probably originated in an incorrect exegetical apprehension of the passage. [Alf., Treg., Tisch. (8th Ed.), omit ; Lach., Lange, and Tisch. (1859) give it with A. C.—E. R. C.]
²⁷ Ver. 18. The reading ἤκμασεν ἡ σταφυλὴ τῆς γῆς, in acc. with B*., *etc.* The easier reading undoubtedly has more
authorities in its favor. But why is this? The question is whether that which is difficult is significant. [Crit. Eds. generally give ἤκμασαν αἱ σταφυλαὶ αὐτῆς, with א. A. B*. C. P. I, Vulg., *etc.*; Tisch. (1859) instead of αὐτῆς reads τῆς γῆς with B*.
7, *etc.*—E. R. C.]
²⁸ Ver. 9. The remarkable reading τὸν μέγαν : the most obvious explanation is that ληνός is *gen. commun.* On the
change of gender in the adjective see Winer, De Wette, Düsterd. [The reading is supported by A. B*. C. P. 6, 8, *etc.*; א. 7,
etc., give τὴν μεγάλην.—E. R. C.]
²⁹ Ch. XV. 1. [There are three words which in the E. V. are translated *wrath : viz. :* θυμός, as here ; ὀργή, ■■ in ver. 10 ;
παροργισμός, which occurs only in Eph. iv. 26. The instances of the occurrence of the first two ■■ follows : Θυμός :
Luke iv. 28 ; Acts xix. 28 ; Rom. ii. 8 (*indignation*) ; 2 Cor. xii. 20 ; Gal. v. 20 ; Eph. iv. 31 ; Col. iii. 8 ; Heb. xi. 27 ; Rev. xii.
12 ; xiv. 8, 10, 19 ; xv. 1, 7 ; xvi. 1, 19 (*fierceness*) ; xviii. 3 ; xix. 15 (*fierceness*) ; Ὀργή : Matt. iii. 7 ; Mark iii. 5 ; Luke iii. 7 ;

gotten the victory [those conquering] over [from] the beast [wild-beast], and over [from] his image, and over his mark [om. and over his mark,][31] *and* [and] over [from] the number of his name, stand [standing] on [or by] the [ins. glassy] sea of

3 glass [om. of glass], having the [om. the][32] harps of God. And they sing the song of Moses the servant of God, and the song of the Lamb, saying, Great and marvellous *are* thy works, [ins. O] Lord [,] God Almighty [,the All-Ruler]; just and true *are*

4 thy ways, thou King of Saints [om. saints—ins. the nations].[33] Who shall [or should][34] not fear thee [om. thee][35] O Lord, and glorify[34] thy name? for *thou* only *art* holy (ὅσιος)[36]: for all [ins. the] nations shall come and worship before thee; for thy judg‧ ments are made manifest [were manifested].

b. The Real Preparation. Equipment of the Angels of Judgment, or the Seven Angels with the Vials of Anger.

5 And after that [these things] I looked [saw], and, behold, [om. , behold][37]—ins. opened was] the temple of the tabernacle of the testimony [witness] in [ins. the] heaven was

6 opened [om. was opened]: And the seven angels came out of [from] the temple, having [or that had][38] the seven plagues, clothed in [ins. linen][39] pure and [and] white [glistening] linen [om. linen], and having their breasts girded [girt around the

7 breasts] with golden girdles. And one of the four beasts [living-beings] gave unto the seven angels seven golden vials full of the wrath [anger] of God, who liveth for

8 ever and ever [into the ages of the ages]. And the temple was filled with smoke[40] from the glory of God, and from his power; and no man [one] was able to enter into the temple, till [until] the seven plagues of the seven angels were fulfilled [should be finished].

xxi. 23; John iii. 36; Rom. i. 18; ii. 5 (bis), 8; iii. 5 (vengeance); iv. 15; v. 9; ix. 22 (bis); xii. 19; xiii. 4, 5; Eph. ii. 3; iv. 31; v. 6; Col. iii. 6, 8 (anger); 1 Thess. i. 10; ii. 16; v. 9; 1 Tim. ii. 8; Heb. iii. 11; iv. 3; Jas. i. 19, 20; Rev. vi. 16, 17; xi. 18; xiv. 10 (indignation); xvi. 19; xix. 15. From a comparison of these passages, especially those in the Apocalypse, it will become apparent that the latter is the *intensive* of the former (see Lange in EXPL. IN DETAIL on ver. 10),—that the effects of θυμός are for the most part experienced in the present life; those of ὀργή in the life to come. In accordance with what he regards as the manifest design of the Spirit to distinguish between the *objectives* of these terms, the Am. Ed. throughout this translation renders the former by *anger* and the latter by *wrath*. It may be objected that this change of the translation of θυμός involves a change in the formula *Vials of wrath* that has become a household phrase. It may be answered that due regard for the distinctions made by the Holy Spirit requires a change here, or in the rendering of ὀργή; and the latter would require an alteration of the formulas—the *wrath* of the Lamb (vi. 16), the great day of His *wrath* (vi. 17), the fierceness of His *wrath* (xvi. 19), the *wrath* of Almighty God, xix. 15.—It should be remarked that in the confused translation of these terms the E. V. closely follows Luther's Version, as it generally does in other instances.—E. R. C.]

[30] Ver. 1. [The translation contemplated is as follows: "Seven angels having seven plagues—the last, for in them is finished the anger of God."—E. R. C.]

[31] Ver. 2. Omitted in the best Codd. [Omitted by א. A. B*. C. P. 6, 7, 14, Vulg., etc.; it is given (see Tisch.) only by 1, 35, 36, 79.—E. R. C.]

[32] Ver. 2. [Crit. Eds. omit the *article* with א. A. C. P.; it is given by B*. 2, 7, etc.—E. R. C.]

[33] Ver. 3. Two variations of the *sons*, of the *saints*. [Crit. Eds. give τῶν ἐθνῶν with א*. A. B*. P. 1, 6, 7, etc.; τῶν ἁγίων with*; א*. C. 18, 95, Vulg., Cl., Fuld., etc., read τῶν αἰώνων. Alford judiciously remarks: "The confusion has apparently arisen from the similarity of ΑΙΘΝΩΝ (ἐθνῶν) and ΑΙΩΝΩΝ; but which was the original, it is impossible, in the conflict of authorities, to decide."—E. R. C.]

[34] Ver. 4. [The construction here is irregular—the *first* verb being φοβηθῇ; the *second*, δοξάσει.—E. R. C.]

[35] Ver. 4. Φοβηθῇ without σε. [So Crit. Eds. with A. B*. C. P. 1, 12, etc., Am., Fuld.; 6, 7, Cl., etc., subjoin σε; א. places it before οὐ φοβ.—E. R. C.]

[36] Ver. 4. [Crit. Eds. give ὅσιος with א. A. C. P. 1, etc.; B*. 6, 7, 8, read ἅγιος.—E. R. C.]

[37] Ver. 5. [The ἰδού is supported only by Vulg., Cop., Prms., Er.; Crit. Eds. omit with א. A. B*. C. P. 1, Syr., Arm., Æth., etc.—E. R. C.]

[38] Ver. 6. [Lange and Tisch. read οἱ ἔχοντες with A. C., etc.; א. B*. 1, etc., omit οἱ; Alf. brackets, Treg. marks with *.—E. R. C.]

[39] Ver. 6. Codd. A. C., etc. [Am., Fuld.] give the difficult reading λίθον; א. B*. [P. Vulg. Cl.] support the Rec. [Lange, Alf., Tisch., give λίνον; Lach. and Treg. λίθον.—E. R. C.]

[40] Ver. 8. Καπνοῦ without ἐκ τοῦ, according to א. A. C. [P.]. [So Crit. Eds. generally; Tisch. (1859) prefixed ἐκ τοῦ with B*.—E. R. C.]

EXEGETICAL AND CRITICAL.

SYNOPTICAL VIEW.

The fundamental idea of the *whole section*, chs. xiv.-xv., is the *End-Judgment in its general form—the same Judgment which subsequently branches into the three special judgments upon Babylon, the Beast, and Satan himself in conjunction with Gog and Magog*. The fundamental idea of this *first division* [chs. xiv., xv.] of our section is the *preparation of the End-Judgment*, or the judgment of the Vials of Anger,* in Heaven. Be‧

* [For the employment of this term rather than *wrath* see TEXT. AND GRAM. (Note 28) on ch. xv. 1. In consequence of

cause this great judgment brings about the final decision, it is preceded by a very great and solemn preparation in Heaven, the description of which runs through two chapters, the judgments then being executed upon the earth itself, in swift succession, by the outpouring of the Vials of Anger (ch. xvi.). Thus, this heavenly proleptical celebration of the End-judgment is analogous to the

the confusion of θυμός and ὀργή in the accepted Version, the same confusion exists in the language of German, as in that of English-speaking, Theologians. As the German *Zorn*, like the English *wrath*, is used to translate both these words; and as it is capable of being rendered by both *anger* and *wrath*, the Am. Ed. takes the liberty of using the one or the other of these English words according as the reference is to θυμός or ὀργή.—E. R. C.]

great proleptical celebration of the Seven Seals of world-history in chs. iv. and v.

The *anger* of God is the manifestation of His love in the forth-going and predominancy of His righteousness unto judgment. God's anger ordains *death* as a punishment for sin—as a reaction against the spiritual death of man, continuous disobedience or germinant apostasy (comp. the art. *Zorn* [anger, wrath] in Herzog's *Real-Encyklopädie*). And inasmuch as anger impels apostasy, or hardening, which is but another form of apostasy, to a crisis, it conducts to eternal death through spiritual death—*i. e.*, it manifests itself in judgment.

But as the very first manifestation of anger was but the climax of a rhythmical succession of chastisements under the reign of long-suffering (Rom. ii. 4, 5), so also the true anger- [or wrath-] period, the great day of anger [or wrath], appears in a succession of constant augmentations.

Great, however, though the anger-judgments may be, so that they wear the aspect of endless and nameless darknesses—as, *e. g.*, in the destruction of Jerusalem, in the fall of Constantinople,—before God they are weighed and measured, and their measure and operation are appointed them by God's faithfulness. Thus, *anger* is contained in *golden vials ;* it is so scrupulously prepared in Heaven, so pondered over, so permeated by the Divine Intelligence, that, as a heroic act of Divine reason, it embodies in itself precisely the opposite to what is described in the heathen pictures of the envy of the gods, and the might of destiny. Our remarks hold good especially in regard to the moderation and limitation of the anger-judgments for the righteous, who are oftentimes externally exposed to the same tempests as the godless—in regard to the cutting short of the troublous days, as the Lord expresses it (see Comm. on *Matthew* xxiv. 22) ; they are, however, also applicable to the operation of judgment in general.

As these Anger-Vials are, on the one hand, akin to the Trumpets, and unmistakably parallel with them (see *Int.*, p. 86), they form, on the other hand, an antithesis to them, in that the Trumpets are predominantly exhibited in the light of judgments in order to awakening (see ch. xi. 13), whilst the Vials of anger generally operate as judgments of hardening (see ch. xvi. 9, 11).

The first great vision in the Heaven-picture of the end of the world is the throng of the elect centre of the Church Triumphant, representative of the Church Triumphant itself. The scene is on *Mount Zion.* That Mount Zion can neither be situate in Heaven, nor be geographically understood of the eminence on which the Temple stood in Jerusalem, is evident from the symbolical import of the expression. Accordingly, Mount Zion is the *real* State of God, in its consummation. The heavenly appearance, ch. i. 12, becomes, ch. iv. 2, the sphere of the heavenly Throne. In ch. vii. 9, the Church Triumphant is depicted *in the process of its growth.* Here we have the picture of its preliminary spiritual consummation. It is still, however, to be conceived of as in the sphere of the *beyond*, for only in ch. xxi. is the union between the Christian further and hither shores consummated in the descent of the heavenly Jerusalem, as the City of God, upon the earth. Then, and not till then, the complete pneumatico-corporeal transfiguration of the world, and the real resurrection, are declared. The spiritual consummation of the Church, however, is declared in this earlier passage—its blessed, secure position above the anger-judgments now about to break upon the earth. The centre of the picture is formed by *the Lamb.* He is surrounded by 144,000 elect souls. To the query as to whether these are the same souls that appear as sealed ones in ch. vii., we would answer : First, that the crisis of trial lies before those sealed ones, whilst these who surround the Lamb have passed it, and are, to the triumphant prophetic gaze, perfected ones, the centre, therefore, of the innumerable throng of ch. vii. 9. Secondly, the symbolical import of the number 144,000 must be carefully regarded in this passage also. We need not, therefore, press the inquiry as to the identity of the two bands as individuals, but may regard as established their identity as a whole ; inasmuch as the sealed elect of this world must also appear in the other world as perfected elect ones. The companions of the Lamb, therefore, are the complete number of the centre of the blessed, representing the entire Church Triumphant.* They have the *Name of Christ* and the *Name of the Father* written on their foreheads, *i. e.*, they are perfected confessors, and hence not such as think they must obscure the Name of the Father by the Name of the Lamb ; nor are they such as act in a converse manner. That the Seer intended to represent this throng as composed exclusively of Jews is an utterly ridiculous assumption, from beginning to end. It is, however, particularly ridiculous when the designation of them as *virgins* is literally understood of celibacy, and the climax of absurdity is reached with the explanatory citation of the Old Testament provision, in accordance with which sexual intercourse rendered unclean for a time. For marriage itself was so far from being represented in the Old Testament as defiling, that, on the contrary, the greatest promises were attached to it. Even Mary, the Mother of our Lord, was obliged to pass through a legal purification, and the Apostle Peter was married. To attribute such a view as the above to the writer of the Apocalypse is to regard him as a dualistic ascetic. Even the Patriarchs and Prophets would, on this ground, be excluded from the number of the elect by this supposed Judaist or *Judaizing non-Judaist*—for the historical interpretation advances even to the latter conception of the Apocalyptist.

This great optical wonder is followed by a great auricular wonder. The *new song* of the consummation of the Church Triumphant bursts, in a grand harmony, from Heaven. It sounds like the *roar of many waters*, for it is the united praise offered to God by the redeemed peoples. It sounds like a *great thunder*, for it is the completed, world-refreshing revelation of God. It sounds like the *harping of harpers*, for all true art has entered

---

into the service of the holy. *And they sing a new song.* These words seem to relate primarily to the harpers, for it is declared' that they sing it before the Throne, before the four Life-shapes and before the Elders. The song, however, is not their property; it is given to them as the perfect blossom of revelation; hence it is also *new* —a marvel of song, which has never before been. We must not overlook the fact that the *new song*, like the State of God, passes through different stages of development before attaining to perfection ; see chs. v. 9; xiv. 3; xv. 3; xix. 6 (comp. Ex. xv.; Ps. xcvi. 1). Even the 144,000 elect must *learn* the song, and they alone *can* learn it, because it presupposes the entire depth and circuit of their experience and the whole state of their being "bought from the earth." *They have not defiled themselves with women.* It is manifest that this can be understood only symbolically, for *virgins* are spoken of. The symbol, however, does not consist of *women* themselves, but of *defilement with women*, by which defilement the women themselves are more particularly characterized (Prov. ix. 13). That illicit intercourse is here referred to, and not marriage, may be understood as a matter of course, in a Book which closes with the Bridal of the Lamb. The Biblical representation of idolatry and apostasy under the figure of harlotry is familiar to all readers of the Sacred Writings, and the idea referred to is the more obvious here, since immediately before the great apostasy has been depicted. The *doing* of these virgin souls was, however, founded upon their *being.** As *virgins*, they have also kept themselves pure from all fanaticism and party-spirit in their piety, for both these forms of the defilement of piety are also, in particular, very fatal forms of subtile idolatry. Their virginity is expressed in the fact that they *follow the Lamb whithersoever He goeth* —follow Him, therefore, in all His historical and heavenly movements and advances, and follow only Him. Absolute, pure obedience in absolute, pure trust, is the sign that they are *bought from among men* as *first-fruits* (see Comm. on *James* i. 18) *unto God and the Lamb.* As, however, the consummation of their electness was based upon redemptive grace, evidence of that electness was given, above all, in the characteristics of uprightness (Prov. ii. 7 ; Eccl. vii. 8) and veracity. Grotius rightly makes mention of the fact that all idolatry is infected with *falsehood* (John iii. 21). The fact that they should not be represented as sinless and having no need of redemption, is manifest from the declaration concerning them, that they stand before the Lamb, that they are bought, and that no falsehood was found in their mouth—no species of untruthfulness—and that they stand as, in every respect, wholly perfected, *blameless*—as is expressly affirmed—before the Throne of God.

After this exhibition of the security of the whole blessed Kingdom of God, the announcement of the Judgment may be made. This Judgment has three sides :

First, it is, for the righteous, final redemption; hence, its proclamation as an everlasting gospel,

the *eschatological gospel* of the final σωτηρία, through the judgment, to eternal blessedness and well-being ([*Heil*] Matt. xxv. ; Luke xxi. 28). This gospel is proclaimed to all *who sit on the earth*, all who are most firmly attached to earth (ver. 6), before the coming of the Judgment itself ; and the proclamation is conjoined with an admonition to voluntary self-humiliation before God, Who is here pertinently designated as the Creator, the Cause and Lord of all things, and particularly also, as the Author of the *fountains of waters*, *i. e.*, all original geniuses.

The Judgment is, secondly, for the world ripe unto perdition, an actual fall into perdition. Hence the proclamation : *Fallen, fallen is Babylon the great!* Be it here observed that in this passage it is not Babylon in the narrower sense of the word, to which reference is had, as in ch. xvii. As in Genesis, ch. i., *water* is at first spoken of in the most general sense, then in a special sense, and finally in the most special sense, so here by Babylon the whole ungodly Anti-christianized world is intended. At the outpouring of the seventh Vial of anger, this ungodly and Antichristian world, represented by Babylon, is divided into three parts (ch. xvi. 19), when the general Judgment branches into the three special judgments : upon the Harlot, or Babylon in the narrower sense ; upon the Beast; and upon Gog and Magog under the leadership of Satan. Concerning the more general Babylon which has, undoubtedly, for a considerable time its culmination-point in the more special Babylon, it is declared : *She gave all the nations* [heathen, Gentiles] *to drink of the wine of the anger* [or *rage*]* *of her fornication.* Antichristianity is a unitous evil mock-growth, which has twined its stifling tendrils throughout humanity, as, on the other hand, the tree of the Kingdom of God has pushed its holy roots throughout the same. The wine of the anger of fornication is only materially identical with the anger of God (see ch. xi. 18); in a formal point of view it forms an antithesis thereto. The wine of the anger of fornication is, as *sin*, passionate, riotous intoxication in apostasy ; as a *judgment*, it is also the wine of the wrath of God, the mind-deranging operation of the death-judgments of God.

Finally, the judgment consists, in the third place, of the sentence which interprets the facts. Thus the actual separation of the sheep and the goats (Matt. xxv.) precedes the sentence passed upon them. The sentence of the Angel is conditioned as follows : *If any one worshippeth the Wild-beast and his image, and receiveth his mark on his forehead or on his hand.* The one implies the other: recognition of the power of the Beast, and appropriation of the false idea of the system, *theocratic* or *practical* testimony. The sentence is as follows : he incurs the internal judgment of having to *drink of the wine of the anger* [or *wrath*] *of God*—deadly derangement of the mind; this is a wine mingled, *i. e.*, here *poured out* (presented, *credenzt*) *unmixed* [οἶνος κεκερασμένος ἄκρατος].† as the strongest and most intoxicating

---

* Schiller: Gemeine *Naturen zahlen mit dem was sie thun*, edle *mit dem was sie sind.*

* [See Text. and Gram. under ch. xiv. 8, note 16.—E. R. C.]

† [See Text. and Gram. under ch. xiv. 10, note 19.—E. R. C.]

beverage, *in the cup*, the self-limiting decree, *of
II's wrath* [ὀργή]. The external *local result* is as follows: *he shall be tormented with fire and brimstone
in the presence of holy angels and in the presence of the Lamb*. The outward and apparent
form of the Judgment is fiery self-consumption
in the ever affluent new elements of fiery irritation. For as, to the righteous, every affluent experience is transformed into the gentle oil of
the Spirit, so, to the wicked, every experience becomes brimstone—fuel for his passion. The *temporal result* of the Judgment is as follows: *the
smoke of their torment ascendeth into ages of ages.*
Smoke rises from fire; not, however, from a
clear fire, but from that which is hemmed in and
dim. Here, doubtless, the fire of hate is particularly referred to—fanatical passionateness
in apostasy. Hence it is further declared: *they
have not rest by day and by night*; this they have
not, not in a good sense (ch. iv. 8), but in a bad
sense, as demonic beings, and the true causality
thereof lies in their very apostasy;—the context
is: *who worship the wild-beast and his image, and
if any one receiveth the mark of his name.* The fact
that the condition of damnation can continue
into the ages denotes, indubitably, the temporal
immensity of that condition, but is also, at the
same time, expressive of æonic figurations and
alterations of it.

At the close of this sentence, we again encounter the saying of ch. xiii. 10, amplified by
the declaration that *the patience* [*endurance*] *of
the saints* is also evidenced in *keeping the commandments of God; their faith*, meanwhile, appearing as a faith in *Jesus*. Only through this
patience or endurance can a man escape that
sentence of æonic fiery death. Here also, as in
ch. xiii. 10, this spirit of blessed calm forms a
contrast to the fire-smoke of the restless (Is.
xlviii. 22). Here again the Seer significantly
insists upon the fact that a vital veneration of
God and faith in Jesus necessarily accompany
each other.

The sentence unto *damnation* is now contrasted with the sentence unto *blessedness.* But
why does not the *Angel* give utterance to the
latter, and not *a voice from Heaven?* We might
reply, because the experience of the celestial
blessedness of proven Christians passes the experience of Angels. According to the context,
this beatitude is pronounced by the *Spirit*, i. e.,
the Spirit of the Church Triumphant; He,
therefore, gives utterance to a testimony of direct experience. The beatitude of the blessed
dead is, however, specially signalized, and com-
mended, as it were, as an inscription for grave-
stones, with the command: *Write.* Although
this precious sentence (ver. 13) holds good for
all times—*blessed are the dead, etc.*—it is of particular moment when regarded in its bearing
upon the last times. Then are the dying, who
die in the Lord as they have lived in Him, to be
accounted particularly blessed, because they are
taken away from the storm of the last days (see
Is. lvii. 1).

We, therefore, interpret ἀπάρτι in the following sense: Such are henceforth peculiarly
blessed, because they attain unto *rest* from their
sore conflicts, whilst the blessing of their *works*,
and also their perfected vocation to ideal acti-

vity, accompany them into the Church Triumphant.

Before passing to a consideration of the three
Angels of the beginning *execution* of the End-
Judgment, we must examine the relation of
these three Angels to the preceding three Angels
of the *announcement* of Judgment. It is natural
to suppose that the first three Angels form an
organic totality (ἄλλος ver. 15, ἄλλος ver. 17,
ἄλλος ver. 18, akin to ἄλλος, ἕτερος, ἄλλος, 1 Cor.
xii. 10), and not that an abstract series of other
and still other Angels is cited. The second angelic triad, then, corresponds to the first, and
the following scheme is formed:

A. THE ANNOUNCEMENT OF THE END. THE
LAMB STANDING ON MOUNT ZION (ver. 1).

1. The ἄλλος ἄγγελος, the proclaimer of the
everlasting Gospel, or the Gospel of eternity
(ver. 6).

2. The ἄλλος δεύτερος ἄγγελος, as the proclaimer of the decided fall of Babylon the Great
(ver. 8).

3. The ἄλλος ἄγγελος τρίτος, the proclaimer of
the judgment upon the worshippers of the Beast
(ver. 9).

4. The *voice from Heaven*: Proclamation of
the blessedness of the dead who die in the Lord.

B. THE ACCOMPLISHMENT OF THE END. AP-
PEARANCE OF THE FORM OF THE SON OF MAN
ON THE WHITE CLOUD (ver. 14).

1. The ἄλλος ἄγγελος, issuing *out of the Temple*,
proclaiming the hour of the Judgment (the beginning of the entire Judgment) as a judgment
upon Babylon (ver. 15).

2. The ἄλλος ἄγγελος, issuing out of the Temple in Heaven, with the sharp sickle for the consummation of the harvest (ver. 17).

3. The ἄλλος ἄγγελος, ver. 18, issuing from
the Altar, having power over the fire of sacrifice
—who challenges the preceding Angel to the
completion of the End-Judgment, as that Angel
(ver. 15) had in his turn challenged the form of
the Son of Man (ver. 14).

We, therefore, distinguish the group of the
proclamation of Judgment (A) and that of the *execution of Judgment* (B). The former is under
the dominion of the Lamb, Who stands fast forever on Mount Zion as the Head of the Church
Triumphant; the latter group is under the dominion of the form of the Son of Man on the
white cloud, with the crown upon His head, and
in His hand the sharp harvest-sickle—under the
Christ, therefore, as He comes for Judgment *upon
the world* (Matt. xxvi. 64; comp. Dan. vii.).

With the *first* Angel, who has *proclaimed* the
eternal Gospel, i. e., the Gospel of a blessed
eternity, the final σωτηρία (ver. 6), corresponds
the *first* Angel of *execution*, in that he notifies
the Son of Man of *the hour* or *time* of harvest,
and summons Him to the harvest; whereupon,
He Who sits upon the cloud, casts His sickle
upon the earth and reaps the earth. This harvest (ver. 16) is, without doubt, the harvest of
the *wheat* (Matt. iii. 12; xiii. 39), with which
the Parousia begins (Matt. xxiv. 31), corresponding to the Gospel of the final redemption, and to
be distinguished from the harvest of judgment
(vers. 19, 20). Distinctive marks: The Angel
of ver. 15 goes forth from the *Temple*, i. e., the
ideal Temple of the ripened Church of God, for

the ripeness of God's Church for redemption is the sign of the ripeness of the world for judgment; this Angel is the symbol of the *decree of the Father* (Acts i. 7). Again, this first harvest is called simply the harvest *of the earth;* it begins with Christ, as the Judge of the world, casting His sickle from the cloud to the earth—that is, with the commencement of His Parousia itself. Here, therefore, the *earth* which is reaped, is to be understood in the more special sense of the term.

With the *second* Angel of *proclamation,* who cries out: Fallen is Babylon (ver. 8), corresponds the *second* Angel of *execution* (ver. 17). This latter Angel issues forth from the Temple of *Heaven,* for the judgment unto judgment is based entirely upon the objective sentence of Divine Righteousness, which decides when the internal corruptness [*Verderben*] of the world must find its judgment in external ruin [*Verderben*]. Even this Angel of judgment, however (who bears a similarity to the import of Michael, the judging Christ), receives the summons to the execution of judgment from another Angel, the *third* Angel of *execution.* This Angel issues from the *Altar;* he has *authority over the fire.* This is what qualifies him to call for the fire of judgment. For every little flame, every fire of sacrifice, has been a pre-exhibition of the great sacrificial burning at the end of the world. Thus with the *third* Angel of *proclamation* (ver. 9), who announced that law of the Kingdom in accordance with which the sentence of damnation (vers. 9–11) *and the Judgment, as a judgment of fire,* ensue, corresponds the Angel of the *actual fiery Judgment,* whose world-historic prefiguration is sacrifice.

We scarcely need mention that this double angelic triad forms a group of symbolical figures; in which the first triad belongs more to the economy of Christ, and the second more to the economy of the Father.

It may appear particularly remarkable that the harvest of judgment is represented ▬▬ a gathering of the *vine*—the *vine* thus, apparently, having an entirely different import here from that assigned it John xv. 1. It might here be suggested that all Antichristianity will be a corrupt and apostate Christianity. There is, however, another motive which lies at the door, *viz.,* that of conforming the entire picture to the central idea of the *wine-press,* Is. lxiii. The wine-press of wrath or deadly judgment brings with it the retribution for the great blood-guiltiness of the world's history—especially as manifested in the history of the martyrs;—this retribution is exhibited in the mighty river of blood in which, at the end of the world, the life of the old humanity pours forth. The *treading* of the wine-press is accomplished *without the city;** an antithesis by which only the City simple, the City of God, can be intended. The depth of the river of blood is indicated by the declaration that it reaches to the *reins* [*Zügel*] *of the horses*—not to the *bits* [*Zäume,* German Version], for in that case the horses would necessarily sink. It is with difficulty, therefore,

---

* [May there not be an allusion to the fact that the crucifixion of Christ, in which the sin and, *par excellence,* the blood-guiltiness of the world culminated, took place *without the city ?*—Tr.]

that the horses of world-development (ch. vi. 2; xix. 14) can labor through this stream; it is only through a great crisis that the new world issues from the old. The bloody stream itself overspreads 1000 *stadia,* the symbol of an æon, by the space of 600 *stadia,* by which an immense extent of further suffering is indicated.

In ch. xv. is represented the *preparation* of this Judgment which is about to be executed through the medium of the Vials of Anger. It might be conjectured that the Earth-picture of the Anger-Vials would begin here, but individual traits are against such a supposition—especially the festival-keeping on the crystal sea. First, then, the Seer beholds *another sign in Heaven,* the *seven Angels* with the *last seven plagues,* or judgment-strokes, with which the anger of God shall be filled up. Again, however, the vision must strengthen the courage of the faithful; the description of the terrible angelic forms is therefore preceded by a picture of the celebration of the Judgment in the congregation of the blessed. The *glassy sea* is here, as in an earlier passage [chap. iv. 6], the completed history of the peoples ▬▬ a history of salvation, *sub specie æterni,* translumined by the Spirit of God; Divinely still and transparent, and Divinely moved. Here, however, it is mingled with the appearance of *fire* (see p. 84); for this new world-form has passed through the sacrificial fire as well ▬▬ through the fire of the universal judgment; moreover, the reflection of the Vials of anger falls upon the crystal splendor of this sea. Hence, the blessed are here designated as *victors over the Beast.* Their victory is detailed. They have vanquished not only the temptation of the *Beast,* but also the temptation of his *Image,* the temptation of his *mark,* the Antichristian symbol; aye, they have overcome even the temptation to a covert [*verblümt*] recognition of him by the assumption of the *number of his name* in a restless pursuit of vanity. And now they all have *harps;* harps *of God,* as Divinely inspired singers and players. The *new song* which they sing is now called *the song of Moses, the servant of God,* and *the song of the Lamb.* Of the two songs, the song of the typical redemption (Ex. xv.) and the song of the real redemption, one unitous, grand anthem of redemption is born. Even the Law is, in the light of the consummation, glorified into a phase of the Gospel; and it is also, in spiritual forms, its very self glorified, elevated—and, by being elevated, in a sense abrogated [*aufgehoben*],—transmuted into celestial custom (Matt. v.). This song has reference to the imminent final Judgment from which they, through the redemption, have escaped, as Israel escaped from the pursuit of Pharaoh. Hence, mention is first made of the *great wonders* of God, particularly as manifest in His conduct of the Final Judgment. Hence, God is again magnified as the *All-Ruler* [Παντοκράτωρ],* and His *ways,* in particular,—His government and providences [*Führungen und Fügungen*=leadings and joinings]—are extolled as *righteous and true;* ▬▬ *righteous* in His world-historic retribution—as *true* in His final fulfillment of all prophecies and threats. Thus

---

* [See on p. 94.—E. R. C.]

He approves Himself the essential *King of the nations* (not simply of the *saints*, after the scantily attested reading).* Thus the *worship* of the true *fear* of God appertains to Him at the end of days as much as, and still more than, in the days of the Old Covenant, for this fear is fundamentally diverse from the fear which is cast out by perfect love. The supreme reason for this worship is expressed in the words: *He only is holy*—words declaratory of the Absolute Personality, not merely as a negation of all impersonal conduct, but also as the Founder and Awakener of the Personal Kingdom of Love, in Whose almighty traction of love *all nations* [*Heiden*, heathen, Gentiles] *shall come and worship before Him* after they have beheld the grand manifestation of His judgments. These words point to a great conversion, to take place amidst the development of the world's judgment.

After this pre-celebration of the Judgment of Anger, the Seer, with new amazement (ver. 5), beholds the equipment of the seven Angels for the execution of the Judgment. The scene opens with the opening of the Temple of the Tabernacle of the Witness, *i. e.*, the Ark of the Covenant—the Holy of Holies, therefore. There the holy Law reposes, which has testified the will of God to the nations; thence, therefore, perfect retribution proceeds, as a punitory providence which itself bears the mark of the Holy of Holies, and hence is to be regarded entirely as a providence in order to the protection of personal life.

This providence issues from the Holy of Holies, under the guidance of the seven Angels who are to execute the seven last plagues. These Angels themselves appear as highly consecrate spirits, clothed with *pure, glistening* (or pearl-beset?†) *linen*, for they accomplish the deliverances of supreme truth and righteousness solely, in executing the sentence of the anger of God; they are no mediums for the outflowings of dark and unfree passion, no ministers of blind and senseless fate-strokes. Hence they are also *girded* for a festal celebration, *about the breast*—not for labor, about the loins; they are girded with *golden girdles*, the signs of Divine strength, self-determination, and bound-abiding faithfulness.

The seven Vials of Anger are given to the Angels by one of the four Life-shapes. Here it is particularly manifest that these Life-shapes cannot be regarded as symbolical forms of creature life.‡ They stand between God and these high Angels—who may not, indeed, be identified with the Archangels—and receive the Vials, which are full of the anger of God. *One* of them distributes the Vials; greater explicitness is not accorded to the vision—hence it would be mere guess-work were we to conjecture that the *Lion* was the recipient and distributer of the Vials.

Why do we here find the expression: *Who liveth into the ages of the ages?* The domination of God's wrath in inflictions of death is conditioned by this life. The manifestation of absolute Life is a decree of death to obstinate sinners.

Furthermore, God withdraws Himself from human view as an angry God. Thenceforth the Temple was *filled with smoke from the glory of God*, so that none could go into the Temple until the seven plagues were fulfilled. This phenomenon cannot be resolved into the more general fact that the glory of God veils itself in the pillar of cloud or in a pillar of smoke (Ex. xl. 34; 1 Kings viii. 10; Matt. xvii. 5), although it is connected with that fact. For the Temple was not previously filled with smoke, to the eye of the Seer; he has even had a mysteriously expressed sight of God. But as God, as the Holy One, in general conceals Himself from the gaze of sinful man, so this is especially the case in His judgments. "He made the darkness about Him His covering—His pavilion round about Him dark waters [*Wassernacht*], clouds upon clouds," Ps. xviii. 11. Thus He covers Himself when He comes with terrors upon His enemies. For the Prophet Isaiah also (Is. vi.), the Temple in which he has seen the glory of Jehovah, afterwards becomes filled with smoke; a sign that this Temple should be burnt, but also an expression of the fact that God is, for the human eye, hidden most in His judgments, most difficult of comprehension therein. That affectionate and familiar boldness which seeks an immediate access into the Temple, to God, shrinks back amid the thunders of majesty; nevertheless, the Mercy-seat is set up in front of the Temple in the person of Jesus Christ for all in the whole world who seek for refuge (Rom. iii.).

[ABSTRACT OF VIEWS, ETC.]
By the American Editor.

[ELLIOTT :* Ch. xiv. 1-5, is parallel with chs. xii., xiii., and presents a view of the true Church gathered around the true Christ (the *Lamb—standing*, not yet enthroned)—in antithesis with the merely *nominal* Church gathered around the enthroned Antichrist, as set forth in those chapters; vers. 2, 3, mark a progression in their condition—they refer to the Reformation;—the *harpers* are the rejoicing members of the churches of the Reformation; the *voice of many waters* and *of a great thunder* implies the uniting of both nations and princes in their rejoicing; the *new song*, the song of the Reformation, as set forth by Luther : "Learn to know CHRIST, Christ crucified, Christ come down from Heaven to dwell with sinners! Learn to sing the NEW SONG, *Thou Jesus art my righteousness; I am Thy sin; Thou hast taken on Thyself what was mine; Thou hast given me what is Thine*."——Vers. 6-8 are parallel with chs. xv., xvi. 1-14 (xi. 15-19), and set forth the missionary advance of the true Church throughout the Era predicted in those passages (see on p. 296).——Vers. 9-20 are connected with ch. xvi. 15 to the end of the Apocalypse (see on p. 297).

---

* [See TEXT. AND GRAMM. under ch. xv. 3, note 33.—E. R. C.]
† On the reading λίθον, see Düsterd. [See also TEXT. AND GRAM.—E. R. C.]
‡ [See ADD. NOTE on pp. 161 sq.—E. R. C.]

* [There is considerable complexity in the last part of Elliott's great work. The whole of chs. xii.-xiv. he regards as a connected revelation written on the *outside* of the Roll, and presenting a revelation parallel with that presented in the other portions of the Apocalypse (*inside* written) to the close of ch. xix. (see ch. v. 1). Chs. xii.-xiv. 5, he regards as extending to what he styles *the primary end* of the period of 1260 days, about A. D., 1789-93 (see p. 260); ch. xiv. 6-8, and 9-20, as above.—E. R. C.]

BARNES: Ch. xiv. contains a succession of symbolical representations, designed to comfort those exposed to the troublous events of chs. xii., xiii., by showing the ultimate result of those events : There is represented by the vision of (1) vers. 1–5, the character and final triumph of all the redeemed ; (2) vers. 6, 7. that the gospel *will* be preached among all nations, and *that* as indicating the near approach of the consummation ; (3) ver. 8, the destruction of Antichristian, Papal Rome ; (4) vers. 9–12, the certain and final destruction of all the upholders of that power; (5) ver. 13, the blessedness of all who die in the Lord ; (6) vers. 14–20, the final overthrow of all the enemies of the Church: the *harvest* representing the righteous to be gathered into the Kingdom ; the *vintage*, the wicked to be destroyed.——Ch. xv. commences the statement of the manner in which the pledges of the preceding chapter would be accomplished, which statement is pursued through the subsequent chapters, giving in detail what is here promised in a general manner—it " is merely introductory to what follows, . . . and designed to introduce the account of those judgments with suitable circumstances of solemnity."

STUART: " The combination of *three* such powerful enemies against Christianity (the *Dragon*, Satan [p. 240]; the *First Beast*, Pagan Rome ; the *Second*, the Pagan Priesthood [p. 261]), was in itself of fearful import. . . . To animate the courage, however, of this noble little band (of Christians), the writer arrests the progress of action in the great drama, in order to hold out the *symbols of ultimate and certain victory*: Symbol *First* is of the Lamb (Christ) on the *earthly* Zion, surrounded by His 144,000 sealed ones—not *forces* to be employed against enemies, but *trophies* of victory already achieved; *Second*, consists of a *triplex* series of *proclamations* of (*a*) the ultimate and certain spread of the gospel throughout the whole world, vers. 6, 7, (*b*) the absolute and certain fall of mystical Babylon (heathen Rome), ver. 8, (*c*) the awful punishment that awaits the followers of the Beast ; *Third*, is constituted of a *triplex* series of *actions*—(*a*) the *reaping*, vers. 14–16 (the harvest which is ripe, *i. e.*, the enemies of the Church whose wickedness is consummated), (*b*) the *gathering*, vers. 17–19 (also the wicked), (*c*) the *treading* of the wine-press, ver. 20.*——Ch. xv. A *Heaven*-scene preceding the infliction of the seven *last plagues* : the martyrs around the Throne sing the song of anticipative triumph, and praise the justice of God as about to be displayed in the overthrow of the Beast, vers. 2–4 ; the *smoke preventing the entrance of any one into the Temple*, ver. 8, indicates that no one is permitted to intercede for those about to be punished, and consequently, that their punishment is certain and inevitable.

WORDSWORTH : Ch. xiv. 1–5. This vision reveals that, although during the sway of the Beast many would fall from the faith, yet the true Catholic Apostolic Church of Christ (the 144,000—the number of *completeness* and *union* in the true doctrine and *discipline* of Christ, as preached by

the *twelve Apostles*) would never fail, and would finally triumph over the power of the Beast, and would *stand* with the *Lamb* on *Mount Zion* (in antithesis to the *rising* of the *Beast* from the *sea*) in His Kingdom, which will never be destroyed (comp. Ps. cxxv. 1, *etc.*); the *virginity* of the 144,000 (ver. 3) indicates that they were not corrupted by the spiritual *harlotries* of Babylon (ver. 8 ; xvii. 1–5); the *song of triumph* (vers. 2, 3), is that of *Angels* chanting the victory of the Church.——Vers. 6, 7 predict the universal proclamation of the gospel (by *literal* Angels?), and *that* as a preparation for the End (compare Matt. xxiv. 4).——Ver. 8 is anticipative of the fall of *Babylon, i. e.*, *Papal Rome*.——Vers. 9–11, a warning (by *literal* Angels?) against worshiping the Beast.——Vers. 14–16, Vision of the Last Judgment, as (1) a *Harvest*, the ingathering of the good; (2) a *Vintage*, the crushing of the wicked.——Ch. xv. 1. " St. John, having been brought in the foregoing chapter to the eve of the Day of Judgment, now *re-ascends*, as usual, to an *earlier* point in the Prophecy ; and enlarges on the judicial chastisements to be inflicted on the Empire of the Beast."——Vers. 2-4. " Anticipations, continued and expanded, of the future *victory* of the faithful over the power of the Beast."——Vers. 5-8. " Preparation for the pouring out of the Seven Vials on the Empire of the Beast."

ALFORD: Ch. xiv. This is not entirely another vision, but an introduction of a new element, one of comfort and joy, upon the scene of the last ; it is *anticipatory*, having reference to two subjects to be treated of afterwards in detail—(1) the mystic Babylon, (2) the consummation of punishment and reward ; it is *general* in its character, reaching forward close to the time of the end, and treating compendiously of the torment of the apostates and the blessedness of the righteous. It naturally divides itself into three *sections :* I. Vers. 1-5. The 144,000 are identical with those of ch. vii. 4, and represent *the people of God ;* their introduction here serves to place before us the Church on *the holy hill of Sion* (" the site of the display of God's chosen ones with Christ " [" the seat of God's true Church and worship ? "]), where God has placed His King, as an introduction to the description of her agency in preaching the gospel, and her faithfulness in persecutions. II. Vers. 6-13. The four *announcements* of this section form the text and the compendium of the rest of the Book—these are of (1) the universal proclamation of the gospel as previous to the final judgments, vers. 6, 7, (2) the fall of *Babylon* (Rome, Pagan and Papal—principally Papal ; see on ch. xvii.), as an encouragement for the patience of the saints, ver. 8 ; (3) the final defeat and torment of the Lord's enemies, vers. 9-12; (4) the blessedness of all who die in the faith and obedience of Christ. III. Vers. 14-16. The *Harvest, i. e.*, the *ingathering of the saints*, answering to the proclamation of the gospel in vers. 6, 7. IV. Vers. 17-20. The *Vintage of Wrath*, fulfilling the denunciations of vers. 8, 11.——Ch. xv. PREFATORY *to the Seven Vials :* Ver. 1, the description of the vision ; vers. 2-4, the song of triumph of the saints victorious over the Beast ; vers. 5 8, the coming forth of the

---

* [The above *seems* to be the division contemplated by Stuart.—E. R, C.]

seven Angels, and delivering to them of the seven Vials. (See also in EXPL. IN DETAIL in loc.) LORD: Ch. xiv. 1-4. The 144,000 are the same as those of ch. vii.; they are also the Witnesses of ch. xi. raised from the dead; they have not belonged to the apostate Church, nor sanctioned the blasphemous usurpations of the Wild Beast, but are pure worshippers of God; they are the first-fruits unto God (distinguished from the complete harvest of vers. 15, 16); the song of ver. 3 is their song.——Ch. xiv. 6, 7. The Angel represents a body and succession of men, who are to bear the everlasting gospel both to the nations of the ten kingdoms, and to all other tribes and languages of earth.——Ch. xiv. 8. Great Babylon is the aggregate of the nationalized hierarchies of the ten kingdoms; she symbolizes the teachers and rulers of the churches, with whom the kings of the earth join in the institution, practice, and dissemination of a false religion; uniting with her in the usurpation of the rights of God as lawgiver, etc.; her fall is her severance from the civil governments, and dejection from her station and power as a combination of national establishments; the Angel is the representative of a body of men, his flight in mid-Heaven denotes their publicity and conspicuity, and his annunciation, that there is to be a public and exalting celebration of her overthrow.——Ch. xiv. 9-13. The warning implies that notwithstanding great Babylon has fallen from her station as a national establishment, men are still worshipping the Wild-beast and its image, and receiving its mark—those Romish hierarchies are still to subsist after their fall, and acknowledge the Pope as their head; the symbol foreshows that after great Babylon has fallen from her station as a combination of nationalized hierarchies, numerous teachers shall arise who shall publicly and strenuously assert the exclusive right of God to enjoin the faith and institute the worship of the Church, etc.——Ch. xiv. 14-16. The one like the Son of Man represents (not Christ but) a human being, raised from the dead in glory, like the human form of Christ in His exaltation—the period of this agency, therefore, is after the revivification of the Witnesses; those harvested by him are the saints, living and mortal.——Ch. xiv. 17-20. The dejection of the vine into the wine-press signifies that those whom the vine symbolizes are to be crushed by the vengeance of the Almighty—the treading of the wine-press outside the city (the symbol of the nationalized hierarchies), denotes that the grapes are from their vineyards—the river of blood symbolizes the vastness and visibility of the destruction; the dejection of the vine into the press is a different work from the treading—the former is the work of the reapers, the latter of the Son of God.——Ch. xv. 1-4. A Heaven-scene wherein the entire mass of witnesses, who throughout the ages have held the testimony of Jesus, and refused submission to Antichristian powers, are represented as praising the wisdom and rectitude of the Almighty.——Ch. xv. 5-8. The introduction to the pouring out of the Vials, indicating that no intercession by the saints on earth for the salvation of Antichristian foes is to be offered during this period.

GLASGOW: Ch. xiv. The 144,000 are the same as those of chap. vii.—they are the first-fruits (comp. Ex. xiii. 15; xxxiv. 20), representing all God's ransomed people; the Angel of ver. 6 symbolizes the ministry of the gospel from the beginning (specially as missionaries to the heathen); the Angel of ver. 8 represents home missionaries, who are more controversial and Protestant than the preceding; the third Angel, ver. 9, symbolizes the Protestant ministry; the dead of ver. 13 are the martyred dead of all ages: the one sitting on the cloud, ver. 14, is Christ in His humanity throughout the gospel dispensation sitting on the cloud (the symbol taken from the cloudy pillar), which ever abides over the Church; the Angel of ver. 15, the whole body of Christ's ministry—the time of their prayer to Christ coincides with the death of the Witnesses, the reaping-time of His compliance with that prayer is that of the resurrection of the witnesses (the Reformation); the Angel of ver. 17 is the Holy Ghost; that of ver. 18 represents persecuted saints; the vintage symbolizes the wasting wars that followed the Reformation.——Ch. xv. The resurrection of the witnesses symbolizes the Reformation, and also presents a general view of the glorious events and retributions that followed.—E. R. C.]

EXPLANATIONS IN DETAIL.

Ch. xiv. 1. **And I saw, and behold.**—Lively introduction of the new, great vision of the heavenly pre-celebration and preparation of the final Judgment. The consummation of the Church, as appearing in the 144,000 virgins, is symptomatic of the consummation of the earth, of its ripeness for judgment.

The Lamb (ch. vii. 17)—here in the radiance of His glorious spoils of victory.

On the Mount Zion.—Is the mountain to be conceived of as in Heaven (in accordance with Grotius, Hengstenberg, Ebrard, et al.)? Or is it, in accordance with De Wette and Düsterd., to be taken in its "proper" acceptation, i. e., literally? Düsterdieck applies the epithet allegoristic to the interpretation of Mount Zion as the Church (after Bede, Calov., et al.), in his chronic misapprehension of what allegorism is. The vision is, evidently, a picture of the Church Triumphant, resident in that spiritual Heaven which pervades Heaven and earth. Mount Zion, however, particularly symbolizes the lofty citadel, the eternal fortress of the people of God.

And with Him a hundred and forty-four thousand.—There is as little foundation for the belief that these 144,000 are composed exclusively of Gentiles (Düsterdieck) as for the assumption that the 144,000 of ch. vii. are Jews exclusively. For a discussion of the question as to the identity (Grot., Vitringa, and many others) or diversity (Bleek, Neander, et al.) of the two assemblies, we refer our readers to the SYNOPTICAL VIEW [also ADD. NOTE, p. 193.—E. R. C.] The 144,000 of the present chapter are, as a whole, the same kernel of the Church of God—a kernel, however, which has developed, from a host of combatants warring on this side of the boundary which divides this life from the life to come, to a host of victors who have crossed the line; as, similarly, the seal on the foreheads of the first has become the open *inscription* of appertinency to God and Christ.

Ver. 2. **A voice from the Heaven**.—The *heavenly* character of the voice is the main thing; the sounds are sounds of perfection. The voices are in part voices of Christian nations (the voice of *great waters*), in part the voices of great Prophets (the voice of *a great thunder*), both the former and the latter being perfected in holy art (the voice of *harpers*). In a certain degree, therefore, the voice from Heaven certainly does represent the 144,000 themselves (Bengel, Hengstenberg, *et al.*); more strictly speaking, however, it is the true fountain of song within the Church of God, whose outflowings pass but gradually to the entire Church:—the *choir* of the celestial Church.—**Great waters** (ch. i. 15).—**The voice of a great thunder** (ch. vi. 1).—**Harps** (or *citherns*).—With all its sublimity, the song, in its spiritual beauty, is as exquisitely delicate as the music of the cithern. [ALFORD comments: "The harpers and the song are in Heaven, the 144,000 on earth; *and no one was able to learn the song, i. e.*, to appreciate its melody and meaning, so as to accompany it and bear part in the chorus." On the other hand LORD remarks: "The Mount Sion on which the 144,000 stood was that of the heavenly tabernacle. . . The song, accordingly, which he heard from Heaven was their song: not the song of the other redeemed or of angels. This is apparent from the representation that it was sung before the Living-creatures and Elders, and that no one was able to learn it but the 144,000. *To suppose it to have been sung by others, is to suppose that they had already learned it.*"—E. R. C.]

Ver. 3. **A new song**.—As the Old Testament is *new* in comparison with the primeval time; as the New Testament is *new* in comparison with the Old Testament; as the eternal gospel is *new* in comparison with the gospel of principial σωτηρία; so the *new song* is *new* in comparison with Moses' song of redemption:—a more developed form is the conjunction of the two songs (ch. xv. 3).—**And no one could learn the song, etc.**—The condition whereon the learning of it is dependent is not artistic talent, but the depth of ethical experience, such as is possessed by the 144,000. The highest æsthetics, the most profound artistic intelligence, in the simplest words.

Vers. 4 and 5. On different attempts to construe the following, see Düsterd.

Attributes of the 144,000: 1. **They are virgins** (παρθένοι, virgin-like [*Jungfräuliche*] the Greek term is applied to men as well as to women) in a religious sense; they have kept themselves pure from idolatry (Coccei., Grot., *et al.*), ideal iconoclasts, who, it may be, even as heathen, perceived the myths to be but symbols. The words [παρθένοι γάρ εἰσιν] have been infelicitously referred to monkish asceticism by Roman Catholic exegetes; to celibacy (Augustine, Bede, Rothe, Düsterdieck); to chastity (Hengstenberg; abstinence from all fornication, De Wette); to the Christians of the last days (Hofmann). And thus the symbolism of the entire Old Testament, bearing upon this point, has been unable to obtain a foothold in the minds of

these commentators. And the flimsy deductions which Neander and others (also Düsterdieck especially, see his note, p. 466) have drawn from the misunderstanding, are a result of this ignoring of the Old Testament symbol, a recognition of which should the more assuredly have been induced by the fact that this virginity forms the extreme contrast to the extreme abomination of idolatry, *viz.*: the worship of the Beast.*

2. **These** (with emphasis) **are they who follow the Lamb**, *etc.*—Düsterdieck and others lay stress upon the present, *follow*, in order to confute the interpretation of the term as a preterite, expressive of the following of Christ to tribulation and death (Grot., Bengel, Hengstenberg). They are the constant attendants of the Lamb, it is declared. The latter thought, however, is inclusive of the former one, even as it is also the result of it. ["If He goes to Gethsemane, they follow Him thither; if He goes to Calvary, they take up their cross and follow Him thither. He is gone to Heaven, and they will be with Him there also." WORDSWORTH.—E. R. C.]

3. **These were bought**.—Emphasis is laid upon the personal worth of these souls by the repetition of οὗτοι. They are redeemed [bought] in a special sense, agreeably to their destination of being an ἀπαρχή for God and the Lamb. ["*Redeemed from among men*—language derived from the Book of Exodus: 'The first-born of my sons I redeem' (Ex. xiii. 15; xxxiv. 20). This exhibits the 144,000 as representing all God's ransomed people."—E. R. C.]

Does ἀπαρχή constitute an antithesis to the entire world (in accordance with De Wette, *et al.*, comp. Jas. i. 18), or, which is more probable, to the general throng of believers (Ewald), or of the blessed (Bengel, Düsterd., *et al.*)? In accordance with the distinction made, ch. vii., between the 144,000 and the innumerable multitude, a special selection is likewise intended here. In this view, the difference between the Augustine-Calvinistic and the Biblical doctrine of election is clearly apparent.

---

* [ALFORD: "There are two ways of understanding these words. Either they may be *figurative*, implying that the pure ones lived in all chastity, whether in single or in married life, and incurred no pollution (see 2 Cor. xi. 2); or they may be meant *literally*, that these purest ones had lived in that state of which St. Paul says, 1 Cor. vii 1, καλὸν ἀνθρώπῳ γυναικὸς μὴ ἅπτεσθαι; and as between these two meanings, I conceive, that the somewhat emphatic position of μετὰ γυναικῶν goes some way to decide. It is not ἐμολύνθησαν, the fact of impurity in allowed intercourse, but μετὰ γυναικῶν that is put forward, the fact of commerce with women. I would therefore believe that in the description of these who are the first fruits from the earth, the feature of virginity is to be taken in its literal meaning. Nor need any difficulty be found in this. It is on all hands granted that he who is married in the Lord enters into holy relations or which the single have no experience, and goes through blessed and elevating degrees of self-sacrifice, and loving allowance, and preferring others before himself. . . But neither on the other hand can it be denied that the state of holy virginity has also its peculiar blessings and exemptions. Of these, the Apostle himself speaks of that absence of distraction from the Lord's work, which is apt to beset the married. busy as they are with the cares of a household and with pleasing one another. And another and primary blessing is, that in them that fountain of carnal desire has never been opened which is so apt to be a channel for unholy thoughts and an access for the tempter. The virgins may thus have missed the victory over the lusts of the flesh; but they have also in great part escaped the conflict. Theirs is not the triumph of the toil-worn and stained soldier, but the calm and the unspottedness of those who have kept from the strife."—E. R. C.]

4. **In their mouth was not found false-hood.**—" The term ψεῦδος (comp. ch. xxi.27) is to be apprehended in its general import, and not to be limited to the falsehood of idolatry (Grot.: *non vocarunt deos, qui dii non sunt,* Bengel), heresy, or a denial of Christ (Hengstenberg)." Düsterdieck. This deliverance is more than half recanted by the remark that a certain antithesis to the sphere of falsehood in which the seducing pseudo-prophet moves, is obvious, (after Ewald, Ebrard). Idolatry is the primary form of falsehood, see Rom. i. Summation of attributes: **For they are blameless.**—Here, again, their æonic disposition is cited as the basis of their temporal conduct; as in ver. 4: *for they are virgins.*

In discussing the design of this vision it must first of all be stated that, in accordance with the construction of the whole Book, the vision has not a backward reference to ch. xiii., but a forward reference to ch. xvi., as a life-picture of the final σωτηρία contrasted with the final Judgment. Church-historical interpretations of particular details—of which are of a remarkable character—see in Düsterdieck, p. 468, and De Wette, p. 143. Christiani's reference of the 144,000 to the Church of the last time agrees better with the context than many another interpretation. A reference to the *Israelitish* Church of the end [Luthardt] belongs to a Judaizing chiliasm.

Vers. 6 and 7. **Another Angel.**—The reference of the expression " *another* Angel " to Angels who have previously appeared upon the scene (De Wette, Düsterdieck), is untenable. The difficulty of ἄλλος was, perhaps, the cause of its omission in Cod. B.; see above.—**Flying.**—Comp. ch. viii. 13.—**In mid-heaven.**—A herald to the whole world.—**An everlasting gospel.**—Ebrard: " The older exegetes, together with Lücke, are probably right in understanding the import of the tidings to be salvation in Christ generally." (Note by the same com.: *"* Of course this apprehension does not in the slightest degree justify the arbitrary allegoristic references of the three Angels to Wickliffe, Huss, and Luther, and the like. Calovius understood by the first two Angels Luther and Chemnitz, most coolly appropriating to himself the honor of being the third."—In conjunction, that is, with the other opponents of syncretism; see De Wette on this passage; also Düsterd., p. 474.) Other interpretations of the three Angels, see collected in De Wette, p. 147 (Peter de Bruis, Wickliffe, Luther, *etc.*). Ebrard refers the Angel of the everlasting Gospel to the preaching of the Gospel amongst the heathen, which, according to Matt. xxiv., precedes the end. But though the old Gospel is, in respect of its purport, an eternal Gospel, it should, as the Gospel of *principial* salvation, be distinguished from the Gospel of the *final* redemption to eternal felicity; and the new proclamation, of which the present passage speaks, is not for the heathen alone, but for the whole earth. One-sided, but not incorrect, is the explanation of Corn. à-Lapide: A message promissory of the eternal good things in Heaven. According to Hengstenberg, the message of the Angel is a Gospel [even for the enemies of God], inasmuch as his exhorta-

tion to repentance is conjoined with the grant of a respite for repentance. But there is no intimation here of a respite for repentance in the strict sense of the words. The last-named commentator interprets the attribute *eternal* as having reference solely to the irrevocability or certainty of this Gospel. On the reference of this Angel to Luther, comp. Hengstenberg, II., p. 133. **To declare glad tidings unto them,** *etc* — The fact that this message is not addressed simply to the *heathen* who may still be left (Ebrard, p. 408), is clearly evident from the further explication of those for whom it is intended: **to every nation,** *etc.* Neither can it be said that the Angel's exhortation to repentance is distinct from his message of joy;—the message in its totality is *the everlasting Gospel,* in the form of a parænesis [παραίνεσις].

The general character of the exhortation:—**Fear God,** *etc.,* rests upon the law that the preaching of the end goes back to the preaching of the beginning; and *that* partly on account of the fact that most Christians have learned very little from Christianity, and that there is now no time to lose. The *fear of God,* according to the text, would be for many the beginning of salvation, as it is elsewhere declared to be the beginning of wisdom. Finally, in the eternal Gospel, the form shall have become transparent for the universal Gospel, and a real worship of God, **Who,** besides **the Heaven, has made the earth and the sea and fountains of waters**—all in a symbolical sense—would be the actual foundation of conversion, the beginning of all Christian development. This Gospel is, certainly, conditioned, but, as conditioned, it is also a real Gospel (see Luke xxi. 28). It cannot be denied that the passage is suggestive of man's absolute dependence upon God, as opposed to a false dependence upon, and subserviency to, the Beast;—the particular truth, however, which it is designed to exhibit is, that the judicial power of God is based upon the fact that He is the Creator of all things.

Ver. 8. **And another, second Angel,** *etc.* —It is not on account of the dramatic vividness of the scene that one Angel follows another (Düsterd.), but because of the rapid succession of particular items in the approaching judgment—a truth of which Grotius was sensible when he commented thus: *Quot rei nunciandæ, totidem nuntii.*

Fallen.—One of the sublimest words of consolation for advanced Christians. Comp. Is. xiv. Before God, the thing is decided; the decision on earth approaches. The passage is, therefore, a proleptical description, in prophetic form, of an imminent event (see ch. xi. 18).—Triumphant certainty is expressed in the repetition: **fallen!**

Babylon the great.—*Babel* was, even in Genesis, the primeval type of a *God-opposed* world-power; in the Prophets, Babel [or Babylon] became the greatest type of the *anti-theocratic* world-power; and here the typical expression is perfected in the type of the *anti-Christian* world-power. Godless self-exaltation (Dan. iv. 30), apparent crushing omnipotence over against the Church of God, and perfect impotence in face of the suddenly approaching storms of Divine judgment—are the individual features of the type. Here, however, as has already been remarked, the reference is, not to Babylon in the narrower sense of the term, but to Babylon in the most general sense, culminating, of course, in Babylon in the more restricted sense.

Who gave all the nations to drink of the wine of the anger [or rage] of her fornication.—*Wine* is a symbol of enthusiasm; *fornication* is a symbol of idolatry; and ϑυμός in this connection is the wrathful [angry] zeal of fanaticism.* As fanaticism, in its lust of rule and its intolerance, corresponds with internal irreligiousness and profligacy, so idolatry itself corresponds with actual unchastity. These characteristics are found combined in the religion of ancient Babylon, and is in process of constant development, corresponding to the increasingly God-opposed character of the world-powers. Various have been the false interpretations of the **wine of anger**, as *e. g.*, *poisoned wine* and *ardent wine*—explanations rightly rejected by Düsterdieck. Yet the expression can not be regarded as significant purely of the wine of the anger of God; rather, together with the anger of the heathen [nations] or the Harlot, the reaction of the Divine anger develops into judgment (see ch. xi. 18; xvii. 4; comp. Rom. i. 21 sqq.). Thus the *fornication* also is not simply "fornication committed with great Babylon" (Düsterdieck), but, above all, the fornication of the Harlot herself (see Jer. xxv. 15; li. 7). De Wette and others assert that this Babylon is pagan Rome solely (Tertull., Augustine, *etc.*); not papal Rome (Vitringa, Bengel, *et al.*), or Jerusalem (Abauzit, Herder, *et al.*), not even the wicked world or world-power (Andreas, Bede, *et al.*). Hengstenberg also confounds Babylon in the wider and Babylon in the narrower sense (ch. xviii.). Similarly Ebrard. It should, indeed, be observed that the judgment upon the great universal world-Babylon commences with the judgment upon Babylon in the narrower sense of the term.

Vers. 9-11. And another, third Angel.— He proclaims the code or norm of judgment in an eschatological form.—**With a great voice.** —This clause is wanting in the description of the *second* Angel. Hengstenberg thinks that this is because the proclamation of the *second* Angel is related to that of the *first* as the particular to the general, whilst the proclamation of the *third* Angel is of a general cast again. The distinction, however, lies also, and in a greater degree, in the purport of the announcements **If any one worshippeth the Wild-beast,** see ch. xiii.—**He also shall drink,** *etc.*—Düsterdieck: "Καὶ αὐτός (comp. ver. 17) represents the individual as incurring judgment equally with the Harlot herself (compare Ewald)" A nearer reference of the καὶ αὐτός would, perhaps, be to the fact that he has previously, in company with the Beast himself drunk the wine of anger of Antichristian fanaticism, and presented the same to others (see ch. ix. 17, 18; xiii. 10; Hengstenberg, II., p. 151). Taken in the abstract, the reference to the Beast would also give a good

sense. The meaning is that none shall be able to excuse himself on the plea that the Beast or the False Prophet seduced him; every one who has worshipped Antichrist shall be personally responsible for the fact—he himself, man for man. An important rule, as opposed to those who hold that individuals belonging to a great mass are personally excused from responsibility. The error is the greater when it includes the belief that the holiness-treasures of a heavily indebted hierarchical system * are available for personal profiting.

Of the anger of God.—Anger for anger— the holy coming as a retribution upon the evil. **Which is mingled** [=poured out—prepared] **unmixed.**—The expression, literally apprehended, contains a contradiction; it must, therefore, be taken as an oxymoron. Now if, with Wetstein and others, we take κεράν in the trite sense of *to pour out*, no distinct point is visible. The explanation of Züllig: "pure essence of mixtures" [spices, *etc.*], needs not to be refuted. Hengstenberg, on the other hand, seems to hit the point: "In the Divine wine of anger, mixture with water corresponds to the element of grace, of compassion. The entire absence of such an element is represented here." Düsterdieck calls this comment artificial. [See Text. AND GRAM., NOTE 19.—E. R. C.] **In the cup of His wrath.**—Here ὀργή appears—the stronger form of ϑυμός. [See Text. AND GRAM., note 29.—E. R. C.] **Tormented with fire and brimstone.**— Ch. ix. 17: xx. 10. "The hell punishment here described may not be resolved, in accordance with Grotius, into pangs of conscience." (Düsterd.). It goes on, however: **In the presence of holy angels and of the Lamb.** Can this be said of the torments of hell, in the strict sense of the term? The torments of hell resultant upon a being cast into the *lake of fire* are spoken of later. Do they not begin, however, in this life, especially at the end of time, where time and eternity come in contact with each other? The *fire* is the glow of passionate self-consumption; the *brimstone* is an envelopment in the fuel of irritability and irritation— a fuel constantly blazing up afresh with new ardor; the pangs of conscience are as yet in the background, or at least form but a part of the torment. On the Old Testament types of punishment by fire, see Hengstenberg, II., p. 150. A leading passage bearing upon the subject is Is. lxvi. 24. ["See ch. xx. 10, and Is. xxxiv. 9, 10, from which the imagery comes. De Wette is certainly wrong in interpreting ἐνώπιον, *nach dem Urtheile—in the judgment of.* It is literal, and the meaning as in Luke xvi. 23 sqq., that the torments are visible to the angels and the Lamb." ALFORD.—E. R. C.] **And the smoke of their torment.**—Ch. xix. 3; Is. xxxiv. 10; Matt. xxv. 41. Smoke is

* [Whether the *indebtedness* has a human or a Divine bearing—*i. e.*, whether it signifies the issue, by the system in question, of more promissory notes than its capital will cover,—or whether it is indicative of a moral involvement toward God—the German leaves undecided (*Heiligkeitsschätze eines schwer verschuldeten hierarchischen Systems*); Dr. Lange's somewhat frequent use of the *equivoque*, however, favors the idea that both aspects of the matter were contemplated by him.—Ta.]

* [See TEXT. AND GRAM. (note 16) *in loc.*—E R.C.]

a phenomenon attendant upon imperfect combustion. If they burned with free devotion in sacrificial fire, they would blaze refulgently, without smoke; the more the flame is restrained by resistance, the thicker and blacker is the smoke which pours forth. Hence, also, βασανισμός is not pure [passive] suffering, but a racking or torturing process. Hengstenberg: "They have no rest day and night from being tormented"—with reference to ch. xx. 10, and in opposition to Vitringa, who interpreted the passage as referring to the torment of conscience.
They have not rest by day and by night.—Absolute unrest or excitement—a frantic condition, therefore—forms the spiritual aspect of their βασανισμός.

Who worship, etc.—The present form of the verb must not be overlooked. The offence continues along with the βασανισμός. It is not: who worshipped. With the punishment, the crime which at the first merited that punishment, endures.

Ver. 12. **Here is the endurance** [Lange: **patience**], etc—Are these words a digression of the Seer, or are they the concluding utterance of the Angel? In accordance with the analogy of ch. xiii. 10 (comp. also ver. 18), they are a practical digression of the Seer. Thus Hengstenberg regards them: "The verse has reference to the point of view, the purpose to which the foregoing is subservient." Does this mean that the warning against this hell-punishment is the source of the patience [endurance] of the saints? This is about the theory maintained by those who occupy a legal stand-point; it was the theory of the Middle Ages, and is still the theory of the most popular Protestant sermons which advocate a turning from sin to holiness principally on the ground of the pain thereby to be escaped. The patience [endurance] of the saints, however, has its source in the righteousness of God, in that sacred and Divine justice which is here depicted in characters of flame (see ch. xiii. 10). The explanation: Here is the place for patience, here it must give proof of itself (De Wette, Hengstenberg, Ebrard), virtually translates ὧδε by hither! which, undoubtedly, in and for itself gives a good sense; it is also mediately to be retained as a challenge, as is evidenced by the subsequent sentence. The construction οἱ τηροῦντες "is informal, like ch. i. 5; ii. 20" (Düsterdieck). In the sense of the Seer, however, a second ὧδε is, probably, presupposed. The expression: **The commandments of God and the faith of Jesus**, is, doubtless, of wider scope than the distinction of Law and Gospel. The whole of revelation is grounded in the eternal righteousness of God, and culminates in the faith of Jesus, which is principially the steadfastness of Jesus Himself.

Ver. 13. **And I heard a voice.**—We cannot fix this voice upon any distinct person [i. e., "saint or Elder" (Hengstenberg)]; nor are there two voices (the first voice and the speaking Spirit, Züllig). It is the voice of God's Spirit Himself in the Church Trumphant, in His sympathy with the Church in the last time. The temptation to apostasy is more prevalent than ever: **Blessed are the dead who die in the Lord.** Düsterdieck (in accordance with

most commentators) rightly distinguishes between the theme, which closes with ἀπάρτι, and the subsequent rationale. On a preposterous reference of ἀπάρτι to the last sentence, see Düsterdieck. With Cocceius and Hammond, we firmly adhere to the view that the proposition does not simply contain a general consolatory truth, but that it has a special bearing upon the last troublous time. Those, however, who die in the Lord are not to be apprehended as martyrs of the old style (Züllig); for the expression is not: die for the Lord's sake (Grotius, et al.), but in Him, in positive fellowship with Him.—**Henceforth** is by Roman Catholic exegetes explained (Stern) as intimating that the intermediate state of purgatory is now [at the end of the world] done away with; by De Wette, Hengstenberg, Düsterdieck, it is interpreted as signifying that the glorious end is near—hence also the perfect beatification of believers. This explanation should be retained only upon the condition that special stress be laid upon μακάριοι, with reference to the temptations and trials of the last time; but precisely this has previously been disallowed by Düsterdieck. Our explanation of the manifoldly interpreted ἵνα is indicated in the translation of the text given in the beginning of this chapter. See the author's Dogmatik, p. 1243.

["The mention of the endurance of the saints brings with it the certainty of persecution unto death. The present proclamation declares the blessedness of all who die not only in persecution, but in any manner in the Lord, in the faith and obedience of Christ. And the special command to write this, conveys special comfort to those in all ages of the Church who should read it. But it is not so easy to assign a fit meaning to ἀπάρτι. That it belongs to the preceding sentence, not to the following one, is, I conceive, plain. . . . . And, thus joined with the former sentence, it must express some reason why this blessedness is to be more completely realized from this time when it was proclaimed than it was before. Now this reason will quickly appear, if we consider the particular time, in connexion with the proclamation which is made. The harvest of the earth is about to be reaped; the vintage of the earth to be gathered. At this time it is, that the complete blessedness of the holy dead commences: when the garner is filled and the chaff cast out. And that not on account of their deliverance from any purgatorial fires, but because of the completion of this number of their brethren, and the full capacities of bliss brought in by the resurrection." ALFORD.—"The language is evidently not to be construed as implying that they who had died in the faith before were not happy, but that in the times of trial and persecution that were to come, they were to be regarded as peculiarly blessed who should escape from these sorrows by a Christian death." BARNES.—E. R. C.]

For [Lange: **But**] **their works follow with them.**—A rejection of the bare idea of reward is detrimental to the idea of retribution itself. The same spirituality of Theology which combats the idea of legal merit as pertaining to works, has also to maintain the truth that those works of believers which have been done in God have become for the performers of them not simply powers and virtues of the new life, but also riches of that life. The κόποι, as such, are left here—from them the blessed *rest;* but as ἔργα, as ideal operations, they pass with them, as their escort, into eternity. Not simply the memory of their deeds accompanies them, but also the love-blessing of this whole world in which they have helped to build the future. [May not the distinction be this : They rest from their *labors* (service rendered with *fatigue* and *pain*), but their *works* (service to be rendered without fatigue and pain) follow them ? See *Add. Comments* on ch. vii. 15, and *foot-note* (*) (2d column), p. 154.—E. R. C.]

Ver. 14. **And I saw, and behold** (a new vision-wonder, the Judgment scene itself).—The Angels of the *announcement* of Judgment are succeeded by the Angels of the *execution* of Judgment; Christ being, as before, at the head. Düsterdieck's superscription of the following section : "further figurative announcements of the now imminent judgment," overlooks the antithesis between this section and the preceding one.—**A white cloud.**—Commencement of Christ's Parousia. The fact that Christ alone can be intended is manifest not only from the attribute of the **golden crown** and the parallelism with Dan. vii. 13; Matt. xxvi. 64, but also from the harmonious contrast between vers. 14 and 1. In the latter passage, Christ stands, as the Lamb, on Mount Sion, keeping holy-day in the midst of the Triumphant Church; in the former, the King Militant appears on the white cloud to execute judgment upon the world. Even the parallelism which the three following Angels of execution sustain toward the three preceding Angels of announcement, serves as evidence that none other than Christ can be intended.* Hence, Düsterdieck rightly rejects the interpretation of the figure as an Angel (Grotius, *et al.*), or as heroic princes, proclaimers of the principles of evangelic truth (Vitringa).—**A sharp sickle.** —The implement of harvest in the hand—a symbol of beginning judgment.

Ver. 15. **Another Angel.**—No reference is had to ver. 14, nor to the preceding Angels (Düsterdieck); the reference is to the two following Angels; see above.—**Send forth thy sickle.**—Such a command is, certainly, not in harmony with the position of a real Angel ; assuredly, however, the decree of the Father (see above) is most aptly set forth in a symbolical Angel.

Ver. 16. **Cast His sickle.**—The commencement of the judgment, therefore, precedes the actual Parousia of Christ.† The Harlot, or Babylon, is first judged through the Beast (ch. xvii. 16) ; then follows the appearance of Christ, for the destruction of the Beast himself (ch. xix. 11). Babylon, or the fallen theocracy, is destroyed by mankind ; the Antichristian bestialization and deification of man is destroyed by Christ; Satan, with his rabble rout, is destroyed

by God the Father.—**And the earth was reaped.**—This is the true harvesting of the fruit, the net produce of the harvest-fields of earth for God (Matt. xxiv. 31).*

Ver. 17. **Another Angel.**—This Angel represents the judgment of reprobation, or the dark side of the Judgment. According to Hengstenberg, this Angel is Christ Himself again. It is wrong to suppose either that Christ only is intended or that a mere ordinary Angel is meant. Why should not the Angel, as a symbolical unit, represent that plurality of Angels, who, according to Matt. xiii. 41, are the executioners of judgment ? The present passage is not identical with ch. xix. 15, nor with Is. lxiii. Certainly, Christ is Himself the Judge in reference to the reprobate as well as to the blessed, but the Angel, as such, is the symbol of a manifestation of Christ which must be distinguished from Christ Himself. Hengstenberg sees in this Angel a terrible warning to those who might suffer themselves to be driven by fear into concessions; he does not say, however, what concessions he means—the expression is so indefinite that it might even mean concessions *against* the hierarchy.

Vers. 18, 19. **And another Angel.**—See chs. viii. 3; xvi. 7. The *altar* here is not the *altar of burnt-offering* on earth, but the *altar of incense* in Heaven.—**Out of the altar;** this can be said only of a symbolical Angel. The mythical idea of a fire-angel (De Wette) must be rejected (see above).

Gather the clusters of the vine of the earth.—Hengstenberg: "Such an antithesis between the *harvest* and the *vintage* as is assumed by Bengel, is not *indicated* by any feature of the description." Manifestly, however, the first harvest, as the fruit harvest [*fruit*—in the primitive sense of that which is profitable and good. —TR.], is characterized by the fact that the harvest-field has become dry or white in appearance; the grapes, on the other hand, are full of grape-blood. See Ebrard, pp. 416-18. Compare Joel iii. 18. The remarkable choice of the figure of the *vine,* the *grape,* and the *blood of the grape* might, primarily, be based upon the fact that the vintage comes later than the wheat-harvest—thus signifying that the judgment upon the wicked is not until after the ingathering of the righteous. To this, however, must be added the consideration that Christ calls Himself ἡ ἄμπελος ἡ ἀληθινή, an expression suggestive of the contrast of a vine which is such in a merely symbolical, unreal sense. Such an one was the Old Testament Theocratic Church at first. The whole vineyard early became corrupted, however, according to Is. v. The vine was laid waste, Ps. lxxx. It became a degenerate vine, Hos. x. 1; Jer. ii. 21; Deut. xxxii. 32. It is to be given over to judgment, Ezek. xvii. 6-10. The fact that the Old Testament vineyard, with its vines, has become a fief [*Lehnsbesitz,* the old feudal term=estate in loan, trust-estate] of the New Testament Church of God, is declared by the parable Matt. xxi. 33 sqq. Christ, the true [*wesentlich*=essential, genuine] Vine, is the author of true [see preceding parenthesis] eternal

---

* [For a different view, see abstract of Lord, p. 283.— E. R. C.]

† [This conclusion does not follow. If the appearance of the Son of Man on the white cloud be the "commencement of Christ's Parousia" (see *comment* on ver. 14), then, manifestly, the *casting forth of the sickle* does not *precede* that Parousia.—E. R. C.]

* [For a contrary view, see abstract of Stuart, p. 282.— E. R. C.]

joy and inspiration; the symbolical vine of the New Testament Church, therefore, in so far as it differs from Christ, is a vine which attains its maturity in spurious enthusiasms, fanatical and untrue joys and festivals. The most terrible thing in its degeneracy, however, is the fact that its clusters acquire their juice [*Blut*] by blood-shed—that it has been the author, to a constantly increasing extent, of demonic joys of bloodthirstiness; hence pure blood flows from it when it is trodden in the wine-press, and the conception *grape-blood* or *juice* is exchanged, with fearful irony, for *blood* (see Is. lxiii. 3). The base lying thought is the following: as much blood as the vine has drunk in, shall be pressed out of it again in **the great wine-press of the anger of God.**

Ver. 20. **Without the city.**—Explained by most commentators of Jerusalem; by others of Rome. In the symbolical apprehension of the passage, only the City of God can be meant. But is this the Church, as Hengstenberg maintains, or the heavenly Jerusalem, as Bede, *et al.*, affirm? The external Church, at all events, can not be intended, since the text treats of the end of the world, a time when the Church is fallen. The visible appearance of the heavenly Jerusalem (ch. xxi. 2), however, is preceded by the Judgment—in the first (ch. xviii. 24; xix. 2), second (ch. xix. 17 sqq.), and even third instance (ch. xx. 9). Nothing, therefore, save the vital Church of God of the last time can be understood—in its quality, incontrovertibly, of passing into the visible appearance of the heavenly Jerusalem and the imperishable City of God (ch. xxi.); as, on the other hand, the treading of the grapes begins with the judgment upon Babylon (to which judgment it seems, also, to have special reference), but extends through the subsequent judgments into the æons. We are of opinion that this æonic duration is that which is denoted by the 1600 stadia (see above). —In view of all this, therefore, the application of *without the City* to the contrast of Heaven is not entirely incorrect, but too external. Curious interpretations of the *reins*, see in Düsterdieck's note, p. 478. [Alford regards the City as that of ch. xi. 2, *viz.*: Jerusalem; so also Barnes, *etc.*; Wordsworth, as the *New* Jerusalem; Lord, as that by which the apostate hierarchies are represented.—E. R. C.]

For a thousand *and* six hundred stadia. —By this we understand a punitory suffering extending beyond this present æon into future æons, a state of misery to which the eye can see no limit. Manifold interpretations of the number, see in De Wette. The complete number 1000 and the age of Noah at the time of the deluge (Andreas). The number 4×400, denoting the expanse of the earth and the four regions of Heaven (Victorinus, *et al.*). The length of Palestine (Bengel, *et al.*), with reference to Jerome. Extension of the Roman dominion (Mede). The British Islands (Brightman: the Reformation; Cranmer: the Angel, ver. 18!). Martyrdom of converted heathen (Alcasar). According to Ebrard, the number should be analyzed by 40. "The number 40 is the number of punishment; 40×40 is, therefore, the number of involved punishment." An involved

19

[mathematical sense] temporal measure of punishment of some 1600 years does not exactly coincide, however, with the æonic succession of judgment.

Ch. xv. 1. **Another sign in the Heaven.** —The Seer has already beheld the unitous phenomenon of the final Judgment; he now sees the historic preparation and development of the same in the succession and intensification of the Anger-Vials or *judgments of hardening.* The antithesis to the sign in ch. xiv. 14 is the pragmatical preparation of the Judgment. The sign, moreover, is a sign *in the Heaven*; it still belongs to the Heaven-picture. "The greatness and marvellousness of the sign does not lie solely in the fact that seven Angels—not Archangels (Züllig, Stern; comp. De Wette)—appear simultaneously, but also in their peculiar equipment: ἔχοντας πληγὰς ἑπτά" (Düsterdieck). Hengstenberg thinks that even before the reception of the Vials they might have been recognized as the Angels of the *seven plagues* by some sign—especially by eyes like flames of fire. Züllig, De Wette, Ebrard, Düsterdieck, rightly regard the vision of ver. 1 as the superscription of the immediately following section, as the Angels themselves do not issue from the Temple until ver. 5 (in opposition to the conception of Hengstenberg). We do not think, however, that the section under this superscription reaches to ch. xvi. 21 (Düsterd.), but hold that it ends at ver. 8, since with ch. xvi. 1 a new picture—the Earth-picture—begins.

The seven plagues—the last.—That is, the eschatological last anger-strokes, which bring in the final Judgment; these plagues are, manifestly, characterized as *judgments of hardening.* **The last:** This term is, on the one hand, not to be construed as having reference to individual life, or to be taken partially (Bengel); but on the other hand, neither should it be confounded with the final Judgment itself (Hengstenberg), as Düsterdieck justly remarks. Ἐτελέσθη denotes not so much the *coming to an end* as the *consummation*, the *full development* of the anger of God. Even in this point the New Testament preserves its *septenary*, in contrast to the *ten* plagues under which Pharaoh and the Egyptians hardened themselves. As, however, those plagues were instrumental to the redemption of the people of Israel, so are these instrumental to the perfect redemption of the New Testament Church of God. For the unitous mass of the earth all plagues do indeed come to an end with the last of these plagues; it is not so in the case of the enemies of Christ.

Vers. 2-4. **And I saw as it were [Lange: an appearance as].**—It might be queried: Is not this a second and therefore superfluous pre-celebration of the Judgment, since we have already had one pre-celebration of it in ch. xiv. 1-5? That, however, was the general pre-celebration of the entire Judgment, with reference to the Church Triumphant and its escape from said Judgment; here we have the more special pre-celebration of the *plagues of anger*, the second part of the Heaven-picture. The antithesis to the fearful stormy succession of those last strokes of anger is formed by the *crystal sea*— the world-history of the saints, calmed and clarified in God; the antithesis to the impenitent world on the earth is formed by the *conquerors* by [on] the crystal sea; the antithesis to the blasphemies of those visited by the plagues is formed by the heavenly celebration in song, and adoration of the righteous judgments of God.

As a glassy [Lange: **crystal**] **sea mingled with fire**, see ch. iv. 6.—Düsterdieck justly remarks, against Ebrard, that the article [before *sea*] must be absent because it is only the *image* of a crystal sea that is spoken of. The greater stress must be laid upon this circumstance, since the idea of a crystal surface of sea mingled with fire does not come within the possibilities of thought, and hence Ewald, in consequence of his insisting upon the reality [materiality] of the image has arrived at the conception of an "ineffably seething and foaming mass, a fiery broth" (see Düsterdieck, p. 484). The image of a crystal-clear sea in Heaven may, however, readily appear as though illuminated and reddened by the fiery glare of the Anger-Vials on earth; and this very reflection is expressed in the song of praise which refers to the judgments of God; moreover, the clarified world-history has itself passed through the fire of earthly world-history (see p. 84 and ch. iv. 6). ["The addition, μεμιγμένην πυρί, is probably made as bringing into the previous celestial imagery an element belonging to this portion of the prophecy, of which *judgment* is the prevailing complexion." ALFORD.—E. R. C.]

And I saw those conquering.—To this passage, again, a great and confused mass of interpretations attaches. De Wette: The multitude and glory of the blessed (And., Areth.). Baptism (Primas., *et al.*). The Divine truth in which believers have their station (Vitringa). Multitude of the heathen (Alcas.). Gentile Christians (Grotius). De Wette: The atmosphere. The last named commentator rejects the reference to the brazen sea in the Temple, but assumes a reference to Israel's passage through the Red Sea. The *fire* has also been variously interpreted: Trial-fire (Andreas; others: temptation, persecution, conflict). Martyrdom (Primas.). Love (Grot.), *etc.* See De Wette, p. 152. According to Düsterdieck, the *crystal sea mingled with fire* denotes the unity of the beatific grace and the judiciary righteousness of God. The *conquerors* are not simply martyrs (in accordance with Eichhorn, Ewald, *et al.*), neither are they (because of the present: νικῶντας) such as are still in the conflict; they are, in a proleptical representation (De Wette), the congregation of victors, especially those of the last time, over against the great plagues of the last time and those who blaspheme under them. 'Εκ τοῦ θηρίον undoubtedly does not mean that they have destroyed the power of the Beast; from this fact, however, it does not follow that it must mean: away from the Beast [*vom Thiere weg*], as if they had kept themselves at a distance from him.

[**On** (or **by**) **the glassy sea** —"Does ἐπί import actually *upon*, so that they stood *on the surface of the sea*, or merely *on the shore of?* On every account the latter seems the more probable, as better suiting the heavenly imagery of ch. iv., and as according with the situation of the children of Israel when they sung the song

to which allusion is presently made. The sense may be constructionally justified by ch. iii. 20, and viii. 3." ALFORD.—E. R. C.]

Harps of God.—Tuned solely for the praise of God (Beng.).

Ver. 3. **And they sing**, *etc.*—The *song of Moses* is the lyrical celebration of the typical redemption by Moses; the *song of the Lamb* the celebration of the real redemption by the Lamb; and the *two songs in their unity* as one song are the lyrical celebration of the Old and New Testament revelation faith, in view of the whole redemption which began with Moses, was decided with Christ, and is now thoroughly consummated through the fiery judgments of God. Not two songs, therefore, sung respectively by Old and New Testament believers (Andr.); not the song of Moses applied to Christ and the things of Christ (Grotius); not a song composed at once by Moses and by the Lamb (Ewald, Düsterd.); but the whole redemption as mediated by Moses and Christ, with a distinct reference to the song of Moses and the passage through the Red Sea, as a type of the passage through those rivers of fire by which the faithful of the last time shall be separated from the hardened sinners of that time.

Great and marvellous, *etc.*—The thought of Vitringa: *Canticum Mosis habet spiritualem et mysticum sensum, secundum quem si accipiatur fit canticum agni*, contains something of truth inasmuch as even in the song of Moses, together with the omnipotence of God, which destroyed the enemy and saved the people of Israel, the manifestation of His holiness is especially magnified, and it is also even intimated that the whole event must make a startling and a relatively awakening impression upon the heathen. Comp. Ex. xv. 14-16 with the conclusion of the song in the Apocalypse.

Vers. 3, 4. The song first glorifies, in an objective *contemplation* of the Judgment, the marvellous, all-swaying, kingly rule of God over the world, in particular over the nations—a governance now attaining its consummate appearance, especially in the righteousness and truth (absolute consistency and faithfulness) of His ways. Then, secondly, it declares the impression made by this rule upon the conquerors: it produces the most sacred awe of the holiness of God, and a joyful enthusiasm which prompts them to praise His name as it shines in the perfection of His revelation. Thirdly, the song expresses the prophetic expectation of the effect which these judgments of God shall produce upon the world of nations;—a genuine New Testament trait ■■ expressive of the hope that many shall yet be converted even under the ministry of the Vials of Anger, Ex. ix. 16, xiv. 7; Ps. cxxvi. 2; Micah vii. 16.—In ver. 4, as well as in ch. xvi. 5, ὅσιος is used "in reference to God, which is unusual."

Ver. 5. **Opened was the Temple.**—It is more precisely defined as the **Temple of the Tabernacle of the witness**. According to Grotius, Ebrard and others, the Holy of Holies is itself intended; according to Ewald and Düsterdieck, the Sanctuary proper is intended, as an adjunct to the Holy of Holies. Hengstenb.: "The Temple in its quality of being the place of the testimony." The Temple as the Sanctuary, in contrast to the Holy of Holies, also needed not now first to be opened; see *Syn. View.*—Be it further observed that the *seven Angels* are symbolical figures of anger in the ramification and course of its domination. ["The *vaός* is the holy place of the Tabernacle, to which latter the appellation *τοῦ μαρτυρίου* is here peculiarly appropriate, seeing that the *witness* and *covenant* of God are about to receive their great fulfillment." ALFORD.—E. R. C.]

Ver. 6. **Clothed in linen pure** *and* **glistening.**—Their adornment is similar to that of Christ. Their import also is, doubtless, connected with that of the Archangel Michael. The reading *λίθον* gives occasion to many debates here (see Düsterdieck, p. 486). Clothed with Christ, the Jewel, or with the ornament of the **vir** ues (Andreas)? This is destitute of all appropriate meaning, and about the same remark may be applied to the explanation that (with reference to Ezek. xxviii. 13) a garment bestudded with precious stones might be understood. In conjunction with such a *λίθος* the adjective *λαμπρός* would be rather superfluous, and *καθαρός*, at all events, would be inappropriate.

Ver. 7. **And one of the four Living-beings** [Lange: **Life-shapes**].—Here, likewise, the false interpretation reappears, according to which the four so-called Beasts are representatives of the *creature*, and hence one of them appears because the plagues concern the whole creation.—**Into the ages.**—The eternity of God surpasses the time of the seven Anger-vials. The Vials of Anger also denote *death*, unceasing and repeated—and over against them stands the eternally *Living One.*

Ver. 8. **With smoke.**—Veiling of the Divine Majesty (Bengel). Also a sign of His unapproachableness in the manifestation of His holiness. See Is. vi.; Ex. xl. 34; 1 Kings viii. 10. Comp. *Syn. View.* Different interpretations, see in De Wette, p. 154; Düsterdieck, p. 484. There are some very curious interpretations amongst those cited, as for instance that of Cocceius: The human ordinances of popery debar men from faith. Or that of Calov.: Symbol of the blindness of unbelief.

["**No one was able to enter into the Temple** (comp. 1 Kings viii. 10, 11; Ex. xl. 34, 35) **until the seven plagues of the seven Angels should be finished.**—The passages above referred to give the reason: because of the unapproachableness of God, when immediately present and working, by any created being. See Ex. xix. 21. When these judgments should be completed, then the wrathful presence and agency of God being withdrawn, He might again be approached."—ALFORD. See also the conclusion of the abstract of Stuart, p. 282.—E. R. C.]

[ADDITIONAL NOTE ON THE SECTION.]

By the American Editor.

[This section consists, as it seems to the writer, of three complete visions, and the beginning of a fourth—each relating to a period still future, and terminating with the consummation of the present æon (the æon immediately preceding the establishment of the Millennial

Kingdom). Each of these visions is independent—each contemplating matters not referred to in any of the others, and each describing events mentioned by all the others, though in a different mode and under different relations.

Vision I., ch. xiv. 1–13, is introduced by the strong disjunctive formula, Καὶ ἴδον, καὶ ἰδού, and consists of several consecutive parts.—Part *first* (vers. 1–5) contemplates the body about to possess the Kingdom—the Lamb with the completed *ἀπαρχή* (see p. 193)—standing on the Mount Sion.* It describes also the condition and character of the chosen companions of Christ.—Part *second* (vers. 6, 7) relates to a universal proclamation of the Gospel preceding the outpouring of the Vials of anger. Whether the *Angel*, in this and the following parts, denotes a *real* Angel, or symbolizes a body of men specially commissioned for the purpose indicated, it is impossible now to determine.—Part *third* (ver. 8) foretells a proclamation of the fall of Babylon (see on ch. xviii. 2).—Part *fourth* contemplates a public *proclamation* of woe to be visited upon the worshippers of the Beast; (the *execution* of the judgments set forth in this and the preceding proclamation is presented in detail in chs. xvi.–xix.)—Part *fifth* is designed for the comfort of the saints. It refers (ver. 12) to the ground of their *endurance*, viz.: the sure destruction of the power of their persecutors; and then declares (ver. 13) their certain blessedness when the trials of this life are ended.

Vision II., ch. xiv. 14–20, is introduced by the same formula as the preceding. It contemplates Christ in the exercise of His office as Ruler over all things (comp. Eph. i. 22)—(1) as gathering His ripened Church from the earth (vers. 15, 16); and (2) as executing judgment upon His enemies. This execution of judgment, as in the preceding vision, is more fully set forth in chs. xvi.–xix.

Vision III., ch. xv. 1-4, is not indeed introduced with the same formula as the preceding; it commences, however, with one equally significant. It is purely a Heaven-scene. It contemplates, on the one hand, the chosen ministers of the judgments about to be executed; and, on the other, the entire glorified Church gathered before the Throne as worshippers, and as spectators of the course of Divine Providence on earth. (Is not this assemblage the same as that mentioned ch. vii. 9? See ADD. NOTE, p. 193.)

Vision IV. begins with ch. xv. 5, and extends to the close of ch. xvii. This vision is introduced with one of the most significant disjunctive formulas employed in the Apocalypse: Καὶ μετὰ ταῦτα ἴδον (see *foot-note*, p. 150, *first column*). It consists of three parts.—Part *first*, ch. xv. 5-8, sets forth the preparation of the ministers of vengeance for their work, and the heavenly

* [It is an interesting question, Where is the Mount Sion here mentioned? Is it earthly or heavenly? In the judgment of the writer, it is heavenly. Christ as Head of the Millennial Kingdom does not come into visible manifestation (on earth) until after the pouring out of the Vials (see ch, xix. 11-16). The earthly Jerusalem and the earthly Sion are types of *places* in the glorious world where Jesus and His disembodied saints now are (comp. John iv. 2, 3; Heb. xii. 22), awaiting the time for the establishment of the Basileia and the manifestation of the Sons of God on earth.—E. R. C.]

events attendant thereupon.—Part *second*, ch. | statement concerning the Harlot and the Beast,
xvi., describes the execution of their work.— | upon whom judgment had been executed.—E.
Part *third*, ch. xvii., contains a supplemental | R. C.]

B.—REAL EARTHLY WORLD-PICTURE OF THE SEVEN VIALS OF ANGER; OR, THE END-JUDGMENT IN GENERAL.

CHAP. XVI.

And I heard a great voice out of the temple saying to the seven angels, Go your ways [om. your ways], and pour out the [ins. seven[1]] vials of the wrath
2 [anger] of God upon [into] the earth. And the first went [departed], and poured out his vial upon [into[2]] the earth; and there fell [came (ἐγένετο)] a noisome [an evil] and grievous sore[3] upon the men which [who] had the mark of the beast
3 [wild-beast], and *upon* them which [who] worshipped his image. And the second angel [om. angel[4]] poured out his vial upon [into] the sea; and it became as the [om. as the] blood [ins. as] of a dead *man* [man]: and every living soul [or soul
4 of life (ψυχὴ ζωῆς)] died [ins. , the things] in the sea. And the third angel [om. angel[5]] poured out his vial upon [into] the rivers and [ins. the] fountains of [ins.
5 the] waters; and they became blood [or there came blood (ἐγένετο[6] αἷμα)]. And I heard the angel of the waters say [saying], Thou art righteous, O Lord, [om. O Lord,] which [who] art, and [ins. who] wast, and shalt be [om. and shalt be[8]—ins. the[9] Holy], [or who art and who wast holy,][9] because thou hast judged thus [didst
6 adjudge these things].[;] For [because] they have [om. have] shed [poured out] the blood of saints and prophets, and thou hast given them blood to drink; for
7 [om. for][10] they are worthy. And I heard another out of [om. another out of][11] the altar say [saying], Even so [Yea], [ins. O] Lord [ins. the] God [ins. , the] Al-
8 mighty [or, All-Ruler[12]], true and righteous *are* thy judgments. And the fourth angel [om. angel[13]] poured out his vial upon (ἐπί) the sun; and power [om. power
9 —ins. it] was given unto him [it] to scorch [ins. the] men with fire. And [ins. the] men were scorched with great heat [scorching], and [ins. they][14] blasphemed the name[15] of God, which [who] hath power [the authority] over these plagues:
10 and they repented not to give him glory. And the fifth angel [om. angel[16]] poured out his vial upon the seat [throne] of the beast [wild-beast]; and his kingdom was full of darkness [became darkened]; and they gnawed their tongues for [be-
11 cause of (ἐκ)—ins. the] pain, and blasphemed the God of [ins. the] heaven because of (ἐκ) their pains and [ins. because of (ἐκ)] their sores, and repented not of (ἐκ) their

---

TEXTUAL AND GRAMMATICAL.

1 Ver. 1. [Crit. Eds. generally give ἑπτά with ℵ. A. B*. C. Vulg., etc.; Lange omits with P. 1, 28, etc.—E. R. C.]
2 Ver. 2. Εἰς instead of ἐπί. [So Crit. Eds. with ℵ*. A. B*. C. P., etc.—E. R. C.]
3 Ver. 2. Ἐπί instead of εἰς. [So Crit. Eds. with ℵ. A. B*. C. P., etc.—E. R. C.]
4 Ver. 3. [Lach., Alf., Treg., Tisch. omit ἄγγελος with ℵ*. A. C. P., Am., Fuld., Demid., Tol., etc.; Lange retains with B*., Clem., etc.—E. R. C.]
5 Ver. 4. [Lach., Alf., Treg., Tisch. omit ἄγγελος with ℵ. A. B*. C. P., Vulg., etc.; Lange retains with 1, 35, etc.—E. R. C.]
6 Ver. 4. [Lange, Alf., Treg., Tisch. give ἐγένετο with ℵ. B*. C. P. 1, Vulg., etc.; Lachmann reads ἐγένοντο with A. 36, 95., etc.—E. R. C.]
7 Ver. 5. [Lach., Alf., Treg., Tisch. omit Κύριε with ℵ. A. B*. C. P. 1, Am., Fuld., Demid., Tol., etc.; Lange retains with Clem., Lips., Æth.—E. R. C.]
8 Ver. 5. Ἐρχόμενος is without authority; all Crit. Eds. read ὅσιος.—E. R. C.]
9 Ver. 5. Ὅσιος without καὶ ὁ. [So also Lach., Alf., Treg., Tisch. (1859), with A. B*. C.; Tisch. (8th Ed.) gives ὁ with ℵ. P.—E. R. C.]
10 Ver. 6. [Crit. Eds. generally omit with A. B*. C. P. etc.; ▓ gives ὅπερ.—E. R. C.]
11 Ver. 7. [Crit. Eds., with A. A. C. P., give simply τοῦ θυσιαστηρίου λέγοντος.—E. R. C.]
12 Ver. 7. [See Additional Comment on ch. i. 8, p. 93.—E. R. C.]
13 Ver. 8. [Crit. Eds. generally omit ἄγγελος with A. B*. C. P., Am., Fuld., Tol., etc.; Lange retains, with ℵ. 1, 6, Clem., etc.—E. R. C.]
14 Ver. 9. [Gb., 8z., Tisch. (1859) insert οἱ ἄνθρωποι with B*.; Lach., Alf., Treg., Tisch. (8th Ed.) read as above, with ℵ. A. C. P. 1, 36, Vulg., etc.—E. R. C.]
15 Ver. 9. [Crit. Eds. generally read τὸ ὄνομα; A. gives ἐνώπιον.—E. R. C.]
16 Ver. 10. [Crit. Eds. generally omit with ℵ. A. B*. C. P., Am., Fuld., Demid., Tol., etc.; it is given in 35, 36, etc., Clem., etc.; Lange brackets.—E. R. C.]

12 deeds [works]. And the sixth angel [om. angel[17]] poured out his vial upon the great river Euphrates[18]; and the water thereof was dried up, that the way of the
13 kings of the east [who are from the sun-rising] might be prepared. And I saw three unclean spirits like frogs come [om. three unclean spirits like frogs come] out of the mouth of the dragon, and out of the mouth of the beast [wild beast], and out
14 of the mouth of the false prophet [ins., three unclean spirits as frogs]. [;] for they are the [om. the] spirits of devils [demons], working miracles [doing signs], which [that][19] go forth unto [upon (ἐπί)] the kings of the earth and [om. of the earth and][20] of the whole world [inhabited world (οἰκουμένης)], to gather them [ins. together] to the battle [war] of that [the] great day of God [ins. the] Almighty
15 [or All-Ruler[12]]. Behold, I come as a thief. Blessed is he that watcheth, and keepeth his garments, lest [that] he walk [ins. not] naked, and they see his shame.
16 And he [or they][21] gathered them together into a [the[22]] place called in the [om.
17 the] Hebrew tongue [om. tongue] Armageddon [or Harmagedon]. And the seventh angel [om. angel[23]] poured out his vial into [upon] the air; and there came a great[24] voice out of[25] the temple of heaven [om. of heaven[26]], from the
18 throne, saying, It is done. And there were (ἐγένετο) [ins. lightnings, and] voices, and thunders, and lightnings [om., and lightnings]; and there was (ἐγένετο) a great earthquake, such as was not since [from the times when] men were [a man was][27] upon the earth, so mighty [such] an earthquake, and [om. and] so great.
19 And the great city was divided [became (ἐγένετο)] into three parts, and the cities of the nations fell: and great [om. great] Babylon [ins. the great] came in remembrance [was remembered] before God, to give unto her the cup of the wine of the
20 fierceness [anger] of his wrath. And every island fled away [om. away], and the
21 [om. the] mountains were not found. And there fell upon men [om. there fell upon men] a great hail [ins. as of a talent in weight descendeth] out of [ins. the] heaven [ins. upon the men], every stone about the weight of a talent [om. every stone about the weight of a talent]; and [ins. the] men blasphemed God because of the plague of the hail; for the plague thereof was exceeding great [because great is the plague of it exceedingly].

[17] Ver. 12. [Crit. Eds. generally omit as in preceding Note; Lange retains.—E. R. C.]
[18] Ver. 12. [Gb., Sz., Tisch. (8th Ed.) omit the article before Euphrates with א. B*. P., etc.; Lach., Alf., Tisch. (1859), Lange, prefix it. with A. C. 1, etc.; Treg. brackets.—E. R. C.]
[19] Ver. 14. The reading ἐκπορεύεσθαι is unimportant. [Alf., Treg., Tisch. read ἃ ἐκπορεύεται. This reading is adopted above.—E. R. C.]
[20] Ver. 14. [Omitted by Crit. Eds. with א. A. B*., Vulg., etc.—E. R. C.]
[21] Ver. 16. [Crit. Eds. read συνήγαγεν with A. B*. C. P., etc.; א. gives -γον. Lange translates he, regarding God as the subject (see in loc.); the more natural reference, however, is to the πνεύματα of ver. 14, which, as a neuter plural, may be the subject of a verb in the singular.—E. R. C.]
[22] Ver. 16. [Lach., Alf., Treg., Tisch. give τόν with A. B*. 1, etc.; Lange omits with א. 14. etc.—E. R. C.]
[23] Ver. 17. [Crit. Eds. generally omit with א*. A. B*., Am., Fuld., Tol., etc.; Lange retains with א*. 1, 23, 35, etc., Clem., etc.—E. R. C.]
[24] Ver. 17. [Lange, Treg., Tisch. give μεγάλη with א. B*., Vulg.; Gb.. Lach., Alf. omit with A. 1, 12, 46.—E. R. C.]
[25] Ver. 17. [Ἀπὸ τοῦ ναοῦ, ἀπὸ τοῦ θρόνου. [So also Tisch. (1859) with B*.; Gb., Lach., Alf., Treg., Tisch. (8th Ed.) give ἐκ instead of the first ἀπό, with א. A. 1, etc. The latter reading is adopted above.—E. R. C.]
[26] Ver. 17. [Τοῦ οὐρανοῦ is omitted by Crit. Eds.: it occurs only in B*. 1, 6, 38, Arm.—E. R. C.]
[27] Ver. 18. Ἄνθρωπος ἐγένετο. [So Crit. Eds. with A. 38, Cop., Arm., Æth.; 1, 7, 8, etc., read οἱ ἄνθρωποι ἐγένοντο.—E. R. C.]

EXEGETICAL AND CRITICAL.

SYNOPTICAL VIEW.

The seven Vials of Anger embrace the collective Earth-picture of the world-judgment in general. Hence the seventh Vial is comprehended together with the rest, and not, like the seventh Seal and the seventh Trumpet, made the basis of a new Seven. The seven Angels of Anger follow each other in rapid succession and with terrible effect; only, between the third and fourth Vials, there occurs a double digression, in a sort as a theodicy of these fearful judgments and for the tranquillization of the startled mind. Now if we hold fast the idea that anger is an infliction of death, death being the decomposition, the dissolution of life, the explanation, in general, of the present section is already established; —especially if we further consider that the anger, or death-judgment, of God is operative through the medium of the anger of the heathen [nations], or the frenzy of false enthusiasm. Once more we are reminded of the lofty consciousness and teleology of the plagues. Only at the command of a great voice from the smoke-filled Temple—at the bidding of God, therefore—do the Angels begin their work. Each one knows, in his quality of Angel, his particular rank in the angelic series, and his particular mission. The following is the succession of the outpourings of anger:

1. Into the earth. This, therefore, is the death, the vital decomposition and dissolution of the New Testament Theocracy, the external phenomenal form of the Church (and relatively of the

Christian State, inasmuch as the old Theocracy embraced both State and Church). (See the *Introduction*, pp. 33 sq.; 2 Thess. ii.) The effect of this first Vial is a malignant *sore*, with which all the worshippers of the Beast are smitten. The consummate idolatrous world-spirit in the Church, in churchly dignities and forms, results in an incurable fiery sore of fanatical self-consumption and self-destruction (2 Tim. ii. 17). The form of this sore is intoxication through the medium of the cup of anger, *i. e.*, the confusing false enthusiasm or fanaticism which it inspires as the product of the denial of all religious and moral principles.

2. *Into the sea.* The worldly life of state and nations likewise becomes the subject of a process of decomposition which leads to death. Consummate passionate subjectivism and party-spirit, in all the forms of senseless self-intoxication, in mercantile, socialistic, absolutist and many other directions, finally rupture all social, popular, and political coherence. The sea becomes *blood* (Ex. vii.), and this blood is as that of a *dead man;* dead blood. All the goods of the social life of the nations lose their vital value, because they have become the property of consummate egoism. They are dead like the men who determine their value, and operate fatally upon every one who would carry on his life in this sea of blood. Every living being, it is declared, died in the sea.

3. *Into the rivers and fountains of waters.* Self-empoisonment of mental currents, and, what is still worse, self-empoisonment of fountains, the original life of geniuses and men of talent. *And there became blood* [ἐγένετο αἷμα]. It is not said that *this* blood was like that of a dead man. The life of minds, of mental culture—pouring forth in an unnatural state of obduracy and frenzied deification of self, frenzied deification and bestialization of man—becomes a nauseous and fatal death-draught for those who would quell their thirst at the fountains and streams of waters. The natural life-fountains and life-rivers of minds have, in the perversion of moral nature to unnaturalness, become fountains and rivers of deadly intoxication and mental distraction.—Now ensues a pause. The Seer hears the *Angel of the waters* speaking. And here let us avoid the pagan and also Rabbinical conception of spirits of nature,—water or fire angels in the literal sense of the term. The Angel of the waters, in this passage, is the Angel who brings anger upon the water, the Angel of the Divine rule as exercised over the surging, social nation-life of men; just as the Angel of the Altar (ver. 7) or of the fire (ch. xiv. 18) is the spirit or teleology of all fire of sacrifice on earth. The Angel of the waters adores the righteousness of God in this terrible judgment upon the waters. Men must now *drink blood*, because they have *shed the blood of Saints and Prophets*, *i. e.*, also, because they have first turned the heavenly fountains of waters on earth, out of which it was designed that they should drink, into blood. The assent of the other Angel from the Altar* designates the natural consequence of the ancient blood-guiltiness

still more decidedly, in accordance with the idea of the *Altar*, as a righteous judgment of God.

4. *Upon the sun.* The sun of revelation itself; not in respect of its essence, but in respect of its shining and effect. The true shining of the sun is as vitalizing life; its effect is healthful vital heat. But how is it when men begin to make Christianity, in great part, a hot-blooded system of confession or negation, a thing of priesthood or of sects!—how is it when churchly fanaticism begins to produce Sicarii, as did Jewish fanaticism in the Jewish war! The fanatical heat of the one class calls forth increasingly the blasphemy of the other, instead of all being horrified at this frightful incapacity for receiving the simple sunshine of Christianity in purity, at this still more frightful capacity for converting the light of revelation into nothing but a misleading and infatuating power and a consuming passion.

5. *Upon the throne of the Beast.* The Beast must still be understood in the general sense, like the City of Babylon (ver. 19), for the branching of the one judgment into three judgments has not yet taken place. The *throne of the Beast* is the government, the system of Antichrist. His *kingdom became darkened;* this means, we think, that it became confused in its contradictions—it lost its consistency. For it was a sphere of spiritual and religious moral darkness from the beginning. Such self-confusion is already to be seen where atheism and spiritism, bigotry and blasphemy, criticism and fanaticism hold high carnival together.—Then a mighty and poignant self-scorn comes over the haughty spirit of the associates of this kingdom, and they *gnaw their tongues* in the pain of their impotence and nothingness. They *blaspheme the God of the Heaven because of their pains.* In so far as they need an object for their blasphemy, therefore, they are still theists. They blaspheme God as *the God of the Heaven*—all that is transcendent is hateful to them because the Beast has become their god on earth.* In so far, also, as Nature reflects the Divine lineaments of her Creator, she too, doubtless, becomes the object of their blasphemy ; indeed she is occasionally blasphemed even now by some who make her the subject of their investigations. *Because of their pains and because of their sores* they blaspheme ; the *sores—i. e.*, the malignant ulcers which do not, as local focuses, eliminate the morbid matter from the system, but which overpower the life, changing it into morbid matter and consuming it—continue, therefore, from the first Anger-vial through all the stages of outpoured anger. This *blasphemy* of despair sets in instead of the *repentance* of faith.

6. *Upon the great river, the Euphrates.* Here also we look upon the *Euphrates* as the line of demarkation between the civilized world and the barbarous and savage world of the nations of the East (ch. xx. ; Ezek. xxxviii. sqq.). We see, accordingly, that the army of horsemen (ch. ix. 14) comes from the *hither* shore of the Eu-

---

* [See EXPLANATIONS IN DETAIL, ver. 7.—E. R. C.]

* [May not a sense of the contrast between their own wretched condition and the condition of the blessed inmates of *Heaven* induce this peculiar form of blasphemy?—TR.]

phrates, from the region of Babylon, the seat of the most ancient *civilization*, the type of all Antichristian world-monarchies (Dan. vii.). On the other hand, the *kings of the East* [*from the sun-rising*] come from *beyond* the Euphrates, as the representatives of all the *barbarism* of the remotest world. The *drying up* of the Euphrates, therefore, signifies that the barrier-line between the civilized world and the rudest and roughest popular life is done away with, in a social as well as a terrestrial sense. In consequence of the mental confusion and distraction resultant upon a false over-refinement, the way is prepared for the hostile attack of rudeness and barbarism upon the seat of culture. Nevertheless, the Eastern barbarian kings come not uncalled. *Three spirits*, resembling *frogs*, proceed out of the mouth of the Dragon, and out of the mouth of the Beast, and out of the mouth of the False Prophet. Thus a frog-clamor with three variations is formed. The key of Satan is contempt of man (Job ii. 4); the key of the Beast is the deification of man (2 Thess. ii.); the key of the False Prophet is a bigoted training of man—a compound of the preceding two elements (ch. xiii. 13, 14). Thus these modern nightingales, the frogs, announce the new spring-time of mankind. As spirits they are spirits of demons, of such demons as engender moral possession; with this effect they come upon the kings of the earth and set on foot the great revolt-alliance for the war of the great day of God, Who, as the All-Ruler, over-rules even this uprising (see ch. xix. 19, xx. 8). As the greatest of catastrophes, this event shall come very suddenly and as in the night-time—hence the admonition of ver. 15. None should abandon himself to spiritual carelessness, as one that sleeps without his garments, for a man so doing might be cast out naked into the night. This admonition applies even to the pious, in reference to the last time. The rebel host gathers, as appointed by God the Judge, at a field of battle called *Harmageddon* [*or*, Armageddon].

The enigmatical name of Harmageddon or Harmagadon gives occasion for a precursory examination of the entire section. The three special judgments following, from chapter xvii. on, are already visible in this general sketch of the judgment. This is manifestly the case with the incipient judgment upon the *Beast* (ver. 10), as compared with the consummate judgment upon the Beast, ch. xix. 19. So, likewise, the judgment upon *Babylon* (chs. xvii. and xviii.) is visible in the judgment of the *first* Anger-vial, poured out upon the earth. The *second* Vial of anger is annexed to the first; the *third* and *fourth* form a transition to the *fifth*. The reflection of the *sixth* Vial of anger we behold in the judgment upon Gog and Magog. When these are said to surround the camp of the Saints and the beloved City, it necessitates the reference of the name Har-Magedon (Mount of Decision or Sentence) to the Mount of Olives in accordance with Zech. xiv 4. The mountains of Israel shall in general, according to Ezek. xxxviii. and xxxix., be *mountains of decision*. A more precise definition of the locality, *the valley of the dead* (ch. xxxix. 11),

leads us into the region between Jerusalem and the Dead Sea—likewise, therefore, into the vicinity of the Mount of Olives. Hence, the Seer may have merely borrowed the name from the northern *waters of Megiddo*, where the Israelites conquered the heathen kings of Canaan (Judges v. 19), and from the southern *plain of Megiddo* (2 Kings xxiii. 29), where Josiah was defeated by the Egyptians,—possibly with the idea that the *mountain of Megiddo* puts an end to the fluctuations between victory and defeat in the wars of the people of God.

7. Upon the air. The air is the vital element of the earth, the sea, the sweet waters, and mankind. With the decomposition of this vital element—which cannot be understood simply of the common spirit-world of humanity, but must be regarded as having reference also to the cosmical vital conditions of men and of the earth, because the end in the former sense necessarily brings with it the end in the latter sense--the death of the old form of the world is decided. Hence a *great voice* resounds from the *Temple* of Heaven and from the *Throne*, saying: *It is done*. This end of the world (see ch. xx. 9 sqq.), however, is not the annihilation of the world, but its setting, in order to a resurrection. Hence the dying of the old world is accomplished amid *lightnings*, and *voices*, and *thunders*, annunciatory of a new world, and together with these comes the *great earthquake* whose like has never been since men were on the earth (see 2 Peter iii.). And now out of the great *general* judgment, the three *special* judgments develop (ver. 19). The *great City* is broken up into *three parts*. The judgment upon great Babylon consists, primarily, in the fact that it is divided into a small, specific, mock-holy Babylon, into the demonic Kingdom of the Beast, and into a brutal, Satanic mob-kingdom (comp. Ezek. xxxviii. 21, 22). The *cities of the nations* [Gentiles] likewise fall—the ancient seats of worldly civilization; the *islands* of small and intimate communities vanish, as do also the towering *mountains;*—great, secluded churches, even proud, firm-based states are sought for now in vain. Equilibrium in the spiritual world as well as in nature is destroyed; all things waver betwixt fiery heat and deathly cold;—hence the formation of *hailstones, of the weight of a talent,* which fall upon men; these hailstones and their fall are, of course, not to be apprehended in a purely material sense, according to which they would dash all men to pieces, but they are still real and terrible enough to provoke the remnants of a recognition of God in the wicked to fresh blasphemy. With the partition of Babylon the Great, the judgment is in reality already decided, there being a reciprocal negation on the side of the parts, and the whole, consequently, being in process of complete dissolution; in like manner the tower-building of ancient Babel was put an end to, and, in its centrality, judged, by the Divine dispersion of those engaged therein.

We call attention once more to the fact that in ver. 19 *the ramification of the great general End-judgment into the three special Judgments now following, is expressed.*

[ELLIOTT: Chs. xvi. 1-14; xi. 15-19; xiv. 6-8; xv., relate to the same period (see on p. 281) —viz.: " The era of the French Revolution, as figured under the first six Vials of the seventh Trumpet," a period extending from A. D. 1789 to A. D. 1848. Chs. xi. 15-19; xv. 1-xvi. 1 is the introduction and commencement of the Vial-outpouring.*—(Note the similarity of the first four Vials to the first four Trumpets. See on p. 201). Ver. 2. The first Vial. The ἕλκος (expressive of the boil that broke forth on the Egyptians, comp. Ex. ix. 9,—probably the plague-spot or the small-pox) figures "some extraordinary outbreak of moral and social evil, the expression of deep-seated disease within, with raging pain and in-flammation as its accompaniment—disease of Egyptian origin perhaps in the Apocalyptic sense of the word Egypt, and alike loathsome, deadly, self-corroding, and infectious—that would arise somewhere in Papal Europe, shortly after the cessation of the Turkish woe, and on the sounding of what might answer to the seventh Trumpet's blast; an evil, too, which would soon overspread and infect the countries of Papal Europe generally and their inhabitants." It symbolizes "that tremendous outbreak of social and moral evil, of democratic fury, atheism, and vice, which was speedily seen to characterize the French Revolution; that of which the ultimate source was in the long and deep-seated corruption and irreligion of the nation; its outward vent, expression and organ in the Jacobin clubs, and their seditious and atheistic publications; its result, the dissolution of all society, all morals, and all religions; with acts of atrocity and horror accompanying scarce paralleled in the history of man; and suffering and anguish of correspondent intensity throbbing throughout the whole social mass, and cor-roding it—that which from France as a centre, spread like a plague, through its affiliated so-cieties, to the other countries of Papal Christen-dom; and proved, wherever its poison was im-bibed, to be as much the punishment as the symptom of the corruption."—Ver. 3. The se-cond Vial. A judgment on the maritime power, commerce, and colonies of the countries of Pa-pal Christendom—i. e., Spain, France and Portu-gal. It symbolizes—(1) The great naval war which continued A. D. 1793-1815, in which " were destroyed near 200 ships of the line, be-tween 300 and 400 frigates, and an almost incal-culable number of smaller vessels of war and ships of commerce. It is most truly stated by Dr. Keith (Signs of Times, ii., p. 209) that the whole history of the world does not present such a period of naval war, destruction, and blood-shed." (2) The revolt of the transatlantic colo-nies and the following bloodshed.—Vers. 4-7. The third Vial. It symbolizes the judgment of war and bloodshed visited on the countries watered by the Rhine and the Danube, and on the sub-Alpine provinces of Piedmont and Lom-

* [Elliott calls attention to the fearful convulsions in na-ture—tempests, hail storms, re-opening volcanoes, earth-quakes (ch. xi. 19)—th t preceded the outbreak of the French Revolution.—E. R. C.]

bardy, A. D. 1792-1805.—Vers. 8, 9.   The fourth Vial. This symbolizes a judgment on the Ger-man Emperor and the other sovereigns of Papal Christendom. Napoleon, A. D. 1806, compelled the renunciation by the Emperor of Austria of the title " Emperor of the Holy Roman Empire and of Germany;" he also deposed the other papal kings, and " scorched men with fire," A. D. 1806-1809. (Comp. the Explanation of the fourth Trumpet, p. 201).—Ver. 10. The fifth Vial. A judgment on Rome (the throne of the seven hills), consecutive on that of the former Vial. Immediately after the battle of Wagram, A. D. 1809, the Pope was subjected to insult and spoliation, his temporal authority over the Ro-man State was abolished, and Rome itself was incorporated with France as the second city of the empire.* — Vers. 10 (last clause). 11 set forth—(1) The severity of sufferings endured; (2) the blasphemy (a) of France in atheism, (b) of Papal countries (subsequently of France also), in ascribing Divine prerogatives to creatures; (3) the continuance in sin of those who had been punished, after the cessation of the pre-ceding judgments.—Ver. 12. The sixth Vial. The first portion symbolizes judgment on the Mo-hammedan Turk, begun A. D. 1820, in the asser-tion of independence by Ali Pacha of Yanina, and the immediately-following Greek insurrec-tion, and continuing in the gradual decay of the empire to the present time. By the kings from the sun-rising are symbolized the Jews; the way for their return to their own land being pre-pared in the decay and fall of the Turkish Em-pire. By the three frogs are figured three un-holy principles, going forth throughout the whole habitable world—viz.: (1) from the Dragon, heathen-like infidelity; (2) from the Beast, popery; (3) from the False Prophet, priestcraft.——Ch. xvi. 15-xxii. 15, together with ch. xiv. 9-20, re-presents " The present and the future, from A. D. 1849 to the Millennium and Final Judgment " —the first portion of which is the æra of the seventh Vial. Ch. xiv. 9-20 presents the primary and briefer series of prefigurations of the æra of the seventh Vial in the part without-written † of the Apocalypse, down to the wine-press tread-ing before the Millennium; this consists of four parts—(1) vers. 9-11, a public and notorious outcry of warning throughout European Chris-

* [BARNES, in support of a similar view, quotes the follow-ing: " In this connection, I may insert here the remarkable calculation of Robert Fleming, in his work entitled Apoca-lyptical Key, or the Pouring out of the Vials, first published in 1701. It is in the following words: 'The fifth Vial (vers. 10, 11), which is to be poured out on the seat of the Beast, or the dominions which more immediately belong to and depend on the Roman See; that, I say, this judgment will probably begin about the year 1794, and expire about A. D. 1848; or that the duration of it upon this supposition will be the space of fifty-four years. For I do suppose that, seeing the Pope received the title of Supreme Bishop no sooner than A. D. 606, he cannot be sup-posed to have any vial poured upon his seat immediately (so as to receive his authority so signally as this judgment must be supposed to call) until the year 1848, which is the date of the twelve hundred and sixty years in prophetical account, when they are reckoned from A. D. 606. But yet we are not to imagine that this will totally destroy the Papacy (though it will ex-ceedingly weaken it), for we find that still in being and alive, wh—n the next Vial is poured out.' p. 68. Ed. New York. It is a circumstance remarkably in accordance with this calculation, that in the year 1848 the Pope was actually driven away to Gaeta, and that at the present time (1851) he is restored, though evidently with diminished power."—E. R. C.]

† [See foot-note, 2d column, p. 201.—E. R. C.]

tendom and its dependencies as to what is meant by the *Beast* and *his image,* and as to the fate of their followers; (2) vers. 12, 13, a deep impression and earnest inculcation, on the part of the true Church, of the near approach of the grand epoch of blessedness predicted in Scripture of departed saints; (3) vers. 11-16, the first grand act of the judgments of the consummation on Antichristendom; (4) vers. 17-20, the last judgment, a judgment unto blood, upon apostate Christendom. Ch. xvi. 15-21 presents "The fuller Apocalyptic figuration, as *within-written,** of the events immediately preparatory to, and those included in, the *seventh Vial;* down to the *wine-press treading,* and destruction of the Beast and False Prophet, immediately before the Millennium;" in it are—(1) ver. 15, an introduction to the outpouring, the warning, indicating increased faithfulness on the part of the ministry in declaring the coming of the Lord and the duty of being prepared to meet Him (?); (2) ver. 16, the success of the unclean spirits in influencing kings and people against Christ and His Church; (3) vers. 17-20, *the seventh Vial* —realities *yet future* are symbolized, viz.: An extraordinary *convulsion, darkening* and *vitiation* of the *moral* and *political* atmosphere of Europe (having, perhaps, a *literal* groundwork in some ominous derangement of the *natural* atmosphere), ministering disease to each body politic, and, perhaps, resolving society for awhile into its primary elements; resulting, finally, in the resolution of the Papal Empire into a tri-partite form, in which form Rome (including its subject *ecclesiastical* State and the *political* tri-partition connected with it), is to receive its peculiar and appalling fate.

BARNES agrees, in the main, with Elliott; he makes, however, the following important differences in interpretation: 1. The pouring out of the fourth Vial upon the sun, *etc.* (ver. 8), indicates "that a scene of calamity and woe would ensue *as if* the sun should be made to pour forth such intense heat that men would be 'scorched,'" the reference being to the wars following the French Revolution.—2. By the kings of the East (ver. 12) are to be understood the rulers of the East (Orient?); "All that is fairly implied in the language here is that the kings of the East would be converted to the true religion," and that the destruction of the Turkish power would be in order thereto.—3. The three malign influences symbolized by the "*frogs*" (ver. 13) are not specifically characterized.—This author quotes largely from Allison's *History of Europe* in support of his interpretations.

STUART regards the Vials as a series of judgments upon the enemies of the Church, terminating primarily in the death of Nero and the destruction of Jerusalem, and ultimately (?) in the destruction of the Pagan power under Constantine. He writes: "The author of the Book has given a sketch which corresponds, with a good degree of exactness, to the state of facts. The persecuting power of the unbelieving Jews ceased in the main with the destruction of Jerusalem. Hence the tempest and earthquake which lay that place in ruins, are the *finale* of the first

catastrophe. But not so with the second. The death of Nero was indeed the destruction of the Beast, for the time being, and it made a temporary end of persecution. But the Beast still came up again from the pit; the contest was renewed, and, with many remissions, continued down to the time of Constantine. Rome, as heathen, then finally ceased to persecute. The Beast was finally slain."

WORDSWORTH regards the visions of the Vials as partially fulfilled, and yet only as "a prelude and specimen of what will be more fully developed." He interprets the εἰς with which the ἐξέχεε of the first three Vials is construed as denoting infusion into and admixture with the object of punishment, and the ἐπί of the last four as indicating the Divine vengeance as trampling *upon* it. His interpretation of the Vials is as follows: 1. This plague is upon men's *persons,* and consists in physical and spiritual disease, the result of the teachings and practices of the Papacy.—2. The sea represents nations in a restless state, and the plague is that carnal men lose the genuine properties of *men* and become mere *things.*—3. This plague is inflicted on the *resources* of the Papacy; those things that once supplied it with wealth and power (*indulgences,* pretended miracles, *etc.*), become occasions and instruments of its suffering and shame.—4. The *temporal splendor* (*sun*) of the Papacy, by the galling exactions through which it is maintained, already scorches its subjects.—5. "The fifth Vial is poured upon the *throne* of the Beast; and his kingdom is darkened. Here is another reference to the plagues of Egypt, *etc.* (No exposition is given.)—6. This plague consists in the decay of *supremacy, secular and spiritual,* which is to Rome, the *spiritual* Babylon, the source of her glory and strength, as was the *literal* Euphrates to the literal Babylon. By the *kings of the East* are symbolized *saints* whose advance Rome has hindered.—7. The destruction of *Rome,* the mystical Babylon, "the capital city of the Empire of the Beast."

ALFORD. This writer remarks generally concerning the Vials: 1. The series reaches on to the time of the end, and the whole of it is to be placed near that time. 2. As in the Seals and the Trumpets there is a marked distinction between the first four and the following three— the objects of the former being the earth, the sea, the springs of water, and the sun, those of the latter being more particularized. 3. As in the other series, so here there is a compendious and anticipatory character about several of the Vials, leading us to believe that those of which this is not so plain, partake of this character also. 4. We have no longer, as in the Trumpets, a *portion* of each element affected, but the *whole.* 5. While by the plague of the fourth Trumpet the sun is partially *darkened,* by that of the fourth Vial its power is *increased.*—He presents no affirmative views as to the nature of the specific plagues, save in the case of the last, which he regards as indicating the destruction of the city of Rome and the execution of vengeance on the mystic Babylon.—For particular remarks see under EXPLANATIONS IN DETAIL.

LORD: The office of the seven Angels is sim-

---

* [See *footnote,* 2d column, p. 201.—E. R. C.]

ply to assist the revelation, by designating the commencement of the seven judgments, and distinguishing them as inflictions of Divine wrath; not to symbolize the agents on earth by whom they are caused. The interpretation of the several Vials is as follows: 1. The *earth*, when distinguished from the sea, etc., denotes the population of an empire under a settled government; the *men* were those who have the mark of the Wild-beast; the *ulcer* symbolizes an analogous disease of the mind; a restlessness and rancor of passion exasperated by agitating and noxious principles and opinions, that fill it with a sense of obstruction, degradation and misery—this ulcer represents the restlessness under injury, the ardor of resentment, hate, and revenge, the noxiousness and contagion of false principles and opinions that marked the commencement of the political disquiets of the European States toward the close of the last century.—2. The *sea* denotes the population of a central kingdom in violent commotion; it is to the animals that live in it what a people is to the monarchs, nobles, ecclesiastics, *etc.*, who owe to them their support. This symbol denotes the second great act in the French Revolution, in which the people slaughtered one another, and exterminated all the influential ranks, king and queen, nobles, *etc.*—3. *Rivers* and *fountains* are to the sea what smaller exterior communities are to a great central nation. This symbol denotes the vast bloodshed in the other Apocalyptic kingdoms, in the insurrections and wars that sprung out of the French Revolution.—4. Those who exercise the government of a kingdom are to the people what the *sun* is to the land and sea. This symbol denotes that the rulers of the people on whom the preceding judgments fell, were to become armed with extraordinary and destructive powers, and to employ them in the most violent and insupportable oppression.—5. The ascription of a *throne and kingdom* to the Wild-beast shows that he is the symbol of the rulers of an empire. The effect of the Vial on the *throne* is not depicted, but only its consequence to the *kingdom;* the subversion of the throne, however, is implied— the event indicated is the subversion of the imperial throne of France, and re-establishment of the Bourbon dynasty in 1814 and 1815.—6. The *Euphrates* is used as a symbol in a relation analogous to that of the literal river to the literal Babylon. The entire symbol indicates that agencies are to be exerted by which vast crowds of the supporters of the nationalized hierarchies (see p. 283) are to be withdrawn from them. This Vial has already begun.—(Vers. 13-16. The *Dragon* is the symbol of the rulers of the Eastern Roman Empire supporting an apostate Church, and arrogating the right of dictating the religion of their subjects, and implies that at the period of this event, a government is to subsist that shall nationalize the religion of that empire as under its last imperial head; the *Wild-beast* is the symbol of the civil rulers of the Kingdoms of the Western Empire; and the *False-Prophet* of the hierarchy of the Papal states. The *unclean spirits* represent ecclesiastics who profess to work miracles, and thus establish a Divine sanction to their mission; they induce the kings of the whole world to

unite in a war to prevent the establishment of Christ's Kingdom. The *Great Day* is the day when Christ shall visibly descend from Heaven and destroy His enemies and establish His Kingdom.)—7. This Vial is to be poured into the *air* which envelopes the globe, indicating that the great changes which follow it are to extend to all nations. *Lightnings, voices,* and *thunders* are symbols of the vehement thoughts and passionate expressions of multitudes, occasioned by the sudden discovery of momentous truth. The *earthquake* denotes a civil revolution in which the whole surface of universal society is to be thrown into disorder, and ancient political institutions to be shaken down. *Great Babylon* (p. 283) is to be divided into three parts. The *cities of the nations* are the hierarchies without the ten kings, as the Russian, Greek, *etc.;* these are to fall. Great Babylon is then to be destroyed. Every smaller combination of men symbolized by the *islands* is to be dissolved, *etc.* These events are to follow the Advent, to precede the vintage and perhaps the harvest, and are to occupy a considerable period.

GLASGOW interprets the Vials: 1. The Vial was poured out by the preaching of Luther in 1517; the woe was executed in the wars waged by Charles V., subsequent to 1519, against France and Rome.—2. Poured out in the great Protest in 1529; the woe executed in the immediately following wars.—3. The rivers and fountains represent the purer Christians that, living in the midst of a nominal Christianity, have spiritual life. The pouring out of this Vial is the shedding of Protestant martyrs' blood, beginning in 1546; followed by the shedding of retributive blood.—4. Symbolizes a stroke (?) upon the ecclesiastical power. It began at the rising of the Tridentine Council in 1564, and was followed by the Popedom of Pius V., the revolution in Holland, the massacre of St. Bartholomew, and the invasion of the English coast by the Spanish Armada, *etc.*, producing what has been styled "the counter-Reformation."—5. The attitude of self-defence assumed by the Protestants against Rome, followed by the Thirty Years' War.—6. The decay of the population and power of the nations that constitute Great Babylon, *i. e.*, the Roman or Latin nations, beginning with the first French revolution.—7. The air represents the *intellectual department of knowledge.* The pouring out of this Vial symbolizes the remarkable changes in political ideas, and revolutions in governments that have taken place and are yet to take place in consequence of the unprecedented advance in Science and Philosophy, to terminate in the destruction of the systems of the heathen world (involved in the fall of *the cities of the nations*) and Romanism (involved in the fall of Babylon or Rome).—E. R. C.]

EXPLANATIONS IN DETAIL.

On the different divisions of the Vials of Anger into four and three, and five and two, compare Düsterdieck, p. 489. The same commentator observes here (in variation from p 21) that "all seven Vials are poured out one after the other without intermission." At all events, the vehement haste of a rapid approach to the end is unmistakable. Though there is no longer question of a fraction that is smitten (first a fourth, then a third), yet the generalness of the phrase, *on the earth, on the sea*, etc., is not to be understood in a literally absolute sense, but only as a universal operation which draws the process of worldly history to a close; otherwise we could hear no more of an emerging Church of God, the Bride of Christ.

Ver. 1. **A great voice.**—"This can belong only to God Himself (Bengel, Züllig, Hengstenberg)." Düsterdieck. The voice speaks, however, of the **Vials of the anger of God.**—The voice **out of the Temple** is the voice of the Temple itself. The house of salvation says: My work upon this hardened race is at an end; now let the reign of anger begin. In like manner it was the spirit of compassion, from the four horns of the Altar, which in its time gave the signal for the loosing of the hosts of horsemen by the Euphrates (see ch. ix. 13). The Apostle Paul makes the entirely analogous declaration (1 Cor. v.): "In the name of our Lord Jesus Christ, I have determined . . . . to deliver the same unto Satan." See Rom. ii. 5.

Into the earth.—Here the *earth* embraces the whole sphere of the Vials of Anger, in distinction from [the *earth* of] ver. 2. Comp. ch. viii. 5.

Ver. 2. **Into the earth.**—The *earth* in a special sense, in accordance with its symbolical import (see above).—**An evil and grievous sore.**—Ex. ix. 10, Deut. xxviii. 35, Job ii. 7. The malignant sore comes upon individual men *from the earth*—from the corrupt mass it fastens upon individuals; the corrupt character of the theocratic authority corrupts those characters that are subject to it, throws them into a condition of moral self-consumption. As they have marked themselves with the χάραγμα of the Beast, they are now, by way of retribution, marked with the sore.

Ver. 3. **Into the sea.**—On the symbolical import of this, see *Syn. View.*—**Blood** ▄▄ of a dead man.—"Not ▄ great pool of blood, as of many slain (ou νεκροῦ as=νεκρῶν, see à-Lapide, Eichh., De Wette, Hengsten., *et al.*), but the horribleness of the fact is increased by the circumstance that the *sea* seems like the coagulated and already putrefying blood of *a dead man* (Bengel, Züllig, *et al.*)." Düsterd. Since the blood of a living person quickly coagulates, the difference does not seem so very great. The main thing is that it is changed as into dead blood of dead men, in which no living being can be without dying. Fearful deadly poisoning of the life of the nations. That which had its being in this sea, lost its life in it. "Tà ἐν τῇ θαλάσσῃ is in apposition" (Ebrard).

Vers. 4-7. **Into the rivers and fountains of waters.**—The drinkableness of this blood, as contrasted with that of the sea, should, we think, not be premised.* Here *the drinking of*

blood is a *punishment;* in ch. xvii. 6 it appears as an *offence* meriting punishment. In the latter passage, the effect of fanatical blood-shedding, intoxicating even to frenzy, is meant; here we have the punishment of men with the drinking, repugnant to nature, of blood—the imbibing of nauseous and pernicious draughts of moral death (ever provocative of greater thirst) which they derive from those very streams and fountains that should give them clear, refreshing, living water.

And I heard the Angel of the waters saying.—This *Angel* is certainly not the guardian Angel of the physical waters (see De Wette, p. 156, with reference to ch. vii. 1—"Angels over the winds"—and ch. xiv. 18—an Angel over fire), but neither is he merely "the Angel who emptied the Vial upon the water" (Grot., Ebrard). As sacrifices and prayers have a divinely ordained mission, represented by the fire-Angel, so *geniuses*—or the source-points of spiritual [*geistig*=intellectual, spiritual, as distinct from material] life—and *spiritual* [*geistig*] *currents* have their divinely-appointed mission. The spirit of the Divine destination of spirits and spirit-currents, therefore, gives utterance to the subsequent deliverance upon the great criminality of those men who have perverted these Divine appointments into the unnatural and horrible opposite of that which they were intended to be—into fountains and rivers of blood and death. According to Düsterdieck, the four Living-beings are analogous to the Angel over the water; he perceives ▄ similarity to them in the Danielic Angel-princes also, whom he mentions (p. 492) in connection with Rabbinical conceptions ("earth-angels, sea-angels, fire-angels and the like)." Hengstenberg violently assumes a connection between our passage and John v. 4.

Who art and Who wast.—"The καὶ ὁ ἐρχόμενος is wanting here as in ch. xi. 17, because the coming to judgment is already in process of fulfilment."—**Holy,** ὅσιος.—In this retribution, God has shown not only His righteousness, but also His ὁσιότης, His holy and pure personal dignity, the Divine humanity of His government, as making visitation in this judgment for the criminal contempt of personal dignity. [The term ὅσιος has reference to the *covenant love and mercy* of Jehovah toward His own people. It is here used as the most fitting ascription to Him who had avenged the blood of His ἅγιοι, His *consecrated ones*, upon their persecutors.*—E. R. C.]—**The blood of saints.**

---

* [Lange has reference, probably, to the following passage in Düsterdieck: "Ταῦτα refers to ver. 4, not to ver. 3, for reference is had (ver. 6) t- drinkable water which is turned into blood, so that the inhabitants of the earth, who have shed the blood of Saints and Prophets (comp. ch. xiii. 7, 10, vi. 10, xi. 7, xvii. 6, xix. 2) are n w constrained to drink blood." Düsterdieck, however, does not assert that the water of the

rivers and fountains is any more drinkable in its transformed state, as blood, than the blo-d of the sea.—Tr.]

* [This is one of the two occurrences of ὅσιος in the Apocalyp-e, the other being in ch. xv. 4. In other portions of the New Testament it appears only in Acts ii. 27; xiii. 34, 35; 1 Tim. ii. 8; Titus i. 8; Heb. vii. 26 (ὁσιότης, Luke i. 75; Eph. iv. 24; ὁσίως, 1 Thess. ii. 10). It is a term of comparatively frequent occurrence in the LXX., and is there generally employed to translate חָסִיד; it is also occasionally used for זָךְ, טָהוֹר, תָּם, תָּמִים. Cremer writes: "The

meaning of חָסִיד is to be defined according to חֶסֶד (see Hupfel on Ps. iv 4). This word, which is=goodness, kindness, is used to denote God's holy love towards His people Israel, 'both as the source and as the result of His sovereign choice and cov-nant with them;' when applied to men 'it does n t den-te the corresponding covenant relationship and feeling of Israel toward God (n t even in 2 Chron. vi. 42 cf.; Isa. lv. 3; lvii. 1), but love and mercifulness towards

—Matt. xxiii. 35; Rev. vi. 10, xvii. 6, xviii. 24, xix. 2.

From the altar.*—The spirit of human destiny is not alone in adoring the righteousness and purity of God in this judgment; the spirit of sacrifice, of reconciliation, of intercession, joins in the sentiments uttered by the former. Over against the praise of Jehovah, the voice from the Altar brings in view the almighty sovereignty of God, the rule of Elohim Sabaoth, and instead of God's holiness it magnifies, together with the *righteousness*, the *truth* in the judgments of God. These do not appear simply at the end, unmediated; they are prepared from the beginning by the prophecies of the Scriptures, of the human conscience, and of history. The bold and hence difficult expression personifying the *Altar*, has been the subject of manifold conjectures and additions, such as the following: Another Angel from the Altar [E. V.]; the Angel who keeps watch over the spirits under the Altar; an inhabitant of Heaven standing by the Altar, *etc.* The explanation of Bede: *Interior affectus sanctorum vel angelorum vel hominum*, does not properly belong in this category of supplements cited by Düsterdieck. See ch. ix. 13. According to Düsterdieck, the idea of the speaking Altar is intelligible from chaps. vi. 10, viii. 3, ix. 13, xiv. 18. But no more than we are at liberty to identify all Altar-visions, may we identify the voice of the Altar itself and the voice of soul-lives *beneath* it crying for vengeance. According to Hengstenberg, "the Altar itself here rejoices at the vengeance" for the "blood shed upon it" (?).

Vers. 8, 9. **Upon the sun.**—Reference is not had to the sun considered by and for itself; but neither is the sun, "in its burning quality," "the figure of the sufferings of this life." The operation of the sun of revelation is intended (comp. ch. viii. 12). This operation—which is Christianity,—from being an enlightening and warming agency of blessing, is, by the anger-fire of fanaticism, over which the anger of God rules in judgment, converted into a glowing *fire-shine* [instead of the former and proper *sun-shine*.—Tr.], which makes men hot with great heat (passive); hereupon men, unable to distinguish between this fervid glow of an externalized Christianity and the *name of God*, Divine revelation itself, *blaspheme the name of the God Who has authority over these plagues*, instead of becoming converted (and so distinguishing between revelation-faith and fanaticism) and *giving Him glory*. This obduracy must be distinguished from impenitency (ch. ix. 20).—It ▬▬ given unto it; *αὐτῷ*—to the sun (De Wette, *et al.*). Bengel and others incorrectly: to the Angel.

Vers. 10, 11. **Upon the throne of the Wild-beast.**—As in the *fourth* Vial of Anger

the judgment upon Babylon, the Harlot, is already foreshadowed, so in this *fifth* Vial the judgment upon the Beast, and in the *sixth* the judgment upon Gog and Magog (see ch. xiii. 2; 2 Thess. ii.) are intimated.—The *throne of the Beast* is the principial system upon which the power of the Antichristian life of the people rests. There is no question of the fact that the principle of the absolute sovereignty of the absolute quantitative majority is the root of the most godless and mischievous confusions and seditious agitations, and that with the loosing of these confusions, induced by the Angel of anger, a great intellectual and social *darkness* must of necessity diffuse itself over that kingdom (not *rulerdom*) of the Beast which, in an ethical sense, was already darkened. That there may be an allusion to the Egyptian darkness is not, indeed, to be denied; it, however, plays no important part here.—**They gnawed their tongues.**—Together with the sensation of torment, the emotion of rage is expressed, as in the wailing and gnashing of teeth.—**Blasphemed the God of the Heaven.**—The blasphemy is directed no longer simply against the *name of God*, revelation, but against the *God of the Heaven*, the primeval revelation of God, and God in His universal revelation—hence, against all that is Divine. They have now reached the stage of recognizing, in the incipient ruin of the bestial kingdom, all the foregoing plagues as plagues, but instead of now, at last, repenting of their works, they pass from their unbelief to that demonic belief in which they do indeed recognize the God of Heaven as the author of their plagues and sores, but recognize Him only consciously to blaspheme Him even in this phase of heavenly omnipotence and glory. Ebrard queries how a darkening or mere withdrawal of light can be conceived of as causing so great torments. The key to this problem is, he thinks, furnished by the locust-plague of the fifth Trumpet—the present darkness being occasioned, as he maintains, by a host of scorpions—and he declares that "any man who is not wilfully blind must be able to see this." The *sores* of ver. 11 are also, as he thinks, distinguished from those of ver. 2, as the consequences of the unmentioned scorpion-stings. The problem as here set forth presupposes sensuous causes and effects; in the spiritual realm, however, there is nothing easier of conception than that the incipient darkening of the Antichristian Kingdom and all the fanatical hopes based upon it should result in the rage and torment of despair.

Vers. 12-16. **Upon the great river** [Lange: the] **Euphrates.**—See Syn. View; comp. ch. ix. 14. Above all things we must distinguish between the starting-point of *this side* of the Euphrates (ch. ix.) and that of *beyond* the Euphrates. Therein is contained not merely a distinction, but also a contrast. It is wrong, therefore, to identify the *Eastern kings* with the four Angels (Ebrard). As little are they iden ical with the ten kings, ch. xvii. 12, who give their power to the Beast (De Wette, Düsterd). The preparation of the judgment upon the Beast was treated of under the fifth Vial of anger. References to Eastern kings or Parthian allies ([confederated with Nero against Rome] Ewald), in the interest of the so-called synchrono-historical

---

interpretation, need no more than a mention. An utter misapprehension of the sixth plague is manifested in Bengel's designation of the imminent judgment upon the kings as itself the plague, into which the kings run. The plague, undoubtedly, culminates in the barely intimated defeat of the kings; but their very coming is a plague also, because, like the Hun and Mongol trains, they sweep away with them to the battle against God all the unsealed men and powers on their road. On account of the laying bare of the Euphrates' bed, an event of historical occurrence in the capture of Babylon by Cyrus, it is maintained by some (Hofmann, Ebrard, De Wette, Brückner) that a battle of the Eastern kings against the spiritual Babylon is intended. To De Wette this passage suggests the passage of Israel through the Jordan. A number of interpretations of the kings see in De Wette, p. 157. Alcasar: The Apostles and Evangelists; Bullinger and others: Believing princes; Grotius: Constantine the Great; Vitringa: The Kingdom of France. Others: The King of Persia, the Barbarians, the Turks, the Flavians. Jews adopting the Christian faith (Herder: the Babylonish Jews who go to the aid of those of Palestine), *etc.*

Out of the mouth of the Dragon, *etc.*— Combined operation of all the evil powers. Out of the three great mouths go forth three unclean spirits, as spirits of seduction. Or rather they have gone forth from these mouths and now exist independently, although at the time of the last battle, in which Gog and Magog are judged, the Beast and the False Prophet are already destroyed (ch. xix. 10). On the other hand, some expositors would fain read in ver. 14 ἐκπορεύεσθαι instead of ἐκπορεύεται, in order, by means of an artificial construction (see Hengstenberg), to gain the missing verb—which would, however, occasion material difficulties. The seed of rebellion lives on in impure spirits in that ring of heathenism which encircles the Millennial Kingdom. Be it, moreover, considered that here we are still in the course of the collective unitous description of the preparation for the General Judgment, and the colors of the three judgments still play into each other.

As frogs.—This similarity is borne by the unclean spirits themselves; it is not their uncleanness simply that is denoted by the ὡς (as according to Hengstenberg). The Egyptian frogs (Ex. viii.) were plaguing spirits because they went everywhere and defiled every thing with their uncleanness; these are plaguing spirits because they go forth to all parts as unclean demons, and seduce the kings of the earth to war against the City of God. They operate as spirits of demons, *i. e.,* through ethico-psychical domination, after the analogy of possession. Even after the judgment upon the centralization of evil in the Harlot, in the Beast, and in the False Prophet, Satanic evil shall continue to exist in a seed of evil reminiscences amongst the heathen, and in demonic operations. The expedition to which they excite the Eastern peoples is not directed against Babylon=Rome, for this has already (chap. xvii. 18) incurred judgment. Hengstenberg says that the expedition is directed against Canaan, *i. e.,* the Church, and that the prediction has reference "not to

something that shall happen at some one future time, but to that which is to be continually repeated." It is also asserted that Rome is not referred to, because all the other plagues have an œcumenical character. As if it were not called *urbs* from *orbis.* That the expedition is really not directed against Babylon-Rome is evident from the order of the judgments. According to Grotius, by the *three frogs* should be understood three forms of superstition to which Maxentius was addicted (the first is *extispicium,* not *exstispicium*); according to Luther, the sophists—namely, Faber, Eck and Emser: according to Vitringa, the Jesuits (the dried Euphrates being France, drained by its kings); according to Calovius, the Jesuits, Capuchins and Calvinists, *etc.* According to Düsterdieck, we should not ask what is to be understood by these three spirits—*i. e.,* they are schematical—importing nothing. According to Artemidor (see De Wette), the frogs are significant of jugglers and buffoons. Aristophanes portrayed their allegorical significance long before the writing of the Apocalypse. The *frog* has been used as a symbol in manifold connections (see Friedrich, *Symbolik und Mythologie der Natur,* p. 611). A lively interpretation of these little impotent, yet withal vociferous, dwellers in slime, see in Ebrard, p. 485. Friedrich brings out the additional fact that frogs have impudent eyes.

Doing signs.—By this can be meant only lying apparent miracles[*]—a description which applies to demonic miracles in general. De Wette speaks of an infatuating eloquence. The charm of eternally-repeated phrases is resident in will-magic, in the overpowering of weak souls by the semblance of assurance.—**The kings of the whole inhabited world.**—This expression is conditioned by the preceding words: the Eastern kings; although these may finally draw yet other powers into their vortex.—**To the war of the great day.**—The *two* days and the *two* battles [wars] (ch. xix. 19, xx. 9) are as yet wrapped together in one—in such a manner, however, that the *last* battle is faintly visible. See Ezek. xxxviii., xxxix.; Dan xii. 1; Zech. xii., xiv.—*The day* of the last end-judgment, properly so-called (Jude 6). Thus Bengel, De Wette, and others. Other interpretations: the *day* is the entire time from the passion of Christ to the end (Bede). "The *day of God* has a comprehensive character, denoting all the phases of God's judgments, *etc.*" (Hengst.) This is an attempt at the obliteration of definities—paving the way for his theory of the Millennial Kingdom.

[The expressions, *day of the Lord, great day of the Lord, etc.,* are of frequent occurrence in the New Testament; see Acts ii. 20; 1 Cor. i. 8; v 5; 2 Cor. i. 14; Phil. i. 6, 10; ii. 16; 1 Thess. v. 2, 4; 2 Thess. ii. 2; 2 Peter iii. 10, 12. These passages (with the exception, perhaps, of those in 2 Peter), together with the one under consideration, seem to refer to the day of Christ's appearing for the establishment of His Millennial Kingdom (comp. ch. xix. 11-21; Matt. xxiv. 30 sqq.), and not to the day of Final Judgment (comp. ch. xx. 11-15; Matt. xxv. 31 sqq) See Excursus on THE FUTURE COMINGS OF THE LORD, p. 339.—E. R. C.]

[* [See *Add. Comment* on ch. xiii. 13, p. 270.—E. R. C.]

Behold, I come as a thief.—A practical, warning digression of the Apostle, as in similar great decisive moments. As a vivid reminder of a saying of the Lord, he introduces the Lord as immediately speaking (see Matt. xxiv. 43, 44, Luke xii. 39, Rev. iii. 3). [Not a digression of the Apocalyptist, but a solemn re-affirmation by the Spirit of the warning of Jesus and His Apostles; comp. Matt. xxiv. 43, 44; Mark xiii. 35, 36; Luke xii. 39; 1 Thess. v. 2, 4; 2 Peter iii. 10.—E. R. C] The peculiar form of Christ's admonition—as recommending *watchfulness*—is doub'less based upon the fact that He is speaking to believing readers. The *keeping* of the *garments* of salvation is an idea which lies the closer at hand since the glance of the Seer passes beyond even the day of the Parousia and the secure years of the Millennial Kingdom.

And He [*or* **they],** *etc.*—The combatants are, without their will or even their knowledge, under the guidance of God, Who brings them to the battle-ground of their defeat (Ezek. xxxix. 2). The subject of συνήγαγεν is God (Hengsten., Ebrard); not the sixth Angel (Bengel), nor the Dragon (Ewald), nor, still less, the unclean spirits (Bleek, De Wette [Düsterdieck]).* **Harmageddon.**—See Syn. View. On the different interpretations of Harmageddon, see Düsterdieck, p. 499. (Etymological interpretations: *Excidium exercitus;* the Capitol; Mount Janiculus. Historical interpretations: The Megiddo of Jud. v. 19, or the Megiddo of Josiah, 2 Kings xxiii. 29; comp. Zech. xii. 11.) Düsterdieck indeed notes the fact that the term *mountain of Megiddo* (כגדו הר) differs from both of the Old Testament appellations—the *waters of Megiddo*, and the *valley* [Germ., *Ebene*=plain] *of Megiddo;* he, however, looks upon this distinction as an accessory circumstance, and thinks that there can be a reference only to the place where the Israelites were victorious over the kings of Canaan (Jud. v. 19). But why should not the fateful name of Megiddo have given occasion to a symbolical compound, with reference to Ezekiel and Zechariah?—denoting, therefore, the mountains of Jerusalem in a symbolical sense. On the repeated reference to *Rome* in Ewald, see Düsterdieck.—In an architectonic aspect it is very noteworthy that the sixth plague conducts us to the place of judgment at Harmageddon, without describing the judgment itself.

[**Harmagedon.**—"It is evidently in the meaning of the *Hebrew* name of this place that its appropriate significance lies. For otherwise why should ἐβραϊστί be prefixed to it? . . . But this circumstance does not deprive the name of geographical reality; and it is most probable on every account that such reality exists here. The words τὸν τόπον τὸν καλούμενον would surely not be used except of a real place habitually so named, or by a name very like this. Nor need we search very far for the place pointed out. הר־כגדו, the *Mountain of Megiddo*, designates at least the neighborhood where the Canaanitish kings were overthrown by Barak, Jud. v. 19; an occasion which gave rise to one of the two triumphal songs of Israel recorded in the Old Testament, and therefore one well worthy of

symbolizing the great final overthrow of the k ngs of the earth leagued against Christ.* That the name slightly differs from that given in the Old Testament, where it is the *plain* (2 Chron. xxxv. 22) or the *waters* (Judg. v. 19) of Megiddo, is of slight consequence, and may be owing to a reason which I shall dwell on below. The LXX. in both places adopt the form which we have here, Μαγεδώ—δών or—δδώ. Nor must it be forgotten that Megiddo was connected with another overthrow and slaughter, *viz.*, that of Josiah by Pharaoh-Necho (2 Kings xxiii. 29; 2 Chron. xxxv. 22), which, though not analogous to this predicted battle in its issue, yet served to keep up the character of the place as one of overthrow and calamity; cf. also Zech. xii. 11, and the striking description, 2 Chron. xxxv. 25, of the ordinance of lamentation for Josiah. At Megiddo also another Jewish king, Ahaziah, died of the wounds received from Jehu, 2 Kings ix. 27. The prefix *Har*, signifying 'mountain,' has its local propriety, see Stanley's description of the plain of Esdraelon, in the opening of his *Sinai and Palestine*, ch. ix. . . . Still there may have been a deeper reason which led to, or, at all events, justified the prefix. As the name now stands, it has a meaning ominous of the great overthrow which is to take place on the spot. Drusius, believing the word to be merely a mystic one, explains it to be חרבא גרהון 'internecio exercitus eorum,' the overthrow of their army. But, conceding and maintaining the geographical reality, must not we suppose that such a name, with such a sound, so associated with the past, bore to a Hebrew ear, when used of the future, its ominous significance of *overthrow?* It is remarkable that in Zech. xii. 11, where the mourning for Josiah is alluded to, the LXX. render not the plain of *Megiddo*, but ἐν πεδίῳ ἐκκοπτομένου, and this agrees with the interpretation of Andreas here, who supposes the name equivalent to διακοπή." Alford.—E. R. C.]

Vers. 17-21. And the seventh Angel poured out his vial upon the air.—The *air* is the common life-sphere of men. The Anger-Vial in the air is, therefore, in the first place a deadly decomposition of the spiritual life-sphere of men, resulting in the falling asunder of great communities. And this is the immediate result depicted in ver. 19. But with the separation of the three powers, Babylon, the Beast, Gog and Magog, is also introduced the cosmical decomposition of the earthly life-sphere—the end of the world.—**From the temple, from the throne.**—The *throne* does not appear to us to be expressive merely of a climax, in order to the more certain indication that the voice comes from God Himself (Düsterd.). *From the Throne* is, primarily, a modification—hence there is no καί to connect it with the preceding sentence. The *Temple* is the Holy of Holies; the *Throne* is the covering of the Ark of the Covenant. The consonance of Temple and Throne is the consonance of the economy of Christ and the economy of the Father. It is, in fine, a unisonous deliverance of the sentiment of the Church of God, as

* [It is worthy of note that the Song of Deborah and Barak is in measure adopted both by David and the Apostle Paul as descriptive (symbolic) of Messianic triumphs; comp. Judges v. 12; Ps. lxviii. 18; Eph. iv. 8.—E. R. C.]

well as of the terrestrial cosmos, through which the voice of God is heard, saying: **It is done!** The end is decided. We take the word absolutely, with Eichhorn and others (*actum est*)—not, however, in the following sense: now is done that which was commanded (in ver. 1) (Bengel, Düsterd., *et al.*). A learned digression explains: *fuit Roma* (Grotius).

And there were lightnings, *etc.*—Ch. xi. 19. Hengstenberg: "We have again reached precisely the same point at which we were already in ch. xi." Approximately true. According to Hofmann, the present vision comes to an end in the midst of ver. 18, and with the words καὶ σεισμός, *etc.*, a new leading vision begins. On the evangelical import of the *lightnings* and *thunders*, see SYN. VIEW.—There follows then **a great earthquake**, such as was never heard of before—a convulsion of earthly relations to their very foundations, so that the Christian world is sundered into three parts, more truly, even, than the Jewish world was thus rent previous to the first Parousia of Christ.—**And the great city.**—We have already more than once pointed out the decisive import of this passage. It contains the key to all that follows, as a summary declaration, namely, of the General Judgment and as a disposition of the three following special judgments (Babylon—the Beast—Gog and Magog). Hence it results also that the *great City*, as such, must comprehend all three parts, and consequently that it can denote neither Christian nor Pagan Rome, though Rome is its highest representative point. Still further from the truth is the reference to Jerusalem (Bengel, Herder, Hofmann, *et al.*). Considered in and for itself, the great City is an ideal City, embracing all Antichristianity in the Occident and in the Orient. According to Hengstenberg (who remarks that two Cities in the Apocalypse bear the title of *great*, Jerusalem and Babylon, *i. e.*, Rome), not only are we to avoid thinking of Jerusalem in this connexion, but we are also to put Christian Rome out of our thoughts—the City, he maintains, can be only a heathen City, heathen Rome. A certain tender care for "Christian" Rome is hardly mistakable here. It is impossible, however, that eschatological Antichristianity should ripen in a heathen City, knowing nothing properly of Christianity.—**Became into three parts**—"The number *three* (comp. ch. viii. 7, 8, 11, 12) has, perchance, a special reference to the *three arch-enemies*, ver. 13" (Ebrard). Düsterdieck: The Beast and the False Prophet, however, are regarded as *one* vanquished power (ch. xix.). The severance of two hostile powers is rightly insisted upon by Ebrard (p. 451); it cannot, however, be said that the third comes direct from the abyss, for the Eastern kings are on the ground; further, the specific Antichrist, in the narrower sense of the term, is the Beast (ch. xix.), not Satan (ch. xx).—**Babylon the great was remembered**, *etc.*—Acts x. 31. *Great Babylon* is but the more definite designation of the *great City*. She receives the anger-wine of the seventh Vial of Anger to drink, and the effect of this wine continues through all the three special judgments now following. The *anger of wrath* [τοῦ θυμοῦ τῆς ὀργῆς] is aptly symbolized by the wine-

cup; *i. e.*, psychical intoxication and drunkenness, spiritual *delirium-tremens*, is the common fundamental trait whence, in all three judgments, death proceeds.—**The cities of the nations** [Lange: *Heiden*], *etc.*—See SYN. VIEW. Ver. 20.—According to Hengstenb., the **islands** and the **mountains** are indicative of kingdoms. "Together with the islands and the mountains" (says the same expositor) "the sea, also, has vanished." In a physical connection this is no necessary consequence, and in a symbolical connection we are constrained to ask: In what respect has the sea vanished?

Ver. 21. **And a great hail. as of a talent in weight,** *etc.*—"Hailstones of the weight of a *mina* are called incredibly great by Diodor. Sic. xix. 45, but our passage mentions hailstones of the weight of a *talent*, which contains sixty minas; they are, therefore, probably of equal weight with the stones used in the catapults" (Düsterdieck; comp. De Wette, p. 161). According to Ebrard, the hail of a hundred-pounds' weight, "symbolizes the tremendous blows of suffering and sorrow which the world sustains in this time of revolution."* *Hail* is a specific devastating atmospheric discharge arising from the tension of the physical extremes of heat and cold, and their conflict. Thus, after the dissolution of human fellowship, the most ruinous conflicts of the extreme parties will arise; most fearful in their effects, however, will be the momentary coalitions that will take place—a truth typically exemplified at the crucifixion of Christ [where Sanhedrin and rabble, Jew and Roman, for the time made common cause.—TR.]. But the great fluctuations of nature in the ageing cosmos are also expressed in this figure.—**And men blasphemed God.**—In order to be able to blaspheme God, they are in a sense become monotheists again [or, rather, the fearful exigency has startled them out of their false systems and brought their inner consciousness of the One Almighty to the surface.—TR.]. It is, certainly, not necessary to suppose that those who are struck by such a hail, blaspheme as they are dying (Hengstenberg). "Some are precipitated lifeless to the earth, others blaspheme" (Düsterdieck). "We are, assuredly, not to imagine that actual natural hail is meant" (Ebrard). This blasphemy is the result of the rage with which they are irritated by a course of worldly affairs which is utterly incomprehensible to them, and by the hostile view of the world which confronts them. Even now not only radicalism, but also liberalism operates thus upon the minds of the hierarchical party; and, *vice versâ*, not only papacy, but even Christianity itself has the like effect upon anarchico-revolutionary spirits. Even in view of the objective world and the course of the times, extremists become increasingly irritated. Especially, not only socialistic, but also absolutist fanaticism is at a loss for money, weapons, wind and weather for the prosecution of extreme party-aims. All-sided pessimism, the issue of optimistic extravagances.—Different historical interpretations of the Vials of Anger, see in Düsterdieck, p. 503.

---

* [GLASGOW finds the *objective* of this prophecy in the tremendous cannon-balls—some of 600 pounds' weight—employed in modern warfare.—E. R. C.]

[ADDITIONAL NOTE ON THE SEVEN VIALS.]

By the American Editor.

[In the judgment of the writer, the vision of the Seven Vials relates to events still future—events the last of which will immediately precede the advent of Christ for the establishment of His Millennial Kingdom. The plagues predicted are to be executed upon the opposers of Christ and His true followers—upon the followers of the Beast (*i. e.*, the world-power, p. 272) and Babylon (*i. e.*, the apostate or world-allied Church, see ADD. NOTE on p. 317); the whole series, possibly, constituting that which in ch. vii. 14 is styled simply " the great tribulation " (see ADD. NOTE, pp. 191 sq.).

The writer is disposed to regard the terms *earth, sea, rivers and fountains*, and *sun*, of the first four Vials (vers. 2-10), as having been used *literally*—the prophecy being that these should be so affected as to cause them to give forth deleterious influences.—If by the Beast is to be understood the *world-power*, then, probably, by the pouring of the *fifth* Vial on his *throne* (ver. 10) we are to understand some influence upon established civil governments—either *destructive*, covering the nations with the darkness of anarchy; or *strengthening*, producing the darkness which flows from tyrannical oppression.—By the *Euphrates* of the *sixth* Vial we are, probably, to understand, with Wordsworth, Lord, and others, that which is to the mystical Babylon what the literal river was to the literal city. If this view be correct, then may we regard the symbol as indicating that current of opinion amongst worldlings in favor of, or those multitudes in the world allied to, the Apostate Church ("many waters"

of ch. xvii. 1 and 15 ?). The drying up of these waters, or their falling away from Babylon, would prepare the way for her destruction set forth, ch. xvii. 16. May it not be that *the kings from the sun-rising* are those mentioned ch. xvii. 12, 13, 16, who are to destroy the Harlot (*i. e.*, Babylon, comp. ch. xvii. 1 and 5)—and who are described as *from the sun-rising* from the fact either that when the Apocalyptist wrote they were below the horizon of vision, *yet to arise* (ch. xvii. 12); or that they were to come from the East? By the *frogs* (vers. 13, 14) we may understand *teachers of evil*, instigated by Satan, and some having *civil* and others *ecclesiastical* authority, and working miracles (see *Additional Comment* on ch. xiii. 13, p. 270), who shall seduce the nations into an assault on Christ and His true Church. For an explanation of *Harmagedon*, see the extract from Alford on p. 302.—The *seventh* Vial poured out upon the *air* may indicate an effect produced upon the literal atmosphere, at once universal in its influence and producing fearful convulsions in the realms of nature and in human society (comp. Isa. xiii. 6-10; Joel ii. 1, 2, 10, 30, 31; iii. 15; Matt. xxiv. 29; Mark xiii. 24, 25; Luke xxi. 25, 26; Acts ii. 19, 20;* Rev. vi. 12-17; see also Note on the *sixth* Seal, p. 179). The destruction of Babylon, here alluded to, is described in the following chapters.—E. R. C.]

* [The Apostle Peter quoted this prophecy of Joel with, out intending to teach that it had received its *ultimate* fulfillment in events attending the Pentecostal effusion. It seems impossible to resist the conclusions that the words of our Lord in Matt. xxiv. 29, *etc.*, have reference to convulsions in nature immediately preceding his second Advent, and that the prophecies of Isaiah and Joel, though they may have already received partial and typical fulfillments, have *ultimate* respect to the same events.—E. R. C.]

SECTION SIXTH.

(Second Division.)

The Seventh Vial of Anger, or the Three Great End-Judgments.

CHAP. XVII. 1—XX. 10.

I.—FIRST SPECIAL END-JUDGMENT.   JUDGMENT UPON BABYLON.

CHAP. XVII.–XVIII.

A.—THE JUDGMENT UPON BABYLON AS A HEAVEN-PICTURE, OR THE HEAVENLY PROPHECY OF THE FALL OF BABYLON.

CHAP. XVII. 1-18.

And there came one of the seven angels which [who] had the seven vials, and talked with me, saying unto me [om. unto me]¹, Come [om. Come] Hither ; I will show unto thee the judgment of the great whore [harlot] that sitteth upon [or ins. 2 the]² many waters ; with whom the kings of the earth have [om. have] committed fornication, and the inhabitants of [they who inhabit] the earth have been [were]

TEXTUAL AND GRAMMATICAL.

¹ Ver. 1. [Crit. Eds. omit μοι with 𝔅 and A.—E. R. C.]
² Ver. 2. [Tisch. inserts τῶν twice with B*.; Lach. and Treg. omit with א. A. P.; Alf. brackets.—E. R. C.]

3 made drunk with the wine of her fornication. So [And] he carried me away in the [om. the] spirit into the [a] wilderness : and I saw a woman sit [sitting] upon a scarlet colored [om. colored] beast [wild-beast], full of [or ins. the]³ names of

4 blasphemy, having seven heads and ten horns. And the woman was arrayed [clothed] in purple and scarlet color [om. color], and⁴ decked [gilded] with gold and precious stones [stone] and pearls, having a golden cup in her hand full of

5 abominations and filthiness [the uncleannesses]⁵ of her fornication⁶ : And upon her forehead was [om. was] a name written, MYSTERY, BABYLON THE GREAT, THE MOTHER OF [ins. THE] HARLOTS AND [ins. OF THE] ABOMI-

6 NATIONS OF THE EARTH. And I saw the woman drunken with the blood of the saints, and with the blood of the martyrs [witnesses] of Jesus : and when I

7 saw her, I wondered with great admiration [wonder]. And the angel said unto me, Wherefore didst thou marvel [wonder]? I will tell thee the mystery of the woman, and of the beast [wild-beast] that carrieth [beareth] her, which [that]

8 hath the seven heads and ten horns. The beast [wild-beast] that thou sawest was, and is not ; and shall [is about to (μέλλει)] ascend out of the bottomless [om. bottomless] pit [abyss] and [ins. to] go⁷ into perdition (ἀπώλειαν) : and they that dwell on the earth shall wonder, whose names were [of whom the name is] not written in [upon] the book [scroll] of life from the foundation of the world, when they behold [see] the beast [wild-beast] that [ins. he] was, and is not, and yet is [om.

9 yet is—ins. shall be present]⁸. And [om. And] Here is the mind which [that] hath wisdom. The seven heads are seven mountains, on which the woman sitteth

10 [or where the woman sitteth upon them]. [,] and there [om. there—ins. they] are seven kings : [ins. the] five are fallen, and [om. and—ins. the]⁹ one is, and [om. and] the other is not yet come ; and when he cometh [is come], he must continue a

11 short space [little while]. And the beast [wild-beast] that was, and is not, even

12 he¹⁰ is the [an] eighth, and is of the seven, and goeth into perdition. And the ten horns which thou sawest are ten kings, which [who] have [ins. not yet]¹¹ received no [om. no—ins. a] kingdom as yet [om. as yet] ; but [ins. they] receive power [authority]

13 as kings one hour [ins. together] with the beast [wild-beast]. These have one mind (γνώμη), and shall [om. shall] give their power and strength [authority] unto

14 the beast [wild-beast]. These shall make [om. make] war with the Lamb, and the Lamb shall overcome [conquer] them : for he is Lord of lords, and King of kings :

15 and they that are with him are [om. are] called, and chosen, and faithful. And he saith unto me, The waters which thou sawest, where the whore [harlot] sitteth,

16 are peoples, and multitudes, and nations, and tongues. And the ten horns which thou sawest upon [om. upon—ins. and]¹² the beast [wild-beast], these shall hate the whore [harlot], and shall make her desolate and naked, and shall eat her flesh, and

17 burn [consume] her with [or in]¹³ fire. For God hath [om. hath] put in [gave into] their hearts to fulfill [perform] his will [mind (γνώμη)], and to agree [perform

---

³ Ver. 3. Tisch. [1859, also Treg.] gives γέμον τὰ ὀνόματα, with Cod. A., etc. [Lach., Tisch. (8th Ed.), Alf. read γέμοντα ὀνόματα ; Tisch. (8th Ed.) declares that P. requires this division. The reading of the participle in the following clause, which, were it certain, would settle the question, is also disputed ; Alf., Tisch. (8th Ed.) read ἔχοντα with א. P. ; Lach., Tisch. (1859), and Treg., ἔχον with B*. 1, etc.—E. R. C.]

⁴ Ver. 4. Lach. gives καί in acc. with A., etc. [So also Treg. and Tisch. (8th Ed.) with א. A., 1, 7, Vulg., etc. ; Tisch. (1859) omits with B*. P. ; Alf. brackets.—E. R. C.]

⁵ Ver. 4. Codd. א A. B*. give τα ἀκάθαρτα.

⁶ Ver. 4. Codd. A. [?] B*., etc., give τῆς γῆς. [So Tisch. (1859) with B*. (not A.) ; Alf., Treg., Tisch. (8th Ed.) give αὐτῆς with A. 1, 7, Vulg., etc. ; א. reads αὐτῆς καὶ τῆς γῆς.—E. R. C.]

⁷ Ver. 8. Codd. A., etc., give ὑπάγει. [So Lach., Alf., and Tisch. (1859) ; Treg. and Tisch. (8th Ed.) give ὑπάγειν with א. B*. P.—E. R. C.]

⁸ Ver. 8. [The "and yet is" is an attempted translation of the printed text of Erasmus, καίπερ ἔστι. This reading, as is now generally conceded, is "an error of Erasmus' copyist" or of the press : it is not found in the original MS. of Erasmus. On this subject Dr. Conant writes (in his article on the Greek Text of the Apocalypse in T e Baptist Quarterly) : "The MS. reads, καὶ πάρ εστι, with εστι slightly removed from the preceding syllable (as often happens in manuscript), but with a distinctly written α in the syllable παρ, and with the accentuation, unquestionably, of καὶ πάρεστι. The copyist, mistaking a for ε in the syllable παρ, and making a wrong division of syllables, wrote καίπερ ἔστι, contrary both to the letters and the accentuation of the MS. There can be no doubt that the true reading is that of the ancient MSS., namely, the Sinaitic (παρεστε—παρεσται), the Alex. (Cod. Eph. is defective here), B. of the Apoc., and the Porphyrian palimpsest, all of which have παρεσται." The reading thus indicated is universally adopted.—E. R. C.]

⁹ Ver. 10. [Crit. Eds. read ὁ εἷσ without καί. in acc. with א. A. B*. P., Vulg., etc.—E. R. C.]

¹⁰ Ver. 11. [Lach., Alf., Tisch. read αὐτός with A. P. 1, Vulg., etc. ; Treg. gives οὗτος with א. B*.—E. R. C.]

¹¹ Ver. 12. The reading οὔπω in acc. with B*. [א*. P., Vulg.], etc. [So Alf., Treg., and Tisch. ; Lach. reads οὐκ with A., Fuld.—E. R. C.]

¹² Ver. 16. [Crit. Eds. read καί with א. A. B*. P. 1, Am., Fuld., Demid., Tol. ; Clem. and Lips. ⁴ ⁶ require ἐπί.—E. R. C.]

¹³ Ver. 16. [Tisch. (8th Ed.) reads πυρί, without ἐν, with א. B*. P. ; Lach., Tisch. (1859), Treg. prefix ἐν with A. ; Alf. brackets.—E. R. C.]

20

one mind ($\pi o \iota \tilde{\eta} \sigma a \iota$ $\mu i a \nu$ $\gamma \nu \omega \mu \eta \nu$)]¹⁴, and [ins. to] give their kingdom unto the beast 18 [wild-beast], until the words¹⁵ of God shall be fulfilled [finished]. And the woman which [that] thou sawest is that [the] great city, which [that] reigneth [hath kingdom] over the kings of the earth.

¹⁴ Ver. 17. [This clause is omitted by Lachm., and bracketed by Alf., in accord. with A. 79, *Vulg.*, etc.; it (or γνώμην μίαν) is given by Treg. and Tisch., with א. B*. P. 1, 7, 14, etc.—E. R. C.]
¹⁵ Ver. 17. Codd. A. B*. [א. P.] give οἱ λόγοι.

EXEGETICAL AND CRITICAL.

SYNOPTICAL VIEW.

When we say : the fall of Babylon as a Heaven-picture, we mean, the fall of Babylon *sub specie æterni*, or, in other words, the phenomenon of Antichristianity in the Church, in all its historical bearings, illuminated by the light of revelation and designated for judgment by the rule of Divine Providence.

We must, above all, keep fast hold of the following points : 1. That the Babylon here spoken of, the Harlot, is to be distinguished from the general Babylon (ch. xvi. 19), and yet that it coincides with the latter as its first [last?]* historical culmination. 2. That the Beast which bears the Harlot is identical with the *Beast out of the sea* (ch. xiii.), as the peculiar antitheocratic and Antichristian organ of Satan ; that, however, it here comes under consideration provisionally in a special aspect only, as bearing the Woman for a time, and, finally, judging her. Hence, also, the history of the Beast is more special here than in ch. xiii. In the latter passage, ver. 3, one of his heads is mortally wounded ; here, the whole Beast disappears for a time (ver. 8).† 3. That the *heads* and *horns* of the Beast here resolve themselves into a special history consisting of two parts—a history which must by no means be confounded with the history of the Beast presented in ch. xiii.

That we are still in the sphere of the seventh Vial of anger is manifest, in the first place, from the bare fact that one of the seven Angels who had the Vials, shows the Seer the judgment of the great Harlot. The latter is preliminarily signalized by two marks : 1. *She sits upon many waters ;* she is an authority based upon many nationalities, many national dispositions, peculiarities and currents. 2. *With her the kings of the earth have committed fornication, and they who inhabit the earth have become drunk with the wine of her fornication.* She herself has become for the *kings of the earth*, of earthly states and seats of culture, an idol, a subject of idolatry which has seduced them to a thousand-fold apostasy from the laws of religion, humanity, truth and righteousness ; and not only have they departed from the true God and served false gods in company and connection with her, but

---

* [It is probable that the *erste* of the German edition is a misprint for *letzte*, as it is only in the latter form that the proposition of our Author can be accepted. It may be remarked that even with this correction the truth of the first part of the proposition is questionable. Is it not probable that by "Babylon the Great" of ch. xvi. 19, the Seer contemplated the *entire Babylon* as "headed up" in the *Babylon of the last days* ; or, in other words, as identical with "Babylon the Great" of ver. 5?—E. R. C.]
† [Is not one and the same event set forth by the figures, "as slain" (xiii. 3), and "is not" (xvii. 3)—*viz.*: the apparent ceasing of the Beast to exist *as Beast*?—E. R. C.]

they have also done the same independently, as her followers and imitators. They have, however, in many respects been swept along in this direction by *those who inhabit the earth*—by absolute hangers-on of the soil and of authority, who have become intoxicated in the fanatical enthusiasm of the bigotry of the world.

The Angel takes the Seer in spirit into *a wilderness*. Here, it seems, we a while ago left the Woman, once clothed with the sun (ch. xii.). And such is indeed the fact: it is the same wilderness, and not the same ; the same Woman, and not the same. History sufficiently instructs us concerning the fact that the holy wilderness of world-renunciation, of asceticism, which so long guarded the integrity of the Woman, became in course of time a wilderness of spiritual and intellectual moral corruption—that the heavenly *flight from* the world was changed into a demonic *seeking of* the world, embodied in the wild career of false monks—that a wilderness of hypocrisy, *pia fraus*, fanatical terrorism and demoralizing dogmas of all kinds was gradually developed. But the Woman—is she, indeed, the same ? Those who cannot understand how the one Woman (ch. xii.) can in the course of time have divided into the two figures of the Harlot and the Bride, should consider the fact that the wheat and the chaff grow on the same ear ; that the same Theocracy which, in respect of its internal essence, bore Christ, also crucified Him, in respect of its external hierarchical figuration ; and that thus the development of the Harlot and the Bride has not been effected in two separate lines, but in an original organic unity, in which the contrast has been continually maturing (see the *foot-note* on p. 25).

The following considerations now successively demand our attention :

1. The Woman and her relation to the Beast.
2. The Beast in his relation to the seven Heads.
3. The seven Heads in relation to the ten Horns.

1. The Woman and her relation to the Beast.

That the Woman here depicted is significant of the fallen Church there can be no doubt, when we consider the import of the Woman (the congregation of God) and of womanhood (religiosity)—(see Rink, p. 238 sqq.). The exclusive reference of this figure to pagan Rome fails to recognize, in the first place, the broad scope of the eschatological vision ; secondly, the fact that even in the time of Domitian, and far more in the time of Nero, it would have been impossible for the Apocalyptist to speak of Rome as cherishing a true Antichristian thirst for the blood of the saints. Thirdly, such a reference misapprehends the idea of Antichristianity, which takes its rise only in corrupt Christianity. From these considerations it will also be evident, first, that not simply the fallen Romish Church,

Rome, is here intended;—this is the further from being the fact since imperial Rome has been transferred to Byzantium and its centre of gravity has been thence removed to Moscow and St. Petersburg; moreover, the hierarchical principle radiates far and wide throughout the Church. It is also further evident, however, that nothing but Christian Rome can constitute the symbolical and historical apex of this whole body of the fallen Church. The Muscovite hierarchism is too rude to be this apex; sporadic hierarchism too theoristic; the mean lies where hierarchism is in its whole demonic depth. Nevertheless, we regard the *seven mountains* whereon the Woman sits, as but an allusion to terrestrial Rome, it being agreeable to the consistency of the Book to take the *seven mountains* as a symbolical figure, of which we must speak further on. The Seer declares that he *wondered* much to see the Woman as he saw her. We apprehend this utterance in the same sense with those expositors who have assigned the contrast of this figure with the appearance in ch. xii. as the ground of the Seer's wonderment. In the earlier passage, we behold a celestial Woman, clothed with the sun, the moon under her feet, adorned with a garland of chosen stars, equipped with eagle's wings. Here we have a Harlot, riding or sitting upon a scarlet Beast, a Beast signalized with the hue of blood and blood-thirstiness (into which the *fiery* hue of the *Dragon* has darkened), and thus herself founded upon the Beast and its blood-thirstiness, *i. e.*, upon an Antichristian world-power and bloody violence. The Beast is *full of the names of blasphemy*—there is no form of irreligion which is not comprehended in the absolute Machiavelism of world-monarchy: religious persecution, contempt of humanity, despotism over consciences, breach of promise, a doctrinal system of faithlessness—and the like—are some of the first articles. The incongruence of the *seven Heads* and *ten Horns* is brought into view here likewise, in order to the signalizing of the power indicated, as possessing the semblance, and but the semblance, of holiness. On this demonic Beast the poor Woman has prepared her a sort of throne for her exaltation; no longer is the moon beneath her feet—vanished are the stars of elect spirits, and the eagle-wings. She herself is clothed with a party-colored double red—with the royal hue of purple and the scarlet of blood—and over this is spread the sheen of gold brocade, of precious stones and pearls, the richest worldly adornment of every sort. In her hand the Woman holds the magical means of her dominion and glory, the *golden cup*, the symbolical vessel of consecrate and holy communion, solace and refreshment—but *full of abominations;* and, together with the cup, *the uncleannesses of the fornication, i. e.,* the idolatry, *of the earth—i. e.,* all those iniquities that follow in the train of idolatry. The *abominations* denote all manner of unnaturalnesses; the *uncleannesses of the fornication of the earth* are all those immoralities which are the consequential issues of the earth's departure from the true God and its service of false divinities. *On her forehead* she has a *name written* as a *mystery; i. e.,* whoever is able to read the name, will read the

following inscription: *Babylon the Great, the Mother of the Harlots and of the Abominations of the Earth.* She herself knows not that her proper escutcheon—absolute sovereignty over the consciences of earth—means only this, and can mean nothing else. Most repulsive is her appearance: *A drunken woman!* Through fanaticism intoxicated to the verge of frenzy! *Drunken with the blood of the saints and with the blood of the witnesses of Jesus!* Blood-guiltiness produces excitement, confusion of the mind; and this remark applies in the fullest sense to that blood-guiltiness whose measure is filled up in the persecution and destruction of the holiest witnesses of God and Christ. Grotius depicts this phenomenon with drastic vividness, like a Dutch genre-picture: *Vidit eam ore rabido, despumante et evomente sanguinem, ut ebrii solent.*—But now arises the question—how can the Beast lend himself to bear the Woman, when it is declared that *the ten Horns and the Beast shall hate the Harlot and make her desolate* (ver. 16)? The weight of the future tense must be observed here. At first the Beast is subject to the Woman, for it is the Woman who helped the Beast out of his apparent annihilation. The absolutism of the hierarchy has promoted the growth of the absolutism of despotism. Finally, however, there is a reversal of the relation, the Beast having made a pupil of the Woman's, the False Prophet, subservient to himself; and in the end it is the deep-lying antagonism between the demonic ground-forms of the two [the Woman and the Beast] which gives occasion to the full outbreak of hostility and the destruction of the Woman—possibly in a conflict in which the Beast will prove himself more human than the Harlot.

The Seer marvels to see the Woman in this situation—or, let us rather say, to see her again. According to the speech of the Angel, that which most surprises John is her fellowship with the Beast, her riding upon him—this most horrible Amazon-equipment. Hence the answer of the Angel [to John's wonderment] has in view an explanation of the origin of this mystery of the fellowship of the Woman and the Beast. The utterance runs thus: *The Beast was, and is not, and shall ascend out of the abyss, in order to go speedily into damnation.** This declaration [of the Beast's vanishment and re-appearance] is, certainly, a parallel to the mortal wounding of a head of the Beast (ch. xiii. 3), but it must be distinguished from the declaration concerning the king who "is not yet come" (ch. xvii. 10). The wounding of the Beast's head is the cause, the disappearance of the Beast the result; the return of the Beast is the transition from the seventh to the eighth head. For at that very moment of the vision [not the moment depicted by the vision, but the time at which the vision was vouchsafed.—Tr.], the Beast *was not*—he seemed to have vanished—whilst the sixth king was in being. We, therefore, understand the declaration of the Angel as of the following import: The Antichristian world-power was in being before Christ; it then seemed, for a period reaching to the time of the

---

* [So Lange here *freely* renders.—E. R. C.]

vision, to be annihilated by the victory of Christ—as indeed it was principially annihilated; it however was to return later as an external apparent power. And it was as the returned Beast that the Beast carried the Woman, for in that interval of his vanishment it was only in the saintly seeming of subserviency to the Woman that he could make his appearance again. But, again, it was also his wonderful re-appearance which induced the Woman to trust herself to him. From the wonder of all people dwelling upon the earth at the apparent invincibility of the Beast—that is, from the renewed belief in the irresistible power of evil—the complete fall of the Woman resulted—the vain fancy that with the help of the Beast, with the help of ungodly and God-opposed state-maxims, she might attain to greatness and ever-increasing glory. Hence this unblest concordat in which, for a long time, the Woman seems to rule the Beast, until she is finally deposed and destroyed by him.

2. The Beast in his relation to the seven Heads.

Hither [let] understanding [come]. The mystery which the Angel here pronounces can be solved only through the union of worldly understanding [or an understanding of the world—*Weltverstand*] and spiritual wisdom. In the application of this problem to the Nero tradition, there would certainly have been no *wisdom;* at most, it could only have contained such an *understanding* as the Apocalyptist would have declared to be devoid of wisdom. To proceed, the seven Heads of the Beast are *seven mountains,* on which the Woman sits, and are *seven kings.* Here our task is, to abide by the laws of symbolism and not take a leap into geography, although we assume that there is an *allusion* to the City of the Seven Hills. Neither is it advisable to regard the sentence, *and are seven kings,* as tautological. As in the Book of Daniel, the world-monarchies (ch. ii.) are, in respect of their bright side, represented in the human image of *metal,* and (ch. vii.) in respect of their dark side, in the *four beasts,* so there is also here, doubtless, an antithesis to be taken for granted. The *seven mountains* are seven forms of empire—in the sacred number, because the State, taken in the abstract, is subservient to the purposes of the Divine Kingdom. The *kings,* however, seem here, in accordance with chs. xvii. 2 and xviii. 3, as despots, to represent the dark side of the world-monarchy, its God and Christ-opposed conduct—hence, pre-eminently, its bestial nature. The reference is not to individual kings; such a reference is impossible on this account, if for no other reason, viz.: because the *kings* must be in exact correspondence with the seven *mountains.* Otherwise the Apocalyptist must necessarily have seen *fourteen* heads, for, in accordance with the laws of allegory, the heads cannot denote two entirely different groups—the seven mountains as diverse from the seven kings. We reckon once more, therefore, the *four* world-monarchies of Daniel and add to them the Roman-Herodian government as the *fifth* monarchy. The *sixth* king is the Roman Empire at the time of the vision, and the Seer proleptically beholds the coming of a *seventh,* a world-monarchy, on

which the Woman can ride for a short time. Then the Beast that was, and is not, again undisguisedly appears. In the *seventh* king it was, to a greater or less extent, the still anonymous bearer of the Woman; in the *eighth,* which issues from all the seven, as their evil extract, it will become the open enemy and destroyer of the Woman, and then, when it has fulfilled its judicial mission, it will *go into perdition.*

3. The Seven Heads and the Ten Horns.

The *ten horns* are distinct from the *seven heads;* they seem finally, however, to be comprehended together above the *eighth* head (*eight* is the number of the world), in which the Beast manifests himself again openly. The number *ten* is the number of the ripe development of the world, in antithesis to the number *seven* as the number of complete Divine order. And so, also, the *horns* denote bare power or force, in antithesis to the *heads* which symbolize the government of intelligence. They, therefore, together with the *eighth* king-picture from the life of the Beast, issue forth as *ten kings* of abstract power, as absolute radicalism. They had hitherto *not yet received a kingdom;* now they obtain, for *one hour,* complete imperial power in the world *together with the Beast.* This *hour* is, again, the great and fear-inspiring hour of the decisive conflict between open Antichristianity and the hypocritically disguised Antichristianity of the Woman. The *ten kings* rule, not successively, but conjointly; they are also not real kings, but mock-kings (ὡς βασιλεῖς),[*] and if they have one *mind,* it is but the spirit of Antichristian coalition. By the declaration: *They shall war with the Lamb, and the Lamb shall conquer them, etc.,* the finale is indicated—the judgment upon the Beast (ch. xix. 19). But to what purpose this interruption here? It explains that hatred of the Woman which finally bursts forth in completeness. A bold change of allegorical images is visible in the first and third verses, where the same Woman is spoken of as sitting upon *many waters,* and as sitting in the *wilderness.* Here [ver. 15] the reference is again to the *waters* on which the Harlot sits (and when we read: *the waters which thou sawest,* this inaccuracy reminds us of similar expressions in the Johannean Gospel). The sovereignty of the Harlot is based not only upon the wilderness and the Beast, but also, through these, upon the *peoples, and multitudes, and nations, and tongues.* And she becomes in the end, by means of the semblance of Christocracy that clings to her, an object of *hatred* to the ten Horns and the Beast. She is destroyed by four principal strokes. In the first place, she is *wasted,* desolated: an allusion to the Harlot as a *city,* or to her false eremite estate. Secondly, she is *stripped,* exposed in her nakedness, a frequently cited punishment of courtesans, whose meretricious adornment has been a means of seduction.

---

[*] [When the Apostle Paul refers to the fact that the Thessalonians treated him *as (ὡς) an Apostle,* does he imply that he was a *mock-apostle?* The well-known force of ὡς is to indicate not mere *similarity* to an individual or a class, but inclusion in a class specified—thus it is declared Matt. xxi. 26, that the people held John *as* a prophet; see also 1 Cor. iv. 1, 14; x. 15; 2 C r. vi. 4. *etc.* And further: "To receive authority as a king," is to be a king, *de facto* if not *de jure.*—E. R. C.]

Thirdly, she is, while still living, *robbed of her flesh*, which her enemies devour: her goods, her territories, all her possessions become the prey of the foe. And fourthly, she is, in a sarcastic *auto da fé*, suggestive of so many like proceedings, *burned with fire;* amid the wrath-fire of open, bold Antichristianity, hypocritical Antichristianity meets its end.—*For God gave into their hearts.* As, in accordance with the grand view of the Seer, in the wrath of the heathen, the wrath of God is manifest in an ironical mode of judgment, so in the *one mind* and unanimity of these kings, the purpose of God is visible, and in the surrender of their kingdom to the Beast, the consummation of the prophetic words of God may be seen, as in that dark hour when Caiaphas and Pilate were made to subserve His Providence (John xi. 51, xix. 11). The Angel at the close comprehends the characteristics of the Woman in one expression: *The Woman that thou sawest is the great city that hath kingdom over the kings of the earth.* In the *Woman*, Great Babylon shall be judged specially as Babylon.

[ABSTRACT OF VIEWS, ETC.]

By the American Editor.

[ELLIOTT:* This chapter contains a vision (vers. 3-6), and a descriptive statement by the Angel (vers. 7-18); both the vision and statement are introductory to the judgment upon Babylon, and explanatory of its causes and reasonableness. *In the Vision*, the Woman represents Papal Rome; the Beast, the Roman Empire under its last or Papal head (see p. 259); the desert, the Roman Campagna. The period of time contemplated in the vision is the 1260 years of the Beast's life under his last head (p. 260).—*In the description*, the Angel contemplates the entire history of both the Woman and the Beast—the former representing Rome, Imperial and Papal (see ver. 18); the latter (identical with the *Beast from the sea* of ch. xiii.), the Roman Empire under all its heads or forms. (It is on the ground of the general nature of this description that Elliott denies that the *burning* of ver. 16 is the *final burning* foretold in ch. xviii. 8. He explains the destruction referred to in the former instance as preceding the vision—as that effected by the ten Gothic powers in the Fifth and Sixth centuries. These *horns* of the Beast (p. 260) then spoiled and burned the City, and so desolated the surrounding Campagna as to produce the ἔρημος or *desert*, in the midst of which Papal Rome arose, and in which (ver. 3) the vision was located.)—The *riding of the Woman on the Beast* (ver. 3) symbolizes that the Western Papal Empire, as a whole, with the power of its ten secular kingdoms and many peoples, should *uphold* and *be ruled by* Papal Rome.—The double character of the Woman, as a *Harlot* with the ten kings and a *tavern-hostess* vending drugged wines to the common people (vers. 1, 2, 4), symbolizes her unholy alliance with the former, and her unholy and corrupting traffic (in indulgences, relics, transubstantiation-

cup, *etc.*) with the latter.—The *adornment* of the Harlot (ver. 4) presents, "as applied to the Romish Church, a picture characteristic and from the life; the dress coloring specified being distinctively that of the Romish ecclesiastical dignitaries, and the ornaments those with which it has been bedecked beyond any Church called Christian."—The word *Mystery*, ver. 5 (allusive to the *mystery of iniquity*, 2 Thess. ii. 7, 8), "was once, if we may repose credit on no vulgar authority, written on the Pope's tiara."*—The title "*Mother of harlots, etc.*," is a parody of the title, "Rome, Mother and Mistress."—The *drunkenness with the blood of saints*, ver. 6, symbolizes the martyr blood shed by Rome throughout the 1260 years of her prosperity.

BARNES: This chapter commences a more detailed description of the judgment inflicted on the Antichristian power referred to in ch. xvi. ; it contains a description of the sequel of the seventh Vial, which is continued (in various forms) to the close of ch. xix. ; it embraces the following: 1. Introduction, vers. 1-3 ; 2. A particular description of this Antichristian power, vers. 3-6 ; 3. An explanation of what is meant by the Woman, and of the design of the representation, which comprises (1), a promise of the Angel that he would explain ; (2) an enigmatical representation of the design of the vision (containing a description of the Beast, *etc.*), vers. 8-14 ; (3) a more literal statement of what is meant by this, vers. 15-18.—The *Harlot* symbolizes Papal Rome ; her *adornment, fornication, cup, drunkenness, many waters*, substantially as Elliott ; her inscription, see EXPL. IN DETAIL, ver. 5.—The *Beast* is identical with that of ch. xiii. 1, and designates the Roman power (see p. 260)—the *period of the vision* being that of the *Eighth* or *Papal* head and the *ten horns*, or ten subordinate kingdoms†—*viz.:* the 1260 years of Papal supremacy.—The *destruction* of vers. 16, 17, is the final destruction of ch. xviii. 8, to be effected by the instrumentality of the ten secular powers who now uphold and are governed by the Harlot.—The ἔρημος, ver. 3, is the Roman Campagna.‡

---

* [*Scaliger*, on the authority of an informant of the Duke of Montmorency whilst at Rome. And so again Francis Le Moyne and Brocardus, on ocular evidence, they assure us; saying that Julius III. removed it. See Daubuz, Vitringa, and Bishop Newton, *ad loc.*" Foot-note by ELLIOTT.—E. R. C.]

† [Barnes agrees with Elliott as to the general interpretation of the *heads* and *horns*, as on p. 259. He understands, however, by the *sixth* head, not the *diademed* emperors whom he includes under the *fifth*, but the Dukedom under the Exarchate of Ravenna, continuing from A. D. 566 to 727.—E. R. C.]

‡ [Barnes agrees with Elliott as to the place indicated by the ἔρημος, but not as to the fact that it was produced by the *destruction* of ver. 16. The following extract which he makes from Gibbon's *Decline and Fall*, ch. xiv., deserves consideration: "Rome had reached, about the close of the sixth century, the lowest period of her depression. By the removal of the seat of empire, and the successive loss of the provinces, the sources of private and public opulence were exhausted; the lofty tree under whose shade the nations of the earth had reposed, was deprived of its leaves and branches, and the sapless trunk left to wither on the ground. The ministers of command and the messengers of victory no longer met on the Appian or Flaminian way ; and the hostile approach of the Lombards was often felt and continually feared. The inhabitants of a potent and peaceful capital, who visit without an anxious thought the garden of the adjacent country, will faintly picture in their fancy the distress of the Romans ; they shut or opened their gates with a trembling hand, beheld from the walls the flames of their

---

* [Elliott is at this point exceedingly obscure. The above is believed to be a fair presentation of the views he designed to express.—E. R. C.]

STUART: Ch. xvii. is wholly occupied with an *explanatory* vision designed for the purpose of making the reader understand whose destruction is going on.—The *Woman* symbolizes the City of Rome, "altogether in the manner of the Old Testament prophets, who everywhere personify great cities by *women*." — "The *Beast* means the Roman Emperors, specifically Nero, of whom the report spread throughout the empire is (was) that he will revive, after being apparently slain, and will come as it were from the abyss or Hades; but he will still perish, and that speedily. The *Beast* symbolizes him of whom it is said, that all the world will wonder at and worship him, when they see him thus returned, as they suppose from the under-world" (see also p. 261).—The *ten horns* denote the subordinate and tributary kings of the empire, who unite with the Beast in persecuting the Church.—Ver. 16 indicates "that tyrants like Nero, and persecutors such as his confederates, would occasion wasting and desolation to Rome, even like that already inflicted by Nero, who had set Rome on fire and consumed a large portion of it. In a description so highly figurative as the one before us, nothing more seems to be necessarily meant."—The ἔρημος of ver. 3, is "appropriate to symbolize the future condition of the Beast."

WORDSWORTH. The views of this commentator concerning the *Woman* and her *session upon the Beast*, coincide generally with those of Elliott and Barnes.—For his interpretation of the *Beast* and the *heads*, see p. 261.—By the *horns* he understands "the kingdoms growing out of the Roman Empire at its dismemberment."—The ἔρημος, he declares, may indicate the Campagna, or the moral wilderness in which Rome is situate, or both.—The *destruction* of ver. 16 he interprets as Barnes.

ALFORD. This commentator also adopts the generally accepted Protestant hypothesis (that advocated by Elliott and Barnes) concerning the *Woman*, her *adornment, fornication, session upon the Beast, etc.*—For his interpretation of the *Beast* and the *seven heads*, see pp. 261 sq.—Concerning the eighth head he writes: "This *eighth*, the last and worst phase of the Beast, is not represented as any one of his heads, but as being the Beast himself in actual embodiment. He is ἐκ τῶν ἑπτά, not 'one of the seven,' but the successor and result of the seven, following and springing out of them. And he εἰς ἀπώλειαν ὑπάγει—does not *fall* like the others, but goes on and meets his own destruction at the hand of the Lord Himself. There can be little doubt in the mind of the student of prophecy, *who* is thus described; that it is the ultimate Antichristian power, prefigured by the *little horn* in Daniel, and expressly announced by St. Paul, 2 Thess. ii. 3 sqq."—He interprets the *ten horns* as "ten European powers, which, in the last time, in concert with and subjection to the Antichristian power, shall make war against Christ. In the precise number and form here indicated, they have not yet arisen."—He regards the *destruction* as the *final destruction* mentioned ch. xviii.

LORD: It is apparent from vers. 1, 2, that the *Woman* had been beheld in a previous but unrecorded vision, sitting where there were *seven mountains* and *many waters*. The scene was the site of Rome; the *seven mountains* were the seven hills of that city, and were symbols of the seven kinds of rulers who had exercised the government of the ancient empire; the *waters* were symbols of the peoples, *etc.*, of the empire; the Woman symbolized the nationalized hierarchies of the Apostate Church, and the actions ascribed to her show that the kings of the earth united with her in her idolatry.—The vision exhibited (vers. 3-6) and the explanation (vers. 7-18) represent the *Woman* in her relations to the *rulers*, first as her *supporters*, and finally as her *destroyers*.—The *Beast* on which the *Woman* was borne, *was*, and *is not*, and *yet is*: it *was*, as the successions of rulers of the ancient empire, which its heads symbolize, had been; it *is not*, as a government of a head is no longer exercised over the empire as anterior to its fall; and *yet it still is*, in an eighth form, inasmuch as the cotemporaneous kings who now reign over the kingdom into which it is divided exert a sway essentially the same—they are a combination of rulers and under their several governments *one*, by exercising their authority on the same principles and on the same authority as the seventh head, and in that respect they are an eighth appropriately symbolized by the same monster under the horns.*—The *names of blasphemy* symbolize the

---

houses, and heard the lamentations of their brethren who were coupled together like dogs, and dragged away into distant slavery beyond the sea and the mountains. Such incessant alarms must annihilate the pleasures and interrupt the labors of rural life; *and the Campagna of Rome was speedily reduced to the state of a dreary* WILDERNESS, *in which the land is barren, the waters are impure, and the air infectious.* Curiosity and ambition no longer attracted the nations to the capital of the world; but if chance or necessity directed the steps of a wandering stranger, he contemplated with horror the *vacancy and solitude of the city; and might be tempted to ask, where is the Senate, and where are the people?* In a season of excessive rains, the Tiber swelled above its banks, and rushed with irresistible violence into the valleys of the seven hills. A pestilential disease arose from the stagnation of the deluge, and so rapid was the contagion that fourscore persons expired in an hour in the midst of a solemn procession which implored the mercy of heaven. A society in which marriage is encouraged, and industry prevails, soon repairs the accidental losses of pestilence and war; but as the far greater part of the Romans was condemned to hopeless indigence and celibacy, *the depopulation was constant and visible, and the gloomy enthusiasts might expect the approaching failure of the human race.* Yet the number of citizens still exceeded the measure of subsistence; their precarious food was supplied from the harvest of Sicily and Egypt; and the frequent repetition of famine betrays the inattention of the emperor to a distant province. *The edifices of Rome were exposed to the same ruin and decay; the mouldering fabrics were easily overthrown by inundations, tempests and earthquakes, and the monks who had occupied the most advantageous stations, exulted in their base triumph over the ruins of antiquity.*... Like Thebes, or Babylon, or Carthage, the name of Rome might have been erased from the earth, if the city had not been animated by a vital principle which again restored her to honor and dominion.... The power as well as the virtue of the Apostles revived with living energy in the breasts of their successors; and the chair of St. Peter, under the reign of Maurice, was occupied by the first and greatest of the name of Gregory.... The sword of the enemy was suspended over Rome; it was averted by the mild eloquence and seasonable gifts of the Pontiff, who commanded the respect of heretics and barbarians."—E. R. C.]

* [Lord regards the Beast as identical with that of ch. xiii. 1. At the time of the *emergence from the sea* (ch. xiii.), the *horns* were diademed, which, in his judgment, indicates that then all the heads should have fallen, although at the *time of the Apocalyptist* but five had fallen. At the *time of the emergence*, and in the passage before us, the Beast represents "the Gothic rulers who established governments in the Western Empire during the Fifth century, and their successors and subjects to the present time" (see p. 262). The Beast in its

arrogation by the rulers of the rights of God, in assuming to dictate the faith and worship of their subjects, legislating over Divine laws, making their will the reason that they are to offer worship, etc.—The *session of the Woman on the Beast* denotes that the combination of hierarchies whom she symbolizes is nationalized and established by the civil rulers.—The *destruction* of ver. 16 has already begun in the disallowance and scorn of the claims of the Established Church in most of the European States, the confiscation of her property in France, the conquest of the Papal States, *etc.;* and these judgments are to be carried on to a greater severity.

GLASGOW. This writer adopts the generally accepted Protestant view that the *Woman* symbolizes Rome ecclesiastical.—The *Beast* he identifies with the Beast of ch. xiii. 1, and the Dragon of ch. xii. (see p. 263), and regards it as symbolizing, in its entirety, the world-power, and at the period contemplated by the vision, the Roman Empire in and after the fall of the Western Empire, A. D., 493.—The *heads* have *here* a double symbolization; they are : 1. *Seven mountains, i. e.,* the seven forms of government through which the Beast (since his emergence from the sea, ch. xiii. 1) has passed, *viz.:* (1) the state of ten horns represented in Italy for a time by Odoacer and Theodoric, (2) the government of Justinian in the West, (3) the Kingdom of the Lombards, (4) that of Pepin and Charlemagne, (5) that of Otho the Great, (6) that of Charles V., (7) that of the Emperors after Protestantism obtained political equality, A. D. 1555 ; 2. *Seven kings, i. e.,* the original kingdoms out of which the Roman power rose, as on p. 242.—The *horns* he interprets as Elliott, see p. 259.—The *session on the Beast* he interprets as Elliott and Protestant interpreters generally.— The *period of the vision* he places in the latter part of the effusion of the seventh Vial; the Woman "is revealed to view in the same condition in which she has existed for a long period." —Ver. 16 foretells the assaults that have from the era of the Emperors been made, from time to time, upon the Romish Church, to result in a complete destruction.

AUBERLEN: This chapter describes the *Harlot* and the *Beast,* ripe for judgment. (For the views of this writer concerning the *Woman* and the *Beast,* generically considered, and the *wilderness,* see pp. 243 sq., and 263 sq.). The *Harlot* is identical with the *Woman* of ch. xii., who symbolizes the Church of God in the world; she is the Church conforming to the world. The identity is established by, 1. The *place* where she is seen, *the wilderness,* comp. xii. 6, 14 ; xvii. 3. 2. The fact that the same expressions are used in chs. xii. and xvii. for *wilderness* and *Woman* (ἔρημος and γυνή). 3. The fact that the Beast in the two chapters is identical;—but Beast and Woman are in both placed in immediate connection ; if the identity of the one is conceded, how is it possible to doubt that of the

other ?* 4. The expression used by the Seer: " When I saw her I wondered : "—the wonder finds its only explanation in the extraordinary change which had passed over the Woman ; the impression made on John may be expressed by the words of Isaiah (i. 21) : " How is the faithful city become a harlot !" 5. The reason which lies in the expressions : *Harlot* (xvii. 1, 5, 15, 16 ; xix. 2), *to commit fornication* (xvii. 2 ; xviii. 3, 9), *fornication* (xiv. 8 ; xvii. 2, 4 ; xviii. 3 ; xix. 2); *Woman* means the Church (see on p. 243); *Harlot* throughout both Testaments the Apostate Church, comp. Jer. ii., iii. ; Ezek. xvi., xxiii. ; Hos. i.-iii. ; Matt. xii. 39; xvi. 4 ; Mark viii. 38; Rev. ii. 21. 6. The objective parallelism between Babylon and New Jerusalem ; both are cities—the one a *harlot,* the other a *bride* (xvii. 1, 3, 5 ; xxi. 9); but as the latter is acknowledged to mean the transfigured Church, it follows that Babylon means the Church in its worldliness. 7. The contrast in xix. 2, 9, between the *Harlot* and the *Wife of the Lamb.* 8. The word *Mystery* on the forehead of the Harlot (ver. 5) ; this word warns us not to adopt a *literal,* but to look for a *spiritual* interpretation of those which follow, an interpretation to which we may be guided by Eph. v. 31, 32.—The word *Harlot* describes the essential character of the false Church ; she retains her human form, remains a *woman,* does not become a *beast*—she has a form of godliness, but denies the power thereof (2 Tim. iii. 8). Her *adultery* "appears in its *proper* form when she wishes herself to be a worldly power, uses politics and diplomacy, makes flesh her arm, uses unholy means for holy ends, spreads her dominions by sword or money, fascinates the hearts of men by sensual ritualism, allows herself to become ' Mistress of ceremonies' to dignitaries of this world, flatters prince or people, the living or the dead—in short, when she, like Israel of old, seeks the help of one worldly power against the danger threatening from another ;" it appears in a less gross form (comp. Matt. v. 28) " whenever she forgets that she is in the world, even as Christ was in the world, as a bearer of the cross and pilgrim, that the world is crucified to her and judged, whenever she regards the world as a reality and lusts after its power and pleasures." " Herein consists the essence of whoredom, in leaning and listening, and conforming to, and relying on the world. Hence, there could not be a better description of it than that given, xvii. 3, 7, 9; the Woman sits on the Beast."† (See also be-

---

* ["It must strike the reader at a first glance that all three expressions, *wilderness, Woman, Beast* (ch. xvii. 3), are without the article, which would be naturally expected here as expressions known from their previous occurrence. But the omission of the article has its good reason. The three expressions are identical and yet in a sense not identical with the former; the heathen world, the Church, and the world-power, have undergone, as we shall see subsequently, great changes, so much so, that John can scarcely recognize them, and sees a beast, a woman, and a wilderness." AUBERLEN.— E. R. C.]

† [Auberlen precedes the statements of which this section is an abstract, with a *résumé* of New Testament prophecy concerning the corruption of the Church. He writes: "Our Lord Himself has given no obscure intimations in the parables which refer to the history of the Church (Matt. xiii.), that when once the gospel, according to its destination, shall have the whole world for its field, . . . the Church would not be pure, but mixed, consisting of good and evil. The xxiv. ch. of Matthew, Christ's eschatological words, in which He

---

entirety symbolizes the Roman Empire in all its forms both before and after the disruption ;—the *heads* representing the different forms of government before the disruption, *viz.:* kings, consuls, dictators, decemvirs, tribunes, Pagan emperors, Christian emperors; the *horns* as above.—E. R. C.]

low).—The Harlot cannot be found exclusively either in the Romish Church, or in the Established State Churches. Christendom (the Church) as a whole, in all its manifold manifestation of sects, is the Harlot; the boundaries between Woman and Harlot are not denominational—true believers are hidden and dispersed, the invisible Church is within the visible, as the kernel within the shell;* nevertheless it is true that the Roman and Greek Churches are in a more peculiar sense the Harlot, than the evangelical Protestant. *"The Roman Catholic Church is not only accidentally and de facto, but in virtue of its very principle, a harlot, . . . whereas the Evangelical (Protestant) Church is, according to her principle and fundamental creed, a chaste woman; the Reformation was a protest of the Woman against the Harlot."*—As yet the mystery of Babylon is not fully developed. Bengel was probably correct in his expectation that Rome will once more rise to power; it is probable that the Greco-Russian Catholicism will likewise become of importance; the adulterous, worldly elements, in all churches and sects, lean towards that false Catholicism, and pave the way for its progress:—and thus may it attain again to power.—In like manner as the *Woman*, the *Beast* also appears in this chapter in a shape other than before; the deadly wound (xiii. 3) is *healed* (see *Extracts* from Auberlen in *foot-notes*, pp. 263 sq.)—he recovers life and returns, but now not only from the *sea* (xiii. 3), but out of the *abyss* (xvii. 8), whence he has drawn new Antichristian strength of Hell; he is now *scarlet-colored*, a symbol of his blood-guiltiness; the *names of blasphemy* formerly on his heads (xiii. 1) now cover his whole body, as a sign that his opposition to God is now to manifest itself perfectly; the *crowns* which were formerly on the horns (xvii. 3) have now disappeared.† In such manner the *Antichristian Kingdom* comes into existence;—"a *new* kingdom in which all the

views simultaneously the destruction of Israel and His Parousia, and hence judgment upon Israel and Christendom, —is based upon the fundamental view that the New Testament Church will become as much a wicked and adulterous generation as the Old Testament congregation; that the Lord dwells upon some symptoms and characteristics of this adultery, as distrust and suspicion, hatred, treachery (vers. 10-12), division into parties (23-26), false doctrine (24). In the light of this chapter the Apostles looked into the future of the Church, see 1 Tim. iv. 1 sqq; 2 Tim. iii. 1 sqq.: iv. 3, 4: 2 Peter ii. 1-3; iii. 3; 1 John ii. 18." Comp. also Luke xvii. 8.—E. R. C.]

* [Auberln quotes as follows from John Michael Hahn (*Briefe u. Lieder über die Offenbarung*, vol. v., sect. 6): "The Harlot is not the city of Rome alone, neither is it only the Roman Catholic Church, to the exclusion of another, but all Churches and every Christian, ours included, viz.: all Christendom that is without the Spirit and life of our Lord Jesus, which calls itself Christian, and has neither Christ's mind nor Spirit. It is called Babylon, that is, confusion, for false Christendom, divided into very many churches and sects, is truly and strictly a confuser. However, in all churches, parties and sects of Christendom, the true Jesus-congregation, the Woman clothed with the sun, lives and is hidden. Co-rupt, lifeless Christendom is the Harlot, whose great aim and rule of life is the pleasure of the flesh, the welfare of the beast-like, sensual humanity, who is open to the influence of all false spirits and teachers, and is governed by the spirit of nature and the world."—E. R. C.]

† ["Is this circumstance intended as an indication that the ten kingdoms into which the Germanic-Sclavonic world is to be divided, will lose their monarchical form in the end? The expression (ver. 2), 'receive power as kings,' speaking of the power which they are to receive along with the Beast in the last time (μίαν ὥραν), seems to be in favor of such a supposition." AUBERLEN.—E. R. C.]

Beast's opposition to God is concentrated, and raised to a power such as it had had never before; therefore we read of an *eighth, which proceeds from the seven* (xvii. 11), and is the full manifestation of the beast-nature." The *final apostasy* will consist in the union of the pseudo-Christian and Antichristian elements, which the Apocalypse expresses by the *Harlot* sitting on the *Beast;* * this alliance likewise appeared in the concluding period of the Old Testament—apostate Israel, which was then the Harlot, formed an alliance with the heathen world-power against Jesus and His Apostles, see Luke xxiii. 12; Acts xvii. 5, 9.—The abominations committed by the Jews, drew down the destruction of Jerusalem by the Romans, that is the judgment of the Harlot by the Beast (Dan. ix. 26, 27)—an exact parallel to the future judgment set forth in vers. 16, 17.—The judgment on the Harlot has already begun; see extract in *foot-note (first* column), p. 264.—E. R. C.]

EXPLANATIONS IN DETAIL.

Ch. XVII. 1, 2. **One of the seven,** *etc.*— *Which,* is not to be determined, though the judgment upon Babylon in the narrower sense is indicated under the fourth Vial of anger.— **Hither,** δεῦρο (comp. ch. xxi. 3).—The reference is not to a local motion, but to a certain direction of the contemplation in accordance with the guidance of the Angel.—**I will show unto thee the judgment.**—"The fulfillment of the promise is not found immediately in ver. 3 (contrary to the opinion of Hengstenberg), nor is it contained at all in ch. xvii." (Düsterdieck). It is doubtless, however, the idea of the Angel that John must already be able to see the *judgment* in *this* appearance of *this* Woman —ch. xvii. being the judgment in a Heaven-picture, and ch. xviii. the same in an Earth-picture. —**Of the great harlot.**—Pagan Rome, according to Düsterdieck. The following description is simply inappropriate to this conception.— **That sitteth** [Lange: **is enthroned**] **upon many waters.**—Pagan Rome did indeed reign over many peoples, but its throne did not rest upon the superstition of those peoples (Jer. li. 13 does not apply here). Still more forcibly does the following pronounce against the application of the passage to pagan Rome.—[Ver. 2]. **With whom the kings of the earth committed fornication.**—Pagan Rome did not allure the kings of the earth by blandishments; she destroyed them. There is *one* case—that of Antony and Cleopatra—which might be recommended, as a make-shift, to the "historical interpretation," but even *there* the genders would have to be reversed before it could properly be regarded as applicable. — **And they who inhabit the earth were made drunk,** *etc.* —Not even this could be said, with reference to pagan Rome, either of the Spaniards, or of the

* [In a preceding paragraph, Auberlen speaks of the *session* of the Woman upon the Beast as symbolizing her *adultery* (see above), but here as indicating the *final apostasy.* Although the former of these is the beginning of, and results in the latter, yet are they distinct as bud and fruit. Is it not more correct to say that the *session* indicates the completed and public alliance of the Church with the world, or world-power?—E. R. C.]

Britons, or of the Germans, or of the Parthians, or of the Jews.

Ver. 3. **And he carried me away in spirit.**—This is to be understood only of a change effected in the ecstatic direction of the *spirit* [of the Seer]. "The confounding of this *wilderness* with that mentioned in ch. xii. 6, 14— a proceeding which, on account of the lack of the article is, even from a mere formal point of view, properly impossible—is in Auberlen's case connected with his view of the identity of the Harlot of ch. xvii. and the Woman of ch. xii."* DUESTERDIECK. Most certainly, the ascetic wilderness in which Jesuitism has its being is, spiritually, utterly diverse from the wilderness of Saint Anthony, and yet the two stand in the relation of historic continuity, and, hence, external unity. In like manner, the relation of the Harlot to the Woman is determined. According to Düsterdieck, *et al.*, the Woman is seen in the wilderness because of the desolation imminent upon her in accordance with ver. 16! The symbolical interpretation of the wilderness is abundantly illustrated both by the Old and the New Testaments (Moses, Elijah, John the Baptist, *etc.*); we must, therefore, wonder at the perverted interpretations of it (Bengel: Europe, especially Italy; other interpretations, see in Düsterdieck, p. 506). The fact that the same Woman who here sits in the wilderness, is subsequently represented as sitting on *many waters*, must necessarily give trouble to the "historical interpretation."—**And I saw a Woman sitting upon a scarlet Beast.**—De Wette and Züllig embellish the Beast with a scarlet *covering*. The Beast must wear the color of blood (Andr., Lyra, *et al.*), just as the Dragon wears the color of flame, which is allied to blood-color. The Woman's attire is variegated; together with the blood-color, the honorable hue of *purple* appears. In general, the Beast of the present passage is identical with that of ch. xiii.; observe, however, the formal distinction that in the latter passage the Beast is spoken of in its general, world-historical shape, whilst here the primary and special reference is to it in its re-appearance after its vanishment, as the bearer, at first, of the Harlot.—**Full of the ▬▬▬▬ of blasphemy.**—The γέμον† with the accusative is remarkable. Hebraizing: An emphatic expression: now filled up with writing; *all* the names of blasphemy. ["The names of blasphemy, which were found before on the heads of the Beast only (xiii. 1), have now spread over its whole surface. As ridden and guided by the Harlot, it is tenfold more blasphemous in its titles and assumptions than before. The heathen world had but its *Divi* in the Cæsars as in other deified men of note; but Christendom has its 'Most Faithful' and 'Most Christian' kings, such as Louis XIV. and Philip II.; its 'Defenders of the Faith,' such as Charles II. and James II.; its society of unprincipled intriguers called after the sacred name of our Lord, and working Satan's work '*ad majorem Dei gloriam;*' its 'holy office' of the Inquisition, with its dens of darkest cruelty; finally its 'Patrimony of St. Peter,' and its 'Holy Roman Empire;' all of

them, and many more, new names of blasphemy, with which the Woman has invested the Beast. Go where we will, and look where we will in Papal Christendom, names of blasphemy meet us. The taverns, the shops, the titles of men and places, the very insurance badges on the houses are full of them." ALFORD.—E. R. C.]

Ver. 4. **And gilded with gold and precious stone and pearls.**—The κεχρυσωμένη is zeugmatical" (Düsterdieck). Both precious stones and pearls, however, must have been set in gold. As a decoration of the Church, such an apparel rudely anticipates the adornment of the celestial congregation.—**A golden cup.**— Even the *cup* [*Kelch*=chalice] or goblet [*Becher* =beaker] would look very strange in the hand of pagan Rome. The *cup* is, apart from the symbolism of measure, here the symbol of fellowship; the *golden* cup symbolizes the holiest fellowship—the fellowship of salvation. But, *filled with abominations*, it is certainly akin to hypocrisy, as in accordance with Bede—a strange equivalent for the "*poculum missaticum*" (Calov.). According to Düsterdieck, the *golden cup* means merely a cup that is golden, agreeably to the "historical interpretation." The accusative καὶ τὰ ἀκάθαρτα is remarkable. The most plausible construction of this is, apparently, that of Düsterdieck, who maintains that ἀκάθαρτα should be taken as parallel with the accusative ποτήριον. It contributes to the characterism of the Woman when it is intimated that together with the cup she has all sorts of other things in her hand— things which the Spirit of truth designates as *uncleannesses*, and which are the issue of the *fornication, i. e.*, idolatry, *of the earth.* ["This language is probably taken from Jer. li. 7, 'Babylon hath been a golden cup in the Lord's hand, that made all the earth drunken; the nations have drunken of the wine, therefore the nations are mad.'" BARNES on xiv. 8.—E. R. C.]

Vers. 5, 6. **A name written.**—The μυστήριον does not belong to the inscription, but it characterizes it—*i. e.*, it is declaratory that the name *Babylon* and the rest of the title—*the mother of the harlots and the abominations, etc.* —is to be symbolically understood. [So also BARNES, STUART, *et al.* On the other hand, HENGSTENB., WORDSWORTH, ALF., *et al.* LILLIE thus powerfully combats the former, and advocates the latter view: "1. While the Apocalypse is full of μυστήρια, in no other instance does the narrator herald one as such. 2. Supposing the *inscription* to have included Μυστήριον, an explanation was thus formally invited which is furnished in ver. 7; and the interpreting Angel is then to be considered as taking up the very word, and as personally (ἐγώ) confronting the difficulty which it announced. 3. As the Angel uses the term is attached not to the *name*, but to the *Woman* herself and her equipment. 4. In that reference it might very well characterize her origin, nature, history, and destination; graciously to know the evil—'the depths of Satan' (ii. 24)—'the *mystery* of iniquity' (2 Thess. ii. 7)—this, not less than the knowledge of the good, requires heavenly teaching and 'an unction from the Holy One' (1 John ii. 20). 5. Even if not intended thus to be itself descriptive of the Woman, Μυστήριον might yet stand in the

---

* [For the view of Auberlen, see *foot-note* (*), p. 311.—E.R.C.]
† [See TEXT. and GRAM., Note 3.—E. R. C.]

inscription as a sort of prelude or index to her name, somewhat like 'Ωδε ἡ σοφία ἐστίν in ch. xiii. 18.''—E. R. C.]

BABYLON THE GREAT.—This symbolism is introduced as early as in Genesis, with the history of the building of the tower, and carried on especially by Isaiah and Jeremiah; this special Babylon, however, must not be identified with the general Babylon (ch. xiv. 8 and ch. xvi. 19), as is ordinarily done.—The **MOTHER OF HARLOTS** has also a more special import; the mother is reflected in spiritually, or rather fleshly, kindred daughters, some of whom compete with the mother in magical power. Grotius is correct in supposing that the aspect of the Woman must proclaim her *drunkenness*—and *that* a drunkenness **with the blood of the saints, even the witnesses of Jesus** (see SYN. VIEW). Prelusive examples of blood-thirstiness and its augmentations are to be found in the old pagan world; this blood-thirstiness, however, is fulfilled in the specific lusting of the Woman after the blood of the witnesses of Jesus, prefigured, it is true, by the death of Abel (see Matt. xxiii.). ["The phraseology is derived from the barbarous custom (still extant among many pagan nations) of drinking the blood of enemies slain in the way of revenge. Here, then, the fury of the persecutors is depicted in a most graphic manner. Blood is drunk by them even to intoxication, *i. e.*, *copiously*, in great quantities. The effect of drinking blood is said to be, to exasperate, and to intoxicate with passion and a desire of vengeance. But the *copiousness* of the draught, and so the extent and bitterness of persecution, is particularly marked by the expression here." STUART.—E. R. C.]—**And I wondered.**—The Seer could hardly have expressed so great astonishment at the blood-thirstiness of pagan Rome—a quality long notorious and, proportionably, not so extraordinary. But this *Woman!* The Jewish hierarchy had, certainly, already nailed Christ to the cross. But that such a Woman could finally be the product of the historical development of the Church of faith then existent, must appear even to the Seer, with his knowledge of the world, a thing unheard of. Düsterdieck here reverts to Auberlen, stating that it is the opinion of the latter that the Seer marvels at recognizing in the Harlot the degenerate Woman of ch. xii. 1. Düsterdieck calls this assumption an "egregious mistake." Not even Auberlen, however, could have looked upon the Woman herself as the Harlot; that which he so regards, is but the Woman's last historical representation—in antithesis to her internal essence, the finally emergent Bride.* Similar utterances of amazement at the degeneracy of the Church are to be found even in the Old Testament, Is. v. 1 [sqq.], Jer. ii. 1 [sqq.], ch. xviii., Ezek. xvi.; Matt. xxiv. 37, 1 Tim. iv., *etc.* According to Bengel, the Seer wondered at the phenomenon of so powerful a Beast being constrained to carry the Woman; according to Züllig, Düsterdieck, *et al.*, he marvelled because he knew not the import of the phenomenon; according to Ebrard, his astonishment was occa-

sioned by the change in the Beast which he had seen in ch. xiii. According to Hengstenberg, who frequently makes a point of discovering moral failings even in the visional moods of the Seer, the wonderment of John is censured as foolish. The object of astonishment is, doubtless, intelligible to the Seer—it is the contrast between the Woman and the Harlot; in regard to the origin and development of this contrast, however, he stands in need of enlightenment from the Angel. [The object of wonder is doubtless the *complex mystery* (the *mysteries*, for each object is in itself a *mystery*) concerning which the Angel gives an explanation, *viz.*: the *Woman*, the *Beast*, and *their relation to each other*. This is evident from the words of the Angel (ver. 7): *Wherefore didst thou wonder? I will tell (explain to) thee the mystery, etc.* The explanation extends through ver. 18.—E. R. C.] According to Düsterdieck, the Beast denotes the *world-kingdom*, and the Woman the *world-city*.

Ver. 7. **I will tell thee the mystery.**—The *mystery* which he is to know, is the relationship betwixt the Woman and the Beast [see above]. How has it come to pass that the Woman could seat herself upon this terrible Beast? Or how is it that the wild-Beast suffered itself to be mounted by the Woman, like a gentle palfrey? In this query lies the key to the dark words that follow. The first explanation is contained in the history of the Beast.

Ver. 8. **The Beast . . . was, and is not, and is about to ascend out of the abyss.**—The historic re-emergence of the world-power, spiritually wounded to death by Christianity—an event proleptically beheld by the Seer at a time when the Beast seemed to be really destroyed—serves as an occasion of offence and fall to the world and, consequently, to the majority of the men in whom the external and visible form of the Woman consists. The earthly-minded *dwellers on the earth, whose names are not written in the Book of Life from the foundation of the world*—who, therefore, do not belong to the selection of the sealed—*shall wonder* when they see this apparent revival and gain of dominion on the part of the Beast. This is the history of the waning faith in the world-overcoming victory of Christ and the simultaneously waxing faith in the omnipotence of the world-power. It is the history of all who can see the Kingdom of God only in a tangible Church, a tangible salvation, a tangible Head of the Church—in a word, in external things. All of these have lost all heart for the powers of the world to come; through them, the Beast rises and the Woman descends, in a spiritual sense, or, in respect of outward appearance, the Woman is elevated on the back of the Beast—by means of a compromise between the two. [For an exposition of the *Abyss*, see Excursus, pp. 364 sqq.—E. R. C.]

Ver. 9. Herewith is connected the history of the Woman. It becomes intelligible only for the **mind** [Lange: **understanding**] **that hath wisdom**, the cultivated connoisseur of world-history, who views the same in the light of the Kingdom of God. The **seven heads** (of the Beast) are, primarily, **seven mountains, on which the Woman sits.** The fact that the Woman sits

---

* [For the view of AUBERLEN, see p. 311.—E. R. C.]

upon the seven mountains is, considered in and for itself, perfectly natural, for *mountains* are Divine political world-ordinances (see Rom. xiii.), and the *seven* mountains constitute the totality of the ground-forms of the political order of the world. But this natural conditionality of the Church upon worldly state ordinances becomes fatal from the fact that the seven *mountains* are at the same time seven *kings*, i. e., here, *despotic powers;* in other words, that the noble human image of metal (Dan. ii.) has a reverse side, in accordance with which it is composed of *four rapacious beasts.* Through the despotism of the world-monarchies, the Woman is continually drawn more and more into the parallel path of hierarchism, and her character becomes more and more corrupt. [See ADD. NOTE, p. 317.—E.R.C.]

Ver. 10. After the general history of the Beast and the Woman, the Angel gives the Seer a world-historical exposition of his stand-point in time. *Five kings, i. e.,* world-monarchies, from a theocratic point of view, *are fallen.* The *one* is now subsisting—the *sixth* king, i. e., the *sixth* world-monarchy, behind which the Beast seems, for the instant, to be annihilated by young Christianity. This view was, assuredly, more entertainable by the Seer at the time of Nerva or even Domitian than at the time of Nero. The *other* king is the *seventh* world-monarchy, the future historico-Christian world-monarchy in a general apprehension, in so far as it, as Beast, bears the Woman upon its back. The Seer, from his distance, beholds, in perspective, the time of the *seventh* king on a reduced scale; *he must continue a little while.* Then, however, the whole Beast reappears in the *eighth* king in his true and undisguised nature. As Satan has embodied himself in the Beast, so the whole Beast, as the sum of all world-historic enormities, embodies itself in the *eighth* monarchy. Hence the Angel speaks of the *eighth* king as proceeding *from the seven,* as, in a sense, the unitous evil genius who was present in separate forms in all his seven predecessors. But because world-historical wickedness is, so to speak, concentrated and sublimated in this monarchy, finally being, as it were, embodied in the personal Antichrist (though the latter may branch into *ten mock-kings*), the stay of this *eighth* king is not long; he appears, he becomes an instrument of judgment upon the Woman, he *goes into perdition.* [See ADD. NOTES, pp. 272 sq., 304 and 317 sq.—E. R. C.]

Hengstenberg correctly regards the *seven mountains* as symbols of *seven kingdoms;* Düsterdieck, on the other hand, with others, understands by them Rome, the City of the Seven Hills. Irrespective of our admission of an allusion to Rome, we consider the *symbolic* apprehension of the mountains as, indubitably, the true one, though, notwithstanding this, a number of other features are decidedly suggestive of the City of the Seven Hills. On the literal interpretation of the *seven kings,* or world-monarchies, as referring to seven persons, see p. 26, and the exegesis of ch. xiii.; comp. Düsterd., p. 512 sqq.— **Seven kings,** this "historical," *i. e.,* literal, exposition [of Düst.] declares, are *merely seven kings* and nothing more. Why then may not the *Beast* be a *real* beast and nothing more? The different modes

of enumerating the kingdoms, see in Düsterd., *ibid.* —**The five are fallen.**—This, it is maintained, means that they are *dead*—in total contradiction to the use of terms. It may be queried: why is the successor of the fifth king not called the sixth, and the seventh, the seventh? Probably because both these numbers are in an eminent sense symbolical; here, however, this symbolism must lie dormant. The *sixth* is, contrary to the nature of *six,* the better, behind whom the Beast seems to have vanished; and the *seventh* is the tame one [*der Zahme,* with reference to the taming of the wild Beast into a palfrey, so to speak, of the Woman.—TR.], in whom the Beast again appears. The expression, **and is of the seven** [ver. 11] is differently interpreted, as: the returning Nero (De Wette, *et al.*); the returning Antiochus Epiphanes (Hofmann); a descendant of the seven (Primas., *et al.*). Düsterdieck, rightly, makes the *eighth* proceed from the *totality of the seven.* This conception is, truly, very difficult in connection with that view of the kings which regards them as significant of so many individuals. A thorough understanding of the subject, in general, is impossible on the basis of this latter view, as is demonstrated by the following note of Düsterdieck: "All interpretations are false, by which the concrete historic reference to the circumstances of the Roman Empire is discarded; thus, for instance, Andreas, who by the ϑηρίον (ver. 8) understands Satan, explains that by the appearance and, especially, the death of Christ, the Beast was brought to a state of *not-being.* Comp. Bede, C. à-Lap., Zeger, *et al.* Marlorat and other Protestants explain: Pagan Rome has passed away; Papal Rome is in present existence, but its world-dominion is in itself nought (οὐκ ἔστιν)." Various enumerations of the kings, in accordance with the synchrono-historical conception, see in Düsterdieck, p. 516. According to this expositor, the Seer did prophesy a little, after first prophesying *ex post facto* concerning kings already known to history; he fore-announced that Vespasian should be succeeded by his two sons: "Titus as the seventh, Domitian as the eighth—that Titus should continue for a short time, and that Domitian should appear as a personification of the whole Beast." Nevertheless, "John was mistaken in the expectation that the Roman world-kingdom would perish with Domitian." Still, Düsterdieck admits that a minimum of prophecy remains notwithstanding this mistake: "The singular error manifests, undoubtedly, a certain imperfectness of the prophetic essence in the Apocalyptist, but by no means entirely (!) abrogates that essence."

Vers. 12 sqq. Now follows the future history of the *ten horns,* in respect of their relation to the Beast and the Woman. For although their war with the Lamb is mentioned here, the principal point of view is the war with the Woman. The war with the Lamb, considered in and for itself, is not announced until ch. xix.; it is introduced here, in this earlier passage [ch. xvii. 14], because the hostility of the radical Antichristian powers against the Woman is directed against the last traces, reminiscences and tokens of Christianity in her nature.

Ver. 12. **The ten horns are ten kings.**—

The number *ten* is the number of the completed course of the world, the completed development of the world. In the *ten kings*, therefore, the political organization of the last phase of world-history is represented. They are all anarchical upstarts, who, thitherto, had **not received the kingdom**. They all cotemporaneously attain to dominion together. They are all, in reality, mock-kings, or, symbolically defined, mock-governments and mock-powers, sporadically diffused over the earth, and for **one hour** only, *i. e.*, for one unitous, great, final, terrible, but short decision-time, do they obtain the government **with the Beast**. This is the specific Antichristian evening of the world, which precedes the Parousia. The fact that they are but quasi-kings, is based not upon the shortness of the time of their supremacy (in accordance with Bengel and Düsterdieck), but upon the anarchical relations of the times. It is the period when the theocratic element in Church and State is laid dead, in accordance with ch. xi.; when the image and mark of the Beast prevail, in accordance with ch. xiii. [See on p. 308.—E. R. C.]

Ver. 13. **These have one mind.**—Not, simply, a common cause, but also a common theory ["one and the same *view* and *intent* and *consent*." ALFORD.—E. R. C.], the system of positive contempt and blasphemy of *the name and tabernacle of God, and the dwellers in the Heaven* (chap. xiii. 6), based upon a threefold perversion of the truth into strong falsehood (the absolute nameless Divine, the absolute religion of this world, and the absolute blessedness of this world). Hence, they stand, from the outset, in connection with the Beast and make themselves, with their masses of peoples, their power and authority, completely its organs.

Ver. 14. **These shall war with the Lamb.** [Together with the Beast, see xix. 19.—E. R. C.]—This announcement has a place here not independently, but as serving as an explanation of their hatred of the Harlot. Because they are enemies of the Lamb, even the dead, despiritualized symbolism, by which the Woman is still suggestive of the Lamb, is a subject of hatred. The Bride they scarcely see, because she is thoroughly *internal, living*, and *human;* she incurs their excommunication only in her individual members; the Harlot, however, they see, because she is thoroughly external, hindering life with her dead forms and denying humanity with her anti-humane statutes.* Hence we here receive, in reference to the Lamb, only the precursory tranquillizing assurance that **He shall conquer** them because **He is Lord of lords and King of kings**. In His conflict and victory His people shall participate; they shall take part therein as truly **called ones**, who, in respect of their eternal ground-trait, are **elect**, and in respect of their character, in its temporal development,† **faithful**. For the description of them is not divisible into three characteristics, but into two—*elect* and *faithful*,

jointly bearing the signature of the truly *called*. This companionship may be predicated of the sealed in this world, who are progressing toward the Parousia, as well as of the trans-mundane retinue of the Lord on Mount Sion, that is to appear with Him in accordance with ch. xix. [14].

["Here is the ground and reason for the victory assigned, and that is taken. 1. From the character of the Lamb: He is King of kings and lord of lords. He has, both by nature and by office, power over all things; all the powers of earth and hell are subject to His check and control. 2. From the character of His followers; *they are called, and chosen, and faithful;* they are *called out* by commission to this warfare; they are *chosen* and fitted for it; and they will be *faithful* in it.—Such an army, under such a Commander, will at length carry all the world before them." M. HENRY.—E. R. C.]

Ver. 15. **And he saith unto me, The waters,** *etc.*—These *waters* serve as an introduction to the judgment upon the Harlot. The Woman has a threefold foundation. Her safest position was in the *wilderness*, in so far as she was spiritually at home there. Pure renunciation of the world is identical with heavenly security. But even the seat upon the *seven mountains*, the seven kingdom-powers of political order, gave her, still, a royal firmness. She is, however, also founded upon the *many waters* of surging popular life, and this foundation has become infinitely fluctuating, since popular life has been set in motion from its very depths, and is sundering into **peoples, and multitudes, and nations, and tongues**, and since the Woman has lost the foundations of genuine asceticism in the wilderness and of the protection of the seven mountains. Hence it is incorrect to say, "in spite of her wide dominion and all her glory, she shall be destroyed" (DUESTERDIECK), for whence should the *ten horns* have their power if they did not establish themselves upon those very masses of peoples that have apostatized from the Woman?

Ver. 16. **And the ten horns . . . . . and the Beast, these shall hate the Harlot.**—This hatred manifests itself in two negative and two positive forms. They *make her desolate*, not in the sense of devastation, but they leave her to herself, they take her at her word, and make her a perfect eremites; moreover, they deprive her of all worldly fulness and covering [*Fülle und Hülle*], so that she appears in all her *nakedness*. To these indignities are added positive damages; they *eat her flesh*, *i. e.*, they wrest all her goods from her, and she herself is destroyed by the *fire* of negative fanaticism, after having so long raged with the fire of positive fanaticism. In all this the Beast, of course, acts through the horns or kings, hence *οὗτοι*. Düsterdieck refers the *flesh-eating* to the figure of the *Woman*, and the *burning* to the figure of the *City*, of course maintaining that Rome is intended.

Ver. 17. **For God gave into their hearts.** Namely, to destroy the Woman. This judicial decree resolves itself into three parts: first, they must, blindly and against their will, execute the counsel of God; secondly, they must, in

---

* [The parallel passage in x¹x. 18, seems to indicate that the attack upon the Lamb and His followers shall be personal and direct.—E. R. C.]

† [*Nach ihrem zeitlich ausgeprägten Charakter.* The idea of the German is not that of an outward character, or form, imposed by the external application of a stamp, but one produced by *internal out-pressing*—by *development.*—E. R. C.]

thus doing, accomplish one purpose; thirdly, they must, in order to this end, surrender their whole power to the Beast until the latter, in like manner as an instrument of judgment, has accomplished all those words of God with which the Apostate Church has been threatened. Here, therefore, as in the crucifixion of Christ, Divine, human, and devilish counsels materially coincide in one, whilst they are formally, in their motives, thoroughly diverse and even opposed to each other. We, with Hengstenberg and others, refer the αὐτοῦ after τὴν γνώμην to God, and not, with Bengel, Düsterd. and others, to the Beast, because this latter idea would then be tautologically expressed—the alliance between the kings and the Beast having previously been intimated. At the close of this chapter, Düsterd. vainly reiterates his assurance that nothing save pagan Rome can possibly be intended (p. 520).*

[Ver. 18. **And the Woman that thou sawest**, etc.—This verse concludes the Angel's explanation of the *mystery* (see ver. 7), and unmistakably presents to us as one and the same, the *Harlot*, the *Great City*, and *Babylon the Great* (comp. vers. 3, 5, 7, 18).—E. R. C.]

[ADDITIONAL NOTE ON CH. XVII.]

By the American Editor.

[This chapter contains a section supplemental to the pouring out of the seventh Vial. It contains: 1. An introduction to the vision, vers. 1, 2; 2. The description of the vision, vers. 3–6; 3. The explanatory remarks of the Angel, vers. 7–18.

In his interpretation of the symbols, the writer agrees in the main with Auberlen, but with variations, as will appear. For his exposition of the Beast, see p. 272. In this chapter the Apostate Church, which, in ch. xvi., was figured by *Babylon* (i. e., the *Great City=Rome*), is presented under the symbol of a *Harlot*. These symbols represent the Church from different stand-points;—the former in her earthly relations as a great, populous, wealthy, powerful world-city; the latter in her relations to Christ, as a once chaste Bride now faithless to her husband;—each of these symbols represents an important truth which is not set forth by the other. In this chapter a portion of the imagery of the city-symbolization is preserved. This, indeed, may be regarded as detracting from the artistic unity of the respective symbols; but upon re-

flection it will be seen not only to unite the two symbols, but to give to each an instructive force that could not otherwise have been given. The *mountains*, the *waters*, and the *wilderness* are taken from the city-symbolization;—the *mountains* relate primarily to the *mountains* on which Rome is situate, which symbolize the seven great world-kingdoms; the *waters*, probably to the Mediterranean—that *great sea* which Rome once dominated, symbolizing the peoples and multitudes subject to the Church; the *wilderness* relates to the present and future *Roman Campagna*, an ἔρημος which aptly symbolizes the moral world-waste around the Church at the period contemplated in the vision—a waste which it was her duty to reclaim and cultivate, but which she has left uncared-for.

The *Vision*, vers. 3–6, is a scene beheld under the seventh Vial; it represents the Church in the last time, in completed unholy alliance with the world-power, and ready for the destruction about to be visited upon her through the instrumentality of the Beast and the *ten horns*. The *Introduction*, vers. 1, 2, and the *Explanation*, vers. 7–18, sweep through the entire period of the Church's history; they represent her as *sitting on the seven mountains* (vers. 9, 10), i. e., as having formed in every epoch of her history an adulterous connection with the then existing world-power—a connection prefiguring, and consummated in, the alliance symbolized in the vision. The parallelism between the *adultery* and the *destruction* foretold in this chapter, and those set forth Hosea ii. 1-13, is manifest upon comparison. Is there not also a parallelism between the *deliverance* of Hosea ii. 14-23 and that alluded to ch. xviii. 4? In the latter case, as in the former, is there not an allusion to the eduction of a life-germ, in the day of destruction, from the corrupt mass, to be the seed of a new organism? The *valley of Achor* has ever been to the *true* Church a door of hope, comp. Hosea ii. 15; Josh. vii. 26; Isa. lxv. 10.*—E. R. C.]

---

* [Elliott also contends that the destruction effected by the *horns* cannot be the *final destruction* set forth in ch. xviii. 8, since the kings of the earth (the horns) are, xix. 9, spoken of as mourning over the burning. He therefore refers the spoiling here mentioned to the destruction of Rome by the Gothic Kings in the Fifth and Sixth centuries (see p. 309). It must be admitted that he brings a weighty consideration in support of his opinion, one that may not be carelessly dismissed. It may be negatived by the fact, however, that men in their wrath often accomplish that over which they mourn in the subsequent hours of reflection. The Roman army destroyed the Temple at the capture of Jerusalem and this fulfilled the purposes of Jehovah. Josephus speaks of the soldier who applied the torch as "being hurried by a certain Divine fury"), and yet that destruction was mourned over by Titus and the army as a calamity.—E. R. C.]

* [The study of this chapter has induced the questions: Is not the range of the seven heads, given on p. 272, too narrow? May not the reference be to the world-powers of the seven great epochs of the Church's history? These are, I. The Antediluvian, ending with the apostasy set forth Gen. vi. 2, 12, and the Deluge. II. The Noachic, terminating in the spiritual adultery alluded to Josh. xxiv. 2, and followed by the call of Abraham. III. The Patriarchal, terminating in the idolatry of Israel in Egypt and the Egyptian oppression; (although not directly stated, it is probable that the spiritual adulteries in Egypt, mentioned Joshua xxiv. 14; Ezek. xx. 8; xxiii. 3, 8, occurred in the days of Israel's prosperity, Ex. i. 7, before her oppression by the Egyptians commenced). IV. The Mosaic, ending in the idolatry mentioned, 1 Sam. ii. 3, and the overthrow and subjection of Israel preceding the day of Mizpeh, 1 Sam. iv. 10, 11; vii. 3-14. V. The Samuelic or Kingly, terminating in the adultery that was followed by the Babylonish captivity. VI. The Restoration, terminating in the alliance between the High Priest and Herod on the one hand and Pilate on the other, and the destruction of Jerusalem. VII. The existing epoch. At the close of each of the first six of these epochs there was on the part of the visible Church an apostasy from God and a completed alliance with the world, followed by a destruction more or less complete of the extant form of the Church and the bringing forth from the corrupt mass of a new life-germ. The prophecy under consideration foretells a similar adulterous alliance, a similar destruction of the visible body, and a similar eduction of the vital germ of a new organism, ch. xviii. 4.—E. R. C.]

B.—EARTH-PICTURE OF THE FALL OF BABYLON.

Ch. XVIII. 1-24.

And [om. And][1] After these things I saw another angel come down [descending] from [ins. the] heaven, having great power [authority] ; and the earth was light-
2 ened [lighted up] with his glory. And he cried mightily [om. mightily] with [in] a strong voice,[2] saying, [ins. Fallen, fallen is] Babylon the great is fallen, is fallen [om. is fallen, is fallen], and is become the [a] habitation of devils [demons], and the [a] hold (φυλακή) of every foul [unclean] spirit, and a cage [hold] of every
3 unclean and hateful [hated] bird. For all nations have drunk of [or fallen by][3] the wine[4] of the wrath [anger or rage][5] of her fornication, and the kings of the earth have [om. have] committed fornication with her, and the merchants of the earth are waxed [became] rich through the abundance [from the power or influence
4 of (δύναμις)] of her delicacies [luxury]. And I heard another voice from [ins. the] heaven, saying, Come [ins. forth] out[6] of her, my people, that ye be not partakers
5 of [partake not in] her sins, and that ye receive not of her plagues. For her sins have reached [heaped together][7] unto [ins. the] heaven, and God hath remembered
6 her iniquities. Reward [Render unto] her even [om. even] as [ins. also] she rewarded [rendered] you [om. you][8], and double unto her [om. unto her—ins. the][9] double according to her works: in the cup which she hath filled [or mingled[10]], fill to [or
7 mingle[10] for] her double. How much she hath [om. hath] glorified herself [herself], and lived deliciously [luxuriated], so much torment and sorrow give her: for she saith in her heart [ins. that][11], I sit a queen, and am no widow [a widow I
8 am not], and shall see no sorrow [sorrow I shall not see]. Therefore shall her plagues come in one day, death, and mourning [sorrow], and famine ; and she shall be utterly burned with fire: for strong is the Lord God who judgeth [judged][12]
9 her. And [ins. there shall weep and wail over her] the kings of the earth, who [ins. with her] have committed fornication and lived deliciously with her, shall bewail her, and lament for her [om. with her, shall bewail her, and lament for
10 her], when they shall [om. shall] see the smoke of her burning, standing afar off for the fear of her torment, saying, Alas [Woe], alas [woe], that [the] great city [,] Babylon, that mighty [the strong] city ! for in one hour is [om. is] thy judgment
11 come [came]. And the merchants of the earth shall [om. shall][13] weep and mourn
12 [sorrow] over her ; for no man buyeth their merchandise [lading] any more : The [om. The][14] merchandise [lading] of gold, and [ins. of] silver, and [ins. of] precious stones [stone], and of pearls, and [ins. of] fine linen, and [ins. of] purple, and [ins. of] silk, and [ins. of] scarlet, and all thyine wood, and all manner vessels of ivory [every ivory article], and all manner vessels [every article] of most

TEXTUAL AND GRAMMATICAL.

1 Ver. 1. Καί is omitted in accordance with ℵ. A. B*. [P.], etc.
2 Ver. 2. The true reading is ἐν ἰσχυρᾷ φωνῇ, in accordance with decisive authorities. [So read Crit. Eds. generally; the ἐν with A. P.; the ἰσχυρᾷ φωνῇ with (ℵ.) A. (B*.) P., etc.—E. R. C.]
3 Ver. 3. [Tisch. reads πέπωκαν, πεπω- (πεπο) with P., -καν with A. C.; Treg. πέπτωκαν with A. C.; Alf. brackets the τ; ℵ. and B*. give πεπτώκασιν.—E. R. C.]
4 Ver. 3. [Tisch. gives τοῦ οἴνου with ℵ. B*., Clem., etc.; Lach. and Alf. omit with A., Am., Fuld., Tol., Lips.; Tregelles brackets.—E. R. C.]
5 Ver. 3. [For the rendering rage, see Note 16 on Chap. xiv., p. 274.—E. R. C.]
6 Ver. 4. There are various forms of this; we, with Lach. [Ed. Maj., Tisch. (1859)], read ἐξέλθε, with B*. C., and also from internal reasons. [Lach. (Ed. Min.), Tisch. (8th Ed.), Treg., Alf. give ἐξέλθατε with ℵ. A.; P. reads ἐξέλθετε.—E. R. C.]
7 Ver. 5. Ἐκολλήθησαν in accordance with ℵ. A. B*. [P.]. De Wette translates: "they have reached unto the heaven."
8 Ver. 6. The ὑμῖν is omitted. [Om. by Crit. Eds. generally with ℵ. A. B*. C. P., Am., Fuld., Demid., Tol., et al.; it appears in 1, 31, 91, 96, Clem., Lips., et al.—E. R. C.]
9 Ver. 6. The αὐτῇ is unfounded. [Om. by Crit. Eds. Tisch. and Treg. insert τά with ℵ. C.; Lach. omits with A. B*. P.; Alf. brackets.—E. R. C.]
10 Ver. 6. [See Note 10 on Chap. xiv., p. 274.—E. R. C.]
11 Ver. 7. [Crit. Eds. give ὅτι with ℵ. A. B* C. P.—E. R. C.]
12 Ver. 8. [Crit. Eds. give κρίνας with ℵ*. A. B*. C. P.; κρίνων is given by ℵ*. 1, 6, etc.—E. R. C.]
13 Ver. 11. [Crit. Eds. generally give κλαίουσιν καί πενθοῦσιν with ℵ. A. C. P.—E. R. C.]
14 Ver. 12. [The article is without authority.—E. R. C.]

13 precious wood, and of brass, and [*ins.* of] iron, and [*ins.* of] marble, and cinnamon,
    [*ins.* and amomum,][15] and odors [incense ($\theta\nu\mu\iota\acute{a}\mu\alpha\tau\alpha$)], and ointments [ointment], and
    fraukincense, and wine, and oil, and fine flour, and wheat, and beasts [cattle], and
    sheep, and [*ins.* of] horses, and [*ins.* of] chariots, and [*ins.* of] slaves [bodies ($\sigma\omega\mu\acute{a}$-
14 $\tau\omega\nu$)], and souls ($\psi\nu\chi\acute{a}\varsigma$) of men.   And the [thy][16] fruits [fruit-time ($\acute{o}\pi\acute{\omega}\rho\alpha$)][17] that
    thy soul lusted after are [*om.* that thy soul lusted after are — *ins.* of the desire of the[16]
    soul is] departed from thee, and all [*ins.* the fat] things [*ins.* and the bright things]
    which were dainty and goodly [*om.* which were dainty and goodly] are [have] de-
    parted from thee, and thou shalt [they[18] shall] find them no [never, never] more
15 at all.[19]   The merchants of these things, which were made [who became] rich by
    her, shall stand afar off for the fear of her torment, weeping and wailing [sorrow-
16 ing], And [*om.* And][20] saying, Alas [Woe], alas [woe], that [the] great city, that
    was clothed in fine linen, and purple, and scarlet. and decked [gilded] with gold,
17 and precious stones [stone], and pearls [pearl]! For [Because] in one hour [*ins.* was
    made desolate] so great riches [wealth] is come to nought [*om.* is come to nought].
    And every shipmaster [pilot], and all the company in ships [every one sailing in
    the region (*or* any whither),][21] and sailors, and as many as trade by [ply the] sea,
18 stood afar off, and cried when they saw [*or* seeing] the smoke of her burning, say-
19 ing, What *city is* [*om. is*] like unto this, the great city! And they cast dust on
    their heads, and cried, weeping and wailing [sorrowing], saying, Alas [Woe], alas
    [woe]. that [the] great city, wherein were made [became] rich all that had ships in
    the sea by reason of her costliness! for in one hour is [was] she made desolate.
20 Rejoice over her, *thou* [O] heaven, and *ye* holy [*om. ye* holy — *ins.* the saints, and
    the] apostles and [*ins.* the] prophets; for God hath avenged you [*om.* hath
    avenged you — *ins.* judged your judgment][22] on her.
21   And a [*or* one] mighty [strong] angel took up a stone like a great millstone, and cast
    it [*om. it*] into the sea, saying, Thus with violence shall [*ins.* be cast] that great city
    [*om.* that great city] Babylon [*ins.* , the great city] be thrown down [*om.* be thrown
22 down], and shall be found no more at all.[23] And the [a] voice of harpers, and [*ins.* of]
    musicians [*or* singers], and of pipers, and [*ins.* of] trumpeters, shall be heard no more
    at all in thee; and no [any] craftsman [artisan], of [*ins.* any art] whatsoever craft *he be*
    [*om.* whatsoever craft *he be*], shall be found any [no] more [*ins.* at all] in thee; and
23 the [a] sound [voice] of a millstone shall be heard no more at all in thee; and the
    [a] light of a candle shall shine no more at all in thee; and the [a] voice of the
    [*om.* the] bridegroom and of the [*om.* the] bride shall be heard no more at all in
    thee: for thy merchants were the great men of the earth;[24] for by thy sorceries
    [sorcery] were all [*ins.* the] nations deceived [seduced *or* misled ($\acute{\epsilon}\pi\lambda\acute{a}\nu\acute{\eta}\theta\eta\sigma\alpha\nu$)].
24 And in her was found the [*om.* the] blood[25] of prophets, and of saints, and of all
    that were [have been] slain upon the earth.

[15] Ver. 13. In accordance with ℵ*. A. C. [P. 6, 11, *Am., Fuld., Tol., Lips.*], etc. In the Rec. ἄμωμον is omitted.
[16] Ver. 14. Codd. ℵ. A. C. read σου τῆς ἐπιθυμίας.
[17] Ver. 14. [The primary meaning of ὀπώρα is, "the part of the year between the rising of Sirius and Arcturus, ...
and so, not so much the Lat. *Auctumnus*, as our *dog-days* or, at most, the *end of summer*. . . It was the proper time for both
the field and tree fruits to ripen" (Liddell and Scott *sub voce*).—E. R. C.]
[18] Ver. 14. [Lach., Alf., Treg., Tisch. (8th Ed.) give εὑρήσουσιν with ℵ. A. C. P. *Vulg.*, etc.; Tisch. (1859) gave εὑρής
with B*.; 7 reads εὑρεῖς.—E. R. C.]
[19] Ver. 14. [The expression *never, never more at all* is adopted as the best idiomatic rendering of the threefold negative
of the original, οὐκέτι οὐ μή.—E. R. C.]
[20] Ver. 16. [Crit. Eds. omit καὶ with ℵ. A. B*. C.; it appears in P., Vulg., Æth., *et al.*—E. R. C.]
[21] Ver. 17. [Crit. Eds. give καὶ πᾶς ὁ ἐπὶ τόπον πλέων with ℵ. A. B* C., *Am., Fuld.*, etc. (B*. inserts τόν before τόπον).
Lange adopts this reading, declaring the Rec. (ἐπὶ τῶν πλοίων ὁ ὅμιλος) to be unfounded; he *translates*, however, *all who sail
to definite places*. Alford translates, *every one who saileth any whither*. The first of the renderings given above is regarded as
most in accordance with the presumptive meaning of the expression ἐπὶ τόπον; see Robinson under Επι, iii. a; and τόπος,
d. (γ).—E. R. C.]
[22] Ver. 20. [Ἔκρινεν—τὸ κρίμα ὑμῶν ἐξ αὐτῆς. Lange translates: *hath executed your sentence upon her.*—E. R. C.]
[23] Ver. 21. [The negatives in this and the following verses are merely double; see NOTE 19.—E. R. C.]
[24] Ver. 23. [Lange translates: *for the princes of the earth were thy merchants.* See on pp. 323, 328 sq.—E. R. C.]
[25] Ver. 24. Cod. B*. gives αἵματα; A. C. [ℵ. P.] give αἷμα. [Tisch. adopts the former reading; Lach., Alf., Treg. the
latter.—E. R. C.]

EXEGETICAL AND CRITICAL.
SYNOPTICAL VIEW.

With the vision of the heavenly counsel of judgment upon Babylon and the ideal judgment itself, is conjoined the proleptical representation

of the actual judgment as taking place on the
earth. Hence, together with the unity of the
two sections, we must also recognize the contrast
between these two pictures of Babylon. In the
light of Heaven, Babylon appears as a *Woman*,
who, in the pomp of false magnificence and

beauty, has lapsed into the extreme of hideousness; a *Harlot*, — drunken with blood — the blood of the saints; bearing still ▪the golden cup of holy consecration, but riding upon the blood-colored Beast of Antichristianity, the organ of the abyss. In her earthly self-sufficiency and in the lament of the earth on her account (ch. xviii.), she is a *Queen*, to whom the kings of the earth have paid homage, who has been magnified by the rich, the merchants, and the sea-farers, glorified by the artisans, and marvelled at, in her splendor, possessions and enjoyment, by the inhabitants of the earth.

A strong *Angel*, who descends from Heaven to earth, comes upon her. His strength is signalized by the fact that *the earth is lighted up by his glory*. There is but one enlightenment for the earth—*viz.*, the light of the gospel; but there is a distinction between the stage of apostolic embassage, that of reformatory confession, dogma and *cultus*, and this spiritual day-light of evangelic truth—appropriated by all good spirits,—which, in Divine-human beauty, in Christian humanity, finally, as in one instant, extends from land to land, and illumines the fallen Woman in all her hatefulness, thus executing upon her the ideal judgment and denouncing (vers. 2, 3) the first real judgment, which appears as a self-judgment of the great Babylon in her internal relations. The ideal judgment is the heavenly proclamation of her fall, loudly promulgated through the earth. *Fallen! fallen!* is the judicial cry of Heaven. The fall agrees in greatness with the height which she claimed as Babylon the Great (see Is. xiv.).

*First Fundamental Form of the Actual Judgment.
Revelation of the Inner Judgment of the Fallen
Church* [vers. 2, 3].

She has become *a habitation* or *dwelling-place of demons;*—does not this, considered in the light of Heaven, signify a sort of Hell on earth? *A watch-tower* [*hold*] *of all manner of unclean spirits;*—does not this mean a concentration of the most diverse evil motives and egoistical characters? *A coop* or *poultry-yard* [*hold*] *of all unclean and hated birds;*—does not this mean ▪ gathering-place of all volatile minds, intent upon the prey of earthly profits? (See Matt. xiii. 32.) The Spirit of prophecy has indicated a firm and exclusive organization by a three-fold term: a fixed habitation, a watch-tower, a secure receptacle for birds.* It is true that φυλακή, in both instances of its occurrence, may be significant of ▪ *prison;* this term would not here have been applicable to the *demons*. The cause of this destruction of Babylon is the *wine of the anger* [or *rage*] *of her fornication*, i. e., the riotous enthusiasm of her anger [rage] or fanaticism in favor of her idolatries, her deifications of all sorts. Of this wine she has given to all nations to drink, and has intoxicated them more or less, instead of truly sobering them for the milk of the Gospel and wholesome nourishment, in accordance with the reiterated instructions of the Apostles Peter and Paul (1 Peter i. 13, iv. 7, v.

8; 1 Cor. xv. 34; 1 Thess. v. 6, 8; 1 Tim. iii. 2, 11; Titus ii. 2; 2 Tim. ii. 26). In distinction from this popular fanaticism, *the kings of the earth*, with the political consciousness of refined worldly-mindedness, *have committed fornication with her*—have deified her, permitted themselves to be deified by her, and shared all manner of other deifications with her.* Another pernicious effect is that *the merchants*, i. e., those speculators of earth who are bent upon mammon, *have become rich through her luxury*. The very one who should equalize earthly relations by the spirit of Christian brotherliness [*i. e.*, the Church], has, by self-deification and the deification of earthly powers, brought to a culmination that false pomp and love of magnificence by which the normal distinction of rich and poor has been perverted into unnatural and pernicious extremes of luxury and pauperism. The poisoning of popular life, of politics, of social ordinances—such is the three-fold and yet unitous effect of her three principal sins: [1] the presentation of the wine of anger [or *rage* (see Notes 5, p. 318; and 16, p. 274).—E. R. C.]; [2] seduction to fornication; [3] luxurious external show.

Second Judgment. Social Judgment of Separation between the People of God and the City of Babylon (vers. 4, 5).

This separation is brought about by the command of ▪ *voice from the Heaven*. Whilst the Angel who descended from Heaven has executed the judgment of the Spirit of truth, this voice comes from the height of Heaven, and, as appears from the context, from the judgment-throne of God Himself. The exode of the people of God from fellowship with Babylon, not only brings her internal judgment to view, but also serves as an introduction to the external judgment, because it is itself the dynamical social judgment. Thus must Noah go forth from the antediluvian race that had incurred the judgment of God; thus Lot must depart from Sodom; thus Israel, from Egypt; thus the primitive Christians, from fallen Jerusalem; *and so on.* This exode, which includes within itself the abrogation of all relations of religious fellowship, is demanded by truth, by righteousness, by fidelity to the Lord. Thus believers execute the minor ban in just reaction against the great ban, and the Church finally goes forth from the Church, in order that it may continue to be the Church (Heb. xiii. 13).† The conservation of human relations of duty will come out all the more clearly, the more religious and moral errors of a false humanism are discarded in pure and strict freedom of spirit. This exode also becomes necessary, however, for the self-preservation of believing souls, as is declared by the warning: *That ye partake not in her sins, and that ye receive not of her plagues.* How easily an accompliceship in guilt originates through implication in the sins of others, the Old Testament has typically demonstrated in the institution of the sin-offering (Lev. v.), as well as in many historical occurrences (Joshua

---

* [In the second and third instances one and the same term is employed, *viz :* φυλακή; and in the first, κατοικη- τήριον.—E. R. C.]

* [For another exposition of the fornication, see *Abstract of Auberlen*, pp. 311 sq.—E. R. C.]
† [See Add. Note and *foot-note*, p. 317.—E. R. C.]

CHAP. XVIII. 1-24. 321

vii.). The modern world's sensorium for these mysterious relations of guilt is much enfeebled. Even an entrance into the heritage of the heaviest ancient blood-debts is performed by many with as little misgiving as if they were stepping into a child's room pervaded with the breath of innocence, or even into a temple of pure spirit, pervaded with spirit-breath. The judgment of God, however, must be executed, because the sins of the City do not simply cry unto Heaven, like the sins of Sodom (Gen. xviii.), but they have become interlinked with each other and *tower up upon each other even to Heaven*, until they have become a demonic offence against the very Throne of God. Hence, *God has become mindful of her iniquities*—not simply of the last and newest, but of the entire series of them. The culmination of these iniquities has—humanly speaking—again made present to Him the whole history of their development, and with these words, the conclusion of His refraining long-suffering and the dawn of His infliction of judgment are expressed. At the basis of the expression in our passage lies a reference to the history of Sodom, the more obviously since here, also, a fiery judgment is at hand.

Third Judgment. The Recompense of Babylon (vers. 6-8).

The command to execute the judgment of retribution is not, like the preceding words, addressed to the people of God, as has been supposed in accordance with the reading of minuscules: *as she rewarded [rendered to] you.** But neither is the command addressed to the Angels of the plagues, as Bleek supposes, for this retribution is, according to ch. xvii. 16, to be executed by the Ten Horns and the Beast. The same judgment which, in the chapter cited, is spoken of as to be accomplished by *them*, is mentioned here, again, in ver. 8. The address is to those to whom she has presented the cup (Matt. vii. 6). De Wette with justice remarks: A challenge to the executioners of the penal judgment. Ἀποδιδόναι has at its second occurrence the meaning of the Hebrew גָּמַל. It shall be done to her as she has done to others. This is the law of historic retribution which runs through the whole of the Sacred Writings (see ch. xiii. 10). It shall, moreover, be recompensed *double to her*. As repentance has a double value in proportion to the punishment which preceded it (Is. xl. 2), so the guilt which is heaped up for the Day of Wrath has, similarly, a double value in reference to the succeeding punishment. So, in particular, the *cup* of the wine of anger is to be *filled double for her*. At the time of judgment, negative fanaticism falls, with double fury, upon the guilt of positive fanaticism.—But not simply the torments which she has inflicted upon men are to be recompensed to her, but also her self-glorification and arrogant ostentation are to be punished, in a corresponding degree, with torment and sorrow. The heavenly voice also gives the ground of this severe sentence. *For*, even now in the hour of judg-

ment, *she*, hardened and without a foreboding of approaching ill, *gives utterance in her heart* to her false security thus: *I sit* [Lange: am enthroned *as*] *a queen, and a widow I am not* (comp. Luke xviii. 3;—not the Church that misses her heavenly Christ on earth), *and sorrow I shall not see*. This obduracy is the motive which doubles her guilt and punishment. *Therefore*, also, *shall her plagues come in one day*—i. e., she does not gradually sink into ruin, but she plunges into it in one grand historic catastrophe. The plagues branch out into the number of the world, the worldly number of completeness, *four: Death, mourning [sorrow], hunger, fire. Death*, doubtless, should not be interpreted as the death of her children (Düsterdieck), but as a presentiment of ruin which now comes over her. With this death, her egoistic *lamentations* correspond, amid which, again, her *hunger* after world-empire is augmented to fury, whilst the *fire* of judgment is already coming upon her. These plagues now attack her with inevitable certitude, for *God has already commenced to judge her* (ὁ κρίνας), *and He is mighty* in His judgments, which He executes through the medium of mighty earthly powers.

Hereupon the heavenly voice denounces a simultaneous judgment upon those classes which have mingled with Great Babylon and involved themselves in her guilt; representing them as mourners over the fallen one (vers. 9-20).

The unitous idea of these lamentations lies in the premise that the mock-holy City has her sympathies, her roots, in the worldliness of the world, especially the great world; that she has, however, brought this world, which it was her duty to convert to God, itself to the brink of perdition. For she has made self-deification, the titanic glorification of her own dignity and authority, the centre of all corruption. She has thereby induced the *kings* or potentates *of the earth* to push their authority also to a degree exceeding a right human measure, to exchange reciprocal deifications with her and either in pride to compete with her, or to make fellowship with her. Thus have been formed the spheres of a morbid luxury, far exceeding the measure of morality, and as the *merchants of the earth*, or the organs of this luxury, have attained to a colossal and morbid greatness, so, likewise, have their riches reached a corresponding grandeur. Even wholesale trade, in the most extensive sense of the term, or supermarine intercourse of the world with the world, has been drawn into this great vortex of feverish worldliness. Thus the most thorough men of the world, far and wide, have lived and sinned with Great Babylon, and are most profoundly shaken and discomfited by her fall. But they care not to share her lot with her; they are faithless to her in her hour of need. *The kings stand afar off for the fear of her torment* (ver. 10). *The merchants stand afar off for the fear of her torment* (ver. 15). *The sea-farers and marine traders stand afar off and cry* (ver. 17). Doubtless, together with the ideas of their participation in her guilt, their grief, and their cowardly desertion of their mistress, there is likewise expressed the fact

* [The ὑμῖν should be omitted. See TEXT. AND GRAM., NOTE 8, ver. 6.—E. R. C.]

21

that Great Babylon is involved in a tremendous conflagration, which illuminates the whole earth, which admits of no remedy, which none dare approach, which, however, is visible from the remotest spots—so far, at least, as its pillar of smoke is concerned—holding all spectators spellbound with fear and amazement. It might be queried: why the great detailedness of the description, especially of articles of luxury (vers. 12-14)? Here we encounter the same masterly skill of the prophetic spirit which is displayed by Isaiah in his portrayal of the luxury of the Hebrew women (Is. iii.). For the worldly mind, this very detail of articles of pomp and pleasure is of supreme importance; the prophecy, therefore, ironically enters into this mode of view—the more since for Babylon every particle of her pleasure becomes a particle of torment. It is, further, characteristic that the kings shall *weep and passionately and loudly lament* (κόπτεσθαι) over the fall of Babylon, yet shall hold themselves aloof even at the ascending of the smoke from the beginning conflagration. That which caused them to become worshippers of the City, were the greatness and (magic) power of it. The *merchants* of the earth weep also; their sorrow, however, takes the form of mourning for the loss which has assailed them. Together with the greatness of the City, its magnificence and wealth have dazzled them. The *sea-farers* express their mourning for Babylon most passionately, in accordance with their life on the water; they were enchained by the incomparableness of the City and the great gain which it brought them.

The first lament is that of *the kings of the earth;* not the kings as such, but those rulers who, by the aid of the Hierarchy, have despotically governed, and, to enable them thus to do, have worked into the hands of the Hierarchy, being, therefore, bearers of a reciprocal deification. The heavenly voice describes the lament of the *merchants* most comprehensively. The splendor of the merchandise of the City is expatiated upon, as consisting of: (1) Precious things [metals, jewels] and splendid stuffs; (2) Costly material (fragrant citron [thyine-] wood) and costly vessels of precious stuffs of all sorts; (3) Spices, ointments, incense; (4) Delicious articles of enjoyment and nourishment; (5) Articles of a princely household, from draught-cattle and flocks of sheep to the souls of slaves—or slavish souls, which are the permanent fundamental condition of every Babylonish power. It might be thought strange that after all this, mention is made of delicious *fruit,* * and that here the enumeration passes into the form of an address to Babylon itself; but in this region the smallest thing is in many respects the greatest, and, moreover, a special category of gastronomical delicacies is in point—those, particularly, which belong to a princely dessert. Whilst *the kings* designated the great disaster of *one hour,* the catastrophe, as a *judgment* upon Babylon, *the merchants* lament that in one hour the great *wealth* of luxury in which Babylon arrayed herself, is destroyed.

Still more openly do *the sea-farers* express their egoistical interest in their cry of woe and lamentation for Great Babylon.

After this fore-description of the special judgments which, with the fall of Babylon, come upon her companions, the judgment upon Babylon herself is represented in a symbolic act.

The heavenly voice replies to all the unworthy lamentations of earth with a cry of exultation. All those who long ago pronounced the spiritual sentence of Babylon's lost state, without its appearing that their sentence was of any value in the actual world, are exhorted to *rejoice.* Now their sentence is ratified by the judgment of God. For such is the meaning of the passage; reference is not again had to the false judgment which they have previously experienced from Babylon, for how would such a reference be applicable to *Heaven?* Babylon has been judged from of old: 1. By the *Heaven* in general, the whole ideal world of God; 2. By the *Saints,* and 3. By the *Apostles*—nay, 4. Even before them, by the *Prophets* of the Old Covenant.

Next follows the symbolic representation of the final consummation of the judgment. *A strong Angel takes up a stone, like a great millstone, and casts it into the sea,* making this act, the violent casting of the stone, the great whirlpool occasioned by it, and the precipitate sinking of the stone, a symbol of the imminent, sudden and violent reprobation of Babylon. The Angel, because he is a fore-runner of the close Parousia of Christ, is conceived of as a personal being (see ch. xix. 9, 10); his action, however, is thoroughly symbolical. The allegorical symbol gains in expressiveness, it becomes typical, if we consider that *the sea* denotes the life of the nations, that *the millstone* is already familiar as the instrument of punishment for offence given (Matt. xviii. 6), that, finally, the proclamation of the strong Angel, in connection with his action, is expressive of the surest certainty of the Spirit of God in His Church. The judgment upon Babylon superinduces a great agitation in the sea of nations. This agitation is occasioned by a great stone of stumbling or most flagrant offence given by Babylon to the world, in particular to the "little ones;" * and it is the Angel of the Christian faith who has in this world awakened the consciousness of the life of the nations in respect of this offence, as is expressed by the fore-runner of Christ from the other world, one, in angelic form, of the glorified ones who shall appear with Christ. The *City,* as Great Babylon, *is destroyed;* as a ruin, as a desert place, *she continues,* for a memorial of terror. Hence the Angel describes her imminent desolation, not simply in order to intimate that her own destruction is illustrated by the destruction of her glory. This has been previously declared. The design is, rather, to sketch the desolation of the ruin of this spiritual Babylon in negative traits, even as Isaiah depicted the desolation of the ancient Asiatic Babylon in positive traits. No *musical sound* from any festivity can be heard any more in the deathly still-

---

* [See TEXT. AND GRAM., NOTE 17.—E. R. C.]

* [Above, the *stone* was the symbol of Babylon; its being *cast into the sea,* the symbol of her punishment by God; but here the *stone* is the symbol of Babylon's sin, and *its casting,* that of her own sinful conduct!—E. R. C.]

ness of Babylon. Not *a single artist of any art* can be found any more in the desert of her ruins. No *sound of a mill* betrays a trace of business or domestic life; *no light of a candle* occasions the inference of life or of a social circle; with *the voice of bridegroom and bride*, every festal presage of a future laden with new life has vanished. And now again, to conclude the picture, the grounds for the judgment are laid before us— *viz.*: Babylon's double guilt. On the one hand, she has fully corrupted the corrupt world. For *the great* of the earth, the possessors of power, were her merchants, *i. e.*, the agents and abettors of her affairs (οἱ ἔμποροι is the predicate, according to Eichhorn; see also Ebrard). Note well the distinction. The ἔμποροι τῆς γῆς (ver. 3) have become rich through the Woman; the μεγιστᾶνες τῆς γῆς have become the ἔμποροί σου, *i. e.*, of the Woman. [See Text. and Gram., Note 24, ver. 23.—E. R. C.] Her love of magnificence has driven luxury to its acme, and converted the dealers in it into great lords; it is still worse, however, that she has made the great of the earth agents of her interests. It was her fault that the merchants* could in many cases become barons and princes—that the princes could in many cases become merchants [*Krämer*]. *e. g.*, of indulgences, hierarchical stocks, and the like. Thus she has instituted a reciprocal action between egoistical mammon-service and egoistical power. The *nations* have been *led astray* by her *sorceries* of all sorts. Thus she has *seduced* the world in its great and little ones. Of the kernel of the Church, however —the Prophets and Saints—not the living images, but the bloody traces of martyrdom, were found in her. The Angel, truly, seems to conclude his accusation in a very hyperbolical manner. Is *the blood of all who have been slain on earth* to be placed to the account of Babylon? We might say: Undoubtedly it is, inasmuch as, at the day of reckoning, Babylon forms the centre of all human guilt and blood-guiltiness. The choice of the verb, however, constitutes a very important item for consideration. Σφάζειν, the verb in question, denotes, at least in a predominant degree, *slaying* from a religious point of view; here, therefore, are indicated the *slain upon the earth* who have been slain as sacrifices to fanaticism in general, and especially in the religious wars and religious criminal courts of earth. The centre of these specific crimes is Babylon; it is manifest, however, that Babylon is not here intended simply as a local centre, for the like blood-guiltinesses make their appearance sporadically all over Christendom—though, indeed, always as fanatical radii, having a fanatical centre.†

[ABSTRACT OF VIEWS, ETC.]
By the American Editor.

[ELLIOTT: (See on pp. 281, 296.) The section extends to the close of chap. xix. 4. In it we have—I. Ver. 1. An angelic proclamation of the approaching destruction of Babylon;—a proclamation, (1) *similar* to that of chap. xiv. 8, but with additional circumstances (ver. 3); (2) *anticipative*, but as immediately preceding the catastrophe. II. A warning voice to Christ's true servants to come out of her; which implies that (1) there would be some of the holy seed in the mystic Babylon, (2) their danger of participation in her destruction would be imminent. III. A vivid description of the catastrophe, in which are depicted: 1. Its nature, (1) *unexpected* (she sits a queen, *etc.*); (2) *instantaneous* (in an hour); (3) *total* (all life destroyed); (4) by *eternal* (superhuman?) *fire* (xix. 3): 2. The *lamentations* over the fall,—(1) of the *kings* who committed fornication with her: (2) of the *merchants*, *etc.*, who were enriched by her IV. The *reasons* for the judgment,—(1) her *deception* of all nations; (2) her persecution of the saints. V. The heavenly song of praise over the destruction,—(1) *twice* by *the heavenly host*, Hallelujah (xix. 1–3); (2) *once* (and it is the last act related of them) by the Elders and Living-beings, Amen—Hallelujah (xix. 4).—From this passage the following conclusions, as to the probable progress of fast-coming future events, may be drawn that—I. The destruction of Rome, the mystic Babylon (comprehending not only the City and the Ecclesiastical State; but, probably, the political tripartition adhering to it, xvi. 19), shall, very soon after the tri-partition, and unexpectedly, be effected by an *earthquake* and *volcanic fire*.* II. Immediately before this event there will be a diffusion of great religious light, and a sounding

<hr>

* [*Krämer*—a word of lower significance than *Kaufleute*, previously translated *merchants*; the latter denotes the great wholesale dealers, whilst the former signifies *retailers*—shop-keepers, as we say in English.—Tr.]
† [See Expla. in Detail, Add. Comment on ver. 24.—E. R. C.]

<hr>

* ["A mode of destruction not obscurely intimated by certain very striking allusive expressions in other prophecies both of the Old and New Testament (Isa. xxxiv. 9, 10; xxx. 33; Jer. li. 25; Luke xvii. 28-32, *etc.*), and thus expected, as we find, alike by ancient Jewish Rabbis and Christian Fathers of the Italian soil has forced on many a mind, in different ages, the thought of its physical preparedness almost for such a catastrophe." Elliott.——Barnes, in support of the probable correctness of this view, writes as follows: "Gibbon (ch. xv.), with his usual accuracy, *as if* commenting on the Apocalypse, has referred to the physical adaptedness of the soil of Rome for such an overthrow. Speaking of the anticipation of the end of the world among the early Christians, he says, 'In the opinion of a general conflagration, the faith of the Christian very happily coincided with the tradition of the East. the philosophy of the stoics, and the analogy of nature; *and even the country, which, from religious motives, had been chosen for the origin and principal scene of this conflagration, was the best adapted for that purpose by natural and physical causes*; by its deep caverns, beds of sulphur, and numerous volcanoes, of which those of Ætna, of Vesuvius, and of Lipari, exhibit a very imperfect representation.' As to the *general* state of Italy in reference to volcanoes, the reader may consult, with advantage, Lyell's *Geology* B. II., chs. ix.-xii. See also Murray's *Encyclopedia of Geography*, II. ii ... . The following extract from a recent traveller will still further confirm this representation: 'I b hold every where—in Rome, near Rome, and through the whole region from Rome to Naples—the most astounding proofs, not merely of the possibility, but the probability, that the whole region of central Italy will one day be destroyed by such a catastrophe (by earthquakes or volcanoes). The soil of Rome is *tufa*, which a volcanic subterranean action is going on. At Naples, the boiling sulphur is to be seen bubbling near the surface of the earth. When I drew a stick along the ground, the sulphurous smoke followed the indentation; and it would never surprise me to hear of the utter destruction of the southern peninsula of Italy. The entire country and district is volcanic. It is saturated with beds of sulphur and the substrata of destruction. It seems as certainly prepared for the flames as the wood and coal on the hearth are prepared for the taper which shall kindle the fire to consume them. The Divine hand alone seems to me to hold the element of fire in check by a miracle as great as that which protected the cities of the plain, till the righteous Lot had made his escape to the mountains.'—*Townsend's Tour in Italy in 1850*."—E. R. C.]

forth of strong appeals on the character and imminent doom of both Rome and the Popedom, alike in the Church and in the world. III. The Jews will probably at, or just after, the catastrophe, be converted (indicated by the *Hebrew* HALLELUJAH—this being the first introduction of a word from that language in *praise*). IV. Down to the time figured by this chorus (a song represented as being in *Heaven*), no translation of the living saints or resurrection of the departed will have taken place.

BARNES: This chapter is a still further *explanatory episode* designed to show the *effect* of the pouring out of the seventh Vial (xvi. 17–21) upon the Antichristian power; the description is that of a rich merchant-city reduced to desolation, and is but carrying out the general idea under a different form. We have—(1) the angelic descent and proclamation, vers. 1–3; (2) a warning to the people of God to be partakers neither of her sins nor plagues, accompanied by a description of the latter, vers. 4–8; (3) lamentation over her fall—by those who had been, (*a*) *connected* with her, (*b*) *corrupted* by her, (*c*) *profited* by her, vers. 9–19; (4) rejoicing over her fall, ver. 20; (5) the final (and total) destruction, vers. 21–24. (Whilst this writer regards the Papacy, and not the *city* of Rome, as the object specially contemplated by the prophecy, he thinks it possible that there may be a *literal* fulfillment of the prophecy *burned with fire*, ver. 8, in the destruction of the *city* as in order to the destruction of the power; for quotations tending to support this view, see the preceding foot-note. For special *comments*, see EXPLANATIONS IN DETAIL *in loc.*)

STUART: In his Introduction to ch. xvii., this commentator remarks: "Before any attack was made upon the Kingdom of the Beast, an Angel proclaimed the fall of great Babylon (*i. e.*, 'persecuting and pagan Rome'), xiv. 8. This, however, was only in general terms. But now the seventh Vial has been poured out, and the city has been shaken to its very foundation, and thus a ruinous state of things has already commenced, ch. xvi. 17–21. Final and utter extinction, however, still remains to be achieved. Accordingly an Angel next appears, and not only renews the proclamation of the fall of Babylon, but describes this in such terms as necessarily to imply its *utter* ruin." *

* [It is exceedingly difficult to determine what is the idea of STUART as to the interpretation of this chapter. This arises from the fact that nowhere in the special comment on it does he define what he means by Babylon; his meaning has to be sought through General and Special and Particular Introductions and through excursuses and textual comments. His comment on xiv. 8 can leave no doubt that *there* he regards Babylon as the City of Rome; that this int rpretation is cont mpla'ed throughout this portion of the Apocalypse, is implied in numerous remarks. But the peculiar scheme of STUART requires him to regard the woe as having been accomplished; and manifestly the City of Rome has never yet become a desolation. The most plausible idea concerning his interpretation is that he regards the prophecy as having its *specific* fulfillment in the destruction of Rome long ago commenced, but not yet accomplished; and its *generic* accomplishment in the overthrow of all Antichristian powers. The view as to the specific fulfillment is suggested by the following remark under xiv. 8: "The reader is not to suppose, that *fallen*, while it denotes absolute certainty, at the same time denotes complete and *instantaneous* excision. The predictions respecting ancient Babylon were fulfilled only in the lapse of several centuries; but they were at last fully accomplished. And so of the tropical Babylon. The

WORDSWORTH: "Fuller description of the future fall of the Mystical Babylon. It is to be carefully observed that though *Babylon* falls, the *Beast* still remains. Therefore, the fall of Papal Rome will *not* be the destruction of Papacy."

ALFORD: Chaps. xviii. 1–xix. 10 relate to the *Destruction of Babylon*. I. Announcement of the destruction (chap. xviii. 1–3). II. Warning to God's people to leave her on account of the greatness of her crimes and coming judgments (4–8). III. Lamentations over her on the part of those who were enriched by her, by (1) the kings of the earth (9, 10); (2) the merchants (11–16); (3) the shipmasters, *etc.* (17–19). IV. The calling of the heavens and God's holy ones to rejoice over her (20). V. Symbolic proclamation of Babylon's ruin (21–24).

LORD: The *Angel* of ver. 1 symbolizes a body of men who shall with resistless *light* unveil the Apostate character of Babylon (*i. e.*, the *nationalized hierarchies*, see pp. 310 sq.). The *fall* of Babylon is her dejection from her nationalized position; it is to be (1) in *consequence* of her idolatry, ver. 3; (2) *followed* by (*a*) her becoming the resort of the most detestable of (human) beings, ver. 2, (*b*) another proclamation by another body of men calling upon those true Christians who remain in her to come out of her, ver. 4; (3) *effected* (*a*) violently, ver. 21; (*b*) by the multitude, and not by the kings and great men who are to mourn over it, vers. 9–19. The *fall* is to be distinguished from the *punishment* (plagues); the latter is speedily and suddenly to follow the former, vers. 4–6. The *destruction* is to be entire, vers. 21–24.

GLASGOW: Ver. 1 introduces an account of what accompanies or follows close upon the full effusion of the seventh Vial. The *Angel* of ver. 1 is the Holy Ghost, who announces the coming fall of Babylon, *i. e.*, the Roman State; the *voice* of ver. 4 is that of Christ. By *the kings* of vers. 9, 10, *the traffickers* of vers. 11–16, *the mariners* of vers. 17–19, are indicated the *three parts* into which the City is divided (ch. xvi. 19); "as ancient Babylon exists now only in the palace of her kings, the temple of Belus, and the tower of Nimrod, so over the fall of the mystic city are heard the wailings of superstitious rulers in the palace, of trafficking priests of simony in their cathedrals, and of far-travelled colonizers and missionaries, propagators of her errors."

AUBERLEN: "The judgment on the Harlot (*i. e.*, Babylon—the apostate Church) is described more minutely in its various aspects (xviii. 1; xix. 5), first by an Angel having great authority; then by another voice from Heaven (vers. 4–20); after this, thirdly, by a strong Angel (21–24); and this is succeeded by great voices of much people in heaven (xix. 1–5), who praise God for the judgment executed.—E. R. C.]

EXPLANATIONS IN DETAIL.

According to Düsterdieck, the judgment upon Babylon is still imminent at the close of ch. xviii. ("note the future $\beta\lambda\eta\theta\acute{\eta}\sigma\epsilon\tau\alpha\iota$"), whilst in

Apocalypse itself gives sufficient intimation of a gradual fulfillment; comp. Rev. xvi. 19–21 with xv.ii. 4–8, 20–24 and xix. 11–21."—E R. C.]

ch. xix. 1 sqq.. it is rejoiced over as actually accomplished. The judgment itself, therefore. [the act of judgment], would not be found in the description. As an external scene, it is, indeed, not to be portrayed. What, however, appertains to a judgment? Is not the heavenly sentence itself the ideal judgment (vers. 2, 3)? Is not the separation of the people of God from Babylon, which must ensue directly upon the heavenly command, the decisive dynamical judgment (vers. 4 and 5)? Next follows the historic recompense; first for Babylon herself (vers. 6, 7). And this is presupposed as an accomplished fact in the lamentation in which all her companions appear as sharers in the stroke which has fallen upon herself, (vers. 9-19). The rejoicing of Heaven and all the saints (ver. 20) clearly expresses the accomplishment of the judgment, and the symbolical act and speech of the Angel (vers. 21-24) are but declarative of the perfect reprobation of Babylon, together with its consequences, her guilt being once more solemnly affirmed. Thus is the judgment executed in four main acts. According to Hengstenberg, the Seer here describes what has already taken place. Exegesis, with him, steers backwards; it, probably, already sights the Millennial Kingdom—and this it is anxious to avoid, as though it were a rocky wall.

Ver. 1. **Another Angel.**—A symbolic angelic form, suggestive of Michael, not precisely Christ (Calov., Hengst.), for the Parousia is not to come until after this. The Holy Ghost (Vitringa), however, is no angel of external events, and Luther's embassage did at least not bring Babylon with violence to her fall. Historically defined, Christianity. in a new, glorious, and therefore mightily efficacious phase of development, must be understood by the Angel. Hence alone is his glory to be explained, which lights up the whole earth. A couple of wretched and disorderly negations can, of course, not be intended by this.

Ver. 2. **Fallen, fallen.**—A certain future, which shall some day become both present and past. The cry of ch. xiv 8 is reflected here; that, however, applied to the universal Babylon. In the first place, doubtless, the complete spiritual fall of Babylon is intended, as is manifest from the context: **and is become,** etc. But along with the complete spiritual fall, her historic fall is also decided. According to Düsterdieck, indeed, the words: **a habitation of demons,** etc., already denote external desolation, like the description Is. xiii. 22. Similarly Hengstenberg, vol. ii , p. 268. Düsterd. even regards it as singular that Ebrard should yet understand the birds "spiritually." A naïve "yet!" According to Bengel, the "unclean spirits" are departed souls, and "this passage very clearly treats of such spirits as, when they appear to the living, are called ghosts." The reverend divine would, however, surely not transfer Babylon to Wurtemberg! According to Hengstenberg, [also Stuart and Alford,—E. R. C.], the φυλακή denotes **a** prison—thus: a prison of unclean spirits and unclean birds. The expression, however, when used with reference to a fallen city, is applicable neither to spirits nor to birds. "The law of their essential character banishes

them thither." To the desert of pagan Rome? This would be the worst that could possibly be affirmed of Christian Rome! In respect of the birds, Hengstenberg cites Ps. cii. 6; Is. xiii. 21, 22; xxxiv. [11, 13] 14 [15]; Jer. l. 39; Zeph. ii. 14.

Ver. 3. **For . . . of the wine,** etc.—This is the offence which is judged primarily by a falling under the dominion of demonic powers. Babylon has offended against three classes of men —the nations, the kings, and a middle class, the merchants of the earth. We must again distinguish these merchants of the earth from the specific merchants whom the Woman has raised up for herself from the great of the earth (ver. 23, see SYN. VIEW). If we examine the arrangements of the Seer, we shall find that he has a more general and a more special arrangement. The more general one distinguishes between the kings, or the mighty of the earth, and the nations. The Woman has seduced the former to the fornication of world-deification, and intoxicated the latter with the rage-wine of fanaticism, according to ch. xvii. 2; xviii. 23. The more special arrangement inserts a third class, the merchants of the earth, a transition-form between the kings and the nations, in which the money-agents can become money-princes, and the princes agents of the Woman. But again, the class of mercantile people is, in our chapter, sub-divided into two classes, viz.: [1] the eminent merchants, who, as immediate servants of the Woman, participate in her luxury, and [2] the ordinary tradespeople of the world, here designated by sea-farers, whose interests are likewise, in a more general sense, involved in the luxury of the Woman. It was clear to the Seer that the super-human exaggeration of magnificence, the pomp of world-seeking in the heart of mankind, in the very place whence the forces of world-renunciation, simplicity and simple culture, should go forth, would place the whole organism of worldly life in a condition of morbid bloatedness, and feverishly egoistic agitation. [See NOTE 16 on chap. xiv., p. 274.—E. R. C.]

From the power (or **influence**) [Lange: **mighty operation**], etc.—According to Düsterdieck (with Grot. et al.), ἐκ τῆς δυνάμεως τοῦ στρήνους refers to the vast wealth [gewaltige Vermögen] of the City, employed in the service of luxury. This would, undoubtedly, be more applicable to pagan than to Christian Rome. Be it well remembered, however, that the "world kingdom" did not become rich through the "world city," but vice versâ. It is also better, from philological considerations, to regard δύναμις as the mighty operation of that central luxury. The interpretation: On account of her powerful luxuriousness (De Wette), really involves an obliteration of δύναμις. ["Δύναμις, copia, ** Vitringa, who remarks, 'alluditur ad Hebræam voce הִיל, cujus hæc significationis vis est, Job xxxi. 5; Ezek. xxviii. 4.' We have πλοῦτον μεγάλου δύναμιν in Jos.: Antt. iii. 2, 4." ALFORD.—E. R. C.]

Ver. 4. **Another voice from the Heaven.** —It is noteworthy that the voice from Heaven, speaking from vers. 4-20, is interposed between the two mighty Angels of ver. 1 and ver. 21. In the two Angels, we behold the denouncer and the executioner of God's judgment upon Babylon, **as** that judgment appears on earth; in the voice from Heaven, we find the cry of the Church Triumphant—the Church not simply in the other world, but also in this world,—addressed to the Church of God on earth. For whilst there is, in the Church on earth, in respect of its individual members, a constant wavering between premature separation from Babylon (by which name even the evangelical Church is designated by sectarian spirits) and a tardy tarrying in the communion of a true Babylon, aggravated by manifold fanatical lapses into the *captivitas Babylonica*, there resides in the heavenly Church the true sense for the determining of the hour of need when the general exode from Babylon before the judgment shall be as necessary as the exode of the Christians of John's time from Jerusalem to Pella. Too early a departure is opposed to humility and love; too late a departure is hostile to faith and fidelity; both acts, that of precipitancy and that of undue delay, are a fanatical opposition to the truth. According to Bengel, the voice from Heaven is the voice of God or Christ, against which Düsterdieck judiciously remarks that such an origin does not accord with the descriptive tone of its discourse. Mediately, of course, every angelic and every heavenly voice is to be referred to God and Christ. **Come forth out of her, my people.**—This can refer only to the complete rupture of religious and churchly fellowship. If we regard the words as having reference to an external departure of the Christians from Rome, all Christian Rome would be a contravention of the heavenly voice. ["In Isa. (xlviii. 20; lii. 11) the circumstances differed, in that being a joyful exodus, this a cautionary one:[*] and thus the warning is brought nearer to that one which our Lord commands in Matt. xxiv. 16, and the cognate warnings in the O. T., viz., that of Lot to come out of Sodom, Gen. xix. 15-22, when her destruction impended, and that of the people of Israel to get them up from the tents of Dathan and Abiram, Num. xvi. 23-26. In Jer. (l. 8; li. 6, 9, 45) we have the same circumstance of Babylon's impending destruction combined with the warning; and from those places probably, especially Jer. li. 45, the words here are taken. The inference has been justly made from them (Elliott IV., pp. 44 sq.), that there shall be even to the last, saints of God in the midst of Rome; and that there will be danger of their being, through a lingering fondness for her, partakers of her coming judgment." ALFORD.—E. R. C.] See Jer. li. 6, 9, 45. **That ye partake not in her sins.**—See Gen xix. 15. This *fellowship of sins* is to be understood in a peculiar sense as a *fellowship in guilt*—a view which Düsterdieck combats, but which finds its sufficient explanation in the distinction between the Biblical ideas of *sin (Sünde)* and *guilt [Schuld=reatus]*.[†] A fellowship of

sins, in the narrower sense (Luthardt), is as little intended as a fellowship in punishment for sins (Düsterd.) is exclusively meant. A guiltless participation in punishment would certainly be akin to propitiatory suffering. Fellowship with *the sinner*, however, on an equal moral footing, without the re-action of discipline, chastisement, excommunication, is fellowship in his *guilt*. Hence the πληγαί are not simply *strokes*; they are *deserved [verschuldete]* strokes (see Josh. vii.; Numb. xvi. 21-24).

["It is implied here that by remaining in Babylon they would lend their sanction to its sins by their presence, and would, in all probability, become contaminated by the influence around them." BARNES.—E. R. C.] Ver. 5. **For her sins have heaped together unto the Heaven.**—See SYN. VIEW. Vers. 6, 7. **Render unto her.**—See SYN. VIEW. Address to those injured by Babylon, as such. [Should we not rather, with Alford, regard these words as "addressed to the executioners of judgment?"—E. R. C.] With *the double measure*, the *qualitative* retribution is expressed in *quantitative* form. See SYN. VIEW. Comp. Is. xl. 2. The expressions διπλώσατε, διπλᾶ, διπλοῦν are, therefore, not simply "rhetorical." The consummation of her punishment is furnished with a three-fold motive, being the punishment (1) Of her evil deeds against the suffering party generally; (2) Of the cup, in particular—by which we are here to understand the cup of bitterness; (3) Of her self-glorification and pride, which involved a like measure of humiliation and oppression for the sufferers. **For she saith in her heart.**—Even now; so unforebodingly secure is she in face of the signs of the times. **A queen.**—Isa. xlvii. 7. **And a widow I am not.**—A widow in the more general sense, as one deserted. See Is. xlvii. 8, 9. Neither is she a *bride* or a *wife* any more, but a *polyandria*. **Sorrow I shall not see.**—Sorrow, particularly, for her many daughters (which, of course, are not the cities and peoples subject to pagan Rome). Thus she also regards herself as elevated above the universal law of earthly vicissitude, elevated above historic dooms.

[These expressions, in addition to reasons presented in *Add. Comm.* on ch. xvii. 18, and ADD. NOTE, p. 317, identify the objective of *Babylon* with that of the *Harlot*. As in ch. xvii., where the main figure was the *Harlot*, a portion of the symbolization was drawn from the *City*,—so here, where the main figure is *Babylon*, a portion of the symbolization is taken from the *Woman*.[*]—E. R. C.]

---

* [A cautionary exodus may be a *joyful* one. The cautioned escapers may rejoice in view of their escape.—E. R. C.]

† [The distinction here referred to seems to be that contemplated by the theologians of the Reformation in the use of the Latin terms *macula* and *reatus potentialis*—the former indicating the *stain* of sin; the latter, the *exposure to punishment* proper to the *persona sinning*. Thus Turretin (Vol. I., p. 654), "*Macula est pollutio spiritualis et ethica, quâ hominis*

anima inficitur. Reatus est obligatio ad pœnam ex prævio delicto. . . . . Duplex oritur reatus; alius qui potentialis dicitur, qui notat meritum intrinsecum pœnæ, quod a peccato inseparabile est; alius verò actualis, qui per Dei misericordiam ab eo separari potest,' etc. As the term *guilt* is habitually employed by a large class of English Theologians as the equivalent of *reatus*, and as it is the term generally employed in the E. V., where *Schuld* occurs in the G. V., it is here adopted. It should be carefully noted, however, that it is employed, not in its ordinary meaning, but in the special sense indicated above.—E. R. C.]

* [The true condition of the Church during the personal absence of her Husband and Head is that of a *widow*, comp. Matt. ix. 15; Mark ii 19, 20; Luke v. 34;—she should ever be looking, with longing, for His appearing, Tit. ii 13. The Am. Ed. cannot resist the thought that these expressions are

Ver. 8. **Therefore shall her plagues come in one day.**—Precisely *therefore* (בְּכֵן). In antithesis to her pride. **Death.**—Since death can not come upon her twice, and since the death of her children is expressed by *sorrow* or *mourning* [ver. 7], the term doubtless embraces the death-doom in general, coming upon her primarily as a presentiment of ruin, and then developing into mourning, hunger, and fiery death. **In one day**—in one great catastrophe (see Isa. xlvii. 9). [*Without succession through a protracted period*—all-together.—E. R. C.] **For strong.**—The whole omnipotence of God opposes itself in judgment to the haughtiness of Babylon, and this judgment has already begun (κρίνας). The whole Providence of God executes the judgment of the **Lord**, for it is as such that God has primarily to do with Babylon.

Vers. 9, 10. **And there shall weep and wail over her.**—In vers. 9–20 [19] are presented the three laments over Babylon, in which the three classes associated in her guilt appear, in antithesis to the people of God, as sharers in the stroke which has fallen upon her. They represent the peripheries of the judgment, forming about its centre. Comp. Ezek. xxvi., xxvii. **The kings of the earth.**—Düsterdieck rightly discards the view of Hengstenberg, who finds in the οὐαί, οὐαί a reference to "*double to her double.*" Highly significant is the kings' **standing afar off**: they will not be burned up with her, for their friendship with Babylon was based upon egoism. They must, however, together with her, be afflicted by the stroke which has descended upon her. Their lamentation is expressive of two things—on the one hand, that they have been dazzled by the grandeur and power of Babylon, and on the other, that they are aware of her guilt, for they speak of her *judgment*, although they do not come to the penitent consciousness that *they* have committed fornication and lived luxuriously with her.

[**Standing afar off.**—"The general sentiment here is that in the final ruin of Papal Rome the kings and governments that had sustained her, and had been sustained by her, would see the source of their power taken away, but that they would not, or could not, attempt her rescue. There have been not a few indications already that this will ultimately occur, and that the Papal power will be left to fall without any attempt on the part of those governments which have been so long in alliance with it, to sustain or restore it." BARNES.—E. R. C.]

Ver. 11. **And the merchants of the earth.**—Second lamentation. Here, egoism is more plainly visible. They **weep and sorrow** because no one will buy their merchandise any more. The vividness of the description is also augmented by the picturesque present: *they weep*, etc., and, no less, by the circumstantiality with which their merchandise, the entire expo-

sition of their secularized industry, is described (see SYN. VIEW). **No one buyeth their lading any more.**—That is, the fall of Babylon is accompanied by a thorough contempt for all splendor and luxury; it ushers in the fashion of simplicity.

Vers. 12–16. The wares are arranged in order (see SYN. VIEW). "The alternation of accusatives and genitives dependent on τὸν γόμον, prevailing till the close of ver. 13, may serve as explanatory of the dubious construction found in ch. xiv. 4" (Düsterd.). The fact that the vision draws the picture of these articles of luxury from the view of antiquity—of ancient Rome for instance—proves nothing for the import of Babylon. On the individual articles comp. the Lexicons. Special consideration, as less known, is demanded by the ξύλον θύϊνον, ἄμωμον, ὀπώρα. The distinction, σώματα and ψυχαὶ ἀνθρώπων, is noted by commentators and differently explained (see Düsterdieck, p. 527); the distinction, at all events, is not a very sharp one, and the second expression is indicative of an augmentation, the extreme consequence of slave-holding. The renewal of these circumstances, even in Christian Babylon, is well known. The strong emphasis laid at the end upon the missing of the favorite *fruit* [*] is highly characteristic as an ironical trait. It is well known that fallen great men often grieve most for the loss of the veriest trifles. Conjoined with these delicacies in the way of fruit, are all sorts of delicious things; "τὰ λιπαρά, literally *the fat*, but its conjunction with τὰ λαμπρά admonishes us to take the expression in the usual unliteral sense (Is. xxx. 23; comp. Hesych., who explains λιπ. as καλόν, ἔλαφρον), with Luther, Bengel, Hengstenberg" (Düsterd.). There seems, however, to be a distinction made between articles of gastronomic and aesthetic taste.

Ver. 15. **The merchants of these things.**—Here the style changes again from a vivid presentation of the Babylonish world-mart to the prophetic future. These merchants [*Kaufleute*] also bemoan the City in a characteristic manner. For them, the greatness of the City consisted, not, as for the kings, in her *power*, but in her outward *splendor*, her *beauty of attire*.

[Vers. 11–16. "The description . . . is perhaps drawn, in its poetic and descriptive features, from the relation of Rome to the world that then was, rather than from its relation at the future time depicted in the prophecy. But it must not for a moment be denied that the character of this lamentation throws a shade of obscurity over the interpretation, otherwise so plain from the explanation given in ch. xvii. 18 (*viz.*, 'that the prophecy regards Rome pagan and papal, but from the figure of an harlot and the very nature of the predictions themselves, more the latter than the former'). The difficulty is, however, not confined to the application of the prophecy to Rome Papal, but extends over the application of it to Rome *at all*. . . . For Rome never has been, and from its position never could be, a great commercial city. I leave this difficulty un-

---

indicative of a state of the Church in which she shall believe and assert that the personal absence of Jesus is no bereavement,—that already as a Queen she has entered upon the possession of the promised Kingdom,—that, during Christ's personal absence, without material hindrance, she is to go on to complete supremacy over the nations. Already in Rome, and to a great extent throughout Christendom, is this cry heard.—E. R. C.]

* [On the meaning of ὀπώρα see the TEXT, and NOTE 17, p. 319. The entire clause is probably figurative, d' claring th? the period of temporal prosperity has passed away.—E. R. C.]

solved, merely requesting the student to bear in mind its true limits, and not to charge it exclusively on that interpretation which only shares it with any other possible one. The main features of the description are taken from that of the destruction of and lamentation over Tyre in Ezek. xxvii., to which city they were strictly applicable. And possibly it may be said that they are also applicable to the Church which has wedded herself to the pride of the earth and its luxuries." ALFORD.—E. R. C.]*

Ver. 17. **And every pilot,** etc.—Marine affairs are sketched as that form of world-commerce and industry which was, proportionally, most remote from the City. Even this general mercantilism is affected by the fall of Babylon, because the blow inflicted upon the kings and upon the luxury of the great world touches it likewise. From the *pilots*, who can sail in all directions, are distinguished those who take ship for definite ports—from these latter, all who do business at sea (τὴν θάλασσαν ἐργάζεσθαι). [See TEXT and NOTE 21, p. 319.—E. R. C.]

Ver. 18. **The smoke of her burning.**—As ver. 9. Not to be confounded with the smoke, ch xiv. 11. The impression which the City has made on them is, proportionally, the most indefinite: she was *incomparable*. If a reference to ch. xiii. 4 was intended, it could yet not be satirical in the mouth of seamen (as Ebrard claims). The expression is, besides, the most general and, therefore, most indefinite form of worldly astonishment. It is thus that popular travellers and seafarers have spoken from time immemorial. [At the same time it should be noted that in reference to both Rome actual and Rome symbolical the expression is strictly true. BARNES comments, "*What city is like unto this great city?*" In her destruction. What calamity has ever come upon a city like this?"—E. R. C.]

Ver. 19. **And they cast dust,** etc.—A well-known sign of passionate mourning. Hence we need not ask, Whence came the dust at sea? The idea may be, however, that they viewed the conflagration from different ports. The narrative has changed to the preterite. The lamentation of these last is particularly passionate, and the egoistic motive is expressly assigned.

Ver. 20. **Rejoice over her.**—In face of the threefold lamentation of the world, the heavenly voice (not John himself) expresses the jubilation of Heaven. We might here discover the indi-

cations of a three-fold jubilation: that of Heaven, with the Saints—that of the Apostles—that of the Prophets. Düsterdieck claims a distinction betwixt "earthly believers"—as Saints, Apostles, Prophets—and Heaven. But even in Nero's time, there were several Apostles in Heaven, to say nothing of Prophets.

For God hath judged your judgment [Lange: executed your sentence] upon her.—We cannot apprehend the judgment [*Urtheilsspruch*=sentence of judgment], κρίμα, passively, with Hengstenb., De Wette, *et al.*, in the sense: God hath recompensed the judgment which ye suffered as martyrs. For how would that apply to *Heaven?* The rejoicing in this form would, moreover, express the satisfaction of the desire for vengeance, in a style savoring somewhat too strongly of the Old Testament. The fitting expression for *that* satisfaction is found in ver. 24, which is a sort of repetition when the above-cited exegesis is adopted. The higher satisfaction, however, which Heaven itself must experience in connection with all the Saints, particularly the Apostles and Prophets, consisted in the fact that their primeval prophetic sentence upon Babylon, accompanying her throughout her historic career, but appearing for so long a mere melancholic fancy, at which the world hooted, has been finally sealed by God Himself through His judgment. The rejoicing over this satisfaction is a rejoicing over the truth and righteousness of God Himself. [ALFORD comments, God "hath exacted from her that judgment of vengeance which is due to you."—E. R. C.]

Ver. 21. **And a** (or one) strong Angel.—On εἰς see Winer, p. 126. As we shall have occasion to recur to this Angel in ch. xix. 9, 10, we may here refer to the predicates there given by the Angel to himself. Düsterd. remarks that the *strength* of the Angel receives mention on account of the action which he is represented as performing **Like a great mill-stone.**—See Jer. li. 63, 64. See SYN. VIEW. **With violence.**—In a catastrophe. **And shall be found no more at all,**—*i. e.*, as the magnificent City which it had been. That, however, it should continue as a desolate ruin, for a memorial of judgment, is evident from the following context. See Ezek. xxvi. 13; Jer. xxv. 10, *et al.*

Ver. 22. **And a voice of harpers.**—Art stood high in Babylon [and in Rome, and in the Visible Church—especially as she increases in worldliness,—E. R. C.]; it was, however, completely under the influence of vanity and in the service of idolatry. With art business vanishes (*the mill*); with business, family life (*the candle*); with family life, family festivals [and relationships] (*bridegroom and bride*).

Ver. 23. **For thy merchants were the great men of the earth** [Lange: the princes of the earth were thy merchants].—The vision closes, most appropriately, with a brief recapitulation of the guilt of Babylon. For this reason, also, we cannot, with Düsterd., Ewald, De Wette and Hengstenberg [also Lillie, Alford, Glasgow, *et al.*,—E. R. C.], read: *thy merchants were the great of the earth.** No leading reproach

---

* [The Am. Ed. entertains the view that by *Babylon* is meant the *City of Rome*, and, still further, that by the *City of Rome* is symbolized the *Visible Church* (apostate in the time of the fulfillment of the prophecy). It seems to him that the difficulties suggested by Alford are imaginary rather than real in reference to both these hypotheses. It should be remembered that, in the days of the Apocalyptist, Rome was not only the centre of the Empire, but in a peculiar sense her boundaries were coterminous with those of the Empire; the commerce of the entire State was hers,—at once resulting from, and ministering to, her wealth and power. A peculiar relation of headship continued to be borne by the City to the nation dwelling within the pale of the old Empire, even after that Empire had been shattered into fragments. Even to the present day she is in a sense the capital of Papal Europe. And still further—the relation of Rome to the peoples of whom she was and is the acknowledged capital, well symbolizes the relation of the Visible Church to Christendom. She is its inspiring centre,—the source, and to a large extent a partaker, of its power and splendor. The commerce of the world is, in a peculiar sense, hers. To Rome actual, and Rome symbolical (in the sense set forth), the description of these verses is applicable.—E. R. C.]

* [The order of the Greek requires this translation. The reproach is, not "that some few money-changers became

would be involved in the statement that some few money-changers became lords and princes under the influence of absolutist luxury. At all events, we should expect first a repetition of the two leading categories of the transgression of Babylon against the world related to her. The first transgression is the seduction of the *kings*, or the *great*, generally, whom she has made her merchants, abettors and brokers (her associates in fornication). The second transgression is against the *nations*, which she has seduced or intoxicated with her sorcery or poison-mixing (= wine of rage). Düsterdieck interprets φαρμακεια as the *love-potions* of the Harlot; "comp. Is. xlvii. 9, 12 sq.; Ewald, De Wette." Our Seer, however, keeps the two categories separate, ch. xvii. 2; xviii. 3. The nations have not been so much intoxicated by love-potions as by rage-potions (of fanaticism). A connection between the two forms is of course unmistakable. [The objective of φαρμακεια may be the instruments of seduction by which she either allures the nations into unholy alliance with herself, or by which she causes them to wander in unrighteous paths. See the TEXT.—E. R. C.]

After the transgression of Babylon against the world, ensues her transgression against *the people of God*—a transgression still greater than the former, yet connected with it.

Ver. 24. See SYNOPTICAL VIEW. Ebrard: "Hengstenberg, who makes the Millennial Kingdom commence with Charlemagne, must, to be consistent with his own view, point out the terrible destruction of Babylon depicted in ch. xviii., ■■ occurring at some period during the time before Charlemagne. Nor does he find this difficult: to be sure, in the City of the Seven Hills the voices of lutists and pipers have never for one moment been silenced; neither is the City thrown into the sea, or burned, nor has an end been put to her commerce and her magnificence, nor has any one mourned over her downfall—on the contrary, she has quietly continued to subsist in the midst of the billows of national migrations: but —'Rome here comes under consideration solely as the pagan mistress of the world'—and as *pagan* she *is* fallen, burned, desolated, *etc:* and all this simply inasmuch as at about the time of Constantine she was gradually transformed from a pagan to a Christian City! In ch. xviii., therefore, we have, according to the exegesis of Hengstenberg, an entirely new portrayal of a—*conversion.*"

[ADDITIONAL NOTE ON CH. XVIII.]

By the American Editor.

[This chapter, introduced by the disjunctive phrase, Μετὰ ταῦτα εἶδον. and immediately followed by a chapter having a similar introduction, forms, apparently, a supplementary section. In it are set forth events preceding the fall of Babylon. The direct vision of that fall occurred during the outpouring of the vials, ch. xvi. 18.

---

princes," but that her merchants, her men of business generally, busied themselves with the affairs of this world, became worldlin.s. and assumed the position of its leaders and great men.—E. R. C.]

19. As, however, that series of visions could not with propriety have been interrupted by the introduction of others descriptive of matters other than the plagues, supplementary visions were vouchsafed descriptive of important matters necessarily omitted, or barely indicated. in the main series. This chapter narrates a series of visions having reference (probably) to "the voices, and thunders, and lightnings, and earthquake" mentioned ch. xvi. 18. It consists of three parts, in which are narrated visions of—I. A glorious, heaven-descended Angel giving a proleptical prediction of the approaching destruction of the City, vers. 1–3. II. A voice from Heaven making a threefold call upon (1) the people of God, who should remain in the doomed City to come out of her, vers. 4, 5; (2) the executioners of judgment to destroy, vers. 6–19; (3) the inhabitants of Heaven to rejoice, ver. 20. III. An Angel giving a symbolic prophecy of the destruction.—An analogue of this section, as to its *subject matter*, is to be found Jer. l., li., where we have a similar threefold division, *viz.:* 1. A proleptical declaration of destruction, l. 2. 2. A call upon (1) the people of God to escape, l. 8; li. 6, 45; (2) the executioners of judgment, li. 14 sqq. 3. A symbolical prophecy of the destruction, li. 63, 64.—One great distinction between the two sections should be noted. The one in the Apocalypse is the record of a *prophecy* of events (including prophecies); that in Jeremiah is simply a record of events (also including prophecies). John prophesied of a Divinely appointed messenger (Angel) who should prophesy. Jeremiah was himself the messenger (Angel) who foretold.

[In the judgment of the writer, the events here symbolized are yet future; nothing in the history of the world has occurred which adequately meets the symbolization. A comparison of this section with the one in Jeremiah, suggests the thought that by the *glorious Angel* of vers. 1-3 may be symbolized a Divinely called and gifted man, or body of men, who, in the spirit of the old Prophets, shall declare the approaching fall of the spiritual Babylon. By the *Voice from Heaven* of ver. 4 may be designated the inspired voice of these latter Prophets uttering the calls foretold; or, as the change in figure (*another voice*) probably indicates a change in instrumentality, by it may be indicated some other Divine influence exerted upon the three classes mentioned. By the *strong Angel casting the millstone into the sea*, ver. 21, may be symbolized some great catastrophe in history or nature—possibly the destruction of the great City that symbolizes the apostate Church.—An objection to the suggested interpretation may arise in the minds of some from the fact that the *Voice* of ver. 4 (an *influence*) and the Angel of ver. 2 (*the agent of a catastrophe*) are both represented in the context as *prophesying*. In answer it may be said that it is altogether in keeping with the dramatic nature of the Apocalypse to represent these symbols of Divine instrumentalities as themselves declaring the results of their agency.—E. R. C.]

II. SECOND SPECIAL END-JUDGMENT. JUDGMENT UPON THE BEAST (ANTICHRIST) AND HIS PRO-
PHET. THE BEAST AND THE MARRIAGE OF THE LAMB; THE MILLENNIAL KINGDOM
AS THE ÆON OF TRANSITION FROM THE EARTHLY TO THE
HEAVENLY WORLD.

CHAP. XIX. 1—XX. 10.

A. IDEAL HEAVENLY WORLD PICTURE OF THE VICTORY OVER THE BEAST; AND
THE MILLENNIAL KINGDOM.

CHAP. XIX. 1-16.

1. *The Harlot and the Bride* (Vers. 1-10).

1   And [om. And][1] After these things I heard [ins. as][2] a great voice of much people, [a great throng (ὄχλου πολλοῦ)] in [ins. the] heaven, saying,[3] Alleluia [Halle-
lujah]; [ins. The] salvation, and [ins. the] glory, and honour [om. and honour],[4] and
2   [ins. the] power, unto the Lord [om. unto the Lord—ins. of] our God : For true and
righteous [just] *are* his judgments; for he hath [om. hath] judged the great whore
[harlot], which did corrupt [that corrupted] the earth with her fornication, and
3   hath [om. hath—ins. he] avenged the blood of his servants at her hand.   And
again [a second time] they said, Alleluia [Hallelujah].   And her smoke rose up
4   [ascendeth] for ever and ever [into the ages of the ages].   And the four and twenty
[twenty-four] elders and the four beasts [living-beings] fell down and worshipped
God that sat [who sitteth] on the throne, saying, Amen ; Alleluia [Hallelujah].
5   And a voice came out [or forth from][5] the throne, saying, Praise [Give praise to]
our God,[6] all ye [om. ye] his servants, and ye [om. and ye][7]—ins. those] that fear him,
6   both [om. both—ins. the] small and [ins. the] great.   And I heard as it were [om. it
were] the [a] voice of a great multitude [throng], and as the [a] voice of many waters,
and as the [a] voice of mighty [strong] thunderings [thunders], saying,[8] Alleluia
[Hallelujah]: for the Lord [ins. our] God omnipotent [om. omnipotent—ins. the All-
7   ruler] reigneth [(ἐβασίλευσεν)—hath assumed the Kingdom][9].   Let us be glad and rejoice [exult] and [or ins. we will][10] give honour [the glory] to him : for the marriage
of the Lamb is come [came], and his wife hath made [om. hath made—ins. prepared]
8   herself ready [om. ready].   And to her was granted [given] that she should be
arrayed [array herself] in fine linen, clean [bright][11] and [and][11] white [pure][11]:
for the fine linen is the righteousness [righteousnesses (τὰ δικαιώματα)] of [ins. the]
9   saints.   And he saith unto me, Write, Blessed *are* they which [who] are called
unto the marriage [om. marriage] supper [ins. of the marriage] of the Lamb.   And

---

[1] Ver. 1. [Καί is omitted by א. A. B. C. P., *et al.*—E. R. C.]

[2] Ver. 1. A. B. C. [א. P.], *et al.*, give ὡς.

[3] Ver. 1. Λεγόντων. [So Crit Eds. with א. A. B. C. P., *et al.*—E. R. C.]

[4] Ver. 1. The readings καὶ ἡ τιμή and κυρίῳ are not based upon secure authorities. [Crit. Eds. give ἡ σωτηρία καὶ ἡ δόξα καὶ ἡ δύναμις τοῦ θεοῦ ἡμῶν with preponderating authorities.—E. R. C.]

[5] Ver. 5. [Tisch. (8th Ed.) gives ἐκ τοῦ with א. P. 1, 31, 32, *et al.*; Lach., Tisch., (1859), Alf. and Treg. give ἀπό with A. B. C., *et al.*—E. R. C.]

[6] Ver. 5. Τῷ θεῷ ἡμῶν in acc. with A. B. C., *et al.* [Crit. Eds. give τῷ θεῷ with א. A. B. C. P., *et al.*—E. R. C.]

[7] Ver. 5. [Tisch. (8th Ed.) omits καί with א. C. P.; Lach., Tisch. (1859) give it with A. B*., 1, 7, 14, 38, *et al.*; Alf. and Treg. bracket it.—E. R. C.]

[8] Ver. 6. Cod. A. [P.], *et al.*, Lach. and Rec. give λεγόντων. [Gb., 8z., Tisch. (1859), Alf. give λέγοντες with B.*; Tisch. (8th Ed.) Treg., λεγόντων.—E. R. C.]

[9] Ver. 7. ["Here is a case where we cannot approach the true sense of the aor. ἐβασίλευσεν but by an English present: '*reigned*' would make the word apply to a past event limited in duration: '*hath reigned*' would even more strongly imply that the reign was over." ALFORD. Still better is Lange's translation *hath assumed the kingdom*, presenting the idea of a *special reign* then begun.—E. R. C.]

[10] Ver. 7. Δώσομεν in acc. with א. and A. [Lach., Tisch. (1859), Alf. give δώσομεν with א*. A. (δωσωμεν) P. 11, 79; Treg., Tisch. (8th Ed.) δῶμεν with א*. B*. 1, 7, *et al.*—E. R. C.]

[11] Ver. 8. [Crit. Eds. give λαμπρὸν καθαρὸν with א. A. P. 7, *et al.*—E. R. C.]

10 he saith unto me, These are the[12] true sayings [words] of God. And I fell at [before] his feet to worship him. And he said [saith] unto me, See *thou do it* [*om.* See *thou do it — ins.* Take heed] not: I am thy [*om.* thy—*ins.* a] fellow servant [*ins.* of thee], [*om.* ,] and of thy brethren that have the testimony [witness] of Jesus : worship God : for the testimony [witness] of Jesus is the spirit of [*ins.* the] prophecy.

2. *The Bridegroom as the Warrior-Prince, prepared to do battle with the Beast.* (Vers. 11-16).

11 And I saw [*ins.* the] heaven opened, and behold a white horse ; and he that sat upon him was [*om. was*] called[13] Faithful and True, and in righteousness he doth
12 judge [judgeth] and make war [warreth]. His[14] eyes *were* as [*om. were* as][15] a flame of fire, and on his head *were* [*om. were*] many crowns [diadems] ; [,] and he had [*om.* and he had—*ins.* having][16] a name written, that no man [one] knew
13 [knoweth] but he [*om.* he] himself. [,] and he *was* [*om.* he *was*] clothed with [in] a vesture dipped in blood : and his name is [has become to be][17] called The Word
14 of God. And the armies *which were* [*om. which were*] in [*ins.* the] heaven followed
15 him upon white horses, clothed in fine linen, white and clean [pure]. And out of his mouth goeth [*ins.* forth] a sharp sword (ῥομφαία), that with it he should smite the nations ; and he shall rule [shepherdize] them with a rod of iron [an iron rod] and he treadeth the winepress [*ins.* of the wine] of the fierceness and [*om.* fierceness and—*ins.* anger of the] wrath[18] of Almighty [*om.* Almighty] God [*ins.* the All-
16 ruler]. And he hath on *his* vesture and on his thigh a name written, KING OF KINGS, AND LORD OF LORDS.

[12] Ver. 9. Οἱ ἀληθινοί: in acc. with A., *et al.*, with the article. [So Lach., Alf., Tisch. (1859) ; but Lach. (8th Ed.) Treg. omit the article with א B*. P., *et al.*—E. R. C.]

[13] Ver. 11. [Treg. and Tisch. give καλούμενος with א.; Lach. omits with A P. 1, 4, 6, *et al.*; Alf. brackets.—E. R. C.]

[14] Ver. 12. [In the original οἱ is followed by δέ. Alf. remarks, "The δέ, as often, is best given in English by an asyndeton, marking a break in the sense, passing from the subjective to the objective description."—E. R. C.]

[15] Ver. 12. Ὡς in acc. with A., *Vulg.*, *et al.*; against it א. B*., *et al.* [Lach. gives it ; Treg. and Tisch. omit with א. B*. P., *et al.*; Alf. brackets.—E. R. C.]

[16] Ver. 12. Cod. B*., *et al.*, have ὀνόματα γεγραμμένα after ἔχων. [So Tisch. (1859) ; but Tisch. (8th Ed.), Lach., Treg., omit with A. P. 1, 7, *Vulg.*, *et al.*; Alf. brackets.—E. R. C.]

[17] Ver. 13. Κέκληται with א. A. B*., *et al.* [So Crit. Eds. generally.—E. R. C.]

[18] Ver. 15. [For this rendering of τοῦ θυμοῦ τῆς ὀργῆς see NOTE 29 on Ch. xv., p. 275.—E. R. C.]

EXEGETICAL AND CRITICAL.

SYNOPTICAL VIEW.

The first great special judgment upon Babylon, or upon Antichristianity in a hypocritical disguise, is now followed by the second great special judgment, the judgment upon the open, bold and specific Antichristianity of the Beast and the false Prophet. After this Antichristianity has accomplished God's judgment upon Babylon, *its* hour likewise comes. It comes, because the downfall and disappearance of the Harlot, "the fallen Church," result in the consummation and appearance of the Bride or the pure Church [Congregation] of God. The alternation of these two womanly forms in their visible appearance, is based both upon ethical and historical laws. When the spirit of idolatry, of deifications—in the form of party and sectarian spirit, as well as in other forms—is destroyed in Christendom ; when, consequently, all hierarchism and sectism are thoroughly annihilated, then, and not until then, can the Church of Christ appear as a Virgin without spot or blemish—as His Bride.[*] Until then, moreover, her simple, retired existence had been historically concealed by the

gaudy and ostentatious form of the Harlot. Hence, also, the investment of the Bride is prepared by a backward glance at the downfall of the Harlot. But the Virgin Church, having no earthly means of defence, stands, armed only with the weapons of the Spirit, opposed to the terrible power of Antichristianity. The hour of tribulation, therefore, is now come —the hour which occasions the return of Christ. He comes in celestial conquering power—for the rescue and emancipation of His Church. Hence His appearing results first in judgment upon the Beast ; this judgment, again, is the preliminary condition of the Marriage of the Lamb, which begins with the Millennial Kingdom.

The heavenly songs of praise, and the pre-celebration of the Marriage, in the description of the Bride and the portrayal of the Bridegroom at the head of His martial train, form the Heaven-picture of the judgment upon the Beast. The heavenly songs of praise are distributed into two choruses. The first chorus, led by the Church Triumphant, finds its lofty finale in the assent of the twenty-four Elders and the four Living-beings ; the second chorus takes an opposite direction, starting from a voice from the Throne, and diffusing itself throughout the spirit-realm. The first chorus is a post-celebration of the downfall of the Harlot ; the second chorus is the pre-celebration of the glorification of the Bride.

The Seer has separated the celestial triumph over the judgment of the Harlot from the vision

---

[*] [The underlying spirit of idolatry, or spiritual adultery, is *worldliness*, which manifests itself in a multitude of other, and more obnoxious forms than those mentioned above. Until this spirit be destroyed, together with all the forms in which it manifests itself. the Church will not be, or appear as, a pure Virgin.—E. R. C.]

of ch. xvii., in which place we should, in accordance with foregoing analogues, have expected it; he has done this for the following excellent reason—that he may constitute this triumph an introd ction to the appearance of the Bride and the Bridegroom. The manner in which he has set forth the antithesis of the Harlot and the Bride—each related to the other, each opposed to the other—leads to very definite conclusions. That the Bride of Christ can be only the true Church of Christ, needs no proof. From this very fact, however, it is evident that she has had a present, but, in her heavenly purity, invisible existence, previous to this—as the *invisible* Church, therefore. Her false image and counterpart, the Harlot, can, in accordance with this, be only the outward and externalized Church, in the consistency of her fall and decay.

How universal and unceasing is the triumph of all good spirits over the fall of Great Babylon! The hosts in Heaven cry, with the unanimity of one voice: Hallelujah! Their rejoicing has reference, above all, to the fact that the glory of God, which had been increasingly obscured by all idolatry, *in* MINOREM *dei gloriam*, is completely restored. Before, at the establishment of the invisible Church in the Heaven of the spirit, the heavenly voice proclaimed: *Now is come* [ἐγένετο] *the salvation, and the power, and the Kingdom of our God, and the authority of His Christ* (ch. xii. 10). Now, however, *glory* supervenes to these; the Kingdom of δόξα is on the point of appearing (ch. xix. 1). Out of the darkness of God's essence-conformed (veritable) and righteous judgments upon the great Harlot, bursts forth the radiance of His glory. The judgment is a double judgment, as a recompense of the great double sin of the Harlot in corrupting the earth with her fornication, i. e., idolatry, and persecuting and slaying the servants of God; on the one hand, it is a judgment of unmasking, and on the other, it is a judgment of avengement of blood. The decisive character of the heavenly sentence is once more expressed in a repeated Hallelujah, based especially upon the fact that the smoke from the burning of Babylon ascends into the æons of the æons. She shall never arise from her ashes. In conjunction with the song of praise of the heavenly hosts, the twenty-four Elders and the four Living-beings utter, worshipping, the Hallelujah, together with an Amen. The four Living-beings are especially called upon to say Amen (see ch. v. 14), because they have been the single factors who have brought about the final result of the judgment, or because the fallen Church was thoroughly at variance with each of these ground-forms of the Divine rule: with ideality (*the eagle*), humanity (*the human image*), with alacrity in sacrifice and suffering (*the bullock*), and with true moral bravery (*the lion*). Heaven has spoken, but God's servants on earth apparently still forbear to utter their sentiments in regard to the fall of Babylon. In face of the kings of the earth, the merchants or mighty men, the international lords of the sea, who are all still lamenting over Babylon—aye, in view of reminiscences of the apparent holiness, the former merits and proud security of Babylon through many centuries, the servants of God, and the truly pious in general, have become reticent and silent. Therefore must a voice from the throne of God issue the command: *Give praise to our God, all His servants* [Lange: *and*] *those* (in general) *that fear Him, the small and the great.* For besides believers, the Seer recognizes fearers of God, not only great ones, but also little ones. With this, a storm of praise is loosed on earth also: *a voice of a great throng*—partly, *a voice of many waters* or peoples; partly, *a voice of strong thunders* or prophetic geniuses—repeats the heavenly Hallelujah. But these loosed tongues still seem timidly to pass by the name of the Harlot—and this so much the more since it is the *world* of the ten horns and the Beast which has destroyed Babylon; they fasten immediately upon the glorious positive result: "*For the Lord our God, the All-Ruler, hath assumed the Kingdom.*" Thus, not the dominion of Christ merely, but the dominion of the Almighty, in the general acceptation of the term, has been obscured by the pseudo-kingdom of Babylon. *Let us be glad and exult*, say the pious on earth, *and we will give to Him the glory* which was so long alienated from Him. And they speak not of foreign things when they introduce the Woman, the Bride of Christ—who, like a Cinderella, if we may venture to make the comparison, has so long been retired from sight and sound—into the field of view, with the announcement: *The Marriage of the Lamb is come, and His Wife hath prepared herself.*

And now the Seer himself takes up the story, speaking first concerning the Woman, and then, in obedience to an angelic voice, concerning her imminent marriage-feast. The appearance of the Woman forms a highly edifying contrast to the appearance of the Harlot. The latter had decked herself with purple and scarlet, and loaded herself with gold and jewels; to the former it is *given* by God *to array herself* in the right adornment, and her vesture is snow-white, shining linen, a *byssus*-robe. The material of her dress, the Seer adds in explanation of its brilliancy and purity, are the δικαιώματα *of the saints*, their final, eschatological judicial acquittals (Matt. xxv. 34 sqq.) which are grounded upon the principial justification (Rom. v. 1), upon the δικαίωμα of Christ, in the most manifold forms of a now manifestly appearing righteousness of life. For this cause, the Marriage can now begin. The herald of it is an *Angel* whom the Seer marks, without further explanation, as one already brought upon the scene of action: *And he saith unto me.* A lack of precision in form which reminds us of similar instances in the Gospel of John. What Angel is meant? This question has been variously answered. Since the reference here is to a personal, and not a symbolical Angel, we do not, with Düsterdieck and others, go back to ch. xvii. 1, as it is one of the seven Angels of the Vials of Anger who there speaks; nor do we think that the Angel of ch. xviii. 1 is referred to; but we hold that the reference is to the Angel who, according to ch. xviii. 21, executed the judgment by a symbolical act, because we here find ourselves in the sphere of the return of Christ, Who is to be surrounded by personal Angels, and also by glorified believers.*

---

* [The most natural reference must certainly is to the Angel of chap. xvii. 1, of whose withdrawal from the Seer

And such an one [a glorified believer] John here sees in the form of an Angel, according to ver. 10; the other world begins to grow visible, in spiritual shapes, in this world. Again is the Seer commanded to write a grand and inviting word of revelation concerning the blessedness of proved believers, as in ch. xiv. 13. *Write : Blessed are they who are called unto the supper of the Marriage of the Lamb.* The great beatitude is strengthened by the addition: *These are the true (veritable.* based deep within the kernel of life) *words of God.*

John describes the impression which the sublime Gospel of the blessedness of the guests at the imminent Marriage has made upon him: *I fell before his feet to worship him.* The Seer cannot have erred in his *inclination* to worship, but he made a mistake in the object of his adoration. It did not seem possible for any but Christ to utter so confident a declaration of so speedy a blessedness. And the Seer was not mistaken in his feeling that the Lord was near. That nearness, however, was announced by a celestial herald; the dividing wall between the hither and the further world [*Diesseits und Jenseits*] is beginning to fall. The herald of the Marriage reveals himself to the Seer as a glorified saint in angelic form. *Take heed not,* might be said by an Angel. And so might, *I am thy fellow-servant.* But the words, *I am one of thy brethren who have the witness of Jesus* [the true rendering is: *I am a fellow-servant of thee and of thy brethren that have the witness of Jesus.* See the text, ver. 10.—E. R. C.], could not suitably be uttered by a real Angel in the literal sense of the term. *Worship God.* This, certainly, is a didactical reprimand and exhortation which is calculated for millions of men; but in the case of John, the words must have reference to something especially calling for worship. And this something is expressed in the words, *for the witness of Jesus is the spirit of the prophecy.* It might, indeed, likewise be said, The spirit of prophecy witnesses of Jesus; but still something particularly worthy of adoration is here expressed in the idea: The witness of and concerning Jesus in His saints is the spirit of prophecy, which is sure of the imminent Marriage. Living, practical Christianity is prophecy from beginning to end. As a witness concerning Jesus, therefore, the Angel is the bearer of, and voucher for, the glorious promise. *Worship God* Who has put the certainty of the most glorious future into the kernel of the life of faith.

Did John perhaps think that Peter, his fellow-servant and one of his brethren of the witness of Jesus, would re-appear as the forerunner of the Parousia of the Lord, to execute judgment upon Great Babylon? However this may be, the conversation of the Angel with John is followed by the Parousia itself. We must of course take it for granted that a period intervenes between the judgment upon the Harlot and the judgment upon the Beast—the period of the

no mention is made. The implication of ver. 8 seems to be that this Angel had continued with the Seer giving him instruction. The reason assigned by our author for denying that the reference is to him, seems to be without foundation, for most certainly the implication of his coming to John and giving him instruction (xvii. 1, *et pass.*) is, that he is a *personal* being.—E. R. C.]

troubled and waiting Church, the hour of heaviness. depicted ch. xiii. 15-17. But in the prophetic perspective, the period vanishes, as, Matt. xxiv., the period between the destruction of Jerusalem and the end of the world; the second judgment follows quickly after the first.

John sees *the Heaven opened.* Again the *white horse* appears, as in ch. vi., now, however, no longer to dominate the course of the world, but to conclude it. The Rider has now, on the one hand, an open name, proved in the history of the world; whilst, on the other hand, the unnambleness of His personality, His mysterious essence, has attained full recognition.* He is called *Faithful and True* (ἀληθινός), the purest consequence and the innermost kernel of world-history, in personal completion ; He is, therefore, entirely the administrator of *righteousness* in the *judgment* which He has just executed, and in the *war* which He is about to begin. With His righteousness corresponds His all-piercing glance ; *His eyes* are as *a flame of fire,* illuminating the object to which He directs them; as this was formerly the case with regard to the fanatical Church at Thyatira (ch. ii. 18), so it is now the case with regard to the whole world. Issuing from many victories, His head is adorned with many wreaths of victory or *diadems,* which, in accordance with the textual variation, may be accompanied by many *names ;* but the full import of His essential name is *known to Himself alone,* in His blissful consciousness. For that which is true of every personality renewed by Christianity—that it has a mysterious, almost anonymous depth (ch. ii. 17)—is true in the highest degree of the Crown of all human personalities. *His* garment, also, is of the color of *blood,* like that of the Babylonish woman; in His case, however, it is the pure blood-color, not offensively mixed with the hue of royalty; it is the color of His own blood, for He has not yet waged an external war with His foes—least of all, by means of an external sword—hence the sense is not the same as that of Isaiah lxiii., although the expression is similar, and the bearings of the two passages are kindred.† One with this perfected glory of beauteous humanity, the adornment of self sacrifice in love, is His mysterious Divine essence which the Church has sought fully to express by the name, THE LOGOS OF GOD. John was, doubtless, perfectly aware that He uttered a mystery of unfathomable depth when, in his Gospel, he called Christ the LOGOS. But now the great Bearer and Forbearer [*Dulder*] comes as a victorious King for judgment upon the world : He has waited sufficiently long to have destroyed every suspicion of passionate reaction [against His injuries]. The world has even accustomed itself to the thought that His crucial passion will never be completely reckoned for. The universal character of His passion and victory appears in His escort—a host of triumphant believers, seated, like Himself, on white horses, and clothed in white and shining linen [*Byssus*],

* [See ADD. NOTE, pp. 178 sq.—E. R. C.]

† [Is not the sense in both cases precisely the same? In both cases, the Conqueror, at His first appearance, is dramatically represented as sprinkled with the blood which He shed in the course of His advance.—E. R. C.]

the color of righteousness, like the Bride of Christ.* His weapons of attack are three-fold: first, the two-edged *sharp sword* which *goeth forth out of His mouth*, and which is designed *to smite the nations* (the modern heathen) (Is. xi. 4; 2 Thess. ii. 8; Heb. iv. 12; Rev. i. 16). From the spiritual victory which He gains with this sword, the symbolism of the Seer distinguishes the fact that He will, secondly, *shepherdize the heathen* [nations] *with an iron rod* (Ps. ii.). This, doubtless, refers to the dynamical, strict social government which Christianity will exercise from the time of the Parousia of Christ. Again, in relation to Antichrist and his company, Christ will, thirdly, manifest Himself as *the Treader of the wine-press* Who *will tread the press of the wine of the anger of the wrath* (wrathful indignation) of God, the All-Ruler (Is. lxiii. 1), *i. e.* execute the actual reprobationary judgment upon Antichristianity in the final catastrophe of the course of the world. It seems enigmatical that He should wear the Name, KING OF KINGS, AND LORD OF LORDS, on His *vesture* and on His *thigh*. The Name is, doubtless, to be apprehended as twice written, not as inscribed simply upon the girdle of the tucked-up garment (as Düsterdieck maintains). We understand this as intimating that the Seer desired doubly to express the idea that it is a small thing for Him to be KING OF KINGS; He wears this Name, not on His crown, not on His brow, but, as a passing decoration, upon His garment. In this place, however, it has deep significance, inasmuch as it is with the blood of His vesture that He has achieved His dominion over the kings of the earth. But why does He bear the name upon His thigh also? Because the generality of kings wear their names there, upon the hilt of the sword, as a title based, for the most part, upon the right of the sword; at least, it is thus with the titles of *the ten kings*, who are from the outset designated as democratic violence-kings. In view of all this, we regard the Name of Christ in this place as expressive of a declaration of war preparatory to the conflict which is now to begin.

[ABSTRACT OF VIEWS, ETC.]
By the American Editor.

[ELLIOTT: Vers. 1-4 are connected with the preceding section, and present the heavenly doxology over the fall of Babylon.—Vers. 5-21 form the concluding portion of the *inside-written* (see *foot-note*. p. 281) prophecy of events under the *Seventh Vial*. The first part of this section contains a hymn of praise, uttered by all God's servants, whose themes are the approaching establishment of Christ's Kingdom and His marriage. (By the *establishment of the Kingdom*, he understands the introduction of the millennial era; by the *Bride*, the completed number of the saints of the old and present dispensations; by *the righteousnesses of the saints*, the badges of their justification; [by *the marriage*, the glorification of the risen saints with Christ?]). The latter part of the chapter describes the glorious personal appearing of Christ and the destruction of Antichrist; which events are subsequent to

the utterance of the hymn, but precede the glorious events pre celebrated therein.

BARNES: "This chapter, as well as the last, is an episode, delaying the final catastrophe, and describing more fully the effect of the destruction of the mystical Babylon." It consists of four parts: I. A hymn of praise of the heavenly hosts in view of this destruction, vers. 1-7. II. The marriage of the Lamb, vers. 8, 9,—*i e.* "the Church is now to triumph and rejoice *as if* in permanent union with her glorious Head and Lord." III. The offered worship of the Seer and the rebuke, ver. 10. IV. The final conquest over the Beast, *etc.* "The general idea here is that these great Antichristian powers which had so long resisted the gospel . . . . would be subdued. The true religion would be as triumphant *as if* the Son of God should go forth as a warrior in His own might. This destruction . . . prepares the way for the millennial reign of the Son of God."

STUART: Vers. 1-9, an episode (delaying the main action) of praise, thanksgiving, and anticipated completion of victory.—Vers. 11 21, the final contest. (This author, in his concluding remarks on chaps. xiii.-xix., writes: "That Nero is mainly characterized in xiii., xvi., xvii., we cannot well doubt. But in chap. xiii., when the beast out of the sea is first presented, he has *seven heads*, and each one of these is itself a king or emperor, xvii. 10. Of course, the beast, *generically considered*, represents many kings, not merely one. Yet as the reigning emperor, for the time being, is the actual manifestation of the beast, or the actual development of it, so the word *beast* is applied, in the chapters named, mainly to Nero, then persecuting the Church. Insensibly almost . . . . this specific meaning appears to be dropped, and the more generic one to be employed again in chap. xviii. sq. . . . That Nero's fall was in the eye of the Apocalyptist here (chap. xvi.), I can hardly doubt. But this was *not* the end of the Church's persecutions; although a respite of some twenty years or more was now given. Farther persecutions were to arise; and so, a *continued* war with the beast, and a still further destruction of great Babylon, are brought in the sequel to our view. . . . As soon as the writer dismisses the case of Nero from his consideration, he deals no longer with anything but *generic* representations. Persecutions will revive. The war will still be waged. At last the great Captain of Salvation will come forth, in all His power, and make an end of the long-protracted war. Then, and not till then, will the millennial day of glory dawn upon the Church. . . . In order to designate the final and certain overthrow of heathenism, as opposed to Christianity, the writer has chosen to represent the whole matter by the symbol of a great contest between the two parties.")

WORDSWORTH: This writer regards the whole section as having respect to the blessed condition of the Church after the destruction of Rome. His comments are of the most general and indeterminate kind.

ALFORD: Vers. 1 10 form the concluding portion of the general section begun ch. xviii. 1, entitled, "The Destruction of Babylon;" vers. 1-8 present "the Church's song of triumph at

---

* [See ADD. NOTE, p. 336.—E. R. C.]

the destruction of Babylon; ver. 9 sets forth the Bride as *the sum of the guests* at the marriage feast. Ver. 11 begins ■ general section extending through ch. xxii. 5, entitled "The End:" the subdivisions of this section are, (1) vers. 11-16, "the triumphal coming forth of the Lord (personal and visible) and His saints to victory; (2) vers. 17-21, the great defeat and destruction of the beast and false prophet and kings of the earth; (3) ch. xx. 1-6, the binding of Satan and the millennial reign; (4) ch. xx. 7-10, the great general judgment; (5) chs. xxi. 1-xxii. 5, the vision of the new heavens and earth, and the glories of the new Jerusalem. (See also *in loc.*)

LORD: Vers. 1-4, the hymn of the heavenly host on the destruction of Babylon. Vers. 5-10, the Marriage of the Lamb, *i. e.* the literal resurrection of departed saints, and their exaltation to the thrones on which they are to serve Christ throughout their endless existence; (the *guests,* ver. 9, "are different persons from the raised and glorified Saints who are denoted by the Bride, and are doubtless the unglorified Saints on Earth"). Ch. xix. 11-21 describes "a personal and visible advent" of Christ, accompanied by the raised and glorified saints, and the subsequent destruction of all His civil, ecclesiastical and military enemies who are to be arrayed in organized and open hostility to him (see Abstracts under following sections).

GLASGOW: Vers. 1-10 show us what transpires among the Saints of God in immediate connection with Babylon's fall; they present a vision of the events that are now begun to be developed in the Church and nation. By the "wife," ver. 7, is to be understood the Church, not merely invisible, but visible; henceforward, she, as a whole, will be honorable and pure, acknowledging the sole supremacy of Christ, and altogether Scriptural in her doctrine, discipline and government; by the γάμος is to be understood the marriage festivities. Vers. 11-16. The opening of the heaven took place only once, and at the beginning of the gospel age,—this scene takes us back to the beginning. In the first seal (ch. iv. 2) Christ appears in His sacerdotal character—here is represented as going forth simultaneously in His office as King; the white horse in both appearances is identical and symbolizes the body of Christian teachers; the entire vision represents Him as going on to complete victory and supremacy.—E. R. C.]

EXPLANATIONS IN DETAIL.

[Vers. 1-8.] Earlier songs of praise may be found chap. iv. 8; v. 9; xi. 15; xv. 3; xvi. 5. ["As each of the great events and judgments in this Book is celebrated by its song of praise in Heaven, so this also; but more solemnly and formally than the others, seeing that this is the great accomplishment of God's judgment on the enemy of His Church." (References ■■ above.) ALFORD.—E. R. C.]

Ver. 1. I heard as ■ great voice —It is, certainly, the voice of a great people, but it is also that of a heavenly people, and hence is to be *compared* with [*as*] the tumult of voices of an earthly multitude. This throng is to be sym-

bolically defined in general as the heavenly Church of God, without further random conjecture concerning those from whom the praise proceeds. Hallelujah.—With this specific shout of joy, the song begins. It is thus from beginning to end a song of praise. In Heaven there is no regret for the fall of Babylon. "It is certainly not unintentional that just here, after the complete judgment upon the enemies of God and of His faithful ones has begun, we find the express Hallelujah, which does not appear any where else in the Apocalypse" (*Footnote:* "Nor is it found in all the rest of the New Testament)." DUEST. A four-fold Hallelujah appears in the New Testament with reference to the fall of Babylon, and is found nowhere else! (for even the Hallelujah of ver. 6 has reference to the fall of Babylon). In the quaternary of the Hallelujah, Hengstenberg discovers God's victory over the *earth,* "whose mark is four," in opposition to which Düsterdieck judiciously remarks that it is not a victory over the earth, but one over the Harlot, that is being celebrated. The salvation.—Comp. ch. vii. 10 and xii. 10.

[Elliott infers from the introduction of the *Hebrew* Hallelujah that at the time contemplated the Jews will have been converted. Wordsworth regards the introduction of the word as "proving that whatever appertained to the devotion and glory of the Ancient People of God is now become the privilege of the *Christian Church.*" The idea of Alford is preferable to either, *viz.:* "The formula must have passed with the Psalter into the Christian Church, being continually found in the LXX.; and its use first here may be quite accounted for by the greatness and finality of this triumph."—E. R. C.]

Ver. 2. For true.—The reason assigned becomes more efficient and solemn when both ὅτι 's are coördinated, in accordance with De Wette and others (see ch. xviii. 23; xi. 18).

Ver. 3. And a second time, *etc.*—We cannot apprehend these words as forming an antistrophe to the foregoing, with De Wette, since a grander antiphone is formed between vers. 1 and 6. Hallelujah.—A Hallelujah based upon the fact that the smoke of Babylon ascends into the æons of the æons! This far surpasses modern sentimentalities. And her smoke, *etc.*—In ch. xviii. 9 and 18, the reference was to the uprising smoke in a historical sense; here the smoke takes a more æonic and metaphorical import, as chap. xiv. 11.

[Into the ages of the ages.—"Another proof that the destruction of the mystical Babylon will be *final,* and that therefore Babylon cannot be heathen Rome." WORDSWORTH.—E. R. C.]

Ver. 4. And the twenty-four Elders and the four Living-beings fell down. *etc.*—The four Life-forms are set above the Elders; hence it is here, also, evident that they should not be regarded as types of creature-life. That as ground-forms of the Divine government in the world they, likewise, *worship* God, occasions no difficulty. The *Amen* corroborates the truth [*Wahrhaftigkeit*], the *Hallelujah,* the Divine authorship of the fact celebrated. [See *foot-note* †, p. 152, and ADD. NOTE, p. 161 sq.—E. R. C.]

Ver. 5. A voice came forth from the throne.—The first voice proceeded from the experience and conviction of the spirit-world; it went from below upwards. The second song is the more developed Amen to the first; it is begun at the Throne of God, and proceeds from above downwards. The expression, **Praise our God**, gives the voice the appearance of issuing from the centre of the Church Triumphant; it is more natural, therefore, to think of the twenty-four Elders, with Düsterdieck, than to refer the voice to Christ, with Hengstenberg, or to the four Living-beings, with Bengel. Everywhere, however, where *one* voice is spoken of, stress is thereby laid upon the *unison*, the *one spirit* of a company; here it is that of the highest company, the one nearest to the Throne (comp. ch. v. 9). The *αἰνεῖν τῷ θεῷ* is the development of the foregoing Hebrew Hallelujah. See Düsterdieck. Comp. Pss. cxv. 18; cxxxv. 1.

Ver. 6. **As a voice**, *etc.*—Quite unique is the harmony in the antithesis of **many waters** and **strong thunders** (see chapter i. 15, xiv. 2; Ezek. i. 24, xliii. 2; Dan. x. 6). The song of praise, now beginning, passes from the post-celebration of the judgment upon the Harlot to the pre-celebration of the marriage of the Bride. ["The triumphant song being ended, an *epithalamium*, or marriage-song, begins." M. Henry. —E. R. C.] The central point of the song lies in the fact that **the Lord our God hath taken to Himself [assumed*] the Kingdom**, *i. e.*, His Kingdom in the hearts of men† (see ch. xi. 17, where, however, the manifest appearing of kingly power in the general judgment is referred to). The Harlot deified herself and robbed God of His glory; the purity of the Bride, on the other hand, consists in the fact that she gives the glory altogether to God.

[**The All-Ruler.**—See *additional comment* on ch. i. 8, p. 93.—E. R. C.]

Ver. 7. **And we will give the glory to Him.**—This is the fountain of the *gladness* and *exultation*, aye, it is the preparation for the marriage itself,—which preparation consists in the right fellowship of human souls, in their participation in a faith—ripening to sight—in the *glory* of God.

Saying (λέγοντες) [Ver. 6].—This grammatical irregularity is based upon the Seer's intention to give prominence to the individual nature of the song of praise, as founded upon subjective heart-truth. It is not merely the jubilation of a sympathetically excited crowd; that which the voice says as *one* voice, they all say singly likewise.

For the marriage of the Lamb came.— This is proleptical, according to De Wette, Hengstenberg and Düsterdieck. In the sense of the vision, however, the judgment upon Babylon, from the consummation of which the vision starts, coincides with the preparedness of the Bride, and the two items are not only preliminary conditions of, but also indices for, the beginning of the marriage.‡ That the terms, *the*

marriage and *the supper of the marriage*, although distinct in themselves, coincide in point of time, should be understood as a matter of course. Züllig, in contradistinguishing the millennial Kingdom from the marriage, as a fore-feast of the Messianic marriage, overlooks the fact that even in the Parables of the Lord His Parousia is designated as the beginning of the marriage. The spiritual marriage is characterized by the moment when the ideal Christian view and the outward appearance coincide in perfect oneness. Hence the first appearance of Christ was the fore-celebration of the marriage (Matt. ix. 15). It is taking a contracted view of this marriage, the idea of which runs through the whole of Sacred Writ (Song of Sol., Isaiah, Ezekiel, Hosea, *etc.*), to understand thereby, "the coming Lord's distribution of the eternal reward of grace to His faithful ones, who then enter, with Him, into the full glory of the heavenly life" [Düsterdieck]. Three elements, above all things, pertain to the constitution of the idea. First, the personal relation between the Lord and His people. Secondly, perfect oneness on the part of His people. Thirdly, their receptivity, conditioned by homogeneousness. Hence it is also evident that the marriage must be blessedness, in the reciprocal operation of a spiritual fellowship of love. **And His Wife.**—The Bride—after the espousal, His Wife (Matt. i. 20; comp. Gen. xxix 21). **Prepared herself.** — That is, adorned herself in a spiritual sense. In active self-appointment, as a free Church, that has attained its majority, she has prepared herself; nevertheless, the material of her readiness is given to her by the grace of God. According to *The Shepherd* of Hermas, the Church, in the form of a woman, undergoes a process of development which is directly opposed to nature. From an aged matron, she is transformed more and more into a youthful appearance. In the end, therefore, when she is free from all spots and wrinkles, she is the perfected Bride of the Lord (Eph. v. 27).

[Additional Note on the Marriage.—Alford most strangely comments *in loc.*: "This figure of a marriage between the Lord and His people is too frequent and familiar to need explanation." Rather, for the very reason assigned, should an explanation be given. Matters most frequent in the Scriptures are matters most important; and those most familiar are often, because of their very familiarity, least studied, and therefore least understood. There are few phrases more frequently on the lips of Christians than "The marriage supper of the Lamb," and it is probable that there are few utterances with which less definite ideas are connected. At first glance, the most natural hypothesis is, that the reference in this verse is to the manifestation of the New Jerusalem, ch. xxi. 2.

Bridegroom (νυμφίος), and His Church the Bride (νύμφη). And if it be necessary to distinguish 'wife' from 'bride,' let it be observed that 'wife' (γυνή) is the word employed in the text: 'His *wife* has prepared herself.'" Glasgow. In his comment on ver. 9 the same writer remarks: "The same festive occasion which in ver. 7 is called the *marriage* is here called the *marriage supper* (τὸ δεῖπνον τοῦ γάμου); which shows that not the marriage ceremony, but the joyous festivities, are meant."—E. R. C.]

This reference, however, necessitates one of two subordinate hypotheses,—either (1) that the visions of chs. xxi., xxii. are merely supplementary; that they do not refer to events to occur after the millennium, but are descriptive of some event mentioned ch. xix. 11—xx. 15; or (2) that the song of triumph now under consideration had respect, not to the *immediate*, but to the *entire* future. The former of these hypotheses seems to be forbidden by the phraseology of the chapter mentioned, which manifestly contemplates a new order of things (*a new Heaven and new earth*), in which there shall be neither sin nor death (see Excursus on the New Jerusalem, pp. 389 sqq.); the latter is hardly admissible in view of the language of the Song, *the marriage is come* (ἦλθεν)—something in the present, or the immediate future seems to be contemplated; we can hardly suppose that a space of at least a thousand years should be grasped by such an expression. The foregoing considerations lead us to seek for something in the events represented as immediately following the Song as the event contemplated therein, and this the writer thinks is found ch. xx. 4-6. Whether the *first resurrection* mentioned in that passage be literal or spiritual (*i. e.*, whether it be a literal resurrection of departed saints, or a more complete deliverance of living saints from the power of sin), it is undeniable that the entire description contemplates the Church as brought into a new condition—a condition of higher spiritual adornment and of closer relation to Christ—one therefore that may be appropriately figured as her marriage to Christ. It is proper here to remark that the writer regards (1) the *resurrection* as literal, (2) the *Bride* as the whole body of the saints (the quick and the dead), at the Second Advent of the Lord, and (3) the *marriage* as the union of this body with a personally present Christ in glory and government (*i. e.*, as the establishment of the Basileia). As to the truth of the first of these hypotheses, see the Excursus on The First Resurrection, p. 352. The second and third hypotheses best satisfy the elements of the marriage relation so beautifully and justly set forth by Lange in the immediately preceding comment; and they are also in perfect consistency with the normal interpretation of ch. xx. 4-6, and of the whole body of Apocalyptic teaching. It should here be distinctly noted, however, that these hypotheses require that the number of those entering into the constitution of the Bride or the New Jerusalem (their identity is admitted) should be complete at the first resurrection, and consequently that the vision of ch. xxi. 1, 2 should refer, not to the *marriage*, but to a *new manifestation* of the Bride. For a discussion of this portion of the subject, see the Excursus on the New Jerusalem.—E R. C.]

Ver. 8. **And to her** ▨▨ **given.**—Her adornment is simply pure and beautiful (*cultus gravis ut matronæ, non pompaticus, qualis meretricis.* Grot.). *Byssus* [fine linen] denotes the most precious of plain, unostentatious, yet elegant, material; a similar character attaches to its hue, ▨▨ opposed to scarlet and purple. A species of contrast is, doubtless, indicated by καθαρός and λαμπρός; the negative purity and positive glory of the new life. **For the fine linen** [byssus],

22

etc.—Even in describing the simple adornment of the Bride, the Seer is anxious to bring out the spiritual import of the same. **The righteous-** ▨▨ ▨▨▨▨ [Lange: *Gerechtigkeitsgüter*=possessions of righteousness].—Τὰ δικαιώματα. The δικαίωμα is always a means by which justice is satisfied or acquittal [*Gerechtsprechung*] is obtained, whether it be the performance of the right, or the expiation of the wrong (by undergoing punishment), or atonement, as the concrete unity of the doing and the suffering of that which is right. Reference is not here had "to the white garment of righteousness before God in Christ (as Beza maintained), which garment the Church does not *first* receive in the last time" (Ebrard). But whether the fulfillment of God's commandments (De Wette, Ebrard, *et al.*) or "righteous deeds" (Düsterd.) be intended, is the question. Righteousness of life is itself established by suitable δικαιώματα and consequent acquittals [or justifications]. Such is the verification of faith treated of Jas. ii. 21 (comp. the Lange *Commentary on James, in loc.*), which, according to Matt. xxv. 31 sqq., ramifies into a multitude of individual verifications. "A delicate allusion to the grace given by God, as the cause and source of the δικαιώματα peculiar to the saints, is contained in the ἐδόθη αὐτῇ ἵνα κτλ." (Düsterdieck). According to Ebrard, it is "thus prophesied that sanctification shall be perfected, that it shall be given to the eschatological Church to put off the last remnant of sin while yet in the flesh." ["The plural -ματα is probably distributive, implying not many δικαιώματα to each one, as if they were merely good deeds, but one δικαίωμα to each of the saints, enveloping him as in a pure white robe of righteousness. Observe that here and everywhere the white robe is not Christ's righteousness imputed or put on, but *the Saints' righteousness*, by virtue of being washed in His blood. It is *their own; inherent, not imputed; but their own by their part in and union to Him.*" Alford.—E. R. C.]

Ver. 9. An analogue of ch. xiv. 13. The two superscriptions of the everlasting Gospel correspond. The former characterizes the existence of the faithful of the last time, with reference to this world; the latter characterizes it with reference to the other world. These two beatitudes of the eschatological Gospel correspond to the beatitudes of the principial Gospel, Matt. v. They are summed up together in the beatitude and superscription, ch. xxi. 3-5.

And he saith unto me.—What Angel is meant? See Syn. View. **They who are called**, *etc.*—The Church in its unitous form is the Bride; in its individual members, it consists of wedding-guests (Matt. xxii. 1; xxv. 1). **These are the true words of God.**—Since all the words of God are ἀληθινοί, the saying can mean only: these are the true [or genuine] words of God in the most special sense; or, to be more definite, in these words are concentrated the true [or genuine] words of promise of God, in analogy with the declaration, "On these two commandments hang all the Law and the Prophets." The highest summit of human consummation-bliss has the highest Divine reality. Different explanations of the sentence, by Hengstenberg ("these words are genuine, are words of God"),

De Wette, Züllig, Düsterdieck (the words of re-velation from ch. xvii. 1 are intended), see in the latter, p. 537.

Ver. 10. **And I fell**, *etc.*—This action of the Seer must be regarded entirely as *a procedure taking place within the vision*—not, therefore, as a subject for moral criticism. There is as little reason, therefore, for Hengstenberg's praising the Seer, on this occasion, for his humility, as for his blaming him elsewhere for visional ac-tions and charging him with faint-heartedness. These, also, are strange words of Hengsten-berg's: "As John here offered (sought to offer) adoration to the Angel, so it befits the Church, that receives this glorious revelation through John, to bow before *him* [John] because of it, and so, also, it befits John to say to her: Take heed not." See Ebrard against Hengstenberg, p. 499. It is remarked, not without reason, by Düsterdieck, that it is probable "that John re-garded the Angel who was speaking with him, not as *a* fellow-servant, but as the Lord Him-self." **Take heed not.**—Properly, *Take heed that thou [do it] not.* Aposiopesy. The whole deli-verance is certainly decisive against all angel-olatry. **A fellow-servant.**—A symbolized Angel could in no case become an object of ado-ration. But neither could a real, personal An-gel. The passage may be so understood that the term σύνδουλος expresses the common character-istic of the angelic and apostolic functions. *I, as an Angel, am a fellow-servant of thee and of thy brethren, etc.* So De Wette and Düsterdieck. Or σύνδουλος is indicative of the category of be-lievers. *I, in angelic form, am a fellow-servant of thee, and one of thy brethren* (Eichhorn, Zül-lig). Against the former apprehension is the consideration that the final sentence, *The witness of Jesus is the spirit of prophecy*, would be idle in this connection. Opposed to the second appre-hension is the fact that it would call for the reading: καὶ ἐκ τῶν ἀδ. We therefore suppose that the meaning of the Angel is as follows: *I, who appear to you as an Angel, am thy fellow-servant, and, as such, a fellow-servant of all who cleave to the witness of Jesus.* **Worship God.**—This does not mean sim-ply, Worship no creature, but also, Thou hast certainly cause to worship God for the revelation that is made to thee, for it is a glorification of the God who has placed the spirit of the prophecy concerning the great marriage-feast of the con-summation, in the witness of [concerning] Jesus. **The witness of Jesus.**—Since the Angel has commenced to instruct the Seer, we cannot see why he should not speak these words also, espe-cially as they are expressive of the profound unity betwixt historical Christianity and the ideo-dynamical development of the world, and characterize Christianity *as* analogue prophecy. According to Düsterdieck (in opposition to Vit-ringa, De Wette, *et al.*), the concluding sentence belongs to John. The declaration contained therein is entirely different from ver. 8. Equally untenable is the assertion of Düsterdieck (in op-position to Vitringa, De Wette, *et al.*) that the genitive τοῦ 'Ιησοῦ must be taken only as sub-jective, signifying *the witness proceeding from Jesus.* That which constitutes the μαρτυρία a μαρτυρία is the very fact that Jesus is its object

(see ch. vi. 9). According to De Wette, indeed, the concluding words simply mean: He who, like thee, confesses Christ, has also the spirit of prophecy; according to Düsterdieck, the mean-ing is: When Christ communicates His revela-tion-witness to a man, He fills him likewise with the spirit of prophecy! According to this latter commentator, an attestation of the prophetic Book of John is contained in these words (and yet he maintains that the Book was not written by John, and that the prophecy is in part *an* er-ror which has not been fulfilled).*

Vers. 11–16. *The Bridegroom in His warlike Forth-going for the Destruction of the Beast, i. e., also, for the Redemption of the Bride.*

Ver. 11. **The Heaven opened.**—Accord-ing to Düsterd. the movement within the visions is very cumbrous. "The Seer was in spirit carried to the earth in ch. xvii. 3 (De Wette)." But in ch. iv. 1 his exaltation to Heaven was identical with his translation into the spirit. **A white horse.**—As in chap. vi. 2. **And He that sat upon him, called**—καλούμενος is in appo-sition [to ὁ καθήμ. κτλ.]. **Faithful.**—The germ and blossom of all Divine life in the history of the world. **True.**—The fulfillment of all world-historical prophecies, especially promises and threats (see ch. iii. 7, 14). **And in righteous-ness** (Isa. xi. 3, 4) **He judgeth and war-reth.**—He must execute His judgment upon Antichrist in *a* warlike form.

Ver. 12. ▓▓ **eyes.**—See ch. i. 14. **Many diadems.**—"If the many royal crowns upon His head are regarded as trophies of victories already won (2 Sam. xii. 30; 1 Macc. xi. 13; Grotius, Wetst., Bengel; comp. also Vitringa), we should necessarily have to conceive of *kings* as conquered—for instance, the *ten kings* of ch. xvii. (Züllig). But judgment is not yet executed upon these. It might also be said that the Lord Who goes forth as a triumphant Conqueror, Who, ch. vi. 2, receives *a* victor's wreath in advance, here appears proleptically decked with the crowns of the kings whom He is to judge. But more obvious is the reference to ver. 16, where Christ is called the βασιλεὺς βασιλέων (Ewald, De Wette, Hengstenb., Bleek, Volkmar, Luthardt"). DÜSTERDIECK. The antithesis thus set forth is based upon deficient, atomistic conceptions. History testifies that Christ, in dynamical ope-ration, has become the King of kings by a grand succession of victories, not necessarily eschato-logical in form, as was evidenced by Constan-tine, and even Julian. **A name.**—A won-drously beautiful designation of the personality of Christ in accordance with its peculiar Divine-human essential name. On the random conjec-tures concerning this name, see Düsterdieck, p. 542 (it is the name given in ver. 18; the name *Jehovah;* no definite name. It is placed on the *forehead*—on the *vesture;* see also De Wette, p. 179). The mystery, however, is sealed only from a worldly understanding, not from the knowledge of love.

Ver. 13. **With a vesture**, *etc.*—The expres-sion of Isa. lxiii. 1, but in a New Testament

---

* [Düsterdieck merely claims that the Book ▓▓▓ not writ-ten by the *Apostle* John.—TR.]

sense. And ▨▨ name hath become to be called.—The theological name of Christ, that which marks His *Divine* nature alone, and which John has also introduced in the most significant manner [in his Gospel?], is therefore in itself more intelligible than the mystery of personal God-manhood. Futile objections to a reference to the Logos, John i. 1, see in Düsterd., p. 75. The Logos is indeed here characterized as τοῦ ϑεοῦ; but His historical mission is here also referred to.

Ver. 14. **And the armies in the heaven**, *etc.*—Not Angels simply (Matt. xxv. 31; Hengstenb., Luth.), but also the perfected righteous (Düsterdieck); nay, these pre-eminently, since they are clothed in pure byssus, and since it is not simply the local Heaven that is intended here, but rather the Heaven of perfected spirit-life.—The byssus of their garments is **white and pure**; they are perfected in innocence and righteousness, and yet their vesture does not shine, like that of Christ.

Ver. 15. **And out of His mouth**, *etc.*—Even in the Old Testament the all-conquering power of the word of Revelation is expressed in figurative forms (Is. xi. 4; Jer. xxiii. 29; comp. 2 Thess. ii. 8; Heb. iv. 12; Rev. i. 16). In the last time, the immediate, spiritually dynamical operations of the word of God coincide with its mediate, physically dynamical operations in a unity which is prefigured Acts v. 5. In Ps. ii., also, the *iron sceptre* has manifestly a symbolical import. **And He treadeth the wine-press.** —Isa. lxiii. 3. The *wine of the anger of the wrath* [Lange: *wrathful indignation*] *of God* is the historic concrete of the wrath of God, on the one hand, and the wrath of the heathen [nations], on the other hand (chap. xi. 18). The judgment of God, in the uprising of "the heathen" [nations], is brought to a decision by Christ by His appearing. Hengstenberg's explanation—The wine-press is the wrath of God; the wine flowing out of it is the blood of His foes—is marvellously *amended* by Düsterd.: "The form of the statement, in which the two figures of the wine-press (ch. xiv. 19) and the cup of wrath (ch. xiv. 10) are combined (De Wette), denotes rather that out of the wine-press trodden by the Lord the wine of the wrathful indignation of God streams, which wine shall be *given* to His enemies *to drink*."

Ver. 16. **On His vesture.**—See SYN. VIEW. Comp. Düsterdieck, p. 543.

[ADDITIONAL NOTE ON THE SECTION.]
By the American Editor.

[This chapter, beginning with the strong disjunctive, Μετὰ ταῦτα ἤκουσα, introduces a new series of visions that flow on in unbroken sequence to the close of the Revelation.

Vers. 1–8 present the heavenly song of triumph over the destruction of the apostate Church, and in prospect of the immediate establishment of the Basileia; it is the hallelujah that marks the beginning of a new æon—*the times of refreshing and restitution* (Acts iii. 19-21). (See *foot-note* † in the following column.)

Vers. 11–16 narrate the vision of the SECOND ADVENT of Jesus, the Advent contemplated ch. i. 7. (See the following NOTE.) In the judg-

ment of the majority of interpreters, the Rider here described is the same as the one of the First Seal. For the views of the Am. Ed. on this point see ADD. NOTE, pp. 177–179.—E. R. C.]

[NOTE ON THE FUTURE ADVENT OF CHRIST.]
By the American Editor.

[It is admitted by all that there is to be a visible Advent of the glorified Messiah. Two views divide the Church ▨ to the time of the Advent—some contending that it is to be Pre-millennial; others, that it is to be synchronous with the Consummation, the general Resurrection and final Judgment.

The advocates of the former hypothesis rely principally on two classes of passages: 1. Those which seem to connect the future Advent with the restoration of Israel, the destruction of Antichrist, or the establishment of a universal kingdom of righteousness on earth, such as Isa. xi.; xii.; lix. 20sqq. (comp. with Rom. xi. 25-27); Jer. xxiii. 5-8; Ezek. xliii. 2sqq.; Dan. vii. 9-27; Joel iii. 16-21; Zech xiv; Rom. xi. 1-27; 2 Thess. i. 1-8;* Acts iii. 19-21.† 2. Those which speak

---

* [The last clause of verse ▨ should not be translated *is at hand*, but *is present.* (See LANGE *Comm.*, Am. Ed., p. 124.) The original is ἐνέστηκεν. It is inconceivable that the Apostle should have spoken of the approaching Advent, elsewhere described as the hope of the Christian Church (Tit. ii. 13), as the ground of distress. His object was to warn them against the false idea that the Advent had already taken place—that the hope that once had cheered them of blessings in the *future* was a vain one.—E. R. C.]

† [The Ἀποκατάστασις. It is universally admitted that the rendering of Acts iii. 19-21 in the E. V. is incorrect. The translation as given in the LANGE *Comm.* is: *Repent ye therefore and be converted, that your sins may be blotted out, in order that the times of refreshing may come from the face of the Lord, and that He may send the Messiah Jesus who was appointed unto you ; whom the heavens must receive until times wherein all things will be restored (times of restitution, χρόνων ἀποκαταστάσεως), which God hath spoken by the mouth of His holy prophets from of old.*

It may at once be remarked that the period here referred to is a lengthened one, as is evident from the use of the plural term, χρόνοι.

To determine what is meant by *times of restitution,* our first appeal must be to the Old Testament Prophets. They are times of which God has spoken *by the mouth of His Prophets.*

The noun ἀποκατάστασις does not occur in the LXX.; its verbal root ἀποκαθίστημι appears however in several important passages, and points unmistakably to an oft-recurring Hebrew word of which it is the translation; see Mal. iv. 6; Jer. xvi. 15; xxiv. 6; I. 19. In the first three of these passages it is the translation of the Hiph. of שוּב, and in the last of the Piel, which, in this verb, is also causative (see Robinson). The verb also occurs Isa. i. 25, 26; lviii. 12; Jer. xxxiii. 7; xxxii. 37; xxiii. 5-8; xxiv. 6, 7; Joel iii. (iv.) 1. The ἀποκατάστασις referred to in these passages seems to be the only one spoken of by the Prophets. That these prophecies were partially and typically fulfilled in the restoration of Israel from Babylon is admitted. It would seem to be manifest, however, that they did not receive their complete fulfilment in that event. And still further, if they were then fulfilled, there were no unfulfilled prophecies of the ἀποκατάστασις in the days of Peter. (Manifestly connected with the passages quoted above, as the completion of the *restitution* herein predicted, are Isa. xi.; lxv. 17—lxvi. 24; compare especially Jer. xxiii. 5-8 with Isa. xi. 10-14. So connected are they that they must be regarded as referring to the same event, although the term under discussion does not appear in them.)

The following seem to be the elements of the *restitution* predicted in the foregoing Scriptures:—1. A restoration of the hearts of the fathers to the children, Mal. iv. 6. 2. The restoration of the rejected seed of Jacob to holiness and the consequent favor of God, Isa. i. 25; Jer. xxiv. 7. 3. The restoration of Israel to their own land, *passim.* 4. The establishment of Israel, not again to be dispersed, Jer. xxiv. 6, 7. 5. The establishment of the Kingdom of righteousness as a visible Kingdom, in power and great glory, with its seat at Jerusalem, Isa. i. 25, 26 (ii. 2, 3); lviii. 12-14; Jer. xxiii. 5-8;

of the coming of the Lord as imminent (in connection with those which declare that there is to be a period of generally diffused peace and righteousness preceding the final consummation), such as Matt. xxiv. 42-44; Mark xiii. 32-37; Luke xii. 35-40; 1 Thess. v. 2, 3; Tit. ii. 11-13; Jas. v. 7, 8.

The upholders of the hypothesis that the Second Advent is not to take place until the final Consummation, base their opinion upon those Scriptures which manifestly connect an Advent with that event. The following is the summation of the argument by Dr. David Brown, one of the most eminent advocates of this view. I. The Church will be absolutely complete at Christ's Coming; 1 Cor. xv. 23; Eph. v. 25-27; 2 Thess. i. 10; Jude 24; Col. i. 22; 1 Thess. iii. 13. II. Christ's Second Coming will exhaust the object of the Scriptures, in reference—(1) to Saints; Luke xix. 13; 2 Pet. i. 19; James v. 7; 1 Pet. i. 13; 2 Tim. iv. 8; Phil. iii. 20: (2) to sinners; 2 Thess. i. 7-10; 2 Pet. iii. 10; Luke xii. 39, 40; xvii. 26, 27, 30. III. The sealing ordinances of the New Testament will disappear at Christ's Second Coming: Baptism; Matt. xxviii. 20: The Lord's Supper; 1 Cor. xi. 26. IV. The Intercession of Christ, and the Work of the Spirit for saving purposes, will cease at the Second Advent —(1) The Intercession of Christ stands intermediate between His first and second Coming; Heb. xi. 12, 24-28: (2) The work of the Spirit is dependent upon the Intercession, and terminates with it; John vii. 38, 39; xiv. 16, 17, 26; xv. 36; xvi. 7, 14; Acts ii. 33; Tit. iii. 5, 6; Rev. iii. 1; v. 6. V. Christ's proper Kingdom is al-

ready in being; commencing formally on His Ascension to the right hand of God, and continuing unchanged, both in character and form, till the final Judgment:—(1) Acts ii. 29-36, comp. with Zech. vi. 12, 13; Rev. v. 6; iii. 7, 8, 12; Isa. xxii. 22; ix. 6, 7: (2) Acts iii. 13-15, 19-21: (3) Acts iv. 25-28, comp. with Ps. ii: (4) Acts v. 29-31 (Him hath God exalted to be a Saviour-Prince, i.e., a Priest upon His Throne): (5) The Apostolic comment on Ps. cx. 1, viz.: Acts ii. 34-36; Heb. x. 12, 13; 1 Cor. xv. 24-26. VI. When Christ comes, the whole Church of God will be "made alive" at once—the dead by resurrection, and the living immediately thereafter by transformation; their "mortality being swallowed up of life;" 1 Cor. xv. 20-23; John vi. 39, 40; xvii. 9, 24. VII. All the wicked will rise from the dead, or be "made alive," at the Coming of Christ; Dan. xii. 2, with John v. 28, 29; 1 Cor. xv. 51, 52, with 1 Thess. iv. 16; Matt. xiii. 43, with Dan. xii. 3; Rev. xx. 11-15; (He interprets the first resurrection of Rev. xx. 4, 5, as "figurative"—indicating "a glorious state of the Church on earth, and in its mortal state"). VIII. The righteous and the wicked will be judged together, and both at the coming of Christ; Matt. x. 32, 33; Mark viii. 38; Rev. xxi. 7, 8; xxii. 12-15; Matt. xvi. 24-27; vii. 21-23; xxv. 10, 11, 31-46; xiii. 30, 38-43; John v. 28, 29; Acts xvii. 31; Rom. ii. 5-16; 2 Cor. v. 9-11; 1 Cor. iv. 5; 2 Thess. i. 6-10; 1 Cor. iii. 12-15; Col. i. 28; Heb. xiii. 17; 1 Thess. ii. 19-20; 1 John ii. 28; iv. 17; Rev. iii. 5; 1 Tim. v. 24, 25; Rom. xiv. 10, 12; 2 Pet. iii. 7, 10, 12; Rev. xx. 11-15; 2 Tim. iv. 1. IX. At Christ's Second Appearing, "the heavens and the earth that are now," being dissolved by fire, shall give place to "new heavens and a new earth wherein dwelleth righteousness" without any mixture of sin; 2 Pet. iii. 7, 10-13; Rev. xx. 11; xxi. 1.

A careful study of all the passages that have been adduced in support of these hypotheses respectively, has induced in the mind of the writer the thought that two Advents still future are predicted—the one for the establishment of the Basileia (at which shall take place a partial resurrection and judgment); the other at the final consummation, at which time shall take place the general judgment.

It will at once be objected that but one future Advent seems to be predicted in the Scripture. To this it may be answered, first, that, whilst this may be true in reference to the earlier portions of the New Testament, in the Apocalypse a twofold Advent seems to be indicated; comp. xix. 11-16 with xx. 11, 12. And in the second place, it may be remarked, that, in deferring a distinct intimation of a twofold Advent to one of the concluding Books of the Canon, the New Testament follows the analogy of the Old.

It is admitted by all that a twofold Advent of the Messiah, one in humiliation and the other in glory, was predicted in the Old Testament. In the earlier prophecies, however, but one Coming seems to have been contemplated. Even in Isaiah, where the Messiah is in one place spoken of as a Man of sorrows, and in another as appearing in royal glory, but one Advent is, in express terms, referred to. The whole of prophecy seems to be cast upon one plane, without refer-

xxxiii. 7 sqq. 6. The gathering of all nations as tributary to Israel or the Church. (For the views of the writer as to the identity of Israel and the Church, see foot-note †, p. 27.) 7. The Palingenesia, Isa. xi.; lxv. 17 sqq.

In the New Testament the noun occurs only in the passage under consideration, and the verbal root only eight times. Two of these instances, however, are of marked significance. In Matt. xvii. 11 Jesus said: "Elias truly shall first come and restore all things (ἀποκαταστήσει πάντα)." That the restoration was future is evident from—(1) the future form of the verb, (2) the fact that the prophecy referred to was not completely fulfilled in the Baptist—he did not restore all things. (The subsequent words of our Lord, ver. 12, are not opposed to this view. They clearly imply that John had not accomplished the work prophesied by Malachi. The Scribes and Pharisees would not receive him as the restorer, Matt. xi. 14; they rejected the counsel of God against themselves, and Elias is yet to come for the fulfilment of the prophecy.)

The verb next occurs Acts i. 6. The disciples asked: "Lord, wilt thou at (in) this time restore again (ἀποκαθιστάνεις) the kingdom to Israel?" Now it seems impossible to suppose that, after forty days' converse with the Great Teacher, during which time "he opened their understanding that they might understand the scriptures" (Luke xxiv. 45), and spake "of the things pertaining to the Kingdom of God" (Acts i. 3), the Apostles should have been in ignorance as to the nature of the restoration. It is equally impossible to suppose that if they had been mistaken, He would not have corrected them. So far from correcting mistake, His answer implies the correctness of their view as to the nature of the restoration. At that time their view was, confessedly, the one now characterized as literal or normal. A few days after (and subsequent to the outpouring of the Spirit at Pentecost) Peter speaks, in the passage under consideration, of an ἀποκατάστασις still future, without the slightest intimation that he had previously been mistaken as to its nature.

The next instance of the occurrence of the term is in the passage now under consideration. The Apostle spoke of a restitution, foretold by the Prophets and manifestly spoken of by our Lord, which he declared to be then future. It seems most natural to connect that restitution with the event spoken of by Paul. Rom. xi. 25-27—a glorious ἀποκατάστασις, in the description of which all the Old Testament Scriptures referred to above seem to have been in the Apostle's mind.—E. R. C.]

ence to the succession of those events, which, we now know, were to be separated by millennia. It is only in the Book of Daniel, and there only obscurely, that a twofold Advent is, in terms, intimated; compare ix. 25, 26, with vii. 13, 14. The hypothesis of a double Advent could have been deduced from the Old Testament Scriptures only from the consideration that things were predicted of the coming Messiah, on the one hand *humiliation* and on the other *exaltation*, that could not be realized in one visit to earth—and this hypothesis exactly satisfies the obscure intimation in the Apocalypse of Daniel. It will also be observed by the careful student that one and the same prophecy sometimes relates to both Advents, in matters in which the first is typical of the second—as, for instance, the prophecy of Joel (ii. 28-32) which had an initial fulfillment on the day of Pentecost (Acts ii. 16-21), but which is to have another and more complete fulfillment in a day yet future (Matt. xxiv. 29; Luke xxi. 11, 25). So also in respect of the prophecies of the New Testament—things are predicted concerning the coming Messiah which cannot find a fulfillment in one Advent,—as, for instance, that He shall establish a Kingdom of righteousness on earth (Acts iii. 21; see preceding *foot-note* on the passage), and that He shall terminate the present order of things in a general judgment (2 Pet. iii. 4-13). These two classes of statement find their best reconciliation in the hypothesis of a twofold Advent—and this hypothesis finds support in a comparison of Matt. xxiv. 30 with xxv. 31, and still more clearly in Rev. xix. 11-16 compared with xx. 11-15.

It is impossible to present the details of this scheme in the present Note. It is submitted with the foregoing general remarks, which sufficiently indicate its leading features, to those interested in prophetic studies. It is proper, in addition to what has already been said, to call attention to the probability that, as certain prophecies of the Old Testament have reference to both the acknowledged Advents, finding an initial fulfillment in the one and being completely fulfilled in the other, so will it be in the prophecies of the New Testament.—E. R. C.]

B.—EARTH-PICTURE OF THE VICTORY OVER THE BEAST. THE PAROUSIA OF CHRIST FOR JUDGMENT.

CHAP. XIX. 17—XX. 5.

a. *The Judgment upon the Beast.*

17 And I saw an [one][1] angel standing in the sun; and he cried with a loud [great] voice, saying to all the fowls that fly in the midst of heaven [mid-heaven], Come and gather yourselves [om. and gather yourselves—*ins.*, be gathered][2] together
18 unto the [*ins.* great][3] supper of the great [om. the great] God; That ye may eat the [om. the][4] flesh of kings, and the [om. the][4] flesh of captains [*ins.* of thousands], and the [om. the][4] flesh of mighty [strong] men, and the [om. the][4] flesh of horses, and of them that sit on them, and the [om. the][4] flesh of all men [om. men], both
19 [om. both] free and [as well as][5] bond, both [and] small and great. And I saw the beast [wild-beast], and the kings of the earth, and their armies, gathered together to make [*ins.* the][6] war against [with] him that sat [the one sitting] on the
20 horse, and against [with] his army. And the beast [wild-beast] was taken, and with him[7] the false prophet that wrought miracles [the signs] before him [in his presence], with which he deceived [seduced *or* misled (ἐπλάνησεν)] them that had [om. had] received the mark of the beast [wild-beast], and them that worshipped his image. [:] These both [the two] were cast alive into a [the] lake of [*ins.* the]
21 fire burning [that burneth] with brimstone. And the remnant were slain with the sword of him that sat [the one sitting] upon the horse, which *sword* proceeded [goeth forth] out of his mouth: and all the fowls [birds] were filled [satiated] with their flesh.

TEXTUAL AND GRAMMATICAL.

[1] Ver. 17. [Crit. Eds. give ἕνα with A. P. 1, *et al*; it is om. by B.*—E. R. C.]
[2] Ver. 17. [Crit. Eds. read συνάχθητε with ℵ. A. B*. P., *et al.*, instead of καὶ συνάγεσθε.—E. R. C.]
[3] Ver. 17. [Crit. Eds. give τὸ δεῖπνον τὸ μέγα with ℵ. A. B*. P. instead of τοῦ μεγάλου with 1, 36, 49, 79.—E. R. C.]
[4] Ver. 18. [These articles do not occur in any Cod., nor are they required by the English idiom.—E. R. C.]
[5] Ver. 18. [Crit. Eds. generally give ἐλευ. τε καί with ℵ. A. B*. P. *et al.*—E. R. C.]
[6] Ver. 19. [Codd. ℵ. A. B*. give the article before πόλεμον. [The reference, doubtless, is to the war predicted chs. xvi. 14; xvii. 14.—E. R. C.]
[7] Ver. 20. [Lach., Treg., Tisch. (8th Ed.) read καὶ μετ' αὐτοῦ ὁ with ℵ. P.; Alf. brackets οἱ before μετ' with A.; Tisch. (1859) reads καὶ ὁ μετ' αὐτοῦ with B*.—E. R. C.]

b. The Millennial Kingdom. (Chap. xx. 1-5.)

1 And I saw an angel come down from [descending out of—*ins.* the] heaven, having the key of the bottomless [*om.* bottomless] pit [abyss] and a great chain in [upon]
2 his hand. And he laid hold on the dragon, that [*or* the] old [ancient] serpent,[8] which [that] is the Devil [*or* Slanderer], and Satan [*or* the Adversary][9], and bound him
3 a thousand years, and cast him into the bottomless [*om.* bottomless] pit [abyss], and shut him up, and set a seal upon [*om.* him up, and set a seal upon—*ins.* and sealed over][10] him, that he should [might] deceive [seduce *or* mislead $(\pi\lambda\alpha\nu\dot{\eta}\sigma\eta)$][11] the nations no more, till the thousand years should be fulfilled [finished]: and [*om.* and][12] after that [these] he must be loosed a little season [time].
4 And I saw thrones, and they sat [*ins.* down][13] upon them, and judgment was given unto them: and *I saw* the souls of them that were [had been] beheaded for [on account of] the witness of Jesus, and for [on account of] the word of God, and which [who] had not [*om.* had not] worshipped [*ins.* not] the beast [wild-beast], neither [nor yet][14] his image, neither had [*om.* neither had—*ins.* and] received [*ins.* not] *his* [*om. his*—*ins.* the] mark upon their [the][15] foreheads, or in [*om.* , or in—*ins.* and upon] their hands [hand]; and they lived and reigned with Christ a[16]
5 thousand years. But [*om.* But][17] The rest of the dead lived not again [*om.* again][18] until [till] the thousand years were [should be] finished. This *is* the first resurrection.

---

[8] Chap. xx., ver. 2. Cod. A. gives the nominative ὁ ὄφις ὁ ἀρχαῖος. Codd. B., *et al.* give the accusative, which is ▬▬▬ in accordance with the text. [Lach., Alf., Treg., Tisch. give the nom. with A.; the acc. is supported by ℵ. B., *et al.*—E. R. C.]

[9] Ver. 3. Lach. [Alf., Treg.] and Tisch. [1859] give ὅς ἐστιν διάβολος καὶ ὁ σατανᾶς in acc. with A. B. *et al.* Cod. ℵ gives the article both times with perfect propriety. [Tisch. (8th Ed) gives ὁ εστιν ὁ διάβολος καὶ ὁ Σατανᾶς; the pronoun ὁ before ἐστιν, and also the article ὁ before διάβολος, with ℵ.—E. R. C.]

[10] Ver. 3. Codd. ℵ, A. B., *et al.* omit αὐτόν after ἐκλεισεν.

[11] Ver. 3. The Rec. πλανῇση is adopted instead of the reading πλανᾷ. [So read Lach., Alf., Treg. Tisch. (8th Ed.), with ℵ. A.; Gb., Sz., Tisch. (1859) give πλανᾷ with B*.—E. R. C.]

[12] Ver. 3. [Crit. Eds. omit καί with ℵ. A. B*.—E. R. C.]

[13] Ver. 4. [The force of ἐκάθισαν can be presented only by the phrase *sat down*. Lange translates *seated themselves*.—E. R. C.]

[14] Ver. 4. [Crit. Eds. read οὐδέ with ℵ. A. B*. *et al.*—E. R. C.]

[15] Ver. 4. [Crit. Eds. generally omit αὐτῶν after μέτωπον in acc. with ℵ. A. B*., *Vulg.*, *et al.*—E. R. C.]

[16] Ver. 4. The article τά before χίλια should be omitted. [The article occurs in B*.; it is omitted, however, by Crit. Eds. with ℵ. A. *et al.*—E. R. C.]

[17] Ver. 5. [Lach., Alf., Tisch., omit the copula with A., *Clem., Am., Fuld., Tol., Lips.*; Treg. reads καὶ οἱ λοιποί with B.* 1, 38, 91, 95, *Memph.*—E. R. C.]

[18] Ver. 5. [Crit. Eds. read ἔζησαν with A. B., *Vulg., et al.*; ἀνέζησαν is without authority.—E. R. C.]

EXEGETICAL AND CRITICAL.

SYNOPTICAL VIEW.

a. The Judgment.

The judgment upon the Beast is accomplished, not in a manner purely of this world and in a form purely historical, like the judgment upon the Harlot, but in a more spiritual form, which is based upon the appearance of Christ from the other world, and which introduces the cosmical transition-form between time and eternity, the Millennial Kingdom.

The first point for consideration is that cosmical change itself, which proceeds from the sun and summons all the birds under the Heaven, all the forces of earthly metamorphosis, to consume all the dead flesh, the exanimate materials which shall be the issue of the great defeat of the Antichristian world—to consume them, in order to convert them into new life.

The second point is ethically mysterious. A decisive act of judgment takes the place of the battle contemplated by the Beast and the Kings. The two leaders and misleaders of the infatuated Antichristian host, the Beast and the False Prophet, are seized. That which seizes them seems to be a judgment of madness, for they are cast alive into the lake of fire burning with brimstone. For them, hell begins in this life; the fire of the fuel in which they have wrapped themselves, surrounds them on all sides—a flame of infinitely wild, fanatical agitation, doomed, in consequence of its absolute worthlessness, to form the pool of a mortal and dead stagnation—the unprogressive and eternally monotonous movement in a circle, or the fiery whirlpool of phrases and curses. In the case of the False Prophet, his guilt is once more noted, in explanation of his judgment; the most bitter reminiscences cling to the perfidy of his apostasy.

The third point is the judgment upon the followers of the Beast. They are not immediately cast into the fiery lake, but are for the time only killed. They are killed by the sword issuing from the mouth of Christ. They are morally judged and annihilated. What remains of them is a world of shadows, a sort of realm of the dead on the surface of this earth itself. All the birds become satiated *with their flesh; i. e.*, all their sensuous and earthly possessions have lost their value and are decayed like the flesh strewed over a field of dead bodies. *All the birds are satiated* with their flesh ; *i. e.*, all the forces of metamorphosis are laboring for their transformation into a new shape. The fullness and manifoldness of the flesh to be devoured by the birds is vividly described in ver. 18. A complete end is to be made of all this.

Though it might with reason be said that because the sun is the symbol of the revelation of salvation, the Angel of judgment, standing in the sun as the angel of the whole salvatory development of revelation, indicates the hour when the work of the revelation of salvation is entirely completed, when the world-clock of the history of salvation in this world has run down—we must not overlook the fact that this moment must coincide with the perfect ripeness of our cosmical system, and that, consequently, a catastrophe must start from the centre of our cosmical system, as well as from the focus of our religious moral system. The harvest of the earth and the harvest of the Kingdom of God coincide, in accordance with the parallelism between spirit and nature, as is declared in the Eschatological Discourse of our Lord (Matt. xxiv. 29), although the Day of the Harvest, the Last Day, stretches out into an æon of a thousand years in a symbolical sense.

The birds of the heaven have, in typical preludes, often been invited to similar feasts upon the slaughter fields of history (Deut. xxviii. 26; Jer. vii. 33; xvi. 4; Ezek. xxxix. 17). In this fact there is not only an expression of irony concerning the vanity of earth's glory, but also an expression of the triumph of life over death. The Kingdom of God is acquainted with a transformation of matter; it is, however, of another and higher sort than that of which modern materialists talk; it does not lie under the curse of an eternal rotation, but is, on the contrary, under the law of the highest life, which changes this lower world of *becoming* into the eternal world of the City of God.

b. *The Millennial Kingdom.*

The prophecy of the thousand years of Christ's reign on earth is, in and for itself, a true pearl of Christian truth and knowledge, because it throws light upon an entire series of difficult Christian conceptions.

In the first place, it mediates an understanding of the Last Day, in that it shows how the latter expands into a Divine Day of a thousand years, in a symbolical sense, i. e., a specific æon; and thus it also casts light backwards upon the import of the days of creation.

Secondly, it mediates the understanding of a catastrophe which is to divide between this life and the life to come, time and eternity, the world of *becoming* and the world of *consummation*, in that it shows how the great and mighty contrast is harmonized by an æonic transition-period, in perfect accordance with the laws of life and vital development, as was clearly explained by Irenæus (see Dorner, *Geschichte der Christologie*, p. 243).

Especially does it mediate the fact of the resurrection, in that it represents a first resurrection as preceding the general resurrection, in harmony with the Apostle Paul (1 Cor. xv. 23). Thus the resurrection is characterized as an affair of *growth* or *progress*, conditioned upon spiritual circumstances. In accordance with this, we apprehend the fact that even in this life the believer advances towards the resurrection

(Phil. iii. 11); that a resurrection-germ gradually develops within him (Rom. viii.); that the beginnings of the resurrection commence with his removal into the other world (2 Cor. vi.); that believers, in their ripening towards the resurrection, are, as blossoms of the general resurrection, a whole æon in advance of the rest of mankind—a fact which is also indicative of a higher form of resurrection; and that Christ must needs have been the firstling and the principle of the whole resurrection (Eph. i. 20).

Thus also the great antithesis is explained which must necessarily exist between the original transruption (*Durchbruch*) of sin or the curse in humanity and the final transruption (*Durchbruch*) of salvation and blessing. As, in the primitive age, pneumatic corruption was for a long time hindered in its outbreak by the resistance of healthy vital substance in the psychical, somatic and cosmical sphere. so in the New Testament time, pneumatic salvation in humanity has had to struggle long with the resistance of evil in the psychical, somatic and cosmical sphere. With the beginning of the Millennial Kingdom, however, begins the transruption of the blessing, in opposition to the old transruption of the curse.

Whilst, on the one hand, the communication of believing humanity with Heaven and its pure spirit-world is spiritually consummated by the Parousia of Christ, and destined to be also physically consummated, the communication between the spiritual sphere of earth and the Satanic sphere of the abyss, on the other hand, is discontinued;—in the first place, because the organic mediators of Satanic operations, the Beast and the False Prophet, as also Great Babylon, are judged and destroyed. Though at the close of the great transition-æon Satan again obtains a foot-hold on the earth, it is the last convulsive struggle of the serpent-nature manifesting itself in a brutal mutiny, which, for the very reason that it is veiled under no spiritual pretexts, like former Satanic efforts, but is the issue of consummate boldness and insolence, is blasted, not by Christological weapons, but by the fire of the Almighty from Heaven.

But of this great effulgent picture of the Millennial Kingdom, the lack of patience and hope in the Christian sphere (Rom. viii. 24, 25) has made the most manifold caricatures.

We distinguish the caricatures of real so-called Chiliasm; the caricatures of the spiritualistic denial of Chiliasm, even to the misapprehension of its primal type—according to this class, the Apocalypse itself is chiliastic, and the same character is finally attributed to the concrete Christian hope; finally, the caricatures of the Millennial Kingdom which were produced by placing it in the past or the present (see the Introduction).

True Chiliasm existed, so far as its element was concerned, long before the doctrinal forth-setting of the χιλια ἔτη, whence it takes its name. It is based upon the great family failing of all Judaizing Christianity; to such Christianity, the cross of Christ is still, more or less, an offence; to such Christianity, the redemption accomplished in the first Parousia of Christ is unsatisfying, and the centre of gravity of the redemption is consequently regarded as situate in the second Parousia, when Christ shall appear in His glory, and shall also promote His people to the state of glory. This Judaizing Christianity has no understanding of the *principial* completion of redemption in its depth and inwardness; hence, only in the *final, peripheral* redemption does it behold the true redemption. According as its ideals of glory are nobler or more base, its eschatological hopes assume a purer or an impurer form, so that a perfect scale of Chiliasms is formed, stretching from an anticipation of the sensuous glorification of Israel to the most carnal orgies in pre-celebration of the return of Christ.[*] This is material Chiliasm proper. It has been rejuvenated in three Anglo-American sects of our own time. The element of truth which is perverted into falsehood and extravagance in it, is the Christian and Biblical expectation of the real, and in a religious sense ever near, coming of Christ.[*]

But material Chiliasm early sought and found a formal supplement, in that it boldly converted the words of the Apostle Peter (2 Pet. iii. 8)—words which, spoken with reference to Ps. cx. 4, were designed as a counteraction against chiliastic impatience—into a chronological article of doctrine, in which it believed that it had discovered the key to the computation of the time of Christ's coming. A Judaizing presupposition was here involved—*viz.*, that God's historical work of salvation would arrive at completion in a Divine week, reflected in the human week. To this was added later the further assumption, that at the first coming of Christ the world had been in existence for about four thousand years. Upon these bases men reckoned, and determined the time of the second Advent. Here another arbitrary assumption arose, converting the Millennial Kingdom into the real Sabbath of God, though the latter is to last forever, whilst the Apocalyptic æon appears as a mere transition-period. In many respects, this formal Chiliasm, whence the system has its name, was subservient to material Chiliasm; in many other respects, however, especially in more modern Theology, formal Chiliasm, as a theological subtilty, detached itself entirely from material tendencies, although it continued to be afflicted with the material infirmity of a somewhat superficial and extravagant conception of the history of salvation.

In face of all these Judaizing conceptions, the spiritualistico-ethnical conception has always considered itself bound, not only to combat true, sensuous Chiliasm, but also to controvert, or at least cast a shade upon, its assumptions—the expectation of the real coming of Christ, for instance; and it has especially felt itself obliged to cast the reproach of Chiliasm upon the putative originator of the same, the Apocalypse. And this, particularly, on account of the *thousand years,* the χίλια ἔτη. The *Tales of a Thousand and One Nights* might, with about equal justice, be denominated a chiliastic composition.

A turbid mixture of both one-sided views is formed by the placing of the Millennial Kingdom in the course of Church History. In refer-

ence to this mixed form, we can distinguish two species. Mediæval Catholicism beheld in the Romish Church the actualized Kingdom of God itself, especially in respect of the papal system. The Old Lutheran orthodox dating back of the Millennial Kingdom into the Middle Ages—a view recently revived by Hengstenberg—was a fruit of the stunting of Eschatology in the era of the Reformation, especially in adherence to utterances of Luther's. We here refer partly to the history of the interpretation of the Apocalypse, as already presented by us, partly to the following exegesis in detail.

The singular opinion of Stier and others, that there is to be a double Parousia, one at the beginning and the other at the end of the Millennial Kingdom, seems desirous of conjoining so-called "Chiliasm" with the older orthodoxy.[*]

With the judgment upon the spiritual motive powers of the Beast, with the destruction of his powerful lies, Satan has lost his foot-hold within the infatuated human race—his right of naturalization, we might say, in this earthly sphere. He is therefore cast into the abyss. An Angel descends from Heaven to execute God's sentence upon him. The office of this Angel reminds us of the offices of Michael; his name, however, is not mentioned. He has the key to the abyss—not simply to the pit of the abyss; this key he has in order that he may *shut* the abyss, *i. e.* entirely shut off Satanic influences from men for the time of the thousand years. This power, however, is connected with the moral fact that all the spiritual pretences contained in the Satanic illusive promise, *eritis sicut deus,* are destroyed by the beauteous reality of the great appearance of the Kingdom. All that Satan falsely promised concerning the path of impatience and guilt, is here attained in the path of pious patience: fulness of blessing, happiness, glory of life of every sort. Thus Satan has come to the end of his Latin, and needs, agreeably to the serpent's tenacity of life, a thousand years to contrive the last desperate stroke of senseless heaven-storming—a procedure which is reported to have been the first act of the revolted Titans of Grecian story.[†] And for this last rebellion a further existence is granted him, for the judgment upon him must be complete. His existence during the thousand years, however, consists in a sojourn in the abyss, betwixt death and damnation (the Realm of the Dead [Hades] and Gehenna), fastened to the chain which the Angel brings with him from Heaven. He has now made an open show of his entire nature, and is therefore called by his various forms and titles, except that the appellation of *Accuser* is no longer given to him—although even this name is contained in the διάβολος. The condemnatory sentence is executed in four acts which follow each other in rapid succession. He is seized, cast chained (not chained to any

---

[*] [See *foot-notes* on pages 3, 58, and 62.—E. R. C.]

---

[*] [See Note on the Future Advent of Christ, pp. 339 sqq.— E. R. C.]

[†] [The slowness of invention which Lange here attributes to the Devil is more in harmony with the character attributed to that personage in numerous popular German tales, —in which he appears as a sort of *Deutscher Michel,* being frequently outwitted and imposed upon by sharp practicers of earth—than with the exalted intellect with which we usually conceive of him as endowed.—Tr.]

object external to himself, but hand to hand, 2 Pet. ii. 4) into the abyss, shut in, and sealed. The *seal* is the symbolic expression for the appointed Divine doom upon him, and is more powerful in its effect than the seal with which the grave of Jesus was sealed. The purpose of all this is that he may not prematurely seduce the heathen, the remnants of heathenism which still constitute the old border of the new world that is in process of *becoming*.

This, then, is the negative side of the Millennial Kingdom. The positive side appears in three features: [1] The first resurrection, [2] the first judgment of restitution, [3] the first period of imperishable triumphal rest and rejoicing and unfading glory in the fellowship of Christ. The first resurrection is represented as a special reward of the faithfulness of Christ's martyrs—above all, the martyrs of the last time, who have not worshipped the Beast; hence these latter constitute a particular class by the side of those slain at an earlier period. They stand in the fore-ground, as representatives of the Victorious Church (see 1 Cor. xv. 23); but we must recollect that this Church is itself of greater extent than here appears. For Christ has come with the hosts of Heaven, according to ch. xix. 14; according to the Epistle of Jude (ver. 14), He is to come with His myriads of saints. With the sphere of this resurrection, the full liberation of the life-power on the sanctified earth is expressed (see Is. lxv. 13 sqq.). The second sphere is the sphere of the preliminary judgment. For the Seer, this occupies the foreground, since Christian longing cries for the removal of all the shame and wrong which, in this world, weigh upon the name of Christ and Christians; hence the Seer first sees the thrones of judgment set. If we consider that the judgment upon the Antichristian host has already been held, and that the last judgment upon the last revolt, which is as yet but germinating deep in the darkness, cannot be anticipated, there results, as a middle domain of judgment, an instruction (*Pädagogik*) and discipline exercised by Heaven upon the human race, as extant at the Parousia, and thus sharing in the cosmical metamorphosis. It is that process of elimination and sanctification which must take place before the perfect appearing of the City of God on this earth; it is a judgment of peace, in accordance with Ps. lxxii. and Matt. xix. 28. The third sphere is the living and reigning with Christ in the glory of a spiritual life which dominates and clarifies all creaturely essence—the organization of earth for its union with Heaven. There is no trace here of an external restoration of Israel in the sense of a privileged people of God, or of a restoration of the Old Testament *cultus* in an inconceivable New Testament sublimation; unless we should apply the subsequent words, *they shall be priests of God and of Christ*, and the words *the beloved City*, to the support of such a theory—in which case the symbolism of the expression must necessarily be discarded. We cannot suppose that there is to be a two-fold heavenly Jerusalem; and the one true Jerusalem is still in Heaven, whence, according to ch. xxi. 2, it does not descend to earth until the end of the thousand years.

[THEORIES CONCERNING THE MILLENNIUM.*]

By the American Editor.

[The word *Millennium* means, etymologically, *a thousand years*, and may with propriety be used in reference to any period of that length. By common consent, however, the specific term THE MILLENNIUM is employed to denote the period mentioned in chap. xx. 4–7. The theories on this subject that have been held in the Church are divisible into two classes—the Preterist and the Futurist—the former of which set forth that the origin of the Millennial period was in the *past;* the latter, that it is in the *future*. Each of these classes consists of two or three generic theories, the respective upholders of which differ amongst themselves on many specific points. It is proper to remark that in the following statement the writer has been greatly indebted to the work of Elliott.

a. *Preterist Theories.*

I. *The Augustinian.* This theory is so styled as it was first propounded by the great Augustine in his *Civitate Dei*, xx. 7–9. It has been upheld in all ages of the Church since its first promulgation, and in modern times by Wordsworth. Its main elements are—1. The period began at the first Advent, when Satan was bound and cast out of the hearts of true Christians and their reign over him (*regnum militiæ*) began: 2. The *Beast* symbolizes the wicked world, and its *image* a hypocritical profession: 3. The *first resurrection* is that of dead souls to spiritual life,[†] a resurrection continued in every true conversion throughout the period: 4. The *thousand years* is a symbolical expression of *completeness* appropriately indicating the entire period of the Messiah's reign:[‡] 5. This period to be followed by a new persecution of the Saints under Antichrist; the destruction of whose hosts by fire from heaven would be followed by the universal resurrection of the good and bad, and the general judgment; after which will begin, *in heaven*, the glorious period of the New Jerusalem.

II. *The Grotian.* This theory was first propounded by Genebrard in the 16th Century; it found its chief advocates, however, in Grotius and Hammond.[§] It differs principally from the preceding in that it makes the reign of Saints to be, not that of the individual Christian in the domain of his own heart, but that of the Church in the world. The elements of this theory are—1. By the *Beast* is denoted Pagan Rome, whose destruction under Constantine was predicted in chap. xix.: 2. The power of Satan was then broken, as was manifested in the establishment of the Christian religion as the religion of the State: 3. The Millennial period began in that

---

† [Wordsworth explains the εζησαν of ver. 4 as the glorified life with Christ *after* martyrdom, and the ἀνάστασις of ver. 5 as spiritual life *begun* in baptism and *completed* at the death of the body.—E. R. C.]
‡ [Augustine himself, probably, held the view that the *thousand years* were *literal*, to terminate with the sixth *chiliad* of the world's existence.—E. R. C.]
§ [A similar theory, indeed the same with specific variations, was propounded by Prof. Bush in a work on the Millennium published in New York in 1832.—E. R. C.]

establishment, it was continued through a thousand years to the 14th Century, and closed with the attack on Christendom by the Ottoman Turks: 4. Gog and Magog denote the Mohammedan power, at the close of whose gradual destruction is to take place—the universal resurrection, the general judgment, and the eternal blessedness of the Saints in heaven.*

III. *The Gippsian.* This view, suggested by Mr. Gipps in 1831, makes the beginning of the period synchronous with the rise of Papal Antichrist. It represents (according to Elliott) "those who lived and reigned with Christ to be men endowed with the spirit of the early Antipagan martyrs, now revived, as it were, to testify for Christ: after which, at the end of the Beast's and witnesses' concurrent (!) Millennial reign, the second and glorious resurrection of the rest of the dead is to be fulfilled in the Jews' conversion and restoration."

b. *Futurist Theories.*

IV. *The Pre-Millennial.* This theory, as to its general features, is the most ancient. It was held by the primitive Fathers, and has been taught with various specific modifications in all ages of the Church. Amongst its most prominent English speaking advocates, in modern times, are Mede, Caryll, Gill, Noell, Elliott, the Bickersteths, the Bonars, Alford, Lord, *etc.* The elements are that—1. The Millennium is to begin in a glorious personal advent of Christ, immediately after the destruction of Antichrist: 2. The binding of Satan is to be "an absolute restriction of the powers of hell from tempting, deceiving, or injuring mankind:" 3. The *duration* is to be one thousand years (literal or symbolical): 4. The *resurrection* is to be a literal resurrection of Saints of the preceding æon (either the martyrs, or the specially faithful, or the entire body): 5. The entire government of the earth is to be exercised by Christ and His risen and transformed Saints, the latter being ὡς ἀγγελοι (Mark xii. 25): 6. Under this government, all false religion having been put down, the Jews and all nations having been converted to Christ, Jerusalem being made the universal capital, righteousness, peace and external prosperity shall prevail throughout the earth: 7. At the close of this period, Satan having been loosed, there shall be a great apostasy, followed by (1) the destruction of the apostates, (2) the universal resurrection of the remaining dead of all dispensations, (3) the general judgment, (4) the consummation.

The principal variation amongst those who hold this theory are as to—1. The *continuance of*

Christ *on earth;*—some holding that it is to be only for the establishment of the Kingdom; others that it is to continue more or less uninterruptedly throughout the whole period: 2. The *duration,* some holding that the thousand years are *literal;* others that they are *symbolic:* 3. The *subjects of the resurrection;*—some holding that they are *all* the saints; others that they are only the martyrs; others still, that they are the specially faithful, including the martyrs: 4. The *relation of the Jews* to the other nations;—some contending that they are to occupy a position of superiority; others denying or modifying this opinion.

V. *The Post-Millennial.* This theory, which is the one most generally adopted by English speaking Protestant Theologians, was first fully developed by Whitby.* Faber, Brown and Barnes have been amongst the most prominent of its advocates. The scheme as set forth by Whitby is as follows:—

" I. I believe that, after the fall of Antichrist, there shall be such a glorious state of the Church, by the conversion of the Jews to the Christian faith, as shall be to it *life from the dead;* that it shall then flourish in peace and plenty, in righteousness and holiness, and in a pious offspring; that then shall begin a glorious and undisturbed reign of Christ over both Jew and Gentile, to continue a thousand years during the time of Satan's binding; and that, as John the Baptist was Elias, because he came *in the spirit and power of* ELIAS,—so shall this be the *church of martyrs,* and of those who had not received the *mark of the Beast,* because of their entire freedom from all doctrines and practices of the Antichristian Church, and because the spirit and purity of the times of the primitive martyrs shall return. And therefore—

1. I agree with the patrons of the Millennium in this, that I believe Satan hath not yet been bound a thousand years, nor will he be so bound till the time of the calling of the Jews, and the time of St. John's Millennium.

2. I agree with them in this, that the true Millennium will not begin till the fall of Antichrist; nor will the Jews be converted till that time, the idolatry of the Roman Church being one great obstacle of their conversion.

3. I agree both with the modern and ancient Millenaries, that then shall be great peace and plenty, and great measures of knowledge and righteousness in the whole Church of God.

I therefore only differ from the ancient Millenaries in three things:

1. In denying Christ's personal reign upon earth during this thousand years; and in this both Dr. Burnet and Mr. Mede expressly have renounced their doctrine.†

* [Elliott writes: "Vitringa, however, who alludes to Whitby's as a work just published, makes brief citations from two earlier writers, Conrad of Mantua and Carolus Gallus, as expressive of the same general view."—E. R. C.]

† [Bush judiciously remarks on this declaration of Whitby: "This may be questioned. These writers have *modified* the creed of the ancients on this subject, without renouncing it." The views of Mede, as expressed by himself, are as follows: "What the quality of this reign should be, which is so singularly differenced from the reign of Christ hitherto, is neither safe nor easy to determine, further than that it should be the reign of our Saviour's victory over His enemies, wherein Satan being bound up from deceiving the nations any more, till the time of His reign be fulfilled, the Church should consequently enjoy a most blissful peace and happy security from the heretical apostasies and calamitous sufferings of former times; but here (if any where) the known shipwrecks of those who have been too venturous should make us most wary and careful, that we admit nothing into our imaginations which may cross or impeach any catholic tenet of the Christian faith, as also to beware of gross and carnal conceits of Epicurean happiness misbeseeming the spiritual purity of Saints. If we conceit any delights, let them be spiritual. The presence of Christ in this Kingdom will no doubt be glorious and evident, yet I dare not so much as imagine (which some ancients seem to have thought) that it will be a visible converse on earth. Yet, we grant, He will appear and be visibly revealed from heaven; especially for the calling and gathering of His ancient people, for whom in the days of old He did so many wonders." Mede believed that Christ would appear literally and gloriously for the establishment of the Millennium, and that in a special sense He would reign throughout the period. In so believing, he held the essential elements of the pre-millennial hypothesis. —E. R. C.]

a [The elder Turretin, P. Mastricht, J. Marckius, Lightfoot, Brightman, and Usher, all teach that the Millennium is past. The continental Theologians suggest as possible eras of its beginning, without deciding which is correct, the Incarnation, the Crucifixion, the Resurrection, the destruction of Jerusalem, the æra of Constantine. Marckius thinks that it may have begun in increased measure at each one of these in succession. These Theologians seem to regard the *binding* as a general weakening of the power of Satan. Lightfoot adopts the view that the origin is to be placed in the first proclamation of the gospel to the Gentiles by Paul and Barnabas, and that the *binding* refers, not to the power of Satan over the Church, but to his influence over the nations. He writes: "There is not a word here of the devil's binding that he should not disturb the Church, but of the devil's binding that he should not deceive the nations." These all agree that the duration of the period was (or was about) one thousand literal years.— E. R. C.]

2. Though I dare not absolutely deny what they all positively affirm, that the City of Jerusalem shall be then rebuilt, and the converted Jews shall return to it, because this probably has been collected from those words of Christ, *Jerusalem shall be trodden down till the time of the Gentiles is come in*, Luke xxi. 24. and all the prophets seem to declare the Jews shall then return to their own land, Jer. xxxi. 38-40; yet do I confidently deny what Barnabas and others of them do contend for, viz.: that the temple of Jerusalem shall be then built again; for this is contrary not only to the plain declaration of St. John, who saith, *I saw no temple in this new Jerusalem*, Rev. xxi. 22, whence I infer there is to be no temple in any part of it; but to the whole design of the Epistle to the Hebrews, which is to show the dissolution of the temple-service, for the weakness and unprofitableness of it; that the Jewish tabernacle was only a figure of the true and the *more perfect tabernacle which the Lord pitched, and not man*; the Jewish sanctuary only a worldly sanctuary, a pattern, and a figure of the heavenly one *into which Christ our High Priest is entered*, Heb. viii. 2; ix. 2, 11, 23, 24. Now, such a temple, such a sanctuary, and such service, cannot be suitable to the most glorious and splendid times of the Christian Church; and therefore the Apostle saith, *The Lord God omnipotent, and the Lamb*, shall be *their Temple*.

3. I differ both from the ancient and the modern Millenaries, as far as they assert that this shall be a reign of such Christians as have suffered under the heathen persecutors, or by the rage of Antichrist; making it only a reign of the converted Jews, and of the Gentiles then flowing in to them, and uniting into one Church with them."

With the above presentation, post-millenarians, in the main, agree. The chief point of difference is as to the return of the Jews to their own land—some holding, with Whitby, that it is to take place; others, denying it. There are also differences as to—1. The nature of the *Second* Resurrection implied in xx. 5,—some, with Vitringa, identifying it with the general resurrection of vers. 12, 13; others, as Whitby, Faber and Brown, explaining it as the uprising of Antichristian principles in the confederacy of Gog and Magog: 2. The New Jerusalem,—some, with Whitby, regarding it as relating to the Millennial condition of the Church; others, as Brown and Faber, understanding by it the *post-millennial* condition of blessedness and glory.—E. R. C.]

EXPLANATIONS IN DETAIL.

Ver. 17. **One angel standing in the sun.** —"*In the sun*, because from this stand-point, fitted, as it also was, to the glory of the Angel, he can best call to the birds, flying ἐν μεσουρανήματι (Ewald I., De Wette, Hengstenberg, Ebrard, Volkmar)." DUESTERDIECK. If this were the motive for the position of the Angel, he might much better have taken his stand in the moon. His position in the sun has an import relative at once to the Kingdom of God and to the Cosmos. The sun, as revelation, is the principle of the spirit-realm of this present life; the sun, as a celestial body, is the domain of this present Cosmos (see SYN. VIEW; comp. Rev. i. 16; Matt. xxiv. 29). **Come, be gathered together.**—See the citations above; comp. also Matt. xxiv. 28. According to Düsterdieck, the slain λοιποί of ver. 21 are the whole mass of the inhabitants of the earth. But whence, then, would come the mutineers at the end of the thousand years? The *Eastern kings* should also be distinguished from the *ten kings*. Gog and Magog have not yet joined the conflict. The λοιποί are, manifestly, the Antichristian host, from which the mass of earth's inhabitants are still to be distinguished. **Unto the great supper of God.**— Antithesis to the Marriage-Supper of the Lamb. At the former, all the flesh of the fleshly-minded

becomes a prey to the birds; at the latter, believers, as heirs of God, become heirs of all things.

Ver. 18. **That ye may eat.**—The prospective complete destruction of the hostile host is set forth in detail.

Ver. 19. **And I saw the wild-beast.**—The war-making, on the part of the Beast, is entirely of this world; it is a march, a drawing up in order of battle, the combatants being provided, perhaps, with the most terrible material weapons. But, opposed to them, stands an *army of God*, partially and predominantly as a host of spirits. And yet more, the στράτευμα of Christ stands contrasted, in its perfect unity, with the internally confused and divided στρατεύματα of the Beast. The attempt at an external conflict is immediately frustrated. The prophetic *chiaroscuro* resting upon this double array and battle cannot be brushed aside. It may only be gathered from the nature of the armies, that upon the side of Christ all the dynamic forces of spiritual humanity are concentrated, whilst upon the side of Antichrist demonic excitement may summon to its aid all the contrivances of craft and violence.

Ver. 20. **And the wild-beast was taken.** —In what way, is reserved for the future to make known. Since there is no mention made of any preceding battle, a spiritual process of dissolution is pre-supposed as taking place in the hostile army—especially a separation between the ring-leaders and the Antichristian host, mediated by Divine terrors. **And with him the false prophet.**—In the crisis of the disunion between Babylon and the Beast, the False Prophet has espoused the side of the Beast; a view which is prepared by the general description in ch. xiii. It is a result of a failure to distinguish between the general judgment-picture of chap. xiii. and the three subsequent pictures of judgment, when Ebrard seeks to distinguish between the pseudo-prophet "in the sixth world-kingdom" and an analogous lying power in "the eighth world-power" (p. 507). **Cast alive into the lake of the fire.**—See chap. xx. 10, 14 and chap. xxi. 8. It is equally incorrect to apprehend *Gehenna* or the lake of fire as a mere internal *condition* of the damned, as to apprehend it purely as a cosmical *region* of punishment. A remark which is true concerning the Apocalyptic Heaven—viz., that it has the import of a spiritual region as well as a corresponding cosmical region—applies also, in antithesis to Heaven, in the first place to Hades, in the second place to the Abyss, and in the third place to Gehenna. Hengstenberg advances a marvellous view. "The term *alive*, without bodily death (comp. ver. 21), confirms the idea that the Beast and the False Prophet are not human individuals, but purely ideal forms. A human individual cannot enter hell *alive*." Against which Ebrard: "If the Beast and the lying Prophet be emblems of mere *powers*, we do not rightly know what the emblematic trait of being cast alive into the lake of fire can mean," *etc.* "In Rev. xx. 12 (comp. John v. 29) the wicked are raised from their graves and re-united to their bodies expressly to the intent that they may be able to endure the flames of eternal torment (ch.

xx. 15) in their bodily natures as well as in their spirits." But, little congruity ■■ there is between purely ideal forms and the lake of fire and brimstone, there is as little necessity to make the possession of a body a preliminary condition of Gehenna suffering. When the *lake of fire* is called "the second death" (chap. xx. 14), this fearful conception stretches, on the one hand, beyond ideal forms, and on the other, beyond ■ corporeal suffering by fire. De Wette judiciously remarks, in respect of the distinctions between the punishment of the two Antichristian forms and the punishment of Satan: "They are judged earlier than Satan—who, chap. xx. 3, is bound but for a thousand years—because their existence and activity have attained their end, whilst, on the other hand, Satan, by virtue of the course of development of things, still has ■ root in the world and must again make his appearance." De Wette has, moreover, not apprehended the term *alive* as corporeally as Hengstenberg most strangely takes it in express connection with *ideal forms.* That the Beast and the False Prophet may be apprehended as collective personalities, is not to be denied; but neither is it to be denied that they converge into symbolically significant units. In the statement that they were cast *alive* into the *lake of fire*, it is doubtless intimated that they could fall under the judgment of Gehenna whilst still on earth. "*Fire* and *brimstone*," remarks Hengstenberg, "as designations of hell torments, have already appeared in chap. xiv. 10, 11. The lake of fire and brimstone is first mentioned here, and then again spoken of in chap. xx. 10, 14, 15; xxi. 8. As the fire and brimstone are suggestive of the destruction of Sodom and Gomorrha (comp. the remarks on chap. xiv. 10), the inference is obvious that the Dead Sea is referred to as the earthly reflection of hell." The term γέεννα, he further observes, is found neither in the Apocalypse nor the Gospel of John, whilst the first three Gospels have it. Ebrard remarks, in opposition to this, that though the Dead Sea owed its origin to a rain of fire and brimstone, it does not burn with brimstone, but consists of brackish water. As it is as little possible to doubt the identity of the two terms, *lake* (or, to use a word which seems to us more applicable, *pool*) *of fire* and *Gehenna*, as it is to doubt the distinction between *Gehenna* and *Sheol*, our next task must be to inquire into the origin of the idea of Gehenna. See *Comm. on Matthew*, p. 114 [Am. Ed.]; *Mark*, p. 90 [Am. Ed.]. If the Dead Sea were the foundation of this figurative principle of doctrine, distinct traces of the fact would necessarily be found in the Old Testament. Besides the fire of Gehinnom, we have, Isa. xxx. 33, a *stream of brimstone*, equally without reference to the Dead Sea. Comp. the article TOPHET in the Lexicons; also in Winer; see also Ps. xi. 6. The marshes and sloughs by the side of the *river of salvation* (Ezek. xlvii. 11) have also, doubtless, contributed to the completeness of the image. That the figure as a whole is an original idea of John's, as a *pool of fire*, is evidenced by the opposite figure of the *crystal sea*. Moreover, the Dead Sea could not well have been employed as an image of hell, without giving rise to the idea that the people of Sodom fell under the judgment of damnation

on the very occasion of their destruction—an idea which the Spirit of Scripture has avoided presenting. Comp. Matt. xi. 23; 1 Pet. iii. 19; see our Introduction, p. 34. [See the Excursus on HADES, p. 364 sqq.—E. R. C.]

Ver. 21. **And the remnant.**—The Antichristian host itself—not the whole remaining human race. **They were slain**—*i. e.*, according to Hengstenberg and Ebrard, they were not cast body and soul into the lake of fire, but they suffered only bodily death, whilst their souls went into Hades. "They are sent into hell," observes Hengstenberg, "only at the universal judgment (comp. chap. xx. 12–15), that is, if they do not in the meantime, whilst they are in the intermediate state, attain unto salvation (1 Pet. iii. 19, 20) ■■ those who have committed only the sin against the Son of Man, and not that against the Holy Ghost." It is questionable, however, whether the slaying of the whole Antichristian host should be apprehended literally or not. They are slain **with the sword of the One sitting upon the horse.**—As this sword **goeth forth out of His mouth**, we should, apprehending the words literally, have to assume that they were all stricken down by the word of Christ, like Ananias and Sapphira (Acts v.). But if this were the case, it would be necessary that they should all have passed through the spiritual experiences of those two. This, however, is by no means supposable; on the contrary, great masses of them are seduced, infatuated, pitiable people—portions of them having even been impressed into the service of the Beast and the False Prophet. We therefore assume that they are *slain* in that they are, in a social respect, rendered absolutely null by that new order of things in the Millennial Kingdom which is instituted by the word of Christ, and, furthermore, that all those properties of theirs that have become utterly valueless (their flesh) become subjects of a metamorphosis in order to their incorporation into the new order of things. According to Düsterdieck, the slaying by the sword of Christ is but significant of a perfectly toil-less conflict [on the part of Christ]. According to Ebrard, the sword slays them as the word of omnipotence.

De Wette remarks on the entire section: "This grand picture of the downfall of Antichristianity has been much weakened by the historical exegetes." Grotius finds here depicted the abolishment of idolatry by the Christian emperors of Rome, and refers ver. 18 to the fall of Julian in the Persian war. The interpretation of Wetstein is the most petty and insignificant: "*Vespasianus cum familia in Domitiano extincta, uti prius familia Cæsarum.*" Ulrich refers this judgment to the unnatural death of persecutors of the Christians. Herder: "The leaders of the insurrection, Simon, the son of Gorion, and John, met with the fate here depicted." For additional particulars see Düsterdieck, p. 545. From amongst other items we quote the following: "Corn. à-Lapide cites authors who relate concerning Luther that he killed himself, and that his funeral was attended not only by a multitude of ravens, but also by devils that came from Holland."

CHAP. XX. 1–5.

The Millennial Kingdom.

This section is by Düsterdieck assigned to the third judgment. Manifestly, however, the Millennial Kingdom is the result of the second judgment. Apart from this, Düsterdieck has a remark which is well worthy of notice—*viz.:* that the order of succession of the individual acts of judgment is the reverse of that in which the Antichristian forms appear. Sequence of the manifestations of Antichristianity: Satan, the Beast with the False Prophet, the Woman. Sequence of the judgments: The Woman, the Beast with the False Prophet, Satan himself. This antithetic parallelism must not, however, be reckoned amongst the organic relations of the Apocalypse, unless we behold the revelation of evil in the corruption of the Woman sketched in the features of the False Prophet; a view which does, indeed, pass muster, insomuch as the False Prophet in the form of a *lamb* seems to represent the Woman herself.

Ver. 1. **I ▬▬ ▬▬ angel descending out of,** *etc.*—Opposed to the spirit-form of Satan there must be a spirit-form from Heaven, just as Christ, the God-man, stood opposed to Antichrist, the Beast. This spirit-form of the Angel has been most diversely interpreted (as Christ; the Holy Ghost; the Apostolate; Constantine the Great; Calixtus II.; Innocent III.; see De Wette, p. 183). As the fallen angel or star of remorse ([*Verzweiflungsbusse*] chap. ix.) opens the pit of the abyss, so it is the Angel of consummate evangelic peace, the Angel of the developed bliss of justification, of blessedness in the Parousia of Christ, who, descending from Heaven, can cast Satan into the abyss, because he has destroyed all his points of appliance in humanity, with the exception of the one consisting of the suppressed rancor of mob-nature, which finally breaks out in Gog and Magog. We have here, therefore, an angelic form representative of the polemical victorious operation of the peace of Christ—a Michaelic form. This is evident from the further fact that he has **the key of the abyss.**—In accordance with chap. i. 18, Christ has the key of death and the realm of the dead [Hades]. We have already seen that the abyss forms the deepest border-region of the realm of the dead; it is contiguous to Gehenna, which latter is not ready for the reception of its guests until the time of the universal judgment. Consequently, Christ possesses the key to the abyss likewise, and hence it is evident that the Angel is significant of a fundamental form of the operation of Christ. **And a great chain.**—The concrete means of fettering Satan—and that, completely, and for a very long time. This is the power of the Spirit of grace and truth, making the genius of malice and falsehood powerless to injure for a whole æon. The key to the pit of the abyss (chap. ix. 1) must not be confounded with the key to the abyss simply. Nothing is more erroneous than, with Ewald, to identify the fallen star (chap. ix. 1sqq.) with this Angel. We translate **in his hand,** instead of *on* his hand (*ἐπί*), for it is not good German to say, *a chain on his hand.* As a

matter of course, the chain is not all contained within the closed hand.

Ver. 2. **And he laid hold on the dragon.** —Great and irresistible turn of sentiments in the spirit-world, concretely expressed—the more so since the consummate spiritual operations likewise become real dynamic operations. **That** [*or* **The**]**ancient serpent.**—See Syn. View. Comp. chap. xii. 9. **And bound him a thousand years.**—The thousand years are a symbolic number, denoting the æon of transition. The millennial binding of Satan is the preliminary condition of the Millennial Kingdom. Those who deny the demonic origin of sin, deriving sin exclusively from the sensual or material nature of man, here meet with a mighty contradiction to their theory. But, on the other hand, those who refer all evil to Satan cannot explain the loosing of the latter.

Ver. 3. **And cast him into the abyss.**— Chap. ix. 1; xi. 7; xvii. 8. A more general idea is presented in 2 Pet. ii. 4, where it is declared that the fallen angels have been cast down to Tartarus, in chains of darkness, held fast or preserved unto judgment. For, first, Tartarus is a more general term for the whole sub-terrestrial region; secondly, the term *ταρταροῦν* is indicative of a hurling away with a constant tendency toward Tartarus; thirdly, the bonds of darkness are those self-perplexings, self-enchainings of evil which impel toward Tartarus; fourthly, the judgment is in prospective here only as a certain future. The various statements concerning the abode of the Devil and bad spirits may readily, if pressed as to the letter of the Scripture, be involved in contradictions, as has been evidenced by Strauss, for instance (see the author's *Positive Dogmatik,* p. 572). But as we must needs distinguish between the dwelling-places and spheres of operation of spirits, so likewise is it necessary to distinguish between the different stages of their history. The abyss may indeed be regarded as the proper dwelling-place of Satan and the fallen angels, inasmuch as it, as the specific region of God-estranged rancor and grief, or despair, denotes the transition from the realm of the dead to hell, or from the sadness of death to damnation. The realm of the dead is only more tormented through the operations of demons than the human world (brooks [E. V.: floods] of Belial [Ps. xviii. 4]); but hell is prepared for the Devil and his angels as the region of final punitive suffering (Matt. xxv. 41). But as Satan is not at home with himself, neither does he stay at home (Jude 6); by nature he is excursive and rambling (Job ii. 2), given to appearing and disappearing, fond of roving about (hence Azazel)—*i. e.,* modes of existence and spheres of operation are to be distinguished especially here. In this relation, Scripture distinguishes Heaven as the pure domain of spirits (Job i. and ii.; Rev. xii.; Luke x. 18); earth, especially the atmospheric sphere, as the sphere of sympathetic and antipathetic world-moods,—and in reference to this sphere of operation, it distinguishes the forms of the *serpent,* or hypocritical craft (Matt. iv.; 2 Cor. xi. 14),

(*ἐπὶ τὴν χεῖρα αὐτοῦ*—*upon his hand*) is preserved. The idea seems to be that the chain was, not held in the hand, but looped *over* it.—E. R. C.]

---

* [In the *text* of the translation, the form of the Greek

and the roaring *lion* of terroristic might (1 Pet. v. 8; Rev. xiii.). The import of the judgment upon Antichrist is that Satan is cast entirely out of the sphere of earth for a thousand years, and shut up in his true home, the abyss. **Shut and sealed over him.**—Expressive of the inviolable Divine determination, manifest in the equally unshakable Divine operation. Likewise an antitype of the impotent sealing of Christ's grave on the part of hell and the world.—**After these he must be loosed.** —This also is a Divine decree—a decree, however, conditioned by the ethical design of causing the remnants of evil, of heathenism, in the sphere of Christ's Kingdom, to appear, and thereby destroying them.—**A little time.** *Little* from the stand-point of triumphant faith. See ch. xvii. 10.

Vers. 4, 5. *Fundamental Traits of the Millennial Kingdom.*

And I saw thrones.—According to Düsterdieck, the θρόνοι "do not come under consideration as kings' thrones (Eichhorn, Züllig), but only as judges' seats (Heinrich, Ewald, De Wette, Hengstenberg, etc.)," as is shown (he declares) by the prefigurement of Daniel vii. 9,* 22, and the κρίμα, expressly mentioned in our passage also. But what then is the force of the words: *They shall be priests of God and of Christ, and shall reign with Him* [ver. 6]? Christ Himself also is amongst the sitters on the thrones as their centre. Moreover, the κρίμα can be understood only in the Old Testament sense, as significant of a princely judicial rule, since the special judgment upon the Antichristian world has been previously executed. It is highly characteristic that the thrones constitute the foreground of the picture. They are significant of the beginning of the Church Triumphant in this world—the visible appearance of the Kingdom of God. Distinct as is the presentment of the thrones themselves, of their occupants it is indefinitely said: **and they sat down [seated themselves] upon them.** Who are meant by *they*? According to Beza, Eichhorn, Ebrard, *et al.*, the martyrs mentioned further on; this view is opposed by De Wette and Düsterdieck. The context also is against it. First, John saw the thrones and those who seated themselves upon them, and then the beheaded ones who revived and reigned with Christ. We must not forget, however, that Christ has not come alone from Heaven, but that He was accompanied by a chosen army (ch. xix. 14). Without doubt, the occupants of the thrones are those who form the peculiar escort of the Lamb (ch. xiv. 4); who even in this world, as sealed ones, constituted the kernel of the Church of God (ch. vii.), the proper centre of which is formed by God's men of revelation [*i. e.* God's revealers], particularly the Apostles (ch. xxi. 14). In considering their position toward Christ, however, something more than mere martyr faithfulness or even mere historic dignity as Prophets or Apostles comes in view—namely, the endowment and destination of the Father, the special election lying at the base of the special glory.

* [The E. V. has here (Dan. vii. 9) "till the thrones were cast down;" the Germ. has "bis dass Stühle gesetzt wurden,"—until seats (or thrones) were set,—Tr.]

These mysterious co-regents of Christ (comp. also Matt. v. 9) have been very variously interpreted (God and Christ; the Angels; the Apostles; the Martyrs; the saints, Dan. vii. 22; the twenty-four Elders [De Wette and Düsterdieck]; Hengstenberg, "the twelve Apostles and the twelve Patriarchs"). Here, however, we have no longer to do with forms that are partially typical [the Elders]; we will simply say: those who in a special sense have been inwardly endowed as joint-heirs with Christ, seated themselves upon the thrones.

And judgment was given unto them.— This κρίμα cannot possibly refer to vers. 1–3 and ch. xix. 20, 21, as Ebrard maintains, since in those passages the sentence of judgment was decided by war, and the execution of judgment was a very brief process. We should hardly expect that Antichrist or Satan himself would have to be sentenced through a trial by jury.

The judgment may be regarded primarily as a two-fold decision—a decision concerning those who are still living (who were not in the Antichristian army), as to whether their lives shall be preserved throughout the thousand years; and a decision concerning those who were beheaded, as to how far they are worthy of being called to the first resurrection. Nevertheless, the antithesis of life and death is now, in a high degree, dynamically, psychically and ethically modified (see Is. lxv. 20), *i. e.* dying and reviving are effects which proceed from within. In general, however, the entire æon is to be conceived of as an æon of separations and eliminations in an ethical and a cosmical sense, separations and eliminations such as are necessary to make manifest and to complete the ideal regulations of life. Of judgments of damnation between the judgment upon Antichrist and the judgment upon Satan, there can be no question; the reference can be only to a critical government and management, preparatory to the final consummation. The whole æon is a crisis which occasions the visible appearance of the Heaven on earth; the whole æon is the great Last Day. We may even conceive of the mutiny which finally breaks out as a result of these separations, for a sort of protest on the part of the wicked was hinted at by Christ in His Eschatological Discourse (Matt. xxv. 44), and the most essential element of the curse in hell is the continuance of revolt, the gnashing of teeth. To the degree in which this can decrease, torment can approach indifference. Opinions concerning this judgment are marvellously at variance. According to Augustine, the reference is to a judgment upon the old earth: *Sedes Præpositorum et ipsi Præpositi intelligendi sunt, per quos ecclesia gubernatur.* According to Hoë, on the other hand, the judgment relates to Heaven itself, as a theological disclosure as to the fate of the souls of the martyrs and others in Heaven, during the thousand years. According to Piscat., De Wette, *et al.*, "the probable idea is that the judgment now held has to decide as to who are worthy to have part in the first resurrection and the Millennial Kingdom."

And (I saw) the souls of them, etc.—Two main points modify the entire picture: *a.* The thrones; *b.* The souls of the martyrs. As these were cut off from the most lively life by a violent death, they abode nearer to life than other dead persons; their more intimate communion with Christ produced the resurrection principle within them; and ■■ men upon whom the ban of the world pre-eminently fell, they must be pre-eminently honored in the Kingdom of God [*als die vorzugsweise Geächteten müssen sie die vorzugsweise Geachteten des Reiches Gottes sein*]. As beheaded, they also accompany Christ from the other world, and though it cannot be said that their category precisely coincides with that of the occupants of the thrones, neither can it be affirmed that they may not be amongst those enthroned ones. The Seer distinguishes three categories of the participants in the first resurrection, or those "that are Christ's in His Parousia" (1 Cor. xv. 23). First, the sitters on the thrones; secondly, the martyrs generally, who were beheaded for Christ's sake; thirdly, all the faithful of the last time, who have worshipped neither the Beast nor his image, nor have assumed his mark. These are the *macrobii* of the last time, who sleep not, but are changed (1 Cor. xv. 51, 52; 2 Cor. v. 4, 5; 1 Thess. iv. 17). Over and above these, as a fourth category, are the remnants of the old humanity that have not belonged to the Antichristian army; the inhabitants of the domain of Gog and Magog, who find themselves only in the periphery of the renewing crisis. It was perhaps on account of the third class that the Seer employed the term ἔζησαν. But even if this is, with reason, made emphatic: *they revived—lived again* (=ἀνέζησαν, De Wette), it does not prove that we should regard the last [third] class (consisting of those who are alive at the time of Christ's appearing), with Düsterd., *et al.*, as having likewise died in the mean time. The expression, [ver. 5] **but the rest of the dead,** finds its antithesis in the martyrs; and the transformation, as well as the awakening, shall lead to the first resurrection.

Ver. 5. The rest of the dead, *etc.*—That is, those not pre-eminently animated by the principle of the life of Christ, not led toward the first resurrection (Rom. viii. 17 sqq.; Eph. i. 19; Phil. iii. 11), and therefore a whole æon deeper under the power of death.

This is the first resurrection.—With these words the Seer constitutes that entire resurrection-process which begins with the Parousia of Christ, a distinct dogmatical conception. We have already discussed the gloriousness and naturalness of this conception. The manifold evasions of this idea, this Christian hope, seem like a general horror—not, however, a horror *vacui*, but a horror *vitæ et spiritus*.

In regard to the **thousand years**, the number, ■■ has already been observed, is symbolical, like all other apocalyptic numbers; it denotes an æon, and is specifically the transition-æon between this present world and the world to come. "The Jews indicate the duration of the Messianic Kingdom by different numbers: according to R. Elieser, however, the days of the Messiah amount to a thousand years; this opinion is based upon the statement, Is. lxiii. 4, 'the day of vengeance was in my mind' [E. V. is in mine heart], and the further declaration, Ps. xc. 4, 'a thousand years in Thy sight are ■■

yesterday,' *etc.* The weightier reason of the *Ep. Barnab. c.* xv. might be added to this, that as God created the world in six days and rested on the seventh day, so in six thousand years all things would be consummated and in the last chiliad a great world-Sabbath would be celebrated." (De Wette.)

The slavish dread of Chiliasm felt by the Old Catholic Church and the mediæval Theology, amounting to an avoidance of the misunderstood Apocalypse itself and a dread of the historical sense of its text, whilst the Old Catholic Church and mediæval Theology were themselves sunk deep in *material* Chiliasm, has found expression in the most diverse interpretations, from Augustine down to Hengstenberg; there is a maximum of excuse for the beginning of the series, but scarcely a minimum for the end of it. On the course of the exegeses see pp. 63 sqq. Likewise Düsterdieck, pp. 554 sqq. In this exegetical party, the elder Lutheran Theology continues most involved in the toils of mediæval tradition. The slavish Theology of the letter has found a support in the view of John Gerhard in particular (Düsterd., p. 556). The Apocalypse, Gerhard declares, is a deutero-canonical book—the Kingdom of Christ will never on earth, not even at the end of the days, be one of external sovereignty (a sentiment dictated, doubtless, by a misunderstanding of Article XVII. of the Augsburg Confession)—all the dead are to arise in *one* day—there is to be but *one* general resurrection of the dead at the Parousia of the Lord. Accordingly, it is further stated, the beginning of the Millennial Kingdom probably falls in the time of Constantine—Gog and Magog are to be regarded as significant of the Turks. A partiality for this prejudiced tradition can in general be regarded only as the sad fruit of partyism. In regard to the view of Hengstenberg in particular, we refer primarily to the notices of Apocalyptic Literature, pp. 69 sq., 71.* The starting point of Hengstenberg's view is by Rinck (*Die Zeichen der letzten Zeit*, p. 333) declared to be the assumption that the Beast can be understood only as the Pagan, not as the Christian, State. This assumption is a proof that Hengstenberg had no just conception of the idea of Antichristianity—which cannot possibly be a product of pure heathenism†—and no idea of the fall of an external State or Church. And yet according to the same commentator, Satan himself is at last to break forth—or rather has broken forth—*immediately*, (in a worse mode, therefore, than in the form of the Beast) in the midst of Christendom.

<hr>

* On Kraussold (*Das tausendjährige Reich*) see Düsterdieck, p. 558. Luthardt, in his work entitled, *Die Offenb. Joh.*, recognizes the futurity of the Millennial Kingdom. Grau, on the other hand, in his lecture on the Contents and Import of the Revelation of John (in *Zur Einführung in das Schriftthum N. T.*), deals in generalities previous to ch. xx.

† Hengstenberg, it is manifest, has entirely lost the idea of Antichristianity by his Eschatology. If Antichristianity is summed up in the Beast, it is also abolished in company with the Beast. Consequently, there can no longer be any Antichristianity. And therefore, according to Hengstenberg, the final outbreak of Satan results in a new heathenism in the original sense of the term. But the world can not fall back into pure heathenism at the end of the days; Antichristianity can be formed only from elements of decomposed Christianity—Christianity that is converted into mighty lies (2 Thess. ii.).

Many arguments employed by Hengstenberg in his article entitled, "The so-called Millennial Kingdom," to be found in the second volume of his commentary, have a very *ad hominem* sound ; for instance, the argument from the inscription on the dome of the royal castle. We are justified in assuming that Hengstenberg was much concerned for the credit of Christian Rome than for the credit of the Christian State (which appears not merely in German, but also in French, Romance, and Slavonic forms), in declaring that the Woman also should be apprehended exclusively as Pagan Rome. Furthermore, the text of the Apocalypse constantly suffers violence at the hands of Hengstenberg. The chaining of Satan (ch. xx. 1–3) ill admits of an assignment to the Middle Ages—hence he explains : "Satan is able to ensnare individual souls during this time, but not the nations as a whole." As if the individual souls of many princes and popes had not had a highly decisive influence in the working of their political and hierarchical systems—Machiavellism, the Inquisition, Dragonnades and the like. Again, the first resurrection, according to the same expositor, can not be apprehended as a bodily resurrection ; it merely denotes the translation of the souls spoken of into that glorious intermediate condition in the other world, where they lived and reigned with Christ. Ἔζησαν, he affirms, is not equivalent to ἀνέζησαν. But, manifestly, this *coming to life* is distinct from the blessed *living-on* in the other world (chs. vii. and xiv.), and prominence is given to it as antithetic to the condition of the dead who did not become alive again during the thousand years. Hengstenberg arrived at a much wished-for result by dating the thousand years from Charlemagne ; the loosing of Satan might thus be assigned to the time of the French Revolution and the movements connected therewith (see Hengst. ii., pp. 367 and 375 sqq. [Ger.]). A series of kindred and opposite constructions of the Millennial Kingdom see noted in De Wette, p. 189 ; Düsterd., p. 555.

According to Düsterdieck (pp. 554 sqq.), the unbiased determination of the exegetical result of the text, and the theological estimate of it, based upon the analogy of Scripture, are two different things. The Millennial Kingdom falls, according to him also, in the time immediately preceding the universal judgment—but he seems to be unable to reconcile the developed Apocalyptic Eschatology with the less developed Eschatology of the other Scriptures of the New Testament. If, however, the one day of the resurrection be regarded as a literal day, rather than as the symbolical term for a period ; if one general resurrection of all the dead, in one day, as an immediate wonder of omnipotence, be regarded as more credible than the profound, organically modified idea of the gradational and hence double resurrection ; and if a sudden annihilation of all evil *at once* be considered more probable than the abolition of it by a succession of judgments ;—the same method of interpretation should, if consistency be at all regarded, be employed in the case of the other portions of Holy Writ, though this would involve a reduction of the living Scripture either to the orthodoxy of the Seventeenth, or the rationalism of the Eighteenth Century—or a taking up with a compound of positive elements and ideal descriptions.

[NOTE ON THE FIRST RESURRECTION.]

By the American Editor.

[The writer believes that he cannot better begin this note than by the presentation of the views of two distinguished writers on the subject,—the one advocating the doctrine of a *literal* resurrection, the other defending the so-called *spiritual* view.

ALFORD, on xx. 4, 5, thus comments:

"It will have been long ago anticipated by the readers of this Commentary, that I cannot consent to distort words from their plain sense and chronological place in the prophecy, on account of any considerations of difficulty, or any risk of abuses which the doctrine of the Millennium may bring with it. Those who lived next to the Apostles, and the whole Church for 300 years, understood them in the plain literal sense; and it is a strange sight in these days to see expositors who are amongst the first in reverence of antiquity, complacently casting aside the most cogent instance of consensus which primitive antiquity presents. As regards the text itself, no legitimate treatment of it will extort what is known as the spiritual interpretation now in fashion. If in a passage where *two resurrections* are mentioned, where certain ψυχαί ἔζησαν at the first, and the rest of the νεκροί ἔζησαν only at the end of a specified period after that first,—if in such a passage the *first resurrection* may be understood to mean spiritual rising with Christ, while the *second* means *literal* rising from the grave ; then there is an end of all significance in language, and Scripture is wiped out as a definite testimony to anything. If the first resurrection is spiritual then so is the second, which I suppose none will be hardy enough to maintain;[*] but if the second is literal, then so is the first, which in common with the whole primitive Church and many of the best modern expositors, I do maintain, and receive as an article of faith and hope."

BROWN, whose work on the Second Advent is, confessedly, one of the ablest that has ever been published on his side of the question, devotes an entire chapter to the discussion of the *Millennial Resurrection*. It is of course impossible to reproduce the entire argument. The following,

---

[*] [Whitby, Faber and Brown, all distinguish between the *second* resurrection implied, ver. 5, in the words *the rest of the dead*, etc., and the *general* resurrection brought to view in vers. 12, 13. Whilst they admit that this general resurrection is literal, they contend that both the *first* and *second* *millennial* resurrections are spiritual,—the former signifying a resuscitation of the martyr spirit at the beginning of the thousand years; the latter, the re-vivification of the spirit of evil in the hosts of Gog and Magog.

Barnes agrees with these commentators save in the last particular. He understands, however, by the *rest of the dead* the *ordinarily pious*. He writes: "*But the rest of the dead.* In contradistinction from the beheaded martyrs, and from those who had kept themselves pure in the times of great temptation. The phrase 'rest of the dead' here would most naturally refer to the *same general class* which was before mentioned—the pious dead. The meaning is, that the martyrs would be honored *as if* they were raised up and the others not; that is, that special respect would be shown to their principles, their memory, and their character. In other words, *special* honor would be shown *to a spirit of eminent piety* during that period, above the *common* and *ordinary* piety which has been manifested in the church. The 'rest of the dead'—the pious dead—would indeed be raised up and rewarded, but they would occupy comparatively humble places, *as if* they did not partake in the exalted triumphs when the world should be subdued to the Saviour. Their places in honor, in rank, and in reward, would be *beneath* that of those who in fiery times had maintained unshaken fidelity to the cause of truth. ¶ *Lived* not. On the word *lived*, see Notes on ver. 4. That is, they lived not during that period in the peculiar sense in which it is said (ver. 4,) that the eminent saints and martyrs lived. They did not come into remembrance ; their principles were not what then characterized the church ; they did not see, as the martyrs did, *their* principles and mode of life in the ascendency, and consequently they had not the augmented happiness and honor which the more eminent saints and martyrs had."—E. R. C.]

however, is presented as a perfectly fair synopsis thereof:

"If the question then be, *Was this celebrated passage* (Rev. xx. 4–6) designed to announce A LITERAL AND GENERAL RESURRECTION OF THE SAINTS? The following appear to me to be strong

PRESUMPTIONS AGAINST IT.

1. It is very strange that the resurrection of the righteous a thousand years before the wicked, if it be a revealed truth, should be directly and explicitly announced in *one* passage only.

2. If this was to be the chosen place for announcing such a prior resurrection, it is surely reasonable to expect that *a clear and unambiguous revelation of it would be made.* (Such a revelation he denies was made in the passage.)

3. If a resurrection of *the righteous in general*—as distinguished from the wicked—be the true sense of this prophecy, the description is very unlike the thing to be described. It is not in the least like any other description of that event in the New Testament. Every other description of the resurrection and glory of the saints as such is *catholic* in its character, while this is *limited.*

NINE INTERNAL EVIDENCES THAT THE MILLENNIAL RESURRECTION IS NOT LITERAL BUT FIGURATIVE.*

1. If the first resurrection mean rising from the grave in *immortal* and *glorified bodies* we do not need the assurance that *on such the second death hath no power* (v. 6), or in other words, that *they shall not perish everlasting'y.* Can it be believed that the Holy Spirit means nothing more than such a truism? But suppose that the first resurrection signifies a glorious condition of mortal men, and the promise becomes intelligible.

2. There are but two alternatives in the prophecy—either to 'have part in the first resurrection,' or to be under the 'power of the second death.' Into which of these classes are we to put the myriads of men who are to people the earth, in flesh and blood during the millennium?

3. The express mention of *how long* this 'life and reign with Christ' will last, viz.: *a thousand years,* if meant to inform us what a long period of *earthly prosperity* the Church is yet destined to enjoy, is intelligible and cheering. But to say that the *risen and glorified* Church is to live and reign with Christ for a period of *a thousand years,* is totally unlike the language of Scripture in every other place.

4. By making the party that 'live and reign with Christ a thousand years' to be the entire Church of God risen from their graves, we are forced to do violence to the whole subsequent context. Thus—(1) *The rest of the dead* must be expected to live again in the same bodily sense '*when* the thousand years are finished.' But we read of no bodily resurrection at all on the expiring of this period. Satan shall then be loosed out of prison, and when we consider the work he has to do, the *little season* of his deceiving the nations can hardly be overstretched by extending it to a century or so. This first millennial period is to be filled up with something else than bodily resurrections. It will indeed be employed in the *raising of a wicked party.* We read of no *bodily* resurrection until after its expiration: (2) None but the *wicked* would remain to be judged in the last judgment, which is inconsistent with the implication of the opening of the Book of Life (v. 12).

5. (This argument is given in the language of Gipps, substantially as follows): The opening of the Book of Life (v. 12) signifies the *manifestation* of those who are written in it. It is inconceivable that this manifestation can take place one moment before what is called the opening of the Book of Life. But the manifestation of the Sons of God will take place at their (bodily) resurrection, Rom. viii. 19, 23. Their bodily resurrection, therefore, will not take place until the general resurrection of v. 12.

6. (Also in the language of Gipps): The omission of any declaration as to the sea, *death* and the *grave, giving up the dead* at the first resurrection, and the making such a declaration respecting 'the dead' in ver. 13, convinces me that 'the first resurrection' is *not* that of the Saints, and also that the dead' in vers. 12, 13, *include all mankind,* both the saints and the ungodly. In every other part of the Word of God the information given concerning the resurrection of the saints is not only much more frequent, but also much more explicit, than concerning the resurrection of the ungodly. I feel convinced, therefore, that in this portion of the Scripture, if it were intended to foretell a resurrection of the saints distinct from that of the ungodly, much more explicit information would be given concerning the *former* than concerning the latter.

7. The clause 'This is the first resurrection' (ver. 5), which is thought to prove it literal, seems to me, if it prove anything, to prove the reverse. It is reasonable—say the premillennialists—to suppose that if the second or last resurrection be literal, the first will be so also—differing from the second only *in time.* Unfortunately for this way of reasoning, what is said in the verse immediately following contradicts it: 'Blessed and holy is he that hath part in the first resurrection; on such the *second death* hath no power ' (ver. 6). Here 'the *first* resurrection ' and 'the *second death* ' are intentionally brought together and contrasted. Is the *first* death, then, of the same nature with the *second?* Does *one* merely precede the other? Now; the first death is that of the body, the second that of both *body and soul;* the first death is common to the righteous and the wicked, the second is the everlasting portion of the wicked and of them alone. To *suffer* the first death for *Christ* is made the ground (not, of course, the meritorious ground) *of exemption* from the power of the second death (see ch ii. 10, 11). Now as exemption from the power of the second death is here made to rest upon a certain *character,* namely, fidelity to Christ even to death, and in our millennial chapter exemption from the power of the second death is made to rest upon *participation in the first resurrection,* is it not reasonable to conclude that this 'first resurrection' is meant to signify a *certain character* in the present life, and not the possession of *bodily resurrection and glory?* . . . To my mind the view of the first resurrection is put beyond doubt by the following words: 'Blessed and *holy* is he that hath part in the first resurrection.' I cannot see what important information is conveyed by these words if 'the first resurrection' mean a restoration to bodily life. To tell us that saints risen from the dead, and reigning in glorified bodies with Christ, are *holy,* seems to me to be very unlike the language of Scripture everywhere else, and very superfluous.

8. It is a fatal objection to the literal sense of this prophecy, as announcing the bodily resurrection of all dead, and the change of all living saints, that it is exclusively a *martyr-scene*—the prophet beholding simply a resurrection of *the slain,* whereas this very circumstance eminently favors the *figurative* sense. The literal sense is utterly inadequate to express the resurrection of the whole Church of God bodily from the grave; the figurative sense is in consonance with the figurative language of Scripture (comp. Rev. xi. 11; Ezek. xxxvii. 12-14; Hos. vi. 2; Isa. xxvi. 19, 14), with that of the best writers in every language and age, and expresses a conception worthy of the Spirit of God to dictate.

9. The literal sense offers no consistent explanation of the 'judgment that was given unto' the slain martyrs. This *judgment* was clearly that referred to in ch. vi. 9-11.* If this be correct, of course *the slain* and *those who slew them,* must be taken in the same sense. If the judgment is to be given to the martyrs *personally* at the millennium, their blood must also be *personally avenged* on them that dwell on the earth. If the *martyrs* are to rise bodily from their graves in order that judgment may be personally given to them, then their persecutors must be raised that vengeance may be rendered to them."

The writer adopts the view of this celebrated passage that is advocated by Alford—the view that has been held in the Church from the earliest ages. It seems to be undeniable that this is the view that results from the normal interpretation of the passage,—a view that should not be set aside but for most cogent reasons. Whilst it is admitted that there is much apparent force in many of the considerations urged by Brown, it is submitted that they are not of sufficient force to overthrow the normal interpretation.

In continuance it should be remarked that the normal interpretation is in line with, and gives special and beautiful significance to, many otherwise inexplicable declarations in the word of God. An anonymous writer in a work entitled CREATION AND REDEMPTION (Edinburgh: Thomas Laurie. 1866. Second Ed.) thus comments:

"It is incumbent on me here to say a few words on the

---

* [Brown thus disposes of a common objection (first urged by Whitby) to the literal view: "It is frequently urged that because '*souls*' (ψυχαί) were seen in this vision, and no mention is made of *bodies* it cannot be a bodily resurrection that is meant. But this is to mistake what the Apostle saw in the vision. He did not see a *resurrection of souls.* He saw 'the souls of them that were slain;' that is, he had a vision of the martyrs themselves in the state of the dead—*after* they were slain, and *just before* their resurrection. Then he saw them rise: 'They lived '—not their souls, but themselves."—E. R. C.]

23

---

* [Is it not rather probable that κρίμα was used in the sense in which it was employed, Matt. vii. 2; John ix. 39; Rom. ii. 2, 3; and that the sentence means, that to the saints, as kings, was given the authority to judge?—E. R. C.]

subject of the First Resurrection, for there is a general impression that the belief in it rests solely upon this passage, (Rev. xx. 6). But this is a great mistake. The truth of a resurrection of some at a different time from that of the general resurrection, is evident from Scripture, independent of this passage in the Apocalypse. Omitting the passages from the Old Testament Scriptures, sustained by the promises of which the Old Testament worthies, as St. Paul says, suffered and served God in the hope of obtaining *a better resurrection*' (Heb. xi. 35), we will state as briefly as may be the conclusion to which we are led by the words of the Lord and His Apostles.

Our Lord makes a distinction between the resurrection which some shall be counted worthy to attain to, and some not, Luke xx. 3, 5. St. Paul says there is a resurrection 'out from among the dead' (ἐξανάστασις) to attain which he strove with all his might as the prize to be gained, Phil. iii. 11. He also expressly tells us, that while as in Adam all die, so in Christ shall all be made alive; yet it shall not be all at once, but 'every man in his own order; Christ the first fruits; afterwards *they that are Christ's at His coming*.' It is particularly to be remarked, that wherever the resurrection of Christ, or of His people, is spoken of in Scripture, it is a 'resurrection *from* the dead;' and wherever the general resurrection is spoken of, it is the 'resurrection *of the dead*.' This distinction, though preserved in many instances in the English translation, is too frequently omitted; but in the Greek the one is always coupled with the preposition ἐκ, *out of*, and the other is without it; and in the Vulgate it is rendered by *à mortuis* or *ex mortuis*, as distinct from *resurrectio mortuorum.* In Rom. viii. 11, 'The Spirit of Him that raised up Jesus from the dead,' it is ἐκ νεκρῶν, *à mortuis.* So in Rom. x. 7; Eph. i. 20; Heb. xiii. 20; 1 Pet. i. 3, 21. So Lazarus

was raised ἐκ νεκρῶν, John xii. 1, 9. Our Lord, in His reply to the Sadducees, made the distinction between the general resurrection of the dead, and the resurrection which some should be accounted worthy to attain to. The children of this age (αἰῶνος) marry, but they who shall be accounted worthy to attain that αἰῶν, and the resurrection from the dead (ἀναστάσεως τῆς ἐκ νεκρῶν), shall not marry (Luke xx. 34, 35). St. Paul, when he spoke of a resurrection to which he strove to attain (Phil. iii. 8, 11), and to which he was with all his might pressing forwards, as the high prize to gain which he was agonizing, and for which he counted all else loss, as if one preposition was not enough to indicate his meaning, uses it doubled, εἰς τὴν ἐξανάστασιν τὴν ἐκ νεκρῶν. '*Si quomodo occurram ad resurrectionem quæ est ex mortuis*.' If St. Paul had been looking only to the general resurrection, he need not have given himself any trouble, or made any sacrifice to attain to that; for to it, all, even Judas and Nero, must come; but to attain to the First Resurrection he had need to press forward for the prize of that calling. And thus in his argument for the resurrection in 1 Cor. xv. (vers. 12, 21), when he speaks of the resurrection generally, he so speaks of the resurrection *of the dead*, (ἀνάστασις νεκρῶν); but when he speaks of our Lord's resurrection, it is ἐκ νεκρῶν, *from the dead*. And he marks the time when Christ's people shall be raised from the dead, namely, 'at Christ's coming,' 'every man in his own order;' 1st, Christ; 2d, Christ's people; 3d, all the remainder, at a more other period, which he terms 'the end,' when the last enemy, death, is to be destroyed, put an end to (ve s. 24-26). And it follows as a matter of course, that if those who are Christ's are to be raised from the dead at His coming, and if He comes previous to the destruction of Antichrist, and to the millennium, this first resurrection must be at least a thousand years before the general resurrection."—E. R. C.]

III. THIRD OR GENERAL END-JUDGMENT.   JUDGMENT UPON SATAN AND ALL HIS COMPANY.   THE SECOND DEATH.

CHAPTER XX. 6–10.

A.—HEAVENLY PROGNOSIS OF THE LAST GENERAL JUDGMENT.

CHAP. XX. 6–8.

6   Blessed and holy *is* he that hath part in the first resurrection: on [over] such the second death hath no power, but they shall be priests of God and of Christ,
7 and [*ins.* they] shall reign with him a [the]' thousand years. And when the thou-
8 sand years are expired [finished], Satan shall be loosed out of his prison, and shall go out to deceive [seduce *or* mislead (πλανῆσαι)] the nations which are in the four quarters [corners] of the earth, Gog and Magog, to gather them together to [the]² battle [war]: the number of whom *is* as the sand of the sea.

TEXTUAL AND GRAMMATICAL.

¹ Ver. 6. [Tisch. (8th Ed.) inserts the article in accordance with ℵ. B*.; Alf. brackets it; Lach. and Tisch. (1859) omit with A.—E. R. C.]

² Ver. 8. Τὸν πόλ., according to Codd. A. B*., *et al.*

EXEGETICAL AND CRITICAL.

SYNOPTICAL VIEW.

The prophecies relative to the three judgments here taper, so to speak, to a point. The most detailed of these prophecies was that which concerned the Harlot; the prophecy concerning the Beast was couched in less ample terms; and this last prophecy of judgment is concentrated in a very little sketch, so that we can scarce perceive the articulations which separate one cycle from another, and divide the heavenly prognosis from the earth-picture. Nevertheless, the breaks in question are still to be found. The words of ver. 6 do indeed glance back to the thousand years; *but this is, manifestly, in order to the introduction of the last judgment, which brings with it the second death.* Even within this diminutive judgment-picture, the antithesis is unmistakable. Vers. 7 and 8 speak of the loosing of Satan and the seduction of Gog and Magog in the future tense. But with ver. 9 the Seer makes a historic presentation, in the prophetic preterite, of the fact which he has before predicted. The plan of the whole Book is, therefore, retained in this case also. The perspective brevity of this section testifies unmistakably to the canonical truth and chasteness of the description. For an apocalyptic *fiction*, the elaboration of this sombre picture of the last revolt of the heathen, the fiery judgment upon Satan, and the second death in the lake of fire, would have possessed the greatest charms. Our Prophet, however, gives only the few features that he has seen—gives them *as* he has seen them, darkly, in well-nigh figureless language. It cannot be said, however, that he is wearied, for soon after follows the picture of the perfected City of God, magnificently developed and vividly distinct.

With a beatitude relative to the sharers in the first resurrection, the perspective of the last judgment is opened. The participants in this resurrection are called *blessed*, as those whose lot is absolutely decided, who have passed their judgment and come forth from it as *holy ones*, forever consecrate to God. This retrospect is occasioned by the prospect of the *second death* as the doom of the third and last judgment. *Over such the second death hath no authority.* The second death (*δεύτερος θάνατος*) is damnation in the pool of fire, according to ver. 14 and ch. xxi. 8: not gradual dissolution and annihilation (Rothe). The term *eternal death* [Düsterdieck] is less explanatory of this mysterious judgment than the figurative expression, *the pool of fire.* It is a fellowship with all those who are in that condition of absolute irritation which is at the same time absolute stagnation, in endless ethical self-consumption and annihilation as a punishment for the persevering negation of God and the personal Kingdom of love. The opposite of this death-peril consists in the fact that the sharers in the first resurrection will be *priests of God and of Christ.* This priesthood, as absolute submission to God in blessedness in Him, stands contrasted with the unblest madness of the pool of fire; and, furthermore, it is perfect submission in reference to the economy of the Father as well as to the economy of redemption. They offer the whole creation, they offer the whole Church, with all the good things of them both, evermore to God and to Christ; and this is the condition whereby an eternal and ever-better possession of these good things is secured—a participation in the dominion of the Lord. Even in the Millennial Kingdom they *shall reign with Christ.*

Not in the vision form, but in prophetic discourse the Seer now announces the loosing of Satan after the thousand years. He *shall be loosed out of his prison*—not break out of it. In accordance with the determination of God, Satan, and with him all evil, must be thoroughly and completely judged. Hitherto judgment has been predominantly accomplished through instrumentalities. The historic judgment upon the Harlot was executed by the Beast, *i. e.*, the preliminary hypocritical instance of evil has been judged by the perfect consistency of evil, in accordance with a very general historic law:—half-way ness succumbs to consistency. Antichristian evil, as a spiritual power, has been judged by the spiritual effect of the personal appearance of Christ, by the terror of His *δόξα* and by the sword out of His mouth. In the end, however, Satan employs the means of resistance still afforded him by his creaturely strength, reviving in a convulsive struggle, in rebellion against God; and with the brutal opposition of consummate Satanity, corresponds the savage sense of strength of the *heathen* [*nations*] *in the corners of the earth,* who have withdrawn

themselves from the sanctifying process of the eschatological economy (the new *οἰκουμένη*), aye, have hardened themselves under it, and have become, especially in their resentment against that heavenly order of things which oversways them, kindred in mind to Satan. It has been asked: whence come these countless heathen, since, according to ch. xix. 21, Christ has slain the Antichristian host? But apart from the fact that He slew them with the breath of His mouth, *i. e.*, morally annihilated them, which might not prevent a continuance of physical vegetation on their part, the terms employed, *the heathen* [nations] *in the four corners of the earth, Gog and Magog,* afford sufficient explanation. Ezekiel prophesied that the people of God should, long after the more familiar anti-theocratic assaults, have to sustain an attack from the circle of the remotest barbaric Orient (Ezek. xxxviii. and xxxix.). This eagle-glance at the future, whose significance trains of Huns, Mongols, Tartars and Turks have already confirmed, could not be missing from our Apocalypse. The present prophecy is heralded in ch. xvi. 12. But whilst Ezekiel, in prophesying of Gog in the land of Magog, referred to distinct Asiatic peoples (see Düst., p. 552), John employs the terms as a universal symbol, in designation of all the barbarous peoples in the corners of the earth—so, however, that the distant Orient plays the principal part. The idea of these last heathen is precisely analogous to the churchly idea. In the earlier days of Christianity, the inhabitants of the villages (*pagani*) or of the heaths, far remote from the great centres of civilization, formed the remnants of the old world—remnants which were both unconverted and difficult of conversion. Thus the entire old world will leave its remnants in a moral, symbolical heathenism, which will surround the Kingdom of Christ not merely as a terrestrial, but also as a spiritual boundary. But the idea that Evil shall at last break out and incur judgment in such a final heathenish mutiny, in a brutal revolt, the stupidity of which is veiled by the innumerable force of the hosts therein concerned, is characteristic of the great Prophet, who sees far above and beyond the learning of the schools.

EXPLANATIONS IN DETAIL.

Ch. xx. 6. Blessed and holy is he, *etc.*— As in the process of the formation of Christian character, the beatitudes of the righteousness of faith condition sanctification or the becoming holy, so in the condition of consummation, blessedness is still more decidedly the eternal source of the renewal of holiness. It is a remarkable fact that even Spinoza had a dim idea of this, that blessedness is itself a virtue and a condition of virtue. Even civic contentment has, in a limited degree, an ennobling influence. By holiness, eternal and complete consecratedness to God is here expressed.— **Over such the second death.** *etc.*—They are beyond temptation, and cannot relapse into sin, and hence cannot fall under the fearful dominion of the second death.— The second death is, ver. 14, declared to be the judgment in the pool of fire: eternal agitation amidst the eternal frustration of plots and attempts: the specific demonic and Satanic suffering. "A dying and an inability to die," ancient expositors were wont to say. The fact is here expressed that the Millennial Kingdom forms only a heavenly circle of culture of the new world within the old earth—in other words, that the heathen [nations], from whom the last rebellion proceeds, form an antithesis to God's people of the first resurrection. The remains of the old humanity will occupy very much the same relation to the new humanity which the remains of the pre-Adamite creation occupy to the human world; although a general recognition of Christ, and, to this extent, the beginning of Christianity amongst all these peoples, is induced by Christ's victory over Antichrist (ch. xix.). The general conversion of the heathen even precedes the Parousia of Christ. **They shall be priests of God and of Christ.**—Because they shall be priests, they shall also be co-regents with Christ, and being *both* throughout the thousand years, they appear unconditionally elevated above the perils of the last Satanic assault.

Ver. 7. **And when the thousand years are finished.**—When the destination of the thousand years is fulfilled (ὅταν τελεσθῇ). **Satan shall be loosed.**—The obedience of the heathen [nations], their Christianity, their faithfulness, must finally undergo a fiery test, after they have long enough been spectators of the Heaven on earth, and enjoyed, in nature and grace, the blessings of the Parousia of Christ. For a similar purpose Satan was permitted to exercise his arts in the first Paradise, to tempt Job, Christ Himself, and His Apostles. Such is the Divine method for the testing and perfecting of the elect, the purification and sifting of the churches, the unveiling of the wicked in order to their judgment, and the inducement of the self-judgment of Satan, resulting in his dynamical destruction. Under this Divine economy, evil *in abstracto* is permitted fully to develop, as is also evil *in concreto*, in wicked individuals, in the fellowship of the wicked, in the father of liars.

Ver. 8. **And shall go out to seduce [or mislead] the nations [Lange: heathen].**— "The difficulty occasioned by the statement that heathen peoples are here once more represented as going up to battle against the saints, after the destruction (ch. xix. 21) of *all* peoples and kings that worshipped the Beast" (Düsterd.), is very simply solved by a distinction between the Antichristian host and the remaining world of peoples, particularly those under the Eastern kings—irrespective of the fact that it is doubtful whether the killing of the *rest* (ch. xix. 21) should be taken literally. Vitringa calls attention to the fact "that the ἔθνη, Gog and Magog, dwell in the uttermost ends of the earth (Ezek. xxxviii. 15 and ver. 9)" * Another difficulty, according to Düsterdieck, consists in the fact that foes belonging to this earthly life fight against the faithful who have part in the first resurrection. This will undoubtedly be a very foolish proceeding, but it will not on that

account be improbable, as those who have passed through the resurrection dwell upon earth in bodily form. Dogs attack lion-, beasts attack men, barbarians and savages attack civilized nations, the foes of Christ attack the Church of God;—all these are wars from motives of sheer instinct, the rationality of which we have not to take upon ourselves to prove. In the antithesis of Cain and Abel, it was, in reality, the mortal who assaulted the immortal. Consider further "that these heathen peoples are seduced to battle against the saints by Satan himself directly." Ch. xvi. 13, it is affirmed, militates against this idea. That passage, however, rather gives an explanation of the manner in which we should conceive of the agitation of Satan. At first, as the red Dragon (ch. xii.), he had no such definite organs as at a later period (ch. xiii.), and yet even then he could work by spiritual influences. And even though the Beast and the False Prophet are destroyed, the *frogs* which went forth from *their* mouths as well as from the mouth of the Dragon, reminiscences of rancor, resentment and rage [*Groll, Gram und Grimm*], can be made effectual for the seduction of the heathen, primarily through their leaders. **In the four corners of the earth.**—Hengstenberg, in the interest of his exegesis, has very ingeniously taken the edge off of the *four corners of the earth* by striving to prove that the corners comprehend that which lies within them, and that hence the four corners of the earth denote the same ground as τὸ πλάτος τῆς γῆς (see his citations, vol. ii., 368 sq. [Eng. Trans.]). But allowing that the four corners might denote, by synecdoche, the complete totality of the land or the people, such a use of the term is entirely different from the present statement, that Satan shall go out to seduce the heathen *in the four corners;* and from the further statement that they *went up upon the breadth* of the earth. **Gog and Magog.**—The following questions arise here: 1. What ethnographical sense did the theocratic world attach to Gog and Magog? 2. How did Gog and Magog become, in the Old Testament, the symbol of the last foes of the theocratic Church of God? 3. How has the Apocalypse taken up this symbol and applied it in manifold forms? 4. How is the same idea reflected in Jewish tradition? [1.] In respect to Biblical ethnography, the name of Magog appears, by the side of Gomer, amongst the sons of Japhet, Gen. x. 2: see *Comm. on Genesis*, p. 348 [Am. Ed.]. Josephus explains Magog as indicative of the Scythians. "Magog seems to be a collective name, denoting the sum of the peoples situate in Media and the Caucasian Mountains, concerning whom a vague report had reached the Hebrews, *etc.*" See Winer, Title MAGOG; Düsterdieck, Note on p. 552. *Gog*, according to Unlemann, as there quoted, and others, means *mountain; Magog* the *dwelling-place*, or *land of Gog.* According to Ezekiel, ch. xxxviii. 2, the prince or the nation is called Gog, the land of the same being denominated Magog, which embraces Rosch,* Mesech and Tubal (see the table of nations). [2.] In the Apocalypse of Ezekiel,

---

* [The G. V. reads here (Ez. k. xxxviii. 15): "Thou shalt come out of thy place, namely, from the *ends* against the north."—Ts.]

* [The LXX. has Ῥώς, but neither the Vulgate, nor the German, nor the English Version, gives it.—E. R. C.]

the spirit of prophecy has, in accordance with a distinct ethical pre-supposition, arrived at the idea that the people of God shall, after all its conflicts with familiar anti-theocratic enemies, after its complete restoration, re-instatement and renewal, have to undergo one more last assault from the rude and brutal enmity of Eastern barbarian nations. These enemies are introduced by Ezekiel under the names of Gog and Magog. Hitzig (*Commentar. zu Ezech.*, p 288) thinks that the Prophet chose the name Gog, the Scythian, on account of its being the name of the most remote peoples ; and adds that the Scythians had appeared in Palestine not so very long prior to the time of Ezekiel's prophecy —two explanations which invalidate each other. On the question as to whether the Scythians had been in Palestine previous to the prophecy, comp. Winer, Title SCYTHIANS. We behold in the name the symbolic term for the rudest and most savage heathenism as contrasted with the perfected Theocracy. Jehovah will curb, subdue and destroy Gog like a wild beast. [3.] In harmony with the same eschatological idea, the Apocalypse took up the symbolical announcement, and to its representation of Gog and Magog as two collateral powers the inducement was given by Ezekiel, in his designation of Magog as a complex of different peoples. In the general judgment picture (Rev. xvi.) these enemies appear as the kings of the east, who come from the region of barbarism beyond the Euphrates. [4.] "In Jewish Theology, also, the two names, of which the first denotes in Ezekiel *l. c.*, the *king* of the *land* and *people* of *Magog*, are found in conjunction as the names of nations : *In fine extremitatis dierum Gog et Magog et exercitus eorum adscendent Hierosolyma et per manus regis Messiæ ipsi cadent, et VII. annos dierum ardebunt filii Israelis ex armis eorum (Targ. Hieros. in Num. xi. 27, etc.).*" DUESTERDIECK. Comp. De Wette, p 191. *Ibid.*, singular interpretations of the names by Augustine, Jerome *et al.*; application to the Goths, Saracens, Turks, all enemies of the Church, Antichrist. "The sorriest interpretation is that of *Bar Cochab* (Weist.)." Hengstenb. (ii. p. 369 [Eng. Tr.]) seems to find a significancy in Brentano's initial juxtaposition of *Gog, Magog* and *Demagog.* A witty reply to the perhaps only seeming desire to discover Gog and Magog in the demagogues of the 19th century, see in Ebrard, Note, p. 517. **To the war.**—That last great war, foretold for ages by Prophecy. **The number of whom is as the sand of the sea.** —According to Ezekiel even, Gog leads with him a mixture of eastern nations (as did, in reality, Attila, Genghis Khan and Timur). At the same time, the figure employed is expressive, on the one hand, of the multitude of sordid human natures, and on the other hand, of a blind trust in this multitude. The salvability of the Scythians, however, is expressly declared by the Apostle Paul, Col. iii. 11.

In the coalition of Satan with the mob of Gog and Magog, the combination of demon and beast, serpent and swine, formed by the dragon figure, is completely realized.

B.—EARTH-PICTURE OF THE LAST JUDGMENT.

CHAP. XX. 9, 10.

9 And they went up on [*om.* on—*ins.* upon] the breadth of the earth, and compassed [encompassed] the camp [army *or* fortification ($\pi\alpha\rho\epsilon\mu\beta\sigma\lambda\dot\eta$)] of the saints about [*om.* about], and the beloved city: and fire came down from God [*or om.* from God][1] out of **10** [*ins.* the] heaven, and devoured them. And the devil that deceived [seduceth *or* misleadeth] them was cast into the lake of [*ins.* the] fire and [*or ins.* the][2] brimstone, where [*ins.* also *are*] the beast and the false prophet *are* [*om. are*], and [*ins.* they] shall be tormented day and night for ever and ever [into the ages of the ages].

TEXTUAL AND GRAMMATICAL.

[1] Ver. 9. 'Aπὸ τοῦ θεοῦ is supported by Codd. א. B*., *et al.*, but is not firmly established. [Treg. inserts; Lach., Alf., Tisch., omit with A.—E. R. C.]

[2] Ver. 10. [Tischendorf (8th Ed.) inserts this article with א.; Lach., Tisch. (1859), Treg., Alford, omit with A. B*. P., *et al.*—E. R. C.]

EXEGETICAL AND CRITICAL.

SYNOPTICAL VIEW.

By the prophetic preterite, as well as by the brevity of the description, the Seer expresses the vanity of this last rebellion, which is aimed directly against God in His people, and which, notwithstanding its terrifically mighty development, is instantaneously annihilated. These enemies, with their creaturely forces, stand opposed, as they think, merely to a city of the children of peace, whilst in reality they are drawn up against all the cosmical powers of Heaven. *And they went up upon the breadth of the earth.* The idea is that they come from the low-lands of the corners of the earth—to destroy the City of God upon the more central, elevated plain of the earth. But that the words are intended to convey the precise idea of a going up against *Jerusalem*, is difficult to suppose, because for the Seer the true Jerusalem, according to chap. xxi., comes down from Heaven, and here only *the beloved city* is spoken of, which, as well as the *camp of the saints*—who are drawn up before the city, in order to its protection—*the enemies encompass*. It cannot be without reason that the Seer has here avoided the name of Jerusalem (although for an Israelitish heart it might be paraphrased by the expression, *the beloved city*), whilst in chap. xxi. he uses the name in the same sense in which it is employed by the Apostle Paul, Gal. iv. 26. At this moment, when the last and, apparently, the most fearful crisis of the world's history is close at hand—a crisis which is all the more fearful, or, we might say, the more demonically unnatural, if we conceive of the glorified Christ as shut in, together with the saints, by the hostile host—there falls from Heaven a *fire* which consumes the foe. An exegetical reading, with the confident feeling that this direct war against God must likewise be put down by God, has added the words, *from God;* viewed in another aspect, however, the latter term *from Heaven* is more effective; Heaven itself, the whole Cosmos, against which they finally rage, must now, for God's sake, react against them, in destroying might, with its fire. And now Satan himself, who *seduceth* the *nations*, is *cast into the pool of the fire and brimstone*, whither the Beast and the False Prophet have preceded him. This view, like the discourse of Christ (Matt. xxv.), is at variance with the mediæval idea that Satan, as a fire-demon and prince of hell, torments souls in hell. *They shall*, it is declared, *be tormented day and night into the æons of the æons* To the essence and spiritual condition of the prince of darkness and his consorts, their sphere and external mode of existence shall correspond. There are in their character no motives for a change; except that through the consummate stagnation of their condition, their consummate irritation must be more and more neutralized.

EXPLANATIONS IN DETAIL.

Chap. xx. 9. **And they went up.**—Hab. i. 6. "The term ἀναβαίνειν, usual where military marches are spoken of (1 Ki. xxii. 4; Ju i. 1), because the position of the attacked is naturally conceived of as on a height (Hengstenberg), is the more fitting here, since the march of the heathen is really directed upward against Jerusalem." DUESTERDIECK. The primary statement is rather, however, that they go up *upon the breadth of the earth*, the symbolic elevated plain of the earth, which, as such, forms the specific antithesis to the symbolic four corners of the earth; it is the highland of the spirit. The object of the attack is then, certainly, defined in accordance with an Old Testament conception (see Zech. xii. 7, 8; comp. Köhler, *Sacharja*, p. 185). The saints have encamped about the beloved city to protect it. All the *forces* of the Kingdom of Heaven form the defence for all its *possessions*. If we glance once more at the passage cited [Zech. xii. 7, 8], Zech. xiv. 1, 2 might seem to afford an explanation as to wherefore the Seer did not call the beloved city Jerusalem. Grotius apprehended the Seven Churches by the camp of the saints, and Constantinople by the beloved city. Others (Augustine, Vitringa, Hengstenberg) have regarded the city as the Church; Bengel and most moderns, as Jerusalem.

And fire came down.—Ezek. xxxix. 6; xxxviii. 22; Gen. xix. 24; Lev. x. 2: Num. xvi. 35; Luke ix. 54. See SYN. VIEW. The fire catastrophe shows that the universal judgment of the world is at hand—the fiery metamorphosis of the earth. **And consumed them.**—To be understood of the destruction of their life in this present world.

Ver. 10. **And the devil that seduceth (or misleadeth) them.**—Πλανῶν, as the present participle, denotes the continuance of sin under punishment. **And they shall be tormented.**—Namely, the Devil, the Beast, and the False Prophet. A preliminary general presentment, see in chap. xiv. 11; the final presentment, chap. xx. 14, 15; xxi. 8.

SECTION SEVENTH.

The New Heaven and the New Earth. The Kingdom of Glory.

CHAP. XX. 11—XXII. 5.

A.—IDEAL HEAVENLY WORLD-PICTURE OF THE CONSUMMATION—ABOUT TO CHANGE TO THE REAL WORLD-PICTURE OF THE NEW EARTH.

CHAP. XX. 11—XXI. 8.

1. *The End of the World; the Resurrection; the Judgment.*

11 And I saw a great white throne, and him that sat on [the one sitting upon] it, from whose face the earth and the heaven fled away [*om.* away]; and there was
12 found no place [place was not found] for them. And I saw the dead, small and

great [the great and the small],[1] stand [standing] before God [om. God—ins. the throne];[2] and the [om. the] books were opened: and another book was opened, which is *the book* of life: and the dead were judged out of those [the] things which
13 were [om. which were] written in the books, according to their works.   And the sea gave up [forth] the dead which were in it; and death and hell [hades] delivered up [gave forth] the dead which were in them: and they were judged every
14 man [each] according to their works.   And death and hell [hades] were cast into the lake of [ins. the] fire.   This is the second death[3] [ins. , the lake of the fire].[4]
15 And whosoever [if any one] was not found written in the book of life [ins. he] was cast into the lake of [ins. the] fire.

2. *The New Heaven and the New Earth.   The Clarified World and the Kingdom of Glory.*

CHAP. XXI. 1-8.

And I saw a new heaven and a new earth: for the first heaven and the first earth were passed away [departed];[5] and there was no more sea [the sea is no more].
2 And I John [om. John][6] saw the holy city, new Jerusalem, coming down from God [om. from God] out of [ins. the] heaven [ins. from God], prepared as a bride
3 adorned for her husband.   And I heard a great voice out of heaven [om. heaven —ins. the throne][7] saying, Behold, the tabernacle of God *is* with men, and he will dwell [tabernacle] with them, and they shall be his people [peoples],[8] and God
4 himself shall be with them, *and be their God [or om. and be their God].*[9]   And God [God or om. God][10] shall wipe away all tears [every tear] from their eyes; and there shall be no more death [death shall be no more], neither sorrow, nor crying, neither shall there be any more pain [nor shall sorrow, nor crying, nor pain, be
5 any more]: for the former [first] things are passed away [departed].   And he that sat [the one sitting] upon the throne said, Behold, I make all things new.   And he said [saith] unto me [or om. unto me].[11]   Write: for these words are true and faith-
6 ful [faithful and true].[12]   And he said unto me, It is [They are] done [or fulfilled].[13] I am [or am][14] [ins. the] Alpha and [ins. the] Omega, the beginning and the end. I will give unto him that is athirst [thirsteth] of the fountain of the water of life
7 freely.   He that overcometh [or conquereth] shall inherit all [om. all—ins. these][15] things; and I will be his [om. his—ins. to him a] God, and he shall be my [om. my—
8 ins. to me a] son.   But [ins. to] the fearful [cowardly], and unbelieving, and[16] the [om. the] abominable, and murderers, and whoremongers [fornicators], and sorcerers, and idolaters, and all [ins. the] liars, shall have [om. shall have] their part [ins. shall be] in the lake which burneth with fire and brimstone: [,] which is the second death.

TEXTUAL AND GRAMMATICAL.

1 Ver. 12. The Recepta inverts the order, giving "small and great."
2 Ver. 12. Codd. A. B*., *et al.*, give θρόνου; the Rec. gives θεοῦ.
3 Ver. 14. A. B*., *et al.*, give οὗτος ὁ θάνατος ὁ δεύτερός ἐστι.
4 Ver. 14. This clause is omitted by the Rec. [Crit. Els. insert it in acc. with א. A. B*. P.—E. R. C.]
5 Chap. xxi. 1. א. A. B*. give ἀπῆλθαν instead of παρῆλθε.
6 Ver. 2. "The words ἐγὼ Ἰωάνν. were interpolated from the Vulgate by Erasmus." (DELITZSCH.)
7 Ver. 3. [Tisch., Treg., Alf. give θρόνου with א. A., *Vulg., et al.*; B.* P. give οὐρανοῦ.—E. R. C.]
8 Ver. 3. Cod. A. and Lachmann [Tisch., Treg., Alf.] give λαοί, Cod. B*., *Vulg., et al.* give the singular, whic his more in accordance with the symbolical expression.
9 Ver. 3. [Tisch. (8th Ed.), Treg. omit with א. B.,* *et al.*; Lach., Tisch. (1859), Alf. give it with A. P., *Vu'g., et al.* —E. R. C.]
10 Ver. 4. [Tisch., omitting the last clause of ver. 3 inserts merely a comma between αὐτῶν and καί.   The rendering of his reading is—*God Himself shall be with them, and shall wipe, etc.*—E. R. C]
11 Ver. 5. [Crit. Eds. generally omit μοι with A. B*.: it is given by א. P.—E. R. C.]
12 Ver. 5. A. B*., *et al.*, give πιστοὶ καὶ ἀληθινοί; the Rec. reads inversely.
13 Ver. 6. There are three readings here: A., *et a'.*, give γέγονα; B.* gives γέγονα ἐγώ, etc.; the Rec. takes its reading from chap. xvi. 17.   [Lach., Tisch. (8th Ed.), Treg. give γέγοναν; Alf. brackets the v.—E. R. C.]
14 Ver. 6. [Tisch. (8th Ed.) omits εἰμι with א. B.* P.; Lach., Treg., Tisch. (1859) insert it with A., *Vulg., et al.*; Alf. brackets.   The reading of the entire passage from γέγονα (v) is exceedingly uncertain.   The possible renderings as given by Alford are: "They (viz.: these words or all things) are fulfilled.   I am the Alpha and the Omega," or "I am become the Alpha and the Omega."—E. R. C]
15 Ver. 7. The reading ταῦτα, in acc. with Codd. A. B*., *et al.*, is given instead of the Rec.
16 Ver. 8. Cod. B., *et al.*, insert καὶ ἁμαρτωλοις.   Since ἀπίστοις is given in a more social sense, ἁμαρτ. might be given in a more special sense also.   On account, however, of the significant totality of terms, it seems to be an addition.

EXEGETICAL AND CRITICAL.

SYNOPTICAL VIEW.

Two points must here be established at the outset.   First, the detachment of the section ch. xx. 11-14 from the foregoing last special judgment, the judgment upon Satan.   Secondly, the distinction, which is carried out here also, of a predominantly heavenly-ideal and a predominantly terrestri real vision-picture, or the distinction of the sections ch. xxi. 1–8 and ch xxi. 9—xxii. 5. In respect to the first point, with the judgment upon Satan the last part of the world-judgment internal to this present world and life, or the outpouring of the Vials of Anger, is accomplished. Though the universal end-judgment is, by the Scriptures and the Church, preeminently denominated the *Dies Iræ*, it lies beyond the proper department of the *Vials* of Anger, since it introduces the eternal dooms, and is a judgment unto life for the blessed, as well as a death-judgment upon the damned; irrespective of the fact that the term of the end judgment is, in Eschatology, summed up together with the foregoing special judgments in one great Day of Wrath, whose prelude is to be beheld in the day of wrath upon Jerusalem. In respect to the second point, we must not overlook the fact that the two finales contained in ch. xxi. 6, 7 and ch. xxii. 4, 5 would, as tautologies, obscure the text, if they were not to be regarded as parallels, in perfect analogy with the parallels ch. xii. 6 and xii. 14. The antithesis does here, indeed, issue in a point in which the two lines are not so strongly distinguished--Heaven descends to earth: earth becomes Heaven—; still, the pause between the visional Heaven-picture and the appearance of the City of God upon earth is distinctly perceptible (chap. xxi. 10).

The present Section A branches into the great antithesis of the end of the old world and the appearance or, primarily, the heavenly development, of the new world.

The centre and causality of the end of the world is the *great white throne* and the Judge enthroned thereon. The adjectives *great* and *white* manifestly denote the majesty and holiness of the Judge and His judgment.

In harmony with the universalism of the judgment and in accordance with vers. 4 and 5, God Himself is to be understood by the *Judge*; not, however, to the exclusion of the fact that Christ is the *appearance of the great judging God* (Tit. ii. 13), and thus His Parousia has here mediated the Last Judgment. With the great appearance of God the Judge, a complete subversion of the old form of the world takes place:—the corporeal world becomes nothing; the spiritual world becomes all. *From His face the earth and the Heaven fled:* and fled without a goal—they vanished. This cannot be apprehended as a real annihilation of the world, as the ancient orthodoxy maintained. And though the idea does essentially coincide with the fiery metamorphosis of 2 Pet. iii. 10–13, it was not the intention of the Seer hyperbolically to express that fact [of the fiery metamorphosis]. Rather, in the antithesis, The corporeal world vanishes, the spiritual world appears, is contained the strongest expression of the thought that at last, under the almighty operation of the absolute personality of God, personal relations, as the true life-principles of the world, must become perfectly manifest. Above all, the old antithesis between Heaven and earth is hereby removed. But as decidedly as worldly relations withdraw, spiritual relations come into prominence. The Seer

beholds *the dead standing before the throne;*—the *great*, because even the greatest is subject to this judgment, and the *small*, because even the smallest shall have perfect justice done him here. And with this the general resurrection is expressed; emphasis is not laid upon it, however, in the same manner as upon the first resurrection, because it is not specifically a resurrection to life. Clearly and positively as *personalities* themselves appear before the throne, just so distinctly are all the *works* of all individuals—works which bear the impress of their characters and which have fixed their destinies—in everlasting remembrance. There are *the books*, which are opened for the revelation of these works, in the unitous character of which latter the judicial sentence is, *de facto*, already extant (Matt. xii. 37). From the *books* the Seer distinguishes *the book*, the book of life, as the book κατ' ἐξοχήν, the Bible of eternity set forth in living Divine images. In this book, that sum total is already made up, for which the books in the plural contain, amongst other things, the material. Those who are *written* in this book have already, in spirit, passed the judgment (John v. 24; Rom. vi.; Gal. ii. 19). The result of the life of other men is contained in the books, but is also summed up in the brief epitome presented in the statement that they have fallen under judgment if their names are *not found in the book of life.* The following antitheses should be noted: 1. The books and the book; 2. The works and the names; 3. The lostness of the names of the lost in the confusion of their works; and the concentration of the works of faith in the names of the faithful, in the perfected characters. *Formally*, therefore, the judgment is general; *all* stand before the throne. And it must all the more be general, since the very separation of the righteous from the mass of the unrighteous is itself the expression and illustration of the judgment. In a material aspect, however, the general judgment, with this very separation of the righteous, brings in view the special judgment of damnation; the more, since the truly perfected Christians, the eschatological Christians, we might say the approved ones of the end-time, with all the martyrs, who represent a spiritual end time through the entire course of the world's history (scarcely those also who have become believers during the thousand years), are already, through the first resurrection, not only exempted from the judgment, but also called to share in its administration.

This general description of the judgment is followed by a specialization which goes back to the beginning. And first in regard to the dead. They come back from every direction out of the condition in which they have been hitherto; through the medium of the general resurrection they are placed before the throne of God. Not even into the abyss could they have sunk so deep as not to appear again. We, therefore, apprehend the detailed description as a gradation. That they are given back by the earth is assumed by the Seer as a matter of course. But also by the *sea*, in whose depths they seemed to have vanished forever; by *death*, by the power of death itself; and by the *realm of the dead*

[Hades]*—are they given up. So far as the immortality of the soul is concerned, these categories are all alike: in whatever way they [as to body] perished, they all [as to soul] live on. Again, so far as death is concerned, they are all dead and in the realm of the dead [Hades]. But in respect of the relation of these categories to a bodily appearance before the throne of God, gradual distinctions are formed. They vanished in the depth of the ocean;—they are here again. They seemed long since a prey to the power of death;—they are living again. They seemed to be floating away as shades in the gloomy land beyond the portals of death;—here they come as entire men in the reality of earthly life, summoned before the judgment throne of God. So they are *judged, each one according to his work.* The judgment is thus thoroughly general and thoroughly individual, and likewise, as the final judgment, characterized as in accordance with the works of those judged (Matt. xxv.). The judgment makes a thorough end of the old form of the world. *Death itself is* cast into the *pool of fire.* As the natural life of the blessed is swallowed up in the spiritual life, so the natural death is merged into the spiritual death. The natural death appertains to the region of *becoming;* with the abolition of this region, it is itself abolished. What remains of it is the sense of continual self-annihilation in the region of an absolutely indifferentized [neutralized] self-tormenting existence. The whole institution of the realm of the dead [Hades], so far as its dark side is concerned, passes into the *pool of fire,* into the condition of a death multiplied into itself, and yet a conscious, living death. Again, together with death and Hades, the spiritually *dead* incur the judgment of the pool of fire. Life, life, life, to infinitude, is denoted when it is said: the name is found in the book of life. The contrast is death, death, death, to infinitude. Middle positions, uncertain, wavering forms, have ceased to be, for it is the harvest of the world.

The pool of fire, or the pond-like, stagnating lake of fire, denotes the entire precipitate of the world and worldly history; hence the new world can unfold itself, over against it, in all its glory. The Seer first beholds the new world in the antithesis of the *new Heaven* and the *new earth,* for the old Heaven and the old earth *have departed, and the sea is not any more.* The sea is the womb of shapeless life, as the nutriment of life that is in process of shaping, and in this respect it is an attribute of the region of *becoming,* but not of the region of *being.* It will be understood that Heaven and earth are intended not in the cosmical sense merely, but also in the spiritual sense, and this may be true of the sea also. For the sea of nations is, in common with the mundane sea, a womb—a womb of characters, as the latter is of creatures. That which is to unite Heaven and earth is the *Holy City,* the *New Jerusalem, prepared in Heaven by God as a bride adorned for her husband.*

Our first business here is to reconcile this Parousia of the perfected Church of God with the Parousia of Christ and His escort (ch. xix.

14). It is impossible to accept the confused notion that another Parousia of Christ from Heaven must ensue here. Consequently, we must distinguish the train of His elect, which has accompanied Him to earth, and has here compacted itself into a whole, from the general constituents of the Church Triumphant; a distinction which was suggested in chs. vii. and xiv. The Church Triumphant in the other world does not consist purely of *warriors of God* [*Gotteskämpfer*] in the narrower sense of that term, and it has found a new home in that other world. Therefore the barrier between Heaven and earth must be in the act of vanishing, if the new earth is to be raised to the dignity of becoming the mother-country of the new Church of God. This, however, seems to be a polar vital law: *Principial* consummation bears upward from earth to Heaven; the *consummate* appearance of life brings back again from Heaven to earth. This may be otherwise expressed as follows: Redemption, as principial, first conducts the redeemed from without inwards; next, as eschatological, from within outwards.

Thus ensues the heavenly consummation of God's Kingdom upon earth. It is proclaimed by a *great voice from the Throne*—hence by a solemn declaration in the name of the Divine government—in a progressive series of theocratic items.

First, the theocratic *cultus* shall find its fulfillment in the consummation of the Kingdom of glory. *Behold, the Tabernacle of God is with men.* That which was typically heralded by the Jewish tabernacle, and, later, by the Temple; that which the Church *principially* realized,—attains now its consummate and visible appearance: a Congregation of God, in which man's communion with God is completely realized.

Secondly, the visible appearance of the full harvest of all pious tear-seed sown throughout the history of the world. *God will wipe away every tear from their eyes.* An image which might have been drawn from the nursery is employed to express the sublimest thought—the transmutation of all the earthly sufferings of the pious into heavenly bliss, through the sensible presence of Divine love and faithfulness. We may also say:—the perfect transfiguration of the cross. *For the first things have departed.* A second, imperishable Kingdom of Life has arisen, in contrast to the second death.

Thirdly, the visible appearance of the renewal of the earth, or rather of the whole earthly Cosmos,—relatively, of the whole universe itself. *Behold, I make all things new.* This promise, too, must be *written;* it becomes, in pursuance of the Divine order, a written bond for the hope of mankind, like the promises in ch. xiv. 13 and ch. xix. 9.

Fourthly, the full realization of all the promissory words of God. *And He said unto me: They are fulfilled.* Namely, the words of which it is declared: *They are trustworthy and true* [veritable]. They have become realized in the new earth, as words creative of God's second, new and eternal world. The surety for them is given by the same God Who *must* be the *Omega* of all life, because He is its *beginning* (see Rom. xi. 36).

---

* [See Excursus at the end of this Section.—E. R. C.]

Fifthly, together with the universal destiny of the world, all individual destinies are fulfilled. For the men of longing, all longing for the eternal will be satisfied. *The fountain of the water of life*—highest life and sense of life, springing forth to infinitude from the depths of the God head—is offered for the *free* enjoyment of all who have thirsted for it.

But as the highest need of the soul, the longing for its true element, has made the thirsters warriors, combatants against all illusions of false satisfaction, and since victory has crowned the constant conflict, the second individualization of the promise runs thus: *He that conquereth* [or *the conqueror*] *shall inherit these things*—namely, the fulfillment of all these promises. And that which constitutes the centre, the sum and substance of this inheritance, is expressed in the words: *I will be his God, and he shall be My son* (1 John iii. 2).

Because the reference is to a conquest and a fulfillment conditioned entirely upon ethical grounds, an antithesis is once more employed. It is highly significant that the lost are designated, above all, as *cowards*. In respect of the measure and vocation of man, in face of eternity and its revelations, faith is, in the first place, heroic bravery and gallantry; on the other hand, unbelief, in its fundamental form, is faint-heartedness, cowardice, despair as to the high calling of God and the high vocation of human nature. Under this characterism, therefore, the *unbeliever* comes, with his timorousness in view of Divine truth; the *sinner*, in the narrower sense of the term, as one who is timorous in regard to the worth of righteousness;* the *murderer*, who was timorous at the calling of love; the *fornicator*, who was timorous at the law of spiritual liberty and purity of life; the *sorcerer*, who was timorous at the sanctity of Nature's laws; the *idolater*, who, in his timorousness, surrendered the glory of the knowledge of God; also the *liar*, who despaired as to the good in truth;—they all cowardly despaired of the Life in life, the Divine word, law and Spirit—hence *their portion shall be in the pool of fire*. Their tendency led, in a straight line, to the perturbation of their being in absolute irritation.

EXPLANATIONS IN DETAIL.

Ch. xx. 11. The pause between the foregoing section and the present one is marked by the announcement of a new vision: καὶ εἶδον.

Ver. 11. **A great white throne.**—The *greatness* and *whiteness* are indicative of the *glory* and *holiness* of the throne (Düsterd.).

And the One sitting upon it.—Who is this? *Answers:* 1. The Messiah (Bengel *et al.*; Matt. xxvi. 31 [64?]); 2. God (De Wette, Hengstenb., Düsterd.: see chap. i. 8; iv. 3; xxi. 5, 6; Dan. vii. 9); 3. God and Christ, "the Two forming *One*, in perfect undividedness" (Ewald). With this modification, *the visible appearance of God in Christ*, No. 3 is entirely correct (Tit. ii. 13; 1 John v. 20).—**The earth and the heaven fled** (see chap. xvi. 20; xxi. 1).—The antithesis between the appearance of God and

the disappearance of the world as world, is represented under the figure of an antagonism and conflict. Before the God Who *maketh all things new* the old form of the world takes to flight.—**And place was not found for them.**—The renewal pervades everything.

Ver. 12. **And I saw.**—The dead have once more taken visible shape.—**The great and the small** (see chap. xi. 18; xiii. 16).—The perfect equality of men before the judgment seat of God is repeatedly declared. The 12th verse, as Düsterdieck judiciously remarks, closes with a general description; ver. 13th then reverts to special items, as in ch. xv. 1 and 6. Bengel and Hengst. apprehend the relation as a continuous unitous description: in that case, the νεκροί of ver. 12 would necessarily go those who are transformed, who have lived to see the day of the Parousia, in contrast to those who are really raised from the dead. Such a view does violence to the text.—**Books were opened.**—(Dan. vii. 10). As there is repeated mention of *books* in the Apocalypse, so likewise is there in the Gospel of John (the Scriptures); see especially ch. xxi. 23. **The book of life** is but one; it is the book of the life of mankind in a concentrated form. Whilst the **books** seem to be journals concerning the works of all, the **book** contains the heavenly result of the history of the world, a register of the treasure, the κλῆρος, the harvest of God, in the names of the blessed. Since the entire decision is briefly contained in the question: Is the name of such an one such a man in the book of life, or not? the *books* occupy the place of vouchers. Thus in Matt. xxv. the one book is illustrated in the statement that Christ places the sheep on H s right hand, and the goats on His left hand; the ensuing discussion of the works of the righteous and the wicked, however, is suggestive of the books.

Ver. 13. **And the sea.**—The *sea* cannot here be understood directly as the sea of nations, although it is thus that Hengstenberg defines even this declaration, maintaining that the reference is to those who have perished in the battles of the nations. According to this, the literal form of the passage would be: the battlefields gave back their dead. In this case, in the subsequent sentence where it speaks of *death* as giving up its dead, we should have to understand those who had fallen on those fields of battle, rather than, with Hengstenberg, unblest dead ones. However, the reference is rather to different conditions of the dead. Personalities of all sorts (ver. 12) must re-appear out of mortal conditions of all sorts (see SYN. VIEW). In regard to the sea, De Wette, after Werstein, groundlessly cites a pagan idea here, according to which those who had been swallowed up in the sea did not enter Hades. According to Düsterdieck, this second presentation [ver. 13] embraces only such as incur the punishment of the second death or the lake of fire. This assumption is based upon the false hypothesis that, according to ver. 5, all believers rose from the dead at the beginning of the Millennial Kingdom. In that case the beginning of the Millennial Kingdom would really have constituted the judgment itself. Any blessed effects of the

---

* See TEXT. AND GRAM. NOTES.

Parousia upon the world of nations would then have been out of the question.

Ver. 14. **And Death and Hades,** *etc.*— "De th and Hades,* presented in ver. 13 (comp. ch. i. 18) as localities, here appear (comp. ch. vi. 8) personified, as demonic powers" (Düsterdieck). The Apocalyptist, however, would probably not father this conception. The inference is, rather, that the pool of fire must not be understood in a purely ethical sense, but that it has also its physical side. And this declaration doubtless imp rts that the two ground-forms of the old morality—first, dying i self, and secondly, the mode of existence of the dead—are merged in their consummation-form, in which nothing remains of them but the second death, the æonic suffering of the lost (see Is. xxv. 8; 1 Cor. xv. 26).

Ver. 15. **And if any one was not,** *etc.*— Literally apprehended, this seems very hard; ideally apprehended it means, where the second, higher life is utterly wanting, there is the second death; the essential and proper fulfillment of death; the natural, and therefore the positive consequence.

Ch. xxi. 1. **And I saw.**—Picture of the consummation—first, as a Heaven-picture. The final goal of the history of the old world; therefore, the final goal of all the longing of all the pious (Rom. viii.), of all revelations of salvation and prophecies, of all the forms and operations of the redemption and of the Kingdom of God, and hence even of all judgments, which at last, in the concentration of the final judgment, were obliged to make room for the eternal City of God. "Augustine (*De Civ. Dei* xx 17) apprehends what follows *de seculo futuro et immortalitate et æternita e sanctorum,* and this opinion of his has, with more justice than others pronounced by him upon the Apocalypse, become authoritative." De Wette. Even Hengstenberg, with a *salto mortale,* touching lightly the last period of the rebellion of Gog and Magog, has leaped from the mediæval Rome into the consummation-time of the new Jerusalem. Grotius, on the contrary, keeps to the period subsequent to Constantine, and Vitringa conceives of the time as still prior to the universal judgment (comp. Düsterd., p. 562, but particularly De Wette, p. 194). From the stand-point of a conception of heavenly felicity as abstractly spiritual, many have been unable to reconcile themselves to this descent of Heaven to earth, in antithesis to a rising of earth to Heaven. "The idea of the Church Triumphant is not that which precisely corresponds with the idea presented here: the conception here presented is that of the Kingdom of God in its consummation—a Kingdom for which Christ has, in His Church, broken the way—a Kingdom which has been gradually actualized—the Kingdom of the whole of redeemed and blessed humanity; the dominion of Christ is merged in that of God, Who is present (ver. 11), and shares His Throne with the Lamb (ch. xxii 1)." De Wette.

A new Heaven and a new earth (Is. lxv. 17; lxvi.; Psalm civ. 30). "The theological question as to whether the old world is to pass

away in such a manner that the new world will arise from it as from a seed, or whether an absolute new creation, following upon the complete destruction of the old world, is to be assumed, can be decided least of all by the Apocalyptic description; this description, however (comp. also 2 Pet. iii. 10 sqq.), is not opposed to the former view, which has greater Scriptural probabilities in its favor than the latter (1 Cor. xv 42 sqq.; Rom. viii. 21; Matt. xix. 28)." Duesterdieck. On the contrary, the Apocalypse alone sets forth the true mediati n of the last metamorphosis of the old world, in the Millennial Kingdom. The idea of the antithesis of an absolute destruction and new creation belongs only to the half-spiritualistic, half-materialistic letter-theology of orthodoxism.

And the sea.—Why is it *no more?* The following *answers* to this inquiry are presented by Düsterdieck: 1. Navigation is no longer necessary (Andr.); 2 It is dried up by the universal conflagration (Bede); 3. As the old world arose out of the water, so the new has arisen out of the fire (De Wette); 4. A horror of the deep sea (Ewald); 5. There was no sea in Paradise either (Züllig); 6. Connection of the sea with the infernal abyss (Ewald II.); 7. The sea as a constituent part of the old world. "The text does not forbid the idea of a new sea accompanying the new earth" (Düsterd.). For our explanation see the SYNOPT. VIEW.

Ver. 2. **The holy City. — New Jerusalem.**—It is related to the ἄνω Ἱερουσαλήμ (Gal. iv. 26) as the resurrection is related to the principle of the new life; or the Palingenesia to the ἀναγέννησις; as the end to the harvest (1 Cor. xv). The heavenly essence of the Church of God, possessed by it even upon earth, here arrives at a heavenly manifestation.— **Coming down from God.**—For a kindred rabbinical conception, cited by Wetstein on the passage in Galatians, see Düsterdieck, p. 563.— **Prepared.**—See ch. xix. 7, 8; 2 Cor. xi. 2; Eph. v. 27; 1 Pet. iii. 3. The new Jerusalem, as the sum of perfected individuals, is the *City of God;* in its unity, it is the *Bride of Christ.* The consummate manhood of all the citizens of the City of God is conditioned by their consummate receptivity, which extends even to perfect unanimity.

Ver. 3. **Behold, the tabernacle of God.**— See Is. ii. 3; iv. 5; Ezek. xxxvii. 27; xliii. 7; 1 Cor. iii. 9; 2 Cor. vi. 16; Eph. ii. 19–22.

Ver. 4. **God shall wipe away.** *etc*—See Ps. cxxvi. 5, 6; Is. xxv. 8; lxv. 19.—**Death**— See ch. xx. 14.—**Sorrow.**—Mourning for the dead, especially.—**Nor crying. nor pain**— Κραυγή is the *acute* form of sorrow ("vehement outcry,—for instance, at the experience of such acts of violence as are indicated in ch. xiii. 10, 17; ii. 10. [Bleek, Ewald; comp Ex. iii 7, 9; Esther iv. 3.]" Duesterd.). The πόνος, pain, or painful labor, is the *chronic* form of the same. —**For the first things** —To be taken in an emphatic sense, like the *first* man (1 Cor. xv. 4, 5 sqq.)—the present æon. In accordance with the entire mass of Holy Scripture, the world is designed to be a succession of two worlds.

Ver. 5. **And the One sitting upon the**

throne, *etc.*—"That which the heavenly voice [ver. 3], interpreting the vision of John, had proclaimed, is now confirmed by the One sitting upon the throne (comp. chap. xx. 11), in two speeches" DUESTERD. The words, **And He saith unto me: Write: for these words**, *etc.*, are, according to Bengel, Züllig, Hengst., and Düsterdieck, an interlogue [*Zwischenrede*= between-speech] on the part of the Angel; these commentators refer to ch. xix. 9 and xxii. 6. Observe, however, the change between ch. xiv. 9 sqq. and ver. 13 [to which also reference is made by Düsterdieck]. There the discourse of the Angel is followed by a speech from Heaven which commands the Seer to write the comforting declaration [ver. 13]. We therefore cannot infer from ch. xix. 9 that an angelic speech here interrupts the voice from the throne. And this inference is the less proper from the fact that it would seem very strange for the speech of an Angel to be made to corroborate the language of God Himself. Moreover, the Divine speech in ver. 6 is too closely connected with ver. 5 for the above-cited view to be tenable.

Ver. 6. **They are fulfilled.**—Comp. chap. xvi. 17. According to Düsterdieck, γέγοναν refers to what John has previously seen. But his visions were sure in themselves. We refer the expression to the λόγοι in the sense of highest realization; they have become facts. The words, **I am the Alpha and the Omega**, *etc.*, contain the proof of the foregoing assertion that the words of God are, on the one hand, words of absolute faithfulness (πιστοί), and, on the other hand, of absolute reality (ἀληθινοί).—**I will give unto him that thirsteth**, *etc.*—In the satisfaction of all true human longing, the height of human blessedness is expressed [blessedness =possession of fullness; comp. the Lexicons).

Ver 7. **He that conquereth.**—(See the Seven Epistles.) Here, towards the end, we are once more carried back to the beginning. For the nucleus of the Seven Churches, considered in their symbolic totality, is the foundation for the glorious City of God which is now about to appear.—God as the inheritance of man; consummate blessedness: man as the son of God; consummate dignity (Matt. v. 9; Rom. viii. 17).

Ver. 8. **But the cowardly.**—Δειλοῖς. "In contrast to ὁ νικῶν, those Christians are meant who elude the painful combat with the world by denying the faithfulness of the faith (Bengel, De Wette, Hengst.)." DUESTERDIECK. This is certainly a much too special and superficial explanation. The category of these *cowards*, who were *cowardly* in the highest relation, embraces all the lost: that is, in other words—in view of the high epic goal of humanity, all lagging behind and being lost is traced back to a lack of specific æonic manly courage, to a shameful straggling from the ranks and a desertion of one's colors. If we apprehend the δειλοῖς as composing a genus, a significant senary of species is formed: 1. *Unbelievers* and the *abominable* (in practice), transgressors against nature (see Rom. i.); 2. *Murderers* and *fornicators* (cruelty and sensuality—a well-known pair); 3. *Sorcerers* and *idolaters*. Even here the affinity is manifest. Now, however, a seventh sort supervenes. apparently,—*liars*. But it is not without import that

an addition is here made—καὶ πᾶσιν—in accordance with which these latter are classed with idolaters. Idolatry is in several instances in the Apocalypse designated as falsity (see ch. xiv. 5; also Grot., ch. xxi. 27; xxii. 15; comp. Rom. i. 25).—**Unbelieving.**—According to Bengel and Ewald: Apostates from the faith. According to Düsterdieck: Inhabitants of the earth hostile to the Christian faith. In the universal judgment, this distinction is no longer of any importance; the heathen is an unbeliever—the unbeliever is a heathen. —**Abominable.**— Those who through the working of abomination have made themselves abominable, ἐβδελυγμένοι, *flagitiis fœdi.*—**Their part.**—Change of construction. We are not to overlook the fact that they have deserved their lot, *i. e.*, have drawn it upon themselves as the penalty of their sin.

[EXCURSUS ON HADES.]
By the American Editor.

[Concerning the souls of the departed, between the periods of their decease and the resurrection of their bodies, there are two questions of acknowledged interest. The one relates to their *moral condition;* the other, to their *local habitation.* The former of these questions it is not intended to discuss at all in this Excursus. The doctrine generally held in Protestant Churches is herein assumed to be true—*viz.:* that at death the period of gracious opportunity and discipline is brought to a close; that the souls of believers in Christ are at once made perfect in holiness and do immediately pass into glory; and that the souls of unbelievers, having sinned away their day of grace, are left hopeless in their sins, and are reserved in misery for public condemnation and everlasting destruction.

The second of these questions—*viz.:* that which relates to the *local habitation* of departed spirits— is one, not only of great interest, but also, in the judgment of all who have given special attention to it, of great difficulty. This difficulty arises, in the judgment of the writer, from three sources. The first and most important of these is the reticence of Scripture on the subject—but little is revealed thereon in the Word of God. More, however, is revealed than is generally supposed.

The second source of difficulty is properly introduced by the preceding remark. Notwithstanding the amount of distinct revelation, the whole matter is obscured to the reader of the English Version of the Bible by the erroneous rendering of the Hebrew term שְׁאוֹל (Sheol) and its Greek equivalent Ἄιδης (Hades). These words which in the original Scriptures have a fixed and definite meaning, indicating a place in the Unseen World distinct from both Heaven and Hell (regarded as the place of final punishment), are constantly rendered by either *grave* or *Hell*. By this mistranslation an idea proper to the Word of God is completely blotted out from the Engl sh Version; and, not only so, but the texts which present that idea are distributed amongst those which set forth two entirely distinct ideas— thus obscuring the teachings of Scripture concerning both *the grave* and *Hell*. But the obscuring and confusing influence of this erroneous translation does not terminate upon those who study only the English Version. The first and most enduring conceptions of the doctrines of Scripture are derived from the Version we read in childhood—conceptions which, even when false, subsequent study often fails to eradicate. And beyond this,—every Version, especially the one in common use, is, to a certain extent, a Commentary, and as such exerts a powerful influence over the minds of students of the original Scriptures. Had the word HADES been reproduced in our Version, much of the confusion that now embarrasses this subject could never have found existence. And here it is in place to remark that even though the Greek and Hebrew words were indefinite, synonymous sometimes with *grave* and sometimes with *Hell*, it would have been well, since the Holy Ghost inspired synonyms, to have preserved their use in our Version.

The third source of difficulty is the general and almost unquestioned assumption that the dwelling-place of the souls of the *righteous* dead has been the same *since* the Resurrection of Christ that it was *before* that event—an assumption opposed, as the effort will be made to show, to distinct intimations in the Word of God. In consequence of this assumption, there have been two schools in the Evangelical Church, each basing its doctrine on the clear and irrefragable teaching of the Scriptures—the one, in view of the ante-resurrection testimony, affirming the existence of an intermediate place, located in Hades, into which the souls of those who *now* die in the Lord are carried; the other, in view of the post-resurrection testimony, denying that there is now, or ever has been, such a place.

It is the desire of the writer to contribute something toward the settlement of this interesting question; and to this end he will endeavor to set forth what seems to him, after careful investigation, to be the Scriptural teaching concerning SHEOL or HADES. To avoid confusion, the Greek term HADES, which is the Septuagint and New Testament equivalent of the Hebrew SHEOL, will be used throughout this article. It may also be remarked that the term HELL will always be employed as indicating *the place of final punishment*.

It will be proper to say something as to the principles and mode of the investigation as conducted in the study. It was assumed, in the first place, that it should be made entirely within the field of the original Scriptures—the Septuagint being used as a door of communication between the Hebrew of the Old Testament and the Greek of the New. It was also assumed that each expression employed in Scripture to indicate a topic of revelation, should be regarded as maintaining one uniform sense throughout the Word of God,—*unless*, indeed, the contexts of different instances of its use should *require* us to put different senses upon it. It is desirable that the limitation of this principle should be distinctly recognized. It was not dogmatically assumed that each expression *must*, at all hazards, be regarded as having only one sense; but that, until the contrary should appear, each passage should be so regarded. Now, the term Hades (Sheol) occurs *sixty five* times in the Old Testa-

ment; in *thirty-one* instances it is rendered in the English Version by *grave*, in *thirty-one* by *Hell*,* and in *three* by *pit*. In the New Testament it occurs *eleven times*; in *one* of these instances it is rendered by *grave*, and in *ten* by *Hell*. It was not assumed that these renderings, or at least one class of them, must be wrong; on the contrary, it was admitted that the very fact that they had been made by the learned Translators carried with it strong probability of their essential correctness—not so strong, indeed, as to make unnecessary an investigation or to show the impropriety of this assumption in order thereto, yet sufficiently strong to make manifest the importance of the limitation.

As to the mode of the investigation—all the passages in which Hades occurs were tabulated and compared together, with the view of determining whether, consistently with the contextual requirements of each, some uniform meaning might not be given to the term. The experiment was successful beyond most sanguine expectation. It resulted in the conviction that by Hades is designated—I. Not *the grave;* II. Not *Hell;* III. Not the *Unseen World*, including Heaven and Hell; IV. Not *the state of death;* V. But—(1) a *Place* in the Unseen World distinct from both Heaven and Hell; (2) having, before the resurrection of Christ, two compartments—one of comfort, the other of misery; (3) to which, antecedent to the resurrection of Christ, the souls of all who died were carried; (4) into which Christ, at His death, descended, delivering the souls of the righteous; (5) to which, since the ascension of Christ, the souls of the wicked, and of the wicked only, have been consigned; (6) in which they are reserved in misery against the day of general judgment; (7) from which they are then to be brought for public judgment previously to their being cast into Hell.

The following argument is designed to commend the foregoing results of private study to others. It will be found to be strictly Scriptural. The truth of the facts on which it is based can be readily tested by any one who has access to the Englishman's Hebrew, the Englishman's Greek, and Cruden's English Concordance.

As a further preliminary it is proper, though scarcely necessary, to state that in conducting the special arguments to prove that Hades is not *the grave*, is not *Hell*, etc., it is not designed to assert that in many particular passages the original term *cannot* bear the meanings denied to them. It is freely admitted that in some instances it may be translated *grave*, and in others *Hell*, without destroying the sense. And so in some instances it might be translated *house*, and in others *ship*. This is but saying that in every passage the context does not determine the meaning of all the terms employed therein. It is contended, first, that in no passage are these meanings *required* by the context; and, secondly, that in many they are excluded thereby. It is also claimed that it will become apparent upon a careful examination that, while the one meaning attributed to the term in this Excursus is *required* by many passages, it is *excluded* by none—that consistently with the context, it may

* [In two of these, the *Margin* reads *grave*.—E. R. C.]

be put upon it in *every* instance of its occurrence in the Word of God.

It is also proper to mention that independent arguments will not be presented in proof of each one of the points included in the last general topic. It is believed that the truth of each will appear in the course of the general discussion.

I. *Hades not the Grave.*

This will be argued, in the first place, from data afforded by the Old Testament; and, secondly, from that afforded by the New.

A. That Hades must be regarded as having been used in the Old Testament to designate something different from *the literal grave*, seems to be evident from the following considerations:

1. It is never construed in the mode, nor with the terms, continually employed in the case of קֶבֶר (or קְבוּרָה), and which unmistakably mark that term as designating the place of the sepulture of the body. Thus קֶבֶר is used in both singular and plural;—it has a territorial location, Ex. xiv. 11; its site is purchased and sold, Gen. xxiii. 4–20; it is possessed by the owner of the soil or by the person buried therein, Gen. l. 5, xxxv. 20; it is dug by human hands, Gen. l. 5; it is connected with the verb signifying *to bury*, Gen. xlvii. 30;—dead *bodies* are buried in it by living men, Gen. l. 13;—it is marked by a monument, Gen. xxxv. 20; it may be touched by living men, Num. xix. 16; literal dead bones are in it, 2 Kings xiii. 21;—it may be opened by men and the bones exhumed, 2 Kings xxiii. 16. Hades is always singular; it is never thus construed; it is not in a single instance thus spoken of.

2. It is spoken of with expressions of comparison utterly inconsistent with the idea of the literal grave. Thus we read of—"The *lowest* Hades," Deut. xxxii. 22, Ps. lxxxvi. 13; "The *depths* of Hades," Prov. ix. 18; "The *midst* of Hades," Ezek. xxxii. 21.

3. It is in two instances clearly distinguished from *the grave*. In Gen. xxxvii. 35, where it first appears in the Bible, Jacob declares—"I will go down into Hades unto my son;" but from verse 33 we learn that the Patriarch was under the impression that Joseph had not, and could not have, a grave; he is there represented as exclaiming, "An evil beast hath devoured him." And in Isaiah xiv. 15 it is declared that Lucifer shall be "brought down to Hades," who, ver. 19, is represented as being "cast out of his (קֶבֶר) *grave.*"

4. It is used in antithesis with Heaven under circumstances which show that the literal grave cannot be intended. "It is as high as Heaven, what canst thou do? deeper than Hades, what canst thou know?" Job xi. 8. "If I ascend up into Heaven, thou art there; if I make my bed in Hades, behold, thou art there," Ps. cxxxix. 8. "Though they dig into Hades, thence shall mine hand take them; though they climb up to Heaven, thence will I bring them down," Amos ix. 2.

5. In the poetical Books it never occurs in one of two parallel clauses, answering to קֶבֶר in the other; nor under any other circumstances which grammatically require us to regard it as a synonym thereof.

6. It is manifestly used as synonymous with two other terms which cannot be regarded as indicating the literal grave—*viz:* בּוֹר* (*pit*) and אֶרֶץ תַּחְתִּיּוֹת *nether parts of the earth.*

The former of these, בּוֹר, occurs fifteen times, and is distinguished from קֶבֶר by all the general characteristics by which Hades is distinguished from it. That it is synonymous with Hades, or that it indicates a compartment thereof, is abundantly evident. In Ps. xxx. 3 the words appear in corresponding hemistiches—"O Lord, thou hast brought my soul from Hades; thou hast kept me alive that I should not go down to the (בּוֹר) *pit.*" The same occurs in Prov. i. 12. "Let us swallow them up alive as Hades; and whole as those who go down to the *pit.*" It is evident upon bare inspection that in Isaiah xiv. 15—"Thou shalt be brought down to Hades, to the sides of the *pit*"—the בּוֹר of the second clause is synonymous with the *Hades* of the first; it is also evident that it is synonymous with the *Hades* of verses 9 and 11, rendered in the former *Hell* and in the latter *grave.* That these words are synonymous will be further evident from an examination of Ezek. xxxi. 14–18. In that passage Hades occurs three times—in ver. 15 it is translated *grave*; and in vers. 16 and 17, *Hell:* בּוֹר occurs twice, in vers. 14 and 16, and in both instances is rendered *pit.* The words translated "*nether parts of the earth,*" in vers. 14, 16 and 18, are תַּחְתִּית אֶרֶץ—a compound term manifestly synonymous with the other two.

The phrase אֶרֶץ תַּחְתִּית or אֶרֶץ תַּחְתִּיּוֹת occurs nine times. In Ezek. xxxi. 14, 16, 18; xxxii. 18, 24; xxvi. 20, it is manifestly synonymous with Hades. In Ps. cxxxix. 15 it is used as a figurative expression for the *womb.* It also appears in Is. xliv. 23 and Ps. lxiii. 9 (10). What does it mean in these passages? Dr Hodge, in his *Commentary on Ephesians* (iv. 9), remarks concerning this phrase that it "is used for the Earth in opposition to Heaven, Is. xliv 23; probably for the grave in Ps. lxiii. 9; as a poetical designation for the womb in Ps. cxxxix. 15; and for Hades or the invisible world, Ezek. xxxi. 24." He gives no reason for any of these interpretations, evidently presuming that their correctness would be manifest upon inspection. No exception can be taken as to the propriety of his opinion in the last two instances, (save as to the judgment concerning the nature of Hades conveyed by the use of the alternative phrase—"or the invisible world"). It should be carefully noted, however, that the phrase appears in Ezekiel, not only in the *one* passage referred to by him, but in *five* others,—in all of which it is manifest that it *must* be synonymous with Hades. This then is not only an established, but is the leading sense of the expression; and we must conclude that it has this sense in the other *three* passages unless the contrary be *required* by the contexts.

---

* [This word should not be confounded with שַׁחַת, also occasionally translated *pit*, as in Psalm xxx. 9, and which is sometimes synonymous with קֶבֶר regarded as the place of physical corruption. The word translated *pit* in Ps. xxx. is בּוֹר as above.—E. R. C.]

Now in Ps. cxxxix. 15 the context *requires* that we should attach to it a figurative meaning. But what is there in the other passages to make it necessary to depart from the leading sense? Most certainly when the Psalmist exclaimed, Ps. lxiii. 9, "Those that seek my soul to destroy it shall go into *the lower parts of the earth*," there is nothing to forbid the idea that he meant they should go into Hades. Nor, on the suppo ition that Hades was a place of conscious existence to which the souls of the departed good as well as of the evil were carried, is there anything unnatural or improbable in supposing that when Isaiah (xliv. 23) wrote, "Sing, O ye heavens, for the Lord hath done it: shout, ye *lower parts of the earth*," he intended to call on Hades to rejoice.

7. Those in Hades are spoken of as being in a state of conscious existence, which never occurs in the case of the occupants of קְבֶר. In Is. xiv. 4–17, the chief ones of the earth who are already imprisoned in Hades, are represented as greeting the King of Babylon at his entrance with the words, "Art thou also become weak as we?" Similar teaching is found in Ezek. xxx. 16, xxxii. 21. With this agrees the idea suggested by the phrases, "sorrows of Hades," 2 Sam. xxii. 6, Ps. xviii. 5 (6); "pains of Hades," Ps. cxvi. 3; and with this agree also the facts that the *womb* (תַּחְתִּיּוֹת אָרֶץ), Ps. cxxxix. 15, and the *belly of the whale* in which Jonah (ii. 2) was imprisoned—both places of conscious existence, though of darkness and confinement—were figured by Hades. All this, it is true, may be attributed to the poetic license—and so any teaching of the poetic Scriptures may thus be attributed. Nevertheless the fact remains that these decl rations are found in the inspired Word of God in connection with Hades, and the further fact that similar expressions are never found in connection with קְבֶר.

In view of all the foregoing considerations it seems rational to conclude that in the Old Testament Scriptures the term Hades was not used to designate *the literal grave*. Certain exegetical objections to this conclusion, may, however, present themselves to the minds of some. These, so far as they are known, or can be imagined, will now be considered.

(1) It may be urged that the declarations of Jacob and his sons concerning the bringing down of *gray hairs* to Hades, Gen. xlii. 38, xliv. 29, 31; and the direction of David to Solomon to bring to Hades the *hoar heads* of Joab and Shimei, 1 Kings ii. 6, 9; seem to imply that Hades was regarded as the resting-place of the *body*. This might be admitted, and at the same time a valid argument be drawn from other Scriptures requiring us to put another than the apparently normal construction upon the words of the Patriarch and David. We are not, however, driven to such a strait as this. Let it be observed that there is nothing in the form of the expressions to forbid our regarding the phrases *gray hairs* and *hoar heads* as indicating men *in a state of old age*. From this point of view there is nothing unnatural in regarding the Hades to which these old men were to be brought as a place of departed spirits. In the case of Jacob, for a reason already given, we cannot regard him

as contemplating under this term the liter l grave.

(2) In several passages, it may also be objected, Hades is spoken of under terms proper only to the *grave*. Ps. vi. 5 (6), "In Hades who shall give thee thanks?" Is. xxxviii. 18, "Hades cannot praise thee, death cannot celebrate thee; they that go down to the pit cannot hope for thy truth;"—Ecc. ix. 10, ' Whatsoever thy hand findeth to do, do it with thy might; for there is no work, nor device, nor knowledge, nor wisdom, in Hades, whither thou goest." * It must be acknowledged that these passages, in themselves, irrespective of the condition of the writers, are consistent with the idea that by the term Hades as employed in them was meant the *literal* grave. This, however, is not a necessary interpretation—and if it be, let it be observed, these texts must be regarded as affirming that the grave is the end of man, as denying the immortality of the soul. But the passages are also consistent with the idea that by Hades is meant *the state of death*, or *Hell*, or *a place of gloom in the Unseen World* distinct from Hell. In the progress of the discussion each of these hypotheses will be considered.

(3) Again, it may be contended that the ideas of *burial* and *consumption*, which are ideas proper only to *the grave*, are presented in the following passages: Ps. xlix. 14 (15), "Like sheep they are laid in Hades, death shall feed on them," etc.; Job xxiv. 19, "Drought and heat consume the snow waters; so doth Hades those which have sinned."

The difficulty in these passages is altogether in the English translation. Dr. J. Addison Alexander translates the former, " Like a flock to the grave (Hades) they drive; death is their shepherd." In Job xxiv. 19, the verb translated *consume* is properly rendered *violently take*, as in the margin; the reference is to the *rapacity* of Hades—not to the consumption of the body. The declaration in the following verse—"the worm shall feed sweetly on him," may refer to the condition of the body when the spirit has been seized by Hades.

(4) It may also be asserted that in the Book of Job, especially in the xvii. chapter, the oneness of Hades with the grave seems to be naturally implied.

In the xvii. of Job, most of the words that have been brought into this discussion are employed: קְבֶר, ver. 1; Hades, ver. 13; שַׁחַת, ver. 14; and בּוֹר, ver. 16. At first glance it would seem as though these terms had been used indiscriminately as synonyms for each other. Careful inspection, however, shows that they may be regarded as indicating the future of the *entire man* —the *body* to the grave, the *spirit* to the place of departed spirits. We, of the present day, sometimes speak of the *grave* as our place after death, and sometimes of the *world of spirits* as our place, without intending thereby to imply our belief that they are one and the same. So is language employed in the book of Job; and in chap. xvii. both forms of expression are introduced. Thus, naturally—and only thus—can the phraseology employed in Job be reconciled with itself and with other Scriptures.

* [It is by no means certain that this pass ge, Ecc. ix. 10, is to be regarded as an inspired utterance.—E. R. C.]

B. The New Testament teaching as to the distinction between Hades and μνῆμα or μνημεῖον (the *grave* or *sepulchre*) is remarkably clear.

The term, as remarked in the Introduction of this Excursus, occurs but *eleven* times in the New Testament, and in every instance save one it is, in the English Version, translated *Hell*. The excepted case is in 1 Cor. xv. 55, "O *grave*, where is thy victory." That in the other instances it will not bear the translation *grave* is evident upon bare inspection. These are as follows: "And thou, Capernaum, which art exalted unto Heaven, shalt be brought down to Hades," Matt. xi. 23: "The gates of Hades shall not prevail against it" (the Church), Matt. xvi. 18; "And thou, Capernaum . . . shalt be thrust down to Hades," Luke x. 15; "And in Hades he (Dives) lifted up his eyes, being in torment," Luke xvi. 23; "Thou wilt not leave my soul in Hades," Acts ii. 27; "His soul was not left in Hades," Acts ii. 31; "I ... have the keys of Hades and of death," Rev. i. 18; "His name was Death and Hades followed with him," Rev. vi. 8; "Death and Hades delivered up the dead that were in them," Rev. xx. 13; "Death and Hades were cast into the lake of fire," Rev. xx. 14.

The New Testament idea of Hades as distinct from the *grave* may be most clearly perceived in the declaration concerning Dives in Luke xvi. 23; and in the didactic teaching of the Apostle Peter, Acts ii. 27–31, concerning the *soul* of Jesus between His death and His resurrection. The Apostle, manifestly, spoke of both the body and the soul of our Lord (comp. vers. 27 and 31), asserting that the former did not see corruption (although it was placed in a *sepulchre*), and that the latter was not left in Hades—implying, of course, that it went to Hades. Unless we adopt the conclusion that the soul sleeps with the dead body in the tomb—in the face of the manifest implications of the Apostle and the whole tenor of the Word of God—Hades must be distinct from the *tomb*. That the soul of Jesus did descend into Hades will, it is believed, more abundantly appear in the course of this Excursus.

Reference has been made to *one* instance in the New Testament in which the E. V. renders Hades by *grave*, *viz.*, 1 Cor. xv. 55. In his comment on this passage, Dr. Hodge writes, in immediate continuance of what has already been quoted—"Here where the special reference is to the bodies of men and to the delivery of them from the power of death, it is properly rendered the *grave*. The Apostle is not speaking of the delivery of souls of men from any intermediate state, but of the redemption of the body." It is indeed true that the *special* reference is to the glorification of the body. But does this forbid the idea that there should be any reference to the soul, that, in the moment of the body's glorification and in essential order thereto, re-animates that body? If indeed there be, or has been, no place of the soul's imprisonment, then, of course, there can be no reference to such a place; but if, on the other hand, there is, or has been, such a place, what more natural than that, in view of the redemption of the body, which involves the complete

deliverance of the soul, reference should be made to that deliverance?[*]

From all that has been said, it seems evident that the New Testament confirms the teaching of the Old as to the distinction between Hades and *the literal grave*.

II. *Hades not Hell regarded as the Place of Final Punishment.*

There are three opinions concerning Hades which it is important should be clearly distinguished from each other: the first, that it is *Hell*; the second, that it is the *Unseen World* including both Heaven and Hell; the third, that it is a term having no reference to *place*, but indicating merely *the state of death*. The first and second of these are often confounded together, and the second and third. That, however, they constitute three essentially distinct doctrines is evident upon reflection. It is designed in this section to show the fallacy of the first.

1. That Hades cannot be regarded as indicating *merely* Hell, is manifest from the fact that it is represented as the dwelling place (antecedent to the resurrection of Jesus) of all the righteous dead.

The Patriarch Jacob declared his expectation of going into Hades, Gen. xxxvii. 35; Job made a like declaration, Job xvii. 13; the inspired David, Ps. xvi. 10, and the righteous Hezekiah, Is. xxxviii. 18, used language which implied that they entertained a similar expectation.

But the location of the spirits of these worthies in Hades locates all the rest of the righteous. Concerning Jacob it is declared, that upon his death he was "gathered unto his people," Gen. xlix. 33. This expression,—and the remark is also true of the similar phrase, "gathered unto his fathers,"—is one having reference to the *spirit*, and not to the *body*. That it is not an euphemism, as some contend, for *being buried*, is evident from three considerations: (1) Concerning Jacob it is declared, that "he gathered up his feet into the bed, and yielded up the ghost, and was gathered unto his people," Gen. xlix. 33. He was "gathered unto his people" immediately upon his death; but he was not buried until long after, Gen. l. 13; (2) Concerning both Abraham, Gen. xxv. 8, 9, and Isaac, Gen. xxxv. 29, it is declared that they *died*, and were *gathered unto their people*, and were *buried*; and (3) To Josiah God declared: "I will gather thee unto thy fathers, and thou shalt be gathered unto thy grave (קֶבֶר) in peace," 2 Kings xxii. 20. Manifestly, being *gathered to one's people* (*or fathers*) was something distinct from both *death* and *burial*; and, further, God gathered to the fathers *man* buried. The expression could have reference only to the spirit, and indicates the fact that all departed souls were carried to one place.

It may appear to some that Acts xiii. 36 mili-

---

* [The preponderance of textual authority, as is well-known, favors the reading θάνατε instead of ᾅδη. If this reading be correct, the passage is, of course, removed from the field of the present investigation. It is to be observed, however, it is to be observed that there is no a single in-stance in the New Testament in which this context even apparently favors the rendering of Hades by the (*literal*) *grave*.—E. R. C.]

tates against the preceding explanation. It is therein declared, that David "fell on sleep, and was laid to his fathers, and saw corruption." The Greek words translated "*laid* to his fathers" (προσετέθη πρὸς τοὺς πατέρας αὐτοῦ) are those used in the Septuagint to translate that oft-recurring Hebrew phrase which is rendered in the English Version: "*gathered* to his fathers." It must be acknowledged that in this passage, at first glance, the phrase seems to be an euphuism for *buried;* and this impression is deepened in the mind of the reader of the English Version by the improper rendering of προσετέθη as *laid to,* instead of *gathered to.* The idea of burial is not merely suggested, but is directly presented by the term employed in translation. This is indeed a possible, though a most unusual, rendering of the verb. In this *Septuagintal* phrase, however, it is manifestly excluded by the fact that in the Septuagint it is the translation of the Hebrew אָסַף, and consequently can have no meaning that the Hebrew verb has not. Now, whilst προσετέθη *may* mean *laid to,* אָסַף never has that meaning. The verse properly translated reads: "David fell asleep, and was *gathered* to his fathers, and saw corruption." This declaration, from bare inspection of it as it occurs in the New Testament, *may* mean either, (1) David died, and his body was buried, and saw corruption—the reference being only to the lower nature; or (2) David died, and his *spirit* went to the place of departed spirits, and his *body* saw corruption—the reference being to the whole man. Nor is there anything in the context that will enable us to decide which of these is the correct interpretation. We must be guided in our determination by the *usus loquendi* of the Hebrews. As we have seen that amongst them that phrase had reference to the spirit, we must place that meaning upon it when employed by the Apostle.

The foregoing argument in proof that the righteous dead were collected in Hades is fully borne out by the parable of Dives and Lazarus, Luke xvi. 19-31. Our Lord does not indeed directly declare that Lazarus was in Hades—concerning Dives only was this declaration made, ver. 23: "And in Hades he lifted up his eyes, being in torments." The whole parable, however, seems to be constructed on the idea that both were there—though in different compartments thereof. The underlying thought seems to be that Hades is a world to which the spirits of all the dead are consigned, having two compartments—one of comfort, and the other of misery—separated by an impassable gulf or chasm, but within speaking distance of each other. That our Lord did not intend to represent Lazarus as in Heaven seems to be evident. The place of his abode is not styled *Heaven,* but *Abraham's bosom;* he is not represented as being carried *up* to it (the general form of expression when Heaven is the terminus), he is simply carried; it is within speaking distance of Dives, being separated from him only by a chasm—but Heaven and Hades are represented as being poles apart: "It is as high as Heaven —deeper than Hades," Job xi. 8; its central figure is not God, but Abraham; God is not

24

there in His glory, nor angels save as ministers of transportation; it is not represented as a place of perfect bliss—Lazarus is merely *comforted* (παρακαλεῖται), a term never used in descriptions of the blessedness of Heaven. The hypothesis that Jesus contemplated Lazarus as in Hades not only gives force and consistency to the whole parable, but is directly in accordance with the natural interpretation of the brief and scattered teachings of the Old Testament concerning the abode of the righteous dead. It presumes that He spoke just as we would suppose that a Jew, acquainted with the sacred Books of his people, would speak. So natural is this hypothesis that there have been interpreters who adopted it, and then attempted to explain our Lord's implied representation of the position of Lazarus as a mere condescension to Jewish prejudices!

In view of all the facts, is it possible to resist the conclusion that in uttering this parable, our Lord recognized the existence of a Jewish belief as to the abode of the righteous in accordance with the natural interpretation of the Old Testament teachings, and that He also recognized the correctness of that belief?[*]

The fact that the pious dead, as well as the wicked, were in Hades, excludes the idea of its being, *in its entirety,* Hell regarded as the place of final punishment.

III. *Hades not the Unseen World including Heaven and Hell.*

The dogma now about to be controverted is to be carefully distinguished from another with which it is too frequently confounded, and which will hereafter be considered, *viz.* that Hades indicates *the state of death.* In the view now before us, it is **a** *place;* in the other, a *condition.*

If Hades be the Unseen World—*a Place* including the *places* HEAVEN and HELL, as Europe includes France and Germany—and if there be no other place included therein, then the *Hades of the wicked* must be *Hell,* and the *Hades of the righteous* must be *Heaven.* The effort will now be made to show that neither of these subordinate hypotheses is scriptural.

1. Hades, as the present abode of the disembodied spirits of the wicked, is not Hell. Throughout the Scriptures it is distinguished from the place of final punishment of devils and men.

In the beginning of this particular investigation, special attention is called to the fact that nowhere in the Bible is it said that fallen angels are in Hades, or that they are to be consigned thereto. The Lucifer, Is. xiv. 15, spoken of as "brought down to Hades," was not the fallen Archangel; but, as we learn from ver. 4 of the same chapter, the King of Babylon. The word translated *Hell* in 2 Pet. ii. 4: "God spared not angels that sinned, but cast them down to Hell," is not Hades. The whole phrase *cast them down to Hell* is the translation of the participle ταρταρώσας—*i. e.* cast them into Tartarus. Devils have another place of punishment than Hades, *viz., Tartarus,* as in the passage just cited; or

---

[*] [The very parable suggests the idea that the phrase *Abraham's bosom* might have been **a** Jewish **name** for the place of departed Saints in Hades.—E. R. C.]

the *abyss*, as in Luke viii. 31, where the legion of unclean spirits cast out from the possessed man in the country of the Gadarenes are represented as beseeching our Lord "that he would not command them to go out into the (ἄβυσσον) *deep.*" This matter, however, will hereafter be more fully considered.

In the Old Testament there is occasionally and dimly set forth the existence of a place of darkness and woe other than Hades, *viz.*, Abaddon (אֲבַדּוֹן), translated in our Version *destruction.* Thus Job xxvi. 6, "Hades is naked before Him, and Abaddon hath no covering;" Job xxviii. 22, "Abaddon and *death* (מָוֶת) say, We have heard the fame thereof;" Job xxxi. 12, "It is a fire that consumeth to Abaddon;" Ps. lxxxviii. 12, "Shall thy loving-kindness be declared in the *grave* (קֶבֶר), or thy faithfulness in Abaddon?" Prov. xv. 11, "Hades and Abaddon are ever before the Lord;" Prov. xxvii. 20, "Hades and Abaddon are never full."

As we enter the New Testament, we perceive that what is but dimly adumbrated in the Old, is therein distinctly declared—though concealed from the readers of the English Version by infelicities of translation.

In Rev. ix. 1–3 an angel to whom was given the key of the pit of *the Abyss* (τὸ φρέαρ τῆς ἀβύσσου—incorrectly translated *bottomless pit*) opens the pit whence come out locusts. These locusts are described, verse 11, as having "a King over them, who is the Angel of the pit of the Abyss, whose name in the Hebrew tongue is Abaddon, but in the Greek tongue hath his name Apollyon." Now, be it remembered that Abaddon is the name of that place of woe mentioned in the Old Testament other than Hades—of which term ἀπώλεια (*Apoleia*) is the Septuagint translation. Does not the name given to this leader beget, to say the least, the *suspicion* that either the pit whence he comes, or the place of woe to which he is to be consigned, should it prove other than the pit, may be the Abaddon shadowed forth in the Old Testament?

In Rev. xvii. 8 reference is made to a Beast that ascends out of the pit of *the abyss* and who is to go into *perdition* (ἀπώλεια); in xix. 20 he is represented as being cast "into the (not *a*) lake of fire burning with brimstone"—manifestly he meets his foretold doom, this lake of fire is the Apoleia, the Abaddon, into which he was to go. In Rev. xx. 8 Satan is represented as being shut up in the *Abyss* for a thousand years; after his imprisonment he is loosed again for a little season, and then, ver. 10, is cast into "the lake of fire and brimstone where the Beast and the False Prophet are"—he also is cast into APOLEIA. Then follows the account of the general judgment (vers. 11–13), after which (vers. 14, 15) "*death* and *Hades*" (or those detained by them) were to be cast into the same lake. This is declared to be *the second death.* It seems unquestionable that this "*lake of fire*" (*Apoleia*=Abaddon), from which both *Hades*, and *the pit of the Abyss* seem to be distinguished, as jails from the penitentiary, is *Hell* regarded as the place of the final and everlasting punishment of devils and ungodly men.

With the instruction thus gathered from the Apocalypse, agree the teachings elsewhere scattered through the New Testament. It is a well known fact that there are two words in the Greek Testament which in the English Version are rendered Hell—*Hades* and *Gehenna.* Our Lord is represented as employing the former of these only three times—in reference to the humiliation of Capernaum, Matt. xi. 23; Luke x. 15; to the deliverance of the Church from its power, Matt. xvi. 18; and to the imprisonment of the *disembodied* spirit of Dives, Luke xvi. 23. When he uttered His fearful threatenings concerning the casting of both *body* and *soul* into Hell, into *unquenchable* fire, the term employed by him was *Gehenna*; see Matt. v. 22, 29, 30; x. 28; xviii. 9; xxiii. 15, 33; Mark ix. 43–47; Luke xii. 5. These passages, especially Mark ix. 43, where Gehenna is described as the place of "the fire that never shall be quenched," immediately connect themselves with Matt. xiii. 42 and xxv. 41, and show that this place of torment is "the furnace of fire"—the "everlasting fire prepared for the Devil and his angels," into which at "the end of the world"—after the judgment—the wicked are to be cast. And these passages are manifestly parallel with Rev. xx. 10-15—"the furnace of fire" and the "everlasting fire prepared for the Devil and his angels" are "the lake of fire" into which the Devil and those delivered up by Hades for judgment shall be cast.

Directly in line with the teachings thus developed are those of the Apostles. Peter and Jude (2 Pet. ii. 4; Jude 6) agree in declaring that the angels who kept not their first estate are "reserved in everlasting chains under darkness unto the judgment of the great day." Are they not in *the pit of the abyss* (with the exception of those permitted for a season to come forth with their leader), reserved for that awful day when, with Satan, they shall be cast into that "everlasting fire prepared for the Devil and his angels?" The "*everlasting destruction*" threatened in 2 Thess. i. 9, is to be inflicted after Jesus has come in flaming fire taking vengeance—after His advent for judgment. Until that time also, when "the Lord cometh with ten thousand of His saints to execute judgment upon all," "is reserved the blackness of darkness forever" which the Apostle Jude teaches us is *reserved* for the ungodly, Jude 11-15. That the ungodly are in *Hades* all admit, but they are not yet in their place of final and everlasting punishment—they are not yet in *Hell.*

Another line of thought bearing on this special subject will now be presented, rather by way of question than of argument. In view of the use of *apoleia* (*abaddon*) in the Old Testament and in the Book of Revelation, may there not be some reference to the place of *final punishment* when it is employed by Jesus and His Apostles—especially when the article is expressed, as is frequently the case? Our Lord declares, Matt. vii. 13, "Broad is the road that leadeth to τὴν ἀπώλειαν. He describes Judas, John xvii. 12, as "the son of τῆς ἀπωλείας. The Apostle Paul, 2 Thess. ii. 3, speaks of the revelation of "the son of τῆς ἀπωλείας. See also Rom. ix. 22; Phil. iii. 19; Heb. x. 39; 1 Tim. vi. 9; 2 Pet. ii. 1, 3; iii. 7. But whatever may be the force of this last consideration, it seems impossible to avoid the conclusion from those previously presented that Hades, so far as it is the prison of the ungodly dead, is not the same as Hell regarded as the everlasting prison of devils and men; as before remarked, it bears to that place of woe a relation similar to that of the jail to the penitentiary.

2. The *Hades of the good* is not *Heaven*. This is evident from the following considerations:

(1) God, angels, Jesus Christ (save during the time between His death and resurrection), are never represented as abiding therein. This is scarce explicable on the hypothesis that Hades is a general term for the Unseen World. It may be said, however, that the term is employed only in reference to the spirits of deceased men. This answer, it will be observed, exceedingly limits the hypothesis we are considering.

(2) Hades, *as an entirety*, is distinguished from Heaven. This is done in two distinct modes. (*a*) By being placed in antithesis therewith, as in Job xi. 8, "It is as high as Heaven; what canst thou do? deeper than Hades; what canst thou know?" See also Ps. cxxx. 8, Amos ix. 2. (*b*) By being *localized* as beneath the surface of the earth. Thus it is described by the synonym "*nether parts of the earth;*" and approach to it is universally described as *a descent* —thus, Num. xvi. 33, Korah and his company are described as going "down alive into Hades" through the opening earth.

(3) Not only is the idea of *situation beneath the earth* presented when the wicked are spoken of, but also when the entrance thereinto of the righteous is described. Not only is it declared that Korah and his company "*went down* alive into (the pit) Hades;" but, also, Jacob exclaimed, Gen. xxxvii. 35, "I will *go down* into Hades unto my son." Not only did Saul ask the witch of Endor "*to bring up* Samuel," (1 Sam. xxviii. 8), thus testifying to the popular belief as to the *descent* of the spirits of the good; and not only did the terrified woman exclaim, (ver. 13) "I *saw* gods *ascending* out of the earth," but the spirit of Samuel (unquestionably his spirit, raised, not by the incantations of the woman, but by the power of God) is represented as saying to the King, (ver. 15) "Why hast thou disquieted me to *bring me up?*" Of Elijah alone of all the Old Testament saints is it said that he *ascended*, and of him alone it is said that he went into Heaven (שָׁמַיִם). Unquestionably the idea of the *Hades of the good* presented in the Old Testament, is that of a *subterranean* place, distinct from Heaven. In strict accordance with the *usus loquendi* of the Old Testament, our Lord when he referred to His own abiding in Hades spoke of it as remaining "three days and nights in the *heart of the earth*," Matt. xii. 40; and the Apostle Paul in referring to the same event, Eph. iv. 9, wrote of Jesus as "descending into the *lower parts of the earth*"—but of this hereafter.

(4) That the *Hades of the good* is not Heaven, is evident from the fact that it is always spoken of as a place, at the best, of imperfect happiness—a place to be delivered from. The pious writer of the xlix. Psalm exclaimed (ver. 15 [16]) "God will redeem my soul from the power of Hades"—as of deliverance from a prison. David, who had bright visions of a future glory after he had seen the face of the Deliverer (Ps. xvii. 15), wrote, not only prophetically concerning the Messiah, but also concerning himself, Ps. xvi. 10, "Thou wilt not leave my soul in Hades." In strict accordance with the idea set forth in these passages that Hades was a prison, are the words in Hosea xiii. 14, referred to by the Apostle Paul in 1 Cor. xv. 54, 55, "I will redeem them from the hand of Hades, I will ransom them from death. O death, I will be thy plagues; O Hades, I will be thy destruction." Here the separation of soul and body seems to be set forth by the appropriate term מָוֶת; the imprisoned condition of the separated soul, by the phrase *hand of Hades*. The promise is of a deliverance of the soul from its prison, and of a re-union of soul and body; or, in other words, of a resurrection of the body.

David also wrote concerning the Hades to which he was about to depart, but from which he was assured that he was in due time to be delivered, Ps. vi. 5 (6), "In Hades who shall give Thee thanks?" Dr. J. A. Alexander in his comment on these words writes: "In *Sheol*, the *grave*, as a general receptacle, here parallel to *death*, and like it meaning the unseen world or state of the dead, who will acknowledge or give thanks to Thee? The Hebrew verb denotes that kind of praise called forth by the experience of goodness.—This verse does not prove that David had no belief or expectation of a future state, nor that the intermediate state is an unconscious one, but only that in this emergency he looks no further than the close of life as the appointed term of thanksgiving and praise. Whatever might eventually follow, it was certain that his death would put an end to the praise of God, in that form and those circumstances to which he had been accustomed." The last remark is certainly true; and yet, is it conceivable that David could have written thus, on the supposition that the departing spirits of the righteous went immediately to Heaven? Could one about to depart immediately to the glorious praises of the land of glory, have penned, under the inspiration of the Spirit, the words "In Hades who shall give Thee thanks," on the supposition either that the *Hades of the good* was Heaven, or that the term indicated merely *the state of death?* Let one imagine, if possible, the Apostle Paul thus writing! The very explanation given by Dr. Alexander, requires that the Hades to which the Psalmist felt that he was to depart should have been a place either of unconsciousness, or of darkness and gloom. The only escape from this conclusion is in the hypothesis, not only that he was not inspired in this utterance, but also that he was in positive error as to the condition of departed saints. It is not enough to suppose that he was in ignorance or doubt as to his own spiritual condition—as to whether *he* was a saint. The implied assertion of the exclamation is universal—"In Hades who shall give Thee thanks?"

In manifest accordance with the teaching of the Old Testament on this subject, is that of the

New. When our Lord referred to the condition of Lazarus, Luke xvi. 25, he did not speak of him as enjoying the fullness of his Father's house, but as being "*comforted;*" a term, as before remarked, never used in reference to the joys of Heaven. And when the Apostle Paul spoke of the condition of the Old Testament worthies, he makes manifest reference to the incompleteness of their blessedness antecedent to the Christian dispensation. He wrote, Heb. xi. 39, 40, " And these all, having received a good report through faith, received not the promise, God having provided some better thing for us, that they without us should not be made perfect." Dr. Owen rejects this view, affirming, " the Apostle treats not here at all about the difference between one sort of men and another after death, as is evident from the very reading of the Epistle." With the highest reverence for the memory of that great man, the writer would remark that the very reading of the Epistle has led him to the opposite conclusion. The special section which includes the words quoted above, begins immediately upon the close of ch. x. 34. In the latter clause of that verse the Apostle had referred to the heavenly inheritance of those to whom he was then writing. The mention of this calls for a special section in which he may incite them to faithfulness in order to the obtaining of that inheritance. He therefore writes, vers. 35, 36, "Cast not away, therefore, your confidence, which hath great recompense of reward; for ye have need of patience, that, after ye have done the will of God, ye might receive the promise." *What* promise ? Manifestly that of the *heavenly* inheritance. He then proceeds to set forth the life of faith, which is in order to this inheritance, by the example of the Old Testament saints who had lived it in the midst of trials and afflictions. The natural apodosis of the recitals of chap. xi. would seem to be, 'These all, having received a good report through faith, having finished the race set before them, *received* the promise;' but not so—" They received *not* the promise; God having provided some better thing for us, that they without us should not be made perfect." Is it not manifest that the Apostle asserts that the old Testament worthies did not receive their *heavenly* inheritance until the Christian dispensation, and that the implied instruction to Christians is, 'You, who are called to earthly patience like theirs, run under better auspices than was vouchsafed to them, even the sure hope of *immediate* blessing ?'

(5) The great argument, however, in proof that the Hades of the righteous *was* not Heaven, is to be found in the fact of their deliverance therefrom at the Resurrection of our Lord. The consideration of this topic, however, more appropriately belongs to the concluding section, in which the effort will be made to establish the affirmative proposition that Hades is a place in the Unseen World distinct from Heaven and Hell.

IV. *Hades not the State of Death.*

The opinion that Hades indicates (at least frequently) a *state* and not a *place*, is one to a great extent entertained in Protestant Churches. This opinion appears to the writer to be unsupported by a single Scriptural passage, the context of which *requires* us to put such an interpretation upon it. The only texts that with apparent plausibility can be cited as teaching this doctrine are Ps. vi. 5 (6), " In Hades who shall give Thee thanks?" Isa. xxxviii. 18, " Hades cannot praise Thee ;" Eccles. ix. 10, " There is no work, nor device, nor wisdom in Hades." These passages, so far as the *immediate* contexts are concerned, are certainly consistent with the idea now under consideration, even as they are consistent with the opinion that by Hades the *literal grave* is intended. But they are also consistent with the idea that by the term is represented a *place of gloom;* and this idea, as we saw in the preceding section, the spiritual condition of the Psalmist requires us to put upon it.

The opinion, thus unsupported by a single unambiguous Scripture, stands opposed to that vast multitude of passages in which Hades is manifestly referred to as a *place*. Many of these texts have already been quoted, and it is unnecessary to re-cite them.

The real grounds of the opinion that Hades is a *state*, and not a *place*, are, as it seems to the writer, philosophical and theological, and not exegetical.

There are those whose psychological views cause them to shrink from any localization of a pure spirit, and who therefore affirm that Hades must indicate a *state*. The same views, it may be remarked, should lead, and in many cases do lead, to the affirmation that the terms Heaven and Hell are indicative, not of *places*, but of mere *conditions* of the soul.

Another ground is what may be styled the *pseudo-scientific*. It seems plain that if the language of Scripture is to be interpreted normally, the location of Hades is in *the heart of the earth*. There are many who shrink from this opinion as though it *must* be false. Why false? If Hades be a place, it must be *somewhere;* and if somewhere, why not in the centre of the Earth as well as elsewhere? True science, which confesses its ignorance concerning the internal condition of our globe, can, on this question, neither affirm nor deny.

Others, still, deny because of their pre-formed opinion that the righteous Patriarchs did depart to perfect blessedness. But manifestly if the Hades of the Old Testament was a *place*, it was a place of gloom. even in the case of the pious. The only refuge from this conclusion is in the opinion that the term has reference merely to the *state* of the soul separated from the body.

The main ground of the opinion, however, is, in the judgment of the writer, the manifest difficulty of harmonizing those texts in the Old Testament which speak of righteous Abraham and Jacob and David, as being in Hades, with those in the New Testament, which on the one hand declare that the righteous are taken to Heaven, and those which on the other hand declare that Hades shall be cast into the lake of fire. The very difficulty naturally suggests the hypothesis that Hades may be an *indefinite* term, meaning sometimes the state of death and sometimes the place of the lost—an hypothesis, however, utterly inconsistent with that mass of Scriptures which require us to *define* it as signifying *a place*. It may further be remarked that if there are intimations in Scripture that, at the Resurrection or Ascension of our Lord, a change was made in the place of abode of the souls of the righteous dead —that a new place in Heaven was prepared, to which those who had previously been consigned to Hades were removed, and to which the souls of those who now die in the Lord are carried— this ground of the hypothesis now contended against, is removed. The attempt will be made in the following section to show that there are such intimations.

V. *Hades a Place in the Unseen World distinct from Heaven and Hell.*

That HADES is such a place logically follows if there has been no fatal mistake in any of the preceding arguments. If it be not the literal Grave, nor Hell, nor the Unseen World including Heaven and Hell, nor the State of Death, then it must be a third place in the Unseen World. The truth of this conclusion would at once be invalidated if a single text of Scripture could be cited which clearly teaches that there are but *two* places in the Unseen World. No such text, however, has been, or, it is believed, can be, adduced. The position of Protestant Theologians who have denied the existence of a third place, so far as is known to the writer, never has been that the Scriptures directly assert that there are but two places, but that they recognize the existence of only two. In this view of the state of the question, the conclusion that the Word of God does teach the existence of a third place might be left to the judgment of the reader without further remark.

There is, however, another argument bearing on the point that should not be omitted, *viz.* that arising from the fact that Christ, between the periods of His death and resurrection, delivered from Hades a captivity detained therein. If it be true that our Lord did perform such a work, then is it evident that Hades is a place distinct from both Heaven and Hell. The fact that He did so, the writer believes to be referred to in several passages of Scripture, and directly taught in Eph. iv. 8, 9: "When He ascended up on high, He led captivity captive, and gave gifts unto men. Now that He ascended, what is it but that He also descended first into the lower parts of the Earth."

That the place to which our Lord ascended, leading "captivity captive" (whatever this phrase may mean), was Heaven, none deny. That the place to which He descended was Hades, and that the "captivity" consisted of the pious dead, seem to the writer to be the natural and legitimate meanings of the terms employed.

That our Lord did at His death go into Hades (whatever Hades may be) is admitted by all. But the phrase, in the passage now under consideration, translated "*lower parts of the earth*" (τὰ κατώτερα μέρη τῆς γῆς) is, as we saw in Section I. of this Excursus, the Greek equivalent for one of the Hebrew synonyms for Hades. Is it not natural to conclude that the Apostle Paul, in using this well-established Old Testament synonym for Hades, had in his mind the same fact to which the Apostle Peter referred when in his Pentecostal sermon he declared

(Acts ii. 31): "His soul was not left in Hades?"

It also seems clear to the writer that, in accordance with Scripture usage, the phrase "*led captivity captive*" must have reference to the deliverance of captured friends. This phrase, *unqualified*, occurs but twice in the Old Testament—once in the Psalm from which the Apostle quotes it, Ps. lxviii. 18; and again in the Song of Deborah and Barak, Judges v. 12: "Arise, Barak, and lead thy captivity captive, thou son of Ahinoam." Regarded merely as a phrase, it may mean either of two things: (1) to lead as prisoners a number of enemies, or (2) to lead as re-captured a number of friends previously captured by an enemy. The latter seems to be its most natural interpretation;[*] and this manifestly is its meaning in Judges v. 12, the only passage in which the context determines the meaning. It is clearly implied, Judg. iv. 16, that Barak took no prisoners, in the words: "All the host of Sisera fell upon the edge of the sword, and there was not a man left." The captivity that Barak led captive *must* have been captured Israel. As this interpretation is manifestly the meaning of the phrase in one of the two instances of its occurrence in the Old Testament, it is but logical to conclude that it is its meaning in the other also. This conclusion is strengthened by the considerations, first, that there is nothing in Ps. lxviii. to forbid our putting this interpretation upon it; and, secondly, that the Song of Deborah and Barak was manifestly in the mind of the inspired writer when he penned the Psalm. This is evident from a comparison of the two passages of Scripture.

This, then, is not only the natural, but the scripturally suggested interpretation of Eph. iv. 8, 9,—that Christ descended into Hades, and then ascended into Heaven (above all Heavens), leading a multitude whom He had delivered (captured) from captivity.

As against the interpretation that by "the lower parts of the earth" the Apostle meant Hades, Dr. Eadie, in his Commentary on this Epistle, queries: "Why not use ᾅδης, when it had been so markedly employed before, had he wished to give it prominence?" It might be retorted: Why use "the lower parts of the earth"—an Old Testament synonym for *Hades*— if he meant simply *the earth?* His own explanation that by the descent of Christ into "the lower parts of the earth" is meant that He was born in a low condition—"born not under fretted roofs and amidst marble halls," *etc.*, is manifestly untenable. The Greek phrase will not bear that interpretation. Two reasons for the Apostle's selection of the phrase, however, may

---

[*] [The words translated "lead captive a captivity" occur a third time in the Scriptures, Num. xxi. 1, under circumstances which show that the *captivity* consisted of the enemies made prisoners. At first glance this fact may seem to militate against the position taken as to the *natural* force of the phrase—a closer examination, however, tends rather to confirm the view of the writer. The phrase in Num. xxi. 1 is not the same as that in the other passages; it is *qualified* by the introduction of the term מִמֶּנּוּ (*a parte ejus*) the whole clause reads וַיִּשְׁבְּ מִמֶּנּוּ שֶׁבִי. This term limits the captivity taken by the Canaanites to have been *of (the number of) Israel.* Its very introduction seems to indicate that without it the clause could not have been thus limited.—E. R. C]

be given—(1) Had he used Hades, the idea of His life on earth would have been obscured; by the phrase, "lower parts of the earth," not only is its O. T. synonym Hades suggested, but also the idea of a descent to earth and through earth is preserved. (2) A second reason may be that on this subject, as on the whole subject of eschatology seems to be the case, it was the design of the Spirit to give an indefinite revelation. A preceding question of Dr. Eadie appears to the writer to be without force. This question is—"Why, if Hades was intended, should the comparative κατώτερος and not the superlative have been used?" In answer it may be said that the idea of the Hebrew is as well expressed by the comparative as by the superlative; and further, to have written that Christ went into the *lowest* part would have implied that He went into the prison of the wicked—the lowest Hades, which it was foreign from the intention of the Apostle, most certainly in this connection, to teach. Another objection of Dr. Eadie to the view presented in this Excursus is—"Those who suppose the captives to be human spirits emancipated from thraldom by Jesus, may hold the view that Christ went to hell (?) to free them, but we have seen that the captives are enemies made prisoners on the field of battle." On turning to the comment on the passage referred to, we find that the *reason* for this opinion is nothing but an unsupported *assertion;* he writes: "'Thou hast led captivity captive.' The meaning of this idiom seems simply to be—thou hast mustered or reviewed thy captives, Judges v. 12." The reference, *as is manifest on examination,* refutes the assertion,—for Barak captured no enemies.

The other objections of Dr. Eadie are involved in the following three presented by Dr. Hodge in his Commentary on the Epistle to the Ephesians.

(1) "In the first place, this idea (the *descensus ad inferos*) is entirely foreign to the meaning of the passage in the Psalm on which the Apostle is commenting." With the greatest veneration for the distinguished and beloved Commentator, it may be asked: In what respect is it more foreign than the idea adopted by himself? It is to be observed that there is no *expressed* reference in the Psalm to Christ. Dr. Hodge remarks on Eph. iv. 8: "... Psalm lxviii. is not Messianic. It does not refer to the Messiah, but to the triumph of God over His enemies." From this point of view, manifestly, *any* idea as to the *terminus ad quem* of the Messiah's descent may be said to be foreign to the meaning of the Psalm; and from this point of view alone could the criticism now under consideration have proceeded. The learned Commentator, however, justifies the application of the Psalm to Christ on three principles which he rightly declares "are applicable not only to this, but also to many similar passages." He writes: "The first is the typical character of the old dispensation. . . . Thus the Psalm quoted by the Apostle is a history of the conquests of God over the enemies of His ancient people, and a prophecy of the conquests of the Messiah. The second principle applicable to this and similar cases is the identity of the Logos or Son manifested in the flesh under the new dispensation with the manifested Jehovah

of the old œconomy. . . . There is still a third principle to be taken into consideration. Many of the historical and prophetic descriptions of the Old Testament are not exhausted by any one application or fulfillment. . . . . The predictions of Isaiah of the redemption of Israel were not exhausted by the deliverance of the people of God from the Babylonish captivity, but had a direct reference to the higher redemption to be effected by Christ... It is, therefore, in perfect accordance with the whole analogy of Scripture that the Apostle applies what is said of Jehovah in Psalm lxviii. as a conqueror, to the work of the Lord Jesus, who, as God manifested in the flesh, ascended on high, leading captivity captive and giving gifts unto men." It is on the platform of these manifestly correct principles that Dr. Hodge declares in his comment on vers. 9, 10: "... the Psalmist must be understood as having included in the scope of his language the most conspicuous and illustrious of God's condescensions and exaltations. All other comings were but typical of His coming in the flesh, and all ascensions were typical of His ascension from the grave." But is it not evident that, on this platform, what must be understood as having been "included in the scope" of the Psalmist's language, in reference to any Divine descent subsequent to the writing of the Psalm, must be determined, not from the language of the Psalm alone, but from that language in connection with those Scriptures which describe the descent? If those subsequent Scriptures teach that the descent was merely to the literal grave, then a descent to the literal grave and an ascent therefrom are all that can be regarded as included within that scope; but if they teach that the descent was to Hades, then a descent thereto must be understood as included. Dr. Hodge has concluded from an examination of the New Testament that Christ's descent was only to the grave; others, from a similar examination, have concluded that it was *ad inferos.* Both these ideas are "foreign" to the language of the Psalm literally interpreted; that one, however, is to be regarded as within "the scope" of its language, which the event, as described by the New Testament writers, shows to have been within the view of the inspiring Spirit, who knows the end from the beginning.

(2) "In the second place," continues Dr. Hodge, "there (in the Psalm) as here, the only descent of which the context speaks is opposed to the ascending to Heaven." This may be freely admitted—although in point of fact the Psalm does not speak of a descent at all; it merely implies one. But what was the *terminus ad quem* of the descent? This the Psalm does not declare. It can be determined only from the Apostle's comment, which declares it to have been *the lower parts of the earth.*

(3) "In the third place this is the opposition so often expressed in other places and in other forms of expression." The writer cannot perceive that the position here assumed is supported by the passages cited. These passages, with the remarks of the Am. Ed., upon them, are as follows: "John iii. 13" ('No man hath ascended up to Heaven, but He that came down from Heaven, even the Son of Man who is in Heaven.') Manifestly there is no allusion

here to the bodily ascension of our Lord. Jesus was not, in this passage, prophesying to Nicodemus that He was to ascend; He was giving a reason why He could instruct concerning heavenly things as no other man could. It was as though He had said, 'No man hath ascended up to Heaven and thence descended to teach; only He can teach you who descended from Heaven, who is still in Heaven' "John vi. 38" ('I came down from Heaven'). Most true. But is this inconsistent with his going still further—into Hades? "John viii. 14" ('I know whence I came and whither I go'). A remark similar to the preceding might here be made. "John xvi. 28" ('I came forth from the Father, and am come info the world; again, I leave the world and go to the Father'). Is there aught here inconsistent with the idea of His going, before His return, to the subterranean world? Because, when on the earth, our Lord spake of a descent from Heaven, are we debarred from supposing that He contemplated descending still further to a place whence also He must ascend?

As before remarked, if the interpretation which the writer contends is the natural one, *viz.*, that Christ went into Hades and delivered captives therein held, be the true one; then, manifestly, Hades as the dwelling-place of the pious must have been a third place in the Unseen World, and not that World itself *in its entirety*, nor Heaven, nor Hell, nor the State of Death.

But whilst the interpretation given by the writer is the most natural, it is admitted that other interpretations may be put upon the passage that has been under discussion. It is not, therefore, contended that by itself, unsupported by other Scriptures, it will establish the doctrine it apparently presents. That the natural interpretation is the true one appears from the facts (1) That the doctrine thereby presented brings into perfect harmony two apparently discrepant classes of Scriptures; and (2) That it sheds light on several obscure passages of the word of God, bringing them, in their natural interpretation and with all their logical implications, into perfect harmony with each other and with the rest of revealed truth.

1. As to the former of these facts.

On the one hand, it cannot be denied that the apparent teaching of many passages of Scripture, written antecedent to the resurrection of Christ, is that Hades is a place distinct from Heaven, to which the souls of the righteous as well as of the wicked were consigned; and, on the other hand, it is clear that all the post-resurrection teachings of the word of God are, not merely that "the souls of believers at their death do immediately pass into glory," but even more specific—that they do immediately pass into Heaven.

It is in place here to consider somewhat at length the latter class of Scriptures. That the post-resurrection teachings of the New Testament are that the souls of believers do immediately pass into Heaven, is evident from the following considerations:

(1) It is implied in all that is said as to the souls of believers going, at their death, to the place where the Lord is, John xiv. 2, 3; "I go to prepare a place for you, and if I go and prepare a place for you, I will come again and receive you unto myself, that where I am, there ye may be also." John xvii. 24, "Father, I will that they also whom thou hast given me be with me where I am, that they may behold my glory." 2 Cor. v. 8, "We are confident, I say, and willing rather to be absent from the body and to be present with the Lord." Phil. i. 23, "To depart and be with Christ." Now, Christ is in Heaven—Him "the Heaven must receive (hold) until the times of the restitution of all things," Acts iii. 21. Believers therefore, *who are with Christ*, must be in Heaven. It is vain to object to this, that believers in Hades may be said to be with Christ, since He is everywhere and He may manifest Himself anywhere. True. As God, He is everywhere; on earth, in Hades, in Hell: and He may make a *spiritual* manifestation of Himself anywhere. He cannot, however, make a *physical* manifestation of Himself (and it is such a manifestation that the texts quoted call for) where He is not, and the Scriptures teach us that He is *physically* in Heaven. True, He has power to convey His human nature anywhere, but the declaration that "the Heaven must receive Him until the times of the restitution of all things," conveys the assurance that He does not and will not convey Himself to Hades. He is in Heaven; the souls of believers are with Him; therefore they are in Heaven—*i. e.*, in one of its "many mansions."

(2) The same doctrine is directly taught, or implied, in such passages as the following: "We know that if our earthly house of this tabernacle were dissolved, we have a building of God, a house not made with hands, eternal in the Heavens," 2 Cor. v. 1. Whatever this heavenly house may be (and that question need not now be discussed) we know that it is in the Heavens. Those, therefore, who inhabit it, must be in Heaven, "with the Lord," as we learn from ver. 8; and thus this verse, which directly teaches that departed believers are in Heaven, by its contextual arrangement confirms the preceding argument that those who "are with the Lord" are in Heaven.

(3) This also is the natural explanation of the record concerning Stephen. Just before his execution he saw "the Heavens opened and the Son of man standing on the right hand of God," Acts vii. 56. Shortly after, in the act of dying, he exclaimed: "Lord Jesus, receive my spirit," as though he still gazed on Him whom a short time before he had been privileged to see at the right hand of the throne of God, Acts vii. 59. The implication of the whole passage is that Jesus, in accordance with His promise—"I will come again and receive you unto Myself," John xiv. 2, revealed Himself unto this dying saint as about to take him into Heaven—to the place in His Father's house He has prepared for His loved ones—that where He, the Saviour, was, there might he, the believer, be.

(4) Is not the same also implied in Heb. xii. 22-24, where, not to seek after the whole meaning, the teaching seems to be that not only are "the spirits of just men" now "made perfect" (comp. xi. 30); but that all such are with angels, and with God the Judge of all, and with Jesus, in the heavenly Jerusalem.

In view of all these Scriptures, the doctrine of the post-resurrection teachings of the New Testament seems to be that the spirits of the just do, on their death, immediately pass into Heaven.

This class of Scriptures seems to present a doctrine in irreconcilable contradiction with that set forth by the former class, on the assumption that each class presents an original and constantly enduring fact in God's treatment of the spirits of the departed dead. In view of the former class there have been many Protestants, as is well known, who have set at naught the manifest teachings of the New Testament on this subject—contending that a soul may be in the *place* Hades, and yet with the Lord; and in view of the latter class, many have utterly ignored the force of Old Testament language, ascribing it (on a matter of pure revelation) to an accommodation to Jewish superstition. Neither of these positions is consistent with due regard to the inspiration of the Word of God. The very conditions of the problem suggest the hypothesis that, at some time about the period of the Resurrection and Ascension of our Lord, there was a change in the condition of the spirits of the righteous dead. This hypothesis receives confirmation from the fact that it is the natural interpretation of Peter's declaration that Christ, between His Death and Resurrection, descended into the place where the Old Testament teaches us that the departed righteous were; and does it not spring to the dignity of an established doctrine upon the discovery of a text which, taken in its literal and most natural sense, teaches that Christ did descend to Hades and thence deliver those therein confined? The text in Ephesians taken in its natural sense brings into perfect and beautiful harmony two apparently conflicting doctrines of the word of God.

2. And more. It sheds light on many detached portions of the Scripture, and brings them, and all their implications, into full harmony with each other, and with the whole body of revealed truth.

(1) The first of these passages that will be noticed is John xiv. 2, "In my Father's house are many mansions; if it were not so I would have told you. I go to prepare a place for you." The implication here is that the future place of His disciples *was not then prepared*. This is inconsistent with the doctrine that the place of the pious dead has always been in Heaven, or that Hades continues to be their place. The implication calls for a change in the place of the pious dead synchronous with our Lord's Ascension.

(2) A second Scripture is Heb. xi. 40, compared with Heb. xii. 23. These passages occur in the same section of the Epistle—that which exhorts believers to patience that they may obtain the promise, i. e., heavenly blessedness. In the former, the spirits of just men who were *not* made perfect (i. e., who did not receive the promise) until the present dispensation, are spoken of. In the latter, these same spirits are manifestly amongst the spirits of just men made perfect. The passage in Ephesians throws beautiful light on both these Scriptures, brings them into harmony with each other, and into perfect

and enlightening harmony with the whole section that includes them.

(3) A third passage is the declaration of our Lord to the dying thief: "This day shalt thou be with me in Paradise," Luke xxiii. 43; compared (a) with those texts that declare he went into Hades, and (b) with 2 Cor. xii. 4, and Rev. ii. 7, which place Paradise in Heaven. The first comparison would seem to indicate that Paradise was a Jewish name for one of the compartments of the place Hades; the second, that it was a name for Heaven, or one of the many mansions thereof. If the natural interpretation of the passage in Ephesians be the true one, then the apparent discrepancy is at once harmonized; at least a mode of reconciliation is at once suggested. If Paradise were the name for the abode of the righteous in Hades, then on their removal to Heaven, to the new place prepared for them, the name of their abode might naturally be transferred to their new home.

(4) The interpretation given to the passage in Ephesians throws light upon, and is supported by 1 Pet. iii. 18-22.

The writer is unable to adopt the common English Protestant view concerning this passage, *viz.*, that the *preaching* mentioned was by the Holy Spirit through Noah to the Antediluvians in the flesh, for the following reasons:

a. On this ground the consistency of the whole passage is destroyed. The Apostle was exhorting believers to the patient endurance of wrong; and he enforces his exhortation by a reference to the case of the God-man, Who by His endurance became a benefactor unto others, and won for Himself a reward of exaltation. Consistency requires that the preaching should follow the death.

b. The modern view requires us to regard the Holy Ghost as indicated by πνεῦμα, notwithstanding the absence of the article, and the manifest antithesis between that term and σάρξ.

c. The use of πνεύματα in this connection requires that we should regard disembodied spirits as the objects of the preaching—the disembodied πνεῦμα (the person dead ἐν σαρκι) preached to πνεύματα.

d. The collocation of the words τοῖς ἐν φυλακῇ πνεύμασι requires us to regard the spirits as in prison when addressed.

e. The term πορευθεὶς of ver. 19 is manifestly parallel with the same term in ver. 22. The implication of the entire passage is that the same person first *went to* the prison, and then *went to* Heaven.

f. The position of ποτέ forbids this interpretation. Thus Bengel writes: "*Si sermo esset de præconio per Noe* τὸ aliquando *aut plane omitteretur aut prædicavit conjungeretur.*"

g. The natural interpretation of the passage, so far from teaching a doctrine at variance with other Scriptures, is manifestly in accord with what is elsewhere taught.

The writer would present the following translation: "For Christ also once suffered for sins, the just for the unjust, in order that He might lead us unto God, being put to death as to flesh, but quickened as to spirit, in which (spirit) also having journeyed, He preached (ἐκήρυξεν = made proclamation) to the spirits in prison, *etc.*"

The passage in Ephesians calls for a φυλακή in which the spirits of the departed, as captives, were held, to which, after His death, Jesus descended, performing a mission of mercy. The passage under immediate consideration represents our Lord as, after His death, journeying to a φυλακή, and there *making proclamation* to the prisoners detained therein. The former passage states nothing as to the *mode* in which His mission was executed; the latter teaches us nothing as to the *results* of the proclamation. But in the confluent light of the two passages can we doubt, not only that they have reference to the same event, but that the *mode* in which the mission was executed (at least in part) was by *proclamation*, and that at least one *result* of that proclamation was the deliverance of those who had been ransomed by the Lord's death?

This interpretation does not require, as some object, that an offer of salvation should have been made to the departed such as is now made to the living, that the gospel should have been preached to them as it is preached to men in the flesh. The term translated *preach* is κηρύσσω, which means simply to *proclaim as herald*. Dr. Mombert, in the EXCURSUS ON THE DESCENSUS AD INFEROS, published in connection with his translation of Fronmüller's Commentary (Lange Series) on 1 Peter, remarks, " it (κηρύσσω) is never used in the sense of judicial announcement, and N. T. usage clothes it with the meaning ' to preach the gospel.' " It is true that it is never used to designate *judicial* announcement, and that for the sufficient reason that it has reference to *heraldic* announcement, which is an essentially different thing. It is also true that the New Testament (E. V.) usage of the word *preach* is almost invariably " *to preach the gospel*." This however is not the case in reference to the use of the *Greek* word κηρύσσω, as is evident from an examination of Mark i. 45 ; v. 20 ; vii. 36; Luke viii. 39; Acts xv. 21; Rom. ii. 21; 2 Cor. iv. 5; Gal. v. 11 ; Rev. v. 2. All that the use of κηρύσσω calls for is the *proclamation* of a fact or facts. These facts, in the case before us, may have been the completion of the work of atonement, and the consequent deliverance of those who had accepted Christ under the types of the old œconomy. Such an announcement would have been a word of life to those who had accepted while in the flesh. In this connection it is proper to remark that if *the preaching of the Gospel to the dead* (εὐηγγελίσθη) of 1 Pet. iv. 6, has reference to the same event as that recorded in the passage under immediate consideration, it would not require us to regard the preaching of the Gospel (glad tidings) as the same as that to men in the flesh—as an offer of salvation. The nature of *good tidings* has respect to the condition of the hearers. To us, sinners in the flesh, the offer of salvation through a Redeemer is *good news*. To captives in Hades who had already performed the conditions of salvation, the announcement of the completion of the atonement and of deliverance consequent thereupon, would be *glad tidings*.

Nor are we forbidden to suppose that the preaching was to those who had already trusted, by the fact that all who were the objects of address are described as " once disobedient " (ἀπειθήσασι = unbelieving). It is to be carefully noted that in this portion of the passage the Apostle is laboring to set forth the gracious effects of the sufferings of Christ. He suffered, the just for the *unjust*, that He might bring us (the unjust) unto God. It was only consistent that the inspired penman should describe the Old Testament recipients of His grace as *sinners*.

It may also be remarked that an objection that may arise in some mind—viz., Why should the Apostle have made special reference to the Antediluvians? presses with equal force upon every conceivable hypothesis of interpretation. Probably the reason of the special reference was that it gave opportunity for the presentation of the Deluge as the type of Baptism. On this point, however, the writer will not enlarge. He does not claim that the hypothesis presented by him explains every difficulty of this most difficult passage of the Word of God. Probably there are allusions therein, as in other Scriptures, to mysteries which will never be understood save in the light of the world to come.

(5) The passage in Ephesians, in connection with the one just considered, throws light on certain expressions in the Old Testament prophecies, especially the following:

Isaiah xliv. 23: "Sing, O ye heavens ; for the Lord hath done it ; shout, ye lower parts of the earth, *etc.*" Not only does it enable us to take the phrase *lower parts of the earth* in its established sense, by showing us that Hades might have cause for rejoicing, but it preserves the antithesis manifestly presented in the passage. It enables us to translate Hosea xiii. 14 (the first clause) literally, and manifests the beautiful propriety of the Hebrew term employed: "I will *deliver* (not ransom) them from the hand of Hades." The verb translated, in the English Version, *ransom*, is פָּדָה which followed by מִן, as in this case, means (see Gesenius) *to let go free—to set free*.

In conclusion of this portion of the Excursus, it may be said, that the proposed interpretation of Eph. iv. 8, 9, which, on the one hand, is manifestly natural; and which, on the other hand, brings into perfect harmony two apparently conflicting classes of Scriptures, and also sheds on many obscure passages a light that brings them into harmony with the whole body of revealed truth—such an interpretation, in the judgment of the writer, must be regarded as the true one.

And in conclusion of the whole subject, it may further be remarked that the passage in Ephesians, interpreted as above, forms the cap-stone of the complex argument which demonstrates that the term HADES indicates a *Place* (and not a mere *state*) distinct from the *grave*, from *Heaven*, and from *Hell;* into which the souls of the righteous were conveyed antecedent to the death of Jesus; but from which they were delivered on His descent thereto, after the completion of His sacrifice on earth.—E. R. C.]

[NOTE ON THE GENERAL RESURRECTION AND
JUDGMENT.]

By the American Editor.

[The Resurrection described in this section is that which is to take place at the close of the Millennium—the Resurrection referred to by the Apostle Paul, 1 Cor. xv. 24, and implied by our Lord in Matt. xxv. 31. The subjects of this Resurrection are the *unraised* of all dispensations preceding the Millennium (the λοιποὶ τῶν νεκρῶν of ver. 5); together with all who shall have lived in the flesh during, and subsequent to, the Millennial period—both the good and the bad.

This Resurrection is immediately to precede, and to be in order to, the General Judgment, when—(1) the present order of things shall pass away, 2 Pet. iii. 10-12; 1 Cor. xv. 24-28; (2) the entire course of human history shall be made manifest to all, Ecc. xii. 14; Matt. xii. 36; Luke xii. 2; Rom. ii. 16; 1 Cor. iii. 13; iv. 5; (3) each (unjudged) individual of the human race, and each fallen spirit, shall be publicly acquitted or condemned, Matt. xxv. 31-46; 2 Cor. v. 10; Jude 6, *etc.*

It is admitted that the majority of the texts bearing on the subject seem to contemplate but *one* future Resurrection and Judgment. Remarks similar to those on the Future Advent of Christ (see Note on THE FUTURE ADVENT OF CHRIST, pp. 339 sqq.) may here be made. The earlier prophecies of the O. T. were cast on one plane, apparently contemplating but *one* Advent, the later prophecies, however, adumbrated *two* Advents; which adumbrations, all now admit, foreshadowed the reality. So with the prophecies concerning the Resurrection and Judgment. In the majority of instances, the prophecies seem to contemplate but *one;* there are other declarations, however, which demand the hypothesis that there are to be *two.* (See the Note on THE FIRST RESUR-RECTION, pp. 352 sqq.)

It may present itself as a difficulty to some minds that the Judge described ver. 11 seems to be God the Father, and not the Son. Alford, who adopts the view that the phrase τὸν καθήμε-νον ἐπ’ αὐτοῦ refers to the Father (see chs. iv. 8; xxi. 5), thus comments: "Be it remembered, that it is the Father who giveth all judgment to the Son: and though He Himself judgeth no man, yet He is ever described as present in the judgment, and mankind as judged before Him. We need not find in this view any difficulty or discrepancy with such passages as Matt. xxv. 31, seeing that our Lord Himself says in ch. iii. 21: 'I . . . am set down with my Father in His Throne.' Nor need we be surprised at the sayings of our Lord, such as that in ch. xxi. 6 (*b*), being uttered by Him that sitteth on the Throne. That throne is now the throne of God and of the Lamb, ch. xxii. 1. Comp. also ch. xxi. 22."

It is sometimes objected to the doctrine of a General Judgment at the close of the present order of things that it is superfluous, since each individual is judged as he leaves this world. In a sense, it is true that each individual is judged immediately upon death; and yet, this should not militate against our reception of the doctrine of a final and general Judgment, so clearly revealed in the word of God. In the first place, our ideas of what may be right or necessary should never lead us to set aside a clear revelation. But, secondly, even on the platform of human reason, such a general Judgment cannot be regarded as superfluous. The objects of public trials by human judges are two: first, to determine the guilt or innocence of the prisoner; and, second, to make manifest the justice of the Judge in acquittal or condemnation. The first of these objects can have no existence where God is the Judge; the second, calls for a public trial before the assembled universe when the present order of things has reached its conclusion. Then, shall all things be discovered, and the righteousness of the Judge be made manifest before all created intelligences.—E. R. C.]

B.—THE HEAVENLY-EARTHLY, IDEO-REAL PICTURE OF THE NEW WORLD. THE KINGDOM OF GLORY.

CHAP. XXI. 9—XXII. 5.

1. The City of God as the Heavenly Jerusalem.

9   And there came unto me [*om.* unto me][1] one of the seven angels which [that] had the seven vials [*ins.*, that were][2] full of the seven last plagues, and talked with me, saying, Come hither, I will shew thee the bride, the Lamb's wife [wife of the

10 Lamb].[3] And he carried me away in the [*om.* the] spirit to a great and high mountain, and shewed me that great [*om.* that great—*ins.* the holy] city, the holy [*om.* the

TEXTUAL AND GRAMMATICAL.

[1] Ver. 9. [Crit. Eds. reject this clause with ℵ. A. B.* P., *et al.*—E. R. C.]

[2] Ver. 9. [The Angels, not the vials, are, grammatically, represented as being *full of the plagues;* the original is Καὶ ἦλθεν εἰς ἐκ τῶν ἑπτὰ ἀγγέλων τῶν ἐχόντων τὰς ἑπτὰ φιάλας τῶν γεμόντων τῶν ἑπτὰ πληγῶν τῶν ἐσχάτων.—E. R. C.]

[3] Ver. 9. We give the reading τὴν νύμφην τὴν γυναῖκα τοῦ ἀρνίου.

11 holy] Jerusalem, descending out of heaven from God, having the glory of God:
and [*om.* and]⁴ her light [light-giver (φωστήρ)]⁵ *was* like unto a stone most pre-
12 cious, even like [as to] a jasper stone, clear as crystal; And [*om.* And] had
[having] a wall great and high, *and* had [having] twelve gates, and at the gates
twelve angels, and names written thereon [inscribed], which are *the names* [*or* the
13 names]⁶ of the twelve tribes of the children [sons] of Israel: On the east three
gates; on the north three gates; on the south three gates; and on the west three
14 gates. And the wall of the city had [having] twelve foundations, and in [upon]
15 them the [*om.* the—*ins.* twelve]⁷ names of the twelve apostles of the Lamb. And
he that talked [spake] with me had [*ins.* a measure,]⁸ a golden reed to [*om.* to—
ins. that he might] measure the city, and the gates thereof [her gates], and the
16 wall thereof [her wall]. And the city lieth foursquare [four-cornered], and the
[her] length is [*is*]⁹ as large [much] as the breadth: and he measured the city with
the reed, [*ins.* to] twelve thousand furlongs [stadia]. The length and the breadth
17 and the height of it [her] are equal. And he measured the wall thereof [her wall],
[*ins.* of] a hundred *and* forty *and* four cubits, *according to* [*om. according to*] the mea-
18 sure of a man, that is, [*om.* that is,—*ins.* which is that] of the [an] angel. And the
building [structure] of the wall of it [her wall] was *of* jasper: and the city *was* pure
19 gold, like unto clear [pure] glass. And [*om.* And]¹⁰ The foundations of the wall of
the city *were* garnished [adorned] with all manner of [every] precious stones [stone].
The first foundation *was* jasper; the second, sapphire; the third, a [*om.* a] chalce-
20 dony; the fourth, an [*om.* an] emerald; the fifth, sardonyx; the sixth, sardius;
the seventh, chrysolite; the eighth, beryl; the ninth, a [*om.* a] topaz; the tenth,
■ [*om.* a] chrysoprasus; the eleventh, a [*om.* a] jacinth; the twelfth, an [*om.* an]
21 amethyst. And the twelve gates *were* twelve pearls; every several gate [each one
severally of the gates] was [*ins.* out] of one pearl: and the street [broad-way
(πλατεῖα)]¹¹ of the city *was* pure gold, as it were transparent [translucent] glass.

2. *The City of God as the Holy City of* all *Believing Gentiles.*

22 And I saw no [not a] temple therein ɪ for the Lord God Almighty [, the All-
Ruler,¹²—*ins.* is the temple of her,] and the Lamb are the temple of it [*om.* are the
23 temple of it]. And the city had [hath] no need of the sun, neither [nor] of the
moon, to shine in [that they should shine for (φαίνωσιν)¹³] it [her]: for the glory
of God did lighten it [lightened her], and the Lamb *is* the light thereof [and her
24 lamp *was* the Lamb]. And the nations of them which are saved [*om.* of them
which are saved]¹⁴ shall walk in [by means of] the light of it [her light]: and the
kings of the earth do [*om.* do] bring their glory and honor [*om.* and honor]¹⁵ into
25 it [her]. And the gates of it [her gates] shall not be shut at all by day: for there
26 shall be no night there [for night shall not be there]. And they shall bring the
27 glory and [*ins.* the] honor of the nations into it [her]. And there shall in no wise
enter into it [her] anything that defileth [*om.* that defileth—*ins.* common], neither
whatsoever worketh abomination, or *maketh* a lie [and that worketh (*or* the one
working) abomination and a lie]: but they which [who] are [have been] written
in the Lamb's [*om.* Lamb's] book of life [*ins.* of the Lamb].

3. *The City of God as the New Universal Paradise—Glorified Nature.*   (*Chap. xxii.* 1–5.)

1 And he showed me a pure [*om.* pure]¹⁶ river of water of life, clear [bright] as
2 crystal, proceeding out of the throne of God and of the Lamb. In the midst of

---

⁴ Ver. 11. [Crit. Eds. omit the copula with 𝕏. A. B*. P.—E. R. C.]
⁵ Ver. 11. [The true meaning of φωστήρ is *that which gives light*.—E. R. C.]
⁶ Ver. 12. [The second] ὀνόματα is omitted by the Rec. [Lange retains. It is given by Lach., Tisch. (1859), with A.
B*., *Vulg., Cop., Syr., et al.*; it is omitted by Tisch. (8th Ed.) with 𝕏. P.; it is bracketed by Alf. and Treg.—E. R. C.]
⁷ Ver. 14. [Crit. Eds. give δώδεκα with 𝕏. A. B*. P., *Vulg., et al.*—E. R. C.]
⁸ Ver. 15. [Codd. A. B*. [𝕏*. P.] give μέτρον.
⁹ Ver. 16. Τοσοῦτόν ἐστιν before ὅσον should be omitted. [So Crit. Eds. with 𝕏. A. B*. P., *et al.*—E. R. C.]
¹⁰ Ver. 19. A. B*. [𝕏*. P.], *et al.* omit καί.
¹¹ Ver. 21. [See *foot-note* †, chap. xi. 8, p. 231.—E. R. C.]
¹² Ver. 22. [See *Add. Comm.* on chap. i. 8, p. 93.—E. R. C.]
¹³ Ver. 23. Codd. A. B*. [𝕏*. P.] *et al.*, omit ἐν after φαίνωσιν.
¹⁴ Ver. 24. The Rec. gives καὶ τὰ ἔθνη τῶν σωζομένων; a reading concocted, most probably, in explanation of the word
ἔθνη. [Τῶν σωζομένων is omitted by 𝕏. A. B*. P., *Vulg., Cop., Syr., Æth., et al.*—E. R. C.]
¹⁵ Ver. 24. The Rec. adds καὶ τὴν τιμήν. [This clause is given in B*., *Vulg., Cop., Syr.*; but is omitted in 𝕏. A. P., *et al.*
—E. R. C.]
■ Chap. xxii. 1. Καθαρόν is unauthorized. [It does not appear in 𝕏. A. B*. P., *Vulg., Cop., Syr., Æth.*—E. R. C.]

the street of it [her broad-way], and on either side [om. on either side] of the river [ins. ₂ on this side and on that side,¹⁷] *was there* the [om. *there* the—ins. a] tree of life, which bare [bearing] twelve *manner of* [om. *manner of*] fruits, *and* [om. *and*] yielded her fruit every month [according to each month yielding its fruit]: and
3 the leaves of the tree *were* [are] for the healing of the nations. And there shall be no more curse [And nothing cursed¹⁸ shall be any more¹⁹]: but [and] the throne of God and of the Lamb shall be in it [her]; and his servants (δοῦλοι) shall serve
4 (λατρεύουσιν) him: and they shall see his face; and his name *shall be* in [upon]
5 their foreheads. And there shall be no night there²⁰ [and night shall not be any more²¹]; and they [ins. have (or shall have) no]²² need no candle [om. no candle— ins. of light²³ of lamp], neither [om. neither—ins. and of] light of the [om. the] sun; for [because] the Lord God giveth them light [shall shine upon them]²⁴: and they shall reign for ever and ever [into the ages of the ages].

¹⁷ Ver. 2. Καὶ ἐκεῖθεν. [Crit. Eds. read ἐντεῦθεν καὶ ἐκεῖθεν with A. B*., *et al.*—E. R. C.]
¹⁸ Ver. 3. Κατάθεμα; comp. Delitzsch, p. 51. [Crit. Eds. so read with אᶜ. A. B*. P.—E. R. C.]
¹⁹ Ver. 3. [Crit. Eds. give the reading ἔσται ἔτι with א. A. P.—E. R. C.]
²⁰ Ver. 5. ᾿Εκεῖ is unfounded.
²¹ Ver. 5. ῎Ετι is supported by א. A., *et al.*; Tischendorf [1859] omits with B*. [but gives it in the 8th Ed. with א. A. P. —E. R. C.]
²² Ver. 5. Tischendorf [1859], with B*., gives οὐ χρεία, etc., which differs from the readings of Lachmann and the Rec. [Lach. and Alf. read οὐχ ἕξουσιν χρείαν with A., *Vulg.*; Tisch (8th Ed.) and Treg. give οὐκ ἔχουσιν χρείαν with א., *Memph.*, *Syr.*; P. also gives ἔχουσιν.—E. R. C.]
²³ Ver. 5. [Lach., Alf., Treg., Tisch. (8th Ed.) give φωτὸς with א. A., *Vulg.*, *et al.*; Tisch. (1859) omitted with B.* P.— E. R. C.]
²⁴ Ver. 5. We give the reading [φωτιεῖ] ἐπ᾽ αὐτούς. [So read Alf., Treg., Tisch. (8th Ed.); φωτιεῖ with א. B.*; ἐπ᾽ αὐτούς with ╫ A. Lach. gives φωτίσει with A. P. ᾿Επ᾽ is omitted by B*. P.—E. R. C.]

EXEGETICAL AND CRITICAL.

SYNOPTICAL VIEW.

As one of the Angels of Anger, or of the Vials of Anger, showed the Seer the wicked world-city under the figure of the Harlot, so it is now again one of the same Angels who shows the Seer the City of God under the name of the adorned Bride. And it seems as if the Spirit of prophecy would hereby illustrate the fact that the anger of God is a flame, divisible into the lightning of righteousness and the light of love.

The great vision-picture which the Angel exhibits to the contemplation of the Seer, after transporting him to a great and high mountain, the lofty stand-point of a perfected gaze into the region of perfection, is, primarily, the appearance of the new creation, the glorified world of eternal *being*, which has taken the place of the first creation, the world of temporal *becoming*. It is, in the next place, that perfected union between Heaven and earth with which the antithesis of life between Heaven and earth, as in accordance with Gen. i., has become the antithesis of a perfected spiritual communion in love. Even this antithesis, the plastic image of religion, finds its fulfillment here. Heaven has assumed the full, fresh, warm and home-like aspect of a familiar and attractive earth; earth is radiant in the heavenly glory of that Throne of God which has now become visible. The new creation is, further, also the new universal Paradise, which has bloomed from the seed of the first Paradise, buried in the soil of the world's history. On this very account this new world is no less the realization of the Great *City of God*, which, first in the camp of Israel and again in the city of Jerusalem, in typical fore-exhibition became a subject of human admiration, longing and hope, and which was subsequently heralded from afar in so many New Testament preludes.

But its most glorious name is contained in the title of *The Bride;* for thereby not only the supremacy of personal life in this new world, not only the perfect unanimity of all blessed spirits, not only their perfect receptivity for the entire self-communication of God, are expressed, but also their Divine dignity, liberty and blessedness in love.

We find in the grand transfiguration-picture of the vision a trilogy, the elements of which are distinctly present even in the Gospel of John: *a.* Transfiguration of the Theocracy, represented by the heavenly Jerusalem (vers. 9–21); *b.* Transfiguration of the believing Gentile world or the universal new humanity (vers. 22–27); *c.* Transfiguration of all nature, or the appearance of the new Paradise (ch. xxii. 1–5). The first section justly forms the foundation of the whole, and is therefore the most detailed; it, again, divides into three parts.

The first part of the first section exhibits the *holiness* of the City of God. In the *Doxa* of God, or the Shekinah, which diffuses its radiance over the whole City, because it is omnipresent throughout it, the Holy of holies is reflected (ver. 11).* In the *high wall* of the City, the economical barrier of the Theocracy is reflected; and the true spirit of that barrier, designed, as it was, to mediate salvation to the whole world, finds its expression in the *twelve gates*, at which *Angels* are posted, symbolical here, doubtless, of true messengers of salvation; for the gates are open by threes toward all the four quarters of the world. Thus a two-fold effect of holiness is expressed—repulsion of everything unholy by the *wall*—free ingress for all that tends to holiness, by the *gates* (vers. 12–14).

The second part gives, in the magnitude of the City, an image of the magnitude of the King-

* [See *additional comment* on chap. xxi. 22, p. 387.—E. R. C.]

dom of God (vers. 15–17). This magnitude is exhibited throughout in forms of perfection. The City has the form of a perfect cube, like the Holy of holies, and appears in this equality of measurement as an expression of the perfect heavenly world.

The third part of the first section unfolds the riches of the City of God in splendor consisting of the most precious materials; these riches, an ideal and spirit-clarified, being exhibited through the medium of precious stones, pearls and shining gold (vers. 18–21).

The second section, likewise, is divisible into three parts. The first part is expressive of the absolute spirituality of the new *cultus*. Since the City has itself become a Holy of holies, a *Temple* within it would, in comparison with itself, seem like a thing of inferior sanctity—a remnant of the old world. Nevertheless, it has a spiritual Temple which surpasses even the City. God, as the All-Ruler, is the infinitude of this Temple; the Lamb is the present definitude of it (vers. 22, 23). The second part of the second section characterizes the City as the great, universal, holy World-City, the City of all redeemed nations and kings, the City of sanctified humanity and of all its moral and eternal properties, yea, the City of the whole heavenly spirit-world and of the eternal radiance of day (vers. 24–26). The third part represents the separation between the sanctified heathen-world and true heathenism throughout the world, here portrayed by the three characteristics: commonness (bestiality), abominableness (transgression against nature), and falsehood (embracing both the former attributes). There is no longer any question of persons here; they have become *neutra* through the obliteration of their personality in their vileness (ver. 27). The *Lamb's Book of Life* has, from the beginning, comprehended this universality of the sphere of salvation.

The third leading section is an unmistakable antitype of the first Paradise. Its general character consists in the fact that all its holiness [*Heiligkeit*] has become pure health [*Heil*] and health-productiveness [*Heilswirkung*]—an infinitely multiplied life-creating, life-renewing and life-preserving Divine life-power. The *river of life* forms the first fundamental feature. It does not issue merely from an Eden, or land of delight, such as encircled the first Paradise (Gen. ii.); nor does it flow merely from the new Temple of Jehovah, like Ezekiel's river of salvation [or healing], (Ezek. xlvii.); it pours forth *from the throne of God and of the Lamb* (Rev. xxii. 1). The second fundamental feature is formed by the *trees of life* which are on both sides of the river, making an avenue with an interminable perspective; fruit-trees of life, so intensively salutiferous that they bear new fruits every month, and that even their leaves serve for the healing (θεραπεία) of the heathen [nations]. So absolute is the health-bringing operation of the trees of life in the City, that in this new Paradise nothing banned can arise—much less shall the new humanity here itself be banned, as were its first parents, through the deceit of the serpent and Satan, in the first Paradise (vers. 2, 3). In the third fundamental feature, the *eritis*

sicut deus is fulfilled in a Divine sense. That which Adam would fain have become, that which he lost in the path of impatience and sin, is now regained in the path of redemption and infinite patience. Now, it is the blessedness of all, that they *serve* [*dienen*] God as His *servants* [*Knechte*] whilst they *see His face* as His blessed children, and are able to look upon His face without being terrified like Adam. Again, this blessed relation has become an eternal condition; their holiness has the character *indelebilis*, the indestructible fixedness of true priests of God.* Whilst the abolition of *night* is again announced here, as ch. xxi. 25, the announcement has here a new significance. In ch. xxi., the reference is to the day of the blessed in a predominantly *spiritual* aspect and considered in the abstract; here, however, the unfadingness of this day is intended, pre-eminently, in the sense of the eternal day of the *glorified world*. That, therefore, which is expressed by the *name of God on the foreheads of the blessed—viz.*, imperishable knowledge of God and consecrateness to God—is supplemented by this declaration. Never again does night come to them, nor any deficiency of light, for *God* Himself *shineth upon them* for ever. This, again, is the eternal basis upon which they shall *reign as kings*, in and with the governance of God, in union with His will, and as organs of His will, eternally free in Him from all the world, for all the world, *into the æons of the æons*.

The magnificence of the entire picture of the new creation, a magnificence which strikes the taste of ordinary humanism as so peculiar, attains for us its entire significance when we look at it in connection with the whole of Sacred Writ—especially that of the Old Testament—as the lofty corona upon the stem of all Biblical typicism.

Our vision, then, is primarily the picture of the consummation and fulfillment of the whole Theocracy.

The revelation of salvation came down from Heaven in many individual items—in voices, in angels, in Theophanies, and lastly in Christ. The fulfillment finally consists in the descent of the entire City of God from Heaven.

The Congregation of God, called into life by the revelation of salvation, was from the beginning destined to be the Bride of God. Now, it is perfected in this destiny.

The *high Mountain*, upon which the City of God is situate, was prepared by Mount Zion, and imported the wide, overtowering and firm order and might of the Divine Kingdom. Now, this Mountain of the eternal order and fastness of God, in spirit beheld by the Prophets (Is. ii. 2; Ezek. xl. 2), towers over the whole world.

The *city of Jerusalem*, after its building and consecration as the royal residence and Temple-city, inherited the ancient typical honors of the previous cities of God, from the camp-city in the wilderness to Shiloh. It was the residence of the Jehovah cultus and of the theocratic constitution. Now, its archetype exists in visible presence—the City in which cultus and culture, in their perfection, have attained their complete union.

---

* [See *additional comment* on ch. xxii. 3, p. 388.—E. R. C.]

The *glory of God*, the Shekinah, manifested itself of old only in transient appearances. The central place of its manifestations was the Holy of holies. Now it spreads, in eternal radiance, over the whole City of God.*

It was formerly exhibited through typical mediums, through visional angelic forms, through the pillars of cloud and of fire, through the cherubim. Now it beams forth from a permanent nucleus of light ($\phi\omega\sigma\tau\dot\eta\rho$). The Parousia of Christ is the Epiphany of God, in brilliancy like the most precious jewel.

Israel, in order to the securement of its holy destiny, was encircled by a hedge, which was designed to separate from it every common thing of heathenism [or the Gentile nations], and by this very process to mediate the future bringing again of the Gentiles through the blessing of Abraham. This barrier—first, theocratic law—then, churchly confession—here appears ideally realized in the *high wall*, which, by means of its insurmountableness, excludes everything common, and by means of its *twelve gates*, kept by Angels, invites and receives all that is akin to God, *i. e.*, all that is akin to God in the twelve-fold character-form of the *Twelve Tribes of Israel*.

The Tribes of Israel were designed to represent in theocratic ground-forms, the fullness of the different human dispositions for the Kingdom of God. These ground-forms are now all fulfilled in the perfecting of the spiritual Israel. Therefore, the gates are adorned with *the names of the Tribes of Israel;* they are indicative of the ground-forms of the people of God in the interior of the City, as well as of the ground-forms of the people of God entering into the City of God from all the quarters of the world.

In so far as the restoration of the people of Israel itself is concerned, a restoration of its kernel, on the platform of perfect Christian equality and liberty, is simply expressed with the typical import of its Tribes; any renewal, however, of Old Testament legal prerogatives is precluded by this same typical import. The same remark applies to the description of the Sealed (chap. vii.). *The sealed ones would not be called after Israel, if Israel were not to form a dynamical power amongst them; the same sealed ones would preclude the idea of elect Gentiles, if they were not to be typically understood.*

The *gates* of the cities of Israel, especially Zion, were, even under the Old Covenant, *open* to the stranger, if he left his heathen practices without. They became the symbols of *ingress* into the holy City, into the sanctuary, into the fellowship of the saints (Ps. c. 4), as well as the symbols of *egress*, in order to the conversion of the world (Isa. lxii. 10), and in order to the bringing in of the King of Glory through its gates (Ps. xxiv. 7; comp. Gen. xxii. 17 [*Comm.*, p. 468, Am. Ed.]).—The new City of God has *twelve* of these gates, in accordance with the sacred number of completeness. She is lacking in no gate of ingress or of egress.

The *stone* at Bethel on which Jacob slept when a wanderer, and where he beheld, in a dream, the heavenly ladder, was consecrated as a monument and altar; the prelude of the foundation stones of the House of God (Bethel, Gen. xxii. 22), and of Christ the Corner Stone (Ps. cxviii. 22; Isa. xxviii. 16; Eph. ii. 20). This stone is, in the consummation, divided again into the *twelve foundation stones* of the wall of the holy City, marked with *the names of the Twelve Apostles.*

The *ground-forms* of Christ's mission to the world, the *Twelve Apostles*, denote, as *Apostles of the Lamb*, also the ground-forms of the world-conquering cross, and, as such, the *foundations* of the City of God.

Sacred *measure* has, in the history of the Temple, an import similar to that possessed, in the Greek view of the world, by the Platonic *Idea* or the Aristotelian *Form;* except that the first unitously represents both the latter in the form of practical energy, as real power (Wisd. xi. 20; comp. the Pythagorean system; Job xxviii. 25–27; Isa. xl. 12).—This power of *Ideal Form* pervades, in perfect supremacy, all the parts of the City of God,—the City and its gates and its walls.

The form of the perfect geometric *square* or cube was the form of the Holy of holies. Now, this same form appears as the symmetry of the City of God. Of old, the Holy of holies was a well-nigh inaccessible sanctuary, guarded by terrors. Here, the great City of God has become a manifest and open Holy of holies.

The magnitude of the City exhibits it, in its *length* and *breadth*, as a World-City; in its *height*, as a Heaven-City.—As the corona of the Temple, the City is the phenomenal image of the Kingdom of God, and thus, at the same time, of the glorified universe.

The holy *wall* which, as a theocratic and a churchly barrier, is an odium of all philosophy of wildness, commonness and indiscipline—here appears in its consummation, built of the material of the most precious jewel, a fact recognized afar off by the Spirit of Prophecy (Isa. liv. 11).

The covering of the Ark of the Covenant, which was, so to speak, the *most* Holy in the Holy of holies, was of pure gold (Ex. xxxvii. 6). Now, the whole City is constructed of *pure gold* so pure that it glitters like crystal. The City is thus, in an unapproachable exaltedness of thought, signalized as God's Sanctuary.

The *jewels* worn by the High Priest in his breast-plate, were significant of the idiocrasies, the charismatic aptitudes of the Tribes of Israel; of their value, spiritual and affectional, for the heart of God, Whom the High Priest represented. Such a Divine heart-affection, in the perfection of the ground-forms of human charisms, is now reflected in all the jewels which form the foundation-stones of the City-wall. The whole City is founded, as it were, upon the breast-plate of the real High Priest.

As the precious stone was early constituted a symbol of a *personal* life, consecrate to God, so the *pearl* was made a symbol of Divine vital wisdom, of that piety which is concentrated in the knowledge or the righteousness of faith. Thus the value of wisdom exceeds that of pearls (Job xxviii. 18; Prov. iii. 15, [viii. 11]);* wisdom,

---

* [See *additional comment* on ch. xxi. 22, p. 387.—E. R. C.]

* [In Job, *l. c*, the G. V. reads: "Ramoth and Gabis are not thought of. Wisdom is of higher value than pearls." In the

however, is also *symbolized* by pearls and is divided, in its individual traits, into a plurality of pearls (Matt. vii. 6), whilst, in its consummate spiritual phase, it is concentrated in the One Pearl of great price, whose value surpasses that of all single pearls (Matt. xiii. 46). But how does the pearl enter into a relation to the gate? In Isaiah liv. 12, we read (in accordance with De Wette's translation): "I make thy battlements of rubies and thy gates of carbuncles (?) and thy whole circuit of costly (precious) stones." The Septuagint distinguishes jasper for the battlements or parapets, crystals for the gates, precious stones for the walls. As the stone for the gates, אֶקְדָּח, is one that does not elsewhere appear, and takes its name from the radiance of fire, but is assuredly not a carbuncle, if it be true that the ruby is of like significance with the carbuncle, we might suppose that John apprehended it as a pearl. The generation of the pearl from a wound in the pearl-oyster, its lodgment in the deep, the rarity and difficulty of obtaining it, are obvious symbolical motives for the use of it. The subsistence of each gate in *one pearl* is a speaking image of that heavenly simplicity which alone finds entrance to the eternal City of God.

In the *golden pavement* of the *streets* of the City, the gold of the buildings is raised to an even higher power. Gold like *translucent crystal.* How far is it from the streets of Jerusalem —consecrated though they were—through Christian city streets and alleys—in which morals and cultivation often, even to this day, carry on a conflict with barbarism—to this goal! Here the lanes and streets are clean; the citizens walk on a pavement of gold, eternally clear and bright as a mirror.

The points which have reference to the perfection of the Theocracy, are followed by the fundamental features of the perfected, believing Gentile world.

As the most pious of the heathen discovered lively signs and traces of the Unknown God, not in their temples, but outside of these, and as the worship of God in spirit and in truth has in all time formed a contrast to the purely local worship on Gerizim and in Jerusalem, so, in accordance with these preludes, a perfect consciousness of the omnipresence of God in His Spirit has been formed. The obscure feeling of God's omnipresence has continually developed more and more, both outside of the revelation of salvation and within it (comp. Gen. xxviii. 16 and Psalm cxxxix. 7 sqq.). Here this feeling is exchanged for the constant contemplation of the presence of God, or, rather, for the perfect manifestation of God.

The universal natural revelation of God (Rom. i. 20) was always, for the heathen, in respect of its fundamental traits, a revelation through the medium, particularly, of the great celestial lights—the *sun* and the *moon*. This revelation is now restored and perfected—sun and moon are outshone by the glory of the Lord. In the spiritual radiance which proceeds from God, through Christ His Light-bearer, the lights of

Heaven seem, as such, to vanish, because they are for the first time effectual in Him in their full import.

The *heathen* [or *Gentiles*] have, in the light of salvation, become *nations* in the purest sense, —types of peoples, which, in their sanctified idiocrasies, conjoin to form the Kingdom of God. In the blessing of Noah, the first sketch of the variant destinations of the tribes of man appeared; at the foot of the tower of Babel, mankind was divided into *gentilisms*. The higher charismatic destination of humanity was, however, not only typically symbolized by the Twelve Tribes of Israel and expressed by the idea of the seventy nations and the number of the seventy disciples, but, moreover, it was the constant task of the Christian Church to work out, from the heathen confusion of peoples, the one people of God; but also, however, to work out from the one Christendom the heavenly family of peoples. Here, this heavenly family has attained a visible existence. *The nations walk* through the light-stream of the Kingdom of God as though they were bathing themselves therein.

Again, that which has ever been represented by *kings*—that of which bad kings were significant as symbolical figures, and which good kings, heroes, approximately realized, in company with the kingly spirits who ruled right royally, though possessing neither crown nor sceptre (Matt. v. 19), potentiated men, as central points of the social organization of humanity —is likewise now fulfilled. *The kings of the earth bring* all the *glory* of the earth, their possessions brought under the service of spirit, into the City of God (Isa. xlix. 23; lx. 16).

Furthermore, the security which man has now and then enjoyed under the protection of the law, in circles of civilization and on the heights of peace, in the bright day-time in antithesis to the night-time, has always been promoted by the Kingdom of God. Here, at last, in the consummation, the "superb repose of Heaven" prevails, secured by the light of eternal day, in the region of eternal sunshine. *The gates* of the City of God are *not shut,* because the day-time is permanent.

As the entire net value of the good things of earth is appropriated to the City of God, so also is the entire net value of humanity, in *the glory of the peoples,* their manifold and various gifts, the whole treasure of human culture. Israel was chosen to be the people of God, in order that it might make the peoples appear again as peoples, in the blessing of Abraham. It is the task of Christianity to this day to take away the covering of sin, of national corruption, from the beauty of the peoples (Isa. xxv. 7). Here is the fulfillment. In contemplating the one glory of Christ, they all come forth in their glory—the treasure, the harvest of God, the triumphal spoils of Christ.

Real heathenism, however, such as disfigured even Judaism (see Rom. ii.), is then eliminated forever from the pure Church of God. Its characteristics are *commonness* [or profaneness, as opposed to consecrateness to God], rudeness, and uncultivation, on the one hand, and, on the other, *abomination,* transgression against nature, including the perverted forms

---

two passages in Proverbs above cited, the word which the E. V. renders *rubies,* is, in the G. V., translated *pearls.*— Tr.]

of mis-culture and over-culture; and the common ground-tone is *falsehood*—the falsification of the high and holy reality of God, the production of mask-like shadows, which in part appear as rude caricatures of reality, in part as caricatures which ape beauty and holiness. At this process of elimination, humanity, in its higher tendency, has labored, by Jewish laws of purification, Græco-Roman justice and police, and by the Christian administration of the keys [*Schlüsselamt*], often amid great and gross distortions of the idea of the ban. Here, however, the City of God has attained to an eternal power of purity, in which, with twelve open gates, it still, in dynamical operation, for ever keeps everything common or ban-laden afar off.

As the circle of the Theocracy is surrounded by the circle of holy humanity, so the latter is surrounded by the circle of glorified nature. Paradise was lost. Lost, however, only as to its visible appearance, and to the world. The grace of God secured the seed of Paradise, and Christ regained that seed for humanity. It lay under the snow, it burst forth again in foretokens and signs in the Promised Land and in Christian civilization.—Here, Paradise is extant again, and how it has grown under the snow! The mysterious garden in Eden has become a glorified universe.

Yonder river of Paradise went out from Eden, the land of delight, and divided into the main rivers of earth. How soon it gathered earthly hues and fell under the doom of transitoriness! And even in Paradise it was no river of *life*. Gradually, indeed, a fountain of salvation burst forth in humanity—burst forth out of the depths, out of the rock of salvation (Ps. xlvi. 5; Is. xii. 3; Jer. ii. 13, *et al.*), being prefigured by the wells of the Patriarchs and the wells of the desert (Ex. xv. 27, *et al.*). Gradually, also, sacred brooks and rivers, Shiloah and Jordan, became streams of blessing, and a great river of life was predicted by Ezekiel.—But here, the mighty, shining river of life bursts forth; it comes from *the throne of God and of the Lamb*, having, even in this present life, been heralded and opened as a fountain (John iv. 7); it abides pure as crystal, it pours forth into infinitude through its one deep channel, and is adorned on either side with *trees of life*.

The one tree of life in Paradise speedily vanished, like a figure in a dream, a celestial apparition. Here it is again. It has become an endless avenue, a glorious grove, and in the plenteousness of its *fruits* and the healing virtue of its *leaves* a power of life is expressed which far exceeds all the conceptions of mortal pilgrims. It is the view of a nature completely elevated to the service of spirit, love and life.

Whilst there is here another reference to the fact that *nothing banned* [*cursed*] has existence in the City, this is certainly not a repetition of the idea set forth in ch. xxi. 27. We are rather reminded, within the domain of glorified nature, that, by virtue of patriarchal custom and Mosaic food-laws, a rigorous ban rested upon a large portion of nature. Christianity paved the way for the acknowledgment that every creature of God is clean that is (and can be) partaken of with thanksgiving. Here, there shall

evermore be nothing banned (literally, *set aside*, καταθεμα, a term which it has been deemed necessary to interpret into καταναθεμα, leaving out of consideration the textual reference). Paradise itself, in whose first rudiment God did, of old, but walk in mysterious appearances, has become a *throne of God and of the Lamb*. The Word once became flesh, that all nature might be spiritualized.

And because there is question here of the holy tillage of the eternal garden, as Adam was called to till the garden of Paradise, and because the task of tilling the field was resumed by the Theocracy and by civilization, Christianity next mediating the holy cultivation of the earth, the sons of God can here once more appear in the most dignified form. But as they shall *serve* [*dienen*] their God as His active *servants* [*Knechte*], so they shall *rest* in the contemplation of *His face* and bear *His name on their foreheads* as a people of high-priests, being ever newly energized by Him through the contemplation of His glory (1 John iii. 2).

And whilst the cessation of the *night-time* is again mentioned here, as in ch. xxii. 23, 25, let us recollect that even this semblance of tautology is done away with by a discrimination of the fact that in ch. xxi. the reference was to glorified humanity, but here it is to glorified Nature. The night side of Nature, diminished by the most manifold torches, lights and inventions for the obtaining of light, is here abolished.

And because God will Himself be the eternal Day-Light of the blessed, they need no more be continually sinking back into the bosom of night. Even under the Old Covenant, the prelude of a holy spirit-life, often emblematized by festal illuminations, flashed through the night-times of nature. The holy birth-night [*Weihnacht*—Christmas] of Christ laid the foundation for the bringing in of eternal day. The Holy Supper became the pre-celebration of the morning of that day. As Christianity is in constant combat with ethical night, so Christendom is in constant combat with the uncomfortable features and distresses of physical night. Here, the eternal *Day* has dawned in the presence of God; therefore do the blessed *reign*,—royally free, without ever losing their consciousness in night,—*into the æons of the æons*.

EXPLANATIONS IN DETAIL.

Ch. xxi. 9. Comp. ch. xvii. 1. Ewald and Düsterdieck have also pointed out the contrast of our passage to that cited, which is couched in similar terms. **The Bride.**—On the change of designations, see Düsterd., p. 565.

Ver. 10. **He carried me away.**—See ch. xvii. 3 (Ezek. iii. 12; xxxvii. 1; xl. 2; Acts viii. 39; 2 Cor. xii. 2). In accordance with the passages mentioned, we have to distinguish between purely spiritual transports and such as are also followed by a corporeal removal, accomplished, as it were, in a dream. **To a great and high mountain.**—According to Düsterdieck, the Seer is taken to this mountain in order that he may obtain a free view of the City. The same exegete remarks that the mountain must be so *great* in order to be so *high*. The Seer, therefore [as Düsterd. maintains], stands on the mountain and looks down upon the City. A splendid view, it is true, but too modern. The symbolical expression points, according to Hengstenberg, *et al.*, back to the fundamental passages in the Old Testament, especially Ezek. xl. 2; xvii. 22, 23; xx. 40; Ps. xlviii. 1, 2; also, particularly, Is. ii. 2. **Descending.**—See Rev. xxi. 2. The difficulties which Hengstenb. and Düsterd. discover in the apparent repetition of ver. 2 vanish when we consider the parallel relation between the Heaven-picture and the Earth-picture.

Ver. 11. **Having,** *etc.*—Or, possessing. The dim radiance in which a large city is always enwrapped at the beginning of night may, on the one hand, have mediated this view; but, on the other hand, it is based upon the idea that the Shekinah no longer hovers over the holy Temple-mount alone, according to the words of the Prophet (Isaiah iv. 5; xl. 5), but shines over the entire Holy City. **Her light-giver** ($\phi\omega\sigma\tau\acute{\eta}\rho$—light-bearer). — Düsterdieck opposes the assumption of Züllig, that the Messiah is intended by the $\phi\omega\sigma\tau\acute{\eta}\rho$, and cites ver. 23 in support of such opposition; that verse, however, is favorable to Züllig's view—as is also Heb. i. 3. **Like unto a stone most precious.**—Comp. ch. iv. 3. **A jasper stone, clear as crystal.**—See pp. 20 and 151. "Comp. Psellus (in Wetstein): $\acute{\eta}$ '$\mathrm{I}\alpha\sigma\pi\iota\varsigma$ $\phi\acute{v}\sigma\epsilon\iota$ $\kappa\rho\nu\sigma\tau\alpha\lambda\lambda o\epsilon\iota\delta\acute{\eta}\varsigma$.'' DUESTERDIECK.

["$\Phi\omega\sigma\tau\acute{\eta}\rho$, from verse 23, is the effect of the Divine glory shining in her: see (also) Gen. i. 14, 16, (LXX.), where it is used for the heavenly bodies." ALFORD.—E. R. C.].

Ver. 12. **Having a wall great and high.** —The measure of the wall, the gates and the City is qualified throughout by the duodecenary; not, therefore, by the number of complete worldly development, *ten*, but by the number of perfection of the people of God. *Twelve* is the number of theocratic perfection; hence it is the number of the Twelve Patriarchs, the Twelve Tribes of Israel, the Twelve Apostles, the perfected Church or heavenly Spirit-World (see p. 15). Here, therefore, there is repeatedly reflected, in all the duodecenaries of the City of God, the quantitative *number of completeness* and the qualitative perfection of the glorified Church of God. It, however, crosses and blends with the number of the world, the quaternary, and indeed is itself composed of three times four, i. e., the God-hallowed world-number. Moreover, the quaternary, as it here appears, continually branches into threes. Thus, we read of *twelve gates*, distributed by *threes* on the *four* sides of the City. And again, the City itself, in its *quadrangular* form, is *thrice* quadrangular—in length, breadth and height—and is thus a cube. The duodecenary is repeated a *thousand* times in the qualification of the *stadia*. The height of the *wall* is defined by the number twelve times twelve, or *a hundred and forty-four*. Even from these numeric proportions alone, the thoroughly symbolic nature of the whole picture of the City is manifest, and the same fact is further evident, in particular, from the *height* of the City.

And at the gates twelve angels.—"Bengel judiciously remarks: 'They keep watch and serve as ornaments.' We are not authorized to seek for a knowledge of any more definite rela-

tions which they may sustain to the City. So soon as we reflect that the new Jerusalem is no longer menaced by enemies, and that it consequently stands in need of no watchmen at its gates, explanations like that of Hengstenberg arise—*viz.*, that these Angels symbolize the Divine protection against all foes 'of which the imagination, filled with the terrors resting upon the Church Militant, can conceive.'" [DUEST.] A most marvellous imagination, truly! As if the blessed inhabitants of Heaven were timid children, or were threatened by empty terrors of the fancy! But even the idea of Angels standing always upon the gates for *ornament* has a singular aspect, and as *watchmen*—who, however, would be superfluous after the final judgment—they would be obliged to stand *in* the gates. We have characterized them above as symbols of the destination of Jerusalem to be the medium of salvation to all the world, to all the four quarters of the world (see Is. xliii. 5; xlix. 6; Matt. viii. 11). DE WETTE: "Guards, probably after Is. lxii. 6 and after the type of the Levitic temple-guards [or 'porters'] (2 Chron. viii. 14)." From this point of view, these Angels would symbolically represent the eternal *security* and inamissibleness of heavenly prosperity or salvation.*

And names inscribed.—The twelve names upon the twelve gates, as the names of the Twelve Tribes of Israel, denote the whole manifoldness of the idiocrasies of the totality of God's people. The typical fore-image is to be found Ezek. xlviii. 30 sqq. Jewish Theology has drawn from this rich symbolism the absurd idea that every Israelitish Tribe of the new Jerusalem shall be permitted to go in and out only of that particular gate which is appointed for it (see De Wette, p. 198). If we were to interpret the sealed out of the Twelve Tribes (ch. vii.) literally, as Jewish Christians, we should here be obliged to go on to the tremendous deduction that the entire heavenly City is to be inhabited solely by Jewish Christians.

Ver. 13. **On the east.**—See the above-cited passage in Ezekiel, ch. xlviii.

Ver. 14. **Twelve foundations** [Lange: foundation-stones].—The twelve gates give rise to twelve sections of the wall, amongst which De Wette and Düsterdieck distribute the foundation-stones. In accordance with this disposition, four are "to be conceived of as mighty corner-stones." Symbolical descriptions, however, should not be pushed beyond the idea which they are designed to convey. It may, at all events, be taken for granted that the twelve foundation-stones are open to view, like corner-stones in the ancient sense of the term. As the

---

* [The *cui bono* argument, if injudiciously pressed, might lead to the conclusion that there are no Angels at all. Angels are described as "ministering spirits sent forth to minister for them who shall be heirs of salvation." 'But,' it may be asked, 'what is the use of them under the government of an infinite God? Are they aught else than symbols of the watchful guardianship which God exercises over His children?' Angels may be unnecessary as watchmen and guards at the gates of the heavenly Jerusalem, and some may object to them as "ornaments;" and yet veritable Angels ministering at the gates of that glorious abode would add to its glory, and might perform other offices than in our present condition it is impossible for us to conceive.—E. R. C.]

whole fullness of the theocratic natural disposition was set forth in the Twelve Patriarchs, so the whole fullness of Christ's Spirit and salvation was manifested in the Apostles. The Apostle John could not, in modesty, have written this, is the cry of an idea-less, snarling criticism. The symbolic expression of the truth, that the celestial City of God is grounded upon the evangelic foundations of the twelve Apostles, can, however, no more lose its ideal value through the one consideration that the name of John is pre-supposed to accompany the names of the other Apostles, than through the other consideration that the name of Paul seems to be omitted from the group; nor is it a necessary inference from the citation of the Twelve Tribes of Israel in our passage, that the modifications in their names (ch. vii.) are to be abolished. Comp. Eph. ii. 20, where a freer apprehension of the symbolic idea already appears: "built upon the foundation of the Apostles *and Prophets*, Jesus Christ Himself being *the corner-stone*."

Ver. 15. **He that spake with me** (see ver. 9) **had a measure.**—Comp. Ezek. xl. 3, 5. The fact that the *discourse* occurring in symbolical representations must be determined by the fundamental thought thereof, is evidenced by Zech. ii. 3 sqq. "The angel who shows John the City (comp. ver. 9) gives him a perfectly distinct idea of its dimensions by actually measuring it before the eyes of the Seer (Bengel, Ewald, De Wette)." DUESTERD.—The *measure* (see ch. xi. 1; Ezek. xlii. 16) denotes the ideality of the eternal Church, the Divine knowledge and appointment of it—qualities which are expressed also in John xvii.; Rom. viii.; Eph. i. The measure is *golden*: through the Divine faithfulness, the ideal Church has become the actualized eternal Church. The Angel performs the measurement in the true sequence: first, the *City* is defined, with reference to the fullness of its inhabitants; next, the proportion of the *gates* and the *wall*.

Ver. 16. **And the City lieth.**—"The fact (ver. 16 a) that the City lies (κεῖται; comp. ch. iv. 2) four-cornered (like ancient Babylon and the new Jerusalem of Ezekiel), rectangular, and with equal length and breadth, and that therefore the ground-plan of it forms a perfect square (comp. Ezek. xlviii. 16), is recognized by John even before the Angel begins to measure." DUESTERD.—**Twelve thousand stadia**, *i. e.*, 300 geographical [German (1384 Eng. statute)] miles. It is a question whether the 12,000 stadia qualify the whole area of the City, so that the dimensions of each side amount to 3,000 stadia (in accordance with Vitringa, *et al.*), or whether the 12,000 stadia are to be taken as applying in their entirety to each of the four sides, and as referring also to the *height* (Bengel, Züllig, *et al.*). In regard to the former hypothesis, the further question arises, whether the *height* also is stated at 3,000 stadia, like the *length* and the *breadth*. De Wette opposes the idea that the *height* of the City amounts to 12,000 stadia. The conception would, in such case, he declares, be that of a lofty fortress, whilst it is manifestly a city that is represented, as mention is made of *streets* (ch. xxii. 2); he even maintains that the

height is determined only by the wall.* Düsterdieck, on the other hand, finds in the 12,000 stadia the measure alike for length, breadth and height (with Bengel, Hengstenberg, *et al.*). Whilst the idea is a prodigious one, we must recollect that we have to do with a thoroughly symbolical description. A height of even 3,000 stadia far exceeds that of the loftiest steeples. If, however, we keep strictly to the text, we find that the measure of the entire square in respect of length and breadth, as the measure of *the City*, is 12,000 stadia; and, accordingly, the height of the City is to be determined by the quarter of this, as 3,000 stadia. The fact that the *wall* will then be considerably lower than the height of the City itself, should not occasion any difficulty. The height of the Kingdom of God towers far above the theocratic barrier. Here, therefore, the typical cube-form of the Tabernacle is realized in the highest sense; and the breadth, length, depth and height of the Divine dispensation of salvation (Eph. iii. 18) are embodied in symbolical significance, in analogy with the incarnation of the Word. (*The Word became flesh* [John i. 14].)

Ver. 17. **Her wall.**—"The height of the City is not the height of the wall, as Bengel also assumes, and therefore maintains that the 144 cubits are equivalent to the 12,000 stadia." DUESTERD.—**The measure of a man.**—The additional clause: **which is that of an angel**, occasions difficulty. De Wette: The Angel has made use of human measure. Ebrard: The measure of glorified men is like the measure of the Angel. Hengstenberg (and Düsterdieck): The measure of the Angel, who makes his measurement for men, is like the measure of men. A reminder of the symbolic import of the act of measuring is probably contained in our passage:—the *human* measure with which the Sanctuary was measured, is here an *angelic* measure, *i. e.*, it has a symbolic, higher import. The Seer frequently inserts similar reminders of the symbolic nature of his forms of speech; see especially chs. i. 20; xiii. 18; xvi. 14; xvii. 9. Now if the *wall* denotes the security of the City of God, and the *cubit* the measure of the Sanctuary, the height of 144 cubits is expressive of the perfect measure of heavenly confirmation or verification: the *theocratic* twelve of the plan of the Kingdom multiplied by the *apostolic* twelve of the consummation of the Kingdom in the fullness of the Spirit of Christ. This symbolical nature of the cubit-measure is expressed in the prophecy of Ezekiel by the fact that every cubit there spoken of is a hand-breadth longer than a common cubit. The figure of the wall approaches the idea of Zechariah (ch. i. 5): "For I, saith the Lord, will be unto her a wall of fire round about, and will be the glory in the midst of her;" [LANGE (not G. V.): "and will manifest my glory in her"]. The prodigious extent of the City is also expressive of an idea—or, rather, of the ideal fact that it extends, with unseen limits, through the universe, and towers up into the height of eternity; that it belongs to Heaven, whence it has descended to

* [De Wette interprets the *Iota*, ver. 16, in reference to the *height*,—viz.: of the *wall*, as he falsely assumes—as *uniform*, because the wall is everywhere 144, *i. e.* 12 × 12, cubits high. Altered from DUESTERDIECK.—TR.]

earth. A discussion of the relative lowness of the wall in proportion to the height of the City, see in Düsterdieck, p. 568.

Ver. 18. **And the structure of her wall.** —The materials. On the rare word ἐνδόμησις, comp. the Lexicons. **Jasper.**—See above, p. 20. The material of the wall is thus of like import with its height,—infinite value in infinite duration, qualities which both appertain to the most precious of precious stones. **The city was pure gold.**—The material of the houses is absolutely pure gold, similar, in consequence of this purity, to pure crystal or glass.

This may be understood as referring either to the transparency of glass, or to the mirror-like brightness of crystal. We adopt the latter signification, retaining it also when διαυγής is predicated of the golden street-pavement [πλατεῖα] (ver. 21). According to Ebrard, there is a prospect that gold itself will really be translucent in the world to come. The genuine heavenly purity and faithfulness of the inhabitants of the City shall, therefore, be reflected in the golden brilliance of their dwellings.

Ver. 19. **The foundations of the wall** etc.—The meaning is, that the foundations or foundation-stones of the City consist of precious stones, as is clearly evident from the following verse (comp. Is. liv. 11). "As the twelve θεμέλιοι have nothing to do with the number of the Israelitish Tribes (comp. ver. 14), that artificial mode of interpretation by which the stones (ver. 19 sq.) are brought into an assumed relation to those worn by the High-priest in his breast-plate (comp. especially Züllig, Excursus II., pp. 456 sqq.; also Ewald II., Luthardt, Volkmar), is to be discarded as decidedly as the vain attempt to assign individual jewels to individual Apostles (Andr., Bengel, et al.)." DUESTERD. If it be proved that a relation exists between the Twelve Tribes of Israel, whose names the High-priest wore in his breast-plate, and the Twelve Apostles,—a relation as between the theocratic plan and the apostolic development,—a general relation will also be assumable between the jewels in the breast-plate and the jewels which constitute the foundations of the Holy City. But if an individual combination of the Twelve Tribes and the Twelve Apostles is impracticable, it will be still less possible to make out a concordance of the stones in the high-priestly breast-plate and the foundation-stones of the New Jerusalem. The general symbolic significance lies in the nature of the precious stones, and also, particularly, in their colors, in the grouping of which they appear as a symbolism of eternal individualities, all, in equal purity, brilliant with the same light, which they refract in the most diverse rays (see Introduction, pp. 20 sq, ; Lange's Miscellaneous Writings, vol. i, p. 15). **The first** . . . .jasper.—Comp. pp. 20 sq. and 151, and ver. 11. **Sapphire.** — Ex. xxiv. 10; xxviii. 18; Ezekiel xxviii. 13; see Winer, Title, PRECIOUS STONES; [also Kitto's Cyclopædia and Smith's Dictionary of the Bible]. "Our sapphire is sky-blue (comp. Ezek. i. 26), translucent, and harder than the ruby. That which the ancients so denominated, must, according to Pliny (37, 39) and Theophr. (ch. vi. 23, 37), have been the lapis lazuli," etc. Winer remarks, in conclusion,

however, that we must suppose the Hebrew word to denote the true sapphire, as is clearly evident from the passages cited from Exodus and Ezekiel. The opinion of Düsterdieck, therefore, who assumes the lapis lazuli to be intended, is incorrect. **Chalcedony.**—Not the agate, precisely. WINER: A chalcedony-agate. **Emerald.**—Grass-green, not very hard, translucent, with double refraction (see Winer, PRECIOUS STONES, No. 3).

Ver. 20. **Sardonyx.**—See Winer, No. 16; comp. No. 1: "Consisting of a combination of onyx and carnelian." **Sardius.**—Or carnelian: it is striped with brown and is not very sharply distinguished from the preceding stone. **Chrysolite.**—See Winer, No. 10: "Pale-green, perfectly translucent, with double refraction. According to Pliny, it is of the color of gold, and hence the topaz has been understood by it." **Beryl.**—Winer, No. 11. **Topaz.**—Winer, No. 2. This seems to have been frequently confounded with the chrysolite. **Chrysoprasus.** —Winer, No. 15: "Pale green, shading into yellowish and brown—translucent." **Jacinth** [**Hyacinth**].—Winer, No. 7. **Amethyst.**—Winer, No. 9.

In respect of color, we distinguish blue stones: Sapphire, chalcedony, amethyst (violet-blue); Green: Emerald, beryl, and, more or less, chrysoprasus; Golden or yellow: Chrysoprasus (see above), chrysolite, topaz; Red: Hyacinth [jacinth], sardonyx, sardius (carnelian). The jasper is, most probably, as a diamond, of the pure hue of light; as an ordinary jasper, it would be non-translucent and of various colors. It is evident from chs. iv. 3, xxi. 12, as well as from the fact that in accordance with New Testament order it stands at the beginning, and in accordance with Old Testament order at the close, that it is to be regarded as the chief or most precious stone. Of the jewels in the breast-plate two names are absent from our catalogue, viz., ruby and the agate, whilst, on the other hand, the names chalcedony and chrysoprasus are wanting in the breast-plate (comp. Introduction, p. 20). For a comparison of the lists, see Ebrard, pp. 533 sqq.; Hengstenberg, vol. ii., pp. 417 sq. [Eng. Trans.]; De Wette. p. 200.

Ver. 21. **Of one pearl.**—Düsterdieck quotes the Jewish tradition from Bava Bathra: "Deus adducet gemmas et margaritas, triginta cubitos longas, totidemque latas." There is, however, a heaven-wide distinction between a great pearl as modified by Christian symbolism, and a great pearl as modified by Jewish Chiliasm. **The broad-way of the city.**—Πλατεῖα [i. e., the flat, as opposed to the elevated, the buildings]. Doubtless significant of the pavement or ground of all the streets and alleys; not merely the market-place (Bengel) or principal street (Züllig). [See foot-note † chap. xi. 8, p. 231.—E. R. C.]. **As it were translucent glass.**—We apprehend this not literally, but poetically, of the mirror-like brightness.

Ver. 22. "The peculiar glory of the City is further described." DUESTERDIECK. That is, the pause is unobserved by him.

[In the old Jerusalem the Temple was at once the dwelling-place and the concealer of Jehovah. Though present, He was not visibly present—in a sense He was *sheltered* by the Temple. The new Jerusalem shall have no place for the shelter of the Lord, for she shall be sheltered by Him. He shall tabernacle over her, ch. vii. 15. Her inhabitants shall dwell under His manifest and sheltering light. *He* shall be *her* Temple. —E. R. C.]

Ver. 23. **The glory of God lightened her.** —See Is. lx. 19. On the distinction between this passage and ver. 11, see above.

Ver. 24. **And the nations** (Is. ii. 3; lx. 11; Ps. lxxii. 11) **shall walk by means of** [Lange: through] **her light.**—Significant future. "This description, drawn from the declarations of the old Prophets, does not justify the idea of those expositors who conceive of the heathen [nations] and the kings as dwelling outside of the City (Ewald, De Wette, Bleek *et. al.*), or who would even attempt to determine what moral condition the heathen [nations] now admitted into the new Jerusalem, occupied during their earthly life (Storr, *etc.*)." Duesterdieck. **Their glory.**—That is, that which the kings possessed of glory. The Apocalyptist knows no political partyism. He recognizes a glory of the kings and also a glory of the peoples (ver. 26).

[Alford: "If then the kings of the earth, and the nations bring their glory and their treasures into her, and if none shall ever enter into her that is not written in the book of life, it follows that these kings, and these nations, are written in the book of life. And so perhaps some light may be thrown on one of the darkest mysteries of redemption. There may be,—I say it with all diffidence,—those who have been saved by Christ without ever forming a part of His visible organized Church."

The conclusion may be granted without recognizing the force of the argument. The distinguished commentator takes for granted that the *kings and nations* are those that lived before the Millennial period, or at least before the great consummation. Is it not rather probable that the great truth is adumbrated in this revelation (see also ch. xx. 2, last clause), that, even after the new creation, the human race is to be continued (ever propagating a holy seed, such as would have been begotten had Adam never sinned) under the government of the glorified Church?—E. R. C.].

Ver. 25. **Her gates shall not be** [Lange: do not be] **shut.**—They stand open uninterruptedly, for the bringing in of all the glory of the kings and the peoples (Is. lx. 11).

Ver. 26. **And they shall bring.**—"An impersonal subject should be supplied to οἴσουσι (comp. chap. xii. 6; x. 11 [the reading λέγουσιν]; Luther, Bengel, De Wette, Hengstenb., Ew. II., *et al.*), not οἱ βασιλεῖς (Ew. I., Züll.)." Duesterd.

Ver. 27. **Anything common.**—See ch. xxi. 8; xxii. 15; Acts x. 14. The elevation of the Apocalypse above Judaistic views is sufficiently evident from this passage alone, which, in connection with the preceding context, thoroughly distinguishes between believing ethnics and the essence of ethnicism, determining the πᾶν κοινόν purely in accordance with moral characteristics.

Chap. xxii. 1. **A river.**—The **water of life** is not to be taken here in a purely spiritual sense, at least not, primarily, as in John iv. 14 and vii.

38. It denotes the stream of spirituo-corporeal life-power which, as an eternal renewing power, ensures the imperishability and vital freshness of the new world (see Ezek. xlvii. 1; Zech. xiv. 8; comp. 1 Pet. i. 4). The unitous spirituo-corporeal operation is especially expressed in the fact that the river **proceeds from the throne of God and of the Lamb**—from the living God, through the glorified Christ, in accordance with the heavenly species of His resurrection-life. The properties of the *river of Paradise*, which operated as a purely *natural* blessing (Gen. ii.), and those of the *spiritual fountain of healing*, first promised by the Prophets and subsequently opened in Christ, are united in this river. As a river, it is *cosmically permanent*, and as a river that proceeds from the throne of God, it is *absolutely permanent*. Its source is not situate under the Temple-mount or under the Temple itself, but in the depths of the Divine revelation of love and life, in the profundities of the Divine government consonant with that revelation. As the *trees of life* are ensured by this eternally clear river, so the river is ensured by the Divine throne itself.

Ver. 2. **In the midst of her broad-way.**— Düsterdieck, with Ewald, refers ἐν μέσῳ to καὶ τοῦ ποταμοῦ also; but how this view can be accompanied by the conception "that the trees stand on both sides of the river," is not clear (see Ezek. xlvii. 7, 12).

A tree [Lange: *Gehölz*=wood] **of life.**— Ξύλον=a wood, a collection of trees, having the common character of *trees of life* (see ch. ii. 7), "generically denotes the entire mass of trees (Bengel, De Wette, Ewald, *et al.*)." Duest. De Wette gives: the *tree* [*Baum*] of life, and adds: "Which produces twelve fruits, bringing forth its fruit every month (Ezek. xlvii. 12);" this, however, can only mean twelve fruit-harvests or fruit twelve times. "Twelve kinds of fruits" (Lutheran Version; ["twelve *manner* of fruits," E. V.]) are, at all events, not intended. *All* the fruits are fruits *of life*.

And the leaves, *etc.*—These words contain, first, an expression of the highest vital efficacy. Even all the *leaves* of all these trees possess a vital energy which can be conducive, as a *healing* power, to the health of even *the heathen* or nations. As extreme views, as opposed the interpretation of Bengel, who holds that reference is had to the conversion of the heathen to whom in this life the Gospel has not been preached; and the interpretation of Hengstenberg, who thinks that the vital forces of the heavenly Jerusalem are intended, as serving in the present age (!) for the conversion of the heathen (Hengst., vol. ii., p. 433 [Eng. Trans.). It is not necessary through fear of an *apocatastasis*, either to do violence to the text, or to place the hope of an infinite healing operation in the leaves of the tree of life—an operation which is expressed by the river, but does not coincide exactly with the restoration-theory. Another contrast is presented in the inclination of Bleek and De Wette, with Ewald and Züllig (also Ebrard), to find a reference to heathen [nations] dwelling outside of the City, and the view of Düsterdieck, who holds that simply the eternal refreshment and beatification of believing heathen [nations] is made prominent. According to Ebrard, the fruits manifestly serve as food for *the inhabitants of the City*, and the leaves for the healing of the ἔθνη without the City; the latter, he continues, do not need such a θεραπεία as to be healed of godlessness and converted therefrom, "but they must be brought from the condition of undeveloped and weak faith and dawning knowledge, to the ripeness of the full stature of men in Christ." It might be queried, how does this interpretation correspond with the distinction of *milk* and *strong meat* [food]? Taken literally, the leaves might be reckoned as strong meat. But let us recollect that we are at present in the third sphere of our description, in which the transfiguration or heavenly glorification of nature is spoken of. Here the expression denotes the highest sanative operation of nature—even the *leaves* of the trees whose *fruits* are the vital nourishment of God's people, serve for the healing [*Therapie*] of the heathen [nations]. We apprehend the word [healing] in the wider sense, and observe, with Düster., that these heathen [nations] have been mentioned before in ch. xxi. 24. The remark of Düsterdieck, that the heavenly enjoyment of life is contrasted with the lack of vital power under which those referred to labored in this present life, is not in itself incorrect, but it gives rise to the question: wherefore are the *leaves* mentioned? As the river of life cannot be restricted to the City, so, also, the trees of life, with their fruits and leaves, can be regarded only as ■ health-giving blessing, stretching out into infinitude; and thus the passage coincides in general with analogous utterances of Paul (1 Cor. xv. 26–28). [See *additional comment* on chap. xxi. 24, p. 388.—E. R. C.]

Ver. 3. **And nothing cursed shall be any more.**—See SYN. VIEW; comp. Zech. xiv. 11.* Ebrard traces the κατάθεμα directly back to the *cherem*, distinguishing, however, as *cherem*, persons and things (in accordance with Lev. xxvii. 28 and other passages). There is yet another distinction to be made, however, between the *cherem* and the κοινόν.

And His servants shall serve Him.— The idea of religious service presented by λατρεύειν does not preclude the idea of ■ service rendered in the heavenly culture of the new Paradise, because, in the glorified world, cultus and culture shall have become one.

[There seems to be a great and blessed truth conveyed by the conjunction of δοῦλοι and λατρεύουσιν. His *slaves* (δοῦλοι) shall be elevated to the dignity of *temple-servitors*. The idea is akin to that presented by our Lord, John xv. 15: "Henceforth I call you not *servants* (δοῦλοι= *slaves*), but I have called you *friends*."—E. R. C.]

Ver. 4. **His face.**—Matt. v. 8; 1 Cor. xiii. 12; 1 John iii. 2.—**His name.**—See chs. iii. 12; xiv. 1.

Ver. 5. **And night shall not be any more.** —This is simply a repetition, according to De Wette, Ebr., Düsterd. (see SYN. VIEW). Hengstenb. discovers here an antithesis harmonizing with the Gospel of John, to wit, the antithesis of *day* as the time of safety and good, and *night*

___

* [The G. V. reads here: "*und wird kein Bann mehr sein*" (and there shall be no more ban).—TR.]

■■ the time of peril and evil (?); he remarks, by way of illustration: "Any one who has lived with a wakeful eye through the year '48 is acquainted with this distinction of day and night." It might be replied: Any one who has become acquainted with it only under such a date, knows it but very imperfectly, to say the least.

And they shall reign.—"In a still higher sense than in ch. xx. 4, 6, says De Wette." To which we query: in what respect? We would remind our readers that reference is here had to the relation of the blessed to the celestial spheres of nature; this fact endows the expression with the import that all dependence upon the power of nature shall be done away with.

Into the ages of the ages.—The antithesis see in ch. xx. 10.—In the region of the damned there continues, according to the same passage, the antithesis of day and night. The æons of the blessed are raised above the vicissitudes of temporality, because in God is eternity, the inexhaustible fountain of holy, festal seasons; and Christ has, in reality, freed even time from the curse of temporality, and made it the rhythmic succession of the fullness of eternity, the development-form of eternal life.

[NOTE ON THE NEW JERUSALEM.]

By the American Editor.

[It was the design of the American Editor to prepare an extended Excursus on this subject. Circumstances, however, over which he has no control, prevent his doing more than present a brief sketch of the views of representative commentators, afterwards indicating those points of his own hypothesis that he did intend thoroughly to discuss.

a. *Sketch of Views.*

So many and variant have been the opinions on this subject that it seems impossible to classify them. The following extract from Elliott will be regarded as a fair exposition of the views of those mentioned by him.

"It has long been a disputed question amongst prophetic expositors, where precisely the New Jerusalem of the xxi. and xxii. chapters of the Apocalypse is to have position; whether *during* or only *after* the Millennium; and if synchronous with it, whether as identical or not with the *glorified Jerusalem* prophesied in the Old Testament. Of the older Fathers alike the pre-millenarian TERTULLIAN, and the anti-pre-millenarian AUGUSTINE, explained the glorified Jerusalem of O. T. prophecy ■■ identical with that of the Apocalypse; the one (TERTULLIAN) however, ■■ symbolic of the risen saints' *millennial* glory, the other (AUGUSTINE) of their *heavenly and everlasting blessedness*. Again, of the moderns . . . WHITBY and VITRINGA, whilst also identifying the two figurations, did yet explain them to signify the *millennial* earthly blessedness of the still living Christian Church. . . . FABER would separate the two, and make Isaiah's *Jerusalem* of the latter day, with its new heaven and earth, *alone* millennial, that of the Apocalypse post-millennial; to which I may add that some expositors, while explaining one or both to prefigure *earthly* glories destined for God's people, make the *restored* and *converted Jews* nationally, not the *Church Catholic* generally, the grand object and chief intended recipients of the coming glory."

ELLIOTT himself (5th edition) "supposes the New Jerusalem to have existence from the commencement, and throughout the progress, of the millennial period." With this opinion the majority of pre-millenarians probably agree, though with vast differences as to particulars. Elliott argues his position from—(1) a comparison of ch. xix. 7, 8, with ch. xxi. 2, 9; (2) a comparison of xix. 10, with xxii. 8, 9, inferring from the coincidence that the same event must have been referred to; (3) what is said concerning the *nations*, chs. xxi. 24; xxii. 2, manifesting that there will be *men in the flesh* during the New Jerusalem, which, he assumes, could not be, after the General Resurrection; (4) a comparison of Dan. vii. 18 (where the saints' *everlasting* reign dates from the fall of Antichrist) with Rev. xxii. 5. He supposes (after Mede and several of the Ancient Fathers) that the entire millennial period constitutes the day (period) of Judgment; that at the beginning of this day, the great White Throne is set up, at which time occurs a partial conflagration; that at the close shall be the casting of death and Hades into the lake of fire, the great conflagration, the new heaven and earth, and the more complete and perfect establishment of the Kingdom.

ALFORD writes: "The whole of the things described in the remaining portion of the Book are subsequent to the General Judgment, and descriptive of the consummation of the triumph and bliss of Christ's people with Him in the eternal kingdom of God. This eternal kingdom is situated on the purified and renewed earth—become the blessed habitation of God with His glorified people."

BARNES (and with him probably the majority of post-millenarians) looks upon chaps. xxi. 1—xxii. 5, as descriptive of the heavenly state of the entire body of the redeemed. He writes: "The whole of ch. xxi., and the first five verses of ch. xxii., relate to scenes beyond the judgment, and are descriptive of the happy and triumphant state of the redeemed Church, when all its conflicts shall have ceased, and all its enemies shall have been destroyed. That happy state is depicted under the image of a beautiful city, of which Jerusalem was the emblem, and it was disclosed to John by a vision of that city—the New Jerusalem—descending from heaven. Jerusalem was regarded as the peculiar dwelling-place of God, and to the Hebrews it became thus the natural emblem or symbol of the heavenly world. The conception having occurred of describing the future condition of the righteous under the image of a beautiful city, all that follows is in *keeping* with that, and is merely a carrying out of the image. It is a city with beautiful walls and gates; a city that has no temple—for it is all a temple; a city that needs no light—for God is its light; a city into which nothing impure ever enters; a city filled with trees, and streams, and fountains, and fruits—the Paradise Regained."

b. *Hypothesis of the American Editor.*

I. The *period* of the New Jerusalem will be subsequent to the General Resurrection and Judgment of ch. xx. 11-15, and the new Creation of ch. xxi. 1. This is, manifestly, the normal sense of the connection between verses 1 and 2 of ch. xxi., and is not to be set aside but for most cogent reasons. This view involves no real difficulties; and, still further, the entire description forbids the thought that the even partial sinfulness that will exist in the subjects of the Millennial Kingdom should have existence under the light of the New Jerusalem, or that its glories should be dimmed by the assaults of Satan and the rebellion of Gog and Magog.

II. Its *seat* will be the *New Earth* (comp. xxi. 1, 2, 24). It is vain for us to speculate as to whether that New Earth will be identical as to substance with the present, or whether it will be different. It is impossible for us to determine whether the present abode of the human race will be simply regenerated by fire, or whether from the universal chaos into which all things *may be* reduced (2 Pet. iii. 10; Rev. xx. 11) some entirely new Earth, or dwelling-place for man, may not be brought forth.

III. It will exist—1. As a real City—the glorious home and capital of a glorified Community (the Bride). 2. As a *Material Symbol* of that Community, its order and glory.*

From the admitted fact that what the Apostle saw was a Symbol, many leap to the conclusion that a real city, or place of abode, could not have been symbolized. It is admitted by all that that which John beheld was a *simulacrum*. He did not directly look upon that which was not to exist for at least three thousand years—he beheld, merely, a VISIONAL SYMBOL. But what was the nature of that Symbol? Was it *immediate?* *i. e.*, did it symbolize a City that is yet to come into existence—or was it *mediate?* *i. e.*, did it symbolize something else than a City, namely (in this instance), a glorified community? In the judgment of the writer it performed the double office set forth in the last paragraph on p. 146. Primarily it was an IMMEDIATE SYMBOL symbolizing a material City; but, secondarily, as the City was itself to be a MATERIAL SYMBOL, of the inhabiting Community, it was a MEDIATE (*Aberrant*) SYMBOL of that Community.

This double use of the Symbol should occasion no surprise. For, in the first place, it is most common in all languages to denote by the same term, as *London*, sometimes the City, sometimes the mass of its inhabitants, and sometimes the complex of the two. This was common amongst the writers of the Scriptures—the Scriptural uses of Zion, Babylon, Tyre, will present themselves as illustrations to the minds of all. And, secondly, a material City is frequently a type of its inhabitants, or of the State of which it is the Capital. No one can visit Rome without being impressed with the fact that, in its combined ruin and grandeur, its death and life, the existing City is itself the type of the existing Roman Church. This in old times was true of Babylon,

---

* [In order to the understanding of this point, the writer would refer the reader to his PRELIMINARY NOTE ON THE SYMBOLISM OF THE VISION, pp. 145 sqq.—E. R. C.]

of Athens, of Tyre, of Rome, and especially of Jerusalem. And, doubtless, it is in great measure owing to this fact that a City and its inhabitants are so generally designated by one and the same name. In the judgment of the writer, as the old Jerusalem symbolized the Israel of which it was the Capital, so the New Jerusalem will symbolize the glorified Community * of whom it will be the abode and Capital.

Concerning the hypothesis that the New Jerusalem will exist as a great City, it may be said: 1. There are many things in the description that have their most natural (their normal) application to such an abode, as is evident upon the bare perusal. 2. This application is supported by the following considerations: (1) A material dwelling-place is as necessary for resurrected saints as was Eden for Adam, or Canaan for Israel. (2) It should occasion no surprise if the same loving care that will raise and glorify the body should prepare a fitting and glorious abode for it. (3) It should be regarded as no strange thing if He who prepares for the body should grant us an inspiring, though general, description of its future abode. (4) On the contrary, the giving of such a description would be but in accordance with Jehovah's dealing with Israel before leading them into Canaan, and in continuance of the information given us by the Prophets concerning the Palingenesia, and especially by the Apostle Paul, Rom. viii. 20, 21.

As to the hypothesis that a *glorified* Community was in some sense symbolized, it may also be said that while there are many things in the description that find their most natural *objective* in a *material City*, there are others that cannot be so regarded; as, for instance, that the New Jerusalem is the Bride of the Lamb. We are shut up to the conclusion that a glorified people were contemplated in the exhibition of the Symbol.

In conclusion of this whole matter it may be remarked that the double hypothesis announced by the writer best satisfies the conditions of the problem; is in accordance with the ordinary and Scriptural use of the names of Cities, especially of Capitals; and is precisely analogous to the Divine declarations concerning the old Jerusalem.

IV. We should distinguish between the *Material City* and the *New Earth*. The former has its situation in the latter, as London in England. We should also distinguish the *citizens of the City* and the *nations* (xxi. 24). The former are risen and glorified Saints, who constitute the *Bride* (ch. xxi. 9), the *governors* (ch. xxii. 5, *last clause*) of the New Creation (see below in V., VI.). The latter are (probably) *men in the flesh*, who walk in the light of the City, who bring their glory and

honor into it, and who are healed (or kept in health) by the leaves of its tree of life (chs. xxi. 24-27; xxii. 2), *i. e.*, who are under its instruction and government (see below in VII.).

V. The term *The Bride* probably identifies the citizens of the New Jerusalem with the subjects of the First Resurrection (see the ADD. NOTE ON THE MARRIAGE, pp. 336 sq.). This body, the Bride (identical probably with the 144,000 of ch. xiv. 1), will probably be completed at the time of the *Marriage*, chap. xix. 7–9. Into that glorious company it is probable that only those who have been partakers of Christ's humiliation and suffering (either personally in company with Him, or throughout the present æon, the period of the humiliation of His body, the Church, Col. i. 24) shall be received (comp. Luke xxii. 28–30; Phil. iii. 10, 11; 2 Thess. i. 5; 2 Tim. ii. 12; Rev. ii. 10, 26; iii. 12, 21; vi. 9-11; xix. 4-6; see also the ADD. NOTE ON THE MARRIAGE, as above.* These are they who sit on Christ's Throne, who are united with Him in authority,—who, as *related to* Him constitute the Bride; as *together with* Him constitute the Kingdom, *i. e.*, the governing power (see EXCURSUS ON THE BASILEIA, II. 1 (4), p. 99).

VI. Chap. xxi. 2, 9, 10, does not refer to the Marriage—that took place at the beginning of the Millennial period (see NOTE ON THE MARRIAGE, pp. 336 sq.), but to a new manifestation of the prophetical Bride, the Wife. Doubtless before, or at the very moment when, "the earth and the heaven fled away" (chap. xx. 11), she was rapt away to the secret place of Jehovah. These verses describe her as descending from the bosom of her God, out of the New Heaven, clothed in new beauty, upon the New Creation, over which she is to dominate.

VII. The *nations* (see above in IV.) will consist (probably) of *men in the flesh*, freed from sin and the curse, begetting a holy seed, and dwelling in blessedness under the government of the New Jerusalem. They will be, not the offspring of the glorified Saints, who "neither marry nor are given in marriage" (Matt. xxii. 30), but the descendants of those who live in the flesh during the period of the Millennial Kingdom. Brown triumphantly asks, "How 'the *inhabitants* of the heavens and earth that now are,' are *tided over* this (the) all enveloping, all reducing deluge of fire, into 'the new heavens and the new earth'?" In answer it may be said, The same Almighty power that conveyed Noah and his family across the waters of the first deluge, can bear other families across the fiery floods of the second, to be the progenitors of the continued race. It may be retorted that there is no promise of such a miracle. That there is no expressed promise is admitted—but the Divine prediction of an event ever implies the promise of a sufficient cause.

VIII. Although the New Jerusalem state is not to be confounded with the Millennial Kingdom, nor to be regarded as a simple continuance thereof, it is to be looked upon as the antitype of that Kingdom. In a sense, it is that Kingdom

---

* [As an Immediate Symbol, the *simulacrum* of the New Jerusalem was probably to a large extent *ideal*. This, doubtless, was the case in the *simulacra* of Angels. We can hardly suppose that the *simulacrum* beheld by John was in all respects *similar* to the City that is to be, and yet it may have been so to a greater extent than we are now prepared to admit. It should here be distinctly noted, what was set forth with great care in the Note on Symbolism, that there is a great difference between an *Immediate ideal* and a *Mediate Symbol*. The former always represents something similar in (apparent) kind to the *simulacrum*, although with differences as to particulars; the latter always represents something different in (apparent) kind, as the *simulacrum* of a *lamb* to represent Christ, and that of a City to symbolize a Church or people.—E. R. C.]

* [The writer expresses no decided op'nion as to whether the *Bride*, the subjects of the First Resurrection, shall consist of the martyrs; or the who le body of the redeemed; or a select portion, including the martyrs—the ἀπαρχή (see p. 193). He inclines, however, to the last mentioned view.—E. R. C.]

raised to a higher plane—completely freed, in its territory and its subjects, from all remains of the curse. The Millennial Kingdom is the reign of the Saints over a race and earth freed indeed from the assaults of Satan, but still, in measure, in sin and under the curse; the New Jerusalem period is that of the reign of the Saints over a race and earth perfectly purified.

IX. The City itself, as it will have placed in it the Throne of God and the Lamb (xxii. 3), will become the noblest of the many mansions of Heaven. Neither it, however, nor the New Earth on which it is situate, including it, will be the totality of Heaven. John saw the Bride descending *out of Heaven* (xxi. 2). The New Earth will be one of the loyal provinces of Heaven, under the light of Heaven, governed by the citizens of Heaven; but it will be the abode of men in the flesh. May it not bear to Heaven a relation similar to that borne by Eden before the fall? Although in it there will be no death, possibly from it will be transported to other scenes its blessed inhabitants, when they have passed through their painless, ennobling pupilage. Possibly, its inhabitants may pass away to other mansions in the Father's House, where dwell, it may be, the Angels who kept their first estate, and the glorified subjects of the Millennial Kingdom, and others glorified who did not attain to the first Resurrection.

X. The prophecies of the Restoration and the Palingenesia (like those of the Advent) have probably a double application. Initially and typically they may refer to the Millennial Kingdom, which is a type of the New Jerusalem. Ultimately and completely, they have respect to the latter, the Kingdom of the Perfect Restoration.

XI. In conclusion, the writer would remark that he feels most keenly that speculation on this subject is dangerous. Speculation, however, to some degree there must be, if there be study,— and study there must be, if we be obedient to the command implied in the benediction, "Blessed is he that readeth and they that hear the words of this prophecy" (chap. i. 3). It may also be remarked that those who hold the current opinion as to the New Jerusalem, *speculate* as really as does the writer. The study of the Divinely given Revelation has convinced him of certain facts concerning this great and glorious subject. These facts, together with certain probable implications, he has stated with trembling, and he trusts with becoming modesty. He now submits them to the considerate construction of his readers.—E. R. C.]*

---

* [The hymnology connected with the New Jerusalem is exceedingly rich. A small work entitled O MOTHER DEAR, JERUSALEM, by *William C. Prime* (A. D. F. Randolph, New York, 1865) gives the entire Poem so named; its history, several of its versions, and also several of the ancient hymns, in Latin and English, whence its sentiments, and in many instances its language, were drawn. To these hymns, embodying as they do the opinions of many of the sainted fathers of the Church, and sung in every land, is due, more than to aught else, the prevalent interpretation of the Apocalyptic description. The original English form of the hymn as it exists in a small volume of poetry, professedly of the age of Queen Elizabeth, in the British Museum, was some years ago published by Dr. Bonar. Modernized by Barnes as to its spelling, it is as follows:

A SONG MADE BY F. B. P.

To the tune of "Diana."

Jerusalem! my happy home!
　When shall I come to thee,
When shall my sorrows have an end,
　Thy joys when shall I see?

O happy harbor of the saints,
　O sweet and pleasant soil,
In thee no sorrow may be found,
　No grief, no care, no toil.

In thee no sickness may be seen,
　No hurt, no ache, no sore;
There is no death, no ugly deil,
　There's life for evermore.

No dampish mist is seen in thee,
　No cold nor darksome night;
There every soul shines as the sun,
　There God Himself gives light.

There lust and lucre cannot dwell,
　There envy bears no sway,
There is no hunger, heat, nor cold,
　But pleasure every way.

Jerusalem! Jerusalem!
　God grant I once may see
Thy endless joys, and of the same,
　Partaker aye to be.

Thy walls are made of precious stones,
　Thy bulwarks diamonds square,
Thy gates are of right orient pearl,
　Exceeding rich and rare.

Thy turrets and thy pinnacles
　With carbuncles do shine,
Thy very streets are paved with gold,
　Surpassing clear and fine.

Thy houses are of ivory,
　Thy windows crystal clear,
Thy tiles are made of beaten gold;
　O God, that I were there!

Within thy gates no thing doth come
　That is not passing clean,
No spider's web, no dirt, no dust,
　No filth may there be seen.

Ah, my sweet home, Jerusalem!
　Would God I were in thee,
Would God my woes were at an end,
　Thy joys that I might see.

Thy saints are crowned with glory great,
　They see God face to face,
They triumph still, they still rejoice,
　Most happy is their case.

We that are here in banishment
　Continually do moan;
We sigh and sob, we weep and wail,
　Perpetually we groan.

Our sweet is mixed with bitter gall,
　Our pleasure is but pain,
Our joys scarce last the looking on,
　Our sorrows still remain.

But there they live in such delight,
　Such pleasure, and such play,
As that to them a thousand years,
　Doth seem as yesterday.

Thy vineyards and thy orchards are
　Most beautiful and fair,
Full furnished with trees and fruits,
　Most wonderful and rare.

Thy gardens and thy gallant walks
　Continually are green;
There grow such sweet and pleasant flowers
　As nowhere else are seen.

There's nectar and ambrosia made,
　There's musk and civet sweet,
There many a fair and dainty drug
　Are trodden under feet.

There cinnamon, there sugar grows,
There nard and balm abound.
What tongue can tell or heart conceive
The joys that there ɯɯɯ found!

Quite through the streets, with silver sound,
The flood of life doth flow,
Upon whose banks, on every side,
The wood of life doth grow.

There trees for evermore bear fruit,
And evermore do spring;
There evermore the angels sit,
And evermore do sing.

There David stands with harp in hand
As master of the choir;
Ten thousand times that man were blest
That might this music hear.

Our lady sings *Magnificat*,
With tune surpassing sweet,
And all the virgins bear their parts,
Sitting above her feet.

Te Deum doth Saint Ambrose sing,
Saint Austine doth the like;
Old Simeon and Zachary
Have not their song to seek.

There Magdalene hath left her moan,
And cheerfully doth sing,
With blessed saints whose harmony
In every street doth ring.

Jerusalem, my happy home!
Would God I were in thee,
Would God my woes were at an end,
Thy joys that I might see!—E. R. C.]

THE EPILOGUE.

CHAP. XXII. 6–21.

1. *The Angel and John; or the Mediators of the Apocalypse.*

6 And he said unto me, These sayings [words] *are* faithful and true: and the Lord
God of the holy [om. holy—*ins.* spirits[1] of the] prophets sent his angel to shew unto his
servants the [what] things which [om. which] must [*ins.* come to pass] shortly be done
7 [om. be done]. [*ins.* And][2] behold, I come quickly: blessed *is* he that keepeth the
8 sayings [words] of the prophecy of this book. And [*ins.* it was] I John [*ins.* who
heard and] saw these things, and heard *them* [om. , and heard *them*]. And when
I had [om. had] heard and seen [saw][4], I fell down to worship before the feet of
9 the angel which [who] shewed me these things. Then saith he [And he saith]
unto me, See *thou do it* [om. See *thou do it*—*ins.* Take heed] not: for [om. for] I
am thy [om. thy—*ins.* a] fellow servant [*ins.* of thee], and of thy brethren the
prophets, and of them which [those who] keep the sayings [words] of this book:
10 worship God. And he saith unto me, Seal not the sayings [words] of the prophecy
11 of this book: for[5] the time is at hand [near]. He that is unjust, let him
be unjust [Let him that doeth injustice, do injustice] still: and he which is filthy,
let him be filthy [and let the polluted[6] pollute himself] still: and he that is
righteous, let him be righteous [and let the righteous work righteousness[7]] still:
and he that is holy, let him be holy [and let the holy (ἅγιος) sanctify himself
(ἁγιασθήτω)] still.

2. *Jesus, the Author of the Apocalypse; the Spirit; and the Bride.*

12 And, [om. And,][8] Behold, I come quickly; and my reward *is* with me, to
give every man according [om. every man according—*ins.* render to each]
13 as his work shall be [om. shall be—*ins.* is].[9] I am [am—*ins.* the] Alpha
and [*ins.* the] Omega, the beginning and the end, [om. the beginning and the
14 end,] the first and the last [*ins.* , the beginning and the end][10]. Blessed *are*
they that do his commandments [om. that do his commandments—*ins.* wash
their robes][11], that they may have [*ins.* the] right to [or authority over (ἡ ἐξουσία

TEXTUAL AND GRAMMATICAL.

1 Ver. 6. We give the reading τῶν πνευμάτων τ. π., in accordance with א. A. B*. [P., *Vulg.* except *Am.*,] *et al.*
2 Ver. 7. Καί, in accordance with A. B*. [א. *Vulg.*, *Syr.*, *Æth.*]
3 Ver. 8. [Gb., Sz., Lach., Tisch. (1859), Alf., Treg., give βλέπων καὶ ἀκούων with A. B*. *Vulg.*, *Syr.*, *Arm.*, *et al.*; Tisch. (8th Ed.) reverses the order with א.—E. R. C.]
4 Ver. 8. B*. gives καὶ ὅτε ἴδον. [So Tisch. (1859).] There are several unimportant variations here. [Lach., Tisch. (8th Ed.), Alf., Treg., read ἔβλεψα with א.—E. R. C.]
5 Ver. 10. א. A. B*., Lachmann [Alf., Treg., Tisch.], insert γὰρ after καιρὸς.
6 Ver. 11. We give the reading ὁ ῥυπαρὸς. [So Crit. Eds. with א. B*.—E. R. C.]
7 Ver. 11. Δικαιοσύνην ποιησάτω, in acc. with א. A. B*.,—an important reading ɯɯ contrasted with δικαιωθήτω.
8 Ver. 12. The καὶ before ἰδοὺ is unauthorized.
9 Ver. 12. א. A. *et al.* give the reading ἐστίν αὐτοῦ.
10 Ver. 13. The sequence of the Rec., which places ἡ ἀρχή. *etc.*, first, is unauthorized.
11 Ver. 14. An important variation occurs here. The reading of א. A. [7, 38, *Vulg.*, *Arm.* mg., *Æth.*], *et al.*, is πλύνοντες τὰς στολὰς αὐτῶν; that of B*. *et al.*, ποιοῦντες τὰς ἐντολὰς αὐτοῦ. Lachmann and Tischendorf give the former. Düsterdieck, with De Wette, prefers the latter reading, because he thinks that it may have been rejected in order to avoid the interruption to Jesus' discourse. The context also is, therefore, in favor of No. 1.

ἐπὶ)], the tree of life, and may enter in through [*om.* in through—*ins.* by] the gates
15 into the city. For [*om.* For][12] Without are [*ins.* the] dogs, and [*ins.* the] sorcerers,
and whoremongers [the fornicators], and [*ins.* the] murderers, and [*ins.* the] idola-
16 ters, and whosoever [every one that] loveth and maketh a lie. I Jesus have [*om.*
have] sent mine [my] angel to testify unto you these things in [concerning] the
churches.[13] I am the root and the offspring of David, and [*om.* and] the bright and
17 [*om.* and—*ins.* , the] morning star. And the Spirit and the bride say, Come [14]
And let him that heareth say, Come.[14] And let him that is athirst [thirsteth]
come.[14] And whosoever [*om.* And][15] whosoever—*ins.* : he that] will, let him take[16]
the water of life freely.

3. *Testimony to the Sanctity of the Apocalypse.*

18 For [*om.* For][17] I testify unto every man [one] that heareth the words of the
prophecy of this book, If any man [one] shall [*om.* shall] add unto these
things [*om.* these things—*ins.* them], God shall add unto him the plagues that are
19 written in this book : And if any man [one] shall [*om.* shall] take away from the
words of the book of this prophecy, God shall take away his part out of [*om.* out
of—*ins.* from] the book [*om.* book—*ins.* tree][18] of life, and out of the holy city, and
from the things [*om.* and *from* the things] which are [have been] written in this book.
20 He which [who] testifieth these things saith, Surely [Yea,] I come quickly : [.]
Amen. [;] Even so, [*om.* Even so,][19] come, Lord Jesus.

Conclusion.

21 The grace of our [*om.* our—*ins.* the][20] Lord Jesus Christ [*om.* Christ][21] *be* with you
[*om.* you][22] all [*or ins.* the saints—*or om.* all *and ins.* the saints][23]. Amen [*or om.*
Amen].[24]

12 Ver. 15. [Crit. Eds. omit the copula with ℵ. A. B.* *Vulg.*, *et al.*—E. R. C.]
13 Ver. 16. We give the very weighty reading, ἐπὶ ταῖς ἐκκλ., in accordance with ℵ. B.* [So Alf., Treg., Tisch.; Lach. gives ἐν with A., *Vulg.*, *et al.* - E. R. C.]
14 Ver. 17. [Crit. Eds. give ἔρχου twice and ἐρχέσθω with ℵ. A. B*, *et al.*—E. R. C.]
15 Ver. 17. Omit καί before ὁ θέλων.
16 Ver. 17. [Crit. Eds. give λαβέτω with ℵ. A. B*.—E. R. C.]
17 Ver. 18. [Crit. Eds. omit the copula with ℵ. A. B*. —E. R. C.]
18 Ver. 19. [Crit. Eds. read ξύλου with ℵ. A. B*., *et al.*—E. R. C.]
19 Ver. 20. A. B*., *et al.* omit καί [and also ναί of the Rec.] before ἔρχου.
20 Ver. 21. Codd. A. B*. [ℵ.] give κυρίου without ἡμῶν.
21 Ver. 21. Codd. A. [ℵ.] give Ἰησοῦ alone; B*. gives Ἰησοῦ Χριστοῦ. [Lach., Tisch., Alf., Treg., give Ἰησοῦ alone. —E. R. C.]
22 Ver. 21. Ὑμῶν is supported by minuscules.
23 Ver. 21. [Lach. and Tisch. read πάντων with A., Am.; Alf. and Treg. τῶν ἁγίων with ℵ., Gb., Sz.; and Lange, πάντων τῶν ἁγίων with B*., Cop., Syr., Arm., *et al.*—E. R. C.]
24 Ver. 21. [Lange reads Ἀμήν with ℵ. B*., Vulg., Cop., Syr., Arm., Æth., *et al.*; Lach., Tisch., Treg., and Alf., omit with A. Alf. gives the subscription Ἀποκάλυψις Ἰωάννου with ℵ. A.—E. R. C.]

EXEGETICAL AND CRITICAL.

SYNOPTICAL VIEW.

The Epilogue of the Apocalypse is strongly suggestive of the Epilogue of the Johannean Gospel, just as the Prologue of the Apocalypse forms a pendant to the Prologue concerning the Logos. In the one case as in the other, the Coming of Christ is a fundamental thought. In the one case as in the other, the Scripture closes with a reflection relative to the Book itself; and in both cases, a mysterious, clare-obscure mode of expression is spread, like a veil, over the whole. The intimate connexion of the *Apocalyptic Epilogue* and *Prologue* is evident upon the most cursory comparison.

Here, again, we distinguish three main divisions. The first, which may be superscribed with the title of the Angel and John, reverts, in vers. 6-11, to the mediators or instrumentalities of the Apocalypse, and accordingly forms a parallel to vers. 1-6 of the Prologue. In the se-cond division Jesus appears, as the Author of the Apocalypse, and over against His revelation is set the longing of the Spirit and the Bride for His Advent (vers. 12-17). The parallel passage in the Prologue is found in vers. 7-10. The third division is formed by the testimony to the inviolable sanctity of the Apocalypse (vers. 18-20). Then follow the closing words—a prayer to the Lord and a wish for a blessing upon all readers.

[Ver. 6.] *And he said unto me.* The conclusion reverts to the beginning. The series of visions is closed—hence, the mediators of the vision once more make their appearance. First, mention is made of the *Angel* of this Revelation (ch. i. 1). According to De Wette, Bleek, Düsterdieck *et al.*, this is the same Angel who speaks in ch. xxi. 9. In other words, the Angel of the entire Revelation is accounted a special Angel from the group of the seven Angels of the Vials of Anger, and we are outside of the visions and yet, again, within them. Thus, too, the incident related ch. xix. 10, is held to be repeated here—either the incident itself or the account of it. The former hypothesis would cast a shade upon the Apostle's aptness to learn; the latter would implicate his ability as a writer. Neither the one nor the other assumption is admissible. In the scene portrayed ch. xix. 10, John believed that he recognized the Lord Himself in the form of the messenger of Christ; here, it is the angelic form in which the Lord manifests Himself to him that he, in his profound reverence, identifies, wrongly, with the Person of Christ. Hence the deprecating words of the two Angels are very different. "I am thy fellow-servant and one of thy brethren who have the witness of Jesus," says one. "I am thy fellow-servant and one of thy brethren the Prophets and of them who keep the words of this Book," speaks the other. As the Angel of the Revelation, he places himself on a line not only with the Prophets, but also with the pious readers of the Apocalypse; this is, doubtless, owing to the fact that Christ assumes His angelic form in the sphere of prophetic, human spirit-life and pious longing for His coming. We translate here, therefore: Worship not the personal medium of the manifestation of Christ; just as we might say, Do not worship the Bible, though it is the medium of the revelation of God. Therefore the Angel further distinguishes the words of the Revelation, whose certainty and reality he affirms, from his mission from the Lord, Whom he identifies with the God of *the spirits of the Prophets.* Here, again, the conceptions of God and Christ run into one, as is frequently the case in the Johannean writings.

We apprehend the words ἐν τάχει, here, as in ch. i. 1, as significant of the rapidity of the course of the things predicted, for the things of the thousand years, which form but one section of the whole eschatological time, can not be conceived of as happening *soon* [or, *shortly*] in the ordinary sense.

Christ identifies Himself with the Angel in the declaration, *Behold, I come soon* [*quickly*], or rapidly, and conjoins with this declaration the beatitude expressive of the truth that he alone preserves the right position toward the Coming of the Lord, who *keeps the words of the prophecy* and makes them his guide.

The Seer now seems to come to himself after his grand visional ecstasy, as was the case, after similar ecstasies, with the Disciples on the Mount of Transfiguration, with the Apostle Peter, Acts xii. 11 and Paul, 2 Cor. xii. 2; he is immediately overpowered, however, by a sense of the great grace which he has been deemed worthy to receive with this Revelation. *And I John*—not any indifferent John—a man by the name of John—*am the hearer and seer of these things.* And now he would fain fall down and worship before the Angel of the Revelation, as he fell down before him like a dead man at the beginning of this Revelation (ch. i. 17). Upon this he receives the prohibition before referred to, because it is his duty to distinguish between the Lord Himself and His angelic appearance, clothed in the materials of prophetic visions and Christian ideals. On the other hand, he receives the direction *not to seal the words of the prophecy.* He is to communicate them to the Churches and to stimulate the reading and exposition of them, because *the times near,* because they are designed to keep Christians awake, and, if they slumber, to rouse them.

And now follows a saying which is peculiarly suggestive of the Gospel of John, especially of the fearful words, *What thou doest* [art about to do], *do quickly* [John xiii. 27]. *Let him that doeth injustice* [or, *unrighteousness*] *do injustice* [or *unrighteousness*] *still.* The meaning of this is that the time is great [weighty with import] and swift, and presses to decision; for every development, in evil and in good, the space granted is but short. The ironical tone which pertains to the first two exhortations is limited, first, by the remark that the following two sentences can have nothing of irony in them, and, further, by the earnest consideration that the seed of evil is peculiarly prospered by being brooded over, in the delusion that there is an endless time before the judgment, if, indeed, there be any judgment at all. The style of speech here employed is, doubtless, in general expressive of the following admonition: Consider that your actions are rapidly progressing to their end. The relation of moral development on both sides is pertinently intimated. The commission of unrighteousness courses into *filthiness,* into a filthy habit of thought and a corresponding mode of conduct; the righteousness of faith, on the other hand, develops, through the practice of right-doing, into a *sanctification* of life.

In the second division of the Epilogue, Jesus Himself is brought to view, with His immediate words. He announces Himself as the Recompenser, with reference to the proclamation of the Angel that the time is near and presses all men to decision. *Behold, I come quickly, and My reward with Me,* He says, in the words in which His Coming is announced by the Prophet Isaiah (ch. xl. 10; lxii. 11; comp. Rev. xi. 18). He will appear as *Judge,* because His life is the principle and ground-law of the history of the world. This He expresses in a threefold manner. Because he is the *Alpha,* He must be the *Omega.* Because He is the *First,* He must be the *Last.* The first formula characterizes Him as the first, and hence the last, *life-idea.* The second formula characterizes Him as the first, and therefore the last, ideal *life-form.* The third formula characterizes Him as the innermost, primarily principial, and therefore, also final *life-power and substance.* Because He is the *Principle,* He must be the *Final Goal.* The bearing of these words upon the judgment (in accordance with Matt. xxv. and Acts xvii. 31) is plainly manifest in the following beatitude.

In comparison with the reading, *Blessed are they who wash their robes,* we cannot possibly regard the other reading, *Blessed are they who keep His commandments,* as correct, although the sense may be the same. We have here to do with a festal symbolic expression, suggestive of the *wedding garment* and the saying, *These have washed their robes in the blood of the Lamb* (ch. vii. 14). These shall enter into the Holy City, with authority to eat of the trees of life. For upon the perfect appropriation of the cross of Christ, rests the putting on of the snow-white robe of righteousness, and this is the condition at once of an eternal vital development and vital joy, and of entrance into the fellowship of eternal life.

The continued existence of a *without*, in contrast to an entrance into the Paradise of life, is expressed by an antithesis in the weightiest of words. Those who are excluded are again, apparently, cited in a group of honor; *six*, but in reality a *quinary* is probably contemplated, as in the figure of the foolish virgins. The arrangement of individual characters also differs from that observed ch. xxi. 8. In the latter passage, the lost were contrasted with the idea of the bravery of the conquerors; hence the *fearful* had the precedence. Here they are contrasted with the picture of heavenly purity—the blessed, arrayed in their robes of honor; hence *dogs* take the precedence, as allegorical figures of spiritual uncleanness and commonness (see Matt. vii. 6; Phil. iii. 2; 2 Pet. ii. 22). *Sorcerers* have profaned and violated nature; *fornicators* have profaned and violated the personal and physical life; *murderers* have profaned and violated the image of God in their neighbor; *idolaters* have profaned and violated the symbols of the Divine and religion itself; *lovers and practicers of falsehood* in general—as a wider class of idolaters—have profaned and violated the consecrated reality and truth of life.

Jesus next definitively distinguishes Himself from the sending of His Angel. He declares that He has Himself sent the Angel to Christians to testify to them of the future in regard to the Churches; the dignity and weight of a *testimony* is thus assigned to His word. The reading chosen by us [ἐπὶ ταῖς ἐκκλ.] we have designated in the TEXT. AND GRAM. NOTES as highly momentous. Even in this expression, which has in many instances failed of being understood, the end reaches back into the beginning. The Apocalypse, namely, is in reality the Book of the future of the Christian Churches, symbolically represented, as they are, by the Seven Churches.

In conclusion, Christ places Himself, as the most glorious Man, the Son of man, over against the longing and expectation of the faithful. *I am the Root and the Offspring of David*, the Kernel in the kernel of the Theocracy, the ideal ground and the ideal blossom of the Davidic line, which rises as prominently in the midst of Israel as chosen Israel amongst the nations. Thus, as the great Promised One, He is the subject of all the longing of Israel, and, no less than this, the *bright star* which has risen upon mankind as the *Morning Star* of a new world. And well does He know that the heart of mankind goes out to Him with throbs of expectation and yearning. The *Spirit* in the Church and the *Church as Bride* answer Him with the cry, *Come!* And every one who hears and understands this cry is directed to join in the cry of longing, *Come!* But all who *thirst*, that is, all men of longing, must first *come to Him* on the platform of the spiritual life, and receive of the *water of life freely* [without price], in order that they may be able to sum up their yearning in that higher eschatological longing which can join in the cry, *Come, Lord Jesus!*

The third division of the Epilogue is the conclu-

ding attestation of the Book, and is suggestive of the attestation of the Johannean Gospel (ch. xxi. 24).

In this attestation we, in company with almost all exegetes, can see the words of the Prophet only; not, with Ebrard, a remark of the Lord concerning the Book of John. In this severe verdict, reference is had not to readings and variations of opinion, but to augmentations or diminutions of the eschatological view of the world here expressed. It is an inviolable vital law that the fanatic, in the same degree in which he heightens the conceptions of judgment above the Biblical measure, loads himself with the judgment of those torments which he has imagined; thus, *e. g.*, the mediæval exaggeration of the idea of hell brought hell torments in abundance upon the fanatics themselves. And on the other hand, similarly, it is a fact that the denier or diminisher of the prospects of Christian hope impairs his own inheritance of hope and bliss, to the same degree in which he takes away from the fullness of the Christian prospect. Every misdemeanor against the truth falls back upon him who commits it (see *Introduction*, p. 63, and Matt. v. 19). The reference is not to transient sentiments, but to maxims which become permanent in a conduct consistently regulated by them. Thus, it is beyond question that consummate fanaticism crystallizes into a disposedness for torment; consummate libertinism into a complete incapacity for even the faintest idea of the conditions of a higher human life of blessedness. These thoroughly true thoughts meet us here as warning verdicts [*vera dicta*], hyperbolically expressed, designed for the protection of this glorious Book, which, in spite of these its guards, has been, and still continues to be, greatly mis-esteemed.

The Seer is sure that, together with himself, Christ attests his Book. He therefore introduces Him also, in the character of a witness, and expresses, in His testimony, the ground-thought of his Book: *Yea, I come quickly.*

Hereupon, giving vent to that which has been the desire of his heart through his whole life, and especially during his old age, he utters the following sentence, by which he takes the Lord at His word in the name of the Church as well as in his own name: *Amen, come, Lord Jesus.*

In conclusion, he pronounces a benediction upon all who, with himself, are awaiting the coming of the Lord, and who constitute the true *Saints of the Latter Days*. The benediction is couched in the following grand and worthy terms: *The grace of the Lord Jesus Christ be with all saints. With all saints*—in this adjunct, the Apocalypse, in its significance, is consistent with itself.

EXPLANATIONS IN DETAIL.

Ver. 6. And he said unto me.—With perfect justice, Ebrard combats the view entertained by most commentators, to the effect that the Angel who is here spoken of is the same who has been the spokesman since ch. xxi. 9; the same exegete maintains that, on the contrary, it is the Angel (of the Revelation) of whom mention is made in ch. i. 1. With this view, however, he conjoins the erroneous assumption that what John here reports, is nothing new, but only a reminiscence of former things; first, of the declaration previously made by the same Angel (ch. xxi. 5) and, secondly, of the certain truth that the entire Revelation is of Divine origin. But visional conditions do not come to an end suddenly any more than they begin suddenly; they die away gradually, even as they began. The face of Moses was still shining when he went down from the mount into the camp.

These words are, *etc.*—By this is meant the entire Revelation now concluded, ■■ in verses 7 and 18.

The Lord God of the spirits of the Prophets.—We apprehend these words as referring to Jehovah as the God of revelation, or, in other words, we find here a concrete summing together of God and Christ, ■■ in the concluding words of 1 John v. 20.

The mission of the Angel is from the Spirit of revelation, as the God of the spirits of the Prophets, the Source and Author of all prophecies, hence also of the Apocalypse (John v. 39; 1 Peter i. 10-12).

The spirits of the Prophets.—According to De Wette, reference is had to the inspiration produced by the Spirit of God, in opposition to which Düsterdieck judiciously remarks that the spirits belonging, respectively, to the different Prophets are intended, which spirits God renders subservient to Himself.

His servants.—See ch. i.

Ver. 7. **And behold, I come quickly.**—Adduction of Christ's word, in corroboration of the expression ἐν τάχει. "As in ver. 6 the Divine authority was cited, so here the main tenor of the Revelation now completed is made prominent. This is effected by the Angel's speaking directly in the name of the coming Lord Himself." DUESTERDIECK. We cannot perceive why the following parænesis should be regarded as "added by the Angel." The Angel utters the whole,—in such a manner, however, as to introduce the Lord as speaking in ver. 7. It is this very fact that gives occasion to what follows—*viz.*, the error, in the entertainment of which the Seer attempts to worship. Finally, we must again call attention to the subtile distinction that is to be made between the Lord Himself and the form of His revelation; not only *personal Angels*, but also *symbolical ones*, are a forbidden object of worship. This is suggestive of the second commandment, "Thou shalt not make unto thee any image," concretely apprehended; it also teaches us how difficult it is for man, in his admiration of the Divine, to leave that and arrive at the perfect worship of God.

Ver. 8. **And** *it was* **I, John.**—The gradual *coming to one's self, e. g.,* out of sleep, out of somnambulic sleep, out of profound contemplation, out of ■■ inspired or demonically excited condition, is a highly interesting phenomenon; its culmination is formed by the gradual return of ordinary consciousness [*Tagesbewusstsein = day-consciousness*] after the ecstasy of the Prophet.*— *And I, John.*—See SYN. VIEW; comp. chap. i.

* See Schiller, *Die Jungfrau von Orleans*, Act IV., Scene IX.:
" *Die Fahne liess ich in dem Heiligthum,*
Nie, nie soll diese Hand sie mehr berühren !
Mir war's als hätt' ich die geliebten Schwestern,
Margot und Louison, gleich einem Traum
An mir vorübergleiten sehen. Ach,
Es war nur eine täuschende Erscheinung."

Who heard and ■■■ [ὁ ἀκούων καὶ βλέπων] **these things.**—On the present form of the participle, see Düsterd. Though the visional unfolding of the things is over, that which the Seer has heard and seen continues to be ever spiritually present before his eyes.

And when I heard.—The reading which adds **and saw**, beautifully brings out the continued astonishment of the Seer.

I fell down to worship.—In ch. xix. 10 he was in danger of identifying a personal Angel or beatified saint with the Lord; here he is in the more subtile peril of confounding a symbolic angelic form with the Lord Himself.

Ver. 9. **Take heed not.**—'Ὅρα μή (see SYN. VIEW).

Ver. 10. **Seal not,** *etc.*—See ch. i. 11, 19; x. 4; Dan. viii. 26; xii. 4, 9. It may be asked, what is the difference between a *sealing* and a *not sealing* in the case of two Books which yet have been diffused in an identical or a similar manner. Irrespective of the fact that there is something symbolical in the expression, which declares, on the one hand, that the Book shall for a long time continue to be obscure and uncomprehended, or, on the other hand, that the Book shall be read, the antithesis also contains ■ distinction for the authors of the Books in question and for the Church. The symbolic mode of presentation is in itself ■ species of *sealing;* a reference to the key of symbolism, such as is frequently to be met with in John, is an *unsealing* (comp. Matt. xiii. 11 sqq.). And thus there is also a difference in the ecclesiastic reservation of the Book and the submission of it for congregational edification. The Hierarchy has sealed the whole Bible; with us, even the Apocalypse is at least freely submitted to the Church for her edification.

For the time is near.—A motive for the diffusion, reading and explanation of the Apocalypse in the Christian Church.

Ver. 11. **He that doeth injustice.**—This form is elucidated by analogies; not only by the already cited address of the Lord to Judas (John xiii. 27), but also by the following passages: Matt. xxiii. 32; xxvi. 45, and, in a less degree, Ezek. iii. 27. And though there may be something of irony in the first two propositions (De Wette, *et al.*), there is nought of that character in the last two, *viz.*, **and let the righteous,** *etc.*—If we seek for a common fundamental thought that shall lie at the basis of all four propositions, it is contained in the following words: "Since the judgment is at the door, let every one quickly prepare himself for it after his own free choice." That this very idea indirectly offers to the wicked the strongest admonition to repent, is self-evident.

Work righteousness still. — The discardure of the erroneous reading δικαιωθήτω is of recognized importance as bearing upon the discussion relative to the meaning of δικαιοῦν.

Vers. 12, 13. **Behold, I come quickly.**—Düsterdieck: "The words of ver. 12 sound like a communication from Christ's own mouth." Most certainly. "Those of ver. 13 (comp. chaps. i. 8; xxi. 5, 6) are as the language of God Himself." But because *God* calls Himself the Alpha and the Omega, it does not follow that *Christ*, the Son of God, may not also so denominate Himself. The Apostle Paul writes concerning God: "Of Him, and through Him, and to Him are all things" (Rom. xi. 36). And again in Colossians i. 16 he writes concerning Christ: "All things were created in Him . . . all things were created through Him and to Him." Because Düsterdieck thinks that this presumed change of speakers must not be hypothesized, he affirms that John speaks these words "after the manner of the ancient Prophets." And yet John here distinguishes his own speech, the speech of the Angel, the express speech of Jesus (ver. 16), and the speech of the Spirit! The motive for this singular retreat upon "the old Prophetic language," (which might itself be called in question, if it were employed with the latitude and inexplicitness which would attach to its use in the present case,) seems to be simply Christ's alleged inability to say: I am the Alpha and the Omega.

Ver. 14. **Blessed are they who wash their robes.**—See SYN. VIEW. The other reading see discussed in Düsterdieck, pp. [574,] 580.

Ver. 18. **Without are the dogs.**—Düsterdieck apprehends the words as a command—*foras sunto. Out with the dogs!* Such a conception, however, does but obscure the clearness of the antithesis; it would be a sort of penal judgment, instead of a representation of the contrast which the region of the lost presents to Paradise —a representation which is a sermon in itself. Be it observed that the term, *the dogs*, is decidedly favorable to the reading, *Blessed are they who wash*, etc. **Dogs.**—"A special reference to sodomites (Eichhorn, who compares Deut. xxiii. 18) is not to be gathered from the context." DÜSTERDIECK.

Ver. 16. **I, Jesus.**—Even these words, according to Düsterdieck, are spoken by *John* in the name of Jesus. And it is possible for him to entertain this opinion after all the distinct intimations which have previously been given concerning the speakers!

To testify unto you.—The ὑμῖν relates to the servants of God, as ver. 6 (comp. chap. i. 1). The servants of God are, through the instrumentality of the Apocalypse, constituted watchmen and warners of the Church. In this sense, even the Seven Epistles are not directly addressed to the Churches. Düsterdieck thinks, with Hengstenberg, that ὑμῖν, in case it is to be retained, refers to the Prophets.

The Root and the Offspring [Lange: *Geschlecht=race*].—The antithesis between root and scion—as the human parallel to the Divine antithesis of Alpha and Omega—is obliterated by the following explanation of Düsterdieck: "That which the first term [ῥίζα] declares figuratively and in accordance with Old Testament precedent (comp. chap. v. 5), is more literally affirmed by the second [γένος]: the *son* (Andr., Ew., *et al.*)." According to Hengstenberg also, the *root* of David is significant of the *product* of the root. The citation of chap. v. 5 proves nothing.

The Bright, the Morning Star.—In meaning, the passage chap. ii. 28, where Christ promises to *give the morning star*, is entirely akin to this. Christ is the bright Morning Star of the coming day of eternity; He therefore also gives the morning star of a spiritual vision of the future (see above, chap. ii. 28).

Ver. 17. **And the Spirit.**—These words, according to De W., Hengstenberg, Düsterdieck, *et al.*, are an answer to the foregoing—an answer which the Apocalyptist is represented as speaking in the name of the Spirit and the Bride. But since John utters his own *Come, Lord Jesus* in ver. 20, we cannot suppose that it was his intention to make so wide a distinction between himself and the Spirit and the Bride; and, moreover, the words, *Let him that thirsteth come, etc.*, are in favor of the assumption that we have here the concluding words of Jesus Himself. A singular view is that of Ebrard, who holds ver. 17 to be a reply to the speech of Jesus, and regards Jesus as again becoming the speaker in ver. 18, with a view to taking the Book under His own patronage.

Let him that thirsteth, *etc.*—See chap. xxi. 6; Isa. lv. 1: Matt. v. 6; John vii. 37.

Freely [gratuitously].—The last full evangelic tone in the New Testament.

Vers. 18, 19. **I testify unto every one**, *etc.* —Testification is a solemn asseveration which binds or makes responsible those to whom it is addressed (Deut. iv. 2; Prov. xxx. 5, 6). We repeat the remark already made by us upon this passage, *viz.*, that, in accordance with the symbolic expression of the Apostle, the reference is not simply to the exegetical treatment of the Apocalypse, as is usually assumed. There are many who add gloom to the Christian view of the world, and many who diminish its depth, without making use of the Apocalypse in thus doing. It is, indeed, also true that any exegetical tampering with the Apocalypse is inadmissible, and the one-sidedness of exegesis are manifoldly connected with the one-sidednesses of fanaticism or spiritualism [*Spiritualismus*]. The paronomasia—ἐπιθῇ, ἐπιθήσει, ἀφέλῃ, ἀφελεῖ—is no mere play upon words; it is indicative, rather, of the fact that transgressions against the purport of the Apocalypse are connected with the inner condition of the guilty one, and hence infallibly rebound upon him, or that, as violations of the Divine faithfulness and truth, they are reflected back in violations of self.

Every one that heareth, *etc.*—That is, every one who is present at the reading aloud of the Book in Church; it is, therefore, designed to be read aloud in Church. According to Vitringa, Bleek, *et al.*, the threat is directed against careless transcribers; according to Ewald and De Wette, against oral inaccuracies of repetition. Düsterdieck justly regards each of these explanations as insufficient, and lays stress upon the keeping of the *contents* of the Book, the revelation of God, maintaining that it is upon the falsification of that revelation that the curse is laid. Luther's words of censure, contained in his preface of 1522, see cited in Düst., p. 582. Bleek is of opinion that Luther was not entirely wrong in taking offence at the words. De Wette also thinks the threat too harsh. Hengstenberg apprehends the words as referring to such additions and omissions as affect the actual kernel of the Book (p. 452 sqq. [Trans.]). According to Ebrard, these words are "the seal which Christ Himself impresses upon the Apocalypse."

Ver. 20. **He who testifieth these things saith.**—Here Jesus is again introduced as speaking. He is brought in, primarily, as a Witness Who supplements the foregoing testimony of John, but at the same time He indirectly appears as a Witness for the whole Apocalypse. He sums up His testimony in the all-corroborating and all-embracing affirmation: **Yea, I come quickly.**

The Seer replies to the word of the Lord with a grand and simple prayer: **Amen; come, Lord Jesus.**

Ver. 21. **The grace.**—See ch. i. 4. The ὑμῶν of the Rec. does, indeed, more nearly agree with ch. i. 4, but it is, on the one hand, not as well supported as our reading, and, on the other hand, the reading **with all saints**, is in perfect harmony with the solemnity of the conclusion.

[ADDITIONAL NOTE ON THE EPILOGUE.]

By the American Editor.

[There are several matters concerning this conclusion of the Book of Divine Revelation which the writer desires to present for consideration:—

I. *The Authorship.*

The entire Epilogue is the utterance of Jesus, by the mouth of His representative Angel (the Angel of chap. xxi. 9), to John—with the exception of the *second clause* of ver. 6, vers. 8, 9, the *last clause* of ver. 20, and ver. 21. In this proposition there are but three points which need discussion, all of which are opposed to the views of our author.

1. *The Angel that addressed John was the Angel of chap. xxi. 9.* That Christ spoke through a representative in ver. 7, is admitted by all; that this was the Angel of xxi. 9 is the point to be proved. The καὶ εἶπέν μοι of ver. 6 shows that the speaker there mentioned must have been the one speaking in the immediately preceding verses—the phraseology forbids the idea that another speaker had been introduced. The καί of ver. 7, together with the absence of any introducing clause, requires the conclusion that the same speaker continued his address; and this conclusion is confirmed by the τοῦ δεικνύντος of ver. 8—manifestly, the Angel at whose feet the Apostle fell was the one who had been *showing* him the things previously described. A difficulty in reference to this interpretation may suggest itself to some minds, arising from the generally received opinion that the Angel of chap. xxi. 9 was (as were all the Angels of the Vials) a *Symbol*; his symbolic character may be regarded as inconsistent with the language of ver. 9, *I am thy fellow servant, etc.* Possibly he was an *Immediate Symbol*—i. e., a *simulacrum*—of a real Angel; possibly, however, real Angels took part in all the scenes described. But however this may have been,—admitting the truth of the first supposition, there was neither impropriety nor incongruity in representing the *simulacrum* of an Angel as using the language of an Angel.

2. *The second clause of ver. 6 is an explanatory remark introduced by John.* It seems to the writer inconceivable, that, if the declaration, *The Lord God sent His Angel to show, etc.*, had been made

to the Apostle, he should immediately after have offered Divine honors to that *creature.* The natural hypothesis seems to be that—(1) in ver. 7, the Angel, as the representative of Jesus, spoke in the first person, *Behold, I come quickly,* and John at once drew the conclusion that the speaker, though in the form of a servant, must be his Lord—a natural mistake and one immediately corrected; and (2) the Apostle in his narrative introduced the explanatory clause of ver. 6.

3. *The address of vers. 18, 19, 20 (first clause), is the utterance of Christ through His Angel, and not a declaration of the Apostle.* This, in the judgment of the writer, is placed beyond doubt by a comparison of the first words of ver. 18 with those of ver. 20; the One who *testifies* is the One who says, *I come quickly.*

II. *The Duty of Studying the Apocalypse.*

That it is the duty of every Christian to study this Book appears from the following declarations of the Epilogue:—1. The Apocalypse was given for the information of the Saints, vers. 6, 16. 2. It was designed to be read in the congregations, ver. 18 (*I testify unto every one that heareth*); see also *comment* on chap. i. 3, p. 90. 3. Its utterances were not *sealed, i. e.,* closed up from individual comprehension (see *foot-note **, first column, p. 193), ver. 10. 4. A blessing is to be bestowed upon those who *keep* the words of the prophecy, ver. 7; which *keeping* requires, of course, preceding *study.* 5. A woe shall be visited upon all who add to, or diminish from, the words of the Book, vers. 18, 19.

The Epilogue, in implying the duty of study, agrees with the Prologue; see chap. i. 3, and the *additional comment* thereon, p. 90.

III. *Angel Worship.*

The Am. Ed. cannot agree with those who hold that in the incident recorded in ver. 8, and in the similar incident mentioned in chap. xix. 10, the Apostle was guilty of an attempt to worship a creature, *knowing him to be such*—i. e., that he was guilty of *idolatry.* Alford, in his comment on chap. xix. 10, takes that position, remarking: "The Angel . . . seems to him worthy of some of that reverence which belongs to God Himself. The reason given by Düsterdieck, that in both cases John imagined the Lord Himself to be speaking to him, is sufficiently contradicted by the plain assertion, here in chap. xvii. 1, and there in chap. xxii. 8 itself, that it was not a Divine Person, but simply an Angel." In answer it may be said—(1) So far as chap. xvii. 1 is concerned, manifestly it is the Apostle's own remark, and probably was not penned until *after* the incident described in chap. xix. 10, *i. e., after* he had received the information that the one who spoke to him was a *mere* Angel; and (2) In reference to chap. xxii. 8, there is nothing in the record to forbid the hypothesis presented above in I. that it was an explanatory clause introduced by the Apostle. It seems utterly inconceivable, first, that John, either as a *Jew* or as an *Apostle of Christ,* could have offered worship to a creature, *knowing him to be such;* and, in the second place, that, if he had done so, he would not have been sharply rebuked for his idolatry. In neither case does the language of the Angel necessarily imply rebuke; in each case it may be interpreted, and most naturally interpreted, **as** a warning against error in conduct, and a rectification of the mistake whence the error was about to proceed. It may also be remarked that, unless the Apostle had been positively informed to the contrary, he might naturally have supposed that one of the Angels of the Vials was Jesus Himself. Let it be observed that, during the pouring out of the Vials, the words of Jesus, *Behold, I come as a thief,* had been uttered—by whom we know not, but the context would lead us to suppose that they were spoken from amongst the Seven Angels (chap. xvi. 15). This might naturally have excited the suspicion that Jesus was there. When the Angel who first came to him used the expression, *These are the true words of God* (chap. xix. 10), it should occasion little surprise that John supposed him to be his Lord. And when another of the Seven, representing Jesus, adopted the language of Jesus, *Behold, I come quickly* (chap. xxii. 7), can we wonder that the Apostle leaped to the conclusion that Jesus in person was with him?

It is scarce necessary to remark that, whatever hypothesis we may adopt as to the subjective condition of John, the words of the Angels convey most positive condemnation of all creature worship.

IV. *The Teaching of Christ as to His Twofold Nature.*

The twofold nature of Jesus is most clearly set forth. His *humanity* in the words, "I am ... the *offspring* (τὸ γένος=race, stock, descent) of David" (ver. 16); His *Divinity,* not less clearly, in vers. 12, 13, 16 (the *root*).

V. *The Time of the Second Advent.*

At first glance, the words of Jesus, *I come quickly* (ver. 7), seem to be inconsistent with the idea that the Advent thus promised is still future. Probably this declaration, more than aught else, has induced the opinion, amongst those who hold it, that the Advent is past.

That the *Coming* mentioned in ver. 7 is the one foretold chap. i. 7 (and also Dan. vii. 13; Matt. xxiv. 27, 30; xxvi. 64; Mark xiv. 62; Acts i. 9, 11, *etc.*), seems to be evident upon comparison; and that that Advent has not taken place seems also to be evident upon an examination of the passages referred to, together with their contexts,—there has been nothing in history that satisfies the description of events accompanying the Advent. We must look for an explanation of the *quickly* (ταχύ) in the declarations of 2 Pet. iii. 18 and Luke xviii. 7, 8. See also *footnote** (first column), p. 89.

VI. *The Final Warning.*

ALFORD comments on vers. 18, 19 as follows: "The adding and taking away are in the application and reception in the heart; and so it is not a mere formal threat to the copier of the Book. . . . . All must be received and realized. This is at least an awful warning both to those who despise and neglect this Book, and to those who add to it by irrelevant and trifling interpretations."

VII. *The Final Prayer.*

In the prayer, *"Amen; come, Lord Jesus"* (ver. 20), the Apostle pours forth the longing of his instructed heart for the realization of "that blessed hope" of the Church—"the glorious Appearing of the great God and our Saviour Jesus Christ" (Tit. ii. 13). In this prayer is summed up all that the Christian heart can desire—the destruction of the power of Satan; the deliverance of the creature from the bondage of corruption; the banishment of sin and sorrow from the individual heart and from the world; the restoration of all things; the establishment of the Kingdom of righteousness; the beholding by Jesus in fullness of the travail of His soul, the bestowment upon Him in completeness of His promised reward.

Let each member of the Church militant, mourning the absence of her Head, but cheered by the promise that He will come again, unite with the Apostle in the longing cry—AMEN; COME, LORD JESUS.—E. R. C.]

SECOND OR DOCTRINO-ETHICAL AND HOMILETICAL DIVISION.*

PRELIMINARY REMARKS.

Since the first thing to be established, in a general work on the Apocalypse, is the EXEGETICAL point of view in which we should regard the Book, it is self-evident that the DOCTRINAL apprehension and the HOMILETICAL application of the Scripture in question are conditioned upon the secure establishment of the Exegetical result. As this result is still, however, to a high degree, a mooted question in Theology, the doctrinal writer cannot, with simple confidence, take his stand upon fluctuating ground; or, to state the case more definitely, he cannot lay the foundations of a structure upon soil that is constantly wavering; and this remark applies with still greater force to the homilist.

It is, for instance, an unquestionable fact that the modern, ostensibly critical, synchrono-historical apprehension of the Book has, in great measure, neutralized and, so to speak, compromised its doctrinal side; thus Schleiermacher, De Wette, *et al.*, assign a very moderate value to this Scripture. This view leaves but a few isolated passages even to Homiletics; and even those passages can be made use of only with a certain inconsistency, the canonical character of the Book being questioned.

The servile adherents of the orthodoxy of the seventeenth century occupy a similar relation toward the Book. According to their assumptions, the idea of a transition-period intervening between the present and the future æon, of a true Millennium, and of a special hope for the return of the people of Israel, is utterly out of the question. The last day must be *one single day*. In this single day, the whole world must be utterly destroyed and replaced by an entirely new world. A Millennium is regarded as conflicting with the XVII. Article of the Augsburg Confession. Gehenna, it is maintained, coincides with the realm of the dead, and is entirely complete and ready for inmates in the midst of Time. Now when it is seen that these and the like assumptions are, contrasted with a vital conception of Holy Scripture, and especially of the Apocalypse, contracted ideas of a servile letter-faith, or an exegetical tradition-faith, the consequence is self-evident: not much secure ground is left in the Apocalypse for doctrinal arguments and homiletical demonstrations. If, nevertheless, a detailed application of the Apocalypse be made from this stand-point, the result will be a doctrinal and homiletical constriction

of this Scripture, similar in degree, though not in kind, to the racking and stretching of the Old Testament in order to make it explicitly declarative of the whole of the New Testament and all the teachings of the Church.

If, again, we consider that more mediate tendency which has viewed the Apocalyptic Book from more liberal stand-points of piety and practice, and has found in it the hope of better times, and even the Millennial Kingdom, we shall find that even here there has not been much doctrinal and ethical ground won, the critics of this school having proceeded upon the platform that the Apocalypse consists of predictions of Church history following each other in chronological succession. Nevertheless, this stand-point is, by reason of the eminent religious appreciation of the Book which it, in comparison with the orthodoxistic and neocritical conceptions of it, manifests, of far greater worth than they.

Even that system of interpretation which professes to regard the Apocalypse as shadowing forth the history of the Kingdom of God, shares in the insecurity of a thorough doctrinal and homiletical application of this Scripture, especially because it has not consistently made its ascertainment of a system of firm Biblico-apocalyptic symbolism its point of departure.

It is our belief that we have labored towards the attainment of this point of view, and we also think that, through the grace of God, our labors have been blessed with some measure of success. But the results which in these pages we offer to our readers are for the present the subject of theological discussion. It will, therefore, be requisite in doctrinal and homiletical comments, to observe caution in making a confident use of even such points as may have been recognized and proved to be true.

We, therefore, do not consider ourselves at liberty to undertake to accompany the whole course of our exegesis with doctrinal and homiletico-practical applications; and we are the more withheld from thus doing by the further consideration, that the object of prime importance at this time is the incitement of our contemporaries to an exposition of the Apocalypse which shall be still simpler and more firmly grounded upon Biblical symbolism than any that have yet appeared. We shall rely upon free citations from authors who admit the allegorical character of the Book, to carry us over the gaps.

But notwithstanding all that we have said, there is still so much to be found on the platform of simple belief in the Bible, so much which such belief, in its various modifications, can accept as sure, as common to all standpoints, and as precious, both for doctrine and life, that, with all the restrictions which we have imposed upon ourselves, we hope still to garner a rich harvest of doctrinal and homiletical truths.

The most convenient arrangement of this treasure will be secured by the division of our remarks into a General and a Special Part. The General Part will contain remarks upon leading points of view; the Special Part will contain remarks upon the leading sections of the Apocalypse. Doctrinal and Ethical, and Homiletical and Practical observations will everywhere be presented under a common caption.

PART FIRST.

GENERAL DOCTRINO-ETHICAL AND HOMILETICAL REMARKS UPON THE APOCALYPSE.

SECTION FIRST.

Doctrinal and Ethical Elements of the Apocalypse.

It was the prejudiced opinion of the elder orthodoxistic school that the Apocalypse must, in respect of its doctrinal and ethical elements, be reduced to the stage of development occupied by the earlier Apostolic Theology, or that it must even be *corrected to suit* that stage. A parallel position is occupied by modern prejudice, as developed in distinct branches. The school of Baur, on the one hand, regards the Book as a genuine writing of the Apostle John, and on that very account also holds it to be the product of an exceedingly contracted and turbid Judo-Christianity; whilst the school of Schleiermacher, on the other hand, maintains that the poverty of the Scripture is connected with its origin from the pen of some non-Apostolic John. The Book is worth little, because it is by the Apostle John—the one class asserts. The Book is of very little value, because it is *not* by the Apostle John—is the declaration of the other class. Those rude assailments of its dignity in which Volkmar permitted himself to indulge, following the tendency of the school of Baur, were preceded by the following frivolous, yet naïve, deliverance of De Wette: "A book, whole chapters of which we must, after pressing out a few drops of juice, cast aside as empty skins, has, at least, not the character of a popular book." (*Introduction*, p. 6.)

On the other hand, some pietisto-chiliastic and theosophic schools have maintained the existence of, in many respects, an entirely new and separate Theology in the Apocalypse; of such a school SWEDENBORG was the founder.

In reply to all these misrepresentations of the true state of the case, it must be maintained: 1. That the Apocalypse contains the same doctrine of Christianity as all the rest of the New Testament, and moreover that it contains it in the Johannean type; 2. That it is to be recognized as the most developed phase of the New Testament doctrine bearing upon its theme—the hope of the Kingdom of God, and the advent of that Kingdom into the world—although it is couched in Biblico-artistic, allegorical and symbolical forms.

There are a great number of opponents of Eschatological Dogmatics who yet claim that they stand upon the basis of firm and assured principles of faith. Their objections against eschatological dogmas may be summed up in the following gradation: 1. No dogmas can be drawn from figurative, allegorical or, in general, poetic representations. 2. The deliverances of Christian hope cannot be turned to dogmatic account. 3. The farther removed the historical elements of Christianity are from the historic centre of the life of Jesus, the more problematical do they become.

So far as the first objection against Christian Eschatology is concerned, it is based upon two false hypotheses. The first of these is that allegorical or symbolical representations cannot be reduced to a didactic or distinct doctrinal idea. The second false hypothesis is that there is in the Bible a region of abstract didactic forms, from which it is possible to mark off the region of figurative forms. It is a singular fact that these same objectors are frequently prone to draw their statements relative to the doctrines of the Old Testament concerning the other world, from poetico-pathological expressions in the Book of Job or the Psalms.

Again, in reply to the attempt to rob the truths of Christian *hope* of true doctrinal evidence, we would state what surely every one should know—that, in a wider sense, the whole Christian faith has the character of hope (Heb. xi. 1); that faith, hope and love substantially coincide with each other (1 Cor. xiii.); that without doctrines of Christian hope, even in the narrower sense of that term, there could be no doctrines at all.

Finally, when an idealistic or spiritualistic [*vom Spiritualismus behaftete*] Christology ascribes less importance to the doctrine of Christ's Resurrection than to that of His historic Life and redemptive Death, it is safe to infer that these unsound individual points of belief are but the superstructure which is erected upon an unsound principial foundation; such an unsound foundation is discoverable in the case of Schleiermacher, in his defective recognition of the personality of the Saviour. Where there is a defect in the idea of the Divine personality, on the one hand, and in that of the human personality, on the other, it is impossible that the idea of the God-Man should subsist in its full, historic import.

Persons who accord a less biased appreciation to the doctrinal significance of the Apocalypse, cannot fail to perceive that the Book in question has not obscured the Christian doctrines of the preceding New Testament Scriptures, but, on the contrary, that it has elucidated them and furnished proofs in their support—nay, that its Theology may be regarded as a mediatory Theology in the best sense of the term. This is true, in the first place, of the eschatological doctrines: —the doctrines concerning death, the intermediate state, the Kingdom of God, the Church Triumphant, Antichristianity the eschatological import of Israel, the Parousia of Christ, the Resurrection, the Last Day, the Kingdom of glory, hell and Heaven. In the second place, the doctrines concerning God, the creation, Christ and His redemptive work, the Christian life in respect of its religious and moral natures, and, finally, Bibliology, are endued with new distinctness.

Let us first examine the first line of dogmas—the eschatological ones.

The doctrine concerning *death* is, assuredly, not obscured, but, rather, enlightened by the fact that the Apocalypse puts forth the idea of the *second death*. The first death is thereby, in measure, degraded to a shadow in its relation to believers—as is the case, likewise, in the Johannean Gospel. Here, Christ has the keys of death, the souls of the departed continue to live, and blessed are the dead who die in the Lord. There is here a more distinct sundering of *Hades*, or the realm of the dead, and *hell*, or the furnace of fire, than is to be found in any other Scripture. In respect of the blessed dead, the bright department of Hades is set forth as a sojourning with the Lord in Heaven; the place of torment within Hades has assumed the form of the *abyss*, and the intermediate region—the realm of the dead, in the narrower sense—is even distinguished by still another separate sphere from the idea of *Gehenna*, which is not yet realized. In the representation of the *souls of the martyrs* as under the altar and *crying to God for recompense*, are expressed the facts that they have a right, and a just impulse, to anticipate their future perfect restitution, or the satisfaction of justice on their behalf; that their life, in accordance with the Divine decree, has been, as it were, sacrificed on the altar, and that they, as followers of Christ, are on the sure road from death to a glorious resurrection. Further, in respect of their resurrection, the bestowal of *white robes* upon them is surely not merely a figure of their justification before God and the world, but is also expressive of the truth that they are developing toward the first resurrection (1 Cor. xv.; 2 Cor. v.).

The *end of the world* or the *Last Day* appears, in ultra-supernaturalistic dogmatics—regarded by their holders as orthodox *par excellence*.—independent, as far as possible, of instrumentality,

or, at least, as owning only that of missions and altered ethical conditions; in harmony with the above, the end of the world is its absolute destruction, and the Last Day is really the last of the days in the astronomical sense of a day. How much more life and organism and instrumentality is displayed in the Apocalyptic presentation, connected, as it is, with less developed intimations throughout the Sacred Writings. Here the picture of the *apostasy*, hinted at by Christ Himself, and more definitely predicted by St. Paul, is completely unrolled; the apostasy is qualified as ripened *Antichristianity*, whose main figure is a demonic bestial formation of Christian national life, and whose secondary figure, in the form of the False Prophet, the apostate, issues from the theocratico-churchly system, so that the latter itself becomes a pseudo-Christian Church, a Church of apostasy.

With this ripening of Antichristianity for the harvest, the ripening of Christianity is implied, although the maturing of the Church into the Bride—assured, indeed, by the 144,000 sealed ones, and illustrated by the 144,000 triumphant ones—almost vanishes behind the scene, behind the manifest Antichristian world. The Church, by reason of the tribulations which it must needs undergo, becomes almost an exclusively invisible Church. Just this unheard of distress or need, however, is the reason of the appearance of Christ (mediated by the maturity of good as well as of evil) in its wondrous and sudden phase. And what a wealth of mediatory instrumentalities is now presented to our view! The *Last Day* itself is exhibited as a Divine day of a thousand years (Ps xc.). The *resurrection of the dead* is exhibited as a vital process, working from within outwards, through an entire æon, from the first glorious blossoms of the resurrection to the last general resurrection; it is thus possible for it to be accomplished in the form of a transformation (in accordance with St. Paul, 1 Cor. xv. 23, 24 [51]). The *judgment* is set forth as a distinct series of judgments, reaching from the war judgment at the return of Christ, through the peace judgment of the thousand years, to the judgment of damnation at the close of those years. The like is true of the *end* of the cosmical *world*. The orthodox school-idea of an actual destruction of the old world and an absolute creation of the new corresponds with the soteriological idea that the new man is the product of an absolute spiritual creation, and as such takes the place of the *natural* and wholly dead man, which latter is identified with the old man; in other words. the former idea is simply the false consequence of the false principle involved in the latter conception.

The doctrine of *Satan* is not only considerably developed in the Apocalypse—especially as regards the conception of him as the *Accuser*—but is also established on a firmer base, inasmuch as Satan enters into the circle of religious experience in this present world by the foundation of Antichristianity.

The end of the world, like the *Parousia* of Christ, is here exhibited in the light of a moral necessity, ensuing, as it does, in order to the crushing of the last mutinous revolt of iniquity against the Church of God on earth. The revival of Evil, apparently long since destroyed and abolished on earth, is thoroughly characteristic of its tough serpent-nature. ' The final stripping of iniquity of all idealistic illusions, such as aided its operation at the time of Antichristianity, is exhibited in its manifestation in the naked conspiracy of the Satanic spirit with human rudeness and brutality. This judgment upon the last revolt is the index for the general judgment, and hence, also, for the general resurrection.

Worthy of note is that ethico-psychological order according to which the Beast, or Antichrist, and the False Prophet are cast a thousand years earlier than Satan into the now ready Gehenna, or lake of fire. This order is in harmony with the idea of life. The Beast and the False Prophet have reached the end of their lives, so far as their powers and arts are concerned, at the Parousia; Satan does not attain the end of his life-term until the completion of the thousand years. It might be said that idealistic evil is judged a thousand years sooner than brutal evil; just as the kernel of humanity as existent at the Parousia is infinitely further developed than the mass of mankind.

So far as it is admissible to speak of an *intermediate state* between the last judgment and the ideal goal of all things, such a state manifestly appears to be for the wicked a series of æons to which the eye can discover no limit. Whither the river of Paradise goes as it flows out of the City of God, is not declared. The mediæval conception of the endless torment of all who have died out of the Church infringes on the liberty of God; the systems of the absolute restoration of all men infringe on the liberty of man; both occupy too positive a position in relation to the hidden secrets of the æons, behind which the mountains of absolute Eternity stand, radiant with the glory of God.

The Apocalypse, despite its figurative presentation, throws light upon the whole mass of the doctrines of our faith. The doctrines of the Trinity of God and of the relation of God to Christ, are here unmistakably raised above all monophysitism, Arianism, and inner-Trinitary subordination. The creation here appears, in the reflex light of the new Paradise, as the original plan of a world of eternal spirit-life. The human race is represented by a selection of elect ones, not in the least prejudicing the great masses of mankind, but forming the centre, the glory and relative support of these, just as Christ is *their* absolute centre, glory and support. How fully, furthermore, are the fundamental traits of Redemption, Reconciliation and Salvation portrayed, in contrast to the gloomy night-side of human life and perdition! Here the Baptism of the Church is reflected in a Baptism of blood; the Supper of the Church is reflected in the Supper of the Spirit; legal excommunication is reflected in dynamical excommunication: the righteousness of faith is reflected in righteousness of life. How richly the different phases of the Church are displayed.—the ground-forms of the internal and external history of the Church, the Kingdom of God, and the world—it is needless particularly to demonstrate, after an earnest consideration of the Revelation.

SECTION SECOND.

Homiletic Application of the Apocalypse.

It must, first of all, be premised that the Apocalypse is not to be laid aside as a *sealed* Book, but that it is to be treated as an *open* Book, and is to be made use of for the edification of the Christian churches (see ch. i. 1-4, ii.—iv., xxii. 10, 16; and the interspersed paræneses).

In the use of the Apocalypse, however, the will of the glorified Lord should be observed, as manifested in His confiding of the Apocalyptic treasury primarily to the *servants* of the Lord— these having to communicate it to the Church— not, indeed, in a tutoring hierarchic spirit, but in pastoral wisdom, with knowledge and understanding. Therefore is the Apocalypse entrusted to the servants (chap. i. 1; comp. chap. xxii. 6, 16).

Hence also the Seer does not write directly to the churches, but to the *angels*[*] of the churches. The responsible nature of this commission is evident from the words of ch. xxii. 18, 19.

The weightiness of these warning words is instanced by the two-fold fact that, despite their stern menace, fanaticism within the Church, and the enthusiastic spirit of entire sects, from the Montanists down to the "Latter Day Saints," have obscured the pure contents of the Revelation by additions, misinterpretations and chiliastic distortions, on the one hand; whilst, on the other hand, spiritualism [=a spiritualizing interpretation] has for ages past not only diminished the effect of the Revelation, through an idle and slavish fear of chiliasm, but has even, in many ways, paralyzed its operations, thus lulling Christian watchmen and Christian vigilance into slumber, and enfeebling the eschatological elements of even the Gospels and the Apostolic Epistles.

It may be laid down as a general principle, that the measure of doctrinal and ethical testimony furnished by the Apocalypse is the index to its homiletic applicability.

In particular, a field for homiletics is afforded by passages whose glory dispels all exegetic scruples; *viz.*, the doxologies, songs of praise, and heaven pictures in general; the Christological items; the soteriological didactic passages; the emphatic alarm-cries and comforting assurances; and, especially, the Seven Epistles, which have already proved such fertile soil for the homilist (see p. 54).

Literature Relating to the Application of the Apocalypse.

Imm. Nitzsch, *Ueber den Kirchlichen Werth und Gebrauch der Apocalypse*, Wittenberg, 1822. Hosse, *Der rechte Standpunkt der Betrachtung der Offenbarung Joh.* (*Monatsschrift für die ev. Kirche der Rheinprovinz und Westfalens*, 12th annual series. No. 7, 1853). Christiani (General Superintendent of Livonia), *Bemerkungen zur Auslegung der Apok., mit besonderer Rücksicht auf die chiliastische Frage*, Riga, Bacmeister. A. F. Schmidt (prebendary deacon in Stuttgart), *Ein Votum*

---

[*] [This would seem to favor the idea, rejected by Lange, that the "angels" are the heads or pastors of the churches.—Tr.]

über die homiletische Behandlung der Apokalypse, Stuttg., 1867. 8. Danz, *Universal-Wörterbuch,* p. 54.

SECTION THIRD.

Starke's Bibelwerk.

We cannot here in silence pass by a *Bible-work* which, in the continuous influence that it has exerted, impelled us to the preparation of our own; although we must, on account of the already noted limits and the atomistic nature of the work in question, restrict ourselves to a brief notice of it.

We find nothing in the *Introduction* of a theocratic bearing specially worthy of mention. Starke's position, in maintaining that the Apocalypse is the most important Book of the Scriptures, is equally one-sided with that of older Lutheran theologians, who regard it as a deutero-canonical Book, or that of modern criticism, which looks upon it as an almost worthless pseudo-prophetic fiction. On the other hand, with what may be called a praiseworthy resignation, Starke almost invariably presents two constructions of the Book, styling one "the system of those who explain it as for the most part *fulfilled,*" and the other "the system of those who explain it as for the most part *to be fulfilled.*" In many sections he sets forth the antithesis of these different views without comment on his own part.

We cite here some observations of Starke on the practical importance of the Apocalypse. "This Book, when rightly understood and faithfully applied, is profitable (1) for the confirmation of our faith in the doctrine of the person, natures, estates and offices of Christ, and in the doctrines of justification, sanctification and the Divine inspiration of the Holy Scriptures; (2) for warning against the great and manifold offence which subsists in Christendom, hidden under so many distresses, heresies and other infirmities of the reason, or by the devil covered up with scandals and sects, so that men stumble against it, or pass false judgment, and thus lose faith in that article of the Christian creed which declares: I believe in one Holy Christian Church; (3) for the powerful arousing of the soldier of Christ to the faithful maintenance of the conflict against sin and the kingdom of darkness within and around him, and to the prosecution of this conflict until the victory is gained;—so often is the admonition given: *He that hath ears, let him hear what the Spirit saith to the churches;* so often do we meet with the words: *He that conquereth, he that conquereth, etc.;* (4) for consolation in suffering, especially that which comes from without, that which the Christian undergoes in and from this wicked world, for the sake of the name and the following of Christ. Of this consoling nature are, especially, those most precious promises which are contained in the Seven Epistles, and which relate to the great and glorious reward which God graciously holds out to the faithful in tribulation; (5) for affording a prospect of troublous times still in the future, in order to the composed awaiting of them in the strength of God, and to encouragement in view of the great decadence of the Church—in face of which the individual believer may feel himself uplifted and supported by the lively hope of the imminent real exchange of darkness for light, which is no small thing to loyal servants and children of God; (6) for the elucidation of the prophetic Scriptures of the Old Testament: for as the Prophets afford us the best key to the Revelation of John, so the latter, viewed in the right light, affords the best key to a true understanding of the Prophets."

SECTION FOURTH.

Literature on the Doctrinal and Ethical and, especially, the Homiletical side of the Apocalypse.

Besides the lists already given in this Commentary (pp. 72 sqq.), and in the Comm. on John (p. 47 [Am. Ed.]), there is noted in Starke's *Bibelwerk* at the close of Revelation, under the caption: *Continuation of the list of exegetical works begun in the first part of this book,* a considerable number of writings on the Apocalypse; most of these, however, are somewhat antiquated.

Of recent works demanding mention here, as bearing upon Apocalyptic dogmatics and homiletics, as well as pertaining to the general literature on the Apocalypse, we name the following: Münchmeyer, *Bibelstunden über die Offenb. Joh.,* Hanover, 1862. *Das Ende der Zeiten, Vorträge über die Offenb. des h. Joh.,* by Emil Steffann, Berlin, 1870. Kienlen, *Commentaire historique et critique sur l'Ap. de Jean,* Paris, 1870 (synchrono-historical, but opposed to Volkmar). O'Sullivan (Rector of Killyman), *The Apostasy predicted by St. Paul,* Dublin, London, 1842 (learned, ingenious, evangelic, anti-papistic: on the Apostasy as set forth 2 Thess. ii.). Thomas Newton (Bishop of Bristol), *Dissertations on the Prophecies which have been remarkably fulfilled, and at this time are fulfilling in the World.* Revised by Dolson, London (a work of interest, evidencing deep reading on the part of its author, who occupies a world and Church-historical stand-point). Garratt, *Commentary on the Revelation of St. John, considered as the Divine Book of History, in which God has delineated what is now past, present and to come and decided beforehand,* London, 1866 (Church-historical and original. By the figure of the Beast, the author understands a council, still future (in 1866), of the united Orient and Occident).

There is a very extensive minor Apocalyptic literature in England, even appearing in the form of periodical papers. The eschatological anticipations of that practical nation have, in many cases, a strong chiliastic flavoring, as is evidenced by Darbyism, Irvingism and similar phenomena.

PART SECOND.

SPECIAL DOCTRINO–ETHICAL AND HOMILETICAL NOTES.

Section First.

Prologue (Chap. i. 1–8).

General.—Of God.—Of Revelation —Of witness [*Martyrium*].—Of visions.—Of Divine service.—Of the Church.—Of the Trinity.—Of salvation.—Of the destination of Christians — Of the Coming of C rist, in order to the complete revelation of God.

Special.—[Ver. 1.] Revelation as the Apocalypse, the end and crown of revelations —The end and crown of the Biblical Books.—The end and crown of the doctrines of the Christian faith. —The end and crown of parœneses.

[Ver. 2.] The Apostles as the great martyrs or witnesses of Christ:—Of His past, present, future [or coming].—John, in respect to his import in a doctrinal and a homiletical point of view.— John as the Seer of spirit in realities (the Gospel) and of realities in spirit (the Apocalypse) —The vision as a sign of the depth of the inner human life, and the height of the ripened Christian life. —[Ver. 3.] Blessedness of the Christian in anticipation of the Coming of Christ.—The always certain nearness of the last time in the rapid course and change of Christian times.—The Coming of Christ in every Christian age — Christian worship in the simple ground-form of readers and hearers.—Common blessedness of the leading and the led in a true cultus.—[Vers. 4, 5.] As the all-embracing idiocrasy of Christ is divided and reflected in the Apostles, so the idiocrasies of the Apostles are divided and reflected in those of the Church.—The Seven Churches in the deepest reality One Church.—The Trinity of God in the glory of its revelation: The Father, as the Primal Source of grace and peace—Who is, Who was, and Who cometh; The Holy Ghost in the manifestations of the Seven Spirits before the Throne of the Divine Rule; The Son of God, as the Faithful Witness, the First-born from the dead; as the Prince of the kings of the earth; as He Who hath loved us and washed us from our sins in His blood.—The *grace* which is *upon* Christians, and the *peace* which is *in* them, an eternally new benedictive greeting from the Triune God.—[Ver. 6.] The high calling of Christians, by which they are made a kingdom of priests; how this calling *is* realized *for* them, and how it *becomes* realized *in* them.—Kings and priests considered in respect of their connection: 1. Kings and priests, in the sense of their degeneracy, alternately war and conspire against each other; 2. Kings and priests, in the sense of the worldly order of things, mutually balance and limit each other; 3. Kings and priests, as servants of God, in the sense of the spiritual life, are one, and mutually condition each other.—A man becomes a *king*, in the service of

God, only when he continually sacrifices or surrenders all things to Him in pure self-renunciation, as a *priest*.—A man becomes a *priest* of the Eternal Spirit only when he can administer *kingly* possessions in *kingly* freedom.—The first doxology: 1. Glory: 2. Dominion; 3. Both to continue into the æons.—Whereby can I perceive that God is glorified on earth? 1. When no earthly glory obscures, like a cloud, this heavenly Sun. 2. When His glory is duly seen and appreciated in the reflected lustre of all that is holy and glorious on earth.—In God's Kingdom, His dominion is based upon His glory, as is His glory upon His dominion.—What is the meaning of *eternities* [æons? the G. V. has: *von Ewigkeit zu Ewigkeit*=from eternity to eternity]? Infinite revelation of the Divine Essence. Infinite unfolding of a blessed life. Infinite development and unveilment of the world.—The Biblical *Amen:* The perfected Personality of Christ; Perfected phase of the Kingdom; Perfected certitude of prayer.—[Ver. 7.] The Theme of the Book: *He cometh.*—Also the theme of worldly history; of religious presentiments; of science and of art.—*With the clouds.* As high and free as are the clouds as they emerge to view out of the depths of Heaven; as hidden and as manifest as the lightning in the cloud; as elevated above the earth, and as surely destined for the earth.—*And every eye shall see Him.* One day these eyes of ours shall show to each and all of us the Lord.—How this announcement finds its incipient fulfilment in every act of worship that we perform: We look up to Him. We perceive ourselves to be guilty in respect of the cross of Christ. We celebrate His Passion and His Death with sacred lamentations for the Dead.—This prophecy shall one day become a completed reality.—With Christ's Coming Sunday comes; true and unceasing worship comes; the word of revelation comes upon the whole earth.—Even His enemies *must* see Him; must recognize their guilt in respect of Him in their guilt in respect of their inmost selves; must join, in one way or another, in the last lamentation over Him.— [Ver. 8.] In the Coming of Christ, God shall perfectly manifest Himself as Jehovah, the Covenant God:—faithful to Himself—faithful to His people—faithful to His justice toward all.— *Alpha and Omega;* or the most profound idea elementarily illustrated. As the whole expression embraces the entire spirit-world, so the Spirit of God comprehends the beginning, the middle, and the end of things.—Import of the fact that God will not perfectly manifest Himself until the end of the course of this world; that He is utterly distinct from (1) fate, (2) despotism, (3) arbitrariness, (4) chance.—On the Martyrs.—On Divine Service.—On the Feast of Trinity.—On Confirmation.

Comp. Ex. xix.; Isa. vi.; Ezek. i.; Dan. vii.; Zech. xii.; Matt. xxiv. 30, *et al.*

STARKE: All revelations of God come to us through Christ.—The most eminent function of an Apostle or Teacher is to testify of Christ.—Such a reading and hearing of Holy Scripture as is pleasing to God, confers blessedness.—*The wish:* [1] The utterer of the wish; [2] The objects of the wish; [3] The subject of the wish; [4] The One to Whom the wish is addressed.—CRAMER: The condition of a Christian a noble condition.—*Nai, ἀμήν est genuina confirmatio, una græca, altera hebraica.*

SANDER (*"Versuch einer Erklärung,"* 1829, see p. 73): If the Revelation of John be compared with the rest of the Sacred Writings, especially those of the Prophets, it will be found that John uses scarce any image that is not contained in these and that might not be explained through them. Compare Rev. i. and Ezek. i. 26; Isa. vi., *etc.* (Moreover, the homogeneousness of the images presupposes the homogeneousness of the facts.) Only in John's writings all those things which in the other Prophets are more scattered, are concentrated; he catches, as it were, in the focus of a burning glass all the rays of individual Prophets, so that it is not to be wondered at that the brightness thence resultant dazzles many.

WAECHTLER (see p. 74): A knowledge of the Revelation of St. John is highly important for all Christians (Rev. i. 1-3).—Grace and peace from God, the inexhaustible Fountain of all comfort (ch. i. 4-6).

BÖHMER (see p. 73): In the Christian creed, the Holy Ghost is placed after the Father and the Son, as proceeding from Them both. John, however, is writing, not a system of divinity, but a sacred history, in which the general point of departure is the all-sovereign eternal God; next are revealed the powers which prepare the way for the fulfillment of His counsel of salvation, and last comes Christ Himself—first, as the true and highest Prophet, the "faithful Witness," then as the "First-born of the dead," and finally as the "Prince of the kings of the earth."

[BARNES: Ver. 7. *And every eye shall see Him.* Every one has this in certain prospect, that he shall see the Son of Man coming as a Judge.]

On the literature (see above, p. 74). LILIENTHAL, *Bibl. Archivarius,* p. 808.—DANZ, p. 57 and *Supplement,* p. 6.

SECTION SECOND.

First Vision. Heaven-picture of the Seven Churches (*Ch. i. 9-20*).

General.—The pastoral fidelity of man here appears in reciprocal action with the pastoral fidelity of God. John on Patmos thinks of his seven churches in the spirit of prayer. But the Lord, through the Spirit of revelation, changes his glance at the seven churches into a vision of the whole future of the Church.—Heavenly blessedness in the midst of earthly martyrdom. —The prophetic visions as the theocratic higher reality of the Platonic ideas, the lofty mysterious source-points of all fundamental spiritual currents, or of the stream of salvation in the history

of the world.—Preliminary conditions of prophecy—external affliction, internal solemn joy, loneliness, prayer.—Forms of revelation.—Development of revelation from the auricular to the ocular wonder.—Appearance of Christ in His glory in respect of its fundamental features. Christ, the Son of God, also eternally the glorified Son of Man.—The shock experienced by the Seer at the appearance of the Lord in His revelation, a species of death, and hence a source of new, high life. How this shock—*a.* In its original form runs through the history of the prophetic callings (Ex. iii. 6; iv. 24; xxxiv. 30-35; Isa. vi. 5; Jer. i. 6; Ezek. iii. 14, 15; Dan. x.); *b.* Is reflected in Jewish tradition (Ju. xiii. 22) and in Greek manticism, in which the manticist himself represents death, whilst the priest who expounds his oracle is representative of new life; *c.* Is shadowed in the history of apostate prophets, especially in that of Balaam (Num. xxiv. 4); *d.* Is crystallized in the fundamental forms of regeneration; repentance and faith—death of the old, resurrection of the new, man. —Doctrine of the kingdom of the dead, and of death.—Hades is to be distinguished from Gehenna.—The appearance of Christ, deadly for the moment, conferring life for ever.—Sacred literature (verse 19).—Key of symbolism (verse 20).

Special.—[Ver. 9.] John, an exile on earth, at home in Heaven.—The great Prophet, a *brother and companion* [fellow-partaker] of all Christians, (1) in tribulation, (2) in the glory of the Kingdom, (3) in the endurance of Jesus.—*Patmos,* so poor in geography, so glorified in the Theocracy, like Bethlehem and Nazareth. The like is true of Palestine and the earth itself. [Ver. 10.] *Sunday* in its apostolic radiance: The day of the spirit; of transport; of complete revelation.—Sunday quiet, absorption of life in its profoundest depths, and thereby, at the same time, in the richest retrospect, and the clearest fore-view.—The sacred *voice.*—[Ver. 11.] The sacred *Book.* —The Bible reposing upon Divine voices and trumpets.—The Christian who, through deep absorption of spirit, finds the three times [the past, present and future] in the present, thereby learns to know God as He Who is, Who was and Who cometh.—The seven churches or representatives of all churches—primarily, of all those in Asia Minor—or the one Church in its seven-fold form.—The sacred septenary of the churches, founded upon the septenary of the Spirits of God, and ever recurring in the subsequent sevens.—[Vers. 12, 13.] Christ is, therefore, here in the midst of the candlesticks, as well as in the other world. The same hierarchism which sunders doctrine and life, belief and morals, clergy and laity, spirit and nature, faith and culture, body and soul, also tears earth and Heaven apart. As the deist confines God to the other world, so the Hierarchy banishes the Lord Jesus Christ thither.—Christ is the living unity of the seven individual golden candlesticks, and through this unity alone is the type of the *one* seven-branched candlestick fulfilled (Ex. xxv. 31-37).—[Vers. 14-16.] The form of Christ, considered in regard to its attributes; or the difference between theocratic symbolism and humanistic æsthetics.—[Ver. 17.] *Fear not,* a ground-word of Christianity from beginning to end (Luke ii. 10; Matt. xxviii. 5; see the *Concordances*, Title, *Fear not*).—The history and operation of the Death and Resurrection of Christ lift all fear from all believers.—[Ver. 18.] Christ, the *Living One*, (1) in respect of His spiritual essence and mission (the First, the Last, the Life of life); (2) in respect of His history (having been dead, and having become alive forever); (3) in respect of His power (having the keys of Death and Hades).—[Ver. 19.] "Write what thou seest." All Scripture a copy of Divine reality.—[Ver. 20.] The key of symbolism must form the starting-point for the disclosure of all Apocalyptic mysteries.— The Angels of the churches, neither presbyteries, nor bishops, nor preachers, but the spirit of the churches in symbolic personification—the spirit which, undoubtedly, *should be* represented by the heads of the churches, but which is very frequently *not* represented by them. This spirit represents their idiocrasy, their ideal, the quality of their spiritual life, and is the local invisible church.—The churches as candlesticks. —Celebration of Sunday.—Bible festivals.—Celebration of Easter.—Festival of the dead.—Celebration of church consecration (or consecration of the angel of a church).—Celebration of the ministry.—See the succession of the visions, ch. iv. 2 (individual items) chap. xvii 3 (individual items).—Parallels: Acts x. 10sqq.; xx. 7; Zech. iv. 2; Dan. vii.; Dan. x.; Isa. xli. 10; xlviii. 12; Mal. ii. 7.*

STARKE: A man is in the Spirit (1) ordinarily, when he permits himself to be governed by the Spirit of God (Rom. viii. 9; Gal. v. 5†); (2) extraordinarily, by transport, and a Divine revelation of things to come (Matt. xxii. 43).— Christ is always present with His Church, to enlighten, sanctify and defend it (Eph. v. 26).— He has, therefore, no need of any vicar.—The Church has for its foundation-pillar the invincible power and strength of Christ.—Christ's servants are in His hand, honored by Him and assured of His help.

RICHTER (see p. 73): In vers. 17 and 18, Jesus declares, in different words, the same thing that is expressed in Matt. xxviii. 18, "All power [authority] is given unto Me in Heaven and on earth," and the same that is expressed in that other saying of His, "I and the Father are one" [John x. 30]. After the lapse of nearly two thousand years, we find ourselves in a different posture toward this saying—so far as belief in it is concerned—from that occupied by the Church in John's time. Has there not been a considerable progress in the setting up of Christ's Kingdom? (It is true that we must not overlook the fact that, together with the furtherances of faith during the course of the centuries, there has been a constant new formation of apparent hindrances.) ⑨

GAERTNER (see p. 73): With the trumpet sound of the voice of Christ, the Revelation was opened for the ear;—with the seven candlesticks, it was opened for the eye.—These seven candlesticks

precisely correspond to the seven lamps on the seven-branched candlestick in the Holy Place of the Tabernacle. The independent candlesticks, having each one its own standard, denote the greater perfection of the New Testament Church; furthermore, the Lord walks in the midst of them, which would be impossible, so far as the figure is concerned, in the case of the one seven-branched candlestick (rather, this fact is declaratory that there shall be, in the New Covenant, no external visible hierarchic unity of the churches). What is there more beautiful and more cheering than a bright light upon a candlestick in a dark and gloomy night! So the Church is a light in the darkness of this world, shining into the gloom and obscurity of mankind. Where there is a church that has the pure word of God and acts in accordance therewith, there is a golden candlestick; just so the faithful Church in Israel was a light to the Gentiles throughout the whole of the Old Testament time. The seven candlesticks are indicative of a perfect Church, into which the Holy Spirit from God's inner world streams seven-fold (sevenfold, and yet singly, through Christ).

[BONAR (Ver. 17): *And when I saw Him, I fell at His feet as dead.* O sinner, learn to know this Christ now as the Saviour, ere the day arrives when you shall see Him as the Judge! His love would save you now; His majesty will crush you then.]

SECTION THIRD.

Earth-picture of the Seven Churches. The Seven Epistles. (Chs. ii., iii.)

General.—The seven Churches as real portraits and at the same time as typical pictures of the whole Church, as regards (1) local extension and (2) chronological development.—The seven Churches as the centre of the seven loosed Seals or unveiled worldly history; as the occasion for the seven penitential Trumpets for the world in the Church and the Church in the world; as the organ of the seven Thunders of awakening and reformation; as the object of the enmity of the kingdom of darkness in the seven Heads of Antichrist; purified and saved by the hardening judgments of the seven Vials of Anger which are poured out upon the Antichristian world, in order to the mediating of Christ's appearing and His union with the Bride, in that one Spirit in Whom the Seven Spirits are united.—The seven Epistles as the all sided sum of all messages of the heavenly Head-Shepherd to the shepherds and congregations of the Church; as the all-sided ensample of pastoral ministry on the part of the shepherds; and, at the same time, as prophetic alarm voices from the Spirit of the Church to the flocks themselves.—The Johannean Theology.—The Johannean Church. —Its historic continuance within Church History.—Its abiding fundamental features.—Its future.

The seven Churches as the seven candlesticks of the earth:—As portraits of the manifold configurations of Christianity.—Parallels and antitheses: Ephesus and Smyrna. Smyrna and Pergamus. Pergamus and Thyatira (Balaam and Jezebel). Thyatira and Sardis. Philadel-

---

* [The G. V. here reads "*Engel*"—angel, instead of the "messenger" of the E. V.—TR.]
† [The G. V. here reads "*im Geist*"—in the Spirit, instead of "*through* the Spirit," as the E. V.—TR.]

phia and Laodicea.—Lights and Shadows: 1. The Metropolis: Growing churchliness, decreasing Christliness. Increased external works at the expense of inwardness—the first love. 2 Smyrna, the Martyr-Church, in conflict with a Judaizing, orthodoxistic tendency. 3. Pergamus, the confessing Church, lax in the exercise of church discipline towards antinomianism. 4. Thyatira, the enthusiastic Church, spotted with immoral fanaticism. 5. Sardis, the Church with a show of churchly life, but spiritually dead. 6. Philadelphia, small and pure—hence also a mission Church. 7. Laodicea, the lukewarm.—How the Lord's threats and promises to the seven Churches have been fulfilled. Historic life-pictures.—The manifold forms of Christ in relation to the seven Churches. All agreeing with individual traits of His total appearance (ch. i.).

Special.—To avoid repetition, we here simply refer to the exegetical department.

1. *Ephesus. The Mother-Church externally and legally faithful, but gathering inward and spiritual darkness.*

How Christ presents Himself to this Church, the metropolis, in accordance with its need (ver. 1). Commendation of the Church: its many virtues (vers. 2, 3). In contrast to these, the one great, threatening want (ver. 4). Corresponding admonition, warning, threat (ver. 5). A hopeful sign, limiting the censure of Christ. In the Church's hatred of Nicolaitanism there remains a trace of the first love (ver. 6). Alarm cry and ethically conditioned promise, in harmony with the Church's stand-point. Ephesus the metropolis, and metropolises in Church History (Jerusalem, Rome, Constantinople, Alexandria, *etc.*).

2. *Smyrna. The Martyr-Church persecuted by Judaism.*

Picture of Christ, in conformity to the needs of this Church (ver. 8). Praise of the Church (ver. 9). Its tribulation in the present and in the future, and the Lord's word of encouragement (vers. 9, 10). The great promise (ver. 10). The alarm cry and the glorious goal, in harmony with the conflict of the Church (ver. 11). Smyrna and other martyr-churches in conflict with the various forms of Judaism and orthodoxism (with the false and the great ban). The synagogue of Satan.

3. *Pergamus. The Martyr-Church persecuted by Heathenism.*

Proclamation: Christ as the possessor of the two-edged sword (ver. 12). Praise of martyr faithfulness in external conflict (ver. 13). Censure of false endurance when there was a call to spiritual conflict (vers. 14, 15). Admonition to repentance and threat of the judicial interference of Christ (ver. 16). Peculiar promise, referring to the relations of the inner, spiritual life (ver. 17). Pergamus, or the libertine Church, defective in the observance of church-discipline towards Nicolaitans and Balaamites Balaam, the type of the false prophet or apostasy. The first Old Testament Judas (followed by Ahithophel and others), a prelude of the last Judas, the false prophet (Rev. xiii.).

4. *Thyatira. The excited Church stained with antinomistic spiritual fanaticism.*

Announcement of the Searcher of hearts and reins in His holy motion (ver. 18). Commendation of the Church's zeal (ver. 19) Censure of its toleration of Jezebel and the antinomistic extravagances of which she is the instigator (vers. 20, 21). Terribly earnest threat of punishment, in perfect harmony with the sin committed (vers. 22, 23). Limitation of the threat by a promise to spare the guiltless (vers. 23 25). Promise of the spirit of holy discipline and of true progress in antithesis to a false advance—in harmony with the situation of the Church (vers. 26-28). The alarm cry comes at the end, instead of preceding the promise, as heretofore. The same change of position between the conditional promise and the alarm cry obtains in the following Epistles. The architectonic distinction hence arising between the first three and the last four Churches may at the same time be suggestive of the antithesis of their geographical position. Smyrna and Pergamus lie to the north of Ephesus; Thyatira, Sardis, Philadelphia and Laodicea, to the south of Pergamus.—Phases of Jezebel in Church History, or the manifold re-appearance of fanatical and immoral sects and schools. Corrupting women in ancient and modern Church History, contrasted with the line of pious women.

5. *Sardis. The Church for the most part spiritually dead.*

Christ addresses Himself to this Church—in which there is a lack of the Spirit—in His whole general sovereignty over the entire Church and in the fullness of His Spirit. He begins by bringing against it the heavy charge of deadness—doubly a crime, since it has the *name* of *living* (ch. iii. 1). Alarm cry, in reference to the still extant remnants of life (vers. 2, 3). Recognition of the few innocent ones, conjoined with a promise corresponding to the fact that they have not defiled their garments (vers. 4, 5). Alarm cry (ver. 6).—Sad instances of dead or dying congregations, and even whole Churches.

6. *Philadelphia. The pearl among the Churches.*

Christ in the solemn aspect of the Administrator of the keys of David, *i. e.* true communion (ver. 7). Great recognition of the Church's faithfulness, and great promise—both in lively alternation (vers. 8-10). Encouragement and extraordinary final promise (vers. 11, 12). Alarm cry (ver. 13).—Characteristic of living Christian Churches and communities: *An open door.* Open outwardly for missions; open inwardly for communion.

7. *Laodicea. The lukewarm Church—nigh unto reprobation.*

The view which we take of Laodicea—*viz.*, that it has fallen into lukewarmness in consequence of its spiritualistic [*spiritualistisch*] tendency—is supported by the characteristic announcement of Christ. He appears here entirely as the historic Christ, and characterizes Himself in this very peculiarity as identical with the ideal primal principle of the creation (ver. 14). The censure of the Church's lukewarmness is immediately conjoined with the threat of the judgment of reprobation (vers. 15, 16). The Lord then discovers the source of the lukewarmness of the Church to be, pride in its supposed spiritual riches, whilst it is in reality, in a state of inexpressible spiritual necessity (vers. 16, 17). With this condition, correspond Christ's searching counsel (ver. 18), the expression of His love and compassion in the censure which He administers (ver. 19), and His peculiar admonition to repentance (ver. 20). The ethically conditioned promise is of as concrete a character as the self-presentation of Christ at the beginning, in perfect accordance with the needs of a church dissolved in spiritualism ([*Spiritualismus*], vers. 20, 21). The closing paragraph concludes both the seventh Epistle and all the foregoing Epistles (ver. 22).—Spiritualistic [*spiritualistisch*] back-ground of the lukewarm Church. An idealistic dream-life as unbelief in the historic power of ideas, or, rather, in the Incarnation of the Word.

Upon glancing over the entire group, we behold in most of the Churches a juxtaposition of light and shade—yet in very different proportions; only Laodicea incurs blame alone, and only Philadelphia is entirely free from censure. This contrast is explained by the spiritual pride of the one, and the humility and modesty of the other. Christ is different and yet the same in His posture toward each individual Church.—The celestially perfect Shepherd of the flock and Physician of the soul.

The wealth of homiletical works upon the Seven Epistles is so immense, and the works in question are so accessible, that, instead of attempting to augment this treasure, we shall refer to what is already extant. Even in more ancient times the Seven Epistles have afforded inducement to manifold dissertations on them, as is evident, *e. g.*, from the list of productions relative to them in Lilienthal's *Biblischer Archivarius*, pp. 811-819. We have cited on p. 74 of the *Introduction* the special works of MEISTER, WICHELHAUS, HEUBNER, ZORN, VAN OOSTERZEE. We have still to mention, among others, Lisko, *Christenspiegel*, *Betrachtungen über die sieben Sendschreiben der Offenb. Joh.*, Berlin, 1837.—To the above may be added the numerous homiletical or generally edifying works upon the whole Apocalypse (see the *Int.*), especially those of Bengel, Hahn, Schulthess, Roos, Wächtler, *et al.* The *Sermons* of Wichelhaus made considerable impression in their time; Wächtler's *Sermons* are energized by study, spirit and fervor; the *Sermons* of Van Oosterzee are especially distinguished by a plenitude of spirit and a grand play of oratory.

STARKE: The title of Christ at the opening of every letter is taken from the vision and description of Christ in ch. i. 11-18; it is, however, not always the same, but varies, on the contrary, in each epistle, corresponding in purpose and appearance with the contents of the epistle and the state of the Church addressed. The promise

which in every epistle is given to the conqueror is adapted to the condition of each Church and to the evil that must be overcome.—*The first love.* The expression is drawn from the first love of married persons, which is wont to be pure and fervid, Jer. ii. 2. (This *first love* is, therefore, the pure bridal phase of religious consciousness —*i. e.* its receptivity, purity [in the sense of being without admixture of foreign or contaminating elements], freedom, warmth and devotion; in one word, genuine earnestness and depth [*wahrhaftige Innigkeit und Innerlichkeit*]). —As common traits of the Old Testament Balaam and the New Testament Nicolaitans may be mentioned: 1. Boasting; 2. Covetousness; 3. Seduction to apostasy; 4. Bringing under judgment.—*Warm or cold.* Warmth is positively wished for; coldness is desired only inasmuch as it is accompanied by less danger and responsibility than lukewarmness.—(Starke allegorizes the names of all the seven Churches—a procedure to which the name of Philadelphia might offer special inducements.)

LAVATER: *Jesus Messias, oder die Zukunft des Herrn nach der Offenb. Joh.* (a poetical work). SMYRNA: *Und der Herrliche rief mir: Schreibe dem Engel in Smyrna: Also der Erste, der Letzte, der todt war und ewiglich lebet: Ich weiss deine Werke, etc.* [And the Glorious One cried unto me: Write to the angel in Smyrna: Thus (saith) the First and Last, Who was dead and eternally liveth. I know thy works, *etc.*]

THE KREUZRITTER ([Knight of the Cross] Von Meyer, *Schlüssel zur Offenb. St. Joh.*; see p. 73). "Be faithful unto death and I will give thee the crown of life." Wreath or crown, it is all the same—except that the crowns of victors were wont to be made of living foliage. The Lord over death and life here demands of His followers such faithfulness and steadfastness as shall go with them even to a violent death. He Himself has won the wreath of victory and the highest crown of eternal life, and His first martyr, Stephen (*i. e.* wreath, crown), in the name that he bears, exhibits, as it were, to all martyrs their heavenly reward.

VAN OOSTERZEE: Let us, then, contemplate the Revelation of the glorified Christ on Patmos: as, for John, never to be forgotten—full of significance for all the centuries of the time following it—rich in instruction for each one of us — Christ stands before you as the Image of the invisible God, the priestly King of the Kingdom of God, the faithful Friend of His servants, the Lord and Judge of the future.—*Smyrna:* Poor Smyrna *enriched; calumniated* Smyrna *honored; threatened* Smyrna *ensured; militant* Smyrna *faithful; triumphant* Smyrna *crowned.*

Literature: TRENCH. *Comm. on the Epistles to the Seven Churches in Asia,* 1867 [New York, 1872].

[From M. HENRY: Ch. ii. 1. *He that holdeth the seven stars in His right hand.* The ministers of Christ are under His special care and protection.—*He walketh in the midst of the seven golden candlesticks.* Christ is in an intimate manner present and conversant with His churches, and knows the state of each one of them.—Ver. 2. *I know thy works and thy labor.* Those that are stars in Christ's hand had need to be always in motion, dispensing light to all about them.—*Thy patience.* It is not enough that we be diligent, but we must be patient, and endure hardness as good soldiers of Christ.—*Thou canst not bear them that are evil.* It consists very well with Christian patience, not to dispense with sin, much less allow it.—Ver. 4. *Nevertheless, I have somewhat against thee.* Those that have much good in them, may have something much amiss in them; and our Lord Jesus, as an impartial Master and Judge, takes notice of both —*Thou hast left thy first love.* Observe, (1) The first affections of men toward Christ, and holiness, and heaven, are usually lively and warm. (2) These lively affections will abate and cool, if great care be not taken, and diligence used, to preserve them in constant exercise. (3) Christ is grieved and displeased with His people when He sees them grow remiss and cold toward Him, and He will one way or other make them sensible that He does not take it well from them.—Ver. 5. *Remember therefore from whence thou art fallen, and repent, and do the first works.* Observe, 1. Those that have lost their first love must remember from whence they are fallen; they must compare their present with their former state, and consider how much better it was with them then than now. 2 They must repent; they must be inwardly grieved and ashamed for their sinful declining, and humbly confess it in the sight of God. 3. They must return and do their first works; they must, as it were, begin again, go back step by step, till they come to the place where they took the first false step; they must endeavor to revive and recover their first zeal, tenderness, and seriousness, and must pray as earnestly, and watch as diligently, as they did when they first set out in the ways of God.—*Or else I will come unto thee quickly,* etc. If the presence of Christ's grace and Spirit be slighted, we may expect the presence of His displeasure.— Ver. 7. *He that hath an ear, let him hear what the Spirit saith unto the churches.* Observe, 1. What is written in the Scriptures is spoken by the Spirit of God. 2. What is said to one church, concerns all the churches, in every place and age. 3. We can never employ our faculty of hearing better than in hearkening to the word of God —*To him that conquereth.* The Christian life is a warfare against sin, Satan, the world, and the flesh. It is not enough that we engage in this warfare, but we must pursue it to the end; we must fight the good fight till we gain the victory; and the warfare and victory shall have a glorious triumph and reward. —*To eat of the tree of life,* etc. They shall have that perfection of holiness, and that confirmation therein, that Adam would have had. If he had gone well through the course of his trial, then he would have eaten of the tree of life which was in the midst of paradise, and that would have been the sacrament of confirmation to him in his holy and happy state. So all who persevere in their Christian trial and warfare, shall derive from Christ, as the Tree of Life, perfection and confirmation in holiness and happiness in the paradise of God; not in the earthly paradise, but the heavenly (ch. xxii. 1, 2).—Ver. 8. Christ *was dead,* and by dying purchased salvation for us; He *is alive,* and by His life applies this salvation to us.—Ver. 9. *I know thy tribulation.*

They who will be faithful to Christ, must expect to go through many tribulations; but Jesus Christ takes particular notice of all their troubles.—*Thy poverty (but thou art rich).* Poor in temporals, but rich in spirituals; poor in spirit, and yet rich in grace; their spiritual riches are set off by their outward poverty. Many who are rich in temporals, are poor in spirituals. Some who are poor outwardly are inwardly rich. Spiritual riches are usually the reward of great diligence; the diligent hand makes rich.—*I know the blasphemy.* He knows the wickedness and falsehood of the enemies of His people.— Ver. 10. He foreknows the future trials of His people, forewarns them of them, and forearms against them. Forearms them, 1. By His counsel. 2. By showing them how their sufferings would be alleviated and limited: (1) They should not be universal; (2) They should not be perpetual; (3) It should be to *try* them, not to destroy them. 3. By promising a glorious reward to their fidelity. Observe, 1. The sureness of this reward: *I will give them.* 2 The suitableness of it: (1) *A crown,* to reward their poverty, fidelity and conflict. (2) *A crown of life,* to reward those who are *faithful even unto death,* are faithful till they die, and who part with life itself, in fidelity to Christ.—Ver. 11. *He that overcometh, shall not be hurt of the second death.* Observe, 1. There is not only a *first,* but a *second* death; a *death* after the body is dead. 2. This *second death* is unspeakably worse than the first *death,* both in agony and in duration—it is *eternal death,* to die, and to be always dying. 3. From this hurtful, this destructive *death,* Christ will save all His faithful servants —Ver. 13. *I know where thou dwellest,* etc. Christ takes notice of the trials and difficulties His people encounter. —Ver. 14. Observe, 1. Corrupt doctrines and a corrupt worship often lead to corrupt conversation. 2. To continue in communion with persons of corrupt principles and practices is displeasing to God, and causes those who thus do to become *partakers of other men's sins* Though the Church, as such, has no power to punish the persons of men, either for heresy or immorality, with corporal penalties, yet it has power to exclude them from its holy communion; and if it do not so, Christ will be displeased with it. —Ver. 19. It should be the ambition and earnest desire of all Christians that their last works may be their best works.—Ver. 21. Observe, 1. Repentance is necessary to prevent the sinner's ruin. 2. Repentance requires time 3. Where God gives space for repentance, He expects *fruits meet for repentance.* 4 Where the space for repentance is lost, the sinner perishes with a double destruction.—Ver. 23 *All the churches shall know,* etc. God is known by *the judgments that He executeth.* Note here. 1 His infallible knowledge *of the hearts* of men. 2 His impartial justice — Ver 28. Christ is *the Morning Star;* He brings day with Him into the soul; the light of grace and of glory —Ch iii. 3. *I will come unto thee as a thief,* etc. Observe, 1. When Christ leaves a people as to His gracious presence, He comes to them in judgment; and His judicial presence will be very dreadful to those who have sinned away His gracious presence. 2. His judicial presence to a dead declining people will be surprising; their deadness will keep them in security, and, as it procures an angry visit from Christ to them, it will prevent their discerning it and preparing for it. 3 Such a visit from Christ will be to their loss; *He will come as a thief,* to strip them of their remaining enjoyments and mercies, not by fraud, but in justice and righteousness, taking the forfeiture they have made of all to Him.—Ver. 4. God takes notice of the smallest number of those who abide with Him; and the fewer they are, the more precious in His sight.—*They shall walk with Me in white, for they are worthy.* In the *stole,* the white robes of justification, and adoption, and comfort; or in the white robes of honor and glory, in the other world. This is an honor proper and suitable to their integrity and fidelity, and no way unbecoming Christ to confer upon them, though it is not a legal, but a gospel worthiness that is ascribed to them; not merit, but meetness.—Ver. 5. *He that overcometh shall be clothed in white raiment.* The purity of grace [ver. 4] shall be rewarded with the perfect purity of glory—*I will not blot his name, etc.* Observe, 1. Christ has His *book of life,* a register and roll of all who shall inherit eternal life: (1) *the book* of eternal election; (2) *the book* of remembrance of all who have lived to God. 2. Christ *will not blot the names* of His chosen and faithful ones *out of this book of life.* 3. Christ will produce this *book of life,* and *confess the names* of the faithful who stand there, *before God, and all the angels;* this He will do as their Judge, and as their Captain and Head.—Ver. 7. *He that is holy, He that is true, He that hath the key of David.* Note here Christ's personal, and His political character.—Observe the acts of His government: 1. *He opens*—a door of opportunity to His churches, a door of utterance to his ministers, a door of entrance, the heart, a door of admission into the visible Church, laying down the terms of communion, and the door of admission into the Church triumphant, according to the terms of salvation fixed by Him. 2. *He shuts* the door; when He pleases, *He shuts* the door of opportunity, and the door of utterance, and leaves obstinate sinners shut up in *the hardness of their hearts; He shuts* the door of church-fellowship against unbelievers and profane persons, and *He shuts* the door of heaven against the foolish virgins who have slept away their day of grace, and against the workers of iniquity, how vain and confident soever they may be.—Ver. 10. Observe, 1. The gospel of Christ is the word of His patience; it is the fruit of the patience of God to a sinful world, it sets before men the exemplary patience of Christ in all His sufferings for men, it calls those who receive it to the exercise of patience in conformity to Christ. 2. This gospel should be carefully kept by all who enjoy it. 3. After a day of patience we must expect an hour of temptation; a day of gospel-peace and liberty is a day of God's patience, and it is seldom so well improved as it should be, and therefore is often followed by a day of trial and temptation. 4. Sometimes the trial is more general and universal; it comes upon all the world. 5. They who keep the gospel in a time of peace shall be kept by Christ in an hour of temptation.—Ver. 16. Lukewarmness or indifference in religion is the worst temper in the world. If religion be a real thing, it is the most excellent thing, and therefore we should be in good earnest in it; if it be not a real thing, it is the vilest imposture, and we should be earnest against it.—*I will spew thee out of my mouth.* As lukewarm water turns the stomach and provokes to a vomit, lukewarm professors turn the heart of Christ against them. . . . They shall be rejected, and finally rejected; far be it from the holy Jesus to return to that which has been thus rejected.—Ver. 17. Here observe what a difference there was between the thoughts that the Laodiceans had of themselves and the thoughts that Christ had of them.—Ver. 19. Sinners ought to take the rebukes of God's word and rod as tokens of His good-will to their souls, and should accordingly repent in good earnest, and turn to Him that smites them.—Ver. 20. Observe, 1. Christ is graciously pleased by His Word and Spirit to come to the door of the heart of sinners. 2. He finds this door shut against Him. 3. When He finds the door shut, He does not immediately withdraw, but He waits to be gracious, even till His head be filled with the dew. 4. He uses all proper means to awaken sinners, and to cause them to open to Him; He calls by His word, and He knocks by the impulses of His Spirit upon their conscience. 5. They who open to Him shall enjoy His presence, to their great comfort and advantage; He will sup with them, He will accept of what is good in them, He will eat His pleasant fruit and He will bring the best part of the entertainment with Him; He will give fresh supplies of graces and comforts, and thereby stir up fresh actings of faith, and love, and delight.—Ver. 21. It is here implied that notwithstanding the lukewarm and self-confident character of this Church, it was possible that by the reproofs and counsels of Christ they might be inspired with fresh zeal and vigor, and come off conquerors in their spiritual warfare. 2. That if they did so, all former faults should be forgiven, and they should have a great reward.—Those who are conformed to Christ in His trials and victories, shall be conformed to Him in His glory.

From THE COMPREHENSIVE COMMENTARY: By a frequent Scripture metaphor a person, living in the defilements of this world, and neglectful of preparation for another, is said to be "dead while he liveth," while he who meets death in the discharge of his Christian duty, is pronounced "living though he die," John xi. 25, 26; 1 Tim. v. 6; 1 John iii. 14; Jude 12. (WOODHOUSE.)

BARNES: Chap. ii. 10. *Ye shall have tribulation ten days.* Affliction in this life, however severe, can be but brief; and in the hope that it will soon end why should we not bear it without murmuring or repining? . . . *Be thou faithful unto death, etc.* It is true of every one who is a Christian, in whatever manner he is to die, that if he is faithful unto death, a crown of life awaits him.—Ch. iii. 3. It is always well for Christians to call to remembrance the "day of their espousals," and their views and feelings when they gave their hearts to the Saviour, and to compare those views with their present condition, especially if their conversion was marked by any thing unusual.—*Thou shalt not know what hour I will come upon thee.* Every man who is warned of the evil of his course, and who refuses or neglects to repent, has reason to believe that God will come suddenly in His wrath and call him to His bar. Prov. xxix. 1.—Ver. 15. *I would thou wert hot or cold.* Any thing better than this condition, where love is professed, but where it does not exist; where vows have been assumed which are not fulfilled.—Ver. 20. *If any one hear My voice.* Any one, of any age, and in any land, would be authorized to apply this to himself, and, under the protection of this invitation, to come to the Saviour, and to plead this promise as one that fairly included himself.—Chaps. ii., iii. Though the churches to which these epistles were addressed have long since passed away, yet the principles laid down in them still live, and they are full of admonition to Christians in all ages and all lands.—From TRENCH: Ch. ii. 2: *I know thy works.* These are words of comfort and strength for all who, amid infinite weakness, are yet able to say, "Search me, O Lord, and know my heart; try me, and know my thoughts, and see if there be any wicked way in me" (Ps. cxxxix. 23, 24), or with St. John, "Lord, Thou knowest all things, Thou knowest that I love Thee" (John xxi. 17); but words of fear for every one who would fain keep back any thing in his outer or inner life from the Lord.—Ch. iii. 4. Observe the gracious manner in which the Lord recognizes and sets His seal of allowance to the good which any where He finds.—From VAUGHAN: Ch. ii. 10. Christ says to each one of us, *Be thou faithful:* use well the talent that I have given thee; forget not Who gave it; forget not Who will call for an account of it.—From BONAR: Ch. iii. 7: *He that hath the keys of David.* The key (1) Of David's house, (2) Of David's castle, (3) Of David's city, (4) Of David's treasure-house, (5) Of David's banqueting-house.—Ver. 20. Note here (1) the *love* of Christ: in the message as addressed to Laodicea, the unloving and unlovable; (2) the *patience* of Christ: *I stand at the door* ; (3) the *earnestness* of Christ: *I knock;* (4) the *appeal* of Christ: *If any man will hear my voice and open the door;* (5) the *promise* of Christ: *I will come in to him and will sup with him, and he with Me.*—Ver. 21. We have here—I. The battle; II. The victory; III. The reward. I. *The battle:* The Christian's life in this world a warfare: (1) Inner warfare; (2) Outer warfare; (3) Daily warfare; (4) Warfare not fought with human arms; (5) Warfare in which we are sharers with Christ. II. *The victory:* multitudinous as is the battle. Sure through Him Who Himself overcame. Individual. III. *The reward:* (1) A throne; (2) Christ's throne.]

SECTION FOURTH.

Second Grand Vision. Heaven-picture of the Seals.
(Chs. iv., v.)

General.—a. Translation of the Seer to Heaven. A vision within a vision, at the same time denoting a momentary translation into the light of the consummation.—The import of *Heaven* in the whole of Sacred Writ, from Gen. i. 1 throughout, is at once cosmical and spiritual. Heaven is, so to speak, the plastic symbol of religion,

and especially of Christianity. God's Kingdom, a Kingdom of Heaven.

b. The Throne, the Sitter thereon, and His Government. The Throne indescribable. The figure of the Enthroned One is—and justly—not depicted, but only symbolized, approximately, by precious stones, having the hue of light and life. —The rainbow, or the glory of the Godhead, visible in the chromatic, seven-fold radiance of revelation, to the spirit-world —The twenty-four Elders on their thrones, or the elect in the lustre of perfect fellowship with God.—The white robes of consummation.—The ground-forms of Divine revelation: Lightnings, voices, thunders; see EXEG. NOTES.—The Seven Spirits of God, under the figure of eternally burning Lamps [Torches], symbols of the eternal living unity of light, life and love.—The glassy sea and the four Life-forms; see EXEG. NOTES.—God's governance under the figure of these Life-forms.—The second doxology (ver. 11) a development of the first (chap. i. 6)—an expression of the ever richer revelation of God.

c. The Sealed Book of the Course of the World. Lamentation and Consolation. The course of the world as a *completed* book, or the counsel of God. As a *sealed* book, or the nocturnal gloom of worldly history. As a *terrible* book, in the apparent impossibility of unsealing it. As a book *full of wonders of salvation,* destined to be opened by the Lion of Judah in His victory. Christ the Crucified and Risen One, the Opener. Explainer and Transfigurer [*Erklärer und Verklärer*] of the book with seven seals. The seals of guilt [*Schuld*=indebtedness to justice], of imputation of guilt, of judgment, of the curse, of death, of the fear of death, and of despair—how Christ looses them and resolves them all into deliverance and mercy, through His redemption. Even the Gospel is to the unenlightened world a dark book of fate, but through the enlightenment which proceeds from Christ, even the dark destiny of the world shall itself become a Gospel.

d. The Lion as the Lamb. The unity of Lion and Lamb, or the absolute victorious power of perfect love and suffering. Divine omnipotence and Divine endurance in their general unity as exhibited in the history of the world, and in their concentrated unity exhibited in Christ. The Lamb, the centre of all life, (1) of the Throne of God, (2) of the four ground-forms of His governance, (3) of the chosen presbyters of the Old and the New Covenant.—The symbolic appearance of the Lamb, see EXEG NOTES.—*As it had been slain,* or the infinite import of the historic phase of Christ and Christianity. Christ has taken the office of solving the riddle of worldly history from the hand of the Father.

e. The Cultus of the Lamb. The third doxology, or the New Song: the type of Christian cultus. An antiphony between the beatified human world and the holy angel-world; a symphony of all good spirits and all creatures, to the praise of the Lamb and the glorification of the all-ruling God.

Special.—[Chs. iv.–v.] The great vision of the Providence of God.—[Chap. iv. 2, 3.] The power of Providence: God on His Throne ; [ver. 4.] the aim of Providence: consummation of the spirit-world, represented by the twenty-four Elders; [ver. 5.] *operations* of Providence: manifestations of the Spirits of God ; [ver. 6.] the *work* of Providence: the glassy sea, the billowy and yet transparent history of the world; [vers. 6 8.] the *organs* of Providence: the four Life-forms, or ground-forms of the Divine governance; [vers. 8–11.] *gloriousness* of Providence: its result a continuous doxology; [chap. iv. 1] *idea* of Providence: the sealed book. [Vers. 2, 3.] *Terrors* and *obscurities* of the *government* of Divine Providence. —[Ver. 4.] The weeping geniuses of humanity.— [Ver. 5.] *Weep not.* How many times these words appear in the New Testament, I ke *fear not*, or *be of good cheer*, an I similar heavenly words of encouragement.—[Vers. 5, 6.] The *light and all enlightening centre* of Providence: Christ as the Lamb and the Lion.—*Christianity*, or the Death and Resurrection of Christ in their infinite operation.— The Redemption [*Erlösung*] as the solving [*Lösung*] of all riddles of worldly history, of humanity and of the world.—The Elders, appearing, in their attributes, as heirs of perfect communion with God, as the trusted witnesses of His rule.— A Presbytery of God: Christological idea of men who are in affinity with God, and who, through Christ, are elevated into the position of heirs of God —[Vers. 8–14.] Third and completely developed doxology.—Every delineation of the Lion is false, which does not, at the same time, permit the Lamb to be clearly recognized. Every delineation of the Lamb is false, behind which the Lion vanishes. Only the Spirit of Christ can grasp this great contrast as a living unity. As so entirely a unity, that the Lion were not without the Lamb's nature, or the Lamb without the Lion's nature.—How Holy Scripture is reflected in the ideal Books which we meet with in the Apocalypse. There are few essential relations at the basis of the Bible which do not here appear in the form of Books.—The Christian cultus, reposing in its truth upon the heavenly cultus of all beings.—Sacred songs and new songs.— All sacred songs are outgushes of the one celestial New Song.—To the song of praise of creation and providence (ch. iv. 11) is added the song of praise of redemption (ch. v. 9).—The groundform of worship an antiphony, in which spirits occupying different stand-points exchange their blessed views.—The Amen in the synagogue and in Christian worship.

STARKE: QUESNEL: One who would know the mysteries of Heaven, must be free from earth.— *The Elders:* This figure here, as in the whole of this vision, is taken from the Temple at Jerusalem, David having instituted twenty-four orders of priests; these held their councils in the outer court of the Temple, the High Priest sitting in the midst upon his seat, and the four and twenty priests or elders sitting in a half-circle around him and before him on their seats. (The Seer has himself, ch xxi., suggested, as the import of the Elders, the twelve heads of the Tribes of Israel and the twelve Apostles; the appointment of the orders [or courses] of priests, however, is itself connected with the original duodecenary.) —The office of the Elders—nay, of all believers —is to comfort the mourning from God's Word and not to leave them without encouragement (Is. xl. 1). He who would emphatically comfort

another, must have sufficient grounds for his consolation to rest upon (John xvi. 33).

THOMAS NEWTON, *Dissertations on the Prophecies*, London, Dove (p. 528): Most of the best commentators divide the Apocalypse or Revelation into two parts—the book, βιβλίον, sealed with seven seals, and the little book, βιβλαρίδιον, as it is called several times. But it happens, unluckily, that according to their division the lesser book is made to contain as much as, or more than, the larger; whereas, in truth, the little book is nothing more than a part of the sealed book, and is added as a codicil or appendix to it.

DE ROUGEMONT, *La Révélation* (see p. 73): Le trône était environné d'un arc-en-ciel, qui avait la couleur de l'émeraude. L'arc-en-ciel est le signe de l'alliance de Dieu avec l'humanité tout entière, issue de Noé, et il annonce ici que les révélations subséquentes auront pour objet l'histoire future des nations. L'émeraude est verte, et le vert est la couleur de l'espérance.

H. W. RINCK (see p. 73): *Die Zeichen der letzten Zeit.—And I wept much, etc.* John had a priestly heart, he was a fellow-partaker in the Kingdom of Christ (chap. i. 9); the Kingdom of God was more to him than his life—"If I forget thee, let my right hand be forgotten" (Ps. cxxxvii. 5 [G. V.]) was the key-note of his soul more truly than it was that of the Babylonish captivity;—he longed for the establishment of Jesus' Kingdom on earth more than did Daniel for the re establishment of Jerusalem and Israel (Dan. ix.). Such being his feelings, we can understand the tears that he wept because none was found worthy to open the Book of the Future.

Literature. ROFFHACK, *Schöpfung und Erlösung nach Offenb.* 4 u. 5., Barmen, 1866.

[From M. HENRY: Chap. iv. 1. Those who well improve the discoveries they have had of God already, are prepared thereby for more and may expect them.—Vers. 8, 9. Note here the object of adoration: 1. One God, *the Lord God Almighty*, unchangeable and everlasting; 2. Three Holies in this one God, the Holy Father, the Holy Son, and the Holy Spirit.—Vers. 10, 11. Observe, 1. The Object of worship—the same as in the preceding verses. 2. The acts of adoration: (1.) *They fell down before Him that sat on the Throne;* they discovered the most profound humility, reverence, and godly fear. (2.) *They cast down their crowns, etc.;* they gave God the glory of the holiness wherewith He had crowned their souls on earth, and the honor and happiness with which He crowns them in Heaven. (3.) The words of adoration: *Thou art worthy, etc.;* a tacit acknowledgment that God was exalted far above all blessing and praise; He was worthy to receive glory, but they were not worthy to praise, nor able to do it according to His infinite excellences. 4. The ground and reason of their adoration, which is three-fold: (1.) He is the Creator of all things, the first Cause. (2.) He is the Preserver of all things, and His preservation is a continual creation. (3.) He is the final Cause of all things; *for Thy pleasure they are and were created* —Chap. v. 5, 6. Christ is a *Lion*, to conquer Satan; a *Lamb*, to satisfy the justice of God.—He appears with the marks of His sufferings upon Him, to show that He intercedes in heaven in the virtue of His satisfaction.—Vers.

8–14. It is just matter of joy to all the world, to see that God does not deal with men in a way of absolute power and strict justice, but in a way of grace and mercy through the Rede·mer. He governs the world, not merely as a Creator and Lawgiver, but as our God and Saviour.—Here observe, 1. The object of worship—*the Lamb.* It is the declared will of God that all men *should honor the Son as they honor the Father;* for He has the same nature. 2. Posture of the worshippers —*they fell down before Him;* gave Him not an inferior sort of worship, but the most profound adoration. 3. The instruments used in their adoration—*harps and vials;* prayer and praise should always go together. 4. The matter of their song. (1.) They acknowledge the infinite fitness and worthiness of the Lord Jesus for the great work of opening the decrees and executing the counsel and purposes of God; *Thou art worthy, etc ;* every way sufficient for the work and deserving of the honor. (2·) They mention the grounds and reasons of this worthiness — Ver. 9. Christ has *redeemed* His people from the bondage of sin, guilt, and Satan; redeemed them *to God ;* set them at liberty to serve Him and to enjoy Him —Ver. 10. He has highly *exalted* them. When the elect of God were made slaves by sin and Satan, in every nation of the world, Christ not only purchased their liberty for them, but the highest honor and preferment, making them *kings,* to rule over their own spirits, and *to overcome the world and the evil one;* and *priests,* giving them access to Himself, and liberty to offer up spiritual sacrifices. And *they shall reign on the earth;* they shall with Him judge the world at the great day —From THE COMPREHENSIVE COMMENTARY: Ch. iv. The Lord Jesus, "having overcome the sharpness of death, hath opened the kingdom of heaven to all believers;" and if we look unto Him by faith, and obediently attend to His voice, whilst He calls us to "set our affections on things above," we shall, by the teaching of the Holy Spirit, behold the glory of our reconciled God on His "throne of grace;" be encouraged by the engagements of His everlasting covenant, and draw nigh in humble boldness with our worship; notwithstanding the terrors of His justice, and the awful curses of His broken law. (SCOTT.)—Chap. v. 9. Redemption by the blood of Christ (mark it well, O my soul!) is the ground-work of the majestic, triumphant song of praise in heaven; and a disposition to join in it, our chief capacity for, and actual happiness in, time and eternity. (ADAMS.)—From VAUGHAN: Chap. iv. We may learn hence the reality of a heavenly world, and of its concern and connection with this;—facts full of confusion and discomfiture to the worldly and sinners, but of comfort and encouragement to the Christian.]

SECTION FIFTH.

Earth-picture of the Seven Seals.   Their opening.
(*Ch. vi.*)

General.—The course of the world in its totality—considered with reference to its predominantly external and predominantly internal phases. Sublime picture of the Four Riders. The cry, as with a voice of thunder, *Come and see! Come and see* that Christ, upon the white horse, precedes the three dark riders, that He has dominion over them, and that He has brought them into His service, into the service of His Kingdom. *Come and see:* the bright fundamental thought of world-history, so dark in respect of its predominant visible aspect. The four Horses, or world-history a *course,* in eternal onward motion. Each horse has its rider, *i. e.,* its idea; its conduct and tendency, regulated by that idea; its goal and purpose. The main tendency of all, however, is regulated and defined by the tendency of Christ. The group of four Riders may be classified under two heads, *viz.,* Christ or personal Victory, contrasted with impersonal War, the desolator of person·l life. For as Christ constitutes the three dark Riders His followers and presses them into His service, so the second Rider may regard the third and fourth as his esquires, War being attended by Dearth, in the first place, and secondly by Pestilence.

1. *History of the world in its predominantly human aspect. First Seal.* Christ, as the Logos, also the dynamic Force, the fundamental and leading Power of worldly history—a Power victorious in holy suffering. The great Victor in all the wars of worldly history—(1.) He has conquered, (2.) He is conquering, (3) He will conquer.—*Second Seal. War.* Its dark side or abnormity. Its light side in the train of Christ. Comp. the author's pamphlet: *Vom Krieg und vom Sieg.*— *Third Seal. Dearth.* Terrestrial sufferings. Social sufferings. Wealth and poverty. Usury and pauperism. Care of the poor. Socinlistic projects. Infinite increase of pauperism through the luxury of those that are at ease; infinite decrease of it through the plainness and simplicity of Christian sentiment and classical culture.— *Fourth Seal. Death.* Circumstances of mortality. Pestilences. Poisons. Wild beasts. Suicides. Lust and cruelty in their reciprocal action. Death of children. Offerings to Moloch. Macrobiotic counter-agencies.—2. *History of the world in its predominantly spiritual aspect. Fifth Seal.* The Martyr-history of the Kingdom, as the kernel of the history of the world: the suffering Christ. The martyrs, beginning with Abel. In respect of human wickedness, slain on the field of the curse, without the sacred camp, on the Place of a Skull; in respect of the Divine counsel, sacrificed on God's altar, buried beneath the altar. Connection of all martyr-sufferings with the holy sacrifice and expiatory sufferings of Christ in the centre. All martyr-sufferings for the sake of God's Word (or for the sake of truth, in the heathen world) cleansed from sin, purified and perfected through the sufferings of Christ. The blood of the heavenly-minded, shed by the earthly-minded, animated by the spirit of intercession, and yet a real historic impulse after justice, demanding recompense. Old Testament martyrologies (Matt. xxiii.). Apostolic martyrologies. Old-Catholic martyrologies. Mediæval Protestant martyrologies. Evangelic martyrologies. The grand history of spiritual martyrdoms. Even John and all like-minded with him, though they died a natural death, are true martyrs. True martyrdom faithfulness in confession, enduring unto death. Witness as confession. There are none save *persecuted* confessions—no *persecuting* ones. Christianity it-

self a confession. Consolation concerning all martyr suffering, and pacification of all martyrs. Pacification in view of the whole matter: *a.* The great company of sufferers; *b.* The Divine counsel concerning the completion of their number; *c.* Rest in patience and in the hope of perfect retribution; *d.* The white robes beyond this life, glistening ever clearer in historic lustre even in this present world. The memory of martyrs is revived even through the canonization of their murderers. The terrors of the Inquisition are, from the fact of their becoming more and more an object of detestation to mankind, also a precursory rehabilitation of the slain. —*Sixth Seal. The triumphant Christ.* Symbolic presages of the Coming of Christ, spiritual and cosmical: the great earthquake. Darkening of the sun and moon (Matt. xxiv.). The sun of the spiritual life veils itself in black; the moon of the natural life becomes as red as blood. The stars of Heaven fall, *i. e.*, our old cosmical system is di solved. The old Heaven and the old earth-phase (mountains, islands) vanish in the process of metamorphosis. Dissolution of the old social order of things: the kings, *etc.*, are afraid (ver. 15). The Coming of the Lord to judgment; a coming to the terror of all the earthly-minded (ver. 16). The great Day of Wrath (see Zeph.) Its convulsing effect. The great Day of Wrath also, however, the great Day of final Redemption. *The Seventh Seal*, yet to be opened, the envelope of all those Trumpets calling to conflict and repentance which, as judgments of God, complement and transrupt the course of the world.

Special.—[Ver. 2.] Attributes of the First Rider, or the individual traits in His appearance.—[Ver. 4.] Symbolic traits of the Second Rider; [ver. 5] of the third; [ver. 8] the fourth. —[Ver. 4.] *War* as a Divine ordinance; to him it was *given* to take peace from the earth. To him a great sword was *given.*—[Ver. 5.] *Famine* or *Dearth* on earth, a distressful state with which the celestial ones are acquainted (ver. 6), which they modify, limit, and direct.—[Ver. 8.] *Death* as a judgment; as a judgment transformed into a blessing. The Death of Christ, the death of Death.—Hades also in the service of Christ.— [Vers. 9 11.] The souls of the martyrs: they are all in existence still, and visible to the eye of the Seer.—How their faithfulness to the Word of God and their witness of Jesus were imputed to them as a crime.—Their common character.— As the avengement of blood contains a germ of righteous retribution, so the judgment of God is a great and holy analogue of unholy avengement of blood.—White robes: a favorite image of John; a favorite adornment of the Church.— Wait a *little* while. Sadness and peace in the consolatory assurance that the sufferers for Christ's sake constitute a great company.—The anxious question of the weak human heart as to how God the All-Ruler, in His holiness which hates evil and in His truth whereby He is the Covenant-God of the pious, can suffer His children, servants, and witnesses to be slain by His enemies —suffer them to be slain for His name's sake, and even make them wait so long for His retribution.—The heavenly answer to this question. —[Ver. 17.] The Day of Wrath, in relation to

its appearances in the Scriptures (or as predicted) and in the history of the world (or as presaged).—The Day of Wrath in its effects.

STARKE: The Rider on the white horse is Christ; this is clearly manifest from ch. xix. 11-16. A white horse was held in particular esteem by the heathen; when the kings of Persia wished to sacrifice to the sun, they offered up a white horse to that luminary. It gave prestige to generals to ride before their armies on white horses; victors used white horses in celebrating their triumphs. and the Romans had their triumphal chariots drawn by white horses.—*Red* is a sign of war; hence the Persians and Lacedemonians wore red garments when they went to war.—The color of the horse in ver. 5 is indicative of hunger, which makes people look black and parched (Lam. iv. 2, 7, 8).—*A balance in his hand.* Such as spices were weighed with. Indicative of want is the fact that provisions are not measured, as usual, by the bushel, but weighed by the scale (Lev. xxvi. 26); not the greatest want and famine are indicated, however, for where it is necessary to weigh out grain, there is, indeed, scarcity, but not yet famine.— Χλωρός, pale, sallow, betokens the pale yellow hue of dry and withering herbs and leaves of trees; thus Constantius was called Chlorus, on account of his paleness. Because Death is commonly called pale, and makes men of a clayey hue, yea, turns them to clay, this figure of a *pale* horse is most appropriate.—On the Fifth Seal. QUESNEL: The saints pray for the second Coming of Christ just as patriarchs and righteous men of old sighed for His first Coming (Ps. xiv. 7; Luke x. 24).—The expressions relative to the occurrences under this Sixth Seal are taken from Isa. ii. 19-21; xiii. 9, 10; xxiv. 23; xxxiv. 2, 4; Ezek. xxxii. 7, 8; Joel iii. 15, 16; Matt. xxiv. 29; Luke xxi. 25.

The exposition of the Seals is placed by Starke on the Church-historical platform, and the alternative is discussed as to whether the first five Seals are already fulfilled, or whether the fulfillment of all the Seals is still future. Starke gives the grounds for (and therefore, relatively against) each hypothesis.

GRAEBER, *Versuch einer historischen Erklärung, etc.* (see p. 73): First Seal. A white, shining horse, and he that sat upon it had a bow, and there was given unto him a crown [*Kranz*= wreath], and he went forth conquering, and that he might (or should) conquer. This first image exhibits to our view not a pagan, but a Christian Victory—to this effect is the super cription which we must give to this picture. The Rider is himself first described, and then his work is set forth. His work is victory. He went forth conquering and to conquer, *i. e.*, he went from one victory to another. His victory was a triumphal procession through the world How sublime and how comfortable is it that the first thing revealed to us concerning the government and dominion of Christ on earth, is His victory. His first procedure is victory, and He goes from one victory to another, and ends with victory! According to this, all that He does is victory. He cannot do otherwise than triumph. Fortune changes not under His government, as it does in the wars of earthly kings, nor are His victories purchased at great expense, like those of earthly sovereigns, b it He conquers always—absolutely. Whoso in these wars will not suffer himself to be gained over to Christ's side as His friend, is judged as His foe. Every one is conquered—these to enjoy everlasting felicity, those to suffer the penalty of eternal damnation.—The *bow* (Ps. vii. 12, 13). He is armed, not with the sword, but with the bow, because the short sword puts the combatant in great danger of being wounded himself, whilst the bow, on the other hand, strikes from afar. (What relation does the "*sword* in His mouth" bear to the "*bow* in His hand?" The sword is, assuredly, His word; the bow, doubtless, is the operation of His Spirit, in its awakening as well as its judging power.)

POLLOCK, [*The Course of Time*]. *Der Lauf der Zeit, ein Gedicht in zehn Gesängen, übersetzt von Hey.* Hamburg, Perthes, 1830. On the Sixth Seal. An attempt to depict the cosmical crisis. ["Meantime the earth gave symptoms of her end; and all the scenery above proclaimed that the great last catastrophe was near. The sun at rising staggered and fell back, *etc.*"] (The idea that in decaying cosmical nature extremes constantly become more sharply prominent, is suggested, but not worked out with sufficient clearness. According to Scripture, moreover, the cosmical convulsion is first perceptible in earthly life.)

VAN OOSTERZEE, *De Oorlogsbode* (the messenger of war): *Tijdpreek in Augustus* 1870, '*s Gravenhage.* On ch. vi. 1-8. The theme: *De Oorlog en zijne ellenden, beschouwd in het licht der christelijke Heilsopenbaring.* "*Op de tweede vraag, wie hem beschikt, dezen rustverstoorder, antwoordt onze tekst veelbeteekenend, dat hem deze macht is gegeven.*

On the seven Seals, and particularly the four Riders, there is a variety of special literature. See LILIENTHAL, *Archivarius*, p. 822. See *Introduction*, p. 74.—L. HOFACKER, *Ueber das weisse Pferd, etc.* Tübingen, 1830.—CUNNINGHAM, *Dissertation on the Seals, etc.* London.

[From M. HENRY: Ver. 16. *The wrath of the Lamb.* Though Christ be a *Lamb*, yet He can be angry, even to wrath, and *the wrath of the Lamb* is exceeding dreadful; for if the Redeemer, that appeases *the wrath of God*, Himself be our wrathful enemy, ("through our rejection of His atonement,") where shall we have a friend to plead for us? *They* perish without remedy, who perish by the wrath of the Redeemer.—Ver. 17. As men have their day of opportunity, and their seasons of grace, so God has His day of righteous wrath; and when that *day comes*, the most stout-hearted sinners will not *be able to stand* before Him.—From BONAR: Ver. 10. *How long?* These words occur frequently in Scripture, and are spoken in various ways: 1. As from man to man; 2. As from man to God; 3. As from God to man. Passing by the first mode of their usage —comp Job viii. 2; xix. 2; Ps. iv. 2; lxii. 3—we come to the other two. 1. *The Words as from man to God;* comp. Ps. vi. 3; xiii. 1; xxxv. 17; lxxiv. 10; lxxix. 5; lxxxix. 46; xc. 13; xciv. 3, 4; Hab. i. 2; Rev. vi. 10. In these passages they are the language, (1) *Of complaint.* Not murmuring or fretting, but what the Psalmist calls "complaining," an expression of weariness

under burdens. (2.) *Submission.* (3.) *Inquiry.* (4.) *Expectation.* 2. *The words as from God to man;* comp. Ex. x. 3; xvi. 28; Josh. xviii. 3; 1 Kings xvii. 21; Ps. lxxxii. 2; Prov. i. 22; vi. 9; Jer. iv. 14. Taking up these words of God as spoken to different classes, we would dwell on the following points: (1). *Long-suffering.* It is this that is expressed in the passage in Jeremiah. (2.) *Expostulation.* How long halt ye between two opinions? (3) *Entreaty.* God beseeches man. (4.) *Earnestness.* (5.) *Sorrow.* (6.) *Upbraiding.* (7.) *Warning.*]

SECTION SIXTH.

Ideal heavenly World picture of the Seven Penitential Trumpets. (Ch. vii.)

General.—The Invisible Church here and beyond: here, the *sealed*—militant conquerors; beyond, blessed conquerors. The Sealing, and its doctrinal import δοκιμή characterized by James as δικαιοῦν; Rom. v. 4; James ii. 21). The neglect of the distinction between justification and sealing has resulted in a sad obscuration of the evangelic fundamental doctrine of justification, especially in three great theological school-circles. According to the idea of the Apostle James, Abraham was *justified*, Gen. xv., and *sealed*, Gen. xxii. Since justification always takes place in a forum of justice, and since there are different sorts of forums (see the Art. by TERSTEEGEN in Herzog's *Encyklopädie*), James could speak of justification *as an imputation of faith as righteousness*, and apply the term of δικαιοῦν to sealing. In the one case, the court of conscience was intended, in the other the forum of the Church contemplated ("and he was called the friend of God"). See the Lange *Com.* on James ii. [and on Rom. v.].—The Sealing has reference not solely to the last time, but, through the whole succession of the New Testament time (which is, indeed, in a general sense denominated the last time), to the assurance of saints in face of the temptations of this world. That is, the Sealing in ch. vii. relates to the Trumpets in ch. viii. That which the four Angels are stationed on the four corners of the earth to accomplish—namely, to loose the four winds of the earth, the spirit of the world in all its ground-forms, upon the earth and the sea, to injure them: upon the theocratic Divine institution, or the Church, and upon national life, to purge them through great temptations—this, we repeat, is fulfilled in the judgments of the Trumpets. In reference, however, to these temptations, which shake and imperil the visible Church, the invisible Church is represented as assured—assured, partly through the sealing effected here and partly through the entry of the blessed into the Church Triumphant beyond. When it is declared that the Angels may not loose the winds of temptation until the sealing is consummated, in the priority of the time of the sealing the priority of strength in the sealed is expressed. They are established through the gift of the grace of steadfastness. In chap. xiv. we learn that their approval was conditioned by uprightness, purity, and the avoidance of falsehood, but we must first know that their sealing is entirely a work of grace.—On the import of the *four winds* from the four corners of the earth, the *earth* itself, the *sea,* the *trees,* the *rising of the sun,* the *injuring,* the number 144,000, see the EXEG. NOTES.

We have already demonstrated that the literal interpretation of the twelve Tribes of Israel as having reference to the Jewish nation in the last time, is utterly untenable. The symbolic designation of the chosen servants of God by the name of the spiritual Israel, is, however, sufficient guaranty for the fact that the Apostle has in view the general hope of a restoration of Israel at the same time that he contemplates a more extended class of elect persons. For as the symbolic name of Israel does not exclude believers from the Gentiles, neither does it shut out believing Jews, or the hope that Israel, as a people, will yet exercise faith in their long neglected Messiah. The well-known Judaistic apprehension of the Sealing—discussed by us in the Exegetical Division—bears upon it not only the exegetical stain of gross literalness, but also the blot of dogmatical error, in maintaining that in the end of the times Israel could again possess national prerogatives in the Kingdom of God, when it was precisely on account of its pretensions to such prerogatives in the midst of the ages that the nation incurred rejection.

Furthermore, the architectonics and symmetry of the table of the sealed plead for its symbolical character. The special duodecenary, running through the general duodecenary and multiplied invariably by the æonic number 1000, is the ever recurring expression of sacred fullness, sacred completeness. Again, the free arrangement and modification of the list of the twelve Tribes (see EXEG. NOTES) are in favor of this symbolical character; and it is no less supported by the perfect coördination of individual Tribes in respect of the number selected from each. We must here repeat the statement previously made elsewhere, namely, that the selection does not exclude further circles of blessed ones. The same literal exegesis which, on the one hand, so exceptionally favors Judaism, would, on the other hand, inflict most serious detriment upon it if it were proposed to apprehend the text as declaring that many Jews should, in the last times, become believers, but that their number, however, should not exceed 144,000. The sealed are the true stand-holders of the living Church throughout the ages of the Church, the pillars, against which many who are weak lean for support.

This truth is immediately expressed by the second part of the vision, the vision of the innumerable throng of blessed ones. These are characterized by the following items: 1. They form a countless throng; in antithesis to doctrinal particularism. 2. They are from all nations and tribes and peoples and tongues; in antithesis to exegetical particularism, which stamps the Apocalypse with a Judaistic tendency. 3. They are perfected; they stand before the Throne of God and the Lamb, clothed in white robes—the adornment of holiness—and palms—as tokens of victory, peace and festival—in their hands; in antithesis to hierarchic particularism, which treats of an immediate entry into blessedness in conformity with mediæval ideas (confining the privilege to martyrs, monks, priests, ascetics

who have built up a holiness of works, and calendar saints). 4 Their cry: The salvation is with our God, etc ;—thoroughly evangelic; it is even a protest against all righteousness of works and doctrine. With our God and the Lamb: in antithesis both to pietistic-exclusive and deistic-exclusive forms of belief. 5. The Amen and the song of praise of the whole angel or spirit world

The great Heaven-picture of the perfected is accompanied by heavenly instructions concerning the origin of the blessed, their endless train, their character and destiny. Even the faith of a John failed to grasp the origin of these innumerable throngs of blessed ones and the height at which they had arrived. But one of the Elders, to whom the depths of the history of the Kingdom are no secret, vouchsafes him an explanation: He explains (1) *whence* they have come—*viz. out of great tribulation.* All come from unknown depths of suffering, of conflict—not simply from visible martyr-sufferings (see Rom. vi.). They have all washed their robes and made them white in the blood of the Lamb With the depth of their experience of suffering corresponds the depth of their experience of salvation: they all recognize and confess the world-reconciling Atonement. But, again, with these depths, corresponds the height of their goal. Thus we have (2) an explanation as to *whither* they have arrived—*viz. before the Throne of God,* to a blessed priestly service. after the type of life in the Temple; to the perfect satisfaction of every longing, and to freedom from all heat, after the image of a life of business toil and wandering (Ps. xxiii.): to the full and comfortable discovery of the joyful harvest of the seed of tears, yea, to the discovery of the heavenly pearl to which every tear has turned (see EXEG. NOTES).

Special.—[Ver. 1] Various forms of the spirit of the world and its temptations.—Temptation as Divine dispensations.—Limited as to time place and degree.—Their design.—[Vers. 2, 3. Different moments in the development of salvation—especially *sealing.* — The awakened man fall; but it is the distinction of the *sealed* that they have made good their faith in the battle of life, particularly in moments of great sacrifice —Men in Christ.—[Vers. 4-8.] The heroes of Israel, the heroes of David, as types of God's heroes.—Chosen stones, flowers, animals, men Christians.—The Twelve Tribes as types of the charisms.—Consecration of a natural gift to gracious gift, through the gift of the Spirit.—Both gifts are gifts of grace in the broader sense of the term—the first as a gift of unmerited creative favor, the second as a gift of unmerited redemptive salvation.—The Twelve Tribes types of the fullness of the charisms in the Kingdom of God.—The choice of them, a type of the personally and historically chosen.—The number 1,000 as a figure of the continual presence of Christ in His Church through the whole æon.—Comparison of particular characteristic Tribes: Judah and Joseph; Simeon and Levi; Joseph and Benjamin.—[Ver. 9.] The visible and the invisible Church.—The two spheres of the invisible Church, in this world and in the Beyond.—In the visible Church, the visible appearance of the Church may be greatly obscured. If the visible Church becomes invisible *as the Church,* the invisible Church emerges into visibility. This remark applies to every time, but is particularly true of the last time.—The heavenly Festival of Palms.—[Ver. 10.] The heavenly confession of the blessed.—Their song.—[Vers. 11, 12.] The song of praise of all spirits concerning the consummation of the blessed.—Doxologies of men and angels.—[Ver. 13.] The catechism of John which the Elder institutes, compared with the catechism of Peter (John xxi.)—[Ver. 14.] Humility of the great Apostle as manifested in his answer to the question of the Elder.—The great, eternal, pilgrim and festal procession of blessed souls from earth to the heavenly Home.—[Ver. 15.] The Throne — Service in the Temple.—The glory of God over them.—Analogous passages: Is. xxv. 4 sqq.; xlix. 10; Pss. xxiii., xci., cxxvi.; Is. lxvi. 13.

STARKE: God has numbered His elect, but their number is known to Him alone. If He has counted the *hairs* of the faithful, He has surely counted their *persons.*—The same number in each Tribe, when there were some Tribes that were more numerous than others, shows that God bears the same gracious will to all believers, of whatsoever race or people they be. (The text, however, has reference to *sealed* persons, and the numbers are symbolical.)—Ver. 13. The best and fittest mode of instruction—especially for those who are young and simple—is by question and answer, Gen. iii. 9; Luke ii. 46, 47 (!).

A. H. W. BRANDT, *Anleitung zum Lesen der Offenb. Joh.* (see p. 73): The sealed. John does not see them even in spirit; much less are they to be seen with the bodily eye in their substantiality on earth. Nevertheless they are a people of God on earth, having His Spirit, and numbered by Him, in the sense of Matt. x. 30. They are described, in prophetic wise, by their Old Testament type, whose names and Tribes are presented not in the single 12, but by 12 × 12, and multiplied by thousands. It is the true Israel, baptized with the Spirit and consisting of all (?) the servants of God who are born of the Spirit.—Vers. 9-12. *And behold! A great multitude.* This excites the astonishment of the Seer, which was not the case with the preceding occurrence; he, indeed, did not see the sealed, but this multitude visibly appears in Heaven. (A highly significant contrast. Concerning the *sealed* on *earth* he learns only the tribal characters and numbers by an *auricular wonder;* the *blessed,* on the other hand, are presented to his contemplation in personal distinctness by an *ocular wonder.*)

[From M. HENRY: Ver. 3. God has particular care and concern for His own servants in times of temptation and corruption, and He has a way to secure them from the common infection: He first establishes them, and then He tries them; He has the timing of their trials in His own hand.—Ver. 9. *Before the throne, and before the Lamb.* In acts of religious worship we come nigh to God, and are to conceive ourselves as in His special presence; and we must come to God by Christ; *the throne* of God would be inaccessible to sinners, were it not for a Mediator. —Vers. 13-17. Here we have a description of

the honor and happiness of those who have faithfully served the Lord Jesus Christ, and suffered for Him. Note, 1. The low and desolate state they had formerly been in. The way to heaven lies through many *tribulations;* but *tribulation,* how *great* soever, shall not *separate us from the love of God.* 2. The means by which they had been prepared for the great honor and happiness they now enjoyed; they had *washed their robes, and made them white in the blood of the Lamb.* It is not the blood of the martyrs themselves but *the blood of the Lamb,* that can wash away sin, and make the soul pure and clean in the sight of God. 3. The blessedness to which they are now advanced, being thus prepared for it. They are happy. (1) In their station, for *they are before the throne of God night and day,* and He *dwells among them;* they are in that *presence where there is fullness of joy.* (2) In their employment, for *they serve* God continually, without weakness, drowsiness, or weariness; heaven is a state of service, though not of suffering; of rest, but not of sloth; it is a praising, delightful rest. (3) In their freedom from all the inconveniences of this present life; *a.* From all want, and sense of want; *They hunger and thirst no more. b.* From all sickness and pain; they shall never be *scorched by the heat of the sun any more.* 4. In the love and conduct of the Lord Jesus; *He shall feed them, He shall lead them to living fountains of waters.* (5) In being delivered from all sorrow, or occasion of it; *God shall wipe away all tears from their eyes.*]

SECTION SEVENTH.

The Seven Penitential Trumpets. Earth-picture.
(*Chaps. viii. 1—ix. 21.*)

General.—Since there is an increase of disagreement in the different expositions of this eighth chapter and by consequence an augmented insecurity attaching to any exposition of it hitherto offered, there is an increased demand for caution in the theoretic and practical application of it.

Many, for instance, consider ch vii. as an episode, and affirm an immediate connection of ch. viii. with ch. vi. We, on the contrary, regard ch. vii. as the heavenly phase of the Earth-picture which follows it in the vision of the Trumpets. Or, in other words the Seven Trumpets are a loosing of the four winds from the four corners of the earth, in order to the injury of the Church and national life (earth and sea). In accordance with this view, we have to do altogether with darkenings of the visible Church, with spiritual occurrences presented under comical forms. These darkenings are agreeably to the conditions of the Church, judgments; for individual Christians, they are temptations [or *testings*]; as dispensations of the Lord, they are admonitions and arousing summonses to repentance and to combat—and, hence, *Trumpets.*

The *silence in Heaven for the space of half an hour* denotes that heavenly bracing and arming for which the whole great *hour of temptation* [chap. iii. 10] gives occasion.

Even the Seven Angels with the Trumpets must restrain themselves and wait for the right moment, like the Four Angels in the preceding chapter. Their waiting has a common purpose with that of the Four Angels. The latter waited for the accomplishment of the Divine work of seal-ing; the former wait for the consummation of the human prayers of the saints, which corres-pond with the work of sealing   Thus the spirit of prayer must constitute the Church's defence against the coming temptations. The prayers which ascend from earth must, however, be com-pleted in Heaven.   Their purification from earthly passion—*e. g.*, of confessionalism or na-tionalism—is first represented in the form of a supplementing with incense, which an Angel with a golden censer, in which much incense is given him for the heavenly altar of incense, adds to the prayers of the saints.   In accordance with Scripture, this figure can be understood solely of the heavenly intercession of the Spirit of Christ.   Next the other function of the Angel is represented—the emptying of the censer, previ-ously filled with fire from the altar, upon the earth.   This is indicative, without doubt, of the missions of the high-priestly Spirit of Christ from Heaven, the effects of which missions are figuratively represented in voices, thunders, lightnings, and earthquake (see the Exeg. Notes).   The two-fold continuance of Christ's work, in His eternal Spirit, consists in a direc-tion towards God in intercession, an I a direction towards the Church on earth in the outpourings of His Spirit, accompanied by the glowing coals of His high-priestly temper of love an I sacrifice.

The First Four Trumpets (see Exeg. Notes). [Ver 7.] The first darkening of the Church owes its origin to fanaticism; this appears as a judgment upon the lack of inward devotion and sincerity.—[Vers. 8, 9.] The second great tempta-tion [or trial] is the spread of fanaticism, in which a great mountain, a theocratic, ecclesiastico-po-litical institution, begins to burn and plunges into the sea—Christian national life.—[Vers. 10, 11.]   This calls forth the reactions of embitter-ment—deviations [or dissents], apostasies, indi-cated by the burning star which falls upon the rivers and fountains.—[Ver. 12.]   A result of these three destructive an I corruptive agencies, which, with all their contrasts, work together, is the great spiritual diminution of the *sunlight* of revelation, the *moonlight* of natural revelation (which, amid all the advances of natural science, may still become obscured), and the light which proceeds from spiritual *stars* in the Church.

The Last Three Trumpets.   These are distin-guished from the first four Trumpets and raised above them, primarily in that they are heralded by an *Eagle*, which flies through the midst of Heaven and proclaims their approach, and se-condly by the Eagle's designation of them as *three woes* upon those who dwell on the earth.   We remark here, by way of addition, that the scope of the first woe is accurately defined as the sphere of the Fifth Trumpet (ch. ix 1 11).   No less definite is the determination of the sphere of the second woe as the sphere of the Sixth Trumpet (ch. ix. 12-21).   As chs. x. and xi. 1-14 relate to the seven sealed Thunders, and in a sense form a real episode between the Trumpets, it might be as well to regard the second woe un-der a formal aspect, as closed with ch. ix. 21, as to conceive of it as continued through ch. x.,—in accordance with the material point of view to which we adhered at p. 226, to the adoption of

which we were particularly influenced by ch. x. 4. The lack of precision in the construction of this portion of the Apocalypse is owing to the fact that the Apocalyptist was in the main desirous of depicting, under the cycle of the Seven Thun-ders only the *activity* of the Two Witnesses, but found occasion to communicate the issue of their history as well.

From the material point of view, the incipient apostasy, depicted ch. xi. 1-14, certainly forms a supplement to the judgment of the Sixth Trumpet. The Eagle's cries of Woe upon the dwellers on the earth, are expressive of the fact that the Spi-rit of prophecy now, in lofty majesty announces th ee universal temptations [trials] which are to come upon all men and which shall be so mighty as to make it manifest from the outset that the majority will fall when exposed to them, whilst the minority, constituted by the sealed, will have to undergo the sorest afflictions and persecutions.

In respect of the Fifth and Sixth Trumpets, we refer to the Exegetical Notes. Although, for our own part, we regard our view as thoroughly grounded (especially by the circumstances that the locusts of the Fifth Trumpet so *torment* men as to plunge them in despair, without killing them, and that the fiery horses of the Sixth Trumpet *kill* men—which must, doubtless, be understood as significant of a spiritual killing), it is requisite that the security of the foundation of this exegesis should be additionally mani-fested before any superstructure is erected upon it.   The founding of homiletical and practical applications upon the traditional Church-histo-rical exposition. *e. g.*, upon the hypothesis that the locusts are Mohammedans and Apollyon the caliphs, and that the horses of the Sixth Trumpet are the second deluge of Mohammedans—the ap-pearance of the Turks (Sander; according to Von Meyer, the locusts denote the mediæval priesthood, the horses being Oriental barbarians in general)—has, like kindred expositions, not such evidence in its favor as evangelical preach-ing and instruction demand.

Especially noteworthy, in our eyes, is the fun damental thought that the destructive agencies depicted in the Seven Trumpets, are set forth in plastic figures of disturbed nature—in part, of the most horrible unnaturalness.   A rain of hai and fire, mingled with blood ; a great mountain plunging, burning, into the sea; a star fa ling from Heaven, and, burning like a torch, poison ing many rivers and fountains ; sun, moon, an stars, shorn of a third of their brightnes —all consternating images of a disturbance of nature.   Under the Fifth Trumpet, however, the most terrific contradictions of nature are exhi bited : locusts that eat no green thing, but, on the contrary, sting men after the manner of scor pions; having hair like the hair of women, an teeth like lions' teeth, *etc.* ; these make their ap pearance as a mere prelude to the fiery horse of the Sixth Trumpet, which seem to drag thei riders along with them, which bite with thei snake-like tails as with mouths, and vomit fro their mouths fire, smoke and brimstone.   Bu not until the Seventh Trumpet is the contradic tion of nature consummated in the figures of th Dragon, the Beast, and the Woman who rides upo the Beast.   With a master-touch at which we ca but marvel, evil is here throughout delineated in extravagant contradictions, as unnaturalness.

Special.—We note only such items as appear to us to be more or less firmly established.—Darkenings of the Church, judgments of God.—The Trumpets of God—Divine judgments upon the unfaithful—as summonses of the faithful to battle, and as calls to awakening and repentance for all.—[Ver. 1.] The silence in Heaven a sign of the great sympathy of the heavenly Church in its foreview of the trials of the Church on earth.—[Vers. 3, 4.] Completion of the prayers of believers by the intercession of Christ in Heaven.—[Ver. 5.] The fire of the health-bringing Spirit, falling from Heaven in order to the vitalizing of the Church, that the fire of *judgment* may not in the end fall upon her from Heaven.—[Ver. 6.] The series of Trumpets of judgment and repentance, a continual climactic succession, in accordance with the increasing development of mankind.—[Ver. 7.] Fanaticism, a mixture of frost and fire (icy coldness of heart and carnal heat of the imagination), mingled with blood.—[Ver. 8.] What can be understood, in a spiritual sense, by a burning mountain, falling into the sea?—[Vers. 10, 11.] Since Satan has been styled a star, falling from Heaven, we may designate the falling star called Wormwood, apostasy, that has its origin in embitterment.—Intellectual or spiritual rivers, currents and fountains in humanity; their destinations and manifold empoisonment.—[Ver. 12.] Darkening of intellectual or spiritual lights of Christendom, and the sins which must have preceded such darkening.—[Ver. 13.] The Eagle of prophecy.—Warning cry of the Spirit of prophecy, concerning the whole earth.—As a woe-cry, it has reference to the earthly-minded.—The great dispensations of woe upon the earth are, incontrovertibly, great general temptations (no cry of woe was heard at the forthgoing of the three sombre horsemen).—[Ch. ix. 1.] The abyss, as the middle region between Hades and hell.—[Vers. 2-11.] The soul-sufferings of humanity, accompanying its development, through the medium of Christianity, in the sphere of all spiritually unsound life.—All spiritual manifestations which, by reason of great internal contradictions, assume a monstrous character, judge themselves. They are, however, the means of the spiritual ruin of the blinded individuals who yield themselves up to them. Examples of such contradiction may be given in abundance, and consist, especially, of pretensions to high spiritual life, conjoined with enslaving ordinances (Montanism); pretensions to high Christian sanctity, conjoined with pitiless severity (Novatianism); pretensions to purity from the influence of world and state, conjoined with a system of robbery (Donatism), etc.—[Vers. 13-19.] Manifestations of *unnaturalness* in the religious and moral world are armies of corruptive and destructive agencies slaying spiritually and, indirectly, also physically.—The horses of corruption and destruction run away with their riders.—[Vers. 20, 21.] Impenitence under the judgments of God, considered under the antithesis of bigotry and the service of sin (see chs. xx. and xxi.). Bigotry and sensuality are prominent features of the most modern forms of corruption.

STARKE: This author gives a singular interpretation of the silence in Heaven as a time immediately succeeding the great judgment and destruction of the Antichristian kingdom, *viz.* the thousand years (a half hour!). In commenting on the consecutive Trumpets, Starke cites, as usual, two adverse explanations; the one class given by those who regard the Trumpets as fulfilled, the other by those who look upon them as to come.

CHRISTOPH PAULUS, *Blicke in die Weissagung, etc.* (see p. 73): Only the first judgment at the time of the first Trumpet, and the last at the time of the seventh Vial of Anger are accomplished by *hail;* they alone, *therefore* (because hail comes from above?), appear as a result of immediate Divine interference, as an immediate demonstration of Divine power. All the other judgments, from the second to the last, bear the stamp of historical occurrences (?).—*Judgment of the fourth Trumpet.* No remarkable occurrence on earth, no historical event distinguishes the time of the fourth Trumpet; nothing of importance happens, but a condition is gradually brought about in which the brightness of all Divine authority on earth is obscured; Church, laws and magistrates lose a considerable portion of their reputation and influence.

Literature.—VETTER, *Die sieben Posaunen,* Breslau, 1860 (see p. 75).

[From M. HENRY: Ch. viii. 3 5. Observe, 1. *All the saints* are a praying people; 2. Times of danger should be praying times, and so should times of great expectation; 3. *The prayers of the saints* themselves stand in need of the *incense* and intercession of Christ to make them acceptable and effectual, and there is provision made by Christ to that purpose; 4. *The prayers of the saints* come up before God in a cloud of *incense;* no prayer thus recommended was ever denied audience and acceptance; 5. These prayers that were thus accepted in heaven produced great changes upon earth in return to them.—Vers. 7-12. Note, 1. When the gospel is coldly received and not permitted to have its proper effect upon heart and life, it is usually followed by dreadful judgments. 2. God gives warning to men of His judgments before He sends them; He sounds an alarm by the written word, by ministers, by men's own consciences, and by the signs of the times; so that if a people be surprised, it is their own fault. 3. The anger of God against a people makes dreadful work with them; it embitters all their comforts, and makes even life itself bitter and burdensome. 4. God does not in this world stir up all His wrath, but sets bounds to the most terrible judgments. 5. Corruptions of doctrine and worship in the Church are themselves great judgments, and the usual causes and tokens of other judgments.—Ch. ix. 2. The Devil carries on his designs by blinding the eyes of men, by extinguishing light and knowledge, and promoting ignorance and error; he first deceives men, and then destroys them; wretched souls follow him in the dark, or they durst not follow him.—Ver. 16. He Who is the Lord of hosts has vast armies at His command, to serve His own purposes.

[From VAUGHAN: Ch. ix. 2. If men will not have heaven open to them, if they will break off the connection between earth and heaven, they must expect to have that between earth and hell opened.]

SECTION EIGHTH.

Veiled Heaven-Picture of the Seven Thunders.
(Ch. x. 1–11.)

General.—Here the mystery of prophecy is raised to a higher power within the mysterious Apocalypse itself. A contrast even is presented consisting in the fact that the Seven Thunders are to be specially sealed (ch. x. 4), whilst the Revelation in general is not to be sealed (ch. xxii. 10). We have already endeavored to explain the motive of this special sealing, and have at the same time set forth the hypothesis that the Seer has in a correspondent *exoteric* form furnished a sketch of the sealed *esoteric* contents of the Seven Thunders (ch. xi. 1-14). For Christianity can in no point be absolutely esoterical. It may also safely be assumed, that the elements of the Seven Thunders are to be found in the Apostolic Epistles and even in the Gospels. There is, *e. g.* (if we regard *thunder* as the symbol of a spiritual purification of the atmosphere and refreshment of life), an oppugnment of orthodoxistic legality in the Epistle of James; a reform of unfree chiliastic externality in the first Epistle of Peter and in both the Epistles to the Thessalonians; libertinism is opposed by the second Epistle of Peter and the Epistle of Jude; the Pauline Epistles reform, in rich gradation, the faith, the Church, Christology, *etc.;* and beyond them there is yet another Johannean reform of Christian gnosis. John not only knew that the Law, as the first reformation of Israel, was given amid thunder and lightning, that the fiery chariot of Elijah had formed a turning point between the legal and the Messianico-prophetic period, but he had also himself been present when Christ's prayer for the glorification of His Father's name was answered with a word of assent that sounded like thunder. And it was in harmony with the development of revelation that thunder, which in the Old Testament was a symbol of the Law, should become for the Son of Thunder, under the New Covenant, a symbol of the Gospel and its seven-fold holy evolutions. In respect of the beautiful, elevated and elevating aspect of thunder, even the Scandinavian mythology is in advance of the standpoint of popular terror, so largely occupied in Christendom with regard to this phenomenon (comp. also Sophocles, *Œdipus at Colonos*).

In referring, at this juncture, to our EXEG. NOTES, it will be understood, as a matter of course, that it is the part of Homiletics to treat the present section of the Seven Thunders with especial caution, although, of course, the phenomena accompanying the voices of the Thunders are not sealed. As to the sealing itself, the expression is to be taken in its broader sense. In a literal sense, written matter is sealed; but here the command is: *write not.*

Special.—*a.* [Vers. 2, 3.] *The Angel of the End-time.* A presage and symbol of the Coming of Christ. 1. His appearance; 2. The little book in his hand relating to the end-time: 3 His dominion and power: his feet planted on the land and the sea; 4. His cry as the roaring

of a lion—the awakening call to the awaking seven Thunders. The word of Christ, the eternal source of all spiritual operations in the Church.—*b.* [Vers. 3-7.] *The Seven Thunders* as mysterious mediations of the end-time. As sealed mysteries. The more complete their sealing as canonical and doctrinal certainties of prophecy, the more powerful their operation upon the religious presentiment, the feelings, the spirit of prayer. The Seven Thunders in nature (Ps. xxix.), emblems of the Seven Thunders of the Kingdom of God.—The mysteries of Christianity, *prefigured* by the mysteries of the Theocratic Sanctuary; *manifest* in the facts and fundamental doctrines of Christianity (1 Tim. iii. 16); *mediated* by the evangelic form of mystery (Matt. x. 27), by mysteries sacramental, Church-historic (*disciplina arcani*), especially those pertaining to the mediæval period of Church history, and by eschatological mysteries. —The sealing of the Thunders, the mystery of mysteries.—The certainty of certainties, or the solemn oath of the Angel concerning the approaching end.—The oaths of God recorded in Holy Writ are Divine assurances which re-echo in the surest certainty of elect human hearts — How is this to be understood—to wit, that the time of Christ's coming is unknown, that it may, in a chronological sense, still be distant, and yet that it is emphatically near? 1. We are in the midst of a constant, uncheckable movement toward that goal; 2. The movement is continually increasing in rapidity, and the catastrophe of this periodic course will come, at all events, more suddenly than we think. The motives of this catastrophe are to be found in the depths of the religious and moral world (*where the carcase, etc.*). Every great event has, from time immemorial, taken men by surprise, like a sort of Last Day.—The time of the Seventh Trumpet, the time of the end.—The blessed secrets intrusted to the servants of God, contrasted with the unblessed secrets of the children of wickedness.—*c.* [Vers. 9-11] *New and second calling of the Seer.*—Command to the Seer to eat the little book. The act itself, and its import. The hearty reception of the prophecy of the last time in its sweet charm and its convulsing and painful effect. (Anguish and terror, especially the terrors of war, not only attack the heart but are frequently the occasion of cholera-like epidemics.)—The converse orders of the operations of the book, as presented by the Angel and by the Seer. Joy and sorrow, says human feeling; sorrow and joy, says the heavenly Spirit.—*Thou must prophesy again,* or the commission to publish the tidings of the last time in the midst of the course of the world, as an imminent Divine doom upon the whole world, peoples and kings.

STARKE: *The Lion roareth*—who shall not fear, examine himself, and truly repent (Amos iii 8)? He that dwelleth in Heaven may keep silence for a while, but in His own time He shall speak so that *both our ears shall tingle* (Ps. ii 5. 1. 21; 1 Sam. iii 11).—Some commentators think that they (the Seven Thunders) discovered the saddest fortunes of the true Church.—Here, also Starke presents the antithetic view of "those who regard this as fulfilled" and "those who deem it to be still future."—The Prophets and Apostles did not write down all things that they saw and heard, but only so much as was necessary for us and as the Holy Ghost commanded them to write.—Although the prophetic predictions remain for a time sealed, when the time of their fulfillment and dénoument arrives, all becomes intelligible and manifest (Dan. xii 9).

JUNG STILLING, *Die Siegesgeschichte der christl. Religion in einer gemeinnützigen Erklärung der Offenb. Joh. (Sämmtliche Schriften, Vol. III. Stuttgart, 1835. On ch. x. 1): *His countenance shineth like the sun,* for He dwells in the light and enlightens all things that He looks upon; since His appearance until now it has been growing brighter and brighter. *About His head the rainbow gleams;* for He is a Messenger of the Covenant,—a Messenger Who is to proclaim the unveiling of the mystery of God, in which mystery God's covenant with Noah and all His promises are to be fulfilled. *He is clothed with a cloud*—which is the chariot and travelling apparel of Him Who is to come in the clouds (Rev. i. 7; Dan. vii. 13) *And His feet are like pillars of fire;* for where He stands, He stands firm; the gates of hell cannot move Him from the spot, and whoso thinks to drive Him away, burns his own fingers. All this is surety to us for the validity of His embassage, for the truth of the little book that He has in His hand, and which John now communicates to us.

RIEMANN, *Die Offenb. St. Joh.* (see p. 73): Every word of God, as heavenly food from the tree of life, is *sweet* when we first receive it in faith, but afterwards, though the sweetness does not cease, it becomes *bitter* also, as a judge of the thoughts and intents of the heart, when the old Adam must sink in death under the sharpness of this two-edged sword: again, this word is doubly sweet when it proclaims the final triumph of Christ over the kingdom of darkness, and yet at the same time it is bitter, for with this proclamation it conjoins lamentation and mourning and woe that sorely come upon the Messianic Church through the last desperate conflict of the prince of darkness with the Kingdom of God.

[From THE COMPREHENSIVE COMMENTARY: Vers. 9-11. It becomes God's servants to digest in their own souls the messages they bring to others in His name, and to be suitably affected therewith themselves: also, to deliver every message with which they are charged, whether pleasing or unpleasing to men. (M. HENRY.)]

SECTION NINTH.

Exoteric Intimations from the Earth-picture of the Seven Thunders. (Chap. xi. 1-14.)

General.—The remarks made by us in reference to the preceding section, apply with equal force to this. The exegetical foundation is not yet sufficiently sure, clear and firm to warrant the erection of a doctrinal and homiletical superstructure. We must distinguish, here as well as elsewhere, between our own firm conviction and the conventional status of exegesis in the Church, which it is not admissible to leave entirely out of consideration in an official undertaking.

We must, first of all, settle the relation which this section bears to the preceding one. *It is not difficult to perceive that the Seven Thunders are recognizable in the procedures of the two Sons of Oil, since fire goes forth from their mouths and they can shut and open Heaven like Elijah*

Another unmistakable fact is that we have here to do with a sketch of those Church-historical circumstances which form a transition to the time of the end.

It is equally certain, furthermore, that in the provision concerning the Temple. vers 1, 2, we have a picture of the Christian Church, and not a prophecy relating to the Temple at Jerusalem, to be apprehended literally and, in such case, manifested to be erroneous In regard to the Temple and the subsequent history of the Two Witnesses, as well as the judgment at the close of the section, we refer to the EXEG. NOTES. A cautious treatment of the subject might be itself upon the following fundamental lines: The inner and outer (or invisible and visible) Church (vers. 1, 2); the New Testament order of God's Kingdom in the antithesis of Church and State (vers. 3-7); the grave prospect that the hemming in of Antichristianity will at some future day be done away with (vers. 7-10; 2 Thess ii.); the certainty that the forms of Church and State, though suffering a temporal extinction, will celebrate their resurrection in the consummation of the Kingdom of God (vers. 11, 12). Finally, the social earthquake connected with the preceding events, which shakes the New Testament City of God of externalized Christian order and, by a precursory judgment, calls many to repentance, whereby such as comply with the call withdraw themselves from the consummate apostasy of the time of the Beast, and are preserved from the final judgment at the Parousia of Christ.

Special.—[Vers. 1, 2.] The Temple arrangements of the Old Covenant, in their symbolic import for the Christian Church. (a) The priestly Sanctuary which has become one with the Holy of Holies; (b) the Altar; (c) the Worshippers; (d) the outer court of the Gentiles.—Import of the outer court: a figurative testimony (1) against that view which reckons the outer court as forming part of the Sanctuary; (2) against the other idea which denominates the outer court the world, simply.

[Ver. 3.] The two ground-forms of witness concerning Christ in the Christian age: The Churchly communion. and the Christian and humane social morals and manners which it inculcates.—[Ver. 4.] The *olive trees,* by which the life of the *sons of oil,* Christians, is, not generated, but mediated.—Olive trees and candlesticks [lamp-stands] at once; *i. e.,* on the one hand, *gifted* with a source of spiritual life (John iv.), and, on the other, *elaborated* into a form favorable for the mediation of the Spirit to men.—The whole Christian age, a time of the one Spirit of Christ in the change of different temporal forms. In the main, the olive trees are at the same time candlesticks [lamp-stands], and the candlesticks [lamp-stands] olive trees; *i. e.,* spiritual life and formal organization. knowledge and practice, run together, in parallel development, through the ages. In individual cases, however, the candlestick [lamp-stand] that should stand beside the olive tree is occasionally missing, and still more frequently the candlestick [lamp-stand] lacks the accompaniment of the olive tree.—[Vers. 5, 6.] Competition of the mediæval Church and State in the training of Christian humanity. Their union. Their terrible severity. Their strainings of authority and their gradual loss of the sympathy of Christian popular life. —[Ver. 7.] The *Beast out of the abyss* as the prelude of Antichristianity or the Beast out of the sea, or how demonic Antichristian dispositions precede the final Antichristian figurations in human characters.—Dying and dead forms of the old order of things (ver. 9) —The Antichristian feasts of the future (ver. 10).—[Vers. 11, 12.] The time of *three days and a half*, or the time of the apparent downfall of the Kingdom of God, always, at the same time, the time of a glorious exaltation of it.—Prospect of the final fulfillment of all Churchly and Stately foretokens in the unity of a heavenly Kingdom.—[Ver. 13.] The Apocalyptic earthquakes in their grand significance: (1) In their spiritual import; (2) In their social import; (3) In their cosmical import.— Fall of the external historic City of God.—Two-fold effect of the judgments and terrors of God: Many *are killed*, the rest *are affrighted and give glory to God*.

STARKE: The true Church should not be judged by its magnitude and visibility, because (just as) the outer court many times surpasses the Temple in length and breadth.—The teachers of the Christian Church must, internally, resemble olive trees, and be filled with the oil of the Holy Spirit, whilst outwardly they must shine as lights, with an irreproachable life.—QUESNEL: When God has used His servants for the sanctification of others, He uses the wicked to purify those servants themselves by suffering and martyrdom.—The world is to be deplored, in that it celebrates its sins with rejoicings, as a public festival.

LÖWE, *Weissagung und Geschichte in ihrer Zusammenstimmung* (see p. 73): [Ver. 3 sqq.] This twofold number, doubtless, denotes a twofold, Divinely commissioned ministry, but not an external condition; thus there are always in existence some few powerful witnesses—testifying of repentance and faith—*of ecclesiastical and secular office and vocation*, in order to the support of Christ's spiritual Kingdom in the world.

WILHELM FRIEDRICH RINCK, *Apokalyptische Forschungen*, Zürich, 1853 (see p. 72): As the Lord sent out His disciples by twos, thus the many witnesses and servants of Christ are here introduced as two messengers (?). Their ministry lasts as long as Jerusalem (the outer court) is trodden down by the Gentiles; the whole time, consequently, from the destruction of Jerusalem to the end of the world.—Two olive trees and two lamp-stands. Oil and lamp-stands belong together.—The city. Neither Jerusalem nor Rome is intended, but an allegorical great city, which lays violent hands on the messengers of God, and even on His own Son. It is impossible that it can be any particular single city when they of the peoples, tribes, tongues and nations are

to see the bodies of the slain witnesses. Con-stance is a part of that great city.*

[From M. HENRY: Ver. 1. Observe, 1. *The temple* was to be measured; the gospel-church in general; whether it be so built, so constituted, as the gospel rule directs. 2. *The altar*. That which was the place of the most solemn acts of worship may be put for religious worship in general; whether the Church has the true altars, both as to substance and situation; as to substance, whether they take Christ for their Altar, and lay down all their offerings there; and in situation, whether the Altar be in *the holiest; that is, whether they worship God in the Spirit and in truth*. 3. *The worshippers*. Whether they make God's glory their end, and His word their rule, in all their acts of worship; and whether they come to God with suitable affections, and whether their *conversation be as becomes the gospel*.]

SECTION TENTH.

Heaven-picture of the Manifestation of Antichris-tianity on Earth. (Ch. xi. 15—xii 12.)

General.—The present section, and also the subsequent chapters, xii. 13—xiii. 18, are peculiarly adapted to illustrate and confirm the construction of the Apocalypse as presented by us. Our section is not readily intelligible without a definite reference to the subsequent Earth-picture, and the development of Antichristianity brought to view in that picture can be apprehended only as illuminated by our Heaven-picture:—as a judgment foreseen in the counsel of God; as an apparent domination of Antichristianity, completely overruled by the victorious power of Heaven, by the triumph of Christ and the victory of His heroic spirit over Satan in the spirit-sphere.

Here, as elsewhere, the heavenly celebration of victory (ch. xi. 15-19) precedes the earthly judgment (ch. xiii. 1 sqq.). The *Woman clothed with the sun*, the Divine Congregation of the Kingdom, appears conformably to her heavenly phase, in full splendor (ch. xii. 1-6); high above her fugitive phase, menaced with mortal peril, on earth (ch. xv. 13-17). The true offspring of her heart (ch. xii. 2-5) is a holy counterpart of the wicked *False Prophet*, who, in the guise of a lamb, comes forth from her terrestrial order, the *earth*. The *great red Dragon* who appears in *Heaven*, the region of spirit, with great seductive power; whose intention it is to destroy the *male Son* and conquer His spirit-host, but who here makes an utterly fruitless attempt against that Son, Who is *caught up to God*,—an utterly abortive attack upon *Michael and his angels*—and is, in consequence, *cast down to earth*,—subsequently appears on earth as a terrible persecutor of the Woman: he vomits forth his water-floods, *i. e.*, masses of peoples, against her; he wars against her individual children; he incarnates himself, with his seven heads, in the seven-headed Antichrist; he helps the horrid Beast, after it has been wounded to death, to an apparent healing; he institutes, by the semblance of demonic omnipotence, devil

---

worship and blasphemies on earth; he draws the False Prophet, with his delusive works, into his service, and attains, for the time being, to a dominion on earth which is, to all appearance, legally organized through the medium of social symbols.

According to the Heaven-picture, the *Woman* is sheltered in the *wilderness*, whither she herself has *fled*, by a *place prepared* for her *by God* (" A stronghold sure "), and there finds food and main enance through her whole trial-time of *a thousand two hundred and sixty days* and days' works. According to the Earth-picture, the *two wings of the great Eagle* must be *given* her for her flight; in the place of refuge to which she has fled, she is sustained through the same period that was before indicated, which, however, is here designated by the ominous number *a time*. (two) *times and a half*—whereby a great, sore and apparently endless time of temptation [trial] is expressed, a period which seems to continue even to hopelessness; she is, moreover, oppressed in a twofold manner by the Serpent. To save herself from being drowned and carried away by the water-floods, the sun-woman must accept the aid of the earth, *by which acceptance her visible existence is itself made dependent upon the earth*; and after the abortive attack upon the kernel of her totality, war is waged against her in *the remainder of her seed*, her individual children.

The high import of the seventh Trumpet, which continues from now to the seven Vials of Anger or to the judgment, is first expressed by a great celebration in Heaven. There is a sublime paradox in the fact that the beginning of Satan's apparent rule on earth is celebrated in Heaven by great voices saying: *The kingdom of the world is become our Lord s and His Christ's, and He shall reign from eternity to eternity.* This epoch of heavenly victory is so completely decided with the appearance of Antichristianity that the heavenly Elders can make the festival already one of thanksgiving. There is a grandeur in the intuition or deduction by which they recognize in the very *wrath of the nations* the forth-breaking of the *Divine anger* (with its Vials of Anger); in the death-time of those who live in and for this world, a new life-time of the [blessed] dead in the world beyond—the beginning epoch of their restoration, which, in accordance with its nature, brings with it destruction for the destroyers of the earth.

Upon this festal antiphony between the heavenly voices and the thanksgiving of the Elders, follow the opening of the heavenly Temple, and the events connected therewith. The full revelation of Satan is anticipated by the perfect revelation of revelation, if we may thus speak. For those who will see with the Seer, *the Temple is opened;* the idea of the Kingdom of God becomes generally intelligible; *the Ark of His Covenant* becomes visible: *i. e.*, the profoundly dark mystery of reconciliation and grace is converted into the clear light of knowledge for all those who see; and the effect of this glorious development of the life of the Church of God cannot fail of supervention; *viz., lightnings* of particulars of revelation, *voices* of proclamation, *thunders* of preaching, *earthquakes* of mental convulsions, and a *great hail storm* of fanatical sentiments originating in the commingling of sultry heat and icy cold.

Together with the glory of revelation, the glory of the Congregation of the Kingdom becomes manifest,—the *Woman clothed with the sun*, in the astral adornment of the terrestrial cosmos.

All the pangs [woes] of earth appear, in connection with the Woman's pangs, as travail-pangs, birth-pangs of the Messiah.

Next appears the enemy, *the great red Dragon*. He is a union of serpent and swine, *"Spottgeburt von Dreck und Feuer,"* resplendent in the gloomy radiance of his fiery nature and bloodguiltiness; he has *seven* mock-holy *heads* instead of the one holy head, and there attaches to him the contradiction of the *ten horns* of his authority, expressive of the fact that that authority reposes entirely upon the decenary of the world, whilst the *crowns* upon his seven heads indicate a legal power falsely gained by the semblance of the sacred seven. Not, however, by the lustre of his crowns, but by the terrible lashings of his tail—apparent power—does he cast the third part, or a spiritual third, of the stars, the geniuses of the spirit-world of Heaven, down to earth, into the earthly service of the ecclesiastico-worldly order of things. The frustration of his plans, however, is expressed in a series of defeats: 1. Christ, in the light of eternity, is caught up as *the Male* into Heaven, to the Throne of God; 2. The Woman is made secure in her place of refuge, and provided for; 3. The Dragon, with his angels, is, by Michael and his angels, precipitated from Heaven to earth. from the sphere of pure spirit of the inner Church to the external Churchly and Stately ordinances; 4. Even in this world an invisible Church Triumphant has been establishing itself, and is as deep and high, as wide and broad, as the perfect joyousness of faith extends in its two fundamental features; faith-righteousness in the Reconciliation, and martyr-faithfulness unto death.

A transition to the Earth-picture is formed by the following thought: The highest weal of the heavenly-minded becomes a woe upon earth and sea, the Hierarchy and popular life.

Special.—Reciprocal action betwixt the development and consummation of the kingdom of darkness, on the one hand, and the Kingdom of God on the other.—[Ch xi. 17, 18] Heavenly rejoicing over earth's last time of need.—Judgment of the wrath of God in the wrath of the nations.—The end-time, a joyful celebration of the justification of all God s witnesses.—[Ver. 19.] Transfiguration of the whole revelation of salvation in knowledge and life: a sure hope of Christendom.—Great effects of this ever more manifest revelation, [ch. 12,] ver. 10.—[Ch. xii. 1]. The Woman clothed with the sun, or the glory of the eternal Congregation of God's Kingdom.—[Ver. 2.] Birth-pangs of the Church of God: 1. The Martyrs of Israel; 2. Christ, the Great Martyr; 3. The Martyrs of the Christian Church.—Christ, even as the universal, eternal Christ, issues from the travail-pangs of the Church of God in Time.—All the sufferings of this present time are not to be compared with the eternal glory.—[Vers 3, 4.] The doctrine of Satan, perfected in the Apocalypse. The great red Dragon (1) as a figurative representa-

tion of Satan; (2) of Satanic or demonic evil;
(3) of evil in general. Unbelief has advanced
from a denial of Satan to a denial of Satanic
evil; from the denial of the latter to a denial of
evil in general. The knowledge of faith must
advance through a deeper-going doctrine of evil
to an apprehension of Satanic evil, and through
the latter to an insight into Divine revelation relative to the existence of Satan and his kingdom.
—*Evil* in the figure of the Dragon: 1. Absolute
hideousness, the Dragon, the monstrous shape, in
its hypocritical pretension to *beauty*, in the pomp
of fiery red, and with its seven crowns; 2. Absolute *falsehood* in the contradiction of horns and
crowns, with its hypocritical pretension to *holy
intelligence* in its seven heads; 3. Absolute *bad-
ness* in its conduct toward the "stars" or spirits
of Heaven, toward God and Christ, toward the
Woman and the destiny of humanity, with the
hypocritical pretension to the *founding of a free
spirit-kingdom* (of fallen stars).—*Satanic evil*, or
conscious enmity to God and Christ.—*Satan and
his kingdom*. The doctrine respecting these has,
by reason of the mediæval classifications of it,
which, in manifold ways, continued to obtain
even in Protestant orthodoxy after the Reformation, called forth a reaction similar to that induced by the gross enhancement of the doctrine of
election, by the fearful exaggeration of the power
of excommunication, of Church discipline, clerical
authority and letter-faith. This doctrine has hence
become a difficult, and more or less, an esoteric,
subject for homiletics. It, nevertheless, must
not be dropped, and still less should it be denied: its true treatment, however, is conditioned
(1) by a prominent setting forth of that spirit-
world which pervades the universe; (2) by the
maintenance of the fact that the origin of sin
consists not in animal sensuality, but in a spiritual abuse of liberty: that a fall of spirits is
assumable neither as having taken place on our
earth *alone* nor throughout the universe; and
that from the earthly fall of spirits, we are,
according to Scripture, to infer a previous fall
of spirits, forming the centre and back-ground
of the evil of this world.

The scattered manifestations of evil on earth,
notwithstanding their plurality, constitute, in
their opposition to the Kingdom of God, a unitous power as the Kingdom of Darkness. A unitous power against the Kingdom of God they
are, but not a united power in themselves, as is
evident from the monster with the seven heads.
—Antitheocratic manifestations in the Old Testament as foreshadowings of Antichristian manifestations in the New Testament and in Church
history.—Satan's work in the invisible world
becomes manifest here in Antichristian facts,
and must be brought to view by means of these.
—The enemy of man, according to John viii. 44,
as a seducer (to spiritual pride, Gen. iii.; to
fanatical fleshly lust, Num. xxv., *etc.*); as
an accuser (Job).—Types of Antichrist: Balaam; Goliath; Ahithophel; Antiochus Epiphanes; Judas.—[Ver. 5.] Satan's plot for the
destruction of Christ defeated by Christ's resurrection and ascension.—[Ver. 7.] The battle
between light and darkness on earth is, in its
decisive centre, a conflict of spirits in the spirit-
realm (see *Comm. on John*, ch. xiii. 31).—[Ver.

9.] The casting of Satan out of the pure sphere
of the Christian spirit into the sphere of earthly
ordinances, (*a*) in the life of Jesus (Matt. iv.;
Luke x. 18; John, *l. c.*); (*b*) in the sphere of
the Church through the medium of the Spirit of
Christ.—Song of triumph over the accuser, ver.
10 (~see Exeg. Notes).

Starke (Lösecken): "It is a noteworthy
circumstance that there is here (ch. xi., vers.
15, 16) no mention of the four Beasts, which
e sewhere throughout the Book precede the
Elders in praising and thanking God (ch. v. 14;
vii. 11). The reason of this seems to be that at
this time the true public ministry of preaching,
represented by the four Beasts (?), will be suppressed to such a degree as to be neither visible
nor appreciable any more." (A little problem
lies before us, but the solution offered is a failure. Possibly the four Life forms [Living-
beings] are omitted because they denote the
fundamental forms of the Divine Governance in
the economy of *salvation*, whilst here a exercise of *judicial* power is celebrated.)—Ver. 19.
*And there occurred lightnings and voices and thun-
ders:* the promulgation of the Law and the Gospel
was set in motion again.—*And an earthquake:* great
commotions arose.—*And a great hail:* with this,
the judgments of God burst upon the Antichristian
kingdom. [*And the Temple, etc.*] The things concerning which there has been so much strife shall
be clearly shown and known—to wit, the Person,
nature and attributes of Christ, the satisfaction
made by Him, the whole nature of the covenant
of grace and of Christ's Kingdom on earth.
After the offence has been taken away, God will
yet give to all nations on earth free access to
His Church and Throne of Grace.—(Ch xii. 3.
"Dragons are said to be the largest of all serpents and beasts, some of them attaining the
length of forty or fifty cubits. Alexander the
Great is said to have had one shown him that
was five hundred feet long.")—Ver. 4. And his
tail, wherein were his greatest power and cunning, *drew*, subdued by cruelty, torture, artifice, flattery, *the third part of the stars*, a great
part of the teachers of mankind.—Ver. 11. This
is the wondrous victory of Christians—to conquer through tribulation and death, to gain in
losing (Rom. viii. 37).—Quesnel: The nearer
we come to the end, the more earnestly does the
devil strive to ruin us, and the more ought we
to watch, pray and work.

N. Von Brunn, *Blicke eines alten Knechts, der
auf seinen Herrn wartet, in die Offenbarung, etc.*
(see p. 73): To us mortals, because of the limitations of our vision, much appears in process
of *coming to pass*, which, by celestial spirits, with
sight unhindered by a veil of flesh, is seen to be
already accomplished. (The Church-historical
system of interpretation is pursued in this work.
The practical remarks are significant and edifying.)

Graeber (see above): "The positions of
Hengstenberg are as untenable with regard to
ch. xi. 19 as in relation to ch. viii. 1. Suppose,
for instance, that the Revelation really definitively
closed here, which, according to Hengstenberg,
is assumable. What! is the entire development
of God's Kingdom on earth to close with a 'great
hail!'—The *wilderness* (ch. xii.). Thus says

Thomas à Kempis: 'If thou wouldest know and learn somewhat that will be useful and profitable to thee, learn what so few know or are able to do—*to be willing to know and to be accounted as nought.*' The *wilderness*, then, is self-renunciation; not simply barrenness, want, poverty, or the concealment of the Kingdom of God in the Middle Ages.) The Lord withdraws His people from the turmoil of the world: a Moses He buries, as it were, for forty years in the wilderness with Jethro; an Elijah He conceals by the brook Cherith, and entombs a Luther in the narrow cell of a cloister, etc."

[From M. HENRY: Ch. xii. 10. *The accuser, etc.* Though Satan hates God's presence, yet he is willing to appear there, to accuse the people of God. Let us therefore take heed that we give him no cause of accusation against us; and that when we have sinned, we presently go in *before the Lord,* and accuse and condemn ourselves, and commit our cause to Christ as our Advocate. —Ver. 11. The servants of God overcame Satan, 1. *By the blood of the Lamb,* as the meritorious cause. Christ by dying *destroyed him that hath the power of death, that is, the Devil.* 2. *By the word of their testimony,* as the great instrument of war; *the sword of the Spirit, which is the word of God;* by a resolute, powerful preaching of the everlasting gospel, *which is mighty, through God, to pull down strongholds;* by their courage and patience in sufferings; *they loved not their lives unto the death,* when *the love of life stood in competition with their loyalty to Christ; they loved not their lives* so well, but they could give them up *to death,* could lay them down in Christ's cause.—From BARNES: Ch. xi. 15. A time is to come when, in the proper sense of the term, God is to *reign* on the earth; when His kingdom is to be universal; when His laws shall be everywhere recognized as binding; when all idolatry shall come to an end; and when the understandings and the hearts of men everywhere shall bow to His authority.—From VAUGHAN: Ch. xii. 11. The three weapons by which the Christian victory is won: The atonement made for all sin in the death of Christ; the word or message of God, to which all true Christians bear in act and in endurance a firm and intelligible testimony; and that spirit of entire self-devotion and self-surrender which perseveres even unto death, and stops not short (if God so require) of the sacrifice of life itself for Christ.]

SECTION ELEVENTH.

Earth-picture of Antichristianity. (*Chap. xii.* 13—*xiii.* 18.)

General.—The climax manifest in the development of Antichristianity on earth, is signalized by the names: the Dragon, Antichrist, and the False Prophet, added to which, as a sort of supplement, is the dominant Antichristian congregation, with its Antichristian symbols of fellowship.

At first, the Dragon has no conscious organs on earth; he does but vomit forth the *water-floods,* as will-less or unfree masses of peoples, *against the Woman, to cause her to be carried away.* Nor can he, after this attempt, at first do more than direct his temptations, in single demonic attacks, against individual believers or isolated communities.

Subsequently, however, he procures a conscious human organ: the *Beast* which rises out of *the sea* of national life, and in which he himself vanishes for a long time. In Antichristianity, which is at first a fellowship of Antichristian sympathies, but which finally becomes personal in geniuses of wickedness who attain their meridian in the Man of Sin, the Satanic essence is reflected in heightened potency. It appears as the consummate compound of all demonic and antitheocratic world-powers, or the four Danielic Beasts. The *names of blasphemy,* visible on its head, must, doubtless, be regarded as *indirect* blasphemies; it assumes many attributes of a blasphemous nature, *e. g.* absolute authority as a ruler and teacher, and the like. With these *names* are also connected the direct blasphemies which are providentially permitted him by the gift of the *mouth speaking great things and blasphemies;* aye, which must aid in the execution of judgment upon God estranged Christendom. That, however, which is in the highest degree conducive to the dominion of Antichristianity, is the apparent perfect revival of it in its ungodly, worldly essence, after the mortal *wound* dealt to it by Christianity in one of its heads (in a special world-power).

Thus are the outward victory of the kingdom of darkness over the saints, and its temporary public rule over the nations, brought about; assuredly, under forms of subtile worldly refinement and by means of the sympathy of infatuated millions. Nor is the devil-worship which is established in the same manner to be regarded as a rude shamanism. The whole submission and homage of the nations arise from *a cowardly recognition of the apparently invincible power of falsehood, hate and violence.*

Violence exercised in the sphere of religion shall, however, meet its judgment; and the more consummate will be that judgment, the more thoroughly the faithful learn. themselves to abstain from all violence contrary to the dictates of conscience and the provisions of justice.

Antichristianity attains its full power, however, only through the medium of the False Prophet, who, at all events *as such,* proceeds from the Church in its external constitution. That he does not conduct the entire institution over to the hostile camp, is evident from the subsequent fact that the Harlot is killed by the Beast; nevertheless, he denotes the true essence of its worldly spirit, the turning-point, subsequent to the appearance of which the familiar relationship between the Woman and the Beast, in which the Beast was at first subservient to the Woman, changes its character, and the Woman is brought into subjection to the Beast. We are thus furnished with a picture of the most disgraceful apostasy, first appearing in back-sliding sympathies, next exhibited in prominent examples of defection, and finally reaching its climax in a perfect genius of perfidy.

The consummate hypocrite then establishes the consummate Antichristian congregation, which exhibits the complete counterpart of the true Church, in that it, like the true Church, has its wonders of revelation, its symbolic cultus, its symbolic marks, and its ban of, excommunication. Its wonders of revelation, however, are delusions; its cultus is a worship of the Beast's Image; its marks are brands of spiritual slavery; and its ban is more than the great ban—it is a social outlawry of the faithful.

The very mark, however, by which the Antichristian is to be recognized, presupposes the continuance of a quiet Church of God in this troublous time, for the benefit of whose members the mark is designed.

Special.—[Chap. xiii.] The Beast and the False Prophet, or the relations, antipathies and sympathies between the secular and the spiritual Babylon.—[Chap. xii. 13.] The Satanic power, the woe-engendering spirit on earth. Also in the domain of the symbolic earth, the institution and order of Church and State.—The spirit of the kingdom of darkness, a spirit of persecution. —[Ver. 14.] The safety of God's Church on earth, ensured by the wildernesses of poverty and renunciation —Holy dwellers in the wilderness: Moses, Elijah, John the Baptist, Christ.— Churches of the wilderness.—The blossoming wilderness.—Borne away on eagles' wings from the persecutors of earth: 1. Israel; 2. The Christian Church; 3. All believing souls.— Preservation and nourishment of the Church even through times of sorest distress.—[Ver. 15.] *And the serpent cast out of his mouth, etc.* The *dragon* now becomes a *serpent*, and again the *serpent* becomes a *dragon.*—The *river [water as a river]* in its symbolical import, in respect of its bright and its dark side.—[Ver. 16.] The *earth* under the same aspects.—Historic dependence of the Church on the earth. Her apparent mergement in the earth. Her solicitude for the earth.—[Ver. 17.] Isolated temptations [trials] of the true children of the Church and witnesses of Jesus. By isolated attacks, it is true, the power of faith is divided, but so, likewise, is the power of evil.—Satan seeks Christians. But for what reason ?—[Chap. xiii. 1.] The Beast out of the sea. His dark intent. His horrible and monstrous appearance. His business (the bringing into vogue of a worship of the Dragon, blasphemy against the Holy One and holy things, and the conquest of holy men [*the saints*]. His history. His success.—His blasphemy, (*a*) indirect, (*b*) direct. *Against* (1) *the Name* of God, (2) His *Tabernacle,* (3) *them that dwell in Heaven* (see EXEG. NOTES).—The great world-monarchies depicted, as regards their bright side, in the human figure of Dan. ii.; as regards their dark side, in the bestial figures of Dan. vii.—Concentration of all ungodly and antigodly principles in the last Antichristian world-power.—*The nature of the Wild beast, nay, of consummate bestiality, in the semblance of, and with the claim to, consummate civilization. The Beast in the antithesis of* (1) *sensuality and blood-thirstiness;* (2) *stupidity and an absolute lack of appreciation of the Divine, and deviceful animal cunning;* (3) *a lust for prey and an impulse to destruction.*—The *Apocalyptic Beast,* in its elegant, spotted *body* resembling the *leopard;* in its heavy and clumsy *paws* resembling the *bear;* in its *heads, horns* and *crowns* perfect monstrosity and deformity —In what respect may we speak of a *conquest of the saints by the Beast,* and in what respect is the ex-

pression an improper one ?—Universalism, or the *international* power of Antichristianity.—Devil-worship in its gross, subtile and extra-subtile forms.—The heavenly *Book of Life.*—Watchword of the Church of God under the persecutions of this world (ver. 10).—[Vers. 11–17.] The False Prophet: 1. His types in Holy Writ; 2 His examples in Church History; 3. His fundamental traits at all times.—Apostasy is a twofold hypocrisy, just as hypocrisy is a twofold apostasy (perfidy at once toward Heaven and hell).—Hypocrisy, the mother of apostasy.—Perfidy, or specific depravity, the brand of apostasy.—Distinction between sinners who are only *wicked* [*Böse*] and those who are depraved [*Schlechte*].— Satan, because he finds his tools in the depraved, calumniates all men as depraved, but in this presupposition he is put to shame (see Job ; Zech. iii.; Matt. iv.).—All tyrants are put to shame when they make the assumption that humanity is rotten and depraved at the core.—God has placed a rock in the midst of the way of worldly history upon which all godlessness must be confounded.—The mock character and work of the apostate. His mock-holiness (*like the Lamb*); his mock-miracles; his mock-cultus; his mock-church.—Horrid picture of the church of Satan. —*Horrible opposites in the nature of evil:* in the nature of the Beast; in the nature of the False Prophet; in the nature of the Antichristian community.—Outlawry of believers in the time of the perfect dominion of unbelief: (1) subtile ; (2) universal.—[Ver. 18.] The mysterious number. Taken as a riddle, it is infinitely obscure (the most diverse interpretations of it have been given). Taken as a symbol, it is clear enough. The Antichristian signature of a life full of endless, vain and frustrated plots, toils, malignities and intrigues.—The mysterious description of the Beast, a great warning for faith—not a great problem for curious investigation.—The grand combinations of the hellish spirit are always confounded by reason of one mistake in his calculation: 1. He holds all to be as depraved as himself; 2. He says: there is no God (Psalm xiv. 1), and he regards the holy and excellent ones that are on earth (Ps. xvi. 3) as chimeras.

STARKE, CRAMER: God has many ways and means of preserving His Church, and can quickly give her wings, that she may easily escape the malice of tyrants—for the Church is to endure forever.—However long or short a space the tribulation of God's faithful ones is to continue, God has beforehand decreed and meted it out.— Ver. 16 (Ps. cxxiv. 1-5). This style of expression is drawn from the natural shutting up of waters in the earth (Ps. xciii. 3, 4).—QUESNEL: No one who is of the true seed of the Church escapes the temptation and persecution of Satan (2 Tim. iii. 11, 12).—A worldly kingdom is called a *Beast* because its government is often conducted with bestial irrationality, tyranny, unrighteous violence and brutish lusts (Dan. vii. 4, 23).— Worldly kingdoms are subject to many and great vicissitudes, for God setteth up and removeth kings (Dan. ii. 21 ; v. 25-28).—As *lions* are of great courage, and very strong and cruel, so the kings of Assyria and Babylon were very haughty, powerful and cruel. As *bears* are indeed very fierce, and yet have something in common with men, in that they eat all sorts of food, and are especially fond of honey, and can be tamed so that they will dance to our music, so certain kings of Persia were very cruel, whilst others, again, were very amiable toward the people of God. As *leopards* are spotted, wily and swift, thus was the Grecian monarchy (ch. xiii. 2).—The Spirit of God speaks in His children, the spirit of the devil speaks, likewise, in his members.—The multitude and high position of those who profess a false religion do not convert error into truth.—The patience of believers in their affliction is their great crown.—The shape of a lamb and the heart of a dragon.—As the Egyptian sorcerers counterfeited some miracles, *etc.*—False religions are set up by violence and cruelty; the Gospel, by humility and patience. We should bear in our bodies the mark of Christ, but not that of the beast (Gal. vi. 17).—The Antichrist practices two kinds of violence; he deprives true believers of life and (or) of freedom, which is as dear as life.—As the Beast is not some individual person but a fellowship of men, so the name of the Beast cannot be the name of a prince, *etc.* The name *Adonikam* would be quite suitable for Antichrist (Ezra ii. 13, *etc.*), since there were 666 of the family of Adonikam that returned out of captivity to their own land. (It is doubtless from this source, or from the still earlier one of Virringa, that Hengstenberg derived his explanation.)—True wisdom consists in knowing how to distinguish the Spirit of God from the spirit of darkness.

LÄMMERT, *Babel, das Thier und der falsche Prophet* (see p 74): Chap. xiii. 1-7. After John has seen the pure Church of God and the Dragon which persecutes her, he is made to behold the Beast out of the sea, the Dragon's representative on earth. This connection obliges us to revert to ch. xii.

H. W. RINCK, *Die Lehre der Heiligen Schrift vom Antichrist* (see p. 73): Interesting communications and dissertations on the subject of the spiritists [*Spiritisten*]. The False Prophet is here regarded as the representative of false science, and is distinguished and separated from the great Harlot Babylon.

SECTION TWELFTH.

Heavenly World-picture of the Seven Vials of Anger, or the Judgment of Anger in its General Form (embracing the Three Special Judgments upon Babylon, the Beast and Satan.) (Chs. xiv., xv.)

General.—The peculiar sublimity of this section is thoroughly manifest only when it is regarded as representative of the heavenly celebration of God's anger-judgments on earth, and when its relation to these is recognized in the treatment of it. The dreadful darkness of these judgments, as they here appear, is pure light above,—aye, it is there resolved into festal radiance. Above, the measures of *Divine anger*, ruling, as a *holy anger* of united love and righteousness, over the *wrath of the heathen* [nations], and, by its ruling, conducting the latter to the judgment of self annihilation, are recognized and magnified, in their holiness and gloriousness, to the glory of God and the Lamb.

In the foreground of the whole festal scene stands the *Lamb, on the Mount Zion*, surrounded by the 144,000 elect, who represent the Church Triumphant. Herein two grand ideas are involved. On the one hand, the Lamb has lifted His heavenly Congregation high above His sphere of anger; and, on the other hand, it is the very righteousness and privilege of the Lamb and His companions by which the wrath of the heathen [nations] is excited, and the holy anger of God at that wrath is superinduced. *Here lies the causality of the Vials of Anger.*

Next follows a description of the perfect heavenly consciousness of the necessity for these judgments, as well as of the ideal import of them—that at the right time they must needs come as the *harvest of the earth*, now that the earth is ripe for harvest,—ripe for a judgment which will be the final redemption, in virtue of its separation betwixt the wheat and the chaff. This entire description is presented in the form of a grand transaction between six Angels, three of whom are charged with the proclamation of the judgment, whilst the three others have the symbolic execution of it. The two divisions are separated by an intervening *voice from Heaven*, declaratory of the blessedness of the dead who die in the Lord. The first herald of the judgment proclaims throughout the universe that the imminent judgment will be an *eternal Gospel*, a Gospel of eternity, for all who *give glory to God*. As a death-judgment, the judgment is divided into two sections, the first consisting of the judgment upon *Babylon the Great*, and the second composed of the judgment upon the *Beast and its worshippers*. These two judgments form two sides of the one general judgment (vers. 19, 20). The transactions of the three executive Angels likewise fall into two divisions. At the head of the three executive Angels appears the seventh, or rather the first, figure of the entire group, the *Man on the white cloud*, or the Lamb, again, in another form. As the Father has reserved to Himself the time and the hour of the final judgment, an Angel represents this reservation on the part of the Father, by summoning the One on the cloud to the harvest of the earth. *Christ casts His sickle upon the earth*, and thus ensues the *harvest* in the truest sense of the term—the harvest of redemption, of the redeemed. This is followed by the harvest of anger. Thus is unfolded the perfect heavenly consciousness concerning the idea, the purpose, the time and the hour of the judgment of anger.

Next follows Act the Third, *the representation of the holy order of the judgment of anger, and its sacred heavenly measures*. The Divine clemency which characterizes the judgment itself is expressed first by the fact that it is septemariously divided; secondly, by the execution of the judicial decrees by seven Angels of God ; and, thirdly, by the circumstance that the result of the judgment once more appears,—the *crystal sea*, the eternal, new humanity,—and that this result is celebrated by a *song*, in which the *song of Moses*, or the song of anger, and the *song of the Lamb*, or the song of love, are united. Worthy of special prominence is the further fact that the Angels go forth from the *Temple of the tabernacle of the witness*, and thus accord with the identity of the Divine Law—a truth which is likewise expressed in their holy adornment [*clothed in pure and white linen*], and in the committal to them of the dispensation of the Divine anger in *golden vials*—in heavenly measures, determined by Divine faithfulness (see EXEG. NOTES).

Special.—[Chs. xiv., xv.] Pre-celebration of the anger-judgment in Heaven.—[Ch. xiv. 1–5.] The Church Triumphant: (*a*) Her stand-point, (*b*) her centre, (*c*) her characteristics, (*d*) her song.—Relation of the 144,000 triumphant ones to the 144,000 sealed ones (ch. vii).—The end-judgment as the harvest of the earth.—The new song: (1) Its newness, (2) its melodies, (3) the singers, (4) the hearers.—[Ver. 6] The eternal [everlasting] Gospel as the Gospel of eternity. Or as the *eschatological* phase of the one *principal* Gospel.—[Ver. 8.] Pre-celebration, in Heaven, of the judgment upon Babylon.—[Vers. 9–11.] Pre-celebration of the judgment upon Antichristianity.—[Ver. 12.] *The patience of the saints*, (1) as endurance in persecution, (2) ▪ forbearance from persecution.—Great warning against Antichristianity (vers. 9–11).—[Ver. 13.] *Blessed are the dead, etc.*, or the heavenly peace-bell, pealing amid the thunders of judgment.—[Vers. 14–20] God's double harvest on earth: I. The proper harvest (the sickle); 2. The improper harvest (the wine-press).—Ch. xv. The heavenly equipment of the seven Angels of Anger in its grand significance: 1. What they effect (ver. 2); 2. What they glorify (ver. 3); 3. What they bring about (ver. 4).—[Ver. 6.] Forth-going of the judgments of God out of His Temple.—The judgments of God in their beauteous heavenly aspect (vers. 6, 7).—[Ver. 8.] Sublime veiling of the majesty of God during the time of His judgments on earth, and the import of that veiling.

STARKE (Chap. xiv.): Christ stands in the midst of His Church, over against Antichristian abominations and cruelties, as a Conqueror (Ps. c. 2), and is ready to help His people (Acts vii. 56).—CRAMER: The holy Christian Church is not founded upon the sand, but upon a mountain (Ps. lxviii. 16), aye, firmer than the seven mountains on which the great city lies (ch. xvii. 9).—Ver. 2. This is to be understood of the true confessors of the Church's doctrine, in which doctrine they, in reference to the corruption of the spiritual Babylon, are emphatic and unanimous. Hence there is ascribed to them a voice of *great waters*, because with their doctrines they instituted many movements; a voice of a *great thunder*, which penetrates and shakes all things, indicates the mighty preaching of the Gospel, Mark iii. 17; and a voice of harmonious *music* teaches that all their doctrines beautifully harmonized in Christ, Col. iii. 16. (All this is, indeed, not yet fulfilled in Protestant theology or the ecclesiastical structures of the Reformation, so far as their outward form is concerned.) This picture is drawn from the service of the Levites in the Old Testament (Ps. cxxxiv.).—Ver. 3. It sounded entirely *new* (as when we hear a new and unknown song, set to a strange and unaccustomed tune), because the faithful bring it with *new* hearts, and because it tells of *new* benefits, *etc*—It is called *new* in antithesis to the *old*.—God's praise must be sung in the Church.—He who would sing the Gospel song aright, must

have a new heart and must have his face set toward God and His Throne.—Ver. 6. The *Angel* with the *everlasting Gospel*. Those who regard this as fulfilled, explain it as follows: This has reference to a remarkable teacher who should reform the Church and purify it in the time of Antichrist; by this Angel, Luther and his associates, who began the Reformation, are intended. Those who regard it as future explain as follows: The voices of these three Angels pertain to the very last time, *etc.*—Ver. 8. This expression is taken from the philters or love-potions of abandoned women, *etc*—Ver. 9. This proves clearly that the Beast cannot be the Harlot, or the Papacy.—Ver. 13. The ancients carefully distinguished between dying *for* the Lord and dying *in* the Lord; the former is peculiar to martyrs, the latter is common to all true Christians. (The distinction, becomes false, however, so soon as it is pressed)—The voice of the Lord which gives command to *write*, also commands men to *read*.—The tears which flow at the departure of pious persons may be wiped away by the diligent contemplation of the bliss to which they have attained.—The Holy Scriptures know of no purgatorial fires; those who have died in the Lord they place, immediately upon their death, in Heaven.—Ver. 15. *And another Angel.* Some understand, by this *other Angel*, the Holy Ghost, Who is sent into the hearts of men and, with strong crying, makes the distress of the faithful known unto Christ.—Ver. 18. Some regard the Angel mentioned here, as the Holy Ghost.—Ver. 20. In the grain harvest there is no sign of anger, but, on the contrary, there is mercy in it, for believers who have remained faithful to Jesus under the domination of the Beast, are then gathered into God's garner because the judgment upon the wicked is at hand (Matt xiii. 30). The vintage is a harvest of anger, for there is express mention of anger in this connection (ver. 19).—Chap. xv. 3. Some apprehend the *song of Moses* as the Law and the *song of the Lamb* as the Gospel (in contra-distinction to those who regard the *song of Moses* as the song of the physical redemption, by means of the passage through the Red Sea, and the *song of the Lamb* as the song of the spiritual redemption from the spiritual Egypt). True servants of God must unite the song of Moses and that of the Lamb—the old and the new.

SABEL (see p. 73): Ch. xiv. 1. He is called *the Lambkin* [τὸ ἀρνίον] in antithesis to the *great red Dragon* (chap. xii. 3) who gave his *great* authority to the Beast (ch. xiii. 2), and in antithesis to the Beast itself, which speaks *great* things and blasphemies (chap. xiii. 5).—Ver. 3. *No one could learn the song, etc.* There are, then, lessons to be learned even in Heaven. That learning will, however, be something different from our more mechanical, discursive learning. Even [in this mortal life] we know the difference between this latter learning and the being *taught of God* (John vi 45).—Ver. 4. Even on the basis of the Apocalypse a literal interpretation of this passage would be productive of great embarrassment. Such an interpretation would exclude from the 144,000 the Apostles themselves—a thing inconceivable according to Matt. xix. 28: the brethren of the Lord—of whom it is related, 1

Cor. ix. 5, that they carried their wives with them on their missionary journeys; and also Philip, one of the deacons, the father of four daughters (Acts xxi. 8, 9). There is, moreover, not the slightest indication to be found in the Old Covenant, from the participants in which the nucleus of the heavenly congregation of the first fruits had been gathered, that celibacy was regarded with any favor in Israel. On the contrary, no eunuch, no impotent man, could enter into the congregation of God (Deut. xxiii. 1), and only of the future system of salvation was it prophesied that not even the eunuch should be shut out from it (Isa. lvi. 3; see Gen. ii. 18; Matt. xix. 4, 5; Eph. v. 23; 2 Cor. xi. 2; 1 Tim. iv. 1–3).—The Angel with the everlasting Gospel. This is the Angel of missions, the representative of all missionary labor, both within apostate Christendom and in heathen lands. (Missions are good and great; but the reference here is to a time when missions must have completed their work, and to a new fact, the end-judgment, in its character of a gospel of a blessed eternity, f·r believers.)

[From M. HENRY: Chap. xiv. 13. *Blessed are the dead who die in the Lord from henceforth, etc.* They are blessed, 1. In their *rest; they rest from* all sin, temptation, sorrow, and persecution. 2. In their recompense, *their works follow them;* they do not go before them as their title or purchase, but *follow them* as their evidence of having lived and *died in the Lord.* 3. In the time of their dying, when they have lived to see God's cause reviving, the peace of the Church returning, and the wrath of God falling upon their idolatrous, cruel enemies.—From THE COMPREHENSIVE COMMENTARY: Chap. xiv. 4. *They follow the Lamb whithersoever He goeth.* Through persecutions and tribulations, into obscurity, or into prisons, with self-denial, obedient faith, and patient hope; "taking up their cross," and copying His example of meekness, purity and love. (SCOTT.)—From BARNES: Ver. 3. To appreciate fully the song of Zion; to understand the language of praise; to enter into the spirit of the truths which pertain to redemption, one must himself have been redeemed by the blood of Christ.—Ver. 11. *And they have no rest, day nor night.* It will be one of the bitterest ingredients in the cup of woe, in the world of despair, that the luxury of *rest* will be denied forever, and that they who enter that gloomy prison sleep no more; never know the respite of a moment—never even lose the consciousness of their heavy doom.—Ver. 13. *Blessed are the dead.* We should be grateful for any system of religion which will enable us thus to speak of those who are dead; which will enable us, with corresponding feeling, to look forward to our own departure from this world.—*Which die in the Lord.* Not all the dead; for God never pronounces the condition of the wicked who die, blessed or happy. The declaration is confined to those who furnish evidence that they are prepared for heaven. "To die in the Lord" implies, 1. That they who thus die are the friends of the Lord Jesus. 2. It would seem also to imply that there should be, at the time, the evidence of His favor and friendship. This would apply (1) to those who die as martyrs; and (2) to those who have the comfort-

ing evidence of His presence and favor on the bed of death.—*That they may rest from their labors.* In view of such eternal rest from toil, we may well endure the labors and toils incident to the short period of the present l fe, for however arduous or difficult, it will soon be ended.—*Their works do follow them.* Note here, 1. That *all* that the righteous do and suffer here will be appropriately recompensed there. 2. This is *all* that can follow a man to eternity. He can take with him none of his gold, his lands, his raiment; none of the honors of this life. none of the means of sensual gratification. All that will go with him will be his character, and the results of his conduct here; and, in this respect, eternity will be but a prolongation of the present life. 3. It is one of the highest honors of our nature that we can make the present affect the future for good; that by our conduct on earth we can lay the foundation for happiness millions of ages hence.—Ver. 15. *For the time is come for Thee to reap.* That is, "the harvest which *Thou* art to reap is ripe; the seed which *Thou* hast sown has grown up; the earth which *Thou* hast cultivated has produced this golden grain, and it is fit that Thou shouldst now gather it in."—From VAUGHAN: Chap. xiv. 7 Till a man fears, he can never know hope. The first call of the everlasting Gospel itself is to fear God and to worship the universal Creator.—Ver. 11. Some rest not day nor night from praise (Rev. iv. 8); others rest not day nor night from suffering.—Ver. 15. As there is a harvest of the earth for good, so also there is a harvest of the soul, an immaturity and a ripeness of the individual Christian.—Ver. 18. So also there is an individual ripening for the vintage of wrath and judgment.—From BONAR: *These are they which follow the Lamb whithersoever He goeth.* We follow Him here in suffering and service, as we shall follow Him hereafter in glory and joy.]

SECTION THIRTEENTH.

Earth-picture of the Seven Vials of Anger, or the End-judgment in its general aspect. (*Ch. xvi.*)

General.—The special homiletical treatment of this section is, like that of others, made more difficult by the disagreement of exegetes. According to Hengstenberg, for instance, the *earth* denotes the earthly-minded; the *sea*, the sea of nations, the unquiet wicked world (in antithesis to the earthly-minded!); the *fountains of waters*, the sources of prosperity; the *sun*, that luminary in its burning quality, the type of the sufferings of this life; the *throne of the Beast*, the government of the Roman emperors; the *Euphrates*, the hinderance to the advance of the God-opposed world-power into the Holy Land, against the Holy City, against the Church.

According to Brandt, the *earth* is the Holy Land, which has become the scene of the world-kingdom of the Dragon; the *sea* is the mass of peoples united under the sceptre of the Beast; the *rivers* and *fountains* are the peoples and families in their still subsistent sunderment; the *sun* is the glowing sun and nothing more; the *throne of the Beast* is the sovereign power of the Beast; the *Euphrates* is the Beast out of the Earth, or Babylon.

The exposition of Sabel is in part b-tter; The *earth* denotes the positive foundations of State and Church; the *sea*, the Gentile-Christian world of nations. Next, however, come some abortive interpretations: The *waters of life* [*rivers*] are the refreshing truths of salvation, and the *fountains of waters* are the schools at which they are taught; the *sun* is the Church of Jesus Christ; the *throne of the Beast* is the Antichristian world —its *darkening* is the confusion and shattering of that world —The *Euphrates* is well characterized as emblematic of the boundary line of the civilized world; the *drying up* of it betokens a change in political wisdom resulting in a new migration of nations, as it were.

The Vials of Anger should, above all, be compared with the Trumpets; and the antithesis between the Trumpets calling to rep-ntance and the judgments of hardening, should be noted. The judgments of hardening may be elucidated by the Egyptian plagues, Isa. vi. 10 and analogous passages. They are indicative of such judgments as ripen corruption—when it has come to be past healing—into its final development and con-ummation, thus resulting in blasphemy, which in itself is damnation (vers. 9, 11, 21), whilst the Trumpets were designed to produce repentance. The first Vial of Anger readily suggests examples of the moral corruption and dissolution of individual states and communities (Babylon, Jerusalem, Rome, *etc.*) as warning signs.

In treating the second Vial of Anger we may touch upon the symptoms of the empoisonment of popular life by writings, tendencies, conspiracies. The symbolic import of the *rivers* is sufficiently attested by Scripture—the Nile, the Euphrates, the Jordan, the brook of Siloah; the same remark applies to the *fountains*. A consideration of poisoned and poisoning, death-dealing currents and fountains or fountain minds, would be appropriate here. The transformation of the *sun* of revelation into a glowing and scorching mass, by human fanaticism, negative as well as positive, is easily intelligible. The *darkening* of the throne and kingdom of *darkness* may be explained by the crumbling of the power of falsehood into contradictions partyisms and suicidal compl ts. The *drying up of the Euphrates*, as the abolition of the boundary line between the civilized and the barbarian world, has a rich significance. Abolition of the distinctions of religions, stations, culture, of the sexes (emancipation of women), *etc.*—Symbolic import of the *frogs.*—The dissolution and decomposition of the common spiritual vital *air* must be a presage that the common existence of those who breathe it is drawing to a close.—The downfall of things in the evening of the world will be, first, a downfall of th spirit-world (ver. 19); secondly, a downfall of nature; thirdly, a downfall of the relation between the human world and the life of nature.

Special.—[Chap. xvi.] The Vials of Anger in comparison with Christ's Cup of Suffering: 1. The similarity; 2. The contrast.—[Ver. 2.] The *noisome sore* in a social and a spiritual sense: Deficit; corruption of morals; mortality, *etc.*—[Vers. 3, 4.] Transformation of the waters into blood, a retribution for the nefarious and mock-holy

shedding of blood (vers. 5-7).—Apology for the avenging righteousness of God.—The blasphemies (vers. 9, 11, 21). How are they punished? Primarily, through themselves, (1) their madness, (2) their impotence, (3) their torment.—[Ver. 12.] The dangers to Christian humanity lying dormant in the Orient. An Orient of mischief over against the Orient of salvation.—[Ver. 13.] The *three frogs.* Even in respect to the terrors of the last time, a sacred irony of the Spirit is manifested, testifying to the freeness of the Spirit.—[Ver. 14] Enthusiasm of those inspired by the frogs.—[Ver. 15.] The Coming of the Lord compared with the coming of a thief: 1. Strangeness of the figure; 2. Design of this strangeness.—[Ver. 16.] *Armageddon,* or the theocratic battle fields. — Battle-fields of the world, from their dark and their bright side.— The last battle-field: Armageddon, the scene of a conflict between the world and the spirit-realm. —[Ver. 17.] *It is done!*—The last glorious revelation of Christ's Spirit in His Church (ver. 18). —[Ver. 19.] The falling of great Babylon into three parts, the announcement of the three judgments.—Crisis of nature in the evening of the world (vers. 20, 21).

STARKE: (This expositor continues his presentation of opposite views.) Ver. 2. Those who regard this as already fulfilled, explain it mystically thus: The *sore* is the manifestly shameful and hurtful condition of the whole papistic Church. (In contrast to this view, there is a *literal* exposition of the empoisonment of earth and of life, and also an *allegorical* interpretation, referring the passage to the bad conscience and anguish of soul of the wicked.)—The wrath of man is greater than his power, but God has power to carry out His wrath (1 Ki. xix. 2, 3).— Ver. 4. Those who regard this plague as fulfilled see in it the blood-thirsty doctrines and counsels of the Pope.—Ver. 6. God, in proportioning His punishments to the sins which have provoked them, teaches us that we should proportion our penitence to our sins.—The blood of saints is precious in God's eyes; He forgetteth it not, but recompenseth it with righteous vengeance.— Ver. 8. Interpretations of the *sun:* [1] The natural sun; [2] A mighty king; [3] The Beast (1 Reinbeck).—Ver. 9. Application to the wars of Charles VIII. and subsequent French kings in Italy.—As all things work together for the good of the pious, so all things, even the beams of the sun, work evil to the wicked (Rom. viii. 28).— QUESNEL: The scourgings of God discover the heart; out of a perverse heart they bring forth blasphemies, out of a penitent heart they bring praise, humility and love.—Ver. 10. Even thrones and majesties are not secure from the chastisement of God. He can in His wrath destroy entire and flourishing kingdoms.—DIMPEL: Misuse not thy tongue for the flattery and excessive exaltation of the lofty, the distinguished and the rich, that thou mayest not afterwards, when God taketh such idols from thee, have to moan and lament, aye, and gnaw thy tongue for vexation; but let thy tongue daily tell of God's righteousness.—Ver. 10. Singular interpretation: The darkening of the Beast's kingdom is the revelation, reaching far and wide, of all the abominations and vices of the Pope and the whole Roman clergy. Opposite (?) interpretation: The kingdom of the Beast despised by men.—Ver. 12. Some: The drying up of the Euphrates is yet to come, although it might seem to be partially fulfilled in the kingdom of France, that being the most powerful kingdom of Europe, and the one that has afforded most protection to the Beast, in the persecution of the Huguenots, etc.—A great religious war is in prospect, the issue of which is greatly to be desired for the true Church.—Ver. 13. The frogs: considered in respect of the Antichristian hellish trinity in which they originate—viz., the Dragon, the Beast and the False Prophet. Many a one who has a horror of the Devil when Scripture calls him a Dragon, listens to him with complacency when he speaks by the mouth of an unchaste woman, or a false teacher or godless babbler. The Devil has his apostles, as well as the Lord.—QUESNEL: Satan has his designs when he assembles armies, men have theirs, and God has His, to the realization of which last all things must conduce (Is. x. 6, 7).

QUESNEL: [Ver. 17.] There is a seventh and last Vial for every individual sinner, but who knows it?—Ver. 18. Some apprehend this mystically as referring to the Church: there shall be voices, open preaching of the Gospel, the thunder of the Divine word, and lightnings, the bright light of the Gospel, shall break forth again with power, and a remarkable movement of men's souls shall be the result.—Ver. 21. How foolish it is to attach ourselves to a world that fleeth away, and, like our desires, vanisheth.—Ver. 21. God's chastisements do not always make men better—they sometimes have a directly opposite effect.

BENGEL, Sechzig erbauliche Reden. The Trumpets make a wide circuit in a long time, but the Vials make quick work of it.—The four holy Beasts [Living-beings] are nearer to the Throne than the Angels in general, and these seven Angels in particular (recte!) [ch. xv. 7].—The earth is Asia, the sea Europe, the rivers Africa (which contains the two principal rivers, the Nile and the Niger, etc.). The sun is the whole surface of the earth (partly, therefore, Asia, Europe and Africa again).—Ver. 10. They still think that the Beast is right, and they become none other than they were, either internally or externally.—Ver. 21. The whole creation is like an organ with many stops, and when one stop after another shall be drawn out as a plague upon the wicked, scorners shall learn somewhat that they look not for.

Briefe über die Offenb. Joh. Ein Buch für die Starken, die schwach heissen (PFENNINGER).—Vers. 1, 2. An evil and poisonous ulcer came upon the men who had the mark of the Beast and who worshipped his image. Another wonderful and repentance-preaching sparing of Christians.—Vers. 8, 9. How strong must be our conviction of the immeliorability of these men.—Vers. 17-21. The great earthquake, greater than any that had ever been, will, judging from ver. 20, bring about those great changes in the shape of the earth, whose embellishment is in prospect, which must precede the time of the Messiah's government. — [Ver. 21.] The last nail: I, for my part, confess that as often as I think of a violent—nay, of the most violent—fever of earth, I can never picture to myself all the symptoms, in their great variety and contrast, in sufficient grandeur and extraordinariness.

[From M. HENRY: Ver. 15. When God's cause comes to be tried, and His battles to be fought, all His people should be ready to stand up for His interest, and be faithful and valiant in His service.—Ver. 21. Note here, 1. The greatest calamities that can befall men will not bring them to repentance without the grace of God working with them. 2. Those that are not made better by the judgments of God, are always the worse for them. 3. To be hardened in sin and enmity against God by His righteous judgments, is a certain token of utter destruction. —From THE COMPREHENSIVE COMMENTARY: Vers. 9, 11, 21. Without the special, preventing grace of God . . . the more men suffer, and the more plainly they see the hand of God in their sufferings, the more furiously they often rage against Him. Let then sinners now seek repentance from Christ, and the grace of the Holy Spirit, or they will hereafter have the anguish and horror of an unhumbled, impenitent and desperate heart, burning with enmity against God, as well as tortured by the fire of His indignation; and thus augmenting guilt and misery to all eternity. (SCOTT.)—Ver. 15. These will be times of great temptation; and therefore Christ, by His apostle, called on His professed servants to expect His sudden coming, and to "watch," that they might retain, and be found in, the garments of salvation, and not "walk naked," and so be put to shame, as apostates or hypocrites; for the blessing would belong only to the watchful. (SCOTT.)—From WORDSWORTH: Vials are holy vessels. . . . Wherever means of grace are not duly used, they recoil on those to whom they have been offered, and become means of punishment.—From VAUGHAN: Ver. 15. The garments of the watcher must not be laid aside; he must have his loins girded about (for action), as well as his lights burning (Luke xii. 35).—The peculiarity of Christ's coming is that everything which seems to defer really brings it near; everything which seems to make it improbable is an argument of its certainty and of its approach. Behold, I come as a thief.—Awake, then, thou that sleepest! Be not found of Him, when He cometh, drowsy and stupefied, overcharged with cares and riches and pleasures of this life; the lamp of grace expiring, or the garment of holiness laid aside.—From BONAR: Ver. 15. These are words for all time, but specially for the last days. They (1) warn, (2) quicken, (3) rouse, (4) comfort. Note here, 1. The coming. Christ comes (1) as Avenger, (2) as Judge, (3) as King, (4) as Bridegroom. "As a thief;"—at midnight; when men are asleep; when darkness lies on earth; when men are least expecting Him; when they have lain down, saying: "Peace and safety." Without warning, though with vengeance for the world in His hand: when all past warnings of judgment have been unheeded. Without further message; for all past messages have been in vain. Like a thief to the world, but like a Bridegroom to the Church. 2. The watching. Not believing, nor hoping, nor waiting merely; but watching. Watch upon your knees. Watch with your Bibles before you. Watch with wide open eye. Watch for Him Whom not having seen you love. 3. *The keeping of the garments.* Do not cast off your raiment either for sleep or for work. Do not let the world strip you of it. Keep it and hold it fast. It is heavenly raiment, and without it you cannot go in with your Lord when He comes. 4. *The blessedness.* It is blessed (1) because it cherishes our love; (2) it is one of the ways of maintaining our intercourse; (3) it is the posture through which He has appointed blessing to come, in His absence, to His waiting Church. 5. *The warning.* Adam was ashamed at being found naked when the Lord came down to meet him; how much more of shame and terror shall be to unready souls at meeting with a returning Lord! O false disciple, come out of your delusion and hypocrisy, lest you be exposed in that day of revelation! O sinner, make ready, for the day of vengeance is at hand!]

Section Fourteenth.

First Special End-Judgment: The Judgment upon Babylon, as a Heaven-picture.

(*Ch. xvii.*)

General.—*Babylon,* in the wider sense of the term, is the entire anti-Godly world, conceived of in its concentration; *Babylon,* in the narrower sense of the term, is the secularized, ungodly and anti-Godly, external Church; a birth-place of Antichristianity, in which the Antichristian essence often appears very undisguisedly, though the Beast, Antichrist himself, does not manifest himself therein. Here, the reference is to Babylon in the narrower sense, and primarily in respect of the heavenly appearance of her judgment.

According to this Heaven-picture of the judgment, the horrible appearance of the Woman is itself the *judgment.* Conformably to her general appearance, she is the *great Harlot* (vers. 1, 2), *i. e.* the object and subject of idolatry, the patroness of, and seducer to, apostasy from the living God. Her appearance is presented in abominable contradictions: 1. A *Woman* in the *wilderness* of a seemingly holy renunciation of the world and asceticism, and yet riding, like an Amazon, upon a royally decorated *Beast,* a many-headed monster, marked with *names of blasphemy.* 2. The Woman in magnificent princely attire, with the *golden cup* in her hand —and yet in, and together with, the cup, *abominations and uncleannesses* of idolatry, and even bearing *on her forehead,* for all who are acquainted with spiritual characters, the following title: *Babylon the Great, the mother of the fornications and abominations of the earth.* 3. The Woman, claiming the purest womanliness, in the religious sense of the term (see ch. xii.), *drunken—with the blood of the saints;* with the blood, even, *of the martyrs of Jesus—of Jesus,* Whose mother, sister, bride, she would fain be called.

The Beast on which she rides has also great contradictions attaching to it. 1. *It was and is not.* The ungodly world-power *was* and is *not*—

is in principle annihilated by Christianity. 2. It is not, and it *will ascend out of the abyss,* to a new development of ungodly worldly glory in face of Christianity. 3. It will ascend, to the end that it may *go* down *into perdition.* 4. It is the hardest riddle to all the pious, the *admiration* of all the *earthly-minded.* 5. Its *seven heads are seven mountains,* which, however, are in reality identical with many ebbing and flowing waters. 6. It goes to destruction in the consecrated septenary of its kings, only to revive again in the profane decenary of kings. 7. It has long borne the Woman on its colossal body, and will at last destroy her with its *ten horns.* 8. The monstrous dividedness of the Beast is transformed into perfect unitedness in the warfare against the Harlot. 9. The Woman goes to destruction through the contradiction of her similarity to the Lamb and her affinity to the Beast.

Special.—[Ver. 1.] *Come, I will show thee the judgment of the great Harlot.* Her appearance itself, therefore, is, primarily, her judgment. We are not to shun speaking of this judgment; but we must not interpret it rudely, in a manner offensive to the legal system of faith and worship. We have, therefore, to distinguish (1) between the Woman and the Beast which bears her; (2) between the symbolic form of the Woman, which embraces a symbolic Babylon, and her historic and most prominent organs and central points; (3) at the same time we are to recognize the fact that the corruption of the Church converges, more or less, to historic nodes, and is therein consummated. Babylon is everywhere in the Church, and yet is nowhere perfectly palpable; it, however, has its historic zenith-points. (Who, for instance, could refuse to reckon consummate Byzantinism, Mormonism and other sects based upon a pretension to inspiration, as forming portions of Babylon?)— As many Antichrists appear in the fore-ground of Antichristianity (1 John ii. 18), so in the foreground of the consummate Babylon of the last time there are many Babylons, especially predominantly spiritual and predominantly secular figures of Babylon.—A leading mark of Babylon is the universal ruinous effect which proceeds from the very city which *pretends to be* and once *was* a teacher and educator of the nations; this effect is two-fold and in many respects antithetic: the seduction of kings to fanatical worldliness, and of nations to fanatical mock-holiness.—[Ver. 2.] *With whom the kings of the earth committed fornication.* An old and yet in many respects new story. History points to a whole series of dynasties which have been ruined by fanaticism, or have at least been brought to the very verge of ruin.—History tells us of nations that *have been made drunk,* and that have more or less, sunk into national ruin. Fallen or sunken Christian kingdoms in the East and West —[Vers. 3, 4.] The similarity and the difference between the picture of ch. xii. and that of the present chapter: 1. Between the phases of the Woman; 2. Between the phases of the wilderness; 3. Between the relative positions of the Woman and the Beast.—Contrast between the wilderness abode of the Woman and her luxury —Contrast between her perilous equestrian seat figuring a taming of the Beast, and her festal attire. (There is also a distinction between war-boots—Eph. vi. 15—and slippers.)—Contrast between the golden cup and the abominations contained in it.—[Ver. 5.] The name on the forehead—manifest and yet a mystery.—The old antithesis: Babylon and Zion. — [Ver. 6.] Amazement of John (see Exeg. Notes).—Horror of the holy mind at a caricature of the holy. —Strange manifestation of unnaturalness in the corruptions of the Church.—Ver. 8. How the earthly-minded are, by the terrible aspect of the Beast, kept in a state of dependence upon the Woman, as long as the latter sits upon the Beast. —Ver. 9. *Hither an understanding that hath wisdom.* Profane learning can only misinterpret this enigmatical phenomenon.—The world-monarchies, see Exeg. Notes.—Waverings of unredeemed humanity between the false unity of the world-monarchy and a dissipation into heathenism, barbarism, savageness.—Continuance of this wavering in the antithesis of the Hierarchy and separatism, absolutism and radicalism. —[Ver. 12] The *ten horns:* Or the fall of religious absolutism is followed by the rule of an irreligious radicalism.—[Ver. 13.] Demonic union of the ten horns. The principle of this union is to be found in their hatred of the Lamb, whose shadow they still persecute in the Woman. —Ver. 14. *The Lamb shall conquer them.* Find the agreement between this and ch. xiii. 7. Of a conquest through [seeming] defeat, and a defeat through [seeming] conquest. What contrasts between the inner and the outer world, between the passing moment and the future, between seeming and being, are contained in the preceding paragraph.—The Beast as the conqueror of the Harlot, conquered by the Lamb.— Comp. the Old Testament prophecies against Babylon, especially Jer. li.—Fearful mission of the ten kings (ver. 17).—[Ver. 16.] Threefold judgment upon the Woman.—[Ver. 12.] The Antichristian power lasts but *one hour, i. e.,* a short time; but it is an *hour* in the theocratico-religious sense, a sore and painful hour of temptation [trial]. The union of the wicked occurs only in special moments of judgment and never, through an abolition of their inner egoistical division, attains to the oneness of the saints.— Ver. 18. in relation to ver. 7. In Heaven, the unnatural appearance of the Woman is itself, already, "the judgment of the great *Harlot.*"

Starke: Application of the judgment upon Babylon to the "idolatrous Church of the Papacy." Reasons for this application: "the great magnificence and ostentation of this Church in the external worship of God: the blandishments and flatteries which it employs to draw people to itself, etc." *Fornication* is interpreted as spiritual adultery, apostasy from Christ, the Husband of the Church. It is easy to learn who this Harlot is, from the description of her, and from her antithesis, the Bride of the Lamb. Her equestrian posture indicates that she derives her might and authority from the Beast and that she rules over it ;—that she has arbitrarily subjected the Roman Empire to herself, has placed herself above emperors and kings, and has instated and deposed them. The crimson and bloody hue [of the Beast] is indicative of the bloodthirstiness excited in it by the persuasions of the Harlot.—[Ver. 4.] *Arrayed in purple and scarlet: purple,* to indicate her usurped royal exaltation and pre-eminence above all potentates; and *scarlet,* to indicate her thirst for the blood of the saints. The true Church is resplendent only in the robe of Christ. There is nothing so abominable and unclean that it cannot be disguised and decorated with a tinsel of this world. —Ver. 5. The whole essence of false religion is a *mystery,* but a *mystery of iniquity* and all godlessness (2 Thess. ii. 7). As the mystery of Christ passes all understanding and incites to godliness, so the mystery of iniquity is conceived by pure serpent-cunning and contains nothing but deception; note, *e. g.,* the miraculous power resident, as the Church of Rome pretends, in certain pictures and images, *etc.*—[Ver. 6.] A leading mark of the false Church: pagan Rome, in the three centuries [of her existence subsequent to the Christian era], shed less blood, by far, than so-called Christian Rome. (Starke adduces the example of France, in particular.)—Ver. 8. *And yet is :* This is not to be understood as referring to Antiochus himself or to such Antichristian regents as stood in the fiercest spirit of Antiochus (*Hoffmann's view ?*).—Ver. 9. *Understanding* and *wisdom* are two different things. There may be understanding without wisdom, but there can be no wisdom without understanding.—(Starke mentions the *seven mountains* of *Rome;* he remarks, however, that the Apocalyptic *seven mountains* have also been interpreted as seven famous Popes.)—Ver. 12. *Marginal gloss,* (Luther): These are the other kings,—for instance, of Hungary, Bohemia, Poland, France (!).—Quesnel: The Lamb suffers and succumbs in His members, and the members, whilst they are oppressed, conquer in the Lamb (Rom. viii. 37).—Ver. 16. This verse is entirely subversive of the opinion that the Beast denotes the Pope. —*Great cities,* great sins; and by the example of such cities, whole countries are seduced (Jer. xxiii. 15).

Auberlen (p. 317 [Eng. Trans.]): The fact that the Harlot is judged first, is not only in harmony with the general principle, that judgment must begin at the house of God (Jer. xxv. 29 ; Ezek. ix. 6 ; 1 Pet. iv. 17), but a restoration of actual truth is also designed. The object which, in effect, alone continues to exist— is recognized as existing—at the time indicated [the time of the judgment of the Harlot], is the world ; for even the Church now courts only *its* favor, even for the Church *it* is the only reality. Against such a Church, the world must carry the day ; and therefore the Harlot is not judged by the Lord Himself, but by the Beast and its kings.

Graeber: [Ver. 5.] A *mother of harlots* is one who brings up others to harlotry.—Ver. 6. It must needs be a subject of highest amazement that Christians, or those who pretend to be Christians, can reach such a pass.—[Ver. 16.] The Catholic States will in great part themselves accomplish the work of the destruction of the papacy.

Laemmert (*Das Thier und der falsche Prophet,* p. 36) : " The origin of Babel [Babylon] is related, Gen. xi. (comp. with ch. x. 8-12). This [Gen. xi.] is the same chapter which, in its second part, gives the genealogy of the chosen

Shemite, Abraham, and closes by describing the exode of Terah and his family from Chaldea and their entrance into Canaan. Here, therefore, we already have the foundation and beginnings of that grand dualism which runs through the whole of the Sacred Writings and the entire history of mankind down to the consummation. The founder of Babel was a grandson of him who scoffed at his father, and his name was *Nimrod*, *i. e.*, rebel. Human arrogance built the city and the tower, *to make itself a name*—not to the honor of God's name; of its own strength and will—not at the behest of God. The inner motives were thoughts of arrogance, of the deification of man and of self."

CHANTEPIE DE LA SAUSSAYE, *De Toekomst*, p. 117. *Man kann zeggen, dat a grond der tegenstelling der beide rijken reeds ligt in de paradijs-belofte. Doch wat daar nog slechts in het allgemeen genœmd wordt het zaad der slang, etc., verkrijgt immer meer kleur en gestalte.*

[From THE COMPREHENSIVE COMMENTARY.— The Lord takes pleasure in satisfying His people concerning the reason and equity of His judgments on His enemies; that they may not be intimidated by the severity of them, or fail to adore and praise Him on that account.—Great prosperity, pomp and splendor, commonly feed the pride and lusts of the human heart; yet they form no security against Divine vengeance.— Those who allure or tempt others to sin, must expect more aggravated punishment, in proportion to the degree of the mischief done by them. (SCOTT.)]

SECTION FIFTEENTH.

First Special End-Judgment; Judgment upon Babylon. Earth-picture. (Ch. xviii.)

General.—That essential judgment of Babylon which lies in her very appearance, and has been manifested in the light of Heaven, is here unfolded on earth in a distinct series of evolutions.

The first Act of the judgment, as executed by the Angel from Heaven, consists of the verdict upon Babylon, the sentence of Divine justice.

The second Act is the incipient execution of the judgment in the social sphere of justice. It is divided into two actions: (1) The people of God go out of Babylon (vers. 4, 6), and (2) the world is commissioned to react against Babylon in pursuance of the same law of violence which she herself has exercised (vers. 6, 8). The universality of her judgment is expressed in the despair and lamentation of all her allies, who are too cowardly to take her part, but yet are stricken with her. The third Act is the complete historic repudiation of Babylon, executed by the strong Angel with a millstone, in a symbolic act.

The whole constitutes the greatest tragedy of the world, complete in *three* or *five* Acts, according to the greater or less prominence bestowed upon the middle items:

1. The guilt of Babylon towards humanity;
2. The exode of the people of God from her;
3. The reaction of the hostile world against her;
4. The lamentation of her friends—a prelude to the final catastrophe:
5. The final catastrophe.

The *Angel* who, *descending from Heaven, lightens the earth with his radiance*, and proclaims the fall of Babylon, is also, without doubt, the actual spiritual author of her judgment. For he has *great authority*, and transports her judgment from Heaven to earth. That is, that judgment which is already declared in the sphere of the celestial Spirit, with the delineation of the character of Babylon, now, through the heavenly illumination proceeding from the Angel, becomes a subject of the universal consciousness of mankind. We hold that the Angel represents evangelic Christianity in the full development of the beauty of its moral and humane principles. For Babylon has outraged all these principles, from liberty of conscience to the recognition of public law. She has perverted her claim to be the educator of mankind into the exact opposite, having become the seducer and destroyer of humanity.

The cry of this Angel is followed by the *voice from Heaven*, the sentence of the heavenly Spirit, the law of the Kingdom of God—declaratory, on the one hand, of the right of the Church (*come forth out of her*) and, on the other hand, of the right of the State (*recompense to her*), and expressing itself, thirdly, as the spirit of history and poetry, in the portrayal of the great lamentations. The tragic coloring of this entire judgment-scene is distinctly brought out in all this; it is particularly prominent, however, in the symbolic execution of the final catastrophe.

Special.—[Ver. 1.] Who is the Angel who comes down from Heaven, and whose glory lightens the earth?—[Ver. 2.] The mighty cry over Babylon. *Fallen! fallen!* or the perfect certainty that Babylon *will fall* on earth, even as she *has already fallen* in the sight of God.—Contrast betwixt what Babylon should be and what she has become.—[Ver. 3.] Babylon's transgression against mankind: (1) against the *nations*, (2) against the *kings*, (3) against the *rich* and *great*.—[Ver. 4.] Call to the people of God, to *come out from Babylon*: 1. Meaning of the call; 2. Motive of the call; 3. Neglect of the call (latitudinarianism); 4. Misinterpretation of the call (separatism).—[Vers. 4, 6.] Diverse conduct of the Church and the world toward guilty Babylon.——Retributory right of the world. This remains pure only in so far as it remains an execution of the right and keeps itself free from fanaticism.—[Ver. 8.] Recompense of corporeal fiery judgments by a social and spiritual judgment of fire.—[Vers. 7, 8.] Contrast between the haughty self-blinding of Babylon and her imminent and great day of judgment.—The City of the Seven Mountains: yesterday and to-day.—[Vers. 9-19.] The three lamentations of the world over the fall of Babylon. Common characteristics of them: 1. A view of her fall; 2. A standing afar off and refraining from taking her part; 3. A participation in the stroke that has fallen upon her—but in the sorrow of this world, with no recognition of the justice of the blow, of its nature as a judgment, or of the Judge Who has inflicted it.—Heaven's judgments, earth's tragedies.—[Vers. 9, 10.] Lamentation of the kings (see EXEG. NOTES).— [Vers. 11, 15-17]. Lamentation of the great the supporters of the luxury of the earth.— [Vers. 17-19]. Lamentation of the pilots o tradesmen.—Community and division of egoistical interests in the lamentations over the fall of Babylon.—Ironical enumeration of the depreciated goods of Babylon (vers. 12-14).—As the Church in its way, and the State in its way, so science and art in their way are concerned in the judgment upon Babylon.—The unspiritual lamentation of the world over the fall of Babylon contains the germ of that judgment which is later to descend upon the world.—[Ver. 21.] The symbolic act of the strong Angel, a representation of the grand final catastrophe itself.— [Vers. 22, 23.] Babylon's desolation. Her spiritual desolation shall be followed by an æsthetic desolation, and to this a desolation of business and of home life shall succeed.—Ver. 24. The summit of Babylon's guilt: she is the murderess of the prophets and saints.—This verse is supplemental to ver. 3.

STARKE: Ver. 2; comp. Is. xxi. 7; Jer. li 8 The repetition of the word [*fallen*] is indicative of the greatness and certainty of the fall.—Ver. 4. This *exode* is based upon a gracious *leading out* on the part of God. There are certain grades in the execution of it, and it is performed as follows: 1. With the *heart*, by a right belief and acknowledgment of the truth, and hatred of false doctrine; 2. With the *mouth*, by a public confession of the truth, and rejection of errors; 3. With the *body*, by a going away from those places in which Babylon has its throne and superstition.—God's people and Church are, partially, still in Babylon, although hidden; otherwise God could not command them to come out. —[Ver. 5.] Sins that cry unto Heaven (Gen. iv. 10), whose measure is full, and upon which final ruin follows.—Ver. 7. These words are taken from Isa. xlvii. 5-10. The greater the security and pride of the wicked, the more terrible is their punishment.—Ver. 8. As Babylon burned innocent martyrs with fire, so shall she herself be burned with fire.—Ver. 10. The fear of torment may cause us (outwardly) to remove far from those with whom we have sinned, but love to God alone can make their sin odious to us.—Ver. 12. QUESNEL: Let us gather treasures that will endure to eternity; nought is eternal save that which is done with a view to eternity. Ver. 16. The world does not mourn over the loss of eternal salvation, but over the loss of riches and external magnificence.—Ver. 20. It is at the downfall of evil, and at Divine vengeance that the pious rejoice; not out of a carnal mind and self-love, but by the ordinance of God and from the love of righteousness (Ps. xci. 8).—Ver. 21. The wicked fall into the abyss of perdition as stones fall into the abyss of the sea. That which the world regards as highly exalted finally meets with the deeper fall (Ezek. xxi. 26).—Ver. 24. The slaughter of true believers under the papacy is like the murder of the saints in the beginning of the world.—Great cities are destroyed on account of the many and enormous sins that are committed in them.—God reckons to the charge of the wicked all the sins of their ancestors, because they tread in their foot-steps (and the guilt of their ancestors attains its consummation and meridian in them).

Schlüssel zur Offenb. Joh. durch einen Kreuzritter (p. 289): The most terrible thing for a human

community is when the salt of the earth, that should preserve it from corruption, is taken out of it by death or emigration, when the props of the rotten building give way, when Lot is led forth from Sodom, because there are not even ten righteous men therein.

[From M. HENRY: Ver. 4. Those that are resolved to partake with wicked men in their sins must receive of their plagues.—Ver. 5. When the sins of a people reach up to heaven, the wrath of God will reach down to earth.— Ver. 7. God will proportion the punishment of sinners to the measure of their wickedness, pride and security.—Vers. 9-19. *The pleasures of sin are but for a season, and they will end in dismal sorrow.*]

SECTION SIXTEENTH.

Second Special End-Judgment, or the Judgment upon the Beast (Antichrist) and his Prophet. **a.** *Heavenly World-picture of the Victory.* (*Ch. xix. 1-16.*)

General.—The heavenly post-celebration of the judgment upon the Harlot issues in a precelebration of the marriage of the Bride. For the Harlot and the Bride bear toward each other the indissoluble relation of a contradictory antithesis. *Heaven*, or the Church Triumphant, and not God's Church on earth, celebrates, pre-eminently, *the judgment of the Harlot*; for an exalted stand-point is requisite for this celebration, and with lesser spirits, vulgar minds, it might easily degenerate into fanaticism. Even in the Heaven of consummate spiritual life, the positive result of that judgment is the thing which is first rejoiced over. *The salvation and the glory and the power are our God's.* Not until after this, is the satisfaction of justice touched upon (ver. 2). The perfect fixedness of the judgment is next set forth (ver. 3). The whole heavenly postcelebration of the judgment is completed in an antiphony, in which the natural relations seem to be inverted, in that the *twenty-four Elders and four Life-forms* utter the *Amen*, which is supplemented by the third *Hallelujah*. Thus a three-fold heavenly Hallelujah is devoted to the rejoicings over the judgment. The Church of God on earth is now commanded to join in the celebration, and her rejoicing assumes the form of a pre-celebration of the *marriage of the Bride.* The delineation of the simple, yet august, adornment of the Bride, and the glorification of the imminent marriage, are followed by the appearance of the Bridegroom, coming from Heaven, on His warlike and victorious march against the Beast.

Special.—[Vers. 1-4.] Three-fold *Hallelujah* of the Church Triumphant over the fall of Babylon. This feature is the more significant, since it is here only that the Hallelujah appears in the Apocalypse. The Hallelujah is also philologically significant; *Jehovah, the Covenant-God,* is glorified, because Babylon obscured His glory and power to the uttermost through her idolatry; in that she, on the one hand, corrupted the earth with her idolatry, and, on the other, killed the servants of God, who sought His glory. The rising of the smoke of her torment becomes a Hallelujah as an eternal visible assurance that the salvation and the glory and the power of God, in redeemed souls, are established forever. —[Ver. 5.] The heavenly order for a general song of praise.—[Vers. 6, 7.] The song of praise: 1. The sound of it; 2. The contents of it.—The marriage of the Lamb. It will essentially consist in the fame of God's glory.—The beholding of the glory of God constitutes the bliss of the beatified. The bliss of the beatified is the highest glorification of God.—Blessed are the pure in heart, for they shall see God.—[Ver. 8.] The Bride in her adornment.—In antithesis to the Harlot in her gorgeous, but blood-colored, attire.—[Ver. 9.] Blessedness of those who are called to the marriage of the Lamb.—Every previous beatitude has this for its end and aim. This is true, above all, of the beatitudes in Matt. v.; and also of that in Rev. xiv. 13.—God's words, pure essential facts: They will be manifested to be the most real realities.—[Ver. 10.] Repeated repudiation of the worship offered by John to angelic beings — comp. chap. xxii. 9. — The measure of inward devotion is the measure of the purity of the worship which we offer to God. This inward devotion, however, is not to be defined simply in accordance with our feeling; least of all, as a mere ecstatic sentiment; but also intellectually, and as an ethical readiness.—The witness of (concerning) Jesus, the real prophecy of this world's history. — [Vers. 11-16.] The Bridegroom, in His going forth for the final redemption and emancipation of the Bride: 1. His forth-going from Heaven; 2. His character; 3. His appearance; 4. His title; 5. His army; 6. His power (ver. 15); 7. His right.

STARKE (ver. 1): *Hallelujah.* There is here, probably, an allusion to the six Psalms, from the cxiii. to the cxviii., which were called the great Hallelujah, and were sung at high festivals, especially at the Feast of Tabernacles (Ps. civ. 35).—Ver. 2, from Deut. xxii. 43. Splendor, power, subtlety, adherents — all cannot save when God wills to punish. He fears none of them.—Ver. 3, from Is. xxxiv. 10.—Ver. 4. The praise of God that issues from a heart that is full of God, fills and kindles other hearts to His praise.—Ver. 6. (This verse Starke interprets as holding forth the prospect of the conversion of the Jews.) Although there are diverse voices and powers, there is yet one Spirit, one faith, one consonance of the whole Church.—Ver. 7. The preparation of the Bride consists in her constantly becoming more qualified for the reception of all the treasures of salvation acquired by her Bridegroom.—Ver. 9. [*Write.*] The Divine authority of the matter to be recorded and of this entire Book is the more strongly indicated, the more frequent the occurrence of this expression (ch. i. 11, 19; ii. 1, 8, 12, 18; iii. 1, 7, 14; xiv. 13).—[Ver. 10.] John was not mistaken in the person of the Angel, for he well knew that he was no Divine person. (Starke here wrongfully assumes that not worship, but only an humble expression of reverence, is here denoted.)—Ver. 11. Heaven opens before Christ, both in the condition of His humiliation and in that of His exaltation.—Ver. 12. Christ has, not *one,* but *many* crowns, because He has gained many victories, and is the

King of kings.—Ver. 14. [In heaven] the faithful are resplendent in white linen, though here they may bear the cross.—Ver. 16. Kings cannot be happier than in yielding themselves subjects of Christ.

SPURGEON, *Stimmen aus der Offenb. Joh.,* p. 132. [Ver. 12. *And on His head many crowns.*] The Saviour's *many crowns.* Oh, ye well know what a *Head* that is; its wondrous history ye have not forgotten. A Head that once reclined, lovely and infantine, on the bosom of a woman. A Head that bowed meekly and willingly in obedience to a carpenter. A Head that in later years became a well of weeping and a fountain of tears (Jer. ix. 1; Heb. v. 7). A Head whose sweat was as it were great drops of blood, falling upon the earth (Luke xxii. 44). A Head that was spit upon, whose hairs were plucked out. A Head which at last, in the fearful death-struggle, wounded by the crown of thorns, gave utterance to the terrific death-cry (Ps. xxii. 1): *Lama Sabachthani!* (The *death-cry* was: *Father, into Thy hands, etc.*) A Head that afterwards slept in the grave; and—to Him Who liveth and was dead, and behold, He is living now forevermore (Rev. i. 18), be glory—a Head that rose again from the grave, and looked down, with beaming eyes of love, upon the woman who stood mourning by the sepulchre.

[From M. HENRY: Ver. 10. This fully condemns the practice of the papists in worshipping the elements of bread and wine, and saints, and angels.—From THE COMPREHENSIVE COMMENTARY: Vers. 1-4. All heaven resounds with the high praises of God, whenever He executes His "true and righteous judgments" on those who corrupt the earth with pernicious principles and ungodly practices, and when He avenges the blood of His servants on their persecutors. Who then are they that throw out insinuations, or openly speak of cruelty and tyranny, on hearing of these righteous judgments, but rebels who blasphemously take part with the enemies of God and plead against His dealings towards them? (SCOTT.)—Ver. 10. If the highest of holy creatures greatly *fear* and decidedly *refuse undue* honor, how humbly should we sinful worms of the earth behave ourselves! (SCOTT.)—From BARNES: Ver. 1. All that there is of honor, glory, power, in the redemption of the world, belongs to God, and should be ascribed to Him. —From BONAR: Ver. 10. *The testimony of Jesus is the spirit of prophecy.* The theme or burden of the Bible is Jesus. Not philosophy, nor science, nor theology, nor metaphysics, nor morality, but *Jesus.* Not mere *history,* but history as containing Jesus. Not mere *poetry,* but poetry embodying Jesus. Not certain future events, dark or bright, presented to the view of the curious or speculative, but Jesus; earthly events and hopes and fears only as linked with Him.]

SECTION SEVENTEENTH.

Second Special End-Judgment. b. *Earth-picture of the Victory over the Beast. The Parousia of Christ for Judgment. The Millennial Kingdom.* (*Ch. xix.* 17—*xx.* 5.)

General.—We must distinguish here: 1. The premise of the last time, the features of which are to be gathered from other passages; 2. Christ's war, in His Parousia, with the Beast and the False Prophet, and the judgment upon them and their Antichristian kingdom; 3. The chaining of Satan, and the Millennial Kingdom thus introduced.

The features of the last time, corresponding to its character as here pre-supposed, are visible throughout the eschatology of the Scriptures. See Matt. xxiv. 22 sqq.; Mark xiii. 16 sqq.; Luke xvii. 26 sqq.; xxi. 26 sqq.; Rom. xi.; 2 Thess. ii. 7 sqq.; 2 Tim. iii. 1 sqq.; 2 Pet. iii.; 1 John ii. 18; Jude 14, 15. Compare especially the terminal points in the cycles of the Apocalypse itself: ch. iii. 20; vi. 12 sqq.; x. 7; xi. 7; xiii.,—beginning, particularly, with ver. 11; xvii. 16. These traits are incipiently set forth in the Old Testament; comp. Is. lxiii. sqq.; Ezek. xxxvi. 33; xxxvii. 21; Dan. ix. 2; Hosea xiv. 6; Joel iii. 1; Zephaniah; Hag. ii. 6; Zech. xii. It should be noted, that in Zechariah as well as in Ezekiel *two* judgments upon the nations are distinguished: *viz.* a more special one, followed by the restoration of Israel, and a general one, with which the end-time closes. Comp. Zech. xii. and xiv., and also Ezek. xxxvi. with xxxviii. and xxxix.

The spiritual situation which superinduces the symptoms of the last time consists in the complete secularization of the Church—the carnal security of Christians, the spiritual lukewarmness of congregations, an extinction of the old foci of Christendom, and a corresponding extension of the Kingdom of God amongst heathen and Jews.

The actual date at which the last time begins corresponds with the fall of Babylon. The consummate Antichristianity of the world has executed judgment upon the wavering Antichristianity in the Church; the former has, however, drawn an apostate of the Church—the False Prophet—into its service, and with his help it obtains a social victory, in that τὸ κατέχον is taken away (2 Thess. ii. 6), or in that the two Sons of Oil (Rev. xi.) are killed.

Antichristian pseudo-Christianity, expressing itself not only in hierarchical, but also in sectarian announcements of *Here is Christ* and *There is Christ*, has turned into pseudo-Christian Antichristianity; practical atheism, or the negation of all faith, has begotten a lying positivism which prosecutes human deification even to the production of the *deified man*, the culmination point of the Antichristian tendency. For human deification is at this juncture no longer a "worship of genius," but the deification of the masses—nay, more, of the *Beast*, of the brutal power and carnal self-seeking of the masses, and this fundamentally depraved generalization must necessarily, through the worship of *agitators*, turn into the worship of *the agitator* κατ᾽ ἐξοχήν.

The actual mark of the last short, but grievous time, is a social terrorism which develops in company with the principles of Antichristianity. The perverted congregation of the Beast seeks to give itself a dogmatical and symbolical shape by its sign of recognition, the mark of the Beast: the faithful fall under the subtile social excommunication of the last time. The characteristics of this grievous time are: a great testing, a great temptation, a great trial of endurance, a great purging, all of which, however, result in a great development of the sealed. The traits of the oppressed Widow thus develop into the traits of the Bride, and the cry of the oppressed forces its way to Heaven (Luke xviii. 1-7).

The Parousia of Christ for war and victory is here, as in the Gospels, heralded by signs in Heaven and earth. With the cosmical sign of the *Angel standing in the sun* and proclaiming the approaching judgment, the cosmical signs in the Eschatological Discourse of the Lord correspond. The ethical sign on earth is the consummate conspiracy of the *kings, i. e.,* the supporters of Antichristianity, and their preparation for battle against Christ. Comp. Ps. ii. In respect of the day of rebellion, the following declaration holds good for ever: *To-day* have I begotten Thee—*i. e.,* set Thee in royal dominion.

As to the battle itself, the Seer intimates that the same turn of affairs takes place here as in the building of the tower of Babel and in the Crucifixion of Christ, and, it might also be said, in the great persecution of the Christians under Diocletian. The point of an external combat is not reached; the Antichristian army seems to be smitten with absolute confusion (ch. xvi. 10). For *the Beast* is *taken,* like an individual malefactor; with him *the False Prophet* is seized, and both are *cast into the lake of fire.* That the *slaying* of the Antichristian army is expressive of a spiritual annihilation, is evident from the fact that they are slain *with the sword which proceeds from the mouth* of Christ.

In respect to the chaining of Satan and to the Angel who accomplishes it, we refer to the Exeg. Notes. We make the same reference in regard to the Millennial Kingdom. The idea of the coming of this pervades the whole of Sacred Writ (see Ps. lxxii.; Isa. lxv., etc.).

The *First Resurrection,* as the blossom of the resurrection time, as the result of the resurrection of Christ (1 Cor. xv.), as the foretoken of the general resurrection, is also a time of great spiritual awakening and resurrection; to this period, doubtless, belongs the prospect of a more general restoration of Israel, for it occurs between the penultimate judgment upon the heathen ([nations] (the οἰκουμένη) and the last judgment (upon Gog and Magog).

With the first resurrection, the first new heavenly order of things is connected: the rule of Christ, in the midst of His people, over the world—a spiritual and social governing and judging as a foretoken of the last judgment.

The *abyss* of the curse *shut,* the *Heaven* of blessing wide *open:* these are the characteristics of the great crisis which makes the σωτηρία visibly manifest throughout an entire æon.

Special.—The appearing of Christ in its two aspects: 1. The war (ch. xix. 17–21); 2. The victory (ch. xx. 1–5).—[Vers. 17, 18.] The Angel in the sun, and the meaning of his outcry.—[Ver. 19.] The Antichristian revolt against the Lord and His army.—The spiritual combat in its form and results.—[Chap. xx. 1–3.] The Angel who chains Satan (see Exeget. Notes).—Satan shall receive his full dues when he shall be let loose again at the end of the thousand years. In other words, evil must live itself out, or completely accomplish its self-annihilation.—[Vers. 4–6.] Import of the first resurrection.—Traits from the picture of the Millennial Kingdom. STARKE (Chap. xix. 18): Those who apprehend this mystically, interpret thus: That ye may spoil the goods, *etc.*—Ver. 20. Those who apprehend this mystically, explain thus: The others, who were seduced [by the False Prophet], were more gently dealt with; they were either conquered and overcome by the sword of Christ's mouth, His word, and willingly *subjected* their life and possessions to Christ, or they lay prostrate, proscribed and despised, as dead bodies. Those who, like birds of prey, have impoverished and devoured others, shall themselves be devoured (2 Sam. xii. 9–11).—Chap. xx. 3. Marginal note by LUTHER: The thousand years must have begun at the time when this Book was written. STARKE, on the other hand: The thousand years are not past, but to come.—Satan has his certain time to be bound and to be loosed. —Ver. 4. Those who regard the thousand years as having already expired, apprehend the resurrection spoken of here ▬ ▪ spiritual resurrection. (Starke adduces another explanation, according to which the resurrection is a physical one, but the life of the risen is in Heaven [2 Tim. ii. 11,12]. The difficulty here originates, probably, in a fear of the ill-understood Seventeenth Article of the Augsburg Confession. The Seventeenth Article, however, negatives the assumption of a millennium (*a*) *before* the Parousia of Christ and the resurrection of the dead; (*b*) a secular kingdom of the righteous, based on the oppression and subjection of the wicked.) RIEMANN, *Die Lehre der Heiligen Schrift vom tausendjährigen Reiche oder vom zukünftigen Reiche Israel* (in opposition to J. Diedrich, Schönebeck, 1858). It is only by caprice that the Millennial Kingdom can here be styled the future kingdom of Israel.—FLÖRKE, *Die Lehre vom tausendjährigen Reiche* (Marburg, 1859). "Our view (of the Millennium) has its point of departure in a difference with the Augsburg Confession." (On this misunderstanding, see the remark in the preceding paragraph.) STEFFANN, in his work entitled: *Das Ende der Zeiten, Vorträge über die Offenb. des heil. Joh.* (Berlin, 1870), also controverts this misunderstanding and Hengstenberg's interpretation: "Ebrard is right in saying that, in drawing up this Article, the Reformers rejected their own view of the Millennial Kingdom and thereby opened the way for a future correct view, *etc.* The rôles are changed, therefore: not those who reject the Millennial Kingdom on the basis of this Article, but we, who teach it in accordance with the permission given us in this Article, stand on the platform of the Augsburg Confession" (p. 336). MUENCHMEYER, on the other hand, intimates with sufficient plainness, in his *Bibelstunden über die Offb. Joh.* (Hanover, 1870,) p. 186,) that orthodoxistic exegetical tradition and the *ill-understood* Seventeenth Article have induced him to place the Millennial Kingdom in the past. He, however, does not reckon the thousand years from the time of John to Gregory VII , with Luther, nor, with others, from the time of Constantine, but from the conversion of Germany—" according to which inter-

pretation the thousand years are now approaching their end, if we have not already entered upon the *little time*" (in which view he resembles Hengstenberg).

HEBART, *Für den Chiliasmus* (Nuremberg, 1859), points to the profitableness of the doctrine of the Millennial Kingdom (p. 24).—*Die chiliastische Doktrin und ihr Verhältniss zur christlichen Glaubenslehre*, by Dr. JOHANN NEPOMUK SCHNEIDER (see p. 73).—*Das tausendjährige Reich* (in opposition to Hengstenberg), Gütersloh, 1860, p. 98. In Ezek. xxxvii. 1–14 the *house of Israel* is spoken of in precisely the same manner (as in chap. xxxvi.), and there is nothing in the chapter which could indicate that in this section the *house of Israel* is not to be apprehended as the natural Israel, but that the prophecy relates to the Church. (See the further remarks on the subject, p. 99. Emphasis is judiciously laid upon the fact that the part which treats of Gog and Magog follows this promise.)

CHRISTIANI, *Bemerkungen zur Auslegung der Apokalypse* (Riga, Bacmeister, p. 28). "Empirical ecclesiasticity must be highly overrated by those who ascribe to such a Church-historical event as the constituting of Christianity the state-religion of the Roman world-kingdom, so high an import in the history of salvation [as to date the Millennial Kingdom therefrom], notwithstanding that the benefits of this event were accompanied by many evils attendant upon the externalization of the Church" (in opposition to Keil).

RINCK, *Die Schriftmässigkeit der Lehre vom tausendjährigen Reich* (in opposition to Hengstenberg, Elberfeld, 1866, p. 35). This expositor places the transformation of the faithful in this time. He also assigns the fulfillment of the following prophecies to the same period: Micah iv. 1-4 ; Isa. xi.; lxv. 17-25; Acts iii. 19-21 ; Rom. xi.; Amos ix. 9-15. Rinck likewise places the people of Israel at the head of the nations in the Millennial Kingdom, and makes them the leading missionary people of the earth. The Judaizing anticipations of Baumgarten, *et al.*, do not, however, appear with any greater distinctness than attaches to them in the view just stated. It is in any case as one-sided to drop the symbolic element in favor of the historic, as to surrender the historic in favor of the symbolic element. Can the following words be understood of the Jewish people in the historical sense: " When the multitude of the sea is converted unto him ?" Israel has already, in the person of the historic Christ, taken the leading place amongst the nations, and in the persons of the Apostles it has become the principal missionary people on earth —this might suffice. According to Rom. xi., all Israel is to be saved, *after* the fullness [full number] of the Gentiles has come in. In the end, only *dynamical* distinctions can be of weight, and when Christ comes to earth with all the elect Gentile Christians of all ages, an external preponderance of the newly converted Jewish people is out of the question. The prospect of the more general conversion of Israel is, doubtless, rightly assigned to the Millennial Kingdom. A Christ in glory will remove the last hindrance of faith for all who have failed to accommodate themselves to the offense of the cross, not out of malice, but through weakness and an obedience to Jewish traditions. For the Israelitish view, moreover, the expectation of a time of the glorification of the Theocracy on earth lay at the door, although this did not involve an approximation to the Christian modification of this doctrine. Yet even Isaiah, viewing the power of evil in the light of the Spirit, perceived that a chasm would intervene between the time of the Messiah's humiliation and sufferings and the time of His glorification. Again, Ezekiel, in distinguishing between the corruption of the central civilized world and that of the remote barbarian world, arrived at the foreview that the victory over anti-Messianism and Israel's restoration should be followed by a late conflict with Gog and Magog.

Volck, *Der Chiliasmus, seiner neuesten Bekämpfung* (Keil, *Kommentar über Ezechiel*) *gegenüber* (Dorpat, 1869). "It may now be seen what importance should be attached to the position of Lünemann, who affirms (commenting on 1 Thess. iv. 14) that the idea of an intervening space between the resurrection of believers and that of other men (Rev. xx.) is entirely foreign to the mind of the Apostle Paul. Precisely the contrary is true. That idea is perfectly familiar to him—a fact which is admitted by Meyer, who remarks on 1 Cor. xv. 24, that Paul, following the example of Christ Himself, has bound up the doctrine of a two-fold resurrection with the Christian faith. Meyer here alludes to the ἀνάστασις τῶν δικαίων, mentioned by the Lord in Luke xiv. 14."

Lavater, *Aussichten in die Ewigkeit.* Our Lord replies to the question of the Sadducees (Luke xx.) in the following terms: "Those who shall be accounted worthy to obtain that world and the resurrection of [E. V.: from] the dead, can die no more," *etc.* From this it is evident that our Lord, in this passage, speaks of the resurrection of the righteous as a felicity which pertains exclusively to them.

[From M. Henry: Chap. xx. 1. Christ never wants proper powers and instruments to break the power of Satan, for He has the powers of heaven, and the keys of hell.]

Section Eighteenth.

Third or General End-Judgment. Judgment upon Satan and all his Associates. The Second Death.
a. *The Heavenly Prognosis. (Ch. xx. 6-8.)*

General.—As we must distinguish between the elect, who have part in the first resurrection, and the general throng of the blessed, we have also to distinguish between the blossom of the earth and of the nations, constituting the Millennial Kingdom, the eschatological οἰκουμένη, and the terrestrial orb in general and its masses of peoples. It is a prophecy corresponding with the most profound anthropology that the rudest constituents of humanity shall at last, at the instigation of Satan, instinctively band themselves together for an assault upon the City of God. The lineaments of this anticipation are distinctly expressed in the passages quoted from Ezekiel. From an ethical point of view, it is the fundamental idea of this anticipation that evil shall, after the annihilation of all its idealistic illusions, make one last attack upon the Kingdom of God, with the convulsive movement of pure brutality, savageness, hostility to, and rebellion against, the holy. From an ethnographical point of view, the remoter heathen Orient appears, in antithesis to the nearer theocratic Orient, as the natural lodgment of the elements for such a final struggle. Already the East has frequently threatened the civilized world of anterior Asia and Europe with its terrors, by its great military incursions. There fanaticism slumbers in millions,—in the diverse forms of Græco-Catholicism, Mohammedanism, and Paganism, the latter of which is further sub-divided into the opposite ground-forms of Brahmanism and Buddhism. Imagine a gigantic Oriental coalition, equipped with the most modern military instruments of the European world, its leaders inspired with the magic song of the three Apocalyptic frogs. In such a case, the ethically monstrous assault against the Church of God must have the aspect of a Titanic cosmical power;—the Divine cosmos, however, must also, infallibly, take upon itself an annihilating counter-agency.

Special.—[Ver. 6.] Glory of the first resurrection. The summit of life is the first resurrection; the summit of death is the second death.—The true priestly domination in the Millennial Kingdom: 1. A domination of all the elect; 2. A domination with Christ.—[Ver. 7.] Sublimity of God's power in the final loosing of Satan.—Last form of evil on earth.—Ver. 8. 1. The absolute majority in conflict against Christ; 2. Rude violence [might] in conflict against the consummate right of His Church; 3. The brutalized power of earth in an assault upon the spirit-kingdom of God from Heaven. Consummate irrationality in its hatred of the consummate Kingdom of light, love and life.—The serpent nature of evil in its last struggle.—The last struggle itself, the foretoken of its destruction.

Starke (ver 8): Satan is the greatest rover; he goes to and fro, in order to seduce men and to do harm. (Job i. 7. In other words: Demonic evil ever and anon issues forth from its dark nothingness, without rule or system, but yet sympathetically, or rather in sympathetic antipathies, and consistently. Oneness in the Kingdom of God is based upon harmony in the Spirit; oneness in the kingdom of darkness is based upon a conspiracy for Antichristian purposes.)

Graeber (p. 357). [Ver. 9.] *And fire came down from Heaven.* This figurative expression indicates that their ruin is brought about by a special event, sent by God, the saints themselves having no hand in the matter. This is described with more particularity, Ezek. xxxviii. 21-23.

[From M. Henry: Ver. 6. None can be *blessed* but they that are *holy;* and all that are *holy* shall be *blessed.*—From Bonar: Ver. 6. The First Resurrection. 1. *When is it to be?* When the Lord comes the second time. (See 1 Cor xv. 23; 1 Thess. iv. 16; 2 Thess. ii. 1). 2. *Whom it is to consist of.* This passage speaks only of the martyrs and the non-worshippers of the Beast; but other passages show that all His saints are to be partakers of this reward. Oneness with Christ now secures for us the glory of that day. 3. *What it does for those who share it.* It brings them (1) *Blessedness.* God only knows how much that word implies, as spoken by Him who cannot lie, who exaggerates nothing, and whose simplest words are His greatest. (2) *Holiness.* They are consecrated to God and purified, both outwardly and inwardly. (3) *Preservation from the second death.* Their connection with death, in every sense, is done forever. (4) *The possession of a heavenly priesthood.* They are made priests unto God and Christ—both to the Father and the Son. Priestly nearness and access; priestly power and honor and service; priestly glory and dignity; —this is their recompense. (5) *The possession of the kingdom.*—Sinner, what is resurrection to bring to you?]

SECTION NINETEENTH.

Third or General End-Judgment. **b.** *Earth-picture of the Last Judgment.* (*Ch. xx.* 9, 10.)

General and Special.—Brief history of the greatest war. 1. The war: (a) *they went up;* (b) *they surrounded the camp of the saints and the beloved city.* 2. The defeat: (a) *fire from Heaven devoured them;* (b) *Satan is cast into the lake of fire.*—Great Heaven as an ally of this little earth.—The Kingdom of the Lord must always be victorious.—The greater the danger which menaces the people of God, the more wondrous their preservation.—The last victory, in its magnitude: Most wonderful (apparently without a weapon of defense), most mysterious (from Heaven), most glorious (destruction of Satan forever).

STARKE: Those who regard this vision as, in part, fulfilled, apprehend it as relating to Turks, Tartars, Scythians and Mohammedans, *etc.* Those who take it, in company with the thousand years, as still future, *etc.* (Confused mingling of the most diverse periods!)—DIMPEL: O wretched hellish trinity! The Beast, the False Prophet and Satan, are tormented in the fiery lake to all eternity.

H. BÖHMER (p. 293): The fact here presented, to wit, that Satan, after having been bound, shall at last be loosed again for a short time, seems to us to constitute a deep and weighty truth; not because sin can be traced only to a seduction through Satan, but because we must naturally suppose that God will, at some future day, permit all who set Him at defiance to unite themselves for the last possible battle against Him and thus prosecute their abuse of liberty to the climax of self-inflicted judgment. We hold this final emergence of Satan to be necessary, because without it there would be no real finale to that conflict which was begun in apostasy from God, and, consequently, no full victory.

[From M. HENRY: God will, in an extraordinary and more immediate manner, fight this last and decisive battle of His people, that the victory may be complete, and the glory redound to Himself.—From VAUGHAN: Upon this gathering, this confederation of infidelity, of ungodliness, and of atheism, will burst the light of Christ's coming, and the devouring fire of God.]

SECTION TWENTIETH.

The New Heaven and the New Earth. The Kingdom of glory. **a.** *Heavenly World-picture of the Consummation.* (*Ch. xx.* 11—*xxi.* 8.)

General.—We here refer to our detailed treatment of the subject in the EXEGET. NOTES (p. 358 sqq.).

Special.—The end of the old world, the natal hour of the new world. This truth is (1) prefigured by life in nature (out of death, life); (2) grounded in the antithesis between the old and the new life of the Christian (the dying of the old man, the rising of the new man); (3) mediated, in its realization, by the verbal prophecies of Scripture and the real prophecies of the development of the Kingdom of God (every apparent down-going, the condition of a glorious resurrection).—The end of the world, a presentiment of all creature-life.—The new world, an object of the aspiration of all the pious.—[Vers. 11-15.]

Individual features of the end of the world: The Judge; the down-going [of the old world]; the resurrection; the judgment; the Book of Life; the lake of fire.—[Ch. xx. 1 sqq.] The new world: A consummate reality; a new Heaven and a new earth; the new Jerusalem; the new habitation of God (ver. 3); the new existence (ver. 4); the new creation (ver. 5).—The *Word* of God, the foundation of the first world (John i. 1 [-3]);—in the explication (and world-historic operation) of His *words,* the foundation of the second world.—Certainty of the new world, (1) in respect of its Founder (ver. 6); (2) in respect of the heritage which it shall afford to the conquerors [ver. 7]; (3) in respect of the certainty of its antithesis [the lake of fire, ver. 8].—The *second death?* Infinitely mysterious in its nature. On the other hand, exceedingly clear as the final consequence, and hence the final punishment, of consistent sin. The *second death,* the last consistent result of the first beginnings of evil.—The contradiction immanent in the figure of *the lake of fire,* in perfect accordance with the essence of godlessness: 1. Extreme agitation and motion; 2. In perfect aimlessness; 3. Hence ethical self-consumption on the basis of physical indissolubleness.—Significant character-portrait of the *lost* under the superscription of *the fearful.* True heroic courage in the light of eternity; and its aim.

STARKE: There are two lines of opinion as to the vision set forth in chs. xxi. and xxii. Some consider that whilst it presents, chiefly, the condition of the Church on earth during the thousand years, a picture of the glorious state of the Church in Heaven is commingled with the former view; others hold that the contents of these two chapters refer particularly to the glorious state of the Church Triumphant in Heaven.—QUESNEL: (Comp. ch. xxi. 4 and John xvi. 20.) O precious tears of penitence and grief shed by the righteous and accounted worthy to be wiped away by the hand of God Himself. (Ver. 6.) God will yet manifest Himself to His Church as *Alpha* and *Omega,* and prove that the promise which He gave in the *beginning,* He will emphatically fulfil in the *end.*—QUESNEL [ver. 8]: There is a *fearfulness* which can condemn us equally with any misdoings.

CLAUS HARMS, *Die Offenb. Joh. gepredigt* (Kiel 1844; p. 183): *The New Jerusalem.* I. It has its name and form from that Jerusalem in Israel. II. But the glory of the new is far greater than the glory of the old. III. Greater, even, than anything the Prophets have predicted in regar to it. IV. Yes, the new Jerusalem surpasses even Heaven and eternal blessedness. V. Christians, have we this glorious city before our eyes? VI. And in our hearts?

HAKEN, *Kosmische Bilder*, Riga, 1862 (p. 190): The new Heaven and the new Earth. Ps. cii. 25, 26; Heb. i. 10. In both passages the terms *pass away* [*perish*] and *change* are promiscuously employed: the Heavens *pass away* only so far as they are *changed*.

[From M. HENRY: Vers. 11-15. Observe, 1. *The throne* and tribunal of judgment, *great* and *white*, very glorious, and perfectly just and righteous. 2. The Judge. 3. The persons to be judged. 4. The rule of judgment settled; *the books were opened.* The book of God's omniscience, and the book of the sinner's conscience; *and another book* shall be *opened—the book* of the scriptures, the statute-book of heaven, the rule *of life.* This book determines matters of right; the other books give evidence of matters of fact. 5. The cause to be tried; *the works of men*, what they have done, and whether it be good or evil. 6. The issue of the trial and judgment; and that will be according to the evidence of fact, and rule of judgment.—Ch. xxi. 3. The presence of God with His people in heaven will not be interrupted as it is on earth, but He will dwell with them continually.—The covenant interest and relation that there are now between God and His people will be filled up and perfected in heaven. *They shall be His people;* their souls shall be assimilated to Him, filled with all the love, honor and delight in God that their relation requires; this shall be their perfect holiness, and He will *be their God;* His immediate presence with them, His love fully manifested to them, and His glory put upon them, will be their perfect happiness.—Ver. 4. Note, 1. All the effects of former trouble shall be done away. God Himself, as their tender Father, with His kind hand, *shall wipe away the tears* of His children; and they would not have been without those *tears* when *God shall come and wipe them away.* 2. All the causes of future sorrow shall be forever removed; *There shall be neither death nor pain;* and therefore *no sorrow nor crying;* these are things incident to that state in which they were before, but now all *former things are passed away.*—Vers. 5, 6. We may and ought to take God's promise as present payment; if He has said, He *makes all things new, it is done.*— *Alpha and Omega, the Beginning and the End.* As it was His glory, that He gave the rise and beginning to the world, and to His Church, it will be His glory to finish the work begun, and not to leave it imperfect.—The desires of His people toward this blessed state [vers. 1-4] are another evidence of the truth and certainty of it; they thirst after a state of sinless perfection, and the uninterrupted enjoyment of God; and God has wrought in them these longing desires which cannot be satisfied with anything else, and therefore would be the torment of the soul if they were disappointed; but it would be inconsistent with God's goodness and His love to His people to create in them holy and heavenly desires, and then deny them their proper satisfaction; and therefore they may be assured when they have overcome their present difficul-

ties, *He will give them of the fountain of the water of life freely.*—Vers. 6-8. The greatness of this future felicity is declared and illustrated, 1. By the freeness of it. 2. The fullness of it; *inherit all things.* 3. By the tenure and title by which God's people enjoy this blessedness; by right of inheritance, as *the sons of God.* 4. By the vastly different state of the wicked.—Ver. 8. Observe, 1. The sins of those who perish. *The fearful* lead the van in this black list; they durst not encounter the difficulties of religion, and their slavish fear proceeded from their unbelief. They, however, were yet so desperate as to run into all manner of abominable wickedness. 2. Their punishment. This misery will be their proper part and portion, and what they have prepared themselves for by their sins. —From THE COMPREHENSIVE COMMENTARY. Ch. xxi. 8. There is then a fearfulness which alone is sufficient to cause our condemnation, as well as the other crimes here mentioned. It is not only that fear which causes us to deny and abandon the faith; but that also which causes us to be wanting to important and essential duties, through fear of hurting our fortunes, our ease, and even our temporal and spiritual interests, and of creating ourselves enemies. True courage is, to fear nothing but God and displeasing Him. Real cowardice is, not to have courage to overcome self, nor renounce the creature, through the hope of enjoying the Creator. (QUESNEL.)—From VAUGHAN: Ch. xxi. 3. To have God with us is to be perfectly safe: to have *God for our God* is to be perfectly happy.—Ver. 8. *The fearful.* O terrible end! O fatal compromise carried on too long and too far with sinners and with sin! O spirit of oversensitiveness, of dislike to trouble, of dread of isolation, of inability to judge decisively and to act courageously, which has brought you, by slow stages, by easy descents, to a level so vile, and a companionship so horrible!—From BONAR: Ch. xx. 12. *Books* are opened—books probably containing *God's* history of the sinner's life, His record of the sinner's deeds. . . . The Divine version of human history . . . how unlike all earthly annals! Most of the leading facts the same, yet how differently told . . . and interpreted. . . . Alongside of these is another book, called the book of life—the register of those whose portion is LIFE eternal.—Ver. 13. *Judged every man according to his works.* God keeps His diary of every soul's doings and sayings and thinkings.—Ver. 14. Of the old prediction in Hosea (ch. xiii. 14): "O death, I will be thy plagues; O grave, I will be thy destruction," John here records the awful (and glorious) fulfillment.]

SECTION TWENTY-FIRST.

Heavenly-Earthly Picture (Earth-Picture) of the New World. The Kingdom of Glory. (Chap. xxi. 9—xxii. 5.)

General.—The Kingdom of glory is the Kingdom of consummation; of the consummate development of all the human capabilities of mankind, as born again through Christianity, together with the consummate development of the renewed cosmos of mankind; the Palingenesia of the human world, founded on the holy Birth and Resurrection of Christ—His Primogeniture from the dead—and mediated by the regeneration and resurrection of the faithful. —Relation of the human cosmos to the universe in general.—This relation is modified by the absolute priority of Christ, resting upon His Divine-human nature, the ideal perfection of His life, the holiness of His cross, the glory of His victory. The consummation itself, however, as eternal, is based upon the super-creaturely, God-related, æonic nature of humanity; upon the eternal foundation, the eternal aim, and the eternal value of the life and work of Christ; and upon the covenant-faithfulness of God and the sureness of His promises.

The promises of God, as *real prophecies*, in nature and in the development of life, as well as in those *verbal prophecies* of the Kingdom of God which hover above this life, have all aimed at that glorious consummation, at the eternalization of the Christian life and its sphere, the eternal City of God. Hence, the domain of the consummation is at the same time the domain of all fulfillments; it is both of these as the Kingdom of glory, the blessed realm of spirits, filled with the life of the Eternal Spirit.

The Kingdom of glory unfolds in three spheres, appearing (1) as the consummation and fulfillment of the Theocracy, or as the *heavenly Jerusalem*, the *City of God* (vers. 9-21); (2) as the consummation and fulfillment of all the truth and all the longing contained in the religious history of mankind, or as the holy Home-City of all believing Gentiles [nations] (vers. 22·27); (3) as the consummation and fulfillment of all the prophecies of nature, or as the Home-Country of all souls, the universal, new Paradise (ch. xxii. 1-5).

Special.—The perfected Kingdom of God, in respect of its different designations and imports: Historic form of the Kingdom of God (ch. xxi. 9-21); the City of God; the heavenly Jerusalem; the Bride.—Blessed prospect of the City of God. Most glorious of all prospects. *"Jerusalem, du hoch gebaute Stadt,"* etc. [" Jerusalem, thou city fair and high "]. *"Ich hab' von ferne, etc."*—Procession of the City of God: 1. From Heaven to earth; 2. From earth to Heaven; 3. Back again, from Heaven to earth.—[Ver. 10.] The descending City of God, or perfected communication between Heaven (the starry world) and earth.—Description of the City of God (vers. 11-21). Its source of light; its walls; its gates; its dimensions and fundamental forms; its fundamental materials.—Spiritual, universal form of the Kingdom of God (vers. 22-27). Its spiritual Temple. Its spiritual Sun. Its spiritual Church. Its spiritual liberty. Its spiritual fullness. Its spiritual purity and consecrateness.—The new Paradise (ch. xxii. 1-5). The *river of life:* 1. Where does it appear? 2. Whence does it come? 3. Whither does it flow?—The *river of life:* 1. In respect of its name; 2. In respect of its beauty (*like crystal*); 3. In respect of its products.—The *trees of life*—the manifestation of highest life: 1. From the Fountain of life to the River of life; 2. From the River of life to the Trees of life; 3. From the Trees of life to their fruits; 4. From the fruits to the

health-producing leaves.—The perfected, pure, consecrated creature (ver. 3).—The laws of purity for creaturely life: a prophecy of the future glorification of the world.—Activity and rest in the Paradise of God (vers. 3, 4).—Perfect union of *culture* and *cultus* in the Paradise of God.—The service (ver. 3).—The blessed rest (the beholding of God [ver. 4]).—The region of eternal sunshine [ver. 5]. — The new world shining in the radiance of the glory of the Lord. —The glorious liberty of the children of God (Rom. viii.), in its eternal duration and renewal.

STARKE: [Ch. xxi. 12.] God is a fiery wall and protection to His Church (Zech. ii. 5).— Ver. 13. Entrance into the Church is free to all people, in all corners of the world, who will but come to the fellowship of the Church (1 Tim. ii. 4).—Ver. 14. The one true Foundation of the Church and of eternal blessedness is Christ alone (1 Cor. iii. 11). This Foundation is laid solely through the Apostles (Eph. ii. 20). (The reconciliation of the apparent contradiction is to be found in the fact that Christ has organically unfolded His fullness in the twelve Apostles.)—On ver. 23, comp. Is. lx. 19, 20.— On ver. 24, comp. Is. lx. 3; see ch. xlix. 23; ii. 2 sq.; Ps. lxxii. 10, 11; also Is. lii. 1; lx. 21; Ezek. xliv. 9.—Ch. xxii. 2. A contrast to ancient Babylon is here presented. As the Euphrates flowed through the midst of Babylon, and as the river of Babylon dried up (ch. xvi. 12), so, on the other hand, the spiritual Jerusalem has the river of the Holy Spirit, which brings water through the midst of the City and which shall never dry up.—Christ is the Tree of life, which has life in itself.—On ver. 3, comp. Zech. xiv. 11.

W. HOFFMANN, *Maranatha (Ruf zum Herrn,* Vol. VIII. Sermon on 2 Pet. iii. 13, 14. P. 180). We shall speak of the new world of the redeemed, as described in our text in the following words: " But we wait for a new Heaven and a new earth." For the first word of revelation from God's mouth runs: " In the beginning God created the Heaven and the earth," and the last word of prophecy is that which we have just read. Thus, between the first *coming into existence* of Heaven and earth and the last everlasting *being* of Heaven and earth, all the Divine economy moves.

[From M. HENRY: Ch. xxi. 10. They who would have clear views of heaven must get as near heaven as they can, into the mount of vision, the mount of meditation and faith, from whence, as from *the top of Pisgah, they may behold the goodly land of the heavenly Canaan.*—Ver. 11. *Having the glory of God;* glorious in her relation to Christ, in His image now perfected in her, and in His favor shining upon her.—Ver. 12. Note, 1. The *wall.* Heaven is a safe state. 2. The *gates.* It is accessible to all those that are sanctified.—Ver. 22. There the saints are above the need of ordinances, which were the means of their preparation for heaven. Perfect and immediate communion with God will more than supply the place of gospel-institutions.—Ver. 23. God in Christ will be an everlasting Fountain of knowledge and joy to the saints in heaven.—Ver. 27. The saints shall have (1) no impure thing remain in them, (2) no impure persons admitted among them.—Ch. xxii. 1. All our springs of grace, comfort, and glory are in God; and all our streams from Him, through the mediation of the Lamb.—Ver. 3. *And there shall be no more curse.* Here is the great excellency of this paradise—the Devil has nothing to do there; he cannot draw the saints from serving God to be subject to himself, as he did our first parents, nor can he so much as disturb them in the service of God.—Vers. 4, 5. Note, 1. There the saints shall see the face of God; there enjoy the beatific vision. 2. God will own them, as having His seal and name on their foreheads. 3. *They shall reign with Him forever;* their service shall be not only freedom, but honor and dominion. 4. They shall be full of wisdom and comfort, continually walking in the light of the Lord.—From THE COMPREHENSIVE COMMENTARY. Ch. xxi. 9-27. "Glorious things are" indeed here "spoken of the City of God" (Ps. lxxxvii. 3); and the whole is well suited to raise our expectations and enlarge our conceptions of its security, peace, splendor, purity and felicity; but, in proportion to our spirituality, we shall be more and more led to contemplate heaven as filled with "the glory of God," and enlightened by the presence of the Lord Jesus, "the Sun of righteousness," and the Redeemer of lost sinners, knowing that "in His presence is fullness of joy, and pleasures at His right hand for evermore." (SCOTT.)—As nothing unclean can enter thither, let us be stirred up, by these glimpses of heavenly things, in giving diligence to "cleanse ourselves from all filthiness of flesh and spirit, perfecting holiness in the fear of God;" that we may be approved as "Israelites indeed, in whom there is no guile," and have a sure evidence that we are "written in the Lamb's book of life." (SCOTT.)—Ch. xxii. 5. In that world of light and glory there will "be no night," no affliction, or dejection, no intermission of service and enjoyments; they will "need no candle;" no diversions or pleasures of man's devising will there be at all wanted; and even the outward comforts which God has provided, suited to our state in this world, will no longer be requisite. (SCOTT.)—From VAUGHAN: Ch. xxi. 22. *The Lord God and the Lamb are the Temple of it.* The worship of heaven is offered directly, not only to God, but in God. It is as if God Himself were the shrine in which man will then adore Him. . . . The blessed will be so included in God that even when they worship, He will be their temple.—If we would hereafter worship in that temple which is God Himself, Christ Himself, we must *know God now by faith;* we must have life now in Christ.—Ch. xxii. 3. If in heaven we would *serve God,* we must begin to be *His servants* here.—From BONAR: Chs. xx., xxi. What a termination to the long, long desert-journey of the Church of God, calling forth from us the exulting shout which broke from the lips of the Crusaders, when first from the neighboring height they caught sight of the holy city: "Jerusalem! Jerusalem!"]

SECTION TWENTY-SECOND.
The Epilogue. (*Ch. xxii.* 6-21.)
General. — The Johannean character of the Epilogue of the Revelation has already been

dwelt upon. A depth of meaning and a festal-ness of mood, conjoined with a somewhat indefinite expression, or a mysterious form, are peculiar to this section as well as to the Epilogue of the Gospel; and the fundamental thought which animates them both is an earnest longing for the Coming of the Lord. In regard to the construction, comp. the EXEG. NOTES.

Special.—The pureness of the Revelation (ver. 6) corroborated by its Author. By its intimate connection with the whole of Holy Writ. By its fulfillment hitherto.—(Ver. 7.) *Behold, I come quickly.* 1. How this saying is misunderstood when it is interpreted in the sense of a secular computation of time. 2. How, for the standpoint of religious sentiment and Christian expectations, it always retains its truth, and, 3, continually gains in weight.—*Blessed is he that keepeth the words of the prophecy.*—Vers. 8, 9. What is the significance of the distinction between the Angel of Christ and Christ Himself (see EXEG. NOTES)?—[Ver. 10.] *Seal not the words of the prophecy of this Book.* Why not? *The time is at hand.*—Earnest and grand character of the course of the world to its end.—*Seal not the Book;* not even by false interpretations —especially, chiliastic darkenings and rationalistic volatilizings.—*Seal not* even the Apocalypse with hierarchic seals, much less then the whole of the Bible.—Ver. 11. Lofty import of these words: What thou doest (wilt do), do quickly! (See EXEG. NOTES.)—Christ's word concerning His Coming (ver. 12). He announces Himself as the righteous Recompenser. — His reward not as the wages of hired service, but an honorarium of love; 2. Not for works of hired service, but for those of the service of love.—Christ as the *Alpha* and *Omega.* Some say: Omega, but not Alpha. Others: Alpha, but not Omega. Whoso, however, rightly says the one, says also the other.—Antithesis of blessedness and damnation (vers. 14, 15).—*Without*—its import (ver. 15).—*Who is without?* Note the pure and purely moral character of these traits.—Christ's testimony regarding His Coming: A testimony to the Church (ver. 16).—Christ in His human and Divine glory (*I am the Root, etc.*).—How His human and Divine glory guarantees His Coming. —[Ver. 17.] The three-fold *Come*—of the Spirit, the Bride, the individual Christian.—He who would greet the Lord with a *Come!* must first hearken to the Lord's call: *Come!*—Our *Welcome* to the Advent of Christ must be based upon His *Welcome* to the reception of salvation.—The clear sound of the *Gospel* may still be heard at the very close of the *Revelation.* Here, also, the declaration is: *Take freely.*—[Ver. 18.] The Apostle's warning in regard to the Apocalypse: It is no subject for haughty cavil, but an enigma for humble meditation. — The mysteries and enigmas of Scripture concluded with a final enigma.—Whoso occupies a wrong position in regard to the future, occupies also a wrong position in regard to the present and the past.— [Ver. 20.] Briefest and most sublime dialogue between the Lord and His people. 1. He says: *I come quickly* 2. We say: *Amen, yea, come, Lord Jesus.*—Who can, with a good courage, say *Amen* to the announcement of His Coming?—

The sum of all human longing, all Christian hope, all Divine promise, in the cry: *Come, Lord Jesus!*—The Apocalypse, a Book of faith; of love; of hope; of longing; of patience; of comfort; of investigation; of knowledge. Of sacred awe, of blessed vision.—Ver. 21. The benediction. Benedictions from the beginning to the end of the Scriptures: In respect (1) of their purport; (2) of their rich development; (3) of their conditionedness; (4) of their glorious operation.

STARKE (ver. 10): No man should be prohibited from reading the Holy Scriptures.—Ver. 11. If the wicked wilfully refuse to follow, God at last suffers them to go their own way (Prov. i. 24 sqq.).—Ver. 12. Comp. Is. xl. 10.—Ver. 17. Because many souls should yet be drawn to Christ—among other things, by the testimonies of this Book concerning the glorious Coming of Christ—John adds these words: *let him that heareth, say, Come.*—Ver. 19. O awful punishment of those who falsify God's word! There is nothing more precious [than the word of God] —hence it needs no addition of worldly eloquence, there is nothing more pure—hence we must take nothing from it.—Ver. 20. Let us say *Amen* and *Yea* to the promises of our Saviour, although as yet we see nothing (?) of their fulfillment.

CALWER *Handbuch der Bibelerklärung.* [Ver. 10.] Although much in the Revelation was not intended to be understood until the times of fulfillment, yet this Book is not a shut (*sealed*) Book, but a Revelation [*Offenbarung*].

LISKO (*Bibelwerk*): [Ver. 16.] He [Christ] is also the bright morning-star, Who caused the day, the whole period of Divine life in mankind, to arise, and issue forth from Himself, and Who now beams upon us from the other world (as the morning-star of the Day of Eternity).

GERLACH (*Bibelwerk*): Ver. 17. To inflame the longing of the faithful for the return of their Saviour, is one of the principal designs of this Book.

[From M. HENRY: Ver. 20. Christ *will come quickly;* let this word be always sounding in our ear, and let us give all diligence, that we may be found of Him in peace, *without spot, and blameless.*—*Surely I come quickly.*—*Amen. Even so, come, Lord Jesus.* What comes from heaven in a promise, should be sent back to heaven in a prayer.—Ver. 21. Nothing should be more desired by us than that the grace of Christ should be with us in this world, to prepare us for the glory of Christ in the other world.— From THE COMPREHENSIVE COMMENTARY: Ver. 16. *The bright and morning star.* Christ's rising, in His incarnation, introduced the gospel-day; His rising in power introduceth the millennial day; His rising in the saving influences of His Spirit introduceth the spiritual day of grace and comfort; and His appearance to judge the world will introduce the eternal day of light, purity and joy. (BROWN.)—"The Spirit," by the sacred Word, and by His convictions and influence in the sinner's conscience, says "Come" to Christ for salvation; "the Bride," or the whole Church

militant and triumphant, says "Come," and share our felicity.. It therefore behooves every man who hears the invitation to call on others to "come." (SCOTT.)—From BARNES: Ver. 11. There is nothing more awful than the idea that a polluted soul will be always polluted; that a heart corrupt will be always corrupt; that the defiled will be put forever beyond the possibility of being cleansed from sin.—Ver. 16. *The bright and morning star.* (Let that star) remind us that the Saviour should be the first object that should draw the eye and the heart on the return of each day.—Ver. 17. *And let him that is athirst, come.* Whoever desires salvation, as the weary pilgrim desires a cooling fountain to allay his thirst, let him come as freely to the gospel as that thirsty man would stoop down at the fountain and drink. —From VAUGHAN: Ver. 7. A special blessing is pronounced by our Lord Jesus Christ upon those who prize, and keep as a precious and sacred deposit, this particular portion of His revealed truth.—Ver. 11. There will come a time to each one of us, when, whatever we are, that we shall be; when the seal of permanence will be set upon the spiritual condition; when the unjust man shall be unjust forever, and the righteous man shall be forever righteous.—Ver. 12. *To give back to each one as his work is.* That is the judgment. It is the reaping of the thing sown. It is the *receiving back the things* themselves that were once *done in the body* (2 Cor. v. 10); receiving back the very acts and deeds themselves, only developed, full-grown, full-blown, ripened unto harvest.—From BONAR: Ver. 14. *Blessed are they that keep His commandments.* It is to a life of such keeping that we are called. By such a life, we partake of blessedness as well as glorify God.—*Enter in through the gates into the city.* (Enter) not over the wall; not by stealth; but as conquerors in triumphal procession, their Lord, as King of glory, at their head.—Ver. 17. Note here, 1. The cry for Christ's advent. 2. The invitation to the sinner. Observe (1) *The inviter;* Christ Himself. He invited once on earth; He now invites from heaven with the same urgency and love. (2) *The persons invited; a. The thirsty.* They who would fain be happy, but know not how; who are seeking rest, but finding none; who are hewing out broken cisterns; betaking themselves to dried-up wells. *b. Whosoever will.* A wide description. It shuts out none. (3) *The blessings invited to;* The water of life. "Water," that which will thoroughly refresh you and quench your thirst; "water of life," living and life-giving. . . . This water is the Holy Ghost Himself, Who comes to us as the bringer of God's free love, with all the joy which that love introduces into the soul. (4) *The price.* Freely Free to each one as he is; though the chief of sinners, the emptiest, wickedest, thirstiest of the sons of men.—Vers. 18, 19. Note here, 1. The perfection of God's word. 2. The honor God puts on it. 3. Our responsibilities in regard to it. 4. The sin and danger of tampering with it.]

INDEX

TO THE

TEN VOLUMES OF LANGE'S COMMENTARY

ON

THE NEW TESTAMENT.

I. GREEK.   II. TOPICAL.

BY

JOHN H. WOODS, A. M.

———

NEW YORK:

CHARLES SCRIBNER'S SONS.

743-745 BROADWAY.

GREEK INDEX.

3

Κερδαίνω, Acts 458.
Κεφαλαιόω, Mark 117.
Κῆνσος, Matt. 319.
Κηρύσσω, Rev. 377.
Κῆτος, Matt. 225.
Κῆφας, Matt. 182, 293.
Κινύρα, Matt. 437.
Κλαίω, John 355.
Κλάσμα, Matt. 266.
Κληρονομέω, 1 Cor. 125.
Κληρονομία, Acts 115.
Κλῆρος, Eph. 41, 1 Pet. 86.
Κληρόω, Eph. 41.
Κλῆσις, 1 Cor. 152.
Κλητός, Rom. 64, 1 Cor. 19.
Κλωπᾶ, John 585.
Κοδράντης, Matt. 114, 195.
Κοιλία, John 255, Phil. 61.
Κοινωνία, 1 Cor. 210, 2 Cor. 139.
Κόπος, Rev. 115.
Κόπτω, Matt. 208, 428.
Κορυφή, Matt. 84.
Κόσμος, Matt. 85, 422, 2 Cor. 67, Eph. 73, Heb. 48, 1 John 63.
Κόφινος, Matt. 266, 289, 290
Κράββατος, Mark 27, John 184.
Κράζω, John 71.
Κράσπεδον, Matt. 275, 406, 410.
Κρέας, Rom. 232.
Κρίμα, Rom. 113, 1 Cor. 125.
Κρίνω, Matt. 118, 138, Luke 105.
Κρίσις, Matt. 113, 412.
Κριτήριον, 1 Cor. 122.
Κρυπτή, Luke 187.
Κρυφαῖος, Matt. 127.
Κτίζω, Rev. 155.
Κτίσις, Rom. 269 sq., 2 Cor. 98.
Κυλλός, Matt. 284.
Κυρήνιος, Luke 31.
Κυρία, 2 John 186 sq.
Κυριακόν, Matt. 293.
Κύριος, Luke 36, Rom. 62, Eph. 216, Note, Thess. 12.
Κωφός, Matt. 222.

Λαλέω, 1 Cor. 183, 2 Cor. 184.
Λαλία, John 166, Note, 291.
Λαμπάς, Rev. 153, Note.
Λατεινός, Rev. 260.
Λατρεύω, Rom. 69, 86.
Λεββαῖος, Matt. 182.
Λέγω, 1 Cor. 183.
Λειτουργέω, Acts 239, Rom. 69.
Λειτουργία, 2 Cor. 157, Note, Phil. 49.
Λεπίς, Acts 169.
Λέπρα, Matt. 150.
Λεπτόν, Mark 127.
Ληνός, Matt. 387.
Λικμάω, Matt. 388.
Λίθος, Matt. 293.
Λίτρα, John 371, Note.
Λογία, 1 Cor. 855.
Λόγιος, Acts 345.
Λόγος, John 52, 54 sqq., Acts 147, Rom. 299, 823, Note, 324.
Λουτρόν, Eph. 199.
Λούω, Rev. 92.
Λυπέω, Rom. 420 sq.
Λύπη, 2 Cor. 30.
Λύτρον, Matt. 365.
Λυχνία, Matt. 104.

Λύχνος, Matt. 104.
Λύω, Matt. 110, Rev. 92.

Μαγαδά, ⎫
Μαγδαλά, ⎬ Matt. 280.
Μαγδαλάν, ⎭
Μαθητεύω, Matt. 555.
Μακάριος, Rom. 86, Note, 144.
Μακροθυμία, 2 Cor. 109 sq.
Μαμωνᾶς, Matt. 133.
Μαστιγόω, Matt. 512.
Μαστίζω, Matt. 512.
Μάστιξ, Matt. 512.
Ματαιότης, Rom. 84, 271.
Μάτην, Matt. 277.
Ματθαῖος, Matt. 182.
Μάχαιρα, Rom. 400.
Μεθύσκω, John 102.
Μέλλω, Acts 221.
Μέλος, Jas. 112.
Μεριμνάω, Matt. 133, 189.
Μέρος, Acts 256, 348.
Μεταμέλεια, 2 Cor. 129, Note.
Μεταμέλομαι, Matt. 501, 2 Cor. 129, Note.
Μετανοέω, Matt. 69, 73, 91, 322, 501, Mark 19, 2 Cor. 129, Note.
Μετάνοια, 2 Cor. 129, Note.
Μεταξύ, Acts 257.
Μετεωρίζω, Luke 194, 201.
Μετρητής, John 106.
Μετριοπαθέω, Heb. 102.
Μή, Matt. 223.
Μὴ γένοιτο, Rom. 112, 117, 200, 201, Gal. 49.
Μήτι, Matt. 223, Rom. 118, Note.
Μικρότερος, Matt. 205 sq.
Μνημονεύω, Thess. 15.
Μογιλάλος, Mark 69.
Μονή, John 434.
Μονογενής, John 74.
Μορφή, Rom. 382, Phil. 33.
Μόρφωσις, Rom. 108 sq.
Μόσχος, Rev. 143.
Μοσχοποιέω, Acts 125.
Μυριάς, Acts 389.
Μυστήριον, Rev. 107, 813.
Μωρός, Matt. 114.

Νέος, Eph. 163.
Νεωκόρος, Acts 361.
Νή, 1 Cor. 330.
Νομίζω, Matt. 108.
Νομικός, Matt. 251, 403.
Νομοδιδάσκαλος, Matt. 251.
Νόμος, Matt. 109, Rom. 121.
Νοσώδης, Matt. 132.
Νουθετέω, 1 Cor. 101.
Νοῦς, Rom. 233, 241, 1 Cor. 28, 63, 287, Eph. 125, Note, 164, Thess. 95, Tit. 10.
Νυχθήμερον, Matt. 226, Luke 187.

Ξέστης, Mark 65.

Ὁδός, Matt. 386, Acts 162.
Οἰκέτης, Rom. 417.
Οἴκημα, Acts 228.
Οἰκονόμης, Luke 205.
Οἰκτείρω, Rom. 313, Note.
Οἰκουμένη, Rev. 131.
Οἰκωδομή, Eph. 99.
Οἰνοπότης, Matt. 208.

Ὀλιγόψυχος, Thess. 90.
Ὁλόκληρος, Matt. 132, Thess. 94 sq.
Ὁλοτελής, Thess. 94.
Ὀμείρομαι, Thess. 31.
Ὁμιλία, 1 Cor. 331.
Ὁμοιόω, Matt. 145.
Ὁμολογία, 2 Cor. 157.
Ὄνομα, Rev. 119, Note.
Ὄνος, Matt. 370.
Ὅπλα, Rom. 210, 215.
Ὀπώρα, Jude 22, Rev. 319, Note.
Ὅπως, Rom. 118, 124.
Ὅραμα, Matt. 308, Luke 154.
Ὀργή, Rom. 80 sq., 98 sq., Thess. 24, Rev. 275 sq.
Ὁρίζω, Rom. 56, 59, 60, 61.
Ὁρμάω, Matt. 166.
Ὁρμή, Acts 262.
Ὅσιος, Matt. 71, Acts 247, Rev. 128, 299, Note.
Ὁσιότης, Eph. 164 sq.
Ὀσμή, 2 Cor. 40.
Ὄστρακον, 2 Cor. 74.
Οὐσία, Matt. 122, 126.
Οὗτος, Heb. 67.
Οὕτως, Matt. 124.
Ὀφείλημα, Matt. 126.
Ὄφελον, Rev. 136.
Ὄχλος, Matt. 173.
Ὀψάριον, John 210.
Ὀψέ, Matt. 544.

Παιδεραστία, Rom. 87.
Παιδεύω, Rev. 138.
Παιδίσκη, Acts 305.
Παῖς, Acts 67.
Παλιγγενεσία, Matt. 349, John 125.
Παντοκράτωρ, Rev. 93.
Παράβασις, Matt. 172.
Παραβολή, Matt. 234, Luke 234, John 317, 318.
Παραδίδωμι, Matt. 90.
Παράδοξος, Matt. 154.
Παράδοσις, Gal. 24, Thess. 144.
Παράκλησις, Acts 292, 293, Thess 29.
Παράκλητος, John 432, 440 sqq., 1 John 43 sq.
Παρακολουθέω, Luke 11.
Παράλυσις, Matt. 152 Luke 86.
Παραλυτικός, Matt. 96, 152.
Παραλύω, Luke 86.
Παράπτωμα, Matt. 126, Rom. 172, 182.
Παράσημος, Acts 470.
Παρασκευή, Matt. 455, 535, 537, John 569.
Παρατηρήσις, Matt. 96, Note.
Παρατίθημι, Acts 272.
Πάρεσις, Rom. 128, 134, Eph. 37.
Παρθένος, John 12, 1 Cor. 159.
Παροιμία, Matt. 233, John 317, Note, 318.
Παροργισμός, Eph. 170, Rev. 11 sq.
Παρουσία, 2 Pet. 18.
Παῤῥησία, Eph. 117.
Πάσχα, Matt. 455, 459.
Πατρίς, Matt. 255.
Παῦλος, Acts 174, Rom. 58.
Παχύνω, Matt. 240.
Πειθός, 1 Cor. 52.
Πειράζω, Matt. 81, 82.
Πειρασμός, Thess. 54, Rev. 130 sq.
Πέλαγος, Matt. 322.
Πένης, Matt. 102, 2 Cor. 155.
Περίεργος, Acts 354.
Περικάθαρμα, 1 Cor. 97.
Περίκειμαι, Acts 474.

Περιπίπτω, Jas. 37.
Περισσεία, Jas. 63.
Περισσεύω, Matt. 113.
Περιχώρησις, John 334, Note.
Περίψημα, 1 Cor. 97.
Περπερεύω, 1 Cor. 269.
Πέτρα, Matt. 182, 293, 296 sqq.
Πέτρος, Matt. 182, 293, 296.
Πηγή, John 149.
Πηλίκος, Gal. 157.
Πινακίδιον, Luke 26.
Πίναξ, Matt. 261.
Πίπτω, Rom. 364.
Πιστικός, Mark 138.
Πίστις, Matt. 412, Rom. 63, 385, Note, 415, Gal. 27, Phil. 13 sq.
Πιστός, Eph. 21.
Πλεονεξία, Eph. 162, Col. 64, Thess. 30.
Πληρόω, Matt. 53, 109, Acts 26, Col. 17, Rev. 125.
Πλήρωμα, John 76, Rom. 369 sq., Eph. 39, 64.
Πληροφορέω, Luke 11.
Πληροφορία, Luke 11.
Πλυῦτος, Rom. 95.
Πνεῦμα, Matt. 480, Rom. 61 sq., 222, 223. 223 sqq., 1 Cor. 62, 283, 287, Gal. 142, Eph. 125, Note, 164, Thess. 95, 98.
Πνευματικός, Eph. 28, Note.
Ποιμαίνω, Matt. 59.
Ποιμήν, Matt. 95.
Ποιέω, Matt. 225.
Πολιτάρχης, Acts 317.
Πολίτευμα, Phil. 61.
Πολυάνδριον, Matt. 164.
Πολυμερῶς, Heb. 23.
Πονηρία, 1 Cor. 116.
Πονηρόν, Matt. 126.
Πονηρός, Matt. 117, 126, 132.
Πορνεία, Gal. 138, Note.
Πόρω, Rom. 362.
Ποταπός, Matt. 159.
Πραγματεύομαι, Luke 290.
Πραιτώριον, Matt. 510, Phil. 19, 20.
Πράκτωρ, Luke 209.
Πραότης, 2 Cor. 163.
Πρασία, Matt. 266.
Πρεσβεύω, 2 Cor. 100.
Πρεσβύτερος, Matt. 95, Acts 222, Eph. 150, Note, Thess. 96.
Πρεσβύτης, Philem. 17.
Προαιτιάομαι, Rom. 120.
Προαύλιον, Matt. 491, 497, 498.
Προβιβάζω, Matt. 261, 263.
Προγινώσκω, Rom. 278 sq.
Πρόγνωσις, Rom. 279, Note.
Προέχω, Rom. 113, 120.
Πρόθεσις, Rom. 278, 289.
Προθεσμία, Gal. 96.
Προορίζω, Rom. 279.
Προσάββατον, Matt. 455, 535.
Προσαγωγή, Rom. 160 sq.
Προσευχή, Matt. 95, Acts 304.
Προσήλυτος, Matt. 151.
Πρόσκαιρος, Matt. 241.
Προσκληρόω, Acts 317.
Προσκοπή, 2 Cor. 108.
Προσκυνέω, Matt. 58, 85, Rev. 267.
Πρόσοδος, Rom. 160 sq.
Προσποιέω, Luke 392.
Προσφάνιον, John 631.
Προσφορά, Eph. 177.

TOPICAL INDEX.

☞ NOTE.—The *Numerals* refer to the pages of the Commentaries on the Books mentioned—which are paged separately in each Volume.

Milton Keynes UK
Ingram Content Group UK Ltd.
UKHW010638220124
436466UK00008B/399